I0589349

EAST OF THE RIVER
~ HOME OF THE SUN CLAN ~

BY T. P. M. THORNE

COVER ART BY T. P. M. THORNE

Published by PaMat Publishing

Copyright © 2015 T. P. M. Thorne

All rights reserved. Apart from any fair dealing for the purpose of private study, research, criticism or review, as permitted under the Copyright, Designs and Patents Act 1988, no part of this work may be reproduced, stored in a retrieval system, or transmitted in any form or by any means – electronic, electrical, chemical, mechanical, optical, photocopying, recording or otherwise – without the express written permission of the copyright owner. Enquiries should be directed to the author of this work.

The author, T. P. M. Thorne, has asserted the right under the Copyright, Designs and Patents Act 1988 to be identified as the author of this work.

Cover art: *an artistic representation of China during the Han Dynasty; the region known as Jiangdong (lit. 'River East', which translates more accurately to 'East of the River') is shaded in light green (it is an approximate representation). The region is also known (more or less) as southern Yang Province, encompassing (clockwise from left) Yuzhang, Danyang, Wu, Guangling and Kuaiji Prefectures. The Sun family (who serve as protagonists in this work) hail from Wu Prefecture (Sun Jian, father of the founder of Eastern Wu, came from Fuchun in Wu).*

TABLE OF CONTENTS

FOREWORD

This is the third work that I have completed that is based in the "Three Kingdoms" era of China that spanned the late 2nd to late 3rd Centuries. It was never my intention to do three books originally, else I would not have had Sun Quan's court in Eastern Wu be so heavily represented in "Crouching Dragon: The Journey of Zhuge Liang". On the other hand, I was keen to avoid the accusation that I had a bias toward the "Shu Han" faction led by Liu Bei and served by Zhuge Liang, and seeing things from the perspective of Shu's ally and rival, Eastern Wu, was key to that. This book is intended as a partial tribute to what was perhaps the most impressive feat of the entire era.

The Sun family were – according to their patriarch and dynastic founder of sorts, Sun Jian – descended from Sun Tzu (or Sunzi), the author of the Chinese military bible "Art of War" (not to be confused with the later Machiavelli work of the same name, though many have). However, by the late 2nd Century, Sun Jian's branch of the Sun clan was serving as minor officials that lived and worked in the mainly impoverished southeast of China. Sun Jian made the most of opportunities that were presented to him in chaotic times, and he was soon a legend of his day, respected and feared by most if not all of the northern warlords, despite being a nominal vassal of the ambitious warlord Yuan Shu. After Sun Jian's death, Sun Ce – Jian's eldest son – would be as tenacious and courageous as his father had been, creating a new and prosperous territory in a previously-neglected part of the land, firstly as a vassal of Yuan Shu like his father and then as an independent warlord: Ce's brother Quan inherited his legacy and built a new nation from that territory that endured for 80 years.

Of the three famous kingdom-founding warlords – Cao Cao (who rose to become Han Prime Minister and paved the way for his son, Cao Pi, to usurp the Han and found the Cao Wei Dynasty), Liu Bei (who ostensibly founded the kingdom of Shu Han to honour the fallen Han Dynasty and continue it), and Sun Quan of Eastern Wu – the last of these is often treated as a tertiary force due to Quan's inconstant alliance with Shu Han, and that is entirely unfair to say when being impartial. The Suns did not have connections to the ruling family to justify a governing mandate as Liu Bei did, nor did they have the Han Emperor as a guarantor and an army that outnumbered their opponents by more than 3-to-1 as Cao Cao did, but nonetheless, Eastern Wu was the last of the Three Kingdoms to perish, and without the unique achievements of the Suns, the 'Three Kingdoms' era would never have happened at all. This work is my researched interpretation – with some justifiable dramatic license, as always – of most of the achievements of the first two of the three patriarchs of Eastern Wu – Sun Jian and Sun Ce – and the people that helped them: I hope that you enjoy it.

T. P. M. Thorne, the author

PROLOGUE: DISCUSSING THE FUTURE

An era of division was about to begin in Eastern Han Dynasty China. An eight-year-long feud between two sibling noblemen had recently ended with the death of one of them, which allowed many to hope that the chaos was now at an end: those that knew the political situation knew that the worst was yet to come.

Two men of the south – a tall, handsome man called Zhou Yu and a short, unimpressive gentleman called Lu Su – left the scene of a barely-diffused incident and retreated to Zhou Yu's home so that they could talk. Both were dressed in statesman's robes, but their concerns were military.

"I'll say it again, Gongjin: for a moment there, I thought it was all for nothing!" Lu Su chuckled as he followed Zhou Yu – whose style/courtesy name was Gongjin – into his living quarters.

"And I'll say this again, Zijing: it was a moment of weakness," Zhou Yu replied. "It isn't the first, and it won't be the last, I accept that... but enough. We need to talk."

"But I thought that was what we were going to talk about," Lu Su replied uneasily.

"No," Zhou Yu said. "That was merely a prompt for me to speak with you now. You and I, we've often discussed the future of the south: now we must do so seriously, for we are the men that will shape that future."

Lu Su grinned and laughed dismissively.

"Stop it, Zijing," Zhou Yu scolded.

"Stop what...?" Lu Su giggled. "I've no rank to speak of! What future am I shaping...?"

"You have my word as your friend, Lu Zijing: I will fight for your recognition as a pillar of this fine new state that we're building," Zhou Yu replied. "Your kindness toward me cannot go unrepaid."

"...The state that you speak of is not so much a state as an idea at the moment," Lu Su suggested. "Jiangdong is still badly underdeveloped, and apart from a fine military it-"

"That will quickly change," Zhou Yu insisted. "Even with all of the threats that we face, that will change. Even though Lord Sun is... not himself... after having to abandon his campaign in Jing Province to deal with this new threat from the regime in Lujiang Prefecture, that will change. Even after what we have just witnessed, that will change."

"Are you talking to me or yourself...?" Lu Su joked.

Zhou Yu was not sure: he had known the charismatic Sun Ce – the son of the hero Sun Jian – for a decade, and the two were more like brothers than friends. Shackles of servitude had been replaced by the pressures of leadership, but the chaos that had enveloped them since their youth was unending, and the latest military and political developments had strained Sun Ce's nerves and temper to their limits. The future of the state of Jiangdong in southern Yang Province was far from secure, and the efforts of thousands of men over fifteen years of nationwide conflict was potentially at risk as new warlords emerged and new boundaries were drawn.

****

ACT I: THE TIGER OF JIANGDONG

1

"...A force to fight a... a 'nationwide peasant rebellion'...?"
The words were part of the mass of bewildered murmurings that could be heard around the public noticeboard in the town of Fuchun, which was located in Wu Prefecture, Yang Province in the southeast of China. Few could scarcely believe it, but the words were true: the Han Empire was now enveloped by chaos caused by the rise of a popular sect called the 'Way of Peace' and the beginnings of militant action by the million-or-more followers of that sect, action that was gradually being dubbed the 'Yellow Turban Rebellion'.
"What should I do?" another voice asked: the question was echoed across the small crowd. The noticeboard carried a call to arms that had been issued by the court in the Han Imperial capital Luoyang: its significance was impossible to overstate.

As always, the world as a whole was enduring change. The vast Roman Empire to the west of China was entering the fourth year of rule by Emperor Commodus, an era that is seen by many scholars as the beginning of the end; in the Parthian Empire to the north of China, Vologases IV was into his fourth decade of rule over a nation that was very stable by contrast. The Chinese Han Empire had enjoyed some trade with Parthia and was looking to trade with Rome, but that was now a faded dream. Two decades of corrupt government had weakened the incumbent emperor Ling, and after a failed military campaign against the warrior-tribal Xianbei Empire on its northern border, famines and economic mismanagement had finally pushed many of the desperate people to their limits and inadvertently forced them to seek salvation in the 'Way of Peace'.

"What can anyone here do?" was another question that was being asked, although it was thought rather than spoken in most cases. The southeast region of the Han Empire was far from the wealthiest, but it had its share of strong and tenacious people: they had to be. Rain battered the land nigh-on unendingly, and vast, hostile marshlands lined the banks of the winding Yangtze River that bisected the country and gave part of the region another name: 'Jiangdong', or 'East of the River'. Other, smaller rivers caused further natural division, and the constant threat of the pirates that all but ruled those waterways was a permanent pressure on the exhausted and under-resourced administration. But the situation was made all the worse by the social divides between north and south.
"Let the northerners sort it out, it's their problem," was another common sentiment. The capital and the influential nobles were mostly – if not all – based to the north of the winding Yangtze River, while the south suffered industrial underdevelopment and general neglect. It could still be said that there was an administrative framework in what was known to the capital as southern Yang Province, but opportunities for advancement would almost certainly mean a move to the north.

A low-ranking official left his place of work and walked to the noticeboard for the second time that day: he had made a decision that would affect not only the rest of his life, but the entire country for the next nine decades. He was a man of strong features, whose past had seen as much combat as it had affairs of the state; that man was *Sun Jian*, and his chosen 'courtesy' or 'style' name – a name by which friends past and future would better come to know him - was 'Wentai'. Like most men of his time and culture, he wore a full-length robe, had straw sandals upon his socked feet and had his uncut hair – which no one willingly parted with as part of their belief in the sanctity of all gifts given by their parents – wound into a ball and secured atop his head: he preferred a small cloth turban for covering, but this day he was wearing a square black cap over his hair. Nothing about his attire was unusual, but he drew stares nonetheless because of who he was.

"What should I do first...?" Sun Jian whispered as he stared at the fateful words on the board.

"...Forgive me, but... it's Mister *Sun Jian*, isn't it...?" a man asked.

Sun Jian turned to the man that had spoken – a handsome, imposing man in smart robes – and smiled politely.

"That sounds like quite a difficult task, I think, Mister Sun... quelling these bandits and cultists," the man continued.

"Oh, I expect that enough people will respond, and the numbers will make a difference," Sun Jian said surely.

"Will *you* respond, I wonder...?" the man prompted.

"I am nearly thirty years of age, and have yet to make my mark on this world," Sun Jian replied. "I have answered the call to quell pirates that threatened a small part of the east; why would I not answer the call to quell traitors that threaten all of us along both sides of the Great River that divides the land...?"

"Well put," the man said. "But you'll never get any sort of valuable commission on your own; you'll need to find a noted general or some other figure of fame, and fight under their banner."

"Actually... I know just the person," Sun Jian replied. "The problem is- ...Actually, I realise that I am being rude in not asking your name, sir. I think that I should do that before we go any further."

With that said, Sun Jian bowed slightly.

"I am as much at fault!" the man said as he returned the bow but lowered himself even further than Sun Jian. "My family name is 'Cheng', name 'Pu', styled 'Demou', originally from Beiping. I am not surprised that you were hesitant in being cordial: a man with your reputation for bravery, a true 'tiger', bowing to me... I am a happy man today, Mister Sun!"

"A man should always be polite, and I am sorry that I failed in that, Cheng Demou," Sun Jian insisted. "And please, call me *Wentai*: today, we are colleagues, and brothers-in-arms."

"You want my help...?" Cheng Pu realised.

"I can tell just by looking at you that you are a man of strong stature and charisma, and such men will inspire others," Sun Jian suggested. "Oh, you might know a bit about warfare, you might not: we'll fix that!"

"The man you spoke of, that you'd be fighting under," Cheng Pu prompted. "Forgive my bluntness, but I hope that it's someone impressive."

"Commander Zhu Jun," Sun Jian revealed.

"C-Commander *Zhu Jun*...? ...One of the three overall commanders of the campaign???" Cheng Pu exclaimed.

"Actually, it humbles me," Sun Jian chuckled. "The thought that I was recommended by Commander Zhu as an 'essential asset' for the expedition: he had said that he considered me a friend of sorts when we last met, but–"

"Wait... wait, but then why were you hesitating?" Cheng Pu wondered. "You're a man that doesn't hesitate when faced with pirates, so why now?"

"The enormity of it," Sun Jian confessed. "Pirates are one thing; a popular uprising is something else altogether, and like it or not, it's a popular uprising. *Very* popular in the north... *very popular*. We'd be fighting the *people*."

"But it is, nonetheless, an anarchic act of treason by a villainous cultist that warps the minds of the weak," Cheng Pu suggested. "It must be ended."

"But we two alone cannot do this, obviously," Sun Jian said. "We need a militia, and quickly. The 'Yellow Turbans' will not wait for us to sort ourselves out."

"Nor will Commander Zhu," Cheng Pu replied dryly. "Forgive this statement, Mister Sun, but I hear that he's a bit of a pedant... I'm not too fond of pedants."

"No, he's just... well, no, maybe you're right," Sun Jian conceded. "Anyhow, we should get a notice up, and–"

As the two had been talking, Cheng Pu had noticed another man watching them.

"That fellow there," Cheng Pu interrupted. "What do you think...? He's built like an ox... a titan, for certain, and doubtless useful!"

Sun Jian turned to look at the tall, swarthy man that Cheng Pu had spotted: the man immediately lowered his gaze and turned to walk away.

"Wait, wait!" Sun Jian said as he ran to the man with no care for the etiquette of the day.

The swarthy man stopped, turned, and faced Sun Jian with humility that contrasted with his imposing features. He bowed politely, and said, "Mister Sun Jian, is it not."

Sun Jian had to catch his breath and was briefly unable to reply.

"...What might your name be...?" Cheng Pu asked as he reached the two men.

"Huang Gai," the swarthy man replied. "I mean... uh... family name, 'Huang'–"

"You've no need to be so formal with us!" Sun Jian wheezed. "I must be more tense than I thought to have been breathless just now... I'm Sun Jian, but call me 'Wentai'... this is Cheng Pu–"

"But you can call me 'Demou'," Cheng Pu interrupted.

"...I'm honoured to meet you both," Huang Gai said as he made a low, humble bow. "My style name, if I have a right to one, is 'Gongfu'."

"Your countenance is odd, if you don't mind me saying," Cheng Pu prompted.

"I... am a very lucky man to be in such good company," Huang Gai replied. "Like the two of you, I am an official... but very, very lucky to be so."

"Are you a local man...?" Sun Jian asked.

"No, I came here from Lingling a few days ago," Huang Gai said.

"Ah, Lingling: all but part of Jing these days," Cheng Pu noted. "I don't think you know of me, but I gather that you know of Sun Wentai."

"Yes, I am aware of his brave exploits against the pirates," Huang Gai said with some reverence. "It is my hope that I can also do good service. I've been loitering around this sign since it was put up, wondering how I can ever be of help... I've read the military texts, but I've never seen a battle, really."

"Yet you have the countenance of a man that's known suffering... I've seen it before," Cheng Pu suggested. "Your 'Huang' line... is it any relation to Huang Zu of Jiangxia...?"

"Are we not all descended from or related to one person or other...?" Huang Gai chuckled miserably. "But no, I'm descended from a senior administrator in Nan County. My family moved to Lingling, but when my father died, well..."

After a few moments of awkward silence, Sun Jian coughed deliberately and said, "Well, if I am truly descended from the great Sun Tzu as some of my clan like to suggest, it didn't get me that far, friend Gongfu! I still need to do something myself, do I not...? I can see you've worked hard for what you have: that means you've earned every bit of it, and should be proud, more proud than men like Yuan Shao of Ru County, who had it handed to them. What do you say to my asking you to help me and Cheng Demou rid the land of some cultists...?"

"Mister Sun Wentai will have us fighting under the banner of *Commander Zhu Jun*, no less," Cheng Pu reported. "That will get you to where you deserve to be."

"...Forgive my bluntness, but... can just the three of us volunteer our services to Commander Zhu...?" Huang Gai replied. "I would think that we need to find some other men to fight with us... if that isn't a pedantic point."

"It *is*," Cheng Pu chortled, "but I'll forgive you, just this once. No, Huang Gongfu, I think you'll find that we're not going to have any trouble finding help...!"

Cheng Pu gestured toward a group of local men that were watching the newly-formed friendship with growing interest.

"...Let's start with *them*!" Sun Jian said with newfound cheer.

A few hours later, Sun Jian, Cheng Pu and Huang Gai were sat in a tavern with two of the men that they had approached, drinking rice wine. Some of the other men were sat at nearby tables, enjoying their own refreshments and alternating between private conversations and eavesdropping on the discussion between their five appointed leaders.

"...So you really don't have a style name...?" Cheng Pu said as he looked at one of the two men, who was a swarthy man dressed in weathered clothes.

"Nope," the man replied. "S'at a problem...?"

"No... no, I mean, if you don't have one, and don't want one, I suppose there's nothing wrong with that," Cheng Pu said uneasily. "But what do we call you...?"

"The name I've got; the name I gave you," the man said bluntly. "*Zu Mao*."

"Zu Mao, I think we shall argue the point no longer!" Sun Jian chuckled.

"*Thanks*," Zu Mao grunted.

"...So you can fight, Mister Zu Mao...?" Huang Gai asked politely.

"Said I could," Zu Mao retorted. "Look, here's how it is: I'm a man o' my word, I always give everythin' my best. No, I'm not a lucky sort that comes from good stock, but I'm a man o' my word, and I guarantee that I'll always watch your back, guard your front, and fight your fight until it's won. If that'll do, then we're done."

Huang Gai coughed awkwardly and said, "Indeed."

Sun Jian's gaze turned to the other man, who was also possessed of a strong build and features, but wore well-kept robes and carried a well-maintained sword at his side.

"Mister Han Dang... or if I may, *Han Yigong*," Sun Jian prompted.

"You're famed in these parts, Sun Wentai," Han Dang replied. "I feel strange talking to a man that's as crazy as you are."

"I *beg your pardon*...?" Cheng Pu said irritably.

"Oh come now, is it not reckless at the very least, what Mister Sun did...?" Han Dang chortled.

"*Brave*, I think," Cheng Pu suggested.

Sun Jian scratched the side of his head and hummed thoughtfully.

"You're thinking about it now, aren't you...?" Han Dang teased.

"Thinking about *what*...?" Huang Gai wondered.

"Sun Jian is renowned amongst these parts for taking down a whole lot o' pirates," Zu Mao chuckled hoarsely. "Charged them headlong, he did, all by himself, and started pointing in all directions, shouting things like '*You men*, from *that* side!' and '*Now*! From *that* side!' to make them think they were surrounded."

"Was that really what you did...?" Cheng Pu asked as he looked at Sun Jian, who nodded sheepishly. Cheng Pu frowned and said, "You're going to get yourself *killed*, doing stupid things like that, Wentai. Why under Heaven did you do it...?"

"I didn't have anyone to help me," Sun Jian admitted. "There were only a few of them, and I thought, 'Why not?'"

"And *you're* the boss," Zu Mao chuckled. "This'll be fun, I reckon."

"Fortunately," Cheng Pu said, "Gongfu and I are both versed in stratagem... so we shouldn't need to resort to suicidal behaviour. I know I said that I detest pedants, but... there are limits to how undisciplined a man should be. What were you trying to prove...?"

"That I'm worthy of my ancestry, for one," Sun Jian confessed. "To be told you're descended from greatness, perhaps the most respected strategist in history, and then you stare into the water, and the man reflected back at you is... ... ...I need to know that I *tried* to be a great man, at the very least."

Every man that was listening fell silent.

"Well put," Zu Mao declared after a thoughtful silence.

"The Yellow Turbans are a menace," Cheng Pu said sternly. "We need to put an end to them... but promise me, Wentai, that you will not throw yourself into the tiger's mouth in the attempt...?"

"No fear of that," Sun Jian said with a smile. "I *am* the tiger. And I'm going to devour them all."

The men were inspired, and they cheered as one.

****

2

Sun Jian returned to his home later that evening, wracked with a sudden sense of guilt. His decision to volunteer his services to the rescue of the Han Empire had not been made lightly, but at the same time, the decision had been made alone, and now he had to explain his decision – and the motivations behind it – to his family.

"**Father!**" Sun Jian's eldest son shouted as soon as he saw the sullen patriarch enter the living quarters. The boy ran toward his father, stopped short, and immediately started to throw punches at the empty air between them. The two enjoyed a short bout of mock sparring before the youth – Sun Ce – hugged his father tightly.

"...I need to speak to the family, Ce'er," Sun Jian ordered.

Sun Ce nodded eagerly and went to the sleeping quarters to summon his mother, Lady Wu.

"What is it, Husband...?" Lady Wu asked as she entered the living quarters; she had with her the second son of Sun Jian, who was two years old. She was an attractive woman, and she had a strong presence that was born from the need to support her brother when their father died without leaving them with a reliable source of income. Lady Wu was the matriarch in every sense, and Sun Jian showed her a degree of private deference for that same strong, supportive nature that she now focussed towards him and the family they were raising together. This did mean, however, that the family they were raising would be very, very different from what was the norm at that time.

"I've... made a decision," Sun Jian said as Sun Ce returned and took a casual seat near the entrance to the sleeping quarters. "I... have decided to-"

"Oh, Husband, *no*," Lady Wu scoffed. "You signed up, didn't you, to fight those cultists... so how many is it, then, exactly...? I have heard that there are *thousands* of them, maybe as many as a *million*; how do you intend to face them alone *this time*...?"

"No, no!" Sun Jian insisted. "I've actually put a militia together this time."

"Well that's *something*, I suppose," Lady Wu grumbled as she wiped the baby boy's face; the oblivious child laughed happily.

"Can *I* go and fight...?" Sun Ce asked eagerly.

"You're *nine*!" Lady Wu scolded. "Save that nonsense for when you're at least five years older! Who's supposed to keep things here...?"

Sun Jian frowned and said, "Your brother-"

"No, he can go with *you*," Lady Wu insisted. "If nothing else, he's level-headed... he'll maybe stop you from doing something reckless."

Sun Ce laughed involuntarily, while his father was suitably awkward.

"This 'militia'... how big is it?" Lady Wu prompted.

Sun Jian smiled sheepishly and said, "I promise, it's a few hundred already; I've met four men, four really good, decent, honest, courageous men that have really helped me inspire people to-"

"Abandon their families and go off on some mad, suicidal mission to kill a load of heretics," Lady Wu interrupted. "Why under Heaven is this not being done by the army...? Why do they need bands of ordinary men like you?"

"I'm *not ordinary*," Sun Jian said with sudden seriousness.

"...Sorry," Lady Wu sighed sadly. "I... I did not mean to belittle you; it's just that I worry, for us all. We're not wealthy... we can't afford any more trouble."

"To answer your question, the army is underfunded and inadequate... a sad sign of how bad things have got," Sun Jian lamented. "This whole region- nay, the whole *country* is badly run, and if I'm honest, I'm surprised that we haven't seen something like this sooner... I'm doing this to stop it *now* before it spreads to the south and endangers us. Anyhow... the fact that I even had to go it alone against those pirates says enough about the state of things for some years, now... there were no soldiers for the people to ask help from *then*, either."

"No... only good people, like *you*," Lady Wu said soberly. After a pause, she smiled and added, "You're far from ordinary, Husband. You're quite amazing, in fact, and I'm sure that you probably *could* defeat them all on your own."

"That's right, he *could*!" Sun Ce proclaimed. "You'll get them *all*, Father! One day, I'm gonna be brave and strong, like *you*, and get them old pirates!"

"Listen to *him*," Lady Wu snickered. "Another one looking for a hero's early grave, and he isn't even ten."

Sun Jian was morbidly silent.

"...Sorry," Lady Wu said quietly. "How long do you think you'll be away, you and your new friends...?"

"A few months, now that I come to think about it," Sun Jian replied miserably. "Are you sure that your brother shouldn't-"

"I said that he should go, and I think that he should; we've all got to do what we can against these dangerous heretics, right...?" Lady Wu suggested. "Off you go, then, Husband."

"I'm not going yet!" Sun Jian chortled. "No, we set out in a few days; tonight, I must gather a few things... but in all, we're going to need supplies, weapons, armour-"

"My goodness, this *is* well-planned, isn't it," Lady Wu chuckled. "I'm already a little less worried."

"And two of the men that I've found, they've read books on warfare as well," Sun Jian explained further. "So that'll be three of us at least that know a bit about strategy. I mean, it was a 'bluff' strategy that I used to scare the pirates, and that worked, so with all of us working together... we can win easily."

"I should like to meet these men," Lady Wu said.

"Uh... yes, perhaps that might help to reassure you further," Sun Jian replied hesitantly. "But, uh... just one thing, my lady..."

Sun Ce awaited his father's request to his mother amid awkward silence.

"Go and play, Ce," Lady Wu ordered, and Sun Ce retreated.

"Forgive me for saying this," Sun Jian murmured, "but-"

"Don't be rude to them...?" Lady Wu giggled. "I am not a fool, Husband. I am well aware that I am a fortunate woman indeed to be married to a man that allows me to speak my mind, even when he'd rather I didn't. I am aware that I must be the dutiful wife in unfamiliar company... have I not done so before...?"

"Always," Sun Jian recalled. "Forgive my asking such a thing, for you're right, you're no fool."

"Your new son is strong, like Ce," Lady Wu said as she wiped drool from the side of her child's mouth. "He dribbles a lot, but I imagine that'll stop when he's older."

"Dada!" the child squealed.

"...Hello," Sun Jian chuckled. "Well, he seems smart enough, as well."

"I wonder," Lady Wu said, "if we can risk thinking about his adult name yet."

"Ce was fine, and I don't agree that it's bad luck to plan ahead," Sun Jian replied. "I think that we can go ahead and call him something if we wish."

"You're his father, so it is your choice," Lady Wu said.

"...'Quan'," Sun Jian declared. "Let's call him 'Quan'."

"Mm... a powerful choice, if I guess you right," Lady Wu giggled.

"We're blessed to have two strong sons already," Sun Jian said. "May we have more."

"... ... ...Well, it's *me* that has to give birth to them, so I can't expect you to understand," Lady Wu sighed. "I think I might be pregnant again, actually, so you may get your wish sooner than you thought."

Sun Jian's smile faded, and he said, "Ah... well, in that case, it would be wrong of me to leave you, so maybe I could-"

"Have you, or have you not, already sent a letter to your friend Zhu Jun, telling him that you're on your way...?" Lady Wu asked.

"...I have, yes," Sun Jian admitted sheepishly.

"Well, then there are no 'maybes'; you're on your way northward," Lady Wu declared. "I have help, so do not fret."

"But your brother could-"

"I already said 'No'!" Lady Wu chortled. "All I have to deal with is some small, rowdy children... there's a big, rowdy *man* that needs watching far more, I think."

"...Alright," Sun Jian conceded. "But I am sorry that I didn't consult you, at least."

"You did the right thing," Lady Wu insisted. "If these men are as decent as you say – and I believe you, you're a good judge – it would not have been sensible to mess them about, and tell them that you needed to ask your wife's permission. You acted quickly. Now you should start preparing to leave. We'll be fine."

Sun Jian looked at Quan, smiled, and said, "He's got your eyes."

"I thought he had *yours*," Lady Wu retorted. "Ce certainly has, and no mistake. He'll follow your path... so make sure you give him a decent one to follow."

"I shall," Sun Jian promised. "This is the beginnings of our path to better things."

Sun Jian then knelt at his desk and focussed on some minor official matters. Lady Wu retired to the sleeping quarters, and silence descended for several minutes.

"...Father, what's up with these 'Yellow Turbans'...?"

Sun Jian sighed miserably, lowered the cloth letter that he had been reading and turned to his son Sun Ce.

"I'd ask Mother again, but she said I should ask *you* last time," Sun Ce continued.

"...Alright," Sun Jian said. "I suppose it'll be useful for you to know; after all, this might go on for years."

"Years...?" Sun Ce exclaimed. "But you said that-"

"I know what I said," Sun Jian interrupted. "Now listen, and listen well. The Yellow Turbans are a cult. They go against everything Confucian that I've raised you to believe in. They are doing things that are deliberately offensive to the emperor."

"...Like what?"

Sun Jian coughed awkwardly and said, "You know your 'Wu Xing'?"

"Fire nourishes earth... an' water... rusts metal...?" Sun Ce replied.

"There's a bit more to it than that, but it'll do for this conversation," Sun Jian chuckled. "But for the sake of the future, Ce'er... study harder."

"I will, Father," Sun Ce said apologetically.

"The Han are represented by red, and fire," Sun Jian continued. "Additionally, the colour yellow is-"

"The imperial colour!" Sun Ce said excitedly.

"...Yes," Sun Jian replied.

"Oh, uh... sorry I interrupted you, Father," Sun Ce said.

"It's fine, just this once," Sun Jian replied. "Now, as I was saying, my son... yellow for the Han is as inauspicious as it is auspicious when used by these cultists."

"I hate cultists," Sun Ce grumbled.

"So you should," Sun Jian said. "We're trying to advance, and such backward groups are going to drag us down. The people that follow them are probably mostly just angry at the government and not proper cultists at all, but that's someone else's fault, not the emperor's... I'll get to that."

"Okay," Sun Ce said. "So why is yellow double-bad?"

"...I don't think that's how I put it," Sun Jian chuckled. "But anyway... first of all, Wu Xing dictates that *earth* – signified by *yellow* – is *nourished by fire*, so part of the cultists choosing yellow is because of that."

"...I get it," Sun Ce said.

"Good," Sun Jian replied. "Secondly, yellow must *never be worn above the head by anyone other than the emperor*. The cult's leader has told everyone to do exactly that, though... which is why they're called 'Yellow Turbans', because that's what they're all wearing deliberately to-"

"That's treason!" Sun Ce exclaimed.

"It is," Sun Jian replied. "But it's worse than normal treason. When Wang Mang usurped the Han over a century ago, he would never have done this. To have the normal people wear yellow isn't just a call to get rid of the emperor; it's a call to get rid of the empire, of everything we know and understand. It's a call to give all of the power under Heaven to *everyone*, not just the emperor."

"...What's wrong with that?" Sun Ce whispered.

"I... admit that it probably doesn't sound wrong to someone your age," Sun Jian replied awkwardly, "but it just *is*, alright...? I want to see people's lives get better, but that isn't what the 'Way of Peace' will give us. They're a cult, and so they'll bring in something loosely based on Taoism, something twisted that will suit the leaders, but not anyone else. But it's the government's fault for making these fanatical idiots seem-"

Sun Ce laughed at his father's words.

"...Hush, my son," Sun Jian pleaded. "I'm being serious."

"Sorry," Sun Ce replied. "S'just that you calling 'em 'idiots' is funny."

"That's what they are," Sun Jian said. "But when they go from place to place 'healing the sick' and spreading that stupid poem, telling people that getting rid of everything that's held this country together for the last four centuries or more is a good thing, they're not just stupid, they're *dangerous*. If we don't stop them, there will be chaos: no one will till the fields, tend the cattle or brew the wine, and there will be famine. They'll ransack everywhere, which means there will be no shops, worthless money, no law; the pirates and bandits that already make things so difficult will be even more dangerous. The Wuhuan, the Qiang, the Northern Xiongnu or the Xianbei – or maybe more than one of them – will sense our disorganisation and invade, and there won't be an army to stop them, especially if the Southern Xiongnu that currently live alongside us decide that we're weak and turn on us too. And if they bring in the nonsense they believe in, most of the people will realise they made a mistake and try and get rid of them... leading to another war almost straight away."

"*Dumb cultists*," Sun Ce grumbled. "I won't *ever* listen to 'em, Father."

"That is very sensible," Sun Jian replied. "Anyway, that's the explanation you wanted about who I'm going to fight. Was that all...?"

"How is it the government's fault?" Sun Ce asked.

"...I'll try and make this quick," Sun Jian sighed.

"Shouldn't I ask?" Sun Ce said.

"You're right to ask, and... and I promised that I'd answer," Sun Jian replied. "The government is currently run by some corrupt people. They... don't help. Money doesn't reach places that need it, and that makes people angry. That's... that's all that I should really say, I think."

"Alright, Father," Sun Ce murmured. "I'll go now."

"Thank you," Sun Jian sighed.

The conversation between father and son had left both with more questions than answers and a shared sense of unease.

****

3

Over the next two days, Sun Jian divided his time between his mundane civil duties and the new, more exciting task that awaited him. On the day of departure, Sun Jian had readied his 1,000 men as best he could and assigned them to his lieutenants Huang Gai, Han Dang and Zu Mao. He wore tired, inexpensive armour and a plain battle helmet that would have rendered him indistinguishable from many of his men had they not been partnered with a vibrant red scarf that he wore around his neck for luck.

"I'm not sure that I should be acting as 'adviser' on this campaign," Cheng Pu said with sudden doubt. "I know that I am a little versed in warfare, but-"

"You'll be the brains," Sun Jian insisted. He then turned to his stoic, hard-featured brother-in-law, Wu Jing, and said, "I can't interest you in a front-line role, my respected brother-in-law...?"

"My sister asked me to keep an eye on you," Wu Jing replied. "I'll act as your second, so I can do that."

"*Aiee*... I am so very, very humbled," Sun Jian sighed.

"In more ways than one!" Cheng Pu joked. "Shall we order the troops to start moving?"

"No... I want my family to see me off," Sun Jian replied. "I want everyone to have a moment with their families, if that's possible."

"A lot of these men don't have families," Cheng Pu suggested.

"...A lot of these men don't have *heads*, either!" Wu Jing chuckled. Some of Sun Jian's recruits had little hair on their heads or none at all, a sign that they had been given a common form of 'capital punishment' – removal of their hair in lieu of actual execution for some serious crime.

"Do not judge them harshly," Sun Jian pleaded.

"I am aware that a lot of soldiers are former convicts, Brother-in-law, and that they render fine service to atone for mast misdemeanours," Wu Jing promised. "So long as they fight alongside us and defend their country, that's all I care about. I was merely jesting, just as Mister Cheng does when he implies that my sister is the master's hand in your family home."

Cheng Pu laughed and said, "Would I do that...?"

Wu Jing smiled dryly.

"So where are we going?" Han Dang asked.

"Southern Yu Province, of course," Cheng Pu replied tersely.

"The Turbans are all over the place, 'Demou'," Han Dang said. "What do you mean by 'of course'...?"

"...I suppose that did sound pedantic," Cheng Pu said with a sigh. "Sorry, my friend. Commander Zhu is based there, and the worst of the threats to the south come from Yu Province. We might go further north if we defeat them there, to Yingchuan, or maybe west, to Nan County in Jing Province."

"It's unbelievable that they've managed to entrench themselves in Jing, Yu, Ji, Yan, Xu, Qing and Yòu," Huang Gai said. "Only the far northwest is spared, then."

"They're in Central Province as well, but there's a ring of defence works around Luoyang," Cheng Pu explained. "And yes, I... I worry. Though I have little love for northern politics, my ancestral home is on the frontier."

"Beiping, near where I hail from," Han Dang noted. "You must've seen a lot o' the Wuhuan when you were up that way too."

"You had it worse in Liaoxi, Yigong!" Cheng Pu chuckled. "But yes, I saw a lot of incursions... and little or nothing done about any of it by the-"

"I... I only narrowly avoided a very similar conversation to the one we're about to start, but with my nine-year-old son," Sun Jian interrupted. "Can we just do what we've been asked to do, and do the politics later?"

"It'll have to come up sooner or later, Wentai," Cheng Pu suggested.

"Later, then, Demou," Sun Jian insisted. "My family's coming to see me off."

Many women and children were approaching: Sun Jian walked to his own family and said, "I'm glad."

"You look amazing!" Sun Ce exclaimed as he looked at his father's armour.

"...In this tatty stuff?" Sun Jian chortled. "Oh, well, I suppose you're young, and the sight of any army is impressive."

"Be careful," Lady Wu said as she struggled with the excitable Sun Quan. "That's all I came to say... be *careful*."

"I will be," Sun Jian promised.

Lady Wu smiled slightly, turned and retreated without waiting to see or speak to her brother.

"*Ayah*... is she already going?" Wu Jing complained as he hurried to Sun Jian's side. "I was in the middle of-"

"Go after her then, Brother-in-law," Sun Jian said. "Perhaps she has last-minute instructions for you."

Wu Jing grimaced and ran after his sister.

"...Are you really so impressed...?" Sun Jian asked as he looked down at his eldest son.

"When I'm older, I wanna be a general," Sun Ce replied. "I'll beat up cultists, pirates, bandits... *anyone*."

"...I'd not say 'anyone', but I'm proud of your spirit," Sun Jian chuckled as he wiggled his son's cloth turban.

"Hey! Don't do that! My hair might fall out!" Sun Ce exclaimed.

"You'd better go, then, before I do it again," Sun Jian said. "Go on... I need to get my men ready to go."

"...Goo'bye, Father," Sun Ce replied.

Wu Jing was returning to the departing army; he was visibly uncomfortable, and he was obviously looking forward to a short dialogue with his feisty nephew Sun Ce.

"...Go on, son," Sun Jian said.

Sun Ce required more prompting before he finally followed his mother: he ran past his uncle Wu Jing without stopping.

"*Ayah*... does no one care what happens to me?" Wu Jing sighed as he reached the sombre Sun Jian.

"He's upset," Sun Jian replied. "Shall we...?"

"Yes, let's get going," Wu Jing agreed.

The two men returned to their small army, unaware that Sun Ce had decided to turn around and watch his father's final retreat. Cheng Pu had prepared a horse with a mostly-white coat for Sun Jian to ride: he mounted it and prepared to make one last horseback address to his small army.

"I hope that every man that had family to say their

farewells too has had their chance," Sun Jian began. **"We've got a long journey ahead of us, and although our enemy is not as fearsome as it could be, it will still be many months before we can come back to our homes. But rest assured, this will be a battle fought together: I have as much chance of coming home as any of you, because I intend to be right out there with you."**

Wu Jing shuddered at the words.

"I know that we had the odd man decide not to go because the enemy is 'the people'," Sun Jian continued. **"Yes, it is... but they've been muddled by lies, taken in when they were scared and angry. Our job isn't to kill everyone, okay...? Our job is to pacify the land. Our job is to stop those that need stopping, and help those that need helping."**

The militia listened silently and carefully.

"We're going to cross the Great River and go through Lujiang Prefecture," Sun Jian continued. **"After that, we'll go west and cut off the enemy advance to the Great River from Runan. Our first objective isn't to save the northerners: it's to protect our own homes. What we do after that is up to the Yellow Turbans and how much they want to come down here; hopefully, they'll take one look at our marshlands and realise that we're doing them a favour."**

Some of the men laughed.

"...Not bad," Zu Mao whispered as he pondered Sun Jian's rhetoric. Cheng Pu brought his horse alongside Sun Jian's and said, "We should get going."

"I know," Sun Jian replied quietly; he then turned his gaze back to his militia and asked, **"Are we ready...?"**

The reassured men spoke as one, yelling, **"Yes, Commander Sun!"**

Sun Jian smiled, raised his sword, and shouted, **"For the Empire!"**

The militia hollered their accord, and the journey out of Fuchun began. Sun Ce watched with a mixture of fear and awe, whispering, "There goes my father...!"

The small southern militia started its long and wearisome journey to Yu Province, a region that sat between Yang Province and Capital Province, where Luoyang was based. Because the army was small, there were not as many of the logistical problems that affected large forces: for one, there was a small baggage train, which would be easier to defend. Secondly, sourcing new food and places of rest was easier for a small army; and thirdly, managing problems such as morale – a factor that could be the make or break of the most numerically-superior or better-equipped force in a heated battle – was easier, as a personal relationship with individual soldiers and officers was easier to cultivate. Sun Jian and his new friends were blessed with the ability to inspire and forge friendships with their men, primarily because they saw them – or, at the very least, treated them – as equals; it was no surprise, then, that the force that arrived at the southern bank of the Yangtze River was enthusiastic, driven, and like a large family that would fight the enemy and protect each other with equal vigour.

"Beautiful," Cheng Pu sighed as he stared at the vast, divisive Yangtze; the commanders were enjoying a brief rest period while scouts surveyed the area and men set up a temporary camp under Han Dang's supervision. Heavy rain was battering the army and the river, so there were few men that shared Cheng Pu's strange observation. Sun Jian, Wu Jing, Cheng Pu and Huang Gai were on horses, but Han Dang and Zu Mao had opted to travel on foot like the rest of the army, and the latter – who was stood next to Sun Jian's horse – was extremely irritable.

"...Have you never seen the river or somethin', Mister Cheng...?" Zu Mao grunted as he wiped rain from his face.

"Of course I have!" Cheng Pu retorted. "It's just that I-!"

"Are we going t'go downriver a bit, now, or are we gonna just go straight across?" Zu Mao asked.

"...We'll need more boats or boat trips than I planned for," Cheng Pu replied. "Our force grew as we travelled... we'll need to..."

The distracted Cheng Pu turned his horse and rode away from the riverbank; the ground was far from stable, and horse and man alike were struggling.

"Imagine the strife the Turbans'll suffer if they get this far," Zu Mao chuckled.

"That's a valid point," Huang Gai said. "If I were a Yellow Turban general, I wouldn't be trying to come into the Jiangdong region from here. I'd want to take southern Jing and cross at a place like Xiakou, or take Guangling to the east and cross to-"

"S'a good job you're not with 'em then, else they'd win," Zu Mao snickered.

"Huang Gongfu is quite right," Sun Jian said as he observed the riverbank on both sides of their position. "They need to take established crossings, like Hengjiang, Wulin, Xiakou; they're not in a position to do that right now, so if we slow them in Runan, prevent them getting into Jiujiang and Guangling to the east and Jiangxia to the west, then we've as good as ruined their chances of crossing the Great River."

"And if we lose, reinforcing Qu'e, Moling, Ba Qiu, Red Cliffs and other places will stop their advance and give the commanders a chance to turn things around," Huang Gai suggested.

"...You're quite the thinker, Huang Gongfu," Sun Jian replied. "I'm fortunate to have such well-rounded men on my team."

Huang Gai smiled modestly, clasped his hands together and bowed slightly, saying, "I only strive to do my utmost, Lord Sun."

"...Call me Wentai, for goodness' sakes, Gongfu... we're *friends*," Sun Jian chortled. He then turned to his brother-in-law Wu Jing and said, "You're quiet."

"I'm enjoying having nothing to be concerned about," Wu Jing replied. "We have a wonderful little army, four good lieutenants, over a dozen good captains, and a trouble-free journey over the Great River awaiting us! That's all auspicious."

"I hope it rains less up north," Zu Mao grumbled. "Or can that horse swim, Mister Sun?"

Sun Jian looked down at his horse's legs and said, "Am I sinking?"

"Not yet," Zu Mao replied as he shook his right leg. "I'd rather be on a horse, in a ways, but then again, maybe not."

"...We should've gone to Wuhu and crossed," Huang Gai said. "Crossing here is-"

"We should go east to Wuhu," Cheng Pu announced as he returned to the gathering. **"There's no danger of the Yellow Turbans being anywhere near here, and we need to make an organised crossing."**
"Great minds think alike, it seems," Sun Jian chuckled. "Alright then, we'll go to Wuhu as soon as we've rested... it isn't far. Do we need to leave men here in signal towers to watch for incursions, do you think...?"
Cheng Pu and Huang Gai voiced simultaneous agreement that scouts and guard towers would not be necessary.
"...I'd like t'see someone light a warning fire in this rain, anyhow," Zu Mao said.

Within two days, Sun Jian's army crossed the Yangtze River and began their journey west through Lujiang Prefecture in northern Yang Province. Han Dang and Zu Mao were now on horses as well, and the men had taken the opportunity to replenish their supplies in the port towns.
"Isn't this area riddled with bandits, Demou?" Huang Gai asked.
"They'll have called a truce with Administrator Lu Kang," Cheng Pu replied.
"The Yellow Turbans' leaders aren't professional crims, they're preachy loons," Zu Mao suggested. "They'll want all the bandits to stop fighting and *pray* and 'reflect on their souls' and all that, which don't sit right, I'd have thought."
"Quite true," Cheng Pu said with a smile.
"So we're safe," Sun Jian supposed.
"I'd say so," Cheng Pu replied. "As Zu Mao has already said in a sense, no proper bandit wants religious fanatics to win a war between people and state; the laws that would follow would be harsh and unforgiving. If anything, we'll probably get some volunteers if we're spotted."
"They'd be appreciated," Sun Jian said.
"...So long as they don't 'revert to type' on the way back," Wu Jing suggested.

Sun Jian would receive a few volunteers, but as the border with Yu Province loomed, every man started to wonder if they were right to be voluntarily adding their presence to the growing chaos. Most stayed on the march, however, and Sun Jian crossed into Yu Province with a force that was still in excess of 1,000 men. He would need every man, because the Yellow Turbans in Runan Prefecture alone reportedly numbered in the tens of thousands, and their local leader, Bo Cai, was almost as charismatic and inspiring as Sun Jian. In fact, two of his lieutenants, Liu Pi and Huang Shao, were quickly becoming as well-known for their skill as leaders, warriors and recruiters, and that made the battle for hearts all the more difficult.

****

4

Sun Jian's small army encountered its first Yellow Turban contingent before a rendezvous with Zhu Jun could be achieved: the Turbans outnumbered them by at least three-to-one, but the majority of their infantry was poorly-trained and driven solely by frustration. Their leader, Liu Pi, had heard of Sun Jian and was making an attempt to turn the new force back with a show of strength before it could threaten the Yellow Turban efforts in northern Runan.

"Blimey," Zu Mao exclaimed as he observed the peasant army. "S'all sorts amongst that lot. Do we have a plan?"

"They've commandeered that village over there as a base," Cheng Pu said as he pointed northward. "The people don't seem to be too happy about it, which is a good thing of course. Our main aim is to push them away from us and simultaneously rescue those poor people."

"We'll split our forces, then," Sun Jian decided. "Huang Gai, Han Dang: you'll take half of the men and make a show of strength here, while Cheng Pu, Zu Mao and I go and-"

"Ayah! You're off already!" Wu Jing cried. "Send your officers to the village and hold here! Swap the orders! You can't-!"

"I'm not going to let the enemy retreat to the village," Sun Jian said. "I'm the commander, and that will reassure the-"

"Ayah! *Fool*! Reckless, death-seeking *fool*!" Wu Jing sobbed. "My sister will-!"

"Forgive me, Brother-in-law, but... I order you to say no more," Sun Jian said sternly. "I'm going, and that's that. Cheng Pu, Zu Mao: let's prepare."

Huang Gai and Han Dang followed their own orders and led a small group forward to distract the Yellow Turbans while their leader readied his team.

"What's the matter with these southern men?" the Yellow Turban officer Liu Pi wondered as he watched Huang Gai and Han Dang's battle with his front-line infantry. "I was hoping they'd come across the river to join us... not fight us! Why would they love the empire so much?"

Liu Pi's subordinates were uncomfortably silent.

"They're good," Liu Pi noted. "You see it too: why couldn't they be on our side???"

Liu Pi's subordinates remained silent; Huang Gai and Han Dang's small militia was carving through the infantry with painful ease, and defeat was a definite possibility.

"...I need to rally them," Liu Pi murmured. After a few moments of thought, he decided to use the infamous sixteen-word mantra that had been passed down by the founder of the 'Way of Peace', Zhang Jue: that small yet memorable statement had been the instrument of recruitment for the sect, and it might, Liu Pi mused, be the saviour of the day.

"...**Han's mandate has passed!**" Liu Pi screamed. His subordinates knew the words as well as they knew the backs of their hands, and they immediately joined in with Liu Pi's recital.

"**Yellow Sky, soon here!**" a larger group of Yellow Turbans bellowed.

"What the-!" Han Dang exclaimed.

"In this renewing year: prosperous all, at last!"

The words were being carried across the ranks of the Yellow Turbans with alarming speed, and they seemed to be doing the desired job of restoring their resolve and making them act as one. The effect on Sun Jian's forces was the exact opposite: the sight of thousands of people uttering the same words as a toneless, synchronised drone was disconcerting and demoralising.

"Han's mandate has passed! Yellow Sky, soon here! In this renewing year: prosperous all, at last!"

The words were repeated over and over by the intimidating mass of Yellow Turbans.

"They're possessed!" one of Huang Gai's men cried. **"They're possessed by a demon... or a god!"**

"Stay calm! Please, stay calm!" Huang Gai said as his men started to falter.

"Damn them! We need to keep them busy for Lord Sun!" Han Dang despaired.

"...Interesting," Sun Jian said as he watched the baying horde of Yellow Turbans. "But why are our men so disturbed? Don't armies chant things anymore?"

"It's what they're chanting, and that they're not an army as such," Cheng Pu suggested. "Watching an army chant simple curses is one thing; watching an organised rabble of ordinary people – just like you, only with no experience of battle to speak of, and some of them women and boys at that – saying the things that they're saying...? Tell me it doesn't make you feel strange."

"...Alright, yes, I admit that it upsets me," Sun Jian replied. "But we have a job to do, and that's that."

"You're a fool... a fool!" Wu Jing whimpered. "How can you ride through them? Look at them! *Listen* to them!"

"That's precisely why I can ride through them," Sun Jian retorted. "Are we ready?"

"...Yes," Cheng Pu replied.

"Right, then!" Sun Jian said. **"Forward!"**

Sun Jian led his men in a sudden, swift – and some might have said 'suicidal' charge at the right flank of the larger Yellow Turban force. The gambit worked: many of the Yellow Turbans were relying on their chanting for strength in the face of fear, and Sun Jian's force was able to stun the peasant army and pass through them with next to no resistance. The smaller Yellow Turban force around the village was far enough away from the main army for the morale-boosting efforts of Liu Pi to mean nothing, and they quickly scattered when Sun Jian's small vanguard of horsemen rushed at them at great speed, hollering cries of support for the Han Empire as they did so.

"Well done, all!" Sun Jian said as his men coalesced. "Now the village is safe."

"I bet they feel lucky that they don't live in a walled city, if only this once," Zu Mao noted. "The Yellow Turbans'd've been mad to try and hold a tiny village of thatched houses like this one."

"It would have ended up being burned to the ground, one way or the other," Cheng Pu supposed. "You're right, Mister Zu; just this once, they might be grateful for their sorry lot, even though that's what started this mess in the first place."

"Enough of that, Demou," Sun Jian sighed.

Grateful villagers started to gather at the entrance of their home; Cheng Pu looked at the weary, relieved people and smiled sadly, saying, "I just hope we restored their faith in order; all we can hope is that the wretched, insatiable thieves in Luoyang learn some sort of lesson and-"

"*Enough*, Demou," Sun Jian pleaded. "Find some good men to stay here and manage the locals against any stragglers from the enemy army; the rest of us will pincer them and force them to retreat."

Cheng Pu nodded obediently and rode away to find reliable men amongst the infantry.

"So now you want to attack that army of heretics head-on, Brother-in-law," Wu Jing complained.

"Here he goes, whining again," Zu Mao grumbled.

"Let him speak," Sun Jian said. "Go on, Brother-in-law: state your case."

"Rushing at them blindly just seems like madness to me," Wu Jing explained. "Isn't there some other way?"

"Like what?" Sun Jian proposed.

"...Fine," Wu Jing sighed. "You can rely on me to fight. My 'whining' is not from cowardice, but from concern for your well-being. I'll protect you if I must."

Some of the villagers were starting to approach the militia to thank them for their relief efforts: Sun Jian turned to face them and said, "**Go back to your homes! Your safety comes first, and we cannot defend you if you are among us! Save your gifts and words of thanks for later, if at all: what we do, we do for the good of everyone!**"

"**Bless you! Bless you, sir!**" the elderly village chieftain cried. "**Come, everyone! Let's go back! But bless that man! Bless him, and bless them all!**"

Many villagers yelled words of thanks and blessings to Sun Jian's men as they retreated. Zu Mao smiled and said, "You certainly know what to say, Mister Sun Jian. Ever thought of becoming a Magistrate, or an Administrator?"

"I just want this nonsense to end so I can go back to Fuchun and be with my family," Sun Jian replied.

"Not looking for adventure anymore, then...?" Zu Mao teased.

Sun Jian smiled and laughed.

Liu Pi cursed involuntarily when a messenger brought word of Sun Jian's pincer attack on his forces.

"**Why are they aiding the criminals in Luoyang???**" Liu Pi cried. "**Do the men of the south know some wealth and comfort that I've not heard about???**"

"Should we ask help from Brother Huang?" one man asked.

"No!" Liu Pi retorted. "We need no help, Hè Yi! Heaven is with us! We will fight back, and we will show these men that joining us or dying are the only options that Heaven has left for them! **Forward! Push them back!**"

"**That's it! Push them back!**"

Sun Jian had finally found his calling. He was filled with pride as he commanded his militia to press forward against the larger

'Yellow Turban' force that was now beginning to falter. Huang Gai and Han Dang rode into the fray, lancing and swiping the more aggressive acolytes and shooing the timid peasant workers that had been convinced that they should join the rebellion.

"**Go home, you fools!**" Zu Mao bellowed as he rode into a large battalion of Yellow Turban infantry and swiped at the air with his sword.

"**Death to the heathen!**" one defiant Yellow Turban officer shouted; Zu Mao was almost pulled from his horse as a rush of the braver Yellow Turbans assaulted his position.

"I'd better go and help him," Sun Jian said to his emotionally-drained brother-in-law Wu Jing.

"You're *mad!*" Wu Jing complained, but he knew better than to expect that his words would have any impact on Sun Jian's decision.

"**Get away, all of you!**" Sun Jian cried as he rode into the rabble, slashed at the acolytes with his sword, and rescued Zu Mao. Wu Jing followed with a small group of horsemen and aided his brother-in-law and commander as best he could.

"Thanks," Zu Mao panted as Sun Jian escorted him back to the front lines.

The militia were now pushing forward with full strength, having been inspired by the reckless charges of their commanders.

"**Heathens!**" Liu Pi cried as he watched his followers' resolve collapse. "We must chant our master's words again! We must do *something*, else...!"

"Should we ask help from Brother Huang?" Hè Yi asked for a second time.

"...No," Liu Pi replied. "We'll have been pushed back by the time he got here anyway. We must move back, and let these heathens think that they've won. But our day will soon come! Let no one think otherwise!"

Liu Pi's followers were no longer sure.

"Han's mandate has passed! That is true enough! The signs are everywhere!" Liu Pi protested. "Why else would the emperor call on this band of robbers and pirates to save him? Where is his army? These men will soon see that, and they'll hear from the local people, and they'll think again! When we meet again, it will surely be as allies! Next time, they'll wear yellow scarves and fight at our side!"

There were a few murmurs of agreement, but for the Yellow Turbans, the day was lost.

The battle was all but over: Han Dang led the last charge and ensured that he gave his all while the other forces consolidated and Cheng Pu ordered more men to go to the nearby village and reinforce it against further attack.

"And just like that, we won," Zu Mao sighed as he watched the last few skirmishes with Sun Jian.

Sun Jian examined Zu Mao's forehead worriedly, and said, "You got a bit beat up there, my friend. Try and be careful."

"This from a man like *you*...!" Zu Mao said with a hoarse laugh. "But... you have my gratitude, and my life's service, Mister Sun Jian... not many'd risk their life for mine... one day, I hope, I'll be able to do the same."

"Okay, but only if you *live*," Sun Jian joked as he turned to mount his horse.

"Ayah… you want to join the battle again!" Wu Jing realised as he approached Sun Jian. "Let your men do it! Stay where you are!"

"Relax, Brother-in-law," Sun Jian chuckled. "I'm just making myself visible for my men; the day's won, and I'm quite satisfied that I've done enough."

Once the Yellow Turban army had retreated completely, Cheng Pu stopped his horse alongside Sun Jian's to report his feelings on the battle.

"Did we do okay, Demou?" Sun Jian asked.

"We lost about a dozen men, I think, maybe a bit more than that, and of course we had injuries," Cheng Pu reported miserably. "It might have been worse; we killed a lot more of them than they did us, but I suggest we use stratagem next time, since they're led by a slightly smarter head than I expected."

"Agreed; I don't want to lose any more men if I can help it," Sun Jian said as he turned and looked at the nearby corpses of some of the men that he had lost in this first battle with the Yellow Turbans.

"Sorry, but… such is war," Cheng Pu said plainly. "You'll see worse if you have the intention of making this type of thing your life."

"True enough," Sun Jian sighed. "Right, let's see what they have for us."

"I've sent scouts, to ensure the way is clear," Cheng Pu explained. "As soon as they report back, we can advance on their camps and push them northward."

"Very good," Sun Jian replied.

"…Can I suggest something…?" Cheng Pu said suddenly.

"Yes, of course, Cheng Demou! Go on," Sun Jian prompted.

Cheng Pu laughed nervously and said, "Do you *have* to wear that scarf?"

Sun Jian touched the bright red scarf that he wore around his neck and said, "It brings me luck. Why should it be a problem?"

"…It makes you stand out," Cheng Pu suggested.

"And that's a problem, is it…? Won't men recognise it and run…?" Sun Jian joked.

"You're *mad*," Zu Mao said with laughter.

****

5

Over the next few weeks, Sun Jian pushed the Yellow Turban forces away from the regions closest to the northern bank of the Yangtze River and made his way northward, toward the area of Runan in Yu Province that was being defended by his immediate commander, Zhu Jun.

"Those southern men again, come to help the Luoyang dogs," Liu Pi complained as a Yellow Turban scout finished a report. He turned to the rest of the officers in his command tent and added, "Why are they not seeing sense...?"

"They're not as aware of the way things are in Jiangdong, perhaps," Liu Pi's ally Huang Shao suggested as he rubbed his short, scruffy beard.

"The south is worse than the frontier!" Liu Pi complained. "Swamps, hovels, pestilence and poverty! They are the people that our master's words should be resonating most with! Must such men be blinded by false visions, rendered deaf by the speeches of the liars in Luoyang, and-"

"They're our enemy, though, Brother Liu, despite all that you say," Huang Shao interrupted. "They bring their end on themselves, then."

Liu Pi nodded silently.

"They've beat us away from the Great River, and now they're set to join up with the others," Huang Shao noted. "If we don't drive them back this time..."

"...I know," Liu Pi sighed.

"So what do we do?" Huang Shao asked. "Do we ask Brother Bo Cai to send us more help?"

"He needs every man he has to keep the rest of our heathen enemies from gaining ground," Liu Pi replied. "I wouldn't ask, and he couldn't offer."

"So we'll meet the southerners together," Huang Shao said.

"...Yes," Liu Pi replied miserably.

Sun Jian and Cheng Pu arranged their men and gave instructions to the other militia leaders before they marched against a ready Yellow Turban force that was camped between them and the forces of their commander Zhu Jun. Liu Pi and Huang Shao inspired a typical round of chanting, but Sun Jian's men were used to – and perhaps a little tired of – the Yellow Turbans' mantra by now, and did not react in any way.

"**Thoughts...?**" Sun Jian asked of Cheng Pu.

Before Cheng Pu could reply, Han Dang said, "**Just this once, I'm going to complain that I am sick of fighting these people.**"

"**Aren't we all?**" Zu Mao suggested.

"**There are several points in their lines that we can exploit,**" Cheng Pu shouted over the din. "**Might I...?**"

"**He asked, didn't he, Mister Strategist...?**" Zu Mao chuckled. "**So what are we doing?**"

"**Huang Gai, Zu Mao, Han Dang, attack where their lines are thinnest,**" Cheng Pu continued. "**Begin with hit-and-run tactics, but if they buckle as I expect them to, lead men**

deep into their lines and scatter them from within. Commander Sun, Wu Jing, I wonder if opportunities might not arise for a direct attack on their leaders... if we can find them among that mess."

Sun Jian and Wu Jing agreed with Cheng Pu's analysis, and had men pass orders to other officers in the battle lines.

The Yellow Turbans were the first to charge, but Sun Jian's militia dispersed the Turban infantry with ease. The Yellow Turbans then started to fire on the Han lines with arrows, but they had few trained archers, so many of the arrows fell short of their targets. Huang Gai and Han Dang then made their first charge, following Cheng Pu's suggestion that the Turban lines should be attacked where they were thinnest. The Turbans reeled as men resorted to instinct and failed to help others if it avoided risking their own survival; their captains ordered the lines to remain as formed as possible, but once the second Han attack on the weak points began, the chance of maintaining order collapsed completely.

"**Do we retreat?**" Huang Shao asked of the silent, mortified Liu Pi.

Sun Jian's infantry burrowed deep into the Yellow Turban lines, and without an array being used to trap those infiltrators, the Yellow Turban forces were doomed to collapse.

"**Do we retreat???**" Huang Shao shrieked, but Liu Pi could not find the words to respond. Some of his more devout followers had started to chant again, but many of the people that had joined the cause out of frustration – and there were more of them than there were true acolytes – were surrendering or fleeing as the situation worsened for them.

"...**RETREAT!**" Huang Shao ordered, and the order was gratefully obeyed.

"Another 'victory'," the gore-covered Sun Jian said half-heartedly.

"More fled than died this time," Cheng Pu suggested. "We–"

"All the same, corpses are corpses," Sun Jian retorted. "Every one of them, ours or theirs, is a life wasted. And where are our friends?"

"I'm sure that they're fine," Cheng Pu said.

"**Ayah! Look at you, Brother-in-law!**" Wu Jing cried as he rode toward the two leaders. "**You sent me to do worthless business so you could endanger your life again! I should have known that-!**"

"**Ah, here are Huang Gongfu and Han Yigong!**" Sun Jian said as he saw Huang Gai and Han Dang approaching on horseback. "**It's good to see that they are unscathed.**"

"And here is Zu Mao," Cheng Pu announced as he looked in another direction.

The six allies met and exchanged respectful bows from atop their horses.

Han Dang laughed gratefully, gestured toward Huang Gai, and said, "This man here saved me from an early grave. His next jar of wine is on me."

The ensemble laughed cheerfully.

"Your ideas were sound, Cheng Demou," Huang Gai said politely.

"Thanks, Gongfu," Cheng Pu replied awkwardly. "I was worried that I might be wrong... if they'd been feigning the disorganisation, then-"

"They *weren't*, which you guessed correctly," Han Dang said reassuringly.

"Quite right," Sun Jian said as he urged his horse to begin a journey back to the camp. "For now, let's rest... we've done a lot today."

"*Yes*, and you nearly got yourself *killed*, *as usual*!" Wu Jing scolded as he rode after Sun Jian. "Look at the state of you! What would my sister say if-"

"Does she even need to know?" Sun Jian countered.

"Does she even need to be *told*???" Wu Jing retorted. "I warned her that it would be pointless! You were never going to listen to me!"

Sun Jian sighed wearily, while his friends laughed at his demeanour.

The way was clear for Sun Jian's forces to advance and meet with Zhu Jun: they hurried northward and found the Han camp – a vast, fenced sea of tents and observation towers – under siege by a small army of Yellow Turbans that was quickly scattered by the two allied forces.

"So Sun Wentai is here!" Zhu Jun said with satisfaction as Sun Jian brought his men into the Han encampment. The commander met Sun Jian in person and brought him to the command tent to speak with him about their future manoeuvres.

"So that's Zhu Jun," Cheng Pu said to Huang Gai as the two men watched their own leader being led away by the famous Han commander. "He looks ordinary."

"I wasn't expecting much from a court-appointed officer," Huang Gai replied. "But he is friendly and courteous enough."

"...A valid point," Cheng Pu conceded. "And his endorsement of Wentai is why we're here at all, so... yes, I will say no more."

Once Sun Jian and Zhu Jun were seated in the latter's personal tent, Sun Jian said, "Your base is impressive."

"Only in that it has kept the wolves from the door," Zhu Jun replied as he gestured to an assistant, who immediately started to prepare dishes of wine for the two officers.

"Wentai, you have done extremely well so far," Zhu Jun praised. "The rebels were looking to start a southern campaign, but thanks to you – amongst others, yes, but mainly you – they are stymied, and we have our first victory over them."

"But they are very powerful in this area," Sun Jian noted. "Is there a plan for dealing with them in any particular way...?"

"Commander Huangfu and I are starting to wonder if our current strategy of engaging them in Jing and Yu simultaneously was not the right way to go," Zhu Jun admitted. "North of here, Cao Cao is doing a magnificent job of keeping Yingchuan City from the rebels, but as for Nan County, in Jing Province... Commander Huangfu cannot hope to save Nan County right now. Zhang Mancheng, the rebel leader there, has outmanoeuvred him several times, and has a force three times the size of his. Only Wan City resists with any effectiveness, and that will fall eventually."

"...So you are wondering if the best move would be for Commander Huangfu to abandon Nan County for now, and concentrate all efforts on helping you to save this province from going the same way as Nan County," Sun Jian supposed.

"That is correct," Zhu Jun replied. "If we can secure Yu Province, we reduce their communications routes considerably; their northern effort in Ji and Yòu Provinces will be less coordinated with the effort in Nan County, and that may help us."

"Well, I'm yours to command," Sun Jian said calmly. "Wherever I'm needed, just tell me and I'll go."

"You are too modest, Wentai," Zhu Jun suggested. "A man like you should be leading men, not following them all the time."

"Alas, I am not of the rank to expect such things... and to be honest, I'm happier following orders, so long as they're sound," Sun Jian replied quietly.

"...Right, well, I'll order a meeting to discuss the plan properly," Zhu Jun said thoughtfully. "It's good to have you here, Sun Wentai; I think we're that little bit closer to winning now."

"You should say such things when I have proven experience and a proven reputation, Commander Zhu," Sun Jian sighed. He then bowed respectfully and departed so that Zhu Jun could plan his upcoming meeting.

As spring gave way to summer, Huangfu Song abandoned the western front at Nan County as expected and joined Zhu Jun in Runan, in Yu Province. With these additional militias, the Han imperial force almost matched the size of the enemy force, which meant that a concentrated campaign against the rebels in Yu Province could now begin.

The important city of Yingchuan in northern Yu Province had been protected from the rebel forces by a coalition of militias led by Cao Cao, the son of a wealthy politician and appointed marquis. For any campaign to liberate the province to work, the rebels had to be removed from the area around this city, which was close to a natural route that led to several places, including the capital Luoyang. Huangfu Song and Zhu Jun moved the camp closer to Yingchuan once their soldiers were organised, a move that was watched with interest by the Yellow Turban commander in Yu Province, Bo Cai.

The mood was changing on both sides, since the messengers from the northern front were bringing unsubstantiated rumours that Zhang Jue – the founder of the 'Way of Peace', and leader of the Yellow Turban Rebellion – was dead, and that his two brothers were under heavy siege. But Bo Cai refused to alter his countenance, and the assaults on Yu Province continued.

Once they were ready, the two Han commanders – Huangfu Song and Zhu Jun – summoned their officers to explain the strategy for the coming weeks. Sun Jian observed the two leaders quietly, but he was aware that there were many resentful stares being aimed in his direction. When the meeting was over, Sun Jian quietly prepared to leave the meeting and return to his small camp to pass on the orders to his subordinates. He expected no friendly conversation, so he was startled when a voice said, "That red scarf... might you be Sun Jian of Fuchun...?"

"Ah... *Cao Cao*, the hero of Yingchuan," Sun Jian hailed as Cao Cao approached him. Cao was fairly tall and had strong features that bore elements of cynicism and mischief. He was, however, quite serious on this occasion, and returned Sun Jian's polite bow without hesitation.

"Your spirited actions in Runan are the talk of the forces," Cao Cao suggested. "I am most impressed by what I have heard about you."

"I have chased away a few men from some battlefields, while you have defended a besieged position against heavy odds," Sun Jian replied. "We have both served well, I think."

Cao Cao bowed once again, and said, "You are most generous. ...I hear that the plan upon the relief of Yingchuan is to announce a second divergence of forces... one commander to go north to Ji, the other, west to Nan County. Others will follow one or the other of them, of course."

"Where will *you* go...?" Sun Jian asked.

"North," Cao Cao replied immediately. "...Oh, well, if I am required to go west, of course I shall go west! ...But my preference is north, to aid Hè Jin against Zhang Jue's followers there."

"Once it is all over, I expect that we can see an end to any coordination, though an end to the chaos may be a little too much to ask for," Sun Jian said.

"I quite agree," Cao Cao replied with a sad smile. "But take heart in the fact that the desperate rebels here in Yingchuan are coalescing for one great battle for Yu."

"A battle that we will win, I think," Sun Jian retorted.

Cao Cao smirked, bowed respectfully and said, "I look forward to our future meetings, Sun Wentai: you're a man with much left to do."

Sun Jian returned the bow and said, "You're too kind," whereupon Cao Cao retreated to join his followers. Sun Jian pondered the encounter, hummed thoughtfully, and left the command tent amid further contemptuous stares from other northern militia leaders.

"Aha! Here he is," Han Dang said as Sun Jian entered the militia's command tent. "So what's the plan, then, Lord Sun?"

"Our main enemy is Bo Cai," Sun Jian said to his assembled officers. "He is currently based close to Yingchuan, which should be our first target. We'll be in charge of attacking the right flank of his army while others engage him directly."

"Tell us something we *don't know*," Zu Mao complained quietly.

"Hush," Cheng Pu ordered. "He means well."

"Methinks you misunderstand Mister Zu, Cheng Demou," Han Dang chuckled. "I think he refers to the real glory belonging to others as usual, despite the fact that we're obviously the most successful militia and therefore most likely to score a victory...?"

"Cao Cao deserves to have the glory," Sun Jian suggested. "After all, he's been forced to watch his men charge and fall against Bo Cai for quite a while with no success to speak of; all we've done is chase away a few rootless bands on various roads, and–"

"That's not a way to build morale," Cheng Pu scolded. "We've fought armies up to three times the size of our own and won with minimal losses. Give us a siege and we'll break it."

"...I'm showing civility toward Cao Cao," Sun Jian sighed. "But will you–"

"What for...?" Zu Mao scoffed. "And why do that at our expense...? Let's just prepare for our small role in what's to come, and stop making giants out of other men just to feel like we're noble."

"...Can I finish...?" Sun Jian pleaded. "There's a grand plan, and perhaps our efficiency is why we're on the right flank... there was an officer called Qu Yi that they've put in charge of strategy, and-"

"He's a veteran of the unrest against the northern tribes," Cheng Pu recalled. "Oh, well; at least they've seen sense and appointed a decent campaign adviser."

"...I will finish if it kills me," Sun Jian chortled. "The plan is to lure them into an assault, and..."

A few days passed before the plan was put into motion. The Han forces left their individual camps and approached the Yellow Turbans, who immediately deployed a large force to obstruct them. Zhu Jun and Huangfu Song took up the rear of the forces, although they ensured that their battle standards were visible to the enemy. The Yellow Turbans were aware of the defeats that Huangfu Song had suffered in Nan County, however, so they heckled the Han forces with cursing chants.

"News that their master is dead ain't hurt 'em none," Zu Mao scoffed. **"P'raps they know something we don't."**

"We know more than them," Sun Jian said as he turned and looked at Qu Yi, who was more impressive than his masters as he held his powerful northern thoroughbred steady with the reins in his right hand and kept a strong grip on a field lance with his left; his armour glistened in the sun and compensated for his drab battle standard and lack of designated subordinates. Though none could see it, Qu Yi was smiling: the day was as good as won, and he knew it.

The Yellow Turban commander, Bo Cai, rode his scruffy brown steed to the front line: he wore a scuffed battle helmet with a crudely-conceived yellow plume protruding from its top, and his armour was as simple as his followers to show solidarity with them. His hard features were all but obscured, but like Qu Yi, he was smiling: he had the numerical advantage, and victory seemed to be certain. Huang Shao held the left flank, and Liu Pi held the right; the few horsemen amongst the throng were pacing and hollering while the infantry inanely recited their supposedly-deceased master's sixteen-word slogan.

"Well, if Zhang Jue wanted his words to outlive him, he got what he wanted," Zu Mao suggested. **"Are we going to attack, or are we waiting for them to charge first?"**

"That's up to the commanders," Cheng Pu replied.

Sun Jian looked to his left: Han Dang was ready. He then turned his gaze rightward: Huang Gai was ready as well. All that was needed was a sign from the commanders, and Sun Jian was secretly as impatient as everyone else. The chanting continued and the morale of the enemy built steadily, but the commanders did nothing. Minutes passed, and the Han coalition's morale started to falter as the unified voice of the tens of thousands of Yellow Turbans filled their minds and hearts with fear and doubt. It seemed to be what Bo Cai had been waiting for: he ordered a charge, and the Yellow Turban infantry surged forward. Huangfu Song's men retreated before the enemy reached them: that sent shockwaves through the Han forces and led to some desertions.

"**Bloody fools!**" Cheng Pu cried. "**What sort of plan is this???**"

"**It isn't what I was told,**" Sun Jian realised. "**Alright, we'll have to improvise.**"

"***Improvise*? Sod that: we have to retreat!**" Zu Mao said. "**We can't fight an army ten times the size of ours!**"

Zhu Jun's men were starting to buckle under the pressure of Bo Cai's assault: within a short time the entire Han force was retreating, including Sun Jian's indignant followers.

The fighting continued, on and off, for many hours: the Yellow Turbans chased the Han forces ever more southward, despite concerns that there might be some trap awaiting them. Bo Cai would hear no dissent: he was certain that the disorganised loyalists had finally become as exhausted as their emperor's mandate to govern. The chase continued to the outskirts of a wood, which the Han forces retreated into.

"We'll burn them out!" Bo Cai chuckled as he observed the scene. "We'll fetch some- …What???"

The front lines were panicking: something was wrong. Bo Cai could not see or hear the problem at first, since the random chants and murmurings of his army had deafened him to the whistling of arrows: suddenly, fire was everywhere, and chants became screams of agony. Flammable liquids and fats had been smeared on the roads as the Han had retreated, but the Yellow turbans had mistaken the slippery terrain for plain mud from recent heavy rain: flaming arrows ignited the ground and any rebel that they touched, and once the panic had started to spread, so did the fire. Bo Cai's vanguard was quickly decimated, and Bo Cai himself was reported to have fallen during an attempted retreat. A second force of men caught the retreating Yellow Turbans in a pincer and increased the fatalities considerably: within an hour, bodies littered the ground and the Han forces were completely victorious.

"**Curse them! Curse them all!**" the Yellow Turban officer Liu Pi cried as he fled the battle with a reduced contingent and his ally Huang Shao. They were now two of many leaders of the scattered rebel forces in Yu Province, but the uprising would not regain Yingchuan.

"**Go on, run, you heretics and bumpkins!**" Zhu Jun bellowed as he rode to the front lines to join the pursuit of the defeated enemy. "**Go back to your hamlets, and reject this unholy nonsense!**"

Sun Jian looked at the mass of bodies and groaned painfully.

"A waste, indeed," Wu Jing agreed.

"They're retreating… all of them," Cheng Pu reported as he regrouped with Sun Jian, Wu Jing and Zu Mao. "Scouts say they're mostly heading southward, to Xihua."

"But this was their grand plan?" Sun Jian exclaimed. "To lure the poor fools into a fire trap and burn them to death…? A simple battle at Yingchuan would have been more merciful and sensible than this!"

"But we might have died," Wu Jing suggested. "This way, the rebels had the most casualties. It may be 'dishonourable', Brother-in-law… but it's also pragmatic."

"...Yes," Sun Jian sighed.

"And now, it's on to Xihua, I suppose," Zu Mao prompted.

"That's... up to Zhu Jun," Sun Jian said as he watched his commander and patron's continued pursuit of the ambush survivors. The entire outcome had left Sun Jian feeling very uncomfortable and praying for a swift end to a campaign that had already gone on for far too long.

****

6

Huangfu Song's ambush had left the Yellow Turbans of Yu Province without a local leader, and the end of that part of the rebellion was apparently within sight. Tens of thousands of demoralised Yellow Turbans gathered at Xihua and prepared to face the Han coalition army that was marching on their position. Huangfu Song and Zhu Jun were at the front of the army this time and ensured that the rebels could plainly see what they were up against. Platoons of archers and crossbowmen readied their weapons, and hordes of infantry and cavalry impatiently awaited the order to charge. Sun Jian's militia was with the attacking force, this time in a vanguard role.

"**What d'you think, Mister Cheng Pu?**" Zu Mao asked.

"**Once again, I see weak points,**" Cheng Pu replied with amusement. "**In fact, the whole of their army is just one big giant weak point now... no leader, no organisation, no morale, and no energy. One big push will break them.**"

The senior Yellow Turban officers, Liu Pi and Huang Shao, rode to the front of their disorganised army of peasant infantry and issued a flat, resigned order to charge; minutes later, the two forces met, and the organised Han loyalist forces ripped into what was left of the enemy.

"**Everyone, forward!**" Zhu Jun ordered with surprising discomfort.

Huangfu Song joined his colleague and shouted, "**Scatter them, quickly, before they are reinforced!**"

"**Reinforced???**" Cheng Pu exclaimed.

"**There must be another army coming here,**" Wu Jing supposed.

"**Then the commander is right!**" Cheng Pu decided. "**If we scatter this force, the second one will withdraw!**"

Sun Jian nodded and rode into the fray once again to face the enemy personally.

"Oh, *for*...!" Wu Jing complained. "**COME BACK, YOU MAD...!**"

"**Actually, we should join him, Wu Jing!**" Cheng Pu said through laughter.

The whole of Sun Jian's militia advanced – along with most of the Han force as a whole – and ploughed into the Yellow Turban army: their efforts disintegrated it completely. Sun Jian took care to spare any women, youths or obvious non-acolytes as he moved, but he slayed several men as he rode deeper and deeper into their collapsing ranks; Zu Mao and Wu Jing followed him quietly and protected the reckless commander from any attacks that he could not anticipate. Suddenly, word spread amongst the ranks of both armies that the second reinforcement army had been routed as it advanced; the remainder of the Yellow Turbans' morale disappeared, and they scattered in all directions. The leaders of the last stand against the Han – Liu Pi and Huang Shao – gathered a large number of their demoralised followers and fled to the northeast.

"**Hè Yi...? Where is Hè Yi's division???**" Liu Pi asked.

"**He went west,**" Huang Shao reported. "**I hope our 'brother' survives!**"

"Surely we should fight to the death!" one junior officer pleaded.
"That isn't what the Great Teacher would want, Hè Man," Liu Pi retorted. **"Teacher Zhang would want us to live to fight another day... and we will."**

"Well done, everyone!" Sun Jian said as his followers gathered around him to watch the Yellow Turbans retreat. **"We were all separated there for a while, but it's nice to see every made it back."**
"Yes, and once again you charged into the thick of it!" Wu Jing scolded.
"Didn't Cao Cao, and our commanders...?" Sun Jian retorted. "This was a critical battle, Brother-in-law: all or nothing."
"...Alright, yes," Wu Jing conceded.
"And don't think that I didn't notice you and Zu Mao covering my back," Sun Jian continued. "For all your whining, you're as brave as any other man here... you worry too much, but that's not really a fault in a sane world."
"A pity, then, that we don't live in one," Zu Mao said with a sigh. "So is it over here in Yu Province, then, d'you reckon...?"
"Some have actually surrendered; others are fleeing to the hills, while others are retreating westward toward the Jing border, probably to join the last resistance around Wan City in Nan County," Cheng Pu reported as he clutched his arm.
"You're hurt, Demou," Sun Jian prompted.
"Not seriously," Cheng Pu insisted. "Anyway, listen: Wan's well-fortified; any man's going to have trouble with those defences. Any ideas, in case we're asked to join that mission...?"
"Siege...?" Zu Mao supposed. "Mind you, that'd be costly... and take a long time."
Suddenly, a voice shouted, **"Mister Sun!"**
Sun Jian, Wu Jing, Cheng Pu and Zu Mao turned to face Commander Zhu Jun, who was riding toward them with three of his staff and three militiamen.
"...Brilliant," Zhu Jun chuckled. "This is easily the fastest, least costly rout that anyone could have expected. You're naturals, and could certainly chase these fools down without anyone looking over your shoulder."
"You are most kind," Sun Jian said as he bowed slightly.
"All that's left is Nan County, now," Zhu Jun continued. "I was hoping that you might join me there, Wentai. Is that something reasonable to ask...?"
"I will go where you feel I am most needed, Commander Zhu," Sun Jian replied.
"Very good; I expect nothing but victory, then!" Zhu Jun chuckled. "The Heavens are with you; truly, you are the progeny of Sun Tzu, for it can be nothing else!"
The group exchanged bows, and Zhu Jun retreated with his entourage.
"That's an incredible compliment," Cheng Pu noted.
"He complimented us *all*," Sun Jian replied.
"You're a rising star, Mister Sun Jian," Zu Mao suggested.
"Oh, *nonsense*...!" Sun Jian chortled. "You all know how it is: we'll get some rice, perhaps a bit of silk and gold, if we're lucky;

officials with contacts, and the commanders, of course, will get the real rewards. I'm doing this because it's the right thing to do-"
"And it proves who you are," Zu Mao suggested further.
"...That too," Sun Jian admitted. "...Yes, that too. But enough of this: their rear guard has retreated, and our scouts are returning, which means we'll get a full report on possible traps and ambushes. Once we know the road is clear-"
"It's on to the west, to *Nan County*," Cheng Pu noted.
"All of you are free to turn back if you feel that is too far from home," Sun Jian said kindly. "I feel that I owe a debt of gratitude to Commander Zhu for offering me this opportunity, but-"
"S'an opportunity for us *all*, Mister Sun Jian," Zu Mao interrupted. "Consider me a barnacle on your backside until this is done and dusted."
Sun Jian laughed at the notion.
"I'd describe myself in less derogatory terms, but I'm with you as well," Cheng Pu chuckled.
"As am I," Huang Gai said. "I want to do my part."
"I'm looking forward to being a part of ending the chaos," Han Dang agreed.
"And I'm not letting you out of my sight," Wu Jing scolded.
Sun Jian laughed again, and said, "Our path is set then, gentlemen! Soon, we'll be going to Jing Province!"

There would be one last battle in Yu Province before the inevitable move west: Liu Pi and Huang Shao had been followed by scouts, and the Han commanders were keen to bring an end to their resistance before reallocating their forces elsewhere. Sun Jian's men were assigned to the task, and they journeyed to the hills that now served as Liu Pi's base. Once a small camp was established, Sun Jian and his officers travelled to the foot of the hills to reconnoitre.
"It occurs to me that we've fought the leader of this lot quite a few times before," Han Dang said.
"We have," Huang Gai replied. "Liu Pi and Huang Shao were commanding the men we fought on the way to Yingchuan."
"So defeating these two is important," Han Dang suggested.
"Defeating... but not killing," Sun Jian said. "Let's not make any more martyrs."
"But if they don't surrender, we won't have a choice," Han Dang proposed.
"...We must give them a choice," Cheng Pu said. "Lord Sun is right: these two have been gathering new followers and making this all a lot harder. People like them: we must publicly crush their will to fight so that others will stop fighting too."
"So then we'll just sit here and let them come to us," Sun Jian decided.
"Uh... they have the high ground, so we weren't really going to do anything else but let them come to us, Lord Sun," Cheng Pu chuckled nervously. "Or did you really intend to charge up there...?"
"I'd have certainly tried it: they wouldn't expect me to, so I'd have the element of surprise on my side," Sun Jian retorted.
"*Ayah*... this is why I whinge!" Wu Jing cried. "I followed you into battle at Xihua, but if you want to charge uphill at these heretics,

then you can do it on your own!"
Sun Jian laughed and replied, "Alright."

Sun Jian's militia was joined by two others, and the resulting blockade left the Yellow Turbans with no way to secure food. Local villagers were either reluctant to show support to the defeated rebels or never supported them in the first place, so it was only a matter of time before Liu Pi and Huang Shao – despite protests from some of their more devout followers – decided to surrender.
"We can't do that!" one officer protested.
"We have to, Shen," Liu Pi insisted.
"We rose up against oppression by the wicked emperor and his heathen ways!" the official Hè Man said. "Teacher Zhang promised us a future where all would be prosperous! We have to keep fighting!"
"What good is a 'prosperous future for all', Hè Man, when we're all *dead*?" Liu Pi replied.
"...That... may be right," Hè Man said.
"It is," Liu Pi insisted. "The only way for our great cause to survive now is to feign surrender, pledge allegiance to their emperor again and-"
"**We would be defying the will of Heaven!**" a third officer cried. "**I say that we fight!**"
A dozen of the other officers agreed: they ignored Liu Pi, Huang Shao and Hè Man's pleas and led a small force of like-minded acolytes down the hill and to certain death.

"What a... what a waste," Han Dang said as he looked down at a defiant young woman that was close to death; he looked at his bloodied sword and tried to reconcile the truth behind his actions.
"We had no choice," Cheng Pu insisted.
Han Dang then turned his gaze to the corpse of a young man and added, "I don't know whether I can do this anymore. It's harming me, Demou."
"I can't say I'm enjoying this anymore than you are," Cheng Pu said as he looked at some of his own victims. "But... but as I said, we had no choice. We *have no choice*."
"**Hold up!**" Zu Mao cried. "**S'another lot coming, I think!**"
Han Dang, Huang Gai and Wu Jing groaned as one: Sun Jian steeled himself for more futile bloodshed and said, "We'll do what we must."
But the second wave of Yellow Turbans was not coming down the hill to fight: they carried no weapons, and many of them were removing their offending yellow headwear as a sign that the battle was over.
"Oh, thank goodness...!" Huang Gai whispered.
"**ENOUGH!**" Liu Pi bellowed. "**Enough... your beloved emperor has won.**"
Zu Mao scowled and shouted, "**We didn't do it for the bloody-!**"
"Hush," Sun Jian ordered.
Liu Pi, Huang Shao and the other surrendered Yellow Turbans were visibly disturbed by the sight of their dead comrades, but none of them contributed any opinions. Instead, Liu Pi threw his turban to the ground, fell to one knee and said, "We're ready to face your emperor's justice."

Most of the other rebels threw or dropped their own turbans to the ground and fell to one knee in reluctant penitence.

"...Alright," Sun Jian sighed. "We'll escort you to the main camp. It isn't up to us to decide what to do with you, it's-"

"**You decided what to do to *them*!**" Hè Man said as he gestured at the corpses of his allies.

"...They decided that for us, and you know it," Sun Jian replied uneasily. "Commander Zhu Jun and Commander Huangfu Song will decide your fate: I'm just a soldier following orders. Rise and follow us, please."

Liu Pi got to his feet, and his allies quickly followed. The journey back to the main camp was silent and sombre as every man and woman present pondered the lasting outcome of the events in Yu Province: others remained behind to give some form of respectful burial to those that had fallen in battle. The discarded yellow scarves were gathered in a sack that one quiet soldier carried: many thought that they would be ceremonially disposed of as a sign to others, but none could be sure.

"You did another amazing job, Wentai," Zhu Jun said as he shared wine with Sun Jian in his personal tent a day later. "Liu Pi and Huang Shao have agreed to cease hostilities and urge others to do the same... for those two to have capitulated is a victory indeed! Already, dozens have handed themselves over for peaceful judgement and burned their turbans! Yu Province is a positive message to the rest of the country."

"...I did little to be praised for, Commander," Sun Jian replied. "I fought when I was told to, retreated when I was told to... the other militias have as great a role to play in things, and they've all achieved great things."

"Your tone leaves little to the imagination," Zhu Jun said. "You're angry at the amount of 'civilian' casualties. Your men are upset at having to kill 'ordinary people'."

Sun Jian nodded silently.

"What's an 'ordinary person'...?" Zhu Jun asked. "A man is a man: is he suddenly transformed from an 'ordinary person' into a farmer because he picks up a rake, or a soldier because he picks up a sword...? We're all men or women. The men and women that chose to fight alongside the Yellow Turbans did so for reasons and excuses that I neither know nor care for. They rose up against *their own people*. Didn't you have to save a village or two full of 'ordinary people' from the Yellow Turbans on the way here...?"

"That's precisely why I didn't turn around and go home," Sun Jian admitted. "I did think about it when I heard about the eunuchs in Luoyang, about the corruption in the local administrations, about the poor, about the famine, when I thought about my own region... every thought led to me thinking 'Go home' until I saw that they were harming people in the name of saving them."

"And when I return to court, Wentai, I swear to you that no matter what it costs me, I'm going to confront those evil eunuchs and their corrupt, destructive allies face-to-face," Zhu Jun replied. "I will petition until my hands seize up from writing, shout until my voice cracks, and cry for the injustices they've caused until my eyes bleed... so will Huangfu Song, Lu Zhi, Yuan Shao, Cao Cao and the multitude of other great men that still have places at

court."
"I'd lend my own voice willingly, but I won't have a place in your court, will I...?" Sun Jian retorted.
"...Probably not, no," Zhu Jun admitted. "I'll certainly petition for you to receive rewards for your service, but I'll be honest, you'll be lucky if they partially reimburse you for your outlays, especially if I'm slandered for challenging the eunuchs."
That's more important," Sun Jian insisted. "Even if it means I get nothing, fighting the 'Ten Attendants' is more important than anything. If they are not removed from the court, this will all happen again."
A messenger entered the tent before Zhu Jun could reply and said, "The officers are gathered for the meeting, Commander."
"...I should go, then," Sun Jian said as Zhu Jun dismissed the soldier. "I'll leave you to prepare for your entrance."
"My thanks, Wentai, for everything," Zhu Jun replied.

Huangfu Song and Zhu Jun had decided to convene one last joint officer's meeting in Yu Province to announce their next moves; Sun Jian left his would-be-benefactor and journeyed to the command tent, where a host of other officers – including the infamous Cao Cao – were waiting patiently. Sun Jian joined his peers, and after a short time, the two commanders arrived to begin their announcement.
"We need to divide our forces now and deal with these last two problems that face us," Huangfu Song explained. "I shall go north and aid Hè Jin in defeating the Yellow Turbans in Ji and Yòu Provinces. While recent reports suggest that Zhang Bao and Zhang Liang have rightly joined their wretched brother in the netherworld, we can be sure of nothing."
"But Zhang Jue is dead...?" Cao Cao prompted.
"His head has been put on display for all to see in Julu, and it has been confirmed that it is he," Huangfu Song promised. "That monster is now very dead."
The militia leaders expressed their relief.
"But his brothers may still live," Zhu Jun noted. "One or both of them might have fled southward, to aid the frustratingly resistant forces in Wan. We'll know more soon, we hope. But Hè Jin has requested help, and Commander Huangfu has volunteered to go north. I, therefore, shall go west to Nan County, and help to aid the relief of Wan. Of course, that means that you gentlemen will need to divide and accompany us; I request Mister Sun Jian's assistance at Wan, if that is not being presumptuous."
Huangfu Song laughed and said, "I will not argue, Commander Zhu."

"Jing Province..."
Cheng Pu pondered the move as he shared heated wine with Sun Jian in the latter's tent on that same evening.
"The Yellow Turbans in Jing Province are no worse an enemy than the ones in Yu were," Sun Jian proposed.
"Ah, but they differ in one way," Cheng Pu retorted. "They've got the advantage of holding Wan City. A smaller, weaker force of men held the place against them for a long time... so how can we hope to uproot them any time soon...?"

"I vowed to my family that I would be home quickly, and I intend to keep that vow," Sun Jian replied. "I promised the men that this campaign would be quick; I will make it quick if it is at all within my power. I have no intention of letting Jing be our burial ground, Demou. We're going to kill the ones that are lost, and save the ones that can be saved, and then we're going home."

"Do me a favour," Cheng Pu said. "In fact, do me two favours: firstly, tell that to the men tomorrow. Secondly... run it past me again. I'm hoping it'll help me get through this myself."

"We'll be fine," Sun Jian promised. "I just know it: we'll be fine."

****

7

Zhu Jun and Sun Jian led the march toward Nan County in Jing Province, clearing any small pockets of resistance and attempts at ambuscades as they went. But the situation started to change as soon as they reached the area around Wan City, which was now the last remaining stronghold of the Yellow Turbans in the west. Once the force reached the Han camp in Nan County, Zhu Jun journeyed to the main command tent to relieve the officers there while Sun Jian assembled his small group of trusted aides for a private conference.

"Wan City is, as Cheng Demou said, considerably fortified," Huang Gai noted miserably. "We cannot hope to siege this place without massive losses."

"Perhaps we can try something," Sun Jian said thoughtfully.

"No!" Wu Jing scolded. "Anything you want to try is always dangerous!"

"But we could end up being here for months, perhaps a year or more, if we don't try *something*!" Sun Jian protested.

"Alright: like what…?" Wu Jing asked bluntly.

"…I didn't say I had an idea, I meant that we should try and think of one," Sun Jian replied eventually. "If I think of one, dear brother-in-law, then I'll propose it."

But no suggestions were made that could be adopted, and the siege of Wan – and the battles around Nan County that inevitably accompanied that siege – took their toll on the Han forces.

Day after day, the siege consisted of sending armies of brave men with tall and flexible wooden ladders to the dry moat around Wan City while archers provided nominal cover. The defenders would pelt the ladder bearers with stones and arrows as they approached the moat and placed their ladders over the moat to cross; the men would have to crawl along the wobbling ladder, all the while hoping that they were not hit by some projectile while they were completely exposed and defenceless. Any that made it across the moat – and many did not – would then face the second stage of the gauntlet. The same ladders would be lifted and moved to the walls of the city, so that the soldiers could climb. Once again, they faced projectiles, but in addition, the defenders might be able to push the ladders away from the walls, roll larger rocks off of the battlements or pour hot liquids like oil or water onto the men as they climbed. A lone climber might have some small defence in the form of flipping the ladder, such that they were underneath it as certain obstacles passed their position, but that did little to save them from boiling oil or heavy rocks that broke the ladder under their enormous weight. The result of this tactic was cruel attrition, pure and simple; it was hoped that the defenders ran out of deterrents before the sieging army ran out of men and ladders.

At the same time, existing and newly-arriving Yellow Turban forces would engage the Han army outside Wan, giving the defenders relief and pressing the already overtaxed loyalist army further. The land battles were less costly than the siege efforts, but they were costly nonetheless. And without the option of other siege tactics, such as siege towers and sappers to tunnel into the city, the Han forces were starting to lose morale. Months went by, and Zhu Jun was quickly running out of supplies and inspiration.

"Wentai, I am at a loss," Zhu Jun admitted as he sat in private conference with Sun Jian in the command tent one evening. "I am close to asking Commander Huangfu to come here and support me, as he did in Yu."
"But all in all, the problem is Wan City, not the battles around it," Sun Jian proposed. "The reason that Commander Huangfu was so successful in Yu – if you'll forgive my apparently dismissing his efforts, for that is not my intention – is because the rebels did not have complete control of Yingchuan or any other major city. Indeed the reason that this province was not regained sooner by us, or lost to them earlier, was because Wan held out for so long."
"I had the same idea, and am glad that we agree on it," Zhu Jun said agreeably. "But Wan is theirs now, and only a sustained siege can break it. But how many more months before we break ourselves...?"
"A shock tactic is needed," Sun Jian decided.
"...By which you mean *what*, Wentai...?" Zhu Jun asked cautiously. "What design do you have for ending this siege so quickly, when we are stuck with the same old solutions to the same old problem...?"
"...Do you trust me?" Sun Jian asked in response.
"Of course," Zhu Jun insisted. "...Wait a moment... are you going to try some sort of madness...?"
Sun Jian smiled sheepishly and said, "I do not consider my plan to be 'madness', rather a tactic that will be unexpected and therefore highly likely to succeed."
Zhu Jun sighed and replied, "I am at a loss, as I said, so if you have a plan, then by all means go ahead and try it. But do not endanger your life needlessly, Sun Wentai; you are a valued pillar of the state."
Sun Jian bowed slightly and said, "I will do all I can to deliver victory, Commander."

Sun Jian returned to his tent, where he was greeted by cynical and disapproving faces; Wu Jing, Cheng Pu, Huang Gai and Han Dang were all visibly worried, while Zu Mao was apparently enjoying the whole affair.
"...What...?" Sun Jian chuckled nervously.
"Reconsider this plan, Brother-in-law," Wu Jing ordered.
Sun Jian looked at Cheng Pu with disappointment and said, "It was a suggestion, *nothing more*. Why did you–"
"Suggestions are suggestions; this is a plan in motion," Cheng Pu scolded. "Sun Wentai, I really cannot approve of it."
"Neither can I," Huang Gai said miserably. "Such recklessness!"
"I admire your bravery, but this is not a task for you," Han Dang suggested.
Sun Jian turned to Zu Mao, who grinned and said, "You're crazy... nobody else I ever met would want to do this. If you insist on it, I'm in."
"**Don't *encourage* him!**" Wu Jing barked.
"Hey, look, I just said 'if he insists on it', Mister Wu," Zu Mao

replied. "If you talk him out of it, I'll say no more."

"And you *can't* talk me out of it, Brother-in-law," Sun Jian insisted. "I have to sit atop a horse every day, shouting orders at men, telling them to run up to those walls and be shot, stoned, crushed, buried alive and fried like market meat. Every day, I walk around the infirmary, and I look at men's eyes as they stare up at me, trying to smile, looking for ample respect and thanks for what they've done, and... and... what level of respect or thanks can ever match such a sacrifice?"

Sun Jian's allies were silent and sombre.

"The real heroes here are those men that run toward those walls day after day," Sun Jian continued. "This war is about 'ridding the land of heretics that intend a new age of theologically-founded anarchy', isn't it, Cheng Demou...?"

Cheng Pu nodded silently.

"It's for the people... and those poor solders are and were people," Sun Jian continued. "They're doing for themselves and their families, not for a small group of corrupt autocrats in Luoyang. If the Yellow Turbans win, they'll kill or persecute anyone that doesn't want to live the way they want to live: that means us, that means our *families*. If we don't stop them, what are we living for...? ...So don't accuse me of being reckless and mad for doing what we expect a lot of other people to do day after day, alright...? If Commander Zhu hadn't recommended us as officers, we'd be 'worthless southern conscripts' and doing it under instruction from someone else eventually anyway."

Cheng Pu sighed heavily and said, "Alright, Wentai. I can't argue with that."

"I should, but... well... I won't tell my sister how you really died if you do," Wu Jing chortled. "I'll say you were killed in a duel with their commander."

"You tell her the *truth*, Wu Jing, if the worst happens," Sun Jian insisted. "Any death here is as meaningful and terrible as another... I won't have you belittling the other men's fates by pretending that it wasn't mine."

After a long silence, Zu Mao said, "When?"

"Tonight," Sun Jian replied. "I want this nonsense over with. Once I'm gone, inform Commander Zhu and have the men ready."

Wu Jing, Cheng Pu and Huang Gai nodded obediently.

"...You're going to take that 'lucky scarf' of yours off to do this, right?" Zu Mao said mischievously.

"Unfortunately, Zu Mao, they're not 'Red Turbans'... so *yes*," Sun Jian chuckled.

That night, two men made their way toward the walls of Wan City under cover of darkness with a scaling ladder. The city walls were sparsely defended in comparison to daylight, and the defenders were less than vigilant. As they reached the dry moat, the two men – Sun Jian and Zu Mao – wrinkled their noses in reaction to the smell of festering bodies in the defensive pit.

"I'm glad we don't have to go in there," Zu Mao whispered.

"It's where we'll end up if we get this wrong," Sun Jian replied. "Remember: any problems, go back if you can."

"*How*?" Zu Mao snickered.

"...Yeah," Sun Jian replied dolefully. "Yeah, you're as dead as I am.

Why did you volunteer for this?"

"Because I reckon I'm as nutty as you are," Zu Mao said with amusement. "C'mon, boss... let's do this."

Sun Jian nodded, and the two lifted the ladder so that they could lower it over the pit. The defenders missed this initial act, and the process of passing the moat began. Sun Jian crossed first; as he crossed, he observed the faint outlines of the corpses below, and grimaced at the thought of how they died. Occasionally, a faint moan could be heard in the quiet of the night, which confirmed a grim truth – somewhere in that sea of corpses in the moat, men were buried alive under their comrades and would slowly waste away without assistance.

"Heaven can be cruel," Sun Jian murmured as he continued his journey.

Once Sun Jian had crossed, Zu Mao began his own journey; Sun Jian alternated his gaze between the moat and the walls and silently prayed that the men atop the walls would fail to spot his friend as he shimmied along the ladder without any protection save his clothing, leather chest plate and leather helmet. But Zu Mao did make it across; at that point, both men took a deep breath and hoped that the next step – which would surely be discovered – would be survived by both of them.

"Okay... now!" Sun Jian whispered, and the two men hoisted the ladder to the wall.

One of the defenders heard the wooden ladder as it came to rest against the wall and peered over the battlements to see what had caused the sound.

"**ENEMY!**" the defender cried as Sun Jian began a speedy climb.

Zu Mao, meanwhile, watched helplessly and wondered what terrible things might await his master. The commotion indicated that there were few men ready to resist the lone infiltrator; eventually, two men came to the wall with some rocks.

"**MOVE!**" Zu Mao shouted, and Sun Jian knew what that meant. He halted, and as the defenders prepared to throw the rocks, he flipped the ladder 180 degrees to the right so that he was underneath it, and continued to climb. The rocks passed him completely, and once he was near the top of the ladder, Sun Jian flipped it again and completed his ascension. There were only five defenders, and one died immediately when the exhausted Sun Jian grabbed the man, pulled the turban from his head, and threw him over the wall. He then drew his sword and ran a second man through; as a group of around 20 men started to make their way toward him from the stone steps inside the wall, Sun Jian parried the attacks of the three men that were near him and made a dash for the nearest set of steps. Once he was at a height that allowed him to land safely, he dropped down to the ground, avoiding the small group of Yellow Turbans that were ascending them to face him, and dashed into a dark space between two buildings. His pursuers passed him; after tying his requisitioned yellow scarf around the plume of his helmet, he left his hiding place, and was ignored by any man that caught sight of him in the poor light. He then made a dash for the main gates, which were only manned by two guards that he killed before they realised who he was. Sun Jian lowered the drawbridge, and Zu Mao joined him to repel any men that attacked them.

"**I really didn't think you'd do it!**" Zu Mao chuckled as they prepared to face a group of six men. "**Bloody mad, you are, but amazing too!**"

"**THE CITY IS OPEN!**" Han Dang announced to a small army that had quietly gathered on the far side of the moat. "**CHARGE!**"

A series of beacons announced to the main Han army that the infiltration had been a success.

"Amazing," Zhu Jun said as he saw the signal fires. "**ALL MEN, ADVANCE!**"

The Han forces charged into the undefended city and defeated the confused and demoralised Yellow Turban forces within an hour. Many were captured and killed, but some were able to flee in the confusion to join forces dotted around Nan County.

"**You are a man among men, Sun Wentai!**" Zhu Jun proclaimed as he met with Sun Jian and Zu Mao. "**How are you not Heaven's will, put here to bring an end to the chaos?**"

The soldiers cheered, and Sun Jian smiled humbly, wheezing, "I... I simply do what I must, Commander. Who has my scarf...?"

"The injuries are minor," a doctor said as he finished examining Sun Jian in the camp infirmary. "A miracle is all it can be."

"Luck," Sun Jian chuckled as he looked around him at the reverent and grateful faces of injured and healthy men alike. "And I didn't even have my scarf on! I must be lucky with or without it, I suppose."

"You are truly a tiger," Cheng Pu said with awe. "I am the lucky man, Lord Sun, to be able to serve a hero such as you."

"I promise that I shall tell my sister nothing," Wu Jing said with a mischievous smile. As Sun Jian frowned and moved to speak, Wu Jing added, "Nothing but the truth, as you asked. Of course I despair at your recklessness, Brother-in-law... but how can I not respect your bravery and skill at the same time...?"

"Zu Mao did his part," Sun Jian insisted.

"Nobody cares about me," Zu Mao joked as his left arm was being examined by the doctor. "Who'll even know who Zu Mao is in a hundred years' time, Mister Sun Jian...? ...But they'll know who you are, that's for sure."

"**A cheer for Major Sun!**" one Han captain suggested. "**A cheer for the man that has shortened this campaign by half a year and guaranteed our success! Now our families will quickly know us again!**"

The soldiers cheered repeatedly, and Sun Jian lowered his head to hide his expression.

The fall of Wan City ended the effective resistance posed by the western contingent of Yellow Turban rebels. The Han forces were able to use the city as a base to finish their work, and within weeks, the rebellion was as good as over. Once the last of the small groups were eliminated, the emperor declared an end to the rebellion, and Sun Jian's men began the long journey home.

"*Husband*...!" Lady Wu said as a battered but proud Sun Jian entered his home one night with Wu Jing and Zu Mao on either side of him.

"He needs a bath and a soft bed, milady," Zu Mao chuckled. "Look after him... he's the finest man in the world."

Lady Wu followed Zu Mao's example of ignoring etiquette as she wrapped her arms around Sun Jian and said, "What have you been up to now...?"

"Later," Sun Jian pleaded. "For now, I want some quiet time with my family."

"My cue to leave!" Zu Mao said with a laugh. "But one more thing, Mister Sun Jian; you saved my life twice over, and more besides, I think... to me, you're family."

Zu Mao departed, and Wu Jing smiled thoughtfully.

"...I've missed you all," Sun Jian whispered as the embrace ended.

"You'd *better have*," Lady Wu replied as she examined her husband from head to foot. "Were you hurt badly...? Brother, what did he do...?"

"What he always does; I cannot and will not criticise," Wu Jing insisted. "You'll hear about it soon enough, my sister; it'll be the talk of the country."

Lady Wu laughed, shook her head, and said, "You're a handful."

"Yes, well, I'd rather not talk about it anymore," Sun Jian pleaded. "I want to rest."

"**FATHER!**" Sun Ce shrieked as he finally entered the room.

"No play-fighting tonight," Sun Jian implored. "I'm very bruised all over; one fight after another, and all the-"

"Enough," Lady Wu insisted. "Ce, Go to bed."

Sun Ce exhaled noisily and went back to his sleeping quarters.

"I shall leave now," Wu Jing suggested. "Good night."

"Yes... good night, dear brother," Lady Wu replied, and Wu Jing departed.

"...I do not know if I shall receive rewards, because people of our level don't get invited to the capital for rewards from the emperor unless it's really something special that you've done," Sun Jian admitted after a short silence. "I am a mid-ranking military officer, *technically*, but the court ordered the disbanding of all militias, so I'm back to being a junior official until another war breaks out."

"That suits me fine," Lady Wu said as she hugged her husband again. But after a long silence, Lady Wu frowned, and without releasing her husband from her embrace, she said, "'Until'...?"

"It's inevitable, my lady," Sun Jian said with a newfound understanding. "It's just a matter of time."

Even with his cynical comprehension of the state of the country, Sun Jian could never have imagined how quickly the fragile peace would make way for war once again: no one was prepared, in fact, for the worse chaos that was to come.

✱✱✱✱✱✱✱✱✱✱✱✱

8

Within months of the end of the Yellow Turban Rebellion supposedly being quelled, the Turbans reappeared and began another swathe of attacks across the land, and within weeks of that, another crisis loomed in Liang Province in the northwest of China. Sun Jian and his allies watched the events with interest, and expected another call to arms against Yellow Turban forces in central China; one and all were set to be surprised when Sun Jian received a letter inviting him to undertake a more far-reaching expedition.

"Lord Sun," Cheng Pu said as he welcomed Sun Jian into his family home.
"...Demou," Sun Jian sighed.
Sun Jian followed Cheng Pu to his living quarters and was directed to sit in the host seat.
"I can't do that," Sun Jian said humbly.
"Sit in the host seat, Lord Sun," Cheng Pu insisted.
Sun Jian conceded and sat down.
"You seem to be troubled," Cheng Pu prompted.
"I have been asked to go to Liang Province and act as an adviser to General *Zhou Shen*, the 'General that strikes fear into the unlawful'," Sun Jian reported.
"...I see," Cheng Pu said thoughtfully.
"But *Liang Province*... that is the other side of the country," Sun Jian said with obvious reluctance. "Do I really want to go all that way to advise some other man on how to fight an enemy I know little about...?"
"I admit, I don't see why you'd be sent all that way when there is a much closer threat from the Yellow Turbans," Cheng Pu replied. "But on the other hand, Liang is in need of heroes, so it's no surprise that you're being asked to do this."
"...Demou, you are a more worthy adviser than I will ever be," Sun Jian said honestly. "Maybe you should accompany me."
"Of course I will, if that's what's best," Cheng Pu replied. "Wu Jing and Zu Mao will no doubt force or be forced upon you... so at least you'll have plenty of support."
"...Right, well... I'd better go and tell my family," Sun Jian sighed.

"Don't tell me," Lady Wu scoffed as Sun Jian entered the living quarters and smiled cheerfully. "I know that look: you've volunteered for something else."
"...Not exactly," Sun Jian replied. "I've been asked to go to Liang Province to-"
"*Liang*???" Lady Wu exclaimed. "That's the *far northwest*!"
"Yes."
"That's the opposite side of the country!"
"It is."
Lady Wu shook her head and said, "But there's no point us talking about this, is there...? Being 'asked' is more a case of being *told*."
"In this case, not really," Sun Jian admitted. "Once again, Zhu Jun has put a good word in for me, and it could mean rewards."
"...Alright," Lady Wu said miserably. "But try and beat them

quickly, else we'll all start to forget what you look like!"
Sun Jian nodded sheepishly and said, "I'll do my best, as always."

Zu Mao and Cheng Pu, meanwhile, were waiting for Sun Jian.
"Aha! Here he comes," Zu Mao said as Sun Jian left his house.
"Should I take Wu Jing?" Sun Jian wondered. "My wife did not suggest it."
"She trusts you... besides, you're an adviser on this one," Zu Mao replied.
"...Quite right," Sun Jian decided. "The three of us will find some good men to help us with our baggage, and set out tomorrow. Wu Jing can ensure that my family are safe, and Mister Huang Gongfu and Mister Han Yigong are busy enough."
"Yes," Cheng Pu said with a smile. "You were right to suggest that they kept our militia alive unofficially; the north is nothing but fools, telling us to disband!"
"And more besides, the way they shafted Mister Sun Jian out of any real rewards," Zu Mao scoffed. "They'd better reward you this time, or by Heaven, they'll have my sword to answer to, the bunch of rotten-"
"Let's get the job done first, shall we...?" Cheng Pu said with laughter.

And so Sun Jian, Cheng Pu, Zu Mao and a small retinue of assistants began a journey north and west to the unstable Liang Province. Once they had crossed the Yangtze into Lujiang Prefecture in northern Yang Province, their journey would take them through Yu Province and the north of Jing Province, where they had already rendered near-thankless service to the empire.
"I really don't want to see Yu Province again, especially not so soon," Sun Jian admitted as the trio and their assistants travelled along a dirt road in the south of Lujiang. "I don't want to see Jing either."
"We're going a little further northward this time," Cheng Pu replied. "Administrator Lu Kang has promised us safe passage and said that we can use his southern residence if we need it."
"A good man, Demou," Sun Jian sighed. "He's done wonders here, hasn't he ...?"
"If someone trusted you with a prefecture, you'd do even better, Mister Sun Jian," Zu Mao suggested. "Look at how many honest men you made out of bad ones! Almost none o' the men you recruited went back to their old ways when we got back to Fuchun... near to none. They respect you, because you're one of them, and you're a hero in all sorts o' ways. 'Administrator Sun Jian' would turn Wu Prefecture around... 'Inspector Sun Jian' could-!"
"Hush, Zu Mao," Sun Jian pleaded. "I know you're trying to help, but... but inadvertently reminding me that we got next to nothing for all the work that we did is... it's too much."

The travellers hurried through Lujiang, crossed into Yu and passed through Runan: former Yellow Turbans and villagers greeted them wherever they went, which only added to their sadness about the situation in Liang Province. The journey into Jing Province was equally uneventful: once again, some village leaders offered lodgings and gifts to Sun Jian to thank him for his recent efforts, which warmed the hearts of the travellers. But once they left Jing Province and crossed into the western region of Central Province, the mood changed.

When the travellers reached the former capital Chang'an – which was east of Liang Province – they wondered if the current capital Luoyang would one day be abandoned by the Han as Chang'an once was, and if the Han would collapse once again, as it had done over a century ago. With each day that passed and each new uprising that occurred, the answer to that question became more and more difficult to determine.

"We've been asked to stop in Chang'an by Tao Qian, Inspector of Xu Province," Sun Jian reported to his allies. "He-"

"He's, uh... he's overstepping his authority a bit, isn't he...? Zu Mao said. "Xu is on the opposite side of the country! Which begs the question, 'Why is he even-'"

"You really are too much sometimes," Sun Jian interrupted. "Let me finish! He's a personal friend of Zhu Jun, and he wants to ensure that we have everything that we need for the journey ahead."

Zu Mao scowled and said, "But-!"

"He's in Chang'an on imperial orders, bolstering the city's defences against the Liang rebels," Cheng Pu explained. "And he's a man with a good reputation, Zu Mao: let him be."

"On the subject of the rebels, Mister Cheng," Zu Mao retorted. "D'you maybe want to explain to this poor, simple man of the south what the hell is going on here...?"

"...Not now," Sun Jian sighed.

"It's... political again, Zu Mao," Cheng Pu said. "The way that I have heard it is that the provincial inspector is a corrupt criminal, and when the Qiang tribes invaded as they often do in Liang, there was no military fund to repel them. The people got frustrated, and-"

"*Again...?*" Zu Mao chortled. "We're fighting the ordinary people *again*???"

"...As before, this isn't 'ordinary people', alright...?" Sun Jian retorted. "The people that have joined the Qiang are not helping anyone that hasn't... they're harming them instead. This is selfish people doing what works for them at everyone else's expense, and that makes them as bad as the eunuchs, the Qiang and the inspector. Now I won't hear any more about it, alright...? We're here to do a job..."

Zu Mao muttered angrily, but he did not contest Sun Jian.

Xu Provincial Inspector Tao Qian was a wiry, grizzled, leathery man whose face appeared to naturally contort into a scowl: neither Cheng Pu nor Zu Mao was left feeling comfortable as Tao approached the heavily-guarded gates of Chang'an, grunted tersely, clasped his hands together, bowed slightly and said, "So you're here, Mister Sun."

"I am glad to meet you at last, Inspector," Sun Jian replied as he bowed low.

"A true hero... not like the other ones," Tao Qian grumbled. "The court has appointed former courtiers as generals... foolishness."

"Perhaps they will prove themselves," Sun Jian suggested.

Tao Qian smiled slightly, grunted a laugh and gestured that Sun Jian and his allies should follow him into the city, which they did.

"So this is the old capital," Zu Mao said as he looked about him. "…Yeah, I s'pose Fuchun must seem like a pig pen to people that live in a place like this."

"They can think what they like," Cheng Pu muttered.

The city had a bustling market that was selling goods from across the empire and beyond: some of the traders were visibly foreign, which prompted Zu Mao to say, "I don't reckon some o' these are even tribes. Where are they from?"

"They're probably from the far north, the places where we get the big horses from," Cheng Pu replied.

"Oh, right," Zu Mao said. "They have funny features, don't they?"

"I'm sure they feel the same about us," Cheng Pu replied. "But at least they can argue that there's a difference to see… a man that can treat a person differently because they have less wealth or didn't get the same opportunities, even if they look the same as they do, is worse."

"…I wasn't really insultin' 'em, Mister Cheng," Zu Mao insisted. "I was just saying that their eyes and noses and everythin' is different; perhaps I shouldn't have said 'funny', because I-"

"I know… what you meant," Cheng Pu said with barely-restrained anger. The group were scruffy, and more than one inhabitant of Chang'an had cast a disparaging look in Cheng Pu's direction that he did not care for.

"…Ah… I see," Zu Mao chuckled. "Ignore 'em."

"Has the last half-year taught them *nothing*?" Cheng Pu despaired; he failed to notice that Sun Jian had stopped speaking to Tao Qian and dropped back to join them. "There's a full-scale peasant rebellion going on just west of here, and they *still*…! …I… I need to calm down, I know that."

"Good; then I don't need to *tell you*, Demou," Sun Jian said admonishingly. "Inspector Tao has invited me for tea, but I've declined since our mission is urgent. We'll depart once we've eaten and rested for a few hours."

"The sooner we advance, the better," Cheng Pu replied. "The north is not to my taste."

Sun Jian did not reply, but his own observations had left him with similar issues with some of the seemingly-oblivious inhabitants of Chang'an. The group stopped in a tavern for a short time and then departed for the western front in Liang Province.

'General that strikes fear into the unlawful' Zhou Shen – a man of average stature with a confident expression and deliberate manners – met Sun Jian and his allies at the gates of the wooden encampment at Mei County in eastern Liang Province.

"Mister Sun Jian," Zhou Shen said with false politeness.

Sun Jian made a bow that was reciprocated, and said, "General Zhou, it is a pleasure to be working with you. I should like to introduce you to-"

"We should both go to speak with Commander Zhang Wen and General Dong Zhuo immediately," Zhou Shen interrupted. "Your servants can find your tent by following that path to my left: a sign marks it clearly."

Zu Mao and Cheng Pu exchanged irritated glances.

"…Alright, well, my *friends* can wait for me there," Sun Jian replied. "Please, lead the way, General."

"GENERAL ZHOU AND MISTER SUN!" a soldier announced as General Zhou prepared to enter the command tent.

"Ah! General Zhou, and Mister Sun Jian!" Commander Zhang Wen hailed as Zhou Shen and Sun Jian approached him.

Zhang Wen was a man of noble stature and inoffensive features, but was otherwise strangely unremarkable. Stood at his side was a man in plain brown robes that had rugged features and a bronzed, muscular physique; that man was Dong Zhuo, the 'General who routs the Despicable'.

Dong Zhuo bowed to Zhou Shen and said, "General Zhou."

"Commander, and General Dong," Zhou Shen said as he bowed to each man in turn.

"Commander," Sun Jian replied with a courteous bow. He then turned to Dong Zhuo, who bowed slightly but said nothing. Sun Jian returned the slight bow and said, "Respected General Dong; it is a pleasure."

"…The same," Dong Zhuo said reluctantly.

"You are invited here for your extraordinary talent, Mister Sun Jian," Zhang Wen said with respect. "We are facing tremendous odds; the Qiang are not to be underestimated, and we have actually lost as many good men to their ranks as their swords, as it were."

"There have been a lot of defections, then?" Sun Jian said with surprise.

"Only of weak, greedy fools that know nothing of loyalty to His Majesty," Dong Zhuo suggested. "They are of no loss to us."

"General Dong is quite right," Zhang Wen said sadly. "But all the same, their numbers are the first problem, and their skill is the second. Now, General Dong has very talented advisers in his employ; General Zhou, regrettably, has been unable to find a talent to assist him, hence you were summoned here. "

"I will serve tirelessly," Sun Jian promised.

"Right, then!" Zhang Wen said with cheer. "Let's start by…"

"*Aiee*… what a bunch of…!" Sun Jian said involuntarily as he entered his tent.

"I can imagine," Zu Mao grumbled. "So when do we fight…?"

"Dong Zhuo will be trouble," Sun Jian said surely. "I've heard rumours; he is greedy, self-serving and cowardly, in contrast to his carefully managed public image. He lost miserably against the Yellow Turbans when forced to fight them; that means that any success here was *bought*."

"So when do we fight…?" Zu Mao asked again.

"…Soon, that's all I know," Sun Jian sighed. "But I do not have high hopes for this campaign. Apparently, the army here will be led by two former Han officials, Han Sui and Bian Zhang."

"Low-level clerks," Cheng Pu supposed.

"A former *Attendant Official* and a former *Magistrate*," Sun Jian chortled.

Cheng Pu frowned and made an unintelligible noise that showed his confusion.

"They're high positions, or high enough that… … …what have we got ourselves into here...?" Zu Mao wondered.

"These 'rebels' are made up of all sorts," Sun Jian explained. "Qiang and Yuezhi peoples made up the initial incursion, but now, it's mostly locals that turned on three successive Inspectors and killed the Administrator of-"

"This *is* a proper uprising against corruption!" Zu Mao groaned. "We're going to be fighting miserable overworked commoners again, and this time they're-!"

"As before, we show *discretion*," Cheng Pu suggested. "But in future... maybe we should refuse these appointments if we can."

Sun Jian nodded slowly.

General Dong Zhuo returned to his command tent with a bitter scowl on his face and a growing tenseness in his chest. Two of his advisers – a small, humble-looking man in plain blue robes and a taller, thin-faced man in purple robes – awaited a summary of the meeting that never happened: Dong Zhuo passed them, sat in his host seat and continued to fight his inner rage with diminishing success. After a short while, the purple-robed adviser looked at his colleague, coughed quietly and whispered, "Shall I ask, Mister Jia Xu...?"

"Allow me, Li Ru," the blue-robed Jia Xu replied, and Li Ru smiled gratefully.

Silence returned while Jia Xu gathered his thoughts: Dong Zhuo glared at the space directly in front of him, and his followers shifted themselves as discreetly as they could to avoid being within his line of sight.

"...I sense that Zhang Wen and Zhou Shen have upset you, my lord," Jia Xu prompted cautiously.

"Them and that idiot *Sun Jian*," Dong Zhuo grumbled. "I'd heard of the fellow, of course, and his 'amazing exploits' during the Yellow Turban Rebellion; he obviously lacks any respect for me, and-"

"Forgive me for interrupting, my lord, but what role is Sun Jian taking...?" Li Ru asked plainly.

"Not the vanguard, for some reason," Dong Zhuo chortled. "No, he's been sent by his friend Zhu Jun to *advise* Zhou Shen... you were obviously right about Zhou, Mister Jia, and Zhu Jun knows it. There's a hope that Zhou will listen to a 'great hero' like Sun Jian... but my opinion of Zhou is poor, and I think he'll fail."

"Scouts report that the rebel army is on its way, led by Bian Zhang and Han Sui," Jia Xu announced. "They're former Han officials, and are exactly what we hoped for. No doubt we'll engage them without stratagem, and nothing will come of it but a stalemate. We'll see how things progress; once an opening appears, we should grasp it firmly and destroy the rebel force. We can worry about repairing the damage to our relationship with the Qiang later; for now, we have possible imperial rewards to consider."

Dong Zhuo almost drooled at the idea and said, "Very good indeed! To hell with Zhou Shen, Sun Jian and Zhang Wen! Glory is ours for the taking!"

"...We should never have come here."

Zu Mao sighed audibly at Sun Jian's comment, while Cheng Pu

hung his head low and grimaced. The night was cold, so Sun Jian's command tent had to be warmed with a fire.

"I'm sorry, truly I am," Sun Jian continued. "But I promise that I won't take any more assignments like this... if we live through this one, at least."

"We will," Zu Mao replied. "We'll hurt, but we'll live."

Cheng Pu looked up and said, "We're not here to fight; we're here to give advice. We'll have to watch others die needlessly."

"Like the siege," Sun Jian murmured.

"Only there won't be any heroics," Cheng Pu retorted. "Let the generals do the fighting, Sun Wentai. Our fight isn't here; it's at home, where we won't have men willing to cross the empire to help us in the way that we've been expected to."

"...You're right," Sun Jian replied. "We need to do something about all the problems in Wu Prefecture. We need to make our own home a better place."

The three men parted company and went to their own personal tents; they knew that they would soon face an alliance of Qiang, Yuezhi and Liang Province inhabitants that would test their faith in the Han Empire, but they could not know that the events would fatefully alter the reputations and destinies of all of the men involved, including the ambitious Dong Zhuo.

****

9

The rebel coalition arrived at Mei County within days and formed battle lines that left Sun Jian, Cheng Pu and Zu Mao close to speechless.
"There's a hundred-thousand, at *least*," Cheng Pu suggested.
Zu Mao shook his head and said, "This is going to be difficult."
Sun Jian surveyed the battle lines around him and said, "The court has learned no lessons; the men are demoralised already, and we haven't even started fighting yet! When was the last time that half of them had a decent meal?"
"Careful with your words, or I might defect," Zu Mao joked.
The enemy commanders ordered a full charge, and Sun Jian readied himself for the inevitable clash of weapons as the Han commanders ordered a limited response and only met the attack with a fraction of the available infantry. The seasoned Qiang were nothing like the Yellow Turban acolytes of the previous campaigns; many Han soldiers buckled under the pressure of the attacks, and the rebels started to gain the advantage.
"I have to do something," Sun Jian muttered.
"What are you-?!" General Zhou Shen exclaimed as Sun Jian rode forward to engage the enemy personally.
"I have to do something!" Sun Jian replied.
"Come back here!" Zhou Shen shouted. **"You're my adviser! COME BACK HERE!"**
Sun Jian halted his horse, grunted angrily, and returned to his master's side.
"How do we deal with them?" Zhou Shen asked.
"By charging them and showing no fear," Sun Jian replied irritably. **"They only respect strength and courage!"**
"Well then, I'll order a full charge!" Zhou Shen replied over the howls of dying men and the clashed of metal blades. **"Where is Dong Zhuo's force?"**
Sun Jian looked around, and realised that Dong Zhuo's banners could not be seen among the warring forces; he turned to look at the army's initial starting point, noted Dong Zhuo's unmoving battle lines and scowled, saying, **"He's just SITTING THERE!"**
Zhou Shen turned his horse enough to look for himself and said, **"You're right! What is this???"**
The battle raged for several minutes more before both side decided to bang their battle gongs and order a complete retreat to their original positions.
"Where is Demou???" Sun Jian barked as Zu Mao approached him on horseback.
"Lost his horse... got hurt," Zu Mao replied. **"He's being seen to, and he'll be fine."**
"Why did you charge???" Sun Jian whined.
"We didn't have much choice!" Zu Mao insisted. **"We saw a group of men that needed getting out of a scrape! Hey, look, at least we were doing something to help them! That bloody Dong Zhuo just-!"**
"I know!" Sun Jian interrupted. **"I know, I... I intend to complain."**

Once the battle was finished, Sun Jian went to Zhang Wen's command tent to protest about Dong Zhuo's procrastination; General Zhou Shen knew his intention and followed him.

"Don't bother with this petition!" Zhou Shen pleaded as he tried to stop Sun Jian outside the tent. "Mister Sun, Dong Zhuo is-"

Sun Jian entered the tent and said, "**Commander Zhang.**"

"Ah, Mister Sun, and General Zhou," Zhang Wen said with strange cheer. "We did not do too badly in this initial skirmish, I think."

"...We could have done better or worse," Sun Jian replied carefully. "Certainly, we might have done even better had General Dong Zhuo actually taken part in the battle! He didn't move until a minute or two before it ended! Was that part of some greater strategy that I was not made aware of...?"

"...No," Zhang Wen said with embarrassment. "I cannot explain why General Dong played such an unenthusiastic role."

"I think that *I* can," Sun Jian declared. "Commander, Dong Zhuo is *corrupt*."

Zhang Wen looked at Zhou Shen, who said nothing.

"Dong Zhuo has obvious ties with the Qiang," Sun Jian continued. "He has lived in this region without harassment while other Han officials have been put to the sword and taken as hostages! I acknowledge that his base beneath the Wei River makes him a harder target than some, but with things as they are, only a corrupt man or an invisible one could be as aloof from the troubles here as he has been!"

"Those are serious accusations that you make," Zhang Wen suggested. "General Dong is now very highly decorated, and he is your superior by many ranks."

"Yes, which means that I cannot directly challenge him; that's why I'm here, Commander," Sun Jian protested. "Eventually, he'll either abandon you or double-cross you; I suggest that you have him removed before he can do that."

Zhou Shen started smiling quietly at Sun Jian's bold frankness.

"...That is not some easy feat, Mister Sun Jian," Zhang Wen retorted. "Dong Zhuo is influential in Liang, you're right; *think*, then, what might happen if I were to petition the court to have him stripped of office. He might become an even greater threat, then, than you propose him to be."

"*Ayah*... he's a *menace*!" Sun Jian pleaded. "Execute him *now*, or suffer *later*!"

"*Execute him*?!" Zhou Shen exclaimed.

"He is guilty of insubordination, misconduct in a public office and military negligence, at the very least," Sun Jian suggested. "His behaviour in that battle led to an increased number of casualties due to the prolonged exchange and reduced numbers; how can that not be considered a form of *treason*?"

"I... I cannot act as you suggest," Zhang Wen said sorrowfully. "General Dong is too well respected, and he will have good reasons for his actions."

"I should like to hear them," Sun Jian retorted.

"And I'm sure that you *will*," Zhang Wen said with a sigh. "Now please, Mister Sun, I have manoeuvres to plan; as do *you*, with the man that you are assigned to as an adviser."

Zhou Shen took the statement as a cue and said, "Mister Sun, let us withdraw to my command tent and plan the rearrangement of

our forces."
"...*Yes*, General Zhou," Sun Jian replied with resignation.

Once Zhou Shen and Sun Jian were within the confines of the former's command tent, the latter said, "General, before we discuss 'manoeuvres', I-"
"We should sit down before we begin," Zhou Shen interrupted.
"...Alright," Sun Jian sighed.
Zhou allowed Sun Jian to sit before he said, "Now, before you proffer advice to me, Mister Sun, I should like to make a suggestion to you."
"...Of course, General," Sun Jian replied.
"I would not try and slander your superiors anymore, Mister Sun," Zhou Shen continued. "General Dong has an illustrious history: he fought alongside the famous general Zhang Huan many years ago, and he has a strong following here in Liang."
"I understand matters very well, General," Sun Jian replied. "I shall say no more: Dong Zhuo isn't my problem, after all, he's-"
"I suggest further that you need to rethink yourself!" Zhou Shen chortled. "Your reputation as a wild tiger is going to your head, methinks, Mister Sun Jian! Dong Zhuo is a respected general of the empire, and showing him such groundless contempt is not something that a cultured man should be doing!"
Sun Jian glared silently.
"...And such a reckless man that does not understand basic protocol cannot be a good adviser, surely," Zhou Shen scoffed. "How can you expect me to listen to you when you act like a mistakenly-elevated peasant and suggest random, knee-jerk solutions to matters that you don't fully understand...? You were sent here to proffer your supposed knowledge of barbarian warfare in the absence of other proven figures like Qu Yi... not give direction on how to deal with political matters that you, as a man from the south, cannot fully comprehend."
"...Yes, General," Sun Jian replied through gritted teeth. "As I said, I understand matters fully. I shall stick to giving military advice, as is my remit."
"That will hopefully be better thought-out than your political advice," Zhou Shen chortled. "So, to begin with, let us discuss the..."

Sun Jian returned to his command tent later that day as an emotionally-battered man; Zu Mao was sat near the host seat, and Cheng Pu was sat at one side of the tent with a bandage around his right arm.
"...Nothing'll be done, then," Zu Mao snickered.
"*No*," Sun Jian said angrily. He then turned to Cheng Pu, and asked, "How are you, Demou...?"
"It isn't serious, but I won't be able to march," Cheng Pu replied. "I'm sorry about Dong Zhuo; are you in danger?"
"If he tries to confront me, I'll *kill him*," Sun Jian said with rage. "I don't care what rank he is, Demou, not when the matter is personal."
"If he's as cowardly as I've heard, won't he send an assassin?" Cheng Pu retorted.
"...They're all fools," Sun Jian decided. "All of the men of the court,

they're all cowards, thieves and fools; our three leaders are two of them fools, and one of them a selfish, corrupt coward. Such men can't win battles, not without a lot of luck. We're going to lose."
"So why are we still here?" Zu Mao said gruffly.
"Because we have to follow their orders," Sun Jian replied.
"What about Dong Zhuo?" Cheng Pu asked impatiently. "What if he-"
"I've done what I've done," Sun Jian interrupted.
Cheng Pu conceded and said no more.

For the next two months, little changed in Liang Province; each side would occasionally challenge the other to battle, have a brief exchange of words or weapons, and withdraw.
One night, as Sun Jian and Zu Mao wandered the Mei County camp and periodically stared upward at the starlit night sky, something strange and almost unbelievable happened.
"**LOOK!**" a soldier cried suddenly.
"Oh, my...!" Zu Mao said as he turned toward the west, and caught sight of the trail of a shooting star. "That... that just...!"
"That looked like that fell on the enemy's camp at Longxi!" Sun Jian said excitedly. "That's an auspicious sign if ever there was one!"
Zu Mao watched the chaos that was erupting around him and said, "We'd better get back, Mister Sun Jian; I reckon we might be ordered to march."
"I'd be surprised if we weren't, Mister Zu!" Sun Jian replied as he started to run back to his tent.

Within an hour, Zhang Wen had been informed of the shooting star by an excited captain, and he ordered a full march on the rebel's Mei County camp. To Sun Jian's annoyance, Dong Zhuo was conspicuously absent from the preparations.
"Before you complain, note something else that Zu Mao's thinking," Cheng Pu said as he tried to put some armour on. "Dong Zhuo's not just quiet... he's not here at all."
"That's what I reckon," Zu Mao said surely. "No banners, none of his men anywhere. The second that meeting was over, he vanished."
"...Quite right," Sun Jian realised. "He's double-timed his way there to get all the glory, after *all the lack of*...!"
Sun Jian's voice trailed as his anger peaked.
"All the same, we need to carry on our preparations," Cheng Pu insisted. "Any glory right now is better than none at all... else coming here was a waste of time, money and lives."

Sun Jian could barely contain his rage when he had his suspicions confirmed; Dong Zhuo had indeed marched at great speed and begun the attack on the rebel camp by the time that the main force led by Zhang Wen arrived.
"**Well, it seems that General Dong was merely saving his strength for a better opportunity!**" Zhang Wen suggested. "**Look; the enemy is routed!**"
"**I'd say that General Dong is a true hero of the era, here for all to see!**" Zhou Shen taunted as he looked at Sun Jian.
"**...It seems that my protestations were premature,**" Sun Jian

said reluctantly.

"Methinks they were," Zhou Shen said with amusement. **"Well, Mister Sun; you're my adviser, so advise me. What now...?"**

"General Dong already has the advantage, so I suggest we simply follow his lead," Sun Jian replied powerlessly.

"CHARGE!" Zhou Shen ordered. **"Let us show them that Dong Zhuo is not the only champion in the ranks of the Han!"**

Sun Jian was on the verge of screaming, and Zu Mao could see it; he gained Sun Jian's attention and said, **"Please steel yourself, Mister Sun Jian: these fools'll come unstuck in the end, you'll see."**

Sun Jian nodded silently and watched as the Han forces swept aside the remnants of the rebel forces that had not fled west.

Once the fighting was over, Zhang Wen ordered a battlefield conference close to the remains of the enemy command tent.

"We must finish them off now," Zhang Wen said to his officers. "They've apparently divided their forces... one force is in Longxi, across the Wei River. General Dong Zhuo, I would like you to take thirty-thousand men and pursue them there."

Dong Zhuo bowed slightly and said, "It has always been my desire to render the best service to His Majesty. I will succeed or face the executioner, Commander."

"Very good," Zhang Wen said with respect. "General Zhou Shen, take another army of thirty-thousand and march on Yuzhong. Take no risks."

"You can rely on me to render good service," Zhou Shen promised.

"Heavens be with you both!" Zhang Wen concluded, and both armies began their journeys.

"...I swear, one day I will expose Dong Zhuo for what he is," Sun Jian muttered as he and Zu Mao rode behind Zhou Shen.

"Don't bet on it; he's a crafty one," Zu Mao sighed. "Just do what you can to survive, Mister Sun Jian, and build your own future."

Sun Jian nodded agreeably; he was about to reply when a disdainful Zhou Shen shouted, **"Mister Sun."**

"Here we go," Sun Jian sighed as he moved alongside Zhou Shen.

"Suggestions...?" Zhou Shen prompted.

"Of course, there is the rule regarding the pursuit of an enemy force in retreat," Sun Jian proposed. "In some cases, it is unwise, but it depends on how well organised the army is, and what sort of leaders it has."

"...I'm aware of it," Zhou Shen retorted. "What do you think...?"

"...I think that this is an army led by Han officials, not barbarian chieftains or Han generals, so their response will be manageable," Sun Jian replied. "If they turn about and attack, we can rout them again; but we might sustain losses in the process if we're not immediately ready for it. We should move carefully, and be cautious."

"...Fine," Zhou Shen said with disappointment. "Not at all what I expected, however, given your reputation; did Dong Zhuo 'move carefully'...?"

"Initially, *yes*," Sun Jian muttered.

The rebels turned about and fought after hours of continual

retreat, but their attack was anticipated and countered; they fled, resoundingly defeated once again.

"**We must pursue!**" Zhou Shen declared over the noise of battle.

"**Before we do anything,**" Sun Jian said, "**we need to cut their supply routes.**"

Zhou Shen was silent.

"**If we do not cut their supply route, they will be able to hold out indefinitely, and we have limited supplies,**" Sun Jian protested. "**In fact, that leads to a second thought; we must double the guard on our own supply train as we move. They will doubtless try and attack it, knowing that we will be left with no choice but to retreat if-**"

"**You presume a lot of these fools!**" Zhou Shen chortled. "**Would we win now, and so terribly easily, if they had brains in their heads? What do they know of sabotaging our supply line? We need our forces in the front, taking enemy heads, not lounging about near the food!**"

"**...At least ensure that their supply line is cut, General Zhou,**" Sun Jian pleaded.

"**We will hit them so hard that they will have no need for food, only coffins,**" Zhou Shen retorted. "**I'm surprised, Mister Sun Jian; I had heard that you were a 'man of action', and yet you come to me with these women's plans of cutting supply lines and holding back! Perhaps the tales of your bold and courageous charges against your enemies are nothing more than that...** *tales.*"

Sun Jian bowed slightly and said, "**You have no need for me, it seems. I shall offer no further advice to you, General, and I will instead do all I can to assist your attack.**"

Zhou Shen sneered, and said, "**Perhaps that would be for the best, Mister Sun.**"

Dong Zhuo advanced directly west and crossed the Wei River to reach Wang Plains, which were northwest of the important city of Tianshui.

"...I don't like this," the adviser Li Ru said worriedly.

Dong Zhuo's army had lost sight of the enemy forces some time before; it was now daylight, and the main Han army was some distance behind them now.

"Don't panic," the adviser Jia Xu pleaded. "First, we must know where we are."

"**We know where we are, Jia Xu!**" Dong Zhuo growled. "**Bloody** *Wang Plains*, **on the** *wrong side of the river*! **How do we get back if-**"

"**REPORT!**" a messenger cried.

"*...Go on,*" Dong Zhuo sighed.

"**The Qiang have armies positioned to the west, northwest and south!**" the messenger sobbed. "**The bridges have been destroyed! There's no way back!**"

"We're effectively surrounded, then," Li Ru realised. "The river behind us, and-"

"**YES, I KNOW THAT!**" Dong Zhuo boomed. "*...Give me a minute to think.*"

"We have to do *something*, Father-in-law," General Niu Fu said pointlessly.

"...Alright, I have it," Dong Zhuo said after a thoughtful pause. "Dam the river."

"They're not likely to let us do that!" Niu Fu whined.

"Calm down...!" Jia Xu chortled. "I understand your plan, my lord... Li Jue, Guo Si, Li Su, order your men to dam the river."

"...If you say so," General Li Jue said cynically as he retreated with his fellow generals to carry out his orders.

"Hua Xiong, Xu Rong, prepare nets," Jia Xu ordered.

"*Nets*...?" General Hua Xiong chortled.

"...Ah, I see!" Li Ru said. "A fine plan, my lord."

"...For *fishing*...!" General Xu Rong realised at last. "Of course... of *course*! **ALL OF YOU MEN, WE'RE FISHING! PREPARE NETS!**" The soldiers looked at one-another with bewilderment, but they began the work nonetheless.

The Qiang watched Dong Zhuo's stranded army, but their situation appeared unchanged to the untrained eye. Dong Zhuo's men fished every day in the bloated section of the river, and cooked meals with a casualness that suggested that Dong Zhuo wanted a confrontation and that he believed that he could win. But Dong Zhuo was secretly thinning his battle lines and sending men back across the river, where no army awaited them due to poor foresight on the part of the enemy. It was only when Dong could no longer hide the tiny size of the force on the west bank of the river that the Qiang realised that they had been deceived and descended on Wang Plains with every man available. But by the time that the Qiang reached the river bank, Dong Zhuo had already crossed with the last of his men, and the dam was being dismantled by a team of saboteurs.

"**FAREWELL, FRIENDS!**" Dong Zhuo bellowed as he began the last stage of his retreat; the Qiang heckled the Han forces from across the river and fired some arrows, but their actions were futile.

"A narrow escape, but an escape nonetheless," Li Ru sighed. "Can we regain their friendship and respect later...?"

"I can think of many ways to do so," Jia Xu replied. "For now, we must be thankful that we lost not a single man and report our situation to Zhang Wen."

"He'll not be happy," Li Ru supposed.

"We'll see; it depends on how well Zhou Shen did, doesn't it...?" Dong Zhuo chuckled.

"That it does," Jia Xu agreed. "And I think they might have done worse."

Zhou Shen's army continued their long march toward the rebel-held stronghold of Yuzhong; the supply train was slow and plodding as supply trains always were, and it remained poorly guarded.

"**What my ancestor would say,**" Sun Jian chuckled miserably as he rode alongside an irritated Zu Mao near the front of the army.

"**This isn't your fault,**" Zu Mao replied as he struggled to steady his agitated horse.

"**Is it not...?**" Sun Jian chortled. "**I am here as an adviser. A man like me... an *adviser*! I am a hero, *supposedly*, so my words should carry greater weight than a little man in a** robe that only reads of war, *presumably*; and yet this 'Zhou Shen' ignores my caution completely, practically dismisses me, and advocates this suicidal advance without taking perfectly logical steps to protect our supplies or hasten their retreat. I never imagined I'd ever say this, but... the man is a witless, reckless idiot, and he just wants a nice big fight to tell the court about, so that he's favourably compared to 'the amazing Dong Zhuo'; he's deliberately ensuring the enemy are fit to face us... I'm sure of it."

"You take risks, sure enough, but never outright stupid ones... only necessary ones, that save lives," Zu Mao noted.

"This man has no sense, Mister Sun Jian. I only hope that he's even the slightest bit right, and the enemy have no strategy whatsoever, else we're doomed before we even get started."

"My ancestor would disown me," Sun Jian sighed. "This is a textbook situation; cut their supply line, safeguard our own, and it'll be over in no time; but *no*, we will-"

Sun Jian's rant was prematurely halted by a commotion at the rear of the army.

"Oh no," Sun Jian groaned. "*Quickly...!*"

Sun Jian and Zu Mao rallied a small group of confused men and hurried to the rear of the military convoy, but it was too late; the blazing flames and plumes of smoke told them that the enemy had successfully destroyed the supplies and ensured that there would be no advance.

"I'll tell him!" Sun Jian shouted to Zu Mao. "Do what you can to calm the troops!"

Zu Mao acknowledged his responsibility, and Sun Jian hurried back to the vanguard.

"What is going on?" General Zhou Shen barked as Sun Jian approached him.

"They hit our supply train... it's gone," Sun Jian reported.

The soldiers within earshot started to panic immediately.

"We have to retreat in an orderly fashion!" Sun Jian pleaded. "The day is lost; we cannot proceed without supplies!"

"Do you think that I do not know that???" Zhou Shen retorted angrily. "I...! ...Mister Sun Jian, I-"

"Order a retreat, General, and quickly," Sun Jian interrupted irritably. "We must now treat the vanguard as the rear, and be ready for attacks to our current position."

"Yes, yes, I... FULL RETREAT! WATCH FOR THE ENEMY!"

Zhou Shen shouted with as much authority as he could muster, but the damage was done; the troops were openly resentful as the army began an ignominious retreat. The rebels attacked repeatedly as the army moved, ensuring that the return to the Han camp would be humiliating and the defeat definitive.

****

10

The officers reported to General Zhang Wen as soon as the final outcomes of both pursuit campaigns were known.

"...*Ayah*," Zhang Wen exclaimed as he looked at Dong Zhuo and Zhou Shen. "I am disappointed, I'll admit: Zhou Shen, you've cost me my job, I think."

Zhou Shen could not look his commander or Sun Jian in the eye.

"To lose most of your men... *shameful*," Zhang Wen sighed. "Mister Sun Jian has been very generous to you as well, I think; three of your captains have told me that he tried to warn you about the baggage train repeatedly, and you ignored him! What good is having sound counsel if you don't heed it...?"

"I am a *disgrace*," Zhou Shen sobbed. "I shall be rightly punished."

"*Yes*, and sadly, Mister Sun Jian and I will be unfairly punished along with you: that's *your* guilt to bear, 'General' Zhou," Zhang Wen scolded. "My main regret is that I did not make you sign a pledge that ensured your execution if you failed."

"I am a *wretch*!" Zhou Shen wailed.

"On the other hand... General Dong, I am ashamed to say that I misjudged you completely," Zhang Wen said humbly. "To be surrounded, and fight your way out of a barbarian horde without losing a single man; you are a hero among men, and deserve the highest accolades. I will certainly ensure that the court hears of your incredible achievements."

"You overpraise me," Dong Zhuo said with no sincerity whatsoever; Sun Jian looked and tried to swallow the imaginary ball of rage that was stuck in his throat.

Sun Jian began a long and miserable journey home that did not take him past the imperial capital. Commander Zhang Wen and General Zhou Shen did travel to Luoyang, however, where they reported their own failures and the supposed successes of General Dong Zhuo, who remained in Liang Province to 'valiantly resist rebel attempts to seize the old capital'.

When Sun Jian's party crossed into Lujiang Prefecture in northern Yang Province, his movements were somehow reported to Administrator Lu Kang, who immediately had a messenger invite Sun Jian to his capital. Sun Jian did not want to delay his return to southern Yang, but he did not want to appear rude, so he accepted the offer. The world-weary, elderly Lu Kang greeted the demoralised Sun Jian at the gates of Huancheng City and had his allies quartered in a respectable tavern while he invited Sun to his own home for tea.

"I have heard much about the Liang campaign from others, Mister Sun," Lu Kang said once the two were seated. "But I wanted to hear it from you."

"...I suppose that I can speak freely, since you're a man that detests the wretched, as I do," Sun Jian replied. "You've opposed the corrupt eunuchs and the like in Luoyang a few times..."

"...I have, in my long sixty years," Lu Kang said with a sigh. "But I paid a heavy price, and coming here, to this place that has so many problems, was the only way to do good while keeping my life and freedom. Some, like the brilliant Cai Yong, paid an even heavier price: he's living in exile somewhere to the east of your home village, and his health is not good."

"The campaign was a disaster because of poor planning and worse leaders, and the campaign wouldn't have been necessary in the first place if the province hadn't been run by such corrupt people!" Sun Jian complained. "They sent what, *three* new inspectors to that place to replace the wicked, greedy fool that they put there originally, and they were all of them either worse or unfit in some other way!"

Lu Kang smiled and said, "The court has been weakened by such things. We lost the war against the Xianbei and nearly lost half the land to the Yellow Turbans, but no lessons were learned. They always promise that they will be, but they never are. But I hear that Dong Zhuo might be promoted to 'Inspector of Bing Province', and-"

Sun Jian groaned involuntarily.

"...I suppose that your experiences are fresh in your mind," Lu Kang said with empathy. "I'll settle for simple answers, then, for my own curiosity."

"Zhang Wen is unfit to be commander of the imperial forces; Zhou Shen is an arrogant mediocrity that failed his forces and his sovereign by closing his ears to sense; and Dong Zhuo... Dong Zhuo is a villain that will harm this country," Sun Jian replied. "Liang has been abandoned, which was entirely the wrong thing to do. Zhang Wen is disgraced for being a poor leader: I don't disagree. Zhou Shen is disgraced for the same: I couldn't agree more. I've been disgraced because my advice was ignored, not because it was wrong, while Dong Zhuo... Dong Zhuo has been venerated because he feigned a success with cowardice."

"Your appraisal of Dong Zhuo is notably harsh," Lu Kang prompted.

"Were it only Dong Zhuo, Administrator Lu... but he is empowered by his advisers and officers," Sun Jian continued. "He was openly rude when we first met, not just to me but to his equals and even his superiors, yet no action was taken. He refused to fight to avoid upsetting his Qiang neighbours, despite being commissioned to do exactly that: is that not treason of some kind? Yet he was spared punishment, so I was told, to avoid upsetting those same Qiang! That, Administrator, is almost a perfect summation of the entire sorry affair."

Lu Kang hummed ambiguously.

"His 'demonstration of super-human ability' at the Wei River was entirely down to subterfuge and an obvious unwillingness by both sides to fight," Sun Jian grumbled. "But when he had an opportunity to rout an army of ordinary people just like he and I are, well that was no assault on his conscience. And his blatant disrespect was gradually reduced, which was good advice, not his own sense, for he has none."

Again, Lu Kang hummed ambiguously.

"Alone, Dong Zhuo would be a loud-mouthed, devious braggart that would expose himself, but the cowards excuse him, the naïve aggrandise him, and his allies aid him, advise him, and fight for him," Sun Jian despaired. "I cannot help but blame the men behind the man as much, if not more for why he is now so powerful. It's the same with the criminals in Luoyang."

"...*Cronyism*," Lu Kang grumbled. "I quite agree, Mister Sun: men that act against the court or state are just men that might be easily thwarted, were it not for the scum that surround and aid them for personal gain. Zhang Jue was one man; it was the horde of greedy, short-sighted idiots that wore his yellow scarves and became his 'acolyte army' that made him a threat. And if Dong Zhuo is, as you say, a devious coward, he is only lord of Mei County and probable 'General of the Van' for the efforts of his counsel and other hirelings. The 'Ten' are the worst cruelty of all: they have their slimy forms encircled around His Majesty like a poisonous miasma, killing the virtuous, obscuring truth and choking justice, and yet their power comes from general inaction and cowardice and from those that are willing to shield them for their own gain."

Sun Jian nodded agreeably.

"In a way, I almost hate the cronies more than the leaders, just as you say, because it is their support that empowers the wicked, not some invisible hand of fate or mystical whimsy," Lu Kang continued. "Let no such man come before me and say 'I was just following orders', not when they know they're wrong to do so. They'll see no civility from me, no matter how plausible their excuses."

"And I, the same," Sun Jian said. "When the world is rid of such people, only then will we know peace, because the lone villains will be unarmed and easily purged."

"...Still, while men like you continue to fight for the right causes, there is always hope, and perhaps that is where we should leave that conversation!" Lu Kang suggested. "I will always greet you when you come this way, though goodness knows, you shouldn't have to do so again for any other reason than to visit friends! Surely the court will sanction you to challenge the problems south of the Great River, closer to your home. There are enough northerners to defend the north, I think."

Sun Jian bowed slightly and said, "Heaven, let that be true."

"And I know that the outcome of that campaign disturbs you, but rest assured that everyone that matters knows that you are a hero of the age, Mister Sun," Lu Kang continued. "Your greatest day is yet to come."

"You are too kind," Sun Jian replied humbly.

Administrator Lu Kang's words were welcome, but they did little to improve Sun Jian's true mood. He was no less melancholy when the group left Huancheng City and resumed their travels, and both Cheng Pu and Zu Mao were determined to find some positive rhetoric to support their lord and friend.

"Be glad of one thing... no, in fact, *three* things," Cheng Pu suggested as the journey neared its end and the Yangtze River was within sight.

"And they are...?" Sun Jian said wearily.

"Firstly, you were not burdened with military expectation, so Zhou Shen is the loser here, not you," Cheng Pu explained. "Secondly, Dong Zhuo was too busy gaining merit to seek revenge for your complaints against him; we are safely home now, and whatever rewards he gains will ensure that he has no time to settle petty debts."

"And thirdly...?" Sun Jian prompted.

"We're all alive, we all survived it," Zu Mao supposed. "Is that it, Mister Cheng...?"

"It is, pretty much," Cheng Pu confirmed. "That's most important of all."

Regardless of the relatively minimal consequences of the Liang Province campaign, Sun Jian was still angry and frustrated, and that was no clearer than when he entered his home days later and bellowed, "**Where is everyone???**"

"Father, what is it?" Sun Ce asked worriedly.

"It... sorry, I shouldn't shout," Sun Jian said wearily. "But why was I not greeted properly...? Why were you not-"

"**Husband!**" Lady Wu cried as she entered the room. "Are you hurt?"

"No, I... well, my pride is very badly battered, but otherwise, I am your husband," Sun Jian replied honestly. "We were made to look like fools: I've been dismissed, technically, though I don't think I'll be punished, since it was all that-"

"You *lost a battle*...?" Sun Ce said with surprise and disappointment.

"I... yes, my son, I lost a battle," Sun Jian conceded. "I cannot always win."

"But... but it wasn't your fault, though, right?" Sun Ce prompted.

"...You're right, it wasn't," Sun Jian replied confidently. "It was the man they put in charge of me, who had me there as an adviser, and then refused to listen to me."

"What a complete waste of your time," Lady Wu scoffed. "The court should be *ashamed*, dear husband, dragging you all that way and misusing you."

"Cheng Pu complains a lot about 'men of the north'... well, they *all do*, really... and they're right," Sun Jian decided. "The men of the north are really, truly fools... the court is a terrible place, run by eunuchs, just as the rumours said."

"*Yuck*," Sun Ce exclaimed. "Why would they let *eunuchs* tell them what to do?"

"Do you know what a eunuch is...?" Lady Wu asked.

"...I dunno... something *terrible*, I guess," Sun Ce replied. "I heard somebody say that they're-"

"*Go and play*," Lady Wu ordered. "Your father and I have to talk."

Sun Ce retreated obediently, and Sun Jian smiled dryly.

"...That boy is such a handful," Lady Wu chuckled. "Still... he takes after you, so that's to be expected. Oh, and we did not greet you because your return was not announced."

"I... I realise that now," Sun Jian said apologetically. "I probably forgot... no, I *did* forget to send someone on to tell you. I've been so *angry*..."

Lady Wu smiled comfortingly and said, "Why did you let them talk you into going all that way, you silly man...?"

Sun Jian scratched his head awkwardly.

"...And making you an *adviser*???" Lady Wu continued. "Just this once, I might have said that you should have been at the front as some sort of warrior, or something; perhaps you might have defeated them all by yourself."

"Thanks," Sun Jian said quietly. "Well, the hero of the day ended up being *Dong Zhuo*, of all people... oh, of course, you don't know who he is, though."

"Another *fool*," Lady Wu suggested.

"Close enough," Sun Jian chuckled. "He used a ruse to escape defeat, and never fought the enemy properly, yet he's a hero because he lost no men. I heard that he might be *promoted*."

"*Disgusting*," Lady Wu grumbled. "Rewarded for *running away*."

"The tribes and lawless rebels now rule Liang Province, so we have had no victory; and we are told that the rest of us 'failed to face the enemy', which I only accept because it sounds better than 'failed to win'," Sun Jian scoffed. "However, the whole thing has inspired rebellions in *Changsha* now, so I heard on the way back... I suppose we'll have to see what idiot the court sends from the north to quell the west."

Lady Wu touched Sun Jian's hand and said, "The people that matter know that you did your best. Forget the whole thing."

Sun Jian nodded silently, but he knew that he would probably be dragged into more irrelevant and unnecessary conflicts that would take him away from his home and family, and the thought of it angered him more than ever.

****

11

The vast region known as Changsha – which was as much a county as a prefecture, but seen as either and both at varying times due to the sparse, scattered populace – was to the west of Sun Jian's hometown of Fuchun in Yang Province, and unlike Liang Province, it was only a relatively short distance away on the same side of the Yangtze River. An uprising by the unchecked bandits or the non-Chinese natives of Changsha could be a direct threat to the safety of the Sun family and of their region in general, and it was a scenario that was feared by all. The expectation was that the court would appoint a member of the ruling Liu family or an ally of the powerful court eunuch clique known as the 'Ten Attendants'; all were to be proved wrong when a letter arrived from the imperial capital bearing surprising news.

"I am to expect a visitor, a messenger," Sun Jian said with surprise. "Zhu Jun... says that I have been...!"

"Been *what*...?" Lady Wu prompted.

"Wait... no, I should not consider this anymore, not until the messenger appears, if he appears at all," Sun Jian decided. "If *this* happens, my lady, this is the beginnings of something at long, long last...!"

"...And you cannot tell me," Lady Wu scoffed.

"I do not wish to curse us," Sun Jian admitted. "You know how it is, my lady."

"Alright," Lady Wu conceded. "When can we expect this 'messenger'...?"

"Soon, apparently," Sun Jian said with poorly-hidden excitement.

"You're edging nearer and nearer to the door, Husband," Lady Wu noted dryly. "Is it that you wish to run away and go and tell your new friends, Cheng Pei and Zu Miao and whatever the other one was called...?"

"...You *know their names*, my lady, so *please*, don't be petty," Sun Jian scolded.

"But you admit that you want to run off and talk to them about this thing that you cannot share with *me*...?" Lady Wu retorted.

"No!" Sun Jian chortled. "I... I don't mean to 'talk' about it... not with all of them. I mean to be *advised* about it... by Cheng Pu. If this thing happens-"

"Oh, for Heavens' sakes, just *tell me*, you *silly man*!" Lady Wu said desperately.

Sun Jian's eyes moved to the entrance to the kitchen, where Sun Ce was standing with his small and unwieldy younger brother Quan, whom Ce was struggling to keep upright. Lady Wu turned, saw her two sons loitering, and dismissed them with a stern stare.

"...I might have been promoted to *Magistrate of Changsha*," Sun Jian whispered.

Lady Wu squealed reflexively, but supressed the gesture as quickly as she could.

"Now do you see why I am so cautious...?" Sun Jian asked pointedly.

Lady Wu smiled broadly and nodded as seriously as she could.

"Note that this is a militarily-guided decision," Sun Jian continued. "They want a tiger in the southwest, baring its teeth and claws to repel the hordes of bandits and barbarians: that's dangerous, and perhaps they couldn't find anyone 'silly' enough in the northern court to do it."

Lady Wu's smile faded ever so slightly, and she nodded slowly.

"There is also the possibility, however slight, that I might fail, and we might lose what little we have, instead of gaining more," Sun Jian continued. "There is also the possibility that this might be a temporary arrangement, and a northern man will be sent to take the post from me as soon as the 'rebellion' is ended."

Lady Wu's smile disappeared completely, and she nodded soberly.

"There is also the possibility that some court lackey or greedy eunuch might override this decision, and have one of their 'friends' appointed instead, in exchange for a favour, or a bribe... that's not uncommon," Sun Jian suggested. "I watch and listen, my lady, and the capital is a cutthroat place: Huangfu Song was a great hero, a man that was revered – as I sometimes am – for his successes in the Yellow Turban Rebellion, and he received even more rewards than I did; he was elevated to one of the highest military posts in the land, in fact. Yet *one mistake* – earning the ire of the eunuchs – reduced him from hero to disgraced pariah in one slanderous gesture. He may regain favour, he may not... I cannot say. But what I can say is that the same uncertainty hovers over my head, only more so, because I am not even a Huangfu Song... in the eyes of the court, I am-"

"I *know*... I *know*," Lady Wu interrupted miserably. "You don't need to say it."

Sun Jian exhaled noisily and turned his gaze away from Lady Wu.

"You should go and plan your responses to this with Cheng Pu," Lady Wu suggested. "I can't help you, Husband, as much as I'd like to be able to."

Sun Jian nodded tersely and departed from the house, leaving Lady Wu to wonder what the future held for her family.

"You seem troubled, Mister Sun," Cheng Pu said as he welcomed Sun Jian into his home and had him take the host seat.

"Please, call me Wentai," Sun Jian replied as he passed the recently-received letter to Cheng Pu, who started to read immediately. After a pause, Sun Jian smiled and added, "That's the least you can do if you're going to keep insisting on me taking the host seat in your own house. How are your family...?"

"Fine," Cheng Pu replied as he studied the correspondence.

"...Good," Sun Jian murmured.

Cheng Pu finished reading the letter, but he could only say "Oh."

"We seem to agree," Sun Jian chortled. "But you might perhaps elaborate on any ideas you have, Demou; I am torn, especially after the disaster in Liang."

"If the messenger does come, accept it," Cheng Pu suggested. "Even if you lost the role afterward to some toady, you'll be a hero thrice over, and you can make your own fortune if the foolish northern court won't reward you amply."

Sun Jian nodded silently.

"Doubts...?" Cheng Pu prompted.

"...Naturally," Sun Jian replied. "How many more times will I answer to this northern court, this den of corruption and ingratitude, and risk my life and the lives of my friends and

countrymen to preserve their existence so thanklessly, as I have until now...?"
"I can't answer that," Cheng Pu sighed. "What I *can* say, though, is that I'd expect the messenger within days."

A messenger did arrive several days later, and Sun Jian was officially told of his new role as Magistrate of Changsha. He hurried from his own office to the office where Cheng Pu worked to inform his friend of the confirmation.
"Well, congratulations, of course," Cheng Pu said warmly. "You'll be going to Changsha alone, or will you take your family with you...?"
Sun Jian's elated expression froze and his eyes darted about as he pondered that previously unconsidered point.
"Stop grinning like that, it looks ridiculous when you're obviously so distressed," Cheng Pu teased.
Sun Jian's smile faded, and as he turned his gaze to Cheng Pu, he tried to find the words to express how he felt, but settled instead on a discontented groan.
"Your eldest is ten or thereabouts... not really a fighting age," Cheng Pu noted. "And you suspect that your wife might be pregnant *again*... it'll be another boy as well, I suppose, you lucky thing."
Sun Jian scratched his head and laughed nervously.
Cheng Pu hummed thoughtfully and said, "Might they stay here, guarded by your brother-in-law, and you go west 'alone'...? I say 'alone', but of course you'll want a second, and I or Zu Mao, Han Dang or Huang Gai could fulfil that role."
"Zu Mao will insist upon it," Sun Jian supposed. "But I'd like us all to go, if I'm honest; this is big, and after Liang Province, I don't want to take any chances."
"You have a big promotion to safeguard this time, after all," Cheng Pu said dryly.
"...I do, yes," Sun Jian admitted. "This could be our moment... not just my family, but all of us, because as Magistrate of Changsha, I'd need good men to help me, and remember that the post allows me to appoint subordinates and pay them what I deem appropriate... we can always come back if-"
"Very good!" Cheng Pu chuckled. "I'll prepare, and let the others know so that they can decide what they want to do. But I imagine that's easy to guess."
"And I shall inform my wife and children!" Sun Jian declared as he got up to leave.
"Wait, wait, *wait*... you came to see me first?" Cheng Pu said with surprise.
"Ah... ... ...yes," Sun Jian realised. "Yes, I... I did, didn't I."
"Go *home*," Cheng Pu chuckled. "Your family should have been the first to know, Lord Sun; *honestly*!"
Sun Jian laughed awkwardly and left Cheng Pu's office after a series of polite bows.

"*Ayah*... you got the job... you got the job...!" Lady Wu said as her feelings darted back and forth between delight, horror and foreboding.
"You should stay here until it's safe for me to summon you," Sun

Jian suggested. "I will need to do all the usual nonsense, like seeing off my predecessor's family, and preparing my residence, and actually fighting the rebels that I've been installed there to fight... but I'm sure that within a few months-"
"As long as it takes," Lady Wu insisted. "Just... just be *careful*."

Sun Jian gathered as many men as he could, and began the journey west toward Changsha County. The journey would take his forces through vast swamplands with simple road networks, through valleys, across rivers, past lakes, and through several underdeveloped or completely undeveloped regions of potentially usable land. As Sun Jian and his allies viewed the land, they wondered to themselves whether the court was doing as much with the south of the country as they could be.

****

12

"**No time given for settling in, then!**" Cheng Pu joked as he parried an attack by a Wuhuan warrior from atop his horse. Sun Jian's forces had come under attack before they had even reached Changsha's capital, and the enemy – a mixture of bandits and opportunity-seizing tribespeople – numbered at least twice the size of his militia. Sun Jian watched as Huang Gai and Han Dang led the wings of his force to damage what little formation existed in the wings of the opposing force and spotted an opportunity.

"**Oh, no, no, for Heaven's sakes, you MUSTN'T...!**" Wu Jing screamed as Sun Jian rode into the central enemy force and started to hack at men left and right with his sword.

"**Yeah, well, you should've stayed in Fuchun, then, if you didn't want to see him do this!**" Zu Mao cackled as he readied his own horse and followed Sun Jian.

"*Aiee... reckless!*" Wu Jing complained. But before Cheng Pu could retort, Wu Jing raised his sword and urged his horse to pursue his brother-in-law into the battle. Wu Jing once again proved to be fairly capable in combat and assisted Zu Mao in defending Sun Jian's back while he dealt severe and unexpected casualties. After an hour of battle, the rebels retreated, and Sun Jian's forces regrouped to assess their performance.

"Next to no losses, even when they had the advantage," Cheng Pu praised. "Still, we're becoming rather good at this, after so many unfortunate encounters."

"So do we pursue...?" Sun Jian panted.

"...*Ayah*! Heartless man!" Wu Jing exclaimed. "Can we not *rest*???"

"Not if there's an opportunity to deal more damage to them," Sun Jian suggested.

"I've sent scouts," Cheng Pu revealed. "If they report that the enemy retreats in a disorganised fashion, then we can pursue double-time and rout them."

"So we *wait*, then," Han Dang said wearily.

The scouts reported no sign of activity other than a full retreat, so Sun Jian gave the order to march. As the forces advanced, a man of average height yet distinguished features ran alongside Huang Gai's horse and said, "Excuse me, Major Huang, but might I have a word...?"

Huang Gai turned and looked down at the man, examined his face for a moment, and said, "I think that I recognise you, sir."

"Major Huang, you might remember me from your work as a clerk for the ducal ministry," the man replied as he jogged to keep up with the horse's steady trot. "My family name is *Zhu*, my given name *Zhi*."

"Ah, yes...! I *do* remember you very well now, Mister Zhu Zhi!" Huang Gai chuckled. "You are always most polite in correspondence... truly the exemplary statesman in the making!"

"You are too kind," Zhu Zhi replied humbly.

"What can I do for you...?" Huang Gai prompted.

"We are about to walk into a trap," Zhu Zhi explained, and Huang Gai stopped immediately; Huang's small force of men stopped as well, since they now considered his instincts as the same as their own. Zhu Zhi noted the concern and added, "Not immediately, of course, else I'd be more worried; the enemy have blockaded the road ahead, and have placed a few primitive ambuscades near that small wood and the valley that we have to pass. It might be wise to have Commander Sun divert a force to the left and outflank them when they attack."

Huang Gai nodded seriously and said, "A thousand thanks... but I think that *you* should be the one to tell him this, Mister Zhu."

"I am but a lowly official, unproven in battle, while you are a hero of the hour," Zhu Zhi replied. "Why should he listen to me?"

"He is an exemplary man, as you are," Huang Gai said sincerely. "We shall speak with him immediately."

"Commander Sun."

"Ah, Huang Gongfu," Sun Jian hailed as Huang Gai and Zhu Zhi approached him. "And that is state official Zhu Zhi, courtesy name *Junli*, I think."

"It is, Magistrate Sun," Zhu Zhi said as he clasped his hands together and bowed slightly. "You have a good memory, since we have only ever crossed paths once."

"I never forget a man of substance," Sun Jian chuckled. "I am glad to see you amongst the ranks of the men that volunteered to help me save this place, and am only disappointed that you did not alert me to your presence sooner. Did you wish to speak with me, Junli...?"

"An ambush lies ahead, laid by Ou Xing's bandit allies," Zhu Zhi reported. "We must slow immediately, and make plans to counteract-"

"*Ambush*...?" Cheng Pu said with confusion. "Strange... the scouts reported a clear road ahead, and the enemy in full retreat."

"They obviously have something resembling a half-decent leader in this 'Ou Xing'," Zu Mao suggested. "How'd you know this, Mister Zhu, if you don't mind me asking...?"

"It is a hobby of mine to read up on warfare," Zhu Zhi admitted. "I took the liberty – excuse me for doing so, Mister Cheng – of making my own enquiries, and upon cautious quizzing of local people, I learned that Ou Xing has a lot of support in the area, and a set of traps was prepared in advance of our arrival. The small wood has a battalion of about a hundred men hiding in it, and the valley has a small contingent of poorly trained bowmen ready to shoot at us as we pass, once we enter... the other end will be blocked as we near it, rather than in advance, so that the scouts report a clear road. One of Ou's closest allies, the bandit chieftain Guo Shi, is leading the ambush party personally, while Ou Xing himself and his ally Zhou Chou are laying siege to the regional capital."

"*Aiee*... I have a lot to learn," Cheng Pu said sadly. "You have my sincerest gratitude for your hard work, Mister Zhu Junli."

"It is easy enough to assume that 'barbarians and bandits' lack leadership and especially sound strategy, but with enough minds pooled – even uneducated ones – ideas can sometimes flourish," Zhu Zhi suggested. "I doubt their ingenuity extends beyond this... and please, sir, don't berate your efforts or your service."

Sun Jian sensed a great measure of talent in Zhu Zhi, and immediately promoted him to an adviser alongside Cheng Pu, who was grateful for the help rather than jealous, threatened or offended. The ambushes were avoided or defeated, and Sun Jian's forces advanced to Changsha's capital, where they attacked the besiegers and forced their way into the city. Sun Jian accepted the seal of office – a stamp that would be used to prove the authenticity of any important documents produced within his administration – and began plans to counter the rebels when they laid siege to the city again.

Zu Mao laughed as he watched Sun Jian, Wu Jing, Cheng Pu, Huang Gai and Zhu Zhi formulate their strategy, and said to Han Dang, "So now we are the defenders! We're getting every kind of experience, aren't we, Mister Han?"

"Yes, we are!" Han Dang replied. "All of it useful, because I can't see it calming down at all… there's rumours around this city that Lingling and Guiyang are probably going to rise up as well."

"Yeah, and just like Liang Province, it's locals and barbarians fighting together, side by side, against the government," Zu Mao noted. "What that means in the end, Heaven only knows… but when the government keeps relying on nasty beggars like Dong Zhuo and idiots like Zhou Shen to be their spokesmen, it can only get worse. All I wonder, is… well…"

"…Whether we should be helping the government…?" Hang Dang snickered.

"Forget I spoke," Zu Mao pleaded.

"S'alright; I wonder the same, from time to time," Han Dang said as he studied the expression on Sun Jian's face. "Makes me wonder if we need to strike out on our own, sometimes… make the south a place of its own. All we need's a leader, and there he is, right there."

"That'd suit me fine," Zu Mao agreed. "Mister Sun Jian is a hero and a statesman, just the sort of man you need at a time like this, and people're flocking to him. I mean, look at the new man, Zhu Zhi."

"A smart one, and no mistake," Han Dang murmured.

"Yeah, and he sees it same as we do; Mister Sun Jian is the *future*," Zu Mao suggested. "You're right, I'm right, we're both right; Mister Sun is going to make the south a place to be proud of, a place to be respected, and we're gonna help him… makes you feel proud, doesn't it…?"

"…But we need more good men, even more than we have already," Han Dang supposed. "We need good men like they were all that there was, to do something like that… still, if it's possible, Sun Wentai is the man to do it!"

The battles continued over the following days.

"Well, here they come again," Cheng Pu sighed as he watched the rebels advance on the city from his vantage point on the high walls of Changsha's capital.

"This time, we end it," Sun Jian decided.

"Not an option," Zhu Zhi said with regret, "but we can give them something to think about. We'll let them set up their ladders and whatnot, and settle in; are Huang Gai and Han Dang ready…?"

"As they'll ever be," Cheng Pu replied.

"Yeah, and so am I," Zu Mao said impatiently. "I can't wait to get out there."

"...And again, they bring no method of assault that really threatens us," Zhu Zhi said as he watched the rebel commanders issue the orders of the day. "Right; signallers at the ready...!"

The rebels began the siege; but as soon as the assault was underway, a hidden signal relay told Han Dang and Huang Gai – who had left the city under cover of darkness, and camped at a distance – that the time had come to spring a trap. Both officers led a force of men against the left and right sides of the rebel camp, throwing it into disarray; as the besiegers turned about to defend their leaders, Sun Jian and Zu Mao led a force out of the main gates and routed them as they fled.

"An excellent result, Mister Zhu Junli," Wu Jing said as he watched the events from the city walls.

"I try," Zhu Zhi replied humbly. "They'll be back, though."

Wu Jing nodded and said, "Yes, but I think we'll win in the end."

Sun Jian's militia broke the siege of Changsha's capital after weeks of solid defence and sporadic ground-based counterattacks. But almost as soon as Changsha was relieved, the neighbouring Lingling and Guiyang regions experienced similar outbreaks of civil defiance, and Sun Jian was forced to send forces to supress those as well; his stay in the central southern 'counties' was destined to be long and devoid of peaceful interludes, but that was a surprise to none. Sun Jian would be created a marquis for his efforts and allowed to remain as Magistrate of Changsha, and that is where he remained as a protector of the Han Empire until the next great disaster befell the country.

****

13

The chaos would bring men from all parts of the country together as allies or enemies; and sometimes, men who lived at opposite ends of the country would one day meet under incredible circumstances. The eastern tip of northern China was part of Qing Province, a place that did not immediately experience the worst of the unrest due to its distance from the capital. In Huangxian, a small city in the Donglai Prefecture of Qing Province, a 20-year-old man of exceptional talent and character was serving in an inconsequential role as a junior official. That man was *Taishi Ci*, styled 'Ziyi', and fate was about to put him on a journey that would one day see him become a significant figure in the land.

"Are you well, Mother...?" Taishi Ci asked as he prepared to leave his home.

"I'll be fine, honestly," Ci's mother insisted. "Go on, you'll be late."

Taishi Ci bowed respectfully, and said, "I shall return on time as always, Mother. Please, be well."

"Go on, go *on*!" Ci's mother cackled. "*Honestly*...!"

Taishi Ci left his home and began his journey to work within the offices of the administrator of the prefecture. But this day, something would happen that would change Taishi Ci's life forever.

"Ah, Official Taishi!" a voice hailed as soon as Taishi Ci entered his office.

"*Ayah*," Taishi Ci groaned. "Am I late, Administrator...?"

"I don't honestly care if you are; please, follow me, we need to talk," the Administrator ordered. Taishi Ci followed his superior to his decorated office and took a seat when invited. However, the Administrator was silent and brooding once the two were seated.

"...Have I done something...?" Taishi Ci said at last.

"No... oh, no, sorry, no!" the Administrator said with a nervous laugh. "It... well, you see, I have a conundrum, and I think that only you – a man of wit, skill, speed and strength that far exceeds the role that you now occupy – can resolve."

"You flatter me undeservedly," Taishi Ci said as he clasped his hands together and bowed humbly.

"No, I don't," the Administrator retorted. "Since a youth, you've been known as an expert horseman, unrivalled in sport, a deft swordsman, a good writer... you're a great talent, and I expect you to go far in life. But that is then and you; this is *now*, and *me*. I need your help, Taishi Ci. Every man answers to someone, as you answer to me. I answer to the Provincial Office. The Inspector's senior officer and I have, for some time, been at odds over a number of local civil matters, and now it seems that the time has come for things to become serious. He has decided to elevate matters to the highest authority, and has written to Luoyang this morning."

Taishi Ci groaned involuntarily.

"Exactly," the Administrator said with a morbid laugh. "You know how it is, Taishi Ci... things were bad enough before the cultists began tearing the country apart; the corruption in the court is beyond belief, and it operates on a simple rule: in a dispute, the first argument is taken as the right one, to save effort. Unfortunately, his office is closer to the capital, so if I don't hurry, I am finished. I have written a letter: I want you to deliver it to Luoyang, and I want you to do *whatever it takes*, Taishi Ci, to ensure that it gets there first."

"Very well," Taishi Ci said without reservation. "Where is the letter...?"

"I do not even have to convince you; truly a worthy man," the Administrator sighed as he took the letter from his waist sash and handed it to Taishi Ci. "Please, do all that you can; remember, Mister Taishi, that the man I work against is-"

"A corrupt wretch," Taishi Ci said as he got to his feet. "I will honour your fair treatment of me and deliver this letter, *whatever it takes*."

The Administrator bowed low and said, "Heavens be with you."

The journey to the capital would be arduous. The Donglai Administrator had provided a fast horse for Taishi Ci to use to begin his journey, but that would not be enough; eventually that horse would tire, and he would need to secure another means of fast transportation if he was to beat his rival from the Provincial Office. He paid a visit to his home before he departed, in order to say goodbye to his family.

"What are you doing back here???" Taishi Ci's mother asked worriedly.

"Never fear, Mother, I have not been dismissed," Taishi Ci replied. "I... ... ...Mother, I have to go on a long journey, to the capital, and-"

"To the *capital*...?" Ci's mother said curiously and with a hint of excitement.

"I haven't time to be stood here," Taishi Ci continued urgently. "Mother, I might not come back to you, so listen; if you need anything, just go straight to the Administrator's office, and tell them who you are: that you are my mother. That will ensure that you are alright."

Ci's mother nodded nervously and said, "Hurry, then, my son. Gods be with you."

Taishi Ci fled his family house at great speed and began a journey to the southwest.

When Taishi's horse did eventually tire, he was east of the capital, and he knew that his rival had a significant head start. The most likely land route that a messenger might take were to go west to Ji'nan and then south into Yan Province by following the Ji River, but any that chose to brave a boat journey could sail down the Ji River from Ji'nan and go straight toward the capital once it met with the Yellow River. After securing a new horse from a travelling trader on the road to the capital, Taishi Ci began a journey west toward the Ji River in the hope of securing a boat. He had already been travelling for several days and nights without proper sleep or nourishment, but he knew that he could not fail.

When Taishi Ci eventually reached Ji'nan, he was already onto his third horse and in desperate need of rest. He found the nearest horse trader and prepared to barter for the animal that he had been using.

"It fast?" the trader asked.

"So-so," Taishi replied.

"It healthy...?"

"It has brought me here from Mount Tai without rest," Taishi Ci replied.

"Not bad!" the trader chuckled. "Alright; how much did you say you wanted fer it, friend...?"

"Enough to get a boat, some rice to fill my stomach, and coin for five journeys," Taishi Ci said impatiently. "I don't care, forgive my abruptness, so long as I can continue my journey, sir."

"...I'll give you a fair price," the trader replied cautiously. "You in a rush...?"

Taishi Ci smiled and said, "I have a letter to deliver. Where can I find a man to take me down the Ji to Chenliu?"

The trader laughed and said, "You'll definitely need me to give you a good price! There're men that'll do that, but it means losing time earning from regular crossings. Actually, you're lucky you came here when you did; nowadays, everyone 'round here that's dangerous is too busy hating our new administrator, same as most of us do. So long as that letter isn't from *Cao Cao*, you'll not have too much trouble; it *isn't*, is it...?"

"I'm from Donglai," Taishi Ci insisted. "It's the Donglai Administrator's letter."

"...He's a good sort, I hear, who runs that place," the trader noted. "Alright, well then you'll get a *very* good price!"

"Great, thank you sir," Taishi Ci replied impatiently.

Taishi Ci's next objective was securing a boat, and that meant haggling with the boatmen that lined the riverbank.

"Chenliu?" a boatman said with surprise.

"Yes," Taishi Ci replied wearily. "Please, I'm in a hurry; you're the third man I've asked, so-"

"You'll pay whatever I ask?" the boatman prompted.

"...Yes," Taishi Ci replied nervously.

"And if we're stopped by pirates, you'll take on all the trouble," the boatman asked further. "Are you a messenger from Cao Cao?"

"*No!*" Taishi Ci chortled. "I'm from *Donglai*, I just want to-"

"Donglai?" the boatman exclaimed. "I have extended family in Donglai! Alright, then, Mister...?"

"Taishi, Taishi Ci, official in the administrator's office," Taishi Ci said impatiently.

"I think it would take time to check!" the boatman chuckled. "Alright, I'm losing a lot of crossing work doing this, but if you're paying... let's go. Where is your luggage?"

"Thank you," Taishi Ci said with relief. "No luggage, I'm delivering a letter."

"I don't want to know," the boatman insisted. "What I don't know, I can't repeat. Let's just go... and you'd better not be working for Cao Cao!"

Taishi Ci travelled down the Ji River with the aid of the boatman; the journey should have offered some sort of rest, but the Ji River – like all rivers in that chaotic age – was continually harassed by pirates, and only a fool would sleep longer than he had to anyway, since he did not truly know the boatman either.

"Well, here we are... Chenliu," the boatman said as he surveyed the waters nervously. "Pay me quickly, so I can get back."

Taishi Ci paid a fairly handsome sum for the journey downriver and jumped onto the dock to begin a search for a place to rest briefly; he knew that his rival had to stop and rest as much as he did, so he asked around for a tavern or inn of some sort.

Taishi Ci finally found a place to rest and approached the owner to request refreshments.

"You look like a man who hasn't slept in days!" the tavern keeper said with amusement as Taishi Ci struggled to keep his weary body upright.

"I just need an hour to *sleep*," Taishi Ci explained. "Nothing else, just *sleep*... oh, well, if you have a little *rice*..."

"Wine?" the tavern keeper prompted.

"No wine... I'm in a hurry," Taishi Ci insisted. "I have a message... deliver to... capital, quickly, *have to*."

"...I'm presuming a lot here, but if you need to rest and move, why not get a carriage?" the tavern keeper suggested. "You have no luggage, right?"

"None," Taishi Ci confirmed. "But... *bandits*...?"

"Pay a man to provide security if you must; but the White Wave Bandits around the capital are really only interested in wealthy travellers, which you most certainly are not," the tavern keeper explained. "I can get you a carriage right now; then you can sleep on the way without losing time."

"Thank you, good sir," Taishi Ci said gratefully. "I need my wits about me..."

"You sound like a man from the northeast," the tavern keeper noted as he turned and gestured to an apprentice behind him. "Qing Province, is it...?"

"*Donglai*," Taishi Ci confirmed.

"...You seem like an honest sort; you get to tell these things in my line of work," the tavern keeper decided. "Alright, well, follow the lad when he comes back, and you'll be on your way west in no time!"

"My... thanks," Taishi Ci said with increasing fatigue.

Although the carriage ride was bumpy, Taishi Ci was able to get some sleep for the first part of the journey; it was only when the open carriage reached Luoyang that the driver was stopped by a gang of swarthy men that wore a mixture of scruffy work clothes and robes under their leather armour.

"Who's in the back?" the leader of the men said to the driver as he stroked the nose of the carthorse.

"J-just some messenger from the east," the driver replied.

"Wh-what...?" Taishi Ci yawned as he sat up and looked at the gang of men that now surrounded him.

"Who're you, then, mate?" the bandit leader asked rudely.

"A messenger from Donglai," Taishi Ci replied as his wits returned. "I'm delivering an urgent letter; it's all I have on me now."

The bandit leader frowned and said, "No money purse?"

"It's empty," Taishi Ci chuckled as he showed the bandit leader his battered leather purse. "Search me if you want... but I spent everything I had getting here."

"...Alright, lads, let's leave him be," the bandit leader said after a moments' reflection. "Off you go, fellows."

The White Wave Bandits backed away from the carriage, and Taishi Ci continued the last part of his journey toward Luoyang.

The vastness of the imperial capital might have overawed Taishi Ci on any other day, but he knew that he had a job to do. Unfortunately, entering the capital would be no easy feat, as recent uprisings and insurrections had led to a massive increase in security checks on any travellers going into or out of the capital.

Taishi Ci leant forward, tapped the driver on the shoulder and said, "You can leave me here, friend... no sense you getting caught up in checks when you don't even want to go in there!"

"My thanks," the carriage driver said, and Taishi Ci disembarked and said his farewells. Once the carriage was gone, Taishi advanced toward the main gate, and noticed an agitated man in official's robes arguing with two soldiers.

"I need to get through!" the man protested. **"I have an urgent petition from the Inspector of Qing Province!"**

Taishi Ci was struck dumb with horror; this was the man that he had been sent to overtake, and now he was in front of him with a considerable advantage.

"And we already told you that you need to wait!" one of the soldiers retorted. "You'll get your turn, Mister whoever-you-are, so please wait!"

"I'll be making a complaint to the Magistrate of Luoyang!" the messenger bellowed.

"You do that," the second solder heckled. "Get in line."

The frustrated messenger turned, observed the queue of people and carriages waiting to pass the human wall of security, and groaned noisily.

"...Right... okay... think... think...!" Taishi Ci said to himself with increasing frustration. He knew that he had only one chance to succeed, but that meant a small moral compromise. After a few moments of wrangling with his conscience, he made his decision and acted upon it.

"You there!"

The messenger turned and observed Taishi Ci, who had tidied himself and haggled with a trader in the queue for an azure silk robe; his new attire and lofty attitude made him look enough like a junior official for the messenger to be fooled. He had a knife tucked into his belt, but the messenger failed to notice it.

"Did you not hear me?" Taishi Ci asked with false irritation. "Aren't you the fellow claiming to be from Qing Province?"

"I am, I am!" the messenger said excitedly. "They-"

"Necessary checks," Taishi Ci insisted. "What is the nature of your request?"

"I have this letter to deliver from the office of the Inspector of Qing Province!" the messenger explained as he produced the wooden tube containing the petition. "This must reach the offices of-"

"That could be anything, and you could be anyone," Taishi Ci chortled. "We're tiring of the false petitions: day after day, the-"

"This is genuine!" the messenger protested as Taishi Ci subtly backed him further and further away from the crowds and further and further away from the gates.

"Isn't everything genuine?" Taishi Ci retorted. "Let me see it."

The messenger was hesitant, so Taishi Ci shook his head and said, "I thought not. You're obviously another fraud, another-"

"Alright, alright!" the messenger whined as he passed the letter to Taishi Ci, who immediately opened the tube, took out the cloth letter, and started to turn around.

"...Mm, well, this is certainly convincing," Taishi Ci said as he held the letter with one hand and quietly reached for the knife in his belt with the other.

"So can I pass?" the messenger said excitedly.

Taishi Ci did not answer; he quickly stabbed the cloth letter with his knife, and cut it down the middle.

"*Ayah!*" the messenger exclaimed as he realised what Taishi Ci was doing. "**HELP! GUARDS! THIS-**"

"You'll be quiet if you don't want to die," Taishi Ci hissed as he spun around and confronted the messenger, who was immediately struck dumb with fear. "You've just handed a piece of official documentation over to a total stranger to be destroyed; think about it."

The messenger allowed Taishi Ci to back him away from the inquisitive crowd.

"*Why...?*" the messenger whined. "No, wait, you... you're from...!"

Taishi Ci smiled and nodded silently.

"Why should I be quiet?" the messenger decided. "You're the guilty man... you have motive... you *tricked me*! You'll just hand over *your* petition now, and-"

"When my superior learns what I did to your petition, he'll not reward me, friend... I'll be in as much trouble as you are," Taishi Ci said calmly. "I stopped you submitting yours; that's all I could do. But now, I'm a fugitive, we *both are*."

The messenger started to sob.

"**Accept your fate!**" Taishi Ci barked. "Now come on: I owe you some help, I think, so let's work together."

The distressed messenger nodded as he sobbed.

"We must both flee immediately," Taishi Ci said as he gestured toward two approaching soldiers. "They know something is amiss: should we run, or would you rather explain what has happened?"

The panicked and confused messenger was only made more frightened by Taishi Ci's ominous words and calm demeanour; he turned and fled, and Taishi Ci followed him.

Taishi Ci was the more athletic of the two men, so it was not long before he overtook his rival; once the two were a distance away from the capital, Taishi Ci stopped running, and the messenger halted moments later.

"I cannot... believe... what is happening," the messenger whined. "What can I do now that you have ruined me???"

Taishi Ci glared at the Provincial Office messenger and replied by asking, "Why did you agree... to defend such a wretched man... over a decent one...?"

The messenger was silent.

"You must... have known his nature!" Taishi said accusingly. "The Donglai Administrator is... is a good man, everyone knows that!"

"It is not my concern!" the messenger retorted. "I was asked to do a job!"

"And you failed," Taishi Ci heckled. "Now you must run, as must I... the sad thing is that I did what I did to defend a good man, and so suffer undeservedly."

"I... I cannot discuss this anymore," the messenger sighed. "Are we far enough away now to be safe...?"

"...No," Taishi Ci replied. "We must keep running. Come on."

Taishi Ci resumed running, and the messenger reluctantly followed; this time, however, Taishi Ci quickly fell behind, and the rival messenger failed to notice it. When he eventually did, the messenger laughed wearily and shouted, **"Where are you, and why do**... you... *not...?"*

The messenger had turned as he had spoken, and he was expecting to see a tired Taishi Ci struggling to keep up with him; but nobody was there. It did not take the messenger long to realise what had happened, and he collapsed to the ground, wailing like a child.

"What's your name, and what do you want?" a soldier barked as he was faced with yet another tired, untidy traveller looking to enter the imperial capital of Luoyang.

The traveller smiled triumphantly and panted, *"Taishi Ci*, of Donglai... I have a petition from... the Administrator... of *Donglai*, Qing Province."

Taishi Ci had succeeded in getting his master's petition submitted before that of the Provincial Office, which meant that his master's life and career were saved. His methods had been unlawful, however, and the wronged messenger was finally able to lodge an official complaint that was taken very seriously; but by that time, Taishi Ci – who would become famous for his actions – had fled the 'mainland' and gone into exile in the Liaodong Peninsula, which was northeast of his old home, across the vast expanse of the Yellow Sea. He would have to remain there for several years, but his journey toward a place in history – and a key role in the founding of an independent kingdom in the south of China – had begun nonetheless.

✱✱✱✱✱✱✱✱✱✱✱

ACT II: THE EASTERN PASS COALITION

14

Three years passed in which the whole of China was rocked by rebellion after rebellion and event after event. In addition to the bandit armies that had formed, the Yellow Turbans reappeared time and again, which kept the government busy in the majority of the land. Further to that, the rebels in northwest Liang Province rose up time and again, killing or recruiting more government officials in the process.

The government had finally despatched one of the heroes of the original Yellow Turban Rebellion, Huangfu Song, to pacify the Liang Province rebels for a second time, and he appeared to be making significant gains, while other heroes like Zhu Jun, Liu Bei, Gongsun Zan and Ding Yuan were seemingly weakening the various groups of rebels, cultists and bandits in the north. Sun Jian, meanwhile, had led his men to Changsha, Guiyang and Lingling and smashed the rebellions in those places with similar vigour and even greater success.

But at the same time, political changes that had been enacted with the best of intentions had weakened the Han court still further. The decision that had the greatest long-term impact was the promotion of certain provincial inspectors to governors with the ability to act almost independently; this made powerful warlords of men like Liu Yan of western Yi Province, Liu Biao of central Jing Province, and Tao Qian of eastern Xu Province, and set the stage for things to come.

Five years after the first Yellow Turban Rebellion that had given Sun Jian his first opportunity, the country was rocked by the announcement that Emperor Ling had died at the age of 33, after 21 years as the ruler of China. A power vacuum was left by his passing that was quickly filled by the late emperor's wife – now Empress Dowager Hè – and her brother, Hè Jin; a brief struggle with the eunuch faction known as the 'Ten Attendants' led to the death of their leader, the partial dissolution of their self-serving, militia-based 'Army of the Western Garden', and the appointment of Emperor Ling's eldest son – and Hè Jin's biological nephew – Liu Bian as Emperor Shao. But in the imperial court, there was no such thing as finality: within a short time, Hè Jin's attempts to eliminate the rest of the 'Ten' had led to his own assassination and a sequence of events that had led to something far worse than anyone had ever imagined possible. Worst of all for Sun Jian and his allies, the greatest beneficiary of the chaos was a man that they loathed and feared.

"A messenger from the imperial court just arrived, Lord Sun," Cheng Pu said as he rushed into the audience hall of the Marquis of Wucheng and Magistrate of Changsha, Sun Jian.
"Not *another one*," Sun Jian complained. "What is it *now*, I wonder...?"
"Let him in, and we'll see," Sun Jian's bodyguard, Zu Mao, suggested dryly.
Sun Jian agreed silently, and Cheng Pu officially announced the imperial messenger, who was greeted by kowtows as he unfurled

a proclamation from Luoyang.

"Dong Zhuo, General of the Van, is hereby promoted to 'Excellency of Works'!" the messenger announced; every man in Sun Jian's court was filled with rage. **"Hua Xiong is promoted to Commander-in-Chief of the army! Wang Yun is promoted to Excellency over the Masses, and Lü Bu to General of Chariots and Cavalry! Other promotions and information are included herein!"**

The messenger passed the proclamation to Zhu Zhi and departed.

"...Do we have to bow and scrape *every time* some little man from the capital comes here, Mister Sun Jian...?" Zu Mao whispered as each man righted himself.

"Afraid so, my friend," Sun Jian sighed; he then turned to his adviser Zhu Zhi and said, **"Mister Zhu, please tell me that was some sort of *joke*!"**

"...I'm afraid not, Lord Sun," Zhu Zhi said as he read through the imperial decree with increasing discomfort. "I don't know what's happened here, but Dong Zhuo's basically running everything, and he's put all of his old friends in high places; I don't know how a man like Wang Yun fits into this; perhaps he's there to give this monstrous government some sort of legitimacy... but overall, they're all there... Hua Xiong, Jia Xu, Li Ru, Li Jue, Guo Si, Li Su, Niu Fu... but who's *Lü Bu*...?"

"I've heard of him," Huang Gai admitted. "He's the- ...Well, I suppose 'bodyguard' is the best description for his actual role... of Bing Province's Inspector, Ding Yuan. He is, by all accounts, one of the most incredible athletes and warriors of our age."

"What's he doing serving *Dong Zhuo*, if he's *Ding Yuan's* bodyguard?" Sun Jian wondered.

"Ding Yuan's *adopted son*," Cheng Pu revealed.

"Oh, wait, yes, now I know who Lü Bu is," Zhu Zhi said apologetically. "Yes, he's the adopted son of Ding Yuan, isn't he... he's been fighting the Black Mountain Bandits to the north of the imperial capital for a few years. But as Lord Sun says, his connection to Dong Zhuo makes no sense; why would a good man like Ding Yuan work with *Dong Zhuo*? ...For that matter, where is Ding Yuan in the list of promotions...? All of his posts have been given to- ...Oh, *no*... I see."

Sun Jian's court awaited an explanation.

"...Ding Yuan's *dead*," Zhu Zhi said as he read the other announcements. "It seems that he is a 'traitor' that 'opposed key government decisions that were critically important to reform'."

"*Ayah*! *Dead*???" Sun Jian exclaimed. "Dong Zhuo has killed a great man!"

"...No, Mister Sun Jian, I think that *Lü Bu* has killed a great man," Zu Mao suggested. "S'obvious what happened here, fellows: Dong Zhuo *bought him*."

"...I want more information about this, not just some piece of Dong Zhuo's self-serving propaganda issued in His Majesty's name," Sun Jian ordered. "That man and I have history – *bad history* – and if he can kill Ding Yuan, he can kill *me*."

"He'd have sent men here to arrest you, or had you demoted," Zhu Zhi insisted. "No, he's up to something... he wants to see who accepts this outrage, and who doesn't. As you say, we need more information; let's get that information, and see where we stand."

Sun Jian turned to a plain-featured man in elaborate official's robes and said, "Mister Huan Jie, you are known for your keen mind and political savvy; do you have an early opinion about this 'northern crisis'…?"

Huan Jie bowed low and said, "It is as Junli has said; but if he is now the court, we might have cause to worry, since he could strip you of all rank if he wished, and–"

"Let's not get too flustered, gentlemen," Zhu Zhi pleaded. "We'll wait and see…"

Many days passed, and more and more information started to emerge about what was going on in the north. Eventually, there was enough information available for Zhu Zhi to explain the situation to a court that was aware of enough of it all to be struck silent before proceedings began.

"Okay… right… *yes*," Zhu Zhi said hesitantly. "Well, uh… as you may or may not know, all of you, this is where things stand as far as current information goes. The former Commander-in-Chief, *Hè Jin*, was assassinated by the 'Ten Attendants', and His Majesty and the Prince of Chenliu abducted by those same eunuchs while they tried to escape Western Garden Army Colonel *Yuan Shao*, who was rampaging through the streets of Luoyang… and even the *palace*… with his cousin Yuan Shu, killing all of their kind."

"Yuan Shao – *the* Yuan Shao, heir to the Ru County Yuan clan estate…?" Cheng Pu exclaimed.

"Yes," Zhu Zhi replied.

"*Yuan Shao* – a descendant of countless court cronies and one of the wealthiest men in the land – entered the imperial palace with an armed militia and killed palace attendants?" Cheng Pu said with increasing alarm.

"…It seems so," Zhu Zhi replied.

"That's *treason*… that's punishable by death!" Cheng Pu noted.

"*Usually*, yes," Zhu Zhi replied. "But this… this is not 'usual'."

Sun Jian shook his head with disbelief.

"Dong Zhuo somehow managed to locate and 'secure' His Majesty and the Prince of Chenliu after they somehow escaped the eunuchs," Zhu Zhi continued. "Reports say that the 'Ten' are all dead… but unfortunately, Dong managed to convince His Majesty to give him temporary regent status."

"*Bastard*," Zu Mao grumbled.

"In the ensuing mayhem, Dong Zhuo apparently announced that he wanted to *depose* His Majesty Shaodi and replace him with the Prince of Chenliu," Zhu Zhi continued. "Ding Yuan objected and threatened to oppose Dong Zhuo, *militarily* if necessarily… in turn, Dong Zhuo managed to convince Ding Yuan's foster son, Lü Bu, to defect to his forces and kill Ding Yuan for him. Lü Bu is now the foster son of Dong Zhuo, and serves him in the same capacity that he once served Ding Yuan. Yuan Shao, who was Hè Jin's deputy of sorts, was forced to flee the capital, and he seems to be deciding whether he is going to attack Dong Zhuo or not; Dong Zhuo has offered Shao a title, so we'll see what happens there. Other former Western Garden Army colonels, like Cao Cao, seem to be waiting to see what Yuan Shao does. In the meantime… Dong Zhuo appears to have put his plan into action."

"What do you mean?" Han Dang asked angrily.

"He's deposed His Majesty Shaodi," Zhu Zhi announced; everyone else in the room gasped at the idea.

"He *can't do that*!" Cheng Pu chortled.

"He has nonetheless, Demou," Zhu Zhi confirmed. "He's having another ascension ceremony for the Prince of Chenliu, and Empress Dowager Hè and the deposed Majesty will be exiled... and then, if all suspicions are correct..."

Zhu Zhi did not continue; after a short silence, Huang Gai said, "Would Dong Zhuo really commit *regicide*...?"

Sun Jian – who had been angrily silent – got to his feet and said, "Dong Zhuo would destroy the sky, the moon or Heaven itself if they were somehow getting in his way! I *warned* that fool Zhang Wen! I *warned* Zhou Shen, I *warned* Zhu Jun! I *said* the man was trouble, and that we'd pay if he wasn't... ... ...alright, I didn't expect *this*, but it was obvious that he was trouble! This is the result of *wilful blindness* to an *obvious danger*!"

"But what can we do...?" the politician Huan Jie said with desperation. "Dong Zhuo *is* the imperial court now; Lord Sun is right to be fearful. Right now, Dong Zhuo is too busy to look to the south, but-"

"Calm down," Zhu Zhi pleaded. "The ray of hope is Yuan Shao."

"Yuan Shao is an elitist do-nothing," Cheng Pu scoffed. "Where was he when the Yellow Turbans were tearing the country apart...?"

"Ah, but it was *he* that slaughtered the eunuchs, and freed the court of their grip," Zhu Zhi proposed. "Had Hè Jin not been assassinated by the 'Ten' and Ding Yuan not betrayed by Lü Bu, then he would be the hero of the hour in an era of peace."

"...A fair point," Cheng Pu conceded. "But what must we do? The time for gathering information has passed; what else is there to know...? It won't be long before Dong Zhuo tests our allegiances, and that is the critical hour."

"Our only options are to resist or yield," Huan Jie suggested.

"I don't care what the consequences are, I'll never yield to him," Sun Jian insisted. "No matter what he said to begin with, eventually he'd make consorts of our wives and daughters, and eunuchs out of our sons. We have to fight him: if needs be, we'll form a southern coalition against him. He has no followers save his usual band, so-"

"Liang Province is with him, Lord Sun," Huan Jie noted. "He has the northwest."

"I *don't care*!" Sun Jian chortled. "*Let him* have the northwest; that was lost ages ago to the Qiang and rebels that he was secretly siding with, so we can hardly be *surprised*! *Leave him* with the northwest! That leaves the whole of the rest of the land! We must find out what men like Tao Qian, Liu Biao, Liu Yan, Liu Dai, Han Fu, and Zhu Jun intend to do; half of them are relatives of the beleaguered Majesty, so- ...Oh wait, I have not heard from my friend and sponsor, General Zhu Jun, for a while... surely he is not...?"

"...Zhu Jun was stripped of his offices and slandered by the 'Ten', but he ekes out an existence to the west of Luoyang," Zhu Zhi explained. "Your sponsor is an isolated man... and soon a dead one, I fear, if the coalition doesn't do more. Huangfu Song is semi-retired, so I hear, and cannot act."

"Zhu Jun will *live*: he *must do*, now that Dong Zhuo threatens to destroy everything!" Sun Jian insisted.

As Sun Jian's court continued to argue about their next move, Zu Mao shook his head and muttered, "A dark day."

As the weeks passed, one man finally acted; the Administrator of Dong Prefecture in Yan Province finally tired of heeding Dong Zhuo's orders and began a public campaign to draw out other administrators and governors against Dong Zhuo, who had by then become 'Chancellor of State', and hence the unopposed power in the capital. The call was mainly answered by many powerful men in the east of the country – including, to the surprise of some, a renegade Xiongnu 'barbarian' chieftain – and Yuan Shao was chosen to lead them. The 'Eastern Pass Coalition' asked for all men to rise up against Dong Zhuo, and Sun Jian was keen to answer.

"The problem," Zhu Zhi said as he addressed Sun Jian's court once again, "is whose banner we will fight under."

"Our own, surely," Han Dang suggested.

"I'm afraid that this coalition is already turning into a political farce," Cheng Pu said with regret. "Each Provincial Governor is fighting under his own banner, and some local Administrators, Magistrates and Chancellors, the same; only *they* can lead named armies against Dong Zhuo. I'm presuming that this is an attempt to prevent more influential militias like their own being born out of all this."

"But Lord Sun's the Magistrate of Changsha," Han Dang noted.

"It may be enough, but we must assume otherwise," Zhu Zhi retorted. "After all, Changsha is ridiculed as a 'southern shire', 'neither this nor that', and an 'undeveloped wasteland'..."

"...Damn the north and its prejudices!" Cheng Pu cried.

"So we must pick a banner," Sun Jian mused. "What are the options...?"

"I'd say the closest is the best place to start," Zhu Zhi replied.

Sun Jian frowned and said, "Wu Prefecture's Administrator, Sheng Xian, is an upstanding gentleman, and Yang is our home..."

"Regrettably, he is not an option," Zhu Zhi replied. "Yang Province's governor is not getting involved, and Sheng Xian can hardly have Wu Prefecture rise up if the governor won't. Yi Province and Jing Province appear to be remaining neutral as well... so our only close choice is Yu Province. The Provincial Inspector, Kong Zhou, is recruiting, so we are most likely going to fight under his banner, or the banner of General of the Rear *Yuan Shu*, who also fights from Yu."

"Kong Zhou, or Yuan Shu," Cheng Pu said ponderously. "What do you think we should do, Zhu Junli...?"

"Honestly, I cannot say," Zhu Zhi replied miserably. "Inspector Liu Dai of Yan and Administrator Zhang Miao of Chenliu are better choices, perhaps; Kong Zhou is Inspector of Yu at Dong Zhuo's decree, so he might not be reliable in the long term, while Yuan Shu... is Yuan Shu."

"By which you mean...?" Han Dang prompted.

"He's a bitter sort," Zhu Zhi explained. "He was set to inherit the Yuan clan fortune and become its head, until his uncle – the then incumbent – adopted Shu's older brother Yuan Shao, making Shao the new future head. Yuan Shu resents that, and has become a very, very unpleasant character... or so I hear. So-"

"Wait, wait," Zu Mao chuckled. "If Yuan Shao is older anyway, then why...?"

"Yuan Shao was the product of an affair between Yuan Shu's father and a maid, before Shu was born," Zhu Zhi continued. "That means Shao is a bastard when looking at the clan hierarchy, and so unable to lead it; when he was adopted by his uncle, he became his uncle's legitimate son, so... there you have it."

"...So Yuan Shu really shouldn't be complaining at all, the way I see it," Zu Mao suggested. "His older brother should get it all anyway, maid for a mum or not... sorry, but Yuan Shu sounds like an arsehole."

"But he is a coalition leader all the same, and General of the Rear, at that," Cheng Pu said thoughtfully. "I, too, am at a loss; my lord, you may have to decide this for yourself."

"Two of you, and I am still forced to be my own counsel!" Sun Jian teased. "But, well, I see your problem; that basically, they're *all* flawed, and not one of them is up to the job. In that case, we might as well tender our services to Inspector Kong Zhou, and after him, Yuan Shu, and then Liu Dai, and after him, Zhang Miao... and so on, until we end up in Ji, fighting under Han Fu, if needs be. But I *will* be part of this, and I *will* kill Dong Zhuo *personally* if I can!"

"...Fine," Zhu Zhi said sombrely. "I'll put things in motion."

"Ah! Here he is! The *Marquis*!" Lady Wu heckled as Sun Jian entered his home after a long day of discussions; two of Sun Jian's younger sons, Quan and Yi, fled when they realised that there might be a confrontation between their parents.

"Not now," Sun Jian sighed as he sat at his study desk and stared at the assorted stationery. "...Where's Ben and Hè?"

"Your nephew and 'nephew' are 'sparring' with *our eldest son*," Lady Wu replied.

"I said 'Not now'!" Sun Jian pleaded. "I have much to think about, my lady, so I don't have time for domestic matters."

"...'Domestic matters'...?" Lady Wu chortled. "I'm a 'domestic matter', now, am I? Oh, well then, I'll just go and be a 'domestic matter' somewhere else!"

"*Aiee*... I have to go to war again!" Sun Jian said as Lady Wu started to walk away. "This is serious! We'll all have to go north to-"

"Why bother taking me?" Lady Wu scoffed as she continued her retreat. "I can stay here and dry up like the old, discarded rag that I am."

"...*Aiee*! I...! B-but...! You...!" Sun Jian protested. "**You have to come with me! Everyone has to come with me! I-!**"

"**Ben! Hè! Your uncle wants to speak with both of you!**" Lady Wu shrieked.

Sun Jian groaned miserably. Seconds later, a tall, strong young man that mildly resembled Sun Jian entered the room and bowed humbly. He was Sun Ben, eldest son of Sun Jian's late twin brother, and he was now part of the household.

"Uncle," Sun Ben said as he bowed low.

A second youth entered the room; he had some similar features, but he was obviously not an extremely close relative. Sun Hè was previously known as Yu Hè, but he had been taken into the household since Sun Jian had the means to support him, and he had additionally been allowed to take the 'Sun' family name.

"Worthy uncle," Sun Hè said as he paid his own respects to his benefactor.

Sun Jian smiled, turned to Sun Ben and said, "Nephew, you'll be accompanying me on this mission." He then turned to face Sun Hè and said, "Hè, you will do all you can to support my lady wife: you, as the oldest man in my and Ben's absence, will be acting as the eldest man of the household while I'm away, since this involves a temporary move north."

"*Mission*...?" Sun Ben prompted.

"A call to arms has been issued," Sun Jian continued. "Sit down, both of you, and I shall explain..."

Eventually, it would be Yuan Shu – General of the Rear and half-brother of the coalition commander Yuan Shao – that would accept Sun Jian's services and take him under his banner. Sun Jian left able men like Huan Jie in charge of Changsha and began a journey northward into Yu Province with his veteran allies and his family; their first stop would be Huancheng, the capital county of Lujiang Prefecture, where many of the families of the fighting men would live while they marched further north to face Dong Zhuo near to the imperial capital Luoyang.

****

15

The situation in the north was evolving quickly. By the time that Sun Jian's was completely moved to the north side of the Yangtze River, Dong Zhuo had been made fully aware of the growing coalition; demoralising rumours were circulating that the families of the coalition leaders had been executed and priceless bronze statues had been melted to produce extra coinage in the wake of the economic effects of the eastern trade blockade. There was no sign of an actual march, however, and that bothered Sun Jian and his allies the most. Many were desperately trying to acquire white and colourless clothing in response to a rumour that the deposed Emperor Shao – who had since been demoted to the 'Prince of Hongnong' and put under house arrest in Luoyang – had now been murdered by Dong Zhuo's agents in response to a demand for his reinstatement.

"They're just... *sitting there*," Sun Jian complained to Zhu Zhi as they travelled side-by-side on horseback at the head of a steadily-growing army. "A Son of Heaven killed... and they just *sit there*."

"It's to be expected," Zhu Zhi suggested. "An attack on the capital puts the life of the new emperor at risk. The latest talk is of Dong trying to *evacuate* Luoyang now."

"And *nobody does anything*???" Sun Jian exclaimed. "Oh, if only we had been *closer*! Cheng Demou was right, they're all do-nothings!"

"None of them are actually anywhere near Luoyang really, except Yuan Shao's vanguard," Zhu Zhi explained. "The rest are blockading important trade routes to starve Dong Zhuo out, as you know, but that means they're not in a position to engage his forces directly."

"But if he desecrates the capital and murders civilians, what else can they do but march on Luoyang quickly and face him...?" Sun Jian said desperately.

As the march continued, the appraisal of the coalition reached a new low when it became clear that no action had been taken at all, despite the collapse of the entire nation's economy as a result of the flood of extra coinage.

"Idiots! Fools! I don't know why we don't just turn back now!" Sun Jian raged as he read the reports coming from the north. His army was now camped near Huancheng City in Lujiang Prefecture, and tensions were high.

"We *could*," Zu Mao suggested. "But you'd never be able to live with yourself, I reckon, Mister Sun Jian. We've got what, *twenty-odd thousand* with us now...? We could attack Dong Zhuo by ourselves if the rest don't want to help us!"

"That's a good point," Cheng Pu agreed. "Hang the coalition, if they won't act; we will, us 'worthless men of the south'. Heh, perhaps His Majesty'll move the capital to Fuchun."

"A capital south of the Yangtze...? That'll be the day, Cheng Demou," Han Dang scoffed.

"I cannot make jokes," Sun Jian said angrily. "This is all ridiculous. *Ridiculous*! What will it take to make these stupid, ritual-obsessed men of the north do something about their own country???"

"Do we turn back...?" Huang Gai asked.

"...No," Sun Jian said. "We'll continue; Dong Zhuo is a threat to me, so I cannot leave him alive. I must try and face him. ... And I won't leave my family here... it's too obvious. We'll go to Shu."

"A sound idea," Zhu Zhi replied.

The march continued.

Sun Jian had his army camp to the north of the walled city of Shu while he entered the city itself and led his large family unit to their new home.

"I prefer the other one," Lady Wu sighed.

"I have to be in the north right now, and I want to be as close to my family as possible," Sun Jian said. "Please, my lady, be fair."

"*Fair*...?" Lady Wu scoffed. "...Well, I suppose you are being fair, allowing me to come here as well as your *new interest*."

Sun Jian scowled and turned away from Lady Wu.

"Yes, I'm sure you're trying to think of something to say, like 'I am serving my country by producing more tigers!' or 'I have needs!'" Lady Wu heckled. "...She's younger, and prettier, and your inflated ego said that the Marquis of Wucheng needed loads of women, and that's all there is to it, Husband."

Wu Jing entered the house, immediately guessed the nature of the discussion and turned around to leave.

"Oh *thank you*!" Lady Wu chortled. "**Thank you, Brother, who I raised like a son, and gave all the-!**"

"**I'm not getting involved!**" Wu Jing insisted as he disappeared from view.

"...Well, I shouldn't be *surprised*, I suppose," Lady Wu grumbled.

"Lady Chen is a consort, and you are my wife," Sun Jian protested. "Name one other man in my position that contents himself with one partner."

"...And that's your best, most well-thought-out argument," Lady Wu chortled. "At least be *honest*, Husband: you used to be, once."

"**Enough of this!**" Sun Jian barked. "I would never elevate Consort Chen's status to equal yours. Yes, I... I do find her more... *enticing*, at times, alright...? But that is the way of things, and yes, I *do* have needs. I'm sorry, but that's how it is. But you'll always be my wife, and my children will always come first."

"And will her children take precedence over mine...?" Lady Wu asked plainly.

"No... they'll be the equal of yours, because at the end of the day, they'll none of them be yours or hers to me... they'll be *mine*, if anyone's, and equals one and all," Sun Jian retorted. "They'll be *ours*, if you'll allow it."

Lady Wu smiled slightly and said, "That was my greatest fear. Discard me from your bed if you will, for my increased age and reduced appeal... but my children must not fall from favour."

Sun Jian fell to one knee and said, "I am a man, and I am a tiger. To meet the needs of both is a weakness, but one I embrace for lack of choice, if I want to continue to be the man that I have to be to get the things that we all need. For that, I'm sorry, but I can do nothing else."

Lady Wu sighed and said, "Get up, you silly man. Someone might see you."

Sun Jian got to his feet.

"I dislike this house, but as you say, necessity comes first," Lady Wu said plainly.

"...I'd rather you didn't keep saying that," Sun Jian complained.

Sun Ce and Sun Quan entered the house together at that moment and looked about them miserably.

"Oh, not you two as well," Sun Jian grumbled. "I need to base you all here! Do you not want to have chances to see me?"

"That isn't it, Father," Sun Ce replied. "S'just that I got pretty used to Changsha; it was exciting, all the bandits and tribes and everything... are there lots of them here to fight as well, or are they all in the capital?"

"*Ayah...* Is that all you want to do, Ce? *Fight...?*" Sun Jian exclaimed.

"Ben's going; I can join you as well, Father!" the 15-year-old Sun Ce said excitedly. "I could help you fight Dong Zhuo!"

"No, no, no!" Sun Jian chortled. "This is far, far too dangerous! You're too young anyway! You're only just turned fifteen!"

"When you were only a year older than me, you fought a whole gang of pirates on your own!" Sun Ce retorted. "Are you saying I couldn't do that too?"

"No, I'm saying that... that... it... ... ...*aiee,*" Sun Jian sighed as he saw his wife's wry expression. "Alright, alright, I was *stupid*. I *am* stupid."

"No you're not, Father, you're *brave,*" Sun Ce insisted.

"No, no, I realise now that I was taking unnecessary and terrible risks," Sun Jian admitted. "My father must have been distraught at what I was doing... if even the thought of you putting yourself in that much danger is making me feel sick."

Lady Wu touched Sun Jian's hand and smiled gratefully at his show of genuine compassion for his family. At that moment, the consort Lady Chen entered the house and immediately lowered her humble gaze; for a moment, Lady Wu could not bring herself to look at the rival for her husband's attention, but after that moment, she smiled and said, "Lady Chen: perhaps we can do something with this house."

Lady Chen smiled and said, "Perhaps we could, Lady Wu."

Lady Wu and Lady Chen went to the parlour together; Sun Jian then turned to his sons and said, "I hope that peace is maintained in my absence."

"That's up to our babysitter, I think, Dad," Sun Ce grumbled as Sun Ben and Sun Hè entered the house. "Here he is; tell *him.*"

"Tell who what, Uncle?" Sun Ben wondered.

"...*Aiee.* I try to be a good man!" Sun Jian complained. "I bring needy distant kin into my home, I support my late brother's family, and yet all I get is hassle!"

"The Yu clan are grateful for your benevolence," Sun Hè said as he bowed low.

"I don't want that from any of you!" Sun Jian insisted. "I just...! ...*Aiee.* Look, I have to prepare to leave now; Sun Hè, as you're older than my son, you will be my spirit while I am not here. Sun Ben, you'll be coming with me."

"Why are you taking Ben but not me?" Sun Ce said.

"He's three years older than you, son!" Sun Jian protested. "Now, as I was saying... Sun Hè...?"

"I shall do you proud, Uncle," Sun Hè promised.

"...Good," Sun Jian said uncomfortably. "Well, then... Ben, we should go."

Sun Ben sighed miserably, smiled at his young relatives and nodded compliantly.

"We'll all be together again soon," Sun Jian promised. "...For now... farewell."

Sun Jian and Sun Ben left the house; Sun Ce then turned to Sun Hè and said, "So what are we doing now, 'Dad'...?"

"Don't be like that, Ce," Sun Hè replied. "I'm doing as I'm asked."

Sun Ce retreated to the rear of the house, muttering, "Yeah... I know."

Sun Quan snorted irritably and followed his brother.

Sun Jian was genuinely surprised when he encountered Administrator Lu Kang as he travelled to his allies' lodgings. The two retired to Lu Kang's Shu residence so that they could discuss the coming conflict.

"Administrator Lu, I shall be brief," Sun Jian said once the two were seated. "I-"

"Before you ask, Mister Sun, no, I am not volunteering anything to this insanity," Lu Kang said. "Don't misunderstand me, however: I know that the coalition has honest motives. But right now there is but one Majesty, and that is Xiandi, and I will not raise a sword to my sovereign's throat for anything."

"...I have to admit that I am swayed by that matter at times," Sun Jian promised. "But rest assured, Administrator Lu, I don't share the ambition of some members of the coalition. I simply want to rescue His Majesty – whichever prince that may be – from the clutches of that villain."

"...You were right, of course, that Dong Zhuo was destined to be the ruin of the country," Lu Kang said. "I saw Cai Yong when I was in the capital... he'd been elevated to 'General of the Household'."

"I heard that," Sun Jian sighed.

"Like you, I despaired," Lu Kang continued. "Like you, I thought, 'Traitor, Cai Yong, for aiding the villain!' But then I thought, 'Perhaps Dong Zhuo is misunderstood, despite Ding Yuan's fate and the matter of succession, which is admittedly very complicated and far from clear'."

"So is Cai Yong his ally or not?" Sun Jian asked plainly.

"He's... trapped," Lu Kang replied. "I swore that I would never forgive a lackey or accept their excuses, but in his case I'll make an exception. He's trapped, Sun Wentai: he cannot leave the capital or his family will be harmed, and he doesn't want to leave the sovereign to that brute's mercy either. That's more than can be said of others, of course... the Magistrate of Luoyang, Zhou Yi, has fled here with family, and the noted scholar Chen Ji took his family and fled to somewhere in Qing or Yòu, so I hear. Excellency Xun retired and fled... the famed appraisers Xu Shao and Xu Jing fled to Xu, or maybe south of the river to Wu Prefecture, I understand... so many have run away from the demon, while others bravely face it, and rightly so."

"'But'...?" Sun Jian supposed.

"But my place is here in Lujiang, stopping the local troubles from adding to the national ones," Lu Kang explained. "In that sense, *I* am trapped... and, perhaps, gratefully so, for I cannot see a correct way to solve this crisis. There are better heroes like you, Mister Sun Wentai, to do what must be done. But show caution! It is Heaven's will that decides the sovereign, not a handful of pampered nobles. Yuan Shao and his like must remember their place just like anyone else."

Sun Jian left Lu Kang's residence a short time later: he was not aided in any way by the Administrator's words since they only reminded him of his own powerlessness.

Sun Jian's militia marched toward Lu County in the north of Lujiang once their families were settled. The army was met by one of Yuan Shu's leading officers, Ji Ling, who had their arrival announced to their new lord and commander while they were forced to wait outside the city.

"...I wonder what he's really like," Zu Mao said.

"Sadly," Sun Jian sighed, "your recent estimation is probably correct."

Zu Mao looked at the tired, irritable soldiers in Yuan Shu's employ and smiled.

"I suppose you'll see this man alone," Cheng Pu said.

"I imagine so," Sun Jian replied.

After a few minutes, the formidable Ji Ling returned and said, "Magistrate Sun, you will now proceed to Lord Yuan's court. Your subordinates will make camp outside the city."

"...As you wish," Sun Jian replied.

Yuan Shu's improvised court was based in the Magistrate's residence. The hall was fairly large, and most of the senior officials and officers had been assembled for a meeting that Sun Jian had assumed to be informal and private like those he enjoyed with Zhu Jun and Lu Kang; he was left demoralised and angry at what would obviously be more of a public grilling than a friendly introduction.

"**Well, well... the 'Tiger of Jiangdong'!**" Yuan Shu bellowed as Sun Jian advanced toward him and fell to one knee.

"I am honoured to be in your service, General Yuan," Sun Jian replied humbly.

"*Naturally,*" Yuan Shu chortled quietly.

Sun Jian raised his eyes and had his first chance to study Yuan Shu: he was a man with a thin, naturally lofty face that obviously spent most of its time contorted into a covetous, bitter scowl. This day, however, Yuan Shu was smiling falsely, and Sun Jian was forced to return the gesture.

"Well, well: today, I have a legend amongst my subordinates," Yuan Shu chuckled. "To have the service of Sun Jian... to have your *total, unwavering allegiance...* is a boon to me."

"I shall serve unwaveringly," Sun Jian promised.

"Yes you shall," Yuan Shu replied icily. "Fine, well! I wonder if you might tell me how many men you've brought here."

"It is my understanding, Lord Yuan, that our ranks have swelled to around twenty-to-thirty thousand since our departure from the south," Sun Jian replied.

Yuan Shu's officials were taken aback; Shu himself smiled eagerly and said, "You add *twenty to thirty thousand men* to my ranks?! ...Well, that surely calls for a position to reflect your contribution... I hereby appoint you 'General who Quells Rebels' – I think that's very fair, since you *have done* – and Inspector of Yu Province."

"*Inspector*...?" Sun Jian exclaimed. "I thought that Kong Zhou-"

"Sadly, Inspector Kong has passed away without worthy issue to inherit his role," Yuan Shu said with no obvious regret. "The position is therefore open, and I think that you are the right man to hold the position. Of course, I expect good service in return."

"...Naturally, I will serve you as a horse would, Lord Yuan!" Sun Jian replied gratefully.

"Very good," Yuan Shu said. "Begin preparations for a march on Luoyang, so that we can show the tyrant who the heroes are!"

Sun Jian kowtowed repeatedly and said, "You shall soon have Dong Zhuo's head as a trophy and as a tribute to your greatness and magnanimity!"

"Very good...!" Yuan Shu giggled strangely. "Greatness and...! Ahem. Dismissed."

Sun Jian then departed to begin his work.

Zhu Zhi was ponderous as Sun Jian returned, and he therefore failed to notice Sun Jian's elated expression.

"Something good has happened," Cheng Pu guessed.

"He's promoted me to 'General who Quells Rebels', and 'Inspector of Yu Province'!" Sun Jian replied excitedly.

"...He can do that...?" Cheng Pu wondered.

"...Oh, no, you're right; you're right, he might have been fobbing me off," Sun Jian realised, and his face fell.

"Mm...? What's going on?" Zhu Zhi asked as he snapped out of his thoughtful trance. He then turned to his master and said, "You're back, Lord Sun; is something bothering you...?"

"He 'promoted me' to 'General who Quells Rebels', and 'Inspector of Yu Province'," Sun Jian reiterated miserably.

"...You suspect that he hasn't the power to do that, but once the situation is resolved, the positions will be upheld, because a man of his stature has to be a man of his word, else he'd have no respect," Zhu Zhi suggested. "Consider the posts as authentic, my lord: after all, you've brought the man nearly thirty thousand men at a critical moment."

"*Critical moment*...?" Sun Jian said with surprise.

"Dong Zhuo seems to be getting a brave streak... well, so long as he isn't the risk taker anyway," Han Dang said with contempt. "Reports are that he's sending an army here in full force; did our wonderful new commander not mention it...?"

"...No, he didn't, but he said that he was glad to have me here... now I see why he was so overly pleased, and quick to hand out rewards," Sun Jian scoffed. "Alright, well, I'm not about to panic; let's train the men, and give Dong's men something to think about when they arrive."

****

16

After a morning of studying at a small private school, Sun Ce wandered the streets of Shu City, sighing miserably every time he passed a house.

"What's the matter, friend...?"

Sun Ce turned to see that he was being addressed by a young man of the same age; his demeanour was strong, and his features were striking.

"...Nothing much really," Sun Ce replied. "Do I know you? I feel as though I've seen you somewhere."

"Yes and no, apparently," the youth chuckled. "*Zhou Yu*... we're in the same class...? We just spent all morning reading from the classics maybe two or three seats away from each other...?"

"Oh, right...!" Sun Ce said with a laugh. "My mind was somewhere else really, during all that introductory stuff... and during the reading too, if I'm honest. We just moved here recently, so my father could go and fight Dong Zhuo, and it was all that I could think about."

"I see," Zhou Yu said thoughtfully.

"Y'don't do all the stuffy nonsense that the oldies do, then...?" Sun Ce snickered. "I really hate all that 'family name, blah, given name, bloo' that we have to do just to start a conversation."

Zhou Yu smiled and said, "So do I, but it has its place. It lets people know that you respect them, doesn't it...?"

"S'pose," Sun Ce sighed. "Oh, uh, yeah... though Dad – Father, I mean – says that it's more about letting the other person know whether you're high up enough in society to be worth talking to, and that's why you give your family name first."

Zhou Yu's smile became a sad one as he admitted, "It *is*, unfortunately, *yes*."

Sun Ce grinned and said, "I'm Sun Ce, but I guess you knew that, though, friend."

Zhou Yu nodded and replied, "I did know your name, yes."

"Sorry I didn't know yours, but like I said, I'm a bit distracted," Sun Ce said honestly.

"Forgive me, but... you're really a 'Sun' as in the son of the 'Tiger of Jiangdong', *Sun Jian*...?" Zhou Yu asked hesitantly.

"Yep," Sun Ce replied casually.

"Well, well...!" Zhou Yu chuckled. "I am truly lucky today! My family has long served the Han, and been well rewarded for it... but there's what *we've* done, and what your father's done, and really, Mister Sun Ce, you're a lucky man to be who you are... but then, I'm sure you know that."

"My friends call me by my courtesy name, 'Bofu'; and actually, I'd prefer everyone did," Sun Ce said suddenly. "Like you said, it shows that people respect you."

"Mine's 'Gongjin'," Zhou Yu replied.

"Well, 'Gongjin', I'm pleased to meet a member of the esteemed Zhou family, 'cause yeah, I have heard your family name bandied about here and there before, same as you've heard mine," Sun Ce admitted. "You live in the big house."

"Since we were forced to flee the capital, yes," Zhou Yu explained.

"Where are you staying at the moment, if you don't mind me

asking...?"

"A really-not-too-pleasant house on the other end of town," Sun Ce explained. "That's what I was sighing about, partly. That, and being annoyed that my father doesn't want me on his campaign."

"Well, I'm stuck here too," Zhou Yu said. "The whole 'Eastern Pass Coalition' thing is a bit messy, so I understand; it's probably better that he does it alone, if he cares what happens to you."

"...S'pose," Sun Ce conceded.

"If that house is really so poor, then please, tell me, and I'll have my father prepare space for you in our house, as honoured guests," Zhou Yu promised.

"I have a big family," Sun Ce replied with amusement. "To make enough space, your dad'd have to move out."

Zhou Yu laughed and said, "Honestly, it's a very big house! I'm sure there's enough space for everyone... and given how badly your father's been treated in the past by some 'men of the north', I'd like to prove that our family knows how to treat people that deserve respect."

"Y'know, I reckon you could be the friend to our family that we've sorely needed," Sun Ce decided. "I'll tell my mother what you said... see what she thinks."

"You do that, Bofu," Zhou Yu insisted. "I won't have the family of a hero living in sub-standard accommodation... it makes a mockery of the world."

Sun Ce laughed, clasped hands with Zhou Yu, and said, "Come with me, and you can tell her yourself."

Zhou Yu nodded agreeably, and the two walked to Sun Ce's home, chatting all the while.

"Mother!" Sun Ce shouted. **"Where are you at?"**

"...You actually talk to her in that way...?" Zhou Yu whispered.

"Sure, we're all very casual," Sun Ce insisted as Lady Wu entered the living quarters. Ce gestured towards his guest and said, "Mother, this is Zhou Gongjin, son of the Magistrate of Luoyang. His family only got here a few weeks before we did!"

"I've heard your father mention as much," Lady Wu replied. She then turned to Zhou Yu and said, "My, you are handsome. Your father must be proud."

Zhou Yu was suddenly very uncomfortable.

"*Mother*...!" Sun Ce whined. "Don't tell the poor man something like that!"

"No, no, it's... it's alright," Zhou Yu chuckled. "I suppose I get a little... well... irritated at being judged on my looks. I play instruments, I read, I am adept with several types of weapons, I compose music and poetry; yet all I ever get is 'You are handsome'. But I need to appreciate the compliment, Bofu, and not feel awkward."

"Certainly not!" Lady Wu chortled. "Any woman will be glad of a husband like you, I can assure you... either of you, in fact."

"Oh, Mother, *no*...!" Sun Ce groaned.

Zhou Yu laughed and said, "Your honesty is a refreshing thing, Lady Wu. We could do with life like that in our home... and would be honoured if you'd leave this drab place and stay with us as our guests."

"In that big house...?" Lady Wu prompted.

"Yes," Zhou Yu said pleasantly. "Will you accept...?"

"Oh, of *course we will*!" Lady Wu chuckled. "Oh, but wait, is that not...?"

"Imposing...?" Zhou Yu guessed. "I would not ask if it was, I assure you. I invite your family as a man that genuinely respects your husband as a hero and an inspiration, Lady Wu; there is not a real man in the land that does not wish they were even half the man that Sun Jian is."

"You're *adorable*!" Lady Wu giggled. "Consider me as already living in your house, my dear. But I warn you... they're all a handful, and 'her' especially."

"...'Her'...?" Zhou Yu said cautiously.

"*Shangxiang*," Sun Ce sighed. "She's surrounded by boys being boys... me, dad, Quan, Yi, Kuang... oh, and the extended family, like Hè and Ben... and so she's kind o' decided to outdo us. It's funny... *sometimes*."

"So *you* say," Lady Wu scoffed. "I have to take responsibility for it all as her mother."

Zhou Yu laughed boisterously and said, "No, really, as soon as you can, move in! I'm really looking forward to it!"

"On your own head be it," Lady Wu chortled. "I'll tell Lady Chen."

As Lady Wu retreated into the bedroom, Zhou Yu whispered, "Do your mother and Lady Chen get on...?"

"*Now, yes*," Sun Ce replied quietly. "Don't worry... we *all* get on. To us – me, Quan, Yi, Kuang, and Shangxiang, I mean – Lady Chen's an auntie, or a second mum... sort of. It really is no bother."

Sun Ce's 6-year-old brother Yi entered the room and started throwing punches at empty air.

"...I was the same," Sun Ce sighed. "Hello, Yi."

"Who's'is, Brother...?" Sun Yi asked as Sun Ce walked to him and ruffled his hair.

"...Gongjin, a friend of mine," Sun Ce said as he turned to the smiling Zhou Yu and grinned. "You're not gonna beat him up, are you, Yi...?"

"Not if he's a friend," Sun Yi replied fearlessly. "Is he who we're gonna go live with? Mumma said we're going to go live somewhere else already! Is this who we're gonna go live with?"

"...*Aiee*... *yes*, Yi, he is," Sun Ce chuckled.

"Alright," Yi said as he turned and went back to the bedrooms.

"...Lively," Zhou Yu mumbled.

"Pray you don't get challenged by Shangxiang," Sun Ce snickered. "Even though she's only three, she's worse than any of us boys."

Zhou Yu shuddered theatrically and said, "You should be quiet, Bofu: I can still change my mind!"

"**Don't you dare!**" Lady Wu shouted from the bedroom; Zhou Yu and Sun Ce laughed together.

****

17

Sun Jian's army advanced to the west of Lu County and camped. Once the perimeter fence was built, the central tents were erected and the work on the guard towers had been started, Sun Jian assembled his senior staff in his command tent.

"Lord Yuan should be pleased when he hears about how organised we are," Sun Jian suggested keenly.

"The idiot confiscated our men," Zu Mao complained. "What if most of them have to stay in Lu County?"

"He's our lord now, so he can do that," Sun Jian replied. "Don't worry, Zu Mao; we won't need them to keep this place."

"What do you have in mind...?" Cheng Pu asked.

"Training begins immediately," Sun Jian ordered. "I want every available moment of every single day spent training: I want the most orderly troops in the country."

"A sound idea, Lord Sun," Zhu Zhi declared.

Zu Mao laughed hoarsely before he said, "That's quite a dream you have, Mister Sun Jian, making that shabby lot into the finest there is! But if it's possible, then I want to be the finest general."

"Never say 'Never'," Sun Jian insisted. "Let's start!"

Sun Jian's demands for discipline were something that the majority of the recruits were not used to; his warm and respectful approach endeared him, however, and the men – many of whom were former bandits, pirates and convicts – did as they were asked and worked without complaint. Yuan Shu was encouraged and delighted by the reports that he received, but some of his vassals were nervous of Sun Jian's obvious talent as a commander and doubted Yuan Shu's ability to retain control over him in the years to come.

Dong Zhuo's army reached the outskirts of Lu County over a week after Sun Jian's camp had been completed; the enemy advance was reported to a calm and indifferent Sun Jian, who dismissed the messenger politely and said to his officers, "They're here at last... I'm surprised that they took so long."

"Are we going to go on full alert?" Huang Gai asked.

"No," Sun Jian replied casually. "My orders are to prepare for a banquet. The soldiers should be–"

"Uh... wait, wait," Zu Mao chuckled. "You're going to have a party? Did I miss something, Mister Sun Jian?"

"...Ah, I see!" Huang Gai chuckled. "I'll get started."

As Huang Gai walked away, Zu Mao scratched his head and said, "I'm missing something, then. Why are you lot all starting to smile? Is there– ...Oh, right! Sorry, friends, me senses left me there. S'a bluff."

"You got there in the end," Sun Jian teased. "We'll see how good you are at matching me cup-for-cup, Zu Mao. In the meantime, we can have the men show our enemies how well I have trained them. Zhu Zhi..."

"I shall order the captains to begin drills," Zhu Zhi replied.

Sun Jian turned to his young nephew Ben and said, "You'll be elsewhere. This banquet will be a rowdy affair with drunken former pirates and whatnot..."

Sun Ben nodded obediently and said, "I shall read in my private tent, Uncle."

Dong Zhuo's vanguard general, Xu Rong, reached a stretch of land to the west of Sun Jian's camp and despatched scouts while he prepared his own temporary encampment.
"Shouldn't we just attack?" a major asked of the mission commander.
"Don't be too hasty," Xu Rong replied. "Sun Jian has quite a reputation; I believe the stories about his exploits, and I have no desire to engage such a man without proper preparation."
"We outnumber him!" another general heckled.
"*Do we*, Hu Zhen...?" Xu Rong scoffed. "He brought twenty-to-thirty thousand from the south, so I hear: just because they're not to be seen, it doesn't mean they're not here. They might be waiting somewhere to ambush us, gentlemen. I advocate patience: let us see what the scouts report."
        When the scouts returned, they brought a story that left the Liang army perplexed.
"The officers are enjoying wine!" one scout explained. "Many of them are falling about drunk, and-!"
"That's *insulting*!" Hu Zhen barked. "We should-!"
"We should *listen*, General Hu," Xu Rong interrupted. "Go on, soldiers."
"General Sun Jian hosts a banquet!" a second scout whined. "The senior officers laugh, sing, gamble, read and play chess!"
Xu Rong pondered silently.
"They're mocking us," Hu Zhen suggested. "It may be a trap, I admit that..."
After a long pause, Xu Rong turned to a third scout and asked, "And what of the men under Sun Jian's command...? Are they equally lax?"
"N-no," the scout replied. "There are a lot of manned guard towers, a well-implemented perimeter guard rota, drills carried out by junior captains, and-"
"Your description of the camp suggests a lot of discipline and contradicts the show of raucousness," Xu Rong interrupted; he then turned to his fellow generals and said, "This is not a trap, gentlemen, it is a *challenge*: Sun Jian is telling us that he can match us, and maybe even beat us. If he can entrust general activity to the lowliest officers and ignore our advance, then he actually tells us with this 'party' he's hosting that he would not need to do anything personally... that bothers me."
"That suggests to me that you want to retreat," Hu Zhen prompted.
"If all of you want to risk a confrontation with Sun Jian here in Lu County, far away from Luoyang, where defeat would mean a complete rout... fine, I shall not contest a majority decision," Xu Rong said calmly. "But if it were left up to me, I would withdraw our main force and allow a more confident and, dare I say it, arrogant Sun Jian to continue his advance: he will eventually reach a place where we will have the advantage, and that is where we will be guaranteed success."
The officers looked at each other silently.
"Well...?" Xu Rong prompted.

"...We should withdraw," Hu Zhen decided. "If our forces are evenly matched, then anything could happen, and as you say, we're in enemy territory. I don't like it, but... the chancellor would punish us if we walked into a trap or did something rash. Perhaps we *should* turn back."
The other officers murmured agreeably.
"A sensible conclusion, gentlemen," Xu Rong insisted. "We shall withdraw: let Sun Jian think he has scared us, because we will certainly have the last laugh."

"DRINK! DRINK! DRINK!"
A mob of baying junior officers urged their commander, Sun Jian, to have one last cup of wine; Sun Jian laughed drunkenly and said, "Alright, but bear in mind that I'll be genuinely out of it if they attack!"
"Don't drink it!" Wu Jing pleaded. "Brother-in-law, *don't*-!"
"REPORT!"
The revelry halted at the very moment that the scout's call was heard; Zhu Zhi turned to the weary young soldier and said, "Make your report."
"The enemy army has turned about!" the scout said with obvious relief. **"The... their whole army has decamped and begun the journey back to Luoyang!"**
"Aha! The cowards flee!" Sun Jian cackled. **"Now we have them!"**
"No... no, we... we shouldn't pursue," Huang Gai pleaded drunkenly. "Blast it, I've had too much to...! ...Cheng... **Cheng Demou... tell him! Tell him!**"
"He knows," Cheng Pu giggled as he prepared to intake an entire dish of wine.
"I'm just glad it worked," Zhu Zhi sighed. "If we'd been attacked, we might not have survived without serious casualties. Now we can rest for a while, ensure that the men are well fed and morale is high, and-"
"If... if we pressed on to Liangdong," Sun Jian interrupted, "we... we could destroy them, and go on to Luoyang."
"Tell him, Demou!" Huang Gai protested.
"...Perhaps he *doesn't* know," Cheng Pu realised. "Look, Sun Wentai, even... even though I'm paralytic, I know that going to... to Luoyang now is suicide! Wait until we're all sober, at least!"
"I meant 'when we're sober'!" Sun Jian cried. "Have some *faith*!"
"So do we stop the party now?" Han Dang wondered.
"*Yes*!" Wu Jing whined. "*Yes, please*, we *should*!"
"*No*... they may still have spies," Sun Jian insisted. "We... we carry on, until we're *sure*."
Han Dang and Wu Jing turned to Zhu Zhi, who nodded seriously and said, "Lord Sun is right: the enemy may still have spies, and if we suddenly stopped all this they might turn around and descend on us. Continue until well after dark."
Wu Jing groaned miserably.
"Suits me!" Zu Mao cackled. **"DRINK! DRINK!"**
Sun Jian grinned as his officers started to chant again; he leant sideways, picked up his empty wine dish, turned to the weary Wu Jing, and said, "Pour."

Once Sun Jian's scouts had reported the full retreat of the enemy army, he sent a man to update his lord Yuan Shu and request further orders.

"This man is incredible!" Yuan Shu said to his advisers with glee. "He repelled that massive army with a show of strength and courage! He truly is a tiger!"

"...We must be careful of such a man," Yuan's adviser Yan Xiang suggested. "We must keep that 'tiger' on a tight leash... as tight as possible."

"Oh, I intend to!" Yuan Shu snickered. "Why do you think I took so many of his men from him? Anyway; he has suggested a march to Liangdong, and proclaims that if he were then allowed to continue on to Luoyang, then he can give me victory over Dong Zhuo in a month."

"*Arrogance*," General Ji Ling scoffed. "You should have let me accompany him, Lord Yuan. He'll hand himself over to the netherworld with an attitude like that. This isn't Yellow Turbans; it's the Liang Province Corps! Dong Zhuo's men are perhaps the second best men in the land after the Danyang Brigades!"

"Ji Ling is right," the adviser Han Yin declared. "I'd allow Sun Jian to march to Liangdong, but no further, and additionally, order him to leave the majority of the men here in Lu County: we should see how he fares and plan accordingly."

"I'll respond by saying as much," Yuan Shu said cautiously. "Hopefully, he'll do as he's told... if he doesn't, then I'll have to tighten the leash even more."

****

18

Sun Jian waited for over a month before he began his northern advance to Liangdong, which brought him very close to the borders with Yan Province in the north and Central Province, where Luoyang was based. Dong Zhuo's general Xu Rong had encamped there after the army had withdrawn from Lu County; he learned of Sun Jian's advance and gathered his officers.

"Hu Zhen and the other senior officers have returned to the region around Luoyang with two thirds of our previous force, so I must manage this troublesome man alone," Xu Rong said seriously. "I now know how many men Sun Jian actually possesses for this march of his, and we outnumber him by at least two-to-one. This time, I suggest that we attack him before he can settle. We march immediately."

Sun Jian's advance army – which numbered around 5,000 men – arrayed on a stretch of barren ground that was to the south of a series of ruins that nature was slowly reclaiming. The actual size of Xu Rong's force startled Cheng Pu and Zhu Zhi.

"**They number at least ten thousand!**" Wu Jing gasped. "**How can we win???**"

"**Numbers mean nothing, Brother-in-law,**" Sun Jian said as he adjusted his red scarf.

"**You're being flippant!**" Cheng Pu replied. "**Wu Jing is right, that army is-**"

"**I thought you hated pedants, Demou,**" Sun Jian sighed.

"**This isn't pedantry!**" Cheng Pu insisted. "**Pitting our little army against Xu Rong's is reckless! It's suicidal!**"

"**I don't expect to lose,**" Sun Jian retorted. "**After all the training we've given them, I think ours is the better force.**"

"**That's only when we're fighting armies of equal size and similar division variants!**" Cheng Pu said. "**We're mainly infantry! Xu Rong has archers, crossbowmen, elite cavalry, and-!**"

"**We'll win,**" Sun Jian insisted. "**Calm down... we'll win.**"

"**I give up!**" Cheng Pu cried. "**Alright, then, fine: we'll face them! ...Aiee!**"

"**ATTACK! ENEMY ATTACK!**" a soldier screamed; the announcement was quickly followed by general panic.

"**Mister Sun Jian, he's here! Xu Rong, he's charged!**" Zu Mao screamed.

Xu Rong had foregone any pre-battle formalities or scouting exercises; he had instead opted to lead his entire infantry and cavalry toward Sun Jian's army in one massive surge.

"*Aiee...* I miscalculated," Sun Jian groaned. "I really thought I'd scared him."

"**Prepare to defend!**" Cheng Pu bellowed. "**Shields, everyone: get the shields up, for arrows, swords and spears alike!**"

Sun Jian turned to Sun Ben and said, "**Nephew, go to the rear line at once!**"

"**I want to stay and help you!**" Sun Ben pleaded.

"**Go!**" Sun Jian barked. "**Lady Wu would kill if I-! ...I said GO!**"

Sun Ben retreated obediently but reluctantly.

Xu Rong's forces had torn into the smaller army before any defences could be organised; Sun Jian's force fell apart, and men scattered in all directions.

"We're surrounded!" Zu Mao reported. **"It's more a case of fighting our way out!"**

"...Cheng Pu, Zhu Zhi, Wu Jing, Huang Gai, Han Dang: do what you can to reorder the lines!" Sun Jian ordered. **"Zu Mao: we must keep Xu Rong busy! Leaders need men, and men need leaders! We all have to survive!"**

"Like I need telling," Zu Mao grumbled. **"And *please*, Mister Sun Jian, will you *take that bloody scarf off*!"**

"It's my lucky scarf!" Sun Jian protested.

"You're *mad*," Zu Mao complained. **"You're *mad*, and we're going to die now because of a *scarf*."**

Xu Rong's northern cavalrymen had routed the elite contingent of infantry that Sun Jian had relied upon for a central defensive wall; Sun Jian was forced to use his small group of horsemen to counter-charge as the enemy approached. Sun Jian cut his way through the horde of infantry and cavalry that surged towards him, but he lost several of his horsemen in the process.

"REPORT!" a Liang scout cried as he approached Xu Rong. **"A man identified as Sun Jian had fled northward!"**

"...*North*...?" Xu Rong chortled. **"He's a dead man, then... I'll lead the pursuit myself. How can he be identified?"**

"He always wears a red scarf!" the scout replied.

"*Still*...?" Xu Rong said with disbelief. **"I thought he'd have been advised against that motif by now... maybe he's just stubborn."**

Xu Rong spurred his horse and gestured for his finest cavalrymen to aid him in the pursuit of the man from Fuchun.

"This is going to be the end for us, Mister Sun Jian!" Zu Mao shouted as he tried to keep his own horse close to his master's.

"...Pessimist!" Sun Jian replied. **"We just need to get a chance to turn and-"**

"HORSES APPROACH!" a soldier shouted.

"Oh great," Zu Mao grumbled. **"There aren't even twenty of us, Mister Sun Jian!"**

Sun Jian stopped and turned his horse.

"You're going to charge them???" Zu Mao exclaimed as he halted his own steed. **"Don't be ridiculous!"**

The ten-strong group of approaching cavalrymen had been part of the initial attack on his position; Sun Jian levelled his spear and rode into their midst, taking one of them down as he passed. The rest scattered; Zu Mao and the rest of the southern horsemen followed their leader, hacking their way through the small group of cavalry. Sun Jian then had his men turn to the west; the area had some tall foliage and remnants of long-destroyed stone monuments to use as cover, but it was sparse and widely spread. Sun Jian had his men stop to plan their next move, but Zu Mao knew that they would have to do something drastic.

"...Look, give me that scarf," Zu Mao said as he stopped alongside Sun Jian.

"Why?" Sun Jian asked.

"Why d'you *think*???" Zu Mao said despairingly. "They know you wear it... they'll follow the man wearing it, thinking it's you. I can take it, and-"

"No," Sun Jian insisted.

"...Please tell me it isn't because you're fond of the scarf, Mister Sun Jian," Zu Mao sighed.

"**Of course not!**" Sun Jian cried. "You're my friend, Zu Mao! I can't let you risk your life for me!"

"You've saved me often enough," Zu Mao retorted. "Now I have a chance to repay the debt; don't worry, I'll be back."

Sun Jian fidgeted nervously.

"Look, there's no *time!*" Zu Mao growled. "**Give me the scarf!**"

"...May Heaven forgive me," Sun Jian whimpered as he pulled the scarf away from his neck and immediately had it snatched from his grasp.

"**Now go on, get back to where Cheng and the others are!**" Zu Mao ordered as he tied the scarf around his own neck. "**I'll be alright, and so will your silly scarf! Go on!**"

Sun Jian turned his horse southward and galloped away.

"**Go with him,**" Zu Mao said to the small group of horsemen.

"No," one of the men replied. "We'll stay and help."

"...You're good blokes," Zu Mao sighed. "But I said 'Go': Lord Sun needs you."

Half of the horsemen reluctantly pursued their commander; some still refused to go.

"...Alright," Zu Mao chortled. "I see that you lot are as daft as me... perhaps it looks more like I'm him if I have guards. Let's get ready, then."

Within a short time, Xu Rong and his horsemen descended on Zu Mao's temporary resting spot; Sun Jian's aide made a point of mimicking the heroic attitude of his master and convincing Xu Rong that he was the genuine article.

"**I want that man's head!**" Xu Rong barked.

Zu Mao retreated to the northwest while his followers did what they could to hold Xu Rong at bay; one by one, they either retreated or fell to Xu Rong's cavalry. The focus was then on Zu Mao: he rode for some time, narrowly dodging attempts to shoot him down by Xu Rong's horseback archers. As darkness fell, he reached an unusual configuration of large, eroded stone pillars and sought shelter in their midst.

"...Mister Sun Jian, I hope you got away," Zu Mao muttered. "Else this was all a waste of my time and my life, wasn't it...?"

Zu Mao looked about for some way to escape his predicament or have a heroic end; he spotted something useful, and smiled.

Sun Jian and his small group of followers rode southward until they came across the beginnings of a survivor's camp; they were greeted at its perimeter by Cheng Pu and Han Dang, who hurried the new arrivals to the improvised infirmary.

"...What a disaster," Sun Jian moaned as a medic inspected him for injuries. "I've lost dozens of good men... I've lost my reputation as a competent military leader... and worst of all, I've lost Zu Mao."

"Xu Rong had his men pursue for a while: we lost between five hundred and a thousand men," Cheng Pu reported. "Huang Gai, Wu Jing and Zhu Zhi are doing what they can to find all the stragglers and-"

"**UNCLE!**"

Sun Jian smiled reflexively as Sun Ben pushed his way past Cheng Pu and fell to his knees, crying, "Uncle, I wanted to search for you, but-!"

"I want to talk, dearest nephew, but right now I need to talk to my advisers," Sun Jian said warmly. "We can talk later."

Sun Ben nodded obediently, said, "I'm just glad that you're safe," and retreated.

"A good lad," Han Dang said quietly.

"He is," Sun Jian agreed: he then turned to Cheng Pu and said, "Where were we, Demou...?"

"...Ah yes, I was telling you what we've done," Cheng Pu replied. "Huang Gai, Wu Jing and Zhu Zhi are doing everything they can to find everyone and reassemble the army, but morale is low."

"Should we retreat?" Han Dang asked.

"I want to, but... Yuan Shu would demote me, take all of you under his command, and send you all back here under someone else," Sun Jian suggested. "We have to hold here, at the very least, and try and win a victory against Xu Rong, so we've chased Dong Zhuo's men out of Yu Province."

"...What happened to Zu Mao?" Cheng Pu asked apprehensively.

"He took my scarf," Sun Jian replied as he touched his bare neck. "He... he used it to lead them away, so I could get back here."

"What a brave man," Cheng Pu said sadly.

"He's not dead... that wouldn't be right," Han Dang suggested.

Sun Jian exhaled noisily and said, "I don't care if I never saw that wretched scarf again... I want Zu Mao to live. I should not have let him do such a thing!"

"He was being pragmatic," Cheng Pu said reluctantly. "He knew that you were more important."

"...It's still wrong," Sun Jian replied quietly.

Xu Rong had retired to his camp to plan another series of attacks, but the new encampment that Sun Jian, Zhu Zhi and Cheng Pu had developed was impressive enough to make Dong Zhuo's general reconsider.

"We just crushed them!" one major complained. "Their leader is probably dead!"

"That's wishful thinking, nothing more," Xu Rong retorted.

"All the same, we crushed them!" the major said. "We-!"

"That was because we caught them off-guard," Xu Rong insisted. "I've been in this sort of situation before. Remember the old saying that 'cornered tigers fight hardest'. It is when things are at their most desperate – like the siege of Wan – that men such as these at their most dangerous. Whoever's in charge there has reorganised his men very quickly and efficiently, and they may be angry. There will be other opportunities."

There was much disappointment and frustration at Xu Rong's decision, but his subordinates did not press the matter any further, and no action was taken.

The assumption amongst the southerners was that Zu Mao had sacrificed his own life to save Sun Jian; but before anyone could begin the official mourning of his passing, he arrived at the gates of the camp as dawn broke, gesturing boldly.

"He's back! He's alive!" Cheng Pu bellowed as he ran into Sun Jian's personal tent, where the latter was sat talking with his nephew Sun Ben.

"...*Zu Mao*...?" Sun Jian exclaimed. "My friend is alive...! Come, Nephew, and let us greet my good friend!"

"Yes, Uncle!" Sun Ben replied cheerfully.

Sun Jian, Sun Ben and Cheng Pu hurried to the gates, where Zu Mao was already surrounded by a cheering mob of surprised and relieved soldiers.

"Ah! Mister Sun Jian!" Zu Mao cackled as Sun Jian fought his way through the soldiers and grabbed Zu Mao's shoulders tightly. Zu smirked and said, "I did bring your silly scarf back."

"I don't care!" Sun Jian said with laughter. "Keep the damn thing!"

"No, no, you can have it back," Zu Mao replied dryly. "You're almost crying."

"Oh, Zu Mao, you're more of a reckless idiot than me!" Sun Jian sighed. "But to see you alive... what happened?"

"They had me cornered in an old ruin," Zu Mao explained. "I saw a pillar that was worn away to about your height... it was misty, so I put the scarf on top of it and hid in some bushes! Xu Rong and his lot rode up, saw the scarf, and panicked... you never saw a group of men so scared! They were slowly moving up that old bit o' cloth on that pillar for ages... making threats, demanding that it should surrender...!"

The audience laughed.

"Then he got close enough to see, and when he saw it wasn't a man, he panicked even more!" Zu Mao chuckled. "That was that: he turned all his men and went away, full gallop! I guess he thought that you'd had a plan to trap him there."

Sun Jian's mood suddenly changed; he frowned and said, "Yes, but Xu Rong really got it wrong, didn't he... he mistook an utter fool for a hero."

"No need to be rude!" Zu Mao joked.

"Not you; me," Sun Jian groaned, having missed the joke entirely. "I insisted on fighting Xu Rong at a numerical disadvantage... this is my fault. So many good men died..."

The crowd of men fell silent.

"...Don't be glum," Zu Mao pleaded. "They lost men too, he's on the defensive now, and you never lost your scarf... so it might have been worse."

"Zu Mao is right," Cheng Pu said as a comforting gesture. "We might have been routed if we'd marched together, or–"

"I'll not ignore good advice again," Sun Jian promised. "As soon as we can, we should advance, and show Xu Rong and his master that we're not done! Next time, things will be different!"

The soldiers cheered heartily.

"...And as for you, my friend... get some rest," Sun Jian said to the weary Zu Mao.

"I intend to," Zu Mao replied.

＊＊＊＊＊＊＊＊＊＊＊

19

The initial defeat at Liangdong had, understandably, lowered morale, but Zu Mao's brave act of self-sacrifice and his subsequent miraculous escape from death had filled the southern army with new confidence and a determination to strike back as soon as it was possible. Once news of Sun Jian's second march northward reached General Xu Rong, the latter retreated from Yu Province and returned to the capital Luoyang.

"I, Rong, have returned to you, Chancellor!" Xu Rong said as he entered the chancellery building's audience hall and neared his master's seat.

"**Why are you back here?**" Dong Zhuo barked as Xu Rong fell to one knee in penitence. "Why didn't you stay and block Sun Jian?"

"It is better that he returned here," the adviser Li Ru suggested.

"My outer camps were harassed by his second advance to Yangren," Xu Rong replied. "It seems that he has secured a larger force now, and-"

"Bah! I'll just have to send my foster son!" Dong Zhuo decided; he turned to a man on his right and said, "Fengxian!"

The tall, imposing man – Lü Bu – got to his feet, bowed humbly, and said, "I shall prepare immediately, my lord and father."

"Uh... Chancellor, why do you send Lü Bu?" Li Ru asked. "Surely he should stay here in Luoyang as your-"

"I intend to send Fengxian to fight Sun Jian, and that is that," Dong Zhuo interrupted. "I shall also send Generals Hua Xiong and Hu Zhen."

"But I have not failed!" Xu Rong protested. "I returned to report and to ask for more troops to-!"

"You have humbled the southern tiger, Xu Rong, and I appreciate that," Dong Zhuo said sincerely. "Now my other generals shall break him, and show the world under Heaven that Dong Zhuo has many, many generals, all of them as good as Xu Rong!"

Xu Rong bowed silently.

"Five thousand of my men should be enough... now that Sun Jian risks giving the others courage, I need the rest to watch for attacks from Suanzao and Henei," Dong Zhuo continued.

"That won't happen," Li Ru insisted. "Give your generals at least ten thousand men, or Sun Jian will defeat them."

"You rate me that poorly, Li Ru?" Lü Bu growled.

"I agree with Fengxian," Dong Zhuo said sternly. "Mister Li, you're usually the cleverest of all; why do you now predict my Fengxian being trounced when Xu Rong was so successful? Why will they think that my General of Chariots and Cavalry and my Commander-in-Chief must be any less formidable than Xu Rong, and not flee with their tails between their legs...?"

"Sun Jian was blunted before; this time, he is sharp," Li Ru retorted. "He does not march calmly with a few thousand men; he marches angrily with as many as ten thousand men, looking to make up for a humiliating defeat. Do not underestimate him now; if he doesn't fear death, he doesn't fear rank."

"I'm sending *three generals*!" Dong Zhuo chortled. "How do I underestimate him?"

"His men are undisciplined southerners," Xu Rong said. "They buckled easily under the lightest pressure, Mister Li; our timidity when he arrived in Lu County was proven unfounded, and I only wish that we'd taken the risk and attacked him then, when his master was only a day's march away once the fool was swept aside."

"Xu Rong's appraisal is enough for me," Dong Zhuo decided. "Fengxian, go and prepare; Li Ru: go and inform Hua Xiong and Hu Zhen of their duties."

Lü Bu left the chancellery, but Li Ru did not move.

"I can see you grimacing, Li Ru," Dong Zhuo said. "This is so straightforward! Where is this pessimism coming from?"

"I shall say no more, and do as you asked," Li Ru replied as he started his retreat.

"...Perhaps I should recall Jia Xu," Dong Zhuo grumbled.

"Leave him with your son-in-law, my lord: you don't need him," the tall, confident general Li Jue suggested. "Mister Li Ru and I are capable enough."

Dong Zhuo snorted a laugh.

Sun Jian pitched camp in the Yangren region and assembled his officers in his command tent.

"So here we are, with mountains between us and Luoyang," Sun Jian began.

"We could go north into Yan Province and then go west," Han Dang suggested.

"Yes, well, that's not our immediate concern," Sun Jian continued. "Dong Zhuo's sent another army: this time, our scouts tell us that he's held Xu Rong back and put Hua Xiong, Hu Zhen and his new foster son Lü Bu in charge."

"Three of his most renowned generals...?" Han Dang exclaimed. "That's... that's dangerous."

"Not necessarily," Zhu Zhi said. "Lü Bu is arrogant and covetous; Hu Zhen is cunning, influential and respected but not as militarily minded as Lü Bu or Hua Xiong; Hua Xiong has a proven record of service and high rank that annoys and threatens Hu Zhen and Lü Bu. The three will contend rather than cooperate."

"...Then we'll attack their camp as soon as they arrive," Sun Jian suggested. "If they are organised, we'll do minor damage and put them on the defensive; if they're arguing, we'll destroy them before their campaign has even started."

"I won't disagree with that," Cheng Pu said.

"Neither shall I," Zhu Zhi said. "Commander Sun, I shall ensure that we know everything that we need to know, and quickly."

Sun Jian nodded silently.

Dong Zhuo's generals Lü Bu, Hua Xiong and Hu Zhen halted their advance to the west of Sun Jian's fenced encampment and observed the southern man's defences with respect.

"He knows what he's doing," Hu Zhen said.

"So do we," Lü Bu retorted.

"...Lü Fengxian, why are you being so terse with me again?" Hu Zhen asked desperately. "Ever since we left Luoyang, you-"

"Who said that you could address me by my courtesy name?" Lü Bu interrupted. "How am I now your friend, Hu Zhen?"

"We are colleagues!" Hu Zhen chortled. "What is this about?"

"Could you two stop it please...?" Hua Xiong sighed. "The enemy are around, and we can't afford to waste time and energy feuding amongst ourselves."

"I need no lecture from you, Hua Xiong," Hu Zhen growled. "I have started nothing."

"So the matter is entirely down to me?" Lü Bu said with anger.

"Who else is to blame?" Hu Zhen replied.

Lü Bu raised his spear; Hu Zhen backed his horse away and raised his own spear in a defensive posture. Hua Xiong and the rest of the army watched the two co-commanders with feelings that ranged from awe and expectation to frustration and despair.

"We must pitch camp!" Hua Xiong protested. "We must safeguard our supplies! We do not have time for this preposterous competitive show of manliness! Remember that I am *Commander-in-Chief*! You *must listen to me*!"

Neither Lü Bu nor Hu Zhen reacted to Hua Xiong's plea, as each man was worried about being distracted if the other chose to act. At the same time, many of the lesser officers and soldiers that were supposed to be working on the construction of a useable camp were now congregating to watch their commanders duel; that meant that there were no defences in place, and very few – if any – were watching for an attack by the enemy.

"Ayah! What is the matter with you two???" Hua Xiong moaned. **"Must I pull rank and intervene? Is that what it will take to-?"**

"ATTACK! ENEMY ATTACK!" a soldier cried as he ran toward the ensemble with clumsiness that indicated true fear.

"*Attack...?*" Hu Zhen said as he lowered his weapon.

"You *fools*!" Hua Xiong sobbed with rage. **"You've let them ambush us!"**

Within minutes, the first of Sun Jian's men were within sight of the three generals; there were no walls to keep them away, and many of Dong Zhuo's soldiers had discarded their weapons when they saw that their leaders were engaged in a personal argument. There was a mad scramble to collect weapons as Cheng Pu, Han Dang, Huang Gai and Sun Jian led independent attacks on parts of the disorganised force; men were cut down, horses were cut loose, and bags of supplies were left as pillars of flame atop the ox-drawn carts they were stacked on.

"Idiots! Fools and idiots!" Hua Xiong cried as he rode toward a group of Sun Jian's infantrymen and hacked them down. **"I am put to work with men with no brains in their heads!"**

"Lü Bu! This is no time for arguments!" Hu Zhen said as he turned his horse. **"If you cut me down when my back is turned, then you wrong the chancellor!"**

Lü Bu snorted contemptuously, turned his own horse and started towards a group of Sun Jian's infantry and cavalry; he used his skill to disarm and dismount three men in a few seconds, and scared the others into adopting a defensive stance. He then embarked on a rampage against the infantry, and several pikemen were his victims before he encountered Han Dang.

"Challenge me!" Lü Bu bellowed; he charged Han Dang and forced him to retreat with a barrage of attacks that Han Dang was unable to match.

"Is there anyone to match Lü Bu???" the foster son of Dong

Zhuo declared.

Sun Jian was alerted to the lack of success against the three commanders: he broke off his attack on the rear guard and started toward the vanguard. Cheng Pu had been injured in a battle with Hua Xiong, and Sun Jian was forced to rescue him.

"You're Sun Jian!" Hua Xiong exclaimed as he spied the familiar red scarf.

Sun Jian raised his weapon instead of answering his opponent; the two had a brief exchange of blows, but Hua Xiong fled when he saw that he was going to be surrounded by a large group of trained cavalry.

"You alright, Demou?" Sun Jian asked of his friend.

"...I keep getting hurt," Cheng Pu complained.

"Zhu Zhi will finish things now," Sun Jian suggested. **"You go and rest."**

Cheng Pu retreated miserably.

"So you're not looking to fight rounds?" Zu Mao asked.

"No, I just want to send them back to Luoyang so I have a clear marching path," Sun Jian replied. **"After Liangdong, I'm not interested in anything other than victory."**

The chancellor's infantry had scattered completely, so all that was left was pockets of cavalry led by the three commanders. Hu Zhen was fighting Huang Gai's men when Lü Bu suddenly appeared with his horsemen and charged at Huang Gai screaming, **"Are you a man worthy of facing Lü Bu?"**

Huang Gai was startled by the reckless attack, and was therefore thrown off-guard; Lü Bu's strikes were fast, fluid and near-impossible to defend against, so Huang Gai retreated at the first opportunity.

"Aha! No man is my equal, Hu Zhen!" Lü Bu heckled as Huang Gai's cavalry followed their leader's flight. **"All men are chaff to Lü Bu!"**

"...We should combine our forces and escape," Hu Zhen suggested.

"*Escape*, Hu Zhen?" Lü Bu chortled. **"*Escape*, when we have the advantage?"**

Hu Zhen observed the mass of fallen comrades and the pyre that had once been the supplies before he shouted, **"We are *not* winning, Lü Bu! Come to your senses!"**

Lü Bu was about to reply when a series of anguished screams interrupted him; arrows were now being used to fell the remnants of the broken army. The two men would be killed or captured if they tried to make a stand: that realisation caused Lü Bu to grunt angrily and flee toward the north.

"...A coward at heart, then, 'Fengxian'," Hu Zhen scoffed as he followed his ally.

Han Dang encountered Hua Xiong and his men as he fled westward; the two officers had a brief exchange of weapons before Han Dang realised that he was outmatched once again. Hua Xiong's force then engaged and defeated several of Han Dang's hesitant cavalrymen and charged the infantry so that they could resume their retreat.

"...Another great warrior," Han Dang sighed.

Wu Jing engaged Hua Xiong as the general neared relative safety; the northern man and his horsemen brushed Wu Jing's men aside with ease and continued on their way, unaware that they were actually riding into a trap. Zhu Zhi smiled as a scout rushed toward him to report Hua Xiong's imminent arrival.

"Fools! Fools, all of them!" Lü Bu said as he smashed his way through the line of men that had been placed to block his retreat; Hu Zhen watched with dismay, and silently wondered why Lü Bu could not have cooperated with his fellow generals in the first place to guarantee a victory. But regardless of any feelings that Hu Zhen might have had about his colleague, the two generals had escaped and they would fight another day.

Sun Jian was delighted by the early reports of the success of his pre-emptive strike: hundreds of Dong Zhuo's men had been killed, and the rest had been forced to retreat.

"We have a surprise guest," Cheng Pu said as he clutched his wounded arm.

"Who...?" Sun Jian prompted.

"You'll be pleased!" Cheng Pu suggested. **"Bring Hua Xiong!"**

"We got Hua Xiong...?" Sun Jian exclaimed.

"You defeated us with cowardly tactics!" Hua Xiong heckled as he was brought before Sun Jian by two smiling soldiers; he was tightly bound with rope.

"You're a despicable man, Hua Xiong," Sun Jian replied. "You helped Dong Zhuo harm the defenceless innocents and murder a fledgling emperor, and now you complain about fairness...?"

"...So what will you do with me then...?" Hua Xiong asked. "You want me to surrender...? Or will you send me back to Dong Zhuo without my ears and nose...?"

Sun Jian smiled and said, **"Guards: death."**

"No! No! I deserve better!" Hua Xiong protested as he was led away. **"Wretched man! Curse you, Sun Jian, you bumpkin! I'm Commander-in-Chief, an Excellency of the realm! I DESERVE BETTER!"**

"Don't bother to bring his head back," Sun Jian ordered.

"NO! DON'T DISRESPECT ME LIKE THIS!" Hua Xiong screamed. **"You mustn't! You CAN'T!"**

"*Bye*...!" Zu Mao cackled.

The other officers laughed.

Once Hua Xiong was gone, Huang Gai asked, "What do we do now, Lord Sun?"

"...Now we advance," Sun Jian declared. "Hua Xiong is dead; Dong Zhuo is next."

****

20

The news of the victory at Yangren was sped to Sun Jian's commander, Yuan Shu.

"...He defeated Hua Xiong...?" Yuan Shu exclaimed. "Then we could have that magnificent warrior in our service as well!"

"General Sun... executed him," the messenger revealed.

"What a waste," the adviser Yan Xiang complained. "Sun Jian should have consulted us before he acted, my lord. But he already shows signs of–"

"**Enough!**" Yuan Shu barked. "I am annoyed that I cannot have Hua Xiong, but I'm sure that my tiger had his reasons. Messenger, please hand over your report to Yan Xiang and withdraw."

Sun Jian's messenger did as he was asked; Yan Xiang read the remainder of the report and said, "He intends to advance on the capital immediately... well, I say 'immediately', but that depends on a lot of things."

"...Such as...?" Yuan Shu prompted.

"Your explicit order would normally be one thing, Lord Yuan, but he seems to be ignoring the need for your instructions; the other main factor is supplies," the adviser Han Yin explained. "If he doesn't receive any supplies, my lord... how can he march...?"

Yuan Shu eyed his advisers cautiously.

"You're suggesting blunting the man, Han Yin," General Ji Ling said with disdain.

"That is surely self-destructive," Yuan Shu suggested.

"Not at all: rather the reverse," Han Yin replied. "If he intends to be another Dong Zhuo, then he must be stopped now, before he seizes the capital. If we halt his supplies, then he cannot advance; he will then request orders, and we can make him understand his place in the scheme of things."

"I agree entirely," Yan Xiang declared. "His report is laced with arrogance: he talks of his *intentions*, my lord, when all he should be speaking of is his desire to follow your commands and be the instrument of *your* intentions!"

"...That bold southern man is not fully aware of the careful way that men of the court word their statements," Yuan Shu suggested. "Is it not the case that he is just excited at his victory, and he shares with me his hunger for an end to this...?"

"We cannot take the risk," Han Yin replied. "Once he is off the leash, there will be no way to capture him again. Put him to the test: make him understand."

"If you do not, and he advances on the capital without knowing that he serves you, then what will we do if he rebels...?" Yan Xiang proposed. "He could join Dong Zhuo, or take the capital after defeating him!"

Yuan Shu pondered his advisers' words carefully. He was a suspicious man by nature, so the suggestions fuelled his paranoia; after a very short amount of time, he nodded agreeably and said, "Cut him off."

"Wretched, treacherous man!" Cheng Pu cried as word reached the camp at Yangren that there would be no more supplies; Sun Jian sat in his host seat within the command tent, but he volunteered no reaction of any kind.

"*Why*???" Zhu Zhi groaned. "Is there any *reason* given, Demou?"

"*None!*" Cheng Pu despaired. "What foolery this man lives by now, no man can say! He just cuts off our supplies, and doesn't even tell us why!"

"...Man's been made to distrust us," Zu Mao suggested.

"That's ridiculous," Han Dang scoffed. "What does Yuan Shu want? We've defeated them, killed one of their famous generals, and-"

"All the effort we've gone to... for nothing," Huang Gai said. "When Dong Zhuo learns of our predicament, he'll send Xu Rong here to rout us again."

"It makes no *sense*," Cheng Pu complained.

"We should have allied ourselves with someone else; I accept full responsibility, gentlemen, for our current crisis," Zhu Zhi declared. "I will-"

Sun Jian suddenly got to his feet and started to put his armour on.

"Uncle...?" Sun Ben prompted; Sun Jian did not respond.

"...What are you doing?" Han Dang asked; Sun Jian did not respond.

"Are we advancing to Luoyang anyway?" Zhu Zhi asked; Sun Jian did not respond.

"You're angry, aren't you?" Zu Mao chuckled; still, Sun Jian did not respond.

"**Answer one of us, will you???**" Wu Jing cried; Sun Jian was silent.

"Where are you going?" Huang Gai asked as Sun Jian finished equipping himself, took up his sword, and started to leave the command tent.

"...**Don't do it, Lord Sun!**" Zhu Zhi cried as Sun Jian disappeared from view. "**Someone go after him!**"

"Why? What do you think that he going to do?" Cheng Pu asked.

"...I don't know, Demou, but whatever it is, someone should stop him!" Zhu Zhi pleaded.

Sun Ben rose and said, "Perhaps I should-!"

"Allow me," Zu Mao said as he ran out of the tent.

Sun Ben sighed powerlessly and sat down again.

"...Should we go as well...?" Cheng Pu asked of Wu Jing.

"No, let Zu Mao try," Wu Jing sighed. "We'll get nowhere."

"What a ridiculous situation," Han Dang grumbled. "We're all stuck serving a man that's his own worst enemy. Yuan Shu is the perfect example of why the world's in such a mess. If anyone wanted to know why we have White Wave Bandits, Yellow Turbans, Black Mountain Bandits, Dong Zhuo and all the rest, there it is right there in that pampered northern donkey's arse."

"...I just hope that Sun Wentai doesn't do anything rash," Cheng Pu said soberly.

"**Mister Sun Jian!**" Zu Mao hailed as he finally located his master; he was climbing onto his horse, and his expression was unreadable. Zu Mao stopped by the horse, tugged Sun Jian's trouser leg, and said, "You can't go to Lu County on your own."

Sun Jian exhaled noisily.

"I thought so," Zu Mao chuckled. "Give me a minute to get a horse, Mister Sun Jian."

"...Alright," Sun Jian replied.

A short time later, Sun Jian, Zu Mao and a small group of cavalry were riding out of the Yangren camp and heading southward, toward Lu County.

"Lord Yuan! Lord Yuan!" Han Yin cried as he ran into Yuan Shu's residence.
"...What is it?" Yuan Shu grumbled. "Don't bother me at home!"
"My lord, you must get ready!" Han Yin said fretfully. "*Sun Jian* is here, my lord!"
"...*Sun Jian*?" Yuan Shu exclaimed. "...*Here*? *Now*...?"
"Here and now!" Han Yin replied. "Hurry!"
Yuan Shu did not know the specific nature of Sun Jian's return to Lu County, and paranoia gripped him once again; he quickly dressed in battle robes and armour and hurried to his court.
When Yuan Shu entered the audience hall of his military headquarters, he found that Sun Jian was waiting for him, surrounded by a horde of armed officers.
"Why are you not in Yangren?" Yuan Shu asked as he sat in his host seat.
"...Where can I go?" Sun Jian replied angrily. "I brought twenty thousand men from the south and pledged allegiance to you. I took the men south, and won and lost battles on your behalf. Recently I won a great victory, and killed one of the enemy's commanders. I do all this for *you*: although he and I have an awkward past, I have no serious personal quarrel with Dong Zhuo. I risk my life and the lives of my men for two reasons only: to remove the traitor for the good of the country, and for you, Lord Yuan, to avenge your personal loss!"
Yuan Shu's eyes darted about wildly as he pondered Sun Jian's words: the affluent and influential Yuan family had been decimated at the very least by Dong Zhuo, so the conflict was very personal for the nobleman and his half-brother Shao.
"Yet my loyalty is met with suspicion," Sun Jian continued as he glared at the gaggle of advisers that were huddled together to the left of Yuan Shu's seat. "I have been slandered, that much I can guess, and so I lost my supplies, and with those supplies my chance to go to Luoyang and do what must be done for the good of the country. I'm here to find out what happens next."
Yuan Shu stared at the furious Sun Jian and pondered carefully. After a few minutes, he sighed theatrically and said, "I have been misled, Sun Wentai!"
The advisers murmured anxiously.
"It is the role of officials to broach every subject and explore every possibility; I do not reproach them for that," Yuan Shu continued. "I was misled by my own suspicious heart! When I thought of the betrayals that my family suffered – in particular, the loss that you speak of – I was distracted! Dong Zhuo was invited to the capital by my brother, Yuan Shao; we invited the murderer of our own clan, a wicked seditionist, to help us to save the emperor! When a man that was called a hero, a man that was given so much trust, turned out to be such a monster... need I go on...?"
Sun Jian grunted unsympathetically and asked, "What now?"
Yuan Shu coughed awkwardly and said, "Your supplies... will be sent. You are hereby given orders to advance to Luoyang and bring us victory."
Sun Jian bowed and said, "As you command, Lord Yuan. Now I

should like to hurry back to Yangren: every moment that Dong Zhuo lives and breathes is a moment to regret."

"Yes, you're quite right," Yuan Shu said tonelessly. "Do that."

Sun Jian bowed for a second time, turned, and retreated.

"...I nearly lost my tiger," Yuan Shu realised; he turned to his advisers and said, "*Fools*! You're lucky that I value your service!"

"It had to be done!" Han Yin insisted. "Now we know his motivations, so the matter is closed!"

"Explain!" Yuan Shu prompted.

"He serves you loyally," Han Yin replied. "He's *your tiger*, as you say; he understands the way of things. When faced with an insult to his person and a risk to his march, all he did was growl and bare his teeth; we now know that he can be controlled, and that was a very important thing to ascertain."

Yuan Shu smiled and said, "I understand. He knows he's mine... that's good to know. Very good indeed!"

Sun Jian prepared for the return to the camp in Yangren, but his heart was heavy.

"He restored our supplies, didn't he...?" Zu Mao asked worriedly.

"...Zu Mao, I belong to Yuan Shu," Sun Jian replied. "Can a man feel pride when he knows that everything he does is for something or someone else...?"

"Apart from nation and family... no," Zu Mao admitted.

"Precisely," Sun Jian scoffed. "He's got his own agenda, that much is obvious... and I'll be made to do things that only benefit him; I can see that as well."

Zu Mao nodded silently.

"I'll have to force myself to believe that I'm doing everything for my lady wife, Lady Chen and the children and the country, or... or I'll die of shame," Sun Jian continued. "Serving Yuan Shu is nothing to be proud of, Zu Mao... nothing to be proud of at all."

"So build your own future if you can," Zu Mao suggested. "If you're clever, you don't need to be tied to him forever: earn merit against Dong Zhuo, and then make your own place in the world where you don't answer to anyone!"

Sun Jian smiled and said, "That would be wonderful... for my family to be able to say that they answer to no lord, not even a rich lord in the north... wonderful indeed."

Unbeknownst to Sun Jian, that dream would one day become a reality. But for the man from Fuchun, the reality was very different: he was the vassal of an ungrateful and untrusting Yuan Shu, and his work was far from done. The self-appointed Chancellor of State, Dong Zhuo, was still in Luoyang, and the future of the Han Dynasty was uncertain for the first time in two centuries. The Eastern Pass Coalition was unmoving, and Dong Zhuo was pondering a retreat to the west, where he would be even more powerful: a hero was needed, and Sun Jian was quietly determined that he would be that hero, shackled or not.

****

21

"**Commander Sun returns!**" a soldier announced as he ran into the command tent of the coalition base in Yangren. Several men were waiting within for the return of their leader: they included Sun Jian's young nephew Ben, Cheng Pu, Huang Gai, Han Dang, Wu Jing and Zhu Zhi.

"...He went to see Yuan Shu," Zhu Zhi said pointlessly.

"He's alive," Han Dang noted. "That means we're alright, I reckon."

Minutes later, Sun Jian entered the tent and said, "What're you lot hanging around for...? Didn't you work out that we're marching to Luoyang?"

"Our supplies are restored?" Cheng Pu exclaimed.

"He was told that I was a threat, which was obvious enough," Sun Jian scoffed. "I think I've managed to convince him that I'm a loyal dog... which, for some reason, I'm supposed to be happy about. So yes, Cheng Demou, our supplies are restored."

"Where's Zu Mao?" Han Dang asked.

Sun Jian tapped his red neck scarf and said, "I'm still wearing it! Zu Mao didn't have to be my decoy again, don't worry. He's readying his troops for departure."

"We should all do the same," Han Dang suggested.

Sun Jian's swift advance was met with anxiety in the blockaded capital, Luoyang. Dong Zhuo summoned his vassals to his chancellery to discuss his next move.

"I thought he was retreating!" Dong Zhuo complained. "Why is he on his way here again???"

"Our spies reported that his supplies were cut off," the adviser Li Ru began. "He-"

"I know his supplies were cut off!" Dong Zhuo snapped. "Does this mean that he has supplies again???"

"...I was about to say that it probably does, yes," Li Ru sighed.

"Sun Jian may have turned on Yuan Shu, and therefore, this march might be a false one, designed to get him closer to the capital so that he can join us," the general and adviser Li Jue suggested.

"I think that's a little far-fetched, Li Jue," Dong Zhuo said with a sneer. "He hates me! He'll surely come here looking to put my head on a spike!"

"It isn't so ridiculous," Li Ru said calmly. "My lord, Sun Jian has been made to look quite stupid by Yuan Shu. He has been very publicly told that he is not trusted, and that he is a vassal, the very lowliest of vassals. That could be advantageous to us."

"...We could have him join us, you mean...?" Dong Zhuo said excitedly.

"Possibly," Li Ru continued. "What I suggest, my lord, is..."

Sun Jian was shocked when he received personal correspondence from the capital; he had been forced to halt while the supply line was reinforced against possible attacks by Dong Zhuo's generals, so he summoned his officials to his command tent to discuss it.

"...A letter," Sun Jian mused as he studied the wooden tube.

"From 'Chancellor of State Dong Zhuo'...?" Han Dang supposed.

"Of course," Cheng Pu scoffed. "He's scared."

Sun Jian continued to study the container as he said, "I wonder what he wants... Dong Zhuo, I mean."

"Whatever it is, it can never be good enough!" Huang Gai barked.

"I quite agree," Sun Jian said as he finally removed the cloth letter from the tube, unfurled it, and started to read.

"...Well?" Cheng Pu prompted after several minutes. "You must have read it by now. What does it say?"

"I... I had to read it three or four times to make sure that I wasn't going mad," Sun Jian chortled as he passed the letter to Cheng Pu. "He actually... he actually has the nerve to suggest a *marriage alliance* between us. He's sending Li Jue here to discuss the idea further."

Sun Ben sneered at the idea.

"He's scared... really scared," Zhu Zhi suggested.

"No good man would want his bloodline tainted by the likes of *him*," Zu Mao muttered.

"...I can hardly believe it myself," Cheng Pu admitted as he passed the letter back to Sun Jian, who immediately handed it to Huang Gai. "What will you do?"

Huang Gai frowned, saying, "Are you suggesting that he-"

"Don't even dare!" Cheng Pu chuckled. "No, I would never suggest thinking it over... I meant the rebuttal... how severe it should be."

Sun Jian shook his head as he said, "My gut instinct is to tell him that I shall meet him and his offspring only to tear them apart with my bare hands, for the good of the state. And I *would* do that..."

"...Only...?" Cheng Pu prompted.

"Only I am the vassal of General Yuan Shu," Sun Jian sighed miserably.

"Don't remind us," Han Dang muttered. "He's almost as bad as Dong Zhuo, the *treacherous-*"

"Enough," Sun Jian pleaded. "I must wonder if this is some plot conceived by his advisers to capitalise on my altercation with Yuan Shu, perhaps instil further resentment... perhaps he actually has the ridiculous belief that I could be convinced to defect."

"*Or...*?" Zhu Zhi said pointedly.

"...Or so that Yuan Shu acts against Lord Sun, eliminating him as a threat that way, under the pretext of a marriage alliance," Cheng Pu realised. "That may also be true... his advisers, Li Ru and Jia Xu, are both wily types that could suggest something like that to make the alliance destroy itself."

Sun Jian nodded and said, "I must be careful."

"This letter is sycophantic rubbish," Huang Gai said with disbelief. "I cannot say anything else, seeing this talk of how you both served in Liang Province together, fighting the wicked barbarians side by side as brothers-in-arms...!"

"*Liar*," Zu Mao grumbled.

"Does he not ally himself with the same 'wicked barbarians' now...?" Zhu Zhi said with amusement. "Perhaps we should tell his allies what he really thinks of them."

"They'd never believe it," Sun Jian lamented. "It is the sad and sorry case that he has ingratiated himself with them somehow, and they consider him to be a most honest and decent individual."

Cheng Pu turned to Huang Gai and asked, "So what would *you* do, Gongfu...?"

"I'd write back quickly, before Li Jue gets here," Huang Gai replied as he passed the letter to a curious Zhu Zhi. "Just tell him 'no' in very formal terms; such coldness will doubtless make him think that you plan his total destruction as a matter of pragmatism, which will scare him far more than an angry rebuke."

Cheng Pu waited for the bemused Zhu Zhi to finish reading and said, "And your view is, Junli...?"

"...I agree with Huang Gongfu," Zhu Zhi said quietly.

"That was my thought, actually, to just say 'no'; I'd never considered such a tone to be menacing, but that only makes it a better plan," Sun Jian replied. "If the fates are with me, I'll definitely kill him, personally, and drag his corpse through the streets on the back of my horse."

"I think he knows that," Han Dang chuckled. "You're a very dangerous man under that quiet façade... he rightly fears you."

But before Sun Jian could send his reply, General Li Jue arrived at Sun Jian's camp and requested an audience.

"**General Li Jue,**" Cheng Pu announced angrily as Dong Zhuo's subordinate strode into the audience hall and paid theatrical respects to Sun Jian.

"You might as well start talking," Sun Jian prompted.

"Marquis Sun, you have been asked about a marriage alliance between your family and the family of Chancellor of State Dong Zhuo, and a possible peace between your faction and the court for the sake of the country," Li Jue replied. "I am here to stress to you the benefits of such an alliance."

"I cannot see any benefits to allying myself with the most hated man in the land, and perhaps of the entire world under Heaven, General," Sun Jian suggested.

"The chancellor is misunderstood," Li Jue responded. "I am aware that you served as an adviser to Zhou Shen during the Liang Province campaign, and gained no merit as a result of being ignored when you provided sound advice."

"...I was," Sun Jian said angrily. "I remember Dong Zhuo doing rather well out of it, and entirely undeservedly! He fought hesitantly and only acted when it benefitted his career! He is lucky that I didn't have the remit to challenge him then!"

"He is aware of your initial appraisal," Li Jue sighed. "But I was an officer in that campaign, Marquis Sun, and I assure you that our situation can be explained. In the initial encounters, the chancellor was hesitant because he and his advisers felt that the approach to the rebels was inappropriate, as you did. He tried, initially, to seek some accord with their leaders, as he has now, but it failed, and so he changed his stance, opting to atone for past reticence with his decisive attack on their camp that ensured initial victory. Had we pressed on together, and not split our forces into three, that might have been the end of it."

"Your lord Dong Zhuo tricked his way out of his predicament!" Sun Jian growled.

"But in doing so, he saved the lives of the men under his command; is that the action of a wicked tyrant, Marquis Sun?" Li Jue retorted. "Why did he not ensure a covenant of silence with his own troops and abandon the supplied troops to the Qiang?"

"...That is a sound point, but there are many answers to it," Sun Jian countered.

"The chancellor turned down becoming the Inspector of Bing Province, opting instead to retain his lesser role and defend Chang'an from rebels that had, by that point, become distanced from the Qiang and sought only anarchy: is that the action of a greedy man...?" Li Jue asked further. "I put it to you also, Marquis, that the chancellor desired the appointment of the Prince of Chenliu as Majesty for the right reasons; his father, His Majesty Han Lingdi, desired the same, viewing the Prince of Hongnong as weak-minded, easily manipulated by his consort-murdering mother, the Empress Dowager Hè, and lacking in any of the traits that made him worthy of the mandate. Indeed, it was the desire of many at court until the chancellor suggested it, and then it was suddenly treason!"

"Discussions before the ascension were one thing," Sun Jian countered. "Deposing His Majesty Shaodi to install the Prince of Chenliu is treason; murdering Shaodi afterward is regicide. Your master is evil, plain and simple. His perversion of General Lü Bu, turning him from noble hero to wicked, impious murderer of fathers, is also of note. His slaughter of the family of my master Yuan Shu yet another of his needless acts of villainy, and his ignorant destruction of the capital's bronze treasures beyond all reasonable doubt."

"...All misunderstandings that can be explained, Marquis Sun, but are of no relevance to our negotiations!" Li Jue insisted desperately. "The chancellor is acting in the best interests of the empire, and besides one group of confused eastern warlords, men willingly serve in a court that serves the will of His Majesty.

"You are the hero of the age, Marquis Sun, and because of bigotry and stupidity and corruption, you have been cruelly undervalued and even ignored. You should have been made an inspector of a province at the very least for your service against the Yellow Turbans, but instead you were appointed as the magistrate of an unimportant place on the outskirts of the land, placed there as an expendable buffer by men that see you as a commoner; and you are surely aware by now of how little your appointment as a marquis of an unimportant place serves you.

"Join us, Marquis Sun, and you will reach the heights that you are supposed to reach! Help the chancellor clear away the chaff and build a new court based on law, order, talent and excellence! A place at his side guarantees important civil or military roles for you and your sons! Surely that is better than being undervalued, fighting on a side destined to lose, for men that would give you no thanks even if you were, by some circumstance, victorious...?"

"You're *serious*...?" Sun Jian chortled angrily. "General, I have heard your long, sprawling mass of dishonest, nonsense rhetoric; in response, he shall have nothing from me but swift, honest clarity. He shall have my response as swiftly and as clearly as it can be delivered!"

Li Jue's optimistic visage disappeared.

"Tell your master that I will advance on Luoyang immediately, and I will accept no surrender, never mind insulting 'bargaining' such as *this*," Sun Jian continued. "I'll track him down, and I'll tear him apart, and then I'll put his corpse on display for the world to see. The dogs will feast upon him, if they can condescend to such self-demeaning horrors."

"*You*...!" Li Jue exclaimed.

"Get out of here, you shameless creature!" Sun Jian bellowed. **"You dare to come here and try to negotiate from a high position, when I have bested many of your generals and have a clear path to Luoyang...? I've killed Hua Xiong and shamed Hu Zhen and Lü Bu; what right have *you*, what strange understanding of the world must you have, to come here and talk to me this way...?"**

Li Jue stepped back and scowled angrily.

"I said *go*, Li Jue!" Sun Jian shouted. **"If you and I have anything else to say, it will be with swords! I won't earn a place in Heaven until I have killed every last one of you and your clans and shown the heads to the gods! You and your master will know nothing but death!"**

Li Jue bowed low, turned, and walked out of the audience hall without saying another word.

"Are you alright, Uncle...?" Sun Ben asked quietly. "You look so angry...!"

"...The *cheek*," Sun Jian said irritably. "Just for that, I will make Dong Zhuo *suffer*, and I am not normally a vindictive man."

"Dong Zhuo brings out the worst in people," Cheng Pu sighed. "So what now...?"

"Now that we have rejected his offer, Dong Zhuo will know that we are unbending," Zhu Zhi declared. "When Li Jue relates your exact response, Dong Zhuo will know that the only option is to fight to the last man. We must go to him, or he will come to us: there is no other choice."

"Have the order issued: we continue our march as soon as it is feasible," Sun Jian replied. "This ends as soon as it possibly can!"

Sun Jian's army advanced to Dagu Pass, a fortified gateway to the south of Luoyang, but that would be as far as he would go due to the unavoidable delays while supplies were received via the long road from Lu County. Dong Zhuo observed Sun Jian's movements with dread, but he did not respond, because there was a sudden change in atmosphere among the northern members of the Eastern Pass Coalition. Cracks were starting to show: the inactive coalition was inexplicably nearing collapse under the weight of needless intrigue.

****

22

Sun Jian's march to Dagu Pass did not solicit the desired reaction from the leader of the Eastern Pass Coalition, Yuan Shao: instead of calling for an all-out attack on the capital, he tried to have Governor Liu Yu of the northern Yòu Province declared as an alternative sovereign. At around the same time, Governor Han Fu of Ji Province, who was the supply commander for the main force, started to reduce the resources that he was contributing to Yuan Shao's main force; that led to Yuan Shu plotting with the northern cavalry commander Gongsun Zan to seize Ji Province from Han Fu. News of those events caused Sun Jian and his allies to delay their advance for even longer, and that in turn gave Dong Zhuo cause to believe that he might win in the end after all.

"...I'm sick of it."
Sun Jian's declaration came after a day of deliberating in his Dagu Pass command tent; his frustration was shared by one and all.
"Dong Zhuo has to be stopped," Sun Jian continued. "I don't care about Yuan Shao and his petty scheming! He can enthrone himself for all I care right now; he's a problem for tomorrow! Dong Zhuo has to be got rid of *today*. I want an immediate march against the capital. We'll prepare at once."
There were no voices of dissent; every officer went to their subordinates and had them prepare the army for an immediate march. But Dong Zhuo had spies in the region, and the activity was reported to the chancellor, who then gave an order that shocked the entire coalition.

"**Lord Sun!**" Zhu Zhi cried as he ran into the command tent with a written report.
"What's happened now...?" Sun Jian despaired.
"Dong Zhuo is doing something... I don't know what exactly, but the capital is in chaos!" Zhu Zhi said. "I think he's trying to evacuate it... *completely*!"
Sun Jian was still; the only other person present was Wu Jing, who was unable to think of an appropriate reaction.
"If he is evacuating, it will be to go west, to his own home territory!" Zhu Zhi continued. "If he gets to Liang Province, or even to Chang'an, he'll be near-unstoppable!"
Wu Jing groaned miserably, turned to Sun Jian, and asked, "What can we do...? We've come this far... but at the same time, we're not fully prepared."
"...We march immediately," Sun Jian decided. "I don't care if we're not fully prepared: I won't let the man get out of the capital!"

Dong Zhuo had ordered an immediate clearance of Luoyang: that action was to be swift, and it would include looting anything and anyone of value. The chancellor had entrusted his foster son Lü Bu with the task, and Bu did not disappoint. Lü Bu had been told to reduce the number of people that would be making the long, perilous journey to Chang'an – the capital of the Han before the infamous Wang Mang ended that dynasty through intrigue and created himself First Emperor of Xin. Dong Zhuo was principally interested in wealth, so in many cases his soldiers dragged the richer families from their homes, slaughtered them, and sacked their homes. But Lü Bu had also been asked to take the wealth from the long-dead, most specifically the previous emperors. And once the looting was completed, Dong Zhuo wanted there to be nothing – not even a worthless city – left for the Eastern Pass Coalition: so Lü Bu had one last order, and that was to raze the city to the ground.

"...Oh... we are in the netherworld!" Zhu Zhi gasped as he observed the area around the southern gates of Luoyang for the first time: there were burning corpses and gutted, burning houses in every direction, and the smells of burning timber, fabrics and flesh filled the air.

"**Where is Dong Zhuo???**" Sun Jian bellowed. "**I'll gut him for this!**"

Sun Jian's army then had their first encounter with Dong Zhuo's troops: Sun Jian, Zu Mao, Cheng Pu, Huang Gai and Han Dang were gripped by rage at the sight of what Dong Zhuo had done, so they were not forgiving to the chancellor's infantry and cavalrymen.

"**Where is Dong Zhuo???**" Sun Jian screamed hysterically. "**Where is he???**"

A terrified major fled in the direction of the Han tombs; Zhu Zhi noted it and said, "**Lord Sun, I think we have to go that way!**"

"...Toward the *tombs*...?" Huang Gai exclaimed. "What would he be there for- ...No. **No! He wouldn't loot the tombs???**"

"**He would, and he does!**" Sun Jian decided. "**Zhu Zhi, Cheng Pu: take a third of the men each and chase these creatures out of Luoyang! Zu Mao, Huang Gai, Han Dang: we'll go to the tombs!**"

"**Let me ride with you, Uncle!**" Sun Ben pleaded.

"**And let you see such things...?**" Sun Jian replied. "**Go back to the camp!**"

Sun Ben returned to relative safety yet again while his uncle charged into the city and toward the greatest danger that he had ever faced.

Dong Zhuo was overseeing the excavation of the treasures in the Han tombs personally; he learned of Sun Jian's approach and shrieked, "**Lü Bu! Li Jue! Where are you??? Where are you when I am in danger???**"

"**You should be calm, Excellency!**" Dong Zhuo's relative and junior officer Dong Yue pleaded. "**Mister Li Ru said that-**"

"**Li Ru is not here either!**" Dong Zhuo said with panic. "**...Lü Bu! Lü Bu! Where have you run off to, you-!**"

"**But I am here, Excellency!**" an officer replied as he rode toward Dong Zhuo.

"...**Duan Wei**," Dong Zhuo muttered. "**Where is Li Jue?**"

"**General Li Jue and General Lü Bu are on their way to intercept Sun Jian,**" Duan Wei replied. "**I have been sent to help with the clearance of the tombs.**"

"**I don't need officers to dig up graves!**" Dong Zhuo barked. "**Go and fight Sun Jian! The more of you there are, the more time it'll take for him to get here! Go on! And get someone to alert Xu Rong and Hu Zhen while you're at it! Xu Rong**

beat him once, so get Xu Rong! Get Xu Rong!"
Duan Wei retreated to carry out his orders; Dong Zhuo looked at the ongoing work on one of the large stone tombs and muttered, "I just need *time*...!"

Sun Jian and his contingent were blocked from reaching the tombs by Lü Bu and his officers Zhang Liao, Gao Shun and Wei Xu, who led a sizeable battalion of infantry and horsemen.
"The tiger from Fuchun!" Lü Bu said with laughter. **"I've been looking forward to a duel with you since I first heard of you... such a shame that we missed each other at Yangren!"**
"Is he serious?" Zu Mao chortled. "He can't really want a duel in the middle of all this...? Does he really not know what he's–"
"Lü Bu!" Sun Jian bellowed. **"Atone and retreat!"**
"Or else *what*, **scabby pirate...?"** Lü Bu retorted angrily. **"You actually think that you can beat me???"**
Sun Jian ordered his forces to charge; Lü Bu did the same. The two forces met and clashed violently; glaive was met with glaive, and spear with spear, and men on horses fought with men on foot. Lü Bu rode through one group of combatants and charged at Sun Jian; his charge was blunted by Zu Mao, but the latter was knocked from his horse after a short, unbalanced exchange. Then Han Dang tried to stop Lü Bu; he was forced to turn his horse and turn his attentions to stopping Major Gao Shun in order to avoid a rout, which left Lü Bu a clear path to Sun Jian.
"I'll have your skin, southern tiger!" Lü Bu screamed. **"Prepare to die!"**
Lü Bu and Sun Jian began an exchange, but Lü Bu was quietly surprised at Sun Jian's ability to hold his ground against his relentless assault. Sun Jian occasionally broke the superior fighter's defences and landed flat-edged blows; that only served to anger Bu, who poured all of his strength into trying to unseat Sun Jian from his horse so that he could deliver a killing blow.
        Zu Mao had recovered from his own defeat at Lü Bu's hands, but he was forced to leave his master to his unwanted duel and assist Han Dang in repelling the combined forces of Lü Bu's senior officers. Han Dang was reeling from a failed attempt to force Zhang Liao to flee, and he welcomed Zu Mao's arrival.
"If you have any ideas, share them!" Han Dang said as the two southern men prepared to face their enemies with their inferior force. But before any of Lu Bu's men could charge, Wu Jing let out a cry and charged at the left flank of Dong Zhuo's force with his horsemen; Han Dang then led his force from the right while Zu Mao fought from the centre, and Gao Shun was forced to order the men to retreat before they were surrounded and routed.
"You're a gift!" Han Dang said to his allies. **"Now we can aid Commander Sun!"**
Wu Jing pursued the enemy officers while Zu Mao and Han Dang rushed to their commander.
        "Coward! You resort to such things because you're no match for me!" Lü Bu complained as Zu Mao and Han Dang's reinforcements arrived to bolster Sun Jian's forces and harass Lü Bu's soldiers. Sun Jian pressed his attack, but he was exhausted, and even an angry, distracted Lü Bu was still the better man when

duelling; Bu almost unseated Sun Jian with a powerful two-handed shove with his spear-handle before he turned his steed and fled to avoid meeting the same fate as Hua Xiong. Lü Bu's soldiers defended his escape for as long as he could, and then they fled as well.

"...That man... may be a moron... but he is truly formidable as a duellist," Sun Jian wheezed as Zu Mao rode to his side. "Your timing was... perfect."

"You lasted longer than anyone else," Zu Mao chuckled. "Now the guard dogs are gone, let's get Dong Zhuo!"

Sun Jian smiled and struggled to catch his breath before the pursuit continued.

"D'AAAAGH! Where is Lü Bu???" Dong Zhuo shrieked as Sun Jian approached the desecrated tombs. **"How did they get past Lü Bu??? Challenge him, Dong Yue, at once!"**

Dong Yue rode forward to challenge Sun Jian, and the two exchanged blows; Zu Mao rode past the battle and charged at Dong Zhuo's bodyguards, who were the best of his cavalry. Sun Jian managed to force Dong Yue to retreat, and as the main forces of both sides finally collided with each other in scattered battles, Sun Jian took the opportunity to charge Dong Zhuo personally.

"TRAITOR!" Sun Jian cried as his spear blade collided with Dong Zhuo's sword.

Dong Zhuo's responses were inarticulate and feral as he tried to block Sun Jian's attacks and save himself; but it was a sudden second attack by Lü Bu and his men that would weaken Sun Jian's force and force its commander to let Dong Zhuo go to save his army. Dong Zhuo sneered and barked retreat orders at his elite bodyguards, who immediately formed a protective shield around his horse so that he could ride to safety. General Li Jue arrived to give additional support, and for the first time, Sun Jian's army fought as one against Dong Zhuo's.

"Wu Jing, Huang Gai: engage the left!" Sun Jian ordered. **"Han Dang, Cheng Pu: engage the right! Zu Mao: with me, at the centre!"**

The two armies piled into one-another for one last time: Li Jue ordered Lü Bu to remain at the battle line and send his generals to engage the enemy officers.

"I am being underused, and I resent it!" Lü Bu complained. **"I am Lü Bu! I should be at the front!"**

"It is the chancellor's orders!" Li Jue retorted. **"You're not to engage them again! You're to block their advance so that he can retreat!"**

Sun Jian tried to charge against Lü Bu, but he was blocked by Zhang Liao; both were tired from their previous exploits, so they were not at their best. Han Dang challenged Gao Shun, but the northern man was more skilled, and Han Dang retreated; Zhu Zhi had an elite cavalry force strike against the front lines of Li Jue's infantry, and both suffered casualties. It quickly became clear that there would be no clear winner, and that both sides would eventually be destroyed if the fighting continued: it would be Li Jue that would eventually decide that the battle had to end and order a full retreat.

"NO!" Lü Bu shrieked. **"They will not beat me! They _cannot_**

beat me! I am Lü Bu! I AM LÜ BU!"

"Obey the chancellor's orders!" Li Jue retorted. **"Pull your men back and retreat at once!"**

Lü Bu could not resist the urge to spur his large brown horse for one last charge against Sun Jian's weary volunteer infantry; they buckled under the pressure, but Bu was ordered to retreat once again, and this time, he complied. Sun Jian ordered a pursuit, but Lü Bu and Gao Shun's spirited defence of the rear forced Sun Jian to order his men to let the enemy go.

"Take heart, Mister Sun Jian," Zu Mao said warmly. "We beat them in the end."

"No we didn't," Sun Jian replied miserably. "Look around you, Zu Mao: look at... look at what they've done."

Sun Jian's force finally had a moment to digest the extent of the damage caused by the Chancellor of State: the once-proud capital was ablaze in every direction, bodies littered the streets, and the imperial tombs were all but destroyed, their contents stolen by Dong Zhuo to fund his new state in the west of the country. Most of the southern men had never seen Luoyang, or even visited the north; yet the sight of their divinely-anointed emperor's capital as a looted funeral pyre was enough to make many of them weep like children.

"We have to pursue," Sun Jian said with tears in his eyes.

"We can't!" Wu Jing protested. **"Lü Bu's force alone has tired us out! We need to secure a supply route and let the men rest!"**

"How can we 'rest', Brother-in-law???" Sun Jian barked.

"Wu Jing is right, Wentai!" Cheng Pu volunteered. **"We're all–"**

"This isn't even just about pursuing Dong Zhuo!" Sun Jian chortled. **"Where can we rest? In this burning ruin???"**

Many of the men were starting to cough and feel nauseous as the noxious smoke started to overwhelm them.

"We must put out the fires before we can pursue, I know that!" Sun Jian continued. **"But then what...? Can we 'rest' in a burnt-out city with no food, no water, no shelter and no gates??? Dong Zhuo could surround us if the rest of this so-called coalition carries on sitting there!"**

"They can't sit there now!" Cheng Pu said optimistically. **"Now that we've acted, they... they *have* to act! They *have to*!"**

Zhu Zhi coughed uncomfortably and said, **"Commander Sun is right: before we do anything else, we must put out the fires! Dong Zhuo's men are too busy retreating right now, so we must use the time we have! Commander, may I issue orders...?"**

Sun Jian looked at the devastation that surrounded him and struggled to find the thoughts and words to rationalise it; after a few moments he gave up, took his helmet off and threw it to the ground, saying, **"Curse him! Curse him to the netherworld, the...!"**

After a silence that was punctuated by sobs and crackling fires, Zhu Zhi said, **"Can I issue orders, Commander Sun...?"**

"...Sorry... sorry, yes, do that," Sun Jian said as Wu Jing picked up his helmet and returned it to him.

Zhu Zhi nodded sternly and turned to the other officers, saying, **"Huang Gai: you're in charge of fire control. Cheng Pu:**

you're in charge of locating survivors. Han Dang: you're in charge of reordering the troops and establishing some defences. I'll try and coordinate where I can and allocate appropriate resting facilities."

"**We can't camp in the ruins!**" one captain heckled.

"**We have no choice!**" Zhu Zhi insisted. "**We can't go back to Dagu Pass! We have to risk staying here! I don't like it any more than any of you... I promise you that.**"

The miserable, demoralised army went about its allocated assignments while Zhu Zhi neared Sun Jian to discuss some other matters.

"Are you going to be okay, my lord...?" Zhu Zhi asked.

"...We have to repair the tombs," Sun Jian said worriedly. "The sovereigns past and present are scrutinising our every move, Zhu Junli. If we don't, they'll-"

"That is why I did not allocate tasks to Wu Jing or Zu Mao," Zhu Zhi interrupted. "I, like you, see the prevailing importance of showing respect to the Sons of Heaven. If we cannot show our loyalty to Heaven, defending ourselves against Dong Zhuo will be hollow indeed."

Sun Jian nodded slowly and said, "I will help with that task personally."

Sun Jian's heroism was noted by the other members of the Eastern Pass Coalition, but the majority continued to hold their positions and made no move to stop Dong Zhuo's slow, laboured retreat to the western capital city of Chang'an. Only one man – Cao Cao, a former colleague of Sun Jian's during the Yellow Turban Rebellion – ignored the consensus and attacked Dong Zhuo's forces at a place called Xingyang. That would be one of Cao Cao's most famous defeats – a later one would eclipse them all – and it would serve, some said, as a lesson to anyone else in the coalition that had ideas about pursuing the chancellor. In the wake of that defeat, Cao Cao retreated to the city of Henei to join his friend and commander Yuan Shao, and his colleagues in Suanzao began to disperse or fight each other: Sun Jian and his allies watched the implosion of the coalition with despair from the ruins of the capital. If they remained in Luoyang, Sun Jian's army could suffer siege attacks from Dong Zhuo's re-established forces; if they retreated, the outcome could be even worse. The heroes from the south were all but trapped, while Dong Zhuo was as free as ever.

****

23

Days passed: Cao Cao's defeat at Xingyang had seemingly cancelled out any morale that Sun Jian's acquisition of Luoyang had generated. The ruins of the capital were no longer ablaze in entirety, but there was little to be found to make use of: food was scarce, and camps had to be erected around the remains of buildings. Sun Jian and his senior officers took shelter in the chancellery building, which now offered little defence from the elements.

"...Am I hearing right, Mister Zhu?" Sun Jian said to Zhu Zhi. "Am I right hearing that Dong Zhuo is courting the other members of this so-called coalition with talk of truces, marriage alliances and the like...?"

"Yes," Zhu Zhi replied indifferently.

Sun Jian held up a letter and said, "An aide to my sponsor and friend, Zhu Jun, risked his life to get this to me, gentlemen; he's got land to the west of here, and he is completely isolated. How is that the case...? How is it the case that Former Colonel Cao Cao charged unaided and nearly died, and a former General of Flying Cavalry is being left to have his bones picked by Dong Zhuo's lackeys...? How is it that we charged out of Dagu Pass, defeated their best men and liberated Luoyang, and we're stuck here, just as Zhu Jun is stuck, waiting to have our bones picked as well...? What is the matter with the majority of these northern men?"

"You can't even call it cowardice," Cheng Pu scoffed.

"I'm been in correspondence with Commander Yuan Shao and Cao Cao," Sun Jian continued. "The latter is as frustrated as we are; apparently, he did everything he could to send me aid, and everything he could to rally all the men in Suanzao to follow my lead. He is the only good one out of all of them; if Cao Cao were the strongest man in the land, gentlemen, then we might see some justice! Instead we are cursed with the Yuan brothers for masters, and two more ineffective men couldn't be wished for! Yuan Shao is 'waiting for the right moment'... Truly, I despair!"

"Let's go home, Mister Sun Jian," Zu Mao suggested. "We can't do any more. So many men have been injured, burned, and killed... loads have got bad coughs now, and some are sick from lack of decent food. The northerners are not going to help us... not the majority, anyway. Let's go back to Changsha."

"I agree," Han Dang grumbled. "This campaign is a waste of everything: time, money, food, lives..."

"...If even a few of them would act...!" Huang Gai groaned. "Instead, they barter for peace, after all that we-!"

"Yuan Shao will not seek peace with Dong Zhuo," Zhu Zhi insisted. "He'll reject the offers. So will everyone else. The problem is that we're increasingly isolated and are therefore in greater danger when Dong Zhuo reacts: the camp at Suanzao has fallen apart since Cao Cao's departure, and they're even killing each other now."

"What...? Explain!" Sun Jian exclaimed.

"Yan Province's governor, Liu Dai, is in charge there, obviously enough," Zhu Zhi continued. "Qiao Mao, the Administrator of Dong Prefecture, was the one that made the call to arms, was he not...?"

"...Yes," Cheng Pu said bemusedly. "What's happened...?"

"Liu Dai 'never liked him'," Zhu Zhi explained. "So he's killed him, and replaced him with a favourite sycophant. Zhang Miao, the Administrator of Chenliu – Cao Cao's friend and, by all accounts, a genuinely nice man – has given up and gone home, and Yuan Shao's cousin, Administrator Yuan Yi, has gone east. Now Suanzao is held together by the incompetent Liu Dai and his toadies. That leaves Wang Kuang's camp at Heyang Ford as the only ally we have to the south of the Yellow River. Everyone else that's even slightly worthy of mention is in Ji Province or across the river in Henei."

"We're a sitting target!" Sun Jian cried. "We've been hung out to dry by those...!"

"...Like I said, we should go home," Zu Mao muttered.

"As long as Wang Kuang is based at Heyang Ford, we can perhaps coordinate with Zhu Jun and try and advance some of our forces to pressure Dong Zhuo," Cheng Pu suggested. "This doesn't have to be over."

"Oh, it isn't, don't you worry," Sun Jian said. "I didn't come all this way to be made a fool of again, like I was in the last campaign that involved that dog Dong Zhuo. He was our enemy then, even when he was supposed to be our ally; this world will never know peace while he's alive. *I* will never know peace while he's alive. None of us will. This is our problem: when you see what he's done to Luoyang, then you know that the stories about him wiping villages off the map are true. This is what he'll do to us, gentlemen, as soon as he's got the resources... but I won't let that happen."

"...Put that way, I can't say I want to give up," Zu Mao replied. "You're right, Mister Sun Jian; we have to keep going."

"And so long as we have Zhu Jun's resistance in the west, Wang Kuang stationed in the near north and something resembling an army based in the far north, there's still a chance," Zhu Zhi declared. "Cao Cao will surely be able to encourage his old Western Garden Army friend to fight: that's the same Yuan Shao that killed the 'Ten Attendants' and saved the emperor! All he needs is proper men around him, encouraging him to act, and not a bunch of robed, self-serving cowards."

"...I'll hold," Sun Jian decided. "Not forever, but... I'll hold. But we'll advance as soon as an opportunity arises."

But the Luoyang camp's optimism was crushed days later, when Wang Kuang – who was a former aide to Hè Jin, the assassinated Commander-in-Chief and uncle to the deposed emperor – was surprised by an attack on Heyang Ford. Dong Zhuo's forces decimated Wang's and forced him to flee to Henei; that left Sun Jian's force in the capital dangerously exposed.

"Here's the situation," Cheng Pu said to the assembled officials. "Dong Zhuo's effectively taken Heyang Ford: that means that we're alone. There are two options available to us now beyond the futile and self-destructive 'Remain here' that nobody advocates: firstly, we can retreat to Dagu Pass and watch for opportunities to regain ground or return to the south; secondly, we can advance some of our army westward to dissuade Dong Zhuo from staying in the region."

"We advance men to Xin'an and Mianchi, then," Sun Jian declared. "If we can push him back far enough, he'll give up on holding onto Luoyang and retreat fully... that's not ideal, but with no allies, it's all that we can hope to achieve. Then, once the imperial tombs are repaired... we're going to blockade Chang'an."
"Another Liang Province campaign," Zu Mao grumbled. "Oh well, it can't be as bad as the last one, I suppose. At least killing Dong Zhuo is actually the main objective this time."

But the Eastern Pass Coalition was still unmoving, even after the attack on Wang Kuang at Heyang Ford; Sun Jian had two forces advance to block key roads that connected the capital to the strategically beneficial cities of Xin'an and Mianchi. Dong Zhuo, in turn, ordered his officers Dong Yue and Duan Wei and his son-in-law Niu Fu to Mianchi and two western defensive positions at Huayin and Anyi. Sun Jian's force at Mianchi did not engage Dong Yue; additional forces were not sent to Huayin or Anyi either, as the former was now guarded by Li Jue and Guo Si, who were two of Dong Zhuo's wealthier and more influential generals, and the latter was receiving the advice of Jia Xu, one of the two men that had engineered much of Dong Zhuo's later career. Sun Jian arranged to meet Zhu Jun before he returned to Luoyang, and the two enjoyed a brief – and final – reunion.
"Dong Zhuo has fled... I can achieve nothing now," Sun Jian complained.
"But what you have already achieved is impressive enough, Wentai," Zhu Jun suggested. "I've requested help from Governor Tao Qian, who was a great boon on your last Liang campaign. He and I are old friends, so he won't refuse like the rest of them."
"But didn't he refuse to join the coalition...?" Sun Jian prompted.
"...He did," Zhu Jun said with a sigh. "He has advisers, as all governors do, and sometimes the decisions they make are for the good of their province, not the good of the land; Yi's governor, Liu Yan, didn't do anything either, but if he had, we might not be seeing Dong Zhuo going west at all... not if he feared a pincer."
"Some of my allies want me to try and get more power; but when I see what nonsense you're burdened with when you have power, I don't want it," Sun Jian replied.
"I've been one of the most influential and powerful military leaders in the whole country," Zhu Jun said wistfully. "Now, I'm a near-powerless landowner... I haven't got the taxable households and vassals that I'd need to fight Dong Zhuo. Lu Zhi and Huangfu Song are equally frustrated; they and we fought an army of a million Yellow Turbans, Wentai! We, along with poor Hè Jin, were the heroes of that campaign, and look at us now: Dong Zhuo holds the power, while we... *aiee*. What a sorry affair."
"The forces I've left at Xin'an and Mianchi will help you, sir," Sun Jian suggested.
"Don't call me 'sir', Wentai... you're a marquis, and in a sane world, you'd be Commander-in-Chief, and besides, we're friends, so call me 'Gongwei'," Zhu Jun replied. "...We both know those forces will be recalled soon, as well, don't we...?"
Sun Jian exhaled noisily and lowered his gaze.
"Yuan Shu wants his army back," Zhu Jun said with desperate laughter. "For what... well, I've heard rumours of things that I

won't burden you with. But you'll be asked to go back to Lu County. And at that time, I'll be out here alone, facing the most vicious of Dong Zhuo's henchmen. If I didn't know better, I'd say that the Yuans were no more interested in preserving my life than Dong Zhuo is."

"I could refuse to obey orders to retreat," Sun Jian suggested as he raised his gaze and looked at Zhu Jun. "Isn't there a military discretion that I can use...? Isn't there something that says 'A commander can act in the field and explain himself later'?"

"You're not a commander," Zhu Jun replied matter-of-factly. "You said that yourself. You told me that Yuan Shu sees you as a vassal, a lackey; if you disobey him, you'll be punished, perhaps executed, and that would be a terrible waste, Sun Wentai... don't let Yuan Shu be the cause of an early death."

"...Alright," Sun Jian conceded. "Anyway, I... I have to go back to Luoyang, and oversee the sealing of the imperial tombs. When that's done... yes, I expect that when Yuan Shu knows that I'm finished doing that, he'll order me back to Lu County. But I swear to you, Zhu Gongwei, that as soon as I have negotiated my release from service, I-"

Zhu Jun smiled and stifled laughter.

"...Why do you laugh?" Sun Jian despaired. "You think that I am bound to that wretched man forever?"

"Just... just don't assume that leaving his service is so easy," Zhu Jun replied.

"Our alliance was for the duration of the Eastern Pass Coalition!" Sun Jian cried.

"And is that coalition dissolved?" Zhu Jun retorted. "No, it is not, and it may never officially be dissolved... not so long as Dong Zhuo lives. And he gave you titles, too. They were a contract between you that will – I *guarantee you* – extend your service beyond the coalition. But I appreciate what you were going to offer to do... thank you."

"...Let's enjoy our wine and tea, and speak about happier things," Sun Jian sighed.

"Yes, let's," Zhu Jun agreed. "After all... it may be some time before we are reunited, Wentai. It might be... a very long time indeed."

Sun Jian returned to the capital and left Zhu Jun to do what he could to reinforce his own borders against the inevitable raids by Dong Zhuo's followers. Yuan Shu sent the inevitable order to withdraw to Yu Province once the tombs were resealed, and Sun Jian reluctantly complied.

"However," Sun Jian said to his officials, "I won't go without aiding my friend Zhu Jun in some small way. Zhu Zhi, you're promoted to Colonel, given a force and tasked with aiding Governor Tao Qian in Xu Province."

"Eh...? Where's this coming from?" Cheng Pu exclaimed.

"If we do that for Tao Qian, then Tao Qian will definitely send the elite aid that Zhu Jun needs to withstand the attacks he'll suffer when we're gone," Sun Jian explained. "We're trading a medium-sized force of our own men for a thousand of Tao Qian's well-trained men. Our men are experts at fighting the Yellow Turbans, and Tao Qian's having a lot of problems with them."

Cheng Pu turned to Zhu Zhi and asked, "Are you alright to do that?"
"It was partly my idea," Zhu Zhi admitted.
"Junli is a genius," Sun Jian said sincerely. "His advice saved us many a time against the tribes in the southern counties, and right now, we need a man that can cultivate ties between ourselves, Zhu Jun and Governor Tao."
"…We'll miss you, Junli," Cheng Pu chuckled sadly. "Now poor Wentai has to rely on my empty head again."
"You're no fool, Demou," Zhu Zhi insisted. "And we'll be reunited soon enough."
"And now," Sun Jian sighed, "we must discuss the other matter… our retreat."

Rumours continued to circulate that the emperor might be dead; others said that the Imperial Seal of Authority had been lost by the emperor's entourage during the evacuation, and that someone – possibly Sun Jian or one of his allies – might have discovered it, and kept it for future times. Those rumours would continue throughout Sun Jian's life and far beyond, but Sun Jian did not speak about it, and nor did those around him. Sun Jian's supporters considered it ridiculous that such a man would keep a royal emblem, and any that harboured the idea that the story of the Seal's discovery might be true assumed that the obedient Sun Jian would immediately tender such an object to his master, Yuan Shu, so that it could one day be returned to the emperor. Something would happen many years later that would add credibility to that theory, but most would never know the truth. Supporters and detractors alike were left to decide for themselves.

****

138

24

Once Sun Jian's forces had finished resealing the tombs of the past emperors and putting out the fires around the capital, he ordered the return to Lu County, where Yuan Shu was waiting for him; the capital was abandoned, and the area around it became a base and playground for the White Wave Bandits – a criminal offshoot of the Yellow Turbans – that had been harassing it in years gone by.

"So the Yellow Turbans won in the end, sort of," Zu Mao suggested as the army slowly and cautiously moved south toward Dagu Pass.

"That thought had occurred to me too," Sun Jian replied bitterly. "It seems as though nothing I did really made a difference now; my successes in Changsha will probably suffer a reversal next."

"Take heart that you did get Dong Zhuo out of Luoyang," Zu Mao suggested further. "It'd be worse if we were retreating and he was still there. We made him run away."

"But he killed so many people, and he looted the imperial tombs!" Sun Jian groaned. "Won't people blame me for that?"

"No, Lord Sun," Cheng Pu replied. "They'll blame the rest of them for letting him sit there for so long making plans and strengthening himself."

"...I suppose so," Sun Jian sighed. "When will we be safe?"

"When we're completely out of Central Province," Cheng Pu replied. "Dong Zhuo isn't going to pursue us through Dagu Pass."

"Hopefully not," Sun Jian said miserably.

The length of the journey from Luoyang to Lu County forced Sun Jian to camp around Yang City, which was a fortified settlement in the southwest of Yingchuan Prefecture in Yan Province. As a result of the changing times and boundary reviews by various administrations, some cities and counties could be considered part of different provinces, and Yang City was one of those places: technically, it could belong to Yu Province – Sun Jian's inspectorate – or it could be part of Yan Province to the north. Since Yan Province was under the jurisdiction of Eastern Pass Coalition ally Liu Dai, no one expected trouble, and security was not as strict as it could have been. Supplies were considered adequate – especially after spending so much time within the ruins of Luoyang – and the morale of the army was low but salvageable.

But while Sun Jian had been marching back to his province, his master Yuan Shu had been the author of a malicious correspondence campaign that was about to change everything.

"**We're under attack!**" Zu Mao said as he ran into Sun Jian's personal tent.

"By *who*?" Sun Jian said as he leapt to his feet and started to put some leggings on.

"...**Some bloke called *Zhou Yu*!**" Zu Mao replied angrily. "**He's got men carrying *Yuan Shao's banners*!**"

"*Yuan Shao*??? ...The *coalition leader*, Yuan Shao...?" Sun Jian asked with growing disbelief. "But I serve his cousin; I'm the only person that's had any success against Dong Zhuo! Is he *demented...?"*

"Worry about that later," Zu Mao grumbled. "Hurry and get ready, Mister Sun!"

But it was too late; Zhou Yu, styled 'Renming' – a former adviser to Cao Cao that had shifted his allegiances to the coalition leader, Yuan Shao – had successfully attacked Sun Jian's army, passed it by, and occupied Yang City. To make matters worse, Zhou Renming's personal banner declared him to be 'Inspector of Yu Province', which was Sun Jian's own title as proclaimed by Yuan Shu. Sun Jian's forces retreated to the south of Yang City, and once they were settled, Sun Jian and his officials did their best to make sense of the new situation.

"...It looks like the Yuans fell out while we were doing all the hard work," Cheng Pu explained to a demoralised audience.

"So this is a personal feud between the Yuans?" Huang Gai exclaimed.

"It is," Cheng Pu sighed. "Our lord Yuan Shu's decided – mainly using *our successes* as a foundation – to declare himself the rightful leader of the Eastern Pass Coalition and the rightful chief of his clan."

Sun Jian screamed angrily and punched the air in front of him.

"That... would be an appropriate response," Cheng Pu continued. "He's not done it in a nice way, by any means; the letters cite Yuan Shao's failings, and call him 'The bastard pretender' and 'A mistake with an opportunistic maidservant'... to give you two of the more pleasant expressions. He's effectively calling for a vote of confidence in Yuan Shao, and as a result, lines have been drawn... battle lines."

The officials were initially silent; eventually, Wu Jing said, "We've been dragged into this without our knowledge; it is therefore unfair for Yuan Shao to send an alternative Inspector here to punish my brother-in-law!"

"It is," Cheng Pu agreed, "but that's exactly what he's done."

"...We all put our resources together for the good of the land, for the purpose – or so I thought – of restoring peace!" Sun Jian said angrily. "We were so close: so *close*! But they did nothing to stop Dong Zhuo... and now this! They won't take up arms against their family's killer, but they'll take up arms against each other??? ...Who in the world can I work with...?"

"Yuan Shu has requested help from Gongsun Zan," Cheng Pu reported.

"But didn't Gongsun Zan help Yuan Shao to take over Ji Province?" Huang Gai said bemusedly. "Why would he now help Yuan Shu to fight Yuan Shao?"

"Don't... don't try and work it out," Cheng Pu suggested. "Let others try and work out what nonsense games they're playing; it's none of our business, so while the help will be nice, let's just recover Yang City, chase this 'Zhou Yu' character out of the province, and tell Yuan Shu that if the coalition is over, then we'd like to return his appointments and go back to Changsha."

"...And, of course, he'll say 'Yes! By all means!' and allow us and our twenty thousand troops to go home and leave him outnumbered against his brother, or cousin, or whatever Yuan Shao is to him," Wu Jing scoffed. "Not likely, Cheng Demou... not

140

likely. We're the reason that he's even had the 'courage' – if you can call it that – to do this."

Sun Jian nodded silently. He was aware that Wu Jing was quite right, but in the interests of maintaining a sliver of morale, he held onto the belief that he would somehow be able to convince Yuan Shu to let him go home.

Sun Ce was frowning as he entered the home of his friend Zhou Yu; Ce was carrying a letter that had been delivered to Shu City by an anxious messenger. His cousin Sun Hè, Zhou Yu, and Yu's father – Luoyang's self-exiled Magistrate Zhou Yi – met him as he passed the banquet hall; Zhou Yu noted his expression and asked, "Something concerns you, Bofu?"

"Dad's stuck in Yingchuan," Sun Ce replied. "He's been pinned there by a 'Zhou Yu' who claims that he's the rightful Inspector of Yu Province."

"...*Zhou Yu*...?" Magistrate Zhou said angrily. "Will your father be alright?"

Sun Ce perused the letter for a second time and said, "Probably... I don't think he's too bothered after all the other stuff that he's been through."

Magistrate Zhou nodded soberly.

"I, uh... I'm sorry if I sounded like I was accusing your family of anything," Sun Ce chuckled nervously. "I'm living in your house, and yet I have the cheek to-"

"I'm not offended," Magistrate Zhou promised. "...This other Zhou Yu must be from the Kuaiji branch of Zhous."

"So this man serves Dong Zhuo," Zhou Yu noted. "How unfortunate it is that I share a spoken name with such a man."

"No, it... is says that the man is with *Yuan Shao*," Sun Ce murmured as he read the letter for a third time. "Wait, that... that can't be right... *can it*...?"

"May I...?" Sun Hè prompted; Sun Ce passed him the letter, and he started to read.

"Well...?" Sun Ce said excitedly.

"You really need to stop skimming through correspondence," Sun Hè sighed. "It's made clear: the Yuans have fallen out."

Sun Hè passed the letter to Zhou Yu, who read on and said, "Your father is being treated as a vassal of Yuan Shu, so Shao's attacked him... what *nonsense*."

"So... so we're not fighting Dong Zhuo anymore?" Sun Ce supposed. "He's... he's dead then, Dong Zhuo...?"

"...No," Zhou Yu exclaimed. "No, he isn't. The madness has worsened. The coalition is fighting itself while the villain has escaped to the west... Luoyang is in ruins...!"

"Our house there is *destroyed then*...!" Magistrate Zhou cried. "Dong Zhuo has left *nothing*...!"

"...I'm sorry to hear that," Sun Ce said miserably.

"It only reinforces that we were right to leave," Magistrate Zhou sighed. "...Yu, your grandfather held two of the three Excellency posts throughout his life; your great-grandfather was Imperial Secretary to two emperors; your elder uncle was Commander-in-Chief. I had always hoped that I would ascend to an Excellency, and that you would then do the same when I died, but... but fate has cruelly contrived otherwise, my son. Perhaps we are being punished for ignoring the evils of the 'Ten Attendants'."

"Nonsense," Zhou Yu insisted. "We're not the only ones to have bad luck! Pity Cai Yong, who was forced to go back to the capital just as we were leaving! He would have been forced to follow Dong Zhuo to Chang'an, and that's a worse fate."

"Yes," Magistrate Zhou agreed. "At least we're in our own ancestral homeland, surrounded by- ... ...*Chang'an*...? ...Yes, that's right, it says that... ... ...so Dong Zhuo is relocating to the old Han Capital...? He truly intends to emulate the old villain Wang Mang, then!"

Zhou Yu nodded silently.

"...But I should like to say that for now, our prayers must be not for ourselves, but for Sun Jian, who is trapped in my father's former provincial holding of Yu, fighting a 'Zhou Yu'," Magistrate Zhou suggested.

"Thank you," Sun Ce replied.

Magistrate Zhou sneered and said, "Thankfully, the 'Zhou Yu' this speaks of is no close relative of ours, the wretch! ...I say again, Bofu, that my prayers are with your father. Wish him well from us all if you get the chance."

Sun Ce bowed respectfully and replied, "I certainly shall, sir."

Magistrate Zhou left Sun Ce, Zhou Yu and Sun Hè to continue the conversation.

"I'm sure your father and cousin will be alright, Bofu," Zhou Yu said reassuringly.

"...I should tell Mum," Sun Ce murmured. "She'll worry... but..."

Sun Hè and Zhou Yu smiled sadly. The family was used to Sun Jian being in mortal danger, but that did not lessen the fear that they felt, and understandably so. This time, Sun Jian was the besieged, and Sun Ben was with him: those factors changed things considerably.

Sun Jian's camp to the south of Yang City was put on full alert when an army of 1,000 cavalry was sighted and found to be approaching at speed; the relief was universal when the horsemen were identified as reinforcements led by Gongsun Yue, the nephew of the northern warlord Gongsun Zan. Sun Jian hurried to the gates of the camp and welcomed his ally personally.

"You're a sight for tired eyes!" Sun Jian said as Gongsun Yue dismounted. The northern warrior was tall, brawny and intimidating: his appearance was almost foreign despite his origins.

"I'm glad that I got here in time to be of use, Inspector Sun," Gongsun Yue replied.

The two men exchanged respectful bows, and Sun Jian led the visitor and his senior officers to his command tent to sit and discuss their tactics.

"Forgive me expecting you to throw yourself into battle without a proper rest, Colonel Gongsun, but the hour is critical," Sun Jian began. "The enemy holds the city and is gradually building forces around it: if we don't uproot him soon, then Yuan Shao will chase me out of the province, and Commander Yuan Shu will be most displeased."

"In other words, he'll put all the blame on you for this disaster he's invited and have you executed for incompetence... to hide his own lack of talent," Gongsun Yue scoffed. "I know of you, Inspector: you're a hero, and a legend. Your manoeuvres against Dong Zhuo and the Yellow Turbans will enshrine you in the future histories as a god among men. I'm truly honoured to be able to fight at your side."

"...I'm unworthy," Sun Jian insisted as he bowed low.

Gongsun Yue laughed and said, "History will say otherwise! ...But enough of that. My uncle has given me command of an elite unit of horsemen that should complement your own formidable forces perfectly: all we need to do is force this cowardly enemy of ours to fight in the open and the day will be ours."

****

25

Sun Jian's forces moved their camp closer to Yang City and made a show of preparing to siege the city; the ploy worked, and Zhou Renming sent his infantry and cavalry to engage their adversaries while his archers lined the battlements. The defending infantry were ill-prepared for a relatively devastating cavalry charge by an elite Wuhuan battalion, and their front lines were decimated.

"**What is going on???**" Zhou Renming shrieked as he watched the battle from the walls of the city. "Since when did Sun Jian have that sort of cavalry???"

"Perhaps they're surrendered Liang men," an archery captain suggested.

"...Perhaps, perhaps not," Zhou Renming muttered as he surveyed the battlefield. "I see a banner reading 'Gongsun Yue'... our northern allies have betrayed us and joined Yuan Shu!"

An infantry captain arrived at the top of the wall and said, "The enemy are routing us, Commander! New orders are requested!"

"...I'll order a full withdrawal," Zhou Renming replied. "We'll get as many of our men into the city as possible... losing the exterior camps is no loss to us. Go and tell the signalmen to sound a full retreat!"

The captain returned to the field.

"...I'm sure that Sun Jian thinks that he has won," Zhou Renming snickered. "He'll regret his overconfidence."

Sun Jian's men cheered as they watched Zhou Renming's forces flee into the city; their celebrations were cut short when arrows were subsequently fired from atop the walls to chase them away. Sun Jian's officers met with Gongsun Yue at the outskirts of the battlefield to discuss their next moves.

"A good first victory," Sun Jian said, "but we'll need to do better if we're to take the city. Sieges are not pleasant, but if the turtle won't stick its head out again, we'll have no choice."

"Cavalry are not a lot of use in a siege, Commander!" Gongsun Yue joked.

"...Quite right," Sun Jian replied. "But in this battle, you were invaluable."

Gongsun Yue bowed respectfully.

"Tomorrow, we begin a siege," Cheng Pu confirmed; there were no voices of dissent. The army retired, leaving the fenceless enemy encampments around the city abandoned.

Sun Jian's men returned to their camp, but within hours, an unexpected retaliatory attack by Zhou Renming forced them to abandon the installation and return to the site that they had advanced from. The decision was made to regain the ground the following day, but Zhou Renming was ready; he arrayed his men outside the city, around his recaptured camps.

"What a fool," Han Dang snickered. "He's led his men out to defend those worthless exterior camps: that gives us the field battle we wanted!"

"...We shouldn't take risks," Cheng Pu suggested.

"Bah! Let them do their worst!" Gongsun Yue chuckled. "Leave this to me, Commander."

Sun Jian nodded as a visible granting of permission; Gongsun Yue rode toward the front line and had his cavalry form several attacking lines in front of Sun Jian's infantry.

"No signs of a trap," Cheng Pu noted. "This man 'Zhou Yu' isn't very good."

Zhou Renming made no move, so Sun Jian ordered a barrage of arrows. Renming ordered his men to put up their shields, so the casualties from the arrow bombardment were minimised, although the infantry were now unprepared for a frontal strike; Gongsun Yue charged, dealing to deal huge damage to the enemy lines.

"I should not have fallen for that!" Zhou Renming cried as he watched the defeat from the walls of Yang City. "**Sound the retreat! Provide cover with arrows!**"

Zhou Renming's battlement archers fired a volley of arrows at the central group of horsemen while his infantry retreated; Sun Jian's archers fired a return volley to try and kill as many of the fleeing soldiers as they could.

"**Aim for their officers! Prioritise the officers!**" Zhou Renming cried desperately.

It was inevitable that some of Gongsun Yue's cavalry would be caught in the crossfire; Yue himself was struck by an enemy arrow as he led his men back to the relative safety of Sun Jian's battle line, and by the time he reached that line, he was slumped lifelessly across his horse.

"...**Retreat... retreat!**" Sun Jian barked emotionally.

"**We should try and hold the camps this time!**" Cheng Pu suggested.

"**We'll be shot at if we stay!**" Sun Jian retorted as he took the reins of Gongsun Yue's horse and tried to lead it away from the battlefield.

"...**What a waste!**" Cheng Pu cried as he turned his horse and gestured to Wu Jing that the signalmen should order a full retreat. The camps around Yang City were won and lost in a painfully short time, and Sun Jian's army were now without a competent leader for Gongsun Zan's donated cavalry. Zhou Renming quickly reoccupied the external camps and started to fortify them, while Sun Jian led his demoralised army back to his own fortified encampment.

The mood was sombre that night: all men wore at least one white article to mourn the sudden, unexpected loss of Gongsun Yue so early into the Yang City campaign. Sun Jian invited his own officers and those that had served Gongsun Yue to his tent in order to prepare for Yue's coffin to be transported to Zhou County.

"...Gongsun Zan will blame me for this!" Sun Jian said with tears in his eyes; he wore a white turban and robe to show how much he was affected. "His nephew is dead because of my carelessness! When I think of how I would feel if it was young Ben lying dead, I...!"

Sun Ben observed his uncle's genuine distress and felt two things: gratitude that he was alive, and gratitude that he had such a benevolent uncle and second father.

"Do not underestimate Lord Gongsun," one of the northern cavalry captains suggested. "We saw what happened, and will report it truthfully: the coward Zhou Yu of Kuaiji ordered him to be shot down after a brave cavalry charge. It is Yuan Shao – Zhou's master – that is to blame for this outrage."

"...I still feel responsible," Sun Jian sighed.

"Most of us will stay here and continue to aid you, because that is what Lord Gongsun would want," the cavalry captain said respectfully. "We will not rest until this murderer is vanquished, Commander Sun."

"He will be," Sun Jian replied. "If Heaven wills it, he will be."

The death of Gongsun Yue had left Sun Jian at a slight disadvantage, since some of the cavalry had to escort the body home for mourning and burial. Yue's uncle Gongsun Zan was furious at Yuan Shao and began a feud with him that would only end with the death of one of them; Zhou Renming, meanwhile, was still in Yang City with an angry Sun Jian looking for an opportunity to expel him from the province.

Sun Jian's attempts to siege the city ended in failure; further attempts to make use of Gongsun's cavalry only served to reduce their numbers further as Zhou Renming increasingly relied on arrows to repel them.

"After everything that we've endured... all the hardships... we're going to be buried in this remote place!" Sun Jian cried as he returned to his command tent after a prolonged battle outside the city.

"Don't assume we're beaten," Cheng Pu pleaded. "That last battle cost him most of the little cavalry that he has... and he has to be running out of food by now."

"I'd imagine so, since *we are*!" Sun Jian barked. "This is *futile*! How can two men born of the same father act like this, especially during a nationwide crisis...? If two sons of mine did what the Yuans were doing now, I'd come back as a ghost and haunt the pair of them day and night!"

"Commander Yuan should be consulted," Cheng Pu said thoughtfully. "Perhaps he can aid us with more resources or a diversionary attack."

"...Sieges aren't working," Sun Jian continued obliviously. "Perhaps I should try what I did at Wan..."

"Don't you *dare*...!" Wu Jing scolded. "You were lucky to come back from *that*! Do you *want* to make a widow of my sister???"

"Wu Jing's right," Zu Mao suggested. "This isn't Yellow Turbans, Mister Sun Jian; this is one of Yuan Shao's trusted advisers. We'll need to show more care."

"You must value your life, Uncle!" Sun Ben cried.

"Yes, I... I know," Sun Jian sighed. "...I'm just glad that Ce isn't here: that mad eldest son of mine would probably do it... like I would have at his age."

"So what *do* we do...?" Wu Jing asked.

"I... don't know," Sun Jian replied powerlessly.

"This is a war of attrition that we must fight," Cheng Pu declared. "It isn't pleasant, but we'll just have to take the losses and whittle this man down. We have more men and a restorable supply route, while he's isolated."

"I can see no other way of proceeding," Huang Gai conceded.

"...Has he sent men out to the exterior camps again?" Sun Jian asked wearily.

"He has," Cheng Pu confirmed.

"...Huang Gai, Han Dang: you'll be in charge of the infantry," Sun Jian ordered. "Zu Mao: we will command a cavalry strike force and look to exploit opportunities as they arise. Wu Jing: you'll command the archery units and signalmen as before. Cheng Pu: hold the camp."

Several battles took place between the forces of Sun Jian and the defenders that were in and around Yang City; at first, it seemed that Zhou Renming would never lose ground, but eventually – after one costly exchange – Sun Jian spotted an opportunity to charge at the city gates while the enemy retreated into the city. Zhou Renming was taken by surprise by the reckless tactic, but Sun Jian and his riders somehow managed to avoid the arrows and deal heavy damage to the unprepared infantry. Zhou Renming ordered a full retreat: Yang City was won.

"Well done... if a little reckless," Cheng Pu said as he met with Sun Jian at the southern gates of Yang.

"I promise I won't do things like that anymore when it isn't necessary," Sun Jian retorted. "Anyway, we've taken the place; but how will we keep it...?"

"By not keeping it," Cheng Pu replied. "The inhabitants look like they've had enough, Commander."

Sun Jian looked in all directions; the emaciated civilians were emerging from their hiding places to see who their current occupiers were, and most of them were grateful to see that it was Sun Jian.

"...If we have food to spare, share something," Sun Jian ordered. "We'll keep a minimal defence force inside the walls, and enhance the external camps to keep the exchanges outside."

The civilians that were within earshot of the announcement voiced their approval; others followed when they realised the cause of the excitement.

"...Now we finally have an advantage, let's push the invader out altogether," Sun Jian continued; his soldiers cheered, and morale was partially restored.

"...So my tiger has recovered his prowess!" Yuan Shu cackled as he read the reports from Yang City. "How long will it be before he humbles the fool Yuan Shao sent to harass him, mm...?"

Yuan Shu's officials murmured agreeably.

"...One day soon, I'll have the glory that I deserve!" Yuan Shu declared.

"Zhou Ang is a threat to our southern interests," the adviser Yan Xiang suggested.

"We'll do something about that," Yuan Shu replied. "We'll go to Jiujiang, and siege Shouchun. Prepare for a march!"

Every battle that Sun Jian fought pushed Zhou Renming further and further away from Yang City, but the cost had been high on both sides. Sun Jian was mulling that point when Cheng Pu entered his command tent to deliver some news.

"Yuan has decided to march on Jiujiang," Cheng Pu reported.

"Oh, *finally*...!" Sun Jian grumbled. "I have heard your constant comments about Yuan Shu doing something to help us, Demou... I

didn't reply because I didn't see the point."
"I knew that," Cheng Pu replied. "We're likely to see Zhou Yu
retreat when the attack is reported to him, since Jiujiang is held
by his brother. Why would he stay here and fight this lost cause
when he could lose a sibling in the process...?"
"I'm glad," Sun Jian said as he finally turned to face Cheng Pu.
"We've lost a lot of good men, Demou... so many of those fine
volunteers from the south have died here, and they won't even
get a decent burial in their hometown... most have rotted on the
battlefield, and all that the family will get back is a few fond
memories and a lump of fragrant wood in a coffin, if the budget
allows for the latter."
"They knew that might be their fate, my lord," Cheng Pu said
comfortingly. "Many of them were men without purpose: convicts
and pirates that you gave a second chance to do something
worthwhile. Compared to being beheaded for a crime, or rotting in
a back alley somewhere after a drunken brawl, this is not so bad:
they died as heroes, men serving their country."
"...You've placated me, Demou," Sun Jian said warmly. "We'll
continue to pressure our enemy until he leaves... no matter how
long that takes."

Zhou Renming fought more battles with Sun Jian, but he was
losing hope of regaining Yang City or the area around it. When a
messenger reported that Yuan Shu had marched against the
capital of Jiujiang Prefecture – one of two prefectures in Yang
province that lay north of the Yangtze River – Renming was forced
to reconsider the future of his campaign in Yu Province, just as so
many had predicted. Within days of learning of his brother's
plight, he began a quiet retreat eastward that was only detected
when his front-line infantry became worthlessly thin.
"Has something happened...?" Sun Jian as Cheng Pu entered his
command tent with a relieved expression on his face.
"...He's fleeing," Cheng Pu reported. "Shall we pursue him...?"
"No," Sun Jian replied. "We've all had enough, I think. The
province is ours again... so now I have the power to give it back to
Yuan Shu. We'll set up local militias, make the province as secure
as we can against any prospectors from Yang in the south or Yan
in the north, and then we'll get out of here."
"Where will we go?" Cheng Pu asked.
"I wish I could say 'Home' and 'The army can be given leave', but
I can't risk Yuan Shu giving me an answer I don't want to hear,"
Sun Jian replied. "We'll march to Jiujiang, with an aim to be
discharged... we'll be a prefectural border away from our families
in Lujiang. We could march southwest, get our families, cross the
Great River, and then that would be it."
Cheng Pu was silent.
"...Of course, we both know that isn't going to happen," Sun Jian
admitted.
"I'll go and talk to the others," Cheng Pu said numbly.
"Yes... do that," Sun Jian replied.
Cheng Pu left Sun Jian alone in his command tent once again. The
man from Fuchun looked at the collection of battle plans,
weapons, bamboo books and cloth letters that were scattered on
his desks and sighed miserably.

"Don't blame yourself, Uncle," Sun Ben said knowingly.

"How can I not, Ben?" Sun Jian retorted. "How can I not... not hate myself for what I have done... I have chained us to a monster."

Once Yu Province was pacified, Sun Jian began the eastward march to Jiujiang with a portion of his army while the rest remained to prepare the provincial militia to fend for itself. He reached Yuan Shu's town-based headquarters within a week and requested an audience that was reluctantly given.

"...My tiger," Yuan Shu murmured as Sun Jian approached him. His officials lined the audience hall of the requisitioned magistrate's house, and many were sneering contemptuously. "Why did you not remain in Yu Province, Sun Jian?" Yuan Shu continued. "Why did you abandon your responsibility and come here in person? I did not ask you to; I hope you reinforced the place first, or you'll need to face punishment."

Sun Jian was irreverent as he replied, "I came here to request that I be discharged from service. I want to return to Fuchun."

The officials snickered derisively at the suggestion, but Yuan Shu was visibly offended and angry.

"You want to go back to the south," Yuan Shu scoffed.

"I did my part, Commander Yuan," Sun Jian declared. "For thanks, I've just been attacked by your cousin, and I've had enough, as have my men. Now that the efforts against Dong Zhuo have apparently ended, I want to take my men and-"

"You *belong to me*," Yuan Shu suggested icily. "You tendered your service to me, Mister Sun Jian, and with that tendered service came rewards... *remember that*."

Sun Jian was suddenly very angry, but he kept it hidden.

"You're Inspector of Yu at *my say-so*... and what I give, I can take away, and there is no magistrate's role in Changsha for you anymore, that role has long since gone to another man," Yuan Shu continued. "The men are not *your* men... they're *my men*. That was the deal, Mister Sun Jian, and it doesn't end just because of the end of hostilities against Dong Zhuo; *you* fight under *my* banner, and in exchange, I reward you. Now, that can be how we carry on... or *not*. What will it be...?"

Sun Jian struggled with his rage as he tried to formulate an appropriate answer.

"...Here he comes," Cheng Pu murmured as Sun Jian stormed into his command tent an hour later with an expression that did nothing to hide his feelings.

"...Sorry, Brother-in-law," Wu Jing said sadly.

Sun Jian screamed angrily and threw his battle helmet to the ground.

"Don't blame yourself, Uncle!" Sun Ben pleaded once again.

"We could desert," Zu Mao suggested.

"And be hunted down by Yuan Shu as well as the rest of the former coalition?" Huang Gai said with disdain. "Zu Mao, I credited you with more sense!"

"Brother-in-law, we're vassals, and that's that," Wu Jing said plainly. "There's no point to being angry or upset, just as there's no point to grieving forever."

Sun Jian's anger prevented him from being able to speak.

"Let's go to Lujiang and visit our families," Han Dang suggested.
"This idiot we're tied to hasn't given us anything to do, I take it,
Lord Sun...?"
Sun Jian shook his head tersely.
"Fine," Cheng Pu said as calmly as he could. "Lord Sun, I know
that there is a part of you that would like to take a force of men to
Yuan Shu's camp and behead him right now, but we both know
that isn't an option."
Sun Jian laughed desperately.
"That's better," Cheng Pu said. "Now try and calm down, Wentai...
this isn't the calm, measured warrior I joined seven years ago."
"A lot... has changed," Sun Jian replied with difficulty.
"You're angry... we're all angry," Cheng Pu said. "Let's go and see
our families, and remind ourselves why we do what we do."
Sun Jian nodded sombrely, and the preparations for a return to
Lujiang began.

****

26

Sun Jian was perturbed by the lack of a welcome by representatives of the Administrator of Lujiang, Lu Kang, as his forces entered Shu City.

"Perhaps he's back in his capital," Cheng Pu suggested.

"No one was sent to greet us, Demou... no one," Sun Jian replied. "And... and I think I know why."

"Go and visit his residence here," Huang Gai urged. "Write to Huancheng City if you must, or-!"

"No, Gongfu," Sun Jian replied. "If he has shunned me for the reasons I suspect, then-"

"Shunned???" Cheng Pu chortled. "Why under Heaven would a great man, a wise man, a hero like Lu Kang that has pacified villains and stray souls as you have, suddenly decide to 'shun' you, Lord Sun?"

"...Because I am a 'lackey' now, a 'crony', a follower of a selfish man whose excuses will not be good enough," Sun Jian replied. "He and I discussed it vividly enough, Demou, and now I am what I most despise, and not just in his eyes. I'm not a tiger now... now, I'm a-"

"Halt right there," Cheng Pu interrupted. "I don't know Administrator Lu as well as you feel you do, but if he's made a decision like that, there's nothing we can do except disprove his beliefs. Maybe we can do that... but for now, we have to visit our families; Lu Kang and his intolerant notions can wait."

Sun Jian nodded silently, and the journey continued in silence.

Sun Jian and Sun Ben entered the home of the Magistrate of Luoyang, Zhou Yi, where he was met by two excited and grateful families.

"**Brother!**" Sun Fu cried as he hugged Sun Ben.

"Did we manage to find a future husband for Shangxiang?" Sun Jian joked as he embraced his eldest son Ce.

"Don't talk to me about that girl!" Lady Wu scoffed as she approached her husband. "She's starting to fight now! She's challenging her brothers all the time, and-!"

"It's nothing to be ashamed of," Sun Jian said as he took Lady Wu's hands in his own. "Our children are truly wonderful."

Lady Wu smiled gratefully.

"It's good to see you, Uncle!" Sun Fu said as he took his turn to embrace Sun Jian.

"It is wonderful indeed, benevolent uncle," Sun Hè said as he bowed low; Sun Jian patted the young man on the arm and smiled gratefully.

"Gongjin, this is great!" Sun Ce said to Zhou Yu. "He's back! He's home at last!"

"Marvellous indeed, Bofu," Zhou Yu replied.

"...You're Zhou Gongjin," Sun Jian said as he caught sight of Zhou Yu. "I have you to thank for this magnificent hospitality; I've yet to repay it, but I will do if I can."

Zhou Yu smiled and bowed humbly.

"Marquis Sun," Lady Chen said warmly; she was cradling a child in her arms.

"...Lady Chen," Sun Jian replied hesitantly. "You are both well?"

"We are," Lady Chen replied.

"...I sense calm," Sun Jian prompted.

"Why argue?" Lady Wu replied without malice. "So you're an inspector of a province now, Husband?"

"I'd... rather not talk about anything that I got from Yuan Shu," Sun Jian admitted.

"At last, at last!" Magistrate Zhou cackled as he advanced toward Sun Jian and took his right hand. "You're the man I've been waiting to meet! General Sun! Marquis Sun! Inspector Sun! ...Which shall I call you...?"

"Call me Wentai if you want, Magistrate," Sun Jian replied. "Your generosity to my family is beyond my ability to thank appropriately. I only hope that I can do something for you one day."

"Your family are wonderful! Wonderful!" Magistrate Zhou insisted. "Your son and my son are like brothers! Our families are one and the same, Sun Wentai!"

Sun Jian looked at his younger sons – Quan, Yi and Kuang – and said, "All of you are growing so fast! I...!"

A skinny infant shoved their way past Lady Wu and stared upward at Sun Jian with eyes that carried a desire for approval and a wilful defiance; Jian's voice trailed as his mind and heart fought over the identity – and gender – of the youth.

"...Is that you, little Shangxiang?" Sun Jian exclaimed. "Why... why are you wearing boy's clothes...?"

Magistrate Zhou and his son laughed involuntarily.

"They not *boy's clothes*!" Shangxiang retorted. "They *strong people's clothes*!"

"... ... ...*Ayah*. Alright, alright: I see what you mean," Sun Jian sighed as he looked at Lady Wu, who refused to reply.

"I'm *strong*!" Shangxiang declared. "I can beat up *Quan*, and-!"

"Don't-! ...Don't embarrass me in front of Father and everyone else, sister," Sun Quan pleaded. "Anyway, how could I be too rough with a four-year-old girl? I went easy on you."

"*Yeah*...?" Shangxiang growled. "Then I wanna '*nother fight*!"

"You'll get no such thing!" Sun Jian said as others laughed. "What's the matter with you, Shangxiang...? I'm as proud of you as any of the rest of them!"

Sun Shangxiang was overcome with joy and embarrassment and fled from her bemused father.

"...What did I do...?" Sun Jian asked desperately.

"...So all I have to do is say that I'm proud of her, and she'll go away and stop picking fights...?" Sun Ce chuckled. "I'll have to remember that."

"Your family is wonderful!" Magistrate Zhou cackled. "Now come! We must have a banquet in your honour! You're a great hero, Sun Wentai!"

Sun Jian smiled humbly as he was led to the banquet hall by Magistrate Zhou and his attendants; Sun Ben, Sun Fu and Sun Hè followed as though they were Jian's own sons.

"*So*, Brother... what did he do this time...?" Lady Wu asked as she grabbed Wu Jing's arm and led him after Sun Jian.

"You *really want to know*...?" Wu Jing chortled.

Lady Chen was visibly isolated; she lowered her gaze and followed the procession with her husband's younger sons behind her and her own child in her arms.

"...He really doesn't consider himself a hero," Zhou Yu sighed. "That is amazing."

"Dad's good like that," Sun Ce replied. "I know Mum doesn't approve of the titles and the fighting and Lady Chen and all the waifs and strays he brings to live with us, but she can see that he's a true hero. He's *my* idol, I know *that*."

"He's mine, in a way, and as much as my father wouldn't like to hear it," Zhou Yu admitted. "You're so lucky to have a father like him, Bofu... I know I'm lucky as well, but *you*... to have *him* to look up to... you are lucky indeed."

"Depends how you look at it, Gongjin," Sun Ce said with a smile. "I have to be at least as great a man as him... think about it. *Me*...? As great as *him*...?"

Zhou Yu nodded slowly and said, "A challenge, for sure. But you're already an amazing fighter, Bofu, so it isn't impossible to say that you'll be as famous as he is one day. Father regrets that he didn't get to be an Excellency, and as a second son, he shouldn't feel that way. I'm a second son too, but I have to live up to him... I don't relish it. So I do know how you feel. *Me*...? *Magistrate of Luoyang*...?"

"You're clever enough, Gongjin," Sun Ce replied. "You read faster than I think."

"Are you two going to stand around nattering all day...?" Lady Wu said as she returned to the entrance hall. "We're supposed to be together as a family!"

"...*Yes*, Mother," Sun Ce replied wearily.

As Lady Wu disappeared again, Sun Ce shook his head and said, "We'd better join the celebrations."

"We should," Zhou Yu replied.

"**And you as well!**" Sun Ce barked at a nearby corridor; a sheepish Shangxiang emerged from a hiding place and shoved Ce playfully as she passed him on her way to the banquet hall.

"...Who'd marry her, Gongjin?" Sun Ce despaired.

"She's a little young for you to be worried about *that*, Bofu," Zhou Yu chuckled.

"Yeah, but she's getting worse, not better!" Sun Ce complained.

"You have over a *decade* before it's a problem, Bofu," Zhou Yu said. "She's a little child! She'll grow out of it..."

"And if she *doesn't*...?" Sun Ce fretted. "When the time comes for her to get married, what do we do? If all she's going to do is beat the poor man up, then-"

Zhou Yu laughed involuntarily.

"...Can you *help me*...?" Sun Ce pleaded.

"Bofu, Bofu; it'll be *fine*," Zhou Yu said with amusement as he led Sun Ce toward the banquet hall. "We're brothers now. So she's *my* sister as much as she's yours, and that means her future means as much to me as it does to you. It'll be fine... by then, you'll have your own county to run, probably, and-"

"Oh, right, yeah... maybe Dad'll have a decent man working for him that'll marry her," Sun Ce replied. "...Even if we have to *force them... pay them*..."

Zhou Yu laughed at Sun Ce's 'dilemma'.

A brief period of peace followed for Sun Jian and his followers while Yuan Shao and Yuan Shu continued their all-consuming private feud. While Gongsun Zan and Yuan Shao fought in the north and Yuan Shu and Zhou Ang fought in the south, Sun Jian's spiritual adversary, Dong Zhuo, reached Chang'an and consolidated his power without any sign of dangerous opposition; that Liang warlord and self-proclaimed Chancellor of State would never face Sun Jian again. The Tiger of Jiangdong's next adversary would be Yuan Shu's next target in his quest to dominate the country: the politically-neutral Governor of Jing Province, Liu Biao.

****

ACT III: THE SHACKLED TIGERS

27

Much had happened to the country since Sun Jian first decided to leave his hometown and fight for the empire. The Yellow Turbans had been defeated within months of their rebellion, but they quickly regained momentum when nothing was done about the root causes of general disaffection. The tribes in the northwest had rebelled as well, which led to the incidental rise to fame of Dong Zhuo, a man whose morals and professional records were highly suspect.

When the subsequent death of the emperor led to a succession debate and then a war between various influential factions in the court, that same Dong Zhuo was invited by the Commander-in-Chief of the army, Hè Jin, and a powerful nobleman, Yuan Shao, to aid them in a political struggle with the powerful palace eunuch faction known as the 'Ten Attendants'. One assassination, one massacre and one kidnapping later, and Dong Zhuo had inadvertently become the most powerful figure in the land, and he demonstrated that power by deposing the young emperor, Shao, and replacing him with his younger half-brother, who became Emperor Xian. The act was met with condemnation, and a so-called 'Eastern Pass Coalition' was formed to blockade the imperial capital and demand Dong Zhuo's removal from office. Sun Jian – who had been made a lesser marquis for his successful work in the south – immediately volunteered his services to the coalition, but he chose to fight under the banner of Yuan Shao's younger brother Shu; early bestowments of high rank suggested it to be a good choice initially, but as Yuan Shu's ambition took greater precedence over the coalition's objectives, the shows of apparent benevolence were obviously closer to a form of gradual entrapment.

Sun Jian had achieved a great victory against three of Dong Zhuo's leading generals, but instead of congratulating him, Yuan Shu had failed to trust him and done everything from confiscating his forces to cutting his supplies off; the coalition commander Yuan Shao created added frustration by failing to act, and the only man that had chosen to follow Sun Jian's lead – Shao's old friend Cao Cao – was left isolated and ultimately routed. When Dong Zhuo decided to burn the capital and flee westward with the city's people and wealth, Sun Jian took a chance and entered the burning capital for a decisive battle with Dong Zhuo's army: his victory was marred by continued lack of support, growing friction between the other members of the fragile coalition, and the discovery that Dong Zhuo had looted the imperial tombs and left nothing alive or of value in his wake. But worse was yet to come.

Being expected to camp in the isolated ruins of Luoyang and provide unsupported harassment to Dong Zhuo's retreating army was initially deemed the worst that Sun Jian's masters could do to him and his brave militiamen, but then he was ordered to withdraw and leave Dong Zhuo with a clear escape route for no apparent reason; and then, as a final insult, Sun Jian retreating force was attacked by Yuan Shao's agents after the Yuan brothers had declared war on each other over a family matter without informing Sun Jian. The battle resulted in the death of the nephew of the powerful northern warlord Gongsun Zan, but the personal feud that it stemmed from would have nationwide consequences for a long time to come.

Sun Jian knew that he was now bound to Yuan Shu – who was seen by many as the worse of the two brothers for having started the feud – and he knew that would give him new enemies – some of whom would be old friends and allies – but he had no choice in the matter. He knew that he was trapped, and he knew that there would be further affronts to his pride in the future: the first arrived quickly in the form of his first assignment as Yuan Shu's vanguard in his war against Yuan Shao.

Sun Jian's principal spouse, Lady Wu, awoke one morning to find that her husband had gone to his study to gather weapons and armour in preparation for leaving their temporary home – his inspector's residence in the Runan Prefectural capital in Yu Province.

"Where are you going at this hour, silly man...?" Lady Wu scoffed. "It's barely dawn!"

"...Yet another campaign," Sun Jian replied irritably.

Lady Wu turned and looked at Lady Chen, who was visibly emotional.

"Where now...?" Lady Wu asked gently.

"Jing Province, probably," Sun Jian replied tersely.

At that moment, Jian's nephew Sun Ben, his adopted nephew Sun Hè and his eldest son Ce entered the study in full battle dress.

"You're taking *Ce*...?" Lady Wu said with sudden, uncharacteristic weakness.

"I don't want to, but I must," Sun Jian replied miserably. "He is old enough, and I must now ensure that he knows the ways of war for... for future times."

Lady Wu stared at Sun Ce with tears in her eyes.

"Don't worry, Mum," Sun Ce chuckled calmly. "I've been training and doing my studies. I know a lot. We'll be back with you in Qu'e before you know it."

"*Qu'e*...?" Lady Wu exclaimed. "You're sending me to Qu'e???"

"*No*," Sun Jian sighed. "Your brother has been given the title 'Administrator of Danyang' by our illustrious leader; so all of our families will be moving to-"

"Qu'e is in *Wu Prefecture*, not Danyang!" Lady Wu heckled. "I am not a fool! I know where things are! Why do you-!"

"*Lie to you*...?" Sun Jian chortled as he turned to face his wife. "I don't: this is like the wonderful appointment as 'Inspector of Yu' that I got. Your brother's been given Danyang as a prize that he must take from the incumbent *Zhou Xin*, who is – coincidentally enough – the brother of *Zhou Yu*, the man that I fought for Yu Province. That's partly why he went to Qu'e... to build an army to take to Danyang. But the place will be safe soon enough, so when Wu Jing is settled, he'll have everyone brought there."

"Why can't we go back to Shu?" Lady Wu asked. "Isn't that closer to Jing Province than Qu'e? Isn't this place closer, for that matter???"

"We... cannot go back to Shu," Sun Jian replied uneasily.

"Gongjin's father wouldn't mind," Sun Ce suggested.

"I'm sure that he wouldn't, but... but others might," Sun Jian retorted.

Sun Ce frowned and asked, "Like who...?"

Sun Jian shook his head and said, "The politics have become-"

"Alright, forget Shu, but why do we have to go all the way to Qu'e???" Lady Wu protested. "Why can't we just go *home*???"

"...I belong to Yuan Shu," Sun Jian replied. "You... you *know that*."

Sun Ben, Sun Hè and Sun Ce despaired silently; Lady Wu fled the room, and Lady Chen followed Lady Wu to comfort her.

"...I'm ready," Sun Jian said to his son and nephews. "Let's go to Lord Yuan."

Sun Jian turned to leave the room, but his son Quan was blocking the way.

"...Nine years of age, and another tiger!" Sun Jian chuckled half-heartedly.

"Am I going to Qu'e as well, Father?" Sun Quan asked.

"Yes, of course," Sun Jian replied. "You'll be schooled here in the south, and one day, you'll be an official; you won't have to fight like us."

Sun Quan sulked silently.

"...We won't be long," Sun Jian said reassuringly.

"You always say that!" Sun Quan snapped. "But you're going to fight somewhere, and that always takes ages! You-!"

"Quan... *stop it*," Sun Ce ordered. "You're my brother, not some whiny mediocrity. War is war, life is life. We all have to be strong for each other as well as ourselves."

Sun Quan was angry, but he understood that his brother was right; he nodded, bowed slightly and said, "Good fortune be with you all, and... and I'll see you all soon. I shall be there for Mother... *and* Lady Chen... and *the other one*... I promise."

Sun Quan fled from the doorway before his father could respond.

"...'The other one'...?" Sun Ce chortled. "Okay, I admit, I found you taking another consort so soon after you got back a little bit difficult, but... to call her 'the other one', especially when she's carrying a little brother or sister... that's-"

"He's not coping, but he'll have to *learn*," Sun Jian insisted. "It is our *way*, son."

Sun Ce nodded silently.

Sun Jian shook his head sorrowfully and added, "Quan is quite right about the time we'll be away for, though; we shall be gone for some time. Sometimes, I left Ben or Hè here to watch over the family, young as they were... but this time, I... perhaps I should leave someone here. Perhaps-"

"Father, we must all go with you," Sun Ce insisted. "Quan and Fu might not be old enough to be considered men, but we're not in as much danger these days... we have servants, money, and lots of allies and friends. Gongjin's family will help if needs be, and-"

"You... you've reassured me, my son," Sun Jian said with pride. "You really are becoming a good, strong man."

"Gongjin's a big help," Sun Ce chuckled. "If not for him, I'd be quite stupid."

The Suns enjoyed the moment of levity, but a moment was all that it was: they then began the journey to see their lord and master in his local residence.

When the Suns reached the gates of Yuan Shu's residence, they were met by Yuan Shu's adviser Yan Xiang, the official-general Chen Ji, a small security force and a small gaggle of junior officials: although Chen Ji and the security men were the only ones that wore armour, all of them were armed with swords.

"This is rude," Sun Ce complained. "Aren't you trusted, even after everything you've done, Father...?"

Sun Jian was too frustrated and embarrassed to answer.

Chen Ji approached the visitors, bowed ever-so-slightly and said, "General Sun," with as toneless a voice as he could muster.

"General Chen," Sun Jian replied.

"When we saw your approach with a force, General Sun, we felt it prudent to be prepared," Chen Ji said unapologetically.

"A 'force'...?" Sun Jian chortled. "It's an escort, not an army!"

"All the same, these are volatile times," Yan Xiang said. "Will you follow me...?"

Sun Jian started to walk, and Sun Ce started to follow his father; Chen Ji frowned and said, "Where are you going, young fellow? Did you really think you're meeting Lord Yuan?"

Sun Ce stopped and glared at Chen Ji with anger; Yan Xiang noted the situation and turned to Sun Jian, saying, "Is this your son, *General*?"

Sun Jian suspected that the emphasis on his rank was a threat as well as a rebuke, so he turned to Sun Ce and Sun Ben and said, "The two of you will stay with the 'force' we brought with us. I shan't be long."

Sun Ben nodded obediently and bowed to show deference; Sun Ce turned his gaze and tried to understand the barrage of new emotions that he was feeling.

"Son...?" Sun Jian prompted.

"...Yes, Father," Sun Ce replied at last.

Sun Jian, Yan Xiang and Chen Ji turned to continue their journey to Yuan Shu's residence; Sun Ce and Sun Ben were left with three of Yuan's junior officials, who studied the youths with curiosity.

"...Something you wanna say?" Sun Ce barked.

One of the officials smiled, bowed, and said, "Nothing at all."

Sun Ce studied the unassuming, plain-robed official; he was not condescending or timid like his peers, and he seemed to be genuinely trying to show respect.

"Why are you hanging about?" Sun Ce asked.

"We're supposed to accompany you to your encampment and review your 'force'," the respectful official replied dryly. "Do not be offended."

"...What's your name?" Sun Ce asked.

"Lü Fan," the official replied.

"*Lü*... you're not a relative of *Lü Bu*, are you...?" Sun Ce asked.

"If we share the same family name, then there is relation somewhere, from some time long gone," Lü Fan replied. "Thankfully, that name is all that we share; I'd sooner be dead than share any traits with a man like Lü Bu."

Sun Ce laughed involuntarily and said, "You're obviously pretty smart... yet you're being used to carry messages and spy on your master's allies...?"

The other officials fidgeted quietly while Sun Ce awaited a response.

"In times like these, men are placed somewhere, and they live accordingly," Lü Fan replied.

"Well then, Mister Lü Fan, let's go and 'review'," Sun Ce replied.

Sun Jian was invited to attend a public meeting in the main audience hall of Yuan Shu's residence. As Sun Jian walked toward his master, he felt condescending eyes boring into him.

"Ah... *Wentai*," Yuan Shu said as Sun Jian halted and bowed respectfully.

"Lord Yuan," Sun Jian replied politely.

"It is good to have you in my service," Yuan Shu chuckled. "To have such a tiger in my employ... is fortuitous indeed! As you know, I have an assignment for you."

"I am ready to serve," Sun Jian replied humbly.

"Very good, very good...!" Yuan Shu cackled. "Listen; I have now formally declared war on Liu Biao of Jing Province. Well, now I must honour my word and bring war upon him. But as you know, Jing is very well fortified. His subordinate, Huang Zu, is quite the dangerous 'crime boss', holding power in the southeast of the province. He must be dealt with before Liu Biao, since he is likely the more dangerous of the two in truth, what with Liu Biao being little more than an appointed lackey of the court."

"I understand," Sun Jian replied.

"I'm glad that you do," Yuan Shu said sternly. "Liu Biao must first be chased out of his holdings in the north. You will his attack his northern capital Xiangyang and its defensive sister city of Fan that sits in its shadow on the north bank of the Han River; Nan County's capital Wan City – which is currently understaffed – will then be isolated and surrender. Now, he'll probably call upon Huang Zu to come up from his holdings in the south to-"

"So you want me to attack from Yu Province...?" Sun Jian realised.

"That's where you are now," Yan Xiang heckled. "Where do you want to attack from, 'Inspector Sun'?"

Sun Jian laughed involuntarily and said, "If Jiangxia's Administrator is the bigger threat, Mister Yan, then-!"

"We'll attack their western border with my domains," Yuan Shu continued; he was visibly annoyed that Sun Jian had interrupted him. "The objective here is to increase my foothold; northern Jing is essential for achieving my ultimate goal of defeating my worthless dog of a brother, 'Yuan' Shao. I presume that you think that I am a fool that does not know my enemy: you will, of course, attack from the rivers, but your ships will sail down the Great River, *through* Jiangxia, up into the Han River and target the *north of Jing specifically*. It is the *north* I want and need right now: the wretched south can *wait*."

"...I understand," Sun Jian said numbly.

"So you keep saying!" Yuan Shu chortled. "Well, anyway, that is that... that is your assignment. Kindly embark on it as soon as you can, *General*."

"I shall, Lord Yuan," Sun Jian replied humbly.

Sun Jian returned to his camp and relayed the confirmation of his assignment to his increasingly irritated followers – his son Sun Ce, his nephews Sun Ben and Sun Hè, and his long-time allies Cheng Pu, Huang Gai, Han Dang and Zu Mao.

"This is self-serving in the extreme!" Cheng Pu complained.

"Naturally," Sun Jian said miserably.

"And if Huang Zu advances on the undefended south from Xiakou in response to an armed fleet passing through his domains...?" Cheng Pu said angrily.

"He was clear," Sun Jian replied. "He wants to expand his own reach, and the 'court lackey' Liu Biao is in his way; that's all there is to it. 'The wretched south can wait', apparently."

"We should not serve this man," Cheng Pu suggested. "He will ruin us with his idiotic acts of small-mindedness and meaningless grudges."

"I am tied to him now," Sun Jian sighed. "A marquis and inspector I might be, but this man is my superior in class and breeding, and I cannot refuse to serve him without becoming a victim of that same petty nature; remember that I am Inspector of this province at his appointment, and 'what he gives, he can easily take away'... leaving me with nothing, since all of my previous appointments were automatically reassigned when I took his ones, just as he said they would be."

"*Aiee*... well, then we should try and make this campaign a grand one, Lord Sun," Cheng Pu suggested. "We can try and force him to give us recognition for more rewards, and push for more autonomy in the south."

"A nice idea," Sun Jian said glumly.

"We could really use Zhu Junli right now," Cheng Pu sighed. "I'm alright against ordinary opponents, but Junli told me that Liu Biao has some really clever advisers... men that could outwit and ruin us. Kuai Liang is-"

"**We can't worry about that!**" Sun Jian barked. "*Please*, Demou, try and understand... as I *constantly try to*... that we are vassals of Yuan Shu, and that worrying about such things... is *pointless*."

Sun Ce was seeing a side to his father that he had never seen before; it pained him and made him hate Yuan Shu and the other northern warlords, although he refrained from voicing his feelings. But Sun Jian was not stupid; he could guess what his son was thinking, and it pained him to know that he was failing him as an infallible idol.

Sun Ce returned to his personal tent once the meeting ended; he was surprised to find one of Yuan Shu's junior officials, Lü Fan, awaiting him at the entrance.

"What now?" Sun Ce grumbled. "Must I let you review my living space now?"

Lü Fan bowed humbly and replied, "I am a man that knows good men when I see them, Master Sun. In addition to the camp inspection, your father was very poorly treated at the meeting, and deliberately so."

Sun Ce fumed silently.

"I cannot justify Yuan Shu when he does these things," Lü Fan continued. "He knows that your father will serve him tirelessly, and that he would never betray his trust, and yet he still insists on humbling him at every opportunity. It is jealousy, Master Sun: he envies your father, because for all of his so-called breeding, he will never be a hero like Sun Jian."

Sun Ce cocked his head sideways and glared at Lü Fan.

"My goodness, what a toady I must sound like!" Lü Fan realised. "I just wanted to assure you that-"

"No, no, you don't sound like a toady," Sun Ce interrupted. "Toadies don't berate their employers, especially not to other vassals. You're as sick of Yuan Shu as I am, aren't you."

"I hail from Runan, where your father is revered for his efforts against the Yellow Turbans," Lü Fan explained. "I ended up as one of Yuan Shu's cronies as a matter of circumstance. But when I see the man that liberated my home region from heretics being treated like dirt by a man who now wages war on his own brother in an effort to steal an inheritance from him, I...!"

Lü Fan stopped himself from saying any more.

"...You *truly respect him*, don't you...!" Sun Ce said with surprise.

"He is a hero," Lü Fan replied. "He *deserves respect*."

"...You're wasted serving Yuan Shu," Sun Ce suggested thoughtfully. "Come in and share a pot of tea with me, and tomorrow, I'll ask Dad – Father – about you joining us when we go to Jing. I'm sure that Yuan'll insist on 'observers' anyway, so why shouldn't you be one of them?"

Lü Fan bowed low and said, "I would be honoured, Master Sun! Truly blessed!"

"...Your style name, please," Sun Ce prompted. "Mine's 'Bofu'."

"I couldn't call you that!" Lü Fan chuckled nervously. "I-!"

"I insist," Sun Ce interrupted. "Style name, please."

"...Ziheng," Lü Fan replied. "But I cannot call you by your-"

"I *insist*, Ziheng," Sun Ce said. "Now let's talk a bit more before you go back."

Lü Fan bowed once again and gratefully accepted the invitation to socialise with the son of a man that was so exalted in his home region. At the same time, Sun Ce was keen to spend time with a man that saw his father as a figure of strength in order to counter the horror of watching him bow and scrape to Yuan Shu and his senior vassals. The two spoke as equals and parted as friends, and Lü Fan secured permission to travel with the Suns when they began their westward march.

****

28

The Sun forces divided to attack Jing Province from land and water: Huang Gai and Han Dang went south to take a fleet of warships and boats down the Yangtze while Sun Jian and Cheng Pu led an infantry force toward the Jing border. As Sun Jian's ground forces advanced through western Yu Province, many of the displaced hero's followers wondered why their families were remaining in Yu Province, being moved out of Lujiang or being sent back to southern Yang.

"It's a valid concern," Cheng Pu said to the increasingly-weary Sun Jian.

"I really am fed up of hinting at this," Sun Jian replied. "The movement out of Lujiang is 'political' and for the best: the families in Yu are probably better off across the river, and-"

"MEN APPROACHING!"

Sun Jian frowned and asked, "Was that one of our-?"

"Scouts...? Yes," Cheng Pu replied. He then turned to the direction the scout had called from and shouted, **"WHICH DIRECTION?"**

"SOUTHEAST!" the scout replied. **"AT LEAST A HUNDRED!"**

Many of the soldiers murmured uneasily.

"I thought the trouble here in Runan had ceased," Cheng Pu said. "It can't be Yellow Turbans or bandits, surely?"

"Even if they're not officially active, they may seek revenge on us," Sun Jian suggested. "Ready the men."

"This is ridiculous!" Cheng Pu scoffed as he signalled to various officers.

"Everything right now is ridiculous," Sun Jian complained. "Yellow Turbans attacking us as we march on neutral Jing Province is hardly the worst nonsense that we're enduring right now, as our previous conversation proved, I think."

The army waited: but as the small militia approached the army it became clear that they had no intention of attacking. Sun Ben and Zu Mao left the main army to confront the men, and they were visibly confused when they returned.

"It's Liu Pi," Sun Ben said. "I know that we were told that the former Yellow Turbans were working for Yuan Shu, but..."

"...He's been asked to supply aid to our march west," Sun Jian supposed. "He isn't going with us as well, is he...?"

"Ask him yourself," Zu Mao grumbled.

Liu Pi and his men had reached the army vanguard: the former rebel bowed humbly and said, "General Sun, I'm grateful for this second, more favourable encounter."

"You work for Yuan Shu now?" Sun Jian asked.

"Not as a proper army," Liu Pi replied. "We're... 'agitators'."

"...*Mercenaries*," Zu Mao scoffed as the conversation continued between Liu Pi, Sun Jian and Cheng Pu.

"Aren't *we*...?" Sun Ben suggested quietly.

"...Yeah, but it's not exactly a religious pursuit, is it?" Zu Mao retorted.

"...And that's really how it is," Liu Pi concluded.

"Right," Sun Jian sighed.

"So I hand-picked these men to accompany you from my own force, and Hè Yi will do the same when you encounter him near

the border," Liu Pi continued. "We're all on the same side now,
General, and I couldn't be happier about that."

Liu Pi smiled, bowed, and turned to retreat: the vast majority of
the men that accompanied him remained and fell to their knees in
a show of deference.

"...I couldn't be more *miserable*," Sun Jian muttered.

"I never thought that we'd end up as mercenaries on the same
side as these religious lunatics," Cheng Pu grumbled as he
prepared to signal a resumption of the march.

"...Father...?" Sun Ce prompted. "Father, are we marching with
Yellow Turbans now?"

"Apparently," Sun Jian replied. "Don't expect me to explain...
because I can't."

The Yellow Turbans were quickly added to the rear of the small
army and the journey to Jing Province resumed.

The Governor of Jing Province, Liu Biao, read the reports of Sun
Jian's advance with dread and summoned his vassals to his court
in Jiangling, his southern capital. His vassals noted his
demeanour: Liu Biao was known as a tall, handsome, charismatic
man that exuded confidence, but the endless unrest of recent
years had prematurely aged him and stripped him of much of his
resolve and vigour.

"We're in an era of flux, that we all knew," Liu Biao began. "Until
now, I worried about pirates in Jiangxia, tribes in the southern
counties, and perhaps losing Wan City – or, perhaps, the whole of
Nan County – to Dong Zhuo's followers."

Many of the officials murmured uneasily; two notable exceptions
to that were Liu Biao's main adviser Kuai Liang and the tall,
unshakeable Administrator of Jiangxia, Huang Zu, who was the
man that held the true power in the south and – in truth – some
of the north of the province as well.

"But now, Yuan Shu sends his prize tiger to devour me," Liu Biao
fretted. "He's the most dangerous man in the land... and nothing
will placate him, I know that. We cannot buy him... Dong Zhuo
tried that, and if an all-powerful Chancellor of State cannot find
his price, what hope has this humble Governor of Jing...? We
cannot fight him and expect to win... even Lü Bu and Hua Xiong
combined were no match for him; he scaled the walls of Wan City
on his own to quell the Yellow Turbans, and slaughtered a band of
twenty pirates single-handed! **What can I do???**"

"There is only one way," Kuai Liang said quietly. "We must isolate
him... and we must *kill him*."

All eyes turned to Huang Zu, who smiled icily and said, "I agree
with Mister Kuai. He's a problem that we have to solve with the
method that will be most effective."

"...I admit, a part of me is loath to destroy a hero of the age,
especially if it is not in pitched battle as he deserves," Liu Biao
replied glumly. "However, if the only other choices are attrition
that will cost me dearly, or that *I* die... then *he* must die."

"Leave him to me," Huang Zu said calmly. "When we speak next,
it will be to say that Sun Jian is an unhappy ghost, and Yuan Shu
is one step closer to defeat."

The Yellow Turban officer-turned-'agitator', Hè Yi, met Sun Jian's

164

forces near the border with eastern Jing Province as promised.
"Defences have been placed near places like Xinye," Hè Yi
reported. "They know you're on your way, and they're scared."
Sun Ce was pleased by the news, but Sun Jian sighed and said,
"When I was here before, it was as a hero, come to- ...Well, uh...
yes, thank you, Hè Yi."
"It's as you almost said," Hè Yi replied. "Last time you were in
Jing, it was to *rightly show us the error of our ways*, and there
isn't a man alive that doesn't know what happened in Nan County:
how strange, then, that this time we're working together to seize
the place for Yuan Shu! Fate works in mysterious ways, and only
Heaven knows why things are as they are."
Sun Jian groaned quietly and said, "It is... it is quite true, what
you say."
"I have selected some fine men to aid you, but I'm staying in Yu
Province," Hè Yi continued. "Heaven be with you, General Sun, as
it has been for so long."
Once Hè Yi had exchanged respectful gestures and retreated, Sun
Jian exhaled noisily, turned to Cheng Pu and said, "Damn this
nonsense. Really, Cheng Demou, I say 'Damn it all'. 'Heaven be
with me as it has been for so long'...? Whether Hè Yi meant it
sincerely or not, I don't believe that Heaven's with me now, if it
ever was before; if it was, I wouldn't be bound to that-!"
"Liu Biao knows we're on our way, which means our stupid master
has threatened him so specifically that he knew to expect us,"
Cheng Pu interrupted. "We must advance cautiously, eliminate the
resistance at Xinye, and-"
"Didn't Xinye welcome us when we were here before...?" Sun Jian
asked. "Didn't we have people thanking us for coming, calling us
'Heroes sent by the gods'...? My ancestor would spit at me... no,
actually, this proves that the family rumour is nothing more than
that. How can I be descended from Sun Tzu? How is that possible,
when-"
"We'll advance to Xinye and deal with Liu Biao's defenders, Lord
Sun," Cheng Pu said.
"...My son has a look on his face that betrays confusion,
disappointment and fear," Sun Jian continued. "Yuan Shu hasn't
just robbed me of my pride, Demou: he's robbed my son of the
man that-"
"Every man here feels the same, but we have to be *calm*," Cheng
Pu insisted. "Do as I do, Lord Sun: reinterpret Liu Biao and give
justification to our campaign. He did nothing while Dong Zhuo
ravaged Luoyang and wronged the people and sovereign. If Yuan
Shu was not sending us here, wouldn't we shun this selfish do-
nothing pedant, at the very least...? Perhaps taking northern Jing
might give us a base to attack Chang'an from."
"...You're right," Sun Jian replied. "You're still the wiser man...
always will be."
"While we're on the subject of our latest enemy, I agree that it's
Huang Zu that probably holds the most power... although it isn't
him I fear most," Cheng Pu continued. "Advisers worry me far
more than leaders and generals."
"You said that a 'Kuai Liang' is the brains behind Liu Biao and
Huang Zu," Sun Jian recalled.
"He has other advisers, but that one is perhaps as wily as Li Ru or

Jia Xu, and that really worries me," Cheng Pu explained. "The combination of an unscrupulous lord and devious adviser has already proved potent: Dong Zhuo, Jia Xu and Li Ru are the rulers of the land now. Liu Biao and Huang Zu might benefit from men like Kuai Liang: his neutrality might be strategic rather than principled."

"…So we cannot assume that he'll adopt a meek, defensive stance forever," Sun Jian supposed. "There may be reason in the argument that he may invade Yu if Yu does not invade Jing first."

"Precisely," Cheng Pu said. "So let's bear that in mind for two reasons: why we're here, and how we operate."

"…What you've said doesn't make working with the Yellow Turbans any easier, but it helps in general," Sun Jian replied. "Let's move on to Xinye as quickly as possible."

Neither Huang Zu nor Liu Biao was present at Xinye: the defence had been left to a young officer called Cai Mao, whose militia was mostly comprised of bandits and pirates. Sun Jian's men camped east of the city, and the officers met to discuss strategy.

"Yuan Shu is moving to take Wan City already," Sun Jian reported. "He expects us to work quickly… but Cai Mao may prove to be a problem."

"Cai Mao's objective is to turn us back here," Cheng Pu suggested. "If not, he intends to block our most obvious routes, in particular the river, hence why our scouts report a mass of boats and ships."

"Jing's navy has proven to be more impressive than I'd expected," Sun Jian lamented. "Hopefully, Huang Gai and Han Dang will be here soon."

"I have to admit, Yuan Shu's blatancy actually benefitted us, whether he intended it or not," Cheng Pu said. "Huang Zu sailed his fleet here and left reduced defences in Jiangxia, so it's likely that our allies will not be impeded at all."

"We'll engage Cai Mao on land at once," Sun Jian ordered. "Cheng Pu: try and acquire boats for a naval attack from the north. We need to push our enemies downriver to secure our supply route."

"I'll depart immediately," Cheng Pu replied.

The stocky, hard-featured Cai Mao arrayed an infantry division to the north of Xinye City and awaited Sun Jian's attack. Sun Jian led the vanguard with his son Ce as a second and placed Sun Hè and Sun Ben in command of the wings of the force; Zu Mao was assigned a free-moving unit that was mostly made up of the Yellow Turbans that had been donated to their force. Both sides chanted and heckled the other, and neither side displayed any genuine professionalism in their ranks: it would, at first sight, be a battle without strategy.

"…Kuai Liang has no role here," Sun Jian scoffed. "Alright, then… let's begin!"

Sun Jian signalled his drummers, and they began to strum a war beat on their large battle drums: his infantry charged at the confident Jing forces and crushed their front lines.

"…Their appearance is just that, then," Cai Mao said as he watched his forces fall apart. He then turned to a junior officer and said, "Nephew, we'll need to lure them onto the water as we planned."

166

The young officer – whose name was Zhang Yun – bowed slightly and said, "I shall alert the naval officers, Uncle."

Sun Ce was becoming impatient as he watched Sun Jian's active infantry from the relative safety of the front line.

"Father, we need to get out there!" Sun Ce pleaded.

"Not at all," Sun Jian replied. "This is just a little taste of things to come…"

Within seconds, panic erupted amongst the rear lines of Cai Mao's force: Zu Mao's unit had moved around the battlefield and engaged them from the south, catching the defenders in a pincer. As soon as it was clear that the defenders were in disarray, Sun Jian signalled for the two wings to press forward and strike: Sun Hè and Sun Ben led their men against the enemy vanguard and dealt heavy casualties.

"**Why are we not *charging*, Father???**" Sun Ce cried.

"For such a small meal…?" Sun Jian retorted playfully. "Think 'tiger': tigers don't eat mice."

Cai Mao observed the situation with surprising stoicism.

"…I should have seen that coming," Cai Mao grumbled.

"**RETREAT! RETREAT AT ONCE!**"

The Jing forces relied on a thin line of archers for protection as they began a retreat to the river; the invading force did not try and pursue at Sun Jian's order.

"…Why didn't you burn their ships?" Sun Jian asked when Zu Mao reached him and halted his excitable horse.

"Too many guards," Zu Mao replied. "He's not so stupid; he wanted to engage us on the water."

"…I thought his infantry management was too poor for a man of his rank," Sun Jian said. "So he's a river-fighter; fine, well, so am I. It'll be nice to show him a thing or two."

"We're gonna fight on the river???" Sun Ce exclaimed.

"…Someone is," Sun Jian chuckled. "Did you do much military naval training while I was away…?"

"We… we did some stuff about keeping balance, managing space, and things like that," Sun Ce replied. "I didn't do badly."

"…Alright then, you can assist me," Sun Jian said. "Zu Mao, Sun Ben: oversee communications for our supply line. Sun Hè: take a force of men along the bank and see if Cheng Pu is on his way here."

As each man went to do his duty, Sun Ce turned to his father and asked, "Why do you not assign anything to *me*, Father…?"

"You're shadowing me," Sun Jian replied. "Do shadows move on their own…?"

"…I'm supposed to watch you, and how you're telling everyone else what to do, so I can do the same," Sun Ce realised. "You think I can lead men like you do, then…?"

"If that's what you decide to do," Sun Jian replied. "I'd rather that you were a scholar or courtier, but I know that some people need to be on the front lines… because that's *my* problem."

While Sun Jian lamented the similarities between him and his son, Ce quietly enjoyed a feeling of empowerment: to him, being told that he was just like his father – especially when he was being told by his father – was the greatest compliment that he could possibly receive.

Cheng Pu had managed to secure some boats for a river pursuit, but they would clearly be no match for the Jing naval detachment led by Cai Mao.

"Many of the better craft were vandalised," Cheng Pu explained as Sun Jian looked at the range of commandeered water vehicles. "We'll be at a definite disadvantage."

"Yes... and the Yellow Turbans will be of no use on the water," Sun Jian noted. "Sun Ben could lead them across the water and go by land... but no, wait, that would be too slow and leave them isolated..."

"Where is Cai Mao now?" Cheng Pu asked.

"He's sailed quite a way downriver," Sun Jian replied. "He's probably picked a spot that he knows well..."

"...If Kuai Liang or any other keen mind is behind all this, we have to be aware that the best naval strategies sometimes involve land-based contributions," Cheng Pu said. "We'll pursue, but we'll need to keep an eye on the topography: if it looks like we'll be lured too close to bankside traps, we'll need to counter them."

The majority of Sun Jian's forces were still made up of former bandits and pirates from the south that were more accustomed to river combat, and they manned the forward units as they moved down the river toward Xiangyang; Zu Mao had the men that were only useful in land engagements take the rear in transport boats and be ready to act as counter-tactical forces should the need arise. Cai Mao was not trying to feign a retreat in any way: when Sun Jian finally caught up with his small fleet, he ordered the smaller boats to advance and engage Sun Jian's men at once.

"**Use your heads, everyone, and take no risks!**" Sun Jian ordered. "**Each of you is as precious as a son! Now forward, and show them what the men of Jiangdong can do!**"

Helmsmen ordered their craft forward to meet the Jing boats: once the opposing sides were able to bring their boats alongside each other, swords and spears were readied for a style of combat that was, to the untrained eye, visibly clumsy, though it required the greatest level of skill. Men duelled while trying to remain standing while their boats bobbed and swayed under their feet, meaning that they had worry about the water as much as their human opponents. Other craft were filled with archers: that stretch of the river was quickly turned into a chaotic struggle for survival that most men feared but others – like Sun Jian and his eldest son Ce – relished for the challenges it offered.

"...**Watch your back, Lang! Left side, Ren, left side!**" Sun Jian barked as he tried to monitor every encounter and preserve as many of his precious followers as he could: Cai Mao was doing the same, although his voice carried no urgency. When one man's precarious situation became too much for Sun Jian to bear, he forgot all thoughts of showing restraint in front of his son and readied his sword.

"**WAIT! NO, WENTAI, COME BACK!**" Cheng Pu pleaded.

Sun Ce was awestruck as he watched his father jump from boat to boat as though they were rigid stones, knocking Jing sailors into the water as he moved: he saved two of his men from death, but Cheng Pu – who showed dexterity that near-equalled his lord – moved to restrain him before he could succumb to the urge to charge Cai Mao's heavily defended position.

"**You're bloody impossible!**" Cheng Pu scolded as he joined Sun Jian in a battle with two enemy boats. "**Now look what you've gotten us into!**"

"**You sound like Wu Jing,**" Sun Jian retorted as he kicked one enemy sailor overboard.

"**Take that back!**" Cheng Pu cackled as he dodged a sword swing and slashed at the assailant's unguarded stomach with his own blade.

Cai Mao observed the battle nervously: it was not proving to be the easy victory that he had hoped for. He looked to the riverbanks, hoping that he could signal to hidden archers if any valuable opponent strayed too close to them: he was shocked to see that the foliage around one of the ambush positions was moving erratically, indicating that it had been compromised by his enemies.

"...**RETREAT!**" Cai Mao shouted. "**MOVE AT ONCE! RETREAT!**"

Cai Mao's rear forces began a frantic withdrawal southward, but the boats that were locked in conflict with Sun Jian's would not escape so easily. The battle continued for the forward units, and some even pressed the invaders with greater vigour.

"**Ben!**" Sun Ce cried when he saw that his cousin was in trouble on a nearby boat: he chanced that he could find the required skill and went to Ben's aid. The two then did what they could to repel the forces around them, but they were outnumbered.

"...**Your *son*, Wentai!**" Cheng Pu exclaimed when he spotted Sun Ce's plight.

"**Damn them!**" Sun Jian cried when he tried to move and had his way blocked by another boatful of Jing sailors. "**Get out of my way!**"

But the way was not clear, and Sun Jian would not be able to reach his son. Sun Hè added his own presence to Sun Ce's position, but that was not enough to repel the experienced Jing sailors: final salvation would come in the form of Zu Mao and three veteran allies.

"**Clear off, you cowards!**" Zu Mao shouted: his boat approached the encirclement at speed and put the Jing men to flight.

"...Thank you," Sun Ben said reluctantly.

"River fighting is about having a lot o' good mates," Zu Mao suggested.

The Jing boatmen were retreating altogether now that they had realised that they had lost their rear support: Sun Jian's weary men cheered with the last of their strength and started to help the men that had fallen into the water during the fighting.

"We forced him back," Cheng Pu sighed.

"But they're good river fighters, better than I'd guessed they would be," Sun Jian replied. "We'll want to wait for Huang Gai and Han Dang before we do that again."

"I agree: let's hope that they give us the choice," Cheng Pu said as he surveyed the reddened waters and pondered the army's next move.

The army camped on the western bank of the river and enjoyed a welcome rest. Sun Ce sat with his father and cousins in the command tent that evening, musing on the events of the day.

"...Are you ever afraid of dying?" Sun Ce asked suddenly.

"That's a strange question!" Sun Jian replied. "I am afraid sometimes, if only for what it might mean for my family... why...?"

Sun Ce stared at the ground as he said, "I... wasn't; is that wrong...?"

"We all die eventually," Sun Jian replied. "Later is better, and when we know we don't leave others at a disadvantage, but it isn't our choice."

"But when we fight, we *are* choosing, in a way," Sun Ce suggested. "But I didn't think about whether Mum might be angry about it, or Quan, or *you*, or... ... ...is that wrong...?"

"All fighting men face that dilemma," Sun Jian replied. "But we do what we do to protect our families. We're here to... here... to..."

Sun Jian's voice faded, his expression turned sour, and he turned his gaze away. His son and nephews could see that the conversation was over, so they quietly got to their feet and retreated to their own tents. Once he was alone, Sun Jian turned his gaze to the easel where his map of the region was displayed. He stared at the map for a while, taking in every line and coloured area, every place-name and marker pin, every proposed line of attack and route of retreat should the need arise.

"...But there's no *point*," Sun Jian whispered. "No point... at *all*."

∗∗∗∗∗∗∗∗∗∗∗∗

29

Cai Mao was obviously eager to have another battle on the river: he sent small teams to harass Sun Jian's camp and gathered his forces on a wide stretch of river so that he could employ his larger ships against Sun Jian's weaker force. Sun Jian summoned his officers to his latest command tent on the southern bank of the river so that they could discuss their next moves against their northern opponents.

"No sign of Huang Gai and Han Dang yet," Cheng Pu fretted.

"Why would they be in trouble?" Sun Jian asked.

"If I'm not mistaken, they have to pass Zhangling and Jiangling," Cheng Pu explained. "Jiangling is the southern capital of Jing, which is self-explanatory; but it and Zhangling are both the responsibility of Kuai Liang's brother Kuai Yue, who is said to be as wily as his elder brother. He once served Hè Jin in a fairly high capacity during the Yellow Turban crisis, and was made Magistrate of Ru County for his efforts."

"…And now he serves the lord of Jing, the sworn enemy of the richest, most powerful man in Ru County," Zu Mao noted. "That's quite a career change, Mister Cheng Pu, just like us going from-"

"I think your point is guessed," Sun Jian chuckled. "So this 'Kuai Yue' might be a serious obstruction to them then, Demou…?"

"Hopefully, that's the worst thing he'd be," Cheng Pu sighed.

"Even if they had to visit us from the netherworld, they'd have found a way to tell us if they'd been routed," Sun Jian suggested. "This 'Kuai Yue' would only do something if they attacked on land, I think. It's more likely that Huang Zu deployed a force to harry and delay them."

"…True," Cheng Pu replied.

"They're natural river men, as good as any pirate or crazy fisherman," Zu Mao said. "Them two could fight their way up the Yellow River if they had to: isn't that right, lads…?"

The officers that were former pirates hollered as agreement with Zu Mao's statement.

"…Whether they're alive and well or not, the biggest problem is that they're not here when we need them," Cheng Pu continued. "This 'Cai Mao' has better ships than we do, better boats than we do, and we have to beat him to advance to Xiangyang before Liu Biao can do too much to fortify it."

"He's had time to dig moats and build mounds, towers and all that," Zu Mao scoffed. "Every man he pulls from Nan County or Jiangxia is a man less to defend the other place: this isn't about time, it's about beating Cai Mao."

"…Alright, yes, I'm solely concerned about beating Cai Mao," Cheng Pu admitted. "And, further to that, maybe I'm concerned that Huang Zu might reinforce his river forces, possibly personally, and Huang is apparently quite formidable."

"If we could beat Lü Bu on land, we can beat Huang Zu on the water," Sun Jian insisted. "We've been told time and again that things were impossible, and we did them anyway."

"**That's right!**" Sun Ce cried. "Dad's absolutely right, old man!"

"…'Old man'…?" Cheng Pu complained. "Lord Sun, I…!"

Sun Jian laughed and said, "You've had worse things said to you,

Demou. What tactics will Cai Mao employ if he can use ships...?"

"He can sail across our positions and fire arrows at us, ram and capsize our smaller boats... the usual things," Cheng Pu replied.

"Precisely; this is just another naval battle, and we have tactics that we can use that will work as well as they always have," Sun Jian said. "Let's turn our attentions to those tactics, Demou... while we quietly wish our comrades well on their journey here to join us."

Cheng Pu smiled, nodded, and turned to the battle map.

"...Do you think that Lord Sun's alright?" Huang Gai asked as he stared at the stretch of the Han River that was in front of him. Han Dang was stood at his side with a strange smile on his face; Huang Gai turned to face him, frowned and said, "Did you hear me, Yigong...?"

"Yeah, I heard you," Han Dang chuckled.

"Have you got some sort of river madness?" Huang Gai asked.

"Maybe," Han Dang replied. "Look at where we are."

The lead ships were about to pass Liu Biao's southern capital, Jiangling, which was to the west of the Han River.

"So far, we've passed an undermanned Three Rivers and an undermanned Xiakou; now we're passing an undermanned Jiangling," Han Dang complained. "All of 'em ripe and easy pickings, but we're sailing up the Han River to Fan to fight everything that Liu Biao can throw at us, and *why*...? Because that bloody Yuan S-!"

"Why are you bothering, Yigong?" Huang Gai interrupted. "All I'm thinking about is our lord and how lucky we are that we got this far without being intercepted... but sad to say, so far as the latter goes, this is it."

"Oh...?" Han Dang exclaimed.

"Look... at our scout boat," Huang Gai said as he pointed at the river ahead: a small fishing boat was approaching, and the 'fisherman' – actually a soldier in disguise – was signalling the approach of several military vessels.

Han Dang groaned and said, "Huang Zu's on to us. How do we play it?"

"It was anticipated," Huang Gai replied. "He can't send many craft to intercept us if Lord Sun hasn't been routed. They expect us to continue until we're met, so let's do something else."

"...A full-speed advance to hit them before they're ready," Han Dang guessed. "I like your way of doing things, Gongfu!"

Huang Gai smiled slightly, picked up a small flag and signalled the other lead ships with an order to increase speed: Huang Zu's forces were caught off-guard, just as Huang Gai had anticipated.

"The Huangs of Jiangxia are no match for our Gongfu!" Han Dang cackled as the flagship crashed into a smaller boat and capsized it with ease, sending its occupants into the freezing water and leaving them completely defenceless.

"What courage," Huang Zu sighed. "These Yang men are... are magnificent. **Begin countermeasures!**"

The Jing ships signalled frantically, and archers were deployed to the rails while some ships at the rear of the force started to retreat upriver. The Sun forces followed their initial strike with a second advance using smaller craft: Huang Gai and Han Dang led their men personally, which impressed Huang Zu still further. The Jing sailors were equally competent, however, so the advantage of surprise quickly gave way to attrition as skill met with skill.

"We're not going to get out of this without pain!" Han Dang shouted to Huang Gai.

Huang Gai had just watched a trusted subordinate fall lifelessly into the water not more than a few feet away: he grimaced and replied, **"It's up to him now!"**

Huang Zu was watching his own trained sailors with a sense of dread. It was not just his own judgement that haunted him: while some leaders and strategists viewed men as expendable and easily replaced, he knew that Kuai Liang and Liu Biao would berate him publicly if he allowed the lives of men that had endured years of training in the art of river combat to be wasted in an initial skirmish.

"Retreat!" Huang Zu ordered. **"Withdraw!"**

"He has sense then," Han Dang said as he watched the enemy retreat under sporadic cover fire. **"Is that good or bad?"**

"Both," Huang Gai replied. **"Let's... let's retrieve our friends and press on. We don't know what he'll do next, any more than he knows what we'll do."**

The painful process of recovering the living and the dead began in earnest, since there was a need to advance quickly and maintain an aggressive stance.

Huang Zu retreated to Xiangyang and sought an audience with Liu Biao, who had relocated there to oversee the defence of his province in person. Kuai Liang hummed thoughtfully as Huang Zu fell to one knee and said, "My lord governor, I failed to repel the fleet that advanced from the Great River. They will doubtless meet with their allies and engage Cai Mao next rather than come here."

"I agree," Kuai Liang said. "My lord governor, we'll need to preserve Cai Mao. He will need support against the bolstered invading force."

"Should I go in person?" Liu Biao asked.

"That would be risky against a man like Sun Jian that takes risks," Kuai Liang replied. "No, General Huang should take a force and engage them after he had fortified the river against a surprise attack. They have to get past Fan in that case, and once they are locked into a siege there, we have them where want them."

"This man specialises in breaking sieges," Liu Biao noted.

"He specialises in surprise, or rather recklessness that no sane man would expect," Kuai Liang retorted. "I know him well enough; he's not going to get the better of us, lord governor."

"I'll depart with river and ground forces at once," Huang Zu said.

"...Do that," Liu Biao replied thoughtfully. "But take no chances: you were wise to allow his officers to win their first river battle rather than lose more men, but next time they must be stopped."

Huang Zu fought frustration as he said, "As you command."

Liu Biao's isolated naval officer Cai Mao was now torn between waiting for reinforcements and striking unexpectedly: his hand was forced when Sun Jian suddenly began a simultaneous advance downriver and across the land. Cai Mao met the river advance with his own ships while he sent word to Fan and sent a meagre ground force to block the roads. The river battle was brief and ended with a mutual decision to withdraw, but the blockade resulted in no battle since the ground forces were wary of possible ambuscades; the situation was a stalemate, and that worried Sun Jian and his allies as they convened in the command tent of a bankside camp.

"He's half-competent," Cheng Pu chuckled when he finished reading the latest reports on Cai Mao's efforts. "But Gongfu and Yigong have broken through Huang Zu's attempt at a blockade, so they're almost here with our proper fleet. At that point, Cai Mao has no chance."

"He'll know that," Sun Jian suggested.

"Knowing you're in trouble and knowing how to get out of trouble are two different things," Cheng Pu retorted. "Let's hit him back with everything we have."

"Alright," Sun Jian replied.

But Cai Mao had the advantage of striking first, and Sun Jian's men were unavoidably weary and demoralised: the next battle was another wasteful river encounter, and the defenders were now taking as many lives as they were losing.

"Ram their ships!" Sun Jian ordered.

"We shouldn't," Cheng Pu replied. "Theirs are stronger. That's eggs against rocks."

"...Well then I have to go and fight again!" Sun Jian decided.

"No, you shouldn't," Cheng Pu replied. "The-"

"We're losing too many people!" Sun Jian barked.

Cheng Pu tried to continue his remonstrations, but Sun Jian was determined: he readied his sword and dashed across the unwieldy boats to engage the enemy sailors in person once again. Zu Mao and Sun Ben joined their lord, but Sun Ce was kept from moving by Sun Hè at his father's request.

"How will I learn?" Sun Ce protested. "How am I a 'shadow' now, when he's over there and I'm-?"

"Dying here won't teach you anything, Cousin," Sun Hè replied. "We're supposed to defend our own craft from saboteurs."

"See yourself as a 'long shadow', Young Master," Cheng Pu joked. "Your father's certainly casting one right now."

Sun Jian's involvement inspired others as it always did, and the tide of the battle started to shift in the invaders' favour once again. Cai Mao's nephew and subordinate Zhang Yun rushed to Cai's side to report on the enemy's newfound vigour and the impact to their own forces.

"...Then I must get involved!" Cai Mao declared.

"Uncle, that's folly," Zhang Yun pleaded. "Sun Jian is-"

"He's a tiger, but we're river dragons!" Cai Mao retorted. "Let's show the southern cur our northern courage!"

Cai Mao led his elite men into battle, and the morale of the defenders rose accordingly.

"...We'll have to do something drastic," Cheng Pu decided. He turned to Sun Hè and asked, "Where's the kindling for the fire arrows?"

"We're going to burn their ships?" Sun Hè exclaimed; he noted Cheng Pu's impatient expression and added, "Uh... it's on the support boats, Major Cheng, as you ordered."

"Right," Cheng Pu said. "Do *exactly as I say*..."

The battle was suddenly halted by an almighty crash. Cai Mao looked to the direction of the noise and gasped involuntarily; Sun Hè had filled a medium-sized craft with kindling, set it alight, and sent it toward the Jing flagship at high speed. The flames climbed up the wooden frame of the damaged ship: the sailors used their keen sense of the situation and chose to abandon their efforts to contain the flames, opting instead to abandon ship.

"The flagship!" Zhang Yun cried. **"They've-!"**

"BREAK FORMATION!" Cai Mao ordered. **"BREAK FORMATION, QUICKLY, YOU BLOODY FOOLS, BEFORE IT SPREADS!"**

Cai Mao's subordinates frantically signalled the other ships, and their captains quickly moved away from the burning vessel before the flames could spread and consume their craft as well. The sight of their flagship disintegrating did little for the morale of the Jing sailors: they started to retreat without waiting for the order.

"PURSUE!" Sun Jian ordered. **"FINISH THEM OFF!"**

"What's going on?" Sun Hè asked as he brought his men back to Cheng Pu. **"We seem to be pursuing the enemy; what-?"**

"Ayah... **your uncle is getting the bloodlust again,"** Cheng Pu grumbled. **"I'd better go and stop him before people start following him."**

"Perhaps we *should* follow!" Sun Ce suggested.

"We have to do something about the fire, and we need to recover our injured and dead!" Cheng Pu retorted. **"Cai Mao will expect a pursuit and be ready for us!"**

Cheng Pu's protestations were similar to those being made by Sun Ben and Zu Mao, who were both trying to restrain the frenzied Sun Jian.

"Cheng Pu can do all that!" Sun Jian insisted. **"I have to-!"**

"We have to let him go!" Zu Mao barked.

"He has to be stopped!" Sun Jian retorted.

"I know you're angry, Mister Sun Jian, but we have to stop!" Zu Mao said. **"What sort of example does this set?"**

Sun Jian froze: his gaze turned in the direction of his son, and after a short deliberation he replied, **"You're right, Mister Zu. HALT! STOP THE PURSUIT!"**

The men followed the order willingly.

Cheng Pu assembled the officers in a bankside command tent for yet another meeting; Sun Jian was visibly irritated that Cai Mao had escaped, and Cheng Pu hoped that he could somehow reason with his lord.

"...I'm tired of this, just like you are," Cheng Pu insisted.

"It's a pity that the fire didn't take all of his ships down, isn't it," Zu Mao said.

"But it was a good decision," Sun Jian admitted. "Cheng Demou, we're fighting a man that isn't afraid to join his men in battle either. Up to now, we've been fighting valiant but untrained men like the Yellow Turbans, or well-trained but cowardly men like Dong Zhuo. I was led to believe that Jing would be a straightforward campaign against a timid coward like Dong Zhuo, who led untrained men like the Yellow Turbans: this is the opposite. The men of Jing know land and river warfare, just as we do: they know war and sacrifice, just as we do. This is a genuine challenge. We'll win, as we always do, but it will cost us."

The junior officers exchanged nervous glances.

"...Cai Mao has halted downriver," Cheng Pu said calmly. "He's licked his wounds, and now he seems to want to reinforce his position. That 'fire trick' won't work again. He'll fight alongside his men again now that he's seen how much it inspires them. And most importantly, Huang Zu's sent extra support from Xiangyang and gone to reinforce the road blockade in person. We'll need to wait for Huang Gai and Han Dang before we do anything else. And... and we've received word from Lord Yuan. He-"

"**He can *bugger off*,**" Zu Mao barked.

The small group of officials that were loyal to Yuan Shu were visibly angry: Sun Jian broke into the outburst of laughter from the veteran junior officers by saying, "**Lord Yuan's words are our guiding force. Please, friends, be silent and let Mister Cheng continue.**"

Once the laughter had died, Cheng Pu turned to the official Huan Jie, who said, "Lord Yuan is dismayed at the fact that we have not taken Fan yet. He urges us to hasten our advance and, 'if possible', send a detachment to Wan."

"Does he want us to do anything else while we're at it?" Zu Mao heckled. "Huan Jie, you crawler, I-!"

"I assure you that I am only relaying the words as they are written!" Huan Jie said as he waved Yuan Shu's cloth-based correspondence like a flag of surrender. "Don't be angry with me, Zu Mao, for-!"

"We... we have to show the utmost deference to our lord, Mister Zu Mao," Sun Jian ordered as he eyes met with those of the officials that Yuan Shu had attached to the expedition. "Mister Huan Jie is doing his job, as we all are."

"This is *humiliating*," Zu Mao muttered.

Sun Jian turned to Huan Jie, smiled and said, "Your role shall be to reply, Mister Huan, and relay our situation with your usual political savvy. Lord Yuan knows that we always do our best, and that our best is usually better than what others bring to the battlefield. We'll take Fan: it'll take time, but we'll do it."

"I'll respond immediately," Huan Jie promised.

"...Which means that we have to blockade the river, defeat Cai Mao, chase Huang Zu back to Fan and then take it 'very quickly'," Cheng Pu noted. "Lord Yuan will be in Nan County very soon: we'll have to hit fast and hard."

Zu Mao snorted angrily and said, "Yeah, and take the sorts of risks that usually get men k-"

"*Mister Zu... Mister Zu, please*," Sun Jian groaned. "Orders are orders. If Lord Yuan did not expect us to achieve it, he wouldn't ask. He has faith in our ability, which is a great compliment from a famous nobleman."

Zu Mao eyed the Yuan loyalists and said, "I feel better already."

Sun Ce frowned at Sun Jian's conciliatory sycophancy: he knew that it was false, but he was still pained by his father's need to show deference to an uncaring and demanding lord that did not, it seemed, have any interest in anyone's welfare save his own.

Cai Mao and Zhang Yun readied their bolstered forces for a third major encounter with Sun Jian's navy. The river force that had defeated Huang Zu had suddenly picked up speed once again, but their imminent arrival did not seem to coincide with an attack by Sun Jian's previously belligerent force to the northeast: that worried Cai Mao, since the lack of an obvious pincer probably meant that his enemies were planning something even worse, whatever that might be. That lack of certainty bled through the ranks and affected everyone in one way or another, such that when Huang Gai and Han Dang launched their attack, Cai Mao's response was blunted and hesitant. The southern sailors pressed their psychological advantage with an attack using smaller vessels, and Cai Mao ordered his fleet to split, sending one part toward Fan and the other in the direction of Sun Jian's other force. It was at that point that Cheng Pu struck: archers on the banks fired regular and flaming arrows at the passing ships and boats, and the larger craft rammed into the smaller Jing craft. The large ships had nowhere to go, and their only option was to retaliate: terrified observers searched for new attempts to burn the ships while archers returned fire and kept manned craft from making boarding attempts. The defensive efforts were doomed to failure once arrows started to run out and the ships were completely surrounded: the smaller craft were overwhelmed by arrow fire and enemy sailors, and the Jing ships finally faced a genuine threat of being boarded.

"What do we do?" Zhang Yun asked of his uncle Cai Mao.

Cai Mao was silent: one ship had already been boarded, and a second had been rammed and breached by a medium-sized craft with a reinforced bow.

"Uncle, what do we do?" Zhang Yun asked again.

"...He's not even *here* this time," Cai Mao muttered.

"Uncle, we've lost two ships!" Zhang Yun protested.

"...Three," Cai Mao said as he watched a third ship start to capsize. "We've lost; our proud navy lost... lost, to a band of volunteer mercenary pirates from Yang. I'll never live it down. Lord Liu will-"

"Uncle!" Zhang Yun cried. **"Uncle, we-!"**

"I... I know," Cai Mao interrupted. **"RETREAT!"**

The remainder of the Jing navy limped away, toward Fan City, leaving a horde of baying, cheering southerners to enjoy a bittersweet victory.

"Huang Zu is all that stands between us and Fan City," Cheng Pu said to his relieved second, Sun Ben. "Let's meet up with Gongfu and Yigong, set up our own blockade, and go and aid our lord on land. We've been on the water long enough."

Huang Zu, meanwhile, was quietly optimistic as he reviewed his infantry and awaited the arrival of his opponents: he learned of Sun Jian's advance and Cai Mao's retreat within hours of each other, and his morale was badly shaken.

"Why didn't he hold???" Huang Zu screamed at the messenger from Cai Mao.

"I... I don't know!" the messenger replied as he sank lower and lower to the ground.

"Why don't you know, you idiot???" Huang Zu cried. **"You're here to tell me what happened, aren't you, you little-!"**

"I-it's all in here, General!" the messenger implored as he proffered a small wooden tube with his shaking hands.

"Give me that," Huang Zu said as he snatched the tube from the messenger. He opened one end, took the cloth letter from within and started to read it. After a short time he snorted angrily, looked down at the messenger and said, "You... you did well to get here so quickly, and at all. Get a drink and a rest, and... and thank you for your efforts."

The messenger rambled inanely and he scrambled out of the command tent on all fours: Huang Zu turned to his officers and said, "He'll be here soon... Sun Jian, I mean. Cai Mao has reinforced the river with what he has left, but the tiger is on land, coming here in person to unblock the road and seize Fan... at which point a river blockade is of limited use. Fan and Xiangyang are interdependent: he must not gain *either of them*, gentlemen, or northern Jing is lost. Ready yourselves."

The officers spoke as one, chanting, "**Death to the invaders!**"

Sun Jian's forces stopped at a crossroads that was fortified with palisades and manned by archers and pike-wielding infantry.

"A fine welcome, indeed," Zu Mao scoffed.

"Tiger traps as far as the eye can see," Sun Jian quipped.

"They won't catch you, though... not so long as I'm alive," Zu Mao retorted. "Are we charging...?"

"I'd say we'll have no choice," Sun Jian replied. "Look over there."

Zu Mao snorted irritably when he saw what Sun Jian was referring to: Huang Zu's forces were approaching at speed.

"Not a lot of horses, and not as many men as there could be," Sun Jian noted. "Let's not give them the chance to get ready."

"We're going to charge a field of stakes and a larger army at the same time?" Zu Mao chortled.

"What else can we do?" Sun Jian retorted.

"We could set up a defensive camp and await Cheng Pu and the others," Huan Jie suggested.

"...On second thoughts, let's charge: the day I agree with a politician is the day my spine's gone," Zu Mao joked.

"We'll rout them easily, Father!" Sun Ce said excitedly.

"You'll be in reserve with Sun Hè," Sun Jian ordered. "Your job is to watch our backs."

Sun Ce groaned disappointedly and said, "But I want to-!"

"You two'll be more vigilant than any other man I could employ," Sun Jian insisted. "Right then, Zu Mao: let's take our friend Huang Zu by surprise! **DIVISIONS ONE THROUGH SIX: CHARGE!**"

"**Ayah! The man is crazy!**" Huang Zu exclaimed as he realised that Sun Jian had charged through his defences and attacked his weary vanguard before they had time to compose themselves. The result was a swift rout; Huang Zu turned and fled, leaving a tenth of his men behind as corpses.

"...If that's all the man's got, Fan'll be ours very soon," Sun Jian said as he watched his enemies run away.

"...'Ours'...?" Zu Mao chortled.

"Yes, yes, I know: don't spoil the moment," Sun Jian grumbled as he turned back to his front line and prepared to address his victorious soldiers.

✱✱✱✱✱✱✱✱✱✱✱✱

30

Sun Jian's advance to the strategic city of Fan gave Yuan Shu's forces an opportunity to attack Nan County, the northernmost part of Liu Biao's province. Once Wan and Fan were taken, a river crossing was all that stood between Sun Jian and a siege of Liu Biao's northern capital, Xiangyang: both sides knew this well. The cities of Fan and Xiangyang were both very close to the banks of the River Han, and there were worries on all sides that the river might swell – as it was well known for – and either flood the city or wash away everything around it, additionally increasing the likelihood of an outbreak of disease. Those extra concerns rivalled or outweighed the worst of all fears for any campaign commander – running out of supplies and having to abandon that campaign.

Sun Jian's force set up a well-fortified camp to the northeast of Fan City, while Huang Zu retreated across the river to Xiangyang City, rendezvoused with Cai Mao, hastily reorganised the Jing forces and prepared to return to Fan while Cai Mao oversaw a series of naval blockades to force Sun Jian to remain on land. Sun Jian's allies learned of the land and river-based approach of Huang Zu's forces and convened a meeting to prepare for their arrival.
"So we're going up against Huang Zu, Cai Mao, and quite possibly the 'amazing' Kuai Liang, all at once," Sun Jian said as Cheng Pu studied a report with increasing concern.
"Why is that a problem, Lord Sun?" Han Dang scoffed. "We've smashed their navy, routed their ground forces and made them look consistently stupid."
"We really do need Zhu Junli," Cheng Pu said worriedly. "If Kuai Liang – or worse yet, him *and* his brother – are brought in to manage this next offensive, I'm concerned that I don't have the wits to match with theirs."
Sun Jian turned to the official Huan Jie and said, "You have impressed me with your political skills, Mister Huan; are you also versed in strategy...?"
Zu Mao, Han Dang and a number of other men quietly scoffed at the notion.
"Please, be honest," Sun Jian prompted.
Huan Jie bowed low and said, "I am not a genius of the age like Zhu Zhi. My ability only extends to winning battles fought with words and pens."
"Then why are you here...?" Han Dang scoffed.
Before Huan Jie could reply, Sun Jian shook his head and said, "I don't want to kill anyone that I don't have to kill. If there is any hope of a bloodless solution to any conflict, you must have men with silk tongues to negotiate. Until I heard that Huang Zu was on his way back here, I'd hoped that I could siege the city, scare them with my reputation for breaking sieges, and have men like Huan Jie talk them into surrendering. Now that Huang Zu is bringing another army here, I fear we're going to be here for a while, and many will suffer needlessly."
"Can't we just siege the city quickly before Huang Zu's new army gets here?" Sun Ce asked.
"Son, I-! ...*Aiee*. But how can I be angry...? You're saying what I'd

have said ten years ago," Sun Jian admitted.

"So why not do it?" Sun Ce asked excitedly.

"Because Huang Zu would trap us between the city, the plains and the river, and we'd be forced to fight our way out," Sun Jian explained. "I got carried away a couple of times on this campaign, I admit that: but this time, we have to be *careful*."

Cheng Pu, Huang Gai, Han Dang and Zu Mao laughed at the notion of Sun Jian championing caution; Zu Mao pointed at Sun Jian and said, "You really *have* changed, haven't you, Mister Sun Jian! When I think of Wan-"

"That's exactly what I'm thinking of," Sun Jian interrupted. "The bodies, the death; I was so driven to win that siege because of what we'd already lost."

The officials stopped laughing as they recalled the campaign.

"Huang Zu's wily and experienced, so I won't risk splitting my forces," Sun Jian continued. "We repel him first, and then – if, for some insane reason, Fan City is holding out – we take Fan, and chase him to Xiangyang."

"You've matured into a great general as well as a hero," Cheng Pu declared. "I'm proud to follow you, Wentai... very proud."

The other officials voiced their own support, and Sun Ce suddenly felt more respect for his embattled father than he had ever felt before.

"...We'll wait for Huang Zu's full force to arrive, and then we'll show him what we can do," Sun Jian concluded. "This will be our greatest victory yet!"

Huang Zu and Sun Jian met on a stretch of land between the cities of Fan and Deng. Both armies numbered in the low thousands, but Sun Jian's men included cavalry that had remained with him after the Yang City campaign and men that had served him since he had left Fuchun; Huang Zu's army was, like Sun Jian's, made up of a lot of ex-pirates, former rebels and convicts, but they had less experience in battle and relied more on training exercises.

"...No proper cavalry, poor arrangement... This'll be easy," Zu Mao snickered as he observed Huang Zu's flawed battle lines. "They're an even more shabby bunch than we used to be. We needn't have worried about them being ready last time, Mister Sun Jian, if this was what they were going to-"

"Take no chances," Cheng Pu replied. "Mad charges are alright when there's a point, like breaking their lines and demoralising them: we should all of us remember that they have archers, please."

"Let me charge them!" Sun Ce said excitedly.

"...Like father, like son," Cheng Pu sighed.

Sun Jian shook his head and said, "Not yet. We mustn't be hasty."

"...Yes, Father," Sun Ce said miserably.

"Han Dang: prepare the cavalry. Sun Ben, Sun Hè: ready the first infantry charge, as I trained you," Sun Jian ordered. "Huang Gai: ready the archers. Cheng Pu: keep me informed of any suspicious activity."

Huang Zu ordered an infantry charge before Sun Jian's forces moved: Han Dang led the cavalry forward to blunt the charge, and then Sun Ben and Sun Hè led the infantry forward to pursue the retreat. Sun Jian had his battle gong sounded, and Han Dang, Sun Ben and Sun Hè stopped their pursuit once they reached the middle of the field; Huang Zu had his signalmen order his infantry to turn about, but Huang Gai ordered a volley of arrows to break that second charge. The outcome was definitive: Huang Zu ordered a retreat from the field, and his forces fell apart.

"**Pursue!**" Sun Jian ordered.

Cheng Pu glared at Sun Jian and said, "**Be mindful, Lord Sun!**"

"Mindful?" Sun Ce scoffed. "This is war!"

The official Lü Fan rode to Sun Ce's side and said, "Mister Cheng is right. Only give chase when they're-"

"In the open," Sun Ce groaned. "I got that hammered into me by Gongjin before we left! I know, okay, Ziheng...? **Let's collect some heads!**"

Sun Jian led an energetic and characteristically open charge, despite the warnings of the advisers; more of the disorganised defenders were hacked down, and Huang Zu was forced to retreat to the banks of the River Han. Sun Ce excelled in horseback combat during the rout, cutting down several men with his glaive and shooting others down with his bow: Sun Jian was filled with pride and left with a sense that his son was a worthy heir to his impressive legacy.

Huang Zu's forces crossed the River Han and took refuge in Xiangyang City with his disappointed master, Liu Biao.

"...Next time, I will be victorious," Huang Zu promised as he looked at the assembly of judgmental officials and Liu Biao himself.

"I hope so," Liu Biao replied dryly. "He's outside now. I really cannot see how you expect to keep the considerable influence that you have if you don't win next time... partly because I'd be forced to doubt your competence, but mainly because I'll lose the province!"

"Calm down, Governor," the adviser Kuai Liang pleaded. "Huang Zu was defeated because Sun Jian is one of the deadliest men of the era. He has one weakness, and that's his inability to avoid taking risks in heated moments. If we ambush him now, he'll take risks. Once he takes risks, we'll have him."

"I... I hope so," Liu Biao reiterated. He could imagine the screams and suffering of the people of Jing Province as Sun Jian laid siege to his capital, and he could imagine the grumbles and voices of dissent. If Sun Jian could not be defeated, Liu Biao knew that someone might throw the gates of the city open, and that Yuan Shu would take possession of his lands. A deep-rooted hatred for Sun Jian was unavoidable, because the man was the instrument of his destruction; he could feel no pity if he was killed, and he could have no inkling of the consequences that would arise from the responsibility for that assassination resting with him. At that moment, survival and the preservation of the independence of his domain was all that could matter, and Huang Zu's next actions would dictate everything.

The mood was optimistic in Sun Jian's encampment around the city of Xiangyang. There were smiles wreathed across most of the faces in the command tent as the commander studied his maps of

Jing Province and shook his head with disbelief.

"We're already close to victory," Sun Jian chuckled.

"Surely the acquisition of northern Jing will be enough to buy our way out from under the boot of Yuan Shu," Huang Gai suggested.

"Oh, that would be something," Sun Jian replied. "I'll be honest and say that I don't think he'd let me go after a victory like this; in fact, the better I do, the more I reckon that he'll want me to remain 'his'."

"Father, don't keep saying that!" Sun Ce pleaded. "Yes, you're his officer, but don't keep saying you're 'his'! It's demoralising!"

Sun Ce's words cut like a knife; Sun Jian's smile disappeared, and he said, "My son, you... you should try and understand the way of things. Whether I am 'his officer', 'his tiger', 'his subordinate', 'his lackey', or 'his whatever-else-you-want-to-call-me', there is a simple truth behind it all... I am 'his'. What I am defined as doesn't matter... I'm his."

Sun Ce exhaled noisily as an involuntary sign of frustration.

"...Huang Gai, Sun Ben, Sun Hè: procure materials to build a ram," Sun Jian ordered. "Han Dang, Zu Mao: prepare the divisions. We should make a show of preparing to siege the city: that will pressure our friend Huang Zu. Let's see if we can make him come out of the city and attack us."

The preparations for an attack lasted for two days, but Huang Zu did not venture out of the city: Cheng Pu started to suspect that his opposite number was up to something and had scouts reconnoitre at regular intervals.

"Well...?" Sun Jian asked as Cheng Pu entered the command tent to make an evening report.

"It... it might be a false alarm, but one of my scouts reports activity from the direction of Mount Xian," Cheng Pu replied.

"From Mount Xian...?" Sun Jian exclaimed. "Might they have sneaked out of the city and...?"

Cheng Pu was silent for a few moments before he said, "Huang Zu is desperate, so an attack from that way is a laboured attempt at an ambush to try and even the odds. We should let them think they've been successful in outflanking us; we can deal more damage that way."

"Very good!" Sun Jian said with laughter.

Sun Ce entered the command tent at that moment; he noticed his father's joyous expression and asked, "Has something good happened?"

"Get ready, Ce," Sun Jian replied. "Huang Zu is about to deliver his head to us!"

"...Be careful, Wentai," Cheng Pu said cautiously. "I know that look... I've seen it far too many times. Don't do anything daft."

"This is as straightforward as it gets, Demou!" Sun Jian retorted. "We should all prepare! Yes, we should get ready! Huang Zu dies now, and Liu Biao yields later! Heaven has dictated it!"

Cheng Pu observed the expressions of the father and son: their excitement and impatience was almost tangible. He sighed, turned, and left the tent.

Huang Zu's approach to Sun Jian's camp later that night was not challenged, but he did not suspect anything. The gates and the guard towers were manned, but visibility was poor and a sudden attack would breach the initial defences before any of the spotters could alert the sleeping commanders.

"...*Now!*" Huang Zu hissed; his small cavalry and 200-strong infantry neared the gates of the enemy camp as silently as they could. Once they were within striking range, Huang Zu bellowed, **"LEAVE NO ONE ALIVE!"**

The gate guards feigned panic and abandoned their posts; Huang Zu's screaming horde broke down the flimsy wooden gates and entered the camp, and the resistance amounted to little more than a few arrows that were being fired from the guard towers. But as Huang Zu reached an area beyond the gates, he halted his horse and gasped with horror: the path to the command tent was protected by a maze of palisades fashioned from sharpened logs. Huang Zu knew immediately that he had been tricked; he started a retreat, but Sun Jian, Sun Ce, Sun Hè, Cheng Pu, Huang Gai and Zu Mao led forces at him from all sides and decimated his small army. Huang Zu broke through the encirclement and escaped with his horsemen, but his infantry had no choices other than surrender or a fight to the death.

"**Wonderful!**" Sun Jian cackled. "**Truly wonderful! Huang Zu's head will not know his neck for much longer!**"

"**...Bloodlust is getting the better of you again, Wentai, and you mustn't let it! You promised that you wouldn't!**" Cheng Pu pleaded. "**We'd be better off getting Huang Zu to surrender, and then-!**"

"**He opposed us on the battlefield and tried to ambush us!**" Sun Jian retorted. "**He'll die, Cheng Demou, for the good of our cause!**"

Cheng Pu did not respond.

"**AFTER THEM!**" Sun Jian bellowed. "**FINISH HIM OFF!**"

"**No! Let him go!**" Cheng Pu protested. "**We have men to-!**"

Sun Jian ignored Cheng Pu's pleas and pursued Huang Zu with a group of cavalry.

"**Here we go again!**" Zu Mao chuckled as he rode after his reckless commander.

"**Not you as well, young lord!**" Cheng Pu barked as Sun Ce tried to follow his father.

"**You can't tell me what to do, old man!**" Sun Ce retorted.

"**Your father would kill me if I let you pursue him!**" Cheng Pu cried. "**He ordered you to guard the camp, and if you pursue him, you-!**"

"**Alright, *alright*!**" Sun Ce interrupted. "**I'll stay here, okay???** ...I'll stay here."

"...Why must he always do this???" Cheng Pu despaired as the sulking Sun Ce turned his horse and rode toward the command tent; Sun Hè followed Ce and tried to calm him down.

Huang Zu and his men fled toward Xiangyang City, but as they neared the edge of Sun Jian's swathe of smaller strategic encampments they were blocked by cavalry and infantry led by Sun Ben and Han Dang. Huang Zu's elite horsemen engaged the two officers, but the battle was pointless; Huang Zu detected Sun Jian's pursuing forces and ordered his men to go west, toward Mount Xian.

"Uncle, why are you here?" Sun Ben asked as Sun Jian stopped his horse in front of him. "I thought we were supposed to push him back towards the main camp!"

"I... ... ...*aiee*. Look, I'm here now, so let's go after him!" Sun Jian replied.

"Pursue him in near darkness to Mount Xian...?" Han Dang exclaimed. **"What sort of madness is that???"**

"He has to be killed!" Sun Jian retorted. **"Come on!"**

Sun Ben and Han Dang looked at Zu Mao, who said, **"I don't have a say, fellows. Let's just get this over with!"**

The four officers chased Huang Zu and his horsemen toward the uneven ground near Mount Xian, but Huang Zu had a small temporary encampment there, and the reserve forces were ready to defend it. Sun Ben and Han Dang became separated from Sun Jian and Zu Mao as the skirmish neared its end and the defenders scattered in all directions; Han Dang returned to the remains of the camp and waited patiently for the others to rendezvous.

"...Major Han!" Sun Ben cried as he brought his men back to the camp a short while later. **"Where is my uncle? Where is Zu Mao?"**

"I don't know, young master," Han Dang admitted.

"...Do we wait???" Sun Ben asked.

"That wouldn't be wise, young master," Han Dang replied. **"We might be ambushed if we stay here."**

Sun Ben sighed and said, **"But can we go back to the camp when-!"**

"He has done things like this before," Han Dang interrupted. **"He is a tiger... do not worry, young master. We should return to the camp and wait for them to return."**

Sun Ben looked to the west, where Mount Xian loomed.

"...We should go back to the camp," Han Dang insisted. **"Come on: Lord Sun will come back victorious, young master, as he always does."**

Sun Ben did not want to abandon his uncle, but Han Dang's words placated him; he nodded silently and ordered his men to begin the journey back to the main camp with a terse gesture.

"...Why must Wentai always worry us like this...?" Han Dang chuckled as he signalled his own retreat.

Cheng Pu, Sun Ce and Huang Gai were waiting at the gates of the main camp when what they supposed to be Sun Jian's pursuit force returned.

"...*Yigong*...?" Huang Gai exclaimed. "B-but... the lord...!"

"Wha-! ...Han Yigong, where is Lord Sun?" Cheng Pu asked. "Where is Wentai?"

"...He's gone on another of his chases," Han Dang grumbled.

"*Again*...?" Huang Gai complained. "I thought he said that he'd stop doing things like that! When did you lose sight of him?"

"We found an enemy camp to the east of the hills around the mountain," Han Dang replied.

"We should not have left him!" Sun Ben decided. "Han Dang, we should not have-!"

"Calm down," Han Dang pleaded. "Apart from the fact that you'll worry the young master needlessly, you'll look a fool when he comes back with Huang Zu's head."

"So what do we do now...?" Sun Ce asked.

"Young lord, your father is... he is a reckless man, sad to say," Cheng Pu replied. "But at the same time, he is a hero. In the past, he's done things like this and he's always come back as the victor. We always worry, but it's always needless, because he's a tiger. Let's just ensure that Liu Biao hasn't got any more tricks for us, and then we should get some rest. We'll probably be sieging Xiangyang tomorrow."

Sun Ce nodded silently and retreated to his personal tent; Sun Hè followed Ce once again to try and keep him calmed.

"You should go and rest as well," Cheng Pu said to the agitated Sun Ben.

"That's easier said than done, Mister Cheng!" Sun Ben suggested. "He's not just the spitting image of my father, or my father's brother... to me, he *is* my father now! He has given me shelter, raised me as his own son! He trusted me, and I left him to-!"

"That's enough of that," Cheng Pu insisted. "Young master Sun Ben, Wentai has been doing things like this for the last seven years! When he scaled the walls of Wan City alone to ruin the Yellow Turbans, our hearts were in our throats! When he disappeared after our defeat at Liangdong, we feared the worst! When he engaged Lü Bu near the tombs of the emperors, even the gods in Heaven held their breath! Every time, he came back... so please, go and rest! Such fretting is pointless."

Sun Ben conceded the point and retired to his personal tent.

"The rest of you: either rest or work, please," Cheng Pu said to the other officers and soldiers, who did as they were asked. Han Dang glanced at Cheng Pu as he passed him on the way to his own personal rest tent, but he said nothing.

"...Are you worried, Cheng Demou?" Huang Gai asked plainly.

"Naturally," Cheng Pu admitted. "But as I said to the young master... what has changed? Isn't this what he always puts us through...?"

Huang Gai smiled and said, "Now *I'm* a little less worried."

"Good: now help me find the same peace of mind!" Cheng Pu joked. "Oh, Huang Gongfu... he promised us that he'd never do this again. And to do this in front of his impressionable and unruly son, after all the complaints about his nature! When he returns, I shall scold him publicly."

Huang Gai agreed silently.

Dawn came, and Sun Jian did not return. The officers gathered at the gate and waited as the sun reached its full height in the sky.

"Where is he...?" Sun Ce fretted. "Mister Cheng, where is he?"

Cheng Pu frowned and said, "I don't know, young lord. We've got scouts out looking, that's all we can do."

"...He's got Zu Mao and some other good men with him," Huang Gai said reassuringly. "And he's very capable, so I'm sure he'll be back soon."

But Han Dang looked into Huang Gai's eyes and saw his true feelings clearly.

"We... we must be *patient*," Cheng Pu insisted.

Sun Ce looked at his cousin Sun Ben and said, "Can't *we* go and look...?"

"*No*, Bofu," Sun Ben insisted. "We should be patient, as Mister

Cheng has said. Uncle is as clever as he is courageous... he'll be back soon. Come on... let's go and play chess, or something."
"Yeah, that's just what I need right now... getting beat at chess," Sun Ce grumbled as he followed Sun Ben's retreat from the gates. "Can't we play something easier?"
"...The young masters are showing enviable stoicism," Cheng Pu chuckled miserably. "I am not finding this easy, even after the countless times that we've done this before."
"As you confess, don't we *always* do this when he doesn't come back?" Han Dang chortled. "So why are you two acting like this...? Demou, Gongfu, why are you being so morbid?"
Cheng Pu and Huang Gai could not answer; both men feared the worst for reasons that they could not explain or justify, but they knew that they had to be optimistic nonetheless.

****

Two days passed, and Sun Jian had still failed to return from pursuing Liu Biao's ally Huang Zu into the hills below Mount Xian. Cheng Pu gathered the officials in the command tent, where the mood was souring.

"He's out there somewhere, and we have to look for him," Sun Ben demanded.

"...We cannot risk it, not while the camp is at risk of attack by Liu Biao," Cheng Pu replied wearily. "Young Master, we-"

"I'm Acting Commander while Uncle is away," Sun Ben said suddenly.

"...Are you serious...?" Sun Ce chortled. "Cousin, that's ridiculous! I might as well be commander, then, since I'm his eldest son and-!"

"I'm the son of Commander Sun's twin brother, and since I was taken into your household, I have become the eldest man when your father is absent," Sun Ben declared. "He left me to be the acting head of the household when he went on campaign before, I served with him when he marched to Luoyang, and-"

"That was before!" Sun Ce heckled. "I'm older now, and besides, we-!"

"And I am older too!" Sun Ben interrupted. "No matter how much older you get, I'll always be three years older than you! And that means that-!"

"Forgive me, young masters, but this isn't a useful conversation," Cheng Pu suggested. "In military matters, Commander Sun always sought my guidance or Zhu Zhi's, and it is my conclusion that we cannot move while a direct attack is imminent. We must await Commander Sun's return."

"And if he *doesn't return*, what then...?" Sun Ben asked plainly.

"...You apologise *now*, Cousin," Sun Ce growled emotionally.

"Sorry, but this is important," Sun Ben said with tears in his eyes. "Bofu, I don't want to think about that any more than you do, but we *have to*! We-!"

"MASTER CHENG! MASTER CHENG!"

All eyes turned to a battered, bloodied soldier whose crazed, distressed eyes said more than any words: he was scrabbling into the tent as though he were trying to ascend a steep hill.

"...Oh no," Huang Gai whispered.

"Master Cheng!" the soldier sobbed. **"Commander Sun, he...! He...!"**

Sun Ben bit his hand; Sun Ce crouched to meet the soldier's gaze and said, "Please, he's my father; tell me he's alive."

The soldier's response was to hang his head and wail; Sun Ce stood up, snorted loudly, and stormed out of the tent.

"Someone go after him, for Heaven's sake," Cheng Pu croaked as he wiped tears from his eyes.

Sun Ben did not move; Sun Hè fought his own grief as he followed Sun Ce.

"We... we need to know," Huang Gai pleaded as he knelt by the soldier. "Tell us... tell us what happened."

The soldier tried to reply, but his babbling was close to incoherent; Cheng Pu nodded at Han Dang, who escorted the distressed man out of the tent. Huang Gai remained in his

kneeling position and had to be helped to his feet by Cheng Pu.
"Somewhere in there, I heard something about the enemy taking... taking his body, after... after whatever happened," Cheng Pu said with difficulty. "We'll need to... to negotiate now, to get him back."
"*Negotiate*?" Huang Gai said with disdain. "If I had my way, I'd-!"
"If I had mine, we'd level Xiangyang and kill every man in there, but that isn't an option now," Cheng Pu insisted. "Mister Huan Jie...?"
The politician Huan Jie awaited his obvious instructions.
"...You will go to Liu Biao, and negotiate the terms of... of whatever we're supposed to call this," Cheng Pu said half-heartedly. "We... *oh, I don't believe I'm going to say this...* we'll exchange the body of our lord Sun Jian for... for a full withdrawal to Yu Province."
Huan Jie frowned and said, "And Lord Yuan...? Shouldn't he be notified, and shouldn't we ascertain his wishes before we negotiate...?"
Huang Gai glared at Huan Jie and said, "Mister Huan, you-!"
"I appreciate that you are trying to foresee potential disagreements, Mister Huan, but right now we have lost our tiger, our emblem, our lord, our friend, and the one thing that the men of Jing have been scared of up until now," Cheng Pu interrupted as he placed a supportive hand on Huang Gai's arm. "Lord Yuan will know that, and he would not suggest our staying here."
"You're probably right," Huan Jie supposed.
"I'm certain that I am, so please follow my orders and save us further humiliation or injury by Liu Biao," Cheng Pu said calmly.
"I will do all that I can," Huan Jie promised.
"Go now," Cheng Pu ordered. "We should not be without his presence for a second longer than we have to be."
As Huan Jie hurried out of the command tent, Sun Ben finally regained some of his composure and said, "We'll go back to Yuan Shu. We... we shouldn't stay here."
Cheng Pu nodded slowly. Everyone agreed, in fact; without their lord, morale was non-existent, and the day was as good as lost.

Liu Biao did all that he could to hide his satisfaction at the sight of Huan Jie all but begging for the return of Sun Jian's corpse; Huang Zu smiled unashamedly throughout the southern official's petition.
"And so I conclude by saying that I can only hope that you have a shred of decency when considering the family of the 'Tiger of Jiangdong', Sun Jian of Fuchun, whose name has been legend for the last seven years," Huan Jie said theatrically. "The decision is now in your venerable hands, Governor Liu."
"What will you do, Governor?" Huang Zu asked rudely.
"...They can have their commander's body back, along with any others that were recovered after the event," Liu Biao decided. "All I ask is that the siege of my northern capital end, which you have promised. The relief of this place is a fine exchange for something that is useless to me. Huan Jie, your terms will be met."
"Thank you, Governor," Huan Jie replied.
Kuai Liang leant closer to Liu Biao, whispered something in his ear and stood upright once again with a slight smile on his face.
"...Your persuasive skills have impressed me, Mister Huan," Liu Biao continued. "Would you consider working for me...?"

188

Huan Jie weighed the situation and bowed humbly, saying, "If my working for you is a desired outcome of this situation, then I would be glad to oblige."

Liu Biao laughed and said, "A wily answer! I'll certainly benefit from your service!"

Huan Jie returned to the command tent of the encampment around Xiangyang City to report the outcome of the meeting to his superiors; Sun Ce was livid at the idea of retreating and made it known as soon as Huan Jie stopped speaking.

"I truly understand and share your pain, young master," Cheng Pu promised. "But-"

"I'm not leaving!" Sun Ce barked. **"The bastards killed my father! I won't leave this place until they're all dead!"**

"We can't do anything," Sun Ben protested.

"Shame on you, Cousin," Sun Ce retorted. "My father trusted you to be his spirit in his absence! Now he's dead, and you want to run away? When did *he* ever run???"

Sun Ben scowled and said, "You're being unfair, Bofu! I-!"

"How cruel is Heaven that you look more like him than I do! That's cruel and wrong! Bohai is more of a 'Sun' than you!" Sun Ce heckled as he gestured toward Sun Hè, who was sobered by the reminder that he was part of the Yu clan and yet so accepted as a Sun. Sun Ce was not finished; he pointed at his cousin Ben as he added, **"Yu Hè deserves to have that name more than you, you craven-!"**

"*Enough*, Bofu," Sun Hè said sadly; he then turned to Sun Ben and said, "Boyang, I agree with Bofu so far as retreating is concerned; I don't agree that you are 'craven', having seen you in battle, but-"

"The men are demoralised, Bohai, and we'll lose now," Sun Ben interrupted. "I'm as upset as either of you, but we have to retreat!"

"The dogs of Jing will never know peace as long as I'm alive," Sun Ce promised as he turned and left the command tent.

"I shall go with him," Sun Hè said as he turned and followed Sun Ce yet again.

Cheng Pu sighed miserably and said, "Huan Jie has done well. We'll collect the fallen from our enemies, and then we'll retreat."

"I shall return to Liu Biao and inform him of your decision," Huan Jie said silkily; Cheng Pu nodded respectfully, and after a bow to all of his colleagues, Huan Jie retreated from the tent.

"...And that's the last we'll see of that snake in the grass," Han Dang grumbled.

"Don't judge him too harshly: there's no point," Cheng Pu said. "He's a politician; he's doing what his politician's instincts tell him to be appropriate. Where is Yuan Shu now, Gongfu...?"

"On his way to Wan City in Nan County," Huang Gai replied.

"He's still coming here to Jing?" Han Dang exclaimed.

"That won't help, of course," Cheng Pu fretted. "I can only hope that we can retrieve our fallen comrades and retreat before Yuan Shu occupies Wan, or we'll be attacked."

"Bastard!" Han Dang cried. "Does he not know what's happened?"

"He knows," Huang Gai replied irritably.

Sun Ce and Sun Hè sat opposite one-another in the former's personal tent.

"...I did not mean to call you 'Yu Hè'," Sun Ce insisted. "Well, I mean, I did, but I meant that-"

"I know what you meant," Sun Hè promised.

"...Your brother's little boy is doing well," Sun Ce said gratefully. "S'funny, thinking about it all... I'm yet to get married, and when I see your boy, and your brother's boy... I suppose that's how Dad felt..."

Sun Ce's contorted expression betrayed the total despair that consumed him.

"...Your father was so good to me," Sun Hè said. "He brought me into your family home, gave me a purpose... in many ways, he is my father too."

"**It's not fair!**" Sun Ce shrieked. "**It's not right! How can he be dead, Bohai???** *How*...? How can he be...?"

Sun Ce fell forward, covered his head with his hands, and howled like an animal as he rocked back and forth; Sun Hè wanted to comfort his cousin, but he was overcome with grief as well, and he cried pitifully. The young official Lü Fan watched from the entrance, but he did not make the Suns aware of his presence; he retreated silently instead, and awaited a better moment to proffer some essential advice.

A day later, Liu Biao's men arrived on two cavalry-escorted ox-drawn carts that were carrying stacked wooden coffins. The Jing soldiers were visibly enjoying the grief of their southern enemies, and no false show of sympathy was made as they dumped the coffins on the ground in front of the camp and retreated a short distance with their weapons readied.

"...No attempt has been made to distinguish one man from another!" Sun Ben despaired as he stared at the tens of cheap, plain, identical boxes.

"...I will check them," Cheng Pu replied. "If you wish to retire, young lord... do so."

"No," Sun Ben insisted. "I am Acting Commander. I must stay and show strength."

"What... what about you, young master?" Cheng Pu asked.

"I'll stay, but I can't look," Sun Ce replied as he glared at the Jing soldiers with a feeling that he had never experienced before: unfettered hatred.

"...Right," Cheng Pu said bravely.

"I shall aid you," Huang Gai said emotionally.

"Me n'all," Han Dang declared with a cracking voice.

The three surviving members of Sun Jian's original group of volunteers examined each box in turn while Sun Ben, Sun Ce, Sun Hè and the junior officers looked on in despair. They found Sun Jian and Zu Mao within twenty examinations, and they also found volunteers from their home regions that they recognised and knew by name; they insisted on checking every casket, and at the end of the ordeal, they were all broken men.

"Oh, this is unfair," Cheng Pu rasped as he clung onto Sun Jian's tatty, dirtied scarf with both hands and tried to supress a flood of tears. "This is... *so unfair*."

"I had so hoped... that it wasn't true...!" Han Dang groaned.

"We've done our checks! You can go now!" Huang Gai barked at the audience of self-satisfied Jing soldiers.

"And *you*...?" the Jing cavalry captain heckled. **"Will *you* go now?"**

Sun Hè was forced to restrain Sun Ce.

"Yes we will!" Cheng Pu cried. **"We gave our word, so of course we will!"**

The Jing troops turned their ox-drawn carts and began the retreat into the city of Xiangyang while Cheng Pu turned to his fellow officers and said, **"The handover is done. Now we must-"**

"I shall take over now, Major Cheng," the 19-year-old Sun Ben suggested; Cheng Pu exhaled noisily and stood aside so that Sun Ben could continue. Sun Ben looked at the demoralised officers and said, **"As Acting Commander, I now order a full retreat. We will go to Yuan Shu, and we will ensure that he knows that we are still his vassals, so that our retreat from Xiangyang is not mistaken for something else. All of you go about your duties: we haven't a moment to lose."**

The majority of the officers dispersed to begin the process of dismantling their camp; Cheng Pu, Huang Gai, Han Dang, Sun Ce and Sun Hè remained to oversee the respectful movement of the coffins. As the work proceeded, Huang Gai and Han Dang touched the scarf in Cheng Pu's hands and tried to find solace in its presence.

"Such disrespect," Sun Ben complained. "They put Uncle in a cheap, unmarked box just like everyone else. He was treated just like the rest."

"It's... what he would have wanted," Cheng Pu suggested.

"...True," Sun Ben conceded. He then turned to the angry Sun Ce and said, "Please don't be angry with me, Bofu; I am doing what must be done. Uncle insisted that I should take charge if something happened, because he was worried that if I didn't, that you would-"

"I know that," Sun Ce interrupted. "I... I get it. Now let's just get this over with."

Cheng Pu suddenly walked to Sun Ce and offered him the red scarf: Ce moved to touch it, but he could not. Cheng Pu forced the scarf into the young man's hands, smiled sadly, and returned to his friends: Sun Ce studied the scarf, stared at the sky, and sobbed silently.

"...Now he must grieve," Cheng Pu said quietly. "Later, then, he can – must – be angry... because we're not done here."

Huang Gai and Han Dang silently agreed.

****

32

The Sun family army broke camp and began a gruelling, lifeless journey to the northeast by water; as they sailed upriver toward Nan County and the Yu-Jing border, Cai Mao's naval forces provided a slow-moving, ominous rear escort. They disembarked at a point where Nan County met the border with Yu Province and prepared to split into groups while Cai Mao's navy finally withdrew.

"I shall take the army to Yuan Shu," Sun Ben said. "Bofu, you shall escort the fallen home to Yang Province."

"...I want to see Yuan Shu," Sun Ce insisted.

"He won't want to see you," Sun Ben retorted.

"Too bad," Sun Ce scoffed. "He sent my father to his death, so the least he can do is give me his time."

"He won't see it like that," Sun Ben protested. "And you cannot confront him!"

"I don't intend to," Sun Ce promised. "There's something that I want to ask him."

"Your duty is to return home with your father!" Sun Ben said emotionally. "I cannot, Bofu, so please don't make me disrespect him further by-!"

"...Alright," Sun Ce conceded. "You're right... you're right. Sorry. But I'll go with you and take care of the camp while you see him. Let me do *that*."

Sun Ben sighed and said, "If you must insist, Bofu: Cheng Pu can come as well. Huang Gai, Sun Hè: continue preparations."

Sun Ce looked at Cheng Pu and said, "You're going to keep an eye on me, then."

"Apparently," Cheng Pu replied unenthusiastically.

Yuan Shu was only a day's march away from Wan City, the seat of power in Nan County; he reluctantly agreed to meet Sun Ben, who approached him quietly.

"...A tiger cub, indeed," Yuan Shu whispered as he stared at the youth, who wore white mourning garments under his armour and a white turban under his helmet.

Sun Ben stopped and bowed respectfully when he was a few paces away from his lord; the officials that surrounded him had as little or less respect for him as they had for Sun Jian and they expressed that in no better way than the total absence of white or colourless articles.

"Speak, then," Yuan Shu prompted.

"I, Ben, have come here as Acting Commander to pledge allegiance to you, Lord Yuan, and to bring with me the army of my late lord, Sun Jian," Sun Ben declared.

"...Very good," Yuan Shu replied tonelessly. "Thank you, Sun Ben, for returning my army to me. It is a shame that no man of talent could hold that army together and continue your campaign in Xiangyang, but if it was a lost cause... so be it. Perhaps I will find a man to finish the campaign one day."

Sun Ben smiled and bowed, but he was privately angry.

"You'll inherit the position of 'Inspector of Yu Province' until or unless a more fitting replacement appears," Yuan Shu added dismissively.

"I thank you, Lord Yuan," Sun Ben replied.

"So you should, boy," Yuan Shu chortled. "Your relative Wu Jing… I can't be bothered to work out what he is to you… the point is that I made him Administrator of Danyang, but he doesn't seem to be doing anything to take the place. Kindly leave long-term mourning to immediate family and help Wu Jing. Tell him that I want the place taken *quickly*, or I will appoint someone else. Is that clear?"

"…It is, Lord Yuan," Sun Ben replied hoarsely.

"Very good," Yuan Shu said. "Other than that, I have nothing more to say for now: you may go as well, 'Inspector Sun'."

Sun Ben bowed low, turned his gaze to each and every one of the irreverent officials that he was surrounded by, and left the tent with far less self-esteem than he had brought with him, despite his unexpected promotion.

"…My Jing campaign has faltered," Yuan Shu complained. "The loss of Sun Jian is a definite setback. The seriousness of his loss must be kept from my enemies for as long as possible: my brother-cousin Shao is fighting Gongsun Zan at the moment, but Cao Cao is only a border away in Yan, to the east; and Dong Zhuo's officers are still active around Luoyang to the north. Sun Jian kept them from my door; his progeny must continue to do so for as long as possible."

Yuan Shu's officials voiced their agreement.

Sun Ce's reaction to Sun Ben's account of the meeting was expected and understood by all.

"**Bastard!**" Sun Ce cried. "I'll-!"

"You'll… you'll do what I did, Bofu: nothing," Sun Ben ordered. "I hate him as much as you do, but he is our master."

"I can't do this," Sun Ce moaned. "Father must have wanted to die rather than be treated like this anymore!"

Cheng Pu exhaled noisily.

"…I have my orders," Sun Ben said calmly. "In a way, you have yours: you'll mourn him, and I'll carry on his legacy until you're ready to."

"I swear to you, all of you, that I will not die a vassal of that man as my father did," Sun Ce declared. "I swear that before any mission that man gives me, I have one: escaping him, and if possible, harming him as he's harmed us."

Lü Fan watched and listened, but he would not speak yet: his words would need to be understood as well as heard, and Sun Ce was still too angry.

The procession passed through Runan in Yu Province: many towns and villages sent people to the roadside to pay respects, and there was barely a moment of the journey where at least one mourner looked on and sobbed as though they were a relative. One surprise came in the form of the former Yellow Turban Liu Pi, who was now a vassal of Yuan Shu: he had a large contingent of his saboteur-militia escort their old enemies for some of the journey and chant words of respect for the man that had once pacified them, and they did so while wearing white turbans and shirts.

But when the procession reached western Lujiang Prefecture, the mood changed.

"...The Administrator, Lu Kang, has... has sent no one to represent him," Cheng Pu said quietly.

"Petty man!" Huang Gai hissed as he watched the oblivious Sun Ce greeting the gathering of civilian mourners. "Even if he views us as vassals of a traitor, the man is dead! Showing no respect to a live 'crony' is one thing, but-!"

"Don't speak too loudly," Cheng Pu implored. "Our late lord's young heir has a fiery temper. Let's not set him on a regrettable path after we did so much to stop him attacking our master."

"...This is unforgiveable!" Huang Gai insisted.

"Yuan Shu harasses Lu Kang regularly, refusing his requests to remain neutral," Cheng Pu recalled. "Sooner or later, Yuan Shu will attack Lu Kang for his stubbornness, and Lu Kang knows it. We might be asked to do it, and Lu Kang knows that too."

Huang Gai nodded sombrely.

"And worse yet, we'll do it; he knows that as well," Cheng Pu continued. "We'll have no choice other than to break the bond between lord and vassal and be accused of wretchedness. Because by betraying Yuan Shu, we betray the brother of our enemy, and we know how these lords often act like madmen."

"...I yearn for simpler times," Huang Gai admitted.

"I think we all do," Cheng Pu replied. "Simpler, saner times, when men like Wentai were invincible, because they were tigers that ran free: how can a shackled tiger truly hope to fight an enemy that can move at will? This was inevitable from the moment we pledged allegiance to that wretched Yuan Shu... the only surprise, sad to say, was that he survived as long as he did."

Huang Gai agreed silently.

Zhou Yu and his magistrate father were part of the civilian gathering: Sun Ce stared at his friend with weary, near-lifeless eyes and smiled feebly.

"...I cannot help him," Zhou Yu whispered.

"A sad day," Magistrate Zhou croaked. "A waste: an awful, terrible waste."

Sun Ce turned suddenly and advanced toward his father's vassals.

"Please let him want something other than what I suspect," Cheng Pu whispered.

Sun Ce stopped in front of Cheng Pu, Huang Gai and Han Dang.

"...Young Master Sun...?" Huang Gai prompted.

"I must speak with Administrator Lu," Sun Ce decided. "My father used to speak to him: I need to speak with now, and-"

"We should hurry onward," Cheng Pu suggested.

"...Father was hesitant about stopping here before he- ...Before we went to Jing," Sun Ce recalled. "What am I unaware of...?"

"...Seek an audience if you must," Cheng Pu replied.

Sun Ce travelled to Lu Kang's office in the prefectural capital, Huancheng City: he was greeted at the door by a low-level clerk that told him to wait while he alerted his superiors. The clerk then hurried to Lu Kang and told him of the new arrival.

"...'Sun Ce, son of Sun Jian'?" Lu Kang scoffed. "I have no time for the famous father; why would I have time for the unknown son?"

"Sun Jian is dead," the junior official replied. "The-"

"I am well aware that he is dead," Lu Kang interrupted.

"Furthermore, I am aware of *how* he died, and what a pitiful end for a man that once seemed not only invincible but incorruptible. That former hero of the age is now just another rebel and bandit, another invader of territories that has died serving an enemy of Heaven that repeatedly demands that I open our grain stores and our treasury to supply his private war with his own cousin while his emperor is a hostage in Chang'an! *Never* will I bend at the knee to such a fool, and *never* will I show respect to a man that does his dirty work without conscience!"

"...So I should rebuke him, then...?" the official asked nervously.

"...Have Registrar Wang entertain him," Lu Kang replied. "Tell him I'm too busy with urgent affairs of state to see him right now."

"...As you wish," the official said apprehensively.

Sun Ce was almost overcome with rage when a registrar appeared, bowed ever-so-slightly and said in a condescending drawl, "Administrator Lu is too busy to meet you, Mister Sun. Will you please follow me?"

"...Yes," Sun Ce replied through gritted teeth.

An hour later, Sun Ce recounted the visit to Lu Kang to an unsurprised Sun Hè.

"...I am the son of General Sun Jian, not some nobody!" Sun Ce said angrily. "I had to sit in the hall with that-!"

"You already told me that, Bofu!" Sun Hè interrupted. "Calm down."

"...For close to an *hour*, he left me with that man, and then I had to leave, like I was a worthless nuisance!" Sun Ce continued. "*Damn* that Lu Kang! How dare that smug, arrogant-!"

"Lu Kang is going senile," Sun Hè insisted. "He's like many men that start off well enough and become something else: he's delusional, lofty, and destined to suffer a terrible end. Let it go."

"...I have no choice, I know that," Sun Ce said bitterly. "But I won't forget him being rude to me; one day I intend to demand an apology."

"I don't doubt it," Sun Hè sighed.

The procession continued on its way to the Yangtze River, where a large boat or ship would be required to take the coffins – filled or otherwise – of the fallen across. The march stopped at a port city and a temporary camp was created for the militiamen while a river crossing was arranged: that evening, Sun Ce sat in his personal tent and looked over his father's military documents with a newfound understanding of the magnitude of what he had chosen to do. He was lost in one of his father's personal journals when Lü Fan entered the tent and bowed humbly.

"...Ziheng...?" Sun Ce asked.

"Yuan Shu's sent a former colleague of mine to inform you that your father's funeral will receive 'adequate representation'," Lü Fan replied. "However, I'd not expect too much."

Sun Ce smiled and said, "You're always honest, Ziheng: I like that honesty, and I need it."

"I'd not insult your intelligence by being anything else, Lord Sun," Lü Fan replied.

Cheng Pu entered the command tent and pushed Lü Fan aside.

"Hey! Don't be rude to Ziheng!" Sun Ce exclaimed.

"...*Ziheng*...?" Cheng Pu said as he looked at Lü Fan. "Sorry, I thought you were some pedant messenger from Yuan Shu's court that had come to gloat and make more empty promises, not a friend of Lord Sun."

"Alas, you're more correct than wrong when you presume my presence here," Lü Fan sighed. "But I assure you, Mister Cheng, that I only deliver the empty promises of others with rank."

It was Cheng Pu's turn to laugh involuntarily before he said, "I like your honesty. Where are you from originally? Your accent suggests Yu Province, perhaps Runan."

"And you would be completely correct," Lü Fan replied. "I know you because of your appearance; the people of Runan all speak of the hero Sun Jian's handsome and courageous strategist Cheng Pu, because your work against the Yellow Turbans there saved many lives and gave them peace."

"Who'd've thought we'd have such a reputation!" Cheng Pu said with surprise. "So were you seconded to us?"

"He was in a really low role, but he's with me now," Sun Ce explained.

"And very gratefully so," Lü Fan said.

Cheng Pu frowned and asked, "How under Heaven did a man as astute as you obviously are come to serve Yuan Shu in such a pitiful capacity?"

"...Fate," Lü Fan replied dryly. "As I said to Mister Sun, men are placed and they live accordingly... like pieces on a chessboard."

"You play chess?" Cheng Pu prompted.

"I do," Lü Fan replied. "And now that you've asked, I'd like an opportunity to demonstrate something, if I may. Lord Sun, might you humour me with a game?"

"...I *hate chess*," Sun Ce muttered.

"All the same, I would like to challenge you," Lü Fan insisted.

The game of *weiqi* was similar to European chess in many respects, including a need to rely heavily on strategy and careful planning. Sun Ce reluctantly accepted Lü Fan's challenge and allowed Cheng Pu to set the board up on his writing desk. Once the pieces were in place, Lü Fan bowed humbly and said, "Please make the first move, Lord Sun."

Sun Ce scratched his head as he looked at the small white pieces that he was ultimately responsible for. Eventually, he moved one piece forward; Cheng Pu smiled, as he considered the move to be fairly acceptable for a man that did not play.

"A terrible opening move," Lü Fan sighed.

"Oh," Sun Ce murmured.

Cheng Pu frowned, pointed at Lü Fan and screamed, "**Pedant! He freshly mourns for his father, you-!**"

"He's not a pedant, Demou," Sun Ce interrupted. "Ziheng, make your point."

"Let me explain," Lü Fan said. "All things are similar in ways that are not immediately clear. In some ways, we are all like the pieces on this board. None of us, Lord Sun, would want to be the one that you just moved."

"I thought I'd done well," Sun Ce said miserably.

"In some ways, yes," Lü Fan replied. "But when a man wants to reach the greatest heights, 'well' is not enough. Some players look to win by any means, and accept the loss of pieces as necessity,

196

like Yuan Shu; others look to preserving as many of their pieces as possible, as though they might play another game with what they have left, because in real life, taken pieces stay taken."

"...Like my father," Sun Ce said weakly.

"I can demonstrate to you that you will lose many pieces, and you will not win, based off of this first move," Lü Fan continued. "You were impatient, and that is always unwise in a game where one must always look ahead; I have seen the entire game from start to finish, based on what you've done, and I can talk you through it if you wish."

"If you've won already, why bother?" Sun Ce complained.

"...Because you'll never learn," Lü Fan replied. "Isn't that right, Mister Cheng?"

Cheng Pu smiled and said, "It is, Lü Ziheng. Kindly continue for both of our sakes; I have much to learn as well, it seems."

Lü Fan smiled, bowed humbly, and said, "I am nothing special. But if I can lend my talent to a worthy master, I do so gladly. Shall we...?"

Sun Ce and Cheng Pu were left surprised and impressed as Lü Fan continued the game, guessing Sun Ce's side of the game with accuracy that left no doubt of his incredible gifts of analysis and foresight. Sun Ce was always aware that the game of *weiqi* was being used to demonstrate Lü Fan's ability as a strategist, and he had done so effortlessly.

Even with his death at the unfortunately young age of 37, Sun Jian of Fuchun would serve as a figure of fear for his enemies and a beacon of hope to his allies. The question was whether any of his children or his relatives could be as great as a man that had done more in 7 years than most had managed in 70; time would tell. For now, Sun Ce had to lead official mourning for the great patriarch of the family, a man who was arguably the first of the founders of what was to come.

****

33

Once the river crossing had been made, Sun Jian's eldest son Sun Ce and Sun Ben, Jian's nephew, led a slow procession along the roads that led to the city of Qu'e in Wu Prefecture, Yang Province. Word had already reached Lady Wu and the rest of Sun Jian's family, and it had left them without hope for the future. Upon arrival in Qu'e, Sun Ce had his father's coffin placed in his uncle Wu Jing's home in the city, and days of tearful lament were carried out by friends and family, who – as ritual demanded – pleaded with the lifeless casket for Sun Jian to have even one more day on the earth. That, of course, would never happen. The city was a sea of white garments as friends, family and admirers came from all corners of the nation to pay their respects to a man that had a unique place in recent history.

One young man that had come to pay his respects was Xu Kun, whose mother was Sun Jian's sister; Sun Ce, Sun Ben and Wu Jing met him at the entrance of the hall and led him to the raised coffin, where the adopted Sun Hè, Sun Ben's younger brother Fu, Sun Jian's younger children and Ladies Wu and Chen were already knelt and sobbing.

"I had wanted to help my uncle," Xu Kun said as he ran his hand down the front of the casket. "Bofu, if I can help at all when mourning is over, you must call on me."

"*Ayah*... another one with bloodlust," Wu Jing complained.

"This is our entire family's fight," Xu Kun retorted. He then turned to Sun Ce and said, "I mean it, Bofu: when you're ready..."

Sun Ce sighed woefully and replied, "Talk to 'Boyang'. He's the head of the clan."

Sun Ben exhaled noisily to show his frustration and despair.

"Come and mourn your father, Ce," Lady Wu said.

Sun Jian's younger brother Jing entered the hall at that moment; his two eldest sons, who were only boys, followed him silently.

"My brother...!" Sun Jing gasped as he saw the coffin and the enormity of the loss overwhelmed him. "Wentai... *Wentai*...!"

Sun Ce stared at Sun Jing and trembled involuntarily at the sight of a man that looked enough like his father at a distance to fool almost anybody; Sun Jing lowered his head and wept bitterly.

Xu Kun scowled angrily and said, "Liu Biao cannot be allowed to-!"

"Not here... not now," Sun Ben pleaded.

Xu Kun agreed, and the mourners focussed their energies on wailing and pining for Sun Jian once again.

Sun Ce had family throughout the region; some were in Guangling, a prefecture that was under the jurisdiction of the Governor of Xu Province, Tao Qian. Sun Ce decided that his new friend Lü Fan could be trusted with the task of retrieving them, so Ce summoned him to make the request. Sun Ben and Sun Hè waited for Lü Fan's arrival and observed Sun Ce with cynicism.

"You'd trust this agent of Yuan Shu so readily...?" Sun Ben said with surprise. "Mister Cheng tells me this man just sauntered into your tent and beat you at chess after you'd just found that... *that*...! How is that the basis for friendship???"

"He's honest," Sun Ce retorted. "You get feelings about people,

Boyang. It was the same when I first met Zhou Gongjin. Lü Ziheng's a good man, and I trust him."

"Zhu Zhi approached Uncle in much the same way," Sun Hè said.

"No he didn't," Sun Ben scoffed. "Zhu Zhi was known to Uncle, and he approached with advice for an active campaign; this pedant Lü Fan approached a grieving son and used his sly ways to get himself a good job!"

"What job?" Sun Ce chortled. "You're the head of the clan at the moment, Boyang, not me. He wanted to escape from Yuan Shu, just like we do. And I knew him *before* the chess game."

"...I just hope you're sure," Sun Ben muttered as Lü Fan entered the room and bowed respectfully to each of the three Suns.

"Ziheng, I'd like you to fetch some of my family from Guangling," Sun Ce said plainly. "Do you mind?"

"I'm honoured that you trust me," Lü Fan replied. "I shall treat them as though they were my own kin, Lord Sun."

"*Bofu*," Sun Ce pleaded. "Call me *Bofu*, Lü Ziheng!"

Lü Fan kowtowed and said, "You are far too kind to me."

"Stop it!" Sun Ce groaned. "You're my *friend*, Ziheng!"

"...All the same, you are too kind," Lü Fan said as he got to his feet. "Tell me where I must go, and I will go there and retrieve your family at once."

While Lü Fan began his mission, the former vassals of the deceased were having a reunion in this most unwanted of circumstances.

"Junli...!" Cheng Pu exclaimed; he rushed to greet Zhu Zhi as he entered the Wu family residence. "*Junli*...!" Cheng Pu said again as he grasped the smaller man's shoulders; Zhu Zhi was smiling strangely, and he seemed to be mute.

"Don't blame yourself for this, Zhu Junli," Huang Gai suggested as he approached Zhu Zhi and guessed the cause of his silence.

"...How can I *not*...?" Zhu Zhi croaked. "I left him to go to-!"

"He ordered you to go to Xu Province," Cheng Pu interrupted. "Now, to steer the conversation in a more constructive direction... how did that go...?"

"I won't be going back," Zhu Zhi replied. "Tao Qian was kind enough to write to the capital to praise me for my work in Xu Province, so the Grand Tutor, Ma Midi, petitioned the court and had me promoted to a Commandant here in Wu Prefecture."

"A fine promotion indeed," Cheng Pu sighed.

"Wu Jing will be Administrator of Danyang if he takes the place," Zhu Zhi noted.

"I wonder what the future holds," Cheng Pu said glumly. "I have a choice to be a vassal of young Sun Ben, who is, in turn, a vassal of *Yuan Shu*."

"So do I," Huang Gai grumbled.

"And me," Han Dang said with as much irritation as his peers. "I could stomach it before, but... but now, without Wentai, I don't honestly know."

"I've said that I've retired," Cheng Pu admitted. "I'll probably go home if Sun Ben remains as the head of the clan."

Huang Gai and Han Dang nodded agreeably.

After a long silence, Zhu Zhi asked, "About Wentai... How...? What *happened*...?"

Han Dang scratched his head and said, "We were all separated after Huang Zu tried an ambush. He went after him into the hills around Mount Xian, with Zu Mao and I don't know... a few riders, maybe twenty, thirty...? ...It weren't enough, anyway, the lot that he took."

"He could have had a *million men* with him, for all that it mattered," Cheng Pu insisted. "What happened had nothing to do with how many men he had with him, Yigong."

Han Dang shook his head and cried, "**But a million could've chased that cowardly bastard Huang Zu down after he...!**"

"...So he was ambushed, then," Zhu Zhi sighed. "How many times did that man ride needlessly into danger...? ...And yet every time, he returned. How sad that the fates made him lucky so many times, and then... so what was it...? Arrows...?"

Cheng Pu shrugged and replied, "We have very little information. He had an arrow in him, but he was... very badly injured otherwise. Does it *matter*, Zhu Junli...?"

"I suppose not," Zhu Zhi conceded. "How a hero dies doesn't matter; the world's still a poorer place for it." After another short silence, Zhu Zhi asked, "What would you all do if Sun Ce took charge of the army?"

"If he is what I suspect... I'd follow him," Cheng Pu replied.

"Same here," Han Dang said.

"I'd follow him too," Huang Gai admitted.

"Well," Zhu Zhi sighed, "what we must do, gentlemen, is wait..."

Sun Ce and Sun Ben were forced to discuss the future of their clan on several occasions, despite the main emphasis being the mourning period. Sun Ce ended one day of debate and returned to his room, where he was confronted by his mother, Lady Wu.

"How are you, Mother...?" Sun Ce asked.

"...'Mother'...!" Lady Wu said with forced laughter. "Oh, how unlike you that is, Ce... but then I suppose you have to talk like that now, don't you, now that... that... that silly, *stupid man*...!"

Sun Ce embraced his heartbroken mother and sobbed quietly; the two remained silent for some time as they tried to decide what to say to the other. Lady Chen watched the two from a doorway; she wondered whether Lady Wu would tolerate her now, and she was fearful that she might meet the terrible fate that was not uncommon to consorts after the death of the master of the house.

"Promise me you'll be strong, Ce," Lady Wu said suddenly.

"Of course," Sun Ce replied.

"Giving your marquisate to Kuang... was a beautiful thing to do," Lady Wu suggested. "You're a good man, Ce... like your father."

"Kuang's the youngest of us first four brothers... Quan and Yi don't need something to give them hope as much as Kuang does," Sun Ce explained. "...But there are eight of us for me to think about... *eight of us*. He had *eight children* in-between being a hero... and with everything there was and is to kill us, we're all still here. I'd never really thought about it before... that's amazing."

"Yes, well, your father was a tiger...!" Lady Wu giggled miserably. "I certainly spent most of my marriage pregnant or nurturing someone... and even with all those healthy children of his own, he brought Ben and Fu into the house when his brother died, and then he adopted Yu Hè... he had a lot of love to give, and there

200

were never enough people to give it to."
"His vassals... are his *friends*," Sun Ce noted. "They miss him... they genuinely miss him... as though they were his brothers."
"You must be the same," Lady Wu insisted. "When it is your turn to shine, Ce, you must be the same; make them your friends and brothers, and always show kindness to them, just like your-"
"Ben is the head of the clan now, isn't he...?" Sun Ce said wearily. "He's 'Inspector of Yu Province', he's commander of the tiny little army we have, he's-"
"He'll yield to you," Lady Wu promised.
Sun Ce was silent.
"He *will*," Lady Wu continued, "and then you will be a great man. Don't let your father's fate sway you; a man must do what his heart tells him that he must do, else he isn't a man. It's the same for women; your sister is who she wants to be, and I wouldn't have her any other way."
Sun Ce snorted loudly.
"I allowed fear to drive me, but not anymore," Lady Wu continued. "I was so scared whenever he left here to go and fight somewhere, so scared that he wouldn't come back, and that I'd be left to manage our family alone. But he left me so many wonderful men that will always be there, always looking out for each other and the family... I know that you'll do the same."
Sun Ce closed his eyes tightly.
"Follow your heart," Lady Wu insisted. "Do not see your father's death; see his life. He'll never truly die, because he's everywhere you look. He's in his children, he's in his friends, his family; he'll never be forgotten. If your heart tells you to be another tiger... then be another tiger."
Sun Ce let out a deep breath, and after a few moments, he whispered, "*Thank you*."

Wu Jing and Sun Ben had to end their mourning for Sun Jian, whether they wanted to or not: they had to quickly take Danyang from its administrator Zhou Xin or lose a useful increase in power and influence. Sun Ce, Lady Wu, Sun Fu and Xu Kun met the army at the gates of Qu'e City on the day of departure, but the mood was desperate and hopeless.
"*Bastard*," Sun Ce muttered. "Can't this wait?"
"Yuan Shu was insistent," Wu Jing replied.
"Allow me to go with you," Xu Kun pleaded.
"You're barely a year or two older than Ce!" Lady Wu admonished.
"So am I, yet I'm burdened with this," Sun Ben suggested.
"So may I go?" Xu Kun asked.
"...Not this," Lady Wu insisted. "You can help my son later on, Kun. My brother does not need you."
Wu Jing whined miserably.
"Why do you make such noises?" Lady Wu asked.
Wu Jing fought tears as he said, "This... this would be easier, so much easier, if-!"
"Do not... do not say it," Lady Wu said with a demanding tone.
Sun Ben felt compelled to take his younger brother's hand and say, "One day, you'll get to decide what you want to do."
"I'll fight too, Brother," Sun Fu replied.
"We should go, and quickly," Wu Jing ordered with as much

strength as he could muster. "Wentai isn't here... so I must earn his respect and do this as *he* would."
Lady Wu smiled silently, but her face was a waterfall of tears.
"...**Sun Ben!**" Wu Jing barked. "**Let's depart!**"
Xu Kun was especially frustrated as he watched the convoy of infantry, cavalry and ox-drawn carts file out of the city gates.
"There'll be other battles, Cousin," Sun Ce said.
"...Yes," Xu Kun replied.
Sun Ce turned to his mother and said, "Shall we go back now?"
Lady Wu was comforting Sun Fu, who had suddenly become distressed at seeing his elder brother going off to war; she nodded silently, and the fractured family returned to the governor's residence to continue mourning Sun Jian.

Sun Ce decided to speak with Cheng Pu and Zhu Zhi, the two men that had served as his father's intellectual support; he did so on the evening after Wu Jing's departure.
"We were hoping that Yuan Shu would be helpful, but he's sent a pretty poor tribute for a man that was his only decent general, and not only that: Sun Ben said that Yuan Shu was rude to him again, and he's confiscated more people," Sun Ce explained bitterly. "What am I supposed to do...?"
Cheng Pu was silent.
"My suggestion, young master, is that you remain in the south and work toward a future of your own," Zhu Zhi said. "For now, you must cultivate relationships with talented men and find sponsors that will aid you with resources. When the time is right, go to Yuan Shu and ask for your father's troops; see how Yuan Shu responds. If he is good-natured and fair to you, then he has understood the times at last, and he is a worthy master after all. If he is the same – and sadly, I suspect that he will be – then you must work for him only until an opportunity to break free of the hereditary shackles presents itself... and then, young master, you must make a base in here in the south, a place that talented men will flock to from all over the land."
"...My thanks," Sun Ce replied sincerely. "Now I have a goal to work toward; I hope that you'll work toward it with me."
"If I can, I shall," Zhu Zhi promised.
"...The same, if Heaven wills it," Cheng Pu said with less conviction. He was yet to be fully convinced, despite his instincts, and he would wait until he was completely sure before he pledged allegiance to such a young, untested and impetuous man.

Sun Ce's new friend, Lü Fan, had no qualms when it came to the future heir to the Sun legacy; he crossed the Yangtze River by chartered boat and completed his journey to Guangling Prefecture, just as Wu Jing and Sun Ben were beginning their fateful attack on Danyang Prefecture to the west. This would change the dynamic between Yuan Shu and Xu Province's Governor Tao Qian, who had once been fairly tolerant neighbours; they would now be rivals for the governance of Yang Province.

****

34

Lü Fan travelled to the capital city of Guangling Prefecture and began asking locals about various members of the Sun family and related clans; word reached subordinates of the Administrator of Guangling, Zhao Yu, who suspected some pre-invasion espionage by Yuan Shu.

"I want this 'Lü Fan' arrested," Administrator Zhao said to his officials. "The funeral of Sun Jian may be part of some wider plan, since Yuan Shu has always been untrustworthy and his recent move against Danyang breaks our covenant. Governor Tao Qian has recently returned from Capital Province, and he will be coming here personally to oversee interrogation."

A city guard captain bowed humbly and left the meeting hall; within hours, Lü Fan was a prisoner of the Administrator of Guangling.

"So you are Lü Fan."

Lü Fan looked up and saw that Administrator Zhao had come to the prison in person; Lü smiled and said, "You are famed for your honesty, Administrator Zhao, and yet you languish here on the borders of your master's territory while he has Ze Rong as his treasurer. What a poor judge of character he is, then!"

"You're a prisoner," Administrator Zhao retorted. "Who are you to slander the good governor when you came here to spy for Yuan Shu...?"

"You're not aware of current events," Lü Fan sighed. "Sun Jian, the hero of the age, is dead, Administrator. His eldest son – who is now a very good friend of mine – asked me to come here and retrieve his family and bring them to the funeral in Qu'e. What's wrong with that?"

"I am instructed that you are to be detained," Administrator Zhao replied weakly.

"And this is the same Tao Qian that praised Zhu Zhi – Sun Jian's tactician – for his aid in repelling the heretics and had him promoted to Commandant of Wu Prefecture!" Lü Fan chuckled. "Why does he favour influential vassals, and then imprison family friends? Who am I? Am I known? Is 'Lü Fan' a known champion?"

"...You're to be questioned," Administrator Zhao said with decreasing certainty.

"Am I?" Lü Fan heckled. "Well then, I hope I am able to give the required answers, or poor Bofu will lose a friend and fail to give his scattered family the chance to-"

"**Enough!**" Administrator Zhao pleaded. "...Governor Tao will discover your intent. I am lacking the talent to see you for who you are."

"No, I think you know, Administrator Zhao," Lü Fan chuckled. "It's Tao Qian that you cannot fathom."

Zhao Yu had heard enough: he turned and fled the prison with unceremonious haste.

Sun Ce took his 9-year-old brother Quan, 8-year-old brother Yi, 6-year-old brother Kuang and 4-year-old sister Shangxiang to their father's grave whenever he could so that the children of Lady Wu

– who best remembered their father – could grieve in their own way; at the end of one of his silent vigils, Quan asked his brother to take him to the home of the Shi family, where Quan's best friend was waiting for him.

"Lord Sun!" Zhu Zhi exclaimed as he left the Shi residence at the very moment that the Suns arrived.

"You know the Shi family, Mister Zhu?" Sun Ce asked.

"They are my relatives," Zhu Zhi replied. "I–"

Suddenly, Sun Quan shouted, "**Ran!**"

The adults stopped talking as an 8-year-old boy joined Zhu Zhi at the entrance to the house; he exuded a surprising amount of maturity, despite his young age.

"...My nephew Ran," Zhu Zhi chuckled. "He's–"

"He's my best friend!" Sun Quan interrupted. "May we go and play, Brother?"

"...Alright, but don't interrupt Mister Zhu or any other adult like that again, okay...?" Sun Ce replied. "Run along."

"Is that okay, esteemed uncle?" Shi Ran asked of Zhu Zhi.

"Of course it is, Zhu Zhi's one of Father's men!" Sun Quan insisted. "Let's go!"

"...Go on, Ran," Zhu Zhi said quietly, and the two boys retreated.

"...My brother has a lot to learn," Sun Ce said apologetically. "But your nephew is really smart; I was nothing but a pair of fists at his age."

"He's something else!" Zhu Zhi chuckled. "I'm yet to have a son, so if I continue to do well, his parents both want me to adopt him as my heir. I said we should wait and see, though; these are volatile times."

Sun Ce nodded silently.

"Heard anything from your friend yet...?" Zhu Zhi asked.

"Uh...? Oh, uh... no," Sun Ce said dolefully. "I trust him, though, Mister Zhu. He said he'd get the rest of my family here, and I know he meant it."

"Things are complicated now," Zhu Zhi sighed. "Your uncle has been ordered to take Danyang, which is currently part of Tao Qian's unofficial holdings; neither Yuan nor Tao have a right to it, but they'll argue, and once again, it's the Suns and Wus that will suffer for it."

"...So Ziheng is in danger...?" Sun Ce realised.

"Hopefully not," Zhu Zhi replied. "Hopefully, he'll be in and out of Guangling before the thought of that place being a future target enters Tao Qian's mind."

Sun Ce nodded silently.

"...I should say again that if there is ever a way to leave Yuan Shu's service, do so," Zhu Zhi continued. "I should also say yet again that I will do all that I can to aid you in the future, young master. Others will do the same if you inspire them... and I believe that you can."

Sun Ce smiled gratefully; the two men exchanged respectful bows, and then they went their separate ways.

Xu Governor Tao Qian arrived in Guangling within a few days of Lü Fan's arrest and had Lü Fan brought to a private interview room within the city prison; once were two were facing each other, the governor glared at his prisoner with probing eyes.

"...Do you see what you were looking for...?" Lü Fan asked.

"Why are you in Guangling?" Tao Qian retorted gruffly.

"I am afraid that my answer is the same," Lü Fan sighed. "I am here to retrieve the family of the fallen hero Sun Jian."

"I have some of them in custody," Tao Qian revealed. "But before I release them – and you – I want to know exactly who you are. Why didn't someone of the Sun clan come here and look for them if it is their private business...?"

"I am trusted by Sun Bofu- ...I mean Sun Ce, the eldest son of Sun Jian," Lü Fan explained. "He entrusted me with the task."

"...Is that so...?" Tao Qian cawed. "Well, well; so you are one of the future tiger's friends... so trusted that you are sent to all manner of places to pass news of the death and bring them to Qu'e... you must be a fine man indeed."

"I don't think I am anything spectacular," Lü Fan said as he caught the gaze of Administrator Zhao Yu. "I am a man that has trust. All I want to do is prove I am worthy of it."

"The Sun clan are finished," Tao Qian suggested. "Even Sun Jian's sponsor, former General Zhu Jun – who is a personal friend of mine, I might add – does not have high hopes for them now."

"Why would I care if Sun Ce is my friend?" Lü Fan countered.

"In such times, men need strong allies and stronger lords, not friends," Tao Qian said. "I need trustworthy men, men of good character. I should like to offer you a role; you can refuse, but then I can only assume that you are an enemy spy, come to discover Guangling's weaknesses so that Yuan Shu can attack it later, as he already covets my interests in Danyang!"

"Your words are without logic," Lü Fan scoffed. "If I were an enemy spy, then recruiting me would be suicide."

"...I am losing patience," Tao Qian growled. "I came from Peng to speak to you, Lü Fan: either show deference to me, or languish here."

"I cannot oblige you," Lü Fan sighed. "I shall have to suffer a criminal's death, it seems... but I would rather do that than abandon my friend."

"So be it," Tao Qian said coldly. The governor then turned to Administrator Zhao Yu, shook his head slowly, and left the room.

"You are a very brave man, Lü Fan, but you are ultimately foolish as well," Administrator Zhao said sadly. "You might not deserve it, but your life is over."

"Don't bet on that," Lü Fan replied calmly.

Weeks later, Sun Ce was preparing for another day of mourning when Sun Hè ran into the hall and said, "**Lü Fan! Lü Fan is back!**"

"Heaven smiles," Zhou Yu – who was visiting his friend Sun Ce at the time – whispered gratefully.

"Who is Lü Fan?" Lady Wu asked in weary tones.

"You don't remember?" Sun Ce exclaimed.

"Oh, yes... that nice young man that agreed to go to Guangling," Lady Wu recalled at last. "So he has come back...? **He has recovered our kin???**"

"He's brought *everyone*!" Sun Hè explained. "He's brought everyone, and he says that Tao Qian imprisoned them, but-!"

"Tao Qian will answer for that later," Sun Ce promised.

"He rescued our family???" Lady Wu shrieked. **"Then this man is family now!"**

"I knew that I could trust him," Sun Ce declared. "In my heart, I knew."

"I want to see him!" Lady Wu insisted. **"Bring this Lü Fan to me! He will be like my own son! Bring him here!"**

"I have another brother," Sun Ce said with pride. "I'll fetch him here myself, Mother: him, and everyone that he saved."

When Sun Ce returned to Wu Jing's home with Lü Fan, the latter was greeted by an ecstatic Lady Wu.

"To me, you are like another son!" Lady Wu said to an embarrassed and emotional Lü Fan.

"You are too kind," Lü Fan replied. "I do not deserve-"

"You're *family*!" Lady Wu barked. "You are family to us now! Now come! You'll sit as one of us, at our family table!"

Zhou Yu smiled mischievously and said, "It's best for you that you obey, Ziheng."

"...Then I shall," Lü Fan chuckled.

The acting heads of the Sun family – Sun Ce and Sun Hè – welcomed Lü Fan to the dining hall and encouraged him to take a privileged place next to Zhou Yu. Sun Hè, Lady Wu, Xu Kun, Sun Ben's brother Fu and Lady Chen took their seats, and the children of Sun Jian – Ce, Quan, Yi, Kuang and Shangxiang – took theirs; once all were seated, Lady Wu had servants pour wine for an increasingly emotional Lü Fan.

"I must insist that I do not deserve this!" Lü Fan cried.

"You're too modest," Sun Ce replied. "You saved some of our farthest-flung family from destruction by Tao Qian."

"That wretch!" Lady Wu said with anger. "He will suffer in the afterlife!"

"Forgive me, but... his actions might be understandable," Lü Fan suggested.

"...I agree," Zhou Yu admitted. "Your arrival in Guangling was concurrent to an 'event' in Danyang; suspicion of your motives came as no surprise to me."

"How did you escape...?" Sun Ce asked. "I know from Bohai that you were put in prison... but how...?"

"Fortunately, the 'event' in Danyang was known to me, so I prepared for the worst," Lü Fan explained. "I had friends that I kept in close contact with, before and after my arrest, by way of bribing or knowing the right people. Tao Qian questioned me without result, and Administrator Zhao dismissed my casual demeanour as bluff or stupidity and left me to my fate. I quickly discovered who had been taken, and when I knew who needed to be freed, I awaited the right moment. Once I knew that Governor Tao Qian was on his way back to his capital, my allies freed me from prison with bribes, and we located and rescued your captured kin. By the time that Administrator Zhao's officials realised that I'd outwitted him, we were already travelling down the Great River to Qu'e."

"And now you are safe," Lady Wu said with gratitude. "From now on, you will come and go as any of the family would. Come and see me whenever you want; I am like your second mother now, and want to be treated as such."

"I am beyond words," Lü Fan replied.

"...And I still think that Tao Qian is a wretch," Lady Wu grumbled. "Why must men that do nothing more than serve their lord be treated so poorly? Why must-"

"Mother... please," Sun Ce interrupted.

Lady Wu sighed sorrowfully as she compared Lü Fan's imprisonment with the death of her beloved spouse; Lady Chen covered her face and started to sob with grief, which solicited a grateful – but slight – smile from Lady Wu.

Zhou Yu frowned thoughtfully and said, "Tao Qian's actions may anger us, but any reprisals will have to wait."

"And another banquet will have to wait as well," Sun Ce replied. "You're going back to Lujiang, aren't you, Gongjin...?"

"Tomorrow," Zhou Yu said. "I don't want to, but... life goes on."

Sun Ce looked at the rest of his grieving family as he replied, "Yeah... it does."

Sun Ce and his closest family would miss much of the next 3 years while they did as ritual demanded and mourned Sun Jian with their entire beings. But for one man who would one day become very well known to Sun Ce, those 3 years would be busy ones.

****

35

While the Sun family mourned Sun Jian, a 24-year-old man of exceptional talent and character was finally becoming accustomed to life on the remote Liaodong peninsula. That man was *Taishi Ci*, styled 'Ziyi', and fate was about to force him to forget any hope of a peaceful life and continue the journey that would one day see him become a significant figure in the land.

Taishi Ci had been trapped and labelled as a fugitive after famously using underhanded tactics to make a successful first petition to the court on behalf of his local administrator. The Administrator of Liaodong was a man named Gongsun Du; he had heard of Taishi Ci from a famed Liaodong intellectual named Bing Yuan, and he had insisted on becoming acquainted with him. Gongsun Du was immediately impressed – as most men that met Taishi were – but there could be no role for him, since he was still a criminal. Hopes were still held, since a general amnesty could be called as part of a change of reign era or some other significant event; Taishi Ci was told to be patient, and fortunately for him, patience was one of his strongest qualities.

Time passed. Since Taishi Ci had arrived in Liaodong, Emperor Ling had died, and his eldest son Liu Bian had become Emperor Shao under the regency of his mother Dowager Hè and her brother, Commander-in-Chief Hè Jin; a general amnesty did not occur. After the destruction of the 'Ten Attendants' that were responsible for much of the corruption – including the 'First petition wins' system that had forced Taishi Ci to become a criminal in the first place – Dong Zhuo had seized the court, outmanoeuvred his opponents, deposed Liu Bian and replaced him with his half-brother Liu Xie, who became Emperor Xian; a general amnesty to calm the incensed aristocrats did not occur. Gongsun Du conducted two campaigns against feudal kingdoms in what was later known to the outside world as Korea, both on the orders of the Chancellor of State, Dong Zhuo; Gongsun Du received rank, but nothing was offered to Taishi Ci, neither a chance to serve nor a pardon. The Eastern Pass Coalition formed and drove Dong Zhuo out of Luoyang; a general amnesty did not occur. The Eastern Pass Coalition fractured into two factions led by the feuding Yuan brothers: in the chaos that followed, Dong Zhuo had completed his move to Chang'an, but no general amnesty was granted to calm the situation in the east. Dong Zhuo was then assassinated and replaced by loyal Han officials, who were in turn replaced by Dong Zhuo's loyalists, led by the scholarly Jia Xu; a general amnesty was expected that would finally give Taishi Ci the opportunity to shine, but it did not happen. Taishi Ci was an inconsequential prisoner of the whims of a state that did not know him and would not grant him what he needed to progress beyond being a fugitive from a broken system. But he was patient nonetheless, and he waited.

5 years in exile had passed. Taishi Ci returned to his simple home after another meeting with Gongsun Du; the people waved and

bowed as he walked, as his good nature made him popular and his infamy made him respected. The intellectual Bing Yuan was with him, having met him on a road as he travelled; the two did not speak until they were indoors.

"Governor Gongsun genuinely respects you," Bing Yuan suggested.

"...But I shall never gain a decent role, Mister Bing," Taishi Ci complained. "I am still 'That criminal conman' to men like Governor Gongsun."

"Not so, Mister Taishi!" Bing Yuan insisted. "He sees you for the hero that you are. But his court is made up of snobs, yes: there are few that have my ability to see the whole. What you did was sneaky, yes, but you got justice!"

"...Nonetheless, there are many moments when I wish I'd said 'No' to the request, Mister Bing, even though my conscience quickly corrects me," Taishi Ci chuckled.

"And that conscience of yours is why you are a hero," Bing Yuan declared with obvious intent.

"...How is your friend Mister Liu?" Taishi Ci asked with growing resignation.

"Alas, Mister Liu Zheng cannot evade Governor Gongsun forever, for I will not be able to shelter him safely," Bing Yuan sighed theatrically. "I wonder, Mister Taishi, if..."

Taishi Ci awaited the request, but Bing Yuan did not continue. The matter was awkward; Liu Zheng had offended Gongsun Du somehow, and the desired punishment was arrest and execution. Many people that were known to be associates of Liu Zheng were arrested when the man himself escaped; Bing Yuan had escaped that fate because of his fame and popularity, but that was about to change.

"Is it true that Governor Gongsun wants to arrest anyone suspected of sheltering Liu Zheng...?" Taishi Ci prompted.

"Alas, yes," Bing Yuan replied. "Because of the level of the decree, my reputation will not serve as a shield. But I do not want to abandon such a fine man to such a cruel fate! Gongsun Du will one day come to forgive or even forget the cause of this feud, but what good will that be, if Liu Zheng is cold bones?"

"...So you want me to rescue him," Taishi Ci guessed.

"I knew that you would understand," Bing Yuan said with delight.

"I have been here for nearly five years now," Taishi Ci realised. "In that time, I have not had a rewarding role, and I have been unhappy, despite being made to feel so welcome by the people. I cannot start a family, and I cannot begin to build a home of my own. There has been no amnesty to allow me to work for Gongsun Du, and I wonder if there would be a job if there were a pardon anyway. But if I do this, Mister Bing, I will become a fugitive again, and this time it would be from Gongsun Du, a man that has subjugated foreign kingdoms."

"But it would be the right thing to do!" Bing Yuan protested.

"And I intend to do it, precisely because it is right," Taishi Ci replied.

"But where will you take Mister Liu...?" Bing Yuan asked.

"You ask me to do this, but you do not have a plan...?" Taishi Ci exclaimed.

"I am forced to admit that I am a mere scholar, versed in the

classics, but that strategy is not my strong point," Bing Yuan
chuckled with embarrassment.
"...I shall go back to the mainland," Taishi Ci decided. "I have been
smuggling letters back to my mother, and she's told me in her
responses that she's been receiving help from Kong Rong, the
Administrator of Beihai."
"What great admirers you have!" Bing Yuan said. "A descendant of
the great philosopher! He obviously sees that you are a man
beyond measure."
"If Kong Rong aids my mother, then I can return to my village and
hide there, once I've saved Liu Zheng," Taishi Ci suggested. "We
should act quickly."
"You are a true hero of the age!" Bing Yuan declared.

Taishi Ci met with Liu Zheng in Bing Yuan's garden and explained
the plan to get him out of Liaodong. The plan was simple enough:
Liaodong's commercial ports were alerted to Liu Zheng, so they
would flee the city under cover of darkness and travel to the
nearest coastal village, where they would procure a boat and
travel back to the mainland. Liu Zheng agreed, for there was little
else that he could do: night fell, and the two men prepared to
start their dangerous journey.
"Ready...?" Taishi Ci asked pointlessly: it did not matter if Liu
Zheng was ready or not, because Gongsun Du would soon begin
his search.
"My life is in your hands, Taishi Ziyi," Liu Zheng replied.
"...Right, then... we'll be off," Taishi Ci sighed.
Taishi Ci was dressed in a robe that concealed light armour, and
he carried two small blades; Liu Zheng carried a short sword for
defence, but he wore no armour since he lacked Taishi Ci's
physical strength and could not risk being impeded by the weight
of extra garments. The two had meagre supplies, because
carrying too much would also slow them down; they would need
to improvise as they went.
        And so the journey began: Taishi Ci walked to the closed
city gates and smiled as the guard – who he knew to be a good
man – bowed in respect of the reputation Taishi had.
"Out for a walk...?" the guard asked.
Taishi Ci laughed and replied, "Oh, you know me and my ways!"
"I do," the guard said as he spied Liu Zheng lurking in the
shadows nearby. "You know that I cannot open the gates if I think
I'm letting Liu Zheng escape. We've been told that-"
"I know," Taishi Ci interrupted. "Open them though... I need to go
out. I have an urgent message to deliver."
"Do you have something from the governor...?" the guard asked.
"...No, it's urgent," Taishi Ci insisted. "I really must insist."
The guard smiled, shook his head, and said, "Go home, Mister
Taishi. Don't harm yourself anymore."
Taishi Ci smiled, turned around, and retreated to the place where
Liu Zheng was hiding; Liu Zheng guessed the situation and said,
"I'm not getting out of here."
"You will," Taishi Ci promised. "I was a fool to think that I'd sneak
you out at night. No, the best way is when the city is at its
busiest..."

The next morning, the gates were thrown open to allow travellers to pass back and forth. Taishi Ci prepared a sack of random goods, disguised Liu Zheng in the clothes of a merchant's assistant, and gained a place on a traveller's cart after paying a considerable sum. When the ox-drawn vehicle reached the gates, there was a tense silence among the passengers as the morning guards inspected the driver's travel documents and moved toward the cargo of people and goods. A child wailed as its mother held it close to her chest; another man with wild beard hair glared at the guards and waited their verdict.

"No sign of Liu Zheng among this lot," one guard whispered.

"Fine," the other said. He then turned to the small militia that was blocking the gateway and shouted, "**THEY CAN PASS!**"

Taishi Ci watched the cart leave the city from a nearby hiding place; minutes later, he made his own way to the gates on foot.

"Ah! Mister Taishi!" one guard exclaimed. "Yen said you were trying to go somewhere last night; where are you off to today...?"

"Same as last night, only not so urgent now," Taishi Ci replied. "The governor wants me to take word about the fugitive Liu Zheng to the other settlements, and then the mainland."

"Aren't you still a fugitive yourself?" the guard prompted.

"If I do this, I'll maybe get a pardon," Taishi Ci replied.

"Oh, well, don't let me stop you!" the guard said excitedly. "Good luck, Mister Taishi!"

No one obstructed Taishi Ci; he passed through the gates and walked down the dirt road as casually as his shattered nerves would permit. Once he was out of sight of the city gates, he put on a burst of speed and started to catch up with the slow ox-drawn cart that carried Liu Zheng. He did so ten minutes later, since the cart had fortuitously stopped so that the ox could rest.

"...You...!" Liu Zheng gasped as Taishi Ci leapt onto the back of the cart; some suspected that Taishi Ci was some sort of thief, so they started to holler and wail.

"**What's going on???**" the cart driver barked as he readied a cheap sword.

"**S'alright!**" Taishi Ci replied. "**It's just another passenger! I have money!**"

Two of the existing passengers whispered excitedly, as they recognised the charismatic Taishi Ci by his voice; the panic subsided, and the smirking driver said, "**Pay me when we get t'the other end, 'Stranger'.**"

Taishi Ci sat next to the terrified Liu Zheng, laughed wearily, and said, "Sorry if I scared anyone."

The journey took the cart to a small coastal village to the east of the thriving city; there would be no checks on the travellers that were coming and going as long as the price was right. Taishi Ci led Liu Zheng to the residence of a couple of notorious fishermen that were known to smuggle things back and forth to the mainland and arranged a boat crossing for a cost that would have made some men choke. An hour later, Taishi Ci took Liu Zheng to the docks to meet his ferrymen.

"Bing Yuan must truly respect you," Taishi Ci said to a relieved Liu Zheng as they prepared to board the boat. "You'll be there soon enough: he's arranged for a 'mutual friend of yours' to be in

Donglai, so I'll see you over, then I'll-"
"Don't come back here!" Liu Zheng said with tears in his eyes.
"You sacrificed your own chances of achieving greatness to save
me from this sorry predicament! Gongsun Du could kill you if he
found out that you helped me!"
"I won't," Taishi Ci replied calmly. "I already decided that."
Liu Zheng's eyes wandered as the enormity of the situation struck
him; he turned to Taishi Ci once again, grasped his hands and
said, "I do not know how I could ever repay you, Taishi Ziyi!
Taishi Ziyi, Taishi Ziyi, I-!"
"I don't do what I do for rewards, just the knowledge that I've
done right," Taishi Ci insisted. "I just hope that we'll be alright..."
Taishi Ci looked at the two unscrupulous fishermen.
"You'll be alright," one of the fishermen replied.
"...Very good," Taishi Ci said. "When you're ready, gentlemen..."

The journey was sombre, but Taishi Ci smiled anyway, since he
had done as he had been asked.
"Prob'ly best y'don't stay," one of the fishermen grumbled. "S'all
goin' bloody mad on the mainland at t'moment. They're all at one-
another's throats, all the gov'nors."
"Yes, I'd heard," Taishi Ci admitted.
"Yeah, well, s'them capital types," the second fisherman
suggested. "No idea about nothin', an' then they go mad, an' start
doin' things like that. They say they got rid o' the Yellow Turbans:
did they...? S'not happened, the way I see it. They're all over Qing
Province, still."
"Volatile times, indeed," Taishi Ci replied. "Who knows what will
happen next..."

That same day, Taishi Ci set a foot on the mainland for the first
time in nearly 5 years; he almost cried at the thought that he was
finally home.
"Six thousand thanks!" Liu Zheng said as he fell to his knees to
kowtow.
"Don't be ridiculous!" Taishi Ci chortled as he pulled Liu Zheng to
his feet.
"But what of Bing Yuan, and my friends...?" Liu Zheng asked. "I
just realised, because I was so selfishly scared for myself... Taishi
Ziyi, what about-"
"They'll search Bing Yuan's home, but they'll find nothing," Taishi
Ci explained. "And in a few days, Bing Yuan will go to speak to
Gongsun Du."
"Why...?" Liu Zheng exclaimed.
"To ensure the release of your allies!" Taishi Ci continued.
"Gongsun Du has failed to capture his 'enemy', Liu Zheng, and
that will be known because you will ensure that *everyone* knows
once you're safe; why hold your blameless friends then...?"
A man approached and signalled to Liu Zheng, who wanted to
thank Taishi Ci one last time: Taishi Ci shook his head and
gestured that he should hurry on. Liu Zheng settled for a low,
humble bow, and then he fled the docks with his ally.
"You going back now...?" one of the fishermen asked.
Taishi Ci felt as though his feet were refusing to lift themselves
from his native soil; after a few moments, he turned, smiled, and

said, "Yes, I'm 'going back'. But not back to Liaodong: I'm going back home, to Huangxian."

"Best o' luck t'ye," the lead fisherman said. "Way things are, yer'll need it."

Taishi Ci laughed, turned, and walked away. He was home: at that moment, it was all that mattered. He walked for a very long time, as though contact with the ground was essential; it was only when he finally tired that he stopped and hitched a ride with the first ox-drawn cart that passed him on the road.

Days later, Liaodong Governor Gongsun Du would pardon and release Liu Zheng's followers at Bing Yuan's request; it was not difficult to guess that Taishi Ci was probably the man that had saved the fugitive, but Gongsun Du did not put out a warrant. The matter was closed, and he left Taishi Ci to the mercy of those on the mainland that still sought him for his original – and far more serious – misdemeanour. But the mainland had too many other problems to worry about Taishi Ci: Qing Province alone was rocked by war between the Yuan family retainers and the sudden appearance of a faction of Yellow Turbans that numbered in the tens of thousands. The latter would soon become the next challenge for Taishi Ci.

＊＊＊＊＊＊＊＊＊＊＊＊

36

Taishi Ci was still familiar to many in his home village of Huangxian, so his return could not be kept secret without considerable effort; he opted to walk for the last part of the journey, so that he could take in the sights and sounds of a place that had been 20 years of his life and 5 years of his memories. He looked forward to seeing his mother in the flesh after so long, but the reunion would be short-lived.

"My son…! My son!" Taishi Ci's mother yelped as he entered her home.
"Is something the matter, Mother…?" Taishi Ci asked worriedly.
"You must hurry and get ready!" Ci's mother cried. **"You have to get ready to leave, and go to-!"**
"Leave…?" Taishi Ci chortled. "I only just got back! Has that official I tricked become powerful…? Is my life in danger?"
"No! It is the life of the Chancellor of Beihai, Kong Rong, a descendant of the great Confucius, that is in danger!" Ci's mother replied excitedly. "You have to go to his aid!"
"…Me…?" Taishi Ci said with disbelief.
"No time! No time!" Ci's mother replied. **"Go! Go!"**
"…Beihai?" Taishi Ci noted. "What's happened in Beihai?"
Ci's mother threw her arms aloft and screamed, **"Heretics! Filthy heretics! Traitors and-!"**
"Yellow Turbans," Taishi Ci guessed. "I'll go as soon as I can, Mother. I shall do you proud again."
"Yes, but try and do it *legally*!" Ci's mother pleaded as Taishi Ci walked to his room to gather some belongings. **"You don't want to end up in exile again!"**
Taishi Ci swept dust from his bed and laughed desperately. He could not believe that he was leaving again, and with such an urgent mission; but then that mission became uppermost in his thoughts, and something occurred to him.
"…**Is there anyone that knows how bad things are?**" Taishi Ci asked suddenly.
Ci's mother entered the room and said, "The tavern. A messenger's staying in the tavern."
"Then I should go there," Taishi Ci replied.

A short while later, Taishi Ci entered the small village tavern and scanned the seating areas for signs of an armoured messenger.
"Taishi Ci!" the tavern keeper exclaimed.
Every pair of eyes locked onto the familiar bronzed figure that had entered; some gasped at the sight of the village's most famous – and notorious – sons.
"No time," Taishi Ci declared. "Where's the man from Beihai?"
The tavern keeper pointed toward a far corner, where a young soldier was staring at Taishi Ci nervously.
"…**You,**" Taishi Ci said as he ran toward the youth. **"What was the situation when you left?"**
"Are you the local militia commander?" the messenger asked.
"No," Taishi Ci replied impatiently. "Please, you have to tell me: what was the situation when you left?"

"They were coming to Duchang, *thousands* and *thousands* of them!" the soldier whined. "They were led by a man called *Guan Hai*, who said he was going to fulfil the dream of-"
"Of their high priest, Zhang Jue, I'd guess," Taishi Ci interrupted. "Yes, well, good luck to him, he'll need it. What were they planning to do when they got to Duchang, do you know?"
"Thousands of them, *tens of thousands*!" the soldier said hysterically. "**Where did they all come from???**"
"That doesn't matter right now," Taishi Ci suggested. "They sound organised; that's bad. The militia here is a volunteer force, no good for something like this; and if they're organised, then they plan to siege the city, like they did in Nan County years ago."
"Maybe," the soldier sobbed. "Maybe, but I don't know. So *many...!*"
"...I have no time to go around raising a militia," Taishi Ci decided. "Who is where at the moment...? I hear there's a war between the Yuans."
"Yuan Tan and Liu Bei are in Pingyuan fighting each other," the soldier recalled.
"... ... ...*Liu Bei*, then," Taishi Ci murmured ambiguously.
"Huh...? Liu Bei...?" the soldier said with confusion.
"No time," Taishi muttered. "I need a horse."
"What's going on...?" the messenger whined as Taishi Ci got up and hurried out of the tavern, intent on retrieving a horse from the village stables. "**Who *are* you, anyway???**"

"*Taishi Ci*!" a teenaged stable-boy exclaimed as the village legend approached him; once again, every pair of eyes turned to Taishi Ci.
"No time," Taishi Ci insisted. "I need a horse."
The confused stable-boy frowned and said, "But... B-but you've only just-!"
"Yes, I know I just got back," Taishi Ci chortled. "I need a horse."
"None to give, none to lend," the stable boy replied sadly. "It's been so difficult, with all the wars, the bandits, the thieves, the... Mister Taishi, I'm sorry, honest I-"
"I'll have to walk," Taishi Ci realised. "...I have to hurry."
People stood and watched as Taishi Ci began the longest walk of his life; he would be going to the city of Duchang, where a hostile army of thousands awaited him.

Taishi Ci would barter for a place on the back of a cart from time to time, and he kept his rests in the settlements that he passed to an hour's sleep, some food and a wash. When he was within sight of Duchang, he could not avoid gasping; the Yellow Turban army had completely surrounded the city with encampments, and they were obviously preparing to conduct a siege. The Yellow Turban leader, Guan Hai, was personally issuing challenges amid the preparations, and the Chancellor, Kong Rong, was despatching forces out of the gates to meet those challenges and provide cover while civilians fled with whatever they could carry. Taishi Ci took the opportunity during one of those encounters to sneak in and demand an audience with his benefactor.
Kong Rong was a slim, frail yet charismatic man in light blue robes. He was nearing the age of 40, but he was

prematurely-aged from the stress of being embroiled directly in some or most of the most important events of recent times – the Partisan Crisis and the other activities of its authors, the 'Ten Attendants'; the original Yellow Turban Rebellion and the subsequent bandit and tribal uprisings; the succession debates following the death of Emperor Ling; and, last and by far the worst, Dong Zhuo's takeover of the imperial court. Kong Rong had narrowly escaped continued service in the capital during that last episode, but his promotion to the role in Qing Province had not spared him from the nationwide unrest.

"...Welcome, Taishi Ziyi," Kong Rong said as Taishi approached his seat in the chancellery. "Is your mother well...?"

Taishi Ci kowtowed repeatedly as he said, "Yes, and only because of your benevolence, Chancellor. I have been absent due to an act of folly, and was unable to be a good son, as your esteemed ancestor dictated that all righteous men should be. I can never truly repay you for sparing me further humiliation."

Kong Rong got up and forced Taishi Ci to get to his feet, saying, "No, no, Taishi Ziyi, you mustn't do that! You mustn't kowtow to me, a pedant that has achieved nothing despite having nothing but my esteemed ancestor's reputation to draw upon! You are a hero: your 'folly' saved a good man from undeserved punishment, and it is I, therefore, that can never repay you for your service to the land! The whole country owes you a debt of gratitude!"

"You flatter me," Taishi Ci insisted. "But we should hurry, Chancellor: the siege preparations are almost complete, and we will be trapped if we do not act now."

"What do you want to do?" Kong Rong asked.

"Give me command of the army," Taishi Ci said. "I will confront them and break their siege before it can be-"

"No-no-no!" Kong Rong replied. "Reinforcements are bound to come if you heard of my plight in such a distant place! I won't let you go out there with what meagre forces I have; you'll be killed, and I'll have that on my already-overburdened conscience as well! We should hold our ground, and do our best to keep them from the walls!"

"...Forgive me, Chancellor, but I must disagree," Taishi Ci retorted. "If we don't stop them from completing their siege preparations, then we will be trapped, and they can starve us out. Let me take the army and face them."

"I understand your concerns, but I must remonstrate again!" Kong Rong insisted. "I cannot let you ride to certain doom! All I have is a few hundred volunteer infantrymen and a small cavalry force! How can you fight tens of thousands with a brigade? You're not a fool, Taishi Ci: why try to smash a rock with-"

"I'm not an egg," Taishi Ci chuckled. "Please, Chancellor, I implore you to trust me."

"Do you know what happened to Sun Wentai, the 'Tiger of Jiangdong'...?" Kong Rong asked.

"...He was the man that broke the siege in Nan County," Taishi Ci recalled.

"Yes, and he's dead," Kong Rong revealed. "He was killed in Jing Province two years ago, trying to do something similarly insane. A man only has so much luck, Taishi Ziyi: you delivered the petition and saved Liu Zheng, but can you do *this*...?"

"Let me find out," Taishi Ci countered.

"No," Kong Rong insisted. "Reinforcements will come... they *must*."

But days passed, and reinforcements did not come. Kong Rong and Taishi Ci travelled to the battlements of the walled city of Duchang every morning and evening to watch with growing dismay as the siege preparations neared and then reached completion: the citizens of Duchang braced themselves for the horrors that would inevitably follow.

"I should have listened to you," Kong Rong admitted. "I'm sorry."

"There's only one thing that we can do now," Taishi Ci suggested. "We must send for help."

"And ask someone to fight through all that???" Kong Rong exclaimed as he surveyed the mass of people in yellow headscarves that were scurrying around on the ground below. "...If there were some way for you to get the remaining civilians out and save your own life, Taishi Ziyi, then that would be a good thing: I deserve to perish behind these walls like the foolish pedant coward that I am."

"Don't talk nonsense," Taishi Ci scoffed. "And we won't be asking anybody to go; *I* will go."

"No!" Kong Rong chortled. "Are you determined to die young??? Are you determined to be even younger than Sun Wentai when you go to your grave???"

"Your constant references to the fate of Sun Jian of Fuchun are relevant, but unfortunate," Taishi Ci suggested. "If he had feared losing every time he acted, he would not have acted. A man can run out of luck at any time... but he should always do what he must, regardless."

"...Never," Kong Rong muttered. "You can't risk that... not without a plan."

"I'll think of something," Taishi Ci promised.

More days passed, and the horrors of the siege began. Hundreds of Yellow Turbans crossed the dry moat and scaled the walls with their ladders; the defenders reacted with rocks and vats of boiling liquids, and the bodies piled up outside the walls. Taishi Ci did what he could to inspire and aid the defenders, and he was forced to personally confront some of the men that managed to reach the top of the wall; the Yellow Turbans did not falter, however, while the supplies in the city started to run out. Taishi Ci saw that Kong Rong was becoming increasingly receptive to ideas, so he approached him again at the end of one hectic day.

"...Ziyi," Kong Rong said numbly. "I have failed, Ziyi."

"Not yet," Taishi Ci replied. "We have one hope: let me do what I suggested before."

"But who would you go to for help...?" Kong Rong asked despairingly. "What allies have I got...?"

"Magistrate Liu Bei, who is stationed in Pingyuan," Taishi Ci suggested.

"...But Liu Bei is locked in combat with Yuan Shao's son Tan for control of this province," Kong Rong noted. "Won't you have to fight your way past Yuan Tan...? And won't you have to ask Liu Bei to hand over men at a moment when he needs them himself...?"

"If the Yellow Turbans win here, that won't benefit either of

them," Taishi Ci countered. "It serves neither Yuan Shao nor Yuan Shu to let an army of religious fanatics take over this city. If the Yellow Turbans took Beihai, then they'd be a stone's throw from Linzi. If they took the provincial capital, and Guan Hai sent a call out to all Yellow Turbans throughout the country that they'd set up an independent state in Qing, how would that suit anyone? Liu Bei isn't a fool... he'll see that too, and he'll definitiely give me the men I need."
"...Alright, Ziyi... alright," Kong Rong conceded. "But how do you plan on getting to Pingyuan when this place is surrounded by the heretics...?"
"I have a plan," Taishi Ci promised.

****

37

Taishi Ci surprised the sieging army by ordering that the western gates of the city should be opened; the Yellow Turban commander Guan Hai expected a messenger to try and make a dash for help, so he sent additional forces to the western wall. But that was not Taishi Ci's plan; he rode out of the city with a small band of horsemen carrying bows. The small band did not try and break through the mass of Yellow Turbans; instead, they started to practice their archery on a piece of forested ground to the northwest of the city. The bizarre spectacle was reported to Guan Hai, who laughed as he tried to understand.

"...So wait, tell me again... a group of men rode out of the west gate, and *practiced archery*...?" Guan Hai said with disbelief. "And *then* what did they do...?"

"They went back into the city," the reporting scout replied.

"They made no attempt to break through...?" Guan Hai prompted.

"None," the scout replied. "They practiced, stopped for a break, resumed, stopped again, and went back into the city."

The Yellow Turban officers exchanged confused glances.

"...Watch them," Guan Hai ordered. "That makes no sense... there are some eccentric noblemen, so maybe this group are just unaware of the danger they're in. Keep me informed."

The scout retreated.

"...Odd," Guan Hai murmured.

Taishi Ci repeated the spectacle again on the following morning and evening; once again, his small force retreated into the city after the short practice sessions. Some of the Yellow Turbans started to see the event as entertainment; they watched as Taishi Ci and his allies hit increasingly difficult targets with great accuracy, and laughed if anyone missed. But the gates were always well guarded when they were opened and closed; the besiegers were never given an opportunity to launch an attack.

"...I really don't get it," Guan Hai complained as he received a report that evening.

"They just went back into the city again," the reporting captain insisted.

"This has to be a trick," Guan Hai said. "Watch them carefully, Captain."

The captain smiled cynically and retreated.

"**I mean it!**" Guan Hai barked. "**Don't get slack!**"

"Shouldn't we just kill them...?" another officer complained.

"Not without knowing who they are and why they're doing what they're doing," Guan Hai insisted. "They're up to something..."

Guan Hai started to pace as he thought about it more carefully.

"...Do they want us to attack the open gates...?" Guan Hai wondered. "Do they want us to chase the men that come out...? Until I know for sure, I don't want anyone to do anything but watch them."

The officers grumbled about the decision, but no one argued.

Taishi came out of the gates again as dawn broke; the Yellow Turbans were waiting for them in lesser numbers, because Guan

Hai's orders were being disobeyed by the arrogant officers that were in charge on the battlefield. Taishi Ci smiled as he rode to the same practice ground to begin his ritual; his plan was working even more quickly than he had expected. He withdrew after a short time, and then he repeated the spectacle in the evening, before the sun set; the numbers that were blocking his escape dwindled further, and Taishi could sense that the following day would give him the opportunity that he had been waiting for, provided that nobody with better sense took over the field operations. Guan Hai did not say anything different, so his increasingly sceptical officers did even less to monitor Taishi Ci.

The following morning, Taishi Ci and his men rode out of the gates for the fourth consecutive day; the Yellow Turbans barely responded, and there were less than a hundred blocking the western road. As Taishi reached a natural junction that led to the west or his selected practice spot, he surprised the observers by going westward; the Yellow Turbans were as stunned as they were embarrassed, and they were as afraid of punishment as they were angry at being tricked. A chase ensued, but Taishi Ci's archers were painfully accurate; they turned and fired as they rode, knocking down man after man until the pursuit ended.

"**Didn't I warn you???**" Guan Hai shrieked at the captain that had been blamed for the debacle. "**I told you to watch them! Am I working with fools??? We have the will of Heaven to work toward! How could you betray Heaven with this act of blatant disobedience, cowardice and laziness???**"
The captain – who was bound with rope – was silent and resigned. "Death to you, heathen," Guan Hai muttered. "You've served the enemies of Heaven today, and have no place among us. Take him away."
Two soldiers pulled the captain to his feet and dragged him away; the condemned man chanted the famous 16-word mantra of the 'Way of Peace' instead of protesting, but Guan Hai and the other officers were unmoved.
"Now we face unwanted interference from more heathens," Guan Hai declared. "We should do all we can to take this place before they arrive."
The other officers agreed silently.

Taishi Ci and his horsemen rode through treacherous terrain, passing bandit forces, small pockets of Yellow Turbans and components of Yuan Tan's extensive supply route before they reached the Ji River.
"I'll go on alone from here," Taishi Ci said to the cavalry captain. "You should wait here for me for six days. If I do not return, then do what you know to be correct."
"Yes, sir," the captain replied.
"...Until we again, then!" Taishi Ci said jovially; the men exchanged respectful bows, and then Taishi started to ride once again.

Taishi Ci commandeered a boat to cross the Ji River, whereupon he was forced to cross more hazardous terrain on foot and cross the energetic Yellow River with another boat; he reached Pingyuan in a day and narrowly avoided the forces of Yuan Tan as he sought the fenced camp belonging to Major Liu Bei, Gongsun Zan's appointed Magistrate of Pingyuan.

Liu Bei was a man of average height that was famed for his large earlobes and regal demeanour; he was descended from a disinherited prince of the realm, which meant that he was, in the direst of circumstances, a potential future emperor. Liu Bei invited Taishi Ci to his command tent and greeted him with respect, but some of Bei's associates were less professional in their conduct.

"Who's this?" one gruff, grizzled man with wiry whiskers asked.

"This is Taishi Ci," Liu Bei sighed. "*Please*, Zhang Fei... please go and do something else if you're going to be in one of your moods."

The whiskered Zhang Fei got to his feet, stared at Taishi Ci, said, "You seem strong," and left the command tent.

"...My captain tells me that you are here to request troops to relieve Duchang," Liu Bei said.

"Thousands, if you can spare them," Taishi Ci replied politely.

Another of Liu Bei's officers – a tall, long-bearded man in green robes – smiled and said, "Am I right in saying that you are the same Taishi Ci that once delivered a petition by treachery and became a fugitive...?"

"Yunchang!" Liu Bei exclaimed.

"I am also a fugitive for doing the right thing, Lord Liu," the long-bearded man continued. "As I, Guan Yu, am a fugitive because of injustice, so is Taishi Ci. I meant no offence."

"...Oh," Liu Bei said with relief. "Mister Taishi Ci, I would love to meet your request, but I cannot spare any of my officers."

"Not even Zhang Fei...?" a thin, disorderly-looking man asked mischievously.

"Not now, Jian Yong," Liu Bei scoffed. "Forgive my officials, Taishi Ci, but we are under a lot of pressure. Yuan Tan is quite effective."

"Yuan Tan is *violent*, nothing more," the long-bearded Guan Yu suggested.

"I won't need officers, just men," Taishi Ci said. "If you can spare three-thousand good troops, Major Liu, then please do: that should be enough to break their siege."

"...How many Yellow Turbans are there, Mister Taishi...?" Guan Yu asked.

"By my estimates, thirty-to-forty thousand," Taishi Ci replied.

"...And you hope to break an army that size with *three thousand*?" Liu Bei chortled.

"It isn't impossible," Guan Yu suggested. "We've done that ourselves."

"...You're very confident, Taishi Ci," Liu Bei noted. "Alright, you can have the three thousand troops, if that's all that you think that you need... because saving the province and preserving the life of the respected Beihai Chancellor Kong Rong – with whom I have recently enjoyed a warm rapport – are very noble endeavours. Guan Yunchang: I leave the preparations with you."

Taishi Ci kowtowed and said, "Thank you, Magistrate. You are as benevolent as men say, and Heaven is surely on your side because of it."

Liu Bei smiled gratefully; once Guan Yu had escorted Taishi Ci from the tent, he turned to the only other man present – Jian

Yong – and said, "Did you see and hear Yunchang? Did you see
the way that Yide wasn't that rude to him?"
"I did," Jian Yong said quietly.
"That Taishi Ci is a talented man that could serve us one day," Liu
Bei decided. "Having just lost Zhao Zilong's service, is it not that
this man is sent by Heaven to bless us further...?"
"Maybe," Jian Yong said thoughtfully. "We'll see what he decides
to do when he brings the troops back."
"Oh, he must stay and help us, surely!" Liu Bei chuckled. "Yes,
Xianhe: Taishi Ci is the next man to join my army of heroes!"
Jian Yong smiled and replied, "Like I said... *maybe*."

Taishi Ci took the 3,000 troops – infantry and cavalry – that Liu
Bei had assigned to him and began the perilous journey back to
Duchang. That journey would take days, and Taishi Ci was quietly
worried that he would not get back in time to save the city: he hid
it well, however, and built a rapport with the borrowed troops that
earned genuine respect.
        The Yellow Turbans were still conducting their siege when
Taishi Ci reached the city. It would not be long, however, before
the Yellow Turbans broke through; Taishi Ci knew that a sudden,
unexpected strike was best, so he had the 1,000-strong cavalry
prepare to launch an attack while the infantry would follow as
quickly as they could. The result amazed the defenders that were
watching from the walls of Duchang, so much so that someone
hurried to fetch Kong Rong.
"Is it true...?" Kong Rong exclaimed as he reached the
battlements; he peered over the walls and laughed hysterically as
he watched Taishi Ci's cavalry scattering the unprepared Turban
forces. "The siege is lifted...!" Kong Rong realised. "We're... we're
saved...!"
Taishi Ci's borrowed infantry then arrived to complete the rout of
the scattered enemy, and the day was won; Yellow Turban
corpses littered the area around the city, and Guan Hai had fled.
Kong Rong had his own small force exit the city to aid in the
pursuit of the enemy, but the majority of the work was done.
Kong Rong himself then journeyed to the western gates to greet
Taishi Ci in person.
"Taishi Ziyi!" Kong Rong cackled. **"Taishi Ziyi, you are a god
among men!"**
"Thank the brave men under the command of Liu Bei of Pingyuan,
in addition to the brave men of this city," Taishi Ci replied. "All I
did was lead them."
"Guan Hai will not be back," Kong Rong said as he surveyed the
grounds around the west gate. "You have destroyed them, Taishi
Ziyi; that was regrettable, but they left us with no choice. What
will you do now...?"
"When we're sure it's over, I must return these fine troops to their
commander," Taishi Ci replied. "After that, I will return home, to
Huangxian."
"You won't fight for our lord ...?" Liu Bei's cavalry captain
exclaimed.
"No," Taishi Ci insisted. "Magistrate Liu is a fine man... but he
already has many fine men. I must go where I am *sorely* needed,
for that is where I am best used... but for now, I must return to

Huangxian and serve my mother as a good son, as Confucius dictated."

"...You are an amazing man," Kong Rong sighed.

Taishi Ci shook his head dismissively, turned to the borrowed forces and said, "We'll ensure that this place is truly safe, and then we'll go back."

Ten days later, Taishi Ci began the journey back to Pingyuan.

"...I am disappointed," Liu Bei admitted. His Pingyuan command tent was silent; Taishi Ci was unmoved by the words, however.

"I must be pious above all else," Taishi Ci insisted. "I have seen my mother's face but once in five long years, Magistrate Liu: she has been supported by Kong Rong for the last five years because I was a fugitive! I must atone for that!"

"*Aiee*... so moral, so just, so very much a man that I want in my service," Liu Bei said miserably. "I thought I had found another Zilong: of course you are every bit his equal, to be fair to you, but for you not to want to serve me... I am truly disappointed."

Taishi Ci bowed humbly and said, "I must go, Magistrate. I want to ensure the safety of Kong Rong one last time, and then I must go home."

"Yes: do not let me keep you from your noble path," Liu Bei replied. "Heaven be with you, Taishi Ci."

Taishi Ci bowed to each of Liu Bei's officers and went on his way once again.

"...What a shame," Liu Bei sighed.

Guan Yu, Zhang Fei and Jian Yong silently agreed.

Taishi Ci returned to Huangxian after his exhaustive exploits, where he received a hero's welcome by the villagers. In addition, he would no longer be considered a fugitive, so he was able to have a career at last; at almost the same time, the eldest son of Sun Jian was ready to begin his own career, and that would change China forever.

****

ACT IV: THE SECOND PRODIGY

38

The beloved patriarch of the Sun family of Fuchun, Sun Jian, had been killed whilst fighting a campaign against the Jing Provincial governor Liu Biao for his master, the nobleman Yuan Shu; just as his siege of the northern Jing capital Xiangyang seemed to be about to deliver victory, Sun Jian pursued Liu Biao's ally Huang Zu into the mountains after a failed counterattack and was felled in an ambush.

Much had changed during the last 7 years of Sun Jian's life: the Yellow Turban Rebellion saw over a million disgruntled peasants turn to a militant religious sect for guidance and rise up against the aloof Emperor Ling, who then died without declaring an heir; the 'Ten Attendants' – eunuchs that dominated court politics and heavily abused that power for personal gain for decades – were subsequently exterminated by Yuan Shao, the head of the noble Yuan family. But just as it seemed that peace may follow, Dong Zhuo – a devious general from the troubled northwest of China – managed to usurp power and become a tyrannical Chancellor of State; the resultant coalition against Dong Zhuo ended in failure, with Sun Jian as the only active member that achieved anything. Sun Jian had then been attacked by former allies when the two eldest brothers of the noble Yuan clan – Shao and Shu – became openly hostile toward each other. It was that last personal war that had cost Sun Jian his life, after all of the heroic exploits and the disasters that he had survived while fighting for the good of the state. His legacy was now left to his eldest son Sun Ce – known to all who respected him as Lord Sun or 'Bofu', his style name – and Sun Ben, the eldest son of Sun Jian's late twin brother. Sun Ben had been appointed as the military clan leader by the ambitious Yuan Shu, but others looked to Bofu as the future of the family and their southern home.

"...Nothing makes sense, Ziheng," Bofu complained as he stood and stared at the courtyard of his maternal uncle's home in Qu'e; that same uncle, Wu Jing, was still away on a campaign against Yuan Shu's chosen rivals, and so the Sun family had chosen to remain there after the mourning ceremonies ended. He was accompanied by his distant cousin Sun Hè and Lü Fan, a young man that he had come to see as his adviser as well as friend in recent times.

"Life rarely does," Lü Fan suggested.

"For such a long time, I've had to listen to what's going on in the outside world without being allowed to venture there," Bofu continued. "My father was a hero: he made history. Me...? Me, I just languish here, while Cousin Ben serves as clan leader instead of me."

"You know that won't be for much longer," Lü Fan said.

"How much longer is 'much longer'???" Bofu asked. "I wanted to avenge my father and prove my worth by defeating all of his enemies and humbling Yuan Shu, but I have to sit and listen while others come and tell me that person after person is doing it all instead of me!"

Lü Fan sighed and said, "Lord Sun... Bofu... I-"

"I really wanted to have my chance to march on Chang'an, fight Dong Zhuo and rescue His Majesty; but now I won't get that chance," Bofu continued.

Dong Zhuo – Sun Jian's enemy and self-appointed Chancellor of State – was assassinated by some of his own vassals within a year of the latter's death, and the resulting coup and counter-coup left a group of Dong Zhuo's loyal followers as the new 'caretakers' of the imperial government while the lead assassin – Dong's own foster son Lü Bu – was left as a wandering fugitive.

"His Majesty is still a prisoner that need rescuing," Sun Hè noted. "The-"

"Yeah, because the men that killed Dong Zhuo were either stupid, like old Wang Yun, or did it for the wrong reasons, like Bu!" Bofu chortled. "If strong, honest men like us had done it, Li Jue and Guo Si wouldn't be running the court!"

Sun Hè sighed and said, "Bofu, the-"

"And Wu Prefecture: what part of the world is called that now?" Bofu continued. "Uncle is trying to annex it all into Danyang, like this bit of it is already, but isn't Zhu Zhi 'Commandant of Wu'? If there's no Wu, won't that rob him of his position? And then there's that 'Xu Gong' bastard that's just invaded the northwest of Wu! Who is *he* working for...? Is it Yuan Shao again, or Yuan Shu playing games, or Tao Qian, or just another one that wants power...?"

"With all due respect, why are we discussing this again?" Sun Hè asked. "Everyone knows what's going on in the land, Bofu; why are we discussing common knowledge?"

"I'm trying to make it make sense!" Bofu retorted. "Dong Zhuo's idiot lackeys run the court now, which makes no sense! There are two, maybe three Wu Prefectures, and I don't know which bit I live in! Liu Biao beat Yuan Shu and chased him out of Jing, and Yuan just fled without fighting for it properly, after my father lost his life getting the place for him!"

Sun Jian's master, Yuan Shu, had secured the northernmost part of Jing Province despite the loss of his best general, but that vital foothold was quickly lost. Liu Biao chased Yuan out of Nan County and into Cao Cao's domains in neighbouring Yan Province, and Cao Cao quickly ensured that Yuan Shu was expelled to Jiujiang thereafter: Lü Fan and Sun Hè both sighed miserably at the thought of it.

"Yeah, and I'm doing more than sighing inside when *I* think about it!" Bofu continued. "And didn't Bu try and get a job with Yuan Shu? Where is the sense in that? Didn't Bu kill loads of Yuan's family? If Huang Zu came to me for a job, I'd tear his face off with my teeth, not-!"

"He rejected the request, and Bu fled Nan County before Yuan Shu could imprison him," Lü Fan recalled.

"He should have captured him when he had him in his courtroom," Bofu said. "Oh well, perhaps Yuan Shu thought it might be fun to let Bu go and then expect me, Cousin Ben or Uncle Wu Jing to lose our lives capturing him, and then he could offer Bu a job afterwards!"

Neither Lü Fan nor Sun Hè disagreed with the statement, since it was entirely plausible when considering Yuan Shu's previous behaviour.

"And now Yuan's attacking Lujiang," Bofu grumbled. "I know I hate Lu Kang – and rightly, given the way he treated me after Dad's death – but the Zhous don't deserve to have their home attacked! I have more to dislike Lu Kang for, and I wouldn't have sieged the place for it!"

Yuan Shu – who still had his sights set on wresting control of his clan from his half-brother Shao – licked his wounds after the loss of Nan County and prepared to build an alternative base from which to grow his own empire. He turned his attentions toward complete control of Yang and Xu Provinces: the eastern Danyang Prefecture in Yang was an obvious first target that Wu Jing was still trying to take, but there was Lujiang Prefecture in the northwest, which was under the popular rule of Administrator Lu Kang. Yuan Shu had repeatedly demanded that Lu Kang publicly join his faction and yield Lujiang, but Lu Kang repeatedly refused, citing that Yuan Shu was guilty of acting against the interests of the nation: Yuan Shu reacted calmly at first, but his mood after the loss of Nan County changed everything, and he quickly ordered a siege of Lujiang's major cities with a view to seizing the prefecture by force. The family of Bofu's friend Zhou Yu – whose benevolence made the Sun family's short stay in Lujiang during the Dong Zhuo crisis a truly pleasant one – were still based in Lujiang, so the situation worried the Sun family greatly.

"What I *really* don't understand," Sun Hè said, "is why the court hasn't ordered him to stop, as they did with Yuan Shao and Gongsun Zan."

Yuan Shao – the head of the noble Yuan clan of Ru County, Yu Province and leader of the failed Eastern Pass Coalition against Dong Zhuo – had resoundingly defeated the northern warlord Gongsun Zan in an epic military confrontation, but the two were subsequently forced to have an armistice by the regency court in Chang'an; Yuan Shao then began a campaign against the Black Mountain Bandits – a million-strong confederacy of smaller criminal gangs – that were still a force for chaos in the north, while Gongsun Zan – whose feud with Yuan Shao still stemmed primarily from a claim that Yuan Shao had reneged on a land-seizure pact and the subsequent death of Zan's nephew while fighting an agent of Shao's in Yu Province – found ways to harry Yuan Shao indirectly, such as supplying clandestine aid to the Black Mountain Bandits.

"Oh, yeah, *that*," Bofu chortled. "See, there's another nonsense: Dad told me about Gongsun Zan's nephew, the one that died at Yang City and caused them two to fight. He said that Gongsun Yue was a future hero, but he died fighting that other Zhou Yu – the one that works for Yuan Shao – just like how my father died in Jing, fighting Huang Zu… and for what…? What is any of it about…? …An *inheritance*. The entire east of the country is being torn apart, and all over which out of two spoiled northern landowner's sons should inherit all the power. But that aside, if I was Gongsun Zan, I wouldn't let the court tell me that I had to stop fighting Yuan Shao after the man wronged me like that. When I get my chance in Jing, Li Jue and Guo Si can send me all the petitions that they want: Huang Zu is a dead man, and so is Liu Biao, if someone else doesn't get to them before I do."

"Perhaps," Sun Hè said, "but my point was-"

"I know your point," Bofu interrupted. "I don't get it either, Bohai."

"I can only surmise that Yuan Shu *was* ordered to stop, but that he refused, and that's why the court sent Liu Yao here to take Yang from Yuan Shu and Tao Qian by force," Lü Fan said.

"And we'll be expected to help our wonderful master repel this 'Liu Yao', won't we," Bofu said. "We'll be asked – no, ordered – to fight a court-appointed governor and-"

"A governor that's been appointed by those immoral so-called 'regents' and their regicide-prone adviser Jia Xu doesn't have a lot of weight, so far as I'm concerned," Lü Fan interrupted. "Yes, we'll probably be asked, but don't consider it to be treason, necessarily."

"It doesn't change the fact that we're on the wrong side," Bofu suggested.

"Is there a 'wrong side'...?" Lü Fan countered. "Or rather, is there a 'right one'...? Yuan Shao started the military aspect of this when he sent his agent to attack your father: there were other, more diplomatic ways to react to Yuan Shu's declaration. Yuan Shao owed your father for his efforts against Dong Zhuo, but he attacked him anyway, seeing Sun Jian as 'a mere vassal of his brother'. Furthermore, other men of finer character, such as Cao Cao, supposedly argued against the attack on your father, and it's obvious that Cao is not benefitting from his current alliance – or should I say 'service' – as much as he could be. He's clearly doing something about it, and that should be our main focus once you are pronounced as head of the clan."

Bofu pondered the point carefully. Cao Cao had recently managed to pacify the majority of the Yellow Turbans in the northeast and turn them into a militia numbering in the hundreds of thousands: it was noted that said militia served Cao Cao and not the faction leader Yuan Shao, and that suggested political friction between the childhood friends.

"You think Cao Cao will break away from Yuan Shao?" Bofu asked.

"Not entirely, but the dynamic will change," Lü Fan replied. "At present, the two men are master and vassal, a leftover of their relationship during the lifetime of the Eastern Pass Coalition when Shao was overall commander; that should have changed when the coalition dissolved, and the two should have gone back to being equals and friends... but that obviously hasn't happened. Cao Cao is still sending communications as 'Acting Inspector of Yan Province', not its governor as one would expect. Yuan Shao hankers for Yan as part of his own expanding domain, and Cao Cao must surely know it. And to say they differ in opinion generally... well, that would be an understatement, I think!"

Bofu hummed agreeably. Cao Cao had been a proponent of a direct attack on Dong Zhuo, just as Sun Jian had been, but Yuan Shao refused to commit his forces to that end; When Sun Jian and Cao Cao were taking their own actions against Dong's forces, Yuan Shao was negotiating the 'seizure by subterfuge' of Ji Province from its appointed governor; and then, when Yuan Shu's petition reached Shao's court, Cao Cao argued for a peaceful solution to the feud that was wilfully rejected without consideration.

At the same time, Yuan Shao had become estranged from Zhang Miao, another childhood friend and Administrator of

Chenliu in Yan Province: Cao Cao had argued for a resolution to their feud but Yuan would not hear of it. To Yuan Shao, all of his old friends were either obedient vassals or hated enemies, and that left little room for sentiment: after being 'put in his place' on a number of occasions, Cao Cao had reduced his communications with Yuan Shao and concentrated on building his armies in Yan Province, seemingly in preparation for going beyond the role of mere vassal to his old friend.

"They're both destructive and stupid," Lü Fan continued. "The Yuans will carry on destroying each other's allies and eroding the nation until one day, when there isn't anything else left to destroy, they'll do one of three things: they'll destroy each other, destroy themselves, or reconcile completely and expect the land and people under Heaven to accept such a thing after all the shed blood."

"So what can we do...?" Sun Hè asked. "When faced with such inevitable misery, what can we do...?"

"Aha! This is not preordained, merely *likely*," Lü Fan replied. "Opportunities will present themselves: if a brave, wise, influential and powerful man were to take them, then a different future will be ahead of us. Who, though, has the courage *and* the way...?"

Bofu sighed miserably: he certainly had the will and the courage, but the 'way' – the military strength, wealth and connections required for such change - did not, at present, sit in his hands. But this was a time of change: just as the seemingly invincible Sun Jian had perished ignominiously in Jing and the tyrant Dong Zhuo had unexpectedly fallen to his own foster son's sword, another man that had enjoyed immense power was about to discover that nothing was certain and that even the simplest of mistakes could be costly.

****

Xu Province's Governor Tao Qian had enjoyed semi-neutrality during the war against Dong Zhuo and had taken control of much of northeast Yang Province when its weak governor proved to be ineffectual in the new, warlord-driven age that had begun; but now Tao Qian was a troubled man.

Yuan Shu had sent Sun Jian's brother-in-law, Wu Jing, to attack his holdings in the Danyang Prefecture; further to that, the new regency court had appointed a new governor, Liu Yao, to Yang Province with a view to stabilising the region in the name of their puppet emperor. Tao Qian was forced to abandon his hopes of taking Yang for himself and send Xue Li, the Chancellor of his capital city of Peng, to the aid of the new governor rather than become another target: it meant that he would still be fighting Yuan Shu for control of Yang Province, but not for himself, and that was a major blow to the old man's ambitions.

And then, in another twist of fate, Yan Province's Governor Cao Cao requested safe passage for his father, Cao Song, to travel southward from Qing Province to his home county of Pei once the Yellow Turbans had been brought under control. Tao Qian accepted the request, but the journey had ended abruptly with the death of Cao Song, the death or capture of Song's entire retinue and the theft of all of their considerable wealth. Tao Qian blamed bandits, but Cao Cao blamed Tao Qian, and the situation quickly turned into an out-and-out war between the two governors that the tactically unconstrained Cao Cao was winning easily.

Cao Cao was killing indiscriminately, and the civilian casualties were mounting daily as Cao wiped entire settlements off of the map in his quest for 'revenge'. Tao Qian looked to his allies – Administrator Wang Lang of Kuaiji, Administrator Zhao Yu of Guangling, Administrator Zhou Xin of Danyang, Peng City's Chancellor Xue Li, and Ze Rong, the chancellor of his eastern stronghold of Xiapi – for assistance, but they all had their own problems or agendas.

The Administrator of Guangling, Zhao Yu, was apparently blessed when the famous Buddhist cleric and Chancellor of Xiapi City, Ze Rong, descended on his capital with a fanatical following that numbered in the tens of thousands. Zhao travelled to the gates to welcome Ze Rong in person.

"Greetings, Master Ze!" Administrator Zhao said as he bowed low.

"Blessings be upon you," Ze Rong replied. "I am glad to see that we are welcome, given that some might consider my being here as an act of treachery."

Ze's appearance was humble: he wore simple robes, cheap sandals on his feet, and he wore no turban, opting to have his hair loosely tied. The vision of such a pious, popular figure delighted Administrator Zhao: no security measures were taken despite rumours that Ze and his closest followers had stolen all of the valuables from Xiapi City before vacating it.

"News of Cao Cao's atrocities in Xu Province is on every person's lips," Administrator Zhao said. "Some have questioned your coming here, yes, but in such times the people must be protected, and the evacuation is completely understandable."

"I am glad that you see my intentions with clear eyes," Ze Rong replied.

"I insist that you join me in a banquet," Administrator Zhao continued.

"I have with me many that are tired and hungry, so a banquet would not be fitting," Ze Rong said with false piousness. "I must decline and live alongside my brothers and sisters under Heaven."

"Your followers will be provided for!" Administrator Zhao promised. "Our granaries are full and our treasury is well-stocked: your being here is no trouble at all!"

"We should not tell him such things," an official whispered.

"He's a man of faith!" Administrator Zhao hissed. "Be silent!"

"You... are doing well here in Guangling...?" Ze Rong prompted.

"Very well," Administrator Zhao replied.

"Well enough to accommodate so many refugees...?" Ze Rong said with disbelief.

"Well enough to cater for all of Xu Province, should the need arise!" Administrator Zhao insisted. "The people must be protected from the evil Cao Cao!"

"...Quite," Ze Rong replied. "Well then, Administrator Zhao, I accept your generous invitation for the purpose of building a strong relationship between us. There are many battles to fight these days..."

"Oh yes!" Administrator Zhao agreed. "Yuan Shu covets Yang and harasses us in the south, while Tao Qian suffers hardships from Cao Cao in the northwest; in addition, bandits, tribal factions and Yellow Turban remnants are everywhere! There is never a moment's peace!"

"Then you and I shall pool our resources and fight for Heaven's banner," Ze Rong suggested. "Let's do what we can to build a new and prosperous future for all, free from war."

"Yes! Let us do that!" Administrator Zhao cried. "But first, let us celebrate your safe passage out of Xu Province!"

That same night, Administrator Zhao Yu had Ze Rong sit as an honoured guest at an ostentatious banquet in his residence. Ze Rong observed the cynical glares of many of Zhao Yu's officials, but he knew that there would be no dissent. Administrator Zhao was showing no caution whatsoever: he carried no weapon, he had no guards of any kind, and he was becoming steadily intoxicated as the night wore on. By the end of the banquet, he was so drunk that he was unable to stand up without assistance.

"You... you mus' come an' see t'city, tomorrow, or soon," Administrator Zhao said as his senior officials tried to escort him out of the hall. "Ze Rong, you are a blessing t'me... blessing!"

"May Heaven protect your honest soul," Ze Rong replied.

The rest of the gathering was no less disturbed by Ze Rong's calm demeanour and dubious intent; the former chancellor of Xiapi got up, bowed to the other invitees and left without ceremony.

Over the next week, Ze Rong was shown the entire capital of Guangling by its administrator, despite repeated warnings against such openness. Several days after the tour of the city's treasury,

Ze Rong reciprocated the administrator's generosity by inviting him to banquet in his own temporary residence.

"This is folly," Guangling's treasurer said as he travelled to Ze Rong's house with his master, Zhao Yu, and the city magistrate in a horse-drawn carriage. "If you must eat at tables with this man, Administrator, then do so on your terms!"

"I agree," the city magistrate said. "We're running the risk of-"

"He is a spiritual man, a man of faith, a living Buddha!" Administrator Zhao protested. "Why would a man that has devoted his life to such a benevolent, all-encompassing faith, a man that loves and cherishes all life, be a threat to me?"

"Ze Rong is his own master, and what he follows is not true Buddhism," the city magistrate retorted. "When does a 'spiritual man' that does not crave material wealth empty the coffers of the city he has been trusted with, and when does 'a man that loves and cherishes all life' flee his home province with his followers, leaving the rest to die a dog's death at the hands of Cao Cao's murderous hordes?"

"You're muddle-headed!" Administrator Zhao said. "You see villains as heroes and priests as demons! This man is-!"

"Your idol Ze Rong amassed Xu Province's commercial and taxation wealth in Xiapi and used it to build a false, self-serving Buddhist utopia... and then he stole all of that wealth when Cao Cao invaded, leaving Governor Tao Qian financially broken," the treasurer interrupted. "It would not surprise me if it was Ze Rong that killed Cao Cao's father for his vast wealth; and if we do not show more caution, we too will be destroyed by this false prophet."

"I won't hear any more," Administrator Zhao barked. "Be silent, both of you! He is not an evil man! He is a Buddha, a living Buddha, and I will not rebuke him because of a few unproven accusations! He is slandered by Taoist acolytes that fear his benevolent message! Now I won't hear any more, do you understand? No more!"

The magistrate and the treasurer sighed and said no more.

The banquet was not as ostentatious as the one thrown by Administrator Zhao, but it was lavish enough that the city officials were left impressed and suspicious. The guest of honour showed no more restraint than he had when he was the host, and Ze Rong was quietly glad of it; within two hours, Zhao Yu was intoxicated and close to being completely incoherent. Ze Rong placated his guests with sutras and other personal thoughts and witticisms while Administrator Zhao watched with drunken awe; at the end of the evening, the majority consensus was that Ze Rong had been a good and gracious host and that he could be trusted. That would soon be proved wrong.

"Oh, what... a shame we've got t'part now," Administrator Zhao said as his city magistrate helped him to his feet. "We... we still have s'much to... to say."

Ze Rong smiled; his attention was divided between the lesser officials that were leaving the banquet and the tipsy city Guard Captain, who had not opted to provide adequate security.

"...We should... do more... I mean, again," Administrator Zhao continued. "There so much... so much to learn if... if I am to become Buddha, and... reach Heaven as complete... y'know... get there good an' be-"

"You're talking *nonsense*," the magistrate hissed.

"His mind is lucid, even if his tongue is tangled," Ze Rong suggested. "He desires true spiritual peace, to become one with Heaven and reach Nirvana. He desires Buddhahood, which is attained through good deeds... great *sacrifice*."

Ze Rong's words were spoken so coldly that the city magistrate was left nervous; Administrator Zhao laughed drunkenly and said, "Yes! That... tha's it! Heaven... I wanna go t'Heaven as a Buddha! I wanna give... an' become a Buddha! Nirvana!"

"You shall certainly go to Heaven, Administrator," Ze Rong said. "You shall certainly give... you'll give all that you have."

Ze Rong had waited until there were only a few guests remaining; he raised his hand, and a throng of acolytes descended leapt out from behind the curtains and set upon on the Guard Captain, the magistrate, the treasurer, the bewildered Administrator and the other guests, killing them all.

"What now, Master?" Ze Rong's lieutenant asked.

"Now, Yu Zi, we go to the treasury," Ze Rong ordered as he stood over the corpse of Administrator Zhao Yu. "Heaven has deemed this place sinful, and in need of cleansing; we shall relieve it of its ill-gotten wealth, so that we might put it to better use."

All of Ze Rong's acolytes, including Yu Zi, clasped their bloodied hands together and bowed at his words.

Ze Rong sacked Guangling's capital and took his horde of followers southward yet again; this time, he crossed the Yangtze River and went to the strategically important city of Moling, which was now under the overall control of Tao Qian's former capital city chancellor, Xue Li.

"Ze Rong is here!" Xue Li announced to his cynical court in Moling. "Show caution, Lord Xue," Moling's magistrate suggested. "We have the Sun family and their allies to worry about: they now hold Qu'e and siege Danyang. If Ze Rong is coming here, we have to ask why! What about Xu Province, or the hospitality he received in Guangling? For what reason does he come here...?"

"We'll know when he arrives!" Xue Li barked. "You men of the south are ignorant, aren't you? You think you know Master Ze better than I, when he was my neighbour? I was and am the Chancellor of Peng, and I truly know Ze Rong! Ze Rong is a living Buddha! Governor Tao Qian allowed him to build a Buddhist Heaven under Heaven in Xiapi, because it was Heaven's will! Master Ze pacified the region, made good men from heretics and brought peace where there was unrest! He no doubt left Xu Province for the same reason that I did; he could do no good against the murderous Cao, but he can help Governor Liu Yao to repel the wicked, covetous Yuan Shu and his brigands!"

The officials were near silent at the proclamation.

"...Yes, I am aware of the fate of the Administrator of Guangling and Master Ze's *supposed* role in it," Xue Li continued. "But I trust him! There is an explanation, and we will soon hear it!"

The officials murmured cynically.

Ze Rong and his acolytes were greeted at the gates of Moling by a trusting Xue Li.

"Master Ze," Xue Li said as he bowed to the Buddhist cultist.

"You are on the way to Buddhahood, Mister Xue," Ze Rong replied. "Your generosity is noted by Heaven and by the great Buddha."

"What happened in Guangling?" one Moling official asked.

"...A sorry thing, indeed," Ze Rong replied as a hundred eyes bored into him, awaiting an answer. "Administrator Zhao had recently suffered incursions by men from Qu'e, such as former agents of Yuan Shu's general Sun Jian. Additionally, bandits run rampant, frenzied by the anarchy and carnage in the north; the Shanyue tribes are also active and looking for easy targets. I do not know which it was, but... the Guard Captain let his guard down whilst in a drunken stupor, and the city fell. Decadence was rife, and so, sadly, it was the will of Heaven that the place suffered as it did. Fortunately, the populace was not harmed, and Administrator Zhao Yu made a considerable donation to our cause beforehand, so he will definitely reach Buddhahood and know everlasting peace."

The Moling officials grumbled cynically.

"Master Ze, you must join us here in Moling," Xue Li insisted. "We need your spiritual guidance, and merely your presence here is surely a boon."

"You have my presence," Ze Rong replied.

"As you may or may not know, we are locked in battle with the vassals of Yuan Shu, who now covets this province," Xue Li continued. "The imperial court assigned Liu Yao as the governor of Yang Province, and it has been decided that the court is to be heard, even though it is currently run by Dong Zhuo's evil lackeys."

"Oh...? So... so you are allied to Liu Yao...?" Ze Rong asked warily.

"Completely," Xue Li replied. "He has forces stationed all around here. This is his provincial capital at present, since Yuan Shu currently holds the north of the province and the true capital Shouchun; but Moling is not really the best place for a capital in the south, so Governor Liu wants to take Qu'e City once the forces there are distracted by other matters."

Ze Rong nodded silently; he had been planning to wrest Moling from Xue Li, but the presence of the local, imperially-appointed governor had just made that impossible to achieve without becoming a wanted man.

"You seem to be haunted, Master Ze," Xue Li prompted.

Ze Rong smiled and said, "I am affected by the turmoil, Mister Xue. But I shall certainly remain here and do all that I can to aid you. Heaven realises that sometimes, even pacifists must take up arms against evil. Governor Liu Yao shall know my support and the support of all of those that have chosen to follow me."

"You are a blessing!" Xue Li cried. "Come with me, Master Ze! We must have a banquet to celebrate your arrival!"

Ze Rong smiled falsely and said, "You are generous, Mister Xue... generous."

Liu Yao, Xue Li and Ze Rong had now formed a strong force to the west of Qu'e, where the majority of the Sun family and their related clans were based. It was against the backdrop of this event and many others that Bofu, the 19-year-old son and heir of the fallen hero Sun Jian, waited for others to give him the opportunity to start his journey toward greatness and a place in history.

****

40

Bofu asked his cousin Sun Ben and his distant cousin Sun Hè to join him in the audience hall of his maternal uncle's home in the city of Qu'e.

"I've been looking forward to your return from the front, Boyang," Bofu began. "Now that you're here, I-"

"I know what this is about," the 22-year-old Sun Ben said. "You want to go to Yuan Shu."

"Yes," Bofu replied.

"...I dreaded this day," Sun Ben admitted. "Not because it means that I'm yielding the army to you, Bofu; that I have no problem with at all. It's the fact that Yuan Shu is a very tactless man: I worry that you'll lose your temper if he says something to you."

"I'm not as hot-headed as I seem, y'know," Bofu promised. "I've had a long, long time to think since Dad died, Boyang. I'm ready for this now."

"Be sure that you are," Sun Ben chortled. "I'm 'Inspector of Yu Province', but am I there...? No, I'm not, because I'm 'unfit for purpose'. He told me that to my face."

"The man's a bitter, incompetent coward and a fool," Sun Hè suggested. "He lost Nan County with pitiful ease a few months ago, so he's in Jiujiang now, no doubt plotting to sneak into Xu Province and take it from Tao Qian now that Cao Cao's softened him up."

"Yes, and we don't want to get dragged into any campaign there," Sun Ben said. "We have to avoid leaving this region, if we can. No Xu, and no more Yu or Jing if that's possible. We should try and stay in Yang Province."

"You're right," Bofu replied. "We need to focus on stabilising Yang Province, secondly."

"*Secondly*...?" Sun Hè said with confusion. "What's first...?"

"I can't do this alone," Bofu replied. "I need Dad's friends to help me do this. Even if I got Yuan Shu to give me what I want, I need more officers. Lü Fan's smart, but I I need Zhu Zhi, Cheng Pu, Huang Gai and Han Dang-"

"I have enough trouble getting the last three to listen to me, and I'm three years older than you," Sun Ben grumbled. "As for the first, recall that His Majesty appointed him as a 'Commandant of Wu Prefecture' shortly before your uncle annexed part of Wu Prefecture into Danyang and Liu Yao took the rest: why would he have to do as you say...? Couldn't Zhu Zhi just go and be an imperial lackey?"

"He gave that role up, once Liu Yao became Governor," Bofu explained. "Why are you being so harsh? He got our family out before Liu Yao took it, didn't he? And he didn't just flee, so there's loyalty there, still..."

"Yes, loyalty to your *father*," Sun Ben countered. "Rescuing a few people is one thing; Huan Jie negotiated the return of the fallen in Jing Province, didn't he, but he still went and served Liu Biao afterward, Bofu."

"Zhu Zhi is different," Bofu insisted. "He's promised me that he's with us. Would he still be in the northwest resisting Xu Gong...? Who's he doing that for...?"

"Yes, well, that still leaves the other three," Sun Ben said.
"Without them, I won't be sure I can do this," Bofu replied. "If they don't want to help me, then maybe I'll leave everything to you and we'll carry on as we are."
"...I'll invite them to Qu'e," Sun Ben said. "I wish you luck, though."
Bofu bowed gratefully.

Five days later, the remaining 3 of the 4 retainers that had seen Sun Jian as a brother and master – Cheng Pu, Huang Gai, and Han Dang – were sat in the governor's audience hall in Qu'e. They all wore white and colourless garments to show that their grief was undiminished.
"I feel no less aggrieved, even after all this time," Cheng Pu said after a long, painful silence.
"...I still wish I'd been there when it happened," Huang Gai said with anger.
"We weren't, though... none of us," Han Dang lamented.
"As I've said enough times, gentlemen... it was unavoidable," Cheng Pu sighed. "Every man has his share of luck, and Sun Wentai's was spent several times over."
Another period of silence began that lasted for several minutes. In that time, each man had their head lowered, their gazes only moving upward to snatch brief glimpses of the expressions of the others before they returned to the floor.
"...What do you think about the lad...?" Huang Gai asked at last.
"He is exceptional; had he only just appeared, I would say that he were the reincarnation of his father," Cheng Pu suggested.
"I just wondered," Huang Gai said forlornly. "He seems quite decent, but-"
"I can't just leave now, if that's where this is going," Han Dang declared. "This isn't over: Yuan Shu, our 'master', sent us on that suicidal mission into Jing, where we were easy kills for that bastard Liu Biao and that craven wretch Huang Zu..."
"...They might have *captured him*!" Huang Gai cried. "Why did they need to kill such a great man...?"
"Because Liu Biao didn't see him as a 'great man', did he, any more than Yuan Shu did!" Han Dang said angrily. "To that lot, to the men who have 'higher bloodlines', all our master ever was... all *we* are to them is... is... 'common peasants'."
"If I seemed to be wavering, then I shall now affirm that I *wasn't*, Han Yigong," Huang Gai promised. "This isn't over... it can't be. Not until Huang Zu is as cold and dead as that great man he killed, and-"
"That's not enough."
The three men turned to the source of the youthful voice, wherein they saw that Bofu had entered the audience hall while they were talking: he was dressed in armour as though he were about to embark on a campaign.
"Lord Sun," Huang Gai said humbly.
"Young Master Sun," Cheng Pu hailed quietly.
Every man then bowed their torso low to show deference or respect to their late master's son.
"I ask that you all call me *Bofu*; I also ask that you stay and help me," Bofu said calmly. "I'm not my father, no, but I'm not a

coward, either. I promise all of you here and now that I have no intention of rolling over. I'm taking down Liu Biao and Huang Zu, and I'm going to finish what my father started; Demou, Gongfu, Yigong... I need you all to help me do that. Will you help me...?"
None of the men needed to think; each man kowtowed and gave their own response.
"I, Cheng Pu, will humbly serve you, Lord Sun Ce!"
"I, Huang Gai, will gladly give my life to your great cause, Lord Sun Ce!"
"I, Han Dang, will give every moment of my life hereafter to aiding you, Lord Sun Ce!"
"...*Aiee*... alright, fine, well, I guess I'm 'Lord Sun Ce', then... for now," Bofu chortled. "I swear, though, that I'll die happier if I get any of you old men to just call me 'Bofu' even once."
"I'm not o-! ...I mean, uh, *yes*, Lord Sun," Cheng Pu said humbly.
"You're old to *me*," Bofu teased. "Anyhow... I'll leave you all now... listen, uh... thank you, all of you, for always being there for Dad, yeah...? He did appreciate it you know; loved you as brothers, one and all. Anyhow, I'll... be off."
Cheng Pu, Huang Gai and Han Dang were left with a newfound sense of loss; they left the house and went to the tomb of their late master, intending to make further tearful lamentations.

Bofu returned to the private audience room, where Sun Ben and Sun Hè were waiting for him.
"So they decided to follow you... *all of them*," Sun Ben said with surprise.
"Even *Cheng Pu* kowtowed to you!" Sun Hè chuckled. "That, I admit, is unexpected. So you're going to see Yuan Shu now, Bofu...?"
"Yep," Bofu replied. "That'll be interesting... but don't worry, either of you. I'm not going to let him get to me."
"I wouldn't blame you if you did," Sun Hè admitted.
"Will you require my presence...?" Sun Ben asked.
"You're the man that's been looking after things up to now, Cousin, so yeah," Bofu replied. "We'll go 'as soon as'; I want to get started."

Shouchun County – and within it, the capital city that was named for that county – was at the north end of Jiujiang Prefecture, so the journey was considerably long; when Sun Ben and Bofu arrived in the city, they immediately demanded an audience with Yuan Shu, who reluctantly agreed to it. When the Suns entered the audience hall they approached their lord without reverence or any other form of intent; as always, Yuan Shu's officials showed little respect.
"...Tiger cubs, indeed," Yuan Shu whispered as he stared at the youths.
Both of the Suns stopped and bowed respectfully when they were a few paces away from their lord.
"So you are Sun Ce," Yuan Shu said as he stared at Bofu.
"I am," Bofu replied.
"...*Tiger cubs*," Yuan Shu muttered once again.
"I, Ce, have here to pledge allegiance to you, Lord Yuan," Bofu declared.
"...Very good," Yuan Shu replied tonelessly. "So why are there two

of you?"

"I am here to ask for command of my father's troops," Bofu said boldly; Yuan Shu's officials either laughed, gasped or groaned as they awaited Yuan Shu's response.

"...Firstly, I shall say that I am impressed, genuinely impressed, at your spirit, and wish that I had such a son," Yuan Shu replied. "Secondly... I have to say that I am equally filled with disdain that a boy such as yourself should have the temerity to ask or demand that you be given *anything* by me. Do I know you...?"

"You knew my father," Bofu retorted. "You knew him as your greatest vanguard general, a hero of the age! I am his son in every way, and he intended for me to inherit his legacy! I do not *demand* anything... Lord Yuan. I *ask* that I be given command of my father's troops so that I can finish what he started. I want to take Jing Province for you, and I want to avenge my father by slaying Huang Zu."

"...Truly a tiger cub," Yuan Shu chuckled. "But a cub all the same! You cannot lead an army, boy; but that brings me to my next point. What 'father's troops' is this that you speak of...? Your father *had no troops*, little tiger cub... they are *my troops*."

Bofu stifled rage.

"...I'll do a deal with you," Yuan Shu said with amusement. "Your uncle Wu Jing is my Administrator of Danyang, is he not...? You can try and recruit your own forces in Danyang, just as your father found men in Wu. That region is famed for its brigades, and is seen a crib for great warriors... men that only respect true strength. Return to me with the same proven ability as your father, and maybe we'll discuss you being allocated more men... but until then... I suggest that you go, so that I might talk with the other one."

Bofu looked at Sun Ben, who was showing no signs of any emotion; Bofu bowed low, turned and left the hall, the sound of snickers and whispered critiques ringing in his ears.

"So where were we...?" Yuan Shu asked theatrically as he turned to the fuming Sun Ben. "Oh, yes! I was going to thank you, Sun Ben, for your enduring service as Inspector of Yu Province. Although it might be better if you were actually there, fulfilling that role that I so generously gave to you, or perhaps in Danyang aiding Wu Jing, instead of escorting Sun Jian's cubs to make demands of me...? ...*Dismissed*."

Sun Ben bowed low, turned, and left the hall.

"Any opinions...?" Yuan Shu prompted.

The adviser Han Yin bowed slightly and said, "My lord, Sun Ce is a truly impressive young man, but he must be kept on a leash like his father, though it may be for different reasons."

"...So you see things as I do," Yuan Shu sighed. "If he does as I have asked, I will give him troops, and have him fight against Liu Yao. Now we must discuss the main matter of the day: Cao Cao's expected second attack on Xu Province seems to be imminent, and Governor Tao Qian is busy preparing to defend what little infrastructure remains in Xu. His Buddhist ally Ze Rong had fled to Yang, taking much of the province's wealth with him, by all accounts; even with the rumoured aid of Liu Bei of Pingyuan, Tao Qian's days as governor are numbered. I want to take the province before Cao Cao takes it: if he got Xu, my wicked brother-cousin would surely snatch it from his grieving grasp and add it to his own dishonest acquisitions, namely Ji and Bing Provinces."

The burly officer Ji Ling bowed slightly and said, "My lord, let me take an army into Xu Province for you. I can seize the new capital Xiapi before Cao Cao returns to the region, and-"

"And then we can waste our resources fighting him again...?" Yuan Shu heckled. "Let Cao Cao burn himself out first fighting Liu Bei and Tao Qian's Danyang Brigades, Ji Ling... *then* we'll go into Xu."

"You're quite right, Lord Yuan," Ji Ling conceded.

Yuan Shu's other officials said nothing to question their lord's judgement.

Cao Cao's second foray into Xu Province would be as violent and unrestrained as the first: his destruction of most of the settlements in the west of the province during his first excursion made his march into the northeast, southeast and north of the region painfully easy. But Tao Qian now had the support of Liu Bei, the man that had recently lent aid to Taishi Ci for the relief of Qing Province, and support of an entirely different kind was about to emerge in Cao Cao's own domain. Yuan Shu watched those developments with hungry eyes, but Bofu could not care less: he was on his way to Danyang Prefecture to gather a force for his future campaigns in the south, and – he hoped – revenge on Liu Biao of Jing Province.

Upon reaching Danyang, Bofu sent a letter to Shu City in Lujiang Prefecture, the home of his close friend Zhou Yu – whose courtesy name, *Gongjin*, was now as preferred as 'Bofu' was to Sun Ce. Gongjin sighed as he read of Bofu's frustration, and muttered, "Yuan Shu will be his own ruin. But take heart, Bofu; your day will soon be here."

****

41

Bofu spent several months gathering a small force in Danyang; at the same time, the general disorder was allowing opportunistic bandit armies to gain the upper hand over the local militias. One of the biggest problems was an army of Shanyue tribespeople and pirates that were led by a man called Zu Lang.

"That bandit is tearing Jing County apart, Nephew!" Wu Jing complained as he marched up and down his audience hall, gesticulating wildly. "That Xu Gong fellow that took the north of Wu has probably pushed all of his problems down here onto me! That's probably where half of the reinforcements have-!"

"Calm down, Uncle," Bofu replied. "I've got a few men now, so I can go and deal with this idiot for you."

"*Ayah*! You are your father's son, alright, with all of his recklessness!" Wu Jing cried. "I cannot allow that, and as the administrator of this place, I forbid it! I could not face my sister if I-!"

"Mum's already said that I should do whatever I think is right," Bofu interrupted. "I have her blessing, Uncle; stop fussing, and don't bother tattling either."

"...Ayah! You are impossible!" Wu Jing whined. "How is it that all the Suns keep trying to kill me with stress when they are not killing themselves with acts of-!"

"Uncle, stop it," Bofu insisted. "C'mon... where's the hero that defeated Zhou Xin and made this prefecture his?"

"...You're right," Wu Jing realised. "It's because I *care*, Nephew; I watched you grow from a tiny child, and... and after what happened to Wentai..."

"I'm not my father, I'm me, and I have my own luck," Bofu chuckled. "A few silly bandits are no worry! This Zu Lang can't be tougher than Liu Yao!"

Bofu left his cynical uncle, met with his friend Lü Fan and travelled to his barracks, where Cheng Pu, Huang Gai and Han Dang were waiting with his small army.

"Hello again, my elderly vassals!" Bofu joked. "I hope that your joints do not ache too much at the moment!"

"...*Lord Sun*," Cheng Pu replied wearily.

Huang Gai smiled silently, as he did not mind Bofu's teasing at all.

"You have a look in your eye that I recognise," Han Dang said worriedly. "What mad thing have you decided on, Lord Sun...?"

"We're going to do something about the bandits in Jing County," Bofu replied.

"Zu Lang has quite a force now," Cheng Pu suggested. "He's allied with the Shanyue tribes, and quite he's likely to be getting help from Liu Yao and Wang Lang as well. We shouldn't try and match them with the little army we have."

"Aw, where's your sense of adventure, old grey hairs?" Bofu chuckled.

"I don't have grey hairs!" Cheng Pu retorted. "I'm barely gone forty, you-! ...I, uh... *ahem*. *Lord Sun*, I apologise."

Bofu grinned and said, "S'alright. You only have a few grey hairs here and there, I admit, but you *do* have them, though."

"Yes, and they're from *worrying about things*," Cheng Pu retorted. "Lord Sun, I do not want to go on an adventure. If we must confront Zu Lang, then we do it with the proper army that we'll get from Yuan Shu."

"We'll be *fine*," Bofu insisted. "We won't even need to get Zhu Junli to help us, since the bandits are hardly likely to have a plan. We'll leave 'as soon as', okay...?"

"...Alright," Cheng Pu sighed.

Bofu and Lü Fan retired to the command tent; Han Dang then turned to his friends and said, "Are we going to be alright?"

"The boy's got the spirit of his father in him, in addition to his own," Huang Gai said surely. "Even if we lose, we'll live: I say we go along with it. If he's no good, why find that out fighting someone more difficult to overcome than Zu Lang?"

"That's a fair point that I agree with," Cheng Pu decided. "We'll let him lead us on this, and see how he does."

Sun Hè was waiting for Bofu and Lü Fan in the command tent.

"I'm really looking forward to this!" Bofu admitted as he sat in the host seat.

"I had noticed," Sun Hè chuckled.

"I was born for the battlefield, Bohai," Bofu continued. "We'll beat this Zu Lang, and then we'll go back to Yuan Shu with a victory under our belts as well as an army! Revenge on Liu Biao and his friend Huang Zu will come next."

"I thought we were stabilising Yang first," Sun Hè said nervously.

"...Just testing," Bofu sighed. "I know we're stuck in Yang Province for now... but it's like I can hear Dad in my head, cousin Bohai, saying 'Avenge me!'"

"Uncle wouldn't burden you with that," Sun Hè insisted.

"Yeah, but I can't help but feel like that," Bofu said. "It's a big hole in the family, Bohai, even after three years: Mum's serious in a bad way, Kuang's so quiet, Yi's having trouble managing his feelings in the way that I used to, Shangxiang's becoming even more strange, and as for Quan... I dunno... something changed when Dad died. He's being funny with me, and he keeps doing things that would really anger me if I didn't know why. Huang Zu's taken something from us, and I want to take something from him; Liu Biao told him to do it, so he pays as well."

"I agree, but only when the time's right," Sun Hè said quietly.

"Now, though, the time's right to go and get Zu Lang out of this prefecture!" Bofu declared. "Get yourself ready for the adventure, Bohai; this'll be fun!"

Sun Hè looked at the silent Lü Fan and said, "You've got a plan?"

"Not really," Lü Fan replied. "We'll see how we do."

Sun Hè was unconvinced, but he did not argue with Bofu or his tactician. Once Sun Hè had left the tent, Bofu turned to Lü Fan and said, "You'll stay here and continue to gather recruits, Ziheng."

"I'd suggest nothing else," Lü Fan replied.

Bofu's younger brother, Sun Quan, was unable to enjoy living and studying in his birthplace in Fuchun, since Liu Yao had taken control of most of the south of Yang Province; small areas around the south bank of the Yangtze River were all that remained of

Yuan Shu's grip on the far south. He often complained about this to his childhood friend Shi Ren; the two were now close to 13 years of age, and they would soon be considered ready for official roles, such as military service, and even governmental posts.

"...Where would I serve?" Sun Quan wondered. "We're losing ground, not gaining it; how humiliating it is, Yifeng, now that I am now looking south to my home and seeing enemy banners raised! We look weak! We've lost Changsha, we've lost Fuchun, we've-!"

"Your brother has been unable to do anything up to now, but that's changing," Shi Ran replied. "Uncle tells me that your brother is going to fight the bandits in Danyang, and then he's going back to Shouchun to demand troops."

"Yuan Shu will say 'No' again," Sun Quan scoffed. "He doesn't respect us."

"He'll learn to," Shi Ran promised.

"...Your uncle writes to you a lot these days," Sun Quan noted.

"He has no son," Shi Ran explained. "He... he wants to adopt me."

"So you'd be called 'Zhu Ran', then...?" Sun Quan teased. "You'll be walking around, and people will shout '**Look here, Zhu Ran!**' and you'll ignore them, thinking, 'Who's this Zhu Ran fellow?'"

Shi Ran laughed and said, "Maybe, at first. But Yu Hè adjusted to being 'Sun Hè', so why can't I adjust to being 'Zhu Ran' after a time...?"

"Oh yes, and aren't we *all* having to adjust to things!" Sun Quan grumbled. "My father is cold bones, a forgotten hero, while his killer laughs and eats well! My hometown is under occupation by an appointed official of a corrupt imperial court run by western barbarian warlords, and my uncle and brother have to kowtow to a greedy, simple-minded northern nobleman that is actually fighting his own brother at the entire nation's expense! My father was shunted from place to place, fighting Yuan Shu's enemies and stealing land for him, but Yuan never had him do right and save the land from Dong Zhuo when the chance was there; now he does the same to my poor brother, so how long before he's brought back to our mother in a coffin?"

Shi Ran sighed and said, "Don't talk that way, Zhongmou."

"I must, for my own sanity!" Sun Quan retorted. "Even though I'm barely a man, I'm shunted from place to place too... just as I always have been! I was born in Fuchun, knowing little of my father 'cause he was always off somewhere fighting... then I was in Changsha, waiting for those howling barbarians to storm the city and kill us... then I was a guest in Zhou Yu's house in Lujiang, feeling like I didn't have a private space to call my own at all... now I'm here in Qu'e, and this isn't home either, and who knows when Liu Yao will seize it and force me to move again...? My father moved about, and my brother moves about, but they both knew who they were from birth, Yifeng. Heroes. Warriors. That's their calling. Who will *I* be...? What's *my* place in the world, Shi Yifeng...? What's *yours*...?"

Shi Ran shrugged and said, "I don't know, Zhongmou. I don't know. I don't know if I'm Shi Ran or Zhu Ran; you don't know if you're a future hero or a just another somebody. I am as frustrated as you... but our fates aren't ours to decide."

"They should be," Sun Quan said angrily. "They *will be*."

A day's marching brought Bofu's small 200-man militia face-to-face with the larger force led by the bandit Zu Lang. Shanyue tribal leaders had lent support in the form of horsemen and countless dozens of intimidating, glaive-wielding infantry; the bandits heckled the tiny militia, and Bofu's allies suddenly wondered if their new leader was doomed to lose or even die as his famous father had.

"I can see your faces, you know," Bofu said as he steadied his horse. **"Why is it that you old men have such a lack of faith in me?"**

"That force is too great for us to defeat!" Cheng Pu replied. **"We should bluff and withdraw!"**

"No, we should bluff and attack!" Bofu cackled. **"Huang Gai, Han Dang: each of you will lead a group to harass their flanks!"**

Huang Gai gazed at the disorderly mass of enemies and said, **"They have flanks?"**

"We'll pretend," Han Dang grumbled as he turned his horse and prepared to issue orders to his regiment.

"Cheng Pu, Sun Hè: we'll harass the centre!" Sun Ce ordered.

"...This is suicidal," Cheng Pu muttered.

The enemy did not expect Bofu's force to attack when the odds were so heavily stacked against them, so the initial shock-induced inaction led to casualties; Zu Lang was not stunned for long, however, and he yelled, **"There's next to none of 'em, lads! Surround 'em and smash 'em!"**

The Shanyue were already counterattacking, and it was only because of the skill of Huang Gai and Han Dang that the flank-harrying forces escaped with few losses. Bofu, Cheng Pu and Sun Hè were surrounded by the main force: Cheng Pu ordered the men to form a defensive ring to keep the enemy back while he tried to formulate a plan. Bofu, on the other hand, was looking for an opening; he saw that there were several places where the ring of enemies was weak due to lack of cohesion between the coalition of tribes and bandits, and he decided to exploit one of them. Bofu charged wildly at one group of men and used his glaive to hack and thrust at them; the men feared for their safety after the first few injuries, and an opening formed in the human wall. Cheng Pu and Sun Hè had their small cavalry ride around and keep the rest of the ring of men occupied while Bofu kept the wall open; their group of a hundred infantrymen then found the courage to make a charge at the broken formation and push their way through. Once there were next to no men trapped within the offensive ring, the men comprising it scattered; Bofu continued to lunge at any men that were obstructing his retreat, and his forces followed his lead.

"Why are they getting out???" Zu Lang cried. **"That was easy! What's the matter with you all???"**

Bofu had lost a small number of his men, and the day was lost: regardless of this, he turned his horse and gestured angrily at Zu Lang' army.

"Boy's *mad*," Zu Lang murmured.

Bofu's force was heckling with the same intensity as the victorious bandits: Bofu himself made beckoning gestures while Cheng Pu and Huang Gai led the injured men away.

"**We pursue?**" a Shanyue tribal chief asked.

"**...No, we won't,**" Zu Lang decided. "**He might have some tricks. Let him go.**"

Zu Lang sneered and laughed at Bofu, as he suspected that the youth's bravado probably was a bluff, despite his unwillingness to test the fact; the bandits started to withdraw, and their Shanyue allies reluctantly followed.

"**...Hold,**" Bofu ordered.

"**What do you mean 'Hold'???**" Han Dang exclaimed. "**We're-!**"

"**Never assume anything,**" Bofu interrupted as he gestured toward a cloud of dust to the north; Wu Jing and Lü Fan had arrived with another force, and the bandits were now caught in a pincer. Zu Lang was unable to control his panicked coalition, and men scattered in all directions: Bofu and his allies led two simultaneous charges, and the enemy force collapsed altogether.

"**And there you have it!**" Bofu shouted as Zu Lang fled the battlefield. "**Go and harass Liu Yao, Zu Lang! He doesn't have teeth and claws!**"

"*Ayah*... you're hurt!" Wu Jing whined as he reached his nephew. "I knew it! You're a man looking to die early!"

"So my arm's cut," Bofu replied. "Did you harass Dad like this?"

"**Yes I did!**" Wu Jing barked. "**And the one time I wasn't there, he-!**"

"Let's not talk like that, Wu Jing," Cheng Pu suggested. "We won. Let's go."

Han Dang and Sun Hè gratefully signalled to the army, and they collectively fled Jing County with an unexpected victory as their first experience of serving under the son of Sun Jian.

Bofu was surprisingly upbeat when he assembled his officers in his Danyang command tent to discuss the battle.

"Why all the glum faces?" Bofu asked.

"...Did we just fight in the same battle?" Cheng Pu scolded. "You were nearly killed!"

"Yep," Bofu replied. "We did okay. And you told Uncle to shut up about it before, so why are you being so fussy now? We did well!"

"Are... are you *serious*?" Cheng Pu exclaimed. "We were encircled! You were trapped, and you might have died! How is that-"

"We were up against a much larger force, and we lost a few men," Bofu interrupted. "But most of us survived, and Zu Lang was put to flight! We fought our way out when we were cornered, so that means we work well as a team, doesn't it?"

Huang Gai hummed thoughtfully.

"You agree with him, Gongfu...?" Cheng Pu chortled as he stared at Huang Gai.

"You have to admit, Cheng Demou, that we did do alright on that first charge, given the odds," Han Dang said. "If Lord Sun was a terrible leader, then we might all be dead now... and we certainly wouldn't have won. He didn't get scared, he didn't give up, and he fought his way out. That's what Wentai would have done. That's what he did do, at least once."

"...That's true," Cheng Pu conceded.

"We bluffed them, and we made them nervous," Bofu suggested. "Uncle only brought another couple o' hundred men, but the whole thing spooked them, and led to a rout. They'll think twice about

making too much fuss now, and when we come back with a bigger force than theirs, they'll surrender rather than fight. The men got a taste of everything out there: failure, despair, urgency, fear, courage, opportunity, hope, and eventually success when the enemy let us go. Okay, so we didn't win decisively, but did we lose...?"
The junior officers mumbled agreeably as they pondered the point; Huang Gai smiled; Han Dang laughed; Cheng Pu shook his head and said, "I sense your influence, Lü Fan."
Lü Fan smiled silently.
"But words have to be heard, and you are obviously a good listener," Cheng Pu continued as he turned his gaze back to Bofu. Cheng Pu reconciled his concerns about Bofu at last and said, "I'm beginning to like you, Lord Sun."
"But you still won't call me Bofu, will you, you stubborn old man," Bofu chuckled.
"...Not so long as you keep calling me 'old', *no... Lord Sun*," Cheng Pu retorted without malice.
"So will you go back to Yuan Shu now, Bofu?" Sun Hè asked.
"Yep," Bofu replied. "He's going to see what sort of men we've trained: men that can fight against the odds and survive. He'll give me troops, and then we'll start to do what we've all been waiting to do: we'll finish what my father started, and then we'll do more... much, much more."
Lü Fan smiled and said, "Indeed we shall."
Cheng Pu, Huang Gai and Han Dang looked at one-another with a newfound sense of optimism: they had found their new tiger, and this one, they decided, would not be shackled to the ungrateful Yuan Shu for long.

****

42

Yuan Shu was pondering a number of situations when Bofu returned to Shouchun: his half-brother Yuan Shao had effectively been blunted by the court, intentionally or not: Shu saw that as a victory for his own coalition.

To the west of Yuan Shu, Jing Province Governor Liu Biao was remaining neutral where possible, although that was becoming increasingly difficult. Yuan Shu and Bofu both had unfinished business in that strategically useful place, but both would have to wait until other matters were resolved.

To the southeast, the minor warlord Xu Gong had ousted the court-appointed Administrator of Wu Prefecture, Sheng Xian, and forced the latter into hiding. The court had opted to recognise Xu Gong as Administrator because he could placate the local Shanyue tribes and provide a stronger buffer against Yuan Shu's local agent Wu Jing; Yuan knew that he would eventually have to bolster the former Commandant of Wu, Zhu Zhi – whose militia was fighting Xu Gong unaided – or risk losing northern Wu Prefecture and ceding greater authority to the court-appointed governor Liu Yao.

To the south, the same Liu Yao was looking to expand his authority in Yang Province, but Yuan Shu held the provincial capital Shouchun: Yao needed a rival capital, and he was quietly preparing to secure one.

At the same time, Yuan Shao's friend and vassal Cao Cao was a twofold problem: he was technically defying Shao by attacking Xu Province without an official order, and his actions were so excessive that Cao's own vassals were on the verge of mutiny. The first assault had left Tao Qian a sick man and caused Tao's 'subordinate', the Buddhist cult leader and Chancellor of Xiapi City, Ze Rong, to flee the the province with most of Xu Province's wealth and tens of thousands of its inhabitants – and inadvertently provide Liu Yao with a new ally – but it had also led to Tao Qian summoning the warlord Liu Bei to assist him: both would have dire consequences.

To make matters worse again, Lü Bu – Dong Zhuo's former bodyguard and assassin – was wandering the northern heartland after being chased out of Chang'an by his former allies. Yuan Shu had rejected Bu's services outright, while Yuan Shao had first recruited him and then attempted to assassinate him for his part in Dong Zhuo's violent purge of the Yuan clan in the former capital: Lü Bu was seen as a threat to stability that could appear anywhere at any moment, and there was plenty of chaos for him to exploit.

But Yuan Shu had one immediate concern that could determine his entire future if mishandled: a young man that he had not expected to see again was now demanding an audience.

"...So Sun Ce has returned," Yuan Shu said as his adviser Han Yin finished announcing Bofu's arrival. "Should I grant him an audience, I wonder...?"
The hall was silent; the officials exchanged glances, but none of them wanted to venture an opinion.

"Will none of you speak...?" Yuan Shu chortled. "Han Yin, Yan Xiang, Chen Ji, Ji Ling...? ...Cousin Yin...? ...What, none, not one of you, has anything to say...?"

Yuan Shu's cousin, Yuan Yin, bowed slightly and said, "There is only one way to decide how to deal with Sun Ce later, and that is by dealing with him now."

"...A fair point, Cousin... a fair point," Yuan Shu said. "Do others agree...?"

"I do," Han Yin said.

"...And Mister Chen...?" Yuan Shu said as he turned to the officer Chen Ji.

"We should measure our words by his achievements," Chen Ji suggested. "Last time, he was a cub; he might be a tiger now."

"Quite right," the adviser Yan Xiang said.

"How many men does Sun Ce bring with him...?" Yuan Shu asked.

"A few hundred," Han Yin replied.

"Not very impressive," General Ji Ling suggested.

"A man of his age with such a small reputation should still be commended for amassing a following of any size," Yan Xiang said. "Mister Han, is it not true that his father's retainers and his cousin Inspector Sun Ben have also pledged their allegiance to him?"

"It is," Han Yin replied.

"...Sun Jian won over the men that followed him," Yuan Shu mused. "They are men that only follow worthy men; untried descendants of worthy men are of no interest to men of the south. If Sun Ce has won them over, then he is also a worthy man... no tiger cub, but a fully grown tiger! Show him in!"

Bofu walked toward Yuan Shu once again: this time, however, there were no derisive comments or condescending sneers. Now Bofu was of interest to Yuan Shu's court: junior and senior officials alike observed him as a future hero that might equal or even eclipse his father.

"I, Ce, come to you once again, and reaffirm my allegiance, Lord Yuan," Bofu said as he fell to one knee before his lord.

"...Tiger... you are a tiger, indeed!" Yuan Shu cackled. "Tigers beget tigers! Seeing you in your armour, I see a warrior, not a boy. Tell me, have your men been tested in combat at all...?"

"We recently fought a battle against the bandit Zu Lang that we almost lost, due to overwhelming odds," Bofu replied honestly. "I was able to break out of the encirclement and win in the end, but we have much to learn."

"But you won against heavy odds," Han Yin said. "Our reports on Zu Lang were giving great concern, so you've achieved something quite impressive."

"...He did indeed," Yuan Shu murmured.

"I have come here once again to ask for troops," Bofu said tactfully.

"...And you shall receive them, Sun Ce," Yuan Shu said with a smile. "I am about to launch a campaign into Xu Province, so that I can save the place from Cao Cao before the feeble Tao Qian loses it. I tell you that in order to help you understand that I cannot grant you more than a thousand troops; I need the rest for my invasion."

"I understand," Bofu replied. "I appreciate your generosity at such a time, Lord Yuan."

"Very good!" Yuan Shu chuckled. "Well then, let's see; I made Sun Ben the Inspector of Yu Province, didn't I, rather than awarding it to you… I would offer you that position now, but I don't like to snatch things from worthy men and grant them to others, you understand."

"I understand," Bofu replied. "I would not deprive my worthy cousin of something, Lord Yuan."

"So noble," Yuan Shu sighed. "Oh, for a son such as you. Anyway, I will instead grant you the role of *Administrator of Jiujiang* as soon as my arrangements for the march into Xu Province are finalised."

Bofu bowed low and said, "I worry that I am unworthy, Lord Yuan, but I shall accept your wise judgement and that of your counsel."

"So noble!" Yuan Shu cackled. "I say again, I would thank Heaven a thousand times for a son such as you! Forgive my bluntness, Mister Sun, but I have matters to discuss with my advisers."

Bofu bowed once again and said, "I shall depart, then, Lord Yuan, and return here at your pleasure."

"Very good! Oh, very good indeed!" Yuan Shu said with delight. "Dismissed!"

Bofu bowed for a third time and retreated from the hall; most the officials were no longer showing contempt now that he had apparently earned their lord's respect.

"He shows respect, but without showing weakness," Han Yin said once Bofu was gone. "In every way, he is his father's son."

"But giving him the role of administrator of the capital prefecture…?" Yan Xiang said despairingly. "Don't we want our tiger to be our agent in the worst of the wilderness? What good will a tiger be, hidden in an office behind stone walls…?"

"I am merely *placating him*, as one should with a tiger that might not be as tame as it appears," Yuan Shu promised. "I will probably grant the role to one of you."

The officials bowed respectfully and silently.

"Now what of the situation in northern Wu Prefecture…?" Yuan Shu asked. "That 'Xu Gong' is acting independently, but will that always be the case…?"

"At present, we have to focus our attention elsewhere," Yan Xiang replied.

"But doesn't Tao Qian's weakness embolden Xu Gong, Mister Yan…?" Yuan Yin said.

"Alas yes, it does," Yan Xiang replied. "But we can do little about that: Cao Cao weakened the old man, not us. At the very worst, Xu Gong will resume his persecution of the former administrator Sheng Xian, which is not our concern."

"But isn't Xu Gong an ally of Liu Yao…?" Chen Ji suggested.

"Inasmuch as Liu Biao is an ally of Cao Cao," Han Yin replied. "Xu Gong's actions were against the court: he is lucky that the land is in turmoil, else he'd have been destroyed rather than accepted. He'll continue to cultivate relationships with the Shanyue tribes, but while Zhu Zhi and Wu Jing do nothing more than harass his southern and western borders, Xu Gong will not be a concern. He'll only join Liu Yao if we force him to."

"Then we shall 'ignore him', in a sense… for now," Yuan Shu decided. "Zhu Zhi and Wu Jing are busy enough, and I cannot spare resources for yet another front against Xu Gong. Let us focus on Liu Yao... and *Tao Qian*. When we have Xu Province, we will be on our way to victory!"

Bofu wandered the streets of Shouchun after his departure from Yuan Shu's court, desperately trying to clear his mind of the frustration that he felt.
"You conducted yourself well, Mister Sun."
Bofu turned to the young officer that had hailed him and said, "Sorry, but I don't know you, uh..."
The young officer bowed and said, "Zhang Xun. I'm a captain. I was Acting Guard Captain during the meeting."
"...Right," Bofu said cautiously. "Well, uh... thank you, Zhang Xun, for your words."
"You don't trust me, I can see that," Zhang Xun sighed. "Like you, I'm a man that is trying hard; let's hope that we're both rewarded for our efforts."
"Agreed, Mister Zhang," Bofu said with a smile.
Zhang Xun bowed for a second time and retreated.
"...Yuan Shu doesn't deserve any of us," Bofu grumbled.

Bofu returned to his base camp outside the city of Shouchun and met with his allies; he was still angry, and the control that he had shown during the meeting itself was all but gone.
"Did it go well...?" Cheng Pu asked after a short silence.
"I... I think I'm really going to hate working for that man," Bofu grumbled. "How you lot grovel to him, I don't know."
"We don't grovel to Yuan Shu, we show expected reverence," Cheng Pu said.
"He's so arrogant," Sun Ce complained. "All that's changed is that I'm his 'tiger' now instead of his 'cub'! He-!"
"Yes, yes, but did he meet your request?" Cheng Pu asked impatiently.
"...We can have a thousand men," Bofu replied. "He needs the rest to invade Xu Province."
"So Danyang was no one-off: Yuan Shu intends to betray Tao Qian completely by seizing his province now," Lü Fan noted. "All untrustworthy... *all of them*."
"That's a fair point," Bofu said. "They're none of them trustworthy, are they? Yuan Shu, Yuan Shao, Cao Cao, Tao Qian... *Liu Biao*..."
"I'm getting angry," Han Dang admitted.
"Which serves no purpose," Huang Gai suggested. "Like it or not, we must serve Yuan Shu and await a moment to fly free. If he has met the request, it is because he fears that you will rebel if he does not, Young Lord. He can see, as we do, that you are no ordinary man; you are another hero, like your father, and that compared to you, he is a hankering mediocrity."
"True or not, we're without a force to realise any vision," Cheng Pu said wearily. "Did he give you any orders...?"
"No, none," Bofu replied. "He said he'd appoint me as Administrator of Jiujiang 'when the right moment presented itself' or some cobblers like that, cackled like a mad old woman for bit, and then he dismissed me."
"Is he demented?" Han Dang wondered.
"Without going over my own personal experiences and his entire

military history... I'd say so," Lü Fan said. "So you're promised the role of 'Administrator of Jiujiang', now, Lord Sun?"

"The Administrator role is 'pending', which means nothing at all when a man like Yuan Shu says it," Cheng Pu noted. "Now that Liu Yao has more allies, we're needed to bolster defences in Danyang, Lord Sun."

Han Dang smiled and said, "So forget staying here, friends, and let's go back."

"I... I don't think we should try and leave," Bofu replied. "I wasn't actually allocated the troops at any point; nobody actually assigned them to me yet. He's holding me here, which may mean any number of things. Let's put on a show for our lord: let's train the men, mingle with the Jiujiang locals – not just here in Shouchun, but all over the prefecture – and prove we're up to administrating it."

"A sound idea, Lord Sun," Cheng Pu said.

While Bofu awaited further instruction from Yuan Shu, his eldest brother Sun Quan continued to live and study in Qu'e. His friend Shi Ran was unusually quiet, and one day, after schooling, he demanded to know the reason why as they walked to the Sun family home.

"Uncle is officially adopting me," Shi Ran explained. "I shall be called 'Zhu Ran' from then on, just as I had expected."

"You make it sound so ominous," Sun Quan teased.

"...It's the timing, I suppose," Shi Ran sighed. "I'm not just losing my carefree life; I'm losing my entire identity. It feels like I'm becoming someone else."

"I've never really thought about that," Sun Quan admitted. "'Yu Hè' became 'Sun Hè', but he never seemed like anyone else but 'Sun Hè' or 'Bohai' to me, probably 'cause I never knew him before. He was already Sun Hè. But his family are still Yus, aren't they... well, I say 'his family', but they're not anymore, technically."

"That's what I mean!" Shi Ran said. "When I become 'Zhu Ran', my mother and my father become my uncle and my aunt, and vice-versa. That... that will not feel right. My parents have been good to me, Zhongmou, so I don't want to lose them."

"You won't be losing them," Sun Quan replied. "They're just... I dunno... becoming a different connection to you, that's all. And Zhu Zhi is alright, isn't he...?"

"He's a wonderful man," Shi Ran conceded. "He has always visited and helped with my tutelage; I'll learn a lot from him. But... he'll be 'Father', not 'Uncle'..."

"Look at it this way," Sun Quan said. "You'll have *two fathers*."

"Oh, I'm sorry," Shi Ran sighed. "I didn't mean to-"

"I know," Sun Quan said. "I was not being snide, just optimistic. I have Uncle Wu Jing, Uncle Sun Jing, and three mothers if I so choose."

"...How are your brothers and sisters?" Shi Ran asked.

"Yi's getting to be more like Ce with every passing day, always running about and throwing punches!" Sun Quan said with laughter. "Kuang is quiet... Shangxiang is Shangxiang... the others, well, they're children: no real personalities there yet."

Shi Ran sensed animosity and asked, "Do you view the children of the consorts differently...?"

"I shouldn't," Sun Quan replied guiltily. "I'm closer to Ben, Fu and Hè than I am or ever will be to the others. I can't help it. My cousins are my cousins... but the children of the consorts... Father cast Mother aside for them. Mother was the person that held it all together, Zifeng... while Father gallivanted about, fighting for this lord and that lord, this cause and that cause, she raised us. Whether we were in Fuchun, Changsha, Shu or here in Qu'e, it was Mother that we all knew and trusted, Mother that was always there. She even raised and supported her own brother. I know I'm not supposed to say things like that, but our family is different to other people's families. My mother kept us as a family, took in whoever Father wanted to take in... and Father cast her aside for Lady Chen, and then-"

"But she is not cast aside," Shi Ran suggested. "Resentment is not healthy, Zhongmou. Look at Yuan Shao and Yuan Shu; is that how you want to end up? Won't any sons that my new father has after adopting me come to see me as an obstacle to their birth-right, and is that right...?"

Sun Quan was silent.

"Family is complicated," Shi Ran continued. "Whatever choices your father made, you mother accepted them. And your siblings were born out of no free will of their own; don't blame them for *what* they are, love them for *who* they are."

"...What you say, it... it's what Mother says," Sun Quan admitted. "Lady Chen... Mother told me that I should see Lady Chen as an aunt, or perhaps a second mother... because, Mother said, anyone that could weep so much for my father... anyone that could be so broken by his death... deserved to be her sister, not her rival. But I cannot see Lady Chen – or the other one – as an aunt or a mother! I'll try, but...!"

"...Try harder, Zhongmou," Shi Ran suggested after a short silence. "I have to see my mother as my aunt: like I said, family is complicated."

Sun Quan sighed miserably and said, "Who am I...?"

"Now *that*," Shi Ran chuckled, "is *your* choice."

Sun Quan nodded thoughtfully.

"Talking to you, I see that having my family name changed is not so bad... I'm still me, whoever that is," Shi Ran continued. "I get to choose who really I am and who I really want to be. Names are names. My father and mother are still my father and mother in my heart... but I'm richer for having two fathers and two mothers. Hopefully, we'll get good jobs soon, and we'll both start building our careers, like your elder brother!"

"...Yes," Sun Quan replied half-heartedly.

The second son of Sun Jian was thinking. Bofu was the heir to the clan, and in the society of that time that left little for subsequent sons to do but serve the heir. Sun Quan empathised with Yuan Shu as, deep down, he felt that there was little to aspire to: he would always be 'the second son of Sun Jian' or 'the younger brother of Sun Ce' unless fate decided otherwise.

****

43

Yuan Shu summoned Bofu to his Shouchun court after weeks of no communication. The young heir to the Sun clan approached his master, knelt humbly, and said, "I, Ce, await your instruction, Lord Yuan."

"Firstly, you will be aware that I have appointed Chen Ji as Administrator of Jiujiang," Yuan Shu declared with a neurotic, aggressive tone that implied some sort of guilt. "You are better placed elsewhere, and Chen Ji is a sound choice for the role."

Chen Ji glared at Bofu and awaited his response.

"I accept your decisions without complaint, my lord," Bofu replied.

"Very good," Yuan Shu replied. "Now, uh… I intend to attack Xu Province now that the situation there has changed. As you may or may not know, Tao Qian has died and left the province to Liu Bei, who is refusing to pledge allegiance to me. In fact, he's in correspondence with my brother-cousin, the traitor! I-!"

"Perhaps Sun Ce does not care about that," the adviser Han Yin suggested pointedly.

"Yes… yes, that's quite right Mister Han Yin; that matter is not your concern, Sun Ce," Yuan Shu continued. "What *is* your concern is a certain Mister Lu Kang, the Administrator of Lujiang."

"I know him," Bofu replied.

"You know that I currently have him besieged…?" Yuan Shu asked.

"I have contacts in Lujiang that inform me of events there," Bofu replied.

"Are you also 'informed', Sun Ce, that he is a wretch, a fool, and a conceited man that dares to defy me?" Yuan Shu asked.

"I have had my own encounters with Lu Kang, my lord," Bofu replied. "His stance toward my late father was poor, and he and I are far from friends."

"That only makes you even more suited to the task!" Yuan Shu cackled. "You will go to Lujiang, and you will uproot and destroy the man for me! I regret that I could not abide by my decision to appoint you to administrate this prefecture, but what is done is done. Do this thing for me, Sun Ce, and you have my word that I will give you Lu Kang's post as a reward."

Yuan Shu's advisers exchanged weary glances.

"I shall gladly accept this task, my lord," Bofu replied.

"Very good! Very good!" Yuan Shu cackled. "I'll give you those hundreds of troops that I promised you now. As I am invading Xu, I need the rest."

"I am aware of it, my lord," Bofu said with a tone that almost betrayed his impatience and contempt.

"Yes, yes, of course you are," Yuan Shu sighed. "Oh, for a son like you… now, then: I asked that doddering cretin for grain for my campaign, so when you secure the province, kindly ensure that my demands are met."

"I shall, my lord," Bofu replied.

"Very good! Dismissed," Yuan Shu said with delight.

Bofu bowed penitently and retreated; once he was gone, Yan Xiang turned to Yuan Shu and said, "Again, my lord, you promise the boy a prefecture. So again I must ask if that is wise."

"Yan Xiang is right, Cousin," Yuan Yin said. "Why did you offer such a thing...?"

"...I am placating him," Yuan Shu promised. "If he is unsuitable, then I will appoint one of you. But if I renege too many times, I am in danger of upsetting him."

"Then stop promising him things!" Yan Xiang chortled. "Make him a general by all means, but do not give him land and taxable households!"

"Remember who is master and who is vassal," Yuan Shu muttered. "...But yes, Yan Xiang, I see your point."

"Mister Sun."

Bofu smiled and turned to face Zhang Xun.

"I didn't see or hear anything, even though I'm a major now, since I was on duty doing something," Zhang Xun continued. "How did your meeting go?"

"We should really go to a tavern to discuss it rather than standing around here, Zhang Xun," Bofu suggested.

"I'll pay," Zhang Xun said.

Bofu and Zhang Xun sat facing one-another in a tavern close to Yuan Shu's estate; Zhang Xun was obviously troubled about something, so Bofu asked, "What is it, Mister Zhang?"

"...I'm climbing the ranks, yet I'm just the son of a shopkeeper," Zhang Xun replied. "You're the son of Sun Jian of Fuchun, a hero of our time, and yet Lord Yuan holds you back. If I make colonel or general, I should like to promote you to a major and give you some power."

Bofu frowned and asked, "Why? You know it'd upset Lord Yuan..."

"You don't judge anyone," Zhang Xun replied. "To you, I'm Zhang Xun. I'm being promoted, but I could lose it all at any time for one mistake, because Lord Yuan does not tolerate failure. You won't fail, so once you're able to rise, you'll soar to the sky. I suppose that I'd like to think that I'd helped you if you needed help. After all, you've been a good friend: we've enjoyed many a drink, and I'm always welcomed into your barracks or residences as a guest."

Bofu risked the possibility that his promised promotion to Administrator of Lujiang might be a rare truth and said, "Your kindness is appreciated, and you know that you've always got a place in my army if I ever soar higher than you. Perhaps, one day, we'll dispense with the formalities and you'll let me call you by your style name as well."

"When I'm a man worthy of having one, perhaps," Zhang Xun replied. "Right now, I feel that I'm being given the opportunities that better men deserve."

"...I need to go, Mister Zhang," Bofu said suddenly. "I have news to take to my allies."

Zhang Xun bowed low and said, "A thousand apologies, Mister Sun! You should have said something sooner!"

"Don't be daft," Bofu chuckled. "But we'll need to all get together one day – you, me, Gongjin, Ziheng, Bohai, all the old men – and sit and have a proper chat. That'll have to wait though, until after the Lujiang campaign."

"Yes," Zhang Xun sighed. "I'm not looking forward to that at all. Lu Kang is formidable; I only hope my commanding officer doesn't send me to my-"

"You're going as well?" Bofu exclaimed.

"...I thought I'd told you already," Zhang Xun replied. "Oh... oh well, at least we can be sure that we can watch each other's backs if things go wrong."

"...Yeah," Bofu replied sombrely. "I'll see you on the march, then." The two men exchanged bows, and Bofu hurried to his camp.

Bofu returned to his barracks, summoned his officials, and explained the latest developments to them with as much optimism as he could muster.

"...So now we're being promised Lujiang," Lü Fan sighed. "I don't trust him, but we've little choice if we want those troops."

"I hate Lu Kang anyway," Bofu said. "Even if he hadn't promised me the man's role, I want to attack him for being rude to me and my father."

"Fine," Cheng Pu replied. "We'll have around five-hundred men in all, so-"

"More than that," Han Dang suggested. "People're joining us all the time, Demou. Lord Sun is as inspiring as his father ever was. We're even getting more pirates giving up their ways and joining us, just like they did for Wentai."

"Incredible," Cheng Pu murmured. "Truly... truly incredible."

"Gongjin's family are still in Lujiang," Bofu recalled. "It'll give me a chance to see him, hopefully."

"There's something else that we need to think about," Lü Fan said. "You need to start putting an effective set of bodyguards together."

"*Bodyguards*...?" Bofu snickered.

"That's a good idea," Cheng Pu said. "My lord, if your father had had a good set of bodyguards, rather than just having poor Zu Mao, he might have-"

"Okay, yeah, I get it," Bofu grumbled as his mood soured again. "None o' you want me to end up like Dad... I get it. I need bodyguards to protect me when I do stupid things... *fine*."

"I meant no offence," Lü Fan pleaded.

"No, Ziheng, I know that," Bofu replied. "Neither o' you want anything else other than to keep me alive a little longer than Dad. So did either o' you have an idea who I should have around me?"

"There are a few really good choices," Lü Fan said. "Wait, Bofu, and I'll introduce them to you."

Lü Fan left the tent; Bofu turned to Cheng Pu and said, "Bodyguards... the idea that I need *bodyguards* makes me feel so... *weak*."

"Your father had Zu Mao," Cheng Pu suggested. "I accept that Mister Zu was not defined as a bodyguard, but he once acted as a decoy to allow your father to escape from a potentially fatal situation. I'm sure that he would have tried to do the same when Huang Zu-"

"Yeah, alright, I get it," Bofu interrupted. "I really don't want to think about Huang Zu right now, okay...? Hearing his name makes my blood boil."

"The point," Cheng Pu continued, "is that it is not a sign of weakness, any more than having an army is. Yes, your father once scaled the walls of Wan and acted alone, and yes, he once bluffed an army of bandits, but most of the time, he accepted that he needed men around him."

"Haven't I accepted that too, Demou?" Bofu sighed.

"By asking us to continue serving you, yes, but in other ways, you clearly want to be a solitary tiger," Cheng Pu replied. "There's no such thing as a lone tiger in war."

Bofu nodded silently and awaited Lü Fan's return. Minutes later, a group of burly men entered the tent and formed an orderly line.

"This lot're pirates!" Han Dang cackled. "Isn't that Zhou Tai and that rascal Jiang Qin that I see?"

Two of the potential bodyguards lowered their heads and closed their eyes. Lü Fan entered the tent moments later and said, "I heard your words, Mister Han, and yes, they're former pirates."

"Look, I'm just being mischievous," Han Dang promised. "Mister Zhou and Mister Jiang are both good blokes. They became pirates for lack of choice; isn't that right, fellows...?"

The tall, intimidating Zhou Tai – who looked like a man that had been on the receiving end of many a beating and survived – and the brawny Jiang Qin – whose simple, austere clothing made him resemble some sort of travelling monk – nodded silently in response to Zu Mao's jovial question.

"...Have they had their tongues cut out?" Bofu chuckled.

"You're free to reply, both of you," Lü Fan prompted.

"We are old friends," Jiang Qin explained. "Yeah, we're old river pirates."

"You're neither of you as old as my father's friends," Bofu observed. "Thirties, maybe...? Still a lot older than me, but-"

"Age is *irrelevant*," Cheng Pu grumbled involuntarily.

Bofu grinned and said, "That's quite right, Demou!"

The small group of would-be bodyguards smiled silently.

"I should not have interrupted you, my lord," Cheng Pu said.

"Like I care," Bofu chuckled.

"So what do you think of the selected men...?" Lü Fan asked.

Bofu turned to look at the men and said, "Here's how it is, gentlemen: I need protecting from myself. You've probably heard about my father... some or maybe all of you worked for him."

Some of the men lost their smiles as they thought of Sun Jian and his untimely death.

"I trust you all, since there's no one that'd still be following me about that weren't either mad or looking to make a difference," Bofu continued. "So here's the deal: I'll let you all be my bodyguards, and in return, you'll try and keep me – and yourselves – alive for as long as possible."

The ensemble of former pirates, convicts and bandits bowed as one and gave vocal acknowledgement of their commitment to serving Bofu.

"Right then, we'll need to have these men become familiar with how I do things," Bofu said calmly. "I suppose that they can't drink when I do, which is a little unfair, but what use would drunk bodyguards be, eh?"

The newly-appointed bodyguards laughed together.

"I'll lead them," Sun Hè suggested.

"You're a Sun," Cheng Pu said.

"No, I'm a 'Yu' that was lucky enough to be made a Sun," Sun Hè retorted. "I want to repay the kindness by being by Bofu's side at all times to guard his life."

"You're not choosing that bloke, though, surely," Han Dang said as he pointed at one tall young man. "He's too young to be throwing himself to the tigers!"

"...You're maybe younger than me," Bofu said as he studied the tall man.

"I am seventeen, my lord," the tall youth replied.

"Tell us about yourself," Bofu said.

The youth bowed humbly and replied, "My family name is Chen, my given name Wu, and my style name is Zilie; I am from Lujiang, but I travelled here to Shouchun when I heard that you were going to begin your career."

Bofu was visibly stunned.

"If I can be of any use at all, Lord Sun, then let me serve," Chen Wu pleaded.

"Mister Chen Wu helped two men fix a broken cart, just as a kindness," Jiang Qin said. "He's as good a man as any could hope t'be, Lord Sun, so you should let him do *something*, if you don't mind me making suggestions."

"No... suggest all that you want," Bofu replied. "Mister Chen Wu... *Zilie*... you're in. I should say that I don't know if you'll all still be bodyguards at the end of the campaign."

"Why not, Lord Sun?" Chen Wu asked.

"I'm not a man that wants men wasted in jobs that don't suit them, Zilie," Bofu explained. "What I want to do is test you all: I want to know if you can lead men, or if strategy is your thing, or whatever. Even if I end up with no bodyguards, I don't care: if I ended up with really good field commanders instead, isn't that better...? I mean, would I need bodyguards if my army never lets the enemy nearly defeat us and get close to me?"

"That's a really simplistic way of looking at it, but it's quite right at the same time," Cheng Pu said. "You're quite a profound thinker, Lord Sun."

"That's me!" Bofu joked. "Right... I suppose the bodyguards have to follow me about as well, so that I get no privacy."

"That's how it tends to work," Cheng Pu said dryly.

Bofu sighed forlornly and said, "Demou, Gongfu, Yigong..."

Cheng Pu, Huang Gai and Han Dang awaited their instructions.

"You three were my father's limbs," Bofu continued. "That means that I don't need to tell you what needs to be done."

Huang Gai bowed humbly and said, "We'll prepare your forces for a march on Lujiang Prefecture."

Bofu turned to Lü Fan and Xu Kun and said, "You two, with me: my bodyguards, of course, have to follow me. I suppose I'll feel a little more popular, eh...?"

Lü Fan smiled and replied, "You just have more friends around you now, Lord Sun."

Once Bofu and his enlarged entourage had left the tent, Cheng Pu turned to Huang Gai and said, "He's definitely his father's son."

"Hey! No time for all that," Han Dang suggested. "Demou, Gongfu: let's get the lad's army ready."

Bofu collapsed into the host seat of his personal tent, as though he were returning from a gruelling campaign; Lü Fan noted the mental fatigue and said, "I didn't think that assigning you bodyguards would make you so miserable."

Bofu looked at the closed entrance; the silhouettes of his new

guardians were visible through the material. He frowned thoughtfully and said, "Maybe we should let 'em all in here and join in; after all, they're going to be with me through everything from now on, so they'll hear a lot of things in the long run anyway..."
Sun Hè and Xu Kun exchanged glances.
"...Like what...?" Lü Fan prompted.
"This is suddenly hitting me, Ziheng: the enormity of it all, I mean," Bofu admitted. "My father was sent to Jing to fight a man that he had never had any quarrel with; in fact, he liberated Wan City in Jing during his first campaign, didn't he?"
"He did," Lü Fan replied.
"Now I'm being sent to attack Lujiang," Bofu continued. "Now it's fair to say that I don't like Lu Kang. He was rude to me, and now that I know that he turned against my father I like him even less. But having a problem with him and attacking the whole prefecture - where my friend Gongjin was born, and where he lives now - that isn't the same. I was schooled there while Dad was fighting Dong Zhuo: I lived in Zhou Yi's house, ate from their table! How can I put them through that after they were forced to flee Luoyang to get away from Dong Zhuo?"
"We won't be harming the Zhou family," Lü Fan replied. "Lu Kang is expecting Yuan Shu to intensify his assault, so he'll advance north and-"
"Wait, so we won't have the advantage of surprise?" Xu Kun said.
"Sadly not," Lü Fan replied. "If I may: Lu Kang will not want his prefectural capital or county capitals harmed. He'll try and engage us on a field near an outlying rural settlement, and he'll assign defence forces to guard all of the prefecture's grain stores. Hefei's main city is a likely place for him to want to fight: It's fairly close to the Jiujiang prefectural border, and although it is a rather poor defensive position, there are good water supplies, a nearby ford and the roads are strategically useful."
"...Fine," Bofu said. "Wherever he intends to challenge us, he's a dead man."
"Because he was *rude to you*...?" Sun Hè chortled.
Bofu sighed and said, "I know that it seems petty, but he knew that I was grieving, he knew who I was and, more importantly, who my father was, and he should have known better. But it isn't just that: now he's refusing to support Yuan Shu, which means that if he isn't dealt with quickly, he'll pledge his allegiance to Liu Yao and we'll lose Lujiang to the 'government forces'. I may not agree with Yuan Shu about a lot of things, and I certainly don't trust him after the way he's treated my father and the way he reneged on giving me Jiujiang, but he's my lord and master, and his problems are my problems. One day, that'll change... but until then, that's how it is."
Sun Hè and Xu Kun offered no arguments, and the smiling Lü Fan offered no additional assessment; Bofu had made his decisions, and they would follow his lead.

****

44

Lujiang Administrator Lu Kang was startled when his officials brought word of the size of Bofu's force, which had numbered in excess of 1,000 before Yuan Shu had allocated any troops to him and grew naturally and considerably with each passing day.

"To think that the boy that once came here demanding an audience now returns with an army to destroy me!" Lu Kang exclaimed. "My principles, however grounded in Confucian decency, might have doomed this place to falling under Yuan Shu's heel! Perhaps I should have shown some small courtesy to Sun Ce at the very least, and then perhaps this disaster could have been averted, for that tiger might well have been convinced to serve his emperor instead of Yuan Shu, or at the very least refused to come here! Where was the careful diplomacy that I am trusted for when it mattered most...?"

Lu Kang's tired officials stared at him with empty eyes and failed to answer. The various sieges had taken their toll on the prefecture already, and the news that the veterans of the Wan City campaign of a decade before were on their way to Liujiang only reinforced the belief that the defenders were doomed.

"I must have a field engagement with this young tiger if I am to have any hope of repelling or at the very least delaying him," Lu Kang continued. "Huang Rang is busy to the south, but there are many other former bandit leaders and worthy men throughout the prefecture that-"

"With all due respect, my lord," one official said, "many of them are either dead or have literally fled to the hills."

"...They respected my 'strength and wisdom'," Lu Kang chortled. "But I have failed, gentlemen, to maintain that façade. We're doomed, and so now I must do all I can to... to do right in this last moment. Send word that Hefei should be doubly fortified against the coming threat, and evacuate your families. Ideally, I and I alone would die here, but at the same time we're defending Lujiang from traitors to the Han, and that is a responsibility that we cannot shirk."

The officials bowed slightly, and one said, "This is a sad day, my lord, but rest assured that we will fight to the last."

Lu Kang left his office and hurried to his home, where his great nephew awaited him. He looked at the frail youth – who was little more than 12 years of age – and said, "Xun, you are as astute as ever. More than fifty years of life may separate our births, but I can see that you understand things before I have even spoken."

Lu Xun nodded and said, "I do, Great Uncle. Who is going, and where shall we go...?"

"To Wu County, across the Great River," Lu Kang replied. "Take everyone."

Lu Xun nodded seriously.

"...And when a proper moment arrives, kindly inform my son Jun that we will not meet again for some time, but that I am proud of him," Lu Kang continued. "And watch over my little Ji... he is a marvellous boy, so thoughtful and wise yet still so young, and no doubt destined to be greater than I, his worthless father."

"You will surely survive!" Lu Xun exclaimed.

"I don't know whether that was a statement or a question, but the answer in any case is 'I shall certainly not'," Lu Kang replied. "But do not hate the man that will inflict this upon me, I beg of you: it is my failure to realise that the world is complex and that the choices a man makes are not always his own true will that is the cause of this calamity. Once, the Lus and Suns were friends: perhaps, if the wise chose to take each man for who he is, that day may come again, and the world will be a better place for it."

"...So it is Sun Ben, or maybe Sun *Ce* that comes here now," Lu Xun said.

"It is Sun Ce," Lu Kang replied.

"...I shall do as you ask, but reluctantly so," Lu Xun said. "That heartless lackey snuffs a great life for his wicked master!"

"But at present, he is not free to do as he chooses," Lu Kang retorted. "If his master orders it, he must kill the sun or sky: that is the relationship between lord and vassal by which he is bound. I forgave Cai Yong, who served *Dong Zhuo*, but not Sun Jian, yet they were both guilty of the same 'crime': lack of choice. If he is as good and kind a man as his father was, then Sun Ce is the most unlucky of us: his is an inherited bondage that only Heaven can deliver him from. My parting words are these: for the world to be a better place, then please, Heaven, act soon."

Lu Xun embraced his elderly guardian and said, "You raised me as though I were your own son. Now I shall repay your kindness by protecting our family as if I were a father to them all: may Heaven give me the strength to do it."

Lu Kang smiled and gently pushed his young relative away: after a moment of silence, Lu Kang retreated and Lu Xun continued the evacuation procedures that, in anticipation of the moment, he had already begun. Over the next few nights, men willingly flocked to Huan City to bolster its defences while families fled its walls under armed protection to seek a safer home elsewhere.

But one man in Shu City had no intention of rushing to the aid of the prefectural administrator.

"...You can *rot*, Lu Kang," Gongjin chuckled as he finished reading the notice that had been placed near the central marketplace; it was late evening, and most men were scurrying around and preparing for the horrors of a possible future siege.

Gongjin's father, Zhou Yi, patted his son's arm and said, "Do not say that too loudly, my son: most here are fearful of your friend's approach."

Gongjin urged his father to follow him back to the family home and replied, "I know how most feel, and I share their pain. But Lu Kang – 'General of Loyalty and Righteousness' – is loyal to a puppet and righteous to a fault, and he brought this upon himself; and he knows it, Father, else we'd have been arrested."

"I reasoned the same," Zhou Yi said.

"I agree with Lu Kang when he says that Yuan Shu is a traitor, but sometimes a man must show sense and choose his moments of defiance carefully, and that is something that Lu Kang could not do when it mattered most," Gongjin continued. "In that he shares a fault with the normally-exceptional Cai Yong, who wept in front of Dong Zhuo's corpse when that was the proper moment to rebuke him, and Wang Yun, who wrongly punished that same Cai Yong too harshly and otherwise showed total intolerance when cautious lenience was required. Bofu knows that opposing Yuan Shu now is not only dangerous but pointless: who will he turn to when the retribution comes...? Liu Yao, who now occupies his home region so disrespectfully...? Xu Gong, who hides behind titles but it little better than a bandit...? Liu Bei, who inherits a grudge against the Sun clan from Tao Qian...? Yuan Shao, who attacked his father...? Liu Biao, who *killed* his father...? Or the 'imperial court', led in truth by Dong Zhuo's petty and vindictive former henchmen that Bofu's father once humbled...?"

"All that you say is true," Zhou Yi sighed.

"This is a case of a stubborn, outclassed, old 'hero' with a misguided allegiance to obvious villains fighting an even-more-obviously leashed tiger whose unwanted master is a malevolent hankerer," Gongjin concluded. "Right and wrong have become an irrelevance: pragmatism is all that remains and it is all that I will show. That said, here is the truth of things: time and again, this city has narrowly avoided long sieges, and now Bofu comes here to finish what his master so incompetently and wrongfully started. He will harm this place, willingly or otherwise, and we shall have to flee until the deed is done."

"Lead the way, and others will follow," Zhou Yi replied.

Bofu's first battle in Lujiang took place on a small plain near the city of Hefei; Bofu struck an early and decisive blow against the defenders when he sent his cavalry – which numbered less than 100 – to harass the defenders' disorganised front lines. Lu Kang's officers tried to use strategy to reverse the situation; Bofu's cousin, Xu Kun, was informed of an attempt at outflanking the army and reported it to Lü Fan.

"Not to worry," Lü Fan replied as Bofu stifled laughter. "I planned for his having a slight amount of sense. We won't-"

"**We cannot sit here!**" Xu Kun shrieked. "**We must counter!**"

Lü Fan groaned and said, "**No, Xu Kun, stay with-!**"

Xu Kun screamed wildly as he left Bofu's side and charged at the small enemy infantry force with his own personal brigade.

"**Come back!**" Cheng Pu cried. "**Impatient...! ...We had a *plan*!**"

"**He means well,**" Bofu chuckled. "**Sun Hè, Chen Wu: assist him!**"

Sun Hè and Chen Wu both hesitated, but Bofu indicated that they should pursue Xu Kun, and they did as they were told.

"**Do you understand the point of bodyguards???**" Cheng Pu said with anger.

"**Yeah,**" Bofu replied. "**But do I need any...? Look at how they're doing.**"

Xu Kun's actions had blunted the attacks from the west, and Sun Hè and Chen Wu had shattered the infantry that were attacking from the east; the enemy were crumbling under the assault.

"...But... **but this isn't how we planned it!**" Cheng Pu despaired. "**We wanted to lure them in closer to-!**"

"**We're still winning, though,**" Bofu retorted. "**And that's all that matters.**"

Yuan Shu was delighted when his adviser Yan Xiang entered his court, stopped in front of him and bowed humbly.

"You have good news; I can tell!" Yuan Shu cackled.

"Hefei has fallen," Yan Xiang reported. "Sun Ce is marching double-time on Huancheng."

"Hefei falling is like telling us that someone ate something," Jiujiang Administrator Chen Ji scoffed. "That place has laughably feeble defences."

"When did it need them?" the adviser Yang Hong said. "It's not on a border with another province, and it isn't so long ago when that would not have been cause to fortify it either."

"My point is unaffected by your rhetoric, Yang Hong," Chen Ji insisted. "Sun Ce has achieved something very minor. When he has done as our colleagues like Chen Lan have done and remains in Lujiang for a year or more without buckling, then-"

"He's been sent there for *precisely that reason*, Mister Chen!" the adviser Han Yin said irritably. "The acquisition of Lujiang should not have taken more than a few months at the most!"

Yuan Shu laughed quietly as he watched his officials bicker.

"Lu Kang is no ordinary man," Chen Ji suggested.

"He's what, seventy years old...?" Yan Xiang scoffed.

"Age is only an obstacle when it is allowed to be," Yuan Yin said. "Men of our family were still fighting battles, attending court and arguing matters in front of their Majesties when they were white-haired and had adult grandsons to be proud of."

Yuan Shu nodded and smiled arrogantly upon hearing his cousin's words.

"That is quite right," Yan Xiang sighed.

"Indeed it is," Yang Hong agreed.

"Qiao Xuan was still formidable at the same age as Lu Kang," Han Yin conceded. "Lu Kang pacified Gaocheng, and nobody had any success there before him. Lujiang's only as peaceful as it is because of that man."

Yuan Shu's expression hardened and he stopped smiling.

"And remember, gentlemen, that his piousness with regard to the state and sovereign was such that he left Lujiang and took tribute to the capital at moments when men would ponder setting foot outside the walls of their city," Han Yin continued.

"That is true," Chen Ji noted; Yuan Shu started to shake angrily.

"He even took tribute to Chang'an, shortly before our military operation against him started, he's that steadfast," Han Yin recalled. "So when we say 'Oh, he is seventy', we should also note that he is a valiant, stalwart character that has won the hearts of bandits, pacified remote settlements where even the children and old women carried weapons for their safety until he did so, and-"

"Your tone suggests that we commit some sort of wrong by harming him now," Yuan Shu growled.

"N-no, my lord," Han Yin insisted. "I merely state that he is formidable, and that we should never have expected an easy, quick victory, not given that he is so loved by-"

"**Enough!**" Yuan Shu barked.

"Your anger is unwarranted, my lord," Yang Hong suggested.

"...Mister Han is merely extending credit where it is due," Yan Xiang said.

"I agree," Chen Ji said. "I ridiculed our enemy, when the classics clearly state that you should always respect your enemy where it is due. Mister Han corrected me rightly, Lord Yuan: do not castigate him for it."

"No harm has been done, noble cousin!" Yuan Yin protested.

"...So long as you all remember that there is one prevailing truth: you are my vassals, and you do my bidding, and that my bidding is that you are to expend no shortage of effort on vanquishing that stubborn old donkey that **dared to defy me!**" Yuan Shu declared. "**I am not some mediocrity that he can turn his nose up at! I am the rightful heir to the estate of the Yuans of Ru County! How dare he come here to Jiujiang with his brats, sit at my banquet table and tell me, in front of my vassals, that I am acting against the will of Heaven! Did I start this???**"

The advisers exchanged nervous glances as they pondered how they should answer.

"I asked a question, in writing, and I posed a challenge, in writing!" Yuan Shu continued. "My brother-cousin Shao responded to my words with violence against my tiger general Sun Jian, and with a groundless claimant to Yu Province! My tiger was chasing Dong Zhuo while Shao and his merry band of school-friends and fawning toadies did nothing but plan land-grabs and usurpations! I withdrew my tiger because he received no help, and because I considered his remaining in the ruins of Luoyang to be killed as an ignominious end and the waste of a valuable resource!"

Many officials cast their glances in random directions as they absorbed the implications in their master's rhetoric.

"So when that old fool Lu Kang had the gall to tell me, to my face and in public, no less, that I am acting against Heaven's will, **how can I not be angered???**" Yuan Shu asked. "**How can I not show frustration at being heckled by an old sack of bones that parleys with bandits and takes gifts to Dong Zhuo's cronies in Chang'an?!**"

Yan Xiang coughed falsely and said, "My lord, I-"

"You'd persist in defending him, I see," Yuan Shu scoffed. "You think that I should leave him be, then...?"

"No," Yan Xiang replied. "He must be coerced into siding with you, because if he remains neutral, he will only be approached – and if necessary, overthrown – by an agent of Yuan Shao's at some point, and we cannot afford to have Lujiang as an enemy base."

"Ah, so you see that, then," Yuan Shu heckled.

"*Ayah*! Did we not all discuss and agree upon it?" Yan Xiang despaired. "I have no problem with uprooting Lu Kang! None of us do! We're sweating blood to achieve it! I came here to report good news of progress against-!"

"Yes... yes, so you did," Yuan Shu sighed.

"...Now, all we can hope is that Sun Ce is a match for the old ox," Yan Xiang continued; the fatigue that he was feeling was evident, and it was shared.

"I am just... tired of being criticised unfairly," Yuan Shu said. "It was not my will that Dong Zhuo fled Luoyang, nor is it my will that we must acknowledge a puppet emperor. It was not my will that the Han is extinguished, its finest sons gone, and that the people will be forced to seek the clan that now possesses the mandate."

The officials looked at each other nervously.

"My wicked, hankering brother-cousin is to blame for it all, and by Heaven, I will smite him for it!" Yuan Shu cried. **"I will destroy him, claim my rightful place as head of our clan, and then – if what I suspect is true – I will do what I must to see this land unified under one sovereign once again!"** Those words made every man shudder.

Within weeks, every major settlement in Lujiang was feeling the pressure of a siege, and Lu Kang was forced to match his wits with the son of a man that he had first respected, then reviled, and finally insulted. The former pacifier of bandits was supported by many of those that he had pacified, but their devotion to a man that had humbled and then embraced them was not enough: supply routes vanished, supply stocks dwindled, projectile weapons were slowly whittled down in number and attempts at repulsion ended in losses of life. As days turned to months, Lu Kang and his allies watched the undaunted besiegers with a growing sense of resignation.

****

45

"This cannot go on!" Lujiang Administrator Lu Kang cried as he stood at the battlements of Huancheng City and stared at the siege preparations below. "Day after day, week after week... curse them! **Damn them all to an end more miserable than ours!**"
The surrounding officials fought tears of hunger and despair.
"**You hear me???**" Lu Kang screamed at the soldiers on the ground below. "**Damn you all, you villains! We'll pile the moat with your bodies, you-!**"
"Don't waste your strength!" an official pleaded. "They can't hear you, and they wouldn't care if they could!"
"...That is truer than I'd like," Lu Kang replied. "Let's retreat... or we're an extra burden to the brave men that guard these walls."
Administrator Lu Kang and his officials withdrew from the wall while his tired, miserable soldiers looked on.

On the ground below, the invaders were divided into two distinct factions: those that pitied the defenders, and those that saw it as just another siege and their lord Yuan Shu's will, and were hence unmoved.
"Yuan Shu's officers really don't care one way or the other," Bofu said to his cousin Sun Hè; they were stood at the entrance to Bofu's command tent having just finished delivering the day's orders to the other officers.
"I thought you hated Lu Kang," Sun Hè replied.
"Not this much!" Bofu retorted. "Not so much as I-!"
"**SUN CE!**" a burly general shouted as he marched toward Bofu's command tent with a retinue of officials.
"*Liang Gang*," Bofu muttered. "Three guesses what he wants."
"What do I win?" Sun Hè chortled.
"I'd love to say 'A boat going home'," Bofu sighed. "I truly would, Bohai, but-"
"**We'd appreciate your militia's assistance with the siege,**" Liang Gang said once he had halted.
"I know that isn't a request, General, but we know our duty," Bofu replied. "I've already sent my men to prepare."
Liang Gang smirked and said, "Will you lead them yourself...?"
"...No," Bofu replied.
"Oh...?" Liang Gang chuckled. "So you're not one for scaling the walls like your father? That's a pity; we'd be leaving here a lot sooner if you were."
Liang Gang laughed falsely, turned and retreated.
"I... really... want... to change sides," Bofu muttered.
"Don't let him goad you," Sun Hè pleaded. "That was so obviously scripted; he's been told to provoke you, I imagine, since-"
"Since making me feel like I'm a fraction of the man my father was might compel me to lose my life trying to outdo him," Bofu interrupted. "But I won't be goaded, Cousin, you can be sure of that; Yuan Shu and Lu Kang aren't worth dying for. I'm saving my greatest strength for *us*."
"I'm relieved to hear it," Sun Hè admitted.
"But I won't lie... it's tough," Bofu added.
But Bofu retained his resolve and ignored any attempts to goad

him into re-enacting his father's acts of heroism. Bofu would occasionally lead a charge against any bandit armies that appeared to defend Lu Kang, but he would never try and scale the walls of the city: he reluctantly left that to his followers, but the sight of their suffering injured him spiritually, just as it had done to his father. And so the siege continued for several weeks more, as did the mutual suffering.

"This... cannot... go on..."
Lu Kang staggered into his command centre – the audience hall of Huancheng City's magistrate's residence – and leant against the right wall. His face was drained of colour and substance, and he knew that he would soon succumb.
"Heartless... *heartless*...!" Lu Kang croaked as he started to slide down the wall.
"**Administrator!**" a young officer cried as he ran into the hall and steadied the old man as best he could. When the old man refused to remain upright, the youth shook him gently and said, "You must stay strong, Administrator!"
"No... point," Lu Kang replied weakly. "Over... over."
"We'll surrender!" the officer suggested.
"N-no...!" Lu Kang retorted angrily.
"But... you'll die!" the youth pleaded.
"You... were... bandit," Lu Kang recalled.
"I... I was," the young man said. "You made me see that-"
"Then... fight on," Lu Kang insisted. "They... are *wrong*."
"But-!"
"I die... not... not matter," Lu Kang wheezed. "Right... must live."
And so there would be no surrender, and the siege would continue for a short while longer.

"...It's killing him... his soul, I mean."
Gongjin spoke the words and shook his head sadly. His father, former Luoyang Magistrate Zhou Yi, sat next to him and said, "How much longer does Bofu think that it will go on for?"
Gongjin placed Bofu's latest correspondence on the desk in front of him, looked at the unfamiliar room around him and said, "I don't know."
The father and son and their family were living in a modest residence in a border town in Jiujiang.
"...Someone flicked their sleeve at me yesterday," Gongjin sighed. "Such public contempt – especially a harsh rebuke like that – means that we are not liked at all by some, and we don't know how else they might choose to show it."
"It's to be expected, my son, but I wouldn't expect violence," Zhou Yi replied.
The reaction to the Zhou family's presence was mixed, since Lu Kang had been a benevolent ruler in neighbouring Lujiang and the people of Jiujiang had equally benefitted from his pacification of the bandit army there.
"Part of me wants to question Bofu's involvement, but... but that's not pragmatic, and I must retain my pragmatism," Gongjin said. "No, of course watching our ancestral home being sieged isn't ideal, and I genuinely abhor the idea of it, but if Yuan Shu doesn't take Lujiang, then someone else – Yuan Shao, Cao Cao, or maybe

even Liu Biao – certainly will. It's too strategically important to enjoy neutrality."

"Spoken like a true pragmatist!" Zhou Yi chuckled.

"If only it were a joke," Gongjin sighed.

"I... I know it pains you, Son," Zhou Yi said. "I know that it pains Bofu too; Lu Kang's pedant attitude to right and wrong annoyed me as well sometimes, but... but he is a principled man at the end of the day, and they're few and far between. He was a hero, but the era of heroes is gone."

"A statement oft-repeated but never devoid of some amount of truthfulness," Gongjin lamented. "Sun Jian is, in a sense, lucky; he won't have to endure the... the..."

"...Humiliation...?" Zhou Yi prompted.

"I don't know if that's a strong enough word for it, Father," Gongjin replied. "One day, I hope to fight alongside my honorary brother Bofu, but... as what...? ...As a nominal vassal-by-proxy of that cretin Yuan Shu...?"

"We'll be his vassals once he takes Lujiang; in fact, we're his vassals right now just by being here in Jiujiang, so far as he's concerned," Zhou Yi suggested. "In fact..."

"...What...?" Gongjin prompted.

"He's... he's already approached my brother with a work offer, and he's invited me to his residence with what can only be the same," Zhou Yi confessed.

"...*Aiee*... then... then the die is cast," Gongjin realised. "I suppose that I'd hoped that somehow, in some way, we-"

Zhou Yi laughed and said, "You hoped that our elevated status would spare us the indignation? I'm now the exiled magistrate of a ruin. Our only path back to that world now is for us to go to Chang'an, and who knows how long that will last...?"

"...Everything has changed," Gongjin murmured.

"Certainty is gone; as you said, there is only pragmatism now," Zhou Yi continued. "I know it as well as you, my son... better, perhaps, for having endured the time of the 'Ten Attendants'... and so I know what must be done. I had to make compromises that would make you physically sick, I think, in order to protect us from those conniving eunuchs; Yuan Shu has none of their talent for stratagem and intrigue. He'll ruin himself, and some greater man will restore order. Until then, we must do whatever we can to still be alive when that day comes."

Gongjin smiled and nodded uneasily. The words did not change anything, they merely reinforced a series of unfortunate inevitabilities; one was that the siege of Lujiang would continue for a short time longer, and another was that the outcome was foregone.

Weeks passed; Bofu was reading a tatty bamboo book when Sun Hè ran into the command tent and said, "**Another bandit army!**"

"...Another one?" Bofu groaned as he tossed to book to one side and got to his feet. "This has to be the last, surely; just how popular is he...?"

Bofu followed Sun Hè to the walls of Huancheng City; lines of men had formed along the base of those walls, preventing any siege from taking place. They hollered for their Administrator to appear at the walls, and after a while, Lu Kang obliged. He was visibly frail, even at a distance, and two officials were obviously doing their utmost to keep him upright.

"He's... he's not got long, the bastard," Bofu said half-heartedly.

"But his bandit following will still defend the city," Sun Hè suggested.

"That... isn't all bandits, Bohai," Bofu replied. "There're local soldiers, too. But we have a job to do, and I can't forget what disrespect that old man showed me! He showed me no pity, so why should he expect any? For Lujiang to be spared misery later, Lu Kang has to be defeated, and we're going to do it now!"

Yuan Shu's generals, Liang Gang and Chen Lan, were already preparing to engage the newly-arrived reinforcements; Bofu hollered for his own subordinates, and the attack began. Lu Kang's officers dragged their emaciated master away from the walls, and as they did so, all that the old man could manage was the occasional faint croak. The siege would continue, but for how much longer, no one could know.

Weeks later, Yuan Shu's adviser Yan Xiang entered his master's courtroom and advanced with an expression that betrayed bewilderment and fear.

"Is this about Sun Ce?" Yuan Shu prompted.

"...He has submitted a full report," Yan Xiang replied.

"*Already*...?" Jiujiang Administrator Chen Ji scoffed. "That proves that he'd have made a mess of the role I now occupy, my lord. The-"

"He won," Yan Xiang said. "He's defeated Lu Kang. Lu himself is dead, the capital has fallen, and the surviving officials have pledged allegiance to Lord Yuan and his cause. Lujiang Prefecture is yours, my lord."

The hall was filled with gasps.

"...A *tiger*!" Yuan Shu exclaimed. "He's another tiger, perhaps more ferocious than the father!"

"Yes, and now he's doubtless planning a journey here to be formally assigned as the Administrator of Lujiang," the adviser Han Yin said with an admonishing tone. "What will you do?"

All eyes turned to Yuan Shu.

"...My lord, you must decide," Yang Hong said. "He was promised Jiujiang Prefecture, but you gave it to Chen Ji. Who will you give Lujiang to...?"

Yuan Shu looked at his officials and hummed thoughtfully.

"My lord, this is not a game!" Han Yin protested. "The young tiger will start to rebel if it isn't fed, but you keep promising the cuts from the family table instead of throwing scraps to the floor as you *should be doing*! Who will you give Lujiang to, I wonder, and where will you send him to next...?"

"I cannot give him Lujiang," Yuan Shu replied. "I cannot have my tiger in a cage. I want it to keep fighting for me; I want it to take more places for me!"

"So what will you tell him?" Han Yin asked.

"I... I will ponder it," Yuan Shu replied.

Yang Hong sighed and said, "For how long, my lord...?"

"As long as it takes, Yang Hong," Yuan Shu retorted. "Do you want me to rush my decision and make needless mistakes...?"

"He will expect a response very, very soon," Yan Xiang said. "I suggest, my lord, that you think *quickly*."

Yuan Shu hummed agreeably and dissolved the courtiers with a terse gesture; within hours, he had formulated a written response and given it to Bofu's messenger to deliver to Bofu's temporary base, the magistrate's residence in Huancheng City.

Bofu read Yuan Shu's response and threw it to one side with contempt. After a moment of silence, he could not resist the anger that was swelling in his chest; Bofu slammed his palm on the ground at his side and cried, "**Bastard! Liar and bastard! I knew that he'd do it, but even though I knew, it... it...!**"

"Go on," Han Dang sighed.

"He's gone and shafted me again!" Bofu said angrily. "He's given Lujiang to a 'Liu Xun'! He's another pampered relative of the emperor, no doubt! **He gave me his word! His *word*!**"

"Perhaps, but we all know that his word is worthless," Lü Fan said.

"Twice now, he's broken a promise," Cheng Pu noted. "Has there been a third?"

"No, his... his letter is very blunt," Bofu said as he tried to calm down. "It's got that 'I know I lied but I will not say sorry' tone about it. No, there're no more promises, but I expect that we'll be told that we have to go and help Uncle at some point. How can he not order me to go to Danyang...?"

"You'd think so," Cheng Pu replied. "But this man is... beyond description."

"We'll prepare for it," Lü Fan suggested. "We'll continue to recruit, and we'll prepare. He won't want to lose ground to Liu Yao, so we'll be sent."

"This 'Liu Xun': he's on his way here...?" Cheng Pu asked.

"Yeah," Bofu replied. "We 'won't be needed here', Yuan says... which means, let's face it, that he doesn't trust me to stay here in case I decide to declare independence like Cao Cao sort of has. He wants me to return to Shouchun."

"...You don't go to Shouchun on the way to Danyang," Cheng Pu said. "He has no intention of sending us to aid Wu Jing."

"No, he doesn't," Lü Fan agreed. "What then...? Does he intend that we help him to take Xu Province...?"

"I'm not sure that I care anymore," Bofu admitted. "Let's just pack up and go to Shouchun. Whatever he wants us to do, we'll be the last to know, and I'm not sure that I want to be here when this 'Liu Xun' arrives... he's going to make me hand the seal of office to him on bended knee, like we did to Lu Kang's man."

"We have to stay and endure the humiliation," Cheng Pu said. "I know that's not ideal, but we have no choice."

"...Zhu Junli was right," Bofu grumbled as he got to his feet to leave the hall. "The sooner we're away from this man, the better: please, Heaven... let it be *soon*."

Lü Fan, Xu Kun, Sun Hè and the bodyguard force followed their lord as he retreated into a private audience chamber; once they were gone, Han Dang turned to Cheng Pu and said, "When will that be, Demou? When will we escape this lying bastard Yuan Shu and have a destiny of our own...?"

"As the lad said, let it be soon," Cheng Pu replied.

Bofu reluctantly awaited the arrival of the man that would be truly rewarded for the acquisition of Lujiang: Liu Xun, the new prefectural Administrator. Liu Xun was a man of average height and average appearance, and his face was contorted into a triumphant smirk; he smirked as Bofu and his followers met him at the gates of Huancheng to proffer the seal of office.

"Don't get angry," Lü Fan pleaded.

"I'm past that," Bofu replied as Liu Xun stepped down from his carriage and sauntered toward him.

"Ah!" Liu Xun chuckled. "Sun Ce, the young tiger; so where is the administrator's seal...?"

The seal was very obvious, since it was the size of an adult fist, wrapped in red silk, and perched on a decorated ceremonial pedestal in Bofu's hands; Cheng Pu was forced to restrain Han Dang and Sun Hè was forced to restrain Xu Kun as Bofu fell to one knee and presented the seal.

"My thanks," Liu Xun said with false sincerity as he took the seal from Bofu's outstretched hands. "Will your forces be here long...?"

"No... we planned to depart as soon as possible, Administrator Liu," Bofu replied as he got to his feet.

"We shall forego a banquet then," Liu Xun said. "Have a safe journey to Shouchun."

Liu Xun returned to his carriage so that he could be driven into the city. Bofu and his followers watched powerlessly before they returned to their new temporary command post: a senior official's house that was within sight of the magistrate's residence that had previously served that purpose.

"You did well to remain calm," Cheng Pu said as Bofu took his host seat in the audience hall. "I wanted to rip the man's throat out with my teeth."

"So did I," Bofu replied. "But... I dunno... it's getting to be so normal that I see how Dad didn't explode. You just... get used to it, sad to say."

"But we shouldn't have to!" Xu Kun cried.

"No, Cousin, we shouldn't, but... our time will come," Bofu said calmly. "It will, I'm sure of it... we just have to be... patient."

Bofu and his force travelled to Shouchun, whereupon Yuan Shu confiscated the troops that he had amassed and ordered him to sit and wait for further instructions. The infuriated yet powerless Bofu agreed, and he sat and he waited; within months, the military and political situations in the north and the south changed, and new opportunities arose.

****

46

The regency court's appointed governor of Yang Province, Liu Yao, finally tired of the humiliation of having no proper capital to govern from. Of the 7 prefectures that made up Yang Province, Liu Yao now controlled Yuzhang, Kuaiji, southern Danyang, most of Wu and Guangling; Yuan Shu held Jiujiang – including the provincial capital of Shouchun – and Lujiang to the north of the Yangtze River, northern Danyang to the south of the river, and the adjacent part of Wu that included Qu'e. Liu Yao felt that the time was right to complete his takeover of Wu Prefecture, since its guardians, the Sun and Wu clans, were busy in Danyang and Jiujiang; Qu'e was deemed the best place to have an alternate provincial capital, and a sudden attack was launched on Wu.

"Lord Sun! Lord Sun!"
Bofu was startled by the sudden arrival of a vaguely familiar face; all eyes in the hall of Bofu's Shouchun residence turned to Sun Quan's childhood friend.
"...*Shi Ran*...?" Bofu exclaimed as the young man fell to his knees before his host seat and tried to catch his breath.
"I'm... called '*Zhu Ran*' now," the youth replied. "But please, my lord, listen! Wu is lost! Qu'e, it's lost! Dan-"
"Wu is lost???" Xu Kun said involuntarily. "That's our home! It-!"
"Calm, please, everyone," Lü Fan ordered. "What happened? Was it Xu Gong?"
"More importantly, is everyone alright...?" Bofu asked.
"The... sorry. Uncle – Father, I mean – he ensured that everyone got out, but Danyang, we lost Danyang as well!" Zhu Ran explained. "The-!"
"So we've lost everything south of the Great River, then," Lü Fan said as nerves started to get the better of the other officials in the hall. "That's unfortunate. What-"
"*Unfortunate*...?" Han Dang chortled. "That's our entire bloody lives taken away from us now, man from Runan!"
"Wait a moment," Cheng Pu said as he tried to control the anger in his gut. "I'm a little behind on events: young man, you're...?"
"Zhu Zhi's adopted son," Bofu explained. "Junli's been planning to adopt him for- ...Hey look, that's not important right now. Where'd everyone go if the southern prefectures are lost...? Where's my brother, my mother, my-"
"Father had them all moved to the north or into hiding," Zhu Ran explained. "Wu Jing and Sun Ben led the army to Liyang."
"That's something, I suppose," Xu Kun murmured as he looked at his cousin Bofu and shared his pain.
Lü Fan cleared his throat, stared at Zhu Ran and said, "I ask again: was it Xu Gong...?"
"N-no," Zhu Ran replied.
"Liu Yao, then," Lü Fan prompted.
"Yes," Zhu Ran replied.
"Liu Yao...?" Bofu exclaimed. "He... Liu Yao... Liu Yao, agent of those bastards in Chang'an, has control of my...?"
"...I can't believe we lost it all...!" Huang Gai said with emotion. "Losing Fuchun was bad enough, for that was where we first

began our careers under Wentai! How can we have lost *Qu'e*, the place where he is-"

"Can we not talk about that, please???" Bofu cried. **"How the hell do think that I feel right now, knowing that my father's burial place is in the hands of his enemies?"**

The hall fell silent.

"Liu Yao is not a fool," Lü Fan suggested. "He didn't order the massacre of the Sun and Wu clans, evidently. He allowed them to flee. So why would he desecrate a grave that cannot harm him...? Sun Jian isn't just the vassal of Yuan Shu; he's the hero of my home region of Runan to name but one place, and the man that fought against Dong Zhuo."

"That's what worries me!" Bofu admitted. "Aren't the imperial regents that control Liu Yao two men called *Li Jue* and *Guo Si*?"

Cheng Pu sighed miserably.

"Yeah, exactly!" Bofu whined. "My dad told Li Jue a few home truths, and he beat him in battle at least once as well, not to mention the feud with his old boss Dong Zhuo! What if-"

"That won't happen," Lü Fan insisted.

"You can't know that, Ziheng," Bofu retorted. "Don't fob me off."

"Alright, fine; I won't," Lü Fan replied disappointedly. "But if I don't 'fob you off', does it change anything, Bofu...?"

"...No," Bofu said. "I... I know that you meant well. I'm sorry."

"Don't be," Lü Fan replied. "Zhu Ran, your father has once again proven that he is a man with few contemporaries. We are eternally grateful that he has saved the clans of the loyal."

Zhu Ran bowed humbly.

"Was it a collaborative effort between Liu Yao and Xu Gong?" Lü Fan asked.

"Father... did not suppose it to be, or at least he did not say such a thing to me," Zhu Ran replied.

"...If that is correct, then Xu Gong is still acting independently, which makes recovering what has been lost far, far easier," Lü Fan said calmly.

Bofu realised that his cousin Sun Hè had not said a word; he turned to him and asked, "You alright, Bohai...?"

"Honestly...? ...No," Sun Hè admitted. "Your father is my father, as I've said often enough... and I worry for our family. Lady Wu, Quan, Shangxiang... It is Heaven's will that they escaped harm, but... I'm furious."

Bofu turned to his officials and said, "I'll ask Yuan Shu for permission to march against Liu Yao. He's got as much to lose as we have; in his own mind, more. How can he say no...?"

Lü Fan's cynical expression answered that question for any that saw it.

"...I can't believe he said no."

Bofu's words cut through the tense atmosphere like a knife; Yuan Shu's dismissal had been terse, cold and uncompromising.

Bofu shook his head with disbelief and said, "He sat there... with no expression on his face *at all*... and he said *no*."

No one could think of anything to say.

"...Where's Zhu Ran...?" Bofu asked of Cheng Pu.

"He was eager to get back to his father," Cheng Pu replied. "I had your thanks put into words for him to take back."

"Oh... well, you see, I wanted to give him a message for Quan," Bofu said. "The others, they'll cope in their own little ways... but Quan, he's... different. I know him; he'll see this as more uprooting, more uncertainty and chaos, more... more of the same. More of everyone... letting him down."

"My lord, we all of us have to retire for now," Lü Fan suggested.

"Yeah, you're right," Bofu said. "I'm so tired."

Bofu and his security entourage left his audience hall once again; Cheng Pu slapped his thighs with his palms and said, "We might not be able to march, but we can assist in other ways. There are refugees that need help, for a start."

"So what *is* Yuan Shu doing...?" Han Dang asked with contempt.

"He's sending Wu Jing and Sun Ben into Danyang with a new army to get it back," Lü Fan explained. "He's not diverted resources away from his planned invasion of Xu Province; I can see why, since Tao Qian's supposed to be dying or dead, there's talk of Liu Bei governing Xu now, and Cao Cao's invasion has turned into something else entirely."

"You sometimes forget that there're a lot of other conflicts to worry about," Cheng Pu said with a sigh. "Yuan Shu's watching the north like a carrion bird; Lü Bu's gone into Yan Province to aid a mutiny by Cao Cao's officials, and old Tao Qian's going or gone with no strong successor. Yuan Shu must think that whoever's in charge might cede the province to *him*."

"*Never*," Lü Fan scoffed. "It'll be one of Tao's sons, or his new friend *Liu Bei*."

"Everywhere you look, it's *Lius*," Han Dang complained. "Forgive me, anyone pious here, but the ruling imperial family are a *pain*. Liu *Biao*, Liu *Yao*, Liu *Xun*... and now Liu *Bei*; all of 'em my *enemies*, I have t'say."

"I won't disagree," Huang Gai said. "Governors Liu Yu, Liu Dai and Liu Yan in the north did nothing good; the first two were incompetents that lost their provinces, and as for Liu Yan... it was his suggestion to have governors instead of inspectors – and create a new era of warlords as a consequence – that led to the mess that we're feeling the effects of now. The Yuans wouldn't be doing all this to become inspectors."

"That's very true," Lü Fan said. "But Liu Bei...? I don't know... we'll see. He may end up being a friend rather than an enemy."

"Not a chance," Han Dang scoffed. "I bet he ends up being as much or more of an enemy than most o' the rest put together."

"Let's hope not, Yigong," Cheng Pu said. "We have enough unsolicited enemies as it is, I think. But Mister Lü, you say he's sending Wu Jing and Sun Ben back into Danyang... so why have all of us languishing here...?"

Lü Fan laughed desperately and said, "I don't know, Mister Cheng... because he *can*...?"

A week passed; Bofu summoned his followers and said, "Ziheng, Demou: kindly tell us what the situation is in Danyang...?"

Lü Fan turned to Cheng Pu and nodded silently.

"Liu Yao's sent forces over the Great River and stationed them at several key points along the riverbank," Cheng Pu reported. "In retaliation, Yuan Shu's appointed his own *Inspector* of Yang Province, some fellow called Hui Qu."

"I know him," Lü Fan said. "I had to work with him once or twice; an obsequious and somewhat ineffectual man, all in all."

"Appointing a rival *inspector* to the court-appointed *governor* is an understandable way of working," Cheng Pu continued. "Yuan Shu would never make a man a governor; he knows that he'd be creating another warlord."

"Yes, and he won't let me help Uncle Wu because he worries that we all might join up and go our own way, probably," Bofu grumbled. "I *would*… oh, I *would*… if I had the right excuse. But I don't. So not sending me to help is daft."

"So we wait," Huang Gai supposed.

"We haven't a choice, Gongfu," Cheng Pu replied. "We shouldn't do anything that might provoke suspicion, like recruiting or amassing weapons, lest Chen Ji report that he 'doesn't like our movements'."

"I'll give him 'movements'," Han Dang growled. "We toil for months to take Lujiang for Yuan Shu, and -!"

"Enough, enough," Bofu ordered. "We're all angry, but repeatedly getting angry and going over the same injustices time and again when we're powerless to do anything about it is just… soul-destroying. Let's just… wait."

Bofu met with his friend Zhang Xun once again and did his best to enjoy a moment of peace in the lively tavern.

"It's a shame that we didn't get a chance to work together during the Lujiang Campaign," Zhang Xun said.

"You got another promotion, though, which is good," Bofu replied.

"…And you got nothing, again, which vexes me," Zhang Xun said. "I did little more than harass outlying settlements and got promoted to colonel; you were the man that broke Lu Kang's defences, and you're still an Acting Major???"

"Perhaps there's some strange wisdom in there somewhere," Bofu joked half-heartedly.

"I am a man that values the lord-vassal rules, and I am bound to them… so I could never betray Lord Yuan knowingly," Zhang Xun said. "But… but at the same time, I am dismayed at his treatment of you and your family."

"Don't lose sleep," Bofu replied. "He'll see sense and post me to the south eventually… and when he does, I'd like you to join me."

"My place is here," Zhang Xun said immediately. "I value the courtesy that you, your family and your friends have shown me, but my place is here in the north. I will always be a penned letter away, ready to help you in any small way that I can, but my fight is in my home region of Huainan, and that is that. I could not bear to be separated from my home. You understand me, of course, because that's your burden… being far from home."

"You're a good man, and I'll hate losing touch with you," Bofu said. "I wish that I could compel you to bring your family to the south and fight under a southern banner, but I understand you and will say no more. But I'll keep in touch, wherever I am: you can count on that."

The two continued to drink and talk for some time, but Bofu was always divided between the conversation and thoughts of his embattled home region.

Shouchun practically overlooked the Yan-Xu and Xu-Yang borders: unrest and bloodshed were normality in the neighbouring territories. Tao Qian's death should have been opportune for Cao Cao, but Cao was now too busy in his own province fighting men that had once called him lord, brother or friend. Those men were led by Dong Zhuo's foster son and assassin, Lü Bu, the Chenliu Administrator Zhang Miao, and one of Cao's former advisers and confidantes; early signs indicated that Cao Cao might lose Yan Province and be left at the mercy of the mutineers and the new governor of Xu Province, Liu Bei. There was much chaos to exploit, and the thought of a march into either of those vulnerable northern territories was almost too much for the hungry Yuan Shu to endure.

****

47

While Wu Jing and Sun Ben did their best to regain the ground lost against Governor Liu Yao, a 28-year-old man of exceptional talent and character was enjoying a deceptive peace in his hometown of Huangxian in northeast Qing Province. That man was *Taishi Ci*, styled 'Ziyi', and fate was about to force him – yet again, and for the last time – to forget any hope of a peaceful life and continue the journey that would one day see him become a significant figure in the land.

Taishi Ci had returned to Huangxian after saving Beihai's Chancellor Kong Rong from destruction at the hands of a faction of Yellow Turban rebels, and since then, he had lived life as a labourer while the system gauged his chances of attaining rank after so many pardoned misdemeanours. Taishi Ci's mother, however, was disappointed at his lack of progress, and one day she made it very clear by frowning at him as he returned home from work. The expression cut into the exhausted hero like a knife, but he was more irritated that ashamed.

"Must I move a mountain...?" Taishi Ci complained.

"Of course I'm amazed and delighted by what you've done," Ci's mother insisted, "but you're not done yet. A man that was born right here in Huangxian is in trouble!"

"...Who...?" Taishi Ci asked miserably.

"Liu Yao, who is now the Governor of Yang Province," Ci's mother said sternly.

"Liu Yao is in trouble?" Taishi said with amazement. "How? I thought that his campaign was going well!"

"I don't know the details, all I know is that you should help a fellow townsman," Ci's mother replied. "By all means rest awhile, my wonderful son, but you were born to be great, and all you'll get here in Huangxian is rough skin and a hatred of vegetables. Always go somewhere that promises you something worthwhile; if Liu Yao does not need or want your help, go back to Kong Rong and find out who else needs help."

"...Very well," Taishi Ci said. "I cannot deny that I crave achievement, and relish helping others. I'll do as you say... once I've had a rest."

Taishi Ci would not rest for long: he journeyed southward within days, working in exchange for food and rest wherever it was required and joining carts of travellers when his worn feet could take no more.

Taishi Ci's first stop was in the capital city of Langya Prefecture.

"Well who's this...?" a tavern keeper asked as Taishi walked toward him and wheezed with exhaustion.

"I... I am here from the northeast, from Huangxian," Taishi Ci replied.

"*Huangxian*?" the tavern keeper said with disbelief. "You didn't walk here, I hope?"

"Not the whole way... but most of it, yes," Taishi Ci replied. "I'm not staying here long... I'm going south, to Yang Province. Wine, please."

Taishi Ci threw some money onto the low table in front of him.

"Welcome to Langya, then," the tavern keeper said politely. "You're looking for a place to stay on your journey, then...?"

"If that's possible," Taishi Ci said gratefully. "I'd also like to know a bit about the state of things at the moment. We don't get much news about the south in Huangxian at the moment."

"Everyone has gone insane," the tavern keeper grumbled as he poured wine for Taishi Ci. "I suppose you've heard that Cao Cao massacred half of Xu Province."

Taishi Ci nodded sadly.

"Some say thousands, some even say close to a *million*," the tavern keeper continued. "Mind you, I didn't think there were a million people to kill in the west of Xu Province. But apparently, it's all gone. Every last house, farm... everything. Then, just when it looked like Xu was doomed, the hero Liu Bei travelled down there. You know who Liu Bei is, right...?"

"I... I've heard of him, yes," Taishi Ci replied cagily.

"Hero; a real hero!" the tavern keeper continued excitedly. "Some say his men – led by his famous long-bearded general Guan Yu – helped Kong Rong!"

Taishi Ci was silent.

"Mind you, others say it was the infamous *Taishi Ci*, that 'man that ripped up the edict' from years back; I thought he was *dead*," the tavern keeper continued. "That's the problem with people: nothing's ever just straightforward! People hear wrong, add their own stories... there're a lot of people around here that like Liu Bei, myself included, so who's right about what, I don't know. But anyway, Liu Bei went to help the Xu governor, and... well, what happened next makes no sense."

"Tell me anyway," Taishi Ci said with cynical fatigue.

"Some say Liu Bei chased Cao Cao out first, or that he left of his own accord; either way, Yan Province's officials all rebelled against Cao Cao!" the tavern keeper continued. "He had to take his entire army home and fight his own followers!"

The tavern keeper found the notion funny, so he started to laugh; eavesdroppers joined in the laughter for a few moments while Taishi Ci waited patiently with a false smile on his face.

"...Sorry, I... it's just that we all hate Cao Cao around here!" the tavern keeper said through dying laughter. "When he was in-"

"Ji'nan," Taishi Ci interrupted. "I travelled through there at the time that he was chancellor; I know all about the man."

"Yeah... we all hate him," the tavern keeper said. "So we're all glad if he gets it from his own friends... they finally wised up, that's what we all say."

The statement was met with murmurs and grunts of accord from nearby patrons.

"What about the far south...?" Taishi Ci wondered.

"It's all connected, my impatient friend!" the tavern keeper joked. "The Yuans are what it's all about, apparently. Well, Yuan Shao is west of here, in Ji Province... Yuan Shu's in the south, fighting Yang's governor, Liu Yao."

Taishi Ci suddenly perked up.

"...Your expression suggests personal interest in that argument," the tavern keeper noted. "Any particular reason...?"

"Oh, uh... well, Liu Yao was born in Huangxian, so it surprised me

that he'd be in the far south," Taishi Ci lied. "Please continue."
"I'm glad to," the tavern keeper said. "Tao Qian's died, and Liu Bei's governor of Xu Province now; Yuan Shu's threatening him, which we don't much like."
The patrons voiced their agreement once again.
"Yuan Shu has a lot of allies," the tavern keeper continued. "The worst used to be *Sun Jian*."
"...He's dead now, isn't he," Taishi Ci prompted.
"Yes," the tavern keeper said without emotion. "But his family are still Yuan Shu's dogs, doing what he tells them; at the moment, the south is all about Yuan Shu and his dogs fighting Liu Yao and his allies; but you know, after all that Qing Province has to put up with – Yuan Shao's son and Tian Kai fighting in the west, bandits and Turbans everywhere, and Cao Cao and Lü Bu hacking each other's men up in Yan, we really don't need to know any more grief from the far south."
"...I'd quite agree, but I've been asked to go there, hence my interest," Taishi Ci replied. "I'm glad of your warnings, friend; I'd rather avoid all of it, but if I had to pick a side, then it would be Liu Yao."
"You're sensible," the tavern keeper said. "When you're ready, I'll show you our rooms: they ain't much, but this ain't Luoyang."
"If it was, I'd be sleeping in rubble," Taishi Ci quipped.
The tavern keeper and his grovelling patrons laughed at the statement; the keeper placed a friendly hand on Taishi's shoulder and said, "I'd forgotten it was burned down! Very fast wit, mate; I like you!"
Taishi Ci smiled silently.

Taishi Ci continued his journey as quickly as he possibly could and made minimal stops once he had crossed into Xu Province; much of the countryside had suffered cataclysmic damage when Cao Cao's forces had attacked it, so Taishi had to find food where he could and sleep in any spot that offered no obstruction.
"...Everywhere... is everywhere like this...?" Taishi Ci wondered. He eventually happened upon one lone wanderer that seemed to be drained of life; he gently coerced the man toward the side of the road that he was shuffling down and asked, "Is everywhere like this...?"
"Not... not Kaiyang," the man replied. "Everywhere else... not Kaiyang."
"Ayah... but I can't stop in Kaiyang!" Taishi Ci exclaimed.
Kaiyang was home to a bandit confederacy led by the minor warlord Zang Ba; his name was legendary in Qing Province. Zang's father had been a prison warden in their hometown, but when he questioned the lack of action being taken against actual criminals and the vast number of innocent men being incarcerated for criticising the local government, he too was arrested and prepared for deportation to the capital. Zang Ba turned, in a moment of desperation, to the men that his father had been campaigning against: the local bandits of Mount Tai. They agreed to help him free his father, and the father and son – now classed as criminal fugitives – fled into the mountains with their unlikely saviours. When the Yellow Turban Rebellion broke out, Emperor Ling's court demanded action, and Zang Ba led the bandits against

the cultists; his success was not amply rewarded, so when the opportunity arose, he seized Kaiyang in the north of Xu Province and founded an independent state that was, to all intents and purposes, governed by bandits.

Kaifang and its rulers were of no use to Taishi Ci, a man that had, like Zang Ba, been wrongly branded as a criminal, but decided, unlike Zang, to remain on the right side of the imperial law where and when possible: he groaned miserably and said, "Are you sure that nowhere nearby is habitable...?"

"A long way east... long way south... that or Kaiyang," the man replied tonelessly.

Taishi Ci shared a small portion of his supplies with the man and allowed him to continue his strange journey northward.

"...Cao Cao... is truly a villain," Taishi Ci sighed.

Whenever Taishi Ci stopped at the remains of a settlement, he watched with dismay as survivors and looters competed for what was left; whenever he was moving, he was forced to avoid the bandits and packs of Yellow Turban cultists that preyed on travellers that might have something to take. Some of Taishi Ci's journey involved boating down the Si River: his boatmen informed him that a part of the river had been literally been dammed by bodies during Cao Cao's attacks, which left Taishi haunted. The boatmen went on to tell him about the former chancellor of Xiapi, Ze Rong, and about how he had fled southward with all of Xu Province's wealth a year before, and that he was now allied to Liu Yao; that left Taishi wondering what sort of man Liu Yao now was.

A sobered Taishi Ci continued his journey by land until he left Xu Province and crossed into Guangling Prefecture in the northeast of Yang Province. Guangling was still held by allies of Liu Yao, but stories of the fate of the previous administrator, Zhao Yu, left Taishi Ci with even more doubts; he could not see how Liu Yao could be allied to Ze Rong, and he was becoming increasingly cynical. Nonetheless, he chartered a boat, crossed the Yangtze, and made his way to Qu'e.

"So this is Qu'e," Taishi Ci muttered as he walked the hostile streets of Liu Yao's capital city and searched for a tavern.

"Who are you?"

Taishi turned to the militia captain that had addressed him and said, "I'm Taishi Ci, from Huangxian. I'm here to give aid to Governor Liu Yao."

The militia captain sniggered and said, "Scruffy bandit! Why would Governor Liu want help from the likes of you?"

"Captain, that's *Taishi Ci*," a soldier whispered. "He's a *hero*!"

"...Oh, right... I thought I knew that name!" the captain said. "So you claim to be *the* 'Taishi Ci' that wreaked havoc in the northeast?"

"*Havoc*...?" Taishi Ci chortled. "I delivered a letter and helped some men with a few problems! How is that 'havoc'?"

"I should arrest you," the captain growled.

"For what...?" Taishi Ci asked. "I've done nothing wrong. I came here from Huangxian to help Governor Liu."

"Are you sure that you're not a friend of that brigand Sun Ce, or a vassal of the traitor Wu Jing?" the captain retorted. "This whole area is riddled with Sun family sympathisers that look and smell like you: so why shouldn't I just assume that you are just another former pirate that wants to make trouble for his master...?"

"I'm sure that Chancellor Kong Rong would have sent a letter for me, or that Governor Liu Bei will vouch for me," Taishi Ci replied. "Is there some way that I can be announced...?"

"I'll certainly inform the governor's officials that you turned up here," the captain said. "I can't arrest you, but I can keep an eye on you."

"Go ahead," Taishi Ci replied.

Governor Liu Yao had the good fortune of being advised by Xu Shao, a famous character appraiser that was well known throughout northern China, especially for his frank and apparently prophetic assessment of a young Cao Cao as a 'Crafty villain in chaotic times'. Word reached Xu Shao that Taishi Ci was in town, and Xu made Liu Yao aware of the development at the next meeting of the Qu'e court.

"Are we sure that this is Taishi Ci...?" Liu Yao asked excitedly.

"I have yet to meet him," Xu Shao admitted. "The captain reports a man that fits the description of Taishi Ci perfectly. If it is Taishi, then Heaven blesses you again, Governor: such a valiant hero will give you certain victory against Yuan Shu's cronies."

Liu Yao could see that his other officials were hesitant, so he did not reply.

"...I can sense that others doubt his talent, doubt his honesty or doubt his worthiness," Xu Shao chuckled. "I shall leave it to you to decide, my lord."

"I'll see this man from my hometown!" Liu Yao insisted. "Someone have him brought before me!"

A rested and bathed Taishi Ci was brought before Liu Yao's court: many of the officials were from noble northern families rather than southern locals, and they eyed Taishi with class-driven contempt.

"Mister Taishi...!" Liu Yao said without condescension. "It is good to see you! How is your mother? Is she well...?"

"She is, Governor," Taishi Ci replied as he bowed low.

"Stop that, stop that!" Liu Yao chuckled as – to the surprise and disgust of some of his haughtier vassals – he got to his feet and forced Taishi Ci to stop bowing.

"Please allow me to show deference, Governor!" Taishi Ci pleaded.

"No! I won't hear of it!" Liu Yao chuckled as he forced a disgruntled official to cede a seat near his own so that Taishi could sit as an honoured guest.

"You flatter me, Governor," Taishi Ci said as he reluctantly accepted the seat.

"You'll call me *Zhengli*," Liu Yao insisted. "Your mother treated me as an honoured guest in her home when I was young, so how can I not do the same?"

"I... I thank you," Taishi Ci said emotionally.

"You have come straight here from Huangxian, I hear," Liu Yao prompted.

"I have," Taishi Ci replied.

"...I have not been home in a very long time," Liu Yao said with nostalgia. "I see the place when I close my eyes sometimes."

"It is much the same," Taishi Ci replied.

"You and I, we're alike in so many ways!" Liu Yao chuckled. "We are both from Huangxian... that makes us brothers. We-"

"Is that so?" an official heckled. "So I should befriend and make kin of every peasant farmer and uncultured washerwoman that I ever passed in the street then, my lord...?"

Many of the officials snickered at the comment.

"**Silence!**" Liu Yao barked. "**Know your place!**"

"I know it," the official retorted. "But I wonder, Governor, if childhood reminiscence clouds your judgement and prevents you from knowing yours... and *his*."

"**Hold your tongue, pedant!**" Xu Shao ordered.

Other officials voiced support for the heckler, so Xu Shao stopped short of further criticism.

"**Silence!**" Liu Yao bellowed. "**I know my place, and it is as your governor!**"

The officials fell silent.

"Now what was I saying...?" Liu Yao said as he turned to the observant, cynical Taishi Ci. "Oh, yes! Ziyi, we both have a sense of duty, a sense of right and wrong... we both do what we must do to be true men."

"You once rescued your abducted uncle, did you not, Governor," Taishi Ci said.

"I did, though I think that your exploits far exceed mine, Ziyi!" Liu Yao replied. "Oh, it is good to have you here, Ziyi... so very, very good indeed."

Xu Shao smiled gladly.

"But that's enough sentiment," Liu Yao said with regret. "Ziyi, it has been suggested to me that I should employ you."

"I would gladly take any role, no matter how great or small, that allows me to serve you and hence the empire," Taishi Ci replied.

Xu Shao looked at Liu Yao with excitement and expectation.

"...Ziyi, we must discuss that privately," Liu Yao said pointedly.

Taishi Ci closed his eyes and lowered his head.

"You do not intend to make proper use of him!" Xu Shao realised.

"**Silence, Mister Xu!**" Liu Yao barked. "**I have my reasons!**"

The court fell silent.

"Please, Taishi Ziyi, follow me to my private meeting room," Liu Yao said.

Taishi Ci observed the indignant faces of Liu Yao's courtiers before he followed the governor's retreat from the main hall.

"...*Aiee*... we are beset with *madness*!" Xu Shao exclaimed.

Once Taishi Ci was seated to Liu Yao's left in the private meeting room, the governor said, "I remember you well, Ziyi, though over a decade separates our times of birth; as a boy, you were honest and good, and one and all could see you were a future gentleman if the state allowed it. Now, your heroism is well known to me and greatly respected, I promise you. But you must understand that there is another view shared by others; you know it well, because you're no fool."

"...I know it, Zhengli," Taishi Ci replied.

"To most out there, the truth is this: your first 'assignment' involved your winning a childish race to the capital to deliver spiteful counter-claims of improper conduct," Liu Yao continued.

"You destroyed official mail; for that, you were forced to hide in Liaodong. But you were not a gracious guest to your gracious host, some say: you helped a wanted man escape justice by smuggling him to the mainland. It is only with your third 'assignment' that you gain something other than notoriety: you aided Chancellor Kong, but that was with a borrowed army. Some say that the borrowed army included borrowed generals; in that case, what is it that you did?"

Taishi Ci sighed woefully.

"I share your distress," Liu Yao promised. "But the situation is out of my hands. To them, you're a man that has had the stain of criminality etched on his soul, if not tattooed on his forehead. To them, I cannot risk trusting a man that destroys correspondence and defies governors by saving local vagabonds. When I challenge them, they'll say, 'What if Taishi decided to smuggle an ally of Sun Ce out of Qu'e tomorrow, simply because his overwhelming sense of morality dictated it'...?"

"...I admit that I cannot answer that," Taishi Ci replied.

"No... and neither can I," Liu Yao continued. "I believe that you would betray me if justice or morality demanded it, Ziyi... and I would not blame you for it. That truth is a truth because you are a true hero... in an age where heroes do not have a place."

Taishi Ci stared at his new benefactor with disbelief.

"The age of heroes is gone," Liu Yao lamented. "All of that – the exploits of Sun Jian, Cao Cao, Zhu Jun, and all the rest – is history. Now, Sun Jian's son is a rebel serving Yuan Shu, Cao Cao is a thief and murderer that stole my poor brother's province after allowing him to be murdered by Yellow Turbans that he now employs as a private army, and Zhu Jun is fodder for the carrion birds that swarm around our poor sovereign as regents. Heroes belong to another age; now, it's about another type of man that knows that he must follow his lord and do as he's told. You can't do that, not if it means doing wrong."

Taishi Ci nodded and said, "You know me very well."

"I *do*, but only because we're alike at heart... the difference is the courage that you have in even greater abundance as a man, but that I... now lack," Liu Yao replied. "I suppose I always lacked it: when poor Lu Kang, who is now dead by Sun Ce's hand, faced slander by the 'Ten', my brother petitioned against them to save him, and I tried to talk him out of it. I felt it was 'good sense', but... but it was cowardice. My brother was right to save Lu Kang, just as you saved your administrator all those years ago. In his own way, he was a hero, and I am not."

Taishi Ci bowed slightly and said, "You are being hard on yourself, Liu Zhengli."

"You are most kind to say so," Liu Yao replied. "I truly hope that an age of heroes comes again, Ziyi, so that you can be the man that you need to be in order to be content. But if I employ you, it must be in a low, nominal capacity in order to avoid two accusations: favouritism, and nurturing fugitives. Xu Shao works for me because, he says, I am a man of fine character; I am truly glad of that. He favours you, Ziyi, because he knows you to be virtuous... but we're both prisoners of our time. To the noblemen beneath me that hold power by favour, I cannot afford to have criminals as generals with the eyes of the imperial court bearing down on me, no matter how illegitimate Li Jue and Guo Si's regency might be in truth."

Taishi Ci nodded silently.

"Yet for all I've said, the court is run by two criminals!" Liu Yao exclaimed. "Li Jue and Guo Si are the worst of monsters... but if they are criminals, Ziyi, then as the court's appointed governor of Yang, what am I, I wonder...?"

Taishi Ci did not reply.

"...I'll see that you're given proper accommodation in the city, Ziyi: that the wretches *cannot* object to, for I do that as a friend," Liu Yao continued. "You should get some proper rest... you've earned it, I think."

Taishi Ci started to get to his feet.

"Stay," Liu Yao said. "I'll have a servant bring tea; we can talk of Huangxian."

Taishi Ci did as he was asked, but in his heart, he was saddened and disappointed by his latest lord and master.

****

ACT V: THE RECLAMATION OF DANYANG

48

The southeast region of China that was known to some as southern Yang Province and others as 'Jiangdong' – East of The River - had seen many years of neglect under many Han Dynasty emperors, but it had produced many heroes to defend that same dynasty. One of the most famous during the successive reigns of Emperors Ling, Shao and Xian was Sun Jian, a man from Fuchun County, Wu Prefecture that had rallied a militia to fight the Yellow Turban rebels that sought an end to imperial rule. Sun Jian – whose style name was 'Wentai' - was one of many men that freed the nation from the cultists' considerable efforts, but he performed feats that were undeniably brave and truly incredible. Sun Jian had then fought against rebels in the northwest Liang Province region, but when he enlisted under the nobleman Yuan Shu to fight the tyrant Dong Zhuo, everything changed. He became, through political naivety, the vassal and property of Yuan Shu, who then sent him to the central Jing Province region to seize it from its appointed governor. The hero of two rebellions would not survive that campaign, but his son Sun Ce – whose style name was 'Bofu' – inherited his spirit and vowed to carry on.

Bofu's lord Yuan Shu had ruined the campaign against Dong Zhuo by starting a personal feud with his own half-brother, Yuan Shao, and that feud had developed into a nationwide struggle for power between ambitious and irreverent warlords. Wu Prefecture experienced a partial takeover by the warlord Xu Gong, and then the regency court's chosen governor, Liu Yao, took most of Jiangdong from Yuan Shu's vassals. Bofu expected an order to take Jiangdong back, but that order did not come: relatives were sent instead, and Bofu was deliberately withheld.

Almost a year had passed since Bofu's uncle Wu Jing and his cousin Sun Ben had begun their attempted recapture of the Danyang and Wu Prefectures in southern Yang; Bofu waited patiently, but the order to aid his uncle and rescue his family home from Liu Yao was still far from forthcoming. His master, Yuan Shu, kept him in his capital Shouchun and gave no indication of how he would be used as the political tensions grew.

In the north, the situation was ever-changing: the warlord-governor Cao Cao had regained Yan Province when an outbreak of famine thwarted the rebellion led by the famous wandering warlord Lü Bu and Cao's childhood friend Zhang Miao; Miao was dead, the rebellion was crushed, and Lü Bu was recovering in western Xu Province with his surviving forces. The recently-appointed governor of Xu, Liu Bei, had decided to give Lü Bu refuge, but Dong Zhuo's former bodyguard and foster son was as capricious as ever; Yuan Shu was in secret correspondence with Bu as part of a long-term plan to seize Xu province from Liu Bei, and the homeless Lü Bu was hoping that he would be allowed to govern it on Yuan's behalf until an opportunity to declare independence arose.

In the west, the regency government led by the late Dong Zhuo's loyalists Li Jue and Guo Si had enjoyed a victory against a planned coup d'état led by Yi Governor Liu Yan and two

Qiang warlords, Ma Teng and Han Sui: Bofu's famous father Sun
Jian had once been deployed to Liang Province to defeat Han Sui,
but now he and Ma Teng were more influential than ever, despite
their defeat. Liu Yan, by contrast, had lost the eldest three of his
four sons to conflict or illness in quick succession: the man whose
advice had deliberately or inadvertently began the era of
governor-warlords succumbed to illness within months of losing
his provincial capital in a freak lightning storm, which left his
province in the hands of his fourth and only surviving son, Liu
Zhang. The only political entities in the west now were the
'barbarian' warlords – such as Ma Teng and Han Sui – and the
regency government, which was on the verge of collapse due to
in-fighting. Li Jue and Guo Si were in the process of purging
anyone that they suspected as having designs on power, but that
included old allies from their days as Dong Zhuo's generals; that
also included each other by design, and there were many officials
in the puppet court that were looking for ways to intensify the
mistrust between the two and liberate the young Emperor Xian
from their grasp. There should have been help from warlords in
the east, such as Yuan Shao, Cao Cao, Yuan Shu, Gongsun Zan
and Liu Bei, but there was too much instability for any help to be
received or offered; the emperor was, to all intents and purposes,
irrelevant and all but forgotten.

Bofu tired of waiting for the order to assist Wu Jing and convened
a meeting of his ever-growing army of officials.
"I'm going to ask to go," Bofu declared.
"Is that wise?" Lü Fan asked. "I already told you that he suspects
us, Bofu."
"Let him!" Bofu retorted. "How can I show no Confucian values
whatsoever? I am betraying not only the state but filial
obligations! I am just sitting here, obeying this selfish, ignorant-"
"Mister Lü is right," Cheng Pu said. "Yuan Shu suspects that we'll
leave his service at the first opportunity, and we'll never get him
to agree. He's on the cusp of sending an army to attack Liu Bei,
that much is obvious; he probably wants to send us northward."
"Yeah, but he's going to have Lü Bu helping him, isn't he?" Bofu
suggested.
"We don't know that," Lü Fan replied.
"You're the one that told me that he's probably writing to Bu!"
Bofu protested.
"Yes, but he'll still need field generals, because Bu is only of use if
Liu Bei does not suspect that Bu is plotting against him," Lü Fan
countered. "If Yuan Shu does not send an adequately-sized army,
Bei might guess that something's going on. I'm sure that Liu Bei
doesn't trust Lü Bu: he'd be a complete idiot if he did, and his
acquisition of Xu Province does not say to me that he's either
naïve or stupid."
"That being the case, he'll suspect Bu anyway," Bofu said.
"But Yuan Shu will still want to send as large an army as possible,
because he will not trust Lü Bu either!" Lü Fan replied. "Bu will
want Xu for himself, much as he wanted Yan!"
"...Of course, that brings up the prickly subject of *Cao Cao*," Huang
Gai said.
"That's the most dangerous man in the country," Lü Fan

suggested. "He's survived every disaster there has been, and now he's gone from the loser in Xingyang to the governor of Yan and master of half-a-million men. Were he a man with a conscience, that would be fine, but he's the villain predicted by Xu Shao."

"Yuan Shu's been defeated by a much weaker Cao Cao than the one he faces now," Cheng Pu recalled. "Perhaps we're being kept here in case Cao Cao marches south."

"All of this is of *no interest to me*!" Bofu cried. "My uncle and my cousin are trapped in Liyang, unable to gain any ground against Liu Yao! Time and again, they've gone into Danyang, and time and again they've been beaten back! I can't take anymore: Cao Cao, Liu Bei, Lü Bu and all of the rest of them can drop dead for all I care! I want to go and fight Liu Yao!"

Cheng Pu and Lü Fan looked at the faces of the officers and officials that surrounded them; Huang Gai, Zhou Tai and Jiang Qin were unreadable, but Bofu, Sun Hè, Xu Kun, Chen Wu and a number of the newer recruits were angry and impatient, and there would be no reasoning with them anymore. Cheng Pu looked at Lü Fan, who shook his head discreetly.

"...Alright," Cheng Pu conceded. "You're going to see him now...?"

"Now," Bofu replied. "I think that we can advance and take down the riverbank defences quickly enough... push them over the Great River, back to places like Qu'e, Moling and Wuhu. Once we've done that, we can cross at different points and rout them."

"...Fine," Cheng Pu said. "If I'm honest, I've wanted to do something for as long as you have; perhaps I doubted our chances of success."

"We'll never know if we don't try," Bofu replied. "Sitting here is achieving nothing. I'll go and see Yuan Shu on my own: all of you get ready to leave."

"But what if he doesn't agree...?" Huang Gai asked.

"I'm not accounting for that," Bofu replied as he got to his feet and left the hall with his bodyguards.

"...I wonder what our 'master' will say," Cheng Pu sighed.

Yuan Shu was rattled by the announcement of Bofu's arrival.

"He wants to leave my service!" Yuan Shu said with the neurotic tone of a man on the edge of sanity. "But that cannot happen! He's my tiger, my-!"

"I imagine that he wants to know if he can help his uncle," the adviser Yan Xiang said.

"I cannot let him go to Liyang!" Yuan Shu cried. "He'll leave my service!"

"Then what will you do...?" Yan Xiang asked.

"...He cannot defeat Liu Yao, even if he does go," Yuan Shu decided. "Zu Lang and Lu Kang were small opponents with no power; Liu Yao has the support of Xue Li and Ze Rong, and the tightest of grips on the lands south of the Great River. I'll give him what he wants... yes... I'll give him what he wants! Show him in!"

The cynical Yan Xiang had Bofu brought into the audience hall.

"I, Ce, come to pay respects to you, Lord Yuan," Bofu said as he fell to one knee.

"You come here in full military dress," Yuan Shu retorted. "That does not suggest to me that you felt like popping in to kowtow. What do you want...?"

"I think that you know, Lord Yuan," Bofu replied. "I have been watching the situation in the south carefully, since so many of my kin and so many places that are of significance to my clan are involved, such as the resting place of my father, who was your loyal, unbending vassal."

"...Go on," Yuan Shu prompted.

"I can see no end in sight," Bofu continued. "At least, I can see no end that benefits your cause, Lord Yuan. Xu Gong has part of Wu; Liu Yao now has the rest of Wu, Yuzhang, Danyang, Kuaiji and Guangling, and is courting Xu Gong as an ally; we possess the whole of Lujiang and most of Jiujiang, but for how much longer...? They are in Jiujiang, sitting on the riverbank, awaiting a moment to advance that we will surely give them by remaining on the defensive. I have come to request troops and permission to march south. This has several benefits: I relieve my uncle, I push the enemy back to the other side of the Great River, I give us opportunities to reclaim that which was lost, and I avenge past insults to us both."

Yan Xiang frowned at the statement and stared at Yuan Shu.

"...Alright," Yuan Shu said. "Sun Ce, I hereby appoint you 'Colonel that Charges and Crushes', and as before, I will assign you men; this time, I will give you a thousand men, fifty of them cavalry."

"I thank you," Bofu said tonelessly.

Yuan Shu was affected by the demeanour of his vassal, since it lacked any signs of any particular intent; he looked at two of his advisers, Yan Xiang and Han Yin, and mistook their disapproving stares for indications that he should further reward his wavering tiger. Yuan Shu slapped his thigh and said, "What good is 'Colonel', mm? How will you inspire others in heated moments? But then I cannot make you a general just yet, Sun Ce... not until you have done more!"

"I am satisfied with any rank," Bofu insisted.

"I am not," Yuan Shu said. "For the purposes of this campaign, I appoint you 'Acting-General that Vanquishes Bandits'. Now-"

Yan Xiang yelped reflexively, but Bofu ignored it.

"...Now you should go and fetch your troops from the barracks, Sun Ce," Yuan Shu continued as he stared at Yan Xiang. "I... I will have word passed to the commander there so that you will encounter no obstruction."

"I will advance to Liyang at once!" Bofu promised.

"...Dismissed," Yuan Shu ordered.

Bofu rose, bowed in all directions – stopping to smile at a surprised and delighted Zhang Xun – and retreated; once he was gone, Han Yin said, "Are you devoid of your wits? 'Acting-General'???"

Zhang Xun frowned at Han Yin's contemptuous statement.

"Remember who is master and who is vassal, Han Yin!" Yuan Shu barked. "I must placate him! He is aware that he is an *acting* general! I have made no false promises!"

"You made him a permanent colonel!" Yang Hong said. "That elevates him enough, Lord Yuan! Men such as Cao Cao and your brother were colonels in the Western Garden Army, and-"

"I DO NOT WANT TO HEAR ABOUT MY BROTHER!" Yuan Shu screamed.

The advisers cowered.

"**I am forced to put my feud with him to one side to manage these petty manoeuvrings!**" Yuan Shu continued. "**When I wrote my rebuke, I did not expect that nearly five years later, I would be stuck here in Jiujiang, besieged on all sides, while he sits comfortably in Ji Province surrounded by advisers, beautiful women and fine wine! He is treacherous and dishonest! He should be dead by now, but instead he enjoys peace while I am fighting on all sides!**"
The officials murmured uneasily.
"...As time passes, we are forgetting what matters," Yuan Shu said. "When will the real matters – my right to command my clan, and appointing the rightful sovereign to govern the world – be resolved...?"

Bofu journeyed to his camp outside Shouchun City and smiled when he realised that his orders had been followed. He entered his command tent – where Lü Fan and Cheng Pu were managing various matters – and said, "All's going well...?"
"Lord Sun!" Cheng Pu exclaimed. "You're smiling... we have permission to go?"
"We do," Bofu replied. "Thanks, Ziheng; you knew what to say to everyone."
Cheng Pu frowned and turned to the smiling Lü Fan.
"Yes, I confess, I am to blame," Lü Fan chuckled. "I gave Bofu all of his nice things to say... not just to Yuan Shu, but to the rest of you as well."
"...So all that anger was part of an act...?" Cheng Pu asked.
"Not at all," Bofu insisted. "I was angry, but the way I said what I had to say was all down to Ziheng: let's face it, Demou, it's like you yourself said... we had to do *something*."
Cheng Pu smiled and said, "You're right... so was I, and... well, I suppose we should move forward now, since we're where we should be. What next...?"
"We've been allocated a thousand men... he doesn't know about the few hundred we gained during the Lujiang campaign, so we have close to two thousand," Bofu explained. "Before we march, I'll write to Gongjin, since I think *this is it now*."
Cheng Pu shuddered.
"...You'd rather it wasn't...?" Bofu prompted.
"No, I... I'm relieved!" Cheng Pu admitted. "I have been a lackey of Yuan Shu's for so long that... that to know we're beginning the process of breaking ties once we've got out of Shouchun... I feel liberated already!"
"You know as well as I do that it'll take time to do it properly," Bofu said. "But if we have you, Ziheng, Gongjin and Junli as our brains, and all the brawn we've accumulated... how can we lose?"
"We *can't*," Lü Fan said; his tone suggested that there were several meanings to his words.
"No... we can't," Bofu replied with full understanding.
"We should get going," Lü Fan added. "I'll come with you to the barracks to fetch the men, Bofu."
"A glorious day," Cheng Pu murmured.
"It is," Bofu chuckled as he prepared to leave the tent. "Free to act at last...!"

Zhang Xun journeyed to Bofu's camp at the first convenient moment to congratulate him; Bofu was alerted to his arrival and went to the gates to welcome him.
"Why are we being so nice to this lackey of Yuan Shu?" Cheng Pu asked of Lü Fan.
"To the outside world, Mister Cheng, we are lackeys of Yuan Shu," Lü Fan replied.
"He's a voluntary lackey!" Cheng Pu despaired.
"He's a complicated fellow," Lü Fan retorted.
Bofu clasped Zhang Xun's hands and said, "My friend, you are welcome, most welcome! Let's all of us enjoy a banquet."
"Your achievements are amazing!" Zhang Xun chuckled. "You are now an Acting General, as you should have been a long time ago!"
As Bofu led Zhang Xun into the camp, Cheng Pu muttered, "If he likes us so much, why does he choose to stay here and work for Yuan Shu...?"
"His entire clan is in Huainan," Lü Fan replied. "I was happy to leave my home region, as you were, Mister Cheng; others are not so flexible. I imagine that Yuan Shu would lose Zhang Xun's service if he ever relocated his capital."
Cheng Pu nodded and said, "A sound point indeed."

Days later, a messenger arrived at the magnificent Zhou family home in Shu City, Lujiang Prefecture; Gongjin was reading in his private study when he was alerted to the arrival by a servant, and he went to the door in person.
"...A letter...?" Gongjin said with surprise as the messenger – who was recognisably a vassal of the Sun family – proffered a document encased in a tube. Gongjin smiled, took the document, opened the tube, unfurled the cloth letter, and started to read.
"...Well, well... so the time is *now*, Bofu," Gongjin said with a smile. "So be it."

****

49

Bofu and his followers began their swift march to Liyang County in southern Jiujiang: every village and town that they passed was welcoming, and many men volunteered their services. Bofu's ranks swelled beyond even his own ambitious expectations: his forces exceeded 5,000 by the time that he completed his march and camped outside the walls of the county capital. Zhu Zhi's spies had spotted the approach of the army, so a welcoming party was at the city gates when Bofu approached them with Lü Fan, Cheng Pu, Xu Kun and his bodyguard force.

"Junli!" Cheng Pu cried as Zhu Zhi bowed to Bofu. "You saved our kin: we're all in your debt!"

"Wu Jing and Sun Ben will be here shortly," Zhu Zhi said. "They insisted on being here to greet you."

Bofu spotted his younger brother Sun Quan, who was now 14 years of age; he was stood next to his friend Zhu Ran, and neither looked particularly happy.

"...Quan," Bofu said quietly.

"Brother," Sun Quan replied. "Will you be seeing the family before you go?"

"Of course I will!" Bofu chortled. "What do you take me for? ...Zhu Ran, I should like to say thank you for your earlier work. You're a credit to your father."

Zhu Ran bowed silently.

"Any sign of Gongjin?" Bofu asked.

"...Zhou Yu?" Zhu Zhi replied. "No, Lord Sun. Is he coming here as well, then?"

"I asked him to bring as many followers as he could," Bofu explained. "This is our moment, Junli."

Zhu Zhi smiled and said, "I hope so, Lord Sun; your clan has been underfoot for too long as it is."

"Too right," Bofu chuckled. "I-!"

"You're Lord Sun Ce!"

Bofu frowned and turned to the source of the unfamiliar voice; a tall man in full battle dress was approaching him with a ragtag band of men of all ages.

"It is! It's Lord Sun Ce!" the militia leader said through laughter. "I have found the tiger at last!"

"...What's your name?" Bofu replied.

"My family name is-"

"Just *tell me*, man, or we'll be here all day," Bofu chuckled.

"Ling Cao," the man said.

"Right," Bofu murmured as he looked at the group of men as a whole. "*Ling Cao...* style name?"

"I... I don't know what I want to use," Ling Cao admitted. "I might be dead soon, so does it matter?"

"What sort of attitude is that???" Han Dang cackled.

"I want to be a hero, but right now, I'm Ling Cao, a nobody," Ling Cao retorted. "I will choose a style name that befits my achievements."

"...Don't wish yourself an early death," Bofu said soberly. "But I like you, Ling Cao, and I hope you decide your style name when we've retaken the south."

"Uh… should we be too open…?" Cheng Pu asked.

"He's a good man; I can tell," Bofu insisted.

"I should like to introduce my family to you, Lord Sun, when it is convenient," Ling Cao pleaded. "We are yours to command, and–"

"Look, you're either my friend or you're not, Mister Ling," Bofu interrupted. "I don't do 'vassals', alright…? Being one myself, I don't much like it."

Ling Cao fell to his knees and said, "You're a magnanimous lord! I'll follow you as a dog or horse would!"

"…Miss the point, why don't you," Bofu sighed as he helped Ling Cao to his feet.

"Oh, uh… apologies, Lord Sun," Ling Cao said.

"Go and meet your new friends," Bofu suggested. "My encampments are quite obvious, so you won't get lost."

"My thanks, Lord Sun!" Ling Cao replied; he gestured to his band of followers, and after more respectful bows from them all, they left Bofu and travelled to the nearby military camps.

"More again," Cheng Pu said with disbelief. "The people are with you, Lord Sun."

Zhu Zhi smiled and said, "Indeed they are, Cheng Demou; indeed they are."

Once Wu Jing and Sun Ben had finished their work and come to the gates, Bofu entered the city, journeyed to the requisitioned governor's residence and enjoyed a reunion with the family that he not seen since he had taken his first army to Shouchun.

"You're so much like your father now!" Lady Wu sobbed as she hugged Bofu.

"Hopefully not too much like him," Wu Jing said. "I appreciate that you're here to help, worthy nephew, but I really could not bear to see you hurt."

"I'll be alright," Bofu promised.

The children of the Sun family formed orderly lines to be greeted by the head of their clan; Bofu turned to the first, Sun Quan, and smiled warmly.

"…It is good that you're back, elder brother," Sun Quan said with a smile.

"We'll need to get you a good job when I've defeated Liu Yao!" Bofu chuckled.

"Be sure and give Zhu Ran a good job too," Quan replied. "He's very smart."

"I will," Bofu promised as he moved his attentions to his next brother, Sun Yi.

"Isn't he the spitting image of you?" Lady Wu said.

Yi was now 11 years of age; Bofu nudged his feisty brother's cheek with his knuckle and said, "Aren't you just! Still fighting empty air at every opportunity, I hope?"

"One day, Elder Brother, I want to go and fight our enemies, like you do," Yi replied.

"…I'd rather you were an official than an officer, so we'll see about that," Bofu suggested. "I want to be the last of us that has to fight, if that's possible."

"Oh, he's more like my darling husband than…!" Lady Wu gasped.

Bofu moved to his third brother, Sun Kuang, who was now 9; he smiled at the boy and said, "How's the little marquis?"

Sun Kuang smiled shyly.

"I suppose I should call you 'Marquis Sun', or 'My lord', shouldn't I?" Bofu teased; Kuang laughed at the idea, since he knew that Bofu had yielded the title to him in a moment of emotional generosity.

"…Hopefully, you're happy to be an official," Bofu prompted.

"I don't like fighting," Kuang admitted. "But I would if I had to."

A small female voice grunted contemptuously; Bofu turned to his eldest sister, Shangxiang, and said, "No change here, then."

Shangxiang harrumphed; she was dressed in trousers and a shirt, and looked more like a boy than a girl.

"You're what… *seven*…?" Bofu said with despair. "What in Heaven's name will you be like when you're-"

"There's still *plenty of time*!" Yi chuckled dryly.

"Yeah… that's what Gongjin always says, but I'm not so sure," Bofu said as he turned his attentions to the 3 younger children, who were gathered around Sun Jian's nervous consort Lady Chen.

"Second Mother," Bofu said politely. "How are you?"

Lady Chen smiled gratefully and said, "I am well, young lord."

"And these are my other brothers and sisters!" Bofu said as he crouched to inspect the small boy and female toddlers that orbited Lady Chen. After giving each child a reassuring smile, Bofu rose to full height, turned to his mother and said, "Where's…? Mother, where's Lady-"

"She… was taken ill, after giving birth, as you know," Lady Wu explained. "She… she became ill, as we fled from Qu'e… but she did not suffer."

Lady Chen smiled sadly and said, "We tried to help."

Sun Quan sneered at the idea of feeling grief for his father's second consort.

"…That's a shame," Bofu said sincerely. "But… but such is life. She, like all those who have suffered at the hands of our enemies, will be avenged."

"I'll help in any way that I can," Lady Wu promised.

Bofu turned his attentions to his cousin Sun Fu; he was nearing his teenage years, and his brother Sun Ben was obviously proud that the athletic Fu was a talented warrior in the making.

"Somehow, Fu, I see that you're going to be joining us on the battlefield whether I approve of it or not," Bofu sighed.

"Are we going to be together long?" Shangxiang asked.

"Oh, so you *can* talk!" Bofu teased.

Shangxiang lunged and threw a punch; Lü Fan stifled laughter as Sun Yi and Sun Fu instinctively restrained her in a manner that appeared to be well practiced.

"…Really, Mother, I'm worried," Bofu said he watched his sister struggle to free herself.

"Is there any *point*…?" Lady Wu asked. "She is who she is."

"Shangxiang, I'll answer your question," Bofu said. "We'll be together today, perhaps tomorrow, and that's it; so shouldn't we make the most of it…?"

Shangxiang stopped struggling and replied, "Yes… yes, we should, Eldest Brother."

Yi and Fu relaxed their grips; Bofu gestured warmly, and after shrugging her captors aside, Shangxiang ran into her eldest brother's arms and smiled gratefully.

"...You smell like Dad," Shangxiang said as he rested her head against her brother's chest.

"Uh... yeah," Bofu replied. "Is... is that a compliment...?"

Lady Wu was crying and laughing at the same time; Bofu stroked his sister's hair and nodded toward Quan, who responded with another smile.

The evening after Bofu's arrival was punctuated with a family banquet; in the morning, Bofu travelled to the northern wall of the city and stared at the seemingly endless landscape while his ever-present bodyguard force – including his cousin Sun Hè – looked on at a distance.

"Are you okay, Bofu...?"

Bofu turned to the approaching Lü Fan and said, "Yeah... I think so, Ziheng. I just wanted to see if I could see Gongjin approaching."

"It's a pity that he couldn't make it here last night," Lü Fan suggested.

"Aw, look, we'll have *another* banquet," Bofu said. "The important thing is that he gets here... we'll need every reliable man for this."

"We shall," Lü Fan replied.

"...While we're here," Bofu said, "could you tell me what you have in mind...?"

"Chasing them back across the Great River isn't enough, because Liu Yao will just insist that they come back again," Lü Fan explained. "We have to launch a decisive attack on them, capture their bases at Hengjiang and Danglikou, and follow up with a swift river crossing before the loss of the northern camps can be reported. We have to take – or at the very least besiege – the cities of Niuzhu and Moling; and then, once Liu Yao's entire supply and communication line is broken, we siege and take Qu'e."

"...That's way beyond what I told Yuan Shu," Bofu noted.

"He'll expect it," Lü Fan scoffed. "My concern isn't that he'll be angry at you for going beyond your remit; my concern is that he'll summon us back out of paranoid fear, or even send his generals to attack us."

"Same here," Bofu admitted. "O' course, I have no intention of obeying an order to return to Shouchun... not while a single man that's loyal to Liu Yao is still based south of the river. Ideally, I'd like to chase him west into Jiangxia... then I could kill him *and* Huang Zu at the same time."

"A wonderful scenario!" Lü Fan chuckled.

The two men stood and stared at the landscape for some time; Wu Jing, Sun Ben and Cheng Pu joined them as the morning gave way to noon.

"Any sign of your friend?" Wu Jing asked pointlessly.

"Nope," Bofu replied. "But I refuse to advance until he gets here."

"We'll be lucky if we can advance at all," Wu Jing complained.

"Nephew, I do admit that your optimism is inspiring, but what do you hope to achieve with a thousand borrowed men...?"

Bofu looked at Cheng Pu and said, "You only told him about the borrowed men...?"

Cheng Pu smiled and nodded silently.

"...You obviously haven't looked at my camps, Uncle," Bofu snickered. "There're a lot more than a thousand... I found a lot of support along the way."

"Close to six thousand, in fact," Cheng Pu said.

"You *are* your father's son, young Ce, for better or worse," Wu Jing sighed.

"Hey... **I see something!**" Sun Ben cried.

Every man looked north; a gathering was approaching with banners aloft.

"...That isn't unfriendly forces," Bofu decided. "It's him... **it's Gongjin!**"

"He's bringing a lot of men!" Wu Jing exclaimed. "Your friends are tigers too!"

"We have to go and meet him," Bofu insisted. "Everyone, we should get to the gates! Find Gongfu, Yigong, Junli, and-!"

"Yes, yes, we know!" Cheng Pu said as he hurried away.

"*Gongjin...!*" Bofu whispered as dashed down the steps that led to the city courtyard.

Gongjin had indeed arrived at Liyang; he had brought a force of approximately 400 volunteers from Shu City and the surrounding settlements. Bofu rushed out of the gates and clasped the hands of his friend and sworn brother, saying, "Gongjin... Gongjin! You're here at last, Gongjin...! With you here, success and greatness are definitely ours!"

"You act as though I am your only reliable friend," Gongjin chuckled nervously.

Bofu turned his gaze to his other allies and said, "Do I treat you all as worthless?"

Many men smiled and indicated that he did not.

"I am just happy to see you, my friend, after far too long," Bofu said as he turned his gaze back to Gongjin. "With you here, we can march; but first, you must see everyone. We're all here: Mother, Yi, the little marquis, Shangxiang-"

Gongjin smirked and said, "Shangxiang... is she still...?"

Bofu sighed and said, "She's *worse*, just as I feared, Gongjin! You said that-!"

"I think we still have time," Gongjin chuckled. "We'll make a lady of the future Lady Sun yet."

"I don't reckon so," Bofu said as he released Gongjin's hands and beckoned him to enter the city. "Still... we have more important concerns."

Gongjin nodded seriously and said, "That we do. Lü Ziheng, I should like to know everything that has happened."

Lü Fan nodded and replied, "I shall talk as we walk, Gongjin."

Despite the urgency of the hour, the second banquet had an even lighter atmosphere than the first; Lady Wu gazed at Lü Fan and Gongjin with a mother's eyes as they ate and talked.

"You two are magnificent boys," Lady Wu sighed. "My son is so lucky to have such handsome and clever friends."

Gongjin nearly choked; Lü Fan smiled awkwardly and said, "I am not usually referred to as 'handsome', Lady Wu."

"Please, call me 'Mother'," Lady Wu insisted. "And no, you're not as handsome as Zhou Yu, but-"

"Mother!" Bofu exclaimed. "Don't talk like that!"

"You're a handsome boy as well!" Lady Wu retorted. "I-!"

"I don't mean that I'm jealous!" Bofu said as Gongjin tried to stop coughing. "You should know by now that Gongjin doesn't want people going on about his looks! We lived with his family for *how long*...?"

"...My apologies," Lady Wu said as she looked at the weary Gongjin.

"And apologise to Ziheng as well," Bofu suggested.

"It's fine," Lü Fan insisted.

"There, see...?" Lady Wu chortled. "I do not have to apologise to him, because he's *fine*."

Lady Chen covered her mouth with her sleeve to hide her smile.

"...It's so wonderful to have us all here together," Sun Ben said suddenly.

Bofu looked around the low table; his mother, Lady Chen, Quan, Yi, Kuang, Shangxiang, Ben, Fu, Wu Jing, Xu Kun, Sun Hè, Lü Fan and Gongjin exchanged warm glances with him and each other.

"We're all older and wiser," Sun Ben continued. "A lot's happened... too much."

"Don't ruin the mood," Bofu pleaded.

"That's right," Wu Jing said as he sipped from his wine dish. "It's usually me that starts whinging, Ben, and I'm trying to get out of the habit."

"Perhaps he's spent too much time with *you*, Brother," Lady Wu suggested.

Bofu, Gongjin, Ben, Xu Kun and Lü Fan started to laugh; Lady Wu noted that Sun Hè was quiet and said, "You're so different, Hè."

"I... I suppose it's my being a bodyguard that's changed me," Sun Hè replied.

"Bohai acts like he isn't my cousin anymore, no matter how much I tell him not to," Bofu complained. "I keep saying that he doesn't need to be so stony, but he's gone and got it into his head that he has to be 'detached'... that he has to stay with the others and watch my every move, be ready to die for me... but-"

"Now who's ruining the mood?" Sun Ben teased. "Bofu, we get the idea; Bohai, lighten up a bit! You're off-duty!"

Sun Hè smiled awkwardly.

"So you have *bodyguards*...?" Lady Wu cawed. "Where are they?"

"Outside," Bofu replied casually. "They're an okay bunch, but oddly *shy*; I'll never get over how funny I find shy pirates."

Quan, Yi, Kuang and Shangxiang laughed together.

"They sound *adorable*!" Lady Wu said. "Invite them in!"

"Mother, they're supposed to be looking after me!" Bofu protested. "Don't start offering them wine and tea, they're-!"

"**Nonsense!**" Lady Wu barked. "I won't have men that are prepared to give their own lives for my son's being treated like nobodies! I was annoyed enough at your silly father never bringing that man Zu Mao to dinner more often!"

"...Put like that, perhaps they can be shown a little more hospitality," Bofu said soberly. "But don't blame me, Mother, they insisted that-"

"Tonight, they're *all* off-duty," Lady Wu insisted. "Your father's friends should be here as well."

"And Zhu Ran...?" Quan asked excitedly.

"I don't know why he isn't here now, you silly boy," Lady Wu replied.

Sun Quan got to his feet and ran out of the banquet hall to find Zhu Ran.

"**Hurry! Hurry! Go and get Cheng Pu, Huang Gai, and Han Dang!**" Lady Wu ordered as Wu Jing, Xu Kun, Sun Ben and Lü Fan jumped to their feet. "**Get *Zhu Zhi*: that man saved us all from death!**"

Shangxiang was amused by the chaos and laughed inanely.

"...We'll need more food," Bofu grumbled as he tried to get to his feet.

"And wine, I think!" Gongjin chuckled as he assisted Bofu.

Lady Wu turned to Lady Chen and said, "Sister, we are blessed to have so many good men around us."

Lady Chen smiled and said, "We are indeed... *sister*."

The remainder of the banquet was a happy affair: morning would be the start of Bofu's career and the beginnings of resistance against enemies and master alike.

****

50

Bofu, Gongjin, Wu Jing, Sun Ben and Yuan Shu's appointed provincial inspector, Hui Qu, led their armies to an area north of the Yangtze River's banks, located halfway between each of the two defensive camps that Liu Yao's forces had in place.

"The most difficult obstacle of the two will be Hengjiang, so I suggest that we eliminate that first," Gongjin said as the commanders viewed the landscape.

"*I* am in charge of this operation," Hui Qu said irritably.

"...Alright," Bofu said calmly. "So what would *you* do, 'Inspector'...?"

"I have known admirable service, 'Acting-General'," Hui Qu retorted. "I am no *acting* general, but a permanent one with a military record!"

"...Where did you serve...? *Fengqiu*...?" Xu Kun asked rudely.

The events that were collectively known as 'The Battle of Fengqiu' included a famous double-rout that was inflicted upon Yuan Shu's forces by Liu Biao and Cao Cao over 2 years earlier; the consequence had been the loss of all of Yuan Shu's holdings in northern Yu Province and northern Jing. The insinuation was clear: Hui Qu's eyes were filled with hate as he pointed at Xu Kun and said, "**You! Who are you, scruffy knave??? How dare you speak to your provincial inspector with such contempt, you-!**"

"Why waste your time arguing with a lackey of a vassal, Inspector Hui?" one of Hui Qu's majors asked snidely. "Let them do the fighting, Inspector: any loss is theirs, and any victory is yours."

Hui Qu smiled at the idea and said, "Very good! Very well, *Acting-General Sun Ce*; the battles are yours to plan, and the responsibility is yours to bear. I will manage the defences in and around our camp, so that we are ready to *retreat*."

Bofu shook his head sorrowfully as Inspector Hui Qu and his followers withdrew.

"I'd gladly kill that man," Xu Kun growled.

"The northern nobles are *cretins*," Cheng Pu chortled. "Hui Qu revels in the notion of our 'inevitable defeat'! Yuan Shu would rather lose everything than deploy us! How, in Heaven's name, did either man ever get anything???"

"Yuan was entitled to his vassals and land by virtue of his birth-right," Gongjin said sadly. "I have followers for much the same reason, Major Cheng, for I am, by my birth, a 'northern noble'. I can only hope that I have more sense than my peers."

Cheng Pu smiled politely and said, "I'm just grumbling. Now, Young Mister Zhou, you should continue telling us your plan."

"I shall," Gongjin said. "First, we should..."

Liu Yao's Hengjiang encampments were commanded by Generals Fan Neng and Yu Mi; neither general was expecting any kind of action, so the sudden, coordinated strikes blunted their ability to retaliate.

"**What do you mean 'Our outlying camps are gone'???**" General Fen Neng barked at a terrified major. "**This is a band of pirates! How can you-!**"

"We're solving nothing by sitting here haranguing our officers, General Fan," General Yu Mi suggested. "The banners tell us that it's Wu Jing and Sun Ben, come back again to lose their heads."
"Yes, but who are 'Sun Ce' and 'Zhou Yu', as if we didn't know…?" Fan Neng retorted. "We'll need to send word to Danglikou, and let General Zhang know that they've hit us."
"Yes, and we'll need to counter their assault," Yu Mi said. "I'll ride out first, and-"
"**We're besieged!**" a captain cried as he ran into the command tent. "**They're attacking our main camp!**"
"**Nonsense!**" Fan Neng barked. "They wouldn't dare!"
"I'll do what I can to repel them!" Yu Mi said as he ran out of the tent with his sword at the ready.

Bofu and Gongjin watched with amusement as their enemies made a desperate attempt to hold onto their own main camp; Xu Kun, Sun Ben, Ling Cao and Chen Wu had led the initial assault, and now they were being joined by a second wave led by Cheng Pu, Huang Gai and Han Dang.
"They're pinned in their camp with nowhere to go but into walls of fire, tips of arrows and spears or the depths of the Great River," Gongjin chuckled. "Ling Cao is already a proven hero on his first outing, and your decision to deploy Chen Wu with a force has proven to be a good one."
"I feel like I should charge as well," Bofu admitted. "I hate being treated like a precious vase. I'm a *warrior*, Gongjin."
"The chances of an ambush are very low, so I don't see why not," Gongjin replied. "Go ahead and feed your bloodlust, Bofu."
"You make me sound like an animal," Bofu chortled as he urged his horse and charged at the enemy camp with his bodyguard force and a team of elite cavalry.

General Yu Mi had managed to gather some men in order to make a spirited counterattack, but the sheer numbers were too much when they were already at a disadvantage. Cheng Pu seemed to be born again, fighting with the ferocity of a man half his age; infantrymen were toppled in every direction as he cut his way through them and aimed for the command tent. But just as the battle was on the verge of being over, General Fan Neng charged out of his command tent to join his fellow general, giving a boost to the defenders' morale and adding one last yet dangerous gasp to the futile effort. Cheng Pu was forced on the defensive, and Bofu suddenly found himself surrounded by angry infantry armed with pikes; they jabbed at his horse and nearly struck his leg. Bofu's bodyguard Zhou Tai made a lone run to clear an escape path while Sun Hè and Jiang Qin rallied the remaining bodyguards and held the pike-wielders at bay; the coordinated effort worked, and Bofu was able to join Cheng Pu and ride to safety. Fan Neng and Yu Mi saw the approach of Ling Cao and engaged his cavalrymen, but Ling's fearless assault scared many of General Fan's infantry and put them to flight.
"…How can I not get involved…?" Gongjin said to himself: he urged his own men forward and rode into the fray. The other officers were too busy to see his efforts, but he proved that he was every bit as skilled a fighter as he was a tactician: Gongjin's militia scattered another unit of Fan Neng's infantry and killed any chance of attacking Bofu's battle line.

"**We must retreat to Danglikou!**" Fan Neng suggested.

Yu Mi did not argue; the two generals escaped a sudden pincer between Xu Kun and Ling Cao and fled the burning ruins of their Hengjiang camp.

"**Where are you two going?**" Han Dang bellowed as he bore down on the retreating generals with a brigade of former pirates; Fan Neng ordered his allies to refuse engagement and continue their retreat, but Huang Gai and his militia were blocking the way.

"...**They're *pirates*!**" Fan Neng cried desperately. "**Since when are pirates so organised???**"

"**Cut through! Cut through!**" Yu Mi ordered; the remainder of the defenders' cavalry charged at Huang Gai, who told his men to offer minimal resistance and let them pass rather than lose their lives needlessly.

"**You let the enemy escape!**" Ling Cao screamed as he rode toward Huang Gai with his sword drawn. "**Are you on their side, or something???**"

Han Dang blocked Ling Cao's way with his spear outstretched and said, "**You watch who you're speaking to, son! Gongfu is a hero! He let them go for a *reason*!**"

"**What *reason*???**" Ling Cao retorted.

"**Cornered tigers fight hardest, Captain Ling,**" Gongjin said as he rode toward the bickering officers with his small army. "**That's why Major Huang let them go.**"

"...I humbly apologise for my attitude, Major Huang," Ling Cao said as he bowed to Huang Gai.

"No need," Huang Gai insisted. "You fought extremely bravely, Captain, if perhaps a little recklessly: please preserve your life for worthier enemies than those two fools that we just routed."

"Yeah, save your strength for later, Captain Ling," Han Dang said as he lowered his spear. "Remember that this is the first battle, not the last."

Bofu, Xu Kun and Cheng Pu joined the officers at that point; Bofu grinned and said, "We kicked them pretty hard, didn't we?"

"Yes, and they'll soon discover that the roads to Danglikou are not to be navigated easily," Gongjin explained. "Wu Jing and Lü Fan have the main roads so tightly guarded that a mouse couldn't get a message to Danglikou."

"Some o' the men we captured are impressed locals," Bofu said sadly. "I didn't have the heart to execute them, so I've said they can go home. Some want to join us, though, so they say."

"Let them," Gongjin replied casually.

"Is that wise...?" Ling Cao asked. "What if they just want to infiltrate us?"

"And learn what...?" Han Dang scoffed. "That we're going to attack Liu Yao really, really hard and kill him if we can...? I think that he knows that."

"I'll let any men that want to join us join Chen Wu's regiments," Bofu decided. "That man is so nice that he could probably get Liu Yao to join us on the right day."

"Yeah," Jiang Qin chuckled. "He insisted on all the captured men getting a drink, and even gave one of 'em a drink from his own flask!"

"So should I do as I said...?" Bofu prompted.

"A sound idea," Gongjin replied. "And Chen Wu is just the right man, as you say. We'd better plan our next attack carefully; if, by any chance, a messenger did slip through..."

"...Then Danglikou will already be prepared," Cheng Pu said. "Then there's the chance that Fan Neng and Yu Mi will fight their way through..."

"Let's hurry to Danglikou, then," Bofu suggested. "Who'll stay in Hengjiang?"

"I'd say that Chen Wu should stay for now and stabilise his new forces, but that isn't enough," Gongjin replied. "We need a man that commands total respect and unshakeable discipline: Major Huang Gai, would you mind...?"

"Not at all, Mister Zhou," Huang Gai said.

"Right, well then I'll start making plans," Gongjin said. "Bofu...?"

"I'm right with you," Bofu promised.

Bofu, Gongjin, Xu Kun and Ling Cao began a withdrawal to their camp; Cheng Pu and Han Dang were noticeably slow to move, and they remained close to the unreadable Huang Gai.

"Are you okay with being bossed about by that pup Zhou Yu?" Cheng Pu asked.

"Of course," Huang Gai replied. "He's young, as we once were. Such is life."

"We could use you in Danglikou," Cheng Pu said. "Why doesn't he leave that idiot Ling Cao here...?"

"Ling Cao is a brave, reckless vanguard general in the making," Huang Gai replied. "He's better used that way than as a guard in Hengjiang."

Cheng Pu nodded slowly.

"You fought like a wild animal, Demou," Huang Gai noted. "I've never see you so... well... reckless, actually."

There was an uncomfortable silence for several moments before Cheng Pu said, "I saw the lad hacking his way out of danger, and I called out to him... and... and I actually found myself nearly calling him *Wentai*."

Han Dang exhaled noisily.

"Of course, that was after I charged, I know that," Cheng Pu continued. "It was... how can I put it... as though I had to fight like that to save Wentai."

"Have you lost your mind...?" Han Dang asked.

"I meant his place of rest," Cheng Pu explained. "That lad has to live with the knowledge that his father's grave is in enemy-occupied territory: so do I, and so do *we*, in fact. I want to be able to pay my respects to my friend. The only way that we're going to be able to do that is-"

"I get it," Han Dang said tersely.

"And you, Gongfu...?" Cheng Pu said. "Do you understand...?"

"I do, Demou, but I say to you what I said to Captain Ling," Huang Gai replied. "We have a lot more battles to fight. Don't expend your energy on these ones."

Cheng Pu bowed slightly and said, "My friend, I wish you well in defending Hengjiang."

"And I you, both of you, in relieving Danglikou," Huang Gai replied as he reciprocated the gesture. The 3 friends then parted ways: Huang Gai went to centre of the ruins of the Hengjiang camp while Cheng Pu and Han Dang pursued Bofu.

The second march was enacted swiftly: the smaller defensive position at Danglikou was commanded by General Zhang Ying, who was still unaware of the situation at Hengjiang when Bofu's forces set upon his outer defences.

"How did they hit us so quickly???" Zhang Ying exclaimed as he stared at the pillars of smoke that marked the remains of his outer camps.

"General Zhang, we should withdraw to Moling!" a major suggested.

"Never!" Zhang Ying insisted. "You'd have me expose my back to a bunch of lucky pirates? They caught us by surprise, that's all! Now I am composed, we'll counterattack and rout them!"

General Zhang Ying had his forces advance against the approaching army; Ling Cao was first to meet them, engaging a cavalry captain and his small band of men with his own mixture of followers.

"Eager as ever," Bofu joked. "He's worse than me."

"By that you mean that you want to charge, of course," Gongjin supposed.

"Look, even Cheng Pu has 'bloodlust' at the moment," Bofu said as he pointed toward his veteran officer; Cheng had charged once again and begun an attack on Zhang Ying's main infantry blockade while Han Dang acted as his rear guard.

"...I'll join you," Gongjin decided.

"You can fight...?" Xu Kun chortled.

"Cousin, you're looking at a very multi-faceted man," Bofu said. "Gongjin can do almost anything he sets his mind to. Shall we all charge, then...?"

"Why not?" Gongjin replied.

Bofu, Gongjin, Xu Kun and Sun Ben led their forces in an all-out attack on the outmatched Zhang Ying; the defending forces disintegrated under the pressure. Gongjin proved his ability by engaging and defeating a major in a horseback duel while Bofu did as he always did and plunged into the fray, making a direct charge on Zhang Ying as soon as he spotted him.

"**What _are_ you???**" Zhang Ying cried as Bofu forced him back with a series of violent spear lunges. Once again, there would be no victory for Liu Yao's forces: Zhang Ying was rescued and given a chance to flee when a young captain distracted Bofu at the cost of his own life. Cheng Pu and Xu Kun smashed their way through the last of the defenders and had their men set the centre of the camp alight, but the battle was already over.

"So what now...?" Sun Hè asked as Bofu jumped from his horse to pick up Zhang Ying's discarded spear.

"We cross the river and take Niuzhu," Bofu replied as he twirled the spear theatrically. "After that, Moling; then whatever else we need to do until we get to Qu'e."

"...Such a waste o' life," Jiang Qin sighed as he looked at the scattered corpses of some of the young recruits that had lost their lives on both sides.

"Some of these boys that died serving Zhang Ying are as young as Quan," Bofu realised. "And they're probably locals, too."

"We've got boys fighting for us, Lord Sun," Jiang Qin said. "That's how it is."

"...I could have _Quan_ out here doing this," Bofu murmured. "I

need to make it so as he'll never have to do this..."
Gongjin rode toward Bofu and jumped down from his horse.
"Another win," Bofu said with a sad smile.
"I don't need to ask; I know your thoughts," Gongjin replied. "Zhu Zhi has the east secured, so Zhang Ying can only go north or south. He'll probably force a fisherman to take him over to Moling or Niuzhu. We need to regroup, leave guards here, and cross as soon as possible. My suggestion is that we bring Chen Wu here, let him liaise, and then bring him with us to Niuzhu."
"Don't forget that we need to tell our wonderful masters, Hui Qu and Yuan Shu, how well we're doing," Bofu grumbled.
"But we shall ensure that neither is aware of our successes until we've crossed the Great River, lest they order a withdrawal to prevent their victory from being too decisive," Gongjin said dryly. "I'll also send word to Lü Fan and Zhu Zhi."
As Gongjin retreated to find some suitable messengers, Sun Ben approached Bofu and stared at him with an unreadable expression.
"...Is this going to be a congratulatory statement or some sort of challenge...?" Bofu asked cautiously.
"I wouldn't challenge you, Bofu," Sun Ben replied. "I... I can see why you wanted to come here. You've managed in days what we couldn't do in a year, your uncle and I; and you knew that you could do it. You're your father's son: I salute you."
Sun Ben bowed low; Bofu grabbed his arm and forced him upright, saying, "There isn't any need for that. Now come on! Here's where we take the fight to Liu Yao. He's had us on the defensive for so long that he won't know what hit him. Then... then we go home."
Sun Ben clasped Bofu's hand and smiled broadly; the victories in Hengjiang and Danglikou had ended months of stalemate, removed Liu Yao's influence on Lujiang and Jiujiang Prefectures and prepared the way for Yuan Shu's vassals to regain the territories to the south of the Yangtze River, and maybe take the entire province.

✳✳✳✳✳✳✳✳✳✳✳✳

51

Liu Yao's court in Qu'e was collectively startled at the news that the generals that had been tasked with securing the northern bank of the Yangtze River were awaiting a chance to report their defeats in person. Every official and concerned person of note – including the unorthodox hero Taishi Ci – gathered in the governor's courtroom and waited. The two that did present themselves – the commanders at Hengjiang, Fan Neng and Yu Mi – were a sorry sight as they entered the hall and approached their lord: they were still wearing the tatty, gore-laden armour that they had been wearing when they were defeated and chased across the river.

"I have… I have just one question for the two of you," Liu Yao said with anger. "How?"

"They broke our communication lines," Fan Neng protested. "Our scouts and outer camps were taken by stealth! The roads between Hengjiang and Danglikou were secured in advance! Our charges were blunted by arrow and stratagem, and our defences were broken by sheer brute force! They sieged our camps and isolated us from the forces in nearby settlements! The people of Hengjiang and Danglikou were with him! How could we hope to defeat him when-"

"*Him??? Him???* **Who is '*him*'???**" Liu Yao bellowed.

"*Sun Ce*, the son of *Sun Jian*!" Yu Mi replied. "Men surrendered! His officers were like tigers, and he has them by the bushel! He has minds, too: men with the wit and intelligence of Zhang Liang and Jiang Ziya of ancient times!"

"**Don't talk *nonsense*!**" Liu Yao barked. "He's a rebel! Sun Jian was a hero, yes, but he became a brave vassal of a fool that charged at arrows and died a fool's death for his lord! What did he know of strategy? How could the son of such a man be so different when nothing has changed? Isn't he still surrounded by unrepentant pirates and rebels? Isn't it the case that you come to me with stories of broken communication lines and the like in an attempt to hide your incompetence?"

"No!" Fan Neng cried. "We were outnumbered and outmatched!"

"Oh, so you were *outnumbered*, now…?" Liu Yao heckled. "So now, you're trying to tell me that he's formed some sort of brigand's alliance!"

"They weren't bands or disorderly men! They were an army, a proper army!" Fan Neng said. "They were… magnificent."

"No, you were incompetent!" Liu Yao retorted. "A few hundred shabby criminals made you look like fools! At least have the decency to admit it!"

"Governor, there were thousands of them, and they were well-armed and organised," Yu Mi insisted. "They are versed in every kind of warfare… infantry formations, cavalry, archery, everything."

The court was filled with anxious murmurs.

"…*Thousands*…?" Liu Yao said with disbelief.

"Yes, Governor, thousands, and they're crossing the Great River to take Niuzhu at this moment," Fan Neng said. "I took the liberty of asking Zhang Ying to go to Niuzhu while we came here, but… but it may even be the case that Niuzhu is already lost."

"...'Already lost'...?" Liu Yao said with obvious desperation. "That's not an option, Fan Neng! Niuzhu is a key supply installation! Niuzhu is a communication stage between Moling and Qu'e! I can't afford to lose Niuzhu!"

"I know, but we had to come here and report, and to ask for troops!" Fan Neng replied. "I-"

"Why didn't you ask for the troops when you first came in here then, you fool???" Liu Yao cried.

"I told the first men that we met, my lord!" Fan Neng protested.

"I can't lose Niuzhu!" Liu Yao whimpered. "I *can't*! *We* can't!"

The court was once again filled with nervous mutterings.

"...My lord, let me go and relieve Niuzhu."

All eyes turned to Taishi Ci.

"No, no, I can't send you," Liu Yao said dismissively.

"Don't be blinded!" the adviser Xu Shao said. "Governor, there is your hero! Send that man to Niuzhu and you will know no more of Sun Ce!"

Liu Yao was hesitant.

"Master Xu Shao is right!" one young official said.

"You can't send a criminal as the vanguard to fight this 'Sun Ce'!" another official cried. **"You have been appointed to govern this province justly and properly! How can you-!"**

"How can you call it 'governing justly and properly' when we fail to send the ablest man to prevent the costliest of defeats?" Xu Shao countered. "How can you talk of criminals being sent to fight for us when this court readily agreed to acknowledging *Xu Gong*???"

"For the *umpteenth time*, Mister Xu Shao, we need to work with Xu Gong!" Liu Yao cried. "Sheng Xian is broken, and we must adapt to circumstances!"

"If we can adapt to using Xu Gong, why not Taishi Ci...?" Xu Shao countered.

Liu Yao was silent.

"Xu Gong has popular support, and is not some lonely rascal!" one official heckled.

Taishi Ci shook his head silently.

"This is suicidal talk, gentlemen," Xu Shao pleaded. "We've already lost our footing on the north bank: do you want to lose your heads now, as well...?"

The majority of the officials heckled, bickered and jeered, although their opinions were increasingly divided and many more were supporting Taishi Ci this time.

"Silence, all of you!" Liu Yao screamed. **"Yes, I will send an army to save Niuzhu, and yes, it will be led by men of obvious merit, not a man that so many of you condemn as a notorious felon!"**

Taishi Ci sighed woefully.

"...I'm sorry," Liu Yao said as he looked at Taishi Ci.

"I know... and I understand," Taishi Ci replied.

"...Fan Neng, Yu Mi: take whatever men you need and relieve Niuzhu," Liu Yao ordered. "Further to that, I want a message sent to Xue Li in Moling... that he must be ready, because they are just as likely to attack him as they are to attack Qu'e, if not more so. Xue Li is my right arm in this dark hour... Master Ze Rong shall be my left, if he condescends to it."

"*Ayah*... Governor, do not use that false cleric," Xu Shao pleaded. "We are still not sure that he didn't-"

"I'll hear no more slander today," Liu Yao said with fatigue. "Fan Neng, have Xue Li ask Master Ze if he would garrison near Moling and prepare for... well... whatever horrors may come our way. A holy man of his grand stature can only be a boon to us in this hour of peril."

Xu Shao realised that a response was pointless, so he settled for a quiet sigh.

"We shall depart for Niuzhu immediately, Governor," Fan Neng said. "And I shall do all that you ask."

"...Good," Liu Yao muttered.

Fan Neng and Yu Mi retreated. Xu Shao looked first at his demoralised governor and then at the disappointed Taishi Ci, but he did not say a word.

But while Fan Neng and Yu Mi sped toward Niuzhu, its appointed defender, Zhang Ying, was taunting Bofu's forces.

"He really is quite stupid," Lü Fan snickered as he read the written challenge from Zhang Ying that had just been delivered by an overconfident messenger.

"Maybe he knows something that we don't," Ling Cao suggested.

"We've scouted thoroughly," Cheng Pu promised. "All he has is that small garrison of troops; we outnumber him, just as we did in the last battle."

"But he didn't have walls and advance warning to protect him last time," Bofu said. "We caught him by surprise. We need to gain some sort of advantage, right, Gongjin?"

Cheng Pu mumbled irritably as Gongjin replied, "We do. If he's so confident that he can defend the place with such a small number of men, then we should have him prove it."

"By siege...?" Bofu asked miserably.

"No... this need not be another Lujiang," Lü Fan said. "A field battle..."

"He's unlikely to take such obvious bait," Cheng Pu suggested.

"Ah! But if he were intelligent enough for that to be true, he would not have sent this challenge!" Lü Fan replied. "I suggest that we reply, gentlemen, saying..."

∗∗∗∗∗∗∗∗∗∗∗∗

52

Liu Yao's generals, Fan Neng and Yu Mi, ordered an immediate retreat when they reached Niuzhu; the entire area surrounding the walled city and the supply depot was defended by an array of camps, which meant that the battle was already over. Scouts reported the approach and withdrawal of Liu Yao's generals to a delighted Bofu, who was now based in the magistrate's residence in Niuzhu City.

"So, Fan Neng and Yu Mi didn't fancy trying their luck again, then!" Bofu joked.

"Against the warriors of the south, what can they do...?" Gongjin said. "You have Xu Kun, Ling Cao and Han Dang as your limbs and Cheng Pu, me, Lü Fan and Zhu Zhi as your brains: Liu Yao has three ineffectual generals for limbs, the cowardly Xue Li and the untrustworthy Ze Rong as dubious foreign appendages..."

Most of the ensemble laughed; Lü Fan did not.

"...And *Xu Shao* is a hidden threat that we cannot ignore," Lü Fan suggested. "I'm surprised at you, Gongjin."

"Because I appear to overlook him...?" Gongjin retorted. "I overlook nothing, Ziheng. I am aware that Xu Shao is the most famous appraiser in the land, but while he knows men's hearts, can he read wise men's minds? Appraisers of character are not strategists, Ziheng."

"But might Xu Shao help Liu Yao employ abler local men to turn his situation around?" Wu Jing suggested.

"He won't," Gongjin insisted. "Liu Yao is incompetent. We've got a lot of support from the locals, and one man has already told me that he's seen Liu Yao; he is no general, no strategist, and no governor. He's surrounded – and influenced – by 'northern nobles' of the kind that Cheng Demou despises: stubborn, classist, ignorant bigots that view 'abler local men' as rustic, criminal deviants that their governor cannot be seen to fraternise with. He'll stick to placing 'the local bumpkins and fools' into his vanguard as fodder."

"I hate Liu Yao already," Jiang Qin grumbled.

"Don't *hate* him, *pity him*," Lü Fan pleaded. "He's been judged as a good man by Xu Shao, and that means a lot: his problem is that while he is a good man, he is not a strong one. By strong, I mean of conviction; he knows right from wrong, but he won't disobey the court or contest the majority."

"Precisely," Gongjin chuckled. "And he's a harsh Confucian disciplinarian that borders on a Legalist despite that timidity, Ziheng; don't forget that! He'll hang every man with a colourful past if he takes this region, mark my words."

"We can't afford to let him do that, and we can't afford to leave the northern bank without proper defences, in case he sends men there while we're here," Bofu said. "We'll need to leave Gongfu on the north bank, but maybe he needs extra hands. Han Yigong...?"

"I shall leave immediately, Lord Sun," Han Dang replied.

"...I'll admit, I'd rather you stayed and helped me get Qu'e back, but I need you to do this for me," Bofu sighed. "I know that... that you and Gongfu wanted to be here to-"

"I'm happy to go," Han Dang insisted. "We're old enough to

understand."

"Thanks," Bofu replied. "I appreciate it... I know Dad was your friend."

Han Dang smiled and said, "Yes, but he was *your father*. You're a great man, Lord Sun! I just needed to tell you that before I go."

Bofu clasped Han Dang's hand and nodded seriously before he allowed his father's friend to leave.

"So now that Huang Gai and Han Dang are guarding the northern bank, we can look to attacking Moling and Qu'e, right...?" Xu Kun said enthusiastically.

"That's right, Cousin," Bofu confirmed. "Gongjin, your scouts reported that Ze Rong's south of Moling and Xue Li's in the city...?"

"They did," Gongjin replied. "Ze Rong's followers are either in the city or dispersed to local towns and villages in an effort to build support."

"That won't do," Cheng Pu said.

"And Ziheng: your intelligence says that Liu Yao is in Qu'e...?" Bofu prompted.

Lü Fan nodded silently.

"So which do we attack first...?" Xu Kun wondered.

"Oh, that's obvious," Cheng Pu replied. "We attack Moling to isolate Qu'e: more specifically, we defeat Ze Rong first and then attack the city."

"Indeed," Gongjin said. "Only a fool or a very, very dangerous man would siege a walled city with an enemy army stationed so close to it."

Cheng Pu sighed at the statement.

"Yes, I know that Sun Jian did something like that once, long ago... the siege of Wan City, during the Yellow Turban Rebellion," Gongjin continued. "While I don't doubt that Bofu could easily match his father's exploits, we can't afford to take any risks. Ze Rong is either very, very badly misrepresented or he is a devious, spiteful, immoral trickster that could do us serious damage if we were careless."

"We'll attack Ze Rong at the first opportunity," Bofu decided. "Xu Kun, Sun Ben, Ling Cao: ready your forces. Cheng Pu, Zhu Zhi, Chen Wu: get as many of the people that have joined us equipped and ready to march with us. Ziheng, Gongjin... I know that you two have a scheme or tactic to plan for, so you just do whatever you need to do... I'll join you after I've met some of our new recruits, if that's alright."

Each man bowed to show respect for their commander.

Bofu wowed the small number of local volunteers by mingling with them and behaving as though he were one of them with absolute sincerity. Bofu then left Cheng Pu, Chen Wu and Zhu Zhi to manage the recruits while he returned to his city residence and joined Gongjin and Lü Fan in a private meeting room.

"So many people!" Bofu chuckled. "I tell you, the people of the south are beautiful, damn near every one of them. After spending so long in Shouchun talking to so many northern snobs, it's nice to be somewhere where the people are people."

"Yes, but we have a very specific problem," Gongjin replied.

"Let's see if I can guess," Bofu said with laughter. "*Superstition*."

"It isn't just the poor, either, though they're the ones that love the

Buddhist message most of all for its egalitarianism," Lü Fan explained. "It'll be men from all backgrounds that like the notions surrounding Buddhism, even if they don't choose to follow the faith... *I* like some of the ideas, I admit... but I, at least, know a fraud when I see one, and others do not. As you know, when I was incarcerated in Guangling I met Governor Tao Qian, and I met the Administrator, Zhao Yu, as well of course. Neither was a fool, but both allowed Ze Rong to do as he pleased in Xu Province because they were in awe of him: he robbed and abandoned the former, and then he murdered and robbed the latter. Despite that obvious truth, a lot of men – such as Xue Li, who served Tao Qian alongside Ze Rong – still refuse to see him as anything other than an earthly Buddha. That won't just be men serving Liu Yao..."
"...It'll be men that serve your clan, Bofu, whether it be for hours or years," Gongjin warned. "We have to be sure of who we take with us. We do not need any men defecting mid-battle."
"We know we can rely on every officer, though," Bofu prompted.
"Your family...? ...Of course. Mister Cheng and Mister Zhu...? ...Of course," Lü Fan replied. "Ling Cao...? Yes, I would say so. Zhou Tai and Jiang Qin... well, I don't know... and they're your bodyguards, so we'll need to be probing in our questioning. Our main concern is the 'common people', if I might use that term for a moment... they're some of them openly devout around the tolerant port settlements like Moling and Niuzhu. We have to find a way to know who to trust, and *quickly*."
Bofu nodded and said, "We'll give people an opportunity to know what's ahead and to choose for themselves. Who will guard against attacks from Qu'e...?"
"Zhu Zhi should hold Niuzhu," Lü Fan suggested. "He's wise and cautious, so we'll be sure to have a besieged Niuzhu to return to rather than a taken one if the worst happens."
"Right then, fellows!" Bofu said with cheer. "Let's get started."

Days later, Ze Rong heard of the approach of Bofu's forces and said to his lieutenant Yu Zi, "This foolish unbeliever will soon know searing pain."
"They appear to be going towards the city," Yu Zi reported.
"Of course," Ze Rong chortled. "They're fools, deprived of Heaven's wisdom. They attack the city and do not regard my camp as a threat to them. But I am doing Heaven's work, so I shall smite them."
"So we shall aid the city...?" Yu Zi supposed.
"...Not immediately," Ze Rong replied. "We are left in the wilderness by the godless governor, and that will not do. Although I am of course an advocate of frugality and penance, we are not invited to live safely within the walls of Moling; rather we are left out here in a fenced camp to be slaughtered, because Liu Yao does not share our beliefs. Xue Li must atone for being complicit in that crime by knowing isolation."
"I understand, Master," Yu Zi said. "And when the enemy come here...?"
"We shall make a proclamation to his soldiers when they come," Ze Rong replied. "Many people from this region have flocked to me already, and there will surely be more now that my life is threatened."

"Let me confront this 'Sun Ce' when his spirit is broken, Master!"
Yu Zi pleaded.
"Of course I shall," Ze Rong replied. "You will then have an even
more important mission: you must make him suffer, and then we
must liberate the innocent of Moling, and punish the wicked Xue Li
if he has not already been punished."
"I will gladly ensure that both Sun Ce and Xue Li suffer, Master,"
Yu Zi declared. "At your word, I will do whatever Heaven desires."
"Heaven bless your piety," Ze Rong replied.

Bofu waited until the last possible moment to turn his forces
toward Ze Rong's encampments; Cheng Pu and Xu Kun led an
advance force to eliminate Ze Rong's scouts and observation
posts, so the subsequent attack – which was led by Sun Ben, Xu
Kun and Bofu himself – was unexpected and devastating.
"**Master! Master!**" Yu Zi screamed as he ran into Ze Rong's
command tent.
"I know," Ze Rong said calmly. "We have been surprised. I require
an escort."
"You cannot address them!" Yu Zi pleaded. "They are frenzied by
demons! Your sagely life would be in peril!"
"I do not intend to address them," Ze Rong replied. "I intend to go
to Moling and enter the city. Heaven's messenger has told me that
I must experience a setback before I experience a victory."
Yu Zi nodded and said, "You shall have your escort, Master, and a
distraction to disguise your journey."
The main camp was surrounded on all sides by the time
that Zu Yi had reported the situation to Ze Rong: Cheng Pu, Xu
Kun, Ling Cao and Bofu were at each of the gates with their own
forces while a secondary force led by Gongjin, Chen Wu, Wu Jing
and Sun Ben was poised to provide support wherever it was
needed. Bofu had a gong sounded, and the forces smashed their
way into the poorly-defended camp; Yu Zi provided his promised
distraction while Ze Rong fought his way past Cheng Pu's forces
and fled through the north gate with a team of riders. Despite the
fact that Ze Rong and his aides had successfully sheltered in
Moling, the outcome was a victory for Bofu: hundreds of Ze
Rong's acolytes were dead, and the camp was in ruins.
"We didn't get anyone important," Gongjin lamented as the
leaders congregated around the ruins of the command tent. "His
aide – a man calling himself Yu Zi – fought well, and allowed Ze
Rong to get to Moling before he retreated."
"Ze Rong got past me... I'm sorry," Cheng Pu said. "I tried to
chase, but the same Yu Zi rushed the rear of my force as I chased
his master. Both got away."
"So Ze Rong has a fairly capable general," Lü Fan mused. "We
should siege the city immediately; if Xue Li and Ze Rong are both
in there, then we'll get both in a stroke and leave Liu Yao with no
allies in Danyang."
Bofu agreed, and the army marched northward to Moling to begin
a siege.

****

53

Word eventually reached Liu Yao that Bofu was operating out of Niuzhu and the city of Moling was on the verge of being lost; he waited until Fan Neng and Yu Mi had returned and called an urgent meeting of his officials to discuss the matter.

"How did Zhang Ying lose Niuzhu so quickly...?" Liu Yao asked irritably.

"He... he boasted that he could hold the city with the men that he had, and allowed himself to be goaded into proving it," Fan Neng replied reluctantly.

"*Ayah*... that's just the sort of behaviour that one expects from low-level officers that lack experience, but not men of Zhang Ying's rank!" Liu Yao complained. "What can I do now???"

"This whole mess has a simple, obvious solution!" Xu Shao said with decreasing patience. "Send Taishi Ziyi! That is the man that can solve all of your problems!"

Some of the officials were already arguing and heckling Xu Shao before he had finished speaking; Liu Yao gestured that he wanted silence and said, "I am glad that Ziyi is not here to hear this. So I am left with the usual choices; General Fan, where is General Zhang Ying now...?"

"He is still recovering from the losses that he sustained during his consecutive defeats," Fan Neng replied. "I left him to prepare for our return."

"But he is fit to fight...?" Liu Yao asked.

"He is, Governor, and he has learned from his earlier mistakes," Fan Neng replied.

"Then I still have my three champions," Liu Yao declared.

The officials that did not favour Taishi Ci started to chatter approvingly.

"...It's like watching farmyard animals awaiting their morning nourishment," Xu Shao said with disgust. "Call yourself officials...? The one man that can solve this mess is denied his moment because of a false perception of his deeds! We could have victory, but no! Why not send Fan, Yu and Zhang to be defeated again!"

"We won't lose this time, Mister Xu," Fan Neng said calmly. "Last time, we were unprepared for what we encountered; this time, we will deal with Sun Ce."

"I certainly hope so," Xu Shao sighed. "I once appraised you as valuable warriors and able leaders... I'd like to be right."

"You are, as always," Yu Mi replied. "We'll surely defeat the enemy this time!"

"What will you do...?" Liu Yao asked.

"Governor, we are not fools," Fan Neng said. "We are not going to attack his main force at Moling. No... *instead*... we'll take Niuzhu."

Liu Yao smiled and said, "Go to it, General."

Bofu's march to Moling was impeded by General Zhang Ying.

"Not this idiot again," Bofu grumbled as his forces halted and prepared for a field battle. "Has he learned nothing from Niuzhu?"

"He's got more men this time," Lü Fan noted.

"And he's challenging again," Gongjin chuckled.

"What does he say...?" Bofu asked.

"It doesn't matter," Lü Fan insisted. "He's looking to save face, and perhaps give Xue Li and Ze Rong more time to ready their forces. He wants to fight a hundred rounds with 'any man that dares'; but we have no time for such theatrics. We need to defeat this man as quickly as possible."

Chen Wu approached Bofu and fell to one knee, saying, "My lord, allow me to remove this obstacle."

"...I dunno... you're tall and strong, but have you the skill to joust with a Han general...?" Bofu wondered.

"Please allow me," Chen Wu said. "I will not disappoint."

"...Get up, ready yourself, and respond to him," Bofu ordered.

"Let *me*!" Ling Cao cried. "Mister Chen is a kind and good man, but he is not a proven match for Zhang Ying!"

"Neither are you," Wu Jing said.

"But I am less valuable!" Ling Cao suggested.

"Tell that to your son," Cheng Pu barked. "How old is he, Ling Cao...?"

"...But is a man's worth measured by his son's age?" Ling Cao retorted. "I cannot win hearts like Chen Wu!"

"You won the hearts of your own followers," Bofu suggested. "This isn't about who's more valuable; I don't want to lose any of you. I'll challenge him myself."

"*Ayah*! That's a worse idea than Chen Wu or Ling Cao!" Wu Jing exclaimed. "*I'll* go then, if we must send someone to do this thing!"

"Can we stop a moment, gentlemen...?" Gongjin asked. "Chen Wu is a match for Zhang Ying, and I can vouch for that. Let him challenge."

Cheng Pu turned to Chen Wu and said, "May Heaven be with you, Chen Zilie."

  Chen Wu rode forth and challenged Zhang Ying.

"**WHO ARE YOU???**" Zhang Ying cried. "**WHO IS 'CHEN WU'? HOW DARE SUN CE SEND SUCH A WORTHLESS MAN AGAINST ME!**"

Chen Wu levelled his spear and waited silently.

"...**FINE!**" Zhang Ying said with a tone that implied offence. "**I WILL SLAY YOUR PIRATE BOY, AND THEN I WILL COME FOR YOUR HEAD, SUN CE! READY YOURSELF FOR THE NETHERWORLD, 'CHEN WU'!**"

Chen Wu and Zhang Ying then charged at each other; Chen Wu held his ground as the two crossed spears for the first time.

"Zhang Ying will not wear him down quickly," Gongjin said to an anxious Bofu.

"I'll admit, I'm impressed," Bofu replied. "Chen Wu's got more training than I was aware of."

The jousters met for a fourth time; neither man gave ground.

"...This might go to fifty," Cheng Pu said to Lü Fan.

"Hopefully not, Mister Cheng," Lü Fan scoffed. "We don't want to be here all day!"

As Zhang Ying and Chen Wu passed one-another for the fifteenth time, Chen Wu lunged with all of his strength and caused Zhang Ying to lose control of his horse. Zhang Ying retreated toward his line, and Chen Wu pursued; Zhang Ying wheeled around once he had control of his horse again, but he was not prepared for a renewed assault. Chen Wu launched a series of attacks on the stationary Zhang Ying, who could neither retreat nor gain an advantage: the battle ended abruptly when Chen Wu used his superior strength to push Zhang Ying's spear to one side and followed with a stabbing attack to the man's stomach. Zhang Ying fell from his horse, and his men immediately broke formation and retreated.

"There is another dragon, another tiger!" Bofu cried. **"VICTORY!"**

Chen Wu's recruits were especially vocal as Chen Wu rode back to his master with Zhang Ying's severed head in one hand and the horse's reins and his battle spear in the other; Bofu could not stop grinning as he slapped Chen Wu's arms and laughed uproariously.

"Now we can advance," Lü Fan shouted to Gongjin, who nodded in response.

"*Aiee*... he's gone," Fan Neng sighed as he scanned Zhang Ying's abandoned encampment to the southeast of Niuzhu.

"What happened...?" Yu Mi wondered. "Was he ambushed?"

"There are no signs of combat," Fan Neng replied. "He's... he's... the fool!"

"He didn't... he didn't go and challenge Sun Ce again?" Yu Mi said.

"He must have," Fan Neng replied. "His arrogance is our undoing yet again! If he'd just waited, we might have taken on the challenge together!"

"He wanted to save face... he told me that," Yu Mi admitted. "He must have tried to obstruct Sun Ce as he marched against Moling."

"Zhang Ying can hold Sun Ce at bay for only so long," Fan Neng said. "Let's hurry, and hope we-"

"We should do as we originally planned," Yu Mi interrupted. "Let's not let Zhang Ying's recklessness sway us from a proper strategy. Niuzhu is our target: let's allow Zhang Ying to fight his personal battle alone."

"...Fool," Fan Neng muttered as he gestured to his cavalry, who immediately resumed their march to Niuzhu.

Xue Li and Ze Rong watched from the battlements of the vast riverside trading city of Moling as Bofu, Gongjin, Lü Fan and Cheng Pu prepared a siege on the eastern end of the long southern wall.

"We cannot just wait!" Xue Li whined as he watched the pile of wooden siege ladders growing in the distance. "He has men going and back and forth with the pace of the imperial forces at their peak! How did he gain such discipline from the wretched sorts that he employs???"

"I, too, employ the weak-minded and mould them into proper men," Ze Rong replied. "The only difference, Chancellor Xue, is that I insist that they repent first; he promises them rewards of the flesh instead."

"We can't let them siege," Xue Li fretted.

"I intend to appeal to them," Ze Rong revealed. "I want archers right the way along the east wall with weapons at the ready: I will go out of the gates and deliver a sermon to them."

"If any man can sway the wicked to the side of virtue, Master Ze, it is you," Xue Li replied. "You'll get whatever you need."

An hour later, Cheng Pu dashed into Bofu's command tent with a worried expression on his face.

"...So the false priest is squawking," Gongjin guessed.

"Yes, and I'm worried that he may actually turn them!" Cheng Pu said. "A lot of men have stopped working! This man is another Zhang Jue!"

"...I take it that he is well defended...?" Lü Fan said.

"Archers on the wall, shoulder to shoulder, a cavalry escort, and two infantry brigades just inside the gates behind him," Cheng Pu reported anxiously.

"We can't let him talk," Bofu said with concern.

"Yes we can," Gongjin chuckled.

"How so, Mister Zhou Yu...?" Cheng Pu asked.

"...Because, Mister Cheng, we made casual enquiries before we set out, and any men that were going to join Ze Rong have already done so," Gongjin insisted. "He was here before we arrived, so he has already won over the winnable. Yes, there's curiosity, but the kind that one has when a bard visits the town or the fellow next door has a new hat. They'll lose interest and get back to work soon enough."

Cheng Pu snorted irritably, turned to leave, and said, "I hope you're right, 'Gongjin'."

"...He doesn't like me," Gongjin said once Cheng Pu had retreated.

"Don't worry about it," Bofu insisted. "Once he sees that you're right, he'll be fine."

Ze Rong returned to the battlements of Moling City after an hour of preaching that had resulted in a handful of desertions amongst Bofu's labourers but little else besides.

"You tried, Master Ze," Xue Li said reassuringly. "They're godless."

"They will be ready to begin their siege soon," Ze Rong replied. "I have failed to delay or prevent it... we must prepare."

"I'm going out there," Xue Li said. "If you can risk your sagely life, Master Ze, then so can I: I can, I must, and I will. I'm going to get my best officers and men, charge out of the gates, and target their siege preparations. Even if I am unable to repel them from the walls, I'll have bought us some time."

Ze Rong bowed and said, "I shall pray for you."

Xue Li bowed lower than Ze Rong had done, and then he retreated from the wall.

Xue Li met the besiegers outside the walls, but his force was too small and ordinary to counter the sheer number of capable officers and enthusiastic volunteers. Xue Li's agents did not manage to affect the siege equipment, as it was too well defended by Bofu and Gongjin; Ling Cao charged at Xue Li and killed one of his senior bodyguards, and Cheng Pu and Xu Kun followed with a full cavalry charge against the isolated vanguard infantry. Ze Rong – who was still atop the wall of Moling – watched as Xue Li tried to withdraw to the city, but his path was blocked by Ling Cao; Xue was forced to flee to the southwest as his army disintegrated. Ze ordered the archers to fire at Bofu's forces, which repelled all attack attempts while the gates were secured.

"That's how it's done!" Bofu cackled as he watched Xue Li ride away. **"Ling Cao, Xu Kun: pursue Xue Li! The rest of you:**

resume preparations for the siege!"

"**Cease firing!**" Ze Rong ordered as Bofu's main force moved out of range.

"What will we do, Master Ze...?" Yu Zi asked.

Ze Rong shook his head as he turned and walked away from the battlements.

"What will we do...?" Yu Zi asked again.

"...Save our strength," Ze Rong replied. "We'll certainly need it now, for Heaven has chosen to test us harshly."

Bofu's siege of Moling began on the following morning, but it was doomed to be rudely interrupted before any serious damage could be done.

"**Bofu!**" Xu Kun cried as he ran into Bofu's personal tent.

"...What's the matter, Cousin...?" Bofu asked wearily. "I only just left the command tent; what's happened now that-"

"Zhou Yu sent me to get you back to the command tent," Xu Kun said. "Please hurry!"

"...I think I know," Bofu sighed. "I'll follow you."

When Bofu reached the command tent, he found that Gongjin and Lü Fan were stood outside the entrance and concluding a nervous conversation with a battered and exhausted messenger. The two advisers were obviously worried, and the cause was likely to be one thing.

"...Niuzhu?" Bofu supposed.

"We need to go back, and *quickly*," Gongjin said. "We can't afford to lose the place or the people guarding it."

Bofu turned and looked at Moling City, which was now a prize that was tantalisingly out of reach.

"**Bofu!**" Gongjin barked. "**We have to hurry! Order a withdrawal!**"

"....**Damn it!**" Bofu cried. "...**Withdraw all forces!**"

Xu Kun retreated to inform the siege commanders.

"I'm sorry," Gongjin said quietly.

"Don't be," Bofu replied. "Let's just hope we get there in time: Ze Rong can wait."

Gongjin hummed purposefully.

"Fan Neng and Yu Mi ...?" Bofu supposed.

"Yes," Lü Fan replied. "Those two are becoming a recurring nuisance."

"They're more than a 'nuisance', Ziheng," Bofu chortled angrily. "They've just cost me a short siege and a quick victory over Ze Rong! I'll grind them into mincemeat!"

Within an hour, the siege was over: Ze Rong watched as Bofu's forces retreated from the walls and started a swift journey back to Niuzhu City.

"Heaven is with us, Master Ze," Yu Zi suggested.

"We must still forge our own path," Ze Rong retorted. "They'll be back; and we must be ready when they return."

****

54

Bofu and his forces descended on the besiegers at Niuzhu and caught them by surprise with an unrestrained attack. For this particular battle, Bofu had elected to give Zhou Tai and Jiang Qin soldiers rather than keep them as his bodyguards; they rushed into battle alongside Ling Cao's vanguard militia and dealt the first decisive blows.

"This Sun Ce has great officers by the bushel!" Fan Neng cried as he watched his rear guard collapse. **"We have to withdraw before they–!"**

"CHARGE!"

Bofu, Cheng Pu, Xu Kun, Wu Jing and Sun Ben led armies from the north and south that tore the wings of Fan Neng and Yu Mi's army apart.

"We're trapped!" Yu Mi gasped.

Zhu Zhi stood on the walls of the city and oversaw volleys of arrows, battle gongs and heckling chants; the enemy army collapsed altogether, forcing the commanders to stage a humiliating retreat with a handful of riders as an escort.

"AFTER THEM!" Bofu screamed.

Bofu and his remaining bodyguards rode after the enemy generals, but he was suddenly ambushed by a concealed unit of cavalry and infantry that were hiding amongst rubble and undergrowth; Wu Jing rode to his rescue, cutting down one of the cavalry captains and forcing the infantry to surrender.

"Are you alright, Nephew?" Wu Jing asked.

"They're getting away!" Bofu screamed; Gongjin, Sun Hè and Sun Ben arrived at that moment and did their best to calm Bofu.

"You nearly died just now!" Wu Jing protested. **"Don't be a fool!"**

"I have to get them!" Bofu replied.

Cheng Pu, Xu Kun and Ling Cao led their own militias toward Bofu.

"No, no, wait, wait!" Gongjin cried. **"Let them go, they're destroyed!"**

"They're destroyed when they're *dead*, Gongjin!" Bofu retorted as he urged his horse for a second time, but Sun Ben and Sun Hè blocked his way and stared at him silently. Ling Cao and Xu Kun were determined to be rid of Liu Yao's generals, so they ignored Gongjin's plea and continued the chase.

"Ling Cao, Xu Kun, you will halt right now!" Cheng Pu bellowed as he rode after his own allies.

Ling Cao stopped his horse and cursed under his breath, but Xu Kun continued.

"Xu Kun!" Cheng Pu shouted. **"Halt at once!"**

Xu Kun did not comply.

"...Xu Kun, stop!" Bofu shouted as he rode alongside Cheng Pu: Xu Kun slowed his horse, but he was torn between following orders and fighting his enemies.

"Captain Xu Kun!" Cheng Pu barked. **"Lord Sun commands that you *halt*!"**

Xu Kun finally ended his chase.

"The most important thing right now is reassuring the war-weary people of Niuzhu and preparing for a swift return to Moling,"

Gongjin said as he reached Bofu and halted his horse. "Those two generals are now humiliated and without an army, Bofu... they'll not be back in a hurry."
Bofu turned his gaze toward the battlefield; Liu Yao's infantry was now reduced to piles of bodies and gaggles of weeping, emotionally-broken captives.
"...Yeah, I know, Gongjin," Bofu said at last. "The local people have suffered too."
"Their army ransacked nearby villages for easy supplies and forced men to join them, because they were desperate," Cheng Pu said. "We've tried to leave the people be, but we're blamed for starting this by some of them."
"Zhu Zhi has rallied the city, but we must do more to win the hearts of the people around here," Gongjin suggested. "This battle was the start of what needs to be done here in Niuzhu. But first we must go back to Moling and break Ze Rong before Liu Yao can muster another army to attack Niuzhu again!"
"Yeah, else it'll be a back and forth, back and forth campaign that'll wear us down and break *us*... we need to defeat one or the other," Bofu grumbled as he turned his horse toward Niuzhu.

While Gongjin and Lü Fan planned the return to Moling, Bofu, Cheng Pu and Chen Wu toured the settlements around Niuzhu in person and distributed food and clothes to the needy; many of the young men feared that Bofu was intending to conscript them to fight for his cause, but he did not. The sight of such a charismatic, affable and sincere youth showing such civility won the hearts of people of all ages, and Bofu soon had the approval of thousands and the service of hundreds of able men. Within a week, Niuzhu was fortified once again, the army had more than doubled in size, and the march west could begin.

"So they're back again," Ze Rong said as he watched the preparations for another siege. "Less than a month... he must be a very capable general, this 'Sun Ce', to relieve Niuzhu and be back here in even greater numbers in such a short time."
"Shall I ride out and challenge him, Master?" Yu Zi asked.
"...Yes," Ze Rong replied. "Try and provoke a full charge... make him careless."
        Yu Zi rode out of the east gates of Moling and charged at Bofu's lines, just as Xue Li had done weeks earlier; Cheng Pu scoffed at the stupidity of repeating a failed tactic and forced Yu Zi to retreat. But Yu Zi did not retreat fully; as Cheng Pu reached the outskirts of Bofu's camp, Yu Zi turned about and charged him, striking his arm and knocking him from his horse.
"Where is a man that can challenge Heaven's General?!" Yu Zi cried as he raced around the camp perimeter and cut down any man that could not avoid his glaive.
        Word of Yu Zi's challenge reached Bofu within minutes.
"I'll kill him myself!" Bofu said with anger.
"No, no, let me take him!" Xu Kun pleaded.
"I'll fight him, Lord Sun!" Ling Cao said.
"And I would gladly do it!" Chen Wu said. "Allow me a second chance to-"
"No!" Bofu cried. **"He's mine!"**

"You mustn't!" Gongjin insisted. "Even if *I* have to fight him, Bofu, you-!"

Bofu did not listen; he rode out of the main camp and dashed toward the front line.

"**Lord Sun! Lord Sun, don't be a fool!**" Jiang Qin cried as he tried to catch up to his master; Sun Hè and Zhou Tai led the remainder of the bodyguards after Jiang Qin, but Bofu was urging his horse to maintain an exhausting pace, and he was some distance away.

"**YU ZI!**" Bofu shrieked as he caught sight of Ze Rong's general. "**Prepare to die!**"

Bofu charged at Yu Zi, and the two clashed blades; but Yu Zi was luring the furious Bofu toward the city, where Ze Rong's archers were waiting.

"**Bofu!**" Gongjin screamed as he reached the front lines. "**What are you doing??? Do you want to end up like your father???**"

Bofu saw Gongjin gesticulating, and although he could not hear his friend's words, something told him what they were; Bofu realised his folly and ended his assault, but he was already too close to the city. Ze Rong gave the order to fire, and arrows rained down from the wall.

"**AHHH! DAMN YOU, ZE RONG!**" Bofu screamed as an arrow hit his right thigh; men were falling all around him as he turned his horse to flee.

"**Sun Ce is struck!**" Yu Zi bellowed. "**Sun Ce is down!**"

A small infantry force rushed out of the gates to inflict further damage to Bofu's demoralised forces; Bofu's soldiers were weeping as they saw that their lord was now slumped forward on the horse that instinctively carried him to safety.

"**Lord Sun!**" Cheng Pu cried with despair. "**Not again! Not again! Lord Sun Ce!**"

"**Sun Ce is wounded!**" Yu Zi shouted. "**Pursue them!**"

An emotional Gongjin pulled Bofu's horse away from the front line.

"...Tell everyone to retreat," Bofu said with surprising strength.

Gongjin gasped.

"*Order a retreat*!" Bofu hissed from his prone position.

"...Yes, yes!" Gongjin whispered with barely-concealed joy; he then assumed a serious expression and shouted, "**RETREAT! RETREAT NOW, EVERYONE!**"

"**LORD SUN!**" Cheng Pu shrieked. "**I FAILED YOU, LORD SUN!**"

"Tell that silly old man to shut up, or we'll be routed," Bofu said as Gongjin led him away from the battlefield.

"**Cheng Pu, come here at once!**" Gongjin ordered. "**Come to your lord! Ling Cao, Sun Hè: sound the gong and lead the men away from the city, quickly!**"

Ze Rong smiled as he watched the disorderly retreat from his safe place atop the walls of Moling. Yu Zi stopped his pursuit when Lü Fan ordered the rear guard and an archery division to cover Bofu's escape, but the defenders' morale was peaked at the thought that Bofu was gravely injured. Gongjin smiled as he led Bofu's horse from the battlefield; he could see Bofu's scheme, and it appealed to him.

Bofu's army retreated and constructed a new camp at a safe

distance away from Moling; once it was safe to relax, there was a congregation of well-wishers in and around Bofu's personal tent that numbered in the hundreds.

"When... when you were *hit*, Lord Sun...!" Cheng Pu whimpered as he sat and stared at the bed-ridden Bofu.

"Sorry it took you so long to be told what happened, old man," Bofu chuckled as a physician fussed over his leg. "I just wish you'd call me Bofu... even at a moment like this, I'm 'Lord Sun'!"

"...I thought it was your father all over again," Wu Jing sighed.

"Yeah, well, it isn't," Bofu retorted. "I'm alive... but Ze Rong doesn't need to know that, does he...?"

"Your quick thinking is to be commended in this matter," Lü Fan said. "A false death ruse is a good idea; it almost makes up for your nearly being actually killed in an act of total, utter recklessness and suicidal foolishness."

"We... we were a little more careless than we should have been in that battle," Bofu conceded as he looked at the faces of his disapproving officials.

"I'm glad that you can see that, even if it is in hindsight," Lü Fan said sadly.

"Never mind," Gongjin chuckled. "It's had some positive outcomes."

"So many have asked us to wish you well," Cheng Pu said with cheer. "You're very popular now, Lord Sun."

"And Ze Rong will now do something stupid, hopefully," Bofu said. "All we have to do is retreat to Niuzhu, put the word out that I didn't make it... and *wait*."

Ze Rong's spies reported news that secretly delighted him: all of Bofu's men were wearing white articles, and there were preparations being made for a full withdrawal to Niuzhu. Ze Rong ordered his subordinate Yu Zi to take most of his forces and launch an attack on Niuzhu, which was more than Bofu could have hoped for.

"The fish have taken the bait," Gongjin said as he stood on the city wall and watched Yu Zi and his soldiers heckle the western gates below.

"So how will we reel them in and make the largest haul...?" Lü Fan asked.

"He has established a camp, so he intends to stay here until we abandon the city," Gongjin replied. "We'll let him think he understands the situation..."

Cheng Pu took a force of 300 men and rode out of the city, shouting, "**Be gone, cultist dogs! Go back to your heretic master!**"

Yu Zi sneered as he observed the poorly concealed white garments and lifeless demeanour that defined his enemies.

"**You're moving like a snake without a head!**" Yu Zi taunted. "**Where is your lord...? Is he well...?**"

"**Bastard!**" Cheng Pu cried with convincing anguish; he lunged at Yu Zi, but he was easily outmanoeuvred.

"**Why do you struggle?**" Yu Zi asked. "**Why do you resist the will of Heaven?**"

Cheng Pu feigned distress and ordered his dozen riders to retreat toward a nearby patch of woodland; the infantry either scattered or did what they could to follow the horsemen.

"Pursue him!" Yu Zi ordered, and he and his men followed Cheng Pu's theatrical retreat.

Cheng Pu halted at the outskirts of the small wood and ordered his men to turn and face their enemies, who outnumbered them considerably when taken as a whole; however, the infantry were far behind Yu Zi and his small cavalry force, all of whom had dashed after Cheng Pu without careful consideration.

"Where can you go?" Yu Zi asked.

"Wherever I please," Cheng Pu chuckled.

Yu Zi and his 30 riders suddenly realised that they were in danger. Yu Zi motioned silently, and his riders began a slow retreat.

"Too late!" Cheng Pu bellowed: a gong sounded, and ambush forces led by Ling Cao and Xu Kun surged out of the wall of trees.

"I have been tricked!" Yu Zi cried as he turned his horse to retreat; but more of Bofu's forces were approaching from the direction of the city, led by Wu Jing, Sun Ben, Sun Hè, Jiang Qin and Zhou Tai.

"Tricking you wasn't hard," Cheng Pu said as he lunged at the distracted Yu Zi and almost knocked him from his horse. What followed was a rout: hundreds of Yu Zi's men perished whilst reciting pieces of Ze Rong's mangled Buddhist doctrine, but Yu Zi fought his way past Ling Cao and escaped once again.

"...Now we finish him off," Cheng Pu muttered.

"...I cannot face Master Ze again!" Yu Zi whimpered as he sat in his command tent and listened to the complaints of his disaffected troops; his captains were silent, expressionless and unsupportive.

"Yu Zi!" Gongjin bellowed as he approached the wooden gates of the camp. **"Yu Zi, why don't you come out?"**

"...**I will redeem myself by smiting the unbelievers!"** Yu Zi cried as he took his sword and ran out of the tent. **"Bring me a horse! Bring me a horse!"**

But when the desperate Yu Zi rode to the gates, a surprise awaited him: at the head of the heckling army was a finely-decorated horse, and sat on that horse was Bofu, who was clearly alive and well.

"*Sun Ce*???" Yu Zi exclaimed.

"He is a demon!" one of Yu Zi's captains yelped.

Cries of pain told Yu Zi that the men in his watchtowers had been shot and killed by Bofu's expert snipers: there would be no second attempt on his life.

"Greetings again, Yu Zi!" Cheng Pu heckled. **"*Here* is our lord! Is he well...?"**

The horrified Yu Zi and his officers retreated to his command tent as Bofu's soldiers began to chant, **"Where is our lord...? Is he well, Yu Zi...? *Here* is our lord! Is he well...?"**

Bofu rode back and forth and laughed, despite the pain that he was suffering: Yu Zi's men lost all hope of a victory and fell into general melancholy. Since defeat was inevitable, Yu Zi waited until the middle of the night and fled through the western gates under cover of darkness.

Yu Zi reluctantly delivered his report to Ze Rong in the audience hall of Moling's grand governor's residence. Yu Zi kowtowed repeatedly as he spoke of the outcome at Niuzhu and the truth that Bofu's reported death was part of a ruse.

"Alive… alive… *alive*…!" Ze Rong muttered as he paced back and forth, disturbing the cushion that served as the host seat with every pass.

"What must we do…?" Yu Zi asked. "Our army is decimated!"

"…We must do what I should have done last time… we must fortify the city," Ze Rong decided. "Do whatever it takes: he does not come back to a mere city, he comes back to a military fortress!"

Yu Zi nodded obediently and got to his feet to retreat.

"Wait," Ze Rong ordered.

"What else can I do for you, Master…?" Yu Zi asked.

"We must re-establish communications with Xue Li and invite him to return here at once," Ze Rong said. "I can only defeat Sun Ce if I have his army."

"He is recruiting in the west," Yu Zi replied. "I shall have a messenger go to him."

"As soon as you can," Ze Rong said.

A week after Yu Zi's force was routed at Niuzhu, Bofu's army marched toward Moling for a third time, and every man was confident that victory would now be swift. But Bofu's jovial mood was immediately replaced by anger and despair when his scouts reported the changes that had been made after Yu Zi's defeat.

"*Trenches*…?" Bofu groaned. "Towers…? Extra walls…? He's turned the place into a military defensive position! **How will we break him quickly now???**"

"We have to try," Gongjin pleaded. "Let's see how bad it really is, and plan accordingly."

Bofu nodded tersely.

Bofu's messengers had actually underestimated the scale of Ze Rong's upgrading of Moling's defences: the city was now one of the most heavily-fortified in the south. Every inch of the wall was either reinforced or manned by archers; the northern side had seen improvements to detect and withstand attacks from the Yangtze River, while the other walls enjoyed a series of trenches to make sieges next to impossible. A single attempt was made to attack the east wall, but after suffering over 100 casualties, Bofu decided that he could do no more. The self-serving Ze Rong would have to wait: Bofu ordered a retreat to Niuzhu so that his strategists could turn their attentions eastward, toward Qu'e.

****

55

Bofu convened a meeting with his officials on the eve of the next stage of the campaign.

"Tomorrow, we all do what we must to regain our homes," Bofu began. "Forgive me for sticking to formal names, friends, but this is a formal occasion. Zhu Zhi, Sun Ben, Chen Wu: you're going to focus on getting Wu Prefecture back; Xu Gong is not likely to be a threat, but I know that you'll also be up against the Shanyue as a separate or joint threat, so if you need extra resource, talk to Zhou Yu and Lü Fan."

Zhu Zhi, Chen Wu and Sun Ben bowed slightly and silently.

"Messengers have gone to Hengjiang and Danglikou," Bofu continued. "Hui Qu doesn't need our help to fortify the northern bank now, so Huang Gai and Han Dang can be here in Danyang and Wu, where they're needed."

Ling Cao bowed humbly and said, "Will they be used to defeat Ze Rong?"

"We have to forget about Ze Rong for now," Bofu replied. "He's dug in deep. The good thing is that he owes no allegiance to anyone but himself, so even if he does manage to build another army, he'll not risk another confrontation to save Liu Yao."

"Quite right," Gongjin said.

"So for now, we're going east and focussing specifically on releasing Danyang and Wu from Liu Yao's control: I thought I should make that clear," Bofu continued. "I am not going to attack Guangling, Kuaiji or Yuzhang… not *yet*, anyway. Hopefully, our actions here will either bring their administrators over to us or inspire those places to be rid of their puppet leaders and get some autonomy back."

"So the rest of us are going to take every place between here and Qu'e," Cheng Pu supposed.

"…I prefer 'liberate', but yes, that's the idea," Bofu replied. "I want to hit Liu Yao hard. I want to be in Qu'e quickly with nothing to get in the way. Zhou Yu, Lü Fan: kindly explain the rest…"

Once the meeting was finished, Bofu invited Sun Ben, Wu Jing, Cheng Pu, Zhu Zhi, Gongjin and Lü Fan to a more private gathering.

"Uncle, Cousin Boyang… I want to apologise to the two of you first," Bofu said humbly. "It must be humiliating for you to be seen to be taking orders from me. But I assure you, I-"

"It's fine," Sun Ben promised. "I already told you that, Bofu."

"You're winning," Wu Jing said. "I'd be a fool to complain if it was bothering me, which it doesn't, I promise."

"Good," Bofu said; he then turned to Cheng Pu, who gestured that he would like to speak next.

"I'm here because I want to be," Cheng Pu insisted. "I don't have a problem taking orders from you or your young friends."

"That is a relief!" Lü Fan admitted. "I still feel awkward, since you are a great hero to me, but to hear you say that is a true relief, Cheng Demou… a true relief."

"Agreed," Gongjin said.

"So now that we are settled on these matters, we can move

forward," Zhu Zhi said as a prompt. "Lord Sun, we must attack with all haste."

"In three days, we march," Bofu promised. "Nothing will delay us."

"Not even your wound...?" Cheng Pu said as he stared at Bofu's right thigh.

"It's not serious at all," Bofu replied. "I almost forget about it sometimes."

"...So long as you're sure," Cheng Pu said warily.

"I am!" Bofu chortled. "Now come on! We have a war to win!"

Governor Liu Yao summoned his aides to a meeting when news of Bofu's swift advance reached Qu'e.

"He's taken Hushu already, and Jiangcheng was on the verge of falling when I received this last letter!" Liu Yao said worriedly. "What will we do?"

"If I must have these words etched on my grave, then so be it, if it means that they will be heeded!" Xu Shao said with despair. "Taishi Ci! Use Taishi Ci!"

Once again, the Qu'e court was filled with the din of fierce arguments.

"...**SHUT UP!**" Liu Yao screamed. "**All of you, shut up!**"

The court fell silent.

"I will have a messenger sent to Administrator Wang Lang in Kuaiji, asking for support, and I will send gifts to the Shanyue to get the help of White Tiger and the other tribal leaders in retaining control of Wu," Liu Yao continued.

The officials were generally agreeable and voiced their accord.

"So you can parley with 'barbarians' and get the approval of these idiots, but not a glimmer of trust in Taishi Ci!" Xu Shao chortled. "I despair, I truly do."

The officials that were sympathetic to Taishi Ci murmured agreeably.

"Taishi Ziyi is my friend, but he is... 'principled', Mister Xu," Liu Yao replied. "Even he cannot be sure of what he will do next, and I cannot risk more complications. He understands."

"I'm so glad that he does," Xu Shao scoffed. "But in the aftermath of that decision, we're back to using Fan and Yu."

Generals Fan Neng and Yu Mi scowled angrily.

"We are," Liu Yao sighed. "Generals, kindly prepare defensive works in and around Qu'e; we cannot let Sun Ce breach the city."

"Be sure to respect the people, Generals!" Xu Shao said. "Sun Ce has already managed to rally close to thirty-thousand men to his side since he took Niuzhu! Don't give him chances to recruit any more, Generals!"

"We shall be careful, Mister Xu," Fan Neng replied irritably.

Once the two generals had bowed and retreated from the hall, Xu Shao said, "What will you tell your friend...?"

Liu Yao eyed Xu Shao angrily.

That evening, Liu Yao invited Taishi Ci to his residence for a private banquet. Once the two were seated, Taishi said, "I hope that you don't intend to lavish me with fine food and wine, Zhengli; enemies will soon be here, and that food is-"

"Spare me!" Liu Yao pleaded. "*Already*, before I've even...!"

"...Sorry," Taishi Ci said after a short silence. "Did you think I wasn't aware of the situation?"

"You're too smart to miss anything," Liu Yao replied. "Ziyi, I cannot use you. You should be our vanguard general, many now say; many more than when you first got here. You're a man that wins friends easily, but that means that you also gain enemies with equal ease, and there are plenty of jealous minds in my court."

"I know this," Taishi Ci said. "You invited me here to tell me this?"

"...No, I invited you here to beg you to heed my instructions," Liu Yao replied. "I cannot have any more wild stallions in the field. I am left with no choice but to work with Xu Gong, grovel to White Tiger, and-"

"White Tiger...? ...The Shanyue khan?" Taishi Ci exclaimed.

"...I suppose he is," Liu Yao said. "But that's not important! What's important is my keeping as much order as possible! Zhang Ying is dead; Niuzhu is lost, Hushu is lost, Jiangcheng is falling as we speak, Moling and Wuhu are isolated; Danyang Prefecture is slipping from my fingers, and if I must use Xu Gong's surprising popularity and White Tiger's armies to keep it, then so be it."

"But you won't use *me*," Taishi Ci sighed.

"Stay in the city," Liu Yao pleaded.

"Let me at least do some scouting for you!" Taishi Ci suggested. "I can assist you by gathering recruits and finding good defensive positions!"

"...Alright, listen," Liu Yao said with trepidation. "You can be assigned as 'Acting Colonel that guards the baggage train', or something, and you can join the army on scouting missions in nearby towns. Help them with recruiting and topography if you can, but do nothing that can earn us scorn."

Taishi Ci bowed low and said, "Thank you, Zhengli. To be of help; that's all I ask."

"...Don't make me regret it," Liu Yao retorted.

Within a week, Bofu's army defeated Liu Yao's forces at Jiangcheng and moved to the outskirts of the region surrounding the city of Qu'e.

"We're almost home!" Bofu said. "Well, I say 'home'... Fuchun's home, but Qu'e... is where... ... ...Sorry, I'm getting lost in myself! Gongjin, Ziheng, what should we do next?"

"We'll camp here and begin scouting the settlements around the city," Gongjin replied. "We'll recruit, seek out defensive positions... that sort of thing."

"I'll go personally," Bofu suggested.

"*Ayah*... you want to be shot again?" Wu Jing heckled.

"I should have sent you to Wu with Zhu Zhi," Bofu grumbled.

"Didn't I save you at Niuzhu?" Wu Jing said. "Why are you now so ungrateful?"

"...Sorry, but Uncle, you whinge too much!" Bofu replied. "If I go scouting, I'll win hearts and minds. Isn't that a good idea?"

Wu Jing conceded the point.

Fate finally brought two heroes together at the town of Shen, near Qu'e. Taishi Ci had separated from the small battalion that he had been seconded to, so he was alone; Bofu, by contrast, was surrounded by Huang Gai, Han Dang and his bodyguards. Bofu

and his followers had finished surveying the area to the south of
the town, and they were now moving along the hills to the east of
it. It was raining heavily, as it often did in the south, so visibility
was poor; the two factions failed to spot each other until it was
too late to avoid a confrontation.

"Who's that man there?" Han Dang asked as he spotted Taishi Ci
in the distance.

"...He isn't one of ours," Huang Gai replied.

Bofu turned to one of his bodyguards and said, "Song Qian, ride
ahead and challenge him."

"Song's one of your bodyguards!" Han Dang protested. "I've been
rotting in Danglikou, so let me go!"

"Song Qian will go," Bofu insisted. "He performed well at Hushu,
and I want to see how he does. There's fourteen of us and one of
him, whoever he is."

Song Qian raised his halberd and charged forward; Taishi Ci
halted his horse and awaited Song Qian's challenge.

"**Who are you?**" Song Qian asked.

"**A man that belongs here,**" Taishi Ci replied. "**Who are you?**"

"The...!" Han Dang said with anger. "I'll-!"

"No, no, wait... this man is interesting," Bofu said.

Taishi Ci observed the entire group of riders that he faced; he saw
that the leader met the description of Bofu and bellowed, "**I will
not fight mediocrities! Sun Ce: why don't you come and
fight?**"

"**How dare he!**" Huang Gai cried.

"**I'll rip his throat out!**" Han Dang barked.

"No, no!" Bofu said with excitement. "This man... I must know his
name! Oh, I hope that Song Qian asks his name!"

"**Will you come forth or not, Sun Ce?**" Taishi Ci asked as he
urged his horse to trot back and forth.

"**Who are you that Lord Sun would fight you if he were
here?**" Song Qian said cautiously.

Taishi Ci raised his glaive and said, "**I am Taishi Ci of
Huangxian! And you are no match for me!**"

Song Qian was overcome by anger: he rode forward and engaged
Taishi Ci, but Bofu screamed, "**RETREAT!**"

Song Qian barely heard the instruction, but he heeded it
immediately.

"...Who is that man?" Bofu asked as Song Qian returned to his
side. "Did I hear right? Did he say 'Taishi Ci'...?"

"He did," Song Qian panted. "He's strong. We should attack
together."

"No," Bofu said as his fighting bloodlust consumed his ability to
reason. "I'll meet his challenge: all of you stay back and watch for
traps."

"You mustn't!" Sun Hè pleaded, but it was to no avail.

Bofu rode forward, levelled his spear, and shouted, "**Here is Sun
Ce! Are you truly Taishi Ci?**"

"**Come and see, villainous pirate!**" Taishi Ci retorted.

Bofu grinned and charged; Taishi Ci met the charge, and the two
clashed repeatedly until their horses started to tire. Bofu ducked
under a swipe, but he swerved too far to the left and fell from his
horse.

"He's exposed!" Sun Hè cried. "We have to-!"

But Taishi Ci did not attack as Bofu's allies expected; instead, Taishi jumped down from his horse and waited for Bofu to retrieve his spear.

"...You're a principled man," Bofu wheezed. "I like that."

"Someone has to be in this age of villains," Taishi Ci retorted. "Else it would be men like you and nothing else."

"...Is that how you see me?" Bofu exclaimed.

"How else can I see you?" Taishi chortled. "Stop talking and fight."

Bofu advanced with his spear, and the two fought for several minutes; both were at the peak of their physical strength, and it seemed that there could be no easy victory for either man. But eventually, the sodden ground gave way under Taishi's feet, and he lost his grip on his halberd; Bofu fought the instinct to capitalise on his opponent's vulnerability and waited for Taishi to get to his feet.

"...Your debt is repaid," Taishi said cautiously. "...But it changes nothing."

"This isn't as simple as you think," Bofu protested. "I-"

"You defy the emperor, and you defy Heaven!" Taishi barked. **"You attack this place and harm the people: how is that not simple???"**

"This is my home!" Bofu shouted. **"Liu Yao chased my uncle from-!"**

Taishi threw his halberd aside and took two hook-ended blades from his belt.

"...You won't listen," Bofu sighed. "That's a shame."

Bofu threw his spear down and took a sword from his belt; the two men then continued their battle with the bladed weapons, each knowing that a mistake by either would lead to a serious wound. But once again, the two were too evenly matched, even though Taishi was nearly 10 years older: eventually, Bofu managed to knock one of Taishi's blades from his hand, but not without Taishi striking the side of his helmet and knocking it from his head. The battle continued for a while longer, but the outcome would soon be decided for them. A horn blared, and Bofu was momentarily startled; Taishi realised that Liu Yao's militia were probably searching for him nearby, so he backed away and picked up Bofu's helmet. Bofu saw that he was close to Taishi's lost blade, so he collected it and hooked it onto his belt before he retreated with his entourage.

"Are you alright, Mister Taishi?" Liu Yao's militia captain asked as he stopped alongside the exhausted Taishi Ci.

"...Yes," Taishi replied uneasily. "Yes, I... I am, thank you."

Taishi Ci pondered telling the captain about Bofu's riders, but he did not.

"What's that you have there?" the captain asked.

"...A general's head," Taishi Ci replied. "Let's get back to Qu'e."

Sun Hè was yelling at Bofu as the two entered their command tent an hour later.

"Stop shouting, we're indoors," Bofu grumbled.

"I won't!" Sun Hè retorted.

"What's the matter?" Gongjin asked. "You're both soaked: why didn't you find shelter?"

"He was too busy proving his worth against some scruffy

mercenary!" Sun Hè said angrily.

"That was *Taishi Ci*," Bofu said with strange pride.

"*Taishi Ci*…?" Lü Fan exclaimed. "*Taishi Ci's* in Qu'e?"

"Whoever he was, our crazy lord insisted on nearly losing his head!" Han Dang said as Bofu took his host seat and took Taishi's blade from his belt to study it.

"Your helmet's gone, Bofu," Gongjin realised. "Were you nearly killed again?"

"Nah," Bofu chuckled. "He's a really honourable man, just as legends say: he's just the man we need to unite the south. Gongjin, Ziheng, I want that man on *my side*."

"Forget it," Lü Fan sighed.

"He came here to help Liu Yao, and the man's not to be turned from anything that he decides to do," Gongjin said with regret. "He is supposedly *unshakeable*, Bofu, and that means there's no winning him around."

"There has to be a way to win him around," Bofu said. "There *has to be*…"

At the same time, the captain of the militia that Taishi Ci had accompanied was concluding his report to Liu Yao: that report included an account of the altercation with Bofu's scouting party that he had coaxed out of Taishi Ci. The reaction was punctuated by excited chatter and a growing demand for Taishi Ci to be made the commander of the armed forces in Yang Province.

"I cannot do as so many of you ask!" Liu Yao protested.

Taishi tightened his grip on Bofu's captured helmet as he said, "Governor Liu, at least listen to my advice if you will not give me rank."

The entire court – including Taishi Ci's shrinking group of detractors – fell silent.

"…Say your piece," Liu Yao urged.

"Governor Liu, Sun Ce is not at all what I expected," Taishi explained. "I expected a coarse, unprincipled wretch that would exploit the weakest of creatures to gain an advantage: instead, I found a man that matches the rumours. He's cultured, skilled, strong, measured and charismatic, and he can gain allies easily with such gifts. If you continue to fight him as if he were a pirate king, you will lose. You must fight him as you would a famous general of the north, like Zhu Jun or Huangfu Song."

"**Preposterous!**" one sceptic said. "So now he's a *hero*? Taishi Ci's found his next master, and his name is Sun Ce!"

The court descended into a mass of noisy arguments yet again; Taishi Ci sighed miserably and waited for Liu Yao to demand their silence.

"**Be quiet!**" Liu Yao barked. "Mister Taishi, your appraisal of Sun Ce is very flattering, and not at all helpful. He is a rebel that commands pirates and criminals, not soldiers, so I think that you have been misled."

"I have not, Governor," Taishi Ci insisted. "He's to be treated with caution. A man with such talent cannot be engaged directly. All successes have been when he has been provoked and outwitted: otherwise, he is very formidable. What we must do, Governor, is–"

"I'm going to attack him soon," Liu Yao revealed. "You can be in charge of the rear guard and the supplies, Mister Taishi."

"Are you listening to me...?" Taishi Ci said through exasperated laughter.

"How can he defeat my army?" Liu Yao replied. "He's strong... that's all. But one strong man cannot win a battle against such odds. I cannot lose."

"Especially not now that I have come here to add my own support," Yuan Shao's appointed Administrator of Danyang, Zhou Xin, said bravely.

"Indeed yes, Mister Zhou!" Liu Yao chuckled.

"...But I am forced to think... for whom do you fight, Mister Zhou...?" Xu Shao asked pointedly.

"We've been fighting the same enemy, but acting separately, and Lord Yuan has seen the folly of that," Zhou Xin explained. "My efforts against the tribes and disaffected of the region were due to my following outdated orders: now Lord Yuan does as he has always done, Mister Xu Shao, and fights for the Han against the wicked elements."

"So he was not avoiding a direct and potentially damaging attack on his brother, then...?" Xu Shao said.

"Yuan Shu is an enemy of all good men, and Lord Yuan Shao is his most active enemy, smiting him whenever the opportunity arises," Zhou Xin retorted. "You need not fear my motives: my loyalty is now to Governor Liu Yao first and Lord Yuan Shao second."

"And with your aid, Administrator Zhou, we cannot lose!" Liu Yao declared. "So you can surely see, Taishi Ziyi, that victory against this man Sun Ce is ours already!"

Taishi Ci looked at Xu Shao: the famous appraiser had given up on making the governor see sense. Taishi Ci had once achieved what Liu Yao now deemed to be impossible, but there would be no debate: there would be a great battle, and the conclusion was inevitable.

****

56

Two battles would be fought to secure the two prefectures that the Sun clan and their allies called home: the battle in Danyang would be fought between Bofu's main army and Governor Liu Yao's state-backed forces, while Zhu Zhi, Sun Ben and Chen Wu were tasked with defeating the state-approved usurper-administrator of Wu Prefecture, Xu Gong; in the latter case, no one knew whether Xu Gong would receive help from the confederacy of Shanyue tribes led by 'White Tiger', but one and all hoped that the tribes would remain neutral.

Bofu's army numbered around 30,000; Liu Yao had been actively recruiting and conscripting since the fall of Niuzhu, so his army numbered close to 100,000, not including the thousands that were fighting because they presumed it to be the will of their spiritual leader, Ze Rong. Taishi Ci took his unsuitable role as the guardian of the supplies and waited with dread; he knew that Bofu would probably win despite the odds, and regardless of his newfound respect for the enemy commander, the thought of Liu Yao's defeat sickened him.

    The chosen battlefield was to the west of Qu'e city; the walls of Qu'e were lined with archers in case of a stealth attack on the city while the main battle took place. Liu Yao arrayed his army carefully: a line of archers was placed at the rear, behind the infantry formations; the front line comprised pike-wielding infantry divisions and cavalry led by Zhou Xin, Fan Neng and Yu Mi. Liu Yao had decided that he would be present at the battle to avoid accusations of cowardice, and he brought his eldest son Liu Ji as an acting field general that he hoped he would not have to use.
"This is foolish," Xu Shao muttered as he watched Bofu's army approach. "The commander should be one great man, and-"
"It's... it's too late for such things, Mister Xu," Liu Yao interrupted. "My army is larger and stronger, and Taishi Ci is still here as a rear guard, so we cannot lose."
    On the opposite side of the battlefield, Bofu convened with Cheng Pu, Gongjin and Lü Fan while Wu Jing, Huang Gai, Xu Kun and Ling Cao readied and arrayed their forces.
"So Liu Yao has managed to build a pretty big army after all," Bofu sighed. "I was hoping this'd be quick."
"It will be," Gongjin promised. "This is all planned for."

Once both armies were arrayed, Governor Liu Yao rode to his front line and found Fan Neng.
"I want this self-proclaimed 'liberator of the south' ground underfoot this time, General Fan," Liu Yao ordered. "No more excuses, no more mistakes, no more failures... crush him."
Fan Neng bowed humbly.
"...Give the order to charge as soon as you're ready," Liu Yao said as he turned his horse and began a retreat to the centre of his force. Fan Neng did not wait for very long: he ordered a full cavalry assault on Bofu's frontline infantry minutes later.
"He doesn't want to parley, then!" Bofu said the enemy started toward his position.

"**Withdraw to the centre!**" Gongjin replied. "**We can't afford to lose you now!**"

"**You won't!**" Bofu replied as he rode forward with his bodyguards and met the cavalry charge.

"...Alright, that's bad, but we anticipated that as well, didn't we," Lü Fan groaned.

"**CHARGE!**" Ling Cao cried; his own forces left the front line and followed Bofu's lead.

"...And *that*...?" Gongjin complained. "...*Aiee.*"

Liu Yao ordered his frontline infantry to begin their advance; Cheng Pu and Lü Fan signalled to the rear of their forces, and a volley of arrows checked the advance.

"You don't need me," Gongjin sighed. "I'll help Bofu!"

Lü Fan nodded, and Gongjin rode onto the battlefield with his halberd raised to chest height and his personal militia in pursuit. Bofu was in grave danger as always, but Gongjin's arrival gave Sun Hè, Song Qian and Zhou Tai the breathing space they needed to cut a path to safety. Bofu had a brief duel with Fan Neng, but the general quickly realised that Bofu was his match and retreated before either could do any damage; Ling Cao engaged Yu Mi and put the general to flight with a characteristic show of reckless courage. Once the third volley of arrows had sent Liu Yao's infantry into a full retreat, Xu Kun and Wu Jing led armies onto the field to pursue and harass them; they only stopped when Liu Yao's own archers started to provide covering fire.

"**This is not how it was supposed to be!**" Liu Yao said as he watched Yu Mi's faltering attempts to reorganise the forces.

"**Let me go forward, Father!**" Liu Ji pleaded.

"**I won't lose my son in this mess!**" Liu Yao cried. "**You'll stay where you are!**"

"**This is your last chance to save your mission, Governor!**" Xu Shao shouted over the din of battle. "**Call Taishi Ci to the front line! Do it now!**"

Liu Yao looked about and tried to find a messenger, but a new development had thrown his forces into a state of chaos: Han Dang has quietly sailed a naval force along the Yangtze and sneaked his forces to a position behind the left wing of Liu Yao's army, and the former bodyguard Jiang Qin had been tasked with taking another force to the south to ambush Liu Yao's right flank. Both of the sneak attacks had succeeded, and Liu Yao's army was now being besieged from 3 sides.

"**No! No, I can't lose!**" Liu Yao shrieked.

"**You must find Taishi Ci!**" Xu Shao barked. "**He can save you!**"

"**But he cannot save my army!**" Liu Yao retorted. "**He is not a super-man! He cannot undo this catastrophe!**"

"**No, but he can save you so that you can fight another day!**" Xu Shao said. "**That's all that you can hope for now!**"

Liu Yao took one last look at the situation before he made his decision; after a tense moment of reflection, he cried out with despair and rode to the east with his closest followers to try and find Taishi Ci.

"**Ziyi! Taishi Ziyi!**" Liu Yao screamed as he spotted his friend and potential saviour; Taishi was fending off attacks by some of Jiang Qin's riders, but the field supply depot was already reduced to a plume of thick black smoke. Liu Ji aided the man from Huangxian and chased the saboteurs away.

"Taishi Ziyi... Taishi *Ziyi*...!" Liu Yao whimpered.

"Why are you here???" Taishi Ci said angrily. **"Go west! Go west! There is nothing for you here in Qu'e now!"**

"I can't lose Qu'e!" Liu Yao cried. **"Qu'e is my capital! It is-!"**

"They planned this too well," Taishi Ci interrupted. **"Come, Governor, and I will help you escape to Moling. You must send advance word there at once, and hope that Ze Rong is the man that you suppose him to be."**

"Master Ze's followers deserted the field, and so have Zhou Xin's!" Liu Yao complained. **"Those-!"**

"Then Ze may already know the outcome of this battle; we can only hope that is good rather than bad," Taishi Ci suggested. **"Now come on: we have no time!"**

Taishi Ci and Liu Ji cleared a path for the faltering governor, and an escape began that would actually take Liu Yao around and past Bofu's army; Xu Shao and Yu Mi joined them as they reached the front lines while Fan Neng provided a distraction by mounting a doomed second offensive.

"The day is won!" Gongjin said. **"Bofu, we've crushed his army in one stroke! Liu Yao's rule in Danyang is over!"**

"I'll agree when Liu Yao is kneeling at my feet!" Bofu retorted. **"Where is he? We have to find him!"**

Bofu led another charge at Fan Neng's thin defensive line, but that was taking his army away from Liu Yao, who was now south of the battlefield and progressing westward with great speed.

Liu Yao's messenger was admitted into Ze Rong's audience hall in Moling; once he had relayed the events in Qu'e to the cultist priest, he kowtowed twice, pressed his head to the ground and awaited instructions.

"Yu Zi, see that this brave man is taken care of," Ze Rong said.

Yu Zi nodded to two burly guards, who took the oblivious messenger away to be quietly murdered.

"Has Xue Li sent anyone yet...?" Ze Rong asked.

"Not yet," Yu Zi replied.

"...We don't have much time," Ze Rong said. "Have Xue Li informed of the outcome at Qu'e, and we'll go to his camp. Ready everyone for evacuation."

"We're abandoning Moling?" one local official exclaimed.

"We have no choice," Ze Rong sighed theatrically. "Today, Heaven has decided that Liu Yao is unworthy; a great smiting will follow, and we must be sure to protect those that do not have the shadow of death above their heads."

The Moling officials chattered excitedly; Ze Rong turned to Yu Zi and nodded purposefully once again, and once again, the gesture was malevolent. There would be two actions taken: Ze Rong's followers would retreat to the southwest with the contents of Moling's treasury, and those deemed 'unworthy' would remain in the city, dead or alive.

At around the same time, the last pockets of resistance around Qu'e were surrendering to Bofu's victorious army. Fan Neng had fled to the west, leaving Bofu and his counsel in no doubt as to Liu Yao's current location.

"We should have blocked the road to Moling!" Bofu complained.

"No," Gongjin insisted. "What about *Ze Rong*?"

"...Yeah," Bofu conceded.

"We were always going to have to deal with Moling at some point," Gongjin continued. "Liu Yao is a mediocrity; this battle proved that. He outnumbered us over three-to-one, and we still won easily. Even if Ze Rong doesn't kill him, he's no threat to us."

"Did we find Taishi Ci?" Bofu asked keenly.

"He probably led the retreat," Lü Fan sighed.

"...I wanted him to surrender!" Bofu groaned.

"Yes, well, he isn't here," Gongjin said. "Let's be glad that he wasn't properly used. Now, we must advance to Qu'e, as we planned. The people must know our intentions."

"Are the surrendered men gathered?" Bofu asked.

"They are," Gongjin replied.

"Then I'll address them," Bofu decided. Gongjin led Bofu to the mass of whimpering, terrified men, who expected that Bofu would order them to be killed: instead, Bofu rode back and forth in front of them on his horse, and said, **"You're all to be released."**

The captives that heard the proclamation murmured inanely; word was carried to the back of the vast ensemble, and the mood lightened as the news sank in.

"Any who served Liu Yao or Ze Rong are guilty of following orders, nothing more," Bofu continued. **"I won't ask you to join me; that's *your* choice. If you want to go home, fine: I'm here to *free* Danyang, not conquer it, and you are not my enemies... you are my neighbours and my kin."**

The captives started to whoop and cheer as they heard and understood Bofu's intentions first or second-hand; he raised his arm in triumph, and he was met with cries of victory or gratitude from every side.

"...There is a great man," Gongjin murmured. "Well *done*, Bofu."

When the road to Moling was in sight, Taishi Ci halted; Liu Yao stopped as well, and turned his horse to challenge his friend.

"I have to stay in this area," Taishi Ci said before Liu Yao could protest. "You'll be alright now that you're on the way to Moling; hurry, Governor, before the enemy find out where you are."

"You have to come with me, Ziyi!" Liu Yao implored.

"I've come as far as I can with you, Zhengli," Taishi Ci with dual meaning. "Go on: I'll defend your retreat if I must."

"...*Ayah*! What have I done???" Liu Yao cried. **"I have lost a battle, lost a friend, lost the province, lost the-!"**

"Enough!" Xu Shao shrieked. **"There isn't time!"**

Liu Ji grabbed the reins of his father's horse and bowed to Taishi Ci; the gesture was reciprocated before Liu Ji led his father away. Xu Shao took one last look at a man that could have been the saviour of Liu Yao's governorship and said, "Truly, I must wonder what will become of the Han if such mistakes can be made."

"Go," Taishi Ci ordered, and the last of Liu Yao's followers turned and continued their retreat to Moling.

****

57

In Wu Prefecture, the forces led by Zhu Zhi, Sun Ben and Chen Wu were suffering in their battle against the forces of the state-recognised administrator Xu Gong and his ally, the Shanyue tribal leader White Tiger. The early stages of the battle had gone well, but the arrival of White Tiger's brother, Yan Yu, had changed the pace; the tall, muscular Yu and his followers charged at Chen Wu's vanguard and inflicted serious casualties as they swung their war axes. Sun Ben's personal cavalry managed to repel Yan Yu's second charge, but the carnage had left the survivors severely demoralised.

"We can't afford to take another strike like that, Commander Sun," Chen Wu complained.

"Zhu Zhi has a plan," Sun Ben promised.

The Shanyue confederacy was preparing for a full charge against the 3,000 men that served Bofu, but Zhu Zhi's attention was focussed on one man: their tall, charismatic leader, White Tiger. The thin, nondescript Xu Gong appeared to be waiting for the outcome of the Shanyue attack, as his small army of 2,000 conscripts did not move; Zhu Zhi smiled, as he now knew that there would be no enemy victory. White Tiger gave the order to charge: the ground shook as the Shanyue infantry and cavalry surged forward like a human tidal wave, but as they were seconds away from being within striking distance, Zhu Zhi signalled with flags and the front line of his spear-wielding infantry became a human palisade. The Shanyue cavalry did all that they could to halt their charge, but momentum carried some of them into the wall of spikes: dozens of men and horses were impaled. Zhu Zhi then ordered a full volley of arrows to hit the confused infantry: the Shanyue attack was converted into a rout, and the tribes fled the field in all directions, their unity having been shattered by the unexpected defeat. White Tiger cried out with anger and abandoned Xu Gong.

"**No, wait, come back!**" Xu Gong pleaded.

"**Go quickly, Master!**" one of Xu Gong's officers urged. "**You mustn't lose your life here! We'll keep them from you!**"

Xu Gong watched as Zhu Zhi ordered a full retaliatory charge against the fleeing Shanyue and Xu Gong's own army: the two sides were almost a match numerically, but Xu Gong knew that he lacked the skilled officers to outwit Zhu Zhi.

"**…Try and survive!**" Xu Gong said as he turned his horse to follow White Tiger. "**I don't want anyone to die needlessly!**"

Chen Wu reached Xu Gong's front line first: he marvelled at the desperate energy that Xu Gong's men had as they fought to their last for their fleeing administrator. Once Xu Gong was safely away, the majority of his forces either fled after him or remained to fight to the last for their allies.

"**Enough!**" Chen Wu ordered. "**Let them go!**"

Chen Wu's soldiers allowed Xu Gong's men to withdraw, and the battle was over.

"**…A noble gesture,**" Zhu Zhi said as Chen Wu returned to his own front line.

"Killing them all was pointless and self-destructive," Chen Wu suggested. "They were fighting like demons; does Xu Gong mean that much to them?"

"He is much respected by his followers... and the local people, it seems, even though he overthrew Sheng Xian with violence," Zhu Zhi replied. "That might be a problem: we should seek his surrender rather than his head, or we might have future worries."

Sun Ben returned from pursuing the last of the Shanyue stragglers and said, "They'd rather die than be caught, those barbarians... have you seen my brother...?"

"...Here he is," Zhu Zhi said as Sun Ben's younger brother Fu approached on horseback with bloodied spear in hand.

"Your first foray has been a success!" Sun Ben said gladly. "But don't overdo it, Brother. Your life is worth more to me than a million Shanyue scalps."

Sun Fu bowed respectfully.

"Their commanders were a handful," Chen Wu sighed. "We must hope that White Tiger has no more brothers like the one that tore into my infantry."

"We won: Xu Gong has fled, and the Shanyue alliance is broken," Zhu Zhi said. "As a former Imperial Commandant of this prefecture, I know the Shanyue well enough to know that White Tiger's leadership was based entirely on strength; it's going to take a while for him and his brother to regain the respect that he lost today. Not long, unfortunately... but long enough."

"And Xu Gong...?" Sun Ben asked.

"Fled with the Shanyue," Zhu Zhi replied. "He'll not be back in quite such a hurry."

"So we have taken Wu...!" Sun Ben said excitedly.

"We have, Commander Sun," Zhu Zhi replied. "I'll write to Lord Sun and tell him the good news."

Chen Wu surveyed the battlefield and said, "So many died today, theirs and ours... are we right to say that we won...? Won't the Shanyue want revenge...? Won't Xu Gong return with another army if he's that respected...?"

"Not yet... not today," Zhu Zhi insisted. "By the time that he does, we'll have stabilised Danyang, and that'll enable us to deal with them properly."

Chen Wu conceded to Zhu Zhi's judgement, and the unpleasant task of clearing the battlefield began.

The former Administrator, Sheng Xian, learned of Zhu Zhi's victory over Xu Gong within days, but he was not pleased at the outcome: Sheng received permission from his host, General Xu Zhao, to use his audience hall and summoned the officials that had joined him in virtual exile to discuss the matter.

"We will not be recognised unless we agree to specifically serve *Yuan Shu*, rather than the Han," Sheng Xian reported. "Even then, gentlemen, we will not be restored to our previous posts."

"That's an outrage, Mister Sheng!" one official cried. "Can't we try and contact Governor Liu again...?"

"The last piece of correspondence that I've received is a notification from Zhu Zhi – my former Commandant! – telling me that Liu Yao is no longer governor, having been recently defeated," Sheng Xian replied. "If Governor Liu has been ousted, then I'm afraid that we will have to accept this humiliation, Mister

Dai Yuan."

"I refuse to serve Yuan Shu!" another official declared. "Mister Sheng, surely you do not intend to bend at the knee to that wretched hankerer...?"

"No, Mister Gui Lan, I do not," Sheng Xian replied. "I cannot fight Zhu Zhi, any more than I could fight Xu Gong; but I will not betray the Han by serving that greedy idiot Yuan Shu or any of his vassals."

Dai Yuan coughed deliberately and asked, "Are the rumours of Xu Gong and White Tiger's impending arrival true, Mister Sheng...?"

Sheng Xian laughed involuntarily and said, "They are, Mister Dai! But fear not: General Xu has assured me that we will have no trouble from either of them, and that they will camp to the north of his estate."

"But Xu Gong tried to kill you!" Gui Lan protested. "We must flee to Xu Province, then, if we cannot-"

"Xu Province is under attack and cannot be considered safe," Sheng Xian interrupted. "Yan Province is ruled by the butcher Cao Cao, and Qing is similarly bereft of peace or order. My friend Kong Rong was only recently rescued from strife by Taishi Ci, the famous 'lone mercenary', but the feud between Yuan Shao and Gongsun Zan has left the province ungovernable. Jing is too far to risk, so that leaves us with no choice but to remain here until Yuan Shu is inevitably defeated."

"*Remain here*...? ...With *Xu Gong*!?" Gui Lan exclaimed.

"And *White Tiger of the Shanyue*???" Dai Yuan cried. "What other villains does Xu Zhao intend to shelter here...? Will we end up with Yuan Shu here as well when he is 'inevitably defeated'...?"

The rest of the officials voiced their frustration and concern.

"Gentlemen, I assure you that I am as perplexed, distressed and weary as you are, but we have no choice!" Sheng Xian chuckled miserably. "We're prisoners of circumstance; let us hope that this is as bad as it gets."

Within days, Xu Gong and his remaining allies arrived at the gates of General Xu Zhao's fortified home city. Archers immediately lined the wall above the new arrivals while their identities were being ascertained.

"...Father, why are we here...?" Xu Gong's teenage son asked. "Isn't Sheng Xian here...?"

"He is, but he's even weaker than I now am, militarily *and* politically," Xu Gong replied. "Remember, my son, that I got rid of him with popular support: he did nothing for Wu Prefecture, and I can't see his doing little things, like giving Cai Yong a form of asylum, as cause for respecting him, not before, not now and not in the future. I did what I did because it needed doing, and-"

"Lord Xu, I think that our host is approaching," one of Xu Gong's aides said.

Xu Gong smiled as he looked to the battlements and saw that the archers had been withdrawn: within minutes, the gates were opened and the retired General Xu Zhao - who was flanked by armed infantry and cavalry from his private militia - approached the potential guests on horseback. Xu Gong and his followers dismounted their horses and bowed to their benefactor, who said, "Welcome, Administrator Xu."

"We are both of us a 'Xu', General, and I like to think that we are reaffirming long-lost family ties today," Xu Gong replied humbly. "I vow that no past enmity between Sheng Xian and I shall-"

"Any man that wants somewhere peaceful to live can come here," Xu Zhao interrupted. "None will judge or harass you, Xu Gong, provided that you do not cause trouble. I am glad of your promises, and as long as you abide by those promises, my home is your home."

Xu Gong clasped his hands together and bowed low once again.

"You shall follow me, Xu Gong, to what will be your home," Xu Zhao ordered.

Xu Zhao turned his horse, and everyone followed him as he went into the city.

"...Is he mad or something...?" Xu Gong's son asked quietly.

"Don't say things like that!" Xu Gong hissed. "He is saving us from our enemies, so let him be mad if he is! ...Once we're settled, we'll summon our kin, and then we will await a moment of opportunity: Sun Ce and his master Yuan Shu cannot hope to keep Wu Prefecture, not when they have ousted the man that the people wanted. The people and the tribes will want to restore things to the way that they were, and when their voices drown out our enemies' voices, we will make our move."

One of Xu Gong's followers asked, "What about Sheng Xian...?"

"What about him...?" Xu Gong chortled. "He lost the prefecture to me because he was incompetent; he had no support then, so why should I worry about him now...?"

The officials snickered derisively, but they still doubted whether Sheng Xian – who was going to be within walking distance from then on – would accept the situation that now faced him.

Whatever Xu Zhao's state of mind was, his actions were plain and clear for all to see: he was now giving refuge to two court-appointed administrators, Sheng Xian and Xu Gong, and that had many possible ramifications in the future.

****

58

The former Chancellor of Xu Province, Xue Li, greeted his former colleague Ze Rong at the gates of his camp to the west of Moling.

"Why have you brought your 'family' to this place...?" Xue Li asked. "Why did you not stay in Moling...?"

"Might we discuss this in your command tent...?" Ze Rong said with silky tones.

"Uh... of course, Master Ze," Xue Li replied. "Follow me..."

Once the two men were inside the command tent, Ze Rong said, "This is a delicate matter, Mister Xue. Liu Yao is on his way, but he has proven himself to be a poor governor and a poor example of piety... he has abandoned the good people of Qu'e and come here to make Moling a futile defensive fortress against the wicked hordes led by Yuan Shu's dog Sun Ce."

"Why did you abandon Moling, then...?" Xue Li asked.

"Liu Yao is not looking for an alliance with me," Ze Rong lied. "He will cast my family out of Moling, as he has already done once... and when one looks back, one sees that he did it with your consent and assistance, Mister Xue."

Xue Li suddenly felt threatened; he looked into Ze Rong's eyes and saw the monster within for the first time. He pointed at Ze Rong and gasped, "You...! You beast! You... you *did* kill Zhao Yu...!"

"Heaven judged him, and others carried out the sentence," Ze Rong said calmly; Xue Li instinctively backed away from the unarmed Ze, but he had nowhere to go.

"...*You're no man of Heaven*!" Xue Li croaked. "Y-you're a *felon*, a *liar* and a *demon*! Heaven *curse you*, Ze Rong! Heaven *curse you*!"

"I don't think that it will," Ze Rong replied.

Ze Rong's aide, Yu Zi, entered the tent and passed his master with blood-stained sword in hand; Xue Li tried to speak, but his voice failed him completely.

"We need your army, Xue Li: you'll provide it, as penance," Ze Rong said as Yu Zi ran Xue Li through with his sword.

"...Heaven... *curse*...!" Xue Li gasped as he lay dying.

"Cut off his head," Ze Rong ordered. "We'll take command of his forces and go at once to Yuzhang Prefecture. We must get there *before Liu Yao does*."

Yu Zi bowed obediently and did as he was asked while Ze Rong pondered his next move against his former ally, Liu Yao.

A triumphant Bofu was greeted by the relieved citizens of Qu'e; the words that he had used to placate Liu Yao's army had been carried to every village, town and city around Qu'e, and the resistance had evaporated completely.

"Yuan Shao's puppet administrator for this prefecture, Zhou Xin, has fled to Kuaiji to join Wang Lang," Lü Fan reported. "Zhu Zhi and Sun Ben have defeated Xu Gong; the Shanyue alliance collapsed after a bad rout, so it was an easy campaign, all in all."

"Forgive me, but... there's something that I need to know," Bofu announced. "I know it's selfish... but..."

"Wentai's grave," Cheng Pu said. "I, too, hope that it is intact."

"But if it is *not*...?" Lü Fan asked.

"...It will be Liu Yao's doing, no one else's," Bofu replied. "I won't

harm a hair on a person's head here in Qu'e, I promise."
"Hundreds are flocking to us," Cheng Pu reported. "Even more of the local people are reconsidering their allegiances now that they've seen that you mean them no harm; thousands of people are with us, and many of them are men of fighting age. They don't hate Liu Yao, though, so we must be careful."
"I can see that he's tried to govern well," Bofu replied. "I think that my father's grave will be untouched... and I think that we will be able to make him and his followers see sense."
"How?" Gongjin scoffed. "We serve *Yuan Shu*, Bofu: so far as that fool's opinion goes, we conquered this place for him, and if we're not careful, that's how people will start to see it."
"Uncle will be reinstated as Administrator of Danyang: that will help them understand, because he governed well," Bofu retorted. "Hui Qu won't come here: he'll stay north of the Great River and 'govern' from Shouchun or Huancheng. This place is ours to manage, and we're planning to do that properly, so what's the worry...?"
"Right now, it's *Ze Rong*," Lü Fan admitted. "He's in Moling, and whether he gets Liu Yao's support or not, he's our next problem."
"We need to rest first," Gongjin said. "Let Ze Rong fortify Moling some more: it'll make it a more effective defensive position for our future campaigns when we take it back."
"Already thinking ahead, mm...?" Lü Fan noted.
"Until Guangling, Kuaiji and Yuzhang are friendly, this isn't over," Gongjin explained. "We'll be ordered to take them even if we didn't need to, remember...? Zhu Hao of Yuzhang and Wang Lang of Kuaiji are the greatest threats, and I would suggest Yuzhang as a first target, since that borders Jing Province."
"Well then," Bofu said, "Zhu Hao of Yuzhang had better start praying to the gods!"

The Administrator of Yuzhang, Zhu Hao, received Ze Rong and his thousands of followers with the same oblivious pleasure that Tao Qian, Zhao Yu, Xue Li and Liu Yao had suffered before him.
"When I received your messenger, I was shocked, Master Ze!" Zhu Hao said as he escorted Ze Rong through the gates and into the city of Yuzhang's capital Nanchang. "You cannot be praised enough, Master, for your efforts in saving the innocent; it is a shame, though, that Xue Li was unable to join you."
"He died fighting for the noblest of causes," Ze Rong lied. "Now it may be the turn of others to do the same, if Heaven decrees it."
"I would rather that we fought gallantly and lived to do further good, Master Ze," Zhu Hao replied. "Come to my official residence, where we can discuss what must be done with the urgency that it deserves."
"I shall," Ze Rong said as he nodded to Yu Zi yet again; within a day, Zhu Hao would be dead, and Yuzhang's capital would be under control of Ze Rong.

"That... *that*...!"
Liu Yao could not find the words to explain his feelings: Moling was drained dry of resources and almost deserted, and everyone knew who was to blame.
"We must advance to Yuzhang at once, Governor," the adviser

and famous appraiser, Xu Shao, suggested sternly.

"...I shall hang on your every word from now on, Xu Zijiang," Liu Yao promised. "I have lost so much from not heeding you before... but then, what good is hindsight?"

"It prevents the same mistakes being repeated, but only when it is heeded," Xu Shao grumbled. "Sadly, I have watched so many, from the highest ministers to the lowliest commoner, as they repeat the same mistakes time and again, with and without hindsight... because every time a wise man tried to use the past to educate on the present, some poor fool – or, sad to say, a man with much to gain from the deliberate repeat of 'mistakes' – laughs and says, 'But this is different'."

"...Ze Rong fooled many men, not just me," Liu Yao said as he stared at the litter-strewn streets of Moling. "He was lauded as more than a man; he was called a 'Living Buddha' by some... no Buddha is he. No... he is something quite different."

"He's the worst of tricksters... a man that uses faith as a weapon to harm the innocent," Xu Shao said. "Everywhere he goes, he leaves death, misery and poverty... he kills the men that govern, steals the wealth that ensures stability, and corrupts the hearts of the commoners that trust him most of all. There is no death too painful for such a creature."

"I sent the messenger to Zhu Hao as you suggested," Liu Yao said. "Once Zhu is aware of how evil and deceitful Ze Rong truly is, he'll capture him for us if he dares venture near the capital."

"Good," Xu Shao replied. "Let's leave this poor place; we can do no good here."

"Fan Neng: prepare for our march to Yuzhang!" Liu Yao ordered. "Yu Mi, Liu Ji: calm the people, and tell them that we'll return and help them when peace is restored."

"...When will that be," Xu Shao wondered.

Liu Yao barely travelled half the distance to Yuzhang's capital when his distressed messenger ran toward his vanguard while clutching a wound on his arm.

"...Who did that to you?" Liu Yao asked. "Bandits...?"

"Ze Rong... has taken Nanchang!" the messenger cried.

"It *can't be*," Xu Shao muttered.

"**Tell me you lie!**" Liu Yao screamed. "**Tell me...!** ...*Again*, I've failed the people! I allowed this! This is *my fault*!"

The messenger kowtowed and said, "Forgive me, my lord! I was too slow!"

"No... *I* was too slow," Liu Yao replied. "We don't have the men and resources to fight Ze Rong right now."

"We have several thousand men, which may be enough," Fan Neng said. "Many that fled the battlefield learned of your movements from allies and men like Taishi Ci of Huangxian, so-"

"**That's the man I need! Ziyi, where are you???**" Liu Yao cried. "**Where are you now, Taishi Ziyi, when I need you to save the whole south from bandits, cults and pirates???**"

"There's no point crying for Taishi Ci now, Father," Liu Ji said. "All that we can do now is gather men and fight Ze Rong."

"...Quite right, my son," Liu Yao conceded. "If we attack Nanchang quickly, we might surprise him. We'll march double-time."

Ze Rong heard of Liu Yao's approach from spies in the villages that lined the route to the capital; he summoned his closest followers and said, "Liu Yao comes here, the godless wretch, to steal this place from us and cast us into the wilderness, after all that we have done to prop up his doomed regime of wanton greed and incompetence! We will never know peace while he lives!"
The acolytes chanted fanatically.
"That's right, my brothers! Open your souls to Heaven!" Ze Rong cried. **"Let us greet our wicked enemy and show him the strength of our word: when he is broken by that, we will show him the power of Heaven's sword!"**
Ze Rong's forces poured out of the gates of Nanchang and dealt a crushing defeat on Liu Yao, the second in as many months: his generals were forced to take him northward to the city of Pengze, where his remaining followers – who now numbered in the hundreds – wondered if there would now be any victories of any kind for the state-appointed governor.
"...I am unworthy, that much Ze Rong has judged correctly," Liu Yao said as he stood on the ramparts and stared southward. "People opposed my being made a 'Magnificent Exemplar', Xu Zijiang, and now I see why. Only one man a year earns that accolade, Zijiang, and it should not have been me. I am not magnificent... not at all. I misjudged every man I ever met."
"You did no such thing," Xu Shao scoffed. "You misused them, which is a similar magnitude of crime, I suppose... but you never misjudged them."
"I misjudged Ze Rong," Liu Yao retorted.
"...As you said, so did many others," Xu Shao sighed. "Perhaps I might have been more vocal, even if I knew that nobody would listen to me."
"We'll build another army and try again," Liu Yao suggested. "I can't let Ze Rong declare himself Administrator of Yuzhang... that's worse than letting Sun Ce take Danyang. I have to right one wrong, and Ze Rong is the worst wrong, I think."
"Agreed," Xu Shao replied. "I have already ordered Fan Neng and Yu Mi to go out to nearby villages; word of Ze Rong's crimes is spreading now, so finding men to fight him will not be hard."

Liu Yao rebuilt his army and struck at Ze Rong for a second time: this time, he was the one with the numerical advantage, and Ze Rong was forced to flee the city of Nanchang while it was being sieged. Liu Yao entered the surrendered city and observed the damage that Ze Rong had done with tangible anger.
"He was truly spiteful," Liu Yao said. "Xu Zijiang, we must pursue that monster immediately, so that he cannot find another army!"
"He won't find another army, not now that he is exposed to the world," Xu Shao suggested. "No... our first concern is the warlord Sun Ce. We must start to build an army to fight him again."
"But can I defeat that man...?" Liu Yao replied. "Have I the men, the resources, the charisma... or the *right*...?"
"You're the appointed governor," Xu Shao said. "The empire has faith in you, and that is all that matters. Rebuild Yuzhang, rebuild your army, and prepare for a return to Danyang. Taishi Ci will help you, Wang Lang will help you, and White Tiger will surely want to exchange more autonomy for help, which is a small price to pay

for ridding the south of Yuan Shu's hirelings. We'll do this, Governor, togeth-!"

The famed appraiser Xu Shao was halted by a fit of coughing: Liu Yao's eyes wandered toward many of his other followers, and he noted that they were also showing signs of illness from travelling across naturally hostile lands during heavy rain. Sickness was the enemy that all men feared, for it could kill at any time, during war or peace, and it knew nothing of class, wealth or worth. But Governor Liu Yao had work to do: he smiled reassuringly and prepared to issue orders to his men.

Ze Rong's retreat took his few remaining followers into the steep hills to the east of Nanchang, where Shanyue tribes maintained a society that was far removed from that of the Han Chinese. Ze Rong noted their apparently 'savage and simple existence' and asked for an audience with the local chief: he got his wish and presented himself and a dozen of his closest followers before the robed chieftain without bringing any customary gifts.

"...**Who are you?**" the chieftain barked. "**Why you come here without gift?**"

"My faith teaches that material wealth is unimportant to the lives of men, especially if they wish to attain immortality in the afterlife," Ze Rong replied without reverence. "If you want to become a Buddha and go to Heaven complete, you must forsake your evil ways and learn the ways that only I can teach you."

The chieftain's aides looked at each other with disbelief.

"...You have plenty wealth," the chieftain heckled. "I see! I am not blind! I am also not stupid!"

"That... was *donated*, for building a place of worship," Ze Rong lied. "Wicked hearts demand money to build our temples for us, so we must provide it, but-"

"**Lie!**" the chieftain bellowed. "**You are liar! You call us evil! You say we are evil! You bring no gift, and call us evil!**"

Ze Rong sensed that he had irrevocably offended the chieftain, and he bowed low from instinctive fear.

"**Death!**" the chieftain screamed; he then took a short sword from his belt and thrust it into Ze Rong's outstretched neck, fatally wounding him.

"**Master Ze!**" Yu Zi cried, but he would not get the chance to act. The chieftain did not even have to issue an order; Ze Rong's followers were cut down where they stood.

"Get their wealth... *ours*, now," the chieftain ordered.

Ze Rong's death and Liu Yao's exile to the southern prefecture of Yuzhang could almost be seen as the end of one period of fighting in the south: Liu Yao petitioned the court to send a new Administrator for Yuzhang while he began preparations for a campaign to reverse his other losses. But for Bofu, the outcome had been positive: after a year of exile in lands to the north of the Yangtze, he was home, and the Danyang and Wu Prefectures were under his – or rather, his lord Yuan Shu's – complete control.

****

ACT VI: THE KUAIJI CAMPAIGN

59

When Sun Jian – the heroic patriarch of the Sun clan – died at the age of 37, he had departed from a nation that was teetering on the edge of chaos. At the age of 16, his eldest son, Sun Ce – also known by his style name, *Bofu* – had inherited a form of serfdom rather than a proper legacy, since his father had been unwittingly bound to serve the northern noble Yuan Shu when he enlisted to fight the tyrannical chancellor of the Han, Dong Zhuo.

Four years had passed since Sun Jian's death, and even more had changed. Bofu's maternal uncle, Wu Jing, had been chased out of his holdings in central Yang Province by the state-appointed provincial governor, Liu Yao; after a year of waiting for an order that never came, Bofu asked Yuan Shu for permission to regain the lost territory. Within months, the parts of Lujiang, Jiujiang, Danyang and Wu prefectures that had been lost were regained, Danyang and Wu were seized completely, and Liu Yao had been forced to make a humiliating retreat to Yuzhang, a prefecture in the southwest of Yang that neighboured Jing Province. Liu Yao managed to gather another army, but his allies were fewer and support for his governorship was fading away in the wake of Bofu's magnanimous return to the region.

In the north, situations evolved: the co-regency of Dong Zhuo's former generals, Li Jue and Guo Si, was coming to an end as courtiers' schemes to divide them finally bore fruit, and Cao Cao, Gongsun Zan, Liu Bei and Yuan Shu's half-brother and mortal enemy, Yuan Shao, were now – by one design or another – the governors of Yan, Yòu, Xu and Ji provinces respectively. Liu Bei's predecessor, Tao Qian, had passed away after a violent feud with his neighbour Cao Cao had left over 100,000 of his people dead; upon taking the mantle of governor, Liu Bei had decided to surrender to Yuan Shao to protect the province from a third ravaging by Cao, although that decision then earned him detractors within Xu and antagonised Yuan Shu. Liu Bei's precarious grip as a puppet governor was weakened further by the arrival of Dong Zhuo's foster son Lü Bu: Bu had fled Yan Province after partaking in a failed attempt to oust Cao Cao that had been instigated by some of Cao's own vassals, and his presence in Xu only served to vex Cao Cao once again. Regardless, Liu Bei allowed Bu to settle on his lands, hoping perhaps that Bu might help him resist the inevitable invasion by Yuan Shu; unbeknownst to Liu Bei, Lü Bu had agreed to help Yuan Shu by taking the provincial capital while Liu Bei was fighting Yuan Shu's generals on the Yang-Xu border. Such was the time: intrigue and betrayal were as commonplace as the wars they spawned.

Bofu, however, was enjoying a brief stability while his vassals repaired the army and the region in the wake of the battles with Liu Yao. Liu Yao's ally, the enigmatic hero Taishi Ci, had disappeared after the last great battle near Qu'e, but Liu Yao himself was already moving north across Yuzhang Prefecture: he was aiming to retake the fortified port city of Moling in Danyang, which was a place that would provide a strong base for attacks on

Qu'e. In the southeast, Kuaiji's administrator Wang Lang was not reacting to any of the events, which only made him more suspicious to Bofu's advisers. But there was another threat: the Shanyue tribes of Wu Prefecture. Their overall leader and king of sorts, White Tiger Yan, challenged the authority of Bofu's allies, and a pacification war was inevitable. With such a long list of enemies – and many worried that the possessive Yuan Shu might be included on that list – the question was who would have to be dealt with first when working toward a lasting peace.

"...Ah, Gongjin... when will it be safe to rest...?"
Bofu asked the question as he stared at the mountains to the west of Qu'e. His friend and sworn brother Zhou Yu – also known as *Gongjin* – smiled and replied, "I find it hard to believe that you want peace, to be honest."
"Of course I do!" Bofu said. "Why wouldn't I? All this fighting is necessary; yeah, I like a good joust or spar, but it doesn't have to end in death. No, I want to be able to look my family in their faces and say 'I made it safe'. I want a family of my own, a new little pack of tiger cubs to carry our story on."
"I am pining for a family life as well, but... Liu Yao in the west, Wang Lang to the south, and White Tiger in our midst," Gongjin mused. "I'm still not sure."
"White Tiger's just looking for attention," Bofu said dismissively. "I don't expect him to do anything yet."
"Liu Yao's stalled near the prefectural border, and some are saying that he's encountering local resistance from remnants of Ze Rong's cult, while others are saying that he's ill," Gongjin reported. "Master Xu Shao's not being mentioned, so... so he's probably dead."
"That bothers you," Bofu guessed.
"He was a good man, Bofu," Gongjin sighed. "It just makes it even harder to reconcile what we are..."
"...*Dogs*, you mean," Bofu prompted.
"I refuse to demean us in that way," Gongjin replied. "But at the same time, I do worry that we're here to do right, but all the time, in the background... is the shadow of Yuan Shu. What if he tried to impose administrators of his own down here, or sends Hui Qu to-"
"Yuan Shu's too busy playing soldiers with Liu Bei," Bofu said dismissively. "Here's how I see things, Gongjin: right now, Yuan Shu controls Jiujiang and Lujiang directly while we are controlling Danyang and Wu for him. That leaves Yuzhang, which is under the administrative control of... Zhu Hao? No, no... that was the last one that Ze Rong probably killed. That royal proclamation we were sent said... uh..."
"*Hua Xin*," Gongjin said helpfully.
"Yeah," Bofu said. "Hua Xin in Yuzhang, and Wang Lang in Kuaiji; I don't reckon that we should be worried about White Tiger in Wu or about Guangling."
"I agree, so far as Guangling goes," Gongjin said.
"Hua Xin's newly settled in Yuzhang, and Liu Yao's no help to him," Bofu continued. "White Tiger is not a problem right now... so that leaves Wang Lang... Wang Lang's the man that we need to go after next."
Gongjin hummed thoughtfully and said, "So we wait for Wu Jing

and Sun Ben to return from reporting our successes to Yuan Shu, and then we advance to Wu to disperse the Shanyue and-"

"Gongjin, I feel like I'm talking to myself!" Bofu interrupted. "White Tiger isn't going to do anything!"

"I don't agree," Gongjin said. "He's harbouring Xu Gong, who will want to-"

"I know that Xu Gong is said to be popular, but in battle he's a mediocrity," Bofu insisted. "He can't persuade White Tiger to risk going up against us so soon. We'll wait for Uncle Wu and Boyang to return from reporting our successes to Yuan Shu, advance to Wu, *ignore* the Shanyue, go around them and into Kuaiji. Once Kuaiji is taken, Xu Gong'll have nowhere to run to, and the Shanyue'll be a single threat with nobody to buy their support anymore."

"...Okay, I'll go with that idea," Gongjin said. "You're really thinking about things, Bofu."

"I don't like to, but I have to, right...?" Bofu replied. "I worry about Uncle and Boyang... let's hope that Yuan Shu doesn't detain them for too long."

****

60

Bofu's uncle, Wu Jing, and his cousin Sun Ben ended the long journey to Shouchun in the north of Yang Province and requested an audience with Yuan Shu that they were granted. The two were met with incredulous stares as they approached their lord: most could scarcely believe what they had come to report, including Yuan Shu.

"...So you are both here," Yuan Shu said hesitantly as Wu Jing and Sun Ben fell to their knees in deference. "Am I correctly informed...? Is your work already done?"

"Were it only *our* work," Wu Jing sighed. "We personally failed to relieve Danyang and Wu: it is your other vassal, Acting-General Sun Ce – my magnificent nephew – that led us to victory against Liu Yao."

Yuan Shu cackled hysterically and said, "I am truly fated to rule!"

The adviser Yan Xiang coughed deliberately and said, "That subject is best kept until *another time*, my lord."

"Oh, yes... yes, I suppose so!" Yuan Shu chuckled. "Liu Yao forced to flee, Xu Gong routed, Ze Rong destroyed, Zhou Xin in hiding... all in such a short amount of time! Sun Ce is quite the tiger... yes... quite the tiger."

Yuan Shu's mood suddenly soured.

"Where is Sun Ce now...?" Yan Xiang asked.

"He is placating the people of Danyang, and he intends to go on to Wu to do the same," Wu Jing explained. "After that, he asked that I convey a wish to advance to Kuaiji Prefecture and defeat Wang Lang for you."

"...For *me*," Yuan Shu replied icily. "Yes, for *me*... of *course*."

Sun Ben noted Yuan Shu's tone and said, "He does what he does for *no one else*, Lord Yuan. He asks humbly, and accepts your judgement. If it pleases you, once we return to Danyang, we-"

"You're not going back to Danyang," Yuan Shu interrupted. "Wu Jing, I hereby appoint you as 'Administrator of Guangling'."

"B-but... but I am already Administrator of Danyang!" Wu Jing protested.

"You dislike promotions?" Yuan Shu barked.

"N-no, my lord," Wu Jing replied. "So I should advance to Guangling at once and seize it...?"

"So glad to see that I don't have to explain," Yuan Shu scoffed. "Sun Ben, you are hereby made Administrator of Yuzhang in addition to your existing rank, but you shall remain here in Shouchun for now. I want a reliable man to guard the city for me when I advance into Xu Province. Your brother – 'Fu', if I recall – can relocate to Luling and act against Hua Xin in your stead."

"I shall do as you ask," Sun Ben replied.

"Your families should relocate to Shouchun, since you will be spending so much time here," Yuan Shu continued. "In fact, I would prefer that the families of Sun Ce, Zhou Yu, Cheng Pu, Zhu Zhi and other prominent vassals of mine should be here... where I can see them. Kindly convey that wish of mine when you advance my reply to his requests."

One of Bofu's few friends in Yuan Shu's court – the senior officer Zhang Xun – stifled a gasp when he heard the demand.

"I shall," Sun Ben said as calmly and politely as he could.

"...We're in trouble."
Bofu was visibly agitated as Cheng Pu, Gongjin and Lü Fan read and re-read Sun Ben's letter; after a fourth review, Gongjin shook his head in response to Lü Fan's words and said, "I expected this, Ziheng."
"And that makes it any less an affront???" Cheng Pu said. "Young man, this is a demand that our lord and all other men of importance to our cause – including *you* – have to send their families to this ungrateful man as hostages! Perhaps that doesn't bother you so much because you have no wife or children yet, but-!"
"I understand the implications, Mister Cheng, and I am as upset as you, since I have other family, if not a wife and children, that this applies to," Gongjin replied. "We don't have a choice though, do we, so what's the use in arguing...?"
"...So what else have we got to endure...?" Cheng Pu asked.
"Wu Jing has been forced to go to Guangling: the place hasn't been the same since Ze Rong pillaged it and killed the last administrator, so taking it will be easier than Danyang was but hard nonetheless," Gongjin suggested. "Boyang's been promoted again – no doubt as a way to divide the two of you, Bofu – but has to stay in Shouchun, which gives us a useful spy, so I wouldn't complain too much; he's in a position of trust, aiding Chen Ji in defending the capital, so he'll learn a lot... including the truth behind this disturbing rumour that Yuan wants to declare himself as a sovereign – a king at the least – at some point."
"If Yuan Shu does *that*, I *quit*," Bofu said angrily.
"If he does 'that', we're *saved*, because we'll instantly be freed from obligation," Lü Fan explained. "I hope it's true, despite the trouble it'll cause."
"So who's the administrator of this place now...?" Cheng Pu asked.
"My uncle Shang," Gongjin replied. "He's a good man, so-"
"Fine," Cheng Pu grunted.
"...Good," Gongjin replied uneasily. "That was it, by the way, so far as 'affronts' go: we're free to advance to Kuaiji and attack Wang Lang, unsurprisingly. But Sun Fu's being sent to *Luling*: what can he do in that remote place...?"
"Yuan Shu's getting worse," Lü Fan noted. "Yuan Shu was demented enough before; now he's openly devoid of etiquette or decency. We'll need to be careful, because he'll probably start wanting to replace people next. He'll wait until Kuaiji's taken, and maybe Guangling and Yuzhang, but-"
"As you say, he'll wait," Bofu interrupted.
"Yes," Gongjin said. "Of course, we don't just have our own master to worry about: Liu Yao may regain momentum, Ze Rong's followers might-"
"Or Taishi Ci might reappear," Bofu suggested. "Don't forget about *that* fellow."
"I *haven't*, believe me," Gongjin said. "Yes, there's him, or Hua Xin may advance from Yuzhang... or *White Tiger* might come into Danyang and-"
"You added that last one to annoy me!" Bofu complained. "White Tiger isn't going to do anything!"

"I'm sure that he won't," Gongjin sighed.

"He won't," Bofu insisted.

Gongjin shook his head, laughed briefly and said, "Oh, yes... have you met your new recruit...?"

"I have *thousands* of new recruits," Bofu said. "Which one are you on about?"

"Zhang Zhao, styled 'Zibu'," Gongjin replied. "He's an intelligent man, and we should make good use of him if he'll join us."

"I know of him," Lü Fan said. "He was once detained by Tao Qian when he was in-"

"Wait a minute: Gongjin, you said he's a recruit, but he *isn't*, is he?" Bofu interrupted. "You're telling me that I have to *ask* this man to join me, aren't you? How old is he?"

"What's that got to do with anything?" Cheng Pu scoffed.

"Am I grovelling to a man that's older, younger, or the same age as me?" Bofu asked. "The answer dictates the type of grovelling."

Gongjin smiled and said, "He's nearly forty."

"Oh-*ho*, another oldie!" Bofu chortled. "Still, that's easier than someone younger. Where is he?"

"In town," Gongjin replied. "I'll invite him to court."

"Did... did he serve Liu Yao when he was here...?" Bofu asked suddenly.

"I honestly don't know, Bofu, and you shouldn't ask him that," Gongjin replied.

"We should invite Mister Quan as well," Lü Fan suggested.

"Alright... oh well, I hope my grovelling works," Bofu mumbled as he adjusted his clothing. "How old's 'Mister Quan', then...?"

Cheng Pu laughed and said, "You really are something, Lord Sun."

Bofu's false joviality hid his anger and fear; he knew that his mother Lady Wu, Lady Chen, his younger brothers and sisters, and the entire families of so many of his followers – thousands in all – would soon be his master's hostages in Shouchun, and that made the inevitable moment of release from Yuan Shu's grip potentially costly.

Bofu held court on the following morning and invited two potential allies to attend: the first, Zhang Zhao, walked into the hall and eyed some of Bofu's more uncouth vassals with disdain.

"...He's just the sort of man we *don't want*," Cheng Pu hissed.

The second man, Quan Rou, was at the very least diplomatic as he entered the hall: he nodded and smiled at men like Huang Gai and Han Dang as he approached Bofu.

"...Better," Cheng Pu muttered.

"So, uh... welcome!" Bofu said as he turned his gaze to Zhang Zhao and Quan Rou in turn. "Mister Zhang, I understand that you are a man who really knows a lot about how to run a state."

"I am versed in the classics, General Sun," Zhang Zhao replied.

"...You're well-read," Bofu said tonelessly. "Okay, well... yeah, I suppose that'll help... of course it will. Of course it will!"

Gongjin bowed ingratiatingly and said, "Master Zhang, it is an honour to receive you here in Qu'e. Your intellect and foresight are well known."

"...I am unworthy of your praise, Mister Zhou Yu," Zhang Zhao replied. "I am, as General Sun has noted, 'well-read, and that is all'. I would relish the opportunity to prove that my learning can be applied practically."

"You'll get that opportunity," Bofu promised. "If Gongjin says you're the man for the job, then you're the man for the job."

"Of *course*," Cheng Pu muttered. "If 'Gongjin' said the sun was *pink*..."

Gongjin heard the quiet rebuke and smiled.

Bofu turned to the second visitor and said, "Now, Mister Quan Rou..."

The middle-aged Quan Rou bowed humbly.

"Mister Quan is a shrewd political mind," Gongjin explained.

"We need loads o' them, really, if we're to govern properly and keep the peace with our neighbours," Bofu said. "Would you help us, Mister Quan...?"

"I would be honoured, Lord Sun," Quan Rou replied.

"Great!" Bofu said. "So we've got new thinkers as well as fighters... I think that we're good to go."

"Go *where*, Lord Sun...?" Han Dang asked.

"We are going to Kuaiji to confront Wang Lang, with the intention of bringing him to our side or replacing him with a man that will not cause further trouble," Gongjin explained. "We've yet to decide who shall be remaining here as a guardian of Danyang while Lord Sun takes the army southward."

The ensemble murmured incoherently.

"Ah, the sound of officials bickering and whinging: now that they're my officials and not someone else's, that chattering has a newfound meaning to me," Bofu said quietly.

Sun Hè – Bofu's ever-present bodyguard and the only man to hear the comment – smiled and said, "Think of it as a sign that you're becoming more important, Cousin."

"We should try and make peace with the imperial court," Zhang Zhao suggested. "If at all possible, that should include the state-appointed administrator of Yuzhang and the state-appointed governor, Liu Yao."

"How do you suppose that we make peace with a man that we just had to kick out of here...?" Cheng Pu asked. "Isn't Inspector Hui Qu in charge now?"

Zhang Zhao bowed slightly and said, "He certainly is, Mister Cheng. But Liu Yao was appointed by His Majesty, while Hui Qu..."

"...Yeah, I think we all get it," Bofu grumbled.

"But this is how it is," Gongjin said. "Mister Zhang, His Majesty is now wandering the northern heartland, his closest aides with begging bowls in hands, while warlords turn their eyes away from his divine light and towards the candlelight of personal glory... our own lord Yuan Shu is not alone in this."

"Alas, we are in a terrible place," Zhang Zhao sighed.

"Before his escape, His Majesty was under the control of Dong Zhuo's evil lieutenants, Li Jue and Guo Si," Gongjin continued. "Any appointments were potentially made at their behest, not the Son of Heaven's own divine will."

"You are wise for your years and quite right, Mister Zhou Yu," Zhang Zhao said.

Cheng Pu stared at Gongjin and hummed thoughtfully.

"I say what I see," Gongjin replied. "His Majesty's very rule was contested by the northern lords, since his appointment is a product of Dong Zhuo's time in the court... but of course, that is

another matter altogether, one that others carry as motivation that we must be aware of."
Cheng Pu nodded slowly.
"We must treat Liu Yao as the agent of Li Jue and Guo Si, not His Majesty," Gongjin added. "If Lord Yuan Shu ever damages the Son of Heaven, then he is an enemy of all men... but right now, he's another warlord in a land ruled by warlords, and as such, we must fight as if there were no emperor, as though we were back in the age of the Warring States that you know so well from your extensive studies."
Zhang Zhao smiled, bowed and said, "You are quite right! Our objective now should be to pacify the unruly and bring stability to the south. Perhaps we will earn recognition from His Majesty if we are successful."
The majority of the officials were convinced by the exchange and mumbled agreeably.
"So on to Kuaiji, then," Cheng Pu said.
"Let's hope Wang Lang sees sense," Bofu replied. "If he doesn't, then... Heaven help him."

****

61

Bofu left Gongjin's uncle, Zhou Shang, and his cousin Xu Kun in charge of Danyang and took his army towards Wu Prefecture. The move confused Cheng Pu, who asked as they moved, "Why are we going this way? Shouldn't we be going into Kuaiji via the southern border with Danyang? Coming into Wu leaves us with no choice but to fight the Shanyue, surely...?"

"We're going *around* the Shanyue," Bofu replied casually. "Don't panic, old man."

"**Stop calling me old!**" Cheng Pu cried. "It's bad enough that you keep taking advice from that pup Zhou Yu before you consult me, but-!"

"*Hey*," Bofu interrupted. "Gongjin isn't a 'pup', he's over twenty now, just like me, 'cause we're born in the same year. Or am *I* a 'pup'...?"

Cheng Pu stared at Gongjin as he said, "I didn't mean to imply that you or your friend was a young dog, Lord Sun: perhaps a better word would be 'youth'."

"That isn't any fairer, even without the 'dog' part," Bofu suggested. "I know that you can't handle taking instructions from me and seeing younger men giving me advice, despite you once telling me otherwise... maybe that's part of why I call you 'old'."

Cheng Pu's eyes wandered.

"Gongjin's clever," Bofu continued. "So is Ziheng. So's Gongfu. So's Junli. So are you. *Age is irrelevant. Your* words, not mine."

"Alright, alright!" Cheng Pu whined. "I... I'll just have to get used to it. So our foray into Wu is part of a carefully thought-out plan...?"

"Of course, we want Wang Lang to think we're going after White Tiger's confederacy," Lü Fan said. "By going into Wu, we achieve that deception."

"Additionally, we need as many allies as we can get," Gongjin said. "We're going to stop in as many towns and cities as we can and rally people."

"Uncle Jing – Father's brother, I mean – is in Wu," Bofu explained. "I'll get him to help, and Zhu Junli can provide help too."

"Junli... how nice it will be to see Junli!" Cheng Pu said. "Heh, I suppose I do sound old when I say things like this, but... I remember when he joined us, perhaps nine or ten years ago, when we were on our way to Changsha. He helped us pacify that place, didn't he, Gongfu?"

"He did," Huang Gai said.

"And now he's holding Wu Prefecture and keeping White Tiger under his watchful eye," Lü Fan said. "He's invaluable."

"And he's a *friend*," Cheng Pu growled.

"What's wrong with you, Demou?" Bofu asked. "Why are you being so aggressive towards Ziheng and Gongjin?"

"I... I just can't believe we're in a worse place, and I cannot rationalise it! I cannot reconcile it!" Cheng Pu admitted. "We're still Yuan Shu's minions, Lord Sun, after six years! *Six years*! It feels like an eternity, a prison sentence! Sometimes I'd rather be at the mercy of the Minister of Public Works, digging roads and building things!"

"Yeah, I know," Bofu sighed. "But how is it their fault? It's *mine*, isn't it?"

"It... it isn't your fault: don't ever think that, Lord Sun," Cheng Pu protested. "I am... I am 'old', I suppose. I can't just shrug it off anymore, not now that he wants to abduct our families. A criminal is incarcerated, serves their sentence, and is released to return to their family... in our case, we are 'free' while our-"

"**Don't-!** ...*Please*," Bofu interrupted. "Everyone keeps telling me to control my temper with Yuan Shu, and yet all you ever do is wind me up!"

"...Sorry," Cheng Pu sighed.

"Let's go to Kuaiji," Lü Fan said. "Let's just keep going, and leave Yuan to fate."

Bofu was about to order an increase in pace when a shout from the direction of his train of followers distracted him.

"...Your brother is here?" Gongjin exclaimed as Sun Quan approached the vanguard on a young horse.

"Believe me, I don't like it," Bofu said as Quan reached him.

"Elder Brother, I want to send someone to Shouchun to tell Mother and Yi about the march!" Quan said excitedly. "What's my rank, by the way?"

"*Rank*?" Cheng Pu chortled as he stared at the short, uninspiring 14-year-old.

"Uh... we'll discuss that when we get to the Wu capital, Quan," Bofu replied.

"Do I get bodyguards?" Quan asked as he stared at Sun Hè and Zhou Tai. "Is Zhu Yifeng with his uncle in Wu?"

"*No* to the first question, *yes* to the second," Bofu replied. "Look, Quan, I... I appreciate that you're excited, but you don't have any experience in battle, and I have a lot of plans to make."

"I'm a tiger as well, Brother," Quan insisted. "I'm as much a tiger as you."

Cheng Pu covered his face with his sleeve.

"Zhou Tai, could you escort my brother back to where he came from?" Bofu asked.

The bodyguard Zhou Tai nodded obediently, turned to Sun Quan and said, "Young lord Sun, kindly follow me."

"Sure," Quan replied. "You were a pirate, weren't you...?"

The ensemble of commanders watched as Zhou Tai led Sun Quan away from them.

"*Aiee*...! I'm a *fool*!" Bofu said as he watched his brother disappear from view. "Why I let myself be talked into bringing him, I really don't know!"

"Let's keep moving," Lü Fan sighed.

****

62

Qu'e had been annexed into Danyang when Wu Jing had conquered it for Yuan Shu years before, so Wu had a new capital, named for the prefecture: Bofu entered that city, whereupon he was greeted by a jubilant Zhu Zhi and his adopted son Zhu Ran.

"Good to see you, Junli!" Bofu said as he clasped the hand of his older friend.

"...Demou, Gongfu, Yigong!" Zhu Zhi exclaimed as he spotted Cheng Pu, Huang Gai and Han Dang. "We're all together again!"

All of the 4 men bowed to one-another as Cheng Pu said, "Good to see you, Junli."

"Is White Tiger planning anything?" Gongjin asked.

"He *isn't going to do anything*!" Bofu cried before Zhu Zhi could respond. "I won't say it again, Gongjin: in all other matters you're right, but White Tiger *isn't going to attack us*!"

"But he may help Wang Lang when we attack Kuaiji, especially since Wang Lang's funding the Shanyue in this area," Gongjin suggested.

"Wang Lang's funding the Shanyue?" Han Dang exclaimed.

"Yes," Zhu Zhi replied. "Liu Yao, for all his supposed decency, was courting the Shanyue; some of Xu Gong's followers are hiding among them. So why wouldn't Wang Lang help them if they are a way to stop us? It isn't as though they have to actually thank the Shanyue when it's over."

"All the same, the funding changes things," Huang Gai said.

"Yes, but when we attack Kuaiji, we'll be cutting off the aid Wang's giving the Shanyue!" Bofu protested. "They won't help Wang Lang, especially not when the aid stops! They'd attack us if we attacked them, but we won't, so they won't!"

"We still need to be mindful of their presence," Gongjin insisted.

Bofu groaned and wrapped his hands around his head.

"...As Lord Sun has suggested, White Tiger and Xu Gong are doing very little at present beside wooing local bandit gangs and pirates," Zhu Zhi said with a smile. "The Shanyue tribes are not looking to make much trouble at present."

"Yeah, *see*...?" Bofu said as he stared at an amused Gongjin. "I watched the tribes in Changsha! I learned from what I saw! White Tiger looks weak to the tribes at the moment, so nobody'll do anything yet unless *we* do, and we're *avoiding them*!"

"Alright, Bofu," Gongjin chuckled. "Mister Zhu, we're going to advance into Kuaiji soon, so we'd better start putting signs up."

Sun Quan pushed his way to the front of the ensemble and placed a friendly hand on Zhu Ran's arm.

"Oh, it's you, Zhongmou!" Zhu Ran said with delight. "How are you? Is everyone well?"

"I feel *alive*, Yifeng!" Quan replied. "I've been talking to one of my brother's bodyguards: he's the man I need as my main bodyguard!"

"What do you need bodyguards for?" Zhu Ran wondered.

"...I'm the eldest brother of the lord of this region," Quan replied with thinly-veiled irritation. "Wouldn't I be a target for attacks as well...?"

"Oh, yes, of course," Zhu Ran replied diplomatically. "Well then,

shall we follow the rest...?"
The local and visiting officials were moving toward the governor's residence: Quan nodded and said, "Yes, we should; I don't want to miss anything important."

Bofu invited Gongjin to share a jar of wine in his private meeting room that night; after a short time, Gongjin said, "Why did you not invite anyone else...?"
"Ziheng... has a family," Bofu replied. "We... don't."
"Ah, yes," Gongjin chuckled miserably.
"That bastard has robbed me of my father, my dignity, and now my mother, brothers, sisters, nieces, nephews... and... and the chance to be a father!" Bofu said with obvious distress. "What's the point???"
"...I know," Gongjin replied. "I lay awake at night, thinking about it sometimes, and I can see no way of rectifying it. Unless we enjoy the 'places of ill repute', as many of our recruits do, we'll not know comfort. And we can hardly father our heirs with prostitutes."
"It's another fool's idea of cunning," Bofu grumbled. "But would Yuan Shu have me if he'd done this to my father...? Doesn't denying me the chance to-"
"You know as well as I do that he wants us to have wives, but that they have to go straight to Shouchun as soon as they're pregnant," Gongjin chortled. "Then they'll know from the cradle 'who their master is'... but he'll get no more slaves from me."
"We need to escape him, Gongjin!" Bofu whined. "I want to be my father's son in all ways, including fathering the next generation! But how can I do that when... when...!"
"...When our eventual defiance might lead to an act of evil hypocrisy," Gongjin said. "Dong Zhuo decimated Yuan Shu's clan, yet he tacitly threatens us with the same for the crime of 'apparent disobedience'. I know, Bofu, I know... it frightens me."
"What if he does something to them and we didn't do anything???" Bofu cried. "What if someone like Hui Qu, Chen Ji or Liu Xun decides to slander us out of spite? Gongjin, what if he-"
"We'd *kill him*, Bofu," Gongjin replied coldly. "But he won't... Heaven has other plans for us."
The placated Bofu nodded slowly and returned to the solace of his drinking dish.

****

The humiliated governor of Yang Province, Liu Yao, was still receiving reports from various parts of the province as he tried to rebuild his forces in Yuzhang. The new Administrator of Yuzhang, Hua Xin, would often try and discuss an approach to attacking Yuan Shu's agents in the south, but Liu Yao was becoming increasingly demoralised.

"I cannot fight him now," Liu Yao said to Hua Xin.

"We must try, Father!" Liu Ji protested. "We can't just give up!"

"Ze Rong was a valuable lesson to me," Liu Yao replied. "I allowed him to fool me as he fooled so many others... but he never fooled Sun Ce, and he never fooled poor Xu Zijiang."

"...I know that you still mourn your adviser, Governor Liu," Hua Xin said, "but-"

"He was more than an adviser, Mister Hua!" Liu Yao barked. "He was one of the geniuses of the age! Such men are irreplaceable! Are you so ignorant that you don't know of his abilities...? He appraised Cao Cao, Yuan Shao, Dong Zhuo, Tao Qian, Ze Rong, Yuan Shu, Fan Neng, Yu Mi, Taishi Ziyi, me, and so many others... and he was right about every single one of them. Cao Cao is a villain, Yuan Shao is an incompetent bumbler, Dong Zhuo was a monster, Tao Qian was false, Ze Rong was an evil fraud, Yuan Shu a talentless hankerer, Fan and Yu are bold but not heroes, while Taishi Ziyi... Taishi Ziyi is a hero... a hero that he repeatedly implored me to use, but I allowed my court of conceited, talentless fools to pressure me into neglecting him! That, perhaps, was Xu Zijiang's only error: rating me as a man of worth! Where are the men that I allowed to bully me now, mm...? Many of them now kowtow to the same Sun Ce that they hurried me to face! Where is Taishi Ci...? Who knows... who knows. And where is Xu Zijiang, the smartest of us all...? ...*Dead*... while unworthy men still walk and breathe air they don't deserve."

Liu Yao started to cough violently as Hua Xin said, "We must coordinate with Wang Lang, Governor, and win the province back from Yuan Shu's minions. Ze Rong is no longer a threat here: the tribal chieftains are calmed, and we have more than sixty-thousand men between us *at least*. If we contact Xu Gong, liaise with the Shanyue, work with Wang Lang-"

Liu Yao could not stop coughing; Hua Xin stopped his remonstrations and left the ailing governor and his son.

"...Father... will you be alright...?" Liu Ji asked.

Liu Yao did not reply, so his son left him alone and returned to the city garrison. Liu Yao then started to weep: he was a broken man that felt that the moment for redemption had passed.

****

Kuaiji Prefecture's administrator, Wang Lang, heard of Bofu's march into Wu Prefecture and summoned his officials to discuss it. Three men were anxious to have their views heard: one was a senior adviser, Officer of Merit Yu Fan; the second was Kuaiji City Magistrate Zhou Xin, who also the former Administrator of Danyang; the last was Xu Jing, the brother of the famous appraiser Xu Shao.

"…Mister Xu, you shall speak first," Wang Lang declared.

"Sun Ce is a menace that surely intends to attack us soon, my lord," Xu Jing said. "He has already made that clear when he drove the rightful governor of Yang Province out of Qu'e, and with him my poor brother, who is now cold bones! While I did not enjoy cordial relations with Zijiang in recent years, he was kin, and he was a genius, and he never hurt a hair on a man's head! Yes, he destroyed men's careers with his *requested* appraisals, but none that didn't deserve it! That thug son of Sun Jian has robbed the world of a much-needed judge of the talented and the virtuous!"

"Ze Rong had as much to do with Xu Shao's lamentable early death as Sun Ce," Yu Fan suggested. "And didn't he also endure the misfortune of proffered advice being ignored…?"

"He was driven to despair by Sun Ce! It is Sun Ce that he wrote of!" Xu Jing retorted. "Don't tell me who killed him! Ze Rong was a final slap to the face after being repeatedly kicked!"

Wang Lang smiled sadly and said, "I regret that I was unable to be his friend as I am yours, Mister Xu. But *can* I fight Sun Ce as you seem to imply that I *should*…?"

"You have no choice," Zhou Xin said. "I have a long and painful history with the Suns of Fuchun and their kin. Sun Ce's father humiliated my brother Renming when he tried to take his rightful place as Inspector of Yu Province, then Wu Jing, the uncle of the upstart, wrenched Danyang from me with cheap tricks and brute force, and then I was forced to flee here by Sun Ce himself. And let us not forget that their master, Yuan Shu, is a hungry wolf that desires all that is not his to have! While his dogs did their work, Yuan Shu personally defeated my other brother, Ang, and took Jiujiang from him! They won't stop with what they have, my lord, and only a fight will prevent your holdings being next."

The prematurely-aged, gaunt Wang Lang nodded thoughtfully.

"Impossible," Yu Fan scoffed. "My lord, we have only a few hundred men as a standing army, and access to a few thousand conscripts! Sun Ce has recruited thousands to his cause; I am hearing that he has tens of thousands of willing followers!"

"Little did I know that the people of Danyang were so heartless and disloyal!" Xu Jing cried. "What sort of age do we live in? His Majesty is a vagrant, the governors and administrators fight each other for land that is not theirs, and the people pledge allegiance to anarchists, cults and pirates! Sun Ce is a criminal: he is a bandit, a thief and a murderer!"

Many of Wang Lang's officials indicated their accord with Xu Jing's emotional outburst.

"And what would you fight the man with, Mister Xu…?" Yu Fan

asked. "We cannot fight him with angry words and bitter tears! We cannot scream and cry this man away! And we must certainly not attack him without provocation! Yes, he took Wu and Danyang, but they are ancestral homes for his clan that-!"

"He's Yuan Shu's attack dog!" Zhou Xin cried. "Did you not hear what I said before? He didn't take those places for his clan; he took them for his *master*!"

"Ignore him and we will lose our homes and our heads, Mister Yu!" Xu Jing said. "We must alert all counties, recruit and if necessary conscript, and we must fight him *when* – not if – he comes into Danyang!"

"...*If* he attacked, then of course, we'd have to defend, and Kuaiji has only a few good points from which we can repel an attack," Yu Fan conceded. "My lord, we should assume that he intends to attack as Mister Zhou supposes, sad to say."

"But the matter of what I must fight them with is unresolved," Wang Lang said. "I could call upon the Shanyue to pincer Sun Ce when he crosses into-"

"*No*," Yu Fan chortled. "It is bad enough that we're aiding their activities in Wu: if we invite any more of them to Kuaiji, they'll take over when Sun Ce is vanquished. We must do as Mister Xu suggested and recruit or conscript locals, and I suggest that we ask men like *Hè Qi*, who has proven his worth as a leader and as guardian *against* the Shanyue that run rampant locally."

Administrator Wang Lang scowled at the thinly-disguised accusation of hypocrisy.

"But we can't hold here," Yu Fan continued. "We must do all that we can to reinforce the Qiantang river line."

"Reinforcing the Qiantang is a good suggestion, Yu Zhongxiang!" Xu Jing said.

There were no objections from the rest of Wang Lang's followers, so Wang said, "Very good: we'll do that, and we'll begin at once."

****

65

Bofu led his army into Kuaiji and quickly realised that Wang Lang had withdrawn to defensive positions on the Qiantang River: after cutting the supply lines and eradicating the supply base that fed the Shanyue, Bofu continued his advance and camped some distance north of the river and sent scouts to review Wang Lang's main camp near the city of Guling. Bofu then gathered his officials in his main camp to discuss tactics.

"The Shanyue in Wu did not react aggressively to the loss of supplies," Lü Fan noted. "Rather, they retreated further north: that means that we are likely to avoid a pincer, as we hoped."

"So Wang Lang is isolated: I say that we should just attack him," Bofu said.

Bofu's uncle, Sun Jing, said, "Wang Lang is another Huang Zu."

"You surely don't rate him as another influential bastard like Huang Zu, Uncle???" Bofu retorted. "Wang Lang is a meek pedant from the imperial court, isn't he?"

"Your uncle has a point, Bofu," Gongjin suggested. "Wang Lang is very clever."

"And he has the loyalty of the brother of the appraiser Xu Shao," Lü Fan noted. "The two are old friends: another of his closest friends is the Chancellor of Beihai, Kong Rong, who's directly descended from Confucius."

"So... so Wang's a nice fellow, then?" Bofu supposed.

"Not at *all*," Gongjin chortled. "I confess that I do not understand why a man like Xu Jing would work for Wang Lang, much less a man like Kong Rong desiring his friendship! Father told me that Wang – who was once an assistant to the Chief of Staff in the palace – was the one that principally advised Tao Qian during the emerging crises six years ago. If that's true, then he advised Tao to remain neutral and pledge allegiance to Dong Zhuo's court, and subsequently to Li Jue and Guo Si's regency. In exchange for that obsequious behaviour, he was awarded the role he has now: had Tao Qian been advised to oppose the usurpers with Yuan Shao, well... who knows."

"So we have this man to thank for the mess we're in now," Han Dang said.

"If it's true, then partially, yes," Gongjin replied. "My point is this: he's got a reputation in some quarters for self-serving acts and devious scheming. That's a man that we shouldn't underestimate, even though he's nowhere near as militarily strong as Huang Zu, since numbers don't always dictate a winner. For example, the-"

"Or in other words," Sun Jing interrupted, "an arrow only needs one man to fire it, and I have no desire to bury you alongside my brother, dearest Nephew. We must show *caution*. I suggest that we try catching him in a pincer, using his own river defences against him."

"...I agree," Gongjin said.

"I do too," Lü Fan said.

"It would involve a covert operation that would doom the force that attempted it if it failed," Cheng Pu suggested. "It's a sound idea, but risky."

"I would gladly lead the infiltration force," Sun Jing declared.

"We'll try attacking him straight on first, before we risk that," Bofu said. "I have no desire to lose my father's brother. If we get nowhere, we try the plan."
Everyone agreed, and preparations began for a series of attacks on Wang Lang's riverside defences.

Bofu's forces outnumbered Wang Lang's considerably, but the defenders had the advantage of terrain. Wang Lang had reinforced all of the walled towns and cities and placed archer towers and ambush units along the river, and his camp was solidly defended by a small cavalry and a determined infantry force that included local Shanyue tribespeople. Bofu took his army to the northern riverbank, and Wang Lang prepared to meet him.
"This isn't great," Bofu said as he observed Wang Lang's Guling camp. "Good organisation, lots of tribespeople to make up for his small conscript army... we may be here a while."
"We *can't afford to be*," Gongjin whispered.
"...White Tiger...?" Bofu supposed.
"Wu and Danyang are both in potential danger, though the signs are early and I might be overreacting," Gongjin replied. "White Tiger is still recruiting, yes, but there's another dangerous element: the 'Bandit King of Haixi', Chen Yu, has been sending people to reconnoitre in Wu, and that worries me."
"Let's see if Wang Lang's army is as strong as it looks," Bofu suggested. "If we have to withdraw to save the other prefectures, then we will, okay...?"
Gongjin nodded silently, and Bofu turned to Cheng Pu and Lü Fan with a calm smile on his face.
"What are your orders...?" Cheng Pu asked as he stared at Gongjin.
"Don't be like that," Bofu pleaded. "Now look, we need to crack and smash Wang Lang like an egg, and the best way to do that is by striking him as a rock would. Ling Cao, Huang Gai, Han Dang: you'll be the vanguard. Cheng Pu, Lü Fan: you're both in charge of logistics, naturally. I want any necessary retreat to be covered, and any of their charges blunted. Now we've got a bigger army, we should think about learning some arrays, I suppose... but that's for later. Archers, pikes... you know the routine, don't you? Now where's Han Yan...?"
A hard-faced, stocky man in weathered battle armour stepped forward from amongst Bofu's officers and bowed humbly, saying, "Han Yan is here, Lord Sun."
"You're our consultant on the southern Shanyue," Bofu said. "There're quite a few on the enemy side, so if there's anything you can tell us, you can tell it to Cheng Pu and Lü Fan."
Han Yan bowed a second time and said, "I will do my very best to repay your faith in me, Lord Sun."
"Great," Bofu replied. "Zhou Yu, Zhou Tai, Jiang Qin, and my worthy uncle Sun Jing: you're the second wave."
Sun Jing bowed and said, "I shall serve as any other man would, worthy nephew."

In Wang Lang's camp, preparations were being made for a field battle. Wang Lang reviewed his forces with quiet optimism, but his adviser Yu Fan was becoming increasingly desperate as he observed the regiments of Shanyue volunteers.

"Those creatures rob villages!" Yu Fan cried. "They steal food and abduct women for their harems! Financing them secretly in Wu is bad enough, my lord: having them openly aiding us here is-!"

"This is a desperate hour," Wang Lang retorted. "Help me or go away, Mister Yu."

Yu Fan exhaled violently and replied, "Fine! I will say no more about it, my lord. I can report that the enemy have the intention of attacking us soon, so we'll need to-"

"I know of it," Wang Lang interrupted. "I intend to meet them when they arrive."

Yu Fan nodded silently.

"Go and reinforce the city," Wang Lang ordered. "I have no need of you here."

Yu Fan looked at Xu Jing, but the famous appraiser was quite happy with the plan to confront Bofu; Yu then turned his gaze to Zhou Xin, but the Magistrate of Kuaiji City was also determined to face his personal enemies in battle.

"...As you command," Yu Fan said.

Wang Lang harrumphed; Yu Fan turned and left the camp with a small retinue of personal assistants, muttering, "I serve a *fool*."

Wang Lang arrayed his men in front of his northern camp and surveyed the enemy force with contempt.

"Yuan Shu's dogs will regret coming here," Wang Lang scoffed.

"Shall I attack...?" Zhou Xin asked.

A battle gong was sounded on Bofu's side before Wang Lang could reply; Ling Cao charged at breakneck speed and led his cavalry and infantry toward Wang Lang's position.

"**Who is this lunatic???**" Wang Lang exclaimed as his bodyguards rushed to repel Ling Cao's charge. "**Protect me, or this day is lost!**"

Ling Cao was repelled, but the attack had left the defenders demoralised; Huang Gai and Han Dang's slower advances were met half-heartedly, and the Shanyue seemed to be slow in reacting to the threat. Wang Lang quickly realised why his Shanyue allies were proving to be so useless: Bofu's consultant, Han Yan, had suggested some simple ways of unnerving and confounding the tribesmen such as wearing specific articles of clothing, riding specific types of horses and using certain battle cries. Some of the smaller Shanyue tribes were retreating altogether, and the remainder of the army was outclassed by the well-trained men that Bofu had deployed.

"**Retreat!**" Wang Lang ordered. "**Retreat into the city!**"

"**I'll retreat to the camp!**" Zhou Xin replied.

Yu Fan provided covering fire from the walls of Guling as Wang Lang led his battered militia through the city gates; Bofu's forces stopped short of the walls and yelled curses at their vanquished opponents.

"Sound a retreat," Gongjin suggested as he watched the city from afar. "We'll not goad him out of there now."

"What about the camps outside...?" Bofu wondered.

"I saw a general returning to the camp," Gongjin replied. "We can try attacking that, but I doubt we'll achieve much there either, at least for today."

"...Fine," Bofu conceded. "**RETREAT! SOUND A RETREAT!**"

Bofu's battle gong signalled to the vanguard, and his army withdrew. Wang Lang had reached the walls of Guling as the last of Ling Cao's men were pulling back; Yu Fan turned to Wang and said, "They'll be back."

"And we'll continue to defend," Wang Lang retorted. "Defending was *your* suggestion, Mister Yu Fan: would you rather that I surrendered...?"

"...Of course not," Yu Fan said. "I was merely commenting on the fact that they are unlikely to withdraw to Danyang."

"I used the battle to open a path for my messenger to go to Wu Prefecture," Wang Lang explained with glee. "He takes with him a letter to White Tiger Yan of the Shanyue... a letter that 'apologises', if you will, for the current situation and requests his participation in a joint attack on Sun Ce and his allies. He shall surely answer me favourably... and until he does, we merely need to hold our positions along the river."

"*Ayah*... 'Apologise'...?" Yu Fan exclaimed. "You *apologise* to these uncultured barbarians, now, my lord...? Write to the court! Write to *Chang'an*, to-"

"And who shall I write to in Chang'an? *Li Jue*? *Guo Si*? They are regents in name only now, and never should have been to begin with, the curs!" Wang Lang retorted. "The north is in chaos! The Son of Heaven has *fled Chang'an* with the remnants of the court, so the question I ask, Yu Fan, is better framed as 'To *where* do I write', actually! The rubble of Luoyang...? The wilderness...? I have no idea what remains of the court or where it is! In such lawless times, one find allies wherever one can!"

"...There must be *someone*!" Yu Fan said. "Someone other than-!"

"**Governor Liu Yao is as good as dead, exhausted and driven to his wit's end by his many defeats at the hands of Sun Ce!**" Wang Lang snapped. "**His allies, Xue Li and Ze Rong, are *dead*, and it's likely one was slain by the other, more's the pity! Xu Gong is vanquished and in hiding with the Shanyue! Hua Xin of Yuzhang and I are the only able ones left now, and Hua Xin has problems of his own! I am a cultured man who once served in the imperial palace and enjoyed the company of men like Kong Rong, Chen Yuanfang and Cai Yong! Do you think that I ally with godless anarchists by *choice*???**"

Yu Fan turned to judgemental gaze to Xu Jing.

"Mister Yu Fan, you can rest assured that I am as aggrieved as you, but Lord Wang is doing what he must," Xu Jing said sternly. "Let it go."

Yu Fan exhaled noisily and said, "I shall, from lack of choice."

"We can only hope that our Shanyue allies here in Kuaiji return, else we are at an even greater disadvantage," Wang Lang sighed.

"I'll... I'll go and oversee the supplies," Yu Fan said.

"Please do that, Mister Yu," Wang Lang replied gratefully.

As Yu Fan left the walls of Guling, he shook his head and said, "I serve a fool... a doomed, isolated *fool*."

****

After several failed attempts to overwhelm Wang Lang's forces at Guling, the frustrated Bofu summoned his officials yet again.

"Alright, I concede... we need to use our wits," Bofu grumbled. "He's not going to be goaded, is he, and I'm sick of narrow misses."

"So am I," Sun Hè sighed. "Being your bodyguard is no fun at all, cousin Bofu."

"I again volunteer to take a force over the river and launch an attack against the rear of their army while you strike from the front," Sun Jing declared. "Please don't ignore my advice again, dear nephew."

"...Everyone else in favour of the *plan*...?" Bofu asked.

The question was met by silence.

"I'll take that as agreement, but Uncle, you're not the right person," Bofu pleaded.

"Who *is*, then, Nephew?" Sun Jing asked. "Who would you send to die in my place?"

"...No man is less worthy than another, right...?" Bofu chortled. "I know it, Uncle, else I wouldn't risk my own life on the field... just be careful, yeah?"

Sun Jing bowed slightly and said, "For you, worthy nephew, I will preserve my life to fight another day. I shall take my sons Hao and Yu with me."

"Only if my dear cousins will try and live as well," Bofu replied. "Go on... show the world that my father wasn't the only mad tiger in the family."

Sun Jing laughed, bowed, and left the tent to begin preparations for his departure. A nervous silence followed; Bofu noted Gongjin's expression and said, "You might as well say whatever you're going to say now, rather than waiting for old Cheng Demou to smack it out of you."

Cheng Pu harrumphed at the notion, but he was smiling at the same time.

"We'll be a lot of men down once your uncle has gone, and that'll be obvious to a sneaky man like Wang Lang," Gongjin suggested. "We've caught three scouts just today, so we must hide this manoeuvre somehow."

"I say that we should learn from the best, and the best, like it or not, includes Dong Zhuo's adviser Jia Xu," Lü Fan said. "I've heard that when he was afraid of Yuan Shao's allies in Luoyang, he used a scheme to fool scouts into thinking he had an army many times larger than in actuality."

"I know of it, Mister Lü," Cheng Pu said. "The 'rotating insignias on repeating marches' ruse, I suppose you could call it. But what about night-time...?"

"Don't fret about that," Bofu replied. "There's an easy way to fool him at night... and it's as easy as *lighting a fire*."

"...Of course!" Cheng Pu chuckled. "Simple, yet effective!"

Wang Lang's scouts would not report anything that would alert him to Sun Jing's infiltration: Bofu had his remaining men light an extra campfire for every missing man, so the army appeared to be the same size to the distant observers. Morning brought daylight, but through the clever use of thinned lines and having the same men conduct the same operations repeatedly with different insignias, Wang Lang was left convinced that Bofu was planning more frontal attacks and nothing more. The expected attack was carried out very carefully, so that Wang Lang would not notice the reduced personnel: but just as Wang expected Bofu to withdraw as he had done before, his messengers reported something that left him quite unnerved.

"They're at *Gaoqian*...?" Wang Lang exclaimed. "That's...! B-but how did they get there without-!"

"We have to retreat," Yu Fan insisted.

"Regrettably, I agree," Xu Jing said. "We cannot win now. We must pull back."

"I can't just give up!" Wang Lang protested. "This is a setback, *nothing more*! Zhou Xin, you must hold here. I will send a relief force to Gaoqian."

"The messenger was clear!" Yu Fan barked as he pointed at the cowering soldier that had delivered the news. "Gaoqian is lost! They now have a camp on our side of the river that we cannot uproot without abandoning this place! We are stuck!"

"Nonsense!" Wang Lang cried. "Zhou Xin, lead a force of men to attack Sun Ce at once! If he's got a massive camp at Gaoqian, then his numbers here are a bluff! We can challenge them and destroy Sun Ce as Huang Zu destroyed his father at Xiangyang! When that happens, won't the rest retreat...?"

Yu Fan could not find the words to retort with.

"*Zhou Xin*: carry out my instructions, please," Wang Lang said with a tone that betrayed his exhaustion.

Zhou Xin bowed humbly and departed from the command room.

"We have to abandon Guling," Yu Fan implored. "Gaoqian is lost, and-"

"You're not much use to me if you're going to cheer for our enemies, Mister Yu Fan!" Wang Lang interrupted. "Either help me or go away!"

Yu Fan looked at Xu Jing, who was still as fanatical about defeating Bofu's army as his master was; Yu Fan lowered his gaze and said nothing more while Wang Lang made plans to continue his resistance.

Zhou Xin led a force northward and camped south of Bofu's. Within hours of his deployment, Bofu had an army ready to confront him. The two forces met near Zhou Xin's camp and prepared for a fight.

"I'll have your head, Sun Ce, for the honour of my brothers!" Zhou Xin screamed as he rode to the front of his battle line. **"Come and face *Zhou Xin*, one against one, and let me avenge the repeated indignities!"**

"*Zhou Xin*...?" Cheng Pu mused. "He's... ah, I see. He's the brother of the Zhou Yu that we fought at Yang City for control of Yu Province."

"So a famous Zhou Yu's brother meets another Zhou Yu that means him harm!" Gongjin chuckled. "...And isn't Zhou Xin the former Administrator of Danyang?"

"Of course, yes!" Cheng Pu said. "Wu Jing evicted him!"

"And then we defeated him again when he allied with Liu Yao at Qu'e," Gongjin noted.

"This is *really* personal for him, then, isn't it," Bofu realised. "I'll fight him."

"You shouldn't," Sun Hè pleaded.

"He's finished, and he knows it!" Bofu replied.

Bofu rode forward with his bodyguard force, which was comprised of Sun Hè, Song Qian and several new additions in light of Zhou Tai and Jiang Qin having been reassigned.

"**COWARD!**" Zhou Xin screeched. "**What kind of man are you?**"

"All of you back away," Bofu said to his bodyguards. "I'll be okay… you do what we agreed on."

Sun Hè nodded obediently, and the bodyguards dropped back by several strides.

"**Here I am!**" Bofu shouted. "**Here is Sun Ce!**"

Zhou Xin met Bofu in single combat: within 6 passes, Zhou Xin realised that he was outmatched, and he retreated to his line. Bofu halted, since he suspected a trap; he laughed and returned to his own line with his bodyguards.

"What do we do?" Huang Gai asked.

"His lines are pathetic," Bofu replied. "Isn't that so, Song Qian…?"

"Yes," Song Qian said. "Weak all along the line: no real leadership at all."

"We outnumber and outclass him," Sun Hè added. "We should charge now and end this nonsense."

"…Cheng Pu, Ling Cao: lead the charge," Bofu ordered. "Jiang Qin, Zhou Tai: you both did really well before, so you'll join the vanguard. Huang Gai, Han Dang: you'll be the second wave this time. Zhou Yu, Sun Hè, Song Qian: we'll follow the charge and get some exercise."

"**For the glory of Lord Sun Ce!**" Ling Cao screamed as he led his horsemen toward Zhou Xin.

"Eager as always, that Ling Cao," Cheng Pu sighed as he urged his own men forward.

The battle was a rout: Magistrate Zhou Xin fell during a confused cavalry skirmish, and Bofu's force advanced on his camp and reduced it to ash.

****

67

"...So Zhou Xin is dead," Wang Lang said soberly; his command room was filled with silent, judgemental figures that glared at him unforgivingly.

"Now we should just accept defeat and flee southward, Administrator," Yu Fan insisted.

"...We'll escape down the river to Dongye," Wang Lang decided. "Yu Fan, you'll coordinate the defences; Xu Jing, you'll journey with me."

"And what word should be sent to the magistrates of the counties?" Yu Fan asked cuttingly. "Or will they learn of this when it is too late to-"

"They'll know that they should join me in Dongye!" Wang Lang barked.

As Wang Lang and Xu Jing retreated to a private room to prepare for their escape, Yu Fan looked at a number of the officials that remained and searched their faces for a sign of their feelings. Many lowered their gazes, and others retreated.

"...I serve a fool," Yu Fan grumbled as he left he command room to prepare the decoy defence of Guling. "I serve a wretched coward and a *fool*."

Yu Fan had made a decision: in his heart, Wang Lang was not his lord anymore.

Bofu's camp was alive with cries of victory when word of Wang Lang's retreat reached them.

"We should attack the city now!" Bofu suggested.

"And if the rumour of his retreat is a ruse...?" Lü Fan asked.

"My scouts are sure," Cheng Pu insisted. "They're not idiots."

"We'll advance across the river and rendezvous with Sun Jing's forces," Gongjin proposed. "If Wang Lang has deceived us, does it matter...? We have the advantage, no matter what."

"Youthful timidity is matched with youthful courage," Cheng Pu heckled. "Shall we get on?"

Gongjin sighed woefully as Cheng Pu retreated from the tent, but Bofu whispered, "Never mind: at least he said you had courage."

Yu Fan watched from atop the walls of the city of Guling as Bofu and his growing army gathered outside and pitched camp.

"What will you do?" one official asked.

"...If you think I'm going to die fighting a tiger to save a rat, then think again," Yu Fan replied. "I'm going to surrender the city and spare us any more bloodshed."

The statement was met with guilty-yet-grateful silence.

An hour later, Yu Fan had the gates thrown open to surrender to the enemy.

"...And that's it? It's over?" Ling Cao chortled.

"Don't sound so disappointed," Bofu said.

"I'm not diappointed," Ling Cao promised. "I'm just surprised."

"Wang Lang's left them with no will to fight," Cheng Pu supposed.

"That or they figured out the truth of things," Bofu retorted. "Let's go and meet the city magistrate or whoever that is at the gates."

Bofu led his officers and a small retinue of soldiers toward the gates: care was taken to maintain watch on the walls for a sudden archery attack, as unlikely as it might have seemed when the city administration was so dangerously exposed.

"General Sun Ce," Yu Fan said as Bofu stopped in front of him; the city magistrate was stood to his left with the seal of office for Guling in his hands. Yu Fan then pressed his right hand to his chest and added, "I am... for what it is worth... the Acting Magistrate of the capital city of all Kuaiji, since Zhou Xin is dead. I'm afraid that I do not have the seal of authority for the prefecture; that's with my master. He took it when he fled."

"Take heart," Bofu said as he looked at the demoralised Yu Fan. "You didn't ask to serve a man like Wang Lang; he was forced on you by Dong Zhuo's cronies. Sadly, you're not the first man to serve an unworthy master: trust me, I know how it feels. What's your name?"

"...Yu Fan."

"Style name...?"

Yu Fan looked at Bofu with evident confusion.

Bofu smiled and repeated the words, "Style name."

"...Zhongxiang," Yu Fan replied uneasily: he stared at the smiling faces of Bofu and his vassals and wondered if this was the first stage of some sadistic ritual.

"Well then Zhongxiang, you've found your new lord," Bofu said, "although I hope that you can view me as your friend as well once you get to know me better. I'd rather you called me 'Bofu', rather than 'Lord Sun', I should say... though the oldies that served my father tend to ignore that fact, just to annoy me. Do you have family here...? Wife, sons...? I bet you have sons!"

Yu Fan laughed nervously and said, "Am I dead...?"

"Don't think so," Bofu snickered. "Come on, relax! It's Wang Lang that I'm after, not you. I can tell that you're a good man, so why would I hurt you...?"

Yu Fan's eyes filled with tears as he finally realised that Bofu was not toying with him: he bowed low and said, "Our true lord has come to us at last! I will gladly serve you, Lord Sun, and so will others when they know who you truly are!"

"Glad to hear it," Bofu said with a grin. "Now up, up! Don't like people bowing and scraping for no good reason! Wang Lang can grovel though, the wretch."

Yu Fan laughed and welcomed Bofu into the city with absolute sincerity that was shared by many of the officials that Wang Lang had so readily abandoned.

****

68

Now that Guling had surrendered and Wang Lang had fled, Bofu's next moves were important: he assembled his officials in the grand audience hall of Guling's governor's residence to discuss the immediate future.

"First, I want to welcome Yu Fan and his colleagues into our fold," Bofu began. "He made a very difficult decision in surrendering the city to us, because I know that I don't have the best of reputations."

"**No! Entirely false!**" Ling Cao cried. "**You are the greatest-!**"

"Just… knock it off, please, Ling Cao," Bofu chuckled. "Save your energy for your constant, fearless charges that pretty much form the whole of *your* reputation."

Some officials laughed; the unoffended Ling Cao smiled silently.

"Now… Uncle has requested that I go to Gaoqian," Bofu continued. "There's some fellow there that's refusing to surrender to him; it seems that he wants to welcome me into Gaoqian personally."

"That sounds dangerous," Sun Hè suggested.

"Perhaps," Bofu replied; he then turned to Yu Fan and said, "Do you perhaps know a tall, inspiring man named *Dong Xi*…?"

"He's a good man," Yu Fan replied. "He's settled in Gaoqian and he's the chief of the village, really, all in all, despite his relatively young age. He isn't what you'd call 'arrogant'… but he wouldn't surrender to your uncle. He came to Shanyin once, looking for work, but there wasn't anything to offer him, despite his considerable skill in martial arts."

"…I want to meet him," Bofu decided. "After that, you suggested going to Yan County, Yu Zhongxiang…?"

"Yes, Lord Sun," Yu Fan replied. "You'll find another friend there, for certain."

"It sounds like I'm going to find a lot of friends here in Kuaiji!" Bofu said with delight. "Tomorrow morning, we go to Gaoqian!"

Bofu left Yu Fan, the consultant Han Yan and Huang Gai to manage Guling while he journeyed to Gaoqian Village. When Bofu and his followers arrived at the surrendered enemy camps around the village, he was greeted by his uncle, Sun Jing.

"You did good work, Uncle," Bofu said. "Father'd be proud of us both, I think."

"I hope so," Sun Jing sighed.

"So where's this 'Dong Xi' fellow that wants to meet me…?" Bofu asked dryly.

"He'll be in the village," Sun Jing replied wearily. "He didn't try and get rid of our forces; he insisted that we didn't raid the village for supplies, but other than that, he's been no trouble at all."

"Lead the way," Bofu said thoughtfully.

Bofu, Gongjin, Lü Fan, Cheng Pu and Bofu's bodyguards followed Sun Jing to the village while Ling Cao and Han Dang pitched a temporary camp. What greeted them was a tall, charismatic man in his mid-30s and a collection of curious villagers: Bofu walked toward the tall man – who wore armour and carried a spear – and said, "Would you be Dong Xi…?"

"I would, General Sun Ce," Dong Xi replied. "I'd like to thank you

and your uncle for invading this region with such etiquette."
Cheng Pu frowned angrily and said, "**What???**"
"You see my being here as an *invasion*...?" Bofu exclaimed.
"Yes, General, I do," Dong Xi said fearlessly. "But it is obvious that you mean no harm to the people when you do so. But in the future, does your *master*...?"
"*Insolent*...!" Cheng Pu cried.
"...I'll match your honesty and admit that I don't know," Bofu replied. "But I assure you that if Lord Yuan Shu does try to harm anyone, I'll oppose it."
"Then I welcome you to Gaoqian," Dong Xi said with a smile. "I'm glad to have such a man as you here, Lord Sun Ce; men like your father are a rare breed these days, and it is nice to see that tigers do occasionally beget tigers."
"I like you, Dong Xi!" Bofu chuckled. "I understand from Mister Yu Fan that you're adept at martial arts."
"I'm flattered that the administrator's adviser knows of me," Dong Xi admitted. "I have studied under some fine tutors in this region, and it certainly helps from time to time when bandits harass us, or the Shanyue come looking for easy pickings; sadly, I have little else to do with everything that I've learned, as rewarding as it is... but that's another story! Please, Lord Sun, accompany me to my home and-"
"No time," Bofu said sadly. "I have a lot to do here in Kuaiji. But I won't go without making sure you've plenty to do. As Administrator of Kuaiji – and I am now – I hereby authorise you to take up the role of Chief Constable and do something about all the bandits; I have someone else in mind to deal with the Shanyue."
Dong Xi fell to his knees and kowtowed, saying, "You will not regret employing me, Lord Sun Ce! I shall-!"
"Up-up-up!" Bofu pleaded as he helped Dong Xi to his feet. "All this is getting tiresome; can't people just tell me their style name, smile and call me 'Bofu'?"
"Yuanshi... my style name is 'Yuanshi'," Dong Xi said.
"Then until more peaceful times that must surely come soon, let's part, Dong Yuanshi," Bofu replied.
Dong Xi bowed one last time, and Bofu turned to his allies, saying, "Have some food distributed for goodwill, and then we'll go back to Guling to fetch Yu Fan."
"Farewell for now, Sun Bofu," Dong Xi murmured as he watched Bofu lead his followers away. "We'll certainly meet again, though sadly not in times of peace."
Dong Xi then turned to his fellow villagers and ushered them back into the village to plan for the days when he would not be there to protect them.

****

69

Once Bofu had returned to Guling and met up with Yu Fan once again, his next journey was to Yan County, a well-managed and well-defended part of Kuaiji Prefecture that was governed by Magistrate Hè Qi.

"Hè Qi will surely join you," Yu Fan said as he rode alongside Bofu. "He's a bit of a character though."

"Isn't everyone that I have working for me?" Bofu chuckled. "That Dong Xi was a character; even the oldies like Cheng Demou are-"

"In what way is this 'Hè Qi' a 'character', Mister Yu...?" Cheng Pu asked gruffly.

"You'll have no problems with him," Yu Fan promised. "Hè Qi's well known for liking things of great value, though he ensures that they all come out of his own purse. He isn't a thief or a liar; he's just fond of nice things."

Bofu looked at the busy farming communities that were on either side of the road and said, "He gets a lot of bandits and tribes attacking the area, I bet."

"Oh, yes," Yu Fan replied. "But he's a very effective magistrate: the people follow him gladly, and he really keeps the wicked elements under control. That's the main reason – one of many – why I detested Wang Lang's alliance with White Tiger so much: what kind of message did it send to the Shanyue that live around here? Men like Hè Qi go to great efforts to quell their uprisings, and then we send aid for them to cause trouble in Wu! What message does it send to *Hè Qi*...?"

"Such double-standards are sadly commonplace these days," Gongjin sighed.

"Yeah, and that's something that I intend to change," Bofu promised. "I want to-"

"We appear to have a welcoming committee coming toward us," Cheng Pu announced.

Bofu's army slowed: Hè Qi had assembled an impressive-looking militia that was now advancing down the road to meet them.

"Who goes there?" Hè Qi bellowed; he was wearing flamboyant armour decorated with all manner of gold elements, a cerise silk cape, and he carried a halberd with gilded rings periodically circling its long handle. His horse's saddle was like that of a feudal prince, and his soldiers were dressed in armour that put the imperial army – and Bofu's – to shame.

"I see what you mean, Yu Zhongxiang," Bofu murmured. "How does he afford to equip the men like that as well?"

"Careful budgeting," Yu Fan said before he rode forward to greet Hè Qi.

"Yu Zhongxiang...?" Hè Qi exclaimed. **"What's going on? I heard that-"**

"Wang Lang has fled," Yu Fan said as he reached his ally. "I've submitted to Sun Ce's army from Danyang. You should too."

"They mean harm if I don't...?" Hè Qi prompted.

"Not at all," Yu Fan replied. "In fact, he doesn't even expect conscripts or donations."

Hè Qi frowned and leant to one side so that he could look past Yu Fan and observe Bofu.

"Quite unbelievable, I know," Yu Fan continued, "but quite true. Sun Bofu is a friend to the south, just as his father was."

"...But we betray the will of the Son of Heaven," Hè Qi suggested as he sat upright and locked his gaze with Yu Fan's.

"*Do we*, Hè Gongmiao?" Yu Fan asked. "Or do we join a man whose father once fought Dong Zhuo to save the sovereign and turn our backs on men that are either followers of the same Dong Zhuo, like the regents who abducted the same sovereign, or complicit to the evil-doings in exchange for personal gain, like Wang Lang?"

Hè Qi hummed thoughtfully.

"Wang had you fighting the Shanyue while he financed White Tiger in Wu," Yu Fan continued. "If even one piece of traded silk or one horse benefitted the Shanyue here, what mockery does that make of all of your efforts...?"

"...Quite right," Hè Qi said with a smile. "I should like to speak with Sun Ce."

"He will want to know all of your names, he is such a man," Yu Fan replied.

"He shall have them," Hè Qi said.

Yu Fan gave way so that Hè Qi could approach Bofu with his weapon lowered.

"Welcome to Yan County, General Sun," Hè Qi declared as he stopped his horse in front of Bofu and jumped down to the dirt road. "I am Hè Qi, style name Gongmiao, and I am the magistrate of Yan County."

Hè Qi bowed low and awaited a response.

"...Gongmiao, I have found in you another champion!" Bofu said with grateful laughter. "Rise, and return to your horse! And call me Bofu, for Heaven's sake! We're all friends here, all friends!"

Hè Qi laughed, mounted his horse, and led Bofu's army toward the nearby capital.

"You are truly a character, just as I was told," Bofu said as he admired the decorative features of Hè Qi's audience hall some hours later. "Everywhere I look, there's finery!"

Hè Qi bowed humbly and said, "I believe in everything looking its best at all times, Lord Sun. Perhaps it is because I know a poorer life and wish to enjoy my newfound success as much as possible."

Bofu's bodyguard Jiang Qin shook his head disappointedly.

"You disagree, sir...?" Hè Qi said as he stared at Jiang Qin.

"Each man has his own way of doing things, Magistrate," Jiang Qin replied. "Mine is frugality."

"Yeah, and he's an ex-pirate!" Bofu chuckled. "Look, I didn't want to start a debate about the rights and wrongs of finery. You look after this place, I can see that: you look after the people from the highest to the lowest, and I like that. You're wasted here, so I'd like to use the fact that I'm pretty much the new Administrator of Kuaiji now to promote you and give you a few things to do."

"You barely know me!" Hè Qi said as he bowed low once again. "How can I repay your kindness?"

"I have a man called Han Yan on my team that I'm putting in charge of harassing Wang Lang," Bofu replied. "We've got a few problems up north that we have to go back and deal with, so I'm not going to be able to carry on following that fool around Kuaiji.

As Magistrate of Yongning, you'll be his second. That'll include a lot of pacifying the Shanyue, much as you do already, but you'll be dealing with whatever else makes this region unstable. Will you help me make the south peaceful by doing this for me...?"
"Gladly!" Hè Qi said.
"Excellent!" Bofu chuckled.
"Lord Sun... what 'problems'?" Han Dang asked.
Lü Fan and Gongjin exchanged nervous glances, but neither they nor Bofu answered the question: instead, Bofu smiled fearlessly and continued to impress his newest recruits with a show of familiarity, wit and intelligence.

Once Bofu's consultant Han Yan and his new assistant, Hè Qi, had been acquainted with each other and their missions in Kuaiji, Bofu ordered the majority of his senior vassals to attend a private meeting while Sun Hè, Huang Gai and Yu Fan kept everybody else entertained and distracted.
"What's going on?" Han Dang asked. "You wouldn't answer me when I asked before, Lord Sun; what's happened...?"
"...I'll explain later, Yigong," Bofu replied. "Gongjin, we have a huge army now, and it seems to me that we have more to worry about now from Yuan Shu... so... so if you don't mind..."
"You'd like me to guard Danyang while you go to Wu," Gongjin supposed.
"It isn't an easy request," Bofu said. "I have Ziheng and Demou to help me, and you and your uncle will coordinate best, I think."
"I shall do as you ask," Gongjin replied.
"And with Han Yan, Yu Fan, Hè Qi and Dong Xi managing things here in Kuaiji, there's no way that we can fail: of that I'm certain," Lü Fan declared.
"*Ooh*...! Will you and your two mates stop prattling on and tell the rest of us what the big emergency is, please, Lord Sun?" Han Dang snapped. "How can we help you if we don't know what we're up against...?"
Bofu sighed sadly, looked at his followers and said, "Any hope we had that Kuaiji was the last big obstacle was wrong... very wrong."
"We're grown men, Lord Sun! Just *tell us*!" Han Dang barked.
"...Alright," Bofu began.
Gongjin nodded at Lü Fan and Cheng Pu before he quietly departed to begin the long journey to Danyang; Lü Fan returned the gesture while Cheng Pu averted his gaze and focussed his attention on Bofu, who was explaining the situation to his angry and unsettled officials. Gongjin shook his head sadly and left.

While Bofu and his allies had been busy in Kuaiji, both Danyang and Wu Prefectures had suddenly come under threat and word had been sent that Bofu's immediate assistance was required in both regions. In Danyang Prefecture, a mysterious rebel faction had formed amongst disaffected people based in the hills of Wuhu County, and they were causing trouble for Administrator Zhou Shang and his aide Xu Kun; in Wu Prefecture, a bandit from Haixi County in Xu Province named Chen Yu – who was known, for ease, as 'Haixi Chen' by his enemies – had decided to lead his immense following southward in an attack on the civil infrastructure. But that was not all when it came to Wu

Prefecture: White Tiger had finally gathered enough tribal and bandit allies to try and vie for control of the region as well, and he was cooperating with Wang Lang to achieve it. The problems in Danyang were serious but manageable; but if Haixi Chen and White Tiger Yan joined forces and overwhelmed Bofu's allies, Wu Prefecture could be lost to what Zhu Zhi called 'A confederacy of anarchists'. Time was against Bofu, and he knew it.

****

ACT VII: THE GREAT PACIFICATION

70

For the vassal-officer Sun Ce – whose courtesy name was Bofu – the signs of victory in his latest campaign had been good, but he had been taken away from his objective at the critical moment. Bofu's opponent – the Han Imperial court's appointed Administrator of Kuaiji Prefecture, Wang Lang – had lost many allies, and some of his subordinates had even defected to Bofu, despite his being the unwilling servant of the power-hungry nobleman-warlord Yuan Shu: such was Bofu's charisma and sincerity in an age when duplicity and opportunism was rife.

Bofu made no secret of his desire to escape Yuan Shu when in the company of trusted people, and he had good cause: despite his famous father's death at the hands of a vassal of Jing Provincial Governor Liu Biao, it was his father's lord, Yuan Shu, that had ordered him to that dangerous place for the sole purpose of increasing his power. Bofu feared a fate not unlike his father's: Sun Jian had once defeated hordes of Yellow Turban rebels and fought the tyrant Dong Zhuo, but he died as an 'Yuan Shu's attack dog' rather than the 'Tiger of Jiangdong' that he had once been known as by those that feared and respected him. Bofu had never known independence from Yuan Shu as his father had, but that did not make his role any less unbearable: he was, like Sun Jian, an 'attack dog', being sent from place to place to fight rebels and royalists alike in a mad race for territory with Yuan Shu's own brother and rightful heir to the clan estate, Yuan Shao, and because Shu now had the families of the senior figures in his capital as guest-hostages – including Bofu's – nobody dared risk dissent. Bofu had already defeated the Han court's appointed Governor of Yang Province, Liu Yao, and seized Lujiang Prefecture to the northwest, and the central prefectures of Danyang and Wu: the southeast region of Kuaiji was supposed to be next, but the weakened Wang Lang would have to wait, because a new coalition of tribal chieftains and bandits had formed in Wu Prefecture that needed to be eliminated before it overwhelmed the regional guardians led by the Bofu's father's chief strategist, Zhu Zhi.

Bofu's return to Wu Prefecture was greeted with relief by Zhu Zhi and his fellow defenders; Bofu could see that his local forces were exhausted as he moved toward the capital, and the ensemble that met him at the city gates – which included Zhu Zhi, Bofu's brother Sun Quan, Zhu Zhi's adopted son Zhu Ran and the young officer Chen Wu – were haggard from lack of sleep and dwindling morale.
"The Shanyue khan White Tiger is causing trouble already, and the bandit king Haixi Chen is moving slowly southward," Zhu Zhi reported as he escorted Bofu toward the governor's residence.
"We've seen a lot more organisation this time around from the Shanyue," Chen Wu said. "The pact with Haixi Chen has given them new spirit, as well."
"Brother!" Sun Quan cried.
"Not now, Quan," Bofu pleaded. "There's a lot to discuss."
"Zhou Tai is with you!" Quan said.
"Major Zhou is one of my best commanders," Bofu replied. "Why wouldn't he be? Go and study or something, and we'll talk later."

"You're a *major* now, Zhou Tai???" Quan exclaimed.

Bofu ignored his brother and continued on his way to the governor's residence: Sun Quan halted and watched his Bofu's entourage – which included the laconic Zhou Tai – with a growing sense of disappointment.

"Well, that's the end of you wanting him for a bodyguard, Zhongmou," Zhu Ran said as he walked to Sun Quan's side. "If he's a major, then-"

"I want that man to work for me," Quan insisted. "My brother's forces are in crisis, and I will be asked to do something to assist, I *know I will.*"

"...And at what point will your brother leave 'one of his best commanders' with you if he needs him to fight the Shanyue?" Zhu Ran said cynically. "Really, Zhongmou, I think that you should just-"

"I know that Zhou Tai is the right man to help me," Quan continued. "When he and I spoke, I knew that he was a noble, honest man that will always do the right thing."

"...Fine," Zhu Ran sighed.

"**HEY!**" Bofu yelled: he had stopped to summon Quan. "**I said we'd talk later, but that didn't mean you wouldn't have to listen to me now!**"

"My brother will give me Zhou Tai," Sun Quan said as he started to pursue Bofu.

Zhu Ran hummed musically and smiled as he followed Quan.

"Right," Bofu said as he took his host seat and received a document from Zhu Zhi. "So this 'Haixi Chen' is coming down here... while White Tiger and his new friends are... there."

"Here, there, what about it???" Han Dang heckled. "My lord, please just answer one question: what are we up against?"

"White Tiger has a considerable following this time," Bofu replied. "Not just his own tribespeople... now he's got bandits, pirates and disaffected 'commoners' aiding him. It seems that a lot of people have been talked into thinking that our being here is bad for them. This other man, 'Haixi Chen', is probably bringing an army of tens of thousands with him to Wu, and his intention is as I already told you: to make Wu into an independent state, like Hanzhong, only for his own kind. He's obviously told the Shanyue that they'll have autonomy too, so they're with him, sort of."

"An independent state...? He can't do that!" Han Dang said.

"Oh, yes he can, Mister Han," Zhu Zhi chortled. "Haven't you heard of *Zang Ba*...?"

"...Zang Ba...?" Han Dang said. "Zang... Ba... that bandit king in Mount Tai...? The one that people talk about that used to be a prison warden's son...?"

"The very same," Zhu Zhi replied. "You... you *are* aware, surely, that he took Mount Tai over, and then moved his followers into northern Xu Province and set up a-"

"Yeah," Han Dang interrupted. "There's so much going on these days that I needed to think for a minute. He's running Kaiyang now... which means you're right, this 'Haixi Chen' could do the same in Wu and get away with it."

"Years ago, that might've appealed," the former pirate Jiang Qin said. "But we can't allow that, Lord Sun. Question is, who do we attack first...?"

Lü Fan coughed deliberately and said, "That's something that Zhou Gongjin and I discussed, and-"

"*Ayah*... I thought that I wouldn't have to hear about that Zhou Yu now that he's in Danyang!" Cheng Pu complained. "He isn't the answer to everything!"

"...I did not say that he was, Mister Cheng," Lü Fan replied.

"And neither are *you*!" Cheng Pu continued. "Zhu Junli and I have brains too, and yet they are never consulted!"

Zhu Zhi smiled and looked at Bofu and Lü Fan in turn.

"Demou has a point," Bofu sighed. "How do we resolve this...?"

"...I was hoping to avoid such things, but here's what we'll do," Lü Fan said disappointedly. "Mister Cheng, let us take a brush and ink, some small pieces of paper, and write on those pieces of paper the answer to the question, 'Who do we attack first', and see if we are all in agreement."

Cheng Pu harrumphed and said, "Fine."

"Do we have time for this?" Chen Wu asked.

"It won't take long," Cheng Pu said as he snatched a piece of cloth paper and inked brush from Lü Fan and scrawled characters onto the paper; he then passed the brush to Zhu Zhi, who smiled dryly and wrote his own answer on his own piece of paper.

"I have already prepared my answer," Lü Fan said. "Shall we all show our thoughts to our lord and each other, gentlemen...?"

"Best answer wins a jar of wine," Bofu joked. "Alright then, children: answers."

Cheng Pu grunted irritably and raised his piece of paper: he had written 'Both at the same time'. Lü Fan raised his paper: he had written the same. Zhu Zhi laughed and revealed that his own contribution was identical.

"...Now of course, that proves a lot of things," Lü Fan said to a humbled Cheng Pu.

"Like what?" Cheng Pu grumbled.

"That we four are all equals among ourselves and betters to the rest," Lü Fan replied.

Cheng Pu smiled, laughed and said, "We certainly are, if 'Gongjin' agreed! So when do we march, Lord Sun...?"

"As soon as possible," Bofu said. "My only concern is that we're leaving our cities undermanned regardless of whether we attack our enemies simultaneously or not. I had to leave nearly a third of the men in Kuaiji with Han Yan and Dong Xi, and Gongjin needs the reserves to reinforce Danyang. Really, we can only have around a thousand men in the bigger cities and smaller militias in key villages."

Sun Quan came forward at that moment and said, "If there is any way that I could be of service, Elder Brother, then please give me your instructions."

"...I shall be bringing you along with me," Bofu replied. "But we need to speak about that *privately*, after this meeting."

Sun Quan smiled excitedly and said, "If I had Zhou Tai as my second, I-!"

"*Later*, Brother," Bofu interrupted. "The most important thing is how we split our forces now. Zhu Zhi, Uncle Sun Jing: you'll be your usual stalwart selves and guard Wu County. Lü Fan, Huang Gai, Han Dang, Jiang Qin, Chen Wu: you'll repel – and if it's at all

possible, *destroy* – the army led by Haixi Chen; you'll go and prepare for that immediately. Cheng Pu, Sun Hè, Ling Cao, Song Qian: we'll fight White Tiger's army; I shall join you shortly."
Zhou Tai was visibly confused at being given no task; each of the named men clasped their hands together in front of their chests and bowed, saying as one, "As you command."
"...Dismissed," Bofu said as he looked at his brother Quan.

Once the meeting was over and Bofu and Quan were alone, Bofu said, "I'm going to place a lot of faith in you, Quan."
"What would you have me do...?" Quan asked.
"We will be marching to Xuan City and using it as an initial base to attack the Shanyue from," Bofu explained. "I... I was pondering leaving you in charge of Xuan City when we're advancing after them. I... I want you to *guard Xuan*. But you have to promise me that you'll do things *properly*."
"Of *course I will*," Quan scoffed.
"No, Quan, don't give me that," Bofu said forcefully. "Since Father died, you've been different. You're less disciplined, and you're becoming-"
"Unreliable...?" Quan interrupted. "Reckless...? *Lazy...?*"
"...Your words, not mine," Bofu retorted. "Quan, you're my brother, and I love you as I love all of my family. But that means that I have to be honest, like Mother and Father always have been. You need to *grow up*."
Quan's eyes steeled.
"Don't get angry; you have no right," Bofu continued. "Father was reckless in battle, *sometimes*, but at home he was *always* a strict disciplinarian. Mother might allow Shangxiang some... 'freedom'... but she'll not tolerate disobedience. I want to be fair, but I have to be tough as well. You can't drink and mess about if I leave you in charge of Xuan."
"I understand your words," Quan replied. "Now *I* have a request, Elder Brother."
"...You seem to have taken a great liking to Zhou Tai," Bofu said knowingly. "I'd hope that if I assigned him to you, you'd learn from his disciplined ways and grow as a person. I'm aware that my newfound status as a 'minor warlord' puts me in danger, and as my brother, you're in danger too... so as much as I need men like Zhou Tai as the vanguard on this campaign... I'll leave him with you when-"
"You're assigning him to me???" Quan said excitedly.
"...*Temporarily*," Bofu replied carefully. "I'll need to have him on campaigns from time to time, but when I don't really need him, he can stay with you."
"You will not regret the decision, Brother!" Quan promised. "He and I will be like brothers and defend Xuan City as though it were our home!"
"...Yes, well, see that I *don't* regret it," Bofu muttered.
"...May I now ask a question...?" Quan said.
"Why not," Bofu sighed.
Quan lowered his head and asked, "Does it still hurt as much...? ...Losing our father, I mean. I feel so much hate for that bastard Huang Zu... and his master, Liu Biao, too. I want to see them cut open and their hearts torn out of their bodies."

"You should already know the answer if you truly know me, Quan," Bofu replied.

"You're hurting as much as me... I know that," Quan said.

"What you really want to know is why I haven't told Yuan Shu that I want to go into Jing... am I right...?" Bofu asked.

Quan snorted quietly and averted his gaze before he replied, "You can't... I know that too. He's your master, and-"

"Once, I had to stand and watch while my father – our father – tried to explain why we were all in Jing, and I remember feeling just like you do now: hurt, offended, angry, and... a-and in a way, I... I-I suppose I was ashamed of him."

Bofu's confession caused Quan to look at him with widened eyes.

"I was ashamed because I didn't understand, and now I do," Bofu continued. "He had no choice but to take us all into Jing, just as I have no choice but to fight here in Yang, doing all this work so that our wonderful lord Yuan Shu can congratulate himself on his amazing talent for stealing territory from the empire. I'm the hireling of a jealous thief."

Quan's eyes filled with tears.

"And I know that makes you ashamed," Bofu chortled. "I know that it makes *me* feel ashamed... I know that Dad was ashamed... but one day, it'll be different."

Quan averted his gaze once again.

"One day, Yuan Shu'll give us the excuse we need to break ties: he can't help it, he's so stupid and greedy and demented," Bofu continued. "And all we have to do to make it happen is to keep winning for him, more and more and more... until we've won so much for him that he'll accidentally set us free. And then we won't need to feel ashamed anymore, Quan: we'll be our own masters, and everything that we won for him will become ours, at least until- ...well, I should explain that later, I think, when the time's right. But until then, you have to trust me. Do you trust me...?"

Quan looked at Bofu and whispered, "Yes, Brother, I do."

"Right: and I'm going to trust you to look after Xuan City for me, you and Zhou Tai," Bofu said with a reassuring smile.

Sun Quan returned the smile, but its sincerity was questionable.

Zhou Tai was not the only man that was surprised by the division of forces.

"Why does the boy separate us when we are more likely to work effectively as a team...?" Han Dang asked of Huang Gai and Cheng Pu as they walked the corridors of the mansion. "Why would I want to take orders from Lü Fan?"

"I think that he makes a point... a valid point," Huang Gai replied. "We like to think of ourselves as the 'veterans', and yet we assume that this is somehow a rebuke of some kind: I see it as something else entirely."

"...Lü Fan might want to learn as much *from* us as he dictates *to* us," Cheng Pu said.

"Yes, and you will be in Xuan to watch over our boisterous young lord rather than a friend that might not remonstrate as you will," Huang Gai continued.

"Put like that, I'm a little less peeved," Han Dang chuckled. "He'd better not boss me about, though, that Lü Fan, or I'll slap him."

"I'm sure that he knows that you would," Cheng Pu replied. "Ah, well... I know we'll get other chances to say it, but good luck to you both."

"We'll be fine, Demou," Huang Gai insisted. "This 'Haixi Chen' will be no problem."

Bofu's armies left Wu County City and went their separate ways: Lü Fan's force went north to intercept Haixi Chen, and Bofu went east to confront White Tiger. The latter force stopped at the city of Xuan and camped in and around its walls: once the preparations were complete, Bofu left the city in the care of Sun Quan and Zhou Tai and advanced on White Tiger's main camp.

"...I wonder how long they'll take," Sun Quan said as he stood on Xuan's battlements and watched Bofu's army move further and further away from the city.

"Lord Sun, we should reinforce the city properly," Zhou Tai suggested. "We should have men outside the city watching for attacks by-"

"I wish that Zhu Yifeng was here too," Quan interrupted. "Still, his 'father' wanted him at his side, and I understand that. Yifeng and I have been friends since we were young children, Major Zhou: did you know that...?"

"You have told me that before, Lord Sun, yes," Zhou Tai replied.

Sun Quan started down the steps that led to the city grounds: as he moved, more and more of the officials that he had been left to command gathered around him and observed his youthful indifference with concern.

"...We need to set up reconnaissance towers and posts around the city," Zhou Tai protested. "Lord Sun, the Shanyue-"

Sun Quan yawned theatrically and said, "I am tired from the long march. Perhaps a banquet will lift our flagging spirits!"

The other officials eyed each other nervously.

"...That's not recommended," Zhou Tai replied. "Please heed my-!"

"Major Zhou, the Shanyue are cowards that are soon to taste the blades of our army," Quan said confidently. "I would like to hear more about your days as a pirate: perhaps you could entertain us at the banquet."

One official sighed involuntarily.

Sun Quan wheeled around and shouted, "**I heard that! What sort of message do we men of the south send to the world by acting as though we're scared of the barbarians, uh...? Only timid pedants sigh at times like these!**"

The guilty official lowered his head and retreated silently.

"There is no need for defence," Quan continued. "Didn't my father once hold banquets and unnerve Xu Rong, Dong Zhuo's deadliest general, with his utter indifference to an impending charge...?"

Zhou Tai frowned and replied, "Yes, but-!"

"We're in a strong position," Sun Quan insisted. "We have *how many men* at our disposal...?"

"...About six-hundred," a guard captain replied. "But they're mostly volun-"

"That's right: about six *hundreds*," Quan said with a tone that made 'hundreds' sound as grand as 'tens of thousands'. "How are we weak...? Father repelled a whole army of bandits *on his own*, they're such cowards. They'd have to attack here in their *millions* for six-hundred to be anything less than *terrifying*."

Zhou Tai motioned to speak, but Quan smiled and added, "And I don't want to hear that anyone went ahead and made plans for camps and the like... I'm the Acting Magistrate at my brother's decree, so I'll be *heeded*, okay...?"
Zhou Tai's shoulders slumped as he replied, "As you command."
The 14-year-old Sun Quan laughed as he turned to walk away, and then he said, "Let's try and show some strength, shall we...? Bandits and barbarians *smell fear*."
"...*Naïve fool*," one local junior officer muttered disdainfully.
Zhou Tai did not respond to the words: instead, he shook his head disappointedly and followed his young master with his elite unit.

****

71

White Tiger's mostly Shanyue tribal forces awaited Bofu's arrival with interest but little concern; Bofu set up a fenced base camp and convened a meeting with Cheng Pu, Sun Hè, Song Qian and Ling Cao.

"We need to finish this campaign as quickly as possible," Bofu began. "Gongjin, Gongjin's uncle Shang and Xu Kun are all writing to say that-"

"We know," Cheng Pu interrupted.

"...It was for Ling Cao's benefit," Bofu continued. "Ling Cao is not aware of the threat posed by the bandits in Danyang. What I want to know is how they're so effective; who's leading them...?"

"I think that 'Gongjin', 'Gongjin's uncle Shang' and your cousin can cope with a few mountain bandits for a while longer," Cheng Pu replied. "How are we finishing this campaign quickly...? How do we break White Tiger...?"

"The old-fashioned way," Bofu said. "We hit them hard."

"...Your friend Lü Fan must have given you some sort of stratagem," Cheng Pu pleaded.

"Not really," Bofu chuckled. "He just said that-"

"But they outnumber us!" Cheng Pu cried. "You didn't even split the forces properly, so we have to rely on your bodyguards as field generals, which leaves you more exposed! We have to have something planned other than 'Charge them', or we'll be destroyed!"

"Panic, panic, panic... Wu Jing would be proud!" Bofu teased.

"*Ayah*! Why do you have to compare me to him whenever I volunteer advice on caution?" Cheng Pu despaired. "White Tiger isn't a normal opponent! He might have Xu Gong aiding him, and Haixi Chen is collaborating with him...!"

"...Or, on the other hand, he could just be a stupid thug that has the same plan as me: 'Hit hard'," Bofu retorted. "Let's see."

"No, let's *not* see!" Cheng Pu cried. "Last time you were flippant, you were shot in the leg! Must I wear white my whole life???"

Bofu's false joviality faded, and he said, "Please don't fret, Demou. We've looked at his battle lines since your scouts reported his numbers, and there're already signs of in-fighting amongst the tribes that he commands. We're going to employ scatter tactics, like the ones my father used against the tribes in Changsha."

"...You discussed it with Junli," Cheng Pu supposed.

"We did; Lü Ziheng and me both," Bofu said. "Oh, and Ziheng asked me to tell you that he is 'in awe of your exploits' whilst serving Dad; he studies your notes and comments 'as if they were composed by Sun Tzu or Wu Qi'."

"...Your friend overpraises me, Lord Sun," Cheng Pu replied apologetically. "Junli was-"

"Don't be modest, Cheng Demou," Bofu said. "I follow your well-trod path because it is stable and proven, and so does Ziheng, who was the one that suggested that you come with me instead of going with 'the others'."

Cheng Pu smiled and said, "Here I am, feeling neglected as usual, and my words are used without prompting as 'guidance'! Very well, Lord Sun... my men are ready, of course, for such things, so a word is all that I and they need."

Bofu grinned and said, "Let's show 'White Tiger' that the son of the 'Tiger of Jiangdong' is here!"

"Let me charge them!" Ling Cao pleaded.

Bofu laughed and replied, "That's what you're here for, Ling Cao."

White Tiger Yan brought his forces close to Bofu's camp and started a routine of heckling and displays of strength; Bofu had his men carry out their drills as normal until the Shanyue warriors tired, at which point Bofu's army left their camp and arrayed professionally.

"...Sun Ce is up to something," White Tiger's brother, Yan Yu, suggested.

"Let him plot!" White Tiger chuckled. "We have a plan too, and we're more and stronger!"

The Shanyue began another show of strength; Ling Cao rode to the front of Bofu's force and shouted, "**HERE IS LING CAO! WHERE IS WHITE TIGER?**"

"...Who is that? Who is 'Ling Cao'?" White Tiger scoffed. "Why does Sun Ce send *that* against me? Is Sun Ce hurt?"

"If he is, we'll win quickly!" Yan Yu replied.

Ling Cao rode back and forth, shouting, "**HERE IS LING CAO! WHY DOESN'T WHITE TIGER FACE ME? IS HE AFRAID...? ARE YOU COWARDS?**"

The Shanyue men that heard the taunt started to holler insults and demand that they be allowed to charge; Yan Yu turned to White Tiger and said, "I'll challenge him."

"Yes!" White Tiger chuckled. "Go."

Yan Yu and his elite unit moved forward to confront Ling Cao.

"Who's this...?" Bofu asked.

"...It must be Yan Yu, White Tiger's brother," Cheng Pu replied. "We should warn Ling Cao; Yan Yu is as fearsome as White Tiger."

"There won't be a need for that," Bofu suggested. "They're letting him know."

The Shanyue were yelping and hollering Yan Yu's name as he moved his horse back and forth and gestured confidently.

"**COME AND FIGHT!**" Ling Cao shrieked.

"**I hope he holds his nerve,**" Cheng Pu shouted over the chorus of battle chants, drums and heckles. "**If he falters, our men might-**"

Ling Cao charged at Yan Yu before Cheng Pu could finish; the two men exchanged blows for several minutes before Ling Cao finally retreated.

"*Aiee...* **we needed a victory there!**" Cheng Pu exclaimed.

"**No we didn't,**" Bofu replied. "**Nobody is fleeing, and they think they've won; it's time to let them have it! Sound the gong, Demou!**"

Cheng Pu ordered the battle-gong to be struck; Ling Cao wheeled around and made another dash at White Tiger's front lines, and most of the rest of Bofu's army followed. Yan Yu held his ground and clashed with Ling Cao again, forcing a second retreat; it was only Cheng Pu's deployment of archers that repelled the Shanyue and forced them to withdraw to their original positions.

"**It's no good!**" Cheng Pu cried. "**They're too many in number and too confident! Yan Yu has given them spirit! We'll have**

to bluff and retreat to camp!"
Bofu gestured toward the Shanyue lines; it was clear that White Tiger was also contemplating a retreat.
"We were lucky today," Cheng Pu said as the Shanyue began a cautious withdrawal.
"...Yeah, we were," Bofu murmured.
"I admit, it complicates things," Cheng Pu replied.
"But we didn't lose," Bofu said. **"That may be important."**
Cheng Pu smiled as he watched the last lines of Shanyue warriors skulking away; he nodded and muttered, "It is. They *respect us*."

The two sides would meet several times, in major battlefield encounters and minor skirmishes; each time, Ling Cao and Yan Yu showed fortitude and ended the encounter as a stalemate.
One night, after a field battle, a messenger from the Shanyue confederacy brought a request from Yan Yu for an audience with Bofu.
"Do we honour the request...?" Bofu asked of Cheng Pu.
"I don't see why they would want to meet," Cheng Pu admitted. "I have a suspicion, but it's too ridiculous to give expression to."
"We're probably sharing that suspicion, Demou, but do I agree to it?" Bofu asked.
"It's entirely up to you, Lord Sun," Cheng Pu replied. "There's only one answer, after all."
"...But so many ways to deliver it," Bofu murmured.
"...Indeed," Cheng Pu said. "Your father had a similar dilemma once, provided my suspicion is correct."
"We'll hear him out as soon as possible," Bofu declared.
Sun Hè grunted quietly.

As dawn broke on the following morning, Yan Yu approached Bofu's camp with a small group of confident Shanyue warriors. Bofu met the subordinate chieftain on the open space in front of his command tent and began discussions by bowing slightly and saying, "Why did you come here, Yan Yu?"
Yan Yu failed to return the bow; he smirked and said, "We outnumber you, Sun Ce. We have Chen Yu from Haixi as a friend with a big army: you had to split yours, we know this. Time after time, I defeated your general."
Ling Cao was restrained by his subordinates, but he managed to shout, **"HERE AND NOW, YAN YU! HERE AND NOW! HERE IS LING CAO: LET'S SETTLE THIS HERE AND NOW!"**
"ENOUGH!" Bofu ordered, and Ling Cao ended his demonstration. Bofu then turned back to Yan Yu and his amused subordinates and said, "Your forces have not won. Mine have not won... yet. You haven't seen what we can do."
"We fight your people all the time!" Yan Yu taunted. "Every time, you turn to silly tricks to get out of trouble! I have never been beaten! That man there, other men that come here... all weak! I fight 'Chen Wu', I fight 'Ling Cao', I fight 'Sun Ben'. But they are all weak! We were always stronger without Chen Yu from Haixi, so with him, aren't we even more strong...? What happens, then, 'Sun Ce', when you run out of tricks...?"
Cheng Pu leant forward and whispered, "End this discussion *now*, Lord Sun."

Bofu smiled, ignored Cheng Pu's plea and said, "When we run out of tricks, we fight harder."

The Shanyue warriors laughed quietly.

"You're strong, we like that," Yan Yu said with a smile. "You're brave, we like that too. Chen Yu from Haixi says, 'Ask if we can all be friends'. White Tiger says, 'We can all be friends'. Perhaps that is better than *dying*, Sun Ce...?"

"... So you came here to suggest an alliance between us...?" Bofu prompted.

"Live side-by-side," Yan Yu replied. "Your people, our people... you don't like the Han, Chen Yu from Haixi does not like the Han, Shanyue don't like the Han, so why argue? Why not forget fighting and work together, live together, trade together? That's what Chen Yu from Haixi says. That's what White Tiger says."

"Uh huh," Bofu said nonchalantly. "You know what *I* say...?"

Sun Hè sensed a sudden change in Bofu's intent and readied himself for something.

"...What do you say...?" Yan Yu retorted cautiously.

Bofu snorted a laugh, turned sideways and looked at the floor; his stance was casual, and gave no warning of the sudden drawing of his sword and the violent slash that followed. Yan Yu was quick enough to recoil and draw his own sword, but Bofu fought his way past the Shanyue warrior's defences, knocked his sword-arm to one side and plunged his own blade into his opponent's stomach. The Shanyue warriors shrank back in horror as Yan Yu – who was not only the brother of their khan, but a champion in his own right – staggered backwards, groaned like an overworked ox and collapsed to the ground.

"I think we understand each other," Bofu said to the surviving Shanyue. "Take him, get out, go back, and tell his brother two things: that he's next, and that there's only room for one tiger in Yang Province, and here it is."

The Shanyue were too shocked to challenge Bofu's followers, who now surrounded them with their swords drawn; they dragged Yan Yu's lifeless body out of the camp and retreated.

"How *dare he*," Bofu scoffed.

"...Lord Sun...!" Ling Cao gasped; his words signalled a chorus of awestruck and respectful chants from the other men.

Cheng Pu gestured to a group of thin, short, unassuming soldiers that then began a quiet retreat from the camp, and then he smiled, bowed humbly and said, "Lord Sun, you are your father's son... but... please, tell me that you were nervous."

"If I was, I was too scared to notice," Bofu quipped as he entered his command tent.

Cheng Pu shook his head and muttered, "I can scarcely believe it."

"Neither can I," Sun Hè said. "That was either the smartest thing he ever did, or an act of self-destructive stupidity: either way, it left an impression."

Cheng Pu and Sun Hè followed their lord into the command tent; Bofu was sat at his host seat, looking over a map. Many soldiers were still chatting excitedly and hollering, so Bofu said, "Any chance of them quietening down a bit...?"

"Not really!" Cheng Pu chuckled. "So what next...?"

"White Tiger has got to decide whether anger or fear wins his heart," Bofu replied. "If it was me, I'd probably descend on this

camp with everything I had. But he might surrender. Either way, he's just lost a man that everyone respects, idolises and fears, and how he died will have left them all feeling rattled."
Cheng Pu stopped smiling, sighed and said, "I think I know that feeling, Lord Sun."
"He won't surrender to 'us'," Sun Hè suggested. "He'd sooner die."
"Then we're going to fight again," Bofu replied. "That's fine: we have the morale advantage now that we were missing before. Demou...?"
"Mm...? Oh, uh... I already sent scouts to pursue and survey, so we won't be caught unawares," Cheng Pu promised.
"Good," Bofu said. "Now our only enemies are luck and stupidity."
Sun Hè hummed thoughtfully and said, "Yes..."

White Tiger reacted angrily and fearfully to the news that his brother had been slain: he had his followers carry out a series of attack on Bofu's camp, but none of them were successful. The Shanyue forces were showing caution, and the sight of Bofu riding to the front line was enough to make some warriors refuse to charge: White Tiger had lost his psychological advantage, just as Bofu had hoped for. As long as nothing went wrong, victory was almost assured.

****

72

While Bofu's Xuan encampment was cautiously enjoying the signs of an impending victory, Xuan City itself was being forced to adopt a casual atmosphere on the orders of its chosen guardian, Sun Quan. The magistrate's mansion was the scene of relatively ostentatious evening banquets hosted by Sun Quan himself, and he additionally insisted upon musicians, dancers and an overly generous supply of wine. That had been the case since Bofu had departed, and this night was no different.

"I *implore you*, Lord Sun, to enhance our defences!" Zhou Tai whispered to a drunk, indifferent Sun Quan. "There are reports that-!"

"Ah, yes... 'Lord Sun'... I like that," Sun Quan sniggered. "Zhou Tai, you're disappointing me! Day after day after day, you whinge! Stop being a pedant like the others! With a show of strength like this, who would dare strike at us?"

Zhou Tai grunted angrily and returned to his meal.

"**More wine!**" Sun Quan giggled. "**More wine, more food!**"

One official leant sideways and said to a colleague, "You'd not think there was a famine not a border away, the way he's acting."

"Hush!" the other official hissed. "You want us both executed???"

Sun Quan was transfixed on the dancing girls; the first official scoffed and said, "He won't notice; is he *really* Sun Ce's brother...?"

Zhou Tai noted the various disdainful conversations that were taking place, but he did nothing to reprimand the guilty; he was more concerned about hidden dangers.

When the banquet finally ended, the irritated officials and officers returned to their appointed residences; some were placed in barracks and tents, but some officials were staying in the homes of mid-ranking Xuan City officials. Zhou Tai escorted his inebriated lord Sun Quan to his quarters, all the while listening for signs of trouble.

"You... worry too much, Zhou Tai," Sun Quan heckled. "You need... to relax! You never drank... any wine... why not...?"

"The whole point of my being assigned as your bodyguard was to watch out for you," Zhou Tai replied with decreasing patience. "Please work with me, my lord, or I will be forced to carry you."

Sun Quan snickered childishly and doubled his efforts to walk.

"I will wait outside your room," Zhou Tai said.

"Don't do that, man!" Sun Quan giggled. "Go and sleep! There's nothing t'be worried about, I told you that!"

"...I will leave momentarily, Lord Sun, and check on defences," Zhou Tai said.

"Go and sleep, Zhou Youping!" Sun Quan protested. "What good are you without sleep?"

Zhou Tai muttered incoherently as he settled Sun Quan onto his raised bed. He turned to the fawning servants and said, "Watch him," and then he retreated.

The five servants formed a human screen across one side of Sun Quan's bed.

"...Go away," Sun Quan ordered, and the servants obeyed.

"Day after day, night after night... the same," one official complained as he walked through the streets of Xuan City with three colleagues. "Open gates in the day, banquets and no guards at night... no guard towers... no checks on traders... nothing. Anything could happen!"

The other officials murmured agreeably. They separated and went to their individual residences, leaving one official to walk alone. But that official did not reach the safety of a house; a sudden din preceded the appearance of a multitude of Shanyue warriors – on foot and on horseback – that cut down anything they saw as they charged through the unguarded city.

"AYAH! HELP! BARBARIANS!" the lone official cried: they were his last words.

The cries of the Shanyue warriors' victims reached Zhou Tai as he was on his way back to the magistrate's residence. He turned back to retrieve a horse from the barracks, knowing that would cost him time; he had no choice, because he did not know what faced him when he reached his lord. The soldiers were completely unprepared for the assault, which began at one wall and quickly became a pincer attack when infiltrators opened all four sets of city gates from inside: soon there were thousands of Shanyue inside and outside of the city, and there would be no easy escape. Zhou Tai rode through the streets at speed, cutting down Shanyue men on foot and horse as he went.

"What's going on???" Sun Quan said as his servants finally roused him: the Shanyue were already inside the residential complex, so he did not have much time.

"Barbarians!" one servant cried as he pulled a mail shirt over Sun Quan's head. **"Quick, Master! Armour, you'll need armour! They'll soon be here!"**

The panic sobered Sun Quan greatly, and he ran into the yard to find his horse; most of his servants were already dead, and the Shanyue were moments away.

"Bastards... **bastards!**" Sun Quan cried as he ran to his horse and leapt into the saddle; the Shanyue arrived at that point, whereupon they cut the last of his servants down and surrounded him as he tried to leave the walled yard.

"Get away! GET AWAY!" Sun Quan shrieked as Shanyue men lunged and swiped with their swords; fortune spared him from wounds, but his saddle was slashed and left close to useless. It was at that point that Zhou Tai and a small band of horsemen finally arrived: Zhou cut his way through the dozens of Shanyue and reached his lord.

"Follow me, Lord Sun!" Zhou Tai ordered.

"I SHALL!" Sun Quan replied hysterically. **"I SHALL, ZHOU TAI, I SHALL!"**

Zhou Tai was already a mess of blood and gore, and some of that blood was his own; he led Sun Quan out of the residential yard and through the streets of Xuan City, hacking men down as he went, and his actions inspired others to do their best to survive the attack together.

"Repel... them... REPEL THEM!" Zhou Tai barked, and the message carried. The newfound unity spread, and small pockets of soldiers and civilians started to turn the tide against the Shanyue attackers; the Shanyue had not expected any resistance, so they started to retreat once their victory would prove costly to them. Zhou Tai left his lord with a small group of his own elite followers, and then he led the final charge against the last of the Shanyue at the northern gate: he chased them as far the dry moat, screaming wildly as he did so. But his efforts had been costly and draining; once all four sides of the city were once again closed to intruders, Zhou Tai rode back to Sun Quan, who was still hysterical.

"…**ZHOU TAI!**" Sun Quan shrieked. "**ZHOU YOUPING! ZHOU YOUPING!**"

"You are… unhurt, Lord… Lord Sun…?" the near-unrecognisable Zhou Tai asked politely.

"**Yes, I… I am alive! I am alive!**" Sun Quan replied.

Some of the survivors exchanged glances that did nothing to hide their anger and frustration.

"…Good," Zhou Tai replied.

"**Zhou Tai… Zh-Zhou Tai! You're hurt, Zhou Tai!**" Sun Quan realised at last.

"I… need rest, Lord Sun," Zhou Tai replied as he fell from his horse and collapsed to his knees on the ground.

"A doctor… **a doctor!**" Sun Quan cried. "**Where is a doctor??? One of you fools get a doctor! If Zhou Tai dies, I…! WHERE IS A DOCTOR???**"

A physician happened to be nearby, treating an official that had a serious facial laceration; the official demanded that Zhou Tai be treated first, so the physician hurried to the fallen hero.

"Will he live…?" Sun Quan asked; when he received no response, he shook the physician and shrieked, "**WILL HE LIVE???**"

"**Yes, Lord Sun! Yes, he will!**" the physician replied angrily. "**Leave me to my work, please! Someone help me get Mister Zhou to the barracks infirmary! And someone take Lord Sun to his home!**"

Four men rushed to Zhou Tai and started to lower him to the ground while two others went to the infirmary to fetch a stretcher to place him on.

"My servants… are *dead*," Sun Quan recalled as two irritated soldiers led him away. "But Zhou Tai, he… … …**DON'T DIE, ZHOU TAI! DON'T DIE! HOW WILL THE WORLD GO ON WITHOUT ZHOU TAI??? ZHOU TAI!**"

"…It could go on without Sun Quan," one official whined as he looked at what was left of his writing hand. "*Damn him*… this didn't have to happen! If only he'd-!"

"Hush," another official said. "He's our lord's brother… we must remember that."

"Someone… someone watch… the young lord," Zhou Tai said deliriously as he was carried to the infirmary. "He… needs… protecting… from… them…"

"Yes, and *we* need protecting from *him*," one stretcher-bearer muttered angrily.

"N-no!" Zhou Tai scolded. "He… made… a mistake. All men… make mistakes…"

****

73

Bofu's reaction to the events in Xuan City was obvious to any that knew him well.

"...**FOOL!**"

Bofu slammed the cloth report onto his writing table and started to breathe noisily; his cousin and bodyguard Sun Hè was watching silently while Cheng Pu tried to think of helpful things to say.

"Bloody... *fool*...!" Sun Ce whined.

"...He's alive," Cheng Pu suggested.

"It's more than he deserves!" Bofu cried. **"He caused one of my best men to be sliced up! My stupid brother nearly ruined the whole campaign – no, he nearly got us all *killed*! If Zhou Tai hadn't been what this report calls 'some kind of super-man', we'd have lost Xuan to the Shanyue and been caught in a pincer with no warning! I've half a mind to disown the little-!"**

"He's your kin," Cheng Pu interrupted. "You're angry now, but-"

"Yeah, I know, I'll forgive him," Bofu wheezed. "I shouldn't, but I will... oh, my... my chest feels like it's going to explode; I haven't felt like this since... since Dad died."

"For some reason, I feel as though I need to apologise," Cheng Pu said suddenly.

"Yeah... so do I!" Bofu chuckled ironically. "Who to, I don't know, but... yeah, I know what you mean. We'll need to go back and reinforce Xuan, then, before White Tiger realises that we have no rear guard."

"I suppose so," Cheng Pu said.

"...I suppose it might have been accidental fate," Bofu said as he got to his feet. "I killed White Tiger's brother unexpectedly, and he nearly got mine; in both cases, the dead brother had it coming through short-sighted, stubborn ignorance. Isn't there something in Buddhism about that...? Things you did wrong coming back to haunt you...?"

"I believe there is," Cheng Pu replied. "I forget what it's called... I can't think straight right now."

"No... neither can I, Demou," Bofu said. "So many died, a lot of them civilians that got no chance to hide, and soldiers that got no chance to defend themselves: I hope that Quan's proud of himself."

"...I'm afraid to ask, Lord Sun, but... will Zhou Tai be alright...?" Cheng Pu prompted.

"Oh, uh... yes, so the doctor says, yeah," Bofu replied. "He's... he's badly cut up, Demou... 'Ten or more bad cuts', it says. I tell you, though, that if he makes it, he'll get more rewards from me than... than... *aiee.*"

"Why groan like that?" Cheng Pu asked.

"Rewards for saving my brother," Bofu chortled. "It... just seemed wrong to say it. Anyhow, I, uh... need a walk. Not outside... just around the camp. I wouldn't want to put anyone in unnecessary danger... not today. Bohai...?"

The silent, ponderous Sun Hè followed Bofu out of the tent.

"The poor lad," Cheng Pu said aloud. "As he just said, he places us all at risk when he does something reckless, just like poor Wentai used to; but *this*..."

"...*Should* I forgive him, Bohai?" Bofu asked as he walked around the camp with his cousin.
"He's like a brother to me too, Bofu," Sun Hè replied. "It's the wrong question."
"Yeah... the real question is, 'Do I trust him with anything else?'" Bofu chortled. "The proper answer to that, of course, is 'No, of course not, because he is a fool', but... but as his brother, and as a warlord – and that is what I'm becoming – I have to appoint him in some role or other, don't I...?"
"Perhaps... perhaps he'll grow up a bit now, Bofu," Sun Hè suggested.
"He's my eldest brother, Bohai, so he has to 'grow up', if that's the actual problem," Bofu replied. "He *has to*: I need him to help me, not... not *ruin us*."

White Tiger's scouts reported Bofu's paced withdrawal to Xuan, whereupon he ordered a full-scale attack; Bofu's forces halted and met the attack with equal ferocity.
"**KILL SUN CE!**" White Tiger shrieked. "**KILL SUN CE! RICHES FOR THE MAN THAT KILLS SUN CE!**"
The Shanyue were motivated by what they perceived to be their enemies' sudden show of weakness, so they charged without fear or restraint.
"**My brother's actions have left us at a disadvantage!**" Bofu complained. "**Curse his idiocy, Bohai! I should make him beg forgiveness for this!**"
Sun Hè was too busy repelling attacks to respond; Bofu was so driven by anger that he was leaving himself open, and his bodyguards bore the brunt of that. Suddenly, Bofu spotted an opportunity to charge at a prominent chieftain and acted on instinct: he broke away from his protectors and galloped toward his target alone.
"**Song Qian!**" Sun Hè cried. "**Song Qian, save him quickly!**"
Bofu's bodyguard Song Qian did as he was asked and rode after his lord; Bofu had already cut down the Shanyue chieftain, but the latter's warriors had not scattered at the sight of it. Song Qian joined his master and aided him in returning to relative safety.
"**Do you know what I'm thinking???**" Sun Hè shrieked at Bofu, who was visibly embarrassed at his own actions. The battle was nearing a natural end, however, and White Tiger called for a general retreat shortly thereafter.
"...We need to hurry to the city, Lord Sun," Cheng Pu said when he reached Bofu.
"Is it under attack again?" Bofu asked worriedly.
"No, but there's the risk of it," Cheng Pu replied. "Without Zhou Tai, the city has no real guardian."
"...Send Song Qian," Bofu ordered. "I'll not be making any more reckless moves, so-"
"Oh, no-no-no," Sun Hè chortled. "You always say that, Cousin. You always say that you're 'not going to do anything else', and then a man couldn't count to ten before-!"
"It's a weakness," Bofu interrupted. "I don't know... maybe we got it from Dad."

Cheng Pu sighed miserably and said, "Perhaps you did, Lord Sun... perhaps you did."

"The city needs Song Qian more than the world needs Sun Ce," Bofu continued, "so until we can organise something more permanent, Song Qian can go and aid the defence of-"

"I shall go as well," Cheng Pu said. "As you say, the city needs defending, and we need the city to hold in order to win. But remember that you have no counsel, so... so please, do whatever bluffing is needed and then withdraw to the city."

"My thanks, Demou," Bofu replied. "We'll meet again soon."

Once Cheng Pu and Song Qian had ridden away to prepare their forces, Bofu groaned miserably.

"...I did not mean to humiliate you, Cousin," Sun Hè said. "I was-"

"It... needed saying," Bofu replied. "We need to set up another camp to fortify against the Shanyue... and hope that we don't lose any more valuable men. Zhou Tai nearly died because of my brother, but... you and Song Qian have almost died here because of me. Zu Mao died at the same time as my father... and then there's the men whose names people won't ever know or remember, except maybe their families; it's like Dad always said, they're all heroes, every one of them. But most of those corpses are just corpses to me... I don't know every man's name... and that's not right."

"I know, Cousin," Sun Hè said gently.

****

74

Bofu was unable to advance to Xuan City, so he turned his army and moved toward the Shanyue once again; the move alarmed Cheng Pu, who wrote to Bofu to demand an explanation.

"What can I do?" Bofu said as he lowered Cheng Pu's correspondence to his table. "He must know that I have no choice! While we were seen to be retreating, we got no peace!"

"He's concerned about the split in our forces," Sun Hè said.

"I know, but I didn't design things to be this way!" Bofu replied.

"He's right to be concerned," Sun Hè continued. "The battle today was almost a rout, had it not been for a few bold men and a few-"

"My lord! Lord Sun!"

Bofu and Sun Hè turned to the command tent's entrance, where an infantry major was kowtowing and whining. Bofu supposed that there was an attack underway, so he leapt to his feet and said, **"Which way are they coming from???"**

"There is no attack!" the major replied. **"A *murder*, Lord Sun! A murder, but I beseech you to hear the facts before-!"**

"Who murdered who???" Bofu cried. **"Don't I have enough problems??? Who is this selfish bastard that ruins my campaign??? ...And who are *you*, for that matter...?"**

"This is Major Yuan," Sun Hè reported. "He's not a direct relation of Lord Yuan Shu, before you ask; he's served since our reclamation of Danyang."

"...Right," Bofu said as calmly as he could. "Alright, Major Yuan: who killed who, and what is it that I 'have to know'...?"

"A man called 'Lü Meng', from Fupo in Runan, is the guilty man, Lord Sun!" Major Yuan replied. "He came to us with a Captain Deng Dang, also from Fupo!"

"Ziheng comes from Runan," Sun Hè said. "...Is he a relation...?"

"Perhaps, perhaps not: there are a lot of Lüs in the world, like *Lü Bu*," Bofu said. "Major Yuan, I'm tired; what happened, exactly...?"

"He was being taunted by an official, a Mister Dai," Major Yuan replied. "He killed him in anger! But his case is unique, Lord Sun! Please, you must-!"

"I have an idea, but you'll need to find Ling Cao and then fetch this man and bring him here, Major," Bofu interrupted; he then turned to Sun Hè and said, "We'll have him brought here so we can hear him out... d'you see anything wrong with that...?"

"Not at all," Sun Hè replied. "Let me assist you, Major."

Sun Hè helped Major Yuan to his feet and ushered him from the tent: the major then hurried to where Lü Meng was being held.

"...What a night," Sun Hè said as he returned to Bofu's side.

"My brother *sends* my men to their graves, I *lead them there*, and then there's this 'Lü Meng' that just kills them himself," Bofu grumbled. "Are we going to win, Bohai, with so much of our own idiocy working against us...?"

"I think I know Deng Dang," Sun Hè replied. "If he's who I think he is, then I think I know this 'Lü Meng', and... and it may be that you need to hear this story."

Bofu hummed thoughtfully and said, "Now I'm curious."

Ling Cao arrived at Bofu's command tent within an hour.

"I have not been too long, I hope," Ling Cao said uneasily.

"I take it that you've been told the story already," Bofu prompted.

"...I have, my lord," Ling Cao replied.

"So go on, then," Bofu prompted. "Tell me the story."

Ling Cao coughed nervously and said, "Lü Meng is Captain Deng Dang's brother-in-law, and he is three years younger than you, Lord Sun. He has no rank, because he is here voluntarily, thus not part of your army."

"Oh...?" Bofu exclaimed. "He wants to fight that badly...?"

"It seems so, Lord Sun," Ling Cao replied. "He is from a poor family, so he 'wants the opportunity to become great'. The men that he fights alongside all call him an inspiration, since he 'fights like a hero' and 'always comes to the aid of men in trouble'... little did I know that I'd met him on the field a few times myself! Captain Deng has tried to send him home repeatedly – home being Danyang, since his family migrated from Fupo – but Lü Meng always refuses to go; additionally, Meng's mother has been convinced – by *Lü Meng himself* – that he is doing the right thing."

"A headstrong man, indeed," Bofu sighed. After a moment of thought, he added, "So why did he kill Mister Dai?"

"Firstly I should say that Mister Dai was a pedant," Ling Cao replied. "He chided Lü Meng at every opportunity, I'm told, calling him a 'boy', a 'pup', and labelling his unrequested acts of recklessness in battle as 'suicidal idiocy'."

Bofu laughed awkwardly and said, "I shouldn't empathise, but I do. So he killed Mister Dai in a fit of rage? I'd never do that, so I can't entirely sympathise."

"Of course," Ling Cao replied. "But he turned himself in to Major Yuan immediately afterward, despite others giving him alternative advice, and Captain Deng has been petitioning to be punished with him, demanding that he be held responsible for allowing Lü Meng to be here at all. Major Yuan and Captain Deng are both outside, waiting to beg for clemency on his behalf."

"And Lü Meng...?" Bofu asked.

"He's outside as you asked," Ling Cao replied. "I know that I should not say this, Lord Sun, but... but he's quite remarkable, and killing him would be a waste."

"...Your valued opinion is noted," Bofu said. "Alright then, I'll-"

"**Lord Sun! Lord Sun! Show mercy, Lord Sun!**" Major Yuan cried as he forced his way into the tent. "**Do not allow that young man to be wasted as a corpse!**"

Captain Deng Dang followed, screaming, "**I must be flogged! Punish me, Lord Sun, for I have harmed your cause by allowing my brother-in-law to-!**"

"**Alright, enough!**" Bofu shouted. "I'll speak with Lü Meng and make my own mind up! You two can go, please!"

"**Mercy, Lord Sun!**" Major Yuan pleaded as Ling Cao ushered him out of the tent.

"**Punish the true wrongdoer!**" Captain Deng said as he followed Ling Cao of his own accord.

"*Aiee*... he'd better be worth all this fuss," Bofu grumbled.

Moments later, Ling Cao escorted a bound Lü Meng into the tent; Meng was athletic, tanned from many hours of outdoor work and strong-featured in a way that gave him an air of maturity beyond his years. His armour was obviously begged and borrowed, but his posture betrayed nothing other than his pride and determination.

Bofu was quietly impressed at the man that had insisted on his presence against all the odds, but he hid it behind a disapproving frown that did not fool Sun Hè at all.

"...You murdered a man in anger," Bofu said. "What have you to say for yourself, Lü Meng?"

"I'm stupid, and therefore had no clever answer to his insults," Lü Meng replied honestly. "All I wanted was a chance to do good like my brother-in-law, and all that man did was harass me for it. I have friends in your army, Lord Sun, and I'd just saved someone, so when that man called me a 'puppy' and said I was going to 'doom men with my'... I forget what word he used, but it was unfair, and I lashed out. I know I was wrong, and I'm here to be punished for it. I'm not afraid to die."

"...I see," Bofu sighed as he hung his head low.

A deafening silence followed; all that could be heard was breathing and the distant cries of Major Yuan, Captain Deng, and the other men that had come to plead for Lü Meng.

"What will you do?" Sun Hè asked eventually.

"...The only thing I can do," Bofu replied.

Another painful silence followed that was eventually broken by Ling Cao, who said, "My lord, I know I shouldn't speak, but-"

"Then please don't," Bofu replied. "It isn't that I don't respect you, as I have said, but this decision is mine alone."

After a third period of silence, Bofu looked up and said, "Lü Meng."

Lü Meng nodded silently.

Aftera short pause, Bofu asked, "Do you have a courtesy name?"

Sun Hè and Ling Cao smiled as one; Lü Meng frowned and said, "I do, Lord Sun, and it is 'Ziming'."

Bofu grinned and said, "Well then, Ziming, we'll need to untie you, decide on your rank, and find some men for you to lead. I won't have good men wasted!"

Ling Cao fought the urge to laugh as he cut the ropes that bound Lü Meng; Meng fell to his knees as soon as he was free, and he said, "You're truly a hero!"

"I hope so," Bofu replied. "The world needs them, and that's for certain! Ling Cao: escort Lü Ziming back to the barracks and please... *please*... make sure that Major Yuan and Captain Deng know the situation? Those two must be crying blood by now."

Ling Cao and Lü Meng left the tent in a jovial mood; once the three men had gone, Bofu chuckled quietly and said, "This is a better day than I'd expected it to be."

Sun Hè smiled and said, "You can forgive Quan now, as well."

"Yeah," Bofu replied. "Everyone make mistakes; it's everything else you do that defines who and what you are. Now... before that Lü Meng business, I wanted to look at maps, didn't I..."

Unbeknownst to all, Bofu had just employed and promoted one of the most important figures of the age. Lü Meng's initial behaviour would give rise to famous idioms, and his later decisions would shape military relations, change boundaries and alter the course of history.

****

75

The war against 'Haixi Chen' had been as tumultuous as the one against 'White Tiger Yan': Lü Fan, Huang Gai and Han Dang were forced to lead many joint assaults against vast armies of pirates on the complex river network while Jiang Qin and Chen Wu fought the bandits and tribal warriors on land. Haixi Chen had not been prepared, however, and his armies were not working in perfect harmony: that meant that he was doomed to failure, despite his numerical advantage. Huang Gai and Han Dang were able to block any river-going routes into the disputed territories, so the final battle would be on land.

"Okay, fellows, this is the moment," Han Dang said to Jiang Qin, Chen Wu and the junior officers that were gathered in his command tent. "Gongfu – Huang Gai, I mean – and Lü Fan are busy maintaining the river security, so they left managing you lot up to me. Gongfu's smarter than me, so it should probably be the other way around, but there you have it; fortunately, 'Haixi Chen' is not that bright either, so I'm hardly outclassed."

Some of the officers laughed for a few moments.

"A merry lot we be," Han Dang chuckled as he turned to the easel that held his battle map. "Right, then, here we are! Haixi's put everything he's got – and since that last rout, his following has halved – into that one camp there, to the north of us. There're still a lot of 'em, but we're going to take them by surprise."

"Mightn't they try the same thing?" Jiang Qin asked.

"They certainly might, my frugal friend," Han Dang replied. "We're going to pull the old trick on them. You're going to hold camp and fortify it against that sort of thing, while Chen Wu and I go and launch a nice surprise attack. And we're not waiting either, we're doing it *tonight*..."

Haixi Chen's scouts reported a drop in the number of soldiers in the opposition camp; he turned to his brother Mu and said, "The scouts report movement to the east, so they're trying to outflank us. I'll lead a force to attack their main camp; you hold here, and when I know where their new camp is, you can go and raid it."

"You can rely on me," Chen Mu replied.

Haixi Chen's forces reached Han Dang's camp at midnight: he readied his men, surrounded the fenced camp and ordered a simultaneous charge on all sides. The few soldiers that they encountered fled, so morale quickly peaked; but when Chen's forces reached the centre of the surprisingly well-lit camp, they were greeted by a sight that many commanders before and after him would suffer.

"**It was a bloody trap!**" Haixi Chen groaned as he stared at the palisades and pits. "**I should have known! Back, back!**"

But it was too late: Jiang Qin's men appeared from the darkness of the nearby tents and attacked the intruders with spears and pikes. Seemingly abandoned guard towers were suddenly manned again, and archers picked off the riders as they tried to find an opening in the walls of defenders. Haixi Chen was an accomplished fighter, so he was able to escape with the aid of trusted men, but his small force was decimated and his retreat was fraught with danger. He expected his return to his camp to be a moment of relative calm, but he was greeted instead by the sight of Bofu's flags above the gates and a jovial Han Dang, who bellowed, "**ARE YOU THAT BLOKE FROM HAIXI?**"

"**Go! Go!**" Haixi Chen ordered, and his small force fled westward.

"Ah, it never gets boring," Han Dang chuckled. "For some it might... but not me. **RIGHT, LADS! LET'S GET COMFORTABLE!**"

Chen Wu led the cheers for Han Dang, and the work of fortifying the camp as a second base against Haixi Chen's dwindling following began.

Haixi Chen found part of his brother's forces to the west of his former camp.

"Where's my brother?" Haixi Chen asked.

"General Chen is to the north," one major reported. "He contacted us shortly before you got here."

"I didn't come all this way to be made to look stupid," Haixi Chen growled. "White Tiger's lot are having trouble too, but I'm not going to let some men from Fuchun make me look stupid! **There's nothing special about them! We can win! And I'm going to make them pay for this! We start gathering everyone straight away, and we have it out with them as soon as we can!**"

Haixi Chen's rhetoric inspired his men, and the preparations for another battle began.

Han Dang and Chen Wu inevitably convened another meeting to discuss their opponent's actions.

"*And...* here we go again," Han Dang chuckled as he stared at a battle map. "Haixi Chen is now to the west of us, approaching with an army of a good few thousand, but I wouldn't worry. He's prepared to fight two armies – one from our main camp and one from the one we're sat in now – but we both know that he's forgotten something. A bad memory can be a terrible thing."

"What are we going to do?" Chen Wu asked.

"You're quite the jouster, if I recall," Han Dang replied. "We'll see if he's prepared to stick his hand in a tiger's mouth: if not, we'll just charge from all sides. This lot haven't got a strategist amongst 'em, so it's the usual brawling. Let's prepare!"

Han Dang's forces were waiting in full formation when Haixi Chen's army arrived. The bandits jeered and gesticulated wildly, but Han Dang's men held their ground and did not respond to the provocation. At the same time, Chen Mu was leading a force toward Han Dang's main camp, which was still being defended by Jiang Qin: Haixi Chen was certain that he would win, since he had the advantage of numbers and no burdens.

"Okay, let's see how stupid he is," Han Dang muttered as he rode to the front line.

"**WHERE IS 'HAN DANG'?**" Haixi Chen bellowed.

"**HERE IS HAN DANG!**" Han Dang replied. "**IS THAT THE HOMELESS BLOKE FROM HAIXI?**"

Han Dang's men started to laugh and heckle the bandit leader. Chen Wu rode to the front moments later and shouted, "**HERE IS CHEN WU, A MAN FROM A BETTER CHEN CLAN THAN THE BANDIT FROM HAIXI! WHO WILL CHALLENGE ME?**"

None of Haixi Chen's men responded; Han Dang sighed and said, "He isn't as stupid as I'd hoped. The second plan it is, then. **ALRIGHT LADS! AS WE PLANNED! GO TO IT!**"

Han Dang and Chen Wu led their men in a charge against Haixi Chen's vanguard; the two sides clashed, and damage was done to both forces. Haixi Chen met Han Dang briefly, but both men were forced to defend themselves against attacks by other people and abandon the idea of a duel. Both sides were starting to tire when Huang Gai brought a third force to the battle and attacked Haixi Chen's rear guard.

"**COWARDS! COWARDS AND BASTARDS!**" Haixi Chen screamed as he tried to fight his way out of the pincer; he fled toward Han Dang's main camp, hoping that he could regain momentum by joining his own battered force with his brother's.

"**Pursue...?**" Chen Wu asked of Han Dang.

Huang Gai approached the two officers and asked the same question: Han Dang nodded and said, "He's finished now."

The battle continued as Haixi Chen retreated; he reunited with his brother, who was staging his own retreat after being ambushed by Jiang Qin's men, so neither had a strong force with high morale.

"**What do we do???**" Chen Mu asked.

"**I won't lose like this!**" Haixi Chen cried. "**Death or victory!**"

Chen's men found some small shred of defiance and joined him in one last push against an enemy that now surrounded them; there was never a hope of regaining an advantage, but when a fourth force appeared that was led by Lü Fan, he finally realised that there could be no victory.

"**ARCHERS, FIRE!**" Lü Fan bellowed. "**CAVALRY, FORWARD!**"

A rain of arrows struck the left side of Haixi Chen's force while a cavalry charge struck at the centre of Chen Mu's regiment: Chen Mu and a number of other senior figures fell to the deluge of arrows, men and horse, and when Haixi Chen learned of his losses, his morale evaporated and he fled northward.

"**BUGGER OFF BACK TO HAIXI!**" Han Dang heckled as he chased the defeated confederacy leader from the battlefield. The battle would continue for a while longer as individual bandit leaders chose to fight on, but Haixi Chen's dream of becoming the Administrator of Wu Prefecture was over.

Han Dang, Huang Gai and Lü Fan held a final meeting to discuss the outcome of the campaign.

"Good performance, lads," Han Dang said to the assembled officers. "Last report says that he's gone north, back to his own territory. He has less a dozen men with him, so I can't see him being a threat anymore: by the time he manages to put together a force like that again, Lord Sun'll have a million men to chase him away again!"

The junior officers cheered at the words.

"It was a great victory," Huang Gai agreed. "Hopefully, White Tiger Yan of the Shanyue will soon be defeated as well. When word reaches him that his bandit allies have been routed, he'll probably retreat straight away. We'll need to leave some sort of force here, but the situation in Danyang has changed, so we'll-"

"Has it?" Han Dang exclaimed. "What the hell's happened now?"

"We're not entirely sure yet, Yigong," Huang Gai replied. "I'll inform everyone as soon as I know more."

"...We're never going to get any peace, are we?" Han Dang scoffed. "If it isn't one problem, it's another..."

Huang Gai turned to Lü Fan and said, "It was a pleasure working with you, Ziheng. I hope that the various demonstrations of naval tactics were of assistance to you."

"If you're going to learn, learn from the best," Lü Fan replied. "I only wish that I could split myself in two, so that I could've seen Han Dang fighting as well!"

"...You're a good sort, Lü Fan," Han Dang conceded. "I understand that your men were the ones that got Chen Mu; good job. You're headed south, aren't you?"

"The Xuan campaign is not going perfectly, shall we say, and I've been summoned," Lü Fan replied. "But I should like to say again, Mister Huang Gai and Mister Han Dang, that I am glad to have had the opportunity to work with heroes such as you."

****

76

Word of Haixi Chen's defeat reached White Tiger at a time when his own forces were at a significant disadvantage against an army that now had officers like Lü Meng and Ling Cao leading fearless, charismatic charges against them; the Shanyue advance faltered, and Bofu was finally able to go to Xuan City and reunite his forces. Sun Quan, Cheng Pu and Song Qian led a welcome that was sombre in tone: the city bore the scars of the earlier incursion, and many scars would never heal.

"*Brother…!*" Sun Quan wheezed as Bofu rode through the eastern gates and glared at him with judging eyes.

"I heard that you've been trying since… since 'then'," Bofu said as he looked at the citizens and military personnel; they were a sea of misery, and many still held a grudge – however small – toward the young man that had caused them so much needless pain.

"I won't be foolish like that again, Brother, I promise!" Sun Quan pleaded. "I have learned my lesson! I would never-!"

"Don't make promises that you can't keep," Bofu interrupted. "Dad said that more times than Cheng Demou, Huang Gongfu and Han Yigong could count, and Cousin Bohai will tell you that I'm no better. Just… just try your best, alright…?"

Sun Quan fought tears and bowed humbly.

"It's good to see you again, Demou," Bofu said as he turned to Cheng Pu. "How bad has it been?"

"They've been back, but we've chased them off," Cheng Pu replied. "Zhou Tai is healing well, but he still isn't strong enough to be moved."

"*Aiee…* I am a wretch!" Sun Quan cried. "Zhou Youping! Zhou Youping, I endangered your life needlessly, and-!"

"Hush, please, that isn't helping matters, and it isn't befitting for a magistrate – acting or otherwise – to whine like a child," Bofu scolded. "Now to business: White Tiger is hesitating, Haixi Chen is defeated, and Huang Gai, Han Dang, Jiang Qin and Chen Wu are able to join us here if needs be. This will hopefully be our last fight with the Shanyue for a while, because we need everything for dealing with the Danyang rebels, Liu Yao and Wang Lang."

"Liu Yao may be dying or dead," Cheng Pu reported. "Nothing's confirmed, as usual, but the signs are – if you'll excuse the wording – 'good'."

"That's too bad," Bofu sighed. "I'd hoped to win him to our cause somehow, but… since our cause is blindly following Yuan Shu… that was never likely, was it."

"Not really," Cheng Pu said. "Should I now oversee fortification of the camps around the city, Lord Sun?"

"Please, yes," Bofu replied. "I should like to talk with my family, so if you, Ling Cao and Lü Meng could-"

"Lü Meng is someone that I've been looking forward to meeting," Cheng Pu said. "I shall aid the preparations: the city interior is as stable as it's ever going to be now."

Sun Quan groaned miserably.

"…Thank you, Demou," Bofu said. "Right then; Quan, Bohai, let's go and… talk."

Cheng Pu thoughtfully watched Bofu, Sun Quan and Sun Hè's

retreat to the magistrate's residence before he joined the officers'
task of reinforcing the camps around Xuan City.

By the time that Lü Fan's speedy journey to Xuan had concluded,
White Tiger brought his remaining allies to Xuan and set up
fenceless camps to the east of the city; Cheng Pu's scouts
reported high numbers of men, but the defenders were relatively
unconcerned.
"Camps with no fences mean easy targets for raids, I think," Bofu
suggested.
"They deserve a taste of what happened here in Xuan City, Lord
Sun," Ling Cao said.
"Taking the fight to them is the best course of action," Lü Fan
said. "At least, that's how I see it... Mister Cheng...?"
Cheng Pu smiled and said, "I agree, Mister Lü."
"Huang Gai and the others are on their way, and they're making
sure that it's known, so we'll hit hard and then shout loud," Bofu
declared. "Cheng Pu, Ling Cao, Song Qian, Lü Meng: ready your
men for raids on their most important subordinate leaders. I'll
challenge White Tiger."
The officers bowed humbly and verbally acknowledged their
instructions for the battle ahead.

That evening, the five contingents struck the five westernmost
Shanyue camps and set them alight. White Tiger's allies were
panicked and forced to make humiliating retreats as the Sun
family retainers tore through their simple bases; White Tiger
himself was alerted to Bofu's arrival, anticipated some sort of ruse
rather than a fair fight, and decided to retreat. Bofu's forces
pursued the remainder of the Shanyue to the remnants of one of
their older camps and prepared for one last confrontation.
"**This time, we humble them!**" Bofu cried. "**CHARGE!**"
The result was a rout; many of the Shanyue tribes fled in all
directions while Ling Cao and Lü Meng led their men on rampages
and felled men left and right. Ling Cao found an opening to
challenge White Tiger, who was totally unprepared.
"**These southern Han men are strong!**" White Tiger exclaimed
as Ling Cao and his riders tore through his first line of defence and
approached at speed.
"**HERE IS LING CAO, THE TIGER HUNTER!**" the officer cried. "**I
WANT YOUR HEAD, WHITE TIGER YAN!**"
Ling Cao lunged at White Tiger, who parried the strike and fled the
field, leaving his bodyguards to do the fighting. Lü Fan had
ordered an archery unit to fire at the only attempt at a
counterattack, and the morale of the Shanyue was gone
completely. White Tiger fled into the hills with some of his
remaining followers, and once he learned of the approach of even
more of Bofu's valiant officers, he made it clear that he was
beaten by withdrawing all of his followers from Wu Prefecture and
placing a wall of primitive defences around the Shanyue domains.

The Wu Prefecture campaign against White Tiger Yan and Haixi
Chen Yu was over: preparations began for yet another march and
yet another battle.
        "...Zhou Youping."

Zhou Tai opened his eyes and shuddered; Bofu was standing over his infirmary bed, smiling strangely.

"I... I failed you, Lord Sun!" Zhou Tai croaked. "Xuan was... almost lost, and-!"

"It was only saved because of your efforts, Youping," Bofu replied. "I didn't believe it when I was told that you consider yourself to be to blame; you're quite the man, more the hero, and not the pirate that you were once. Furthermore, you saved my brother, fool that he was, and I couldn't be more grateful for that."

"I failed him!" Zhou Tai insisted. "It... was my job to-"

"I left you here to protect him, not do his job for him," Bofu interrupted. "He was Acting Magistrate: he should have known better. He should have known a lot better. The 'Crisis management classes' that he'd have done at school during his studies on civil administration would've given him all the guidance there is, and he deliberately ignored the lessons and acted like a Han prince instead. It cost lives, resources, confidence, morale, time... there're some that would rather die than serve him now."

"You... did not forgive him, then," Zhou Tai said. "My... my fault."

"You're more stubborn than I am!" Bofu chortled. "Fine, blame yourself: I blame me, he blames him, you blame you... we're all at fault, and that's that. But I did forgive him. And now I'm rewarding you."

"Lord Sun, you shouldn't!" Zhou Tai pleaded. "I-!"

"If... if ever I'm free to appoint men properly, maybe I'll make you a duke," Bofu said. "I'm going to recommend you to Yuan Shu as a county Magistrate."

Zhou Tai coughed uncomfortably and said, "How am I a-!"

"You'll accept it, and you'll like it," Bofu insisted. "The way you rallied the people here before and during... 'that'... and inspired my brother to become remotely competent at his job proves that while you weren't assigned to him to do his job, you did, and you did it well. You're wasted as a bodyguard, Zhou Youping, be it mine or his. You're a leader and statesman."

Zhou Tai groaned painfully and said, "I'm a... fool pirate...!"

"If you say so," Bofu replied as he patted Zhou Tai's arm. "I say you're a fine officer and an even greater hero. But you carry on beating yourself up all you want."

Bofu stood up, smiled and left the infirmary.

On the day before the departure from Xuan, Bofu called a meeting of his officers.

"We'll leave forces here in Wu, reinforce Danyang against this mystery troublemaker, and deal with the problems in Kuaiji now," Bofu declared.

"Wang Lang...?" the newly-arrived Han Dang said.

"Yes, Yigong: Wang Lang and his new ally Zhang Ya, and the bandits Huang Longluo and Zhou Bo that Dong Xi's been up against," Bofu replied.

"But you mentioned bolstering Danyang," Ling Cao said.

Bofu shook his head and said, "We haven't a choice: the rebels there are organised and doing serious damage to our forces."

"The *Danyang bandits*...?" Han Dang chortled. "Look, enough is enough: who is leading them that they're suddenly such a big problem for us?"

"I don't know, but I have a hunch that I won't share," Bofu replied. "Whoever it is has rallied everyone that we didn't get through to and turned the hills of Danyang into a natural fortress. It isn't quite the Black Mountain Bandits that have had Yuan Shao tied up in knots for the last goodness-knows-how-long, but it's pretty bad. Our 'mystery enemy' is cunning, ingenious, and more stubborn than any of us: we need to get back to Danyang and whittle down his followers using tactics, else we'll lose Danyang like we almost lost Wu. Whoever it is doesn't seem to be working with Liu Yao's forces... we'll see when we look into it more closely."
"So we're going to leave a credible show of strength here to dissuade White Tiger from coming back – and, incidentally, frighten our other problem, Xu Gong, into remaining in hiding – and go back to Danyang and Kuaiji quickly," Cheng Pu said. "Wang Lang probably can't be chased away like White Tiger and Haixi Chen: he'll need to be rooted out."
"We should try and coerce Wang to join us," Bofu suggested.
"He's not someone we should want, Lord Sun," Cheng Pu said. "He's of poor character, if what Yu Fan says is true. We should just catch and kill him."
"If we have to, but he's court-appointed, and I hear that he has a lot of influential friends," Bofu noted. "If it's at all possible that we can keep him alive, we should."
"Alive, maybe, but we should send him home to the north if we catch him, or imprison him quietly," Lü Fan said.
"We will do whatever we have to do," Bofu replied. "Right, then: on to Danyang."

****

77

The uprising by mountain-based rebel forces in Danyang had initially seemed to be a backlash against the obtrusive military operations rather than an organised revolt: that had changed over a relatively short time in a startling fashion. The rebel army grew and grew and their incursions became more and more destructive, putting unbelievable pressure on Gongjin, Zhou Shang and Xu Kun's defence forces. The rebel force was as well-organised as any professional army, brutally effective, and it was on the verge of doing serious damage to Bofu's regime in Danyang: the leader was of especial interest to Bofu and his counsel, and one name that was being bandied about was Taishi Ci, who had not been seen since Liu Yao's defeat.

"What... the...!"
The like of Cheng Pu's exclamation was echoed throughout Bofu's army as they marched toward Danyang's capital; the region's defensive works were visibly battered by weeks of attacks, and the signs were that the enemy was matching the defenders at the very least.
"If it really is Taishi Ci, then he is some sort of champion of the age, that much cannot be denied," Lü Fan said as he turned in all directions to view the damage to nearby settlements. "Taishi – or whoever it is – must be conducting raids on a daily basis to leave everywhere looking like this."
"Whoever it is has to be killed," Cheng Pu declared. "To let them escape would be idiocy: they'd only gather another force and appear somewhere else, and we can't afford to keep seeing this sort of thing."
"I'm still worried about Wu Prefecture," Bofu admitted.
"Zhu Junli and Han Yigong are capable enough," Cheng Pu insisted. "If they need help, they'll hold out and ask for it. As for Kuaiji, your uncle Sun Jing has gone on ahead to form a western barrier between Liu Yao and Wang Lang as suggested."
"Speaking of uncles, I hope that Wu Jing is alright," Bofu said.
"I'm sure that he's fine," Cheng Pu replied.

There was no attack underway when Bofu's army reached the walls of Danyang's capital: the main force camped around the city while Bofu and his senior officials met with Gongjin, Zhou Shang and Xu Kun to discuss the situation properly.
"I don't know how much you know about the north, but bear with me, because it has relevance," Gongjin began. "While you've been in Kuaiji and Wu, the entire political landscape has changed."
"I know bits of it, but go ahead," Bofu prompted.
"His Majesty has been 'rescued' by Cao Cao, and is now either in Luoyang's ruins or on his way to Yan Province, depending on which rumour you believe," Gongjin continued. "Liu Bei, I understand, is trapped in one of his own cities by Ji Ling after being double-crossed by his sitting tenant Lü Bu."
"...Pardon?" Cheng Pu exclaimed.
"So Lü Bu is now running Xu Province?" Bofu said.
"I suppose so," Gongjin replied. "That may benefit us, of course,

because it means that Wu Jing is now fighting Liu Bei loyalists that might stop fighting soon or that Wu Jing may be recalled by Yuan Shu because there is no longer a need for a campaign there. We'll have to see, but let's face it, Lü Bu is 'changeable', and we could end up fighting Bu instead."

"...They're all mad in the north," Cheng Pu complained.

"The regency is ended, which is a good thing," Lü Fan noted. "Whatever we may think of Cao Cao, he once spoke of our lord's father as the greatest hero under Heaven, while Li Jue and Guo Si were bitter enemies of ours. If those monsters have finally been humbled, then we might be about to see stability at last."

"Or not, Ziheng," Bofu said. "If Cao has His Majesty, and Cao is the best friend of Yuan Shao, doesn't that make our lord an enemy of the Son of Heaven? And that being the case, doesn't that mean we're...?"

"The thought had occurred to me," Lü Fan said. "One possible advantage is that it might force our master's hand and make him do that thing we've all been waiting for: that will only benefit us. If Cao doesn't use His Majesty to force Yuan Shu to make peace with his brother-stroke-cousin, then yes, I admit that we'll be in trouble if Yuan doesn't capitulate of his own will. It all rests with Cao and our master, and what they are *really after*."

"That's all important, but it has to wait while we deal with Wang Lang and what seems to be Taishi Ci," Gongjin said. "So-"

"Why did you raise the matter, then...?" Cheng Pu asked gruffly.

"...Because it is important, Elder Cheng," Gongjin replied.

"D'AAAGH! I am *not old*!" Cheng Pu bellowed. **"You little pedant, I-!"**

"Hey, hey!" Bofu shouted. **"No arguing! We have wars to win!** ...Gongjin, we appreciate the necessary update on the north. Where is the rebel army now?"

"Their leaders must have learned of your arrival and withdrawn their forces as a cautionary measure," Gongjin replied. "Our enemy is a clever one..."

"Yes, 'Gongjin', but now that Lü Fan and I are here, we might see a better match of wits," Cheng Pu said cuttingly. "You go back to your northern poetry and essential criticism of southern musicians, and gathering gossip from across the river to-"

"Demou!" Bofu chortled. "Please remember that Gongjin is my friend! Please remember that his family showed us great courtesy and generosity in Lujiang!"

Cheng Pu glared at Gongjin and Zhou Shang, grunted irritably and said, "Please excuse this prematurely grey-haired fool for his unwarranted frustration."

"Now who's wasting time?" Bofu asked of Cheng Pu, who merely grunted again.

"Taishi Ci - or whoever it is that leads these rebels from the shadows - must wait," Lü Fan suggested. "The situation in Kuaiji is worsening, so we'll have to act quickly. Han Yan needs more men if he's to defeat Wang Lang any time soon or at all."

"...We'll go southward immediately, then," Cheng Pu said.

The events in the south were being closely watched by Bofu's lord, Yuan Shu, who was still based in his city stronghold in the Yang Provincial capital Shouchun. But however positively Bofu and his allies might have expected Yuan Shu to feel about the successes that had been enjoyed, paranoia was still paramount in the nobleman's mind.

"I am concerned, gentlemen, about my young tiger."

Yuan Shu glared at each of the senior officials in his court in turn as he spoke.

"How, I ask, can I be sure that he is loyal…?" Yuan Shu continued as he held his gaze on one unlikely recipient of the address: Bofu's cousin, Sun Ben.

"My lord, Cousin Ce has faced obstacle after obstacle and conquered them all for you and you alone," Sun Ben pleaded. "Why do you now doubt his sincerity again at such a critical moment? With Wu Prefecture only barely calmed after Wang Lang and Liu Yao's long-distance intriguing with the Shanyue, a huge rebel army is attacking Danyang, and-"

"I find some of the stories that I'm hearing a tad preposterous, Sun Ben," Yuan Shu interrupted. "Sun Ce is not a super-man! Yet I'm hearing stories of victories against ridiculous odds and making senior officers out of courageous youths that just happened to be tagging along with his army! If he is so amazing, then why is Liu Yao sitting unchecked on the eastern border of Yuzhang? How is it that Hua Xin still administrates that same Yuzhang? Why is Wang Lang not dealt with?"

"He cannot be everywhere at once!" Sun Ben retorted. "Lord Yuan, he is doing everything that he can because yes, he is not superhuman! He is a man, and he is having to gain allies in various regions in order to-"

"Ah, yes, that's another point," Yuan Shu said. "I should be aware of every man that works for me, Sun Ben: they are not 'his allies', they are 'my vassals'. Who are these people? How can I be expected to trust him when he makes friends that he does not want to tell me about…?"

Sun Ben did not reply.

"Your silence is damning," Yuan Shu chortled. "Han Yin…"

The adviser Han Yin bowed theatrically.

"Sun Ce is a callous man indeed to be plotting fission when I have his and his officers' families in my custody," Yuan Shu suggested.

"If that is what he is planning," Han Yin replied, "then yes, he is most callous."

"He plans *nothing*!" Sun Ben pleaded. "He follows orders – your orders, Lord Yuan – to pacify the south and bring it under your control!"

"…Your protests have some shred of sincerity in them, Mister Sun Ben," Yuan Shu decided.

"But we should, perhaps, consider alternative administration if we are not certain, lord and cousin," the adviser Yuan Yin said.

"And you, dear cousin, are the right man for it," Yuan Shu replied. "You will begin preparations to travel southward: I will provide you with a letter demanding that Zhou Shang relinquish Danyang's seal of office."

"He has not wronged you!" Sun Ben cried.

"**SILENCE!**" Yuan Shu barked. "**How dare you address me thus??? Know your place or lose it!**"

"…Forgive my outburst, Lord Yuan," Sun Ben replied meekly.

Yuan Shu turned his gaze back to his cousin and said, "Yuan Yin,

you will do as I have already asked: additionally, I want Zhou Shang and Zhou Yu to move to Shouchun as soon as you arrive."
"But that will- ...*Aiee*," Sun Ben whispered.
"What are you muttering about, Sun Ben?" Yuan Shu asked.
"...Zhou Yu advises Cousin Ce and has been instrumental in his victories," Sun Ben explained. "To bring him here would-"
"If Zhou Yu is that clever, then he should be here, advising his true master," Yuan Shu interrupted. "Your words only increase my desire to have him here in Shouchun. You may retire from the court, Sun Ben: in fact, all lower-ranking officials may go. Yan Xiang, Han Yin: to my private audience room."
As Sun Ben retreated from the hall, he muttered involuntarily and struggled with the urge to make his true feelings known to his master.
"Mister Sun Ben, I'm sorry."
Sun Ben turned to Bofu's friend Zhang Xun and said, "It wasn't your fault, General Zhang, so why apologise...?"
"I... don't know," Zhang Xun replied. "Please tell Sun Ce that I am glad that we are still friends despite my stubborn allegiance."
"...I shall," Sun Ben promised; Zhang Xun retreated, and Ben journeyed to the current home of Lady Wu and the rest of the Sun clan so that he could inform them of the latest developments.

"Wretched man!" Lady Wu exclaimed once Sun Ben had informed her of the outcome of the latest meeting. "O, Heaven, why do you make my son kneel to such a miserable-!"
"Be careful of what you say and how loudly you say it," Sun Ben pleaded. "Remember that many of your servants might really serve Yuan Shu."
"...He is drawing men away from my son!" Lady Wu hissed. "Every time that Yuan gains ground he does something that ensures that he will lose it! What good will come from taking young Zhou Yu away from-"
"Lord Yuan... is demented," Sun Ben whispered. "It is only a matter of time before he does something quite ridiculous. At that moment, we have to hope that I have the resources and contacts to evacuate everyone before he can shut the doors and trap us all here. Perhaps... perhaps having Zhou Gongjin here might be good rather than bad... perhaps... perhaps our idiot lord has given us just what we needed...!"

****

78

At the same time that Bofu was preparing to join his allies in Kuaiji Prefecture, their problems worsened. In Kuaiji's capital region of Shanyin, Chief Constable Dong Xi was under constant attack from a bandit confederacy led by notorious criminals named Huang Longluo and Zhou Bo; and further to the south in Hougan County, Commandant Han Yan and his subordinate Hè Qi were confronted by an alliance of rebels, Shanyue warriors and followers of the former Administrator, Wang Lang.

"…Ah, Mister Hè, you are like a ray of sunshine when you come here in those clothes," Han Yan chuckled as Yongning Magistrate Hè Qi entered his Hougan command tent. Hè Qi was, as ever, dressed in finery and equipped with shining, immaculate armour; many of Han Yan's officers had mistaken Qi for one of Yuan Shu's senior generals as he walked through the camp and shown needless deference.

"You want to make a final push against Wang Lang, I understand," Hè Qi said.

"I do," Han Yan replied. "Lord Sun trusted me with this role, and if I dally any longer Wang Lang will have the tribes coming up here from Jiaozhi and bandits from every foul orifice in the prefecture. He outnumbers us, Magistrate, but I have to take the risk, since Lord Sun may take time to arrive, what with all the problems in Danyang at the moment."

"You have my full cooperation," Hè Qi promised. "In fact, I'd be glad to be the vanguard against that vile Wang."

"I was hoping you'd say that!" Han Yan replied. "We'll prepare immediately."

Han Yan's army met Wang Lang's on a piece of waste ground. Wang Lang was accompanied by his adviser Xu Jing, the Magistrate of Hougan and a local rebel leader called Zhang Ya.

"…Magistrate Hao, ready your men for the strategic manoeuvres that we discussed," Wang Lang ordered.

"Yes, Administrator," Magistrate Hao replied.

Wang Lang turned to Zhang Ya and said, "Mister Zhang, your support is, as I have said a countless times, invaluable."

"And as *I've* said countless times, *Administrator*, honouring your promises is all I ask in return," Zhang Ya retorted. "You do more, I'll do more."

"Then kindly have your followers lead the first charge," Wang Lang said politely.

Zhang Ya eyed Magistrate Hao with contempt and rode away to give orders to his various officers; Xu Jing then turned to Wang Lang and said, "We must not renege."

"I am aware of that, Mister Xu," Wang Lang replied coldly.

Commandant Han Yan observed Wang Lang's battle lines with renewed discomfort.

"They are greatly reinforced somehow," Han Yan fretted. "I knew he had a small amount of Shanyue support and maybe a few bandits, but… what's *this*?"

"There are a lot more men than the scouts initially reported," Hè Qi sighed.

"Thousands more... and worse still, organised," Han Yan noted. "We'll have to-"

"**REPORT!**" a messenger cried as he ran to and fell to his knees before Han Yan's horse. "**ENEMY FORCES ARE APPROACHING FROM WEST AND NORTH!**"

Han Yan groaned miserably and said, "Dash it! We've been lured into a-!"

"**COMMANDER!**" a scout captain cried. "**THE ENEMY CHARGES!**" A Shanyue tribal alliance descended onto the rear of Han Yan's right flank; at the same time, an army of rebels attacked the left flank and caused panic to spread through the ranks. Zhang Ya's charge at the vanguard was a final pressure that caused the majority of Han Yan's army to scatter; Hè Qi held his gaudy and conspicuous units on the battlefield and engaged Zhang Ya personally.

"**Who's this dandy?**" Zhang Ya heckled as Hè Qi lunged with his decorated spear.

"**Here is Hè Qi!**" He Qi retorted. "**Do you know me?**"

"**Father-in-law, that's the famous 'Bandit smasher' Hè Qi!**" a rebel cavalry officer screamed. "**Be careful!**"

"**Oh-ho! So you're Hè Qi... but where is your master?**" Zhang Ya taunted as a wall of infantry and cavalry came between him and Hè Qi.

"**Come back and fight!**" Hè Qi bellowed as he swung his spear left and right, scattering the rebel infantry.

"**Another day!**" Zhang Ya said as he turned and galloped away.

"*Aiee...* **Commandant Han! Commandant Han!**" Hè Qi shouted as he and his men scoured the battlefield for Han Yan, scattering the rebels as they did so.

"**Who is that fanciful character?**" Magistrate Hao complained as he watched Hè Qi's men break the spirit of the rebel vanguard.

"**Hè Qi of Shanyin,**" Xu Jing reported. "**He's Magistrate of-**"

"**He's ruining things!**" Magistrate Hao cried. "**We have to try and shoot him!**"

"**We can't risk an archery attack right now, in case we hit Zhang Ya's men!**" Wang Lang said. "**Do you want to destroy our alliance???**"

Hè Qi found Han Yan in the midst of the right flank; the Shanyue were winning, but the sight of Hè Qi's extravagant men fooled the tribal leaders into thinking that some mighty reinforcement had arrived, so many of them fled.

"**Y-you're Heaven... sent... Hè Gongmiao,**" Han Yan panted.

"**You're hurt, Commandant,**" Hè Qi noted.

"**I am unbroken!**" Han Yin retorted as he put on a show of renewed vigour. "**We have to break this enemy quickly. Let's fight them together!**"

Han Yan and Hè Qi led a spirited counterattack against the rebels attacking the left flank, and suddenly it was Wang Lang that was at a disadvantage.

"**They're... they're winning,**" Wang Lang said nervously. "**They're winning, Xu Jing! Do something, Xu Jing, or we'll be routed again!**"

"**You there! Zhang Ya!**" Magistrate Hao heckled as he caught sight of the rebel leader loitering nearby. "**Why are you not at the forefront?**"

"**Why aren't *you*, Han crony?**" Zhang Ya retorted. "**I'm organising a-** ...Why should I explain myself...? **DO SOMETHING YOURSELF!**"

"**Rude peasant!**" Magistrate Hao cried. "**I'll-!**"

"**Shut up, you fool!**" Wang Lang shrieked. "**Go and join Han Yan, why don't you???**"

"**The rebels are moving back,**" Xu Jing said. "**Archers! Magistrate Hao, THE ARCHERS, AT ONCE!**"

Magistrate Hao regained his senses and signalled to the archer division; Han Yan and Hè Qi had begun a charge, but it was immediately blunted when Han Yan was struck.

"**COVER FIRE! COVER FIRE!**" Hè Qi barked at one of his captains, who immediately started a signal relay to the archery division; Hè Qi leapt from his horse and personally hoisted the wounded Han Yan back onto his horse so that a swift retreat could be made.

"**Han Yan must be down,**" Xu Jing said as he watched the charge disintegrate. "**Have Zhang Ya charge again! We have them, we-!**"

"**He's already charging,**" Wang Lang said with a smile. "**I think we just had our first victory, Mister Xu... Sun Ce will not know his head for much longer!**"

"**Dratted scum!**" Hè Qi cried as he was forced to defend Han Yan's slumped body from attacks by rebel infantry and cavalry. "**Someone come and fetch Commandant Han! I'm needed elsewhere!**"

One of Han Yan's personal guardsmen led the wounded commander away while Hè Qi concentrated his efforts on repelling Zhang Ya's charge; but within minutes, the rebels were retreating once again as Hè Qi's requested archery attack finally began.

"Too clever," Xu Jing complained. "**WITHDRAW!**"

"...Very well," Wang Lang muttered: he then turned to his officials and shouted, "**SIGNAL A RETREAT!**"

"...Damn it," Zhang Ya muttered as he watched Wang Lang and Magistrate Hao withdraw their personnel. "Han court toadies... worthless to the last."

Zhang Ya's son-in-law rode to his side and asked, "**Are we retreating as well, Father-in-law?**"

"**Of course, Liao!**" Zhang Ya chortled.

Both sides withdrew, leaving a battlefield strewn with corpses.

That same afternoon, Han Yan's camp infirmary was the scene of a pivotal transfer of responsibility.

"...Hè Qi... Hè... *Gongmiao*...!"

Han Yan was close to death; the attending physician stood up, frowned thoughtfully and turned to Hè Qi, saying, "Hours at the most, Magistrate."

"Seal... sword... Hè Qi...!" Han Yan croaked.

"...Isn't there another man who shines brighter than I...?" Hè Qi asked humbly.

Han Yan smiled involuntarily, coughed blood and replied, "Funny... but... no."

Hè Qi knelt beside Han Yan and said, "I will take your seal and sword temporarily, until a better man is found by our lord Sun Ce. I shall write to him immediately, informing him of our situation,

and I have already ensured that the camps are-"
"See...?" Han Yan whispered. "Who else... Gongmiao... could..."
Han Yan now lacked the strength to speak; he mouthed, "Lead them," and closed his eyes slowly.
"...I want him to be comfortable until the end," Hè Qi ordered. "And as for Wang Lang and Zhang Ya... I will offer their heads to your shrine, Han Yan."
Han Yan exhaled slowly and smiled; he would be dead by evening, and the responsibility of pursuing and destroying the former administrator of Kuaiji was now Acting Commandant Hè Qi's.

"I sometimes wonder if Heaven despises me," Bofu chortled as he read a report from Hougan. He then turned to the officials that filled his roadside command tent to capacity and said, "Han Yan was a good man. Wang Lang has wronged the world again, but what can I do...? Liu Biao, Huang Zu, Wang Lang, Zhang Ya, Liu Yao, Hua Xin... like Dong Zhuo and his lackeys before them, I'm always stuck doing something else and unable to deal with them! Why does something Heaven-sent always delay justice???"
Lü Fan – who had already read the report – smiled encouragingly and said, "Han Yan's passing is sad, Lord Sun, but Hè Qi is proving to be a marvellous leader. His ostentatious behaviour often proves confusing to the tribes and bewildering to everyone else; it's a pity that we cannot afford to dress all of our men in such finery, for we'd win every battle before it ever started if we could."
Major Lü Meng hummed thoughtfully – but quietly – at the words.
"Well we can't, Ziheng, so we have to watch good men shed blood instead," Bofu grumbled. "Still, I take it you agree with me that Gongmiao is best made the permanent Commandant and left to carry on...?"
"Yes, and I don't think he'll need further support," Lü Fan replied. "Dong Xi, however, cannot-"
"I know he's struggling against that massive bandit army that's sprung up in Shanyin," Bofu said. "I'll send aid to him as soon as we have the men to spare."
"Will the capital be alright?" Cheng Pu asked. "Are Xu Kun, 'Gongjin' and a legion of pedants going to be enough...? Shouldn't we have left others there to-"
"Gongjin is capable of holding the region now that the worst of the rebel forces have been pushed back," Bofu replied. "I have faith in him, Demou."
Cheng Pu grunted irritably and said, "I had noticed."

As they continued the journey to Kuaiji, Bofu's army learned that Liu Yao had passed away, leaving his sizeable army to be led by his son Liu Ji and the Administrator of Yuzhang, Hua Xin; they did not know what sort of repercussions that might have and they could not afford to think about it. The only thing that mattered was the defeat of Wang Lang and Zhang Ya.

****

79

In Jing Province, Governor Liu Biao watched the developments that now surrounded him with increasing discomfort. He summoned his counsel to a private meeting and asked, "Just when I thought that peace might be imminent, the situation has worsened! Sun Ce haunts my southern borders, I have the ineffective Liu Zhang and the cultist Zhang Lu as my neighbours in the west, Yuan Shu is yapping at my eastern gates, and Dong Zhuo's lackeys are squatting in Nan County! But despite my neutrality, what stance does Cao Cao take…? Does he thank me for my work against Yuan Shu…? No, he declares war on me in the name of the Son of Heaven and threatens to send an army to 'pacify me'! What must be done?"

"About what…?" the adviser Kuai Liang retorted. "Lord Liu, your neutrality might not be as ideal as one might hope, but it is your saving grace! While you have been accused of doing no right, you have also done no wrong."

"Tell that to Sun Ce of Fuchun!" Liu Biao cried. "He grows before my eyes, Mister Kuai, and I know that it is only a matter of time before his wicked master orders him back here with his father's retainers to claim my head in 'revenge', unless he decides to take it upon himself to-!"

"He's busy… very, very busy… and therefore unable to act, and I've devised a way to keep him busier still, *should the need arise*," Kuai Liang promised. "My brother sends me regular reports: Wang Lang is refusing to buckle in Kuaiji, and the situation in Danyang is as tumultuous as ever. Yuan Shu is the terrible lord he's always been, and it won't be long before Sun Ce breaks away from him. At that point, we will doubtless be able to reason with-"

"Forgive me, old friend, but I cannot agree," Liu Biao chortled.

"…Sun Ce will never have the required manpower for a successful invasion of Jing," Kuai Liang insisted. "We have a fine navy-"

"His father smashed our navy!" Liu Biao shrieked as he pointed at a visibly embarrassed Cai Mao. **"That man there remembers, so why don't you???"**

"…Of course we all remember, but we were defending against a coordinated land-and-river offensive," Kuai Liang insisted.

"Forgive my interruption, but I was Sun Jian's diplomat during that affair, and I can tell you that their successes were more luck than skill," Huan Jie said. "He exploited your underestimation of his ability: if you do not underestimate his son, you cannot lose."

"…You had better be right, gentlemen," Liu Biao scoffed. He then turned to a pasty, obviously-distracted youth in pale blue robes and said, "'Mister' Wang Can, I was kind enough to give you work: could you stop staring at that scroll and provide an opinion…?"

Kuai Liang peered over Wang Can's shoulder, looked at the scroll, turned to face his lord again and smiled.

"What distracts you, Mister Wang…?" Liu Biao asked snidely.

"It has a fine drawing of a donkey on it, Lord Liu," Wang Can said as he returned his attentions to the meeting.

"…And I wonder why I lose," Liu Biao despaired. "You were a disciple of Cai Yong??? I have never met a man that cannot focus in the presence of donkeys – even a *drawing* of a bloody donkey!"

"It's not so much their appearance, Lord Liu," Wang Can replied.
"I like their braying, it calms me, and-"
"Will that drawing bray, do you think...?" Liu Biao heckled.
"No!" Wang Can said cheerfully. "But you didn't need me to contribute anyway: Kuai Liang was going to suggest that you reinforce Jiangxia's riverbanks and ponder harassing northwest Yang in order to show strength against Sun Ce should the need arise, and with regard to our 'squatters' in Nan County, I imagine that our policy is to support them only if we must. The cowardly Liu Zhang has Zhang Lu's family as hostages and therefore neither is an immediate concern, and Cao Cao's threatened march may never happen, but if he did we would have to-"
"*Thank you*, Mister Wang," Liu Biao interrupted. "Mister Kuai, please enlighten us with your *experienced views*."
"...Mister Wang reads me correctly," Kuai Liang admitted.
"You actually propose that I attack Sun Ce?" Liu Biao exclaimed.
"*If* the absolute *need* arises, and even *then* only in a sense, since they are not his domains," Kuai Liang replied. "They are Han domains that you would be protecting from Yuan Shu's criminal allies, just as you have to protect the Jing-Yu border against those hireling Yellow Turbans that obviously work for Yuan Shu."
"...Understood," Liu Biao said. "Should Huang Zu manage this?"
"I suggest not," Kuai Liang replied. "It is a mission to defend Han territories from incursions and insurrections, so a clansman should lead the effort."
"...My son Qi?" Liu Biao prompted.
"Not in this instance," Kuai Liang replied. "Your eldest son is too young and inexperienced to fight the sort of rabble that Sun Ce will deploy in response, so I suggest that your nephew Pan lead all necessary efforts while Huang Zu and Cai Mao focus on training the navy and recruiting more men. We have many enemies, and we must be ready for them all. Liu Zhang is, as Wang Can said, not a concern, and nor is his reluctant subordinate Zhang Lu. The regents in Chang'an are finished, and Jia Xu and Zhang Xiu are quite happy to hide in Nan County and provide us with muscle to keep Yuan Shu from invading again. If Cao Cao attacks us, he'll start with Jia and Zhang because of their connection to Dong Zhuo, and we can adapt our own stance according to his success."
Liu Biao hummed thoughtfully and said, "I will accord with everything. I shall have my nephew reinforce the riverbanks and then – if needs be – cross the Great River to Yang, and I shall write to Huang Zu with orders to bolster our navy and recruit for land defence as well. Cai Mao, Zhang Yun: you'll enhance your recruitment and training exercises as well."
Cai Mao and his nephew Zhang Yun bowed humbly.
"All matters are discussed," Kuai Liang said optimistically.
"Sun Ce still worries me," Liu Biao admitted. "What will he do...?"
But despite those worries, Liu Biao's nephew Pan led a militia to Jiangxia and began preparations for a possible harassment campaign against military installations and settlements that supported the Sun clan or Yuan Shu.

****

Bofu was prevented from marching to Kuaiji at speed by a series of rebel ambushes and Shanyue attacks; but in Hougan County in Kuaiji, Bofu's new Southern Commandant Hè Qi was enjoying success after success against the former administrator Wang Lang, the rebel leader Zhang Ya and the wavering magistrate. Wang Lang and Xu Jing travelled westward to the Kuaiji-Yuzhang prefectural border with the intention of coaxing some of the late governor Liu Yao's men to his side, but that left Magistrate Hao and Zhang Ya as the leaders of the defence forces in Hougan. Hè Qi noted the change of atmosphere and reduced effectiveness and sensed an opportunity: he launched a series of attacks against the unlikely coalition of rebel and establishment, causing massive casualties to both.

"I've had enough!" Magistrate Hao cried as he fled the battlements of his capital city and sought refuge in his residential audience hall: the rebel leader Zhang Ya and his son-in-law Liao followed, and neither was sympathetic to the magistrate's plight.

"Are we somehow immune to what's happening?" Zhang Ya asked. "You know, I'd never been inside a magistrate's mansion until this 'alliance', and all I can say is that I can see where all the money's going. But an Administrator's residence is probably nicer still, mm...? I'm sure you feel hard done by, having to make do with plain silk drapes."

"Shut up, you peasant!" Magistrate Hao retorted. **"What man of breeding respects needless frugality? We're fighting a man that dresses his men like kings! If visitors to a magistrate's mansion were greeted by a hovel with filth on the floor and served bowls of damp rice with dead bugs floating in it, they'd-!"**

"I... think I understand your view of things," Zhang Ya chortled.

"...I didn't mean to offend you by resorting to an exaggerated caricature of a poorer existence, Zhang Ya," Magistrate Hao continued. "I don't have contempt for normal people like you. But I can't live frugally just to avoid upsetting people that get paid less than I do! I get paid well because I work hard to manage the whole county, and I am expected to have a nice home, and... *aiee*. Your expression is enough."

"Good," Zhang Ya said coldly. "Now tell me what you meant by 'I have had enough', please, Magistrate."

"You don't like Wang Lang, and neither do I," Magistrate Hao said. "Our defence is ostensibly of Hougan, but in truth it is of Wang Lang specifically! Where is Sun Ce harming people? I think that this place has suffered enough."

"You're scared of Hè Qi, and that's all there is to it," Zhang Ya heckled.

"Alright, yes, I'm scared of Hè Qi!" Magistrate Hao barked. "But why should I risk my life or anyone else's life, mm...? You want some sort of rebel paradise, and Wang Lang wants a human shield! In both cases, I'm fighting causes that harm me!"

"You mean to surrender," Zhang Ya realised.

"I don't care what you do, but Hougan's administration is not going to fight this pointless battle anymore," Magistrate Hao retorted. "Please leave me be."

Zhang Ya bowed slightly and gestured to his son-in-law: the two men retreated to the streets of the city and convened a meeting of their officers.

"He's writing the letter of surrender as I speak," Zhang Ya reported. "We need to decide, friends, what to do."

"Hè Qi's men are treated well, Father-in-law," Liao noted.

"Can he afford to dress us all like princes and dukes?" Zhang Ya retorted. "He'll fund that by paying everyone else less than they deserve. That means, hard though it is to believe, that he's probably – no, definitely – worse than old Hao. So here's the idea, friends: we take the city for ourselves. We take the county for ourselves."

"What about Wang Lang?" Liao asked.

"That coward won't argue," Zhang Ya scoffed. "He'll crawl and offer us whatever we want in exchange for our continued support."

"Well then we kill old Hao and take the city," one officer said. "If we surrender, what will Hè Qi do to us?"

The other officers mumbled agreeably.

"...Leave it with me," Zhang Ya said.

Wang Lang and Xu Jing were on their way back to Hougan after a disappointing end to their recruitment mission when news of Zhang Ya's insurrection reached them.

"*Ayah*! First we are prevented from gaining help, and now that bandit seizes Hougan!" Wang Lang exclaimed.

"A bandit – or rather rebel – that we've already been dealing with," Xu Jing said. "I wouldn't worry just yet, Lord Wang. Let's see what Zhang Ya's conditions are now that he is self-appointed Magistrate of Hougan."

"...**I have created another Ze Rong, another Zang Ba!**" Wang Lang cried. "**He'll want Hougan for an independent state! He'll-!**"

"Promise Zhang Ya whatever he asks for, and we'll worry about obliging or reneging when we've defeated Hè Qi," Xu Jing suggested. "We're forced to act according to circumstance: Sun Ce's vile following is our foremost concern."

Wang Lang returned to Hougan's capital and visited Zhang Ya in the unchanged magistrate's residence: Zhang was surrounded by family and friends, and the atmosphere was surprisingly calm.

"Greetings, Administrator Wang!" Zhang Ya chuckled.

"...You have adjusted to the role well," Wang Lang said cuttingly.

Zhang Ya frowned angrily.

"Be civil, Lord Wang!" Xu Jing whispered.

"...By which I mean, of course, that your efforts since taking charge have been beyond expectations, Mister Zhang," Wang Lang said ingratiatingly. "Was it my imagination, or has Hè Qi retreated a considerable distance...?"

Zhang Ya's expression softened: he smiled and said, "Yeah... *yes*. But there's still a lot of work to do, Administrator. I've managed to rally more people to our cause; how was your trip to the Yuzhang border...?"

"There is no sense in lying to you: I was unsuccessful," Wang

Lang replied. "It is, therefore, vital that we learn to work as friends as well as allies. Consider yourself the permanent Magistrate if that's what you wish, and we'll-"

"I may need to be considered as more than that," Zhang Ya said. "For now, though, I'll take the Han title: it'll help me get support. What will you do now?"

"I intend to liaise with the Governor of Jiaozhi, Shi Xie, and see whether we can come to some agreement," Wang Lang explained. "My forces are still considerable, and I'm sure that we'll both gain support now that Hè Qi is proven to be human."

"...Perhaps," Zhang Ya said with a smirk.

Wang Lang bowed slightly and said, "I shall leave you, Magistrate Zhang, as I have need of rest. We shall meet again soon."

"I'll look forward to it," Zhang Ya chuckled.

Once Wang Lang and Xu Jing were gone, Liao turned to Zhang Ya and said, "When you become Administrator or Governor of Hougan State, what will I be, Father-in-law...?"

Zhang Ya snorted a laugh and replied, "You'll be grateful that you married into my clan."

"I helped to secure this for you!" Liao barked. **"I'm your son-in-law! I-!"**

"So you want rank just because you married my daughter?" Zhang Ya heckled. "Go and inspect the walls again, Liao: we'll continue this conversation another time."

"...You're riding for a fall, Zhang Ya!" Liao bellowed as he marched out of the hall with his irritated kin.

"And who's going to topple me, Liao? YOU???" Zhang Ya retorted.

Zhang Ya's brother coughed deliberately and said, "You should make it up with him. His family's not that small."

"For now, yes, but I might find my daughter a better husband," Zhang Ya sighed.

Hè Qi was startled by the sudden increase in effectiveness that Zhang Ya brought to the reformed Hougan coalition: the number of rebels grew daily, and Hè Qi was pushed further and further back. After a week of reversals, Hè Qi wrote to Gongjin and Lü Fan to request further instruction, but the political situation in Danyang had just taken a nasty turn: Yuan Yin had reached the capital with the intention of taking control of the prefecture on behalf of his cousin Shu.

****

81

Yuan Shu's cousin Yin stopped his entourage in front of the gates of Danyang's capital and awaited a welcome: Bofu's cousin Xu Kun, Gongjin and the latter's uncle, Administrator Zhou Shang, peered over the battlements and watched the increasingly impatient Yuan Yin with irritation and fear.

"...So what will we do?" Xu Kun asked of Gongjin. "I asked Zhang Zhao, and all he does is babble about 'surrender options'; Quan Rou is nice enough but insists that we should probably 'capitulate'. That isn't your view, or we'd have opened the gates already... so what do you want to do...?

"There are two things that we must do here," Gongjin replied. "The first is to repel him: the other is to accept his demands."

"...Isn't that a nonsense?" Xu Kun asked.

Gongjin smiled and said, "If we refuse him, we risk war with Yuan Shu and losing Danyang later. If we accept him, we lose Danyang now, and Yuan Shu will contrive a reason to destroy us later on. If we take a third, 'nonsense' route that gets rid of him temporarily and gives us an opportunity to plead our case to Yuan Shu, then we might be able to turn this apparently no-win situation to our advantage."

"...That still sounds like nonsense, but alright," Xu Kun replied. "What do we do, then...?"

"The way to deal with this situation is for each of us to act separately and divide responsibility," Gongjin explained. "Firstly, Xu Kun, you will..."

An hour later – and shortly before Yuan Yin was about to make a fourth and final demand to be let into the city – Xu Kun ordered that the gates be opened and rode out of the city with a unit of cavalry.

"**HOW DARE YOU!**" Yuan Yin shrieked as Xu Kun drove the official's men away from the wall. "**I AM YOUR LORD AND MASTER'S-!**"

"**BE GONE!**" Xu Kun boomed. "**BE GONE, DECEITFUL STRANGER, OR I WILL KILL YOU!**"

The terrified Yuan Yin cried out and fled, and his ill-equipped entourage followed.

"...Well, Nephew, there they go," Zhou Shang sighed he watched the scene from the battlements with Gongjin. "What now?"

"I already told you, Uncle," Gongjin chuckled. "You and I will go to him and..."

Gongjin and Zhou Shang waited for several hours and then pursued Yuan Yin to the small village to the west of the capital that the official had chosen as a refuge.

"**You're all doomed!**" Yuan Yin screamed as Gongjin and Zhou Shang entered his temporary residence in the village inn; he then pointed at both men in turn and added, "**When I report this to Cousin Yuan, you-!**"

"You misunderstand the matter, Mister Yuan," Gongjin said.

"What is there to misunderstand???" Yuan Yin exclaimed.

"My young nephew speaks truthfully," Zhou Shang said. "The fault is entirely mine. I left Xu Kun in charge and told him that with

rebel saboteurs and tricksters about – rumoured to be led by the wily *Taishi Ci*, no less – none were to be given access to the city."
"But isn't the word that Taishi died defending Liu Yao at Qu'e?" Yuan Yin retorted. "So your lies are wasted on me, Zhou Shang! This only proves my lord's suspicions that Sun Ce intends to-"
"Would Sun Ce be so obvious when he is in such a weak position?" Zhou Shang asked.
Yuan Yin frowned and said, "Weak position...?"
"Sun Ce intends no insurrection," Zhou Shang insisted. "It is as I said: our latest information tells us that Taishi Ci is alive and leading this 'uprising', and if he is, Taishi is a known trickster and knave, and he has surprised smarter men than any of us before. He made a fool of Gongsun Du in Liaodong and outwitted an army of a million Yellow Turbans in Beihai: why shouldn't he feign weakness and take Danyang's capital while our lord is distracted? And then there's Liu Yao's following, Wang Lang, the threat of the resurgence of trouble in Wu..."
Yuan Yin sighed and said, "That's all plausible. But now that you know who I am, there is no further need for trouble. Let me into the capital, and there will be no further-"
"Ah, but you see, there's an additional problem," Zhou Shang said. "I told Xu Kun that none should be admitted, for my intention was to go east and oversee reinforcement of cities there against the Shanyue: I realised that I had forgotten some important documents – including, Heaven forgive me, the Administrator's seal! Now Xu Kun will not even allow me into the city, fearing me to be another rebel trick! When – if – the rebels are truly routed, then there will be no problem, but-"
"This is nonsense!" Yuan Yin chortled. "**I came here from Shouchun! From SHOUCHUN! I crossed the Great River to be here! Where do you two expect me to go???**"
"...Shouchun?" Gongjin said dryly.
"You shut up, you schemer!" Yuan Yin retorted. "I sense young mischief-makers at work, and most likely *you*, Zhou Yu, son of Luoyang's magistrate and supposed 'genius'!"
"Oh...?" Gongjin chuckled. "Am I considered a genius, then...?"
Yuan Yin flicked his sleeve, harrumphed and said, "Lord Yuan has somehow been convinced of your 'great worth', but-! ...Wait."
Yuan Yin's countenance changed.
"...Your expression betrays awkwardness, but I imagine that your sleeve-flick was a mistake in a heated moment," Gongjin said with false warmth.
"...Uh... it is true that I had, in my anger, forgotten that there was a second request from Lord Yuan," Yuan Yin replied. "You are to travel to Shouchun and join Lord Yuan's court. Perhaps, under the circumstances, it would be better if we went together so that I can explain the... 'situation'... here in Danyang."
"Fate works in mysterious ways," Gongjin said. "I have to write to Lord Sun Ce and inform him of my relocation: if you can wait until I have done that, we can leave tomorrow. Uncle can remain here and try and find some way to-"
"I am in no rush now," Yuan Yin grumbled. "But for your sakes, this had better not be some sort of ruse; Lord Yuan distrusts you all enough as it is."
Gongjin and his uncle left the residence and retreated to the

village gates. As they walked, Zhou Shang said, "Be careful."
"I can outwit Yuan Shu," Gongjin insisted. "And this may, in fact, be to our advantage..."

As the weeks passed, Southern Commandant Hè Qi was trying to play a patient game of his own. One day, a messenger came to his packed Hougan command tent and said, "The agent reports success, Commander."
"Ah! At last!" Hè Qi chuckled.
"What has happened?" one officer asked.
"Gentlemen, you must have noticed the sudden drop in proficiency that our enemies exhibited during our last few encounters," Hè Qi began. "Well, I decided to find out what the 'problem' could be, and to my surprise, it wasn't a split between Zhang and Wang! It seems that our friend Zhang Ya has domestic issues: his most trusted subordinate is also his son-in-law, and since the takeover of Hougan, the two have ceased to be allies and become more like rivals. Wang Lang has actually had to mediate between them at least once."
"So what have you done?" the officer asked.
"I've sown the seeds of doubt and mistrust," Hè Qi explained. "I placed a number of agents in their ranks: it was painfully easy, since they assume us to be something that we're not because we dress so well. Now one of those agents has managed to worsen the problems between Mister Zhang and his son-in-law, and it won't be long before we can act! The two are now at war with one-another, gentlemen!"
The officials chattered excitedly.
"All that we need to do now is to wait for an agent in one camp or the other to report their man preparing for an attack against the other, and we'll act," Hè Qi concluded. "It will be as easy as taking something out of a sack: and when Zhang Ya is broken, Wang Lang is finished."

Suddenly, two serious situations – one in Danyang, and one in Kuaiji – were on the verge of being suddenly and gratefully resolved. That should have been well received in Shouchun, the capital of Yang Province and base of Bofu's lord Yuan Shu, but Yuan had other, far more self-destructive thoughts in mind: he had learned of Gongjin's imminent arrival and the return of Yuan Yin, and the latter greatly displeased him.
How dare they turn away my cousin!" Yuan Shu shrieked.
"We must not act rashly, Lord Yuan!" the adviser Yang Hong pleaded.
"And what is 'rashly', Yang Hong?" Yuan Shu retorted. "What is 'rash' compared to a vassal – a lowly vassal, a vassal so lowly that his name is not only unknown to me, but *irrelevant* – chases his lord's cousin away from the city that he has been designated to inhabit, and worse still, the prefectural capital that he is designated to administrate on his lord's behalf...?"
Sun Ben bowed low and said, "My lord, there is more to this, as you know from Zhou Yu's correspondence that I have relayed to you already. Rebels numbering in the tens of thousands are currently causing havoc in Danyang, and the Shanyue are rampant everywhere else. The-"

418

"Do I not know these things…?" Yuan Shu heckled. "These things are the reasons behind my tolerating your headstrong cousin's continued presence in that region! If I had my way, he'd be somewhere else – anywhere else – and I would have men that I know and trust – not 'Hè Qi', 'Zhou Yu', and 'Cheng Pu', and all these other people that he writes to me about – acting as magistrates, administrators and commandants! What has a few rebels got to do with turning away my cousin by force…?"

"It's explained already!" Sun Ben protested.

"And it still makes no sense on the thousandth recital!" Yuan Shu barked. **"Tell me, Sun Ben, why I shouldn't just have you all arrested!"**

"…Because we're loyal, Lord Yuan, and you can make good use of us," Sun Ben replied carefully. "When the rebellion is eradicated and the Shanyue contained, solid foundations for government can be built in Danyang. Until then, we must not give our nomadic, ubiquitous enemies anything tangible to harm us."

"A fine way of putting it, but when can we expect the things you speak of?" the adviser Han Yin asked.

"I can no more predict that than the next harvest or plague," Sun Ben retorted. "All that I can do is pass on what I have been told to pass on: that they continue to do everything in their power, and that we must… wait."

"I'm a patient man, gentlemen," Yuan Shu said bitterly. "I'll wait… for in the end, it shall all be *mine*."

In Hougan, Commandant Hè Qi's patience was finally rewarded.

"Report!" a soldier cried as he ran into Hè Qi's busy command tent. "Zhang is planning to attack Liao within the next few hours!"

"Aha! Now is the moment, gentlemen!" Hè Qi declared. "We'll divide as we planned! Wang Lang's limbs are about to harm each other, but let us ensure they are severed!"

Zhang Ya led the majority of his forces out of Hougan's capital and moved at speed toward his son-in-law's new encampment around a nearby village; Wang Lang's protests fell on deaf ears, and Hougan City – which was now lacking defenders – prepared for the worst.

Zhang Ya struck quickly and powerfully, scattering his unprepared son-in-law's forces and putting them to flight. But as he chased the survivors across Hougan's landscape, his own army was set upon by most of Hè Qi's.

"How can this be???" Zhang Ya cried. **"We'll have to forget our grudges and team up again!"**

"Liao's dead, I think," Zhang Ya's brother reported. **"We shouldn't have done this!"**

"I… **I know!**" Zhang Ya replied as he tried to think of a plan. But there would be no victory now: his scouts quickly reported the destruction of most of his camps around Hougan. Hè Qi had won, and Wang Lang was once again humbled.

****

82

"Hè Qi's brilliance gives us much-needed breathing space," Lü Fan said to a gathering of officials in Bofu's command tent. "Instead of going to Hougan, we can go and end the trouble in Shanyin."
"But shouldn't we make sure that Wang Lang is crushed first?" Bofu asked.
"The uprising in Shanyin has to be put down," Cheng Pu said. "If you insist on going to Hougan, I won't disagree, but who will go and aid Dong Xi and Yu Fan in defeating those bandits...?"
"I'll go personally," Bofu replied. "The Shanyue in Danyang and Wu are all hiding; the rebels in Danyang are a problem, yes, but manageable if we leave enough people here; and Hè Qi seems to have found a way of managing Wang Lang's friends..."
"Who will go with you?" Lü Fan asked.
"You, naturally," Bofu replied. "Huang Gai and Chen Wu can join me as well. Cheng Pu, Jiang Qin, Ling Cao and Lü Meng can remain here to provide backup to whoever might need it and react to the rebel armies as they appear."
"We'll depart immediately then," Lü Fan said.

Chief Constable Dong Xi and Officer of Merit Yu Fan greeted their lord at the gates of Shanyin's capital.
"Aren't you going to ask if we had trouble getting here?" Bofu joked as he jumped down from his horse.
"Your timing couldn't be better, Administrator Sun," Yu Fan replied. "We-"
"Ayah... that's worse than 'Lord Sun'!" Bofu complained.
"...Lord Sun, then," Yu Fan continued. "Huang Longluo issued a challenge yesterday, but-"
"Is 'Bofu' so difficult, Yu Zhongxiang?" Bofu sighed.
"...The bandits are really making life difficult," Yu Fan said.
"*Aiee*... alright, fine, I'm 'Lord Sun'," Bofu grumbled. "You know, I do nothing but fight. I never thought I'd hear myself say this, but I am tired of non-stop fighting, and so's everyone else. These bandits had better surrender, because-"
"Killing them would be no loss to society, Lord Sun," Dong Xi said. "Did you see what they've been doing?"
"I have, Yuanshi," Bofu replied. "They're animals."
"And they'll soon be dealt with, Lord Sun," Lü Fan suggested. "We'll divide our forces and be ready at their next likely targets."
"That's the problem, Mister Lü Fan," Yu Fan said. "They attack at random, even hitting places more than once that have nothing left to take: how will we know where they'll strike next?"
"Even random strikes have some small pattern," Lü Fan replied. "Men need food, water, and other supplies, so in a lot of ways, they'll tell us what we want to know."
"Ah... I see your reasoning!" Dong Xi said. "Let's end it, then."
Huang Longluo and Zhou Bo had split their bandit army between them, so they could potentially double the number of targets that they could attack: but just as Lü Fan had suggested, they had fallen into a subconscious pattern of always following an attack on a new target with an adjacent old one or the converse. Dong Xi, Yu Fan and Chen Wu were waiting in an area that Huang

Longluo was known to frequent, while Bofu, Lü Fan and Huang Gai awaited a raid by Zhou Bo in another part of the county. Huang Longluo was intercepted within two days, and his forces were routed by a combination of cavalry and archery tactics; Zhou Bo evaded Bofu for a further day, but he was defeated and chased away from a village by a full deployment of everything that Bofu currently had at his disposal. The bandits consolidated at that point and issued a challenge, which was exactly what the defenders had hoped for: Bofu and his allies regrouped in Shanyin's capital and awaited the approach of the entire bandit army with strange delight.

"They couldn't make it easier for us!" Lü Fan said to an audience of officials. "All that we have to do is fight them as we have every other army of savages, be they Shanyue or bandit."

"I would like to be in the vanguard," Dong Xi said. "I have a lot of poor performances to make up for."

"Don't be so hard on yourself," Bofu replied. "If you want to be the van, fine: you show them what you can do."

Dong Xi rode to the front of the defending army and faced the two bandit leaders that had caused so much misery in Shanyin. Huang Longluo rode back and forth along his front line and rallied his vast horde with chants, while Zhou Bo made mock charges and heckled the defenders directly: neither expected Dong Xi to attack first, but that is exactly what he did. He galloped toward Zhou Bo as the latter was retreating from another series of taunts: after a brief exchange of weapons, Dong Xi ran Zhou through with his spear and pulled the dying bandit from his horse with his free hand. The bandits immediately panicked at the sight of one of their leaders being killed with such ease: Huang Longluo quickly urged anger instead of panic, and ordered a charge. But instead of retreating to Bofu's front line to gather backup, Dong Xi and his elite riders left their infantry colleagues behind and charged at Huang Longluo.

"**Magnificent...!**" Lü Fan exclaimed.

"**We just keep finding more and more talents, don't we Ziheng?**" Bofu chuckled. "**Let's all-out charge and smash the rest of them.**"

Bofu's entire army charged at the disorganised bandits: Dong Xi had, in the meantime, broken the defensive circle around Huang Longluo and leapt from his horse to fight the bandit on foot while his followers scattered Huang's guards. Huang Longluo lunged at Dong Xi with his poorly-maintained sword, but Dong Xi was too swift and skilled for the seasoned brawler. Dong Xi dodged this way and that, and when Huang Longluo left an opening, Dong Xi ran him through. With both bandit leaders dead, the criminal coalition largely disintegrated: Bofu's officers killed every man that tried to rally the bandits for a counterattack, and the rest either fled or surrendered.

In the wake of the swift victory in Shanyin, Bofu held a banquet: Dong Xi was singled out for his elimination of the bandit leaders.

"I deserve no praise!" Dong Xi pleaded modestly.

"You do, Yuanshi, and you know it," Bofu chuckled. "The way you rallied the men – including some of mine – and charged straight at those bandits was just what was needed. Yu Zhongxiang agrees, and he's been telling me all about some of your exploits. You two would have won within a few weeks anyway, I think!"

"I am no hero," Dong Xi insisted. "I just-"

"You have so few men under your command that it's insulting," Bofu continued. "I'm giving you a few thousand, and I'm promoting you to a major. In addition, I-"

"You mustn't, Lord Sun!" Dong Xi pleaded. "I'm not worthy!"

"...Where's the brave, defiant man that insisted that I accept your surrender in person, Dong Yuanshi?" Bofu retorted. "I suppose it's because you're worried that you're becoming arrogant or reckless. Your achievements here make any man that accuses you of being arrogant a fool, and as for 'reckless'... well, I'm reckless, so I for one won't be saying too much about it!"

"Quite right," Sun Hè chortled.

"So you'll accept my promotion, and you'll accept the additional title of 'Commandant that dispenses Martial Might'," Bofu continued. "The bandits were routed, but there are other problems here in Shanyin."

Lü Fan coughed loudly.

"...Excuse me," Bofu chuckled as he turned to Lü Fan.

"On the subject of 'other problems', we should go back to our southern Danyang camp immediately," Lü Fan suggested. "The rebels have been pressurising us, and the defenders need help..."

"...And we need to consolidate before we march to Hougan, of course," Bofu sighed. "Okay, we'll hurry back."

****

83

While Bofu's forces began a speedy journey back to southern Danyang, the newly-appointed 'Major of a Separate Command' and 'Commandant that dispenses Martial Might', Dong Xi, and Yu Fan returned to the process of pacification in Shanyin; and in Hougan, Acting Southern Commandant Hè Qi continued to pile pressure on the increasingly isolated former Administrator of Kuaiji, Wang Lang. But once again, Bofu's lord and master – Yuan Shu of Ru County – was more concerned with the situation in the north and guiltlessly claimed the southern successes as his own.

"I… I am destined for greatness!" Yuan Shu cackled as he read a report from the north. "Cao Cao plans to abandon his emperor to go north and fight Zhang Xiu and Jia Xu! He publicly declares that he intends to punish Liu Biao as well!"

The adviser Han Yin coughed deliberately and asked, "How do you interpret the move as advantageous, if I might be so bold as to ask, my lord…?"

"I can only win!" Yuan Shu replied. "Zhang and Jia are in Nan County, are they not…? If Cao attacks them, it leaves Liu Biao vulnerable! If Cao wins, I will go west and take Xiangyang and Fan, or perhaps south, to take Jiangxia! If Cao loses, well… that's even better, for reasons that I needn't explain!"

"…How could he lose?" the adviser Yan Xiang scoffed. "I know that Jia Xu is enviably cunning, but Zhang Xiu is, in comparison to his formidable uncle that actually seized the place before dying, a mediocrity that cannot hope to defeat the Han Imperial Army when it is led – personally – by one of the most talented men of the day!"

"You overpraise Cao Cao, I think," Yuan Shu growled.

"Are we sure that Cao Cao will be leading the army personally?" Jiujiang Administrator Chen Ji asked.

"He led the army against Liu Pi and Huang Shao personally," Han Yin noted.

"That was an unfortunate loss, as was Yufuluo," Yuan Shu sighed.

"Yes, and perhaps we should see that as inauspicious when pondering the 'other matter'!" Yan Xiang said carefully.

"Is that still being discussed…?" Bofu's cousin Sun Ben exclaimed. "Lord Yuan, I have already relayed the Sun clan's position on that matter, and-"

"**Don't dictate terms to me, Sun Ben!**" Yuan Shu barked. "**Remember who is lord and who is vassal!**"

Sun Ben exchanged weary glances with Gongjin – who was now part of Yuan Shu's court as well – before he replied, "My apologies, Lord Yuan."

Yuan Shu harrumphed and said, "Mister Han Yin, your observation about Cao's intention to lead his army on every campaign – the same reckless behaviour that led to his defeat at Xingyang – is an observation shared and hoped for by your lord. I want to know when he is definitely out of the capital."

"…Uh… why do you think that Cao Cao will let you invade Jing after he defeats Zhang Xiu…?" Yang Hong asked.

"He will have no choice but to withdraw after the losses that he'll sustain against Jing's navy!" Yuan Shu replied. "His role, as

defined by the fates, is to soften the prey before I capture and consume it... and with Jing under my control – the throat of the nation – I will choke my enemies and fulfil my heavenly destiny!"
Yuan Shu started to laugh while his officials looked on silently.

Once the meeting was over, Sun Ben and Gongjin left the hall together.
"He's every bit as deranged as you implied," Gongjin said as the two walked the streets of Shouchun.
"Yes, and you've heard it for yourself: day after day, he moves closer and closer to... to... to that thing I daren't say for fear of angering Heaven!" Sun Ben despaired. "What can we do?"
"My observations are that he has mistreated the people and mismanaged the administration of Jiujiang, his chosen capital, never mind everywhere else," Gongjin scoffed. "How he can think that he's... 'mandated'... Heaven forgive me for even referring to it... is ridiculous. At least Cao Cao could argue something like that because he's actually done a good job in Xuchang, from what I hear."
"Most of Yuan's following will desert him," Sun Ben said.
"Oh, naturally they will," Gongjin replied. "It's one thing to have your own militia, claim ancestral lands as personal domains, challenge your clan leader, claim other people's lands, and even indulge in clandestine support for bandits and terrorists... but it is another thing altogether to do as he intends. He'll be isolated and destroyed for it, and rightly so."
"You sound confident," Sun Ben noted. "You have a plan then, for... for 'that time', when it happens...?"
"Yes, and I'm certain that it will work," Gongjin replied. "So, like so many are having to do these days... we must wait."

Bofu returned to his main camp on the Danyang-Kuaiji border and prepared to march: during that time, word reached him that Liu Bei had capitulated to Lü Bu and allowed the latter to become the Governor of Xu Province in exchange for being rescued from Yuan Shu's general Ji Ling; and to the surprise of all, Cao Cao's newly-instated imperial court in Yan Province recognised Bu publicly. He also learned of Liu Pi and Huang Shao's reformed faction of Yellow Turbans in Yu Province and their subsequent defeat, and Cao Cao's recent declaration of war against Liu Biao.
"So Huang Shao is dead: can't say I'll miss him," Cheng Pu scoffed. "It's a pity that Cao Cao spared Liu Pi: every single one of that bunch of heretics deserves death."
"But still... they were working for Yuan Shu, so what happened...?" Sun Hè asked.
"...Cunning," Lü Fan said as he read the latest reports from the north. "Yuan Shu's allowed them to become Yellow Turbans again so that he couldn't be blamed for their actions, but he won't fool Cao Cao; the Black Mountain Bandits and their Southern Xiongnu allies were also being paid by Yuan, and I think he may have added the White Wave Bandits to his cause too."
"But the White Waves were defeated by Cao at Luoyang, weren't they...?" Huang Gai said. "And wasn't Yufuluo killed...?"
"The White Wave leaders fled into Yu Province," Cheng Pu explained. "But yes, Yufuluo's dead, one way or the other, and his

band of renegade Xiongnu have supposedly gone back to Bing Province to be part of the main tribal confederacy. The Black Mountain Bandits are weaker now, but who knows what'll happen there... but yes, for all of our criticism of others like Wang Lang, 'Lord' Yuan probably funds more bandits, pirates, crime families and cultists than the rest put together."

"...We work for a crime boss," Bofu muttered.

"There's no sense in saying things like that," Cheng Pu said.

"It concerns me, though, when thinking about... the future," Bofu admitted. "Still, as you say often, we're in the here and now, and our main focus is Wang Lang. When was the last report from Kuaiji received...?"

"A week ago, roughly, and Hè Qi was reporting that Zhang Ya was probably dead," Lü Fan replied. "If he is, we can count the days before that slimy pedant Wang tries to flee, probably to Jiaozhi: I think that we need to hasten our preparations for a march to Kuaiji Prefecture."

"If that's what you and Demou agree on, we'll speed up our departure," Bofu said.

The Kuaiji Prefecture campaign against its former Administrator, Wang Lang, was about to come to an end: Acting Southern Commandant Hè Qi had received more local support since the defeat of the rebel leader Zhang Ya, and there was now next to no chance of Wang regaining his grip on power. Wang Lang was also trapped in Hougan County's capital, which only added to his woes.

"Where will I go???" Wang Lang asked of his adviser Xu Jing. "What can I do???"

Xu Jing did not reply: the two were in the relative calm of the hall of the magistrate's residence, but the sounds of siege preparations were everywhere.

"You have to have an answer, Xu Jing!" Wang Lang pleaded. ***"Save me!"***

"...This isn't just about *you*, Mister Wang," Xu Jing replied.

"I know, I know, I... I apologise, Mister Xu," Wang Lang sighed.

"I joined you to revenge my brother's death, but now I am a pitiful fugitive," Xu Jing continued. "How far we've come, Wang Lang, since those days in the capital when we were all young, free-spirited scholars..."

"Don't say such things!" Wang Lang replied. "Your words are drenched in finality!"

"There is finality in our next move," Xu Jing said. "You are finished here in Kuaiji, Mister Wang, and I am finished too. The north is a place of uncertainty where we might find that old friends are now our enemies: besides, it's too far, and requires travelling through the places where Sun Ce and his master are strongest. Our only hope is Jiaozhi."

"...Seeking aid from that godforsaken place is one thing, but living there is another!" Wang Lang replied. "Is that truly our only option, Mister Xu?"

"Zhang Ya is either dead or in hiding, and so is his extended family," Xu Jing said. "They were our last remaining source of allies: that self-styled talent Dong Xi and the treacherous Yu Fan have apparently destroyed the bandit uprising in central Shanyin with Sun Ce's help, and the Shanyue are not responding to my attempts at re-establishing communications with them at all."

"We could go to Hua Xin!" Wang Lang suggested.

"He's a mediocrity that has failed to get an alliance with Liu Yao's followers," Xu Jing replied. "The tribes in that area are probably going to rise up soon, and at that point, we're dead. Besides, we have to pass through-"

"I know, I know: places where Hè Qi is very influential, places where Sun Ce's uncle is operating, places that chose to rebuke me even before this catastrophic loss," Wang Lang grumbled. "There is nowhere to go but to the south."

"I shall go on ahead at speed and arrange for an armed escort," Xu Jing said. "The city must be fortified in such a way as to prevent our enemies from suspecting and following: you must make appearances and rally the men while preparing for your escape, which you should begin ten days after I have gone."

"Heaven speed you, Mister Xu," Wang Lang replied. "Let us hope that we can salvage something in the long term, however, from such a... humiliation."

Xu Jing grunted irritably and left the hall.

"...How far, indeed, we have come since those days when we were all in Luoyang, with bright futures ahead of us...!" Wang Lang chortled. "Now, I am a fugitive from a wretched pirate king... yet I thought I was destined for so much more than this..."

Wang Lang waited awhile before he went to his commanders to issue his final series of orders: in the meantime, Xu Jing prepared his small entourage and fled under cover of darkness on the same night. Wang Lang's hope was that Governor Shi Xie would not only risk giving refuge to him, but that he would somehow agree to form an army capable of retaking Kuaiji; Xu Jing had more modest hopes as he hurried to the border, little knowing that he would never see Yang Province – or the east of China – again.

****

84

Gongjin's time in Shouchun had introduced him to a small, visually-unimpressive man in his mid-twenties that would prove to be a pillar of future endeavours. The two had quickly become friends since they shared scholarly pursuits: the man's name was Lu Su, and his style name was 'Zijing'.

"Ah, Gongjin, what times we live in," Lu Su said as the two enjoyed a kettle of heated wine in a city tavern. "Other men with my education have served in ten administrative roles by my age, but I've done nothing."

"Forgive how this is going to sound, Zijing, but neither have any of the rest of your family," Gongjin replied.

Lu Su groaned miserably and said, "You're right, Gongjin! We're all failures!"

Gongjin laughed and said, "It depends on what you consider to be success, Zijing. Do you look at me – the descendant of countless senior Han officials, including 'Excellency' post-holders – and see a better man...?"

"Yes!" Lu Su replied honestly.

"You shouldn't," Gongjin insisted. "You might have noticed the weathered sleeves of this robe I'm wearing... and no doubt you thought that I simply cherish it for some reason, perhaps as a reminder of loved ones that have aged, grown sick and died."

"I don't really stare at people's sleeves, Gongjin," Lu Su chuckled.

"...So my point is lost," Gongjin sighed.

"Did you want to elaborate?" Lu Su asked politely.

"No," Gongjin replied. "We should, instead, discuss the current political situation."

"Ah, yes," Lu Su said. "I came here with every last coin of my wealth, every last bit of property, in order to pledge it to Lord Yuan Shu. But now I'm hearing from men with looser tongues than yours that he's not a particularly benevolent man."

"Go home, then," Gongjin suggested.

Lu Su laughed awkwardly and said, "I would, but... well..."

"...You didn't," Gongjin exclaimed.

"I suppose I should have mentioned it before," Lu Su said.

"Maybe!" Gongjin chortled. "You sold your family land???"

Lu Su nodded slowly.

"*Ayah*... Zijing, land is land, while coin is only as valuable as the idiots and schemers that regulate it!" Gongjin despaired. "What have you done with your money?"

"I bought two granaries," Lu Su replied.

"...That isn't so foolish," Gongjin conceded. "Grain is more valuable than gold in some places at the moment, especially since that locust plague... but now you are shackled here, and what if Yuan Shu confiscates your granaries...?"

"The thought occurred to me, but since I came here to serve him, I decided that his taking them is the same as me sharing them," Lu Su replied. "But anyway, haven't we digressed...? The political landscape is complicated at present: Liu Zhang in the west, a worthless type that will inevitably lose Yi to Zhang Lu and-or Liu Biao..."

"I hope not," Gongjin chortled. "My friend Bofu hates Liu Biao."

"Ah yes, Sun Ce of Fuchun… you know some very impressive people in addition to being one yourself, Gongjin," Lu Su said enviously. "I have wanted to ask for some time: is he as belligerent, reckless and short-tempered as people say? I suppose that his famous father's death was rather ignominious in addition to being unexpected, so he has a right to be like that if he is."

"…Are you always that tactless?" Gongjin retorted.

"*Aiee*… I meant no offence, Gongjin," Lu Su pleaded. "I had heard that-!"

"Never mind," Gongjin chuckled. "Why don't you return to your original point?"

"Liu Biao will take Yi, and then you have Li Jue and Guo Si in Liang, Cao Cao, Yuan Shu and Yuan Shao in the central territories, Gongsun Zan in the northeast and Lü Bu in the east," Lu Su said. "Bu is a fool, so one out of Cao Cao or the Yuans will take Xu Province eventually; Gongsun Zan is brave but flawed, so he'll lose Yòu Province and Qing Province to Yuan Shao eventually; when Li Jue and Guo Si inevitably turn on each other again, that region will either fall to the Qiang tribes, Cao Cao, Liu Biao or Yuan Shao; the number of warlords will shrink, and the territories that the survivors hold will get bigger…"

"You've given it a lot of thought since our last chat, I see," Gongjin said.

"Oh, yes," Lu Su replied. "I know that none of the warlords are perfect, but a man has to decide on a master and follow him in such an age. If I'd stayed where I was, I might have ended up in Lü Bu's court: what an awful thought!"

Gongjin laughed and said, "I quite agree, Zijing."

"So that left Yuan Shao, Yuan Shu, Cao Cao and Liu Biao, since I didn't fancy going to Yi and that mediocrity Liu Zhang is doomed anyway," Lu Su continued. "At present, it would take a self-inflicted disaster of quite ridiculous proportions to turn Yuan Shu from a hero to a vagrant, so he was a certain choice."

Gongjin smiled and hummed knowingly.

"…Did I say something stupid?" Lu Su asked.

"No, no!" Gongjin replied. "Do go on, Zijing."

"Yuan Shao is a wealthy, shrewd political and military powerhouse, so he's going to be a major figure for some time to come," Lu Su continued. "Cao Cao is still underestimated by many, I think: nobody thought he'd still be around, and yet he's Excellency of something-or-other now. At present, there seems to be an inevitable move toward four 'super-warlords'. That won't last, because it can't: at some point, one will fall to one of the others, and then there will be three, and *that's* when it becomes interesting. What isn't clear to me yet is who the first to fall will be… they all seem to be so unshakable…"

Gongjin risked making a suggestion: he coughed falsely and asked, "What if Yuan Shu were to be the one that fell first…?"

Lu Su grinned and started to laugh.

"I mean it," Gongjin insisted.

Lu Su fought the involuntary laughter and said, "He'd have to be the biggest idiot alive to lose everything he has now!"

"Just assume that he is, as you say, an unbelievable fool for a moment, *hypothetically*," Gongjin pleaded.

Lu Su stopped laughing, shook his head and said, "*I'd* have been an idiot to buy granaries here."

"Look, forget the granaries!" Gongjin chortled. "What, in your opinion, would be the division of power then…?"

"…Mm… it's so unlikely that I hadn't considered it," Lu Su admitted. "But… if something did happen to Yuan Shu, then… his vassals would have to go to new lords… unless they were powerful enough to become a warlord themselves."

"In that scenario, where would you place my lor- I mean, my friend, Sun Ce?" Gongjin asked.

"…Sun Ce…?" Lu Su exclaimed. "Well, uh… my own understanding is that he has a temper that he needs to control, but… well… if he were to be released from service right now, he would be able to consolidate the south against the others quite easily. He wouldn't be able to retain Lujiang and Jiujiang – Cao Cao or Yuan Shao would seize them for certain – and he may not keep Guangling either, but… but everything south of the Great River would be his to govern. With the Great River as a barrier, he could form his own state and me almost impossible to defeat. My goodness… if that happened, why, that could upset everything…!"

"In what way…?" Gongjin prompted.

"How would the mightiest reunify the land if there were a man like Sun Ce sitting beyond the Great River?" Lu Su replied. "If the south were properly developed, then it could become a second state, a new and independent region that the Han would have trouble controlling: it could be like Kaiyang, only mightier, better, and run by better men… that would cause fission that would last a hundred years or more, at the very least, depending on whether there were one or two super-warlords to the north of the river."

"A splendid conceit, Lu Zijing!" Gongjin chuckled.

"But that's all it is," Lu Su insisted. "Yuan Shu is Sun Ce's master, and he insists on retaining power – and a capital – in the north. Sun Ce will never betray the lord-vassal covenant, so my previous theory holds."

"I agree," Gongjin said cheerfully. "After all… how could that other nonsense ever happen…?"

"What a thing!" Lu Su cackled. "An independent south…!"

Gongjin's smile was an honest one: he knew, unlike Lu Su, that Yuan Shu was poised to destroy himself, and that Lu Su's 'nonsense vision' was a very possible reality.

✳✳✳✳✳✳✳✳✳✳✳✳

Bofu led an army southward and intercepted Wang Lang before he could cross the provincial border and find relative safety in Jiaozhi, a region that encompassed part of would later be called, amongst other things, Northern Vietnam. A campaign into that vast, hostile region would have been costly, so Wang Lang's capture was a relief to all.

Wang Lang was brought unbound before a temporary tent court for what he presumed to be final disposition. Wang's former subordinate Yu Fan was present in addition to Bofu, Lü Fan and Hè Qi; none of the men regarded Wang as the famed talent that he professed to be and Wang knew it well. There was a long silence as each man awaited words from the other, but it would be the son of Sun Jian that would speak first.

"…Wang Lang," Bofu said tonelessly. "What have you to say for yourself…?"

"Before he answers that, I have a more pertinent question when looking to the future as well as the present," Lü Fan said. "Wang Lang, where is your adviser, Xu Jing…?"

"He went into Jiaozhi ahead of me, Mister Lü Fan, in an attempt to seek an audience with Governor Shi," Wang Lang replied calmly. "He hoped to gain a promise of sanctuary, but Heaven has deemed – for reasons unfathomable to me – that his sagely life was preserved while mine was netted for destruction."

Hè Qi and Yu Fan harrumphed angrily.

"You are said to be a friend of Kong Rong and student of some of the capital's most famous scholars," Lü Fan said. "You knew Cai Yong, Qiao Xuan, Yang Si, and more; how, then, did a man who was once called a *xiaolian* come to advising deference to Dong Zhuo, funding tribal insurrections and fraternising with murderous bandits, tribes and rebels to destabilise his own region…?"

Wang Lang smiled falsely and said, "Xu Jing might have been a fine appraiser, but his advice was not to the standard of his famous brother Xu Shao. Xu Jing served me in order to revenge his brother, but that same brother – and the shrewder of the two – deliberately avoided entering my service as well as Tao Qian's, since he unexpectedly – and, I insist, undeservedly – presumed my character to match Tao's, which he famously rated poorly."

Lü Fan harrumphed and said, "I had heard as much, Lord Sun: that's how Xu Shao ended up in Liu Yao's service."

"And such a loss to the world Liu Yao was as well, Mister Lü," Wang Lang continued. "Our loss is Heaven's gain: Xu Shao was a man that I knew, and now he is cold bones as well! Who else can say that they knew him, I wonder; and in addition I ask, who here can or cannot say that they inadvertently or intentionally killed him, indirectly perhaps but nonetheless culpable…?"

"Southern Commandant Han Yan was a good man, and you and your rebel friend Zhang Ya killed him," Bofu said. "How do you feel about that, Wang Lang?"

"Why do you demand explanations from me?" Wang Lang retorted. "Don't you intend my death no matter what I say…?"

"…I came here to secure your *surrender*, Wang Lang," Bofu said. "If I wanted you dead, you'd have been dead a long time ago."

"To serve you, as Yu Fan lowers himself to...? To serve you is to serve Yuan Shu, which I cannot do!" Wang Lang replied. "Spare me and I will retire from public life and dedicate my existence to reading the classics and praying for forgiveness for failing in my public duty to serve the Han and smash the rebels, Sun Ce! You will have no more trouble from me! Wang Lang is consigned to the past! But others will pick up where I left off! Yuan Shu will not escape righteous torment!"

"So you have no intention of defending your position with anything remotely convincing, then...?" Lü Fan heckled. "Don't you feel like a wretch that has left a legacy that contradicts your alleged promise...?"

"...I am, like all men in this chaotic age, a victim of circumstance!" Wang Lang cried. "I could not bear to remain in the capital when my benefactor Yang Si died! I later had the fortune of entering the service of the famous Tao Qian, but by then he was like most men of this era: trapped on a path that only led to contentious decision-making! I did what I could, but when Dong Zhuo began his career in Luoyang my lord was suffering domestic problems that had to take priority! I only advised him as anyone else would have!"

"...And that got you Kuaiji," Bofu scoffed. "Men like my father were opposing Dong Zhuo with no territory or with territories more besieged than Xu Province was! Tao Qian stole part of Yang! He was never in any danger!"

"It was take or be taken!" Wang Lang retorted. "And I was awarded Kuaiji for more than ingratiating myself with Dong Zhuo! I had a distinguished record!"

"That you've now tainted by acting like an underworld figure," Yu Fan said. "The colluding with the Shanyue bad enough: Zhang Ya was an enemy of the people! What were you thinking???"

"I had no choice, Yu Fan, and you more than anyone else here will know what I was up against!" Wang Lang barked. "The imperial court ordered me to resist Yuan Shu, and that is what I did with the meagre resources at my disposal! You surrendered instead! How can you-!"

Wang Lang stopped suddenly and reviewed the faces of his judges: he saw nothing but contempt.

"...What must be understood, gentlemen, is that I did as I was asked, and nothing more," Wang Lang continued. "I am aware that some of my decisions were poor. That is why I lost. As I have already said, Xu Jing has rightly escaped, and I am caught. I am not worthy of my previous responsibilities here in the south, where I am perceived to be a cause of misery. I will return to the north, and if I cannot find a minor post in some small place then I will retire altogether."

Bofu looked to each of the men around him: none of them were gesturing in a way that suggested that they wanted him to push for Wang Lang's service.

"...That would be best," Bofu said. "You may go."

Wang Lang bowed and retreated with his guards.

"I'll ensure that he is escorted to the Great River," Lü Fan said.

"Yeah... I'd like to throw him in it, and watch him drown, but I think we have to show him mercy because of his court connections," Bofu replied.

"So sad," Yu Fan sighed. "I had heard so much about him, but that is what we got. The north is welcome to him."

"I agree," Hè Qi grumbled. He then turned to Bofu and said, "Lord Sun, my work is done. Who will now take my place as permanent Southern Commandant?"

"Are you serious?" Bofu chortled. "Who else would I get?"

"I'm unworthy," Hè Qi insisted.

"You're Southern Commandant now, and that's that," Bofu retorted. "Wang Lang is defeated, but Xu Jing might come back, or Zhang Ya might reappear. I need a man that can deal with them, and you are that man. Please don't refuse."

"I... I won't," Hè Qi replied. "I'll serve you unyieldingly, Lord Sun, for placing such faith in me."

"...And we, sad to say, must go back now without pausing to celebrate our victory over Wang Lang," Bofu said wearily. "It seems as though we – I – will not get any rest until the final end, whenever that may be. So many left to fight... so many..."

Wang Lang's adviser – the famous appraiser Xu Jing – could not and did not try to rescue his former master: he remained in Jiaozhi for a short time and then fled to the west. His next master would be Governor Liu Zhang of Yi Province, and after him the warlord Liu Bei, whose actions in Yi would near-rival those of the Sun clan that Xu Jing despised so much.

Wang Lang returned to the north and disappeared from public life. For some time, it was presumed that Wang Lang would never be seen again, but in truth his proper career had yet to begin: within two years he would be in Cao Cao's court in Xuchang, and he and his descendants would shape China in ways that none could have foreseen.

****

86

Bofu's friend Gongjin was starting to fret. He was now maintaining a militia in Yang's capital Shouchun, but his once-influential clan was running out of money, and without funds, his small army would inevitably fall apart. His new friend Lu Su was due to visit his home, so he had to decide whether to discuss his finances openly: he had still failed to come to a decision when Lu Su arrived with a small, unsolicited gift of dried meat.

"Ah, Lu Zijing, Lu Zijing... please, come in," Gongjin bleated as he ushered Lu Su into his home: he then spied the gift in Lu Su's hands and bellowed, "**Chen!**"

A servant hurried to the door, took the dried meat from Lu Su and retreated silently.

"You look so miserable!" Lu Su chuckled.

"Yes, well, laughing isn't the best response to identifying that someone is upset about something, but I'm used to your ways now," Gongjin grumbled as he invited Lu Su to sit at his side.

"Ah, right, yes... sorry," Lu Su replied. "Did you want to talk about it, Gongjin?"

"Not really," Gongjin replied. "How is your family?"

"...Shall I go?" Lu Su asked.

"Please forgive my demeanour; and no, I don't want you to go," Gongjin replied. "I have a lot on my mind: letters from Bofu, family matters to arrange..."

"You sound too busy for my visit to be convenient, Gongjin," Lu Su suggested.

"Stay!" Gongjin chortled. "I'll... I'll get wine."

Gongjin clapped his hands together, and two timid servants brought wine dishes and a small jar of wine. Once the servants were gone, the wine was poured into the wine kettle and the kettle was boiling, Gongjin said, "I suppose I should have asked whether you wanted it hot or not."

Lu Su was looking around the room: he spied Gongjin's *qin* – which was a form of zither – and hawed respectfully.

"Ah, yes," Gongjin chuckled. "I forgot to mention that I play the qin, didn't I."

"...Why aren't you married?" Lu Su asked suddenly. "You're an enviously handsome man with a list of talents that would make any man jealous, and yet you don't have a wife. Is there any particular reason?"

"What kind of question is that?" Gongjin chortled.

"...I didn't mean to offend," Lu Su pleaded. "I just-!"

"I pine for a family, but... I cannot, not right now," Gongjin said. "There's a political reason for it."

"...Political...?" Lu Su exclaimed. "Has Yuan Shu forbidden you from-?"

"Alright, fine, I didn't want to, but I'll come straight to the point," Gongjin said. "I'm... poor."

Lu Su grinned and said, "That's ridiculous!"

"Lu Zijing, the world is changing," Gongjin replied. "My family is a shrunken, broken thing indeed. We've had no real income since fleeing Luoyang, and I'm funding a militia on Yuan Shu's orders."

Lu Su frowned and said, "Why did he make you do that? Doesn't

he know that you can't afford it? Why didn't you tell him...?"
"I... I don't think you're ready for that revelation yet, Zijing,"
Gongjin replied. "I'll simply say that I am overestimated."
"...I don't know what to say," Lu Su admitted.
"That's better than one of your usual tactless comments, Zijing,"
Gongjin replied. "Anyway, you got your answer. Can we change
the subject now...?"
"...No, we cannot," Lu Su said seriously. "I won't enquire further if
you so wish it, but... I'd like to help you financially."
"*Ayah*... Don't be ridiculous!" Gongjin whined. "I couldn't-!"
"Please accept a further gift beyond the dried meat, Zhou
Gongjin," Lu Su said. "You have been so kind to me since I got
here: I am a man that sometimes offends unintentionally, and you
have been most patient. In addition, I am a man that comes from
a family that had wealth and land, but no prospects: to most men
of your noble birth that would be enough for you to turn your
head at the sight of me, but you welcomed me into your house...
and you'd rather be a beggar than exercise your class superiority
over me and demand that I help. How can I ignore such true
nobility, the nobility of the heart rather than social breeding...?"
"...You can be quite eloquent when you want to be," Gongjin
sighed miserably.
"You are a good man, Zhou Gongjin, and while I will not enquire
about other matters, I am starting to suspect that all is not well
here in Shouchun, and that we will inevitably discuss those things
on another occasion," Lu Su continued. "For now, I will be
satisfied by your accepting my second gift."
"...What do you propose...?" Gongjin asked apprehensively.
"I am a small man with a small appetite," Lu Su said. "I have no
militia, only a desire to serve a good lord well: you're not my lord,
but you're my friend and a man that serves our lord directly, so it
would be terrible for you to fail him through no fault of your own.
Accept one of my granaries as-"
"I cannot!" Gongjin exclaimed.
Lu Su bowed and said, "I insist that you do. Your hired men must
eat, Gongjin."
"...Lu Zijing, you are a man with a heart the size of Mount Tai!"
Gongjin said as his eyes filled with grateful tears. "I can never
truly repay you for such benevolence!"
"Repay me by being the same man that you are now, and never
being tempted to waver from it," Lu Su replied jovially. "Now,
perhaps, we should have that meat that I brought here to enjoy
with our wine!"
Gongjin laughed like a man that had been relieved of a great
burden: he bowed low and said, "Lu Zijing, you shall have only
the finest food in this house! Today, I have found another hero!"
"I wouldn't go that far!" Lu Su replied.

Gongjin visited Bofu's cousin Sun Ben on the following morning.
"Lady Wu is anxious to see you," Sun Ben said as he led Gongjin
into the house.
"Oh...?" Gongjin exclaimed. "Has something happened?"
"There's nothing wrong... nothing different, anyway," Sun Ben
sighed.
"I keep meaning to ask: how is your brother doing?" Gongjin

asked. "Does he write often?"

"I encouraged Fu to be simple in his communication, in order to avoid undue suspicion, and that appears to have been interpreted as 'Write very rarely'," Sun Ben chuckled. "Luling is remote, unsafe, tedious, but he fares well enough, and I think that he may get a moment to shine when-"

"Ah! Zhou Gongjin is here!" Bofu's mother, Lady Wu, shrieked as she stepped out of her sleeping quarters and caught sight of her visitor.

"It is always a pleasure," Gongjin replied. "When Boyang told me you were anxious to see me, I was worried: after all, am I not here more than I am at home...?"

"You're still wearing that scruffy robe," Lady Wu said. "Why?"

"I'm... being frugal," Gongjin replied. "I could spend money on new robes, but I need the coin for my men."

"I can find nobody that enjoys living here, and I include myself!" Lady Wu complained. "That fool Yuan Shu treats his 'subjects' like dirt, and-!"

"Don't... use the word 'subject'," Gongjin pleaded. "I'm not ready, so if he-"

"Alright, alright," Lady Wu said. "But are your finances really so grave...?"

"Aren't we all having to be careful...?" Gongjin replied. "But something quite unexpected has come to pass: you'll recall that I mentioned a Mister Lu Su...?"

"That little man with the strange ways," Lady Wu giggled.

"He's tactless, and maybe a little naïve in funny ways... yes, I suppose he's odd," Gongjin replied. "But he's honest and kind, too: he's just donated an entire granary to me."

Sun Ben nearly choked with shock.

"What a wonderful man!" Lady Wu cooed. "Bring him here to-"

"He's very, very tactless," Gongjin chuckled awkwardly. "I daren't risk it."

"...I'll trust you on that, but he has my gratitude," Lady Wu said. "You're like a son to me, Gongjin, and a brother to my dear Ce, wherever the poor boy is now."

"He's in Danyang... I think," Gongjin replied. "Liu Biao and Huang Zu are amassing naval forces around Xiakou, which might mean an attack on the northwest; I imagine that Bofu wants to confront them at some point soon."

Lady Wu sighed miserably and said, "That wretched man took my husband – my children's father – from me. If I were able, I'd take up arms and fight Liu Biao myself. All of my children would fight him, and knowing that he could but can't is probably tearing my poor Ce's soul apart."

"It is," Gongjin replied. "He and I have discussed it often."

"We're all upset," Sun Ben said. "We're all angry. But this latest action by Cao Cao may give us hope."

"Ah, yes, the 'Nan County Campaign' that he's just carried out," Gongjin replied.

"Against Liu Biao?" Lady Wu said excitedly.

"Cao Cao has attacked Nan County in northern Jing, which is currently occupied by two of Dong Zhuo's loyalists, Jia Xu and Zhang Xiu, the nephew of General Zhang Ji," Gongjin explained. "I say 'attacked', but it was more a case of his marching there and

Jia Xu advising surrender. Cao Cao's just sitting there now, presumably while he decides whether to turn south and bring Liu Biao under control – which would be amusing, for sure, but not necessarily good for us – or to turn west and destroy Li Jue and Guo Si, which Cao Cao might not want to do since that potentially pits him against the Qiang warlords as well."

"…I see," Lady Wu replied. "I'd like to know more about these things in future, Gongjin: it brings me closer to my son."

"In that case, Lady Wu, I will keep you informed on everything from now on," Gongjin promised. "I'll start by telling you about the recent events in the south…"

Bofu's victory over Wang Lang was far from the end of the story: Liu Yao's son, Liu Ji, was sitting on the Yuzhang-Danyang border with 10,000 of his father's followers; Ze Rong's remaining acolytes were active in Yuzhang; Yuzhang's Administrator, Hua Xin, was hostile toward Yuan Shu and his vassals, including the Sun family; the various tribes were still rising up intermittently against whoever governed over them; and worst of all, the mysterious rebel army in Danyang was growing by the day. It was well-known that Taishi Ci was, at the very least, some sort of spiritual focus for the rebels, but most suspected his personal involvement: there would come a time when the Danyang Rebels would have to be dealt with, but a greater problem loomed in the form of Yuan Shu's growing ambitions.

****

87

"*Aiee...* The problems are unending," Bofu said to his miserable followers as they endured another day in a besieged camp in the centre of Danyang; the rebel attacks had suddenly intensified once word of Bofu's presence in the area had reached their leadership. The son of Sun Jian turned to Lü Fan and asked, "Ziheng, what word from Shouchun or Danyang's capital?"

"Gongjin's in Shouchun; Yuan Yin's whereabouts are currently unknown to me, but we have to presume that he went back to Shouchun to demand military action against Xu Kun and Zhou Shang," Lü Fan replied. "Xu Kun and Gongjin did the right thing, I suppose, when they opposed Yuan Yin, but it makes life difficult. I trust Gongjin when he says that he will placate Yuan Shu, but we've still got to have Yuan Yin as Administrator of Danyang at some point, which is not ideal. It means that Yuan will inevitably send men like Yang Hong, Yan Xiang, Han Yin and Yuan Huan to the other prefectures, including Guangling."

"Yeah, and I can guess why, too," Bofu grumbled. "He really means to do it..."

"...He's sent another 'prompt', then," Lü Fan sighed.

"I didn't want to say anything, but... yeah," Bofu admitted. "I ask you, Ziheng: is he living in the same world as we are? He's writing to me about 'his successes in the south', when they're all down to me! He's telling me about my own campaigns! And worse than that, he's talking about-!"

"We should discuss this privately," Lü Fan suggested.

"...Yeah," Bofu conceded. "After the main meeting, then..."

When the general concerns were concluded, Bofu, Lü Fan Cheng Pu and Sun Hè continued their political discussion in the privacy of Bofu's personal tent.

"Yuan Shu's talking about 'his vast domains', Ziheng," Bofu complained. "He holds Lujiang through terror, and from the carefully-worded stuff I'm getting from Gongjin and Boyang – and even Zhang Xun hints at it accidentally at times, come to think of it – it sounds like he's pushing the Huai region too far as well. Yuan claims that he's 'uncontested in Yu Province' just weeks after Cao Cao strolled over the border with an army and crushed his sponsored Yellow Turban 'agitators'; and Liu Pi wasn't doing too well against little village militias before that, so I hear."

"I heard the same," Lü Fan admitted. "Liu Pi is quite pathetic."

"Yuan Shu is pathetic as well," Bofu scoffed. "He's claiming that he rules 'all of Guangling' when he only has the half that Uncle Wu took for him, and he's still going on about 'signs'. I've warned him – *again* – that I can't serve a man guilty of treason against the Han, but it's looking increasingly likely that he'll announce it soon, even with everything that's going wrong for him."

"Let him," Lü Fan said.

"Agreed," Cheng Pu grunted.

"The problems are still the same," Bofu retorted. "He has our families, and now he's trying to place his loyal cronies in charge of Jiangdong. How can we turn on him if it means doing everything all over again and losing our families...? Can we repeat the victories we've just had against Zu Lang, Lu Kang, Xue Li, Ze Rong, Liu Yao, White Tiger, Haixi Chen, Wang Lang, Zhang Ya, Huang-"

"You don't need to list them all!" Cheng Pu chuckled. "I was there for most of them, and so was your friend!"

"...But you see my point?" Bofu asked.

"Yes!" Cheng Pu said.

"Of course I do," Lü Fan replied. "If we had to, could we retake the prefectures from Yuan Shu...? Yes, of course, but we probably won't have to."

Bofu frowned and sighed, saying, "But if we did-"

"If we did, Lord Sun, we'd have a host of new talents to help us that we didn't have before," Lü Fan said. "In addition, we're popular now, whereas before, we were fighting a court-appointed governor with a good reputation... and we were the villains. If Yuan Shu did what he intends, we'd then be the heroes, fighting on the side of the Han. We might even have this 'rebel army' on our side."

Bofu sighed anxiously and said, "But our families-"

"Gongjin will get them out," Lü Fan insisted. "He and I discussed it, and he can do what I once did when I retrieved your kin from Guangling. Tao Qian was smarter than Yuan Shu, and I succeeded nonetheless."

Bofu exhaled fiercely.

"Let us hope Lord Yuan's famous impatience compels him to make his historic mistake before he sends his lackeys to overthrow us," Lü Fan said. "Because *then*, Lord Sun, after so, so long... we'll be *free*."

Bofu and Cheng Pu both smiled cynically.

Gongjin was certain that Lu Su was a worthy future ally, so he invited him to his home once again.

"I didn't bring anything this time," Lu Su said as he sat on Gongjin's guest seat.

"I think the granary was an ample gift that will do me fine for now," Gongjin joked as he sat down. Once the servants had brought the refreshments and retreated, Gongjin asked, "Do you trust me, Zijing...?"

"...Of course," Lu Su replied cautiously. "Haven't I given you a-"

"There is a difference between generosity and trust," Gongjin suggested. "We all do charitable things for men we do not trust. You pitied my situation, and I am grateful for that... but do you trust me...?"

"And I repeat, 'Yes'," Lu Su said irritably. "Why do you suddenly challenge me in this hostile manner?"

"It isn't because I want your other granary," Gongjin promised. "The matters that I have not discussed before, Zijing... I must discuss them now, for both our sakes, but I can only do so if we trust each other completely."

"You make it sound like Heaven is about to fall," Lu Su joked.

"...It may well be," Gongjin replied seriously. "I must ask you to keep our words to yourself: share them with no one, not even your closest family."

"What... what is the matter...?" Lu Su asked.

"We discussed a hypothetical scenario wherein Yuan Shu

destroyed himself with an act of idiocy," Gongjin said. "Lu Zijing, it is not fantasy. He intends such an act, and very soon."
Lu Su's eyes wandered.
"I feel awkward when I say these words, but... I have been in his court and heard it for myself, and so have Sun Bofu and his cousin Sun Boyang," Gongjin continued. "Yuan Shu is quite mad, and-"
"I... am unprepared for this," Lu Su interrupted.
"Please hear me out," Gongjin said. "I genuinely consider you to be my friend, Zijing, and I want to give you a change to realign yourself before the worst occurs."
"'Realign'...?" Lu Su chortled. "To your childhood friend Sun Ce, I presume."
"Naturally," Gongjin replied. "He will be the new force in Jiangdong when-"
"I... I know that I am sometimes taken for a fool, but... this is a tad too much," Lu Su said disdainfully. "I gave you a granary, and now you're trying to poach me – and my other granary – for your friend!"
"No, Zijing, that isn't it!" Gongjin protested. "*Ayah*; this is why I asked you if you trusted me, and evidently you either lied to me or were deceiving yourself."
Lu Su was getting up to leave: he froze for a moment, pondered Gongjin's retort, sighed miserably and sat down again.
"...What now...?" Gongjin prompted.
"I... I trust you, Gongjin, and I am sorry if my panic-driven words were... 'poorly chosen'," Lu Su replied. "It isn't that I suspect you or your friend Sun Ce of duplicity, it's... that I'm not ready for what you are saying. I came here to serve Yuan Shu. I gave up my ancestral lands and everything and everyone I knew to come here and pledge allegiance to a lord that – you now inform me – is about to commit political suicide. What does he intend???"
"I need to tell you...?" Gongjin asked.
Lu Su pondered some small changes in administration, strange rumours of large fabric orders, apparently-needless food rationing and muted whispers about angry officials and desertions from Yuan Shu's elite forces. Suddenly, it struck him: his eyes widened, and he said, "You... y-you can't mean that he intends to...!"
Gongjin nodded slowly.
"...And you're sure...?" Lu Su prompted.
"He openly discusses the prospect at court, and his advisers are constantly forced to rein his ideas in," Gongjin replied. "Sun Bofu is plagued by letters that demand his opinion – all of Yuan's senior vassals are – and despite their protests, the man is not to be swayed. What began as an obsession with being the head of his clan has become an obsession with... with possessing a 'proven, substantial mandate'."
"Ayah! He will bring disaster upon every poor fool that pledged themselves to his service!" Lu Su cried. "Zhou Gongjin, the-!"
"It will not happen today or tomorrow, but it will happen soon," Gongjin continued. "At that time, I must rescue the families of my friends and allies and ensure that they reach safety in Jiangdong. After that, we'll be at war with him, and I couldn't bear to see you harmed. I urge you, Zijing: join Sun Ce of Fuchun! If Yuan Shu delays his plans for the next ten years, you'll be serving him by proxy; if he does it next week, you will be behind a shield of men

that will fight him justly."
Lu Su whined painfully.
"I know it is a difficult decision, but I had to give you the opportunity to choose," Gongjin continued. "You're my benefactor, Lu Zijing. You saved me: let me now save you."
"I'll... I'll sell that other granary building, and transport the grain to somewhere on the riverbank," Lu Su said.
Gongjin smiled with relief and said, "Juchao. Send it to Juchao. I'm shortly to become Juchao's magistrate, and I can oversee the transportation of you and your resources to Jiangdong."
"You're a born schemer and orator, Gongjin," Lu Su sighed. "You knew you'd win me over."
"I didn't, Zijing, I assure you," Gongjin replied. "What I have just achieved is beyond my expectations... but then the cause of my actions is more ridiculous than anything else."
"...Mandated to rule...?" Lu Su exclaimed. "Never in all my years did I dream that I would know another Wang Mang in my lifetime; who knows what else could happen in such a chaotic world as this...?"
Gongjin laughed and said, "Who indeed...?"

A rare break in region-wide hostility between influential warlord-officials had begun, but it would not last for long. Some areas in the south never found peace, even without the likes of Liu Yao, Wang Lang, Hua Xin and Ze Rong: Bofu and his allies continued to deal with tribal uprisings, rebel insurrections and the remnants of Ze Rong and Liu Yao's followings that could not bring themselves to yield to a vassal of Yuan Shu. To some, the 'usual worries' being the only worries signalled a possible cessation of hostilities between the warlords in the north as well, although the more informed never entertained such a blindly optimistic notion. Those that knew the truth of things knew that Yuan Shu was doing more than posturing: he had been gathering resources, preparing regalia, drawing up documents and readying various militias for a grand proclamation that would shock the country. Yuan was waiting for a catalyst or an excuse, and it would be Cao Cao, the current guardian of the young Han Emperor Xian, that would inadvertently give him a very good excuse while excessively enjoying his victory over Zhang Xiu and Jia Xu in Nan County's capital, Wan City.

****

ACT VIII: PARTINGS AND MEETINGS

88

Sun Ce – style name 'Bofu' – had barely had a chance to rest since beginning his career six years before: he was immediately thrust onto the front line of a violent inheritance feud between his late father's lord, Yuan Shu, and Shu's half-brother and cousin by adoption, Yuan Shao, who was the chosen chieftain of the influential Yuan clan of Ru County, Yu Province. The Yuan feud had allowed the infamous tyrant chancellor Dong Zhuo to ransack and then destroy the capital Luoyang and escape with the young Han emperor, Xian, and the entire Imperial court as hostages: Sun Jian and Yuan Shao's childhood friend Cao Cao were the only men to raise arms against Dong Zhuo during the tenure of the ill-fated 'Eastern Pass Coalition' that Yuan Shao spearheaded, but the two men's efforts had been for nothing. Cao Cao would become a vassal of his friend Shao, while Sun Jian would become unexpectedly and undesirably bound to Yuan Shu as an unappreciated warrior vassal: but while the former used his growing pool of advisers and talented officers to earn fame, military rank and the governorship of Yan Province, Sun Jian endured thankless assignments that were solely designed to increase his lord's already impressive domain.

It was while Bofu's father Sun Jian was in Jing Province – known by some as the 'throat of the nation' for its geographical centricity and large number of open land borders with other provinces – that he had met his end whilst fighting the governor's wily lieutenant Huang Zu. Sun Jian's loyal vassals eventually pledged allegiance to the teenaged Bofu, but his cousin Sun Ben and maternal uncle, Wu Jing, were initially assigned as the military replacements for Bofu's father. To the horror of Cheng Pu, Huang Gai, Han Dang and Zhu Zhi – who were Sun Jian's first comrades and later his trusted friends – Yuan Shu had no intention of releasing the powerful Sun clan from servitude: he intended to use them to seize the whole of the southeast of China while he tried to seize the north with his own forces.

When Bofu finally assumed the mantle of Sun clan leader, he immediately proved his worth by confronting the bandit king Zu Lang and subsequently uprooting the formidable veteran bandit pacifier and Administrator of Lujiang, Lu Kang; but when Liu Yao, the regency court's appointed governor, took the upper Jiangdong region from Wu Jing, Bofu had to argue for an opportunity to retake it. The paranoid Yuan Shu did eventually give Bofu the troops and remit that he had asked for, and within two years, Governor Liu Yao, Kuaiji's Administrator Wang Lang, Xu Provincial Governor Tao Qian's former Chancellor Xue Li, the powerful cultist-warlord Ze Rong, a multitude of Shanyue tribal alliances and bandit confederacies and the infamous lone wolf hero Taishi Ci had been defeated in battle. Bofu had also proved to be a charismatic figure that retained the loyal service of his father's vassals and earned many new allies and confidantes, including the nobleman Zhou Yu – whose style name was 'Gongjin' – and the young genius Lü Fan; but instead of being grateful, Yuan Shu tried to force puppet administrators on the liberated regions and continued with plans to elevate himself to more than a warlord. Patience was wearing thin: Bofu, his close friend Gongjin and his other allies were longing for the day when Yuan Shu would release them from service – intentionally or otherwise – but had to tolerate his increasingly taxing demands until that day came.

In the west of the country, in the original Han capital Chang'an, Emperor Xian suffered the indignity of being a puppet to Dong Zhuo and then to Dong's subordinates Li Jue and Guo Si, who formed a regency government when Dong Zhuo was assassinated by his own foster son, the unpredictable warrior-prodigy Lü Bu. When the regents finally turned on each other, Emperor Xian convinced them to allow him to return to the husk of his former capital Luoyang: that resulted in over a year of living in adverse conditions before Yan Provincial Governor Cao Cao – who had only recently fought a battle with his own former friends and subordinates for control of Yan – rescued the court and brought it to the city of Xuchang, which was then named as the new capital while the process of rebuilding Luoyang was underway. Yuan Shao – who had actually declined an opportunity to shelter Emperor Xian himself – was suddenly suspicious of his old friend Cao Cao, and when Acting Commander-in-Chief Cao tried to appease him by appointing him as 'Excellency of Works', Yuan reacted angrily, despite the 'Three Excellences' – 'Excellency of Works', 'Commander-in-Chief' and 'Excellency over the Masses' – being the highest posts in the land; Yuan considered himself to be more deserving of the title that Cao Cao had, so Cao switched their roles and planned for the inevitable day when the two would meet on a battlefield.

Cao Cao had once been labelled as a 'Hero of Chaos' or 'Crafty Villain' by the famous appraiser Xu Shao, and it was a moniker that he relished and reviled between his varying moods. When Cao Cao scored an early victory against the resurgent Yellow Turbans in neighbouring Yu Province, he decided to go further straight away and declared war against Zhang Xiu and Jia Xu, the current rulers of Nan County in northern Jing Province: both men were known as former subordinates of Dong Zhuo, and Jia Xu was especially notorious for being Dong's senior adviser during his rise to power. Cao Cao gained a swift surrender, but his arrogance apparently peaked in the wake of such an easy victory, and he began to abuse his authority over Zhang Xiu in ways that could not be excused, even when considering the crimes perpetrated by Dong's regime: everything that happened next – the battle, its outcome and its repercussions – was as historic as it was shocking.

"Excellency Cao… has been *defeated by Zhang Xiu*," Bofu's friend and adviser, Lü Fan, reported to a shocked audience in Danyang. The field command tent was silent: Cao Cao was the acting commander of the Imperial armed forces, so his defeat was Emperor Xian's as well.

"*How…?*" Bofu asked incredulously.

"Cao Cao… *lost*, and that's all there is to it," Lü Fan replied. "It doesn't matter how he lost the battle, Lord Sun: he lost it, and now we can expect a reaction from his enemies."

The veteran Sun family retainer Cheng Pu frowned and said, "I've heard nothing like this since the days of serving your father, Lord Sun. This is as preposterous as when we heard that Dong Zhuo had seized power, and Jia Xu was behind that feat as well: is Jia Xu a wizard...?"

"No, Mister Cheng, he's just an exceptionally gifted schemer," Lü Fan replied.

Cheng Pu's long-time ally Huang Gai said, "What surprises me is that Cao Cao has talents like Cheng Yu and Xun Yu; how did he lose so easily when...?"

"...Vice," Lü Fan revealed.

Bofu's 15-year-old brother Sun Quan laughed and said, "Why not tell us, Mister Lü? We're not prudes here!"

"Stop it, Quan," Bofu scolded.

"Your brother is right, Lord Sun," Lü Fan said. "I should tell everyone: this is of national significance, after all. Cao Cao appears to be a 'Crafty Villain' after all. In fact, he committed an act of contempt that one would have expected from Dong Zhuo."

"He took someone's wife for a mistress," Cheng Pu supposed.

"Not just anyone's wife," Lü Fan chuckled. "Zhang Xiu's aunt: Zhang Ji's widow."

Bofu and many other men laughed hysterically.

"...Oh, Cao Cao, you are a man without peer for comedy!" Cheng Pu cackled. "Taking the famous beauty Lady Zhou, right under her nephew's eyes! Really, Ziheng, did he do such a thing...?"

"And he enjoyed her in her nephew's bed, too," Lü Fan said. "He really is without boundaries."

"Give me that report!" Cheng Pu said through laughter. "I must read it for myself!"

Lü Fan passed the letter to Cheng Pu, who read it and started to laugh again.

"It gets *worse*...?" Bofu exclaimed.

"He had a live-in prostitute that he shared with his bodyguard!" Cheng Pu giggled. "He slept with Lady Zhou in Zhang Xiu's house, in Zhang Xiu's bed, while Zhang Xiu was evicted and lived in his office...! Oh, Cao Cao, you are a famous heckler and deviant now, as well as a 'Hero of Chaos'!"

"If anyone deserved humiliating, it's the servants of Dong Zhuo, even if the method is morally questionable," Lü Fan said.

Huang Gai was all smiles as he asked, "So how did it end?"

"...Ah... goodness!" Cheng Pu gasped: his smile disappeared, and he said, "Jia Xu is a man that we must never cross if we are to know future success!"

"I agree," Lü Fan sighed.

"Why? What happened?" Bofu prompted.

"He successfully ambushed Cao Cao, and – despite being at an enormous numerical disadvantage – managed to claim the heads of Cao's famous bodyguard, Dian Wei, *and* Cao's eldest son and heir as well," Lü Fan reported.

"Incredible!" the young officer Ling Cao said. "Is it really true?"

"...If this report is genuine, then Cao Cao – the *Excellency of Works* – is harmed politically, personally and militarily," Cheng Pu said as he read the letter for a second time. "There is no way that Yuan Shu can be seeing this and not..."

The tent fell silent.

"...It will be soon, then," Bofu sighed.

"We can expect it within weeks, I think, if Gongjin's intelligence is correct," Lü Fan replied.

"Cao Cao, you *fool*...!" Cheng Pu cried. "Do you even know, mad idiot, what your wretched behaviour has unleashed???"

"He isn't here, so don't waste your breath, Cheng Demou," Bofu said. "It's done now, and while it gave us a good laugh for a minute or two there, it... it gives us something to think about, to worry about."

"...Like what...?" Ling Cao asked. "How do we manage rumours and-?"

"Say nothing to anyone below the rank of major," Lü Fan ordered. "This has to be contained until we know for sure that he's said it, done it and which man thinks what of it. We'll have little time..."

"And we have to rely on 'Gongjin'," Cheng Pu scoffed. "Where is he now?"

"He's succeeding in his plans," Lü Fan promised. "Everything will... be *fine*."

Bofu's friend Gongjin – or as most knew him, Zhou Yu of the noble Zhou clan that had once served Han emperors as senior officials and Excellences – prepared to make a journey southward from Yuan Shu's capital Shouchun. He was being assisted in the endeavour by Bofu's older cousin Sun Ben and his new friend and benefactor, Lu Su of Dongcheng.

"How he was convinced to make you Magistrate of Juchao, I'll never know," Sun Ben said. "You're a wily one, Gongjin."

"He trusts me," Gongjin replied as he lifted a heavy sack of belongings onto a cart.

"Shouldn't you be leaving your servants to do all this, Gongjin?" Lu Su asked.

"I'm a man that likes to 'muck in', Lu Su," Gongjin chuckled. "Now, Boyang: are we in accord about what comes next...?"

"Leave everything in Shouchun to me," Sun Ben replied. "Messengers are ready to hurry to Juchao or Jiangdong, depending on the timing of the announcement, and preparations for the rest are underway as we agreed."

"...Gentlemen, we're about to begin a new and frightening journey into the unknown, and I wish us all luck," Gongjin said. "Good luck, Boyang, and may we meet again soon, here on this world under Heaven."

Sun Ben bowed and replied, "Good luck, Zhou Gongjin, and Mister Lu Zijing."

"*Ayah*... 'Good luck', indeed! This is *madness*!" Lu Su said as he bowed to each man, turned sharply and walked toward the lead carriage at speed.

"He's more reliable than he seems, Boyang... I promise!" Gongjin joked as he followed Lu Su.

"I wonder, though, how we'll really fare when it happens," Sun Ben muttered.

There had been no successful usurpation of the Han in over a century: the notorious Han retainer Wang Mang had declared his own Xin Dynasty that came and went in a relatively short amount of time, and the Han Dynasty was restored.

When the Taoist cultist Zhang Jue triggered the

nationwide Yellow Turban Rebellion against Emperor Ling and his self-serving eunuch confidantes, China was rocked to its foundations and its borders were closed while private militias did the pacification work that the underfunded and neglected Imperial Army could not; when Dong Zhuo murdered Emperor Ling's eldest son Emperor Shao – whom he had already demoted to a prince and replaced with his younger brother – the Eastern Pass Coalition that had formed to force a restoration of the toppled sovereign was left collectively speechless; when that same coalition then suggested alternative Han emperors to Dong Zhuo's puppet Emperor Xian, many balked at the idea; even when the emperor was wandering the northern region without a place to call home, none dared claim to be the new mandated ruler.

Wang Mang had created the notion of the 'Mandate of Heaven' to allow other clans – including his own – to succeed the existing dynasty, but there were few that were willing to risk announcing their own worthiness or the incumbent's lack of worth. But the list of recent insults against the Han Dynasty was long, and all it took was one man to state was what secretly on many men's minds: after over 300 years the Han was fading, and there was always the option to let the dynasty die and replace it with something new. The first question was, of course, whether 'new' would evolve into 'the same' or 'different', and if it was the latter, would it then evolve into 'better' or 'worse': Yuan Shu offered little hope of 'better' to those that knew him well. The second question was who would accept the declaration, because it was obvious that there would be numerous detractors, not least Cao Cao and Yuan Shu's half-brother Shao; if Yuan Shu received a large amount of unexpected support, the resulting civil war could drag on for decades, but if he was universally rebuked, he could expect to last no more than three years. Now that the announcement was an impending reality, Bofu's advisers could ponder nothing else.

****

89

Lü Fan rushed into the command tent of Bofu's camp in the middle of Danyang Prefecture and shouted, "**He's done it! He's done it, my lord!**"
Every man in the tent – all of whom were senior officials and officers – froze.
"...Just to clarify, since I don't want to be mistaken, Ziheng, he's, uh... he's done 'it'...?" Bofu asked hesitantly. "He's... he's declared that he's... *emperor*...?"
Lü Fan laughed excitedly and said, "He has!"
"*Ayah*... I can't believe it, even after all the preparation for it," Cheng Pu said.
"I... wait, who's he told?" Bofu asked.
"That's it: he's just telling us at the moment," Lü Fan replied breathlessly. "He's... he's sending a man to-"
"I don't want to, but I have to warn him not to, one last time, don't I?" Bofu asked.
"Say your piece!" Lü Fan chuckled. "The fool will do it anyway!"
"Our families are in his custody!" Cheng Pu cried. "How will we save them???"
"Gongjin and Boyang are dealing with that," Lü Fan promised. "Yuan Shu has sent an 'Imperial messenger' here with a 'formal decree', but our own messenger has maybe a three-day advantage: we have to decide whether-"
"I am not bowing and scraping to some pedant underling of Yuan Shu's that has enjoyed a sudden and fraudulent elevation to an 'Imperial messenger'!" Cheng Pu barked. "How can you even entertain the idea, Lü Fan???"
"That's right," Huang Gai said. "Even the act of deference toward a false representative of the Son of Heaven is an act of treason."
"...That's quite true," Lü Fan realised. "Forgive my excitement robbing me of my wits, gentlemen. We cannot show any kind of deference... in fact, we cannot give him an audience, can we...?"
"He must be detained until we decide how to respond," Bofu decided. "And we cannot respond at all, of course, until we know that our families are safe."
"I'm quite glad that I didn't need to reiterate that point," Cheng Pu said coldly.
Bofu noticed that his brother Quan was silent and serious, so he said, "When the meeting's over, we need to talk."
Sun Quan nodded silently.
"This... is truly beyond my ability to rationalise," Cheng Pu admitted. "Oh, we've known it might happen, but... but... but I..."
"After deaths of great men that seemed invincible, it is only such things as this that are truly shocking," Lü Fan said.

Sun Quan had questions for his brother, and Bofu was initially happy to answer them as they sat down for a private discussion.
"I'm not world-wise, but I'm not stupid either," Sun Quan began. "I have wondered something for a while now: how...? How did he control you, and how did he control Father...?"
Bofu coughed awkwardly and replied, "I... I used to wonder about it too, Quan, when I was on the outside. Yuan Shu's counsel was

obviously a lot more cunning than him; it began with feigned respect and offers of rewards for good service, and once Father had severed ties with anyone or anything that could help him escape, Yuan Shu showed his true nature and met defiance or criticism with threats."

"Threats of what...?" Sun Quan asked.

"I need to explain...?" Bofu chortled. "He's mad! He withdrew Dad from Luoyang but didn't allow him to reach safety before he sent that public rebuke to his brother; he knew that Dad would be attacked! He knew, and he didn't care! I don't know, maybe Dad wasn't supposed to live: he did, though, and when he tried to argue, Yuan threatened to take everything away that he'd given to him. That meant the loss of the inspectorate in Yu Province, but it also meant the military rank: Dad would have had to come back home with nothing."

"He was still the court-appointed Marquis of Wucheng and the Magistrate of Changsha!" Sun Quan retorted.

"Dad's marquisate was the lowest marquis rank that the court can appoint, if I have to be brutally honest for a moment... so it meant very little socially," Bofu replied. "Changsha was taken from him when he accepted the inspectorate, but even if it hadn't been, Quan, it's isolated, and being its magistrate isn't really good when there are bandits and tribes that can be 'encouraged'."

"...You're saying that Yuan Shu might've paid people to make Dad's life difficult," Sun Quan prompted.

"Yes, and we have the proof now," Bofu replied. "He's funded or still funding the White Wave Bandits, the Runan Yellow Turbans, the renegade Southern Xiongnu and the Black Mountain Bandits."

"...So if you'd 'betrayed him', he'd probably have turned to White Tiger and had those scum fighting us *for* him, after sending us there to defeat them!" Sun Quan realised. "Brother, I didn't really understand!"

"It's better that such nasty games don't immediately make sense to you, Brother: it means you're not naturally evil," Bofu said encouragingly. "Dad was forced to accept the ranks because the only other option was to lose everything and be harassed for the rest of his days, and he had us to provide for. He was tricked, and it's a shame that he was. But when Yuan Shu did what he did, it closed the door on Dad being able to go to other warlords too... not without losing loved ones. After all, who'd have got to us faster if Dad had tried to defect: him or Yuan Shu...?"

Sun Quan nodded slowly.

"That's how Yuan's controlled us recently... by having our families as hostages," Bofu continued. "Before, it was like when Dad first joined him: confiscating troops and being rude or aloof, and then feigning benevolence and promising titles when we were reaching breaking point. As soon as he had things over us, he reverted to threats, and we had no choice but to accept the situation stoically. Even now, we can't do anything militarily while our loved ones are in danger: that's what Gongjin is taking care of at the moment. We'll be able to complain, say that we're unable to serve a traitor as we have suggested before, but we cannot unite with the other warlords that will definitely condemn him for this."

"So what will we do...?" Quan asked.

"If we have to, we'll follow the example set by the toadies of the imperial clan, Liu Biao and Liu Zhang," Bofu replied. "They have survived with cries of 'neutrality', and that is what we might do. If we can't guarantee our families' safety, we'll dissociate ourselves from Yuan Shu but refrain from pledging support to his enemies. Of course, Cao Cao may demand our help with an imperial decree, but we'll deal with that if it happens."

Bofu's final written remonstration was, as expected, ignored: Yuan Shu subsequently announced to the world that the Han Dynasty's mandate had expired and that he, as the only man of integrity and worth, was chosen by Heaven to begin his own imperial line, known as the Zhong Dynasty. The announcement was, as expected, met with a rare moment of unity by the northern warlords: they put aside their personal grudges momentarily and rebuked Yuan Shu as one. While Yuan Shao – who was not keen on the idea of killing his half-brother despite the already-sizeable human cost of their six-year feud – quickly resumed his long-running dispute with Gongsun Zan, while Jing Governor Liu Biao refrained from pledging military support to an imperial government that had recently sanctioned attacking him. Excellency Cao Cao would be fighting the pretender with the Imperial Army that was, in reality, his own, and his only substantial external aid would come from the exiled former Governor of Xu Province, Liu Bei, and the incumbent governor of Xu Province, Lü Bu.

Lü Fan, Cheng Pu and Bofu met for one of their regular private meetings: Bofu began proceedings by asking, "What word from Shouchun?"
"It's exactly as we suspected," Lü Fan replied. "Chen Ji, Ji Ling, Han Yin, Yuan Yin, Yan Xiang and the like – most of his following, in fact – have remained loyal; the adviser Yuan Huan and Generals Lei Bo and Chen Lan deserted or defected almost immediately. But security in Shouchun is in disarray: there are public shows of disobedience, people throwing themselves under carriages and hanging themselves from things, marches, riots... getting out of there unnoticed wouldn't be hard, even if you were the height of a mountain."
"The northern warlords have all shown a united front against him," Cheng Pu said. "He's isolated, so we're the least of his worries. But how are we viewed by those same northern lords...? Will they see that we're not the same as him?"
"I think so," Lü Fan replied. "They'll send messengers with offers of titles soon enough, and if we know our families are safe then we should accept them. Cao Cao doesn't want Yuan Shao taking control of the coalition against his own relative, because this isn't the family feud that it was until recently anymore: now Yuan Shu is a traitor, a heretic, a criminal that has wronged Heaven. Yuan Shao wanted his half-brother humbled for his public letter, not killed: now he must die, and Shao will do everything he can to ensure that Shu escapes when the end is nigh."
"...If that's true, then the feud that the entire nation has suffered was needless," Bofu said. "Oh, we all know it was anyway, but... but if he can now save Yuan Shu after all the lives that have been lost in the last six years, then the two of them both deserve to die

a dog's death."
"We should go back to Qu'e," Lü Fan suggested.
"I agree," Cheng Pu said. "I know that we still have to deal with the rebels and whatnot – though you'd hope they will stop attacking us once we dissociate ourselves from Yuan Shu – but our main concern is fortifying the Great River crossing points against Yuan Shu."
"And preparing for a new wave of cultivated unrest," Lü Fan suggested. "Yuan Shu will not like our 'betrayal', and he will court our enemies: he'll talk to the Shanyue and the bandits, and-"
"And even if the rebels that have been attacking us stopped, we have to fight the Shanyue and the bandits again anyway!" Bofu exclaimed.
"...Huang Longluo, Zhou Bo, Haixi Chen and Zhang Ya are dead or fled, Wang Lang is exiled, Ze Rong is dead; our only concerns are Xu Gong, White Tiger, Zu Lang, and whoever it is that leads the Danyang uprising," Lü Fan replied.
"Xu Gong and White Tiger are both hiding with Xu Zhao and Sheng Xian," Cheng Pu noted. "Wu Prefecture is under threat while those four are alive."
"General Xu is sheltering Shang Xian and Xu Gong, two men with no cause to form an alliance," Bofu retorted. "Zhu Junli tells me that Shang Xian will never work with the man that ousted him, any more than he would work with us. Xu Zhao is just a man that has an honourable streak that gets the better of him."
"I have to say that I agree, Mister Cheng," Lü Fan said. "Xu Zhao did not join any of the alliances against us, and Sheng Xian has not been proven to have any involvement in anything either."
"...I hope you're right, Mister Lü, because things that are left to grow become bigger problems later on," Cheng Pu suggested. "What's happening in Guangling at the moment...?"
"Exactly what was to be expected," Lü Fan replied.

Yuan Shu's appointed Administrator of Guangling, Wu Jing, summoned his officials to his command tent and said, "As you all know by now, Yuan Shu has committed the worst of treasons by declaring that he is a mandated emperor: we cannot serve him and know peace in the afterlife, so we must and will be breaking ties with him at once."
The officials voiced their satisfaction.
"We're ending hostilities with the Han forces and leaving at once," Wu Jing continued. "We can't dally, or else our 'ally', the pirate king Xue Zhao, might have a chance to attack us: we don't know if he will be ordered to by Yuan Shu, after all."
One official in his mid-thirties coughed deliberately and said, "Will we be offering an opportunity to anyone that doesn't want to stay and be governed by Lü Bu?"
"Of course, Lü Dinggong," Wu Jing replied. "Did you have anyone in mind...?"
Lü Dai – whose style name was 'Dinggong' – smiled and said, "Zhang Hong, the brother of Zhang Zhao that is already in Jiangdong, and Qin Song, Zhang Hong's friend. They have received invitations, but I wanted to be sure that they might travel with us."
"Every man – whether it's you, Dinggong, that volunteered your

services here and now, or able talents like Zhang Zigang and Qin Wenbiao – are welcome in Jiangdong, and may travel now or later," Wu Jing promised.
"Then let us hurry to our new home," Lü Dai replied.

While Bofu's maternal uncle Wu Jing and the rest of the Guangling campaign forces began a careful retreat, Bofu's cousin Sun Ben concluded a clandestine evacuation of the families of Bofu's loyalists from the chaos of Yuan Shu's capital Shouchun. The eldest boys and Sun Ben's close family were the only ones left to leave, but there were still many obstacles to pass before being safe, not least crossing the Yangtze River.
"...I won't be sad to see the back of this place," Sun Ben said to his teenaged cousin Sun Yi. "Finally, we'll all be together again."
"And I can finally think about being able to fight alongside my brother," Sun Yi replied.
"...You're barely thirteen years of age, Shubi," Sun Ben chortled. "You don't just look like Bofu... you think just like him too."
Sun Yi grinned and said, "Yeah, well, he can't be wrong, can he, so why's being like him a bad thing? Anyhow, Dad was fighting at my age."
"He wasn't," Sun Ben insisted. "Fifteen or sixteen, *maybe*."
"There are loads of boys my age fighting, and I want a piece of Yuan Shu after he's had us all locked up here for all this time, Cousin," Sun Yi retorted. "I-!"
"Until we get out of here, he's 'Divine Majesty the First Emperor of Zhong', or some other similar thing," Sun Ben said sternly. "We can be rude and call him all the names we want once we're back at home."
Sun Yi sighed and said, "Yeah, I know, you don't need to tell me."
A youth ran up to the two and said, "Are we going?"
"...You are indeed, Cheng Zi... you are indeed," Sun Ben replied. "A few at a time... but yes, you are."
Cheng Pu's son Cheng Zi turned and retreated to the last convoy.
"Why the hesitation, Cousin...?" Sun Yi asked. "And you said 'you', not 'we'... why...?"
"You haven't had any dealings with Yuan Shu: I have," Sun Ben replied. "He's a terrible man, and he's constantly suspicious. I have been summoned to a meeting, and if I do not attend I risk your safety. You'll lead the penultimate retreat on my behalf, Shubi, and I'll catch up with my wife and children when I can."
Sun Yi fidgeted nervously.
"...Go on!" Sun Ben ordered.
"Alright, but... you're like a brother, Boyang, and I don't want to see you hurt," Sun Yi replied warmly. "You go and listen to him one more time and then get out, yeah...?"
"Yes, yes! Now go!" Sun Ben said desperately.
"...Don't make me fight my way back in here to get you," Sun Yi pleaded.
Sun Ben groaned and said, "If I have to say it once more, then-!"
"I'm going, I'm going," Sun Yi promised as he turned and followed Cheng Yi.
"...So am I... into a netherworld under Heaven," Sun Ben muttered as he turned to walk toward the 'palace' of the 'First Emperor of Zhong': he was constantly jostled by people that were frantically

packing or protesting, and Yuan Shu's forces were visibly struggling to maintain order.

Yuan Shu was now wearing dragon-patterned robes and a mortarboard hat with rows of beads at back and front, just as a Han emperor would; in addition, many of Yuan's senior courtiers had changed their attire to match the uniform dress of officials that were in the presence of their monarch, and the grand hall had been decorated with drapes and ceremonial lamp stands. There were noticeably fewer officials, however, since so many had deserted after the proclamation for fear of being punished by the heavenly gods for being party to treason. The advisers Yuan Yin, Yan Xiang, Han Yin and Yang Hong were close to their ruler, and the 'crown prince' Yuan Yao was sat to the left of his father and dressed in elegant, expensive robes. Sun Ben was, like some others of a lower rank, unprepared for the extent of the changes and had worn his regular robes to the gathering.

"Sun Ben," Yuan Shu bellowed. **"Why do you not dress appropriately for this court? Why do you not show full acceptance of our authority...?"**

Sun Ben was aware that he was not the only guilty party: he frowned momentarily, but when the loyal vassals indicated their anger at his stance he reluctantly kowtowed and said, "Your Majesty, I... uh... my unworthy self is guilty of a great insult unintentionally, and I beg forgiveness."

"...So you should," Yuan Shu scoffed.

Sun Ben noticed that a screen had been erected at the back of the hall; the silhouettes of Lady Feng – now 'Empress Fang' in Yuan Shu's pretender court – and Shu's eldest daughter Lady Yuan were visible.

"We have received no recent correspondence from our Administrator of Guangling, Wu Jing, and our 'Acting General that Routs Bandits' or whatever we called your cousin Sun Ce," Yuan Shu continued. "Where is the confirmation that our authority is recognised? What do your relatives intend?"

"...I cannot say, but communications might well be suffering from disruption, and their previous protestations are well-known to this court, Your Majesty," Sun Ben replied carefully. "I could-"

"Get out," Yuan Shu ordered. "You are improperly dressed, uninformed and otherwise useless. You can consider your role as 'Inspector of Yu Province' to be under review: we may make it a principality to be governed directly by our crown prince. Go on, get out. And do not return without the proper dress and some understanding of things! Now... **you there! Why are you dressed thus?"**

Sun Ben fought the urge to smile as he turned and left the court: Yu Province was under assault by Cao Cao's forces and was all but lost, so the inspector's title was utterly meaningless. Yuan Shu had turned his attentions to heckling others, and was clearly deranged: Sun Ben returned to his residence calmly and slowly to ensure that he was not suspected of anything. But when he reached the street that led to his home, a servant from his home suddenly appeared and tapped his arm.

"You must flee!" the servant said before Sun Ben could speak. "They have your lady wife and your children, Master, but you

452

mustn't stay!"

"How can I leave, you fool???" Sun Ben retorted angrily. "Who took them? When? Why? How???"

"Men came and said that they had to move closer to the 'palace'!" the servant replied. "Your lady wife ordered me to tell you to go: she said that you had to live and fight on, and that they would-!"

"I cannot hear any more!" Sun Ben whined. "I... I have to give myself up, then, and-!"

"Your lady wife made me tell you to go to the south," the servant insisted. "She said that she would rather die than keep you here, and that it is better that someone lives than everyone dies."

"...But the others, they'll be discovered... I must warn them that he might be pursuing soon," Sun Ben decided. "My family... if he harms them, I'll come back here and kill him."

"We must go!" the servant pleaded.

Sun Ben reluctantly fled Shouchun City with his loyal servant, leaving his family to the mercy – if, indeed, he possessed any – of Yuan Shu. The self-proclaimed emperor would not learn of the loss of the rest of his valuable hostages until they were some distance away from the capital, but his 'revenge' would have to wait: all of his northern interests were under heavy, sustained attack by Cao Cao's forces, and his only theoretical ally was Lü Bu, the Governor of Xu Province.

∗∗∗∗∗∗∗∗∗∗∗∗

90

Every one of the many dozens of escapees from Shouchun was headed for Juchao, where Gongjin had already arranged for boats to take them to Danyang Prefecture: Gongjin was aided in that venture by Sun Jian's old friend Zhu Zhi, who had travelled from Wu to assist the younger man in the difficult task.

"So near and yet so far," Gongjin said as he awaited the last convoy, which would contain – at Bofu's insistence – the Sun family. "I understand that he wanted to prove that every one of his vassals' families was important, but risking his own when they were guaranteed to be punished, where others could bargain…"

"But it was the only way," Zhu Zhi replied.

"I know, Junli… I know," Gongjin chortled. "It would be the Sun clan that Yuan Shu would want paraded to prove that there was no mass escape underway… and if they could not be produced, the rest would probably be killed. I knew that, and yet I said what I said… because I still hold onto the proven nonsense that Yuan Shu is in any way different to Dong Zhuo."

"They are almost here, and then our work is done," Zhu Zhi said. "You've achieved something quite impressive, 'Young Zhou': you've fooled Yuan Shu, rescued our families, and somehow managed to convince Yuan Shu that you are still his loyal vassal throughout. I'm sure that you could contrive a plausible excuse for this evacuation if you had to."

"Let's hope that I don't have to, Mister Zhu," Gongjin replied. "I don't share your estimation of my talent."

"…He'll react badly to this, of course," Zhu Zhi said. "He'll send or create some sort of force to hound us as punishment. Will he ask the Guangling pirates, the Wu and Danyang Shanyue, or the bandits of Jing County…? Might he waste valuable resources bribing them all to harass us, so that we have to expend our own precious resources defeating them all again…?"

"You ask these things of a vengeful, spiteful lunatic," Gongjin replied. "Like Dong Zhuo before him, I consider nothing to be beyond him; he'll seek help from any that agree to view him as 'First Emperor of Zhong', be they pirate, bandit, mercenary, cultist or barbarian… which is the only help that he'll get."

"…Which means that this will go on for as long as he has money to buy that paid help," Zhu Zhi said. "He's kept up the feud with his brother for six years; how long can he be a false emperor for…?"

"A year or two at the most!" Gongjin chuckled. "He's wasted a fortune on redecorating the centre of Shouchun as his imperial capital: he'll lose Yu Province, and with it his home county, where his loyalist support is strongest. After that, he's dependent on paid help that will continually 'up their fees'. He won't win, thankfully, because if he did, the country would be a lawless mess of independent states run by the dregs of society, and he'd be the penniless, isolated emperor of Shouchun and little else."

"Sun Ce! Sun Ce, you ungrateful dog!" Yuan Shu cried as Yan Xiang finished reading the last piece of cordial correspondence that he would ever receive from Bofu. **"I-! …I-I mean *we* have nurtured that nest of southern rats for eight years, and this**

is how they repay us??? We might not have their families anymore, but is everyone beyond our grasp? Where is Sun Ben? Where is that wretched cousin of the southern dog?"

Yan Xiang coughed nervously and said, "With the exception of Sun Ben's family, every single one of them is gone, Lord Yuan; we–"

"**'LORD YUAN'???**" Yuan Shu shrieked.

Yan Xiang kowtowed repeatedly and said, "Your Majesty! Your Majesty, Your Majesty!"

Yuan Shu had swapped his cumbersome and impractical new emperor's clothes for gilded armour and purple clothing; he huffed irritably and said, "We can understand the slip of the tongue, given we are not dressed as a sovereign should be. Why has the alert not been confirmed as over, Grand General Zhang?"

The newly-instated Grand General, Zhang Xun, bowed humbly and said, "Your Majesty, the unrest in the east of the city has still not been quelled."

Jiujiang Prefecture's Administrator, Chen Ji, flicked his sleeve and said, "So says the shopkeeper's boy. You're in charge of restoring order, so restore it! …Or do we need to reconsider your surprising appointment and find an abler man…?"

Zhang Xun smiled meekly and said, "Your estimation of me is rightly low, since I have not served with His Majesty as long as others have. But I vow that order will be restored quickly."

"…Mister Chen makes a fine point," Yuan Shu said. "Your inability to police the city contributed to the loss of the hostages. We appreciate your worth, General, but if we do not see greater expediency you'll be demoted."

"I shall personally command the troops and bring an end to this incident, Your Majesty," Zhang Xun replied; he then kowtowed repeatedly and backed out of the hall.

"…If only we didn't need so many others in trouble spots," Yan Xiang sighed. "Zhang's a man of the pen, not the sword, if truth be known."

"General Zhang has proved himself time without number on the battlefield, therefore his promotions are deserved," Yang Hong said. "In fact, I would go so far as to say that he has been every bit an equal in prowess to Sun Ce, and–"

"And he got on *rather well* with Sun Ce, if I recall," Han Yin said. "Were – are – the two not *friends*, Mister Yang?"

"…*Friends*?" Yuan Shu exclaimed. "Then… then he might have aided the rebel in-! …**Why has nobody mentioned this important matter before???**"

"Your Majesty, I can vouch for him," Yang Hong said. "General Zhang is a very amiable gentleman that is on good terms with a lot of people, and his loyalty to Your Majesty outweighs any friendship."

"…It has to be noted that he is loyal beyond belief," Yuan Shu admitted. "Sun Ce is gone, Yuan Huan is gone, Chen Lan is gone, Lei Bo is gone; Qi Ji and Qin Yi went before we had even declared our divine status; but Zhang Xun has stayed, gentlemen, just as you all have. He is… *loyal*."

"He is," Yang Hong continued. "Our concern right now is not Sun Ce's *acquaintances*, but Sun Ce: how do we deal with him?"

"We have Sun Ben's family, who should be executed," Yuan Yin suggested. "That way, the Sun clan will know the penalty for–"

"I disagree," Yan Xiang said. "If we kill Sun Ben's family, it will enrage them and drive them closer to Cao. They should be kept as hostages to ensure, at worst, Sun Ben's neutrality. At best, we might hope for Sun Ce's neutrality, or even his return to service..."
Yuan Shu hummed thoughtfully.
"Sun Ce is an asset that we should try to reacquire, Your Majesty," Yang Hong ventured. "Will we perhaps try and reach out to him, and perhaps offer him considerable rank in exchange for-"
"We cannot grovel to a pirate king!" Yuan Shu chortled. "He'll suffer for his actions: Sun Ben's family shall be spared, but they are to be kept under constant guard by men that cannot be bought. In addition, we want correspondence sent to the Shanyue tribes in the east of southern Yang and the rebel confederacy leader Zu Lang in Jing County."
"Zu Lang?" Yang Hong exclaimed. "He's not a rebel leader, Your Majesty, he's a bandit king! We might as well court Sun Ce if we're going to lower ourselves to cooperate with that-"
"We will hear no more dissent," Yuan Shu ordered. "The Shanyue and the 'bandits' of Jing County shall be offered their own semi-autonomous domains and-or rank if they destroy Sun Ce."
"*Ayah*... Don't do *that*!" Yang Hong pleaded. "Your Majesty, we-"
"Enough about Sun Ce: our will is known and shall be acted upon," Yuan Shu said. "We must now know more about our success in courting *Lü Bu* as an ally..."

As the last of the rescued hostages boarded boats to southern Yang, Sun Ben stared at the vast Yangtze River and stifled tears of frustration and despair; Gongjin, Sun Yi, Zhu Zhi and Lu Su were stood to his left, and each of them was desperately trying to think of something to say.
"...My wife... my children...!" Sun Ben whimpered.
"We won't leave them to languish, Boyang," Gongjin promised.
"I say we go back," Sun Yi urged. "We should-!"
"No, Cousin, I... I cannot betray them like that," Sun Ben said. "My lady wife understood our dilemma; she could not live as a good person with values if we lived in Shouchun and kowtowed to Yuan Shu as emperor. She could not watch as her sons blindly served a heretic, and that's if we were allowed to live. It is more likely that Yuan Shu would execute us if I were to go back, whereas he will spare them if I am then a threat to Bofu's plans to oppose him."
Sun Yi exhaled angrily.
"I know, Shubi... I know," Sun Ben sighed.
"He's always tried to divide the Sun family," Gongjin noted. "He gave promotion after promotion to you, Boyang, while giving nominal reward to Bofu: he always saw you as a way of neutering Bofu, since you yielded the chieftainship of the clan to him in a way that Yuan Shu could never do himself... he went to war for a right to chieftainship that he didn't have, after all!"
"I yielded to Bofu rightly and sincerely," Sun Ben insisted. "I didn't stand in his way then, and I won't now. Perhaps my own reluctance to stand up to Yuan Shu in those earlier days is why we were only just freed from servitude: perhaps, in some small way, this is ironic punishment for being 'cowardly'."
"Don't say that!" Sun Yi cried. "*Never* say that, Boyang! And we shouldn't leave them! We should go back, I say, and-!"

"Leave it, Shubi," Sun Ben insisted. "He will not harm them if we go... and when he is defeated, they will be freed."

"...When the boats come back, it will be our turn to bid farewell to the north," Gongjin declared. "Whether we will return or not, I cannot say: but we've made more friends in recent days, and many are trying to escape Yuan Shu's rule. When he is defeated, we may be able to come back here and get some sort of foothold."

Zhu Zhi smiled and said, "Lord Sun intends to build a state, then."

"The south has been a wasteland for long enough," Gongjin replied. "I have met some wonderful people since I crossed the river, in Lujiang and Jiujiang both; wise men, fine women and gifted children, all of them keen to be in a place where they can grow... and in the south, one and all cry out for it. Bofu wants to build a southern state that families can prosper in: he wants a fine army, a grand navy, ample agriculture, solid cities, excellent academic facilities, and an infrastructure devoid of the corrosive corruption that kills the northern courts from within. He wants the south to be as good, or better, than the north, and if it possible, then I will help him build it."

"And he shall have the help of Lu Su of Dongcheng," Lu Su promised. "I shall miss the Huai region, but why shouldn't a man call any place his home...?"

"...It has long been my dream to see the south become a place where people can live instead of exist," Zhu Zhi said. "Every undeveloped piece of waste ground, every sodden marshland, every disease-ridden village near a stagnant pond... hurts me. I saw Xu Province, and I saw what a place could be like: Ze Rong's 'utopia' aside, I saw the good that Tao Qian had done, and then I saw the bad... which was avoidable. If we learn from the best and ignore the worst, we can quell the dissent, placate the tribes, pacify the bandits, reintegrate the pirates and make Yang Province a place that the north looks straight at, not down to. Even before Yuan Shu is defeated, we must prioritise that."

"And we shall," Gongjin replied.

Sun Yi looked at the mortified Sun Ben and asked, "Are you really alright with abandoning them, Cousin...?"

"...Like you, Shubi, I want to go back to Shouchun and tear down the walls, but it would be suicide," Sun Ben replied. "I am resigned to the way of things, so... so let's just go back to Jiangdong, reunite those that escaped with their loved ones, and see our losses as... as part of life. We all of us had to accept your father's death, as we had no choice in that either."

"But we'll get Huang Zu and Liu Biao for it one day though, right...?" Sun Yi asked. "That's how we have to be, isn't it...? We have to wait."

Sun Ben nodded slowly and said, "Yes, Shubi; we have to wait..."

Secret messengers were hurrying to Wu and Danyang Prefectures while the escapees completed their own journeys: Yuan Shu's various incentives would begin a new cycle of violence in those regions and provide yet another obstacle to peace in the south.

****

91

Bofu and his allies welcomed their families at the banks of the Yangtze River.

"Bofu...!" Lady Wu cried as she hugged her rugged, weary son.

"...Mother," Bofu replied emotionally.

"It is so good to see you, again, Brother!" Sun Fu said as he embraced his haunted brother Ben; after a moment, Fu closed his eyes and added, "I... I know that-"

"Do not speak of it, Brother," Sun Ben replied quietly. "Your nephews and nieces are safe so long as we do not place ourselves in the tiger's mouth."

"Brother!" Sun Yi cried as he hugged Sun Quan tightly.

"You... are as strong as Bofu!" Sun Quan exclaimed as Yi's vice-like embrace forced the wind from his lungs.

"...The little marquis," Bofu said as he turned his attentions to the 11-year-old Sun Kuang.

"I don't deserve the title, Brother," Sun Kuang replied. "You deserve it, and always did."

"You're keeping it anyway," Bofu said with a smile; he then turned to his tomboy sister and said, "Ah... *Shangxiang*... if I weren't so glad to see you, I'd probably cry with fright!"

The 10-year-old Shangxiang scowled, tugged at the left leg of her trousers, and said, "Why won't anyone let me be...?"

"Uh... because you won't get a husband if you act like that," Bofu replied uneasily. "Really, you... you need to change your choice of clothes, dear sister, and maybe be a little less aggressive, and all at some point in the next four or five years, preferably."

"My husband will let me live as I choose!" Shangxiang retorted.

"*Ayah*... what man is that...?" Lu Su said involuntarily.

Bofu raised an eyebrow, turned to Lu Su and said, "You're that fellow that lent a granary to Gongjin, aren't you?"

"*Gave*," Gongjin noted.

"...Lent, gave... that granary's in Shouchun, Gongjin, and we're in Jiangdong," Bofu retorted; he then turned back to the nervous Lu Su and said, "I appreciate that you helped Gongjin, but, uh... so far as my little sister goes, Mister Lu Su, it's for me to criticise and you to accept."

"Y-yes, Lord Sun," Lu Su replied meekly.

"*Aiee*... well done, Zijing," Gongjin muttered as Bofu turned his attention to Sun Yi. "He's unlikely to want to give you a large role now, no matter how much I value your friendship!"

"I am my own undoing," Lu Su whined. "I all too often speak before I think, but I mean no harm!"

Bofu finished speaking to Sun Yi and turned to his father's consort, Lady Chen; she reflexively lowered her gaze, which prompted him to say, "Second Mother, how have you been...?"

Lady Wu smiled at the gesture; Lady Chen smiled gratefully, looked into Bofu's eyes and replied, "I have been well, and I am glad to see that you are well too... my dear Ce."

"...The little ladies and Lang look well enough," Bofu said as he crouched to greet his three younger siblings, all of whom were no less than seven years of age.

"They are strong and bright," Lady Chen replied as Bofu rose and placed an affectionate hand on her arm.

"And you, Second Mother, are a credit to us for your strength alone," Bofu replied.

Sun Quan scowled at the attention that was being given to Lady Chen; he then turned to say something to his brother Kuang, but he was jostled by Shangxiang, who said, "I heard you fought; so why are you still so weak?"

"Ayah! Why are you attacking me, Shangxiang???" Quan cried. "I have waited so long to see you, and-!"

"Tell me about the fights!" Sun Yi asked of Bofu.

"...I'm really tired of fights, Shubi," Bofu replied. "My whole time down here has been one big fight, and now I have to go and fight Zu Lang and the Shanyue, so-"

"You're going to fight soon???" Sun Yi exclaimed. "I'm going too!"

"You're *not*," Wu Jing scoffed.

"Uncle is right," Bofu said. "You're going to have to train first, Shubi. As strong as you are from the sports you obviously play, you have to undergo-"

"Military training???" Sun Yi exclaimed. "That's good enough! When can I start?"

Wu Jing groaned, turned to his sister Lady Wu and said, "What did you do wrong...? The girls are like boys, the boys are all obsessed with-"

"They are all *themselves*," Lady Wu retorted. "Every one of them is who they *want to be*, Brother, and that isn't 'wrong'."

"...My apologies," Wu Jing said. "I just... worry, as I always do."

Bofu finally turned his attentions to Sun Ben; he smiled awkwardly, placed a supportive hand on Ben's arm and said, "What do you want to do...?"

Sun Ben sighed miserably and replied, "Fight him, Bofu. I don't know if I can give my all, but... you, you have to fight him. He's wronged the empire, not just with what he's just done but with everything he's done. You'll have to fight his hirelings first, of course..."

Bofu grunted angrily and said, "Yeah, which will be like some cruel reliving of horrors; Quan nearly lost me Zhou Tai, and I nearly lost a lot of people their lives too, just as needlessly and more times than I want to think about. Fighting White Tiger and Zu Lang again is something I never wanted to think about, never mind *do*."

"What about Taishi Ci?" Sun Ben asked. "I heard that-"

"He's rumoured, but not proven, to be leading the rebels here in Danyang, though I'm hoping he'll come over to us soon and give us some peace, if it *is* him," Bofu explained. "Even without Yuan Shu bribing troublemakers, I have problems on every side, Boyang: that's why things have to change here in the south. We need to do more than wrap the festering wounds every now and then, Boyang: we need to find the medicines and heal them."

"Zhou Yu and Zhu Zhi were discussing it before we got here," Sun Ben replied. "It won't be easy, but you're right: we need to make the south strong. Wu, Danyang, Kuaiji and Yuzhang could be-"

"To be secure, Gongjin reckons that we need to have Guangling, Lujiang and Jiujiang, in other words the *whole of Yang Province*," Bofu interrupted.

Sun Ben frowned and said, "Won't that pit us against Cao Cao...?"

"If he knows what's good for him, he'll appoint one of us as

provincial governor," Bofu replied. "I don't care if it's you, Uncle Jing, Gongjin or whoever; it's only right. If we're fighting Yuan Shu for the empire, and for Dad to be properly honoured with the hereditary honours that he never received while he was alive, it's only right."
Sun Ben grunted ambiguously.
"Boyang, he was the hero of the Dong Zhuo Campaign!" Bofu continued. "He was the man that relieved Jing Province from the Yellow Turbans, as well!"
"...You're justifying an awful lot, Bofu," Sun Ben said cautiously.
"...Yeah, well, now isn't the time, anyway," Bofu grumbled. "We'll have a banquet, and then we'll deal with Yuan Shu's new pets."
At around the same time, Cheng Pu and his young son Cheng Yi found Gongjin and Lu Su amongst the crowd and bowed low to Gongjin as a joint sign of gratitude.
"There's really no need!" Gongjin chuckled awkwardly.
"You... you saved my family, Young Zhou," Cheng Pu insisted. "I doubted your ability, and perhaps I still don't consider you to be infallible enough to trust completely on every matter, but... but neither am I, and what you did was... amazing. You have earned respect, Zhou Yu."
Cheng Pu and Cheng Yi bowed once again and retreated to join their family; Lu Su then turned to Gongjin and said, "Is that an improvement in your relationship?"
"Cheng Pu thinks that I'm a spoiled, overrated northern mediocrity, a hereditary dandy that enjoys social status purely because of the imperial court's corrupt, blindly nepotistic tendencies," Gongjin replied. "That'll probably never change, Zijing... but any small shred of respect that I've earned is a step in the right direction."
"So he's a bit of a stubborn 'noble-hating bumpkin' type, then," Lu Su said.
"...Actually, Lu Zijing, he's a man from Beiping, all the way to the north on the undeveloped frontier, that came here to become a success, but found his roots and chosen home to be burdens," Gongjin replied. "He studied hard, trained hard, and was a limb to Bofu's father; he, like Zhu Zhi, Huang Gai and Han Dang, is responsible for much of the progress that has been made up to now. My fellow 'tactician' and a wiser man than I am, Lü Ziheng, practically idolises him, and I have to confess that his respect would mean a lot, more than any reward from the court."
"...I know that was another rebuke, and I also know that I brought it upon myself," Lu Su said. "I am going to learn to be more diplomatic, even if it kills me!"
"You'll have plenty of time to practice in whatever nominal role you're given, Zijing," Gongjin teased.
        "So we're reunited, Zhongmou," Zhu Zhi's adopted son, Zhu Ran, said as he bowed to his friend Sun Quan.
"There's no need for such formality with me, Yifeng!" Sun Quan replied as he clasped his friend's hands. "It's good to see you! How were things in Wu when you left...?"
"The same as my last letter to you, sadly," Zhu Ran sighed. After a pause, he added, "I'm glad that our families are safe. I missed mine greatly anyway, but..."
"As you say, they're safe," Sun Quan said. "Let's just enjoy the

evening and worry about bad things tomorrow."
"After so long facing nothing but violence, I shall agree, if only this once!" Zhu Ran replied.

The Sun clan and their allies enjoyed a night of celebration in the governor's mansion in Qu'e City, but the festivities were, at times, half-hearted: Sun Ben's family was still imprisoned in Shouchun City and Yuan Shu's actions had left the country divided and damaged once again.
"You'll need to introduce me to all the new people tomorrow," Bofu said to Lü Fan, who was sat to his left.
"I considered inviting all of them to this banquet, but we haven't the room," Lü Fan replied. "I did, however, invite Zhang Hong, since his brother was already working for you."
Bofu looked at a pale, gaunt man that was sat to the left of the official Zhang Zhao and said, "So that's Zhang Hong, is it…? Didn't you say they were both special?"
"They were known as 'The Two Zhangs' as youths for their amazing talents at reciting the classics and commenting on the affairs of the day," Lü Fan explained. "We're most fortunate to have them both in our service."
Gongjin – who was sat to Bofu's right – smiled and said, "Indeed we are, Ziheng."
"…It's been too long since we've all been together like this," Bofu said. "Seeing my mother again, and my brothers and sisters, and Lady Chen; seeing how the children have grown, even if it's only by a little; Yuan Shu robbed us of so much, and now we can finally 'repay the kindness in full'."
"More importantly, Bofu," Lü Fan said as he sipped from his wine dish, "we can finally consider the other matter… the one that has waited far, far too long."
Bofu shuddered.
"…Have I spoken out of turn…?" Lü Fan asked.
"You meant… you meant going after Liu Biao, didn't you Ziheng?" Bofu prompted.
"Naturally," Lü Fan replied. "He's escaped justice for far too long: when the last of Yuan Shu's mercenaries and rented mobs is dealt with, we should launch an attack on Huang Zu and finally avenge your father."
Bofu smiled icily.
"I agree with Ziheng," Gongjin said. "We'll destroy them both, avenge the dead, and annex Jing into your holdings. Why should Cao Cao have it as a gift for one of his useless children, or to put another of the Son of Heaven's treacherous 'extended family' in there? Do we want Liu Zhang or Liu Bei to end up with it?"
"…I don't know," Bofu sighed. "Revenge, maybe… but… now I've thought about it more… wouldn't land-grabbing make me no better than Yuan Shu?"
"So you genuinely haven't considered it properly," Lü Fan asked.
"Of course I have!" Bofu admitted. "The governorship of Jing should be reparation for what our clan was put through, not just by Liu Biao but by Yuan Shu as well, and by Yuan Shao. Dad was the Magistrate of Changsha, yet that's ended up as someone else's due to a nonsense technicality; the four counties south of Jing are part of Jing, so our clan has a hereditary right to preside

over Changsha at the very least. But Dad liberated Wan City single-handed too: doesn't Liu Biao owe us Nan County? He let Yuan Shu squat there for months, and he's let Zhang Xiu and Jia Xu – Jia Xu! – live there as well, but he begrudges the progeny of the hero of the Dong Zhuo campaign and Yellow Turban Rebellion that made his region safe to live in...?"

Many of the closer attendees – including Sun Quan – were quietly listening to what their lord Bofu had to say, and most of them agreed with him.

"...*Aiee*... But at the same time, it's land-grabbing," Bofu continued. "My arguments are the same arguments that Yuan Shu used to seize Yu Province, send us here to take Yang Province, attack Tao Qian in Xu Province, and send Dad to die in Jing Province; Yuan Shao's just as bad. Gongsun Zan wrote to me a few times, trying to have some sort of direct relationship with us instead of through Yuan Shu, and he was always saying that Yuan Shao tricked him into attacking Ji Province so that Shao could overthrow Han Fu. Now, Yuan's using the Black Mountain Bandits as an excuse to move more and more of his lackeys into Bing Province, and his feud with Gongsun Zan would give him Yòu and Qing Provinces if he won."

"Forgive my intrusion, Lord Sun," Huang Gai said, "but Gongsun Zan overthrew Liu Yu unjustly, and so his 'governorship' of Yòu is no more correct than Yuan Shu's governance of Yang."

"Oh, I know that, Gongfu," Bofu replied. "Gongsun Zan is no better than the Yuan brothers, Liu Biao or Cao Cao. I know that Liu Biao is eyeing northern Yuzhang, so we might have to 'push back', but 'pushing back' and invading Jiangxia are two different things: one's defence... and the other is invasion. Dad never wanted to go to Jing Province: he told me that. I wouldn't go if I didn't have to... I'll go to revenge Dad, but I don't know about staying there afterwards..."

"If you don't take the place, his surviving allies will come after you," Cheng Pu warned. "Cao Cao will appoint another man, maybe one of the Kuai brothers, or a member of the Jiangxia Huangs or the Cais, or perhaps his new friend Liu Bei, who is known to believe very strongly in the right of scions of the imperial house to govern provinces, and he'll resent 'the likes of us' harming a fellow scion."

"The boundaries are an administrative nonsense," Gongjin said. "Jiangxia should be a part of what we call Jiangdong: it shouldn't be a part of Jing."

"...But aren't Lujiang and Jiujiang parts of Yu and Xu Provinces, then, by that same argument...?" Bofu countered.

"...And wasn't your father made 'Inspector of Yu Province' by a member of the Eastern Pass Coalition...?" Gongjin replied. "Even if Sun Ben's appointment was Yuan Shu's illegal doings – and I hope you'll forgive me for saying so, Boyang..."

Sun Ben snorted miserably and said, "It's true, Gongjin, so why not say it...?"

"...Then Sun Jian was accepted as 'Inspector of Yu Province' by the coalition as a whole, and the coalition was formed in the name of the Son of Heaven to liberate His Majesty from Dong Zhuo, hence making that coalition the legitimate law-passing authority at the time," Gongjin continued. "It was Yuan Shao's irrational spite that

denied it to him, Bofu, and you know it."
Bofu exhaled fiercely.
"I don't think that I'm being presumptuous," Gongjin insisted.
"Sun Jian was made 'Magistrate of Changsha', 'Marquis of
Wucheng', and 'Inspector of Yu Province' by the *recognised
authorities of the land* in his short and incredible career: why
shouldn't all of those titles be legitimate? Cao Cao is 'Marquis of
Wuping', 'Governor of Yan Province', 'Excellency of Works' and
'Acting Commander-in-Chief' right now, so don't tell me that a
man can't have many titles."
Bofu hummed thoughtfully; Bofu's other advisers – Lü Fan, Cheng
Pu, Huang Gai, Zhu Zhi, Zhang Zhao, Zhang Hong and Quan Rou
– listened intently but showed no emotion.
"And if, by my own arguments, we should have administrative
control of Yang Province, Yu Province and Jing Province, where is
the ambiguity?" Gongjin continued. "Whether Lujiang and Jiujiang
are part of Yu or Yang is irrelevant, because your father had – and
by hereditary right, *you have* – the right to govern both provinces
anyway. And it isn't land-grabbing, Bofu: you'd be governing them
by court appointment. If Yuan Shao can govern Ji, Bing, Qing and
most of Central Province, then don't tell me that a man can only
govern one province."
Bofu laughed and said, "Are you after being made a 'Sun',
Gongjin?"
The majority of those that heard Bofu's remark were compelled to
laugh at it, but the strategists and politicians were noticeably
sombre. When the laughter faded and many returned to their
private conversations and meals, Gongjin asked, "Why did you
deflect me, Bofu? We're among friends."
"I trust everyone here, but I don't want to talk about land grabs
all night," Bofu replied dismissively. "It all has political
implications: 'The Two Zhangs', Quan Rou, Demou, Gongfu, you,
Ziheng and whoever else you want to bring on my staff, like that
little rude man that gave you grain, can discuss it tomorrow. This
is supposed to be a party!"
"...I... I know that Lu Su is... 'tactless', but I really wouldn't call him
'rude', Bofu," Gongjin pleaded.
"Gongjin, to most people, 'tactless' and 'rude' are more or less the
same thing," Bofu retorted as he bit into a piece of pork. "If he
was 'honest in a polite way', that would be fine, but he's not, is
he, or you'd have let Mum meet him in Shouchun."
"...Alright, yes, he's completely without the ability to find a polite
or delicate way of saying important things and not saying anything
else, but... he's a good man," Gongjin protested. "Don't leave him
without a suitable role because he's tactless."
"How about an envoy...?" Bofu replied sarcastically.
Gongjin groaned miserably.
"...Look, he can be in charge of supply management or
something," Bofu continued. "Just don't give the man a role where
he's got to debate with others in any way, Gongjin, or he'll
probably start a needless war; despite what everyone thinks, I
don't want to do any more fighting than I have to."
"He's got a lot of ideas in his head," Gongjin pleaded.
"*Ayah*... Look, can we discuss Lu Su *tomorrow*...?" Bofu asked
desperately. "No more talk about war, recruits, Liu Biao... for just

this one night, let's not give them our time."
"...Alright," Gongjin replied.
Sun Quan had listened to every word, and many of the ideas and
names that had been bandied about intrigued him. He wondered
what his own role would be in the new state that his brother
intended to build, but his thoughts also turned to Zhou Tai, the
man that had almost died saving his life; word had reached Quan
that Zhou was ready to return to active service, and Quan was
looking forward to working with the former pirate once again.

When the banquet ended, each family went to their home – be it
new, temporary or familiar – and enjoyed being together again.
The peace would soon be shattered, but the next day would be a
day of meeting new allies and forming new bonds of friendship;
and although he could not know it for certain, Bofu would be
meeting some more of the talented men that would help his family
shape the southern state in times to come.

****

92

Bofu had every one of his many senior allies that were present in Qu'e – his brother Quan, his maternal uncle Wu Jing, his paternal uncle Sun Jing, his cousins Sun Ben, Sun Fu, Sun Hao, Sun Yu and Xu Kun, his friends and advisers Gongjin and Lü Fan, his father's former retainers Cheng Pu, Huang Gai and Zhu Zhi, the politicians Zhang Zhao and Quan Rou, and the officers Ling Cao, Chen Wu and Lü Meng – attend a meeting in the audience hall of the governor's residence. The military officers – who included Gongjin – and Sun Jian's veterans sat to Bofu's left, while the politicians and family members sat to his right.

"Before we get down to business, I should like to update the court on a few matters," Lü Fan said. "Lü Bu wants to liaise with us... we'll need to respond."

"We shouldn't need to, not with the past between us," Cheng Pu complained.

"Nonetheless, the need is there," Lü Fan sighed.

"We can't risk annoying him, I suppose," Huang Gai said. "The man is so easily 'provoked into changing his allegiances', after all..."

"...That's true," Cheng Pu replied. "We don't want to be blamed for driving him toward betraying the coalition."

"...Alright, that was the first matter," Lü Fan said. "I shall continue to the next: Hè Qi has pacified the bandits that were hounding the villages to the north of Hougan, so he might be able to join us personally on our next endeavour; Lord Sun's uncle Sun Jing and his sons have already joined us now that Kuaiji is more stable; Dong Xi and Yu Fan are having to deal with the remainder of Zhou Bo's men, but they weren't very organised when they had a leader, so that shouldn't be problematic; as for Hua Xin... he wasn't making any aggressive noises before you left Yuzhang, was he, Mister Sun Fu...?"

"You make him sound like a dog, Mister Lü!" Sun Fu chuckled. "But yes, he wasn't giving the impression that he wanted a fight: like Liu Ji, he appears to be waiting to see what the next political developments are."

"...But shouldn't Liu Ji and Administrator Hua Xin be prioritised...?" Zhang Zhao asked.

"I don't see why, Mister Zhang," Quan Rou suggested.

"So Liu Ji being the son of the ousted – and deceased – court-appointed governor, Liu Yao, is not a serious cause for concern," Zhang Zhao scoffed.

"Until Danyang is pacified and the extent of Yuan Shu's spreading of poison is known, why are we going to attack a man that seems to be quietly observing and rile up an army of ten-thousand against us...?" Quan Rou retorted. "We suspect that Hua Xin is unpopular, but attacking him might cause others to rally around him that would not have done so otherwise."

"...You are quite right, and I apologise for a moment of 'undue caution'," Zhang Zhao replied. "I shall say no more."

"...So was that it, Ziheng?" Bofu asked hopefully.

"Oh, don't be so optimistic!" Lü Fan chortled. "Zu Lang is, as expected, showing signs of hostility, so we can expect the need for a campaign. The rebellion here in Danyang has apparently softened its actions against us, perhaps due to the 'leadership' wanting to assess who their enemies are now; the Shanyue have no clear leader, but the individual tribes are making trouble, which may be harder to deal with than a confederacy. The bandits in Wu are also carrying out minor raids that don't appear to be connected to the rebels, so we'll have to deal with that whether it has anything to do with Yuan Shu or not."

"Han Yigong and Jiang Qin can cope, can't they?" Cheng Pu asked.

"I'm going back there soon," Zhu Zhi said. "We might need more support if it reaches the point where figures like Xu Gong and White Tiger reappear."

"I still say that we should attack Xu Zhao and eliminate all of the men that he's sheltering," Cheng Pu declared. "If we leave Sheng Xian, Xu Gong and White Tiger to grow their armies of supporters, we–"

"General Xu Zhao is another Zhu Jun that is too kind for his own good; former Administrator Sheng Xian is an over-principled pedant, another Lu Kang, and an unlikely source of trouble; White Tiger is powerless whilst hiding, for his following is based on public shows of strength; and Xu Gong is only popular with the people that benefitted from his takeover of the region from Sheng Xian," Gongjin suggested. "We may need to revisit them later, but right now, they're of more concern to each other than us."

"I shall concede to your superior understanding of the situation, Zhou Gongjin!" Cheng Pu said sarcastically. "Zhu Zhi, might you also show deference to Young Zhou, whose–"

"Mister Cheng, I am not trying to belittle the understanding of the situation in Wu that is possessed by esteemed veterans such as yourself and Mister Zhu," Gongjin protested. "I am trying to apply my own understanding of the northern court and the men that it deployed to the regions as well as your own well-known appraisals. Sheng Xian is the court-appointed Administrator of Wu Prefecture, appointed at a time when the eunuchs ruled the court, and his actual performance in the role is questionable: Xu Gong overthrew Sheng Xian using an alliance of the many disaffected inhabitants of the region and bandits, and Sheng fled to the estate that Xu Zhao was given as his reward for military service. We, in turn overthrew Xu Gong because he chose to ally himself with the regency's appointed governor Liu Yao, but Sheng Xian, with his simple view of things, fails to see that the enemy of his enemy is his ally: he saw us, as vassals of Yuan Shu, to be invaders, just like Xu Gong, and he was technically right. Now that we are once again in the service of the Han Dynasty – or, at worst, Cao Cao, who claims to be a Han loyalist – I propose that we now try and mediate with Sheng before we resort to assassinating him, as you appear to be suggesting."

"What, and let him regain control of Wu Prefecture, after all that we've done to pacify the place...?" Cheng Pu retorted. "That's nonsense! Sheng Xian is a eunuch stooge that is unpopular with the people! Xu Gong betrayed the people's trust with his self-serving ways and happiness with aligning himself with the pillaging Shanyue and bandits, both the worst of scum! Neither man deserves a voice, never mind power!"

"Perhaps, or perhaps not, Mister Cheng," Zhang Zhao said. "But my lord, this conversation detracts from the true reason for this meeting."

"Agreed," Bofu said. "I have a headache already... and I haven't even met anyone yet. I have a whole load of new names to remember, and now all I can think about is Sheng Xian, Xu Gong, Xu Zhao, White Tiger and Zu Lang! No more of that until we've met the new people!"

"And, I think, they've been waiting long enough," Lü Fan said apologetically. "Lord Sun, I shall now summon Lü Dai, Zhang Hong, Qin Song and Li Shu."

"...Another Lü?" Bofu chuckled as Lü Fan departed from the hall to fetch the newest of the potential recruits.

"Lü Dai, styled 'Donggong', is a man from Guangling," Wu Jing explained.

"I must have every Lü clan in the land working for me now, except for Lü Bu's of course," Bofu joked. "Still, there's another 'Zhang' to remember as well..."

Four slim officials in pale blue robes entered the hall with Lü Fan and bowed humbly.

"Couldn't you dress more individually?" Bofu complained.

Lü Fan sighed and said, "Lord Sun, the man on the far right is Mister Zhang Hong, styled 'Zigang'."

"I saw you at last night's banquet, Zigang," Bofu said. "Welcome to the south; I hope that you and Zhang Zibu will help me build it into a place that men will come from all around the country to reside in."

"I shall serve tirelessly to enhance the glory of this cruelly-forgotten corner of the empire!" Zhang Hong replied.

"...And the man to the left of Zhang Hong is Qin Song, styled 'Wenbiao'," Lu Fan announced. "He, too, is a scholar and talent of the age."

"You are too kind," Qin Song said; he then turned and bowed to Bofu, adding, "I shall exhaust my energies for your cause if needs be, Lord Sun."

"Let's hope that won't be necessary, Wenbiao!" Bofu chuckled. "Welcome to the south. Who's next, Ziheng...?"

"...The third man, Lord Sun, is Lü Dai, styled 'Dinggong', from Guangling," Lü Fan said.

"If Heaven wills it, I will be a rock on which a new and prosperous south is built, Lord Sun," Lü Dai declared.

"Your aid is appreciated, Dinggong, even before it is seen," Bofu promised. "So who do we have last...? Li Shu, wasn't it...?"

"It is," Li Shu replied. "I am from the south, not Guangling. I am a practical man, Lord Sun, and not one for familiarity, if you can excuse that. My desire is to serve in your army – as I have been doing, in a minor capacity – and restore order to the land, if only to repay you for your kindness and live up to the benevolent feats carried out by you and your esteemed father."

"...Okay, well, you've impressed me with your attitude, so we'll make sure you have men to command, Mister Li," Bofu replied. "You should join my court at once, all of you, but if nobody minds, I'd like a break."

"It's your court, Lord Sun," Lü Fan chuckled. "Gongjin, didn't you want to discuss something anyway...?"

Cheng Pu sneered and muttered, "'Gongjin'...! 'Gongjin'...!"

"I did, Ziheng," Gongjin said as he looked at the weary Bofu. "It's... another introduction, actually."
"Have you found me a wife?" Bofu chortled as he got to his feet and started toward the private meeting room that was behind the hall; Sun Hè followed quietly.
"...Sadly, no," Gongjin sighed as he got to his feet to follow Bofu.
Cheng Pu glared at Lü Fan as he gestured toward an amused Zhu Zhi and Huang Gai and asked gruffly, "Are *we* invited?"
"**Yes!**" Bofu bellowed. "You too, Ziheng."
Lü Fan smiled dryly and followed Bofu.

A slim, emotionless man in his early thirties was sat waiting for Bofu when he entered his private meeting room; Bofu lent sideways and whispered to Gongjin, "Is he shy, or something...?"
"No, but I wanted to show him special courtesy," Gongjin replied.
The young scholar bowed humbly and said, "I am glad to meet you, Lord Sun."
Bofu laughed uneasily and replied, "I'm glad to meet you, uh..."
"...This is *Gu Yong*, a man I met in Lujiang," Gongjin explained.
"Aha... well, welcome to the team then, Mister Gu Yong," Bofu chuckled. "What can you do...? You must be impressive for Gongjin to go to this much trouble."
Gongjin groaned quietly.
Gu Yong coughed to clear his throat and said, "I have studied the classics, primarily, and I am aware of all the matters of civil governance that will be essential to you in stabilising and expanding your influence, Lord Sun."
"...Right," Bofu with surprise. "You, uh... you seem to have a real sense of confidence about you, proper confidence... that comes with knowing yourself."
"He studied under *Cai Yong*," Gongjin said excitedly.
"...Alright," Bofu said with less enthusiasm.
"Cai Yong is... *was*... one of the most brilliant minds of our age," Cheng Pu said with reverence. "You are very lucky to have studied under him, Mister Gu."
"Lucky indeed," Gu Yong replied. "I am not so privileged otherwise, Mister Cheng: and I benefitted, sad to say, from his twelve-year exile in Wu."
"...When Master Cai was forced to hide from the 'Ten Attendants'," Huang Gai recalled. "So he really did teach the people of Wu...?"
"Even the underprivileged, so-called 'underclass', for Master Cai was a man that saw talent, not class, and that was his greatest lesson," Gu Yong replied.
"I like you already," Cheng Pu said with a smile. "Do you have a courtesy name, perchance...?"
"'Yuantan'," Gu Yong replied.
"Well then, Yuantan, I shall look forward to future discussions!" Cheng Pu said cheerfully. "Young Zhou, you were right to show respect to this marvellous young man."
Gongjin smiled and bowed slightly.
"...Cai Yong's death still haunts you," Huang Gai said as he stared at the unreadable Gu Yong.
"I saw him leave Wu by carriage with his family," Gu Yong replied. "He did not live long after that. It saddens me, but he was wrong to mourn Dong Zhuo."

Bofu noted the increasingly sombre mood and said, "We should have a cup of wine together, all of us, to celebrate your joining us, Gu Yuantan!"

"I don't drink wine, Lord Sun," Gu Yong replied.

"Uh... alright," Bofu said as he looked at a desperate Gongjin.

"You dislike me, Lord Sun," Gu Yong supposed.

"No, no, it's just that... well, you don't seem like you're gonna be much *fun*, if I'm honest," Bofu said disappointedly.

"*Ayah*...! Is he here to have fun...?" Gongjin asked desperately.

"But that's okay, sure and that's okay," Bofu rambled. "I mean, it's not *everyone* that's fun, right...?"

"Right," Gu Yong replied.

"...You really are like that, aren't you...?" Bofu realised. "You're not just trying to impress me with your piety... you really are no fun at all, Yuantan."

Gongjin, Lü Fan, Cheng Pu and Zhu Zhi covered their faces with their sleeves.

"I am honest, hard-working, careful, and versed in skills that will aid you," Gu Yong replied. "I hope that will be enough."

Bofu sighed, bowed slightly, and said, "Sorry, Yuantan... you're quite right. I'm being foolish; men like you will build our state. Welcome aboard, and... *well*... maybe we can have heated *tea*, or something."

Gongjin coughed deliberately.

"I mean it, we don't have to drink wine," Bofu insisted.

"I do not drink as a personal choice," Gu Yong explained. "I am happy to join you at a table and watch you drink, Lord Sun, but I do not drink myself. That is all."

"Oh, well, that's alright then!" Bofu said cheerfully. "Let's do *that*!"

Gongjin shook his head and exhaled noisily.

"But first, we need to conclude the court, and I need to finish my break before I can go back in there and listen to any more politics," Bofu said as he clutched his forehead. "Gongjin, Demou, Ziheng, Gongfu, Junli... why don't you take Gu Yuantan to meet the others...? I want a minute or two to rest my brain."

Cheng Pu laughed and said, "As you wish, Lord Sun. Gu Yuantan...?"

Gu Yong bowed slightly and followed Cheng Pu, Huang Gai and Zhu Zhi as they retreated from the room; Gongjin, Lü Fan and Sun Hè remained, which prompted Bofu to say, "Go on, all of you. I don't need bodyguards or advisers right now."

"Are you worried about the impending problems?" Gongjin asked.

"Of course I am!" Bofu replied. "How could I not be? This is *madness*, Gongjin: a few days ago, I was the man's pet dog that attacked his enemies for him, and now I'm the one that's going to be attacked, and by the very people that he used to send me off to fight!"

"Things have been relatively straightforward until now," Gongjin said. "Now, Bofu, you're a warlord, which means that you have to endure first-hand what you only suffered the consequences of whilst serving Yuan Shu: *intrigue*."

Bofu chuckled miserably.

"Oh, it'll get worse; but that's why you need so many advisers," Gongjin continued. "Zhang Zhao's sudden outburst might have seemed to be 'undue caution', as he put it, but it'll be those sorts of questions that will save us trouble. And even though I argued against taking action against Xu Zhao and Sheng Xian, that is my current assessment; that may change if I learn something new. We must continually re-evaluate every man and situation from now on."

"Sad to say, that's the truth of it," Lü Fan sighed.

Bofu shook his head, got to his feet and said, "In that case, any attempt at resting my brain now is pointless. I'll go back in there, hear what needs to be heard, and rest later. Come on."

Bofu returned to his court and endured a long discussion about the various problems that may or may not beset the Jiangdong region. A man that had once relied on one or two voices now had Gongjin, Lü Fan, Cheng Pu, Huang Gai, Zhu Zhi, Gu Yong, Zhang Zhao, Zhang Hong, Quan Rou, Qin Song, Yu Fan and Lü Dai as his senior counsel, and more would be added with every passing day. But they were needed for more than the removal of threats: there was a vast region to govern, and Bofu would need hundreds, if not thousands of men of a similar calibre if he hoped to turn the south into a powerful, self-sufficient state.

****

93

Bofu would have to make use of his large and relatively dependable family while he sought his future courtiers: it meant that he would once again have to trust his eldest brother Quan, although that would be difficult given the result of his last assignment in Xuan City. After a lot of deliberation, Bofu appointed Sun Quan as a county magistrate, but the decision was not without its detractors.

Bofu invited Gongjin and Lü Fan to join him for a private drink before they began their campaign against the Shanyue tribes in Danyang and Wu Prefectures. After an hour of conspicuously muted drinking, Lü Fan said, "What bothers you, Lord Sun?"
"...Away from the court, please don't call me 'Lord Sun'," Bofu pleaded. "We're old friends, Ziheng: six years of 'Lord Sun' is-"
Lü Fan laughed and said, "I apologise, though you must be fair and note that I remember to do so most of the time: what bothers you, *Bofu*?"
"...I was about to ask you the same question," Bofu replied. "I saw your face when I appointed Quan as the Magistrate of Yangxian."
"Mine, I hope, was equally telling," Gongjin said bluntly.
"...It was," Bofu sighed.
"...Quan is, shall we say, 'not very world-wise'," Lü Fan suggested. "Bofu, I really think that you should find someone else."
"I've made the appointment now: would you have me renege, like Yuan Shu?" Bofu asked pointedly.
"You're right," Gongjin conceded. "All we can hope is that he finds good help."
"He's my brother," Bofu chuckled. "He'll find it, like I would!"
Gongjin and Lü Fan exchanged cynical glances.
"...Alright, I admit that he's still not as responsible as I'd like," Bofu continued. "But he really did learn from that mess in Xuan... I just know that he did. One day, he'll be a better civil administrator than I could ever be, because that's what he's studied for. As I keep saying, he's just having trouble adjusting at the moment; that's why I think that a bit of peacetime responsibility will be good for him."
"Yangxian is in Wu, and Wu is, amongst other things, beset by the Shanyue, the same Shanyue that he failed to deal with last time," Lü Fan said plainly. "I know that he's your brother, and as a frequent guest in your home, I do not like to be so rude, but-"
"But if he shows even the slightest signs of making another mess of things, you want me to remove him immediately," Bofu interrupted.
"...I apologise," Lü Fan said meekly.
"Don't," Bofu insisted. "He's my brother, but he's also a Han vassal, like I am, and I will treat him like any other Han vassal. If he falters, he'll be replaced, and he'll have to accept it. He'll get no special treatment."
"...To change to another subject, I think that Zu Lang is planning something, and that we should prioritise him," Gongjin said. "In fact, I think that you should send others after the Shanyue for now and concentrate on Zu Lang."

"Mm… Zu Lang was my first opponent after I took over the military responsibilities from Boyang," Bofu recalled. "Beating him will be like… closing a circle for me, in a way."

"And I'd like to make a suggestion about the situation in Wu Prefecture, if may," Gongjin said.

"Go ahead," Bofu prompted.

Gongjin cleared his throat and said, "Sheng Xian is the former Administrator, and-"

"He's already refused to work with us before," Bofu interrupted. "What's changed?"

"What's changed, Bofu, is what I have discussed before," Gongjin replied. "You're not a vassal of Yuan Shu anymore: you're a servant of the Han again."

"In that case, isn't it up to Cao Cao, His Majesty's 'Excellency of all things', to write to Sheng Xian and offer him his old role back?" Bofu said.

"…That's unlikely to happen," Gongjin replied. "Cao Cao will want to court us, and as such, he won't want to upset conciliation between us by putting Sheng Xian – or Xu Gong – back in charge in Wu. What we must do, Bofu, is act as the Han's guardians of this region, and offer – as Han's guardians – Sheng Xian a significant administrative role. Yes, he was far from universally popular, but-"

"Xu Gong was more popular, as you have already said," Bofu retorted. "If I must recognise *Sheng*, what rank should I give *Xu*…?"

"…We might have to give Xu Gong rank," Lü Fan suggested. "Our objective right now should be to unify the various factions: firstly as a way to prevent them allying with Yuan Shu, and then as a way of consolidating the south against those that will want to return it to its former state once the crisis is over."

Bofu groaned miserably and said, "It isn't ever going to end, is it…? With every enemy we defeat, we seem to earn or find another one!"

"With power comes two things," Gongjin replied. "The first is responsibility, and the second is, to simplify it, 'jealousy'. By that I mean that you now have something to take, and there will never be a shortage of people that will want to take what you have. People like Lü Bu wanted to challenge your father purely to steal his reputation, so why are you surprised…?"

"…So you want to talk to Sheng Xian again…?" Bofu said.

"We can but try," Gongjin replied. "And we *should* try, Bofu: as Mister Gu Yuantan has sternly reminded me recently, Sheng Xian sheltered Cai Yong – which would have infuriated the eunuchs that I accused him of potentially being allied to – and he did try to govern justly, even if the embittered multitude that followed Xu Gong failed to see or feel it. Sheng Xian's support would benefit us greatly, primarily as a way of legitimising our future ventures."

"Alright, write to him," Bofu said. "We'll be marching soon, so we should spend a bit more time with our families… and in my case, I really need to speak with my mother and Quan."

"That's a good idea," Lü Fan replied.

Sun Quan was initially excited when Bofu invited him to discuss his new role as Magistrate of Yangxian County, but his mood soured when he realised that his mother, Lady Wu, had been invited to the meeting and that it was going to be a lecture on responsibility.

"I've learned my lesson!" Sun Quan protested.

"...Quan, your father named you optimistically, but he would sigh if he were here now, after what happened in Xuan," Lady Wu said.

"Forgive me, Mother, but state affairs are not your concern," Sun Quan retorted. "I love you dearly, but these are men's matters, and so I don't see why-"

"You...!" Bofu exclaimed angrily.

Lady Wu laughed and said, "So you're a man now, are you, Quan...?"

Sun Quan was suddenly humble and silent.

"...Only just, and in fact, the state should be a matter for everyone that has the capability to understand the way of things, which – as the widow of a national hero and mother to the future heroes and statesmen of the south – I understand quite well, I'll have you know," Lady Wu continued. "I insisted on being made aware of everything that was going on around me, and so I am well placed to have an opinion. I'm shocked, Quan, that you should be so ignorant, after everything that I've tried to instil in you and your brothers... and *sisters*."

Quan remained silent; Bofu noted his brother's discomfort and said, "Yeah, well, I do complain a lot about Shangxiang, Mother, which I know I shouldn't do. I'm quick enough to defend her when others criticise, so I know I'm wrong to do it."

Lady Wu smiled and said, "Yes, *you* know. But do *you* know, Quan...?"

"...I am at fault," Sun Quan replied. "Forgive me, Mother, for patronising you. Will you be more involved in state affairs from now on...?"

"Inasmuch as the ignorance of others permits," Lady Wu said. "And to return to my original point... your behaviour in Xuan was reckless. I think that you were trying to emulate your father's bluff tactics at Lu County, but 'General Xu Rong' and 'a load of barbarians' are two different things. Your father did not bluff the tribes when he was Magistrate of Changsha; as he often told me, they don't react to weakness by being suspicious of traps and retreating, they interpret it as weakness and attack. Such a 'bluff' should, in fact, be a way of luring them into a trap, contrary to what a normal general would suspect."

Sun Quan nodded silently.

"...Zhou Tai will be returning to active duty soon, but I need him for my campaign against- ...Uh, well, I shouldn't discuss that yet," Bofu said. "Suffice to say, Quan, that I won't be 'giving him back to you'. Part of your role in Yangxian – besides making sure that not just the county capital, but the entire county is amply protected against the Shanyue – is to start recruiting men to our cause. Some will obviously follow you directly, but if there are any minds that would be wasted if they're confined to one county, send them to me and Gongjin, so that they can work towards the entire state."

"Who will be my military support as Magistrate, Elder Brother?" Sun Quan asked tonelessly.

"You'll be assigned men, and it's up to you to find more Zhou

Tais," Bofu replied. "Once again, though, don't keep the dragons and tigers for yourself: you don't need such men to guard one county, but the state needs them to keep the packs of wolves from the door."

"...Will everyone else get such a lecture?" Sun Quan asked bitterly.

"Has 'everyone else' proved needy of it...?" Lady Wu retorted.

Sun Quan sighed and said, "I understand. There will be no more disasters."

"I... I don't like doing things in this way, but I have others to reassure," Bofu admitted. "Please, Quan, don't let me down. Don't let *us* down."

"May I go now, Mother...?" Sun Quan asked in a deliberately childlike tone.

"...*Aiee*... Do you know how often I am reprimanded?" Bofu asked. "Do you...? On the day that I heard what you did, I nearly got myself killed, and Bohai was screaming at me! Uncle was always shouting at Dad, but...!"

Bofu whined like an animal as his thoughts suddenly turned to the sight of his father's plain wooden coffin and the heckling Jing soldiers; the knowing Sun Quan fought tears and said, "I vow, Brother, that I won't be a fool again: Yangxian will know a magistrate that's fair, honest and sensible."

"...I know you will," Bofu replied as Lady Wu touched his hand and smiled encouragingly.

"You're going after Huang Zu soon, aren't you," Sun Quan said. "That's what you need Zhou Tai for."

"...When... when Yuan Shu's troublemakers are put down, it has to end," Bofu replied. "I tolerated that man sitting across the river in Xiakou, laughing at us, for nearly six years while Yuan Shu was my master; now that I'm my own master, I'll be damned if he's going to enjoy another day of peace, not unless I want Dad to start sighing at *me*."

"But you won't be taking me when you go to Jing Province," Sun Quan supposed.

"It... depends," Bofu replied. "I want to throw everything and everyone at it if I can, but despite what I just said, I may have to wait until Yuan Shu is defeated, I may have other problems; right now, I can't answer that."

"...So when do you go to Jing *County*...?" Sun Quan asked.

"...Actually, I'm going to west, to Lingyang, and I'm leaving tomorrow morning," Bofu replied. "You'll go to Yangxian as soon as you're ready."

"I'm ready now," Sun Quan insisted. "I'd go this very minute if I could."

"...In that case, I can have a staff and militia ready for tomorrow afternoon," Bofu said. "That look in your eyes, Quan, it tells me that you're truly ready for this... so I won't ask any more of you. I'll stick to wishing you good luck."

"And I wish the same to you, Brother," Sun Quan replied.

Lady Wu wiped a tear from her eye and said, "You're both going again. We've only been together for a handful of days, not even a month, and now Yuan Shu and the rest of the wretched creatures are forcing us apart again. I'd fight them myself if I-"

"We know, Mother, for you're always telling us," Bofu chuckled. "This won't take long; we'll be back before you know it."

Lady Wu knew that Bofu was deliberately understating the time and effort that the campaign would demand to placate her, but she smiled nonetheless.

The former Administrator of Wu Prefecture, Sheng Xian, shook his head and sighed when he read the latest correspondence from Bofu's appointed Administrator, Zhu Zhi, but he did not speak; his assembled officials and fellow exiles filled the audience hall of General Xu Zhao's mansion with anxious murmurs while they awaited a response.

"What insults do Yuan Shu's dogs throw at us now, Mister Sheng?" the official Dai Yuan asked angrily.

"Yes, Mister Sheng, we have to know!" the official Gui Lan demanded.

"Gentlemen, this is not from any dog of Yuan Shu's... not anymore," Sheng Xian replied at last; the hall fell silent.

"...But it is from Zhu Zhi...?" Dai Yuan prompted.

"Sun Ce has broken away from Yuan Shu and declared a form of independence... or so this says," Sheng Xian said as waved Zhu Zhi's letter back and forth. "But otherwise, nothing has changed: it is obvious that there is anxiety amongst his counsel that I will turn to others, so they have sent this thinly-veiled demand for a pledge."

"A pledge...? To *Sun Ce*...?" Gui Lan scoffed.

"That is the obvious inference that one can make," Sheng Xian replied. "He can mean nothing else, as far as I am concerned. We can expect to remain in exile if we do not acknowledge Sun Ce as the Lord of Wu... if not all of Yang."

"Preposterous!" Dai Yuan cried. "Write to Excellency Cao!"

"I have done, but so far, I have had no response," Sheng Xian revealed. "Once again, politics outweighs justice: Cao Cao needs Sun Ce's support to destroy the pretender Yuan Shu, so how can he threaten him...?"

"...That cannot be right!" Dai Yuan protested.

"It isn't, but that's the current political situation," Sheng Xian replied. "I suggest that you resign yourselves to it, gentlemen, as I have."

"...Perhaps we should join forces with White Tiger," Gui Lan grumbled. "Everyone else has gone mad, so why shouldn't we...?"

Sheng Xian laughed and said, "I have to confess that a tiny shred of my soul yearns for an act of madness, but we should do as we have. Xu Gong and White Tiger are probably behind the latest unrest – White Tiger undoubtedly is – but I will not aid the insurgents, for they are obviously working for Yuan Shu."

"...Ah, yes, indeed they are," Gui Lan realised. "Such times..."

"This is a storm that we must weather as servants of His Majesty," Sheng Xian declared. "When Yuan Shu is inevitably defeated – I say that again for he will be – then His Majesty will once again be in full control of the northern provinces, and at that point, Sun Ce will either capitulate or rebel; it does not matter what he does, however, because either way, Han rule will be restored in northern Yang, and our previous titles will be restored to us. It is only a matter of time."

"So what will you tell Sun Ce's lackey...?" Dai Yuan asked.

"I'll tell him the truth," Sheng Xian replied. "It will vex them, but I do not care: a traitor is a traitor, and a hankerer is a hankerer. They cannot divert resources to harass me at present, and by the time that they can, they dare not. So let them know the truth, gentlemen, for once."

The officials were not reassured, but Sheng Xian did not care; he replied to Zhu Zhi's letter, and none were in doubt as to where he stood politically. But Sheng Xian was quite right when he said that there would be no immediate repercussions: Bofu was engaged in a struggle for control of Lingyang with the bandit king Zu Lang, and Bofu's allies throughout the province were at war with ethnic tribes and other criminal and rebel confederacies, all of whom were being funded by the ever-more-desperate 'First Emperor of Zhong', Yuan Shu.

****

94

Bofu's forces divided in order to deal with the multitude of problems that the region now faced: Sun Ben, Sun Fu, Sun Jing, Sun Jing's sons, the official Quan Rou and the officers Li Shu, Hè Qi and Lü Meng crossed the Yangtze River and journeyed to southern Jiujiang, where they began to attack Yuan Shu's officials directly, despite the threat that posed to Sun Ben's family; Dong Xi and Yu Fan continued their pacification work in Kuaiji but were working toward joining the campaigns further north as soon as it was feasible; Gongjin, Wu Jing, Zhang Zhao, Zhang Hong, Gu Yong, Lü Dai and Xu Kun fortified eastern Danyang against the continuing rebel threat; Bofu himself had arrived in Lingyang – which was in the west of Danyang – for the second campaign against Zu Lang since inheriting his father's legacy.

The fighting in Lingyang began almost immediately, but those smaller armies of bandits that dared to fight the organised Sun forces were quickly swept aside. Zu Lang did not confront the Sun army until many of his smaller allies had been eliminated, but his total following still exceeded 10,000, and at least half of that force met their enemies on a piece of waste ground close to the main town. Bofu surveyed his opponent's clumsy battle lines and smiled: the bandits were heckling the Sun army, and some of Ling Cao's men were matching the din with their own taunts.

"This time, we must defeat him once and for all, Lord Sun," Lü Fan said.

"Defeating him will be easy enough this time," Bofu replied.

"I reiterate: '*Once and for all*'," Lü Fan said. **"We're not here to temporarily pacify him, we're here to break him."**

"...Alright," Bofu chuckled.

"We have to be pragmatic," Lü Fan continued. **"Zu Lang is being paid to fight for Yuan Shu this time, so his military incompetence is compensated for by a large amount of hired help and, perhaps, some borrowed advice or even advisers from Shouchun. This isn't Zu Lang we're fighting, it's *Yuan Shu*."**

"I do get it," Bofu insisted. **"It's just that I didn't intend to do what you're suggesting, really."**

"What then...?" Lü Fan asked.

Bofu did not get the chance to reply: Zu Lang rode to the centre of his army and yelled, **"CHARGE! CHARGE NOW! SHOW 'EM WHO THE REAL MEN ARE, DOWN HERE IN THE SOUTH!"**

The bandits surged forward with their array of weapons drawn and flailing. Lü Fan raised a small wooden fan that he carried specifically for the purpose of issuing orders: a nearby signalling captain watched and interpreted Lü Fan's subtle gestures and immediately sent a coded message to Ling Cao's men using hand-held flags. Minutes later, Ling Cao countered the bandits' charge.

"WHERE IS SUN CE?!" Zu Lang shrieked as he rode about and hacked at the Sun infantry. **"COME AND FIGHT, SUN CE!"**

Word of Zu Lang's challenges reached Bofu as the lines pulled back temporarily; he shook his head and said, **"I vowed that I wouldn't rush in, and... as much as I want to, and Heaven only knows I want to... I won't."**

Sun Hè grunted cynically and said, "**Not straight away, Cousin!**" A bandit army captain reported that Bofu had remained stationary during the initial charge; the revelation startled Zu Lang, who muttered, "This... isn't the same man."

"**Are we gonna charge again, then, Zu?**" one minor bandit chieftain asked.

"**...Yeah,**" Zu Lang replied. "**We should-**"

"**Enemy attacks coming from the sides and rear!**" a bandit captain cried.

"**What???**" Zu Lang exclaimed.

Cheng Pu, Huang Gai and Song Qian had suddenly led attacks on Zu Lang's army and broken its formation completely: bandits were scattering in all directions, and it was only when there was no more order in the enemy ranks that the impatient Bofu finally charged with his bodyguard force.

"**You lied!**" Sun Hè complained as he followed Bofu into the centre of a crescent-shaped cluster of enemy infantry.

"**I'd thought you'd be glad that you were right!**" Bofu retorted as he rode left and right and cut down any man that left himself exposed.

"**We're done – finished!**" Zu Lang cried as he tried to fight his way out of the battlefield. "**How could I-?**"

"**Sun Ce has charged!**" a bandit rider reported.

"**About bloody time!**" Zu Lang replied. "**Where is he?**"

"**To the northwest!**" the rider replied.

"**Pass it on: a man's weight in gold – no, an ox's weight in gold for the bloke that kills Sun Ce!**" Zu Lang bellowed to the few men that could hear him over the din of battle. Zu's offer reached many ears, and the allure of wealth gave a lot of men new vigour and compelled them to resume fighting: the primary target was Bofu, who had lost himself in the mass of combatants.

"**Yet again, you've done this to us!**" Sun Hè scolded as he fought off a crowd of bandits and tried to clear a path for Bofu to return to his front lines. "**Why couldn't you just stay where you were???**"

"**I'm sorry, Bohai!**" Bofu replied as he lunged at a cavalryman with his spear.

"**We could still win this!**" Zu Lang bellowed. "**We could-!**"

"**Death to the criminals!**" Ling Cao declared: he and his elite riders had fought their way through the thick lines of men that had been protecting Zu Lang and his chieftain allies, and they were now poised to hit those leaders.

"**We have to get out of here!**" one bandit chief said as another fell to Ling Cao's spear.

"**Cover us! Cover us!**" Zu Lang shrieked at his bodyguards.

Ling Cao managed to kill another one of Zu Lang's allies, but Zu Lang himself had already turned his horse and galloped away.

"**Spineless wretches!**" Ling Cao heckled as the surviving leaders fled. "**Where are your tigers, Zu Lang? All that I can see is rats and mice!**"

At around the same time, Cheng Pu hacked his way through the bandits that were surrounding Bofu and stopped his horse alongside his lord.

"**I know I've left myself exposed, and I'm sorry!**" Bofu said. "**But aren't we winning generally?**"

Cheng Pu harrumphed and replied, "**We are.**"

Zu Lang had fled; the bandits gradually dispersed as Ling Cao's men intensified their targeted strikes, and within minutes the battle was over.

"...He didn't get into the town, did he...?" Bofu asked of a surprisingly calm Lü Fan.

"I secured the town," Lü Fan replied. "Zu Lang will have to run to the nearest hills, where we can trap him and force him to submit."

Cheng Pu laughed and said, "It's Liu Pi and the Yellow Turbans all over again!"

"As you get older, you start to despair at seeing the same things over and over again," Huang Gai suggested. "It's better to die young, when you feel that the world is fresh and exciting, than wait until our age and older and realise the extent of the repetition and monotony. We'll see it all again, you know."

"You sound like me, Gongfu!" Cheng Pu joked.

"So are we going to camp under the hills now, Ziheng and Demou?" Bofu asked.

"I yield to you, Mister Lü," Cheng Pu said dryly.

Lü Fan smiled and said, "Now: Zu Lang must be dealt with."

"...Something bothers me," Bofu said suddenly. "Why Lingyang...?"

"I agree that his moving west is perplexing, since he had a lot of support in Jing County," Lü Fan replied. "It could be because Yuan Shu ordered him to secure Lingyang for strategic reasons, or... or one other strong possibility is 'eviction from the home by a mightier hand'. But that's unimportant at this moment. We should pursue Zu Lang at once, and we should write to Qu'e and let Gongjin know that we're about to have a victory, so that resources can be planned in advance for our next move."

"Can't we do our own resource management?" Cheng Pu asked. "Why do I need to ask 'Gongjin' to-"

Bofu sighed and said, "Not now, Demou! Let's get Zu Lang!"

An imperial edict from Cao Cao's court in Xuchang arrived before Bofu could pursue Zu Lang: the entire camp was forced to show deference as the robed messenger strolled toward Bofu's command tent and awaited his audience.

"...I hate all this," Bofu muttered as he gestured for Lü Fan to admit the messenger.

"Bear it stoically, as your father did," Cheng Pu implored.

Every man then had to bow as low as he could; the messenger then entered the tent, unfurled his cloth document, cleared his throat, and prepared to speak.

"**This herald of the court of His Majesty Xiandi addresses Sun Ce, loyal vassal of the Han! His Majesty is grateful for your public rebuke of the great traitor, the heretic and pretender Yuan Shu, and further asks that greater military opposition be shown henceforth! To legitimise your role, His Majesty now bestows upon you the noble title, 'Marquis of Wu', and the military rank of 'Rebellion-supressing General'! Furthermore, Wu Jing has been appointed as 'General who spreads Martial Might' and confirmed as 'Administrator of Danyang'! Sun Ce, come forth and receive the official seals!**"

The messenger proffered two small signature seals wrapped in

coloured silk; a stunned Bofu accepted them humbly and silently.
"This representative of the court of His Majesty Xiandi hereby concludes our meeting!" the messenger said proudly. **"May Heaven guide you to victory for His Majesty, Marquis-General Sun!"**
The ensemble kowtowed and voiced their loyalty to the emperor: the messenger then retreated, and the moment was over.
"...'Marquis of Wu'... '*General*'...!" Cheng Pu cackled. "Oh, Lord Sun – *Marquis Sun – General Sun* – this is a great day indeed! Just this once, the northern court will know a good word from me! Cao Cao might be an occasional fool, but he has honoured your father and undone all of the harm caused to your clan! He has elevated you to where you belong, Lord Sun!"
"I... can scarcely believe it myself," Bofu replied as he inspected the official seals. "Another title, and I'm a proper general at last; I'm angry that Father wasn't given these things, but this will do. And Uncle is now a general and the recognised Administrator of Danyang... which is good as well. Now we can finish hunting down Zu Lang and the rest of Yuan Shu's puppets."
"We'll... need... to respond to the court," Lü Fan said quietly.
"...We will," Bofu replied. "I will... at once, at once! Someone stop the messenger and get him refreshments! I'll write back immediately! Someone get me pen, paper and ink! I must ensure that the court knows that I am true!"
Bofu's followers wanted to celebrate the development with a banquet, but Zu Lang was still at large: once the imperial messenger had been entertained and given a response for Excellency of Works Cao Cao – the true author of the court's decision – Bofu postponed the festivities until a more appropriate time and continued the chase.

Gongjin and Lu Su met in the latter's new home in Qu'e in order to discuss the new appointments from the Han court.
"Lord Sun Ce must be pleased!" Lu Su suggested.
"Oh, I imagine that he is," Gongjin replied. "My interest resides with the motive: Cao Cao has courted Bofu with this action, and what we must ascertain is whether Cao has done it because he respects or fears Bofu."
"...I understand your point completely, Zhou Gongjin," Lu Su said. "That conversation that we once had about what would happen if Yuan Shu destroyed himself... included a highly theoretical discussion about Lord Sun becoming lord of an independent south. Cao Cao will doubtless be wondering whether our future plans involve such a thing."
"If His Majesty is saved from Yuan Shu and Cao Cao remains in his role as a loyal vassal, then we would not need to do anything of the sort," Gongjin replied. "But if Cao Cao is tempted by the allure of greater power, as Dong Zhuo and Yuan Shu have been, then we will be left with no choice."
"...I agree," Lu Su admitted. "I don't like to talk about the Son of Heaven's predicament for fear of being cursed, but my approach, I realise, is harmless to me. I have thought about the court in Xuchang, and what I see does not bode well."
"Most of His Majesty's loyalists died during the flight from Luoyang, the time spent in Chang'an and the return to Luoyang,"

Gongjin noted. "The court in Xuchang is Cao Cao's, as many have said before: that would not be a problem if Cao was a good sort, but his recent behaviour suggests that his true nature is vile indeed. Once Yuan Shu is destroyed – for which Cao will be rewarded handsomely, with a duchy, perhaps, or the 'Nine Dignitaries' – it will not be long before Cao insists that a close relative is made a senior consort to His Majesty, and it would not surprise me at all if he contrived a way to make her Empress. At that time – or before, hopefully – the few remaining loyalists will rise up, and although they will pay a heavy price, a call to face Cao Cao would be answered by the remaining warlords, who would be anxious to show their loyalty."

"...At that point, Yuan Shu's domains would be absorbed into Cao's," Lu Su suggested. "Liang Province is returned to a state of chaos, which leaves Liu Zhang and Zhang Lu – who will do nothing – in the far west, Liu Biao in Jing, Lü Bu in Xu, Yuan Shao and Gongsun Zan in the north, and Lord Sun in the south as the only other warlords in the land. Seven warlords and a cultist...? That is too many by far. It will reduce further. Someone will destroy Liu Zhang and seize Yi: maybe Cao, Zhang Lu, the Qiang, Liu Biao-"

"Naturally, I'd prefer that Bofu took Jing," Gongjin interrupted.

"Naturally," Lu Su replied dryly. "But Liu Biao will not go down without a fight. At present, I think that there is one clear scenario that won't change unless someone else decides to become suicidal: Liu Biao, Lord Sun, Yuan Shao and Cao Cao will become the four dominant forces. Yuan Shao will defeat Gongsun Zan and take Bing, Ji, Qing and Yòu Provinces under his command; Cao Cao will annex Xu, part or all of Yu and part of northern Yang-"

"We would take northern Yang," Gongjin insisted. "I won't have Cao Cao governing Lujiang, and we need Guangling for security."

"...Naturally, that's preferred," Lu Su said. "That's why I said 'part', Gongjin. In any case, the far west will, eventually, be taken by Yuan, Cao or Liu, since we lack the manpower for a march to Liang, Yi or Hanzhong. Part of southern Jing will probably come under our control during this scenario, which means that Lord Sun will have almost everything to the south and east of the Great River and some of the land above it. We could also go south and ally with or demand subservience from Jiaozhi, but that's another matter. Whatever happens then, the four-warlord situation cannot last: someone would have to be destroyed, at which point the three survivors would enter a stalemate that could last for years."

"...And Yuan Shao or Cao Cao will be the ones that contend for that coveted place as third warlord, while Liu and Sun guard their borders," Gongjin suggested.

"That's my view also," Lu Su admitted. "Yuan Shao hates Cao Cao now, and desires the role as His Majesty's guardian – and main recipient of rewards – for himself: those two will fight eventually, especially if Cao kills his brother, and in a fight like that, Cao is doomed unless he can intrigue his way to victory."

"...What a tumultuous era," Gongjin sighed.

"And the worst of the storms are yet to come," Lu Su replied.

****

95

To the surprise of all, Zu Lang regrouped his forces and challenged Bofu again: the two armies met in a field to the southeast of Lingyang.

"He can't think he'll win, not after last time," Bofu said.

"He tried some traps, but our scouts have foiled them," Lü Fan replied. "This time, Lord Sun, he has to be defeated: we cannot risk his fleeing to the hills and prolonging this, not with the rebels that are in the hills already."

"Yeah, but the rebels haven't given Zu Lang aid, which means they're not affiliated," Bofu said. "That only makes it clearer that-"

"Later, Lord Sun!" Lü Fan interrupted. "They're charging!"

The bandit army was smaller but more organised; Zu Lang ordered the front lines to retreat once Ling Cao and the other front-line officers were drawn out, but the ruse was obvious, and Bofu's men withdrew amid heckling from the bandits.

"What's the matter, Sun Ce?" Zu Lang shouted. "Why won't you come and face Zu Lang?"

Ling Cao rode forward and said in retort, "You again? Must I teach you another lesson, scruffy criminal?"

Zu Lang's followers had a brief skirmish with Ling Cao's, but the latter's men were too well trained. After a few minutes of fighting for his life, Zu Lang realised that Bofu would not be goaded for a second time and returned to his front line.

"Why do you run, Zu Lang?" Ling Cao heckled as bandit archers fired on his position.

"COME BACK HERE, LING CAO!" Bofu shrieked. "DO YOU WANT TO DIE???"

"Hit him with everything!" Zu Lang bellowed. "Don't let them get to us!"

The bandit army pushed forward and Ling Cao retreated, but Ling's men had successfully demoralised Zu Lang, who groaned miserably, grimaced at the thought of another defeat and said, "How do you catch a tiger that won't be trapped...?"

"That don't solve anythin'!" one bandit chieftain said. "What are you gonna do?"

"I don't know!" Zu Lang replied. "We'll have to-"

"They're running away now!" another bandit chief announced. "Look, lads! Chasing their man off worked: we've broken 'em!"

Zu Lang laughed when he realised that his subordinate-colleague was apparently right: Bofu's vanguard troops had been ordered to abandon their weapons, armour and supply packs and flee the battlefield.

"After them!" Zu Lang ordered. "Advance and rout them!"

The bandit army did advance, but the majority of the men were more interested in the abandoned goods than finishing their rout.

"Leave the bloody stuff!" Zu Lang barked at his fellow leaders. "Tell your men to leave the stuff and-!"

"AMBUSH...!"

The bandit captain's announcement caused Zu Lang's distracted forces to collapse almost immediately; Bofu's forces were attacking the bandits from all sides.

"**They tricked us!**" Zu Lang whined. "**They left that stuff to...! ...We have to turn this around, you hear??? Turn it around! TURN IT AROUND!**"

Nobody was listening to Zu Lang anymore: two bandit leaders fled with their small followings, which prompted Zu Lang to cry, "**Not again! Sun Ce, you bastard! You will die a dog's death if I have anything to do with it, you boy pirate!**"

"**We'll have to run an' all, Boss!**" one of Zu Lang's burly minders said.

"**Not this time!**" Zu Lang barked. "**If I run again, they'll all desert me! We have to show we've got balls! Come on, lads!**"

Despite widespread protest, Zu Lang ordered his men to charge in all directions and meet the armies that now surrounded them: the action was self-destructive, however, and Zu Lang was quickly isolated.

"**Damn you, Sun Ce!**" Zu Lang cried as he swung his sword erratically in an effort to fend off the infantry and cavalrymen that surrounded his horse. "**You'll burn in the netherworld the same as me, you pirate in noble's clothing! You wait and see if you don't!**"

But words were a feeble defence against overwhelming odds: the last of Zu Lang's men surrendered, fled or died, and Zu himself was caught, tied roughly with coarse rope and taken to Bofu's camp.

"Magnificent!" Lü Fan chuckled. "A great threat is eliminated!"

"Not the worst, though," Bofu suggested.

"No, but his defeat marks a turning point in Danyang," Lu Fan retorted. "We'll let him suffer awhile, and then–"

"I know what I want to do with him, Ziheng," Bofu interrupted. "Let's rest for now, though, and deal with him later."

Lü Fan nodded seriously, and the southern army enjoyed a moment of peace.

The former scourge of Jing County, Zu Lang, and his senior allies were herded into the corral that served as an open-air prison in Bofu's camp; Zu endured a night of misery that was accentuated by threats and taunts from his frustrated allies, and when dawn came, the Sun family soldiers enjoyed a session of heckling that pushed the bandits to the edge of despair.

"**Kill me, you bastards!**" Zu Lang cried through angry tears; he spied Ling Cao patrolling nearby and shouted, "**You there, you that challenged me! Kill me now! Don't put me in here like a horse or pig!**"

"**Oy! So is that what *we* are, then, is it, Zu?**" another bandit chief heckled.

"**No, you idiot!**" Zu Lang replied. "**We none of us should be in here! We deserve to die like men!**"

Ling Cao smiled coldly, approached the corral and said, "**You'll wait until Lord Sun decides what to do with you, Zu Lang; I hope he lets us officers decide how to dispose of you.**"

"**We deserve better!**" Zu Lang protested. "**We've had no food! How are we supposed to 'do things' in here with any dignity?! I don't want to 'go in the corner' like an animal!**"

"**Oh...? So you're *hungry*, are you, you bandits...?**" Ling Cao retorted. "**But if you don't want to have to 'go in the corner', why do you want food...?**"

"**Pirate!**" Zu Lang shrieked as Ling Cao and his men walked away laughing. "***Pirates, all o' you*, no better'n us! You'll all die too! You watch! YOU WATCH!**"

"I've got to go to a meeting to decide his fate," Ling Cao said to his men once they were some distance away from the corral. "Hopefully, we'll be taking them out and beheading them one by one by the end of the morning."

"Hopefully, sir!" one of the captains replied as Ling Cao walked toward the command tent on his own.

"...What are we going to do with him...?"

Cheng Pu's question about Zu Lang and his allies was a common one in the mind of the men in Bofu's command tent.

"I know that there's a lot of you that want to 'see justice done', but I have to think about the future," Bofu said as he caught Lü Fan's eye.

"...Another intervention by 'Gongjin', I suppose...?" Cheng Pu asked snidely.

"No, rather that I thought about it a while, and I reckon that Zu Lang should be spoken to before we do anything," Bofu replied. "Gongjin would probably agree that I should just order Zu Lang's death, but I will treat him like a defeated general."

"You're giving the man too much importance!" Cheng Pu said. "Mister Lü Fan, if you're not behind this decision then talk to Lord Sun and-!"

"In this matter, Lord Sun acts alone," Lü Fan replied ambiguously.

Bofu looked at the frustrated Ling Cao and said, "Please bring Zu Lang here."

"He's a criminal, not at all like Jiang Qin or the others!" Ling Cao retorted. "Just kill him, Lord Sun! He doesn't deserve to be in your presence as you suggest-"

"Bring him here *now*, *please*, Ling Cao," Bofu ordered, and this time, Ling Cao did as he was asked.

"Is he worth upsetting loyal officers for...?" Sun Hè asked quietly.

"If I have my way, a worse one will follow soon," Bofu replied. "I have to get them used to my way of doing things."

Sun Hè did not fully understand Bofu's response, but he did not speak further.

Minutes later, Zu Lang was brought to Bofu's command tent by Ling Cao and some prison guards.

"The prisoner, General Sun," Ling Cao announced.

"...So here we are," Bofu said as he stared at Zu Lang. "What do you have to say for yourself, Zu Lang...?"

"Second time lucky," Zu Lang heckled as Bofu's military court stared at him. "But all that's changed is that I've lost men and you've gained them! Who we are, that's the same! **You're all a bunch of pirates and bandits, same as me!**"

"You don't intend to beg, then," Cheng Pu said coldly.

"For what...?" Zu Lang chortled. "Oh yeah, because you're not with Yuan Shu anymore, then so you're 'Han' now, I s'pose, and I'm a dirty bandit for doing what you used to do: take money and orders from Yuan Shu."

Ling Cao glared at Bofu and said, "Lord Sun, why take this-?!"

"Let him speak," Bofu ordered. "This is his chosen defence."

Zu Lang grinned and said, "So what happens now then, uh...? ...You gonna brand my forehead and cut my hands off for being a naughty old rascally bandit, then, 'General Sun'...?"

"That's the legal sentence available, but I think that would be the waste of a talented man," Bofu replied. "Zu Lang, many if not all of us were 'dissidents by circumstance': I'm offering you a chance to do something *valuable*."

Zu Lang frowned and asked, "You what?"

"You could die now, yes, and be remembered as 'Zu Lang, short-lived bandit king of Jing County that died serving a heretic', or you could live on as a field general, working for – no, *with* – me, and everyone else that you see here," Bofu said plainly. "We could build a better south together. What say you...?"

"...You'd spare me, even after I tried to kill you before...?" Zu Lang asked cautiously. "I mean, I work for Yuan Shu now, the 'big traitor', the 'heretic'! Is this some sort of joke...?"

"On matters like this, I don't joke," Bofu replied. "You're a man that can rally people, and it's people like you that I need to have on my side to get other people to listen to me. Yuan Shu offered you a lot of rewards to fight me, I know that. He trapped my father with insincere promises."

Zu Lang grunted.

"...I don't know what that gesture meant, but believe me, there are a lot of people around us right now – not just Ling Cao – that probably would've been happier if I'd just said 'Guards: death' as soon as you were brought here, if not before," Bofu continued. "I'm a practical man, Zu Lang. If you think you can work with me, then say the word; if you can't, then you'll get the death you expected."

"...To pardon me, after all I've done, and trust me... takes a man with more going on in his head than I'll ever have," Zu Lang replied. "For being prepared to trust me, Sun Ce... *Lord Sun*... I swear that I'll serve you as well as any other man here in this tent. I'll fight on your front line, and I'll help you build your better south. I'd rather give that a try than die like a mad dog."

"I'm glad to hear it," Bofu said. "Ling Cao, Chen Wu: untie Zu Lang and escort him to the barracks. Release his men, and allocate them space on the outer part of the camp."

Ling Cao and Chen Wu were obviously hesitant, but they did as they were asked and freed Zu Lang from his rope bonds; to the further surprise of all, Zu threw himself to the ground as soon as he was freed and cried, "You are sent by Heaven! I'm reborn today, Lord Sun, and I shall serve until my death!"

"...There's no need for that," Bofu said as he helped Zu Lang to his feet. "You're one of us now: go and find your allies."

"You won't regret this, I promise," Zu Lang replied as Ling Cao escorted him from the tent. "I'll fight harder than anyone! **You wait and see!**"

"...When will we be putting his vows to the test, Lord Sun?" Cheng Pu asked cynically.

"Demou, we have a lot of ex-pirates and bandits working for us, like the pious Jiang Gongyi, who now fights the Shanyue for us, and Zhou Youping, who shielded my brother with his body and nearly died," Bofu retorted. "Why shouldn't I give Zu Lang another chance...?"

"My question is unanswered, Lord Sun," Cheng Pu said tonelessly.

"...We'll go and deal with the Shanyue now," Bofu replied miserably. "He'll come with us and fight in the vanguard, alongside Chen Wu. Ling Cao can stay here and fight any rebels that appear."

Cheng Pu smiled and said, "That's all that I wanted to know, Lord Sun. If you had suggested leaving him here while we fought the Shanyue, then I might have doubted your judgement a little. He can inspire a rethink amongst the bandit elements of our next enemy, whereas here in Danyang, he'd have been open to further bribery by Yuan Shu or the rebels."

"Yes... the next target is the Shanyue... *again*," Bofu grumbled.

"But this time, we're operating as servants of the Han, so why wouldn't we get more support from the locals and followers of previous administrations in Wu and Danyang?" Lü Fan asked.

"We tried asking Sheng Xian to support us, and he said 'No' in the most polite-yet-contemptuous way possible," Cheng Pu said. "As I've said before, we should-"

"We'll try again," Bofu insisted. "I'm not hoping for much, but we have to keep trying as our circumstances change. I'm 'Marquis of Wu' and 'Rebellion-supressing General' now, not a newly-independent warlord with vague intentions."

"He'll rebuke us again," Cheng Pu replied. "Like it or not, his fate is sealed."

"...I'm still going to try," Bofu retorted.

Within a day, the march to Wu Prefecture began.

****

96

While Bofu began his campaign to defeat the Shanyue, his eldest brother was enjoying his new status as Magistrate of Yangxian. Day after day, Sun Quan wandered the streets of his county capital with a sense of pride. At 15, he had what men like his own father had struggled for 2 decades or more to attain: he had his own domain, and men had to obey him. One day, he noticed that a man in fine clothing was being dogged by an older man in shabbier clothing: he stopped and stared at the strange altercation, and his weary vassals were forced to stop and wait behind him.

"You *must* hear me out, Mister Pan Zhang!" the older man protested feebly.

"Later, later!" the well-dressed Pan Zhang said with suffocating confidence. "I am a man of my word, I assure you, and I will not stand for accusations to the contrary!"

"**But the *money*…!**" the older man cried.

"You are hollering without cause," Pan Zhang insisted. "I have already said, and yet I shall say again, sir, that I am a man of my word!"

Pan Zhang stopped and loomed over the older man: Pan was tall and well-built in addition to being confident, and his older, weaker pursuer had no allies to support him.

"I am a *patient man*, Pan Zhang!" the older man said as he started to back away.

Pan Zhang laughed and said, "And I am no liar. You'll know your money again, and in good time!"

"…Who is that man, gentlemen…?" Sun Quan asked as he stared at Pan Zhang.

"Pardon, Magistrate…?" one of Sun Quan's officials prompted.

"I want to speak with that fine man there, the one in the fine clothes!" Sun Quan ordered. "I want him brought to my office!"

Sun Quan turned about and started toward his office; two of his officials stared at one-another with a sense of foreboding before one of them approached Pan Zhang.

That afternoon, Pan Zhang entered Sun Quan's office and bowed humbly.

"Aha! Mister Pan! It's Mister Pan Zhang, isn't it!" Sun Quan said excitedly.

"You have heard of me, Magistrate," Pan Zhang replied: his words carried none of the strength and confidence that his earlier confrontation had demonstrated.

"In a sense!" Sun Quan chuckled.

"Before we discuss monies owed and the suchlike, Magistrate, may I offer words in my own defence…?" Pan Zhang pleaded.

Sun Quan was confused: he leant forward and said, "Monies…? *Defence…?*"

"Magistrate, it can be said that I am a man that enjoys life, for that is what Heaven intended for all men," Pan Zhang explained. "I am a man that enjoys a drink, and I have to confess that I am also far from averse to placing the odd bet."

"What real man *isn't*?" Sun Quan said with a youth's bravado.

The notorious drunk, gambler and dandy, Pan Zhang, raised his eyes and had his first proper look at the new county magistrate that he had expected to punish him for his amassed debts and carefree ways; he realised that he was dealing with an excitable teenaged boy, and he calmed slightly.

"Magistrate Sun, why do you waste time on this individual?" one official asked.

"I will be my own counsel in this matter!" Sun Quan snapped.

Pan Zhang frowned thoughtfully, realised that the new magistrate was almost certainly a relation of the Sun clan of Wu Prefecture, and planned his next sentence accordingly.

"I will listen to this man, and that is that," Sun Quan declared; he then turned to Pan Zhang and said, "Please continue, Mister Pang."

"…I am a man that sometimes relies on the generosity of others to place some of my bets, but I am a man that always repays what he owes!" Pan Zhang continued theatrically. "Pan Zhang is a man of honour, Magistrate: when I am not being a real man in the pursuit of wine and whiling away idle hours, I am dealing justice to wrongdoers, like the legendary Sun Jian of Fuchun!"

"You… you are a hero, like my father!" Sun Quan said with delight.

"Father…?" Pan Zhang exclaimed. "Then… then you would be a son of the tiger! Yes, and I can see it now, when I look at you!"

The officials groaned quietly and powerlessly as they watched Pan Zhang win their naïve magistrate around.

"Tell me, Pan Zhang: how old are you?" Sun Quan asked.

"Oh, I am not your esteemed father's age, rather I am in my late twenties," Pan Zhang replied. "I look older because I have lived so vigorously."

"You are tall, strong, and confident," Sun Quan noted with envy.

"I am nowhere near to being the tall, fierce tiger that lives in my heart! But I need men around me all the same. Tell me, Mister Pan Zhang, where you hail from and what military experience you've had."

"…I'm from Dong Prefecture, Yan Province, and as for military experience, well I'm not exactly an officer, but I've led men on one or two things," Pan Zhang replied. "This is an age of bandits, heretics and all sorts, and every man has to do their bit, don't they, Magistrate Sun?"

"They do," Sun Quan said. "You see, I'm looking for men such as yourself to act as captains of my-"

"Ayah! We-!"

Sun Quan stopped and turned to the official that had cried out: that man was now covering his face with his sleeve while the official to his left bowed meekly and hoped that his attempt at silencing his colleague had saved their careers and lives.

"…I am not suitable for such things," Pan Zhang said as he fell to the floor and kowtowed. "I am an 'everyman', Magistrate, unsuitable for-!"

"Ignore my officials, Mister Pan, for they do not know manners," Sun Quan said sternly. "I am a decisive man by nature, and I know a great man when I see one. A man that dresses in such a dignified and resplendent manner and speaks with such flair and confidence can only be a man of the finest calibre! I hereby appoint you as a captain of my forces, and-"

Many of Sun Quan's officials were forced to stifle groans and whines of despair.

"You do not know me!" Pan Zhang cried. "Do not rush in your judgement, Magistrate!"

"I have faith that you shall grow, Pan Zhang," Sun Quan insisted.

Pan Zhang hesitated.

"All men walk a narrow path, and how hard it is," Sun Quan said sadly. "But as a man cannot hope to stay on the path at all times, a man can do his best to follow it as best he can. I wish I could say I thought of it, but a friend of my brother told me that. Will you walk the path well for me, Pan Zhang...?"

Pan Zhang looked at the irritated and frustrated officials and wondered if they would let him serve or not; he then moved his gaze to Sun Quan, who was smiling reassuringly and awaiting an answer.

"...Magistrate Sun, I shall certainly try," Pan Zhang declared. "If you'd have me work for you, then I will try my damnedest, I swear to Heaven that I will! I'll work like a horse or donkey, and make this county the safest in the empire!"

"Very good!" Sun Quan chuckled.

Pan Zhang kowtowed repeatedly, but many of the county officials were doubtful that a man known for poor restraint and excessive vice was capable of the loyalty that he now promised.

Within weeks, reports of the events in Jiangdong reached Jing Governor Liu Biao's court in his southern capital Jiangling.

"...So Sun Ce is now a Han general and a higher-level marquis than his father was," Liu Biao said tonelessly. "Cao Cao will not forgive my squatters or me for the death of his heir and favourite bodyguard, yet I cannot uproot Zhang Xiu as I did with Yuan Shu: his ally Jia Xu is a man that can fight giants with twigs! But don't I have to remove them to restore my standing with His Majesty? And all the while, Sun Ce is growing and growing... until one day, one terrible day, he will come here – perhaps with Han authority this time – to destroy me!"

"...This might seem convenient, but the 'Han authority' that you speak of is the will of another tyrant, namely Cao Cao, the 'Crafty Villain'," the adviser Kuai Liang said calmly. "We're to bow and scrape to a randy, feckless drunk that would probably want to sleep with your wife in your bed – or perhaps sleep with your aunt in your bed, whichever appeals to him at any given moment – were he to somehow defeat you...? Cao Cao's only claim to authority is 'rescuing' His Majesty from the rubble of Luoyang, planting His Majesty in his own province, and then surrounding His Majesty with his own hand-picked toadies. Are his appointments genuinely the wishes of the Son of Heaven? Yuan Shao certainly doesn't think so."

Liu Biao hummed thoughtfully.

"I know why you called this meeting," Kuai Liang continued. "Huang Zu has, as you have, expressed doubts about who we oppose now. Is resisting – or even attacking – the Han-appointed 'Rebellion-suppressing General Sun Ce' an act of survival or an act of treason...? Well, since Cao Cao is content to contrive excuses to lead punitive expeditions against you – you, a Han-appointed provincial governor that he cannot justifiably remove from office – why should we worry about a distant general with a dubious past

whose appointment was a matter of circumstance...? Would Cao
Cao be courting that undisciplined thug if he didn't need the help
to fight Yuan Shu...? If you remember that Cao Cao also
aggrandises *Lü Bu* at present, the question answers itself."
Liu Biao laughed and said, "Your words are comforting, Kuai
Zirou: it's at moments like these that you prove why I consider
you to be my finest friend and counsel. We should then intensify
our defence and perhaps attack Sun Ce's northwest holdings...?"
"I genuinely think that we should," Kuai Liang replied. "It's
something that myself, Mister Huan Jie, the Misters Pang, Mister
Wang, my brother Yue – in fact, everyone – agrees as a sound
approach when considering all of the facts. Sun Ce is not going to
be on good terms with Cao Cao for long, while your irremovable
status as a scion of the imperial house will restore you to favour
when Cao Cao's power is diminished by his own inevitable, self-
destructive actions."
The named officials murmured agreeably.
"...Then I am resolved," Liu Biao said. "My nephew will personally
lead the attacks on the Yang Provincial counties, and Huang Zu
will ready the navy. Sun Ce will lose his ill-gotten gains and then
his head!"

The self-styled 'First Emperor of the Zhong Dynasty', Yuan Shu,
was angered and dismayed in equal measure by Bofu's court
appointments, and he made that clear to a small gathering of his
most trustworthy advisers.
"...Lü Bu mocks us, but he can and must be courted for an
alliance, both military and through marriage," Yuan Shu said. "But
Sun Ce... is perhaps lost to us. Lü Bu is insatiable by normal
standards, and so the Han court cannot hope to buy him with
ordinary seals and titles; Sun Ce, by contrast, hates us, and
sentimental principles outweigh his desire for power."
The adviser Yuan Yin smiled and said, "We must retain Sun Ben's
family but treat them well, Cousin and Majesty, as Yang Hong has
already suggested. When our victories outweigh our setbacks,
then Sun Ce will want to regain the favour that he enjoyed before,
Your Majesty. The 'Han court' is an invention of Cao Cao's, built on
that most ridiculous of foundations – the legitimacy of Dong
Zhuo's puppet usurper, the Prince of Chenliu, that Cao himself
once refused to recognise – and that so-called court is, as Your
Majesty has said, the true heresy. The Han Dynasty died with
Emperor Shao: the Mandate of Heaven has passed to a worthy
hero of the age, one that can unite this fractured nation as no
other has managed, and Cao Cao, the lecherous and undisciplined
fool that he is, will soon know the will of Heaven."
"Indeed, yes," Yuan Shu chuckled. "We will soon cast aside the
illusion of legitimacy that he shrouds his puppet with! Men will
flock to us when they know our greatness truly! Even Sun Ce, with
all of his misguided feelings toward our pragmatic military
relationship, will understand that there is a place for every man
and that he was no worse treated as our vassal than he would be
or has been by any other lord! I'll spare his cousin's family, so
that they can one day be reunited and serve me willingly together!
Let Cao Cao award him: it means nothing!"

"…Let Cao Cao award Sun Ce of Fuchun: it means nothing," the ousted Administrator of Wu Prefecture, Sheng Xian, said to his assembled allies; they were still hiding on the estate of General Xu Zhao, and by refusing an alliance with Bofu, that would be where they would remain.

"How dare Cao Cao ignore us!" the official Gui Lan cried. "There's even talk of *Xu Gong* being recognised, isn't there???"

"There… is, yes, but I do **not consider it to be a popular concept!**" Sheng Xian shouted over a growing, united voice of discontent.

"**How can you be so optimistic?**" the official Dai Yuan asked. "**We are being abandoned by all sides in favour of barbarians, criminals and deviants!**"

"**Gentlemen, please, I can barely hear myself think!**" Sheng Xian bellowed; once the din had subsided, he said, "I cannot answer your questions about Cao Cao, but I can answer your concerns about Sun Ce's latest demands for deference: my answer to him is exactly the same as before. Cao Cao is making politically-motivated appointments at present, and once Sun Ce can be targeted, he will be, for he is no less the pirate king that is overthrowing the appointed governors and administrators than he was before. He has not invited Wang Lang back to Kuaiji, I'm sure, and Liu Yao's grieving son will not be named Governor of Yang, either. When Yuan Shu is defeated, Cao Cao will quickly demand greater deference from Sun Ce that he will not receive, at which point Sun Ce will become the greatest threat to peace."

"So there will be no peace with Sun Ce…?" Dai Yuan prompted.

"Gentlemen, there will be no peace with Sun Ce *or* Xu Gong," Sheng Xian promised. "I am a man that some may call 'stubborn': I call it 'principled'. Lu Kang died for his principles, and I'm prepared to die for mine: Sun Ce and Xu Gong are both hankering bandits, and I will serve in no court that calls them otherwise."

"We are with you, Mister Sheng!" Gui Lan declared.

Other men voiced their support for their isolated former administrator: there would, as before, be no peace with Bofu or his new regime, and that was something that Bofu – who was nearby, fighting the Shanyue – lamented upon learning of it.

****

97

Bofu had left Gongjin to preside over the military situation in Danyang Prefecture: Bofu's counsel in Wu Prefecture was, as always, his friend Lü Fan and his father's trusted aide Cheng Pu, but his late father's senior adviser Zhu Zhi was contributing his own unique understanding of the region as well. Bofu had, in addition, left the veteran Huang Gai and his valiant vanguard officer Ling Cao as extra military might in the region, as he had the veteran Han Dang, the former pirate Jiang Qin, the young prodigy Chen Wu and his newest recruit, the former bandit Zu Lang, for his fight with the reorganised Shanyue tribes.

The Shanyue were being led, ostensibly, by a confederacy of tribal leaders that had once pledged allegiance to White Tiger: Bofu's advisers sensed the clandestine involvement of White Tiger and, perhaps, his intermittent ally Xu Gong, but it did not really matter, as a show of indomitable strength, rather than eliminating specific leaders, was the key to ending the Shanyue threat in the region.

"We've beaten them back from Xuan City… *again*," Cheng Pu reported to Bofu and Lü Fan.

"Everyone's doing a great job," Bofu said to the ensemble in his command tent. "How is Zu Lang faring against the ones that tried to attack the villages to the south of Xuan City?"

"I… was wrong about him," Cheng Pu admitted. "He's been an asset, and he never tires of praising your… well, I was going to say 'magnanimity', but his words for it are 'good heart', which is simple and right. He's even rallied others to our cause, just as you said that he would."

"…I hope to be right about someone else," Bofu replied.

"Who…?" Cheng Pu asked.

"It's… obvious, Demou, but not important right now," Bofu replied. "For now, let's focus on getting these tribes to stop making trouble: I wish it was as easy as saying 'Yuan Shu is a lying madman that will tell you whatever you want to hear and then kill you all when he has no need of your help anymore', but they wouldn't listen."

"…Back to business!" Lü Fan said with false cheer. "Mister Cheng, how does Han Dang fare against the bandits to the north?"

"He's complaining about the repetition of it all, but yes, he's beating them back, just as he did with 'Haixi Chen'," Cheng Pu replied. "Chen Wu is dealing with the Shanyue to the east of his position, Lord Sun's brother's militia has repelled an attack on Yangxian, and-"

"Quan hasn't let me down!" Bofu chuckled. "Oh, that's good. Sorry, Demou, carry on."

Cheng Pu smiled and said, "I'm glad too, Lord Sun. But as I was saying, Jiang Qin was able to rout the force that attacked Fuchun, so there was no need for you to go there yourself after all."

Bofu scowled and said, "If they'd harmed my father's hometown, I'd have-!"

"Their attacks are, like the pirate attacks, a fact of life," Cheng Pu interrupted. "That's hopefully due to change, but there's no point to getting angry about something that's commonplace. We all carried weapons or knew where to find one at short notice: that's just 'what you did'."

"...Yeah, sorry," Bofu sighed.

"The important thing, Lord Sun, is that we're winning," Lü Fan said. "There are signs that the tribal leaders are going to try a large-scale attack against Wu County City to demoralise us, and that's a battle that you should fight personally."

Bofu's cousin and bodyguard, Sun Hè, groaned and said, *"Must he*, Ziheng?"

"Let me have my moment!" Bofu retorted. "A great general-"

"'A great general never fights a battle from the stationary saddle or the safety of his command tent'," Sun Hè interrupted. "It's something you like to say, and I'll not argue, 'General Sun'."

Bofu grinned and said, "Glad to hear it. These tribes have got to see that I'm the same Sun Ce that pacified Zu Lang, beat Wang Lang and cut off their supply of food and money, killed White Tiger's fearsome brother and made White Tiger run away. How do I do that by hiding?"

"For just this one type of opponent, reckless courage and strength are all that matter, and we all know that, including you, Bohai," Lü Fan said. "Lord Sun has to do this: there's no other way."

Sun Hè turned to his fellow bodyguard Song Qian and said, "I hope you're feeling alert, Mister Song."

Song Qian smiled and replied, "Aren't we used to it all now?"

The northern front in Jiujiang was a scene of shared frustration as news of Lü Bu's military movements – or rather, the lack of them – reached the Sun faction.

"He can't be planning to betray us all again, can he?" Sun Ben asked of his campaign adviser Quan Rou.

"Who is to say?" Quan Rou replied. "His is not a political mind, so I cannot read it easily."

"We have to find out what Bu intends, Nephew," Sun Jing said. "If he joins Yuan Shu, we have our backs to the Great River, and we're isolated."

"I... I know, Uncle," Sun Ben replied. "We have spies in Shouchun, and it appears that Yuan Shu is trying to establish cordial communications with Bu: he can't buy him with rank, so it has to be a promise of a high status."

"It's all nonsense," Quan Rou scoffed. "High status...? In a pretender's court, that is a meaningless thing. We should try and open our own communications channels with Bu and try and sway him from doing something rash."

"If his own advisers cannot keep him from straying, no one can," Sun Ben replied. "Everything south of Juchao is secured, thanks to Gongjin's careful planning; if we have to retreat, we will only be facing attacks from the north and west, and that's manageable. Of course, brave men would have to hold the enemy off..."

Li Shu bowed and said, "I am glad to fight to the last man should the need arise, and I don't doubt that others would do the same, Colonel Sun."

"My life and sword are here, of course," Hè Qi said.

"I, too, am willing to die if I must, whether it is during an attack or a retreat," Lü Meng said; other officers then added their own brave voices to a brief chorus of defiance.

"...You are all fine men," Sun Ben replied. "Let's hope that Bu doesn't force us to waste our lives, after all that we've achieved..."

Lü Bu's obvious hesitation was also causing alarm to the south, in Danyang Prefecture's capital.

"Lü Bu is the great danger of the age!" Zhang Zhao cried. "Such a man must be removed for the land to know sanity again!"

Gongjin smiled and said, "I agree." He then turned to Wu Jing and said, "Administrator Wu, we should–"

"To me, Gongjin, you are like family, so don't be so formal," Wu Jing insisted. "I know what you're thinking, by the way: we should ensure that there are boats and supplementary forces available for our allies, just in case Bu switches his allegiance."

Gongjin bowed slightly and said, "You are a wise man that does not need my help in such matters."

"But I'll need you help against the 'rebels' here in Danyang, if that's what we should even be calling them now!" Wu Jing despaired. "Why are they resuming their attacks on us? We're serving the Han now, not Yuan Shu!"

"The rebels are obviously uninterested in serving anyone," Gongjin replied. "That's strange, I admit, because we'd assumed that their leader was Taishi Ci, whose main reason for coming to this region was to help Liu Yao, the *court-appointed governor*... making this make no sense at all."

"It makes perfect sense," Zhang Zhao suggested. "Taishi Ci is, therefore, exactly what wise men of this region claimed him to be: a criminal. He is famed for acts that appear pious in intent but have no legitimacy in perpetration. He aided his regional administrator because he hoped for a promotion; he aided the fugitive scholar because he was promised handsome rewards that never came; he aided Kong Rong purely to erase his past misdemeanours; he aided Liu Yao when aiding Kong Rong failed to produce the desired results. He has now resigned himself to a life of banditry, and that is all there is to it!"

"My brother is right," Zhang Hong said. "Taishi Ci is an example of 'a vigilante mistaken for an altruistic pragmatist': he is always careful to make his actions seem justifiable, if only just so, but when one looks at his methods – treason by destroying official correspondence, trafficking people using illegal transport routes, borrowing a warlord's men for acts of unrestrained violence and the terror tactics that he employs here in Jiangdong – one can see that he finds it difficult, if not impossible, to do things in a clean, honest fashion. He is drawn to the shadows by a lust for danger, and such a man is a mad dog that must be killed."

Gongjin looked at the prodigy Gu Yong, who said nothing.

"...Bofu would not agree, Zhang Hong," Gongjin sighed.

"My nephew has his heart set on winning over men like Zu Lang and Taishi Ci, but some people cannot be made to understand," Wu Jing suggested.

"But if the rebels cannot be pacified with reason, what are we to do?" Gongjin asked. "There are so many of them: violence would result in a halving of men in Danyang at the least, which would leave us dangerously exposed to our enemies, like Huang Zu, Yuan Shu, Liu Xun, and maybe Cao Cao as well!"

"Why would Excellency Cao attack us?" Zhang Zhao scoffed. "I respect you, Mister Zhou Yu, but you are not always lucid. The Han have bestowed rank and titles on our lord and Mister Wu Jing, so why would he then attack us...?"

"Things are not as simple as you assume them to be," Gongjin replied. "You, as a politician, should know that things are rarely straightforward. Besides, do you actually credit Cao Cao with any sense at all after his wanton, disastrous actions in Nan County...?"

Zhang Zhao grunted and said, "He is, as you say, flawed."

"The Han is in decline, and we cannot, therefore, apply the rules of the last three-hundred or more years to today," Gongjin continued. "Cao Cao is either the hero that he was when he fought courageously – yet lost due to poor planning – at Xingyang, or he is the person that molested Zhang Xiu's aunt, led an army into Xu Province to massacre a hundred-thousand people over a personal matter, and-"

Zhang Zhao bowed slightly and said, "I stand corrected, Mister Zhou. I was imprisoned briefly by Tao Qian, Governor of Xu Province, who was a man that had a very good reputation indeed, yet Cao was supposedly – I might argue likely, given my own experience – wronged by Tao. Nothing, as you say, is simple."

"This may be the beginning of an era akin to the Age of Warring States, just as you once told my brother, Mister Zhou," Zhang Hong suggested quietly.

"It might, Mister Zhang," Gongjin replied. "And in such an era, outcomes of all kinds are possible."

Bofu learned of a mass gathering of Shanyue near Wu County City and met the advance with most of the forces that were available to him in Wu Prefecture.

"This is the end of it... again, for now, until next time," Lü Fan joked.

"Let's make this defeat impact for a little longer, Mister Lü," Cheng Pu replied.

The disorderly horde of Shanyue warriors hollered and heckled, but the seasoned Sun army was not affected.

"So do I ride forward, then...?" Bofu asked of his advisers.

"There are cavalry units, archers and elite infantry units readied for any action on their part," Lü Fan replied. **"Be careful, of course, but yes, you should challenge them."**

"Oh, well, if I absolutely *must* go forth...!" Bofu joked.

"I'm sure that you're terrified at the prospect, Cousin Bofu!" Sun Hè said sarcastically.

Bofu, Sun Hè, Song Qian and the rest of Bofu's elite guards rode forward on their groomed, partially-armoured horses and made themselves visible to the enemy.

"HERE IS GENERAL SUN CE, WHO QUELLED WHITE TIGER!" Bofu screamed. **"HERE IS REBELLION-SUPRESSING GENERAL SUN CE, WHO KILLED YAN YU! WHO CHALLENGES ME?"**

There was a tense atmosphere as the Shanyue warriors that heard the challenge hurriedly relayed it to their allies.

"...I wonder what will happen," Cheng Pu murmured.

The atmosphere suddenly changed: the Shanyue intensified their taunts and posturing.

"They're not going to retreat, then," Lü Fan said.

One young tribal leader's son galloped toward Bofu and bellowed,

"I challenge you, Han dog!"
Bofu met the lone warrior for a horseback duel using spears: both men were trained to fight in the saddle, but the Shanyue were known – less so than the Xiongnu, but reputed nonetheless – for their prowess as cavalrymen, and many of Bofu's followers were concerned at the pressure that the chieftain's son was piling on their young leader.
"HE SHOULD RETREAT!" Cheng Pu cried.
"No, he has to fight or they'll charge!" Lü Fan said.
"I KNOW THAT!" Cheng Pu retorted. "I... I know that... I know."
Bofu met every lunge with a parry or counter-lunge, and his Shanyue opponent was visibly surprised at how well Bofu matched his aggressive attacks. Both men were young, but both men were starting to tire: the outcome would be decided by the first mistake, and it was the Shanyue 'prince' that faltered.
"KILL HIM! KILL HIM!" Cheng Pu shrieked as Bofu knocked his opponent's spear from his hands.
"CHARGE!" one of the Shanyue leaders ordered.
"Cowards!" Cheng Pu cried. **"They won't let it end the way that Heaven wanted it!"**
"COUNTER!" Lü Fan barked to a signaller, and Chen Wu led the vanguard forward to meet the Shanyue charge. The result was a meeting of hundreds of men and horse, and for many long and painful minutes there was carnage.
"What a mess!" Lü Fan complained. **"We'll lose a lot of able, decent men in this!"**
Cheng Pu was almost oblivious to Lü Fan's words: he was preoccupied with trying to spot Bofu amongst the combatants, but his young master was nowhere to be seen.
"...I'll have to find Lord Sun!" Cheng Pu said.
"We have to hold our main line, to show strength!" Lü Fan protested. **"He has Bohai and his bodyguards! He'll be fine!"**
"He's my friend's SON!" Cheng Pu replied angrily.
"Yes, and he's my friend!" Lü Fan retorted. **"He stands a better chance if we hold!"**
"...I know," Cheng Pu replied.
Two more armies suddenly appeared to the north and south.
"Curses!" Cheng Pu exclaimed. **"They have reinforcements!"**
"Accounted for, Mister Cheng, and this is not at all as bad as it seems!" Lü Fan insisted. **"To the north, Shanyue; but to the south...!"**
Cheng Pu smiled when he realised that the southern army was led by Zu Lang; his force of former bandits and volunteers rushed toward the Shanyue and dealt them a powerful blow. The Shanyue tribes were once again humbled, and the leaders began a quiet retreat while their warriors provided cover.
"To the hills with ya!" Zu Lang cackled as he pursued one minor chieftain.
"A sound choice," Cheng Pu admitted. "Sparing him... was a very sound choice."

Once the Shanyue were driven back to the hills that they used for refuge, Bofu convened a meeting in the audience hall of Wu County City's governor's mansion.
"That, I think, was that," Bofu began. "They're making the noises

that they always make when we've broken their spirit."
"Are we going to try and find White Tiger and Xu Gong now...?"
Chen Wu asked.
"We don't know if that was orchestrated by White Tiger, since he never showed his face, but he's known to be encouraging the tribes to attack us, so he was at least partly to blame for the numbers," Bofu said. "As for Xu Gong... well, we can't be sure about him either, but we have to do something to ensure that we don't have anywhere near as much trouble from the Shanyue in the near future."
"They've had a good kicking, worse than the one you gave me," Zu Lang suggested.
"Yes, Zu Lang, but you reasoned and joined us," Bofu replied. "The Shanyue won't join us, not ever. They'll keep on making trouble, whether it's because of offers from traitors like Wang Lang and Yuan Shu, or just because they hate us. It's personal for White Tiger, too, since I killed his famous brother and made him look weaker."
"And for Xu Gong, this is equally personal," Zhu Zhi suggested. "We ousted him."
"Yeah, but he ousted Sheng Xian, so why complain...?" Bofu chuckled.
"Mister Sheng won't work with us, but Xu Gong might, hard as that will be to stomach," Lü Fan said. "Xu Gong is popular, and I suspect that he didn't lend aid to this uprising for fear of angering the Han government again. Overthrowing Sheng Xian is one thing: supporting a pretender is another."
"I know *I* regret it," Zu Lang sighed.
"So we're going to talk to *Xu Gong*," Cheng Pu grumbled.
"We have no choice," Lü Fan suggested. "He should be offered rank here in Wu Prefecture, not Administrator perhaps but something significant."
"...I don't like it, but alright," Cheng Pu replied.
"I don't like it either, but we may have to work with *Lü Bu* and *Cao Cao*," Bofu said. "My only exception is the administration in Jing Province. Huang Zu, Liu Biao, the Kuai brothers, Huan Jie, Cai Mao... *never*."
"I'll write to Xu Zhao," Lü Fan said. "After that, we need to deal with the problem in Danyang, do we not, Lord Sun."
Bofu smiled and nodded silently.

The fugitive Xu Gong was surprised and delighted when he received Bofu's indirect request for cooperation between them: Xu Gong summoned his vassals, told them of his intention to agree to Bofu's suggestions, and began preparations for a second term as a local politician and civil government agent in Wu Prefecture. Sheng Xian's followers were angry but not surprised, while Sheng Xian was stoic: he would have to watch for a second time as Xu Gong took a public office in a prefecture that was his to administrate by royal appointment, and he could do nothing about it that could coexist with his lofty principles.

****

98

Bofu convened a meeting on the eve of his urgent departure from Wu Prefecture.

"I know that many of you were expecting me to announce that I was going to bolster our forces in Jiujiang, but we're not going to be able to divide our forces between our enemies this time," Bofu declared. "The next one'll require almost everybody: in fact, I wish that I could recall the people in Jiujiang to help us."

"Is this the Danyang Bandits?" Han Dang asked.

"Yes, and we can be certain now that they're being led by Taishi Ci," Bofu replied. "He's finally emerged... and declared himself the rightful Administrator of Danyang."

The officials were understandably surprised.

"He *dares*???" Song Qian exclaimed. "How can he think that he can do that?"

"I... don't know," Bofu replied as he caught Lü Fan's gaze. "We're with His Majesty now, so... I really don't understand. What I do understand, though, is that he's intent on destroying us."

"So once again, we're going to leave a credible show of strength here to dissuade White Tiger from coming back, and go back to Danyang quickly," Cheng Pu said. "Taishi Ci probably can't be chased away like White Tiger and Haixi Chen: he'll need to be rooted out and eliminated."

"Or convinced that we're who he should be working with," Bofu suggested.

"That's hardly likely, Lord Sun, not if he's still determined to fight us when we're court-appointed now," Cheng Pu retorted.

"Don't be so sure," Bofu insisted. "You said that about Zu Lang, and there he is in our midst as a friend."

Zu Lang laughed and said, "I can scarcely believe it myself!"

"The point is," Bofu continued, "that we have to-"

"I was right about Wang Lang, Lord Sun," Cheng Pu said. "We must approach every man individually and uniquely, and Taishi is not like Zu Lang!"

"He's not like Wang Lang either," Bofu retorted. "Yu Fan, Dong Xi and Hè Qi are with us, Zu Lang is with us, and some of Liu Yao's former officials are as well. Taishi Ci had chances to kill me and he didn't take them, which means he was thinking... and I think that we can make him think some more."

"If you want to try, fine, but we don't risk lives over it, Lord Sun," Cheng Pu replied.

"I'm cynical about the idea of Taishi Ci joining us too," Lü Fan said, "but we can certainly appeal to him."

"We will," Bofu insisted. "Right, then: back to Danyang."

The Sun army in Jiujiang was rocked by a piece of news that was as expected as it was unexpected, and as disappointing as it was frightening.

"He... plans defection to Yuan Shu, then...!" Sun Ben whimpered as he read a despatch from an agent based in the north.

"Lü Bu...?" Ben's brother Fu prompted.

"Who else but that inconstant madman...?" Sun Ben replied.

"We cannot afford to have an army of that calibre suddenly

coming here and joining forces with Hui Qu!" Quan Rou said. "We must hope that Lü Bu's aides are not entirely stupid and-or uninfluential."

"...Perhaps we should smash Hui Qu with a sudden strike on his camps," Sun Ben said desperately. "If Hui Qu were defeated before Bu got here..."

"Might I see the despatch...?" Quan Rou asked.

Sun Ben smiled meekly and passed the letter to Quan Rou.

"...All is not lost," Quan Rou said once he had finished reading the despatch. "Bu's daughter has to reach Shouchun for this to have any tangibility to it, and I hazard a guess that she will not."

"Oh...?" Sun Ben exclaimed. "What do you think will happen?"

Quan Rou smiled and said, "I have discussed this extensively with the two Zhangs, Gu Yong, Lü Fan and Zhou Yu. Lü Bu has a staggering *seven* principal advisers: Chen Gong, who facilitated his invasion of Yan Province; Wang Kai and Xu Si, Chen Gong's collaborators; Chen Gui and Chen Deng, father-and-son chieftains of the influential Chens of Xiapi; and lastly he has Chen Yuanfang and Chen Qun, a father-and-son team of respected scholars originating from Yingchuan. The five Chens have nothing more in common than ancestry, as they all have different agendas: Chen Gui and Chen Deng will want to retain their power in Xu Province; Chen Yuanfang and Chen Qun will want to atone for their treacherous defection from Liu Bei that allowed Bu to seize the province, and so will be working with or hoping to work with Cao Cao covertly; Chen Gong, by contrast, will be terrified of Bu losing his grip in Xu, because that will leave him exposed to Cao Cao, who will, naturally, want revenge for the rebellion in Yan, and Wang Kai and Xu Si will be similarly determined to keep Cao Cao out of Xu Province."

"...So Chen Gong, Wang Kai and Xu Si are behind this marriage idea," Sun Ben supposed. "...And the other four Chens will try and reverse it."

"Bu is an idiot," Quan Rou replied. "Any one of those four Chens could plant the seed of doubt in such an untrusting mind, and it only takes one moment of hesitation to undo the entire thing."

"Oh, let's hope so," Sun Ben said. "We can beat Hui Qu and his friends easily enough, but not Lü Bu, not without more help."

Bofu could not resist the urge to visit his brother Quan in Yangxian before he returned to Danyang, despite the urgency of the situation: Quan welcomed Bofu into Yangxian and gave him a brief tour of the city that left him surprised and impressed.

"Such order!" Bofu chuckled. "You know what you're doing, Brother."

"...It certainly seems to be a well-run city," Lü Fan said cautiously.

"It does," Bofu said. "Quan, I like what I see so far."

"It's a collaborative effort, Elder Brother," Sun Quan replied graciously. "My officials are hardworking, diligent and wise."

The officials were visibly glad that they were being heeded more often than not, but many could not resist turning their eyes toward the tall, gaudily-dressed Pan Zhang; Bofu eventually noticed this and turned to look at his younger brother's new ally.

"I am grateful to be in your presence at last, Lord Sun," Pan Zhang said meekly.

"...I see a man that likes the finer things in life," Bofu replied coldly. "I'm sure that such humility does not come easy for you."
"Mister Pan has been invaluable!" Sun Quan protested. "He is a lover of finery, yes, much like the 'Hè Qi' that I have heard so much about!"
"So everything is always paid for properly, then...?" Bofu asked knowingly.
"I... I do have what you might call a 'generous relationship' with my creditors," Pan Zhang replied awkwardly. "I do, at times, postpone payments for items, but-"
I wish I had time to stay here and dig deeper into how Yangxian is being run," Bofu said as he turned to the irritated Sun Quan. "When this latest crisis is over, I'll be back, and I hope that I like what I find."
Bofu turned and walked back to the gates of the city: once he was no longer likely to hear what Quan had to say, the latter turned to his officials and said, "You might have cost me my role here with your snide behaviour!"
"We none of us said or did anything," one official replied. "If anyone is at fault, Magistrate, then it is Pan Zhang!"
Another official turned to Pan Zhang and said, "You should be grateful, Mister Pan, that Lord Sun was not accosted by one of your 'creditors' at any point: did you have them all arrested before he arrived...?"
Pan Zhang glared at the officials and said, "I won't be provoked. I do my job, gentlemen: the bandits don't come here anymore, and the Shanyue were repelled. If I have faults, then they are outweighed by my virtues."
"...The bandits do well enough," a third official mumbled.
"I believe in you, Mister Pan," Sun Quan announced. "Let us pursue my brother, before I am accused of failing to give him a proper send-off."

Bofu was waiting patiently when Sun Quan and his staff – minus Pan Zhang, who had notably declined to join the farewell committee – reached the gates of Yangxian. Bofu laughed and said, "Your friend the 'lover of finery' has other matters to attend to, I presume, Magistrate Sun...?"
"Mister Pan is in charge of policing the city," Sun Quan replied. "His time is wasted on civil ceremony."
"...I won't need any of your men for the Danyang campaign," Bofu said irritably. "I meant what I said before, though, Quan: I'll be coming back here, and I want to know what's being spent on what. And if your new friend is found to be misusing public funds – or is, himself, a misuse of public funds – I'll have him dragged into the market and flogged, and I'm sure there are a lot of 'creditors' that would like a turn with the whip."
Sun Quan's eyes steeled, and he replied, "That won't be necessary. Everything will be in order, brother and lord."
"...I hope so, I really do, because it looks like you've been doing a good job, and... I'm proud of that, and don't want the moment spoiled," Bofu said honestly.
Sun Quan's expression softened: he smiled and said, "As I said, you can trust me. And... and I'm glad that you are proud of what you've seen."
Bofu patted his brother's arm and turned to mount his horse.

"...Please be careful when fighting Taishi Ci," Sun Quan added.
"If I have my way, he'll be a friend of ours soon," Bofu chuckled.
"Farewell for now, dear brother."
Bofu and his entourage left Yangxian, and a grateful Sun Quan returned to his duties as the county magistrate.
"Cousin, do you think that Quan's doing a good job...?" Sun Hè asked as he rode alongside Bofu.
"...I honestly don't know, so all I can do is hope so," Bofu replied. "I don't warm to Pan Zhang, but I don't really like Zu Lang either, truth all told: I just have to hope that the officials were just dismayed by his ways rather than scared of what it all leads to."
"Forgive my intrusion," Lü Fan said, "but I have heard about Pan Zhang. We must be cautious, yet optimistic: such a man can either bring out the worst in others or have the best brought out in him, and young Master Quan's obvious trust might do that, just as our trust has brought out the best in Zu Lang."
"The signs are good," Bofu suggested.
"They are, Lord Sun," Lü Fan replied.
"...But I wasted valuable time coming here," Bofu declared. "We'd better hurry to Danyang, before Taishi Ci does something too impressive."

When Bofu's army did reach Danyang's capital, they were left more aghast than the first time that they had returned to face the rebels' actions: it was obvious that the enemy had grown in number and confidence, and the capital's formidable outer defences had barely survived a recent attack against them.
"Tell me that he should be spared," Cheng Pu challenged.
"...I still say that he can be won around," Bofu retorted.
But Bofu's view was not widely shared: after many, many months of careful preparation, Taishi Ci had wreaked his vengeance on his enemies, and he would be a force to be reckoned with as his efforts to destroy Bofu and his allies intensified.

Once the officials were assembled in the audience hall of the governor's mansion, Bofu said, "Ziheng, I can see that you want to start proceedings."
"Taishi Ci will want to know what forces we have brought before he challenges us," Lü Fan suggested. "He has, once again, withdrawn temporarily in order to assess the strength of our returning army, but now that he's calling himself the prefectural administrator, we can be sure that he won't stay quiet for long. Our lord is his primary target, so I imagine that the attacks will worsen – if that's at all possible – now that we're here. What we must decide is whether we are to simply defend and appeal to his honour or take the fight to his hilltop strongholds and humble him. The problem is that technically, this man has never known defeat: his 'Letter ruse' was a complete success, his 'River rescue' was a success, and his defence of Beihai against ridiculous odds was a feat worthy of our lord's father."
"Yeah, that what's bothers me most, Ziheng," Bofu admitted. "This is like... like fighting my dad at his peak."
Cheng Pu grunted and said, "You mustn't see the man like that, Lord Sun."
"Your father would not hide in the hills and randomly raid defenceless settlements as Taishi does," Huang Gai agreed. "He

would demand a face-to-face encounter."

Danyang's Administrator, Zhou Shang, sighed miserably.

"...He's challenged us in some way amid these cowardly raids...?" Cheng Pu asked.

"He's claiming that he has proof of humbling Lord Sun before, and that he will do so again," Zhou Shang replied. "Furthermore, he has increased his support in recent days: you may or may not have seen the Shanyue on your way here..."

"We just pacified the Shanyue," Cheng Pu said.

"The Shanyue of Wu Prefecture, perhaps, but not the tribes that live here in Danyang that were not part of the last uprising," Gongjin said. "They're very much active and very much on the side of Taishi Ci."

"He commands bandits, pirates, the common people and the Shanyue against us???" Bofu exclaimed. "Why, though...? We're fighting for the Han now... so *why*...?"

The official Zhang Zhao coughed deliberately and said, "Lord Sun, such why and wherefores are not worth further discussion. Somehow – and it does not matter how – he has managed to rally officials – some of them senior – from Liu Yao's former administration in the-"

Cheng Pu laughed miserably and said, "This would not have happened if we were not allied to Yuan Shu before! Taishi's got an entire alternative regime consisting of the muddled and the stubborn!"

"He has to win, though, for that to have a point, and he won't," Bofu insisted. "Huang Gai, Chen Wu, Ling Cao, Jiang Qin, Song Qian, Zu Lang: ready your forces. Cheng Pu, Lü Fan, Zhou Yu: I want your forces readied and your elite reconnaissance units out there gathering every last bit of information on where Taishi is operating from."

"What are we going to do?" Cheng Pu asked.

"I know his men are operating out of the Wuhu hills, but where is *he*...?" Bofu said. "What's his appointed capital, if he says that he's the 'Administrator of Danyang'...? As much as he'd like to, he can't have officials preparing to run an alternative regime out of an open-air hillside camp."

"...I agree, of course, but once again, I sense 'Gongjin' when I hear you speak," Cheng Pu replied.

"You're right that I needed help working that all out, but why's that a bad thing...?" Bofu retorted. "Yes, Gongjin and Ziheng advised me, and I imagine that Zhang Zhao and Quan Rou played their part too."

"...I'll send men southward to scout," Cheng Pu said. "I have my suspicions..."

Many eyes turned to the former bandit Zu Lang, who said, "I reckon you'd be right, Mister Cheng. The rebels were dead set on keeping me out of Jing County when I wouldn't join 'em, so that's a fairly safe bet that's he's setting up there. I dunno, though: s'just a thought, friends, but when you think about why he's not backing down, d'you think it was because *I* joined you...?"

"...Maybe, Mister Zu, but I believe that there's got to be more to it," Lü Fan replied. "Taishi prides himself on being a symbol of justice in a corrupt world... yet he's waited until we were recognised by the Han court before he declared himself as a rival administrator. That implies no interest in Cao Cao's regime in Xuchang..."

"...Or a desire to oppose the Han with the like-minded...?" Zhang Hong suggested.

"Mister Zhang Hong, you're suggesting that – after all the trouble he gave us before, serving Liu Yao – he might be working with *Yuan Shu*...?" Bofu chortled.

"No, rather that he intends to build an independent state here, a plan much like the one that is being bandied about by some of your more enterprising followers, Lord Sun," Zhang Hong replied. "If he has 'lost faith in the Han', that is entirely possible."

"Liu Ji hasn't supported him," Gongjin said. "That's a sign that Taishi is operating alone. Perhaps his wits have left him; perhaps the intriguing has left him unable to tell one thing from another. Perhaps he's building a state here before you can, and he thinks that he's doing it for the Han. Who knows...? All that's certain is that he has to be stopped before he can do any more harm."

Four very different people now threatened the security of the Jiangdong region: the first was Liu Biao, whose forces were harassing the northwest despite the Han appointments that the Sun regime now enjoyed; the second was self-proclaimed Zhong Emperor Yuan Shu, who was determined to either humble or destroy his former vassals in the south; the third was Taishi Ci, whose motivations could be fathomed by none in Bofu's court; and lastly, there was the Governor of Xu Province, Lü Bu, who was Bing Provincial Inspector Ding Yuan's former foster son, tyrant chancellor Dong Zhuo's former foster son and bodyguard, the murderer of both of the aforementioned figures and a man known for a general lack of consistency.

Yuan Shu has sent his senior adviser Han Yin to liaise with Lü Bu's agents and collect Bu's daughter from a border settlement for an impending marriage to his 'crown prince', Yuan Yao: if the affair concluded successfully, Bu would be the brother-in-law of the pretender and a grandfather to any future Zhong Dynasty emperors, and with a man like Bu to help him, Yuan Shu might well succeed where he had previously been doomed to failure. The future of the country was now in the hands of the most unreliable warlord in the land for the fourth time in eight years, and there were many that had decided – provided, of course, that Bu made another of his famous turnabouts and denied Yuan his empire – that there would be no fifth pivotal moment, and that Lü Bu – the 'Man among men' – had to be destroyed once and for all. That would, however, be the responsibility of the 'Men of the north', for in the south, the greatest threat was, of all men, Taishi Ci of Huangxian, a man known for forthrightness and consistency, and therefore a complete contrast to Lü Bu: Bofu was still determined to keep such a man alive and coerce him into joining his own cause, but that still seemed to be highly unlikely to happen as Bofu prepared to drive Taishi's rebel allies away from Danyang's capital.

****

99

Time passed, and in the south of Yang Province, a surprising first victory was being struck against the exasperated Taishi Ci. Bofu, Gongjin, Ling Cao, Chen Wu and Zu Lang led their ground forces against the mixture of Shanyue, bandits and disaffected people that Taishi had rallied while a naval detachment led by Huang Gai and Jiang Qin dealt with the pirates that were harassing the port cities from the water. News of the double-rout reached Taishi Ci's base to the south of Qu'e – a small city that had served as the latest rallying post before an assault on the surrounding region that might have driven Bofu's allies away. Now the plans would need to be revised.

"He's only just reached Danyang, and he's tearing my forces apart!" Taishi Ci complained as he read report after report from his officials. "Are the Shanyue somehow unable to move? Why have they been so ineffective?"

"He's... probably scared them, Lord Taishi," one official replied. "He's just humbled them for a second time in Wu, and-"

"The tribes of the Shanyue are, like all tribes, united only when it suits them!" Taishi Ci retorted. "How many times did I meet the Danyang chieftains and frankly broach that subject? They assured me that they would not be shaken if Sun Ce defeated the Wu tribes again!"

The officials mumbled nervously.

"We'll... need to move again," Taishi Ci said miserably. "To Jing County... Zu Lang's bandits have joined Sun Ce now, but we still have enough men to... to... to do something, at least, for a while, at least... ... ...*aiee*."

"Shall we prepare immediately...?" a second official asked.

"We were so close!" Taishi Ci cried. "So close to Qu'e, so close to taking the prefecture and...!"

After a short silence, the second official coughed nervously and repeated his question.

"...Please, yes, prepare immediately," Taishi Ci replied. "I'll... I'll try and think of something."

But Taishi Ci was haunted: he had never been defeated before, and in his mind he could only wonder why. He started to ponder the idea that not only might he have underestimated the young Sun Ce's military might; he wondered if the charismatic warlord might be a future figure of benevolence rather than a villain. The idea clashed with his mother's request, Liu Yao's allegiances and, most importantly, the infamous nature of the Sun clan's former master Yuan Shu, but it was somehow valid nonetheless: how else, he wondered, could his unfailing track record for fighting for the side of righteousness and winning be so easily broken. But then there was the fact that it was an initial defeat and much was still required of both sides before any real outcome could be declared: Taishi Ci resolved to stay true to those that had placed faith in him – including the Han Emperor, whose instructions were behind Liu Yao's actions – and fight on. But that fight would be difficult: Bofu had regained the north of Danyang with relative ease, and he had only just begun.

To the north, Yuan Shu's appointed Inspector of Yang Province, Hui Qu, and Bofu's cousin Sun Ben both received news that affected them very differently: Xu Governor Lü Bu had, as many had anticipated, changed his mind yet again.

"Let Hui Qu ruminate this until his teeth fall out!" Quan Rou said after he had finished reading a report to the officials within Sun Ben's command tent in southern Jiujiang. "It is as Heaven decreed!"

"Bu is, indeed, a man that leaves men with frayed nerves," Sun Ben chuckled. "So he has retrieved his daughter, captured Han Yin, and sent him to Cao Cao: what will happen next...?"

The young officer Lü Meng frowned and said, "Perhaps he might change his mind again."

"How can he, Mister Lü?" Quan Rou teased. "Han Yin is or was a pillar of Yuan Shu's nonsense state! Yuan Shu has been humiliated now, and Han Yin will probably lose his head when he gets to Xuchang! Lü Bu cannot go back now, silly man, not after this!"

Lü Meng smiled awkwardly and said, "I'm not very smart, Mister Quan, so all this 'intrigue' goes over my head. I wouldn't know what to do if I were him."

"Fortunately, you're loyal and constant, Major Lü, and Bu is neither of those," Sun Ben suggested. "...Bu has angered Yuan Shu with this, and he's also blunted Hui Qu: if Yuan now has to prioritise fighting Bu, we've as good as won now! I'd better write to Danyang and let them know that the threat Bu posed is no more."

"They'll be glad to hear of it," Quan Rou replied. "Taishi Ci has been repelled from the capital, but that fight is far from over."

Sun Ben had a second messenger despatched to Danyang within days of sending the first: Yuan Shu had, as most had expected, prioritised Lü Bu, but he had employed the services of the White Wave Bandits and allowed the entire confederacy – which still numbered in the tens of thousands – to pass through Yu Province, Lujiang Prefecture and Jiujiang Prefecture and join his own forces on the Xu-Yang border. Bofu's friend, Yuan Shu's Grand General Zhang Xun, had been deployed to Xu as well, and he would be joined by Jiujiang Administrator Chen Ji and Generals Liang Gang and Qiao Rui.

"I still wonder whether Heaven despises me," Bofu chortled as he read the second of Sun Ben's reports. He then turned to the officials that filled his roadside command tent to capacity and said, "I am trapped in a cycle of violence and powerlessness. Liu Pan harasses the river border with Jiangxia, but I haven't the generals to spare to send there. Yuan Shu has sent most of his forces to Xu Province, but Boyang daren't risk attacking Shouchun with such a small force, when that would not only end it but make us the heroes of the campaign! All over this province, bandits and tribes are making trouble, but I have my hands full with a pro-Han rebel that's attacking men on his own side! Why does *Taishi Ci*, of all men, delay justice???"

Lü Fan sighed and said, "It is, I agree, a shame that we cannot deal with Liu Pan or march on Shouchun, but our lot is our lot."

"I do worry about losing the northwest," Cheng Pu admitted.

"Zhou Tai insisted on going there in an administrative-stroke-consultancy capacity, despite his still being far from recovered," Lü Fan said. "I believe that he can inspire them to hold on for a little longer."

"Liu Pan and Huang Zu are both poised to do more, and so long as we're stuck here and they know it, we're in serious danger," Cheng Pu replied.

"I know the northwest force is struggling, but what can I do...?" Bofu said. "I'll send aid as soon as this stubborn Taishi is made to see sense!"

"So you're still determined to recruit him," Cheng Pu sighed. "Whose lives is he worth trading for, I wonder...?"

"I won't see any more good men wasted if I can help it, Demou," Bofu insisted. "I lost Han Yan to a lesser man, and that's regrettable, and I know that gaining Zu Lang wasn't without cost."

Zu Lang sighed miserably.

"...But I can get Taishi Ci, I *know I can*, and I will not stop trying until he makes that impossible!" Bofu vowed.

"And we must be positive," Lü Fan suggested. "Lü Bu is not an enemy at present, which means that we do not need to reinforce the border with Guangling, and Hui Qu will not get any more help either, so we don't need to bolster Sun Ben. We can safely focus on Taishi Ci, which will only make defeating him easier and quicker."

"Then let's hurry, before there are any more unforeseen developments," Cheng Pu said. "Let us charge and smash this man's defences and end this once and for all. Danyang has suffered enough, and so have we!"

Taishi Ci's forces had blockaded the roads to Jing County and received additional support from the local Shanyue tribes: Bofu deployed Cheng Pu, Huang Gai, Chen Wu, Jiang Qin, Ling Cao and Zu Lang simultaneously to attack different parts of the mass of barricades and infantry divisions.

"For the south!" one of the rebel officers cried as he led a force of villagers and bandits toward Chen Wu's ordered phalanx; the nearby Shanyue did not lend their support to the attack, opting instead for an attack on Bofu's thin front line.

"Morons," Sun Hè scoffed as he watched the tribal warriors approach at speed.

"I heard that!" Bofu chuckled. **"But how can I disagree?"**

Song Qian rode forward and formed a line of men and horse to keep the Shanyue away from his lord.

"What will we do?" Bofu's brother Sun Yi asked.

"You're doing nothing, Yi: you're here to watch, and that's it!" Bofu replied. **"Lü Fan: countermeasures!"**

Lü Fan signalled to the archers, and a limited volley put the Shanyue to flight. The rebels that had attacked Chen Wu were already routed, and Chen had moved to support Ling Cao. A second wave of Shanyue appeared from the east that Huang Gai and Jiang Qin engaged together; Zu Lang and his riders galloped about, harassing rebel and bandit positions with random attacks from all directions and throwing them into a panic; Cheng Pu had charged straight into a pack of bandits, and despite being injured yet again he had successfully repelled them.

"Old Cheng really has still got it," Bofu suggested.

"I don't think he likes you calling him that!" Sun Hè chuckled.
"Jiang Qin's men are setting fire to the southern barricades," Bofu noted. **"This is almost over."**
"And Huang Gai and I dealt with the attack on the baggage train," Lü Fan declared.
"Baggage train…?" Bofu exclaimed as he turned to look behind his battle lines.
"Stay focussed on the enemy in front of you!" Lü Fan scolded. **"I said that we dealt with it, my lord!"**
"…Dad would kick me," Bofu murmured. "How did I forget that…?"
        The battle for the road to Jing County City ended within the hour, and the march resumed.
"I can't believe that I neglected the baggage train after everything Dad said about the Liang campaign!" Bofu said miserably.
"Don't worry about it," Cheng Pu insisted. "Such things are for your advisers to worry about. You don't have to worry that you're not another Zhou Shen!"
"It's a good job that I have so many good advisers," Bofu sighed.
"Huang Gongfu's men are so disciplined that it makes me jealous sometimes!" Cheng Pu admitted. "It took a tiny squad to repel all those bandits… I'd have had a legion posted around the carts and taken needed men away from the front."
Huang Gai bowed slightly and said, "You overpraise me, Demou."
"What surprises me," Lü Fan said, "is how… well… forgive me for wording in in precisely this way, but… how *easy this is*. This is *Taishi Ci*."
Bofu, Huang Gai and Cheng Pu hummed agreeably.
"His traps have been easily spotted, his forces easily dispersed… have we missed something, I wonder…?" Lü Fan continued. "Mister Cheng, Mister Huang: are we being baited into something terrible that I cannot see…?"
Huang Gai was silent; Cheng Pu hummed thoughtfully and replied, "I wrote to Zhu Junli in Wu, expressing my own concerns, and he said that his own sources point to a genuine inability on the part of Taishi Ci to match our forces for cohesion. Taishi's army is made up of the disaffected, but there are many, often competing, sources and causes of disaffection. Some of the rebels hate the Shanyue and bandit contingents of his forces for their village raids, the Shanyue hate our people – including the bandits and rebels – and see them as encroaching on their ancestral territory, the bandits see the rebels as Han collaborators, and… well, I needn't go on, since we all know this!"
Lü Fan turned to Huang Gai and said, "What are your thoughts, Mister Huang?"
"Surrendered rebels that I've spoken to are reflective of what has been said, Mister Lü," Huang Gai replied. "Taishi Ci's supporters are a fractured lot."
"So it is our united opinion that we are not being tricked," Lü Fan noted. "That's good."
"Have we asked 'Gongjin'?" Cheng Pu asked with false enthusiasm.
Bofu groaned desperately and covered his face with his hands.
"You really are letting that young man get to you, Demou!" Huang Gai chuckled.
"Whatever do you mean, Gongfu?" Cheng Pu said with false

innocence. "Perhaps I am merely basking in his light, and–"
"Yes, I've asked Zhou Yu, and he didn't think we had cause to worry either," Lü Fan replied patiently.
Bofu lowered his hands from his face and stared at Cheng Pu.
"...Then all of the minds are in agreement," Cheng Pu said. "That's fine, but on a more serious note: what concerns me, gentlemen, is that the current narrative inevitably leads to..."
The mood darkened.
"...A siege," Bofu sighed. "*Another one*; must Taishi Ci insist on being another Lu Kang...?"
"Sad to say, there's a risk of it," Lü Fan said.

Bofu's army was met by heavy resistance from Jing County locals that were especially keen on keeping Zu Lang – a menace that they remembered well – from taking control of any part of the region: the unoffended Zu Lang was ordered to station his forces outside of Jing County while the rest of the army advanced.

At the same time, the infamous Governor of Xu Province, Lü Bu, was enduring a siege of his ill-gotten holdings by a combined army of White Wave Bandits and Yuan Shu's loyal forces. Bu was outnumbered, and his cause appeared to be lost: now, Bofu and his allies were hoping that the self-styled 'Man among men' would somehow reverse the situation militarily rather than make another political turnabout to avoid destruction.

****

100

The atmosphere in Jing County's capital was sombre: the famous vigilante, rebel leader and self-proclaimed 'Administrator of Danyang Prefecture', Taishi Ci, read the reports on Bofu's advance and sighed woefully.

"What will we do?" one officer asked.

"…Major, I've no choice," Taishi Ci replied. "I allowed myself to be talked into hiding in here and coordinating everything from afar like a warlord-governor, when I knew all along that it was doing that very thing that doomed Liu Yao. I must confront Sun Ce personally and lead from the front."

"**Ayah! You mustn't, Lord Taishi!**" an official cried. "**If you were lost-!**"

"If I was lost, then Heaven wills it so," Taishi Ci retorted. "Liu Yao's death gave you Taishi Ci; Taishi Ci's death will give you someone else if that's what Heaven decrees. Isn't that why Sun Jian's death gave the world Sun Ce…?"

The officials were silent.

"…I'll get ready at once," Taishi Ci continued. "If I can, I'll meet Sun Ce in battle again, and finish what I started when I took this."

Taishi Ci took Bofu's battle helmet from the ground at his right side and held it aloft for his followers to see.

"Is that…?" one officer gasped.

"This, gentlemen, is the battle helmet that I took from Sun Ce when we fought a duel in the rain near Shen Town," Taishi Ci explained. "He took my blade, I took his helmet; there are people that will say that there are omens attached to such things. Taking my blade meant that he will steal military victories from me, and that he has certainly done; my taking his helmet points to my taking the head it once covered, and if that is Heaven's will, then I surely will at the next battle!"

The officers' morale was boosted by the rhetoric: they cried as one, "**Victory for Commander Taishi!**" The officers that had previously served under Liu Yao and other administrations added, "**Glory to the Han!**" but that was met with sneers and grunts of disapproval by the bandit and rebel officers that had tired of the Han regime and turned against it long ago.

"…Let us want victory as one, and… and strive to achieve it as *one*," Taishi Ci said as he noted the divisions with disdain. His relatively simple vision of the world as a place of benevolent heroes and malevolent villains had been completely shattered now, and with it his indefatigable resolve.

The two armies met on the road to the county capital: the city itself would be within sight on a clear day, but the sky was cloudy and it was raining as it often did.

"…**What I'd give for some sort of parasol hat,**" Lü Fan grumbled.

"**Invent one,**" Cheng Pu joked. He mopped the rain from his face, strained his eyes to get a clearer view of the enemy army and added, "**This lot are more organised… and… and that means only one thing: Taishi has decided to join his army. So he** *was – is –* in Jing County after all. Lord Sun, this might be an opportunity to end it quickly!"

"Yes, well, *you* won't be challenging him, Demou, not with that wound you got last time," Bofu replied. "It rained when we met before... when..."

Bofu had brought the blade that he had taken from Taishi Ci to the battle: he took it from his belt and studied it as though he had never seen it before.

"**Don't you dare, Lord Sun!**" Song Qian cried. "**Please, somebody, tell Lord Sun that he mustn't!**"

Cheng Pu spied the confiscated blade and said, "**Lord Sun, you should not engage him here!**"

"**If fate wills it, I will!**" Bofu replied.

Taishi Ci ordered an infantry charge, but the slippery ground was unfavourable to his newer, poorly-trained volunteers: the men that he had trained during his time in the hills were constantly impeded by the sliding and stumbling amateurs, and some of Bofu's men were compelled to laugh at the sight of it.

"**Where are the Shanyue???**" Taishi Ci barked. "**We need them, damn it: where are they???**"

The Shanyue tribes were to the north, waiting and watching: Lü Fan and Cheng Pu's spies had reported it, and both men had prepared a scheme to take advantage of the selfish reticence. Jiang Qin led a force of men against the Shanyue and struck at them with such force that they scattered; at the same time, Bofu ordered the rest of his officers to charge at Taishi's disorderly forces rather than await them.

"**I should stay at your side!**" Song Qian protested.

"**I have Bohai!**" Bofu replied. "**Go on, man, and earn a reputation!**"

Song Qian charged as instructed, but he deliberately kept a relay of men active to warn him of attacks against the front line.

"...He's... charging?" Taishi Ci exclaimed. "**Then I must meet them personally!**"

Taishi Ci ignored the pleas of his officials and rode out to confront Chen Wu: the two duelled, but Taishi Ci was the more cunning. Chen Wu was, like everyone else, distracted by the pounding rain: he missed a lunge, and Taishi Ci grabbed his spear and used Chen's own momentum to unseat him from his horse.

"**Chen Zilie!**" Ling Cao cried: he abandoned his position and rode to Chen Wu's aid, but Taishi Ci deflected his initial strike and galloped toward Bofu.

"**He must not reach Lord Sun!**" Chen Wu screamed as he got to his feet and prepared to engage the enemy infantry. "**Pursue him, Ling Cao!**"

Ling Cao rode after Taishi Ci, but Taishi had selected a horse that was swift and capable, even in the wet conditions that he now faced: Ling Cao's horse was not moving confidently, and he stood no chance of catching up to Taishi Ci.

"**The lord! PROTECT THE LORD!**" Ling Cao shrieked, despite the total impossibility of his being heard.

"**An attack!**" Sun Hè exclaimed as Taishi Ci and six riders suddenly appeared: he rode forward instinctively and engaged Taishi, but he was no match for the wandering hero.

"**Bohai!**" Cheng Pu cried: he forgot his wound and rode to Sun

Hè's aid.

"**Let me challenge him!**" Bofu pleaded, but Sun Hè's men had formed a barrier around him that was two-way at Hè's instruction.

"**Blast it!**" Cheng Pu cried as his wound opened and prevented him from continuing his fight with Taishi Ci's wily riders; but at the same time, Song Qian had been alerted to the situation and had returned to aid a grateful Sun Hè. Taishi Ci did not have the men or the skill to repel Sun Hè and Song Qian when they worked as a team, so he reluctantly retreated to his own lines.

"*Damn it,*" Taishi Ci muttered. "There was the chance!"

"**That was the chance to end it quickly!**" Bofu complained to Sun Hè, Song Qian and Cheng Pu. "**Him or me, deciding things, as it should be! Why didn't you let me fight him???**"

"**Is he your nemesis?**" Cheng Pu retorted. "**Why lose here when Huang Zu and Liu Biao are still breathing? Play the long game, Lord Sun!**"

Bofu conceded the point and nodded dolefully.

"**Lord Taishi, you're alive!**" an official squealed when Taishi Ci finally reached his front line.

"**He's surrounded by good men!**" Taishi Ci replied enviously. "**We have to throw everything we have at him, and-!**"

"**ENEMY CHARGE!**" a captain shrieked.

Ling Cao had broken through Taishi Ci's charge and launched a direct assault on Taishi's front line: Bofu's forces had all but concluded their rout.

"**Heaven, what is your design???**" Taishi Ci cried as he fought his way out of Ling Cao's encirclement and began a humiliating retreat to the safety of the capital's fortified walls.

"**It's over: Taishi's fled,**" Lü Fan reported to a visibly disappointed Bofu.

"**Yeah, and now we have to attack the city,**" Bofu replied as he tucked Taishi's blade into his belt once again. "**He knew it and I knew it: this was a way to have it out without-!**"

"**It's sad that men have to repeat themselves to make a point understood, but isn't it that old case of 'Two tigers fighting'...?**" Lü Fan retorted.

Bofu looked at the wounded Cheng Pu, sighed and said, "Yeah... **'When two tigers fight, one of them is sure to be hurt'. And you're right, I know that, but... another siege, Ziheng...** another *siege.*"

"**It was unavoidable,**" Cheng Pu suggested. "**This battle was never going to decide anything: if Taishi had died, you can bet that he's either found someone to take over or that someone would carry the fight on anyway, perhaps one of Liu Yao's men.**"

"...Yeah," Bofu sighed. He was about to continue when a triumphant chant broke his concentration: he turned to look at the approaching Ling Cao, adopted a false smile and said, "**Now I have some men to congratulate!**"

Bofu held a modest banquet for the officers to celebrate breaking the enemy's most recent show of defiance.

"Is this banquet wise...?" Lü Fan wondered.

"It was your idea," Bofu chuckled.

"Yes, but now I'm not sure," Lü Fan admitted.

"I've organised the security personally," Cheng Pu said. "We can get politely drunk if we wish: Jiang Qin has agreed to forego his place here, and Sun Hè and Song Qian refuse to join our revelry." Bofu turned to look at the solemn Sun Hè and frowned thoughtfully.

"It's good for morale, Cousin," Sun Hè said. "I'm happy to watch."

"...Alright, if you're sure," Bofu said as he turned back to his wine dish. "I won't drink too much though... in case Taishi tries something, like I would."

"He won't," Lü Fan insisted. "He lacks the cohesion. The Shanyue have left his coalition, and his public support has dwindled after some raids his allies carried out. Once he's surrounded, it's over."

"...But what about bandits?" Bofu asked. "The-"

"Now that Zu Lang is with us...?" Lü Fan chuckled. "Unlikely."

Taishi Ci tried – in a moment of desperation – to enlist the support of a local bandit leader, but the written response was so unambiguous and coarse that Taishi was forced to smile.

"How can you be jovial at a moment like this, Lord Taishi???" an officer cried.

Taishi Ci laughed miserably and replied, "I... I'm sorry, but... but I've never actually seen someone put that in writing! It... it's quite something to see. But... why should I be upset? Did I want to receive help from such people...?"

"What about Zu Lang?" one young infantry captain asked.

"How can you ask that, you... you man from Qu'e!" a local man replied angrily.

"...Zu Lang's not come into Jing County because that would cause the people to add more support to us," Taishi Ci replied. "If we turned to such a man, we'd lose more friends than we'd gain."

"Then we are finished," an official whined.

"Maybe, maybe not," Taishi Ci replied. "I have no kind words for you, gentlemen, no encouraging rhetoric... just a promise that I will die fighting Sun Ce if I must."

But as Taishi himself had said, the words were of no encouragement: the people of Jing County's capital – be they residents or guests brought by war – would have to prepare for a siege. Taishi Ci devoted time to coaxing the vulnerable and innocent into leaving, but there were some that would not go. As ever, there would be those that would be harmed simply because they refused to leave their home: Taishi Ci fought the urge to blame himself as well as his opponents, but he was becoming increasingly convinced that he might have a made a terrible – and potentially irredeemable – mistake.

In the north, Sun Ben read the reports from the border with Xu Province and frowned miserably. 'Inspector' Hui Qu had launched a failed attack on his camp the day before, but morale was low because of bad weather, harsh rationing and the knowledge that Lü Bu's destruction would allow the enormous confederation of White Wave Bandits and 'Zhong Dynasty' forces to be deployed southward.

"What can happen...?" Sun Ben sighed.

"Have faith in Lü Bu's counsel," Quan Rou replied. "With the hope of reconciliation gone, Chen Gong will now work toward preserving

his protector from Yuan's wrath. With all of the man's advisers working together as one, something can be contrived."
"...But what would Zhang Xun do if he did get the order to march southward...?" Sun Ben wondered. "Bofu talks of Zhang as a friend, but as Grand General of Yuan's armies, he's now, let us be blunt, potentially the greatest threat that we'll face. Two questions haunt me: would Zhang sacrifice Bofu's friendship and kill us for his lord, and would Bofu forgive us if we killed Zhang...?"
"Zhang Xun is, if you'll forgive me for saying so, a bit too simple-minded, while Lord Sun understands the times well enough and knows you to act appropriately," Quan Rou replied. "The answer to both questions is 'Yes', Commander Sun, but your chances of defeating an army of that size is low, so my advice is that you should hope for the best and plan for the worst."
"...You're right," Sun Ben said. "I'll write to Zhou Gongjin and ensure that he is ready to provide us with any support that we need should Bu die."

Gongjin received Sun Ben's correspondence a week later and discussed it at length with Bofu's growing pool of advisers and politicians.
"We should, of course, fortify the riverbanks once we know that Bu has fallen," Zhang Zhao said.
"Guangling will have to be secured," Lü Dai suggested.
"Perhaps we should do that anyway," Zhang Hong said.
"And Sun Ben...?" Gongjin chortled. "Gentlemen, this discussion is about more than fortifying Jiangdong and occupying Guangling! We need to ensure the safety of our allies if the worst occurs!"
"What should we do then, in your opinion, Mister Zhou...?" Zhang Zhao asked.
"...I don't know, because I don't want to think that after all we've achieved, that... that Yuan Shu is going to be able to send an army of godless criminals down here to tear Jiangdong apart!" Gongjin replied desperately. "We'd... we'd need to have boats ready, of course, but I've already dealt with that. I... I suppose that we've done all that we can do... haven't we...?"
Gongjin turned to look at the young prodigy Gu Yong, who nodded and said, "Our shared fate is, unfortunately, in the hands of Lü Bu now, Mister Zhou."
Gongjin's friend and benefactor, Lu Su – who was among a throng of voiceless junior officials – looked on powerlessly.

Later that day, Gongjin invited his friend Lu Su to his residence so that he could discuss – and complain about – the military situation in the north.
"*Lü Bu*... our 'shared fate' is *Lü Bu's* to decide...!" Gongjin cried. "This is *ridiculous*, Zijing! How can we be dependent on whether that-"
"I know how frustrated you must feel, Gongjin, but Gu Yong was right," Lu Su suggested. "Tell Lord Sun, double-check your boats, and hope that Heaven's design is kind to us."
"...What frustrates me, of course, is that it affects everything that I had hoped – *we* had hoped – to see," Gongjin replied. "Yuan Shu was on the verge of self-destruction, and the stage was set for Bofu to become one of the great warlords: now Yuan has suddenly

won the support of the White Wave Bandits, and, well... Bu aside, the bandits are the real problem. If Yuan can rely on them, then perhaps all is lost, and maybe there will be a 'Zhong Dynasty' after all."

Lu Su exhaled loudly and slapped his thighs.

"...But then, perhaps I am being too pessimistic," Gongjin realised. After a short pause, he smiled and said, "How can Yuan send his new criminal army to fight us when he must first defeat Cao Cao in Yu Province...!"

"So we will have time to prepare," Lu Su supposed.

"'Prepare' for what...?" Gongjin chortled. "Oh, yes, Cao Cao was crushed by Jia Xu, but only because he was distracted and muddle-headed: the Cao Cao in Yu Province is the other Cao Cao, the one that deserves the title, 'Hero of Chaos'. Yuan's forces are losing in Yu, and he will need those White Wave Bandits there, not here; but Cao Cao is an expert at fighting such enemies, and he has defeated the White Waves once already, when he rescued the emperor from Luoyang! No, all is well, Zijing... all is well! Yuan Shu will still lose, and Sun Bofu will still rise to greatness as he deserves to! Heaven is with us!"

Lu Su smiled dryly and said, "You sound certain, and I'm happy to agree with you!"

But Cao Cao would not have to face the White Wave Bandits for a second time: something unexpected was about to happen in Xu Province that would surprise everyone yet again.

****

101

The siege of Jing County City was an unwanted stalemate. Day after day, Bofu sent men to the walls, and time after time, Taishi Ci personally managed the walls and kept the attackers from breaching them.

"We need rams, fire, towers, and a million men if we stand a chance of beating this hero of the age!" Bofu cried as he watched another force of men retreat from the walls: it was evening, and the light was poor.

"You must keep your head, Lord Sun!" Cheng Pu barked.

"Sieges are not pleasant, but they're a part of warfare," Lü Fan protested.

"He's keeping me from other matters!" Bofu replied. **"Dong Xi needs help, Zhu Zhi needs help, the northwest needs help *and* a leader, Liu Yao's ghost is more likely to do something about his army in Yuzhang than I am, and what's going on in Jiujiang now, exactly???"**

"I... don't know," Lü Fan sighed. "But-"

"I know I'm sounding like a hypocrite," Bofu said. "I know that I've had two chances to kill Taishi, and that there are a lot of people that resent the fact that I didn't allow it. Maybe I'll allow the next man that sees an opportunity to exploit it: I do understand that there's no point gaining one champion at the expense of several others. It's just that... if we were to have *Taishi Ci* with us...!"

"His reputation is worth a few champions," Lü Fan admitted. "But in saying that I do not mean that he is worth losing champions for. Now, if we may return to business: we have an opportunity to cut his support, and I suggest that we take it."

"Go to it," Bofu replied: when Lü Fan did nothing in reaction, Bofu grinned and asked, "Do I need to know what you're doing...?"

"It seems that the Shanyue are *almost* removed from his list of allies," Lü Fan replied. "Whatever the cause, they're coming back. We need to scare them away."

"The Shanyue are starting to tire me," Bofu grumbled. "What do you have in mind...? Are we sending Jiang Qin after them again?"

"This time, I want *you* to challenge them," Lü Fan said. "I know it means that you're being taken away from here, but I fear that it will take the man that humbled White Tiger to get rid of them. Of course, we don't want Taishi knowing you're not here, but-"

"On the contrary," Cheng Pu chuckled.

Lü Fan only needed a moment to think: he smiled and said, "How foolish of me. We'll ensure he knows, but too late!"

Four days later, Taishi Ci was taking a much-needed rest from the walls of Jing County City when a messenger rushed into the magistrate's residential hall and shouted, **"REPORT! Sun Ce has left the area and gone to challenge the Shanyue!"**

"Oh...?" Taishi Ci exclaimed. "That... that's the moment I've sought! Yes, it's probably cowardly, but... but... yes! Messenger, go to the barracks and inform the captain that I intend to charge out of the southern gate!"

"Yes, Commander!" the messenger replied as he turned about and scurried away.

"...When you return to this place, Sun Ce, you'll find your defeat," Taishi Ci muttered.

Taishi Ci had the southern gates of the city opened and led the charge against the north entrance of Bofu's camp: Ling Cao had been left in charge, and he put on a convincing show of being unprepared.

"DEATH TO SUN CE, THAT DOG THAT SERVES VILLAINS!" Taishi Ci screamed as he rode through Bofu's camp, slashing at men and knocking torch-stands and cooking pots over. But when he reached the southern end of the camp, he recoiled in horror: the exit had been barricaded with palisades and archers, and there were two cavalry units led by Huang Gai and Chen Wu to his left and right.

"Why don't you surrender?" Ling Cao bellowed as he charged at the rear of Taishi's force.

"Wretched dogs, all of you!" Taishi Ci cried as he turned about and began a desperate fight to escape the camp.

"Huang Gai will take you down, Taishi Ci!" Huang Gai taunted.

"No, Chen Wu will tame the beast!" Chen Wu joked.

"D'AAAAGH! ALL OF YOU WILL BURN IN THE NETHERWORLD!" Taishi Ci shrieked as he moved through the maze of tents, cutting down any man that challenged him.

"Why are you running, man from Huangxian?" Song Qian heckled.

"Here is Jiang Qin!" the thrifty pirate said as he tried to block Taishi Ci's way: Taishi turned his well-trained horse and took another route.

"Where are you going?" Cheng Pu shouted as he blocked yet another path.

"...He has champions by the bushel!" Taishi Ci said involuntarily as he turned and fled yet again.

"Did my father not stop you?" Cheng Pu's son, Cheng Yi, shouted as he blocked Taishi's way yet again with a force of protective elite men from his father's unit.

"Heaven abandons me!" Taishi Ci complained as he made one final effort to escape the camp with his remaining riders: he managed to fight his way out of the eastern entrance, but as he cleared the gate he was met with a sight that made his blood boil.

"Here is Sun Ce of Fuchun!" Bofu shouted: he was at the head of a large army, and he had obviously been waiting for Taishi for some time.

"YOU TRICKED ME, YOU DOG!" Taishi Ci screamed as he turned and fled toward the city.

"Let him go!" Lü Fan pleaded as Sun Hè blocked Bofu's path.

"I thought we wanted him out of the city!" Bofu retorted. **"I thought that the whole point was to lure him out so we could-!"**

"We've harmed his reputation," Lü Fan said. **"Our saboteurs exploited his absence to destroy the main supply depot in the city, and his water supplies are now limited. We've just scattered his Shanyue allies once and for all, and the last of his outlying camps are gone. It's only a matter of time now, Lord Sun, and we have-"**

"We had him isolated!" Bofu whined. **"We-!"**

"**It's a matter of time,**" Lü Fan insisted. "**His people are hungry and tired, and we have shown him that we have too many champions for him to deal with. All we need to do now is show some *patience*!**"

Bofu was about to reply when Cheng Pu arrived and said, "**Where is he? Who got him?**"

Bofu turned and looked at Cheng Pu with weary eyes.

"...**You stupid little pedant!**" Cheng Pu screamed at Lü Fan. "**We had him! We-!**"

"**If we want him alive, we have to *wait*!**" Lu Fan protested.

"***Do* we want him alive?**" Cheng Pu retorted. "**Do you know how many have-!**"

"**We want him alive, Demou... so... so Ziheng was right to allow him to flee,**" Bofu decided. "**We'll continue the siege works, and... and wait.**"

Sun Ben's command tent was a scene of celebration after a messenger brought welcome news: Lü Bu's advisers had somehow convinced the White Wave Bandits to turn on Yuan Shu's forces and drive them back into Jiujiang, and 'Inspector' Hui Qu – who now faced being caught in a pincer – had been ordered to withdraw to the capital, Shouchun, and aid its defence.

"We might now have the dubious pleasure of assistance from the White Wave Bandits, gentlemen, but compared to annihilation, I do not care!" Sun Ben said to his assembled officials. "Yuan Shu might not last a month now!"

"...But Bu is the hero of the hour, which is disconcerting," Sun Fu suggested.

"Don't ruin the moment, Brother!" Sun Ben chuckled.

"I agree," Quan Rou said. "The important thing now is that Lü Bu is now on the offensive, pushing ever further southward into Yang: if we were to push northward now, we could pincer the capital and rid the land of the pretender ourselves."

"We'll prepare to advance, then!" Sun Ben declared. "Let's end this once and for all!"

The officials chattered excitedly and discussed their preparations amongst themselves: Sun Fu, meanwhile, turned to his brother and asked, "What about my sister-in-law, and my nieces and nephews, Brother?"

"...I am concerned, but I must think of more than them," Sun Ben replied. "If Yuan Shu is not stopped, the chaos will never end and they'll live and die as his hostages. Even if he kills them out of spite... he won't live to relish it."

Sun Fu nodded sadly.

Weeks had passed in Jing County. Taishi Ci summoned his followers and prepared to make a statement. His countenance was humble, weak and resigned, so his audience guessed the tone of the impending announcement with ease.

"...**You mustn't!**" one officer cried before Taishi could speak.

"You'd fight on?" Taishi Ci asked of his audience.

"To the end!" one former Liu Yao official declared. "The Sun clan are wicked creatures that must be purged from the world!"

"...But I am harming the populace," Taishi Ci suggested.

"Unavoidable!" another official said. "We can't allow Sun Ce to-!"

A terrified soldier ended the discussion when he ran in and screamed, **"Commander! Commander, the… the city is breached!"**

"The people must have opened the gates for them!" Taishi Ci exclaimed. "Did I not say that-!"

"We must defend our positions!" a second officer declared.

"Y-yes… yes, we must!" Taishi Ci said. **"To… to the end!"**

One last battle was fought between the defenders led by Taishi Ci and the vanguard of the sieging army led by Ling Cao and Chen Wu: civilians fled to their homes as men fought in the streets and left them awash with blood. Bofu's officers did what they could to spare lives when they could, and many of their opponents surrendered: Taishi Ci was chased back to the governor's residence and captured after a violent scuffle that left a number of Ling Cao's men wounded or dead.

"So… so we have him, then… we have Taishi Ci," Bofu said to his assembled officers.

"Yes, and I must once again request that we just put him to death before news of his capture inspires an attempt to free him," Cheng Pu replied.

"I… I can't do that to a man like Taishi Ci of Huangxian, a man that has been a folk hero for the last decade," Bofu insisted. "I want to try and reason with him."

"…*Aiee*… fine, well, be it on your own head!" Cheng Pu scolded.

Bofu produced Taishi's captured blade and said, "I have to return this to him at the very least."

"He had your helmet," Ling Cao reported.

"…He kept it?" Bofu exclaimed.

"He no doubt intended to put your severed head back inside it at some point!" Cheng Pu heckled. "Just kill the man, Lord Sun, or we'll have no respite from chaos!"

"You're proposing that I kill a famous tiger because he threatens my door, Cheng Demou," Bofu retorted. "I never took you for a Kuai Liang."

Huang Gai groaned reflexively.

"…Don't compare this man to your father," Cheng Pu pleaded. "Your father was not like this man."

"He's similar enough," Bofu replied. "Please arrange for him to be brought to me in the audience hall of the city's governor's residence."

"…Very well," Cheng Pu sighed.

Two hours later, Taishi Ci was brought before Bofu for final disposal.

"How dare you bring me to this last bastion of defence against your evil!" Taishi Ci heckled. **"You soil this place, hankering dogs!"**

"Here is Taishi Ci," Cheng Pu said tonelessly.

"Get your work done, Sun Ce, and let me make my final journey!" Taishi Ci added before Bofu could speak.

"Must we fight…?" Bofu asked. "I'm not allied to Yuan Shu now, so why do you oppose me…? I have court appointments, and-"

"Cao Cao is another tyrant in the making!" Taishi Ci retorted. "I have seen his handiwork first-hand! All that you have done is swap one villain for anoth-!"

518

"It isn't stupidity, pride or weakness that makes me obey my lords without question, Taishi Ci," Bofu insisted. "It's... it's *necessity*."

Taishi Ci grunted contemptuously and said, "Is that so...?"

"My father pledged his service, along with all of his clan members and vassals, during the Dong Zhuo crisis," Bofu continued. "My father was a hero."

"Yes, 'was'," Taishi Ci scoffed. "My travels brought me into contact with a lot of people in the north that despised him and still despise your family for serving Yuan Shu. Sun Jian's earlier exploits are outweighed by a disservice to the empire that is continued by your bending at the knee to the 'Crafty Villain'. I don't care if Cao's 'fighting Yuan Shu': Cao's an evil man, and who will he harm when Yuan is gone...?"

Cheng Pu snorted angrily, and Huang Gai sighed woefully.

"Taishi Ci, I won't kill you," Bofu insisted. "Your reservations are grounded, I confess, but at present I am unable to address them as I would like. I trust that you know what I mean by that."

"...I may do," Taishi Ci said cagily. "So what will you do with me?"

"You will be kept comfortable, but under constant guard," Bofu replied. "We'll talk again, when I have the time."

"Summon me here all you want, but it will change nothing," Taishi Ci retorted.

"...Guards, take him to his room, please," Bofu ordered.

Once Taishi Ci had been escorted from the hall, Cheng Pu turned to Bofu and said, "You're still harbouring this mad idea that he can be recruited, even after what he just said to you...?"

"Liu Yao is dead, and Wang Lang proved himself to be no hero," Bofu replied. "I intend to allow Taishi Ci to ask questions of his guards, the servants, and anyone else that he 'happens to encounter'. I can sway him... I know I can."

Taishi Ci's capture was a positive occurrence, but in the north, Lü Bu exhibited more of his self-serving behaviour and caused Sun Ben to halt his enthusiastic advance. The White Wave Bandits had used the incursion into Jiujiang as an excuse to rampage and loot any village or town that they came across, so Lü Bu did not enjoy any local support; and then, just as Bu was about to cross the Huai River and siege Shouchun, the bandits started to disperse and return to southern Xu Province. The White Wave Bandits had provided the bulk of Bu's numbers, and their withdrawal was therefore going to leave Bu at a major disadvantage: so after an empty show of strength, Bu returned to Xu Province as well. The main winners in the whole affair were the White Wave Bandits – who now had a new region to pillage – and Lü Bu, who had the bandits as a buffer against Yuan Shu; the obvious losers were Generals Zhang Xun and Qiao Rui – who both suffered demotions as punishment for their perceived failures – and the people of Jiujiang and southern Xu Province, who would now suffer raids by the untethered White Wave Bandits.

****

102

Three days later, Taishi Ci was brought before Bofu and his senior vassals once again.

"I hope that you have been comfortable," Bofu said.

"As a caged animal can be, Sun Ce," Taishi Ci retorted.

Bofu produced a blade – the same blade that he had taken from Taishi during their duel at Shen Town some time ago – and said, "You recognise this, of course."

"...I do," Taishi Ci replied.

"My men report that you kept my helmet," Bofu said. "Why?"

"For what reason did you keep my blade?" Taishi Ci asked.

"It reminds me that you're another worthy man in the world," Bofu replied. "You didn't kill me when you had the chance."

"**I _should have_!**" Taishi Ci barked.

"...And if I returned this blade to you now, would you try and kill me...?" Bofu asked.

"I _would_!" Taishi Ci replied defiantly.

"...So why did you keep my helmet, then?" Bofu asked again.

"To remind me that I had a mad tiger to slay," Taishi Ci replied. "You've driven a lot of good men to despair and death, Sun Ce, and I intend to avenge them."

"Liu Yao was regrettable, and so was Xu Shao," Bofu sighed.

"Are they the only ones?" Taishi Ci heckled.

"...Of course not," Bofu replied. "But if Liu Yao had defeated me, what would he have done next...?"

Taishi Ci was silent.

"I think that he'd have done as I have done," Bofu continued. "The Shanyue and the bandits had to be pacified. White Tiger, Haixi Chen, Zu Lang... they would still be a problem, wouldn't they...? And I understand that Governor Liu was a 'disciplinarian', so wouldn't he have gone on a campaign of 'righteous punishment' that would have harmed all sorts, and maybe even led to, I don't know... someone with a strong sense of justice deciding to rise up against him...?"

Taishi Ci did not reply.

"The problem is, Mister Taishi, that Liu Yao – a _xiaolian_ candidate – was funding White Tiger in the north," Bofu continued. "Kuaiji's appointed Administrator, Wang Lang, Liu Yao's ally – and another _xiaolian_ candidate, I believe – was funding the tribes in the north _and_ south, and was using the notorious rebel army led by Zhang Ya to harm not only my friends, but ordinary villagers when they needed supplies and carried out violent raids to acquire them. And as far as dodgy alliances go, you don't do too bad yourself these days: weren't you allied to the Danyang Shanyue...?"

"**...I had no _choice_!**" Taishi Ci cried involuntarily.

"Is that so...?" Lü Fan snickered.

Bofu hid a smile when he noted a small change in his prisoner's countenance: Taishi had realised that he had just publicly confessed to being as trapped by circumstance as the man he addressed, and, Bofu supposed, it was the first time that Taishi had truly had a moment to contemplate it properly.

"The court that appointed the governor you revere and his friend Wang was the court of Li Jue and Guo Si – two of the most evil men of recent times," Bofu said. "Li and Guo were Dong Zhuo's lieutenants; they drove my father's patron – General Zhu Jun – to an early grave, and there isn't a person alive that doesn't know what their master did. Have I sliced the skin from men or boiled them alive...? Have I razed entire villages or abducted women and children to use as slaves...?"

"...No," Taishi Ci replied.

"And just as many of Liu Yao's followers now serve me as sided with you," Bofu continued. "Everything these days is about perspectives, and I think you know that."

Taishi Ci sighed miserably and said, "I do."

"I know you do," Bofu said. "Ask Yu Fan, Hè Qi, Dong Xi, Zhang Zhao, Quan Rou; there are a lot of men – and women, and children – that know I mean only the best for the south, while your master and his friends gave power to *Ze Rong*."

Taishi Ci nodded silently.

"...I have a few things to discuss with my advisers, because political situations are changing across the land and I must be kept abreast of them at all times," Bofu continued. "We'll talk again, Taishi Ci; until then, your needs – except your need to take my head for Liu Yao's temple, of course – will be met."

"You... are a difficult man to fathom, Sun Ce," Taishi Ci said as he was led away. **"But I shall!"**

"...*Aiee*... really my lord, just lock him up and be done with it," Cheng Pu said. "He won't see sense! He's too stubborn for that!"

"Some people require gentle persuasion, and he's one of them," Bofu retorted. "I know what I'm doing."

Yangxian's Magistrate, Sun Quan, was surprised and delighted when his childhood friend Zhu Ran paid a visit to his capital: he hurried to the gates and had Zhu Ran escorted to his mansion by a force of officials and soldiers.

"You've done a wonderful job, Zhongmou!" Zhu Ran chuckled.

"Thank you, thank you," Sun Quan replied. "My brother's happy with my work here too. My friend and invaluable ally, Mister Pan Zhang, is, at present, fighting a small army of bandits that harassed a village south of here, else he would have been the very first person that I would have introduced you to. How long will you be staying for, Yifeng...?"

"Not long, sadly," Zhu Ran said. "But I couldn't keep writing. I long for a moment when we'll have some peace here in the south... but everything is still so tense."

"Yes, I know," Sun Quan replied. "Lü Bu in the north, who, last I heard, was thinking about joining up with Yuan and then changed his mind, and then there's Taishi Ci, who my brother's been sieging for weeks now... Yuan himself, and all the bandits and barbarians, too... there's little chance of peace."

"...And Liu Biao," Zhu Ran prompted.

"I... try not to think about Liu Biao and Huang Zu," Sun Quan retorted. "Like my brother, I am frustrated at the lack of opportunities to-"

Sun Quan was suddenly halted by a vicious cough.

"...Are you sick...?" Zhu Ran fretted.

"No, no!" Sun Quan insisted. "Nothing that some wine won't fix, Yifeng: once we're settled, I'll have some of the best stuff brought

for us!"
"I... haven't interrupted your civil duties...?" Zhu Ran prompted.
"They can manage without me, I think!" Sun Quan chuckled.
The officials in the entourage grumbled quietly.
"You're an honoured guest, and etiquette dictates that I must entertain you," Sun Quan continued. "We can't have you going back to your uncle in Wu County and saying that I treated you badly, uh...? Ha-ha!"
Zhu Ran noticed that Sun Quan's pallor was somehow different, but he did not comment on it as the procession ended at the gates of the magistrate's mansion.

Six days after his last confrontation with Taishi Ci, Bofu – who was now dressed in armour – invited Taishi to the audience hall of Jing County City once again.
"We have little time, as I have military matters to attend to," Bofu began. "I only have one more thing to say to you, and then it's up to you where we go from there."
Taishi Ci nodded silently.
"I know why I do things... most of the time," Bofu continued. "When I came here to Danyang, it was to secure my father's grave, rescue my clan's homeland and do my lord's bidding... in that order. When I encountered you at Shen Town, I acted instinctively; we met, we fought, we extended courtesy to each other, and then we retreated with trophies in hand. Since then, not a day has passed when I haven't thought about that encounter... because it was the day when a tiger met a dragon."
Taishi Ci turned his eyes sideways and exhaled noisily.
"I think I know you, Taishi Ci," Bofu continued. "You're not a soft-hearted man: when you outfoxed the messenger and delivered your petition, you cared nothing for his reputation because you knew him to be wrong. When you rescued the fugitive from Liaodong, you lied and cheated because you knew your cause was right. When you deceived the Yellow Turbans at Beihai and borrowed the troops from Liu Bei to defeat them, you showed no mercy for them, man or woman, because you knew them to be acolytes of a wicked cult that harmed the innocent."
Taishi Ci turned his gaze back to Bofu and said, "You've studied me well."
"Well enough to know that when we met at Shen, you had at least four chances to kill me, and yet you didn't take them," Bofu continued. "Men that don't know you assumed it to be misguided honour, but you're a man that does what's necessary... by your own words, you do whatever it takes when you lack choices... and I know that to be true, because I'm the same. You didn't spare me because you're too honourable; you spared me because something told you that I wasn't what you'd been led to expect."
After a short silence, Taishi Ci laughed sadly and replied, "That is true, Sun Ce of Fuchun."
The court was stunned; Bofu smiled and said, "I could tell straight away. I hear that you argued for a different approach against me after our encounter, and had it been adopted, I'd be dead now; do you regret that your words weren't heeded...?"
"...I cannot answer that," Taishi Ci replied.
Bofu laughed and said, "You're hard work, Taishi Ci! But here's my

last offer. You've been mistreated by your past employers, who used you without caring for your well-being. The administrator you defended ensured no pardon for you; the fugitive scholar that you saved returned to his life, while you were left a fugitive twice over; Kong Rong and Liu Bei had ways of repaying you, but they were concerned only with recruiting you for your selflessness and heroism, and you know it; Liu Yao ignored you time and again, and you came here with the notion that you'd be helping a pious man fight a wicked one... not aiding a governor appointed by Liang Province criminals in his quest to ruin an ambitious noble's territory expansion plans."

"Nothing's as it should be," Taishi Ci replied. "It is as Liu Yao once said: the age of heroes is gone."

"No it isn't," Bofu said. "It's just that right now, the heroes are shackled to the ground or to unworthy lords that misuse them. You're a dragon, Taishi Ci, and dragons belong in the sky. You're in need of a base, and I would gladly be that base if you'd let me. In fact, I'd consider it to be an honour."

Taishi Ci frowned cynically.

"...I see that you're still wary, so here is my very last plea to you," Bofu said as he got to his feet and bowed low.

Cheng Pu moved aggressively, saying, "**Ayah! Don't-!**"

"Let him," Huang Gai said as he restrained Cheng Pu.

"Taishi Ci, you are a man that should be a friend to me and my family, and cruel fate and greedy fools have prevented it... until today, if you'll allow it," Bofu said as he fell to one knee before his shocked audience. "Please do not refuse."

Taishi Ci looked at the emotional faces around him, gazed at Bofu and said, "Never... never have I seen such a thing as this, or met such a lord as you. You are proud, but you'd bend at the knee to me... I will not have it!"

"You push me to it, but it's worth it to know you," Bofu replied.

Taishi pulled Bofu to his feet and then kowtowed, saying, "I, Taishi Ci, yield to you, Lord Sun Ce! I shall aid you in your cause!"

Bofu helped Taishi Ci to his feet and said, "You're not my vassal; you're my ally at the least, if not my friend."

Taishi Ci sighed desperately and said, "I did not expect this! I cannot-!"

"What's your courtesy name...?" Bofu asked.

"...Ziyi," Taishi Ci replied. "It... is 'Ziyi'."

"Ziyi, we have a lot to do," Bofu continued. "I know that I push my luck, having only just recruited you, but I have three labours for you."

"You'd give me assignments straight away?" Taishi Ci exclaimed.

"I would, if you would hear them," Bofu said.

"Name them," Taishi Ci replied immediately.

"I shall only give you the first, for now," Bofu said. "Liu Yao has sadly passed... I know that he was a good man at heart, but-"

"I am resolved on that matter," Taishi Ci insisted. "Please, instruct me, Lord Sun Ce."

"...Liu Yao's forces number close to thirty-thousand men now, or so I'm told," Bofu continued. "I want you to visit them for me, and tell them that I will gladly have their assistance as guardians of Jiangdong. I am not demanding service... they can do as they please. It is merely a request."

"I will do that and more," Taishi Ci promised. "I will gather my own supporters from around Danyang and Yuzhang as well. My only condition is that I be given sixty days to return, for the task is far from simple."

"Sixty days???" Ling Cao cried. **"That's enough for-!"**

"Hush, please, Ling Cao," Bofu ordered. "Taishi Ziyi, you shall have your sixty days. I shall await your return with a jar of wine to celebrate our finally being on the same side. How many men will you take with you on this task...?"

"I only need ten," Taishi Ci insisted. "I know just the men, and can gather them as soon as I am allowed to leave."

"Ling Cao will accompany you to the holding cells when you go to fetch your allies," Bofu said.

"I shall depart immediately, if you so allow it, Lord Sun Ce," Taishi Ci said excitedly.

"If that's your desire, so be it," Bofu replied, and Taishi Ci left the hall with his former guards and an exasperated Ling Cao.

"...Please tell me that you gave Ling Cao secret orders to behead him on the way to the cells, Lord Sun," Cheng Pu sighed as he stared at Bofu.

"Why would I do something so unnecessary...?" Bofu replied.

"You've gone soft in the head, Cousin!" Sun Hè scolded. "Catching that man was an effort that cost lives! If he allies with Liu Yao's thirty-thousand and comes back here, he'll-!"

"He won't betray me," Bofu insisted.

"That's a nice thought, but I say that we pursue him immediately," Cheng Pu said. "Don't be so naïve! Your show of obeisance won't have won him over!"

"I meant it, and he knew it," Bofu insisted.

"*Ayah*... it doesn't matter whether he believed it or not!" Cheng Pu cried. "He's not a dragon, he's a snake, a very dangerous snake, and we just let it back into the grass to bite us another day! *Weeks*, it took us! *Weeks* of espionage, hilltop sieges, city sieges, ground battles! *Weeks* of wearing him down, and you let him walk away... *aiee*."

"Ziyi is a hero of the time, Demou," Bofu insisted. "He won't break his word."

"...I hope so," Lü Fan said. "But we have other matters to deal with, of course: the bandits in other parts of Jiangdong that need reminding of our strength, our plans for developing the region, and, of course, the hostility stemming from Jiangxia."

"Firstly, we should return to Qu'e," Bofu replied. "Taishi Ziyi is no threat now; the Shanyue in Danyang and Wu are all hiding; we can divert and reassign our forces generally, and we have to. Yuan Shu is the main threat now."

"We'll depart immediately then," Lü Fan said.

And in the space of one day, two heroes that had just been seen to join forces were once again forced to go their separate ways: a reinvigorated Taishi Ci went west to Yuzhang to carry out the first of his three labours, and Bofu went back to his capital to reorganise his forces for the difficult times ahead.

＊＊＊＊＊＊＊＊＊＊＊＊

ACT IX: A GRAND DESIGN

103

For 13 years, the Sun family name had symbolised great strength against great adversity. From the day that Sun Jian – a near-fearless natural warrior and leader – had left his hometown of Fuchun to fight the millions-strong Yellow Turban rebel armies that threatened the Han Dynasty, his name would become part of history: he went on to fight the tyrant Dong Zhuo, whose faction had seized control of the imperial court, but Sun had chosen to fight under the banner of the nobleman Yuan Shu, whose half-brother Shao was clan chieftain and leader of the warlord coalition opposing Dong Zhuo, and that choice would have unforeseen consequences. Yuan Shu was possessive and neurotic, which strained the relationship between lord and vassal at the best of times: but when Yuan Shu decided to declare his right to lead his clan and publicly rebuked Yuan Shao, Sun Jian and his allies would be the first to suffer Shao's malice as the coalition collapsed and was replaced by a sibling feud that would engulf most of the east of the country.

Yuan Shu was not content with fighting Yuan Shao for titles: he had Sun Jian embark on a dangerous campaign against the powerful governor of Jing Province, Liu Biao, so that he might take that strategically important region for the grand future that Shu was planning for, and it was in Jing that Sun Jian perished during an ambush. Sun Jian's nephew, Sun Ben, took control of the clan temporarily, as Jian's eldest son Ce – whose style name was *Bofu* – was considered to be too young and inexperienced at the time. The Sun clan were forced to postpone revenge against Liu Biao and his ally Huang Zu, as their master Yuan Shu had other plans for them: he wanted to possess the whole of Yang Province, which encompassed the entire southeast of China, and the Sun family were tasked with achieving it.

Sun Ben and Bofu toiled thanklessly, seizing Lujiang Prefecture to the northwest from the respected elder statesman Lu Kang and defeating the regency court's appointed governor, Liu Yao, to take Danyang Prefecture in the eastern centre of Yang. Further campaigns saw Bofu defeat Shanyue tribes and bandit armies to pacify Wu Prefecture in the northeast and outwit the devious Wang Lang to capture Kuaiji Prefecture in the southeast, which left Guangling Prefecture to the far east-northeast of the province and Yuzhang Prefecture to the far southwest as the only areas that Yuan Shu could not call his own. The campaigns had created new enemies for the Sun family, and none were more dangerous than the Shanyue and Taishi Ci, the infamous vigilante from Huangxian in Qing Province: Yuan Shu's claims to the province were unfounded, and the Suns were seen as his puppets. That all changed when Yuan Shu's hubris peaked and he declared that he was the First Emperor of the Zhong Dynasty: the Han Emperor, Xian, had recently escaped the clutches of Dong Zhuo's former retainers – the self-proclaimed regents, Li Jue and Guo Si – and the young monarch had been enjoying relative stability under the protection of the warlord Cao Cao, leading most to assume until then that the dynastic crisis was nearing an end. The bickering warlords rose up as one to condemn Yuan Shu, and the Suns were finally free to govern the part of Yang Province that lay to the south of the Yangtze River – a region they called 'Jiangdong', or 'East of The River' – as servants of a legitimate, recognised Han regime. The last pacification campaigns against the Shanyue, the bandit king Zu Lang and Taishi Ci had brought the latter two under the Sun family banner and ensured that Yuan Shu had no jurisdiction anymore: only Yuzhang and Guangling prefectures were potentially hostile, and Bofu had plans for both.

Yuan Shu was now surrounded by enemies and becoming increasingly desperate: his Yellow Turban army had been humbled, and one of its leaders killed; the Southern Xiongnu tribal renegade Yufuluo had died and his followers had abandoned their activities in Yan Province and the surrounding regions; the million-strong Black Mountain Bandits were now losing ground to Shu's brother and rival Yuan Shao, and their presence outside of Bing Province to the north had diminished significantly; the White Wave Bandits that Yuan Shu had turned to as allies against Xu Provincial Governor Lü Bu had abandoned his cause and settled in the south of Xu Province, their only communication being in the form of the occasional raid in the Huai River region that Yuan still controlled; Cao Cao had gained significant ground in Yu Province, which had been where Shu had once been at his most influential; Lü Bu was now extremely hostile in the wake of Shu's attempted takeover of Xu Province, and there appeared to be no way to restore good relations; the Sun family and their allies were gratefully opposing their former lord and gradually taking the south of Jiujiang; none of the bandits or rebels in the Jiangdong region wanted to assist him anymore, and the majority of the ethnic tribes were recovering from the punishment for previous demonstrations of unity; and to the west, Liu Biao of Jing Province was watching unsympathetically but otherwise focussing on harassing the Sun faction. Yuan Shu's financial situation was deteriorating as well, and that would ultimately decide his fate more than anything. One way or another, a man that had once been considered as one of, if not the most powerful warlords in China was doomed to destruction, and was already becoming an irrelevance as people looked to the future.

Once the twin threats of an attack by Lü Bu – whose brief and violently terminated alliance with Yuan Shu had almost culminated in a marriage between the two men's children – and an invasion by the White Wave Bandits were known to have passed, Bofu's cousin Sun Ben turned his attentions to one of Yuan Shu's few remaining allies: Liu Xun, the Administrator of Lujiang Prefecture. Xun's adviser, Liu Yè – who was also distantly-related to the royal house of Han, but not directly to Liu Xun – demanded that the situation be discussed properly, and a senior-level meeting was convened in the governor's mansion in Lujiang Prefecture's capital, Huancheng.
"Your youthful exuberance is inspiring, Mister Liu, but there are times when I wonder if I should listen to you so much," Liu Xun scoffed. "Sun Ben and Sun Fu are hardly the best forces that Sun Ce has at his disposal! Their deployments are incompetent and

they number only a few!"
Some of the older officials murmured agreeably.
"Be warned that the first of those two men was – and you should
remember this anyway, my lord – the head of the Sun clan after
Sun Jian's death," Liu Yè retorted. "Yes, they're young – so am I,
and I can see that being in my twenties is suddenly a bad thing,
when there are fourteen-year-old county magistrates!"
"I was wrong to raise the subject of your age, for you are right, it
has no meaning," Liu Xun replied apologetically. "But our greatest
concerns are Cao Cao, Liu Biao, Lü Bu and *Sun Ce himself*, not
Sun Ce's hirelings and cousins! His best men are in Jiangdong,
and are therefore not as much of a concern as Cao Cao, who
looms in the north, poised to-!"
"Cao Cao is, as you say, a serious threat, but closer threats are
worthy of mention, and Sun Ben is underestimated," Liu Yè
retorted. "If we do not treat him as being as capable as his more
famous cousin, we will lose Huancheng."
Some of the officials laughed at the suggestion, but Liu Xun was
noticeably sombre.
"You know that I am a shrewd man, and people have suddenly
forgotten my achievements," Liu Yè continued. "Was *Zhen Bao*
nothing much to mention...?"
Every single heckler fell silent and stopped smiling at the mention
of an officer that had tried to intimidate the local administration in
the Huainan region: Liu Yè had feigned weakness and killed Zhen
Bao during a hosted banquet, placing control of the thousands-
strong Huainan forces firmly in Liu Xun's hands.
"...You're right, Ziyang, and I'm sorry that I allowed you to be
ridiculed," Liu Xun said. "Were it not for you, I would be forced to
pay homage to private landlords and crime families, and my
generals would be telling me what to do. If you say that I must be
wary of Sun Ben and Sun Fu, then I will."
"I'll be honest: it will be difficult to defeat these enemies even
when we do not underestimate them," Liu Yè replied. "But we will,
at least, hold the capital, and with that comes hope. I agree that
we will not suffer as your predecessor Lu Kang did, not unless Sun
Ce comes here... but we must chase these men back to Jiujiang at
once. We must also be wary of Lei Bo and Chen Lan, His Majesty's
former generals, who are building a rebel army in the remote
regions of this prefecture."
"I will do everything that you suggest," Liu Xun replied.

Liu Xun led an army to the outskirts of the Huancheng region,
where Sun Ben and Sun Fu had amassed forces for an attack on
the capital city. Liu Xun was taken aback by the organisation,
numbers and diversity of unit types that he faced: he turned to
Liu Yè and said, "They're an impressive force, just as you said
they were, Ziyang."
"We must be very careful," Liu Yè replied.
Sun Ben and Sun Fu finished inspecting their battle lines and rode
toward the campaign adviser Quan Rou for further guidance.
"Why do we need to ask for help...?" Sun Fu asked.
"This isn't bandits, it's Liu Xun," Sun Ben replied. "Up to now, our
enemies haven't been too bright; we're up against smarter men
now, and we might need to use tactics or even formations."

Sun Fu hummed thoughtfully, and the two brothers continued their journey. When they found Quan Rou, Sun Ben asked, "What now, Mister Quan?"

"I've got a bit of an understanding about tactics and formations," Quan Rou replied. "Not much – I'm no Zhou Gongjin or Lü Ziheng – but they explained a few things to me, and I've done a bit of reading myself."

"So we'll employ an array, then?" Sun Fu said excitedly.

"Alas, no," Quan Rou replied. "The men haven't been trained in arrays, but we can use simpler tactics that should work just as well. Liu Yè might know arrays, though, so we should be careful!"

"...So what did you have in mind, Mister Quan?" Sun Ben asked.

"We could be a little less intimidating, for a start, for a show of weakness will play on the enemy's arrogance and make them careless," Quan Rou explained. "We should have the men at the front be aggressive, disorderly, and do a lot of crude heckling."

"...And make him think that we're still a bunch of 'scabby pirates'," Sun Ben chuckled. "I like it! We'll pass the word to the captains."

Sun Ben's forces could not be missed as they suddenly started to hurl a chorus of abuse at Liu Xun's army, but the other deliberate lapses in order might have been missed without reconnaissance that was swiftly carried out after the din began: one of Liu Xun's captains reported the change in general behaviour to his delighted master, who said, **"Aha! So that initial orderliness was only while they were confident! They've seen our neat, professional lines and-"**

"I'm not so sure, Lord Liu," Liu Yè interrupted. **"I sense a trick, and I advise continued caution."**

"Sun Ben and his untalented brother are galloping back and forth down their lines, trying to calm them!" Liu Xun cackled. **"They're hopeless, Mister Liu Yè, and the day is won!"**

"*Aiee...* **This is no novice that we're dealing with!"** Liu Yè protested. **"It's a trick, Lord Liu! If we charge, they'll-!"**

"The enemy charges!" a second captain announced.

Sun Ben's front-line forces were advancing, but there was no order to their actions whatsoever.

"Aha! There, see...? There is your genius, Mister Liu Yè!" Liu Xun heckled. **"I – or rather, *you* – gave this boy unwarranted praise! Now we shall rout him and deliver Lujiang from the clutches of a particularly clumsy carrion bird!"**

"It's a trick!" Liu Yè retorted. **"Don't be goaded! They'll-!"**

"You're giving them undeserved respect!" one of Liu Xun's other officials said.

"I agree!" Liu Xun declared. **"We've as good as won!"**

"Never have I seen such pathetic management of men!" one of Liu Xun's generals scoffed. **"I'll charge them, Lord Liu, for your glory!"**

"Go to it!" Liu Xun chuckled, and the complacent general led his promised charge.

"...AAAH! You are sending your men to their deaths, Lord Liu! You have to recall them at once!" Liu Yè pleaded.

But it was already too late: the general led his men into the centre of Sun Ben's disorderly forces, but once they were entrenched the feigned incompetence vanished and Liu Xun's men were hopelessly surrounded.

"What will you do now, Liu Xun?" Sun Ben challenged as he and his brother rode forward with their cavalry to personally participate in the rout.

"*Ayah*! What is this???" Liu Xun exclaimed.

"Where is Liu Xun?!" Li Shu screamed as he led a second force from the south; the semi-pincer caused most of Liu Xun's men to panic and flee in all directions.

"AAAAGH! Where did *he* come from???" Liu Xun cried.

"Here is Lü Meng!" the young warrior from Fupo said as he led his own force from the north to trap Liu Xun.

"Another one?!" Liu Xun exclaimed. **"Where have-?"**

"Did you not scout as I suggested???" Liu Yè retorted.

"I...! I...! D'AAAAAGH! AAAAAH! WRETCHED PIRATES!" Liu Xun screamed as he watched his forces collapse altogether.

"Wretched *self*, Lord Liu, for being careless after all that I said!" Liu Yè suggested angrily. **"Withdraw now or we'll die!"**

"But I...! I...! HOW CAN I RETREAT???" Liu Xun screeched.

"How can you stay?" Liu Yè retorted.

Liu Xun observed the battlefield, conceded to Liu Yè and retreated with what was left of his army: Sun Ben did not pursue.

"A marvellous first victory," Sun Ben said to his officials once he had gathered them in his command tent. "That fool won't dare challenge us on the battlefield again without planning it first..."

"We should hope that he doesn't come back with another army and better counsel, Commander Sun, and that he sticks to hiding in Huancheng City," Quan Rou suggested. "There was enough order in his ranks to suggest that a better understanding of strategy would have resulted in an entirely different outcome. In addition, we have to remember the rules of advancement through these kinds of territories: the smaller settlements will capitulate quickly, either to avoid bloodshed or because they feel disenfranchised, while the large cities will fight to the last and require sieges to break."

Sun Ben's smile disappeared, and he said, "I agree, sad to say. We were lucky that our opponent was a conceited, ignorant nobleman that mistook us for common, simple-minded animals in this encounter, but next time he might... mm. I'll write to Bofu and request more resources for the attacks on major settlements."

"That would be wise," Quan Rou replied. "Liu Xun lost this battle, and he will certainly lose towns and villages where the Sun family name still carries weight of fear and-or respect, but Liu Xun will not give up this prefecture in its entirety without a long struggle."

"I'll write at once," Sun Ben said soberly.

Liu Xun's continued defence of Lujiang would be spirited, and his major cities would remain under his control, but the smaller settlements in the southeast of Lujiang – where Yuan Shu's declaration of sovereignty had not been quite as popular – fell easily as Sun Ben advanced westward by land and river.

****

104

Sun Jian's widow Lady Wu invited her brother Wu Jing and her eldest son Bofu to a private discussion in the garden of the governor's mansion in Danyang Prefecture's capital city.

"Is this about me getting married...?" Bofu asked.

"I'd like you to, but you're very busy right now, and I understand that," Lady Wu replied. "I would like some grandchildren, though. But no, that isn't why I wanted to talk to you both. I wanted to talk about the future of this region firstly."

"That's a matter for the court as a whole, Mother," Bofu retorted.

"Bofu is right, and you know it yourself," Wu Jing said. "Why have you insisted on this meeting when you-"

"Brother, I am, as people will never fail to notice, a woman," Lady Wu interrupted. "As a woman, I have no place in the court, and that seems to me to be ridiculous since I act as an adviser."

"Don't take this the wrong way, but... envoys would mock us," Wu Jing said carefully. "The land is run in a particular way, and we are not in a position to dictate our own culture and processes."

"Jiangdong accounts for a quarter of the empire," Lady Wu retorted. "At a time when the people are openly rejecting Han rule, the-"

"*Ayah*! Don't say things like that!" Wu Jing cried. "Such words have no place in a court comprised of Han loyalists! You want to have a place in court when you harbour opinions like that and are willing to vocalise them...? A *man* wouldn't be-!"

"I am observing the state of things, Brother, not defaming His Majesty," Lady Wu insisted. "The Yellow Turban Rebellion was a popular uprising against the Han. The Liang Rebellion was partly so. His Majesty was a prisoner in Chang'an for four years and the only man that attacked the city was an army led by western tribal chiefs, rebels and a seditious relative who wanted to steal the throne. The eastern warlords left His Majesty in the wilderness for months without conscience or fear. A person – man or woman – cannot see such things and not say 'People are openly rejecting Han rule', because it is true: whether it is right or wrong was not part of my point."

Bofu grinned and said, "You could give Zhang Zhao trouble!"

"Not that I would, since he is a very charming man, and so is his brother," Lady Wu replied. "But we are drifting away from the point: I want to sit in the court and have a voice. Alright, I will accept that I must not be present when visitors attend from elsewhere, but when we are among friends, why should we behave falsely...?"

"...In small, private meetings, I can see no problem," Wu Jing said. "I daren't risk your attending larger gatherings, since they often include people that-"

"Small private meetings will do," Lady Wu replied.

"You said 'firstly'," Bofu asked reluctantly. "Please don't tell me that you want Shangxiang to join the army."

Lady Wu laughed and said, "Don't be silly! I want her to be a wife and mother as much as you do, because she will benefit from it. But I do think that while she insists on being... well... 'as she is'... we should accommodate her."

Wu Jing groaned desperately.

"Don't do that, Brother!" Lady Wu complained.

"She wants to dress like a boy and learn martial arts," Wu Jing retorted. "What do you want me to do...?"

"...The clothes, and the occasional bit of banter, I can live with," Bofu said. "But now she wants to learn to *train*...? *Why*???"

"She wants to give any girl that wants to learn such things the chance to do so," Lady Wu replied. "She has some friends, and they've-"

"Oh... *no*," Bofu groaned. "Mother, you-! ...You haven't let her start spreading her ways to her *friends*...!"

"They all enjoy the dance-like nature of it," Lady Wu said casually.

"So have her learn to *dance*!" Bofu chortled. "What official or officer will appreciate us training their future wives and consorts in the art of *violence*???"

"Some of the girls' fathers have voiced no problem with it," Lady Wu retorted. "In fact, with the amount of dangers that a girl faces in a region riddled with pirates, tribes and bandits, some of them welcome it: your father taught me how to defend myself, and it's almost been necessary once or twice."

"...Alright, I see that, especially with a lecher like Cao Cao as the most important minister in the country: there's no telling when we might get a visit," Bofu conceded. "So what does she want?"

"Somewhere for her and her friends to gather, and if needs be, ask questions from someone that knows what they're doing," Lady Wu replied.

"...A training gym for girl fighters," Wu Jing scoffed. "What a thing to be supporting in our first hours away from Yuan Shu...!"

"There are loads of abandoned temples," Bofu suggested. "I have no interest in the cults that founded them claiming them back, so she can use one of them until she has a home of an adequate size with a courtyard."

"She's what, *ten*, if that???" Wu Jing exclaimed. "When will she have a house???"

"Not for many years, but I'm thinking ahead," Bofu replied. "Mother's right, Uncle: we should do this our way, rather than copying the Han court. After all: did their way work...?"

Lady Wu smiled proudly.

"...So my eldest niece will be a violent thug that beats her husband up in years to come, and my sister will be my counsel," Wu Jing said with a sigh. "People will look back at Danyang's Administrator Wu Jing and say... what *will* they say...? Or will they just laugh...?"

"You're being ridiculous," Lady Wu scoffed. "Shangxiang is, as you say, still a child, and when she is five or six years older, this region – and, if Heaven wills it, the whole country – will hopefully be a lot more stable, and she will have seen her role in the world. As for me being an adviser of sorts, well, I know that some of the sheltered, oblivious Empress Dowagers that have ruled this country from behind screens were complete idiots, just like most of the officials, and I appreciate that they don't help to change opinions, but I know real life, and I can give good advice. If I didn't think so, I wouldn't suggest it."

"...Of course, this all depends on whether we are allowed to make our own choices," Wu Jing said. "As Bofu has said, 'Excellency Cao Cao' is a famous villain, and when Yuan Shu is gone, will we be targeted next...?"

"Why...? Did we kill his eldest son and favourite bodyguard, or did Liu Biao's accepted guardian of Nan County – I forget his name – plot those deaths and that defeat that went with them...?" Lady Wu challenged. "Like us, Cao will want to destroy Jing. By the time that he came around to attacking us, we'd be established, provided we actually *do something* between now and then."

"...*Ayah*. Bofu is right: Zhang Zhao and Zhang Hong, here is your match!" Wu Jing cried.

"By the way, I understand that your friend Lü Fan has gone to visit Quan," Lady Wu prompted as she turned her attention to the smiling Bofu.

"Yeah," Bofu replied. "I said that I would go, but I don't know if might need to be here to greet Taishi Ci when he returns, or if cousin Boyang needs help in Lujiang."

"I hope that he's doing things properly," Lady Wu sighed.

Bofu's face fell, and he said, "So do I, Mother... I wouldn't know what to say if... if he was letting us down."

Bofu's best friend Zhou Yu – known to Bofu by his style name, *Gongjin* – invited his benefactor and friend Lu Su to his home for a private banquet two days later: Lu Su could not stop giggling when Gongjin informed him of the decision to allow Lady Wu to attend smaller meetings, so Gongjin was forced to say, "Do you want a better job, Zijing...? Or do you *want* to be a nonentity...?"

Lu Su stopped laughing.

"You gave me a granary to feed my troops, but so far as Bofu is concerned, you're rude and unlikeable, and you're doing little to change that by laughing as you do now," Gongjin continued.

Lu Su frowned and said, "What did you expect me to do...? Will everyone bring their wife and mother to important meetings in years to come?"

"Lady Wu is wise beyond her years," Gongjin retorted.

"With a famous boy-like daughter that fights her siblings," Lu Su chuckled.

"...I didn't invite you here to discuss that," Gongjin said. "Liu Bei has executed the leaders of the White Wave Bandits, and Lü Bu is now hostile toward him again."

"I never understood that situation anyway," Lu Su scoffed. "Liu Bei, the former governor, is a tenant of Lü Bu, the man that ousted him, and Bei did nothing when Yuan Shu invaded – nothing at all!"

"Ziheng – Lü Fan, I mean – believes that Cao Cao will kill Bu soon, and I agree," Gongjin said. "That troublemaker has to be militarily emasculated at the very least."

"And hasn't the lord's cousin done quite well in Lujiang, and the lord's officer Hè Qi in Jiujiang...?" Lu Su prompted.

"Yes to both," Gongjin replied. "...Incidentally, I have heard that the famous 'Elder Qiao' is in Lujiang at the moment, probably in Huancheng."

"Oh...?" Lu Su exclaimed. "Well there's only one reason why you're excited about that! His daughters are rumoured to be two of the most beautiful women in the country, aren't they, perhaps more than Zhang Ji's wife Lady Zhou was when she was younger, though Cao Cao obviously felt that–"

"You're prattling," Gongjin interrupted.

"…Why do you care that the Qiaos are living in Lujiang, then…?"
Lu Su asked.

"…I… I don't know," Gongjin sighed. "…You're right, I suppose… a romantic nonsense, perhaps…"

"They'd be quite the match for you and Lord Sun, wouldn't they?" Lu Su chuckled. "Two beauties for two heroes, two sisters for two sworn brothers; what a shame, then, that they'll probably end up married to Yuan Shu's-"

"*Forget*… that I mentioned it, Zijing," Gongjin insisted.

Lü Fan's visit to Yangxian County's capital was met with frostiness that surprised Fan, given his status as a trusted friend and frequent honoured guest in the Sun family home: he was given accommodation in a hotel rather than Quan's own residence, and he was not given any preferential seating during the nightly banquets. Pan Zhang, by contrast, was hailed as a hero of the age, and Sun Quan would often demand that toasts be made in his honour. Lü Fan immediately suspected that the banquets were being funded by county tax funds rather than from Quan's own purse, so he decided that he would check the treasury: the tour of the treasury office was personally supervised by Sun Quan, who finally asked, "Do you not trust me, Mister Lü…?"

"…I might ask the same question, Magistrate Sun," Lü Fan replied. "I have served your brother for well over five years, and have known him a little longer; I rescued a large part of your clan from Guangling; I have been trusted for some time with financial affairs, but above all I am treated like family by Lady Wu. Why, then, have I been treated like a visiting toady from Xuchang…?"

"You've come here to check on me!" Sun Quan retorted. "How is that reasonable, 'Lü Ziheng', when, as you say, my mother treats you like a son…?"

"I… have come here to ensure that everything is well, yes," Lü Fan admitted. "But I do so because-"

"And is everything well…?" Sun Quan asked snidely.

"…Apparently so," Lü Fan replied. "…Lady Wu hopes that you will visit Danyang soon, Lord Sun, and I promised that I would bring her a response."

"I will visit soon," Sun Quan replied. "You can tell them that when you return, Mister Lü."

"*Aiee*… you mistake concern for contempt, Quan!" Lü Fan pleaded.

"Do I, 'Fan'…?" Sun Quan replied.

"You know that you do, Zhongmou," Lü Fan replied: his deliberate and uncharacteristic use of Sun Quan's style name reminded the 15-year-old of more peaceful times when the two had been like cousins.

"…I will ensure that you get the recognition that you deserve, Lü Ziheng, before you go," Sun Quan promised. "I… I apologise if I have seemed to be aloof, but I wanted you to see that I not only govern well, but that I reward achievement and acknowledge the officials and future heroes that aid me. If you feel that my rewards and celebrations of achievement are excessive, then-"

"I dare not - and would not - question," Lü Fan said as he looked into the faces of every official that was present: they were obviously a lot happier than they had been in the past, which indicated that Quan was improving as a statesman.

"...You should feel that you can, and I am at fault for being too defensive, Ziheng," Sun Quan replied. "I still remember the harm I caused to Zhou Youping... which reminds me... is he well...?"

"He gets better with every day that passes," Lü Fan replied warmly. "He speaks of you, Lord Sun, often asking how you are and wishing you well."

"...But I'm guessing that he doesn't often mention that he would like to work for me again," Sun Quan sighed.

"When I return to Danyang, I will be reporting a success, Lord Sun," Lü Fan promised. "There are no soft words necessary: I will say what I have seen, and they will be glad of it. In fact, I should probably go today, since Lord Sun Ce will probably want me to be there when Taishi Ci returns from Yuzhang."

"I was delighted to hear of his surrender," Sun Quan said. "Shall we go to the house, then, and enjoy an afternoon banquet to honour your visit...?"

"I have been here for five days, and I have enjoyed your hospitality," Lü Fan replied politely. "You have done enough for me, I think! I shall go now."

Sun Quan nodded silently, sent a man ahead at speed to arrange for transport, and joined a ten-strong escort to the city gates, where a requested carriage was waiting.

"...You're sure that you won't stay another day...?" Sun Quan asked meekly.

"You have done enough!" Lü Fan reiterated as he climbed into the carriage.

"...Have a safe journey then, Lü Ziheng," Sun Quan said quietly.

The charismatic county constable Pan Zhang joined the entourage at that moment with a small group of armed men.

"You have served the region well, Mister Pan," Lü Fan said.

"I live to serve," Pan Zhang replied.

"...Farewell, Lord Sun, until we meet again," Lü Fan said.

Sun Quan bowed slightly, turned and gestured to the carriage driver, who lashed his horse and started the journey to the capital of Jiangdong.

"...Your face says it all, Lord Sun," Pan Zhang chortled.

Sun Quan watched the carriage for a while before he snorted irritably and said, "I need a drink, Wengui. The scheduled meeting can wait until later."

The officials bowed humbly and allowed their magistrate to walk away with his friend Pan Zhang.

"...Should we have said something...?" one junior official asked.

"One way or another, Yangxian is peaceful," a senior colleague replied. "Why risk that peace for a few flaws...? What will we get instead...?"

The officials murmured agreeably: despite any reservations that any of them might have had, Sun Quan's tenure as magistrate had been free of disasters, and that, in a world of chaos, was gratefully acknowledged.

****

Over fifty days had passed since Taishi Ci had surrendered and travelled westward to carry out the first of the three labours that Bofu had given him: word reached Danyang's capital that a large army was on its way, so the veteran Cheng Pu alerted the internal defence forces and ordered the army that was still stationed around the walls to be ready for a decisive battle.

"It's Taishi Ziyi, and we shouldn't be so hostile!" Bofu implored as he followed Cheng Pu around the western camps. "You have to refrain from sending the wrong message, Cheng Demou!"

Cheng Pu groaned theatrically and said, "You're impossible, Lord Sun! Impossible! You might, in fact, be more impossible than Wentai ever was, Heaven rest his soul! You fight so hard to gain ground, and then you-!"

"Hold, Mister Cheng," Lü Fan pleaded. "Taishi's men are not marching in a way that provides them with a useable advantage. He's bringing them to us."

"...Are you sure...?" Cheng Pu exclaimed.

"Almost," Lü Fan replied. "That should not be enough, I know that, but... something tells me that it is."

Cheng Pu looked at Gongjin, who smiled, bowed slightly and said, "I'm sure that you don't care for my opinion, Mister Cheng."

"But if I *did*...?" Cheng Pu retorted.

"Then it would be the same as Ziheng's," Gongjin replied.

"Alright then... Lord Sun, I apologise for my gruffness and obstinacy in this matter," Cheng Pu said humbly. "You judged this man Taishi Ci correctly."

"I simply took him to be what everyone that's met him has said that he is, Demou," Bofu replied. "It's me that had to prove something, not him. For all of his famed duplicity, he's always been the one with nothing to prove at all."

Cheng Pu snorted a laugh and said, "Now that you say it, that's... that's quite right."

Bofu led a welcoming committee out of the city and clasped hands with his former rival Taishi Ci as soon as the opportunity arose.

"My lord, release my hand so that I might kneel before you and reaffirm my allegiance," Taishi Ci pleaded. "Though I have taken a little less than the sixty days that I promised, I have still taken altogether too long to return, and-"

"Not so, not so!" Bofu chuckled. "You-! ...Wait, do I see... *Liu Ji*???"

Governor Liu Yao's son stepped forth from amongst the throng of officers and bowed humbly, saying, "I, Liu Ji, pledge my service to you in your mission to pacify the south and restore stability, Lord Sun Ce."

Gongjin and Lü Fan smiled silently.

"...This has to be a trick," Cheng Pu muttered. "It *has to be*."

"I, uh... I accept your pledge, Mister Liu, although I'm surprised that you would want to work with me," Bofu said cautiously.

"My father was driven by circumstance, Lord Sun, just as you are," Liu Ji replied. "Taishi Ziyi and my father were friends, born in the same town, but prejudice toward Ziyi prevented them from serving the Han Empire together. Father served the men that claimed to represent the Son of Heaven, but he always knew the truth of things; now His Majesty is in Xuchang, under the protection of Governor Cao Cao, and all of the past appointments are uncertainties. What *is* certain, Lord Sun, is that Taishi Ziyi forgave any part that you may have had in my father's persecution, and if he can forgive then I can forgive, because Taishi Ziyi is a man of unparalleled principle. His word is as good as my father's."

"*Aiee*… now I feel like the greatest wretch under Heaven," Bofu sighed. "Your father's death will always haunt me. His, and Lu Kang's, and Xu Shao's… although I did not act as a free agent at the time, my lord's directed actions were still my own."

"Times have changed, and you are free to be the hero that you want to be now, Lord Sun," Liu Ji replied. "You care for the people of the south, and Heaven only knows, it's about time that they had someone doing things for them."

"What happened to Generals Fan Neng and Yu Mi…?" Bofu asked.

"Fan Neng perished in a battle with Ze Rong's former followers, and Yu Mi was killed in a skirmish with the tribes around Yuzhang's capital," Liu Ji reported. "It is a shame, for despite their apparent ineptness they were both valiant generals."

"I quite agree, and I was looking forward to giving them both posts as guardians of Danyang," Bofu said. "Fate is not being kind to any of us. I hope that changes."

"As for myself, I only ask that I not be given military rank, for I fear that I am no military leader, Lord Sun," Liu Ji volunteered. "I am a man of the pen, as was my father's preference."

"He *doesn't want military rank*…?" Cheng Pu murmured. "Then he's… he's *genuine*…!"

"…If you're sure, then I shall give you civil administrative rank," Bofu said. "Don't think that you have to refuse to command men to earn my trust, Mister Liu Ji… you have it."

Liu Ji bowed low and said, "You are as wise and magnanimous as Ziyi says, and just as Father conceded in his last days! I will serve your just administration diligently!"

"…Please, rise," Bofu asked quietly. "Don't bow and scrape to me, Mister Liu Ji."

Taishi Ci noted the increasingly sombre mood and said, "I am now ready for the second task, Lord Sun."

Liu Ji smiled, stepped aside and said, "Please continue your operations, Lord Sun."

"Ah, yes!" Bofu chuckled gratefully. "Ziyi, you have travelled far, and although I feel like a terrible lord for asking you to go all the way back to Yuzhang, that is what I am going to do."

"…Why did you assign him only one of the labours when at least two involved going to Yuzhang, my lord…?" Huang Gai asked.

"I imagine that Lord Sun was being careful not to tell me too much about his future plans," Taishi Ci suggested dryly. "There is only one thing of interest in Yuzhang now: Hua Xin, the Administrator of Yuzhang."

"Quite right," Lü Fan said involuntarily.

"…Ah, I see it now," Cheng Pu muttered. "This is a well-laid scheme, indeed."

"My second request, Ziyi, is that you return to Yuzhang and enter the court of Hua Xin, taking care to note his successes and failures in that region," Bofu said. "When you return, I want you to tell me your honest expert military opinion about how best to secure Yuzhang against further problems."

"...Hua Xin is not a man that I liked," Liu Ji admitted. "His civil administration was in disarray at all times and in ways that the vile cultist Ze Rong and the local tribes had no responsibility for. Be careful, Taishi Ziyi, of a man whose role was probably bought, not earned."

"He was one of the regency court's last appointments before it collapsed, so he's probably a crony of some kind," Lü Fan said with disdain. "If we must oust him by force, then so be it, but friends are always better than subordinates."

"I understand," Taishi Ci promised. "I shall depart immediately. Shall I return here when my task is completed...?"

"Write to us with your conclusions and continue to observe him unless you have no choice in the matter," Bofu replied.

"Then I shall leave immediately, Lord Sun!" Taishi Ci cried. After one last respectful bow, the man from Huangxian turned and began a sprint away from the city walls.

"...Such stamina," Cheng Pu sighed. "Truly another man among men, just like Lord Sun, and his father, my dear friend Wentai..."

"And Lü Bu," Bofu chuckled. "He loves referring to himself as-"

"*Aiee...* don't mention that creature!" Cheng Pu pleaded. "Your father and the rest of us had so many unpleasant encounters with him, and now he's Governor of Xu, constantly shifting this way and that!"

"But Lü Bu is, I understand, a bit of an odd one," Lü Fan said. "He's taking commissions from the new imperial capital in Luoyang and *still* contemplating liaising with Yuan Shu at the same time, even after that last battle they had. He's as unpredictable as ever..."

"And not our immediate concern, Ziheng," Bofu said. "He can be Cao Cao's problem. I'm still concerned about more paid threats from our old master, and the best way to combat them is by beginning our work."

"...And start building a proper nation here in the south," Cheng Pu said gratefully. "I, for one, will work as hard as ten men."

"...I propose that we discuss the future of the region and plan new deployments while we wait for Taishi Ci to complete the second of his three tasks," Lü Fan declared. "Perhaps Lord Sun should visit Yangxian County as well."

"I'd like to," Bofu admitted as he gestured for his younger brother Yi to join the discussion. "I believe you, Ziheng, but I want to see it for myself."

Gongjin - who had been silently observing the events and subsequent discussions - smiled and said, "Who will make that journey...?"

"I shall remain here," Cheng Pu suggested. "You and your two friends should go to Yangxian together, Lord Sun."

"Yangxian...?" Sun Yi exclaimed.

"...A fine idea, Cheng Demou," Bofu replied. "I'll let my mother know that we're going, since she'll probably want me to take gifts and letters with me."

"I'll go too, Brother!" Sun Yi said enthusiastically. "Let's all go! You, me, Kuang, Shang-"

"Alright," Bofu replied. "There will be other opportunities for us all to reunite, Brother, and I think that Kuang and *especially Shangxiang* should be staying here."

Sun Yi smiled and said, "I won't argue. Our sister would probably want to join the army, or beat Quan up in front of his staff, wouldn't she...!"

"I'm glad that I'm not the only one that understands," Bofu sighed.

"She'll change," Gongjin chuckled.

"*Will she...?*" Bofu retorted.

Cheng Pu coughed purposefully and said, "We should keep our conversation to civil matters and the like, Lord Sun... though I mean no offence to Mister Liu Ji."

"I am not offended," Liu Ji insisted. "My lord's family matters are not for untrusted ears, and I understand that completely."

Bofu turned to Liu Ji and said, "I want you to feel trusted, Mister Liu, because you are: if you want to write to Excellency Cao and enquire about inheriting your father's position, or you want to join my counsel... you're free to act as you wish."

Liu Ji bowed humbly and said, "I am happy to work with you, Lord Sun. Say no more of the past."

Bofu travelled to Yangxian County with Sun Yi, Sun Hè, Lü Fan, Gongjin and his elite bodyguards. Bofu's eldest brother, Yangxian Magistrate Sun Quan, journeyed to the gates of the city and greeted his visitors without fear or irritation: he was accompanied by a group of officials that included his deputy-of-sorts Pan Zhang, who was wearing an expensive silk robe that was emblazoned with images of animals.

"It appears that we have another Hè Qi!" Gongjin joked.

"If I can ever be compared to a great man like Hè Qi, I will be content to die thereafter, knowing that I truly lived," Pan Zhang replied. "Suffice to say that I have some way to go before I can enjoy such praise."

Lü Fan hummed thoughtfully.

"Nothing will be spared in the cause of celebrating recent victories and our reunion, Brother!" Sun Quan promised. "I-!"

"Just ensure that it is properly budgeted," Bofu chuckled. "When in doubt, ask Ziheng: he is now my chancellor."

Sun Quan smiled coldly and turned to Lü Fan, who asked, "Why do you stare at me so...?"

"Ziheng had nothing but good things to say," Bofu promised.

"He praised you, Elder Brother Quan, so don't be so unfriendly," Sun Yi said.

"...I merely wondered whether he wanted to advise me on the budget for this banquet," Sun Quan replied.

"You're obviously doing fine," Bofu said. "I was just commenting."

"Then shall we go to my residence...?" Sun Quan asked.

For the next two days, Sun Quan entertained his brothers, Gongjin and Lü Fan with banquets and tours of his relatively stable county: Bofu was disturbed at the level of frivolous spending, but he was also pleased to see that the people were happy and the troublemakers were being kept under control.

"...I won't attend the banquet tomorrow evening," Lü Fan said to

Bofu as they prepared to go their separate ways after a night of entertainment; the sober Sun Hè – who refused to abandon his role as bodyguard to his cousin – watched silently.

"Yeah, I guessed you'd say that," Bofu replied. "It's prob- ...Probably for the best. That wine he's serving us could knock out a horse!"

"You're not doing too badly," Lu Fan joked.

"...Gongjin was being a bit... what's the word... 'picky'," Bofu noted. "Yeah, I know that Quan's musicians aren't the best, but I... I started to feel sorry for them when he started glaring at them whenever they got a note wrong."

"He's really fussy about music, Bofu," Lü Fan replied. "Where is he, by the way...?"

"He's more drunk than I am," Bofu chuckled. "He... he prob'ly went for a walk."

"Your brother intends to continue the banquet regardless of our absence, and he was going to order more wine," Lü Fan said thoughtfully. "I... I think I might go to the treasury. I want to see the ledgers."

"You want to study ledgers with a head full of wine!?" Bofu cackled.

"...You're right, I shouldn't," Lü Fan conceded. "But I want to know what he's paying himself and his followers that he can afford such-"

"Look, Ziheng, I trust you, and I'll leave it with you, but can we not talk about it while I'm drunk...?" Bofu pleaded.

"...I apologise," Lü Fan replied.

"Don't apologise, you-! ...I... I think I need a walk as well," Bofu said. "I... I think I might try and find Gongjin."

"I, meanwhile, shall retire," Lü Fan replied. "Goodnight, Bofu."

Bofu and Sun Hè found Gongjin by the city's main well: Sun Hè stood guard while the two friends talked freely.

"...This wine is not walking off," Gongjin complained. "Quan certainly gets a strong brew. He must have innards like leather, Bofu."

"Yeah, and he's years away from being twenty," Bofu replied. "I'm worried that... that he's got that friend of his, Pan Zhang, that-"

"Pan Zhang is a fraud," Gongjin interrupted. "I heard two officials whispering about... hold on, I need to focus... ... ...that's better. I heard two officials saying that he killed someone that he owed money to."

"*Aiee*...! That's it then, Gongjin!" Bofu groaned. "I have to go back and-!"

"We don't know that it's true, and your brother respects him," Gongjin warned.

"He's turning my brother into a pirate!" Bofu complained. "He-!"

"He isn't the only one, Bofu," Gongjin suggested. "Before Pan Zhang, there were others. Your brother has always liked to 'safely live dangerously', hasn't he...?"

"...For the last two years at least, yeah," Bofu admitted. "Why can't he be more like Yi...? Yi is learning the best as well as the worst from the scabby lot we sometimes have around us, but Quan is... is... *aiee*."

"He's... different to you, that much is true," Gongjin said. "You're

540

all different, all of you... that's the price of your upbringing I suppose... or maybe not. Who taught Cao Cao to be a homicidal deviant...?"
Bofu grinned and said, "True enough, Gongjin. He is what he is... we all are."
"...We're getting on now age-wise, you and me," Gongjin noted. "We're both twenty-two and unmarried..."
"...Dad was twenty when I was born, and I... I have no idea how many children he had that died before me," Bofu realised. "Yuan Shu, the bastard... robbed me of at least six years of my life! And you, you silly idiot, following me instead o' finding a better friend, you ended up the same as me!"
"A hero's lot isn't an easy one," Gongjin suggested. "Lü Bu will be dead soon... Liu Bei, Cao Cao, Yuan Shao, they're all fighting every step of the way."
"They're all married, Gongjin," Bofu grumbled. "No more, you hear me...? You and me, we're going to find wives in the next year, alright...?"
"I hope my future bride has an ear for music!" Gongjin joked.
"Why, so's you can both heckle the court musicians...?" Bofu retorted.
"Maybe we'll produce the next generation of musicians, and they'll be better than those tone-deaf fools your brother's employed," Gongjin said. "Are there no better musicians in Yangxian? I could do better in the state I'm in now!"
"...We should go to our rooms," Bofu suggested. "It's dark, and... and Wu being Wu, I don't know if we're completely safe."
"You, championing caution... is always funny, Bofu," Gongjin giggled. "Alright, I'll go to my room: perhaps I can work on that new tune I'm writing."
"Let me know when you finish it," Bofu said as he began the walk back to the governor's mansion.

****

106

In the north, situations evolved and men rose and fell: Yuan Shao had finally dealt enough damage to the Black Mountain Bandits in Bing Province to force them into hiding, which allowed him to begin a campaign against his long-time rival Gongsun Zan; once word reached Cao Cao that his friend-turned-rival Yuan Shao had departed from his capital, Cao launched a campaign of his own against Xu Provincial Governor Lü Bu. For Cao Cao, it was personal now: his treasured 'cousin' Xiahou Dun had been shot in the face by one of Bu's generals and had lost an eye as a result; his aide on the campaign, the former Xu Provincial Governor Liu Bei, already viewed the campaign as personal after having suffered two crippling military defeats at Bu's hands in recent times and suffering two years of humiliation at his hands prior to that. In addition to the obvious foes that he faced, Lü Bu was surrounded by Cao's agents, most notably the father-and-son team Chen Gui and Chen Deng: Bu's end was inevitable unless he could somehow forge a new alliance with Yuan Shu, who was also doomed if he could not find a powerful ally.

"...When Yuan Shu and Lü Bu are gone, there will be a new age," Gongjin said as he shared a kettle of tea with Bofu and Lü Fan; the three men had been in Yangxian for a week, and they were contemplating a return to Danyang's capital.
"Those two might join forces at the last, in which case we'll not be able to see what happens next," Lü Fan suggested.
"Oh, I hope not," Gongjin replied. "With Yuan Shao having advanced to Yòu Province to destroy Gongsun Zan, there will be other opportunity available to Cao Cao: if he attacked Bu under any other circumstance, Shao would attack Yan Province and snatch His Majesty from Xuchang."
"...They treat the Son of Heaven like a bag of money," Bofu said. "It's Dong Zhuo all over again, isn't it?"
"And this time, we won't have anyone telling us who we can and cannot attack," Gongjin suggested. "If we have to attack Cao or Yuan for the empire, we'll do it."
"...Quan intends a lavish banquet to commemorate our departure," Lü Fan said after a short silence.
"He can't make them any more lavish, can he...?" Bofu groaned. "I'm not going to be able to think straight if I keep drinking that wine he gives us!"
Lü Fan got to his feet and said, "I'm going to the treasury. I want to check the ledgers now, and–"
"Who am I to keep you from your vices...?" Bofu teased. "Go and enjoy yourself, Ziheng, but don't overindulge on revenue figures!"
"Ha... ha... ha," Lü Fan retorted as he left the room.
"...Ziheng is right to worry," Gongjin suggested.
"I know he is," Bofu replied. "That's why I didn't stop him."

An official reported Lü Fan's impromptu visit to the treasury to Sun Quan, who shouted, **"The pedant! Why does he keep trying to undermine me???"**
"Perhaps you need to have a word with Lord Sun," Pan Zhang

suggested.

"...I will," Sun Quan replied. "That man is insulting me!"

Sun Quan asked for and received a private meeting with Bofu in the former's private meeting room.

"...Why does Lü Fan inspect my treasury without informing me...?" Sun Quan asked gruffly.

"He's my chancellor," Bofu replied casually. "As the chancellor of Jiangdong, he has the right to check any treasury at any time."

"Yes, he's your chancellor, but am I not your *brother*???" Sun Quan retorted.

"...So if he'd found some evidence of fraud, why would that be a bad thing, then, *Brother*...?" Bofu asked.

"...Lü Fan should not have done what he did without informing me!" Sun Quan protested. "It implies distrust!"

"And when would you have liked him to inform you, Magistrate...?" Bofu asked.

"What kind of question is that?" Sun Quan scoffed.

"You are surrounded by men that you trust, Quan, whether they deserve such trust or not," Bofu explained calmly. "Ziheng is family... which is something that you appear to have forgotten at some point."

Sun Quan snorted irritably.

"He didn't make a fuss about it, but I was angry at the way that you treated him on the last time he came here," Bofu continued. "You lavished praise on that wandering con-man that you've befriended, and treated Ziheng like a-"

"Pan Zhang is a hero!" Sun Quan insisted. "All you go on about is how well I'm managing things, yet you won't trust the man that makes it so! Pan Zhang is the one that the bandits fear!"

"...So you've said," Bofu replied. "But does finding him mean losing Ziheng...?"

"...Alright, I get it," Sun Quan grumbled. "I was rude, I suppose, and I apologise. But did it give him the right to start inspecting my affairs as though I am untrustworthy? Does he treat Jiang Qin, Cheng Pu, Yi, or Hè Qi like this...?"

"Yi...?" Bofu chortled. "Yi's barely old enough to have any responsibilities that need auditing, so what's he got to do with it?"

"The others, then!" Sun Quan snapped.

"...Every one of the men that you mention accepts Ziheng's scrutiny, since they have to delegate responsibility at times, and even if they are completely trustworthy, others that they employ might have deceived them," Bofu explained. "Hè Qi worried me because of his ostentatious lifestyle, but he has time and again proved that he sources the wealth legitimately without harming others."

"...And I don't...?" Sun Quan chortled.

"You might, but does every man...?" Bofu retorted. "Yes, Pan Zhang is a 'hero', you say, that quells bandits, but he also likes to amass debts... so naturally, I like to ensure that he pays them properly rather than exploit your respect... and his is but one possible scenario. And while we're on the subject of your lifestyle..."

"So now, after saying that I am not the problem, you admit that I am," Sun Quan chuckled irritably. "Yes, I enjoy an exciting life, like everyone else gets to."

"...Quan, I'm unmarried and spend my entire time fighting," Bofu scolded. "Lü Fan actually enjoys reviewing ledgers and legal documents, I think, Gu Yong blends into the walls a lot of the time, the Zhang brothers are pedants beyond belief; what 'exciting life' are you talking about...?"

Sun Quan was silent.

"...Yes, I do admit that the taverns and brothels are a temptation," Bofu continued.

Sun Quan grinned and said, "I'm more than happy to be-!"

"Just... don't forget who you are," Bofu continued. "You're the second son of Sun Jian of Fuchun, the 'Tiger of Jiangdong': Dad wouldn't be very impressed with a man that spent all day in taverns, gambling houses and brothels."

"...I'm only human!" Sun Quan cried.

"And I'm not...?" Bofu retorted. "I'm just... just... look, just be sure to place trust in others only when you have to or can be certain that you can, Quan. Men like Ziheng, Gongjin, Demou, Gongfu and Junli are few and far between, and I'm lucky to know so many men like them. Don't judge a man on his military achievements, alright...? Zu Lang is a great fighter, but I wouldn't let him near the treasury."

"...I will be careful in who I place faith," Sun Quan replied dryly.

"And you won't castigate Ziheng...?" Bofu prompted.

"No, I won't," Sun Quan replied coldly.

"...He's your family too, Quan," Bofu sighed sadly.

"...You're leaving tomorrow," Sun Quan prompted.

"I am," Bofu replied.

"...Must I change my ways as well if I am to remain in this post...?" Sun Quan asked.

"So long as you don't become another Cao Cao, I don't care what you do," Bofu insisted. "I almost succumb a lot myself, but... but I have too much to do."

Sun Quan hummed thoughtfully.

"...Lecture over," Bofu chuckled. "You can go now, naughty boy."

Sun Quan smiled humbly and said, "Thank you, Elder Brother, for caring... I can see that you do. I'll improve... I'll keep on improving... until I'm worthy of being a Sun. I promise."

"You're not unworthy, you're just... flawed, like everyone else," Bofu suggested.

"...And you should find a wife, Brother," Sun Quan replied. "Where will the next tigers come from if you don't provide them...?"

"I agree, and I intend to start looking," Bofu promised.

"I look forward to meeting my nephews and nieces!" Sun Quan chuckled.

Bofu patted Quan's arm, and the two parted company as friends.

When Bofu returned to his quarters, he found Gongjin, Lü Fan, Sun Hè and his brother Yi waiting for him.

"...Why did Quan demand an audience with you...?" Sun Yi asked.

"He actually meant to scold me for allowing Ziheng to inspect the treasury!" Bofu complained. "But he's said that he won't press the matter further."

"...Why is he being such an idiot...?" Sun Yi chortled. "Has he got something to hide...?"

"I hope not," Bofu replied.

"...I can see that you don't want to talk about it, Bofu," Sun Yi said. "I won't say anymore, and I won't talk to him about it either. I'll pretend I don't know."

Bofu smiled and said, "You, you're like me... thanks, Yi."

"If you're grateful, you'll take me on a campaign as soon as I'm considered to be old enough," Sun Yi replied. "I want to be in the vanguard."

"*Another one*," Sun Hè muttered.

Bofu laughed and said, "You really are just like me, Yi! You have my word that you'll have your moment soon enough."

"If I could, I'd fight Yuan Shu *and* Liu Biao, right *now*!" Sun Yi declared. "I'd make them pay for everything that they've done to us Suns!"

"...I'd fight them too, Yi," Bofu replied glumly. "I'd fight them too."

Bofu and his entourage undertook a swift journey back to Danyang; upon their return, Bofu and his counsel learned that a messenger from Taishi Ci had just delivered a report from Yuzhang Prefecture. Once Bofu and his senior counsel – Lü Fan, Gongjin, Wu Jing, Cheng Pu, Huang Gai, Gu Yong, Zhang Zhao, Zhang Hong, Qin Song and Lü Dai – had retired to the private meeting room and been joined by an enthusiastic Lady Wu, Lü Fan read Taishi's report on Hua Xin's administration.

"Well...?" Bofu asked.

"Let him read," Lady Wu said quietly.

"...So we must march on Yuzhang," Lü Fan said when he finished reading the written report. "I shall have to speed a messenger to Luling as well."

"Now...?" Bofu exclaimed. "Has Ziyi judged Hua Xin as a serious military threat?"

"Quite the opposite," Lü Fan chuckled.

"...So... so our army is marching to Yuzhang to convince him to surrender," Qin Song supposed.

"That is it, Mister Qin," Lü Fan replied. "We'll prepare at once."

Once again, Wu Jing, Gongjin and Xu Kun were left to guard Danyang while Bofu took Lü Fan, Chen Wu, Ling Cao and Liu Ji on a campaign: but this time, there would be next to no resistance as they travelled.

****

107

Hua Xin's administration in Yuzhang collapsed altogether when news of Bofu's army reached the prefectural capital; village after village, town after town and city after city surrendered without a struggle, leaving Bofu with a clear marching path.

"...**Why does Sun Ce march against me so easily???**" Hua Xin cried as he looked at his remaining vassals and his guest Taishi Ci. Hua Xin rose from his cushion and started to pace back and forth; he stopped after traversing the floor three times and said, "He's going to be here within days, perhaps hours, and my defence forces are either fleeing or surrendering! And there are rumours that he has Liu Yao's son at his side and most of Liu Yao's court in his service!"

Some officials turned their eyes toward Taishi Ci; Hua Xin noted their gestures and said, "Ah, yes, Taishi Ziyi! You're a hero of the age, and I'm privileged to have you here. All those ugly rumours about you being the one that recruited those men for Sun Ce–"

"Were true," Taishi Ci declared; the court was filled with gasps.

"...You...! Y-you... you...!" Hua Xin stammered. "Knave! T-traitor! I-I'll kill you myself!"

"Why?" Taishi Ci asked as Hua Xin ran to the pedestal that held his sword. "You have no following, so why don't you just give up and join Sun Ce? He's the hero in the south, Hua Xin. Whom do you fight for now...?"

Hua Xin looked at his exhausted vassals and sighed miserably.

"I switched my allegiance to Lord Sun Ce because he is a future hero, newly released from service to Yuan Shu," Taishi Ci continued. "He is gaining the support of men that have seen the truth, and the truth is that our country is changing. We cannot look to old rules as our guide when the Son of Heaven spent a year as a vagrant while his lords openly contended for his lands and egregious rapists and murderers were Chancellors and Regents for quite a while before that. Something is happening, Administrator Hua, and whatever it is will divide men into survivors and victims. Which will you be, and what will you do?"

Hua Xin pondered for few moments, groaned in resignation and said, "Someone get a pen and some paper, please..."

One night later, Bofu held a banquet for Taishi Ci in the command tent of his camp.

"Magnificent! Taishi Ziyi, you are a man with few peers!" Bofu said. "It may have cost grain and time, but not men and blood! Hua Xin is pacified and placated, and your task is completed!"

"So now I want to know what my third and final task will be," Taishi Ci prompted.

"Ah, well... sorry, but this one is the hardest one, Ziyi," Bofu sighed. "You can have a short rest first before I–"

"I am a man that cannot live without a challenge, Lord Sun," Taishi Ci replied. "Give me your orders and I will begin immediately."

"...Liu Biao is obviously worried about my increasing strength in this region, because he's sent his nephew Liu Pan to harass the northwest region," Bofu explained.

"I know of the situation," Taishi Ci said.

"It's something that I've been forced to ignore, what with everything else that I've had to deal with, but now that Yuzhang, Kuaiji, Danyang and Wu are pacified and Southern Guangling has been taken by my uncle, now is the time," Bofu continued. "I'm appointing you as the guardian of the six counties that he is threatening and despatching you to repel him."

"I shall leave immediately," Taishi Ci replied.

Bofu laughed and said, "You don't have to-!"

Taishi Ci got to his feet, bowed to his peers and left the tent.

"...Go right now, Ziyi," Bofu sighed.

"He obviously disagrees, Lord Sun!" Ling Cao snickered.

"*Aiee*... he really means it when he says that he lives for challenges," Bofu said. "But can any of us afford to stop? Ziheng, what word from Lujiang?"

"Liu Xun is refusing to cede Huancheng, and the other major cities are equally well defended, but the outer districts are ours," Lü Fan replied. "You shouldn't need to reinforce them personally. The Jiujiang campaign is stalling, but it doesn't matter, since Cao Cao is getting closer and closer to Shouchun and will probably rout him within six months."

"Yuan Shu's running out of money, land and friends," Bofu said. "Soon, we can do what I've wanted to do for so, so long..."

"...Jing Province," Lü Fan sighed.

"Provided that nothing gets in my way, yes," Bofu continued.

"Your father's death eats at you, which I understand," Liu Ji said. "But is there no opportunity for reconciliation with Liu Biao...?"

Many of the other diners stopped talking and awaited Bofu's response.

"...I wish that I could say 'Yes', but I cannot," Bofu said. "You see, Mister Liu, I did not witness any regret at what was done to my father. He, like me, was following orders, and capturing him was an option. Even if he had to die, as they would no doubt claim, the least they could have done is show some remorse! That...! ...That friend of his, Huang Zu, is worse still, and... and...!"

"...Your posture is forced, I can see that," Liu Ji replied. "I in no way compare our father's fates: you did not shoot my father down from the shadows, and you did not laugh at the coffin. Liu Biao has proved himself most undeserving of his ties to the royal house, and I detest the idea of our sharing lineage."

"You're... a good man, Mister Liu," Bofu said with difficulty. "Now, perhaps... we can change the subject. If I had my way, Liu Biao and Huang Zu would not exist, and I would like to pretend that they don't."

"Why don't we toast Taishi Ci again?" Lü Fan suggested.

"Yes!" Bofu agreed. "To Taishi Ci, a toast: were we all of us under Heaven like him, what a world it would be!"

When the banquet ended, Bofu, Sun Hè and Lü Fan retired to Bofu's personal tent.

"Liu Ji upset you unintentionally," Lü Fan said.

"I just want this to end, Ziheng," Bofu complained. "Liu Xun holds Lujiang, Yuan Shu holds northern Jiujiang and Lü Bu is in Xu Province: while those three are alive and able to aid each other, what peace can I know...?"

"Lü Bu will be dead soon, and Yuan Shu will not last long after that," Lü Fan insisted. "Liu Xun is surrounded by able men, but he is an arrogant mediocrity that be destroyed by turning his own self-importance against him."

"Yuan Shu, my old master, can't die soon enough," Bofu grumbled. "He's held out for so many months more than I'd ever thought he could."

"All the same, he'll die," Lü Fan said.

"...And after that...?" Bofu asked. "Who must I fight after that...?"

"Who can say...?" Lü Fan replied. "We're free, we're popular, and we're many more in number now: whoever we must face, Lord Sun, we'd have Taishi Ci, Liu Yao's son and a host of new talents to help us that we didn't have before."

Bofu laughed miserably and said, "Whatever happens, we'll not know peace. When will I be able to do other things...?"

"Do not despair," Lü Fan pleaded. "Fate has a way of being as cruel as it is kind, and as kind as it is cruel, with no way of knowing what will come next. After such hardships, you are sure, as a hero that has, if you'll forgive me saying so, equalled or perhaps surpassed your father-"

"I...! ...I know you're being kind, Ziheng, but I could never surpass Dad, no matter how hard I tried," Bofu interrupted. "I refuse to accept that I've equalled him, either."

"But you have," Lü Fan insisted. "He'd be proud that you have surpassed him, so why not embrace it...? Most of Jiangdong is yours to govern properly, you're free of Yuan Shu, and you've not only gained new heroes like Chen Wu and Lu Meng: you've pacified Taishi Ci and Zu Lang, and managed to earn the respect and service of all of your father's vassals! Do you know how hard those men will find taking orders from their former lord's son, a man half their age...?"

"...I know," Bofu replied.

"Embrace your talent and ability, and embrace your achievements, Bofu," Lü Fan continued. "If your father could talk to you now, he would say that he was proud to be your father. Doesn't Lady Wu always say that...?"

Bofu smiled and said, "Yeah, she does."

"And, to return to my original point, that qualifies you for some good luck, 'Marquis Sun Ce of Wu, Rebellion-supressing General'," Lü Fan continued. "Don't stray from your path, and you'll soon get what you want and need."

Bofu bowed slightly and said, "You're a good friend, Ziheng."

"Now, to another emerging development," Lü Fan said. "Cao Cao has written to us again, saying that he has 'found a man to help us in our fight with Yuan Shu in Jiujiang'..."

"Oh...? Why's he done that?" Bofu exclaimed.

"I suspect that he's unsure of our motives, which is a problem in itself," Lü Fan replied. "The main problem, however, is the name he's given us for this 'help'."

"...Why do I get the feeling that I'm going to groan when I hear this name...?" Bofu chortled. "Go on: who has the 'Crafty Villain' found to 'help us'...?"

"...Does the name 'Chen Yu' sound familiar...?" Lü Fan asked dryly.

"...Chen Yu... Chen Yu... Chen- ...Wait, no, not...! ...*Haixi Chen*???" Bofu exclaimed. "Are you sure that he didn't say 'Cheng Yu'?"

"This was *written*, and there's no way to get 'Chen' and 'Cheng' confused, unless he dictated the letter whilst drunk," Lü Fan replied dryly.

"It has to be another Chen Yu," Sun Hè suggested. "It *can't be that bandit*."

"Hasn't Cao Cao got an army of 'former Yellow Turban rebels' working for him that regularly forget that they're not Yellow Turban rebels anymore…?" Lü Fan retorted. "If he can employ them as his 'Qing Province Corps', he can employ Haixi Chen for… for whatever purpose he has in mind."

"…This has to be a joke," Bofu pleaded.

"It might be a different Chen Yu, as Bohai suggested," Lü Fan said. "I'll take my elite unit and some trusted captains and meet this man while you return to Danyang."

"Where are you to meet him?" Bofu asked.

Lü Fan smirked and said, "Wu Prefecture, on the border with-"

"*Ayah*! It *is* Haixi Chen!" Bofu groaned.

"Leave it with me," Lü Fan chuckled. "I'll go and deal with it one way or another."

"If it's him, then your unit killed his relative, and someone else should go," Bofu retorted. "Have Ling Cao go, or-"

"No offence to Ling Cao, but a restrained man with quick wit is needed," Lü Fan insisted. "It's either Gongjin or me, and I prefer to go myself."

"…Cao Cao sent that man here to 'help us'…?" Bofu chortled. "He's our future enemy now, that much is clear: only another Yuan Shu would employ villains like that."

"Leave it with me!" Lü Fan said through laughter. "I'll go and rest now… goodnight, Bofu."

"…Yeah," Bofu murmured as Lü Fan left the tent.

"*Haixi Chen*…?" Sun Hè exclaimed.

"…It'll be another Chen Yu, it… it *has to be*," Bofu replied.

Bofu summoned his officials to the command tent at dawn.

"Lü Fan has gone ahead to… to liaise with someone sent by Cao Cao," Bofu reported. "We're going back to Danyang: a few people will be left here to watch Hua Xin, but he'll be allowed to continue in his post until we find someone else."

"And is it true that Hè Qi is advancing eastward to manage the Shanyue in Wu, Lord Sun…?" Ling Cao asked.

"It is, Colonel Ling," Bofu replied. "My uncle and his sons are perfectly capable of holding the northern front in Jiujiang since Hui Qu's retreat, and Zhu Junli and Xu Gong are in need of an officer that knows how to intimidate the Shanyue: Hè Qi's gaudy lot certainly have that effect."

"So who will be going to Lujiang?" Chen Wu asked.

"I don't know right now," Bofu replied. "Boyang and Guoyi are managing Liu Xun well enough… but that's all up for discussion later. For now, let's just get home to Danyang."

One and all agreed, and Bofu's army left the pacified Yuzhang Prefecture in the closely-monitored hands of the man that had surrendered it to them.

＊＊＊＊＊＊＊＊＊＊＊

108

The balance of power changed yet again over the following weeks: Lü Bu made one last, desperate attempt to forge an alliance with Yuan Shu, but his efforts to resume the marriage of his daughter to Yuan Shu's son were thwarted, and Bu retreated to the inner depths of his capital Xiapi while enemies besieged him on all sides. His end would be ignominious: after 9 years of notoriety, the former foster son of Ding Yuan and Dong Zhuo, usurper of power in Yan Province and then Xu Province, abductor and then self-styled saviour of Emperor Xian, accomplice to regicide, mass-murder, torture and tomb-robbing, and self-proclaimed 'Man among men', Lü Bu, was betrayed by some of his own disgruntled followers and condemned to a deliberately inappropriate form of execution by Cao Cao. General Zhang Yang, Administrator of Henei and the only man that might have helped Lü Bu – and, by proxy, Yuan Shu – out of a strange sense of loyalty had been assassinated as well, and Gongsun Zan had been repeatedly defeated by Yuan Shao; Yuan Shu was now completely isolated, and most were glad of it.

"...'Am I being selfish?', he writes," Bofu chortled as he threw a piece of correspondence from his cousin Sun Ben to the floor in front of him; he then turned to Gongjin – his only company in his private audience room – and said, "Is Boyang being selfish...?"

"You obviously don't think so, and neither do I," Gongjin replied. "He fears for his family, and he is right to do so."

"...But would he falter if he had to choose between facing Yuan Shu and saving his wife and children...?" Bofu wondered. "I know that I couldn't trust myself; isn't that how Yuan Shu controlled us for all those years, making us kill good men and conquer places for him...?"

"It was," Gongjin conceded. "Do you want to replace Sun Ben as commander in Lujiang, then...?"

"...No, Gongjin, I couldn't do that to him," Bofu replied. "He was very good when he ceded control of the clan and the army to me, and he's never challenged me since: he was just voicing his concerns, and that's all."

"On another subject, how is Lü Ziheng faring...?" Gongjin asked.

"He writes, 'Do not ask'," Bofu scoffed. "Cao Cao is a deceitful bastard. How dare he send a man here to try and destroy me!"

"He'll never confess to it," Gongjin supposed.

"No, no, he won't," Bofu sighed. "He'll send apologies, Ziheng reckons."

"Oh, I agree!" Gongjin chuckled. "He'll say 'I was taken in', and other such things. But Chen Yu was no friend, and now he's not a problem for us either, and that's good. Our only problems now are the Shanyue tribes as usual – and they're being dealt with very effectively by Zhu Zhi, Jiang Qin, Hè Qi, Yu Fan, Dong Xi and Zu Lang – and Yuan Shu. Yuan can't fund any more trouble here in Jiangdong now, and with Lü Bu dead and Cao Cao at the Shouchun County border, and Sun Ben and Sun Fu poised to strike Huancheng City, it'll all be over soon..."

"...And in the meantime, I can finally go after Liu Biao!" Bofu said with glee. "I bet that Old Cheng and all the other doubters are

regretting their words now, uh…? Taishi Ziyi made a fool of Liu Pan and drove him out of three of the six counties in no time at all! With Zhou Tai ready to return to service, and little else to worry about, I say that we get ready for an attack on-"
"We should go to Huancheng first, Bofu," Gongjin suggested. "I think that-"
"I'm not replacing Boyang!" Bofu chortled. "Come on, Gongjin, you know me better than anyone else alive! You're my best friend! You know that if I say that I'm not going to do something, then-!"
"There's someone there that we have to meet," Gongjin interrupted. "We'd not be going there to fight."
Bofu frowned and asked, "Why then…?"
Gongjin smiled, leant forward and said, "Have you ever heard – I ask sarcastically, of course – of the Qiao sisters…?"
"*Ooh… they're supposed to be… … …Are they in Lujiang???*" Bofu exclaimed.
"I thought that you knew," Gongjin replied. "They and their father wandered there at some point or other, and they've ended up in our care. I know that it sounds ridiculous, but…"
"…But might they be what we've been waiting for…?" Bofu said.
"Precisely," Gongjin replied. "Fate does, indeed, work in mysterious ways, Bofu: call me a foolish dreamer if you want, but they were *born for us*, they *must have been*."
"Oh, but if they went to that region, wasn't it probably for a marriage to Yuan Yao, or Liu Xun's son, or something…?" Bofu groaned.
"They're available," Gongjin promised. "We should go at once."
"…Yes," Bofu replied excitedly. "We'll go to Huancheng as soon as a boat can be arranged, then, and-!"
"I arranged it already," Gongjin admitted sheepishly.
Bofu grinned and said, "That's why you're my friend! Let's be off!"

Sun Ben and Sun Fu welcomed Bofu, Gongjin and Lü Fan at the gates of their fenced camp in the Huancheng countryside.
"I hope that we haven't taken you away from urgent matters in Jiangdong," Sun Ben said as the group of men and their subordinates journeyed to the command tent.
"This area is important too," Bofu replied. "Besides, it's all very quiet… well, compared to before it is, anyway."
"To have Zu Lang, Taishi Ci, *Hua Xin* and *Liu Ji* as vanguard champions of our cause in Jiangdong is… well, it's almost unbelievable!" Sun Ben chuckled. "Truly, Bofu, I believe that you could win around almost anyone. Perhaps you should try and recruit Liu Xun!"
Bofu laughed and said, "If I could, I would, as much as I hate him for the way he treated us after we took this place from Lu Kang. You seem to have done well yourself as far as recruitment and gaining surrenders is concerned."
"So many places surrendered without a fight because they like *you*, not me," Sun Ben replied. "Your name is synonymous with justice and heroism."
"That's good," Gongjin chuckled. "All the better for why we're here…"
Sun Ben smiled and said, "Ah, yes… the Qiaos. Gongjin, you're not as subtle as I thought you were."

"Why should I pretend?" Gongjin retorted. "For too long, we-!"

"I... I know how you feel, in a sense, being deprived of an existing family," Sun Ben said with obvious despair. "Your enthusiasm to find your future brides is entirely understandable. Bofu, Gongjin, you'll find them in the town to the south of here. We've been sure to treat everyone well, not just them, so you'll find a very good atmosphere generally."

Bofu stopped suddenly and asked, "Shall we go now?"

The entire entourage halted.

"There is no military emergency here, Bofu," Sun Ben replied. "The Jiujiang front is quiet, and Liu Xun is trapped. Go and see whether Heaven has been kind to you both at last."

Bofu bowed and said, "You are a hero of the age, Cousin, and kind and thoughtful with it. We'll not be long, and then we'll come and help you smash Liu Xun!"

"Don't be ridiculous," Sun Ben replied. "If all goes well, there will be weddings, and Liu Xun can wait: Yuan Shu is... is finished, isn't he, and so is Liu Xun!"

Sun Fu sighed miserably and whispered, "Brother...!"

"...I'm fine," Sun Ben insisted. "Yuan Shu has good men around him, even if he a wretch himself. Isn't that right, Bofu...?"

"As soon as Yuan Shu falls, I imagine that Zhang Xun will take over at least part of his remaining forces, at which point we have a new ally," Bofu replied. "There's no sense in harming my cousins, not if Yuan Shu wants to know any kind of peace after he's defeated."

"So why should I be too concerned...?" Sun Ben chuckled falsely. "Go on, Bofu, and Gongjin: meet these famous beauties you crave so much."

"*Aiee*... you make us sound like *Cao Cao*," Gongjin grumbled as he turned and walked away.

Bofu laughed, turned to follow Gongjin and said, "One's enough for me!"

"For now," Lü Fan teased as he followed Bofu.

"After seeing how Lady Chen made my mother feel at first...?" Bofu chortled. "My mother would probably... well, I don't know, Ziheng. But-!"

"I was joking," Lü Fan insisted.

Sun Fu watched Bofu and his friends walk away and said, "Are you sure that you're alright, Brother...?"

"...I have no choice but to be 'alright'," Sun Ben replied. "My loyalty to Bofu exceeds any other concern... even my family. They would have it no other way, for there is no victory to be had by betraying what I believe in for their sake."

"I know that, Brother, I... I was just... asking," Sun Fu sighed.

"...I wonder if the father of these famous sisters will want Bofu and Gongjin as his sons-in-law," Sun Ben said.

"They are certainly beautiful, those Qiao ladies," Sun Fu sighed.

"There will be many a man that would envy Bofu and Gongjin for being married to such radiant beauties, and I confess that I will be one of them," Sun Ben chuckled. "I shouldn't be so, but... married or not, I'm still a man."

Bofu and Gongjin travelled southward and met with 'Elder Qiao', the father of the young women that the two men had set their sights on meeting. The Qiaos were staying in a hotel, and so the meeting between Bofu, Gongjin and the man that they hoped would become their father-in-law would take place in a garden space to the rear of the hotel.

"Well, well… two magnificent young men, indeed!" Elder Qiao cackled as he sat and stared at Bofu and Gongjin. "Two heroes of the age and no mistake: two sons of great men as well as great men in their own right!"

Gongjin smiled sheepishly, bowed humbly and said, "You flatter me, Elder Qiao."

"I'm quite old, and so I've seen a lot," Elder Qiao continued. "Sixty years, I've been alive, and so I've seen a lot. I've lived, loved, lost… my two girls are very precious to me, as precious as the hair my parents gave me that I would not cut for any man. I've traversed the land, looking for somewhere safe for us to rest our weary bodies, and somehow, I've ended up here in Huancheng, where we're surrounded by violence."

Bofu bowed and said, "I must bear responsibility for that, Elder Qiao. I-"

"Nonsense!" Elder Qiao scoffed. "I'll not hear it! I won't! Yuan Shu, that wretch, that cowardly, heretical hankerer, he declared that he was the Son of Heaven! And don't you think I've heard things, mm…? Don't you think that I know that Liu Xun came here and took Lujiang from you after you fought Lu Kang for it…?"

"…And how do you feel about my treatment of Lu Kang, Elder Qiao…?" Bofu asked nervously.

"You were forced to do it, and everyone knows it," Elder Qiao replied. "Oh, there are some that will never forgive you, but who are they, mm…? Lu Kang brought it on himself by not living in the age! He should have either capitulated to Yuan Shu or allied with Yuan Shao! How did he think that he could sit there and pontificate when there was no law in the land anymore…?"

"You are… very generous to me, Elder Qiao," Bofu said.

"Nonsense!" Elder Qiao replied. "How am I generous by stating the truth, mm…? As I said, I've lived a long time. I've seen the Han crumble under His Majesty Lingdi, and the Yellow Turbans that your father so heroically faced and bested; I've seen His Majesty Xiandi pushed and pulled this way and that by villains while warlords hummed tunes and looked the other way; everything is different now. What I see, truthfully, is two handsome and talented young men: one, Sun Ce, is the son of Sun Wentai, the hero of the last age that crushed the Yellow Turbans, fought Dong Zhuo, freed the capital and resealed the imperial tombs; then there is-"

"And… and you pay no heed to the ugly rumours…?" Bofu asked.

"Don't mention that," Gongjin whispered.

"Oh, the nonsense that Yuan Shu's friends are spreading about the Imperial Seal, you mean…?" Elder Qiao cackled. "The story that your father purloined it from a well in Luoyang and was forced to give it to Yuan, who took it as the first of many signs of his own magnificence…? The purpose of the tale answers the question, and I'll hear no more of it!"

Bofu smiled and said, "My thanks, Elder Qiao. I could not bear to-"

"No more, you hear?" Elder Qiao continued. "Now where was I, mm…? …Oh yes! Zhou Yu."

The humbled Gongjin dreaded Elder Qiao's assessment, despite the signs that it was going to be extremely positive.

"Zhou Yu, second son of Luoyang's magistrate, who bravely aided the exposure and political assassination of the vile 'Ten' that manipulated the throne for so long," Elder Qiao continued. "The Zhous have long served the Han loyally, as the Suns have in an undeservedly lesser capacity: no, your lineages are enviable."

"You are too kind!" Gongjin exclaimed involuntarily.

"Nonsense!" Elder Qiao cackled. "And now, we come to the two of you… and what father – or father-in-law – could fail to be proud…?"

Bofu and Gongjin felt as sick as they felt grateful as the enormity of the moment started to sink in for both of them.

"Sun Bofu, you inherited your father's daunting legacy at such a young age, but my, look at how much you've done!" Elder Qiao continued. "As a warrior and charismatic leader of men, you have no peer: you've pacified the bandits, quelled the tribes, broken the shackles and opposed the pretender, put fear in the heart of your father's killers and forced the mighty Cao Cao to acknowledge you in your own right when he would probably prefer not to! And you, Zhou Gongjin, are as talented in all of the arts as you are handsome, and as adept with a sword as you are with a pen. Yuan Shu craved your guidance, but yet you easily outwitted him and his entire counsel, and even Cao Cao's famed advisers will come to fear you if they do not already. Jiangdong is already affected by law for the first time in so, so long, and yet you've neither of you even started! That's what I hear, and that's what I know from seeing you two here now. You've suffered hardship and servitude to a monster, known nothing but war and persecution, and now you want to know happiness; my daughters are, like me, possessed of hearts, and if they can bring happiness into your lives, why, they would do so gladly."

"…I am content already!" Gongjin admitted. "Just knowing, is… Elder Qiao, if you would truly condescend to allowing your daughters to meet us, then-"

"Right now, if you wish," Elder Qiao declared.

"I… would be glad to!" Bofu replied. "Oh, but wait: aren't we supposed to do all that 'matchmaker' stuff…?"

Gongjin frowned and sighed, saying, "Ah, yes, I'd actually forgotten about that."

Elder Qiao smiled and said, "If you both insist on all the formalities, that's fine, but since you're here, and they've already come to greet you…"

Bofu and Gongjin shuddered involuntarily.

"They will be a lot more nervous than you, I think!" Elder Qiao whispered.

Gongjin was the first to turn his gaze toward the entrance to the garden: he groaned involuntarily as soon as he caught sight of the sisters, who - despite the both of them being dressed in plain gowns and straw sandals – were two of the loveliest things that he had ever seen. Both of the young women smiled shyly and covered their blushing faces with their sleeves; Bofu turned and stifled a gasp when he saw how attractive the Qiao sisters were.

"What are your thoughts…?" Elder Qiao asked nervously.

"…A man sighs upon the sight of such beauty with such a groan…

for he knows his heart's forever given, and no more his own,"
Gongjin replied as he stared at the younger Lady Qiao.
"Is that so...?" Elder Qiao teased.
"Oh!" Gongjin gasped. "Forgive my speaking of your daughters in
such a way, Elder Qiao, but-!"
"You admire them, and I am not offended, for you will, Heaven
willing, shortly be married to them, and everyone will be happy,"
Elder Qiao interrupted. "Daughters, you should retire."
The younger Lady Qiao smiled at Gongjin and said, "Farewell,
Mister Zhou Yu, and Lord Sun Ce."
"I, uh... yes! Yes, indeed! F-farewell, for now, Lady Qiao, and, uh,
Lady Qiao," Gongjin bumbled as he tried to bow and found that he
had lost some of his coordination through nerves.
Bofu was silently besotted with the elder Lady Qiao, who said,
"Farewell, Lord Sun Ce, and Mister Zhou Yu."
"...For *now*, yeah...!" Bofu replied casually. Gongjin coughed
deliberately, and Bofu immediately bowed and added, "Oh! Wait,
no, no, I-! Yes, farewell, fair ladies, until we meet again, which
will be soon. I hope. Ladies."
The two Qiaos stifled giggles and retired to their room; Elder Qiao
– who was also stifling laughter – shook his head and said, "I
always feared such days when men ogled my daughters so, but in
your case, gentlemen, I am glad that they will know such devotion
from their future husbands."
Gongjin turned to Elder Qiao and replied, "My home will be your
own, and my heart and soul your daughter's, just as my mind is
the state's and my loyalty belongs to my friend Sun Bofu. I feel
five years younger, even just from...!"
Gongjin paused.
"...And you, Lord Sun...?" Elder Qiao asked as he looked at the
bemused Bofu.
"I... I've seen beautiful girls before, but never like... ... ...sorry,"
Bofu murmured.
"Bofu!" Gongjin scolded.
Bofu turned to Gongjin and snapped, "Hey, look, you're talking a
load of fancy nonsense, so don't have a go at-!"
Elder Qiao started to laugh.
"...*Aiee*... we've undone ourselves at the critical moment!" Bofu
despaired.
"You've done no such thing, Lord Sun!" Elder Qiao promised. "Go
and arrange your matchmakers, as my daughters already have
me to act for them."
"If my father is still too ill, then my uncle Shang can act for me,"
Gongjin said.
"...Who do I get...?" Bofu wondered: his face fell, and he added,
"M-my father... was who would always... oh, how I wish he was...!"
Elder Qiao smiled sadly and said, "You are both so full of
emotion... if you would prefer that we did not concern ourselves
with formalities..."
"No, I can have my father's brother Sun Jing or my mother's
brother Wu Jing act for me," Bofu replied. "You have been most
kind for allowing us to meet your wonderful, beautiful daughters,
and... and I hope that you will all join us on our return trip to
Danyang, where we can... well, you know, do all the 'formalities'."
"Well put," Gongjin whispered.

"Well put indeed!" Elder Qiao teased. "We shall meet again soon, future sons-in-law. Until then, do not allow yourselves to come to harm. My daughters want you as handsome and impressive as you are now."

"*Aiee*… I-I mean, uh, yes, thank you, Elder Qiao," Gongjin replied. "Forgive my- I, uh, I mean, you see, I've never much liked being reminded of my looks, for I've often felt that it compromised my ability to be respected by-"

"It does you no harm on this occasion," Elder Qiao suggested.

"We should go," Bofu supposed.

"For now, yes," Elder Qiao replied. "Farewell to you both."

Bofu and Gongjin rose, exchanged bows with Elder Qiao and said as one, "Farewell until next time, Elder Qiao."

Elder Qiao bowed slightly, and the two young suitors retreated from the hotel.

"We nearly messed that up a few times, Gongjin," Bofu sighed as the friends walked through the streets.

"I've… never been caught off-guard like that," Gongjin replied. "I didn't know where to look! My heart was in my throat! I had silly poems in my head and no sensible words to go with them!"

"Yeah, well, at least we didn't say anything stupid to them," Bofu suggested.

"…Were you not spirited away by them…?" Gongjin asked.

"Don't ask me that!" Bofu whined.

"But I've been honest with you, Bofu," Gongjin retorted.

"Of course I was 'spirited away'!" Bofu replied desperately. "They were perfect! They were so perfect that I couldn't think straight! It… it scared me."

"…It scared you to be enraptured by your future wife…?" Gongjin chortled.

"No, it…! …It… it scared me to be distracted," Bofu admitted. "I'll be thinking about them all day, now… if I needed to lead an army, I wouldn't be able to concentrate."

"…We'll learn to live with that I think," Gongjin said. "Don't other men with wives as beautiful as that…?"

"Yeah, but then aren't we becoming less 'enraptured'…?" Bofu retorted.

"Not at all, no!" Gongjin insisted. "It… I mean… the…!"

"…We're both completely muddle-headed," Bofu complained. "The oldies will laugh at us… in fact, won't everyone laugh at us?"

"Not when they see why," Gongjin replied. "Now enough of that, Bofu… let's get our matchmakers sorted out and plan for the journey back."

"…What about Shangxiang?" Bofu asked suddenly. "She might-!"

"Oh, don't start worrying about Shangxiang now!" Gongjin pleaded. "Nothing will go wrong! Calm down!"

"…*Aiee*; I've climbed walls, run at horses, crawled through a river of bodies, braved arrows, had duels with Shanyue chiefs… but never, *never* have I felt as sick, as nervous – no, as *terrified* – as I do now," Bofu admitted. "Did Dad feel like this, I wonder…? Seeing him with Mum, and how she could talk to him… maybe, yeah. But… but does that mean I'll be letting Lady Qiao talk to *me* like that…?"

"If you love someone, and I think that our feelings will turn to true

love very quickly – I know that mine will – you are utterly candid, truly free in their company, and you find a comfort that we cannot find in even the best of friends," Gongjin replied. "I have long pined for the day that I could have such companionship, for... and please excuse me for saying this, friend and brother... nothing else is like it."
"Hark at you, Mister Soppy!" Bofu chuckled. "Don't let Cheng Demou hear you say that!"
"Right now, even the snide asides that I can expect from Cheng Pu are not going to ruin how I feel," Gongjin retorted. "I've too much to look forward to."
"...Yeah," Bofu said. "Yeah, I... I'm looking forward to it too."

Bofu and Gongjin were still distracted by thoughts of the Qiao sisters when they returned to Danyang by boat: that was something that amused their allies immensely after several years of seeing them both as almost unshakable.

****

Bofu and Gongjin were decidedly nervous as they entered the great hall of the Sun family residence: most of their Danyang-based relations were in attendance, including Bofu's siblings Yi, Kuang and Shangxiang, Bofu's mother Lady Wu and his late father's consort Lady Chen, Bofu's cousin Xu Kun, Bofu's maternal uncle Wu Jing and Gongjin's uncle Zhou Shang.

"My son...!" Lady Wu cried.

"...Mother," Bofu replied humbly.

Lady Wu hugged Bofu tightly once he was within range.

"You're gonna get *married*?" Shangxiang scoffed. "Is she weak...?"

"Shangxiang!" Lady Wu exclaimed.

"If, by 'weak', you mean that she wears women's clothes and doesn't beat everyone up all the time, then yeah, little sister, she's weak," Bofu replied.

"...Is she pretty?" Shangxiang asked.

"Oh, she's more than pretty," Bofu replied carelessly. "She's...! ...Uh, she's... she's 'pretty', Shangxiang, she's pretty."

"...There were two, right...? How did you choose which one you were going to have?" Shangxiang asked snidely.

"Ayah! Don't ask that in front of-! ...I-I mean, look, I suppose you feel that it was all a bit unfair for them, and maybe if we'd not liked each other, then it would have been," Bofu replied awkwardly. "Sister, I... look, Gongjin, you talk to her."

Gongjin smiled and said, "Shangxiang, when we met – the Qiao sisters, your brother and I – we were able to see each other and make decisions. Bofu and I were besotted straight away, and they seemed to like us very much, too."

"Why wouldn't they?" Lady Wu scoffed. "You're both so handsome!"

Gongjin groaned and covered his face with his sleeve.

"Sit, sit!" Lady Wu ordered as she turned and took her place to the left of the host seat: Bofu took the host seat, and Gongjin sat to his right.

"What do they like...?" Shangxiang asked once everyone was seated.

"...*Gongjin*...?" Bofu whispered desperately.

Gongjin laughed and said, "They are both readers, and they like poetry and music, as most people do, Shangxiang. The younger Lady Qiao – my choice – shares an interest in fine art, poetry and music, while the elder Lady Qiao – who Bofu couldn't take his eyes away from – is also an admirer of music and poetry."

"...Ce can't write poems, or sing, or play an instrument that well: all he can do is fight," Shangxiang noted.

"I like poetry!" Bofu retorted. "I'll read other people's stuff to her! I'll have a musician play for us if I can't learn to play an instrument! *Aiee*... why are you being like this...?"

"I just want to know that she'll like you properly, so you'll be happy, Big Brother," Shangxiang replied. "When she isn't as pretty and you're not as strong, what then?"

"...Mother, help me!" Bofu cried.

"Silly boy," Lady Wu chortled. "Shangxiang, your father and I were... never really able to spend much time together. Lady Qiao will be a mother, and raise her children. That's how-"

"Will you get another younger, prettier wife when she gets old, like Father did when Mother got old...?" Shangxiang asked as she looked at Lady Chen.

"**Now that's enough!**" Lady Wu shouted. "**Apologise to my honorary sister!**"

"...I am sorry, Lady Chen," Shangxiang said quietly.

"I am not offended," Lady Chen promised. "But sister, Shangxiang has a right to ask. I was not popular when I first came into your household, and-"

"Now, you are my sister, and I'll not have you slandered," Lady Wu insisted. "If Bofu decides, at a later date, to take another wife, or a *hundred wives*, then so be-"

"*Ayah*! I don't even have *one* wife yet! Give me a chance, everyone!" Bofu pleaded.

Wu Jing laughed and said, "Nephew, I am delighted to see you wed at last. You have been so cruelly held from such things for so long, you and your friend..."

Wu Jing turned to his eldest son, Wu Fen, who said, "Cousin, you're shaking!"

"Am I...?" Bofu chuckled. "I must be... cold."

"You and I both if you are, Bofu," Gongjin said. "Are we gathered here for a banquet?"

"I will have food brought, yes," Lady Wu replied. "When will I meet my daughter-in-law, Bofu...?"

"...They're on their way," Bofu replied cautiously.

"Ah... I know that tone," Lady Wu said. "I will not call you 'Bofu' in front of Elder Qiao or either of his lovely daughters, and I will not do anything that is against etiquette... not, at least, until after you are wed!"

"...But after that, anything goes," Bofu sighed.

"Everyone will have to accept the way things are done here in Jiangdong, and also the little things that make us imperfect," Lady Wu retorted. "Or do you intend to live a lie once you are married...?"

Bofu turned to look at Shangxiang and said, "As much as I'd like to hide some people permanently... I suppose you're right."

Shangxiang stuck her tongue out and shouted, "**How many wives will you have?**"

"*One*, alright, *one*, if it'll mean that you'll leave me alone!" Bofu replied.

Shangxiang smirked and said, "I don't believe you. Gongjin is sensitive, but *you're not.*"

Gongjin stifled laughter.

"...I'm not sensitive...?" Bofu asked with mock offence.

"You're like *all the boys*!" Shangxiang giggled. "You're like *Quan*, and *Yi*, and-!"

"**Hey!**" the frail Sun Kuang exclaimed. "*I'm* sensitive! What have I ever-?"

"*Speaking*... of *Quan*... we need to summon him here, do we not...?" Lady Wu noted. "He, as your eldest brother, cannot miss this, Bofu."

"I'll write to him personally," Bofu promised.

Marriage preparations began immediately, and everything was

ready by the time that Sun Ben – who left subordinates at the front in Lujiang – had personally escorted the Qiao family to a hotel in Danyang's capital. The Qiao sisters were visited by Lady Wu, who had successfully argued that she should act as matchmaker for her son: she returned to the family home in a strange mood.

"...Why that face....?" Bofu asked as his mother took her seat in the grand hall.

"She... they... are like Heaven-sent creatures, Bofu," Lady Wu replied. "What can I say...? They melt the heart, and even the older men that have learned manners are forced to look as they pass. I can see why they have had such an effect on you and Gongjin... but thankfully, I see no 'Daji' lurking in either of them. They are very pleasant, in fact: enviably beautiful yet charmingly good-natured, devoid of the vanity that one would expect to go with such looks."

"Gongjin's quite funny," Bofu chuckled. "He starts composing poems at random these days, saying that Younger Lady Qiao 'inspires him'. But... well, I shouldn't laugh, since I think about little else at the moment than Elder Lady Qiao's smile."

"Their father is very nice also," Lady Wu said. "They are almost too good to be true, aren't they...? And yet they are exactly what they appear to be: Heaven-sent for two young heroes that deserve some luck after so long. Ah yes! Quan..."

"...I've written to Quan, and I expect him to come here straight away rather than reply first," Bofu replied. "I should warn you, though, that..."

"...That he's grown up as a result of his role in Yangxian, but that I might not recognise him...?" Lady Wu said tactfully.

"...That's a very nice way of putting it," Bofu sighed.

"Every parent has that moment when they wonder who their children are," Lady Wu suggested. "Every person is an individual: I did not raise any of you to be another me or a copy of your father, and I would not have gotten copies of us if I'd tried to. Quan is Quan: he's still my son, and that is that."

"...As long as you know, I've done my part," Bofu replied.

Gongjin travelled to Lu Su's home and enjoyed a quiet afternoon with his friend and benefactor.

"You, ready to join the ranks of the married men...!" Lu Su teased.

"So you've said twice already, Zijing," Gongjin sighed.

"When is it, again...?" Lu Su asked.

"I never said," Gongjin replied.

"...I know you didn't," Lu Su said awkwardly. "Can it be that I will not be invited to attend, Gongjin...?"

"You'll be there, and as an honoured guest," Gongjin replied. "But it changes nothing politically, Zijing: you'll not enjoy high rank from Bofu."

"Oh, look, I really don't care," Lu Su chuckled. "I'm happy here in Jiangdong! My family is happy! I may not have high rank, but I still have some of my fortune, so we're not going to starve any time soon. And perhaps, one day, I'll do something to win over your friend and my lord, and then things will change."

"Perhaps," Gongjin replied.

"...It feels a bit strange that we're celebrating two weddings in the middle of a dynastic crisis, but I suppose that life goes on," Lu Su said. "How does Taishi Ci fare against Liu... Pan, was it...?"

"It was," Gongjin replied. "Taishi's employing all of his famed tactics against Liu Pan. He's an asset that we cannot now imagine living without, I'm surprised to say."

"So Taishi is routing Liu Pan, Liu Xun is isolated, and Yuan Shu is near to defeat," Lu Su noted. "My, how things have moved on! Lü Bu is gone, Zhang Yang is gone, Li Jue and Guo Si are gone, Gongsun Zan is close to defeat too... and all the time, Lord Sun, Cao Cao and Yuan Shao grow and grow, and Liu Biao remains static. There's still *four*..."

"Ah, yes, your 'Tripod Theorem'," Gongjin chuckled.

"It isn't nonsense!" Lu Su insisted. "If, as we both suspect, the Han's power has near-irreversibly deteriorated, there are only two directions: one, a super-warlord becomes the guardian of the Han and nurtures it until it recovers; two, a super-warlord vanquishes all of his opponents and cultivates his own dynasty to supplant an exhausted Han. In either case, a warlord must be triumphant, and four will not sustain anything but chaos."

"And three is somehow a wonderful thing...?" Gongjin teased.

"Listen, listen!" Lu Su pleaded. "If, say, Yuan Shao were next to go, then there would be Liu Biao, Cao Cao and Lord Sun. If not Yuan, then Cao. Either way, those two are destined to come to blows, as we have discussed before. The end result is one super-warlord that governs Yan, Xu, Yu, Qing, Ji, Bing, Yòu and Central Provinces. That leaves the barbarian-run Liang, toady-run Yi, cultist-run Hanzhong, Liu Biao's Jing and Lord Sun in Jiangdong."

Gongjin frowned and said, "You're right about the outcome of the feud between Yuan and Cao... that would, as you say, leave a man with control of almost everything! How did I not see it???"

"You've been busy," Lu Su suggested.

"That's no excuse," Gongjin replied. "I'm Bofu's adviser! Alright, I know that Ziheng is more the Chief Strategist than I am, but I should have seen this! Jiangdong is vast, but can we hope to oppose a region with access to immense quantities of resource, trade with the foreign powers to the north, and up to half-a-million men-at-arms? The population of Jiangdong is so sparse that we'd struggle to amass fifty-thousand! If the victor of that Yuan-Cao feud turned their hungry gaze this way, we would be in serious trouble!"

"That's why there must be three," Lu Su insisted. "If there were three powers that hated each other, but had to have an option for alliances with one of the others, then we might stand a chance against that mighty power that will be Yuan or Cao."

"...Your idea is too dependent on luck and intriguing for my tastes," Gongjin retorted. "No, we must instead look at an alliance of Jiangdong, northern Yang, Yi, Hanzhong, Liang and Jing under a confederacy of like-minded warlords or under Lord Sun's sole command."

"And where are these 'like-minded warlords' now...?" Lu Su countered. "Liu Zhang...? Zhang Lu...? Ma Teng, Han Sui and Song Jian...? *Liu Bia-*"

"Your theory is no less outlandish," Gongjin scoffed. "Doesn't it imply an alliance between Lord Sun and Liu Biao...?"

"Your idea involves making promises to the untrustworthy, and having barbarians and cultists as our western pincer, which *doesn't work*!" Lu Su protested. "Liu Biao alone will be forced to make concessions to us, and-"

"And, if I recall, your plan involves either him or Bofu annexing Yi Province without, somehow, triggering any kind of response from Zhang Lu, the Qiang warlords in Liang Province, or the Nanman – remember them? – who will try and seize the place as soon as Liu Biao or Bofu stepped over the border," Gongjin heckled. "Zijing, leave it. Strategy is, like diplomacy, not one of your strong points."

"...I'm right," Lu Su insisted.

Gongjin exhaled fiercely and said, "Maybe you are, maybe you're not, but I'll be honest and say that right now, Zijing, I would rather think about my future wife and the quite-obviously-short time that we will have together before the insanity draws me in again."

"*Aiee*... Once again, I have been loose-tongued and ruined a happy moment!" Lu Su cried. "I am cursed to forever be a tactless idiot with no good employment!"

Gongjin smiled, laughed and said, "Oh, I don't know... maybe we'll need a well-paid fool as the court grows. You'd certainly entertain people if they thought you were joking."

****

110

The joint wedding of Bofu and Gongjin to the beautiful Qiao sisters was a grand affair, despite the troubles that surrounded Danyang. There were some that would not be able to attend: Taishi Ci was busy fighting Liu Pan in the northwest of Jiangdong; Bofu's friend Zhang Xun was too closely tied to Yuan Shu and besieged in Shouchun along with his master; Xu Gong and Hè Qi were once again forced to pacify a minor Shanyue rebellion in Wu Prefecture that had been encouraged by the fugitive White Tiger Yan; Sun Quan's friend Pan Zhang stayed away at Quan's recommendation and acted as guardian of Yangxian County in its magistrate's absence; Yuzhang Administrator Hua Xin stayed away for political reasons. But at the same time, most of Bofu's family and allies were able to be in Danyang, and that reunited old friends.

"Here we all are, to see the son of our lord and friend wedded at last!" Cheng Pu said to Huang Gai, Han Dang and Zhu Zhi. "To see you all again, it warms my heart; we've all gone grey, though!"

Han Dang rubbed his beard and said, "So we have, Demou."

"Our sons are all growing fast, Demou," Huang Gai noted. "Soon, we'll be passing our legacy on to them as Wentai did, only not so terribly early."

"Oh, I'll be fighting until I'm *white-haired*, Gongfu!" Cheng Pu chuckled. "Death is the only thing that will take me away from what we're doing!"

"So what about the whole thing being a double wedding, uh…?" Han Dang asked.

"Lord Sun Ce and Zhou Yu are like brothers," Zhu Zhi replied. "It seems that Lord Sun Quan and my own son Ran are much the same, which is nice."

"Yeah, but them marrying a pair of sisters is a little odd," Han Dang said.

"Not really," Huang Gai suggested. "There have been men that have married multiple sisters, have there not…?"

"Yeah, s'pose, but that's one man doing that: this is them two marrying sisters, but then how will their children marry each other, as friends like them often like to see?" Han Dang proposed. "They couldn't, could they?"

"They obviously see themselves as true brothers," Zhu Zhi replied.

"I admit, I still don't like 'Gongjin'," Cheng Pu muttered.

Zhu Zhi laughed and said, "He has not mellowed you, yet, then, Demou…?"

"That little pedant criticised the musicians at the last banquet I held!" Cheng Pu retorted. "Little creep, he stopped them in the middle of a nice piece and when asked why, he said, 'They got a note wrong'. My guests were all so embarrassed!"

"All of them…?" Zhu Zhi teased.

"…Well no, but *I was*!" Cheng Pu grumbled. "So what if they got a note wrong? He was drunk anyway, so how can we be sure that he even heard right…?"

"Young Zhou does, it has to be said, have a flawless ear," Huang Gai said. "And when he plays the *qin* himself, it is quite magnificent. I don't know if there's another man alive that could keep pace when he does a 'free-style' piece that goes this way and that: completely improvised, and yet perfect, note after note after note."

"...Enough about 'Gongjin'!" Cheng Pu pleaded. "I care nothing for that northern pedant! Let him marry the spare sister! I'm here for Lord Sun!"

Zhu Zhi and Huang Gai snickered quietly.

"Are they really as beautiful as I've heard...?" Han Dang asked.

"...Whatever you heard, treble it," Cheng Pu replied. "Lord Sun and 'Gongjin' have really been blessed."

"What would truly bless them," Zhu Zhi said seriously, "is if we no longer needed to rely on the likes of Xu Gong, and if Yuan Shu would kindly consign himself to history a little faster, and if Cao Cao, Yuan Shao and Liu Biao would kindly do the same so the Sun family can share their brilliance with the rest of the country."

"That's a valid point: no sooner are those two married than they'll be hurled into an inevitable battle between the warlords after Yuan Shu dies," Cheng Pu said. "But with us grey-haired men to be his brains, boots, sword and shield, Lord Sun will not need to fight as hard as his father if he doesn't want to."

"He does, of course, have the next generation to help him as well," Zhu Zhi suggested. "He has my son Ran, Jiang Qin, Zhou Tai, Chen Wu, Ling Cao, Lü Meng, Dong Xi, Hè Qi, Li Shu, Yu Fan..."

"And a wealth of new advisers and politicians of all ages, like the two Zhangs, Gu Yong, Quan Rou, Qin Song and Lü Dai," Huang Gai said.

"We are still his most experienced minds," Cheng Pu retorted. "There is no substitute for experience."

"We all agree, Demou, and so does Lord Sun," Zhu Zhi insisted. "Now let us retire to our rooms and prepare for this most wonderful of occasions."

Sun Quan met with his friend Zhu Ran and walked the grounds of the Sun family estate with him.

"I wonder when I will find my Heaven-sent beauty, Yifeng," Sun Quan sighed.

"You'll find the right person when the time is right, Zhongmou," Zhu Ran replied. "Now, if you don't mind me asking..."

After a short silence, Sun Quan laughed condescendingly and said, "Ask, then!"

"...You do not look well," Zhu Ran noted. "Is there a reason that you can share with a concerned friend...?"

Sun Quan was pallid, and his complexion was poor; he grunted irritably and replied, "I do not get to go out in the fresh air much these days, what with work and... and what I now see as 'play'."

"...Ah, so you are merely a victim of enclosure through your lifestyle," Zhu Ran chuckled. "I was worried that you might be stricken with something!"

Sun Quan smiled gratefully and said, "You... were not going to remonstrate...?"

"It wouldn't be my place, even if it were necessary, Zhongmou," Zhu Ran replied. "I am aware that we are, in a sense, lord and vassal as well as friends, and I wouldn't dare be so vulgar as to reprimand my lord for life choices."

"It's friends like you that I need!" Sun Quan declared. "People like

Lü Fan, they act as though they are the lord rather than the vassal, or perhaps a judgemental parent! I am the younger brother of Sun Ce, and yet that pedant acts like I am a naughty nephew just because my mother extended him too much courtesy! You understand the way of things, and he does not!"
Zhu Ran hummed thoughtfully.
"We two must work together more often in the future," Sun Quan continued. "We must- ...Oh, but is that...! ...It is! **ZHOU YOUPING!**"
Sun Quan had spotted Zhou Tai arriving at the estate: he abandoned any noble graces and ran toward the former pirate, almost tripping on his own gown several times as he did so.
"...Lord Sun Quan," Zhou Tai said as Sun Quan stopped in front of him and grabbed his arms tightly.
"Zhou Youping...! Zhou Youping...!" Sun Quan gasped. "You look so well! Oh, how I worried that you would-!"
"**Ah, Youping,**" Bofu hailed.
Sun Quan's eyes dimmed; he released Zhou Tai and stepped aside so that his elder brother could greet his visitor.
"Lord Sun," Zhou Tai said humbly.
"You've made a full recovery, as you'd insisted," Bofu replied. "That's good... and I see that my brother ran over here to greet you and no doubt apologise for taking you away from the action for so long. But it isn't necessary, since we all make mistakes!"
"Lord Sun Quan was not at fault!" Zhou Tai protested.
"No, Zhou Youping... I was," Sun Quan said. "You almost lost your life because I was... being a fool."
Zhu Ran had arrived moments before: he bowed to Bofu and said, "Lord Sun, congratulations."
"My thanks," Bofu replied. "Quan, you-"
"I shall leave you to talk with Zhou Tai," Sun Quan interrupted: he then turned to Zhou Tai, bowed slightly and said, "It is good that you are well again. May you be given a more worthy master next time."
Sun Quan turned about and walked away without paying respects to Bofu; Zhu Ran bowed twice as though he were doing so for both of them and followed his friend.
"...Zhou Youping, you've suffered greatly due to my errors of judgement," Bofu suggested. "In the future, you can expect those rewards of official posts that I promised you some time ago. You'll lead elite groups of men until the trouble is ended, and then you'll enjoy a quieter time."
"I would sweat blood if I had to, Lord Sun!" Zhou Tai insisted. "I am happy to remain on the front lines!"
"...If you insist, then I want you to be part of my vanguard when I attack Liu Biao," Bofu replied. "We'll discuss it closer to the time. Is that a gift you're holding...?"
Zhou Tai smiled meekly and said, "It isn't much, Lord Sun, but...!"
"...Etiquette aside, you needn't have, Youping," Bofu replied. "You gave me 'your life in the balance' when you protected my brother from himself... that's a gift that will never leave me."
"Lord Sun...!" Zhou Tai wheezed.
Bofu patted Zhou Tai's arm and said, "Come and meet my mother, Youping: she's been wanting to thank you for quite a while now."

Lü Fan met with Gongjin, Dong Xi, Gu Yong and Lu Su in a tavern.

"...Still no big role, then, Lu Su...?" Lü Fan teased.

"No," Lu Su replied quietly.

Gu Yong sipped his heated tea and said, "In the future, there will be the need for more and more men of talent and-or good nature."

"...I wish those men luck," Lu Su grumbled.

Gongjin laughed and said, "You'll get to where you should be eventually, Zijing. Now, what's this I hear about more potential recruits to the political and advisory wing of our growing enterprise...?"

"A young man by the name of Lu Xun, and a fellow by the name of Zhuge Jin have come to my attention," Lü Fan replied. "I'm hoping to use the first court session after the wedding to bring them into the fold."

"...Lu Xun...?" Gongjin prompted.

"Neither man comes without problems," Gu Yong said plainly.

"Oh...?" Gongjin exclaimed. "In what way are they problematic, and if so, then why do we consider them...?"

"Lu Xun is a future genius, as is his cousin, who is even more problematic," Gu Yong said.

"Why are we worried about problematic people...?" Lu Su chortled.

Gongjin glared at Lu Su.

"...*Aiee*... *I* am problematic, and yet I say such things aloud!" Lu Su cried.

"In what way are they problematic?" Dong Xi prompted.

Lü Fan sipped his wine and said, "Lu Xun is the great nephew of *Lu Kang*, the former Administrator of Lujiang."

"*That* Lu Xun??? ...Why do we consider him then, for Heaven's sake???" Gongjin exclaimed.

"He is, as I have said, a genius worthy of employ," Gu Yong replied. "If we do not recruit him, others will. The same goes for Lu Kang's young son, who is here in Jiangdong with Lu Xun. Neither bears a grudge, and we would be fools to ignore them, just as we would have been fools to reject Liu Ji."

"...Fine," Gongjin sighed. "And Zhuge Jin...?"

"He is a relation of the former Administrator of Mount Tai, I presume...?" Lu Su said.

"And a relation of a former Administrator of Yuzhang," Lü Fan replied. "The Zhuge clan are mid-to-high-ranking Han officials historically, but they appear to have suffered from the changes of recent years, as the Zhou clan have."

"I empathise, then," Gongjin sighed. "So why is he problematic...?"

"...It's where he's come from to find work, but we can worry about that later," Lü Fan suggested. "We're here to toast your fortune, Gongjin, and discuss positive things for a while."

"Then we shall do so," Gongjin replied. "Two days now..."

The Sun family estate was a scene of great joy when the wedding day arrived at last: red was the most prominent colour on show, as was the custom, and there were red flags billowing in every visible direction. Bofu's mother Lady Wu, Gongjin's uncle, Zhou Shang, and Elder Qiao sat in host seats as the matchmakers; the guests were seated according to their prominence in the

Jiangdong regime, with close family and figures like Cheng Pu, Zhang Zhao, Zhang Hong, Zhu Zhi and Lü Fan enjoying seats close to the matchmakers. A Taoist priest in plain robes awaited his moment silently and proudly.

The grooms arrived individually, and the Qiao sisters arrived together: once all four were present, they walked through the grounds, into the hall, and presented themselves to the matchmakers and the priest that would bless their unions. Both brides and both grooms were dressed in red, elaborately-patterned robes; the women wore red veils, while the men wore black mortarboard hats. The priest immediately gave his blessings, and then the two couples sat before their matchmakers. After the customary declarations of devotion to their parents and to the heavens, the last vows were taken, and the event was over: Bofu was now married to the older sister – known sometimes as 'Daqiao', or 'Older/Bigger Qiao' – and Gongjin was married to the younger sister, who was sometimes referred to as 'Xiaoqiao' or 'Younger/Smaller Qiao'. Celebrations began across the city, and the newlyweds enjoyed their first days together as though the world was at peace.

"...I am content."
Gongjin laughed softly after saying the words and continued to strum the strings of his *qin* while his wife Xiaoqiao looked on with loving eyes.
"...You and I, we were paired by Heaven," Gongjin continued. "It can only be so, it is all that makes sense, for... for I feel too undeserving."
"You are a wonderful man!" Xiaoqiao replied. "Your skills are without number, and everyone loves you..."
"...Except Cheng Pu," Gongjin joked. "He even sneered at me after we gave our vows. He'd be glad to see me buried at the earliest opportunity, I think. But I don't care! We have been married for two days only, and yet I feel like there is nothing left to do, even with everything that must still be done. If someone asked me right now, I would smile and say 'Everything is perfect'."
"...But you will have to go away soon," Xiaoqiao supposed.
"Oh, no-no-no!" Gongjin chuckled. "Not for a few days, or even a few weeks: Sun Ben and Sun Fu have returned to Lujiang, Dong Xi and Yu Fan will soon return to Kuaiji, and so on and so on, but Bofu and I have the opportunity to rest, for once. It is not selfish, I think: every other man has had his moment to build a family, and now we are to have ours."
"It feels strange being away from my sister," Xiaoqiao admitted.
"...A union is often paired with a parting," Gongjin replied. "It is the way of things... Heaven deems it so. One can never have everything, not all at once at least. One must leave some things behind to go forward, or leave one home to join another. It is not like the day before: your sister is not far from here, and you will have plenty of opportunities to be reunited, for Bofu and I are like brothers, and in peacetime, we are at ease when sharing a kettle of wine in the same room."
"...But I am happy," Xiaoqiao promised. "Like you, I am happier."
Gongjin stopped playing, looked at Xiaoqiao and said, "Heaven denies us words for how we truly feel, so 'happy'... which does not

begin to tell the story... will have to do."

That same night, Bofu was stood at the back of the Sun family estate, staring at the sky. Daqiao approached him and asked, "Are you not happy...?"
"That's the problem," Bofu replied. "I'm *too happy*... which doesn't seem right."
Daqiao grasped his right arm tightly.
"...My father was denied seeing this by Huang Zu, Kuai Liang, Cai Mao, Liu Biao, and Yuan Shu," Bofu continued. "He should be here. But he isn't. And that hurts, even though I'm happy. Do you see...? I'm happy, angry and sad at the same time, so... so I'm confused."
"But you are not disappointed...?" Daqiao prompted.
Bofu looked down and into Daqiao's eyes as he replied, "That would be impossible, my lady. You... you make me feel like I got a part of myself back that I never knew I had."
Daqiao smiled gratefully.
"...It's just... that I have to try and focus on what's left to do," Bofu said as he returned his gaze to the night sky. "However 'complete' I might feel, it's all still to do. Yuan Shu, Liu Biao... Cao Cao... and whoever and whatever else is out there. Part of me wants to just hand it all over to someone else, but... only I can do this. Maybe one day, I can trust Yi with some of it, but... not yet."
"...So when will you be starting again...?" Daqiao asked.
"Not for a few days, and even then it'll be court stuff," Bofu replied. "I have some new people to meet, but I won't be fighting for a long time yet."
Daqiao closed her eyes and whispered, "Good."
"...I have a future to build," Bofu continued, "and you're more a part of that than any fight, any meeting, any enemy, or any friend. Family – including Gongjin, who is my brother in all but blood and name – comes before everything."
"I want us to have a big family," Daqiao announced.
"...That won't be a problem," Bofu chuckled. "So do I; I wouldn't have it any other way."

For Bofu and Gongjin, life would never be the same again: both of the ambitious young heroes of the coming age could now start to build their lives and legacies completely, while their master Yuan Shu's grip on everything that he had been born into – financial wealth, social status and political power – continued to slip away.

****

111

Taishi Ci had been gaining ground against Liu Biao's nephew Liu Pan, but he was anxious to bring the campaign to an end.

"...I missed my friend's wedding, and that is the last insult," Taishi Ci said to his assembled officials. "Are our agents in place...?"

"They are, Commander Taishi," an officer replied.

"Liu Pan and Huang Zu will both wish they had stayed in Jiangxia and stuck to playing pirates with their friends," Taishi Ci continued. "We'll bait the trap today."

Liu Pan brought an elite force to a small fishing village on the bank of the Yangtze and prepared to advance to one of the larger settlements; he had a small fleet of boats docked along the bank to provide offensive and defensive cover and began the usual process of locating and seizing resources.

"All goes well," a captain reported.

"And no sign of any resistance whatsoever this time!" Liu Pan chuckled. "It looks like Taishi Ci has given up, his reputation tarnished forever by our superior forces! How long will it be, I wonder, before the counties that we lost are regained...?"

"The people are just handing everything that we ask for over, so I think we've broken them," the captain added.

"We're looking at a new addition to Jing Province!" Liu Pan cackled. "Uncle will be most pleased!"

The preparations continued, and nothing prevented them.

Liu Pan began his eastward march on schedule, and nothing opposed it. He stopped at the first town that he reached, and once again, there was no resistance at all.

"...I don't like it," one adviser said.

"What's not to like?" Liu Pan chuckled. "We've broken them! That's all there is to it!"

"But there's word that their lord Sun Ce has begun marriage preparations and started to build a state," the adviser retorted.

"Then what we're seeing is a misallocation of resources that will cost Sun Ce dearly!" Liu Pan replied. "He's either lost the support of these people from undertaking in self-indulgent activity, or he's diverted men away from here – including Taishi, perhaps – for his wedding! Either is fatal!"

"...Taishi Ci is known for his cunning," the adviser suggested.

"And where was his cunning when Sun Ce defeated him and forced him to work for him?" Liu Pan retorted. "Maybe Taishi has let us take this place to spite his unwanted master!"

The adviser sighed desperately and ceased his remonstrations.

"We'll sack this place and move on, since there is nobody to fight us!" Liu Pan declared. "We'll charge at the heart of this place and seize it for Governor Liu!"

Liu Pan's officials mumbled disconcertedly, but they did not offer arguments either.

Liu Pan's forces were advancing from different settlements along the eastern bank of the Yangtze as it wound from north to south: none of those forces were reporting any resistance as they moved deeper and deeper into northwest Yang. Taishi Ci waited until the enemy had stretched their forces and moved them far from the safety of the riverbank before he finally gave the order to retaliate: that operation would take place at night, when the complacent Liu Pan was asleep in his field command tent.

    "FIRE!"

"Wha-uh...? What...? *Fire*...?" Liu Pan mumbled sleepily.

The captain that had raised the alarm pulled Liu Pan from his bed and shook him violently, saying, **"Fire, Commander Liu! FIRE!"**

"Fire!" Liu Pan exclaimed. "We've been tricked after all!"

Liu Pan left his tent and surveyed the camp: many of the outer tents were ablaze, and Taishi's horsemen were galloping about, cutting down his men in every direction.

"*Ayah*! He's made an idiot of me!" Liu Pan whined. **"We have to flee!"**

A frantic retreat began while a few brave men fought Taishi's ambush force and protected the rest.

"Now he'll see what a real commander is!" Taishi Ci declared as he stopped outside the abandoned command tent: a ring of men surrounded the enclosure, but it did not fool Taishi Ci, who said, **"Liu Pan's not there and I know it, so don't bother! Put your weapons down, men of Jing Province! He isn't worth your lives!"**

The Jing soldiers surrendered quietly.

Liu Pan's retreat brought him to a village that he had recently sacked. This time, however, the villagers were armed, and they chased the demoralised Jing men away with arrows and an improvised infantry battalion armed with farming tools.

"D'AAAAGH! Taishi has made lions out of mice!" Liu Pan cried as he was forced, yet again, to turn and flee.

Liu Pan's forces had not been able to secure any of their ill-gotten supplies before they had fled: they were becoming increasingly desperate, and they vowed that the next settlement would succumb so that they could eat and rest. But at every village and town that they stopped at, the situation was the same: Taishi Ci had supplied the people with defence training, and they were effective enough to force the Jing invaders to retreat. The various forces gradually coalesced as they neared their bases by the riverbank, and they stopped close to one defiant town to set up a field camp and rest.

"...Taishi Ci will die for this," Lui Pan muttered.

"We suffered the same fate as you, Commander," a major said. "Every place we went through offered no resistance until we reached a city, and then it all changed."

"Taishi might think that he is clever, but when we have reorganised, he will know differently!" Liu Pan replied angrily. "I swear, gentlemen, that-!"

"AMBUSH!"

"...No," Liu Pan bleated. "He- He couldn't have caught up with us...!"

"An ambush is an ambush! Who cares if it's him or not?" a second major grumbled as he got to his feet and ran out of the command tent to rally his men.

"...**Go, the rest of you, go!**" Liu Pan ordered. "**I will follow!**"
Every military officer fled the tent, leaving Liu Pan and his team of three irritated advisers.
"...We'll turn this around," Liu Pan insisted feebly.
"But for now, we should retreat to the boats," his lead adviser suggested.
"I... I should have listened to you before," Liu Pan replied. "Alright, we'll retreat to the river..."
Liu Pan fled once again as his men defended the camp against an attack by a small contingent of Taishi's trained cavalry and local townspeople armed with whatever they could find: this humiliating defeat weighed heavy on Liu Pan as he continued his flight to the riverbank.

"No... **NO, HE...!** ...*He*...!" Liu Pan whined when he saw the destruction for himself: his scouts had already reported that a large number of his boats had been sabotaged, but he had not expected that the small fleet had, in fact, been decimated.
"We're most of us trapped here now without these boats, and when the low-ranking soldiers figure out that it will be 'important figures get to leave, the rest can stay and die', there will be mutiny," the lead adviser suggested.
"...Taishi has ruined me," Liu Pan replied. "If the men hacked my body to pieces, it would make no difference now: my reputation is already in pieces, and that means I'm good for nothing now."
"That sort of thinking doesn't save lives!" the adviser hissed. "*Do something*!"
"We'll need to have help," Liu Pan replied. "Huang Zu and Kuai Yue can help us. A force of men – of ranks high and low, for fairness – will take the boats and go to Xiakou, while the rest of us fortify the bank and move inland to avoid being trapped with our backs to the water, and wait for help. Taishi was with the force that attacked us first, so he's not far behind us and sure to be here soon."
"That'll do," the adviser sighed. "We'll begin preparations."

Taishi Ci was quietly impressed by the late show of organisation by Liu Pan's battered forces: he smiled and said, "I'll not kill him here, but I've won all the same."
One cavalry captain smirked and said, "Shall we charge?"
"...Keep your eyes open, but yes," Taishi Ci replied. "I'll come with you. **Infantry will hold, in case this man is now listening to his advisers a little too well. FORWARD!**"

****

Bofu's court received the report on Taishi Ci's success and Liu Pan's humiliation a week later.

"...My first day back at court, and I get good news like this: a very good start!" Bofu chuckled.

"Everything is going very well," Lü Fan agreed. "And today, we hope to add a few more names to our list of talents."

Zhang Zhao smiled falsely and said, "Might they include 'Lu Xun' and 'Zhuge Jin', Mister Lü Fan...?"

Lü Fan's eyes steeled as he replied, "They would, Mister Zhang."

Bofu noticed that Sun Quan – who had delayed his return to Yangxian County – was not completely awake or sober: Bofu leant sideways, nudged his brother and whispered, "What's your explanation...?"

"...That we're not in Yangxian...?" Sun Quan retorted.

Bofu harrumphed and turned his attention back to the meeting: three men had entered the hall and were awaiting introduction.

"My lord, may I first introduce Mister Lu Xun and Mister Zhuge Jin," Lü Fan declared as he gestured toward the two robed men that were stood to his right.

Bofu frowned and said, "Two names for three men...?"

"Mister Wei is being elevated for good work," Lü Fan replied as he gestured toward the small and unremarkable man to his left.

"I see," Bofu said as he viewed his latest recruits with interest: one man had a long head that was strangely reminiscent of an equine form, and the other had round, boyish features that did not do him credit as a future leader of men.

"...My lord...?" Lü Fan prompted nervously.

"Zhuge Jin... 'Zhuge' is an interesting name," Bofu said as he stared at the long-headed man in his late 20s. "Do you always look so miserable?"

The other officials stifled laughter or tried to hide their despair at their ruler's enduring frankness by covering their faces.

"Yes," Zhuge Jin replied.

"I meant no offence, Mister Zhuge: it's just that I want everyone to be happy!" Bofu said cheerfully.

Lü Fan smiled and asked with mock ignorance, "So are you in any way, perchance, related to the former Administrator of Yuzhang, Zhuge Xuan?"

"He was my uncle," Zhuge Jin replied. "My father, who is also deceased, was once in an official role in Mount Tai Prefecture."

"...Mount Tai...? That's in Qing Province," Bofu noted. "You Zhuges get about! Your father and uncle were officials at opposite ends of the country! So whatever happened to your uncle then?"

"He... he journeyed to Jing Province," Zhuge Jin admitted.

Bofu's expression changed.

"Don't judge him!" Lü Fan pleaded.

"If he's got a really good reason why I shouldn't send his head back to Liu Biao, whole or in pieces, then I won't," Bofu growled.

"When the wicked villain Cao Cao attacked Xu Province, the suffering spilt into Qing!" Zhuge Jin explained desperately. "Our family had enjoyed status, yes, under the *Han*! We have always been loyal to the *Han*! We fled to the only place that enjoyed neutrality in the north, Jing Province, and settled in Longzhong! But my father died, and my uncle was forced to travel northward to raise us, for we were too young to-"

"You're far too old to need raising," Bofu scoffed.

"...Sorry, my haste made me mix events up," Zhuge Jin said.

"*Fear*, you mean," Zhang Zhao heckled.

"Stop it, Zhang Zhao," Lü Fan scolded. He then turned to the nervous Zhuge Jin and said with warmth, "Please, Mister Zhuge, continue your explanation."

"My uncle was forced to leave his post here in Jiangdong when I was nineteen... that would be eight years ago or thereabouts," Zhuge Jin said carefully. "That was when my father died... Mother died three years before that. So our uncle raised the five of us."

"You needed 'raising' at nineteen?" Zhang Zhao cackled. "Mister Zhuge, you make a mockery of northern men! Were you infirm?"

Some of the southern officials laughed unsympathetically.

"Amusing, but *petty*, Zhang Zhao," Bofu chortled. "Mister Zhuge, please carry on."

Zhuge Jin sighed and said, "If only for your amusement, Lord Sun. My younger brother, Liang, was left grief stricken, since he had to mourn both parents in quick succession; I have to confess, the loss of a mother that we loved and a father that we... that we *idolised*, Lord Sun... was heart-breaking, and yes... perhaps we were left like lost children. Even I, at nineteen, was left... empty."

Bofu pondered his own feelings of loss and said, "Anyone still laughing should stop."

That order only applied to Zhang Zhao, who lowered his head and feared for his safety.

"Go on, Mister Zhuge," Bofu said. "I know the loss of a much-loved father, and what it can do to a man's soul."

Zhuge Jin bowed humbly and said, "We were surviving, once the grief became manageable... and then Cao Cao invaded Xu Province. When we heard of the things that he did to the people of Xu, and that our own home was in danger, we feared the worst: and then, when he left the place, we heard that he'd left... well, nothing. Nothing at all."

"Taishi Ci is but one of many men that can verify that, having seen it with his own eyes as he travelled to Yang Province," Lü Fan noted helpfully.

Cheng Pu shook his head and said, "There was a time when Cao Cao was the talk of the land for his heroism, like Sun Wentai; now, he is the worst of villains, perhaps worse than Dong Zhuo. What can good men do...?"

"That's another conversation, Demou," Bofu said pointedly.

"Of course," Cheng Pu sighed.

"Go on, Mister Zhuge," Bofu said soberly. "We both know that Cao Cao went back again, and that Lü Bu, my father's enemy, decided to do good for once in his wretched life. Am I right in saying that it was the fight between those two that led your family to flee Qing and go to Jing?"

"You would be, Lord Sun," Zhuge Jin replied. "When we got there, Uncle immediately sought service with Liu Biao so that we would be provided for, little knowing - or, in our desperation, caring - for your feud with the man; Liu Biao proved to be petty and insincere, and he did not offer my uncle a high post. Not long after that, the stress of low rank compared to his previous appointments, coupled with the energy he expended bringing us across the country... wore him out, and after an illness, he died."

"A truly terrible thing," Bofu sighed.

"My thanks for saying so, my lord," Zhuge Jin said. "After that, I became the head of the household, and I knew that I had to ensure our family survived: my two sisters were blessed with good looks, so finding them husbands was not difficult."

"...Might I ask to whom they were married...?" Lü Fan said after a conspicuous silence.

Zhuge Jin laughed miserably and said, "I was afraid you'd ask that. One is married to a man of the prestigious Pang family, while the other is married to a member of the Kuai clan."

Bofu's expression changed again as he asked, "The same Kuai clan that formed the plan that...?"

"...I assume you refer to a 'plan' that led to your father's death," Zhuge Jin replied uneasily. "I'm afraid that I do mean the Kuais that advise Liu Biao. But I assure you, my lord, that it was intended to be a way to ensure their survival. But it did not lead to offers of work for me, so I left and came here."

"To be a *spy*...!" Zhang Zhao heckled. "**Spy!** You're here to serve your kinsman by marriage, Kuai Liang, and deliver another Sun corpse to Huang Zu!"

"Not so! Not so!" Zhuge Jin insisted. "I was ignored, so I left my home and my brothers Liang and Jun, and I came here to seek work! That is all there is to it! I am a servant of the Han, as my uncle was when he administrated Yuzhang!"

"Meaningless!" Zhang Zhao said. "Go back to Jing, fool! Your slow wits and loose tongue will not serve your master here!"

A few officials started to aid Zhang Zhao in heckling Zhuge Jin.

"**Wait,**" Bofu ordered.

The room fell silent.

"You'll get no high rank from me," Bofu said as he stared at Zhuge Jin. "But somewhere in you, I sense honesty and decency... I'm not the only one that sees it."

Lü Fan nodded silently.

"So here's the deal," Bofu continued. "You will serve me in a small capacity, and I'll pay you a low official's wage. If your brothers want work, then they can come here, but expect no high rank for them either. You'll be watched, and you'll not know *my* business or *your* privacy... understand...?"

Zhuge Jin kowtowed and said, "I am grateful for any help that I can get in aiding my family until the farm in Longzhong is profitable. The Pangs and Kuais offer no aid, for they doubt us as you do, perhaps because our uncle once administrated here in the south; when the farm is profitable, I promise that I shall go home and work there, and never bother you again."

"...Fine," Bofu said coldly. "You may go."

Zhuge Jin got to his feet and retreated silently and penitently.

"That wasn't a bad man," Bofu decided. "Watch him, as I said... if he ever proves that he's as honest as I suspect, then we'll employ him in a higher capacity."

"Don't do that!" Zhang Zhao protested. "He's-!"

"He's not a man of Jing: his family are Han retainers, like Gongjin's family," Bofu interrupted. "If they're that poor, then they weren't greedy and either gave away or abandoned the wealth when they fled Qing... the uncle could have brought them to the south, but instead he gave up his rank to care for them... that says something."

Many officials voiced their agreement.

"But his sister married a *Kuai*!" Zhang Zhao cried.

"*Enough*, Zhang Zhao," Bofu ordered. "If there's any way that we can find out more, do it: if he's sincere, then the Zhuge family could be of use to us in the future. Now, might we move on to the other fellow...? Lu Xun, wasn't it...?"

"He's fifteen if he's a day, sixteen at most," Zhang Zhao scoffed. "How can he be a politician?"

Sun Quan sat up, looked at Zhang Zhao and asked, "So what about *me*?"

"...That is quite right, my lord," Zhang Zhao conceded.

Bofu laughed, looked at the mortified Lü Fan and said, "Ziheng looks like he'd rather defer this introduction to another day. Who are *you* connected to, then, Mister Lu Xun...?"

The 15-year-old Lu Xun bowed low, smiled dryly, and said, "Lu Kang, the former Administrator of Lujiang: he was my grandfather's brother. Shall I leave now...?"

Many eyes turned to Lü Fan, who laughed nervously and said, "He is a great talent, Lord Sun, and he bears no-"

"Lü Fan has obviously given leave to his wits!" Zhang Zhao heckled. "First he gives us Zhuge Jin, a horse-faced spy from Liu Biao, and now *this*! How can we employ the great nephew of a man that our lord is blamed for ruining?"

"My brother is right!" Zhang Hong cried. "How can we do such a thing, Lord Sun?"

Liu Ji coughed deliberately and said, "How indeed, Brothers Zhang. We'll be employing the *sons* of such men next."

Cheng Pu started to laugh at the Zhangs, who were two men that he regarded as the worst of pedants.

"I... am merely concerned," Zhang Zhao insisted. "The welfare of Jiangdong is my only concern."

"...Lu Xun, I... I am truly touched that you would work with me after the terrible events in Huancheng," Bofu said sincerely. "I am, sadly, very much to blame for Lu Kang's early death, so if I can support your clan, I will."

"Lord Sun, Great Uncle Lu Kang made me promise to understand everything properly, and I do," Lu Xun insisted. "The monster Yuan Shu drove events at that time, and no man was free to act as they pleased. I agree that I am too young to take a place as an influential statesman, but I can certainly learn from the talents you have and become the next generation, if you so will it, Lord Sun. If you do not trust me, I completely understand: my life is in your hands."

"...I'd rather you put it in a different way," Bofu said awkwardly. "But, uh... we can certainly find a place for you in the civil administration. Perhaps Lü Fan would like to organise that, since he acquainted you with us...?"

"It would be my pleasure," Lü Fan insisted.

"Depart for now, then, and we'll meet again," Bofu said warmly, and after a series of polite bows, Lu Xun departed.

"...Is that man there going to introduce himself, or are we done for today...?" Bofu asked as he gestured toward the last of the three men that Lü Fan had brought to the court.

"Mister Wei Teng has been recommended as an Officer of Merit for his exemplary work," Lü Fan explained. "He has served for some time, and his work is indeed good."

Bofu smiled and said, "That's what I like to hear! You've obviously earned praise and reward, Mister Wei Teng."

"He will now be an even greater asset to us," Zhang Zhao said.

"I, Teng, am honoured to be serving my lord in a higher capacity," Wei Teng replied humbly.

"Keep working and you might continue to rise," Bofu said. "You may join your colleagues now, and thanks for your efforts."

Wei Teng bowed low before he joined the senior officials.

"Right, well... I know that a lot of you are going to be making your way back to your own domains over the coming days, so... so thank you all for coming, and may the fates be with us as we move forward," Bofu continued. "If there's nothing else...?"

"Anxious to be reunited with Lady Qiao, I imagine!" Wu Jing teased. "I shall take over the proceedings, Nephew: you go and enjoy married life."

"Might Gongjin also be excused, gentlemen...?" Bofu asked as he looked at his friend.

"...It's your court, Lord Sun," Gu Yong suggested.

The newly-appointed Officer of Merit Wei Teng gestured that he would like to speak, but he lowered his hand after receiving a stern glare from Lü Fan.

"So it is, Yuantan!" Bofu snickered. "C'mon, Gongjin: you look as bored as I am."

"I'm not bored, I'm *tired*," Gongjin whispered as the two men left the court together.

"...Ah, to be that age again," Zhu Zhi sighed.

"So does Lü Fan have any more enemy agents and silly-looking men to introduce, or will we be moving on to other matters now...?" Zhang Zhao asked snidely.

"Shut up, you snivelling pedant!" Cheng Pu barked. **"You're another Huan Jie! You criticise others, but at the first sign of trouble you'll-!"**

"That's enough, Demou," Zhu Zhi pleaded. "Mister Wu Jing, please continue."

Sun Quan got to his feet and left the hall via the rear entrance that led to the private meeting room once the proceedings had begun again: Lü Fan frowned at the lack of etiquette but did not interrupt the discussions.

****

113

Another week passed: Bofu arranged a senior-level meeting in his small private hall that would include his mother Lady Wu and her 'sister', the consort Lady Chen.

"...So what are we here to discuss, Bofu...?" Lady Wu asked.

"I think that the time for an attack on our enemy Liu Biao is coming," Bofu replied.

"Is it wise...?" Zhang Zhao asked.

"Is *anything* wise to you...?" Cheng Pu growled.

"Mister Cheng, I know you to be an incredibly brave and charming man that was a right arm to my dear, departed husband, but you are being unfair to Mister Zhang Zhao, who merely serves to ensure that there is proper debate rather than rash action that costs lives," Lady Wu said politely.

"But in answer to the question, the answer is 'I don't care one way or the other'," Bofu replied coldly. "Liu Biao killed my father."

"And I don't wish to now give him my son," Lady Wu retorted. "If there are reasons why it is unwise to attack him now, I should like to hear them."

"Yuan Shu is still alive, though reports suggest he won't last long," Zhang Zhao explained. "Cao Cao's intent is unknown, the tribes are still rising up in eastern Danyang and Wu, we have no idea what Cao Cao's appointed Administrator of Guangling, Chen Deng, is up to, Hua Xin's also untrustworthy, and there are still a lot of bandits and pirates that have refused to be pacified or recruited. If we attack Jing Province now, we risk being caught in a pincer at the very least."

"So I should just accept that he launched an attack on Yang Province that Taishi Ci's been fending off for us, and let him think he can do things like that and go unpunished...?" Bofu retorted. "And then there's the matter of who he might ally with in the future: Mister Zhang, it isn't even that you're being cowardly: you're just not thinking!"

"I agree," Cheng Pu said. "Jing Province is our neighbour, and the lord of that place is our enemy. That cannot continue."

"The future is all that we can focus on now," Gongjin volunteered. "If we sit here and do nothing about Liu Biao, he will either annex Yi, becoming a super-warlord like Cao Cao that will contend with Cao for this place or he will be swallowed by Cao, who will then turn his attentions to us."

"It is Chen Deng that I worry about, because he is a famous inconstant that betrayed Tao Qian, Liu Bei and Lü Bu in quick succession, but Cao Cao is the Han's most powerful statesman!" Zhang Zhao countered. "Yes, he has his faults, but he is, at present, the voice of the Han!"

"I have to concur!" Zhang Hong said. "To talk about opposing Excellency Cao is-!"

"There you go," Cheng Pu scoffed. "Didn't I say they'd act like this...? So much for 'The Two Zhangs are loyal to the last': if we have to fight Cao Cao, you can say goodbye to those little-"

"Mister Cheng, the Zhangs are most upright figures, spiritual as well as intellectual," Lady Wu interrupted. "Please do not be so discourteous."

"...*Spiritual*...?" Bofu said as he glared at the timid Zhang brothers.
"That's unimportant now," Lü Fan suggested. "Mister Zhang Zhao,
Lady Wu: Gongjin and I have discussed it at length in the past,
and in recent times, Mister Cheng Pu and Mister Huang Gai have
been kind enough to add their own ideas. This is not just about
revenge anymore: Liu Biao has attacked us. Liu Biao has sent men
into Yang Province and attacked villages and towns. He's done it
once, and even after Taishi Ci's chased them away, they'll do it
again. And again. And again, and again, and again, until we are
chipped down by it or retaliate, and if we dally, then yes, the
other threats that you speak of will rear their heads more
dangerously. Nobody wants a war with Liu Biao, but he's brought
it on himself with repeated insults and incursions!"
"...As you have stated, Jiangdong's security is threatened by Liu
Biao, perhaps by him more than anyone, and when put like that, I
cannot offer further remonstrance without making a mockery of
my role as political defender of Jiangdong," Zhang Zhao declared.
"If we are to do this thing, ladies and gentlemen, then it must be
safely done: every border watched, every bandit and pirate
accounted for and bribed to keep quiet if needs be, and everything
put to the best use."
"Well said, admittedly," Cheng Pu grumbled. "Who will stay and
who will go?"
"I want to throw as much at Liu Biao as I can," Bofu replied. "If I
could, I'd have all you oldies, and Ling Cao, Lü Meng, Hè Qi, Chen
Wu, Jiang Qin, Zhou Tai and Dong Xi, and Ziheng and Gongjin too,
of course: if Wu Jing, Xu Kun and Zhou Shang can hold Danyang,
and if Xu Gong held Wu, and Yu Fan held Kuaiji-"
"*Xu Gong*...?" Cheng Pu chortled. "Hè Qi can stay on duty and
keep an eye on him, and I think that Zhu Zhi should too, if I'm
really honest! That region is crawling with Shanyue, and Gong's
already teamed up with White Tiger once before!"
"And we haven't discussed the remit of this campaign," Zhang
Hong noted.
"I reluctantly agree," Gu Yong said. "Are we teaching Liu Biao a
lesson, or are we invading Jing Province with a view to annexing it
into Lord Sun's domains? The latter would not be appreciated by
the Han court."
"By *Cao Cao*, you mean," Bofu chuckled. "He's the Han court,
whether the Han court likes it or not."
"Whether we like Cao Cao or not, he is the man that represents
the Han, and I don't think that the Son of Heaven would like us
invading Jing either!" Zhang Zhao said.
"His Majesty didn't mind Cao Cao attacking Liu Biao, and we would
be doing it for the same reason: to pacify the region and bring a
traitor to justice," Gongjin suggested. "If Cao doesn't want Lord
Sun to govern Jing afterwards, fine: but slapping Huang Zu's face
and coming back home won't solve anything. Yes, ladies and
gentlemen, we have to, if you want to call it that, 'invade' Jing
Province, starting with Xiakou."
The last statement Bent was met with silence.
"...We all agree, or at least decline to disagree, then," Lü Fan
noted. "Then let us move on to the formalities... we'll want to be
ready the moment that Liu Pan and Huang Zu retreat, ideally."
Lady Wu turned to Lady Chen and whispered, "I hope that

everything makes sense so far."

"There is nothing difficult to understand, except for why I am here," Lady Chen replied quietly.

"My son... my and our sons... and grandsons, eventually... need guidance," Lady Wu explained. "We both need to be ready to offer that guidance."

Lady Chen understood quite well that the older Lady Wu was preparing for a day when she might not be there as a matriarch for the Sun family: she nodded slowly and said, "Some will not accept me."

"That will change," Lady Wu insisted. "It has to, and they know it, so it will change."

Gongjin visited his friend Lu Su after the meeting rather than going straight home.

"Ah! Gongjin, this is a nice surprise!" Lu Su chuckled as he guided Gongjin into his living quarters and had him sit opposite the host seat for an informal meeting.

"Let it not be said that I forget friends," Gongjin replied.

Lu Su sat down, sighed theatrically and said, "That Zhuge Jin fellow has started his new job, and I'm keeping an eye on him as you asked, though I thought that Lord Sun would want to-"

"I've asked you to see that he is treated properly," Gongjin interrupted. "Spying on him is other men's work."

"...What is Lord Sun afraid of?" Lu Su wondered. "Aren't a lot of his new vassals former servants of enemies past and present...? How can he employ Zu Lang and Xu Gong but turn away such a decent man as-?"

"Liu Biao is a special case," Gongjin explained. "Kuai Liang and the other advisers are very cunning: there is a worry that everything – including the convenient 'cover story' regarding the Zhuges being snubbed – is just that, a cover story, since you don't snub the wholesale service of a talented, socially-respected clan and then marry their women to your top officials and risk 'pillow talk'. As infatuated as I am with Lady Qiao, I would not have gone through with the marriage – or allowed Bofu to do the same – if they had been potential spies for Yuan Shu, Cao Cao, Liu Biao or any of our other concerns. But at the same time, Zhuge Jin intrigues me: he has a strange sincerity about him that compels me to think that he is, at worst, an unwitting innocent in a scheme of Kuai Liang's, and at best a future asset. If we were to win him around, the Zhuges could then be providing us with information about Liu Biao, which would be advantageous indeed!"

"Well, I'll keep an eye out for him, then, and make sure he doesn't suffer too much sleeve-flicking," Lu Su promised. "I don't need to ask whether you're enjoying married life, since you obviously are, even after such a short time, so I'll ask about political things. I'm hearing rumours from my own contacts about a possible flight from Shouchun: Cao Cao is about to make his final push, and Yuan Shu cannot survive it."

"He'll hold out for a few months more," Gongjin suggested. "The 'First Emperor of Zhong' didn't do all this to buckle at the first breach of his capital! He'll probably try and make some deals, but who with... I don't know. Liu Biao hates him, Gongsun Zan will soon be dead, the Black Mountain Bandits are fragmented, the

White Wave Bandits have disintegrated since Liu Bei killed their leaders, Yufuluo's dead and his Southern Xiongnu renegades are re-assimilated into the main tribal alliance that serves the Han, Liu Pi and his Yellow Turbans are newly broken and under constant watch by Cao Cao, Xue Zhou's pirate confederacy is dependent on the Guangling waterways and of no use outside that region, Haixi Chen is a broken man that's fled to Yuan Shao, Zu Lang's with us now, the Qiang, Di and Shanyue tribes are only interested in defending their own territories, Ma Teng and Han Sui are too far away, the cowardly Liu Zhang's loudly pledged allegiance to Cao's court, Zhang Lu daren't risk supporting rebels while his family are Liu Zhang's hostages, Lü Bu is gone, Liu Bei is now indebted to Cao Cao and wouldn't betray him, Yuan Shao can't risk being seen to aid a traitor..."

"...So it's almost over," Lu Su said. "Liu Xun of Lujiang is his only remaining ally, unless Xu Gong surprises us."

"Xu Gong is a friend of such shining lights as Kong Rong, the former Chancellor of Beihai," Gongjin replied. "He won't betray the Han... although there is one concern that I have only just acknowledged, now that you remind me... *Wang Lang*."

"...The former Administrator of Kuaiji...?" Lu Su exclaimed.

"Kong Rong invited him to serve in Cao Cao's court, so he's out of retirement and based in Xuchang, and slowly working his way up the ranks, no doubt, with his particular brand of 'constructive counsel'," Gongjin said bitterly. "There's a future enemy of ours, and no mistake: even if Cao Cao did not intend to turn his sword against us later, there's a man that might convince him to eliminate us, citing his own experiences."

"...And yet you still want to risk action against Liu Biao?" Lu Su prompted.

"That realisation only reinforces the need for it," Gongjin retorted. "What if Wang Lang proposed an amnesty for Liu Biao on the condition that he aided a campaign against us? That's always a possibility. We're a bigger force than Liu Biao's now, Zijing, and therefore a 'greater threat to stability'. We'll have to be proactive or risk losing everything."

Lu Su sighed and said, "Oh well; at least you've found happiness for a while before the chaos resumes, Gongjin. If there's any way that I can help you, say so."

Gongjin bowed and replied, "And when the moment arrives, I vow that I will fight for you to have a prominent place in the government. Bofu is stubborn, but he will forgive your little ways and employ you in a higher capacity eventually."

Lu Su smiled, bowed, and offered to pour Gongjin another dish of heated wine.

****

114

Days passed. Lü Fan made one of his now-routine visits to the state treasury, assuming that his obedient and trustworthy staff would be as pleasant, cooperative and unruffled as ever: he was therefore surprised to find the staff to be awkward, timid and incoherent. But that was only the beginning: he was then mildly surprised and greatly disappointed when he entered the treasury storeroom and discovered Bofu's eldest brother Sun Quan – who was mildly intoxicated – taking coins from the tax coffers and stuffing them into a silk purse.

"**What are you doing?**" Lü Fan barked.

"...Oh, *you*," Sun Quan scoffed. "Look, I'm your master's brother. This is his domain, isn't it? So isn't this his money, which he would gladly give to me?"

"No, young master, it's the *state's money*, collected to spend on the *state*," Lü Fan retorted. "The stability of the state depends on that money."

"...**You wretched pedant!**" Sun Quan cried. "**You dare to speak to me thus???**"

Lü Fan turned to the officials and dismissed them all with a wave of his hand.

"So you *do* have some sense then, Lü Fan!" Sun Quan cackled once he and Lü Fan were alone. "Now, we'll-"

"I have sense enough to see that you assume that your bluff has worked," Lü Fan interrupted. "It has not, however, because-"

"Y-you're going to cross me, even knowing that *your lord* is *my brother*...?" Sun Quan heckled defensively.

"Your brother is my lord, yes, but he is also my friend," Lü Fan replied calmly. "He insists that I call him 'Bofu'; I eat with your family, and Lady Wu treats me as she would her own kin; you know that, so why do you call me a wretch and a pedant, and worse yet, threaten me with empty promises of punishment?"

Sun Quan was silent.

"You have no right to take that money, young master, and you knew that, else you would not sneak in here while your brother was busy to steal it," Lü Fan continued.

"They're my brother's officials, not yours!" Sun Quan retorted. "We collect those taxes from the nobles and peasants to-!"

"'*Peasants*'...?" Lü Fan said with disdain. "Oh, dear..."

"...My elder brother is Marquis of Wu, my younger brother the Marquis of Wucheng!" Sun Quan protested. "We've earned our place, and-!"

"And you feel that you can just walk in here and help yourself to state funds whenever your own considerable magistrate's salary cannot cover your extravagance," Lü Fan said dryly. "Why, then, as I have noted already, did you sneak in here like a common thief if you've a Heaven-bestowed right to the money...?"

"**I did not 'sneak in here'!**" Sun Quan barked. "**Weren't there men here???**"

"Yes, and they – unlike me – were too scared to 'cross you'," Lü Fan retorted. "You knew that, alas, and played on their fear to commit theft."

"...Don't tell my brother," Sun Quan pleaded.

"How can I not...?" Lü Fan asked. "Audits are a commonplace thing, and at some point or another, the ledgers are going to be matched against collection records and the discrepancies will-"

"For a *few coins*???" Sun Quan chortled.

"...The ledgers are going to be matched to the collection records, and they're not going to make sense, and the ledgers will be wrong, and it will be obvious," Lü Fan continued.

"You're the chancellor, aren't you?" Sun Quan retorted. "We can change the ledgers, and then nobody will notice anything! Are you seriously telling me that the 'state' is going to miss *this*?"

Sun Quan jangled his heavy purse in a theatrical manner to accentuate his point.

"Every coin that is taken is not there to be given to a worthy cause," Lü Fan retorted.

"So I am not a worthy cause...?" Sun Quan heckled.

"Your desperation is evident, because you know your brother's views on proper governance and yet you still did this foolish thing," Lü Fan lamented. "Alas, young master, I am an honest man by nature, and I cannot allow you to do this. *No*, I will not change the ledgers or expect others to do so in order for you to have extra spending money. *No*, I will not let you take the money you have in your hand, because once you've gotten away with it once, you'll want to make a habit of it. *Yes*, I will tell your brother, because he would never forgive me if I did not."

"You'll *regret it*!" Sun Quan growled. "I won't forget it, you pedant! You-!"

"So what false allegations will you contrive to have me arrested in order to silence me, and how will you explain it to your brother...?" Lü Fan asked.

Sun Quan shook violently.

"Put the money back, please," Lü Fan said with disdain. "And then I shall escort you out of here, young master... and give instruction that you are never to be allowed in here again without an escort."

"**Pedant!**" Sun Quan said with tears in his eyes. "You'd tattle on me, like a child, and ban me from my brother's treasury?! I won't forget! **I won't forget, Lü Fan!**"

"I'd hope not," Lü Fan replied. "If I am to be punished for my honesty, then so be it, but I would hope that you'll understand one day. Now please return the money."

Sun Quan accepted defeat and returned the stolen money to its proper place.

Lü Fan reported his unfortunate to discovery to Bofu and Gongjin in a hastily-arranged private meeting an hour later.

"He was *openly stealing tax money*...?" Bofu said with disbelief. "He's been problematic, but... I never thought that it'd come to *that*, Ziheng."

"No, Lord Sun," Lü Fan replied nervously.

"I believe you, Ziheng," Bofu promised. "You did the right thing. I'll have a word with him: I'd wanted to entrust him with more when he got older, but I can't do that if he's going to do dishonest, stupid things like this. Can I let him return to his duties as the Magistrate of Yangxian after this...?"

"You asked a similar question after Xuan, Bofu, and that 'mistake' was far worse," Gongjin noted.

"Should I get rid of Pan Zhang...?" Bofu wondered.

"He had no Pan Zhang with him when he stole that money," Lü Fan suggested. "We should keep an eye on that obvious vagabond, of course, but at the same time we must treat him as we do Zu Lang."

"I agree," Gongjin admitted.

"I suppose I should tell Mum as well... she'll be upset, but she'll probably get further with him than me," Bofu sighed.

Lü Fan nodded silently.

"...What's he spending the money on?" Bofu wondered.

"Vice is rampant," Lü Fan replied honestly. "It could be anything."

"That was always the problem with him being surrounded by so many 'reformed' pirates and convicts... they're only so reformed," Bofu said. "So many of them are still chronic gamblers, drinkers, addicts and womanisers, Ziheng, and so I can't be surprised if he's seeing all that and wanting to join in. But he can do it with the money he's earned or given."

"...You're quite the ruler, Bofu," Lü Fan chuckled. "Your father would be proud."

"That's what I'd hope," Bofu replied. "In a way, I *am* Quan's father now. I *have to be*, now that Dad's gone. He needs me, and I'm going to help him."

Sun Quan was understandably hesitant when Bofu summoned him for a private meeting between the two of them.

"...You know about the money," Sun Quan supposed.

"Of course I know about the money," Bofu muttered.

"...Lü Fan should not have tattled on me like a child!" Sun Quan protested. "It was such a small amount of money that-!"

"Do you remember what bad years were like...?" Bofu asked.

"Yes, of course," Sun Quan scoffed.

"And the people that those taxes are collected from still have those bad years, months and days, Quan," Bofu continued. "If they knew that you'd used their tax money for... for whatever it is that you're spending it on, and I'm not sure that *I* want to know, they might be angry, just as we'd have been angry when-"

"Yeah, yeah, I get it," Sun Quan grumbled. "And to answer the question, I enjoy an exciting life, like everyone else gets to."

"...That same argument again," Bofu scolded. "I'm married now, and that's all that's changed: so once again I have to ask you what exiting life it is that 'everyone else enjoys except you'."

Sun Quan was silent.

"Once again, Quan, I'll say this: don't forget who you are," Bofu continued. "You're the second son of Sun Jian of Fuchun: Dad wouldn't be very impressed with a man that spent all day in taverns, gambling houses and brothels when he had a job to-"

"...I'm only human!" Sun Quan cried.

"...Have you any idea how repetitious we sound, and how much worse you are than me...?" Bofu retorted. "You said exactly the same thing last time! I would never... *never* raid the city treasury to pay for women and drink, Quan: I'm not a bandit or a scrounger, and you shouldn't be either. If you think you deserve an increase in pay, ask and it'll be discussed; if you cannot afford your lifestyle, change it. ...Or should we just allow any bandit that feels entitled to a better life just take whatever they don't

have...?"
"...You even *sound* like Father now," Sun Quan replied glumly.
"...Alright, Elder Brother, I promise that I won't do anything like that again."
"And you won't hold it against Lü Ziheng...?" Bofu prompted.
"I... I cannot abide pedants!" Sun Quan whined.
"Yes, and he cannot abide *thieves*," Bofu retorted.
"...Alright... I forgive him," Sun Quan muttered.
"You 'forgive him'...?" Bofu chortled. "You asked him to aid you in committing fraud! You tried to bully the poor man into sacrificing every principle that he has in order to-!"
"I... I understand what he did, and bear no grudge," Sun Quan said at last.
"I hope so," Bofu sighed.
"...I'm leaving tomorrow," Sun Quan sighed. "...That is, if I'm still the Magistrate of Yangxian after what I've done."
"...You are," Bofu replied reluctantly.
"And... and you're going to have someone accompany me to Yangxian in order to keep an eye on me, I suppose," Sun Quan prompted.
"When your stupidity almost got Zhou Tai killed, you got smarter," Bofu replied. "Now that you've been embarrassed with your own weakness, you'll get stronger. So why should I have you watched...? You learn from your mistakes, Quan, and that means that you can only become a better man."
"I am glad to be getting another chance," Sun Quan said with as much humility as he could muster.
"...And what about the 'excess'...?" Bofu asked.
"I'll have no choice but to cut down if I can't afford it all," Sun Quan replied. "But I need to enjoy life, Elder Brother. Don't make me live like a hermit."
"As long as it doesn't affect your work, I don't care what you do," Bofu insisted. "As I've said before, I almost succumbed a lot myself at bad times, but... but I had too much to do. I still do, and I need your help."
Sun Quan hummed thoughtfully.
"...Lecture over," Bofu continued.
"I am rightly humbled, and I will learn from this," Sun Quan promised. "Thank you, Elder Brother, for your patience with this unworthy brother of yours. I'll improve... I'll keep on improving... until I'm-"
"Worthy of being a Sun," Bofu said with obvious disappointment. "You said that before. And I'll even match you with the same reply: you're not unworthy. You're flawed, like everyone else. That, I think, is where we should leave it."
"...Must Mother know...?" Sun Quan asked.
"Ah! I wondered when you'd ask that," Bofu chortled. "She's been made aware, but left it to me. She's... she's aware of it."
"...And she's disappointed... disgusted, even!" Sun Quan whined. "I have-!"
"Let's just put it behind us, Quan," Bofu insisted. "What's done is done, and what's undone is undone. Go back to Yangxian and carry on being a good magistrate."
"I... I look forward to meeting my nephews and nieces," Sun Quan said as one last conciliatory – and familiar – statement.

"Yeah," Bofu sighed. "We're working on it."
Bofu patted Quan's arm, and the two parted company as brothers.

Bofu waited for a while and then summoned Gongjin, Lü Fan, Sun Hè and his brother Sun Yi to the meeting room.
"...Is it true...?" Sun Yi asked. "Did Quan really steal money...?"
"I-! ...*Aiee*. It makes it harder to forgive him when it is just said in that way!" Bofu groaned. "Yes, Yi, he... he stole money from the treasury. But he is sorry, and he has returned it all."
"...'It all'...?" Sun Yi chortled. "How much did he steal?"
"In total...? I... don't know," Bofu replied. "I was scared to ask."
"...I think that was it, Bofu," Lü Fan said. "There were no other visible discrepancies. He probably hoped that he'd be halfway to Yangxian by the time someone reported it to me."
Bofu groaned and said, "Why has he gotten worse like this...?"
"...And why have I been invited to a meeting to discuss it...?" Sun Yi asked.
"Yi, I... I'm not invincible," Bofu replied.
Gongjin exhaled noisily at the words.
"...What do you mean...?" Sun Yi asked nervously.
Bofu noted Gongjin's obvious interpretation of his previous words as foreboding and said, "All that I meant was that I can't be everywhere, and you're soon going to be old enough to accompany me on campaigns or stay behind as a guardian. Like it or not, I need to make you aware of Quan's... flaws... since you'll be acting as a substitute for me... at times."
"So what role will I play in the Jing campaign...?" Yi asked.
"That's still being decided," Bofu admitted. "A lot is still undecided. This is a big moment, after all; revenge at last."
"If I had my way, I'd be in the vanguard," Sun Yi replied.
Bofu smiled and said, "We'll see. You have the right to be, but... we'll see."

Later that same evening, Bofu met with Lady Wu and Lady Chen, the women that had played the largest role in Quan's upbringing.
"Just this once, I... I feel that I have made a mistake," Lady Wu admitted.
"It is a shared mistake if it is a mistake!" Lady Chen protested.
"...You're kind to say so, sister, but he is my son, raised by me primarily," Lady Wu retorted. "Somewhere, somehow, a moral fibre has been lost, and-"
"Yi, Kuang and Shangxiang are all as honest as the day is long," Bofu interrupted. "I'm disgusted by what he did, same as you are: it's like you've always said, Mother... 'Every person is an individual, and can only be shaped so much'."
"...But to think that I have brought a thief into the world!" Lady Wu cried.
"He's... flawed, and has been since Dad died," Bofu insisted. "It affected us all differently, but him, it... it made him bitter, resentful. He blames everything and everyone, feels that he's been wronged in all sorts of ways."
"Like Yuan Shu...?" Lady Wu chortled.
"I would never compare Quan to that animal," Bofu replied. "Yes, he's got 'issues', but he's not like that man. He'd never do the things that Yuan Shu's done. He saw Dad with pirates and thought

it was all fun; he saw me with the likes of Jiang Qin and Zhou Tai and got his own Zhou Tai called Pan Zhang. Perhaps it was my fault for not giving him a bodyguard with some sense when I sent him to Yangxian; Zhou Tai was unavailable, but if I'd given him Song Qian or Jiang Qin, then-"

"Then you'd be yet another good officer down, and he'd probably have got that poor man hurt as well," Lady Wu suggested. "Perhaps... ... ...perhaps we'd better keep him close and not use him too much."

"He'll learn," Bofu replied. "I was stupid in different ways, but I'm learning. I'm not perfect either."

"But you're not a drunken thief!" Lady Wu sobbed.

"Calm down, Mother... please," Bofu said quietly. "He'll learn."

"...Go and spend some time with Daqiao before the poor girl forgets what you like," Lady Wu replied. "We've wasted enough time on Quan today."

Bofu bowed to his two mothers – actual and honorary – before he retreated.

"...Bofu needs every bit of help that he can find," Lady Wu said angrily. "How *dare* Quan be so *selfish*!? Didn't we *all* lose his father???"

Lady Chen did what she could to provide support to the furious, distressed and desperate Lady Wu: age and the stresses of life were taking their toll on the Sun family matriarch, and she would soon start to search for ways to ease the burden.

On the next morning, Sun Quan was invited to a private meeting that he assumed to be with his mother: he was surprised and angered to find that it was his father's consort Lady Chen that awaited him.

"So now you feel that you have the right to scold me as well...?" Sun Quan growled.

"Perhaps I do, Quan, but that isn't why we're here," Lady Chen replied. "Your mother is angry and disappointed at what happened, but I have argued that you are to be properly understood."

Sun Quan frowned.

"You do not like me, I know that," Lady Chen continued. "I am mother to some of your younger brothers and sisters, however, and your mother has made it clear that I am to be her spiritual successor should the sad day come when she is unable to be there for you. As such, I do not want us to be enemies."

"So you defended me in order to win me around, then," Sun Quan heckled.

"I am not so stupid as I would think that such a thing would work, and would not insult you by trying such a thing," Lady Chen insisted. "I am as upset by what you did as Lady Wu is, but I observed our household after Lord Sun Jian's death. His death harmed us all: I would have cried blood if I could have, because he treated me very well, better than many consorts, and I knew only love in every direction that I turned. Such a man cannot die and not be missed... and I still miss him now."

"...I am being unfair," Sun Quan realised. "I can never truly see you as a mother because of my love for my actual mother, but when I think of others that must see aunts, cousins or even strangers as their mother because they have been adopted, like 'Zhu Ran', and... and perhaps I see now that I am resentful for selfish reasons."

"I took your father from your mother," Lady Chen sighed.

"No, no, you didn't," Sun Quan said. "Nobody made Father bring you into our household. He did that, and I was so angry after he was killed that I tried to blame every little thing I didn't like or accept on someone else because he couldn't be flawed, just like my attempts to blame others for my own actions because I don't want to admit that I am... far from perfect. Nobody made me take – no, steal – that money and it was wrong for me to hate Lü Fan for exposing me. Father brought you into our home, and I chose to take what I saw to be his rejection of my mother out on you, when... when it was his decision alone. But I couldn't bring myself to hate him, so I chose to... to hate you. But I can't, I shouldn't hate you. You've done nothing wrong."

Lady Chen smiled sadly.

"You've borne my behaviour for years and never complained," Sun Quan continued. "You were always like a second mother, no matter how much I pushed you away... and you're still trying to be one now, even after everything else. Mother's right: you're part of our family, and... and... if I may, I shall call you 'Aunt'. I know that is not the same, but..."

Lady Chen bowed slightly and said, "It is enough."

"...Will Mother ever truly forgive me, do you think...?" Sun Quan asked worriedly.

"She wants to, so very, very much, Quan," Lady Chen replied. "She only wants you to be the greatest man that you can be."

Sun Quan snorted loudly and said, "I can never be like Elder Brother."

"Nobody asks you to be," Lady Chen insisted. "No more than I ask you to see me as your mother, or than people demand more gentility of Shangxiang; each is their own. You're your own man, destined to be great in your own way, Quan: don't live in your brother's shadow, cast your own."

Sun Quan fought tears as he said, "Lady Chen, I have wronged you! I will grow as a person, and I swear that one day, I will call you Second Mother! I... I cannot, not now, not while I fight with myself, but...!"

"You must learn to overcome the judgements of others, Quan," Lady Chen replied. "It is not easy... Heaven knows, it is not easy... but you must, and you will. Your mother and I love you, and we believe in you: now you must believe – *truly believe* – in yourself."

"...I do not deserve my family, but I will do all I can to earn it," Sun Quan said as he took Lady Chen's right hand in both of his own. "Thank you... thank you."

Lady Chen nodded and smiled silently: after a few tense moments, Sun Quan released Lady Chen's hand and retreated from the room.

"...He could not do the right thing and call you 'Second Mother', not even at the last, after everything you said, and that saddens me," Lady Wu said as she emerged from behind a screen.

"He is tormented, confused, unable to fathom things," Lady Chen protested. "We must give him time to-"

"He is my son, and yet I cannot fight for him as you do right now," Lady Wu admitted. "I want to, but he spits in the face of decency, and... ... ...perhaps we should just say no more. If he is destined to 'grow', as he keeps promising to do, then he will, and if he doesn't, then... then so be it. But he will still be my son."

Sun Quan returned to Yangxian County in Wu Prefecture, where he would remain as Magistrate: he kept his word and endeavoured to be a better man in the wake of his behaviour in Danyang's capital. Bofu would smile as reports of his administrative professionalism reached him in later days, but neither brother could know that in the future, it would be Sun Quan – a man whose early reputation was far from exemplary – that would be the central pillar of the emerging southern state.

****

115

After a few weeks of enjoying married life, Bofu assembled his officials in the audience hall in Danyang's capital.

"We're marching, aren't we?" Lü Fan said before Bofu could speak.

"Yes, but not to Lujiang," Bofu replied.

"No one expected you to say 'Lujiang'," Cheng Pu chuckled. "No one wanted you to, either, no one that truly fights for what we fight for."

"And what do we fight for, Mister Cheng...?" Officer of Merit Wei Teng asked.

"I beg your pardon...?" Cheng Pu retorted. "You've enjoyed a few days' fair treatment, and now you think that you can-!"

"Mister Wei Teng asks a valid question!" Zhang Hong protested.

"It was a pedant's question!" Cheng Pu barked. **"You're all the same, you little cowardly toadies: 'robed rats', that's what you are! How dare a man that enjoys sudden elevation for doing his job properly – and little else – come here and berate our mission to avenge Wentai!"**

"...Lord Sun...!" Zhang Hong whined as he turned to Bofu.

"I agree with Demou," Bofu admitted.

"*Ayah*... so this entire state's entire purpose is to avenge the death of one man?" Wei Teng said desperately. "Are there no other reasons for us being here...?"

"How dare you!" Bofu screamed. **"I've known you for a very short time, Wei Teng, and already you're getting on my-!"**

"*Lord Sun*, Wei Teng and Zhang Hong are just expressing the views of the majority of the people in Jiangdong!" Qin Song said. "I don't profess to be in full agreement, but we must consider the consensus before we force men to march west against an enemy that will fight a costly war of attrition with us!"

"We must be logical!" Zhang Zhao declared.

Bofu shuddered angrily.

"So it comes to this," Cheng Pu scoffed. "I knew that it would: when we had one little Huan Jie, we were safe: now we have whole nests of them in our midst, fomenting cowardly and self-serving opinions and-"

"Forgive my interruption, Mister Cheng, but we must be pragmatic," Lü Fan said. "I saw Lord Sun Jian with my own eyes, and as a frequent guest in my lord's home I cannot be unemotional when discussing this, so know that what I say is said with the utmost understanding of the whole situation."

Cheng Pu smiled and replied, "I know you now, Ziheng. Say your piece."

"*Ziheng*...?" Bofu exclaimed.

"He's accepted one of us, then," Gongjin sighed.

"To the detractors, I say this: Liu Biao intends us harm, and that is clear, irrefutable fact," Lü Fan continued. "I want war with Jing as much as anyone – not at all – and I dare any man to say that Lord Sun Ce does this due to bloodlust. We have Taishi Ci to thank for Danyang's safety: Liu Pan was repelled while attempting to invade Jiangdong, and that is irrefutable fact. Liu Biao has latched onto the Sun-Liu feud with as tight a grip as any Sun: he uses it as justification for 'getting us before we get him', and he will certainly try and attack us again. In fact, Huang Zu bolsters the naval force at Xiakou yet again as we speak: another irrefutable fact."

"Could it not be for defence only...?" Zhang Hong asked.

"Why are you here, Zhang, and not in Jiangling with your master Liu Biao???" Cheng Pu shrieked as he leapt to his feet and tried to approach Zhang Hong: Huang Gai was barely able to restrain him.

"What is the point of a court when no man is allowed to question matters???" Zhang Hong retorted. "Why summon us here, then, if our counsel is not even to be heard, never mind heeded???"

"...Because you're wrong," Bofu replied. "Demou, please return to your seat."

Cheng Pu shrugged Huang Gai off and sat down again.

"You're wrong because your counsel is being heard, Zhang Hong," Bofu continued. "I cannot promise to heed it, but not because I am a fool or a belligerent. This is about more than my father's life now. It is, as Ziheng has said, about the removal of a threat to Jiangdong. I did not fight all those pacification wars just to allow Liu Biao to come here now and return us to chaos. If Liu Biao takes Jiangdong, Cao Cao will march against him in retaliation: remember, gentlemen, that Cao was heading for Jing's capital before his sexual misdemeanours caught up with him at Wan City, and had he kept his libido under control, Jing would be under imperial control now."

"...That is true," Zhang Zhao conceded.

"Yes, and you craven pedants and toadies knew that, because we've discussed this a hundred times before, and every time you've said the same things and been beaten back by the same proven arguments!" Cheng Pu heckled. "Lord Sun, please just announce the march and order an end to discussion about it, else we'll have to do this all again on every day between now and the march!"

"...It shall be as you say, Demou," Bofu announced. "We are going to deploy a full military force – army and navy – against Jiangxia Prefecture in Jing Province. We are going to destroy Huang Zu and rid that region of a vile criminal figure that has ruled it for far too long. There will be no further discussion."

"And what will we tell the imperial court, the only true authority in the land...?" Wei Teng asked.

Bofu started to rise in anger, but Gongjin grasped his arm and glared at him insistently: Bofu slowly sat down again, and after a few moments he said, "Cao Cao will get an explanation, Mister Wei. Let your words be the last ones that go against my judgement."

There were no more remonstrative words from Bofu's court: a date for a march was set, and the preparations for war with Liu Biao and Huang Zu began.

****

116

Jing Governor Liu Biao assembled the majority of his courtiers in the main residential hall of his southern capital Jiangling and said, "I suppose you've all heard the news by now: Sun Ce has finally begun a march against us. He's taking his time to cross Yuzhang, but that only frightens me more, since that means he doesn't feel the need for surprise; such casual behaviour can only be bad."

"My brother requests aid, but we cannot risk a sudden incursion by Yuan Shu's retainers into our eastern region," the adviser Kuai Liang said. "Jiangxia must hold with what it has: Huang Zu will have to recruit additional forces."

"Can he hope to repel Sun Ce with untrained and unreliable pirate brigades?" the politician and former Sun family retainer Huan Jie asked.

"He has little choice," Kuai Liang insisted. "Yuan Shu might be on the verge of defeat and likely death, but that doesn't mean he's not a threat: if his forces decide to abandon Shouchun and Yu Province and flee westward to our eastern counties, we'll have him entrenched there for goodness knows how long, giving Cao Cao the excuse he needs to invade the province again."

"...But what if Jiangxia is lost???" Liu Biao cried.

"It's a risk that we must take," Kuai Liang replied. "Yuan Shu still has assets that he can use to barter for aid at the desperate hour..."

"Like what...?" Liu Biao scoffed.

"Kinship with Yuan Shao and the Imperial Seal that he claims to have," Kuai Liang replied. "Neither is to be considered unlikely as a weapon or shield."

"...Kinship with-? ...How can that be?" Liu Biao chuckled. "How could Yuan Shao rescue him or ally with him now...?"

"If not for sentimental reasons, then the Imperial Seal that Shu claims to have," Kuai Liang replied. "Yuan Shao is like every other warlord we share space with, Lord Liu: if Yuan Shu cites kinship and proffers the Seal – whether it exists or not – then Yuan Shao will save him."

"Yuan Shao would become as much of a rebel and traitor as Shu if he were seen to rescue him," Huan Jie suggested.

"Yuan Shao has plans that account for it and schemers that can twist the narrative to suit," Kuai Liang retorted. "The point, gentlemen, is that he might have one more gasp, and Jing might become a temporary base while he negotiates, which is a wholly unacceptable scenario."

"...Quite right," Liu Biao decided. "Cai Mao: continue to ensure that the north of Jing is fortified, especially to the east, and hold your forces here unless developments force a change of tactics."

The naval commander Cai Mao bowed humbly and said, "I shall continue with our current approach, Lord Liu."

"I want to be kept informed, even if I must be dragged from my bed in the middle of the night," Liu Biao ordered. "Mister Kuai, our fate rests with your keen mind."

"Your faith is well-placed," Kuai Liang replied.

While Liu Biao prepared to defend his domains against an angry

Bofu, the latter's former master, Yuan Shu, was preparing to bid farewell to Shouchun.

"We... I... am ruined."

Yuan Shu was stood in the centre of his grand palace's residential hall: his elite forces were busy stripping the walls of the remaining finery in preparation for a humiliating retreat.

"...Yan Xiang, Ji Ling... *gone*," Yuan Shu continued. "Yuan Huan: *defected*... Chen Lan, Lei Bo: *deserted*... Hui Qu, Chen Ji: *no word*... My... my army...!"

"Your Majesty, we will soon be departing," Yuan's loyal former Grand General, Zhang Xun, said quietly.

"You must ready your family at once," the adviser Yang Hong said.

"...Where will I go...?" Yuan Shu bleated.

"I say again that we might try contacting Sun Ce, Your Majesty," Zhang Xun replied. "He is a magnanimous, honest-"

"I cannot go to Sun Ce!" Yuan Shu cried. "How can I go to Sun Ce? He hates me, Zhang Xun!"

"Our options are limited, and time is precious," Yang Hong said. "Sad to say, I agree with His Majesty, Zhang Xun. Your friendship with Sun Ce blinds you to the threat he will pose to His Majesty's life: he will not acknowledge His Majesty as sovereign, and-"

"**Stop calling me that!**" Yuan Shu shrieked: many of the soldiers halted their work and turned to stare at their self-destructive master.

"...**Back to work!**" Yang Hong ordered, and the work resumed.

"I am no majesty," Yuan Shu continued. "I am a fool that mistook measured fortune for signs of future ascension. No emperor am I, Yang Hong. This place will soon be ash, and with it any visible sign that I made such a claim. But men have memories, and they all know, and will not forgive..."

"Forgive me, but that's unimportant right now!" Yang Hong hissed. "Your Majesty, Lord Yuan, whatever you wish to be called now... we have to flee."

"...To where do we go, if not Danyang...?" Yuan Shu asked. "What about Lujiang...?"

"Sun Ce's lackeys siege the place day and night," Yang Hong reported.

"If we tell him that the war is over, he'll stop!" Zhang Xun pleaded. "He knows when and when not to bear grudges! He'll give you shelter, and-!"

"We cannot parley with my former tiger!" Yuan Shu insisted. "He'll demand that I apologise for past treatment, demand that I be his court fool, wed my daughters to his lowest vassals as an insult, and-"

"We're going to the Qian Hills," Yang Hong said. "Lei Bo and Chen Lan are no more tolerated by Cao Cao than we are, so they'll want an alliance for the purpose of self-preservation at the least."

"To think that I must now ally with my own deserted vassals, and maybe bow to them as equals...!" Yuan Shu chortled. "O, Heaven, your punishments are harsh and humiliating indeed!"

"...But I will not abandon you, Lord Yuan," Zhang Xun promised. "I was taught that the bond between lord and vassal must never be broken."

"Not even when your lord is a traitor, a heretic and a *pauper*...?" Yuan Shu giggled.

Yang Hong sighed miserably: the last of the wealth in Shouchun would be spent on food and military equipment, and then Yuan Shu would be no wealthier than his lowest infantrymen.

"Men lose and gain reputations and fortunes," Zhang Xun replied. "You gave me opportunities to be a greater man than I ever hoped to be, and I must repay that."

"...While others, like Sun Ce, punish me for inflicting the very opposite upon them," Yuan Shu said glumly. "People will not call me a man that ruled evenly."

"Father, we are ready to go," Yuan Yao said as he approached Yuan Shu with his own force of elite men.

"...No tiger is he, but a man nonetheless," Yuan Shu murmured.

"Father...?" Yuan Yao prompted.

"N-nothing," Yuan Shu said. "I said nothing... nothing important, anyway. We should go. I cannot bear to see this place alight, not when... not when so much went into building it."

"There will be opportunities to rebuild," Zhang Xun suggested.

"My next ostentatious enclosure will be my tomb, if I am allowed to have one," Yuan Shu retorted. "Until then, I will have to make do with a hillside command tent, will I not...?"

Yang Hong and Zhang Xun did not reply: Yuan Shu snorted miserably and began the last journey out of his bare-walled imperial palace. Within an hour, the self-proclaimed Zhong Emperor was atop a plain brown horse and undertaking a gruelling trek into the Qian Hills while a portion of his followers – led by his cousin, Yuan Yin – remained in Shouchun to set alight to all of the administrative buildings, including the palace, and turn the remnants into a decoy defensive position. That marked an end of an era in itself: the Zhong Dynasty existed only in the heart of Yuan Shu, who now had no palace, no capital, no lands, no money and no home. Much of Shouchun's population was forced to flee, but not all of the refugees from the Jiujiang capital were loyal to Yuan Shu: many – including the family of Bofu's cousin Sun Ben – were glad to be freed from Yuan's grip at last, and they journeyed southward, toward the Yangtze River and a new life as citizens of Jiangdong.

****

117

Jiangxia Administrator Huang Zu received his Governor Liu Biao's letter and immediately summoned his court.

"This is nonsense!" Huang Zu barked. **"He says that I must 'hold with what I have'! He says that Yuan Shu is a threat! Well then, let us fear every bird, dog and mouse in the country if we must now fear Yuan Shu! In all our years of cooperation, I never thought that I would one day be faced with such hesitation and cowardice!"**

"You speak this way of our *lord*," the adviser Kuai Yue noted.

"…And of your brother's unhelpful interference!" Huang Zu retorted. "Isn't this so-called 'advice' his…? Who else would advocate abandoning me to-!"

"My brother Liang and I converse regularly," Kuai Yue interrupted. "You are not being abandoned: Cao Cao could turn his attentions this way again once Yuan Shu is defeated, or the squatters in Nan County could try and expand their foothold after their victory against Cao Cao, or Yuan Shu could flee westward and-"

"All conjecture and theory: you'll be telling me that we're worried about Liu Zhang next!" Huang Zu heckled. "Forget who might come here or who might be a threat; Sun Ce is definitely on his way here, and after the humiliating defeat his vassal Taishi Ci inflicted on the governor's nephew, I thought that he'd care more than he obviously does!"

"Sun Ce has got to bring his navy down the Great River from Danyang, and that will slow him down," Kuai Yue said. "To truly threaten Jiangxia, he must employ a pincer strategy, and he cannot do that easily. Southern Jiangxia borders Yuzhang to the south and east and Changsha County to the west: everything in-between is hostile and populated by people loyal to us and tribes that are loyal to whoever promises them freedom. Even if he were to get as far as Red Cliffs, Wulin's marshy terrain is unfriendly to invaders, so he cannot get far. Northern Jiangxia is across the Great River from any position that he can seize, and the river is an obstacle enough: by reinforcing Three Rivers and other major settlements along the northern bank, we have prevented him gaining a foothold to the east of here, and even if he did somehow manage to overcome the defences of any of those places, Xiakou is heavily fortified, and the riverbank is lined with signal towers, so what have we to fear…? He cannot pass such defences without serious loss."

"…You're suggesting that I just sit here and let him bring his entire navy to my door…?" Huang Zu scoffed. "It's easier to see why Hè Jin died now, I think, if he had men like you advising him. Han Xi, Huang Yi…"

A rugged naval commander in a suit of weathered leather armour bowed humbly and said, "Here is Han Xi, Administrator: what are your orders…?"

A robed man in his twenties struck his chest with his fist and said, "Here I am, Father! Your word is my command!"

"…Han Xi, Huang Yi, you'll take a small fleet of ships, sail east to Three Rivers and engage Sun Ce to test his strength," Huang Zu ordered. "Further fortify the land on either side of the river as you

go. Show caution, but at the same time show strength: once we know what we're up against, we can plan for what we're actually going to do, since waiting for assistance from Kuai Liang is obviously not an option."
Kuai Yue sighed and said, "Mister Huang, my brother is-!"
"A pedant toady, like all of you so-called 'advisers'," Huang Zu grumbled. "Isn't his craven suggestion that we lure Sun Jian into an ambush instead of killing the man in a fair fight why we're even fighting Sun Ce...?"
"And who, among you and your officers, was Sun Jian's equal...?" Kuai Yue retorted. "You went along with that plan willingly, Mister Huang, because you knew that it was the only-"
"Alright, alright, shut up!" Huang Zu barked. **"Han Xi, Huang Yi, get going! You don't have much time to prepare!"**
Kuai Yue exhaled loudly as he watched Han Xi and Huang Yi depart to carry out their orders. Huang Zu then turned to another officer and said, "Su Fei."
Su Fei bowed silently and awaited his orders.
"...Su Fei, you will take your force and fortify the riverbanks at Wulin and Red Cliffs," Huang Zu ordered. "Leave no place exposed."
"I shall do as you ask, Lord Huang: none will pass my force," Su Fei promised.

Bofu's vanguard sailed down the Great River to the port of Hukou in northwest Yuzhang: he and his entourage disembarked, journeyed to a conspicuous riverbank camp and was finally reunited with Taishi Ci. The two former rivals clasped hands, and Bofu said, "Ziyi, are you well...?"
"I am, Lord Sun," Taishi Ci replied. "The-"
"I insist that you call me 'Bofu'."
Taishi Ci shook his head and said, "I cannot, for-"
"No protocol should exist between friends," Bofu insisted. "Please, Ziyi..."
"...I am well... *Bofu*," Taishi Ci said with obvious difficulty.
"I wish that we could celebrate our reunion and your successes against Liu Pan, but time is against us and I have much that I want to do," Bofu explained. "I've left Li Shu – did you meet him? – to continue our siege of Lujiang, and I've brought my cousins here that I'm sure you haven't encountered, Boyang and Guoyi. They're like brothers to me, since we all grew up together: Boyang's family is still captive in Shouchun, though I've heard that Yuan might give up the place and flee... I don't know how that'll work out, but-"
Cheng Pu coughed loudly and deliberately.
"I'm rambling, Ziyi!" Bofu chuckled. "In short, I've brought most of the clan here for this, because it's personal as well as strategic."
"I am well aware of the history," Taishi Ci replied. "I've had men procuring and constructing small boats."
"And I've had lake-based facilities set up at Po," Bofu said excitedly. "A huge fleet is being brought down the Great River from Danyang. It's amazing what we've managed to achieve! Huang Zu doesn't stand a chance!"
"His lands to the south of the Great River are poorly fortified, so

we could risk a land crossing to reinforce the river assault," Taishi
Ci reported. "Wulin is too treacherous for a landing, so we'll need
to seize Three Rivers and risk a two-pronged pincer from river and
land. Is there any risk from Lujiang, which would be to the north
and east of that northern landing...?"
Gongjin and Lü Fan laughed quietly.
"This is why I wanted you to join my cause, Ziyi!" Bofu chuckled.
"There's no need for reconnaissance because you've done it all
already!"
"You must not rely entirely on my work!" Taishi Ci said as he
bowed low.
"We could, I think!" Gongjin joked.
"But we won't, of course," Cheng Pu said. "Your efforts are
impossible to criticise, Mister Taishi, but every man can miss
something. Zhou Yu, Lü Fan: we will conduct our own
reconnaissance and see if our findings concur with Mister Taishi's."
Gongjin and Lü Fan bowed silently.
"So close now... so close...!" Bofu said excitedly.
"We have a lot to do, and with only one point of entry to Jing that
we can use," Gongjin noted. "Your father had the advantage of
being able to bring a naval force down the Great River as we do
and attacking the north at the same time from Yu Province.
Without that vital second pincer in the far north to guarantee
dividing Liu Biao's forces, we risk-"
"Relax, Gongjin!" Bofu said. "You worry too much. Our sources
say that Liu Biao's too scared to move his whole army down here,
remember...?"
"...Yes, I remember, because that source was mine," Gongjin
retorted. "But situations can change, and we don't need Cai Mao
and Kuai Liang suddenly adding a lot of extra brawn and brains to
the enemy force!"
"How many talented officers do we have...?" Bofu asked.
"...More than him," Gongjin conceded, "but-!"
"Right, so relax," Bofu said. "Liu Biao has Huang Zu, Cai Mao,
Zhang Yun, Han Xi, Huang Yi, Liu Pan, Liu Qi, Kuai Yue, Kuai Liang
and that traitor Huan Jie that he got from us: we have Ling Cao,
Lü Meng, Zhou Tai and Taishi Ci for a vanguard, Lü Fan, you,
Cheng Pu and-"
"I... I see your angle, but I cannot agree completely," Gongjin
retorted. "Bofu, we're going to have our backs to Lujiang. If
anything changes there-"
"I know all the potential problems, Gongjin!" Bofu chuckled. "Now
come on: we have a couple of villains to kill!"
"*Aiee*... I only want to avoid history repeating itself," Gongjin
sighed as Bofu walked away to inspect a battalion of infantrymen.
"Can the forest be the same without its tigers...?"
Cheng Pu hummed agreeably but quietly.

While Bofu prepared to begin his multi-pronged incursion into
southern Jing Province, Yuan Shu was ending a journey to the part
of the Huai River that bordered Xu Province: he had once fought
Lü Bu at that same location as the numerically-stronger warlord,
but now he had a force numbering less than a hundred. His plan
was simple enough: he had sent a man ahead to negotiate a truce
and rescue attempt with none other than his brother and cousin

by adoption, Yuan Shao, and his chosen bargaining tool was the Imperial Seal that he claimed to possess. For reasons and purposes that could be known only to Yuan Shao, an agreement had been swiftly reached and Shao's eldest son Tan had been sent to meet with his uncle Yuan Shu and escort him through Xu Province and into Qing Province. Yuan Tan only needed to get to the Huai River, and Yuan Shu was safe: but Cao Cao had somehow learned of the plot, and he had immediately ordered that the armed rescue attempt be countered with a military blockade.

"So... so all is lost..."

Yuan Shu sat and stared at the messenger that had brought the news that everyone had dreaded: his attempted escape had been thwarted by an army led by former Xu Provincial governor Liu Bei and Cao Cao's officer Zhu Ling.

"That was our last... *my* last chance," Yuan Shu continued. "Oh, to be looking at this river yet again... and now it means something so very different..."

"We can try and break through, surely...?" Zhang Xun protested.

"You couldn't win a battle here when you had an army, Zhang Xun," Yuan Shu chortled. "How do you now hope to smash a rock with an egg...?"

Zhang Xun stared at the Huai River and said, "But we cannot just...!"

"...Lord Yuan is right, General," Yang Hong suggested.

"...Curse my worthlessness as a general!" Zhang Xun cried. "Had I been more capable before, Xu Province might be ours and-!"

"The funniest part," Yuan Shu said suddenly, "is not that an imperial scion leads one half of this army that obstructs me beyond that river: it is that my way is also blocked by *Zhu Ling*, one of my brother's former officers!"

Yuan Tan's messenger kowtowed and said, "Lord Yuan, there are many-!"

"I... I heard you the first time, young man," Yuan Shu interrupted. "I'm not deaf, just as... just as you're not a coward. I'd have someone provide refreshments, but... but we can barely feed ourselves."

The following minutes were silent save for the occasional sob.

"...Go back to my nephew, and tell him that I am going back to Shouchun," Yuan Shu ordered. "Tell him to withdraw before he is attacked... and tell him not to mourn his uncle, for the tears are wasted on me."

"I cannot say that!" the messenger cried.

"...Then tell him whatever rubbish that you want to tell him, so long as he understands that I'm not advancing," Yuan Shu retorted. "I can go no further, for as you see, my army shrinks with every passing day. Soon I'll have nobody, so how can I fight my way past Liu Bei and Zhu Ling...?"

"Yuan Tan is a tiger," Zhang Xun suggested.

"So is Sun Ce, who will come here as soon as his spies report that I am trapped here, and once I am in a pincer it is done," Yuan Shu said. "No, I am not muddled at this moment in time; go please, messenger, and do your duty."

The messenger retreated.

"...It almost worked, though!" Yuan Shu chuckled. "It almost worked: oh yes, I know that my brother is only after the Imperial Seal that I offered him, and that he did not do all this for any other reason... but safety is safety."

"*Can* we go back to Shouchun...?" Yang Hong asked.

"...There is no other option," Yuan Shu insisted. "O Heavenly gods, you have an intelligent sense of humour! You even give me a pile of burning rubble for a capital, just like the Han Emperor that I wanted to replace! In Sun Ce I have my own Lü Bu, and in Cao Cao my own Dong Zhuo! But do I have my own Wang Yun in Liu Xun, I wonder, if I cannot stay in my capital...?"

"Our only true option now is to go to Sun Ce," Zhang Xun pleaded.

"No, our only option now is to go back to Shouchun, resist Cao Cao, and open communications with Liu Xun," Yuan Shu insisted. "I can never go to Sun Ce. I can never... ... ...no. I cannot. It is impossible. Do not suggest it again."

Yuan Yao sighed desperately and said, "But Father-!"

"We would be humiliated, my son!" Yuan Shu chortled. "He will lure us into thinking that we are safe, and then he would turn us over to Cao Cao!"

"I don't believe that he would, Lord Yuan!" Zhang Xun protested.

Yuan Shu smiled and said, "Your greatest strength is loyalty, Zhang Xun, but it is also your greatest weakness. Sun Ce is, as you say, an honourable man, but he is not as forgiving as you would like to believe. He blames me for the death of his father: if I give him the opportunity, he will destroy me and relish it. Where is he now...? On his way to Jing, isn't he...? If he has not forgotten Liu Biao's part in it, he will not have forgotten mine. Now please, Zhang Xun, say no more of going to Sun Ce."

Zhang Xun bowed slowly and said, "As you command, Lord Yuan."

"We'll go back to Shouchun... yes, we'll go and we'll go now," Yuan Shu ordered. "We'll... we'll go now."

Yuan Shu and his senior retainers looked at the faces of their subordinates and saw nothing but fear, despair and anger in their expressions. The greatest threats to the former warlord were desertion, mutiny, hunger, malnutrition and disease, but he had no choice other than to turn his small force and begin the journey back to the smouldering ruins of Shouchun City, where Cao Cao's forces awaited him.

As the days passed and various situations changed and intensified, the former Administrator of Wu Prefecture, Sheng Xian, summoned a dozen of his most loyal followers to his home for a private discussion.

"I cannot risk a larger gathering," Sheng Xian explained once everyone was seated. "Yuan Shu has fled Shouchun, been thwarted by Liu Bei and Cao Cao, and turned back to the west of Jiujiang, toward Shouchun or maybe his family seat in Ru County. Soon, there will be no Yuan Shu..."

The former official Dai Yuan coughed deliberately and said, "So you have received official communications from Cao Cao, talking about the future, then...?"

"...No, I have not," Sheng Xian replied bitterly. "Rather, I have received yet another request for a pledge, this time from Sun Ce's lackey Zhu Zhi. How dare they, gentlemen! What role would they give me, mm...? A subordinate to Xu Gong, the man that stole my job and currently occupies it illegally, and for an insulting second time...?"

"You refused, I hope," the former official Gui Lan prompted.

"As I always do, but I called you here to implore you all to leave me now," Sheng Xian replied. "I am finished, gentlemen. I shall never be more than I am now. You have spent these last three years or more here in exile with me, and I wholeheartedly respect and appreciate that loyalty, but enough is enough! I was ousted, I now realise, because I was unpopular. Perhaps I deserved it... I cannot say. But you've all suffered enough for being my officials, so-"

"You are wrong in this matter, Administrator!" Dai Yuan protested: the other men added their own near-incoherent remonstrations to Dai's.

"I am still finished, whether I am right or wrong!" Sheng Xian replied. **"Gentlemen, please hush... and let me speak."**

The exiled officials fell silent.

"...Go, all of you, and find work," Sheng Xian pleaded. "You cannot continue to raise families and live on this estate, not while White Tiger Yan recovers his strength and General Xu ages and weakens. When this place ceases to be a refuge, what then...? You all intend to die at my side, when all I ever was to you was a manager, a superior...? I am not your lord, and you are not my vassals!"

"All the same, you treated us well, and we cannot abandon you," Gui Lan insisted. "You supported us and encouraged us and nurtured us, Mister Sheng, and so we owe you our loyalty. We'll defend you, fight for you, and even die for you if needs be. What has a Confucian got if he does not have the principles that he was raised with? If not for duty, loyalty, honesty, righteousness and such, what does he have...?"

The officials murmured agreeably.

"...You are all too good to me," Sheng Xian replied. "Perhaps all will be well: perhaps Sun Ce will be appointed officially, and then working with him becomes a possibility, or maybe my friends in the capital will find some way to resolve this. It cannot go on much longer, surely..."

Since Sheng Xian's faction had been ousted by Xu Gong, they had seemed to be something of an irrelevance: many disregarded them as hardly worth a mention, although others, such as Cheng Pu, advocated eliminating them in order to remove the threat that they theoretically posed to the Sun family. Bofu had opted for leaving Sheng Xian alone: in the future, the Sun regime would take a different stance, and that would set a chain of events in motion that would leave the Sun clan with wounds that would never fully heal: for the next year, they remained an irrelevance.

✳✳✳✳✳✳✳✳✳✳✳✳

118

The two men that had been selected to lead the initial defence of Jiangxia's waterways – Administrator Huang Zu's son Yi and the officer Han Xi – were at the helm of the naval force that hoped to blockade the route to Three Rivers and prevent Bofu's navy from establishing any kind of foothold in Jing Province: they stationed their boats to the west of Hukou and awaited Bofu's response.

"Word is that the majority of the latest recruits are pirates," Gongjin reported to Bofu, who was stood on the deck of his flagship and observing the enemy fleet.

"So are ours," Bofu replied casually. "But does he have anyone like Zhou Tai, I wonder...?"

Zhou Tai bowed slightly and said, "You are too kind, Lord Sun."

"Huang Gai and Han Dang are almost here, Jiang Qin brings the smaller boats as requested and will be here even sooner, and Zu Lang is camped in Yuzhang and ready to reinforce us if he's needed," Lü Fan reported.

"What a day and age," Cheng Pu sighed. "Zu Lang as our reserve... Taishi Ci as our vanguard...!"

"Who is this 'Han Xi' that he tries to go up against us...?" Bofu scoffed. "I'd never heard of him until now. And 'Huang Yi' is his scrubby, untalented son: Huang Zu has no worthy officers, and Jiangxia is as good as ours."

"He even delivers it to us quickly!" Ling Cao chuckled.

Han Xi had ordered an advance: Bofu laughed, gestured to his officers, and turned to Sun Hè, saying, "I want to get involved."

"Let your officers deal with this until we know the riverbanks aren't lined with traps," Cheng Pu suggested. "You were in Xiangyang, Lord Sun, and you fought in naval battles there, so you know what-"

"Yes, old man, I remember," Bofu grumbled as he watched Ling Cao, Lü Meng, Zhou Tai and Taishi Ci's joint preparations for a river skirmish: the four officers left the flagship and took their places on the lead boats that would meet Han Xi's.

Taishi Ci surprised everyone when he outpaced Ling Cao and engaged Han Xi in one-on-one combat: the former roaming vigilante was as adept at river warfare as he was on land, and Han Xi, though competent, was forced on an immediate defensive. Ling Cao and Lü Meng passed Han Xi's boat and attacked the others, which left Han Xi surrounded: Zhou Tai, meanwhile, led a force down the southern bank and began the essential search for hidden snipers.

"*Ayah*... Lü Meng passes out more brains in a morning's relief than he keeps in his head!" Cheng Pu complained. **"What is he doing???"**

Lü Meng had been tasked with securing the northern riverbank, but bloodlust had drawn him away from that task and into a battle with one of Huang Yi's subordinates that was drawing him and his crew further and further away from safety.

"I'll have to go and get him!" Bofu suggested.

"You'll stay where you are!" Cheng Pu barked. **"If he wants to die, fine!"**

Jiang Qin, Sun Ben, Sun Fu and Xu Kun arrived as part of a force of small boats at that point: Lü Meng was saved from his dilemma and suddenly became part of a pincer attack that forced Huang Yi to withdraw his boats.

"**He might be stupid, but he's also lucky!**" Bofu joked.

"**The 'stupid' part is still a worry,**" Cheng Pu replied. "**He hasn't moved back, so I'm going to have to lead my men down there to do his job for him before we lose anyone important.**"

"*You're* **important!**" Bofu protested. "**Besides, you're-!**"

"**I'm *not old*!**" Cheng Pu barked. "**And you're more important, Lord Sun! Zhou Yu, Lü Fan, Sun Hè, Song Qian, please ensure that he doesn't-**"

"**We will,**" Gongjin promised.

Cheng Pu added his own veteran presence to the river battle and immediately ended an attempted attack on the flagship by saboteurs that Ling Cao and Taishi Ci had been unable to intercept: he then turned his attention to the southern riverbank while his elite men engaged any individual boats that tried to approach him or the ships.

"**...It's over,**" Lü Fan reported.

"*Already*...?" Bofu exclaimed: he turned his gaze to the enemy ships and saw that they were beginning a withdrawal westward, toward Three Rivers.

"**That showed them!**" Bofu cried excitedly. "**Huang Zu, your head will soon be mine to present to my father's tomb!**"

"**...You shouldn't celebrate so soon, Bofu,**" Lü Fan suggested. "**One little skirmish-**"

"**We've crushed them!**" Bofu insisted.

"**They're *testing our strength*!**" Gongjin said. "**He has other officers!**"

"...So what do you suggest that we do, then...?" Bofu asked.

"We must send scouts to ascertain their response to this 'test result'," Gongjin replied. "If we do not, we risk being countered. Kuai Yue is with Huang Zu, and Kuai Liang sends advice from Liu Biao's northern capital: those two alone are enough of a worry."

"...Alright," Bofu said as he watched his boatmen chase Han Xi's forces away.

The short battle ended, and the various leaders of Bofu's army and navy prepared for a meeting to discuss their next moves. But before that meeting could take place, an elated Sun Ben boarded the flagship, ran into the command room and said, "**They're back! A messenger sent word that-! ...He *released them*, Cousin Bofu! My family, they...!**"

Bofu, Sun Yi and Sun Hè approached Ben with smiles on their faces, and Bofu grasped Ben's shoulders.

"It must soon be over then!" Sun Ben continued. "If... if he freed them, then-!"

"They're alive and safe, and right now, that's all that you should be thinking about, Boyang," Bofu suggested. "Why and how, they're for the advisers to ponder. Did you want to leave the front and-?"

"No, Bofu, no: I only just got here, anyway!" Sun Ben replied insistently. "Liu Biao is my enemy as much as he's yours. I remember that time in Xiangyang as well as you do, and my

family will just have to understand that his destruction must come first. If they can understand my abandoning them to be hostages, then they can understand that."
Sun Fu had followed his brother to the command room: he frowned and said, "Don't say such things! You didn't abandon them, Brother!"
"...I feel like I did," Sun Ben replied. "But they're safe, and Yuan Shu is close to destruction in that case... ... ...I wonder if I have Zhang Xun to thank for this."
"He's my friend, but at the same time, his pedantic loyalty to that evil man annoys me and makes it hard to like him," Bofu admitted. "If we do have Zhang to thank, then it's too little, too late so far as I'm concerned. He should have abandoned Shu a long time ago and come over to us! He could have brought his family with him from Huainan, and-!"
"We could have done a lot of things differently, Bofu," Sun Ben retorted. "Don't judge the man yet, not until we know what he's spared us from."
"...Quite true," Bofu sighed.
"Word's coming from the far north that Gongsun Zan is dead or as good as," Sun Fu reported. "Yuan Shao will return to the main political stage then; I wonder what he'll make of his brother being hounded to death by us and-"
"We did nothing to Shu," Sun Ben said. "We left his service and harassed Liu Xun, but his death is down to Liu Bei and Cao Cao."
"...Are you sure that you don't want to go to Danyang?" Bofu asked.
"I'm certain," Sun Ben chuckled. "Your wife is pregnant, Bofu, but you're here, even though you worry for her and the child she carries; my family is precious, yes, but no more than yours. My place is here, defending Jiangdong from Huang Zu."
"Then let's hurry and destroy our enemies so that we can go home," Sun Yi said excitedly. "I want to see my cousins, Bofu!"
"Huang Zu and Liu Biao will not keep us here long, not after such a boost to morale," Bofu replied. "Whatever happens, and however long it takes, we cannot lose!"
One and all agreed.

Yuan Shu's small army of followers were dogged by bad weather and dwindling supplies as they neared Shouchun: Shu was stricken by illness and was transferred from a horse to a stretcher as his condition worsened.
"...To... end... like...!" Yuan Shu gasped as he stared at the darkened sky above: it was raining, as it very often did, and the cold water pierced his body like thousands of icy arrows.
"Save your strength," General Zhang Xun pleaded.
"We're almost there now!" the adviser Yang Hong said encouragingly.
"...Almost... end," Yuan Shu replied. "Yes... almost..."
His occasional exclamations were replaced by laboured breathing for the remainder of his time, which amounted to a few hours. Nobody noticed that he had expired straight away, as they were too focussed on moving through the unfriendly terrain that they were forced to pass through in order to avoid the numerous enemies of their disgraced lord: when they did realise that Yuan

Shu was gone, their determination was replaced by a sudden liberation from service – which some enjoyed by deserting immediately – and a need to find a new purpose, which others pondered as they continued their journey to Shouchun. This was the end of an era: after eight years of being a source of unrest and instability, Yuan Shu of Ru County was dead, and there was now one less warlord in China.

Once the small group led by Zhang Xun and Yang Hong had reached Shouchun, they entered the besieged city and met with Yuan Shu's cousin Yin in the ruins of Shu's imperial palace.
"...I am close to speechless," Yuan Yin said as he stared at Yuan Shu's hastily-procured, cheap wooden coffin.
"What are we to do, Lord Yuan...?" Zhang Xun asked of Yuan Shu's son Yao, who was too affected by his father's recent death to answer.
"I will act in my late cousin's stead," Yuan Yin declared. "We have no time to mourn: Cao Cao has heard the news and wants to inflict one last insult upon our lord by seizing his coffin and the Imperial Seal. We must-"
"Wait... it was real, then...?" Zhang Xun exclaimed.
"...Was *what* real...?" Yuan Yin asked defensively.
"The Imperial Seal," Zhang Xun replied.
"**Are you accusing my father of lying???**" Yuan Yao shrieked.
Zhang Xun bowed humbly and said, "N-no, Lord Yuan, but-"
"You harboured *doubts*, then, Zhang Xun...?" Yuan Yin heckled. "You doubted the word of our *lord*, Zhang Xun...? Why, because Sun Ce is your *friend*, and he promised you that-"
"No!" Zhang Xun protested. "I have not been allowed to see the Seal as we travelled, and I supposed it lost by the last Han emperor, and I supposed that the common rumours that Lord Yuan had another made to-"
"You suppose a lot for a shopkeeper's boy that benefitted from his lord's generosity!" Yuan Yin retorted. "Some Grand General you are, that you-!"
"I thought that we had no time for anything but flight," Yang Hong prompted. "The Imperial Seal's authenticity is irrelevant at this point, Zhang Xun!"
Zhang Xun averted his gaze and murmured, "I suppose so..."
"Do you job, General Zhang, and escort the late Lord Yuan's family to Lujiang," Yuan Yin ordered. "Yang Hong will accompany you. I shall take up the rear of the force, since the army trusts me."
"...Alright, Mister Yuan," Zhang Xun replied.
Zhang Xun and Yang Hong led the retreat from Shouchun: as they travelled, Yang Hong said, "You may be right to doubt the authenticity of the Imperial Seal, General Zhang, but do not raise it in front of the young lord again."
"It was a mistake," Zhang Xun replied apologetically. "I am torn between being a friend to Sun Ce and a vassal to the Yuan clan."
"Your lord must always come first, and the subject of going to Sun Ce has been discussed and resolved already," Yang Hong retorted.
"Forgive me for how I say this, but Lord Yuan Shu's death has changed everything," Zhang Xun replied.
"How so...?" Yang Hong asked.

"Any grudge was against Lord Yuan Shu specifically, and I can prove it with Sun Ce's other actions," Zhang Xun explained. "Sun Ce now employs *Lu Xun*, nephew of *Lu Kang*, and *Liu Ji*, the son of *Liu Yao*!"
Yang Hong hummed thoughtfully.
"He takes each man on his individual merits, and so I doubt that he will harm the young lord!" Zhang Xun continued.
"...But he'd expect service," Yang Hong supposed.
"Liu Ji enjoys high rank and is a guest at the family home on special occasions," Zhang Xun replied. "I don't believe that Sun Ce would want to humiliate the young lord."
"...You don't need to convince me further," Yang Hong admitted. "I detest the idea of being 'protected' by an arrogant hankerer like Liu Xun: and unlike Yuan Yin, I don't trust the man. His connection to the royal house inflates his ego: if he were to come into possession of an artefact like the Imperial Seal that we possess, then real or not, he would probably decide that it was his by divine will and contest the Han throne, thereby beginning another era of trouble for us."
"...So we must be wary of Liu Xun," Zhang Xun prompted.
"Naturally," Yang Hong replied. "We must make many decisions, you and I: do we go to Sun Ce, or do we trust Liu Xun...? Do we now serve the young lord Yuan Yao or do we serve his self-appointed protector Yuan Yin...?"
Zhang Xun hummed thoughtfully.
"...After what you've said, my instinct is to trust Sun Ce, I must confess," Yang Hong continued. "We will open communications when we reach Lujiang."
Zhang Xun smiled and said, "We can trust him, Mister Yang... I know we can."

The subjugated Administrator of Wu Prefecture, Xu Gong, was one of many men that met with Bofu's representative in Wu Prefecture, Zhu Zhi, to discuss the evolving political situation.
"As you'll know by now, Yuan Shu is dead," Zhu Zhi said to a numbed audience. "I understand that he died on route back to Shouchun after a failed escape attempt... but when and how he died is actually unimportant. He's dead, and that changes everything here in Wu Prefecture, just as it changes everything everywhere else."
Xu Gong cleared his throat and said, "In what way, Mister Zhu?"
"For one, it frees up the majority of Cao Cao's army," Zhu Zhi replied. "We do not know what he intends to do with that army."
"When you say, 'Cao Cao's army', you mean the *Han Imperial Army*," Xu Gong retorted. "Cao Cao is a loyal supporter of His Majesty. But what are 'we'...?"
Some of Bofu's followers started to grumbled disconcertedly.
"Hold your tongue, Xu Gong!" Zhu Ran barked. "My father is-!"
"Your father is quite capable of answering for himself, Ran," Zhu Zhi said. "Mister Xu Gong, 'we' are also loyal subjects of the Han. Everything that we now do is done for the sake of the Han, and so it shall remain. Our former lord, vile man that he was, is dead, and we are no longer prisoners of the past. In the future, we'll only know service to the empire."
"If anyone has anything to be worried about, Xu Gong, it's *you*!"

one of Hè Qi's majors heckled. "Excellency Cao might want to put Sheng Xian back in office here in Wu, and what of you then, I wonder...?"

Xu Gong snorted a laugh and said, "What then...? I'll *tell you*... the people will demand that he be removed again. I've been recognised by Excellency Cao, who hates the men that benefitted from the 'Ten Attendants' running Luoyang as much as I do: Sheng Xian's friends orbit the Excellency of Works like flies around dung, but none of them can convince the court to give Sheng anything but promises that he won't be harmed."

Xu Gong's growing following murmured agreeably: Zhu Zhi harrumphed nervously and asked, "What do you want to say, Mister Xu?"

"I have said it," Xu Gong replied. "I have no quarrel with men that want to follow the Han regime that Cao Cao represents. If Sun Ce does not want an argument, then I can see no-"

"He is 'Lord Sun Ce' to you, Xu Gong!" Commandant Hè Qi bellowed.

"...He is not my lord," Xu Gong retorted. "I pledged allegiance to the Han, not to Sun Ce. I allied myself to Sun Ce and his vassals, and that is all. My allegiance is to the Han, and if I sense anything to the contrary from Sun Ce, I will be compelled to report it to Excellency Cao."

"...For a man that had supposedly said everything that he wanted to say, you certainly had a lot to add, Xu Gong," Zhu Zhi grumbled. "I won't deny that I find a man that overthrew the appointed administrator with an army of barbarians and bandits slightly amusing when he speaks with such pomposity, but your points are noted: Lord Sun is not intending any rebellion against the Han, and never has."

"What is the purpose of his current campaign in Jing Province...?" Xu Gong asked.

"...It is not, as some have claimed, for petty revenge," Zhu Zhi replied cautiously. "Liu Biao has been targeted by Cao Cao before in the name of His Majesty, so Lord Sun merely acts in his capacity as 'Rebellion-supressing General' while Cao Cao is distracted by Yuan Shu's loyalists in Yu and northern Yang. What is the problem there...?"

"...There is no problem, apparently," Xu Gong said politely. "I am satisfied that I deal with a man of high integrity."

Zhu Zhi found it difficult to take his eyes off of the smirking Xu Gong as he continued the discussion. There were some that were determined to be rid of Xu Gong, but Bofu insisted upon toleration of his controversial ally: in the future, Xu Gong's actions and the reaction to them would set a chain of events in motion that would significantly harm the Sun clan, but for now, he was little more than a controversial ally.

****

119

Yuan Shu's appointed Administrator of Lujiang Prefecture, Liu Xun, first learned of the impending arrival of his 'guests' from Shouchun when Yang Hong's messenger delivered an urgent request for a military escort to his embattled capital, Huancheng.

"...**You may go and rest,**" Liu Xun said to the messenger, who immediately kowtowed, turned and fled the hall with his two soldier escorts.

"We should ponder this," one adviser suggested.

"Ponder *what*...?" Liu Xun asked. "I am sieged continually by this 'Li Shu' that Sun Ce left here to oversee my destruction, and Cao Cao – once a man that I worked in the court with and might have called a friend until the Yuan feud – now looms large and threatens to devour me for my allegiance to Lord Yuan! Now I am expected to 'ponder' something when everything is so clear...?"

"Lord Liu, you are a scion of the imperial house that has supported a usurper, thereby harming your own right to a higher existence," the adviser continued. "You did so out of loyalty to Yuan Shu, but Yuan is dead now. By harbouring his coffin and his family, you continue to wrong your own clan, the Liu clan, and the Han Emperor that you are kin to!"

Some of the other advisers murmured agreeably.

"That boy on the throne is not the legitimate heir," Liu Xun scoffed. "I-"

"By dying a pauper with his capital in ruins, Yuan Shu has proved that he was no legitimate successor with the Mandate of Heaven," the adviser Liu Yè said. "Like you, Lord Liu, I am related to the ruling Liu clan, and like you, I doubted the authenticity of Cao Cao's puppet... I still do. But Cao Cao is an old acquaintance to us both, and negotiations might be considered. On the other hand, we have to ponder our loyalty to Yuan Yao, the son of our deceased lord, and Yuan Yin, the cousin of our deceased lord and 'guardian' of sorts to Yuan Yao, despite his being a man and not requiring one."

Some of the officials sniggered at the dry remark.

"...All that you say is true in one way or another," Liu Xun said.

Liu Yè smiled and said, "Yuan Yin guards the rear while Zhang Xun and Yang Hong hurry here with what's left of Yuan Shu's army and, I understand, not only the lord's coffin but his rumoured 'Imperial Seal' that failed to serve as a trade for his safety."

The other officials mumbled nervously; Liu Xun leant forward and asked, "Is that so, Mister Liu Yè...?"

"Real or not, that Seal is on its way here, and while it sounds like we may lose Yuan Yin and-or the lord's coffin, the rest of the party will make it to the Lujiang border," Liu Yè replied.

"Well then," Liu Xun said, "we'd better make them welcome, hadn't we...?"

A few days later, a messenger ran into the command room of Bofu's naval flagship and shouted, "**REPORT!**"

"Ah! The scouts are back!" Bofu chuckled.

"...He's not a scout," Cheng Pu said fretfully. "He's Li Shu's man."

"**Reports from northern Yang!**" the messenger began. "**The-!**"

"...This had better not be a distraction," Bofu said angrily. "We're so *close*, and-!"

"*Hush*, and let the messenger speak," Cheng Pu suggested.

"Go on, messenger," Lü Fan prompted.

"Yuan Shu is now confirmed as dead!" the messenger began: he was immediately interrupted by a chorus of cheers and other celebratory exchanges that Lü Fan was forced to silence. After a few moments, the messenger added, "Yuan Shu died on his way back to Shouchun after fleeing east to the Xu-Yang border! Yuan Yin has abandoned Shouchun, and Cao Cao is now fortifying the region! Yuan Shu's family have been escorted to Lujiang's capital Huancheng by Yuan Yin, General Zhang Xun and Mister Yang Hong: General Zhang and Mister Yang have requested dialogue with Lord Sun! But-!"

"Of *course* my friend Zhang Xun can talk to me!" Bofu chuckled. "Go back now, man, and tell him that-!"

"The messenger isn't finished," Lü Fan said sombrely.

Bofu looked at the miserable messenger and said, "Go on, then. What else is there?"

"...But Liu Xun, the self-appointed Administrator of Lujiang, has taken Yuan Yin, Yang Hong, Zhang Xun and Yuan Shu's surviving family as captives, and has declared that he is now an independent warlord with the right to govern Yang Province now that Yuan Shu is gone!" the messenger reported. "Commander Li Shu has withdrawn to the Jiujiang border because he is unable to resist the new combined force of Yuan Shu's impressed troops and Liu Xun's own men without further help! Liu Xun has begun preparations for an attack on Haihun, and-!"

"We risk losing Li Shu...?" Lü Fan murmured.

"And Liu Xun plans an attack on Haihun???" Gongjin exclaimed. "We must turn about at once and-!"

"D'AAAAAGH! WHY, WHY, WHY AM I ALWAYS CONFOUNDED AT THE CRITICAL MOMENT???" Bofu screamed. **"WHY MUST I NOW ALLOW MY FATHER'S MURDERER TO ESCAPE AND-!"**

"Bofu, you must *calm down*!" Gongjin pleaded. **"You must-!"**

"Calm down???" Bofu retorted. **"Huang Zu is alive, and you want me to *calm down*??? Liu Biao is laughing and thanking the gods for saving his rotten hide yet again, and you want me to *calm down*???"**

Lü Fan turned to the cowering messenger and asked, "Was there anything else...?"

"N-no, Mister Lü," the messenger replied.

"Go and rest then," Lü Fan ordered, and the messenger retreated. Fan then turned to Bofu – who was still raving incoherently, and bellowed, **"We have to go back and that's that, Lord Sun!"**

"...You too, Ziheng...?" Bofu croaked. "You'd let him-?"

"We... we have to go back," Cheng Pu said with obvious difficulty. "If Liu Xun is about to rally the remnants of Yuan Shu's army under a new, untainted banner and try and take northern Yang, then Li Shu will not be able to cope alone. We must deal one last blow to Huang Zu with our vanguard force and then retreat, citing that our purpose was to punish him for attacking Yuzhang. He'll think twice before doing that again, and we can return when our other problems are dealt with."

Taishi Ci shook his head sorrowfully and said, "I feel that my sluggishness in dealing with Liu Pan led us to this. Let me take the vanguard, Lord Sun, and deal that last blow that Mister Cheng speaks of."

"You have no need to reproach yourself, Mister Taishi," Cheng Pu insisted. "I, grey-haired fool that I am, took you for a criminal and wanted you dead, but we'd still be pushing Liu Pan out of Yuzhang if not for you. At least we've scared them, and-"

"We can't just *leave*!" Bofu chortled. "You've all lost your minds! Let Liu Xun take Haihun! What good will it do him??? Once Liu Biao is dead, we'll-!"

"All that we've managed to achieve is one small naval victory, Lord Sun, in quite a considerable time!" Cheng Pu scolded. "You're talking about going into Jing and eliminating Huang Zu, Cai Mao, Kuai Liang, Liu Biao and the rest of them as though it were a matter of scattering a few rebels! It was underestimating them last time that cost us your father! We cannot rush into this or we'll suffer more pain! How can we attack northern Jiangxia when Liu Xun will be at our backs the entire time...? We have to go back to Danyang, secure the Yuzhang riverbank and go to Lujiang to stop Liu Xun before he-!"

"I KNOW, ALRIGHT??? I... I *know*," Bofu replied. "But... we were so close...! I... I thought that after all we'd achieved, that-!"

"This is a story that must remain incomplete for now, Lord Sun," Cheng Pu said. "I ache too, believe you me... we all do."

Huang Gai nodded slowly and sadly.

"...But we've had to stomach Liu Biao and Huang Zu's persisting existence for as long as you have, and yet we understand that other things must come first," Cheng Pu continued. "We'll go now, Lord Sun... the sooner we deal with Liu Xun, the sooner we can return and finish what we've started."

Bofu was unable to respond for a few moments: he looked at the faces of his family and retainers and realised that he was far from alone in wanting to stay, but at the same time he saw the same understanding that the fates had spoken and retreat was a necessity.

"I had to order the withdrawal last time, Bofu, and... and I know how it feels, but it has to be done," Sun Ben protested. "Liu Biao, like it or not, *can* wait, while Liu Xun *cannot*."

"...Lü Fan, give the general order to withdraw," Bofu said. "Taishi Ci, Ling Cao: you'll put on a show of strength and smash Han Xi's forward units while the rest go back. Gongjin, find an able man with wit and have him convey our false intentions to Huang Zu as soon as Taishi and Ling have done their work. We'll go back to Danyang first, ready ourselves, and try and use some sort of scheme against Liu Xun rather than rush at him, since a third siege of Huancheng is the last thing that any of us want, and we'd then have Huang Zu at our backs... everyone is dismissed."

The command room slowly emptied: only Bofu, Sun Hè, Sun Ben, Sun Yi and Bofu's bodyguard force remained.

"...Whatever I need to do to get us back here quickly, I'll do it," Bofu said. "But I swear... Liu Xun is doubly dead. I swear it. For taking me away from this, he'll-"

"Bofu, let it go," Sun Ben pleaded. "You'll be unable to fight Liu Xun if you're this angry when we get to Lujiang, and his adviser Liu Yè is as dangerous as Kuai Liang! We all need to calm down

and go back with clear heads."
Bofu sighed and said, "I can't promise that, Boyang... I'm sorry."

Huang Zu received Bofu's messenger, heard the reasons given for the sudden withdrawal and dismissed the messenger without harming him.
"We should have sent the man's head back in a box!" Han Xi protested.
"Han Xi is right, Father!" Huang Yi said. "We should kill the messenger and-!"
"And *what*...?" Huang Zu interrupted. "My son, I have not held Jiangxia for all this time by luck alone: I do have some shred of understanding of military and political matters, and I now see, once again, the need for heeding counsel. Mister Kuai...?"
All eyes turned to the adviser Kuai Yue, who said, "We are fortunate. Yuan Shu's death must have changed the political situation in northern Yang in a way that somehow threatens the Sun family. Perhaps Liu Xun, Yuan Yin or Yang Hong has managed to establish their own foothold with the intent of using Yuan Shu's army to recapture Jiangdong. I shall look into it."
"If there's an alliance to be had, find it and secure it," Huang Zu ordered.
"...I would need to consult Governor Liu first," Kuai Yue suggested.
"Of course," Huang Zu said. "But it is your view that this retreat is genuine...?"
"Oh, certainly," Kuai Yue replied. "Sun Ce is a fearless, reckless hero, like his father: he wouldn't say he's retreating and then attack, because he'd consider that to be cowardly. He's gone, though probably not for the reason he's given: we all know that he'll never let go of his hatred for you, Mister Huang, and that he wants Jing. This was no punishment for our incursion into Yuzhang... no, it's something else."
"Whatever it was, it saved us a lot of trouble," Huang Zu said. "I shall write to Governor Liu and tell him what's happened. There will, as you say, be a 'next time', and we must be far readier for it than we are now..."

When Bofu reached Danyang's capital, he found that a strange new atmosphere existed: people were talking about miracles and sermons by a mysterious figure that was known only as 'Gan Ji'. Bofu ordered an immediate investigation, but he was shocked to find that his senior officials were all aware of the Taoist preacher.
"...So let me see if I understand this correctly," Bofu said to his packed court. "I was away for a few months, and in that time, all that anyone could find to do was allow this Taoist cultist fraud to enter Jiangdong and start spreading his nonsense...?"
"...My lord, Gan Ji is a renowned figure, a living Taoist *saint*, and he is benevolent and good," Zhang Zhao insisted.
"Indeed he is!" Zhang Hong said. "He heals the sick, gives hope to those who despair, brings-!"
"You're describing another Zhang Jue or Ze Rong!" Bofu heckled. "Didn't Zhang Jue 'heal the sick' and additionally spread that mantra that turned sensible people into gibbering fanatics that my poor father – whose death goes unavenged while I deal with such nonsense – had to go halfway across the country to pacify...? And

wasn't that murdering liar Ze Rong a 'living Buddhist saint'...?
...I'm angry. I won't deny that, I'm angry. I-"
"But my lord Sun Ce, even your mother Lady Wu speaks well of
Gan Ji, and agrees with the consensus that he can only be a
saint!" Zhang Zhao declared. "Lady Chen has also spoken well of
his calming words and feats of Heavenly wonder!"
"...Oh, no," Gongjin whispered as he stared at Bofu, who was
becoming increasingly unable to contain his rage.
"...Zhang Zhao, my nephew is obviously unhappy to hear that my
sister converses with this Taoist man," Wu Jing said. "You should-"
"Most agree that he has performed genuine miracles!" Zhang
Zhao continued. "He spreads nothing but love, and a message
that we could all-"
Bofu slammed his palm onto the writing desk in front of him and
shouted, "**Who allowed this man near my mother???**"
"Not I!" Wu Jing replied instinctively.
"...My lord, he is benevolent and good," Zhang Zhao whimpered.
Bofu looked at his nervous officials, laughed disdainfully and said,
"You're all fools! **Fools!** How many of them must there be?"
"We are not all complicit in this," Gu Yong insisted.
"No, Yuantan, I know you to have more sense!" Bofu chortled.
"Zhang Zhao: I brought you and your brother here to advise me,
not to send my mother and aunt mad with talk of Taoist saints!"
"Others agree!" Zhang Zhao protested. "Gan Ji is-"
"Can we even be sure this man *is* Gan Ji?" Lü Fan suggested. "He
is far too young, surely, to be Gan Ji."
"People speak of him finding ways to extend his life!" Zhang Zhao
retorted. "His knowledge of the Taoist teachings is-"
"I really do not believe this," Bofu said angrily. "You are a
simpleton! It is men like you that allowed Zhang Lu to take over
Hanzhong and Ze Rong to take over half of Xu Province! What did
I say not once, not twice, but more times than I can count? No
more saints! No more healers! If it isn't nonsense, then they mean
no good anyway, else the world under Heaven would be peaceful!"
"...He's a good man, even if he isn't a saint," Zhang Zhao insisted.
"Based on what?" Bofu chortled. "Do you truly know this man any
better than Tao Qian knew Ze Rong, or Liu Yan knew Zhang Lu?"
"So what do you want to do?" Lü Fan asked.
"Ziheng, I am not a vicious man," Bofu said desperately. "All I ask
is that people do as they're told. We fought long and hard to make
the south what it is now, and I am not about to have it ruined by
a religious fraudster! Zhang Zhao, I trusted you with matters of
state, and yet you bring this man into the fold! I don't care if he is
Gan Ji or not... I want him arrested."
Some of Zhang Zhao's supporters gasped and groaned at the
proclamation.
"You mustn't, Lord Sun Ce!" Zhang Zhao pleaded. "We will be
punished by Heaven!"
"So you want to allow this man to poison the minds of the people
and return the south to its original state, Zhang Zhao?" Bofu
heckled. "The Yellow Turbans, the Way of Five Pecks, they're all
the same... no progress is made. I am a follower of Confucius, who
taught that the good of the state is paramount, and the state is
people and system both. That means that anything that can harm
the state, be it a corrupt official in the system or a heretic or

anarchist amongst the people, must be purged. This man will be arrested and asked to leave Jiangdong: if he agrees, then he will be politely escorted to the border with Jiangxia and sent to Huang Zu, for I'm sure that the two will get along very well; if he refuses, he will be publicly put to death to send a message to any more of these types that want to make trouble here."

"**Lord *Sun Ce*!**" Zhang Zhao cried.

"That's my name," Bofu quipped. "Kindly do as I ask... for *once*."

There was no more dissent: the man claiming to be Gan Ji – a famous Taoist priest and philosopher – was apprehended and placed in the main prison.

Lady Wu and Lady Chen summoned Bofu to an urgent meeting two hours after 'Gan Ji' had been arrested.

"I know what this is about," Bofu said dismissively. "No more frauds, Mother. I-"

"He is good and kind!" Lady Wu insisted. "Do you have any idea how many he's brought hope to...? The Zhangs are inundated with demands for Gan Ji's release already! So many women came to me to beg me to speak to you! He has nothing to say that is wicked or provocative, and-"

"They always begin with kind words," Bofu interrupted. "Every one of them does, Mother... Zhang Lu, Ze Rong, Zhang Jue... but in the end, they all want the same thing. The real Gan Ji is probably dead, the man is so old, and that man I've just visited is barely ten years older than me. He cannot answer simple questions and instead resorts to riddles and phrases that sound intelligent and insightful but are, in fact, meaningless nonsense designed to make clever men look stupid to the less intelligent, who are additionally compelled to agree for fear of looking stupid. Father warned me against men like that a long time ago, Mother... so why do you now let him muddle your mind...?"

"...He comforts the troubled!" Lady Wu sobbed.

"I've heard nothing that indicates that he means anything but good!" Lady Chen protested.

"Ah... I see... he plays on your distress over Dad and what Quan did recently," Bofu said. "That's all the more reason to kill him."

"You mustn't, Bofu!" Lady Wu pleaded. "If you harm a man that thousands regard as a living saint, you will be hated! You will make enemies from the highest to the lowest! Men you've never met will plot your death!"

"'Men I've never met' already plot my death!" Bofu retorted. "Cao Cao will be looking to kill me, Mother, and Yuan Shao too! Every soldier that Liu Biao, Huang Zu, Liu Xun, or whoever else I've angered will want me dead, and how many of them have I met, mm...? What's a few more if it means that I halt another mass uprising of heretics...?"

"...You won't be swayed, I can see that," Lady Wu said. "But Zhang Zhao and Zhang Hong... you won't hold it against them that they introduced me to Gan Ji at my request...?"

"No more than I want Quan holding it against Ziheng for reporting the theft," Bofu replied. "The Zhangs thought they were helping... I see that. But 'Gan Ji' – or whatever his real name is – must be removed from Jiangdong one way or the other. If he won't leave, he dies."

"...You're angry that you were forced to withdraw from Jing," Lady Chen prompted.

"Yes, Second Mother, but I am not running to men like 'Gan Ji' to find the hope that I need to carry on," Bofu replied. "I-"

"**Elder Brother!**" Shangxiang said as she entered the room with Kuang and Lady Chen's children.

"All of you go back to your rooms at once!" Lady Wu ordered.

"Let Shangxiang greet her brother," Bofu chuckled as he embraced each of the children in turn. "Still wearing trousers, I see, Shangxiang. But they suit you!"

"...Thank you, Brother," Shangxiang whispered.

"I'd better go," Bofu continued. "What we discussed, Mother, is resolved. No more trouble. I have a Lujiang campaign to plan for, and I don't need to be worrying about another 'Way of Peace' springing up while I'm there."

"...It isn't worth the risk, and I understand that," Lady Wu replied. "But in other matters, Bofu, I shall continue to challenge you. You're angry, and I know what that means... I won't let you destroy yourself and everything that-"

"I'd better go to Daqiao before she forgets what I look like," Bofu interrupted. "We'll all have a banquet before I go, maybe..."

Once Bofu had departed, Lady Wu turned to Shangxiang and Kuang and said, "Children: go back to your rooms. Kuang... remain, please."

The thin, frail Kuang awaited his mother's words while the others retreated.

"...Soon you'll be ready to take up an office," Lady Wu continued. "You're not a fighting man like Bofu and Shubi. You're like Quan... well, not quite. You're an honest man of the pen, and Bofu will need to find you a good role."

"I am content with whatever I am offered," Kuang replied.

"Such a good lad," Lady Wu sighed. "Go and return to your studies."

Sun Kuang bowed humbly and retreated.

"...Will you really let Bofu kill Gan Ji...?" Lady Chen asked.

"His argument made sense," Lady Wu replied. "Like it or not, it made sense, and we cannot risk everything for a man that might be a fraud. His 'miracles' might be medicines, and his words, however benevolent they might seem at present, might be a precursor to something else. My son knows what he's doing in this instance, I think, but... but I hope he does not let his anger lead him to do something stupid. It certainly could, and... and then we'd lose everything. Hopefully, he'll chase 'Gan Ji' to the border and then go on to Lujiang without further incident, but... but I'm scared, sister... I'm scared."

Bofu ordered the execution of the man that called himself Gan Ji as soon as he was seated in his court on the following morning: the decision was accepted, but many were silently affected by it: the Taoist wanderer met his end on the same afternoon, and the people of Jiangdong were left to make their own judgements.

****

120

There had been a moment when it had seemed that the circle was about to be closed. After years of being forced to serve the nobleman Yuan Shu, the Sun clan had been freed by Yuan Shu's claim to the throne and his subsequent fall and demise; after years of the southern region of Jiangdong – 'East of the River' – being regarded poorly by the north, it was growing as a state with every passing day; and after years of Sun Jian's assassination by Huang Zu's agents being unavenged, the Jiangdong navy had scored a minor first victory against the Jing navy and advanced into hostile waters. Yuan Shu was dead, and Jiangdong was growing, but the third matter – Sun Jian's untimely death and destroying the men held responsible – had been delayed once again by the Lujiang warlord Liu Xun's decision to become a new force in the region above the Great River. Bofu could not drive his anger at the missed opportunity from his mind, and as the moment of departure for Lujiang approached, he became ever more bitter and hate-filled.

Bofu walked into his packed court and sat in his host seat for another day of non-stop deliberations: his fretful uncle, Wu Jing, coughed deliberately and said, "Well, uh... now that my esteemed nephew is here, we can begin, I suppo-"
"I was so close," Bofu declared. "For years, I've dreamed of the moment when I would go to Jing and settle my score with Liu Biao, and just when I thought that Yuan Shu and his underlings couldn't stand in my way anymore, Liu Xun interrupts me at the critical moment! I swear, gentlemen, that-!"
"Forgive me for saying so, my lord, but wasn't the Jing campaign 'sold to us', as it were, on the premise that it was for border security...?" Officer of Merit Wei Teng asked bluntly and impatiently. "Why, then, is that same border poorly policed now, if it was in such terrible danger...? Is Taishi Ci enough if we are still in so much danger...?"
Cheng Pu was expected to be the first to retort, but Bofu was faster: everyone was taken aback when Bofu leapt from his seat, pushed Wu Jing to one side with surprising force, charged at the terrified Wei Teng and said, "**You have just crossed a very clear line, you wretched little man! Now you're going to answer for it here and now, you-!**"
"**Bofu, STOP!**" Lü Fan protested as he shuffled across the room.
"**You have to calm down, Cousin!**" Sun Hè cried as he tried to restrain Bofu.
"**Release me at once, Sun Hè, if you are truly my cousin!**" Bofu shrieked, and the offended Sun Hè complied.
"*Ayah*... must I do this?" Gongjin muttered as he shoved Sun Hè to one side.
"**Every time you open your mouth, it's *poison*!**" Bofu said as he loomed over Wei Teng.
"**Don't ruin yourself now, my friend!**" Gongjin pleaded as he restrained Bofu.
"**Let go of me!**" Bofu cried. "**I am your lord as well as your friend, Gongjin, so let me go at once!**"

"**But I'm your friend first, and I won't let you pull down everything we've built together for the sake of one verbally-incontinent pedant!**" Gongjin retorted.

"**He insulted me!**" Bofu said. "**Father-!**"

"**Your father died building a future for the people of Jiangdong, Bofu, and he wouldn't be very happy right now!**" Gongjin implored.

"...The lad's right," Cheng Pu muttered.

"**Let me go, Gongjin!**" Bofu screamed. "**He's insulted me once too often!**"

"**SOMEBODY SPEAK FOR ME!**" Wei Teng pleaded.

Huang Gai started to move, but Cheng Pu stopped him and said, "I'll help Gongjin."

Huang Gai frowned and said, "Alright."

"**You mustn't do this, Lord Sun!**" Cheng Pu said as he aided Gongjin's efforts to restrain Bofu. "It was my instinct too, but I'm a grey-haired old fool! You're the guardian and founder of Jiangdong... so please... stop."

Bofu stopped struggling and dropped his sword, which was quickly retrieved by Lü Fan: Gongjin and Cheng Pu released their lord, who retreated slightly but kept his gaze fixed on Wei Teng.

"Forgive my tactlessness, Lord Sun!" Wei Teng pleaded: Cheng Pu and Gongjin groaned in unison, because they knew that Wei's daring to speak would reignite Bofu's hatred for him.

"...No," Bofu growled.

"The 'Gan Ji Incident' was a mistake that I don't want to see repeated," Gongjin whispered to Lü Fan. "We need Lady Wu to deal with this."

Lü Fan nodded and retreated from the hall using the private door at the rear that led to the private audience chambers.

"...No, Wei Teng, I can't let men treat me with such contempt," Bofu said after a long silence. "Wei Teng, you were given your role because of your skill with a pen, but someone should have taken your loose and venomous tongue into account before they recommended you to me."

Gongjin's friend Lu Su – who was among the mid-level officials – was silently thankful that he had not been promoted.

"I'll not let anyone mock me," Bofu continued. "I govern a fifth of the empire now, and you have the cheek to talk to me as though I'm some boy...?"

"I-it was not intended as an insult, Lord Sun!" Wei Teng protested. "Others can vouch for me: I only sought a rational discussion! Others can vouch for me, Lord Sun... **others can speak in my defence!**"

The repeated prompts for support were met with silence: Zhang Zhao, Zhang Hong, Gu Yong, Qin Song, Lü Dai and the rest of the officials offered no words.

"...You seem to be lacking the defence that you speak of," Bofu chuckled icily. "I think it is a case of men 'knowing when to be silent'. What a pity, Wei Teng, that you were not raised with any sense. **Guards...!**"

There were several soldiers present, but none of them responded to the call.

"Bofu, *no*," Gongjin pleaded quietly. "You mustn't do this, not so soon after 'Gan Ji'! Forgive him, demote him, *imprison him* if you absolutely *must*, but do not-!"

"**GUARDS!**" Bofu shrieked: even Gongjin and Cheng Pu were startled and unnerved by the anger in his voice.

"...Listen to your friend," Cheng Pu said gently. "This isn't the way, Lord Sun Ce."

"The 'way' can go to hell, Demou," Bofu replied. "**GUARDS!**"

Two soldiers finally answered their lord's summons and approached with weapons in hand.

"...*Bofu*...!" Gongjin whispered.

"... ... ...*Death*," Bofu ordered as he pointed at Wei Teng.

The guards looked to Gongjin and Cheng Pu, but neither man said a word.

"...Did I not speak...?" Bofu asked angrily.

The guards pulled Wei Teng to his feet and started to drag him from the hall.

"**PLEASE, LORD SUN!**" Wei Teng screeched. "**I MEANT NO HARM! I MEANT NO HARM! I MEANT NO HARM! I MEANT NO-!**"

"**SHUT UP AND DIE, YOU WRETCH!**" Bofu yelled. "**JUST SHUT UP AND DIE LIKE A MAN!**"

The other officials were struck dumb: Zhang Zhao turned his gaze to his brother and grimaced, and Zhang Hong nodded purposefully in response.

"I'll watch this man die," Bofu grumbled. "I still suspect that someone let that other bastard 'Gan Ji' free and lied to me... but there won't be any ambiguity this time."

Bofu then marched out of the hall with Sun Hè and Song Qian at either side of him.

"...*Aiee*... This could harm us, Gongjin," Cheng Pu said quietly.

Gongjin was taken aback that Cheng Pu had used his style name to address him: he quickly regained his senses and said, "I've had Ziheng fetch Lady Wu, so-"

"I know, I saw," Cheng Pu interrupted. "Quick thinking that's to be commended: let us hope that Lady Wu can sway him before it's too late..."

Gongjin hummed agreeably, and the two men followed their lord to the designated execution site: a stretch of public ground by a water-well. The other officials followed, and many were, understandably, reconsidering their options.

"One stroke if you can," Bofu said to the designated executioner.

"This is wrong," Gongjin pleaded.

Wei Teng had lost his voice: he was croaking hoarsely and sobbing as he awaited his end. Bofu smiled and said, "**This should serve as a lesson to any that feel that they can-**"

"**STOP!**"

All eyes turned to Lady Wu, who was stood by the well with Lady Chen, Bofu's wife Daqiao, Wu Jing, Sun Yi and Lü Fan.

"**I won't let you do this, Bofu... not again,**" Lady Wu continued.

"**Stay out of this, Mother!**" Bofu ordered. "**This isn't your business!**"

"Isn't it...?" Lady Wu retorted. "**You're the ruler of Jiangdong, and now you're poised to take Lujiang and Jiujiang, and maybe Guangling as well... Jiangxia, if you can... a state**

that the world will view with envy and respect. But there is
still so, so much that you haven't done, so much that you
have to do. I know that Wei Teng is frank and, perhaps, a
little tactless... but that does not make him evil, and only
evil men deserve what you're about to do now for no other
reason than misdirected anger."
Bofu turned his gaze to the crumpled, quivering Wei Teng.
"He's talented, honest, hard-working and diligent," Lady Wu
continued as she casually circled the well with Lady Chen at her
side. "Men like Wei Teng are not flawless, but neither are
they so flawed that they deserve death for simple words! If
I were to accept the fate of the man people called 'Gan Ji',
it would be because I understood your arguments about
the threat he posed: what threat does Wei Teng pose to the
state...?"
Bofu exhaled fiercely.
"You should treat men like him with respect, Bofu, forgive
any flaws that they might have, appreciate their strengths,
and reward them for their service," Lady Wu continued. "Is it
not true that Wei Teng has worked hard for the state...?"
"...It is true," Bofu replied numbly.
"So Officer of Merit Wei Teng has been working hard,
serving the state, and his reward is being dragged into the
street to be beheaded like a common thief," Lady Wu said.
"What, then, should we do with thieves...?"
Bofu shuddered as he thought of his brother Quan's recent
actions: tears formed in the corners of his eyes as his raw anger
at being torn away from his Jing campaign was finally outweighed
by his usual understanding of right and wrong.
"Officer Wei is a good, hard-working man," Lady Wu
continued as she sat on the edge of the well. "He's done work
that few can criticise. If you kill him today, then others will
turn away from you tomorrow, or perhaps sooner."
Bofu turned to look at the ensemble of officials: some, like
Gongjin and Cheng Pu, were obviously steadfast in their loyalty,
but others, like the outspoken Zhang brothers, were obviously
unsure about the future.
"I've watched your father and his friends build an army and
a family, and I've watched you and your friends build a
family and a state," Lady Wu said calmly. "I've watched so
much building, so much growing, so much... cold a word as
it is, 'progress'... that to see what you're about to do now,
it pains me. I can't endure another disaster, Bofu. I can't."
Bofu whined miserably and said, "Mother, I-!"
"So I'm going to ensure that I don't have to endure another
disaster in the only way that I can, Bofu," Lady Wu continued.
"I'm going to throw myself down this well."
"What???" Wu Jing exclaimed.
"You'll all stay back!" Lady Wu ordered. "This is all I can do!"
Gongjin, Lü Fan, Cheng Pu and Huang Gai stifled smiles, because
they were certain that it was a stunt to sway Bofu from his
reckless actions.
"WAIT, NO, STOP!" Bofu shrieked: he pulled Wei Teng to his
feet, dusted him down and said, "Look, here is Wei Teng! His
head still knows his neck! He's alive, and... and I won't

harm him further! He... he'll get a raise! I... I... *AIEE*! I've damn near ruined everything because I was prevented from avenging my father! Wei Teng, I have wronged you for saying what had to be said, and... and I can never undo what I've done!"

Wei Teng was still bereft of a healthy voice, but he smiled and bowed slightly to show that he would not hold the day's events against his impetuous lord.

"You should not forgive me... and... and I do not deserve such men in my service," Bofu sobbed. "I... I have done nothing today to-"

"Enough," Wei Teng croaked.

"...*Mother*...!" Bofu cried as Lady Wu approached him with her mixed entourage of family and officials. "Mother, you would not have thrown yourself in the-!"

"I would," Lady Wu said as she stopped next to Wei Teng. "I would do anything for the good of my children, Bofu... *anything*. In that, your father and I were and are the same."

"...Bravo," Cheng Pu murmured.

"You stopped me from committing a terrible crime against a decent, honest man," Bofu said as he stared into his mother's eyes. "I... I still have a lot to learn... my temper and my haste to do things are still... still very, very bad problems."

"They are," Lady Wu replied. "But you have to remember that they cost your father his life and must learn *control*... so some poor lad doesn't have to go somewhere to avenge *you* in ten years' time, and when I might not be here to stop them making similar mistakes. You want poor Daqiao to have to worry...?"

Bofu looked at his pregnant wife and said, "No, I don't."

Lady Wu turned to Wei Teng and said, "Go home and rest, Mister Wei, and we'll discuss how best to apologise for what happened here today."

Wei Teng shook his head insistently.

"I owe everyone an apology, not just Mister Wei," Bofu declared. "I tried to deny it, but my main aim in Jing was avenging my father: Wei Teng was right, and I didn't like it. When I became an animal that lashed out against men for speaking their minds, I became Yuan Shu: perhaps he got inside my head for a moment there to undo me, or maybe I'm just stupid."

Some of the officials laughed nervously.

"...There's no need to be scared of me now," Bofu promised. "I... I faltered. But I vow to you all that I won't ever allow myself to be such a fool again. I earned your support by being honest, and for a while there I wasn't being honest because I was scared that the truth made me selfish... and it did. But in the future, I'll be open, as I have been until recently... and I won't put personal matters before the state again."

"Lady Wu, you have long sought a greater role in state affairs, and there are none that can deny that you have proved your worth as an orator and debater," Zhang Zhao suggested humbly. "Let the envoys mock us! It is their loss."

The officials laughed fearlessly.

"And with regard to Lord Sun's late father... today I've seen how much he meant to so many people, and I've had my eyes opened," Zhang Zhao continued. "We all have... and we have to remember that we're all men with hearts and souls. Lord Sun, my brother and I will never heartlessly obstruct your desire to punish Liu Biao for his wrongdoings: we never intended to before, but I can see that we were too pragmatic in our approach to our arguments and failed to see that he will continue the feud that he started regardless of what we choose to do. Return to your home and be with your lovely lady wife, and we will plan the proper defence of Yuzhang and the required resources for our advance to Lujiang."

Daqiao approached Bofu and said, "You should do as Mister Zhang suggests."

"...I will," Bofu replied calmly. "Let's not waste another minute together, my lady... for I'll be gone a long time."

Once Bofu had retreated, Cheng Pu turned to Gongjin and said, "Don't assume that my softened stance means that I like you. You're still a pedant that criticises my musicians."

Gongjin laughed and said, "I cannot help it, Mister Cheng."

"...Call me 'Demou'... 'Mister Cheng' puts years on me," Cheng Pu replied as he turned to walk away.

"...'Demou' it is!" Gongjin chuckled.

"*Aiee*... What a calamity that nearly was!" Lu Su said as he approached Gongjin. "Wei Teng was crouched over, the sword at his neck... a few more minutes and-!"

"A few more minutes and the state of Jiangdong would have been a dream," Gongjin replied sombrely. "You and I should walk back to my home, Mister Lu Zijing: we need to talk... about the *future*."

****

EPILOGUE: EVALUATING THE PRESENT

Lu Su – whose style name was Zijing – and Zhou Yu – whose style name was Gongjin – were sat in the living quarters of the latter's home, quietly digesting the 'Wei Teng incident' that Lady Wu, the mother of Sun Ce, the lord of Jiangdong, had averted from becoming something unmanageable and costly. Zhou Yu had been struck silent as he thought about everything at once: eventually, Lu Su said, "You wanted to discuss the future, Gongjin…?"

Zhou Yu sighed and said, "I'd like to, but… first, we must discuss the present. Zijing, we're about to go to Lujiang… again. Liu Xun will be ready for us. I don't know what Liu Biao will do. After today, I don't know what Bofu will do, either."

"…I know what I said, but Lord Sun spared Wei Teng in the end," Lu Su noted.

"Only after an interjection by his mother!" Zhou Yu chortled. "Ziheng, we won't be bringing Lady Wu with us to Lujiang, Jing, Guangling, or wherever else might demand our attention in the years to come: and, like it or not, I have to think about the time when some people might not be there. When I said that I wanted to discuss the future, that… that was what I meant."

"…The lord's mother is in her forties and in good health," Lu Su said. "Lord Sun is in his twenties and in good health; Cheng Pu, Huang Gai, Zhu Zhi and the others are all in their forties and in good health; Lü Fan, yourself, and all the rest are-"

"That can change," Zhou Yu replied. "None of us are invincible… Sun Jian's fate proves that. Bofu is no more invincible than his famous father was, and he makes mistakes. He should not have executed 'Gan Ji', but I could not stop him! Wei Teng was almost cold bones, and I could do nothing to stop him! Others will rile and provoke Bofu, and he'll deal with them in the same way, even when that isn't appropriate. Wei Teng is not Yan Yu, and neither was 'Gan Ji': one does not treat officials and clerics like barbarian champions, but that is what's been done. If Bofu continues to make enemies, his life becomes harder to protect, and now, it isn't just about him anymore… it's about Jiangdong. Southern Yang - the state of Jiangdong - is ours to govern now, and if what I've just heard is right, 'Excellency' Cao Cao – and, by proxy, the Han Imperial court that he represents – is willing to accept it for the sake of peace."

"…But there will be no peace!" Lu Su insisted. "Yuan Shu and Gongsun Zan are gone, yes: but that leaves Yuan Shao, Cao Cao, Lord Sun Ce, Liu Xun in Lujiang Prefecture, the Qiang warlords in Liang Province, Liu Zhang in Yi Province, Zhang Lu in Hanzhong, and Liu Biao in Jing Province! Cao Cao controls northern Jiujiang, Yu, Yan, Xu and some of Central Province; Yuan Shao controls Ji, Bing, Yòu, Qing and the parts of Central Province that Cao does not control! Those two will soon clash, and-!"

"I know that you're right, Zijing, about that if not about other things," Zhou Yu said. "Cao Cao will want us to aid him in his fight against Yuan Shao, which we might do if others don't sway our allegiance with strong arguments. Cao is not invincible either, and he has a lot of enemies as well. This story is far from told, and we two will be two of many that will tell it, Zijing."

"Lord Sun will not give me rank," Lu Su replied.

"He will, one day, I am certain of it," Zhou Yu said. "Jiangdong is vast and surrounded by enemies: he'll need good men to defend it. You and I, we are two of many pillars of a new state, emerged from the ashes of a Han damaged by hostile fires: none thought it possible, but it happened. We'll grow, consume our enemies, and become something else again, Zijing: this story is far from told, and it will be a story that none will forget. If we are careful in what we do now, then the future is ours to write, and what a future it will be!"

Lu Su and Zhou Yu continued their discussions to a late hour: both men knew that they were now part of a new era of history. Jiangdong – 'East of the River' – was, after years of neglect, an emergent state in an era fraught with chaos. Yuan Shao and Cao Cao would, as many predicted, lock horns in a titanic struggle that is known to history as the Battle of Guandu, but not before Cao Cao had been attacked yet again by men that he thought to be allies and friends: Cao's progeny would go on to found their own state, just as the Suns had done in the south.

Sun Ce had one last triumph before an inevitable tragedy, and then it would be the turn of others to determine the fate of the state of Jiangdong. A river battle between the Suns and Cao Cao would eclipse Guandu in terms of fame, entering history as the Battle of Red Cliffs: Jiangdong would then be the foundation of a larger state – the state of Eastern Wu – that would endure until the late 3rd Century. And for every famous name that had emerged during the years, more would appear from every quarter to steer the nation toward further division, the era known as 'Three Kingdoms', and – as many a scholar foresaw – the reunification that must inevitably follow division. The story was, indeed, far from told, but Sun Jian and Sun Ce – who had often changed the direction that story took in ways that none could predict – had already earned their place in one of the most well-known periods in Chinese history, and Jiangdong – once an economic and political irrelevance – had become the home of generations of scholars and heroes.

****

CHARACTER PROFILES AND NAME PRONUNCIATION GUIDE

It may or may not come as a surprise that the author of a novel about China cannot actually read, write or converse in Chinese (yes, that is still the case for anyone that read 'Crouching Dragon' or '"Yellow Sky"' – I know a few words for the purpose of research and that's it): that could be seen as an indication of how interesting this era can be regardless of knowing the language or culture well, but it severely reduces what you can find in the way of further reading or information. The Three Kingdoms era is very popular in Far East Asia, so there are a lot of works based on the period, although there are only a few that have been translated to English and other European languages. But even when you find the work in your language, there is the pronunciation hurdle to jump; this is a (admittedly simplistic) guide for the completely uninitiated to at least get started, although I should note that I am not a professional historian, language teacher or linguist of any kind and that my guide is not meant to be a professional start of a Chinese language course. That said, here we go.

Pronunciation of Chinese names can be very awkward, since the spellings generated by the Hanyu-Pinyin system are sometimes misleading. Cao Cao, for example, is often thought to be 'Cow Cow' at first. The first attempt at translating *Three Kingdoms* by C. H. Brewitt-Taylor used a different method for pronunciation, known as the Wade-Giles system, wherein Cao Cao was spelt T'sao T'sao: the modern approach assumes awareness of 'C' never being used as a 'K' (as in, say, *continue*), but always as an 'Ts' (similar to its usage in *central*). The pronunciation guide below does not use either Wade-Giles or Pinyin, and might itself be open to interpretation: hopefully, it will serve as a rough guide for English speakers. The characters are ordered alphabetically rather than by order of appearance or affiliation. Place names are completely translated or partially translated depending on what I felt worked best.

In every case, the family name is first, the given name second: nobles often take on a 'style name' in addition, which is often used to differentiate the friend, focus of respect, or ally from a stranger or enemy in conversation, hence I say 'in familiar terms' after the style name. Some of the details have been rewritten or corrected where mistakes were found post-publishing the previous books (I'll say this and no more: I'm only human).

Some of the information provided along with the name – intended as a refresher, as an explanation as to what happened to them after they disappeared from the narrative, or to elaborate where the person was only mentioned in some context – can sometimes spoil surprises for a first-time reader. **You have been warned.**

NB: 'ow' on its own or after an apostrophe in a compound should be pronounced as it is in 'cow', 'ay' as in 'pay' and 'eye' as is. 'X' is a tough one, as is 'J': I vary my approach to the latter quite a bit, since it is a soft 'ch' that's almost a 'j' (just as 'B' is a soft 'P' and 'G' is a soft 'k'), but 'X' can be seen as 'Sh' or 'Hs' (I use 'Sh' because it best reflected it so far as my research went).

Name [Pronunciation] – *brief refresher on who the person was.*
**Any other name they were known by, typically their style name.*

PEOPLE

Bian Zhang [P'ee-arn Ch'arng] - *Han official-turned-rebel in Liang Province: he is an early minor opponent of Sun Jian in this work.*

Bing Yuan [P'ing Yoo-arn] – *noted scholar that lives in the Liaodong Peninsula; he befriends the fugitive Taishi Ci.*

Bo Cai [P'oh Ts'eye] – *Yellow Turban rebel general based in Yu Province; he is a major antagonist to Sun Jian during the Yellow Turban campaign.*

Cai Mao [Ts'eye Mah-oh] – *senior vassal of Jing Governor Liu Biao and his future brother-in-law; he is an antagonist during Sun Jian's ill-fated Jing campaign. His sister later arranged a marriage between her niece and Liu Biao's second son Liu Cong [Lee-oo Ts'ong] and planned for Cong to inherit the province instead of Biao's eldest son Liu Qi: Cai Mao became very powerful and influential, and when Huang Zu and then Liu Biao died within a short time he aided his sister's plan, supported Liu Cong and surrendered to Cao Cao. His historical fate is vague at best, but in popular fiction Cao Cao is tricked into executing him (and hence weakening Cao Cao's naval capability) by Zhou Yu (Gongjin) during the 'Battle of Red Cliffs' timeframe.*

Cai Yong [Ts'eye Yong] – *famous polymath and Han official that was responsible for saving the unaltered works of many classical literati by petitioning the court for the creation of the Xiping Stones; he later earned the ire of the 'Ten Attendants' and suffered a long period of exile in the north and east of the country. During his stay in the east, he educated Gu Yong, one of the men that helped the Sun family to found the state of Eastern Wu. He is responsible for launching the careers of many other men, including Chang'an magistrate and calligrapher Zhong Yao and scholar-prodigy Wang Can, who was the author of the Cao Wei Empire's official histories and a vassal to Liu Biao in his younger days. Dong Zhuo invited Cai Yong back to the court during his usurpation of power, and he accepted after less-than-gentle prodding; this would have fatal consequences when Dong Zhuo was finally murdered and his allies scrutinised. Cai Yong was named as one of those that tolerated and even assisted Dong Zhuo, and he was executed for it. His prodigious daughter Cai Wenji [Ts'eye Wern-jee] – who had been abducted and forcibly married to a Xiongnu tribal chieftain – was later saved by Cao Cao, who felt personal grief at the fate of her famous father and wanted to right what he believed to be an unforgivable wrong Cai Wenji is a possible mother to the founder of the Han Zhao state of the so-called 'Sixteen Kingdoms' era that followed the Jin Dynasty's brief reunification of China.*
**Known by the courtesy name Bojie [Boh-Jee-eh]*

Cao Cao [Ts'ao Ts'ao] – *famous and significant figure of the era; he is Sun Jian's colleague during the Yellow Turban Campaign and Eastern Pass Coalition but serves as an off-stage political rival to Sun Ce later on. He was the son of a marquis, and adopted grandson of a favoured palace eunuch. Cao lived a relatively charmed life, suffering far less than his contemporaries for acts of mischief and outright defiance. He had many influential friends, served successfully against the Yellow Turban rebels and was appointed one of the colonels of the 'Army of the Western Garden' shortly before the death of Emperor Ling. He then served as a field general in the anti-Dong Zhuo coalition, and was appointed as Governor of Yan Province. He later took Emperor Xian from the ruins of the capital and kept him in his own capital, Xuchang and locked horns with Yuan Shu, the Sun clan's master when Shu declared that he was the next emperor. The act of bringing Emperor Xian to his own province prompted many to accuse him of sedition, and he was then forced to face former friend and ally Yuan Shao and defeat him. Cao Cao then waged war on all of the remaining warlords in China, and by the last quarter of the first decade of the 3rd Century, only the exiled and disinherited Jing heir Liu Qi, wandering warlord Liu Bei and Wu ruler Sun Quan were prepared to oppose him. The famous 'Battle of Red Cliffs' resulted in a famous victory for the rebel warlords that forced Cao Cao on the defensive and lost him southern Jing. By the time of Cao Cao's death at the end of the second decade of the 3rd Century, he was Prime Minister of the Han, King of Wei, and perfectly placed to seize the imperial mandate, but it would be his son, Cao Pi, that would actually depose the Han Emperor and begin the era known as 'Three Kingdoms'.*
*Known by the courtesy name Mengde [Mung-der].
*Also known as A'Man [Ah-Marn] as a child and for varying reasons in adulthood, from affectionate to derisive.
*Once labelled a *jianxiong* [jee-arn-shee-ong] (which the author translates at various point as 'Crafty Villain' and 'Hero of Chaos', as either might apply) by the appraiser Xu Shao.

Chen Ji [Ch'en Jee] – *a senior vassal of Yuan Shu that is later appointed as Administrator of Jiujiang instead of Sun Ce*

Chen Ji [Ch'en Jee] – *known as Chen Yuanfang throughout the work (with the exception of certain dialogue) to make him stand out and also to distinguish him from the Chen Ji that served Yuan Shu. The scholar and author Chen Ji was the son of disgraced statesman Chen Shi and father of Chen Qun. He studied diligently whilst in exile in his youth, and when the 'Partisan Crisis' ended he became an official in the Han Court. He briefly served Dong Zhuo in the capital before fleeing to Qing Province with his family and serving Pingyuan Magistrate Liu Bei. He then followed Liu Bei to Xu Province. He is covered more extensively in the author's other work '"Yellow Sky": Crisis for the Han Dynasty'.*
*Known by the courtesy name Yuanfang [Yoo-arn-farng]

Chen Lan [Ch'en Larn] – *officer serving Yuan Shu that later becomes a bandit*

Chen Mu [Ch'en Moo] – *a vassal (and possible relative) of the bandit king Chen Yu – in this work he is described as Yu's brother*

Chen Woo [Ch'en Woo] – *early ally of Sun Ce that became a formidable vanguard officer; he was supposedly very popular due to his good nature*
*Known by the courtesy name Zilie [Tz'ee-lee-er]

Chen Yu [Ch'en Yoo] – *bandit king from the Haixi region: in this work he is referred to mainly as 'Haixi Chen'. The work refers to a 'Chen Yu' being sent to assist Sun Ce by Cao Cao that has to be defeated due to ill intent: this is deliberately vague during the work as Cao Cao's involvement is unknown, it might be a different Chen Yu and the tale may be fictional*
*Known in the text as 'Haixi [H'eye-shee] Chen'

Cheng Pu [Ch'erng Poo] – *a well-known ally and close friend of Sun Jian from his first days as a military officer: he may have known Sun Jian before that, but the author has them meeting as the opening event in chapter 1. Cheng Pu went on to serve Sun Jian's eldest sons in turn: he served Sun Ce until the latter's death as a senior adviser and officer and then became an elder statesman during the early years of Sun Quan's reign, passing away at some point after the famous 'Battle of Red Cliffs' and the siege of Jiangling that followed.*
*Known by the courtesy name Demou [T'er-moh]

Cheng Yi [Ch'erng Yee] – *Cheng Yu's son: he is given a minor background role to indicate that the progeny of the founders are going to be just as active later on.*

Cheng Yu [Ch'erng Yoo] – *a respected scholar that later became Cao Cao's adviser. He was quite old, relatively speaking, when he joined Cao Cao (around 50), and he was known in earlier years of service for being cantankerous, frank and devoid of conscience when matters required it; he is only referred to in this work, but he would later advise Cao Cao during his ill-fated campaign against Sun Quan.*
*Known by the courtesy name Zhongde [Ch'ong-der]

Dai Yuan [T'eye Yoo-arn] – *a subordinate of ousted Wu Administrator Sheng Xian (and, perhaps, a former county magistrate – that is what the author implies): he appears to be an overblown character in this work, but he goes on to kill a significant member of the Sun regime as revenge for Sheng Xian's assassination.*

Daqiao [T'ah-chee-ow] – *see Lady Qiao (Older)*

Deng Dang [T'erng T'arng] – *the brother-in-law of the famous Sun family vassal Lü Meng; Meng followed him into Sun Ce's service.*

Ding Yuan [T'ing Yoo-arn] – *a Han official and Inspector of Bing Province at the time of the Liang Province Rebellion and the Black Mountain Bandit attacks in the north; he later discovered and*

recruited the warrior Lü Bu. He was murdered by Bu, who then joined Dong Zhuo.
*Known by the courtesy name Jianyang [Jee-arn-yarng]

Dong Xi [T'ong Shee] – *self-appointed defender of Gaoqian that joined Sun Ce during the latter's pacification of Kuaiji Prefecture: he went on to become a senior figure in the regimes of Sun Ce and Sun Quan.*
*Known by the courtesy name Yuanshi [Yoo-arn-shee]

Dong Yue [T'ong Yoo-er] – *relative and vassal of Dong Zhuo*

Dong Zhuo [T'ong Ch'oo-oh] – *The infamous tyrant that seized the capital after the deaths of Emperor Ling, Commander Hè Jin and the 'Ten Attendants' and ruled villainously, protected by his foster son Lü Bu. Sun Jian encountered Dong Zhuo twice during his career – once in Liang, during the rebellion there, and again after Dong Zhuo seized power – and can be considered as one of his fiercest rivals and enemies. Dong Zhuo deposed the eldest son of Emperor Ling and placed his younger brother on the throne as Emperor Xian, an act that led to the majority of the warlords in the east of the country forming a coalition against him; that coalition later collapsed, but not before Sun Jian had forced Dong Zhuo to abandon the capital Luoyang and flee westward, toward the former Han capital Chang'an. Dong Zhuo remained in Chang'an with the young emperor as a hostage and enjoyed a life of vice and luxury while the warlords fought amongst themselves; eventually, a small group of officials managed to convince an ever-more frustrated Lü Bu to betray and kill Dong Zhuo. His reign is part of the narrative of '"Yellow Sky"'.*
*Known by the courtesy name Zhongying [Ch'ong-ying]

Duan Wei [T'oo-arn Way] – *officer that served Dong Zhuo and then the regents Li Jue and Guo Si*

"Elder Qiao" [Chee-ow] - *father of the famous Qiao sisters that married Sun Ce and Zhou Yu: he is identified by some fictional works as Qiao Xuan, a famous Han official, but Xuan died before the Yellow Turban Rebellion*

Emperor Ling of the Han [Ling] – *Liu Hong, Marquis of Jieduting was selected – at the age of 12 – as the successor to Emperor Huan, who had no issue. Some blame him for the fall of the Han. He was Emperor during one of the most famous events in 'pre-Three Kingdoms era' history and folklore, the 'Yellow Turban Rebellion'. His death was followed by the rise of Dong Zhuo and the fission that resulted from that. He is only briefly mentioned in this work, but he is covered more extensively in '"Yellow Sky"'.*
*Also known as (Han) Lingdi [(Harn) Ling-t'ee] (lit. Han Emperor Ling) when Lingdi is a better option for conciseness.
*Known as Liu Hong [Lee-oo Hong], Marquis of Jieduting [Jee-er-doo-ting]) before being created Emperor.

Emperor Shao of Han [S'ah-oh] – *Emperor Ling's eldest son, born to Empress Hè. Liu Bian became Emperor shortly after the death*

of his father, but when Dong Zhuo came to power in the capital the young emperor was deposed, created the Prince of Hongnong and replaced by his younger brother Liu Xie, who became Emperor Xian, the last Emperor of the Han Dynasty. Bian was murdered by Dong Zhuo's agents during the crisis that followed his deposition.
*Known alternatively within the text as (Han) Shaodi [(Harn) S'ah-oh-t'ee] (lit. Han Emperor Shao) when Shaodi is a better option for conciseness.
*Known as Liu Bian [Lee-oo P'ee-arn], Prince of Hongnong [Hong-nong] after being deposed by Dong Zhuo.

Emperor Xian of Han [Shee-an] – *Emperor Ling's second son, Liu Xie was born to Consort Wang rather than Empress Hè: the jealous empress then poisoned his mother. There were a lot of inauspicious prognostications being made at that point in time, so Emperor Ling had his sons 'adopted' to others prior to their coming of age; Liu Xie was entrusted to his grandmother, Empress Dowager Dong. He was first created the Prince of Bohai and then the Prince of Chenliu after the 'adoption' period ended, but despite being a second son by a consort, he would later become Emperor Xian after a series of extraordinary events in the court. It is no secret or 'plot spoiler' that the Han Dynasty was finally eradicated in the early 3rd Century; Xiandi was the last Han Emperor and had the 'privilege' of overseeing the final years of the decline. He is said to have lived for over a decade after abdicating as the Duke of Shanyang; his given date of death is unusually close to – as in not long after – the death of Zhuge Liang, Chancellor/Prime Minister of the independent state of Shu Han, whose mission it was to restore the Han in some form. He is never seen in this work, but he is covered extensively in the author's other work, '"Yellow Sky"'.*
*Also known as (Han) Xiandi [(Harn) Shee-an-t'ee] (lit. Han Emperor Xian) when Xiandi is a better option for conciseness.
*Known as Liu Xie [Lee-oo Shee-er], Prince of Bohai [P'oh-high] after leaving his grandmother's direct care.
*Known as Liu Xie [Lee-oo Shee-er], Prince of Chenliu [Ch'en-lee-oo] prior to his ascension.

Empress Dowager Hè [Her] – *the second empress taken by Emperor Ling; her brother, Hè Jin, would go on to become Commander-in-Chief. She was the mother of Liu Bian, later Emperor Shao and Prince of Hongnong. She was later murdered by Dong Zhuo's agents. She is only mentioned in this work, but she is covered extensively in '"Yellow Sky"'.*
*Known as Empress Hè before the death of Emperor Ling.
*Known as Lady/Consort Hè prior to being created Empress.

"Excellency Xun" [Shoon] – *'loosely based' on the historical figure Xun Shuang [Shoon S'oo-arng], who was uncle to the famous adviser Xun Yu (Wenruo) that served Cao Cao. He is only mentioned in this work, but he is featured in the author's other work, '"Yellow Sky"'.*

Fan Neng [Farn Nung] – *a general that served the regency court's appointed Governor of Yang Province, Liu Yao: he serves as an antagonist to Sun Ce during the latter's reclamation of Danyang.*

"Gan Ji" [K'arn Ch'ee] – the author will either relish or regret the addition of this character! The stories surrounding Sun Ce's death are many and vivid, and one of the most famous is the one that partially or entirely blames his untimely end on the Taoist 'saint', Gan/Yu Ji. The historical Gan Ji gave his teachings to a mid-2nd Century Han Emperor, so by the time that he is supposed to have appeared in Jiangdong – 2 years before the dawn of the 3rd Century – he would have to have been very old indeed. The popular tales state that Sun Ce had this popular healer and philosopher put to death for heresy and that his spirit then exacted a revenge of sorts by hounding Ce while he was recovering from an assassination attempt: the author plays with this myth and the popular debunking by having the text's Gan Ji be an almost certain fraud and tying Sun Ce's decision to his inherited distaste for cults and spiritualists.
*Known as Yu Ji [Yoo Ch'ee] in some works.

Gao Shun [K'ao S'oon] – *a subordinate of Lü Bu; he remained with Bu until his death, but the two men had a difficult working relationship. Gao Shun was known for his honesty and attempts at giving advice that was rarely wanted or heeded. He was also a very competent field commander. His encounters with Sun Jian are minimised in this work, but he would have been prominent whenever Bu was.*

Gongsun Du [K'ong-soon T'oo] – *warlord that operated in the northeast of China: he engaged the neighbouring Korean Goguryeo Kingdom/Empire to protect Han interests in the far northeast. He was governing the Liaodong Peninsula at the time of Taishi Ci's self-imposed exile, and he reputedly respected Taishi very much: Taishi rescued a man from Du's wrath, however, leading to Taishi becoming a fugitive twice over.*

Gongsun Yue [K'ong-soon Yoo-er] – *a much-loved nephew of Gongsun Zan; he was sent to assist Sun Jian at the Battle of Yang City, but he was struck down during that conflict. Gongsun Zan held Yuan Shao personally responsible for the incident.*

Gongsun Zan [K'ong-soon Tz'arn] – *a military officer, county magistrate, self-appointed governor and warlord in the last two decades of the 2nd Century; he was a friend of the warlord Liu Bei, and was known for his tumultuous relationship with the Ru County Yuan clan. He collaborated with Yuan Shu from time to time and briefly worked with Yuan Shao, but he later became fiercely antagonistic toward the latter for a number of reasons. He then fought Yuan Shao for control of Ji, Qing and Yòu provinces. He once sent his nephew to aid Sun Jian. Gongsun Zan was defeated and killed by Yuan Shao, and his ill-gotten holdings became Shao's.*
*Known by the courtesy name Bogui [P'oh-goo-ee]

Gu Yong [K'oo Yong] – *a student of the famed scholar Cai Yong while the latter was in exile in Yang Province; Gu joined Sun Ce*

and became one of the men that helped Ce and his brother Quan to build the state of Eastern Wu.
*Known by the courtesy name Yuantan [Yoo-arn-tarn]

Guan Hai [K'oo-arn H'eye] – *a Yellow Turban rebel that attacked Beihai City in Qing Province 2 years after Dong Zhuo's retreat to Luoyang. Taishi Ci employed his usual cunning and a small unit of Liu Bei's troops to defeat him.*

Guan Yu [K'oo-arn Yoo] – *an early ally of Liu Bei who is famous in his own right; he is known for his long beard, his green robes, his learnedness, his lofty demeanour, his 'Green Dragon' weapon (which the author has retained despite its being a possible fiction), his fictional inheritance of the equally-fictional 'Red Hare' warhorse from Lü Bu, and his similarly fictional unmatched skill in battle, although his historical skill is still quite impressive. He is revered by the lawful and the lawless alike, since he is seen as a man that applied morals when and where appropriate to achieve an ultimate end. He is briefly featured during Taishi Ci's relief of Beihai, his early career is covered in '"Yellow Sky"', and his later career is chronicled in 'Crouching Dragon: the Journey of Zhuge Liang'.*
*Known by the courtesy name Yunchang [Yoon-charng]

Gui Lan [K'oo-ee Larn] – *loyal vassal of ousted Wu Prefecture Administrator Sheng Xian; he is, like Dai Yuan, named and featured with apparent needlessness, but he goes on to assassinate a prominent member of the Sun faction as revenge for Sheng Xian's assassination.*

Guo Shi [K'oo-oh S'ee] – *a leader of the bandit and tribal uprising in Changsha County that Sun Jian was sent to quell upon his return from Liang Province.*

Guo Si [K'oo-oh See] – *a general serving Dong Zhuo; he later cooperates with fellow Liang Province general Li Jue and becomes co-regent after Dong Zhuo's death. He later fought with Li Jue after external provocations by unwitting agents of the emperor's loyalists that included Guo Si's own wife: Emperor Xian fled the capital and the regents – minus their vital hostage – quickly lost power and were killed by their own vassals. Guo Si died first.*

'Haixi Chen' [H'eye-shee T'ern] – *see Chen Yu*

Han Dang [Harn T'arng] – *one of the first men to join Sun Jian when he began his military career: he is not as prominent a figure as Zhu Zhi, Cheng Pu and Huang Gai, but the author makes extensive use of him early on. His son goes on, regrettably, to be less of an asset to the Sun regime.*
*Known by the courtesy name Yigong [Yee-k'ong]

Han Fu [Harn Foo] – *the Governor of Ji Province; Han Fu later lent his forces to the campaign against Dong Zhuo. He is ousted by Yuan Shao during the course of Act III.*
*Known by the courtesy name Wenjie [Wern-jee-er]

Han Sui [Harn Soo-ee] – *Attendant Official of the Liang Province administration at the time of the major rebellion in the year 185; he serves as an antagonist during the Liang Campaign.*
*Known by the courtesy name Wenyue [Wern-yoo-er]

Han Xi [Harn Shee] – *an officer serving Jiangxia Administrator Huang Zu. He fought Sun Ce at least once, but the author has him fight Sun Ce at the end of the work in a possibly fictional encounter. Sun Ce would later slay him during a naval battle.*

Han Yan [Harn Yarn] – *an officer serving Sun Ce: the author could find little about this man, who was made Southern Commandant during Sun Ce's Kuaiji campaign and tasked with pacifying the local tribes and defeating Administrator Wang Lang. His death led to the promotion of the more famous Hè Qi.*

Han Yin [Harn Yin] – *adviser to the warlord Yuan Shu; he serves as a distant and indirect antagonist to the Sun faction. He met his end when acting as a go-between for a marriage alliance between Yuan Shu and Lü Bu: Bu made one of his famous political turnarounds and sent Han Yin to Cao Cao for disposal.*

Hè Jin [Her Jin] – *the brother of Empress Hè; the Hè family were not at all wealthy or influential, but Lady Hè's beauty elevated Hè Jin from a butcher to the head of the Imperial army within a few years. After the Yellow Turban Rebellion, Hè Jin tried to change the structure of the court, and in particular to reduce the influence of a eunuch faction known as the 'Ten Attendants'; his feud with the eunuchs had a number of unforeseen consequences. Hè Jin invited Dong Zhuo to the capital Luoyang and began a plan to slaughter the 'Ten', but they learned of his intentions and were able to strike first, slaying him in the palace gardens while he was unarmed, alone and vulnerable. Hè Jin's ally Yuan Shao avenged his death by leading a purge of the palace eunuchs, but it was too late to undo the political damage. When Dong Zhuo arrived, he saw the chaos that had resulted from Hè Jin's death and exploited it, taking over the imperial court and beginning the next dynastic crisis. His son went on to serve the Han in a lesser capacity.*
*Known by the courtesy name Suigao [Soo-ee-gah-oh]

Hè Man [Her Marn] – *a Yellow Turban rebel officer that was part of Liu Pi and Huang Shao's faction based in Yu Province; he may be related to Hè Yi, but the author declined to speculate.*

Hè Qi [Her Chee] – *a Kuaiji Prefectural official that defected to Sun Ce during the latter's Kuaiji campaign against the Administrator Wang Lang. He was adept at pacifying the ethnic tribes and famous for his ostentatious lifestyle, generosity and careful budgeting.*
*Known by the courtesy name Gongmiao [K'ong-mee-ow]

Hè Yi [Her Yee] – *a Yellow Turban rebel officer that was part of Liu Pi and Huang Shao's faction based in Yu Province; he may be related to Hè Man, but that is not considered at any point.*

Hu Zhen [Hoo Ch'ern] – *an influential Liang Province general serving Dong Zhuo; he had a minor rivalry with Lü Bu that was not always friendly and led to a rout at the hands of Sun Jian's army. He later served the regents Li Jue and Guo Si but met his end during their rule.*
*Known by the courtesy name Wencai [Wern-ts'eye]

Hua Xin [Hoo'ah Shin] – *appointed Administrator of Yuzhang after his predecessor was murdered; he was initially allied to Liu Yao but went on to serve Sun Ce, Sun Quan and then Cao Cao.*
*Known by the courtesy name Zuyi [Tz'oo-yee]

Hua Xiong [Hoo-ah Shee-ong] – *a general serving Dong Zhuo; he is most famous for how he was killed in fiction. In 'Sanguo Yanyi' (Romance of the Three Kingdoms), Hua Xiong was depicted as second only to Lü Bu (whose strength is also greatly exaggerated); he bests every general sent to challenge him, including the formidable Sun Jian, but he is finally killed with ease during a duel with Guan Yu. Historically, Hua Xiong is far less exciting, and it is this Hua Xiong that the author has chosen for the sake of producing a more factual work: he is captured during a rout and sentenced to death by Sun Jian.*

Huan Jie [Hoo'arn Ch'ee-er] – *a politician and diplomat that served Sun Jian until the latter's death in Jing Province, whereupon he negotiated the return of Sun Jian's body to the Sun family and then defected to Jing Governor Liu Biao. He later served Cao Cao and may, according to some sources, have been a vocal proponent of the last Han Emperor's abdication in favour of Cao Cao's heir Cao Pi.*
*Known by the courtesy name Boxu [P'oh-shoo]

Huang Gai [Hoo-arng K'eye] - *an early ally of Sun Jian and veteran officer to Sun Ce and Sun Quan: he is most famous for his key role in the Battle of Red Cliffs, where he feigned defection to Cao Cao's forces and guided several boats containing flammable articles toward Cao's fleet, destroying it. He was injured in that battle, but he continued to serve Wu for some time afterward (until his death).*
*Known by the courtesy name Gongfu [K'ong-foo]

Huang Longluo [Hoo-arng Long-loo-oh] – *a bandit chieftain in Shanyin County,the capital region of Kuaiji Prefecture; he rose up against Sun Ce with his ally Zhou Ba, but both were killed by Sun Ce's champion Dong Xi.*

Huang Shao [Hoo-arng S'ah-oh] – *a Yellow Turban leader in Yu Province: he initially served under Bo Cai, but after Bo's death he formed an alliance with Liu Pi that lasted until his own death.*

Huang Yi [Hoo-arng Yee] – *Jiangxia Administrator Huang Zu's son and a serving officer in Jing's armed forces: he fought Sun Ce at least once, but for story-telling purposes he engages Sun Ce's fleet in the final act and is defeated.*

Huang Zu [Hoo-arng Tz'oo] – *Administrator of Jiangxia Prefecture in southeast Jing Province and the head of a powerful family in its own right; he effectively ruled Jiangxia, despite being in the service of Jing governor Liu Biao. He is considered to be the man that orchestrated the death of Sun Jian. He was eventually defeated by Sun Quan prior to the famous 'Battle of Red Cliffs'.*

Huangfu Song [Hoo-arng-foo Song] – *a prominent general of the Han Dynasty army; he was extremely effective against the Yellow Turbans, and he was renowned for his upstanding moral values and generous nature. He challenged the 'Ten Attendants' and therefore suffered a temporary downturn in his career, but he had one last significant victory against the Qiang rebels that was then impacted by concurrent events in the capital. He died in relative obscurity during the Li Jue/Guo Si regency period.*
*Known by the courtesy name Yizhen [Yee-ch'ern]

Hui Qu [Hoo-ee Choo] – *a vassal of Yuan Shu that was later appointed as 'Inspector of Yang Province' to rival the court's appointee Liu Yao*

Ji Ling [Jee Ling] – *a high-ranking officer serving Yuan Shu; he does little within the scope of this work, but he was a dangerous antagonist to the warlord Liu Bei.*

Jia Xu [Jee-ah Shoo] – *an adviser and politician; Jia Xu served the infamous Dong Zhuo until the latter's death, at which point he aided Dong's generals Li Jue and Guo Si when they tried to govern as co-regents to the emperor. He is probably one of the most divisive and decisive figures of the period, and is, it might be argued, one of the greatest strategists of the time, an equal or perhaps superior to more famous figures such as Zhuge Liang, Pang Tong, Zhou Yu, Lü Meng, Lu Xun, Sima Yi and Guo Jia. He is covered more extensively in '"Yellow Sky"': here, he achieves a remarkable off-stage victory against Cao Cao at the 'Battle of Wan City' that the author cites as a catalyst for Yuan Shu's declaration of divine anointment.*
*Known by the courtesy name Wenhe [Wern-her]

Jian Yong [Jee-arn Yong] – *an ally of imperial scion Liu Bei who is said, in some accounts, to have travelled with him from the earliest days of his career; he was said to be vulgar and direct, so the author tends to use Jian Yong as a means for lightening the mood. He receives a cameo of sorts during Taishi Ci's relief of Beihai as part of Liu Bei's court; he features in '"Yellow Sky"' as a constant companion to Liu Bei, but his most active years are story threads in the author's earlier work 'Crouching Dragon'*
*Known by the courtesy name Xianhe [Shee-an-her]

Jiang Qin [Jee-arng Chin] – *a reformed pirate that initially serves as a bodyguard to Sun Ce and eventually becomes a renowned officer to Ce and his brother Quan; he was known for his frugal ways once he gave up on criminality*
*Known by the courtesy name Gongyi [K'ong-yee]

Kong Rong [Kong Rong] – *a descendant of the famous philosopher Confucius; he assumed many respectable roles, including Chancellor of Beihai in Qing Province, and was an acquaintance of men such as Cai Yong, Sheng Xian, Wang Lang, Liu Bei and Yuan Shao. At some point after Emperor Xian escaped his regents and found relative safety in Xuchang, Kong Rong was forced to flee his role as Chancellor of Beihai – a role that brought him into contact with the famous vigilante Taishi Ci, who saved him from Yellow Turbans – and take a role in the Han court. He became an outspoken critic, and one of his targets was Cao Cao, who eventually tired of him and eliminated him.*
*Known by the courtesy name Wenju [Wern-joo]

Kong Zhou [Kong Ch'oh] – *appointed Inspector of Yu Province by Han loyalists during the build-up to the Campaign against Dong Zhuo; he seems to have passed away by the time that Sun Jian pledges service to Yuan Shu, since his role is then given to Jian as a barbed gesture by Yuan Shu.*
*Known by the courtesy name Gongxu [K'ong-shoo]

Kuai Liang [Koo-eye Lee-arng] – *Jing Governor Liu Biao's senior adviser; he is cited as a likely contributor to the plan that led to Sun Jian's death*
*Known by the courtesy name Zirou [Tz'ee-roh]

Kuai Yue [Koo-eye Yoo-er] – *brother of the adviser Kuai Liang and guardian of Zhangling, a region to the east of Jing's southern capital: the author uses him as an adviser to Huang Zu in lieu of any named figures. He is said to have served He Jin in an administrative capacity, although the author did not use or refer to him in '"Yellow Sky"' to reduce an already large cast.*
*Known by the courtesy name Yidu [Yee-t'oo]

Lady Chen [T'ern] – *Sun Jian's consort and mother to some of Sun Jian's younger children. In 'Crouching Dragon', a 'State Mother Wu' is present during Sun Shangxiang's marriage to Liu Bei, but this could not be Shangxiang's mother Lady Wu since she was already dead: the author has taken the liberty of modifying the mythical version (that has State Mother Wu as Lady Wu's sister) to have Lady Chen be elevated to an 'honorary sister' to Lady Wu and 'Second Mother' to Sun Quan that can then be State Mother Wu later on.*

Lady Qiao [Chee-ow] (Older) – *the elder of two beautiful sisters; Sun Ce and Zhou Yu learn of the Qiao sisters and court them a short time after the two men have broken away from Yuan Shu's regime. The older Lady Qiao (who is more commonly called 'Daqiao' in the text for narrative simplicity) married Sun Ce, while her younger sister married Zhou Yu. Sun Ce died young, but he had at least 3-4 children (a son and 2-3 daughters) in the year (or less) that he was married to Daqiao: Daqiao may have been the mother of them all, and the author assumes this to avoid controversy (Sun Ce and Daqiao are popularly portrayed as a devout loving couple, and the polygamy practiced by most Chinese men of the time – including Sun Ce's father – tends to*

debunk the sentiment in modern times).
*Known as Daqiao [T'a-chee-ow] (lit. Big/Older Qiao)

Lady Qiao [Chee-ow] (Younger) – *the younger of two beautiful sisters; Sun Ce and Zhou Yu learn of the Qiao sisters and court them a short time after the two men have broken away from Yuan Shu's regime. The younger Lady Qiao (who is more commonly called 'Xiaoqiao' in the text for narrative simplicity) married Zhou Yu, while her older sister married Sun Ce. At the time of the 'Battle of Red Cliffs', Xiaoqiao is happily married to Zhou Yu while her sister is an early widow: the two women are the subject of various tales, and one well-known element of the Red Cliffs fictional narrative is Cao Cao's supposed obsession with them. Cao Cao was renowned for lechery, and he coincidentally orders the construction of a 'Bronze Bird Tower' with two 'qiao' (bridges) linking the structure: some interpret the 'two qiao' to be 'the two Qiaos', and Zhuge Liang employs this rumour to anger Zhou Yu is many popular retellings. Whether Cao actually commissioned the tower before he declared war on Sun Quan is for historians to ponder, as is what Cao actually meant by 'two qiao': that story cemented the Qiao sisters in history and gave rise to the many romantic depictions of the two couples. Zhou Yu may have had consorts, but the author has not given him any, opting instead to portray Zhou Yu as having Xiaoqiao as his sole muse and being completely infatuated with her.*
*Known as Xiaoqiao [Shee-ow-chee-ow] (lit. Small/Younger Qiao)

Lady [Woo] – *Sun Jian's wife and mother of Sun Ce, Sun Quan, Sun Yi, Sun Kuang and Sun Shangxiang; she later becomes a strong voice in the administration of the region and was known as 'State Mother Wu' after the establishment of a more tangible southern state, although this is more of a posthumous honour since Lady Wu died before the 'Battle of Xiakou' and 'Battle of Red Cliffs' that allowed Sun Quan to establish Wu. Lady Wu was a strong-willed woman that had even been forced to support her brother, Wu Jing, when he was in dire straits. She raised Sun Jian's children to be courageous and wilful, and that is most evident in Lady Sun (known as Shangxiang in this work), the famous tomboy that later married the warlord Liu Bei. Lady Wu died shortly after Sun Quan assumed the role of head of the clan; in 'Crouching Dragon: The Journey of Zhuge Liang', a 'State Mother Wu' is seen at Lady Sun's wedding to Liu Bei a decade later, but it is explained here as Lady Chen, Sun Jian's consort, having been given that status for the purpose of continuity.*

Lady Zhou [Ch'oh] – *the beautiful wife of Dong Zhuo's general Zhang Ji; Cao Cao's taking her as a consort (whether this was voluntary or not is disputable) triggered the 'Battle of Wan City'*

Lei Bo [Lay P'oh] – *military officer serving Yuan Shu that left Yuan's service after the latter announced that he was a new emperor; he became a bandit in northern Yang with his former colleague Chen Lan.*

Li Jue [Lee Joo-er] – *one of Dong Zhuo's subordinate officers; he*

sometimes served in an advisory or emissary capacity in addition to having a personal army and acting as one of Dong Zhuo's most trusted generals. He later took charge of Chang'an with fellow officer Guo Si after Dong Zhuo's death and became a co-regent. He later clashed with his co-regent and lost the emperor when he was tricked into allowing the court to return to Luoyang under escort. Once Li Jue had no emperor to hide behind his power disappeared, and he was later killed by a subordinate.
*Known by the courtesy name Zhiran [Ch'ee-rarn]

Li Ru [Lee Roo] – *an adviser to the warlord Dong Zhuo; he usually worked alongside the more famous Jia Xu.*
*Known by the courtesy name Wenyou [Wern-yoh]

Li Su [Lee Soo] – *a cavalry officer serving Dong Zhuo; he later participated in a plot to kill Dong Zhuo, and was one of the men that actually dealt killing strikes. He was finally executed for incompetence for failing to defeat Dong Zhuo's son-in-law, Niu Fu.*

Liang Gang [Lee-arng Garng] – *officer serving Yuan Shu*

'Liao' [Lee-ow] – *NAMED FOR NARRATIVE COHESION; son-in-law of the Kuaiji rebel leader Zhang Ya*

Ling Cao [Ling Ts'ah-oh] – *an early volunteer in Sun Ce's army; he later became known for his bold charges and general heroism. He was succeeded by his more famous son, Ling Tong [Ling Tong], who is briefly referred to, though not by name.*

Liu Bei [Lee-oo P'ay] – *a member of the Liu family that ruled China as the Han Dynasty; his ancestors were disinherited after committing an offence, so Bei was forced into a life of weaving straw shoes and mats. He was later pitied and advanced by a wealthier relative, and quickly made friends in high places. He gained initial notoriety for his victories against the Yellow Turbans, and made many acquaintances that would become famous in their own right. He was said to have had imperial ambitions as a youth and eventually became one of the three dynastic founders of the 'Three Kingdoms' era. He joined forces with the young Sun Quan to fight Cao Cao at the 'Battle of Red Cliffs', and then had an uneasy alliance with the Sun family for over a decade: Sun Quan and Liu Bei eventually came to blows over Jing Province. He later marched against Sun Quan's state of Eastern Wu to avenge a personal matter and was defeated by Commander-in-Chief Lu Xun in the so-called 'Battle of Xiaoting'; he died shortly thereafter, leaving his mission to reunify the country to his trusted Prime Minister, Zhuge Liang. Liu Bei appears only briefly in this work as a collaborator for Taishi Ci: Bei's early career is a story thread in '"Yellow Sky"', and he is dealt with more specifically in 'Crouching Dragon: The Journey of Zhuge Liang', where he is the title character's first lord.*
*Known by the courtesy name Xuande [Shoo-arn-der]

Liu Biao [Lee-oo P'ee-ow] – *a scion of the Liu family that ruled China as the Han Dynasty; he was Governor of the 'artery region'*

of Jing Province at the time of Sun Jian's pledge of allegiance to Yuan Shu. Liu Biao is a major antagonist for the Sun family due to his role in Sun Jian's early death: Biao's final years and the fate of his strategically-important province are a central story thread in 'Crouching Dragon: The Journey of Zhuge Liang'.
*Known by the courtesy name Jingsheng [Ch'ing-s'erng]

Liu Dai [Lee-oo T'eye] - *a scion of the Liu family that ruled China as the Han Dynasty and brother of Liu Yao; he was Governor of Yan Province at the time of the Eastern Pass Coalition against Dong Zhuo. Liu Dai had Cao Cao as a vassal, but he would eventually cede the province to Cao with his death at the hands of Yellow Turban rebels, providing the 'Hero of Chaos' with his first foothold. He risked his life when he publicly defended the veteran hero Lu Kang from the 'Ten Attendants' at one point in his early career. Liu Dai's career forms part of a story thread in the sister work '"Yellow Sky": Crisis for the Han Dynasty'.*
*Known by the courtesy name Gongshan [K'ong-s'arn]

Liu Ji [Lee-oo Ch'ee] – *son and heir of the court-appointed Governor of Yang Province, Liu Yao: he went on to serve the Sun clan in the south, despite his father being at odds with Sun Ce and dying in disgrace after losing the provincial capital to the young warlord. Some accounts suggest that it was Taishi Ci that convinced Liu Ji to join Sun Ce.*

Liu Pan [Lee-oo Parn] – *Jing Governor Liu Biao's nephew and a serving officer; he spearheaded a campaign to seize Yuzhang Prefecture from Sun Ce while the latter was preoccupied with other military matters, but he was overcome by the newly-recruited Taishi Ci and chased back to Jiangxia.*

Liu Pi [Lee-oo Pee] – *a Yellow Turban leader in Yu Province: he initially served under Bo Cai, but after Bo's death he formed an alliance with fellow subordinate Huang Shao that lasted until Shao's death. Unlike Huang Shao, he has two possible death dates: the author chooses the later one (during the 'Girdle Edict Crisis' that occurs outside the timeframe of this work, rather than dying alongside Huang Shao during Cao Cao's pacification of Yu Province that occurs after Cao has retrieved Emperor Xian from the ruins of Luoyang).*

Liu Qi [Lee-oo Chee] – *Jing Governor Liu Biao's eldest and a serving officer in his later years; Liu Qi's military career and the related crises are part of a central story thread in 'Crouching Dragon: The Journey of Zhuge Liang'.*

Liu Xun [Lee-oo Shoon] - *a scion of the Liu family that ruled China as the Han Dynasty; he was a vassal of Yuan Shu that was later elevated to Administrator of Lujiang Prefecture after Sun Ce had defeated the incumbent Lu Kang. Liu Xun only becomes prominent after Yuan Shu's death: as depicted in the last act of this work, he seizes Yuan Shu's family and declares independence, which forces Sun Ce to abandon a campaign against Jing Governor Liu Biao and return home to bolster Jiangdong's defences. Sun Ce later*

636

outwitted Liu Xun, defeated him and forced him to flee to his acquaintance Cao Cao: Xun then served as an official until his inherent arrogance angered Cao and ended his career.
*Known by the courtesy name Zitai [Tz'ee-T'eye]

Liu Yan [Lee-oo Yarn] – *a scion of the Liu family that ruled China as the Han Dynasty; he managed to convince Emperor Ling that the Provincial Inspectorate system was inadequate for dealing with the nationwide rebellions, and he was then made one of the first Provincial Governors. As Governor of Yi Province to the far west, he exercised near-total autonomy and immediately had the cultist Zhang Lu carry out a takeover of the neighbouring Hanzhong: he later challenged the regents but was humiliated, losing two of his four sons in battle. He then lost a third to illness and became ill himself: he died a miserable man, and his legacy was inherited by his timid fourth son Liu Zhang. Liu Yan's career forms part of a story thread in '"Yellow Sky"'.*
*Known by the courtesy name Junlang [Ch'un-Larng]

Liu Yao [Lee-oo Ya-oh] – *a scion of the Liu family that ruled China as the Han Dynasty and brother of Liu Dai; he was promoted to Governor of Yang Province by the Han Regency court and sent to the region to deal with the ambitious Yuan Shu. Liu Yao seized Danyang Prefecture and part of Wu Prefecture, which riled Sun Ce and led to a bitter rivalry: Sun Ce emerged as the victor after Liu Yao repeatedly ignored sound advice and made poor use of his followers, who included prodigy and friend Taishi Ci. Liu Yao died in technical exile, and his son Liu Ji inherited his army. Liu Yao's career also forms part of a story thread in '"Yellow Sky": Crisis for the Han Dynasty'.*
*Known by the courtesy name Zhengli [Ch'erng-lee]

Liu Yè [Lee-oo Yer] – *Lujiang Administrator Liu Xun's senior adviser and later an adviser to Cao Cao*
*Known by the courtesy name Ziyang [Tz'ee-yarng]

Liu Yu [Lee-oo Yoo] – *a scion of the Liu family that ruled China as the Han Dynasty; he was promoted to Governor of Yòu Province by the Han Emperor Ling and ordered to quell an uprising. He remained as governor until Emperor Ling died, Emperor Shao succeeded him and Dong Zhuo seized power: he then became embroiled in the schemes of Dong Zhuo and Yuan Shao, and when Yuan tried to name him as a possible replacement for Dong Zhuo's Emperor Xian, he refused to comply. He had a complex political relationship with his vassal Gongsun Zan, who eventually ousted and killed him. Liu Yu's tenure in Yòu Province is shown in '"Yellow Sky": Crisis for the Han Dynasty'.*
*Known by the courtesy name Bo'an [P'oh-arn]

Liu Zhang [Lee-oo Ch'arng] – *Yi Governor Liu Yan's fourth and only surviving son after a series of misfortunes; he inherited the governorship of Yi Province when his father died. Liu Zhang is not seen but is often referred to when discussing the future of the nation: he is viewed as timid, obsequious, incompetent and cowardly by his contemporaries, and he is usually seen as a weak*

ruler that is destined to be usurped. Liu Zhang's military career - and prophesied defeat – forms part of a central story thread in 'Crouching Dragon: The Journey of Zhuge Liang'.
*Known by the courtesy name Jiyu [Ch'ee-yoo]

Liu Zheng [Lee-oo Ch'erng] - a respected intellectual in Liaodong Peninsula that angers the ruler Gongsun Du somehow; he is then rescued by the wandering lone hero Taishi Ci.

Lu Ji [Loo Ch'ee] – the younger son of ousted Lujiang Administrator Lu Kang, cousin to Sun Quan's famous fourth Chief Commander Lu Xun, a long-serving vassal of the Sun clan in his own right and one of the '24 Filial Exemplars' in Chinese history; he is never seen and only referred to in this work, but he later joins Sun Quan's government.
*Known by the courtesy name Gongji [K'ong-k'ong]

Lu Jun [Loo Ch'oon] – the elder son of ousted Lujiang Administrator Lu Kang that is referred to during the text but never seen: he was supposedly rewarded with rank by the Han court (or, more accurately, the regency court or Cao Cao's regime, depending on when any appointments were made) for his late father's loyalty in the face of Yuan Shu's siege, but his fate is unknown at the time of writing.

Lu Kang [Loo Karng] – a long-serving vassal of the Han Dynasty; his grandfather was a victim of a slander campaign against his father additionally suffered through his stubborn refusal to accept a role thereafter. Kang was known throughout his career for being principled and honest, even when that was going to get him into trouble: he was, however, a natural negotiator when he wanted to be, and he successfully pacified at least two troubled regions that others have given up as lost. He criticised the corrupt and powerful eunuch faction known as the 'Ten Attendants' and was arrested: Liu Dai and others argued for his release and reinstatement, and he then took on the role of 'Administrator of Lujiang Prefecture'. When Dong Zhuo seized power and ousted the young emperor Shao in favour of his brother Xian, Lu Kang opted to recognise Xian, refused to join the Eastern Pass Coalition against Dong Zhuo and braved hostile regions to take tributes to the capital. When the coalition dissolved and the Yuan brothers, Shao and Shu, began their 8-year-long feud, Lu Kang refused to serve either, citing loyalty to the Han: Yuan Shu refused to accept his stance and attacked him. Lu Kang – who was in his late sixties at this point – held out until Sun Ce was deployed to siege his capital: accounts suggest that the siege lasted 2 years (the author found that time frame was unworkable when taking other events into account and adjusted it somewhat), but regardless of the actual time, Lu Kang succumbed to the pressure. Lu Kang died and the prefectural capital fell to Sun Ce, who was then forced to cede it to Yuan Shu's chosen Administrator, Liu Xun. Lu Kang's younger son Lu Ji would go on to be one of the '24 Filial Exemplars' and a vassal of the Sun clan, while Lu Kang's great nephew Lu Xun would go on to be one of Sun Quan's greatest strategists and military commanders, going on to marry one of

Sun Ce's daughters and become the Prime Minister of Eastern Wu.
*Known by the courtesy name Jining [Ch'ee-ning]

Lu Shang [Loo S'arng] – *the grandson of the elder son of ousted Lujiang Administrator Lu Kang: he was supposedly rewarded with rank by the Han court for his late grandfather's pacification of a rebel uprising in Lujiang.*

Lu Su [Loo Soo] – *a vassal of the Sun clan; he befriended Zhou Yu (Gongjin) in Jiujiang and travelled to Jiangdong with him when Yuan Shu declared his right to rule. He did not achieve high rank under Sun Ce, despite famously donating an entire granary to Zhou Yu's underfunded militia (the author alludes to the fictional depiction of Lu Su as a social buffoon and provides tactlessness as an explanation). Lu Su is a major character in 'Crouching Dragon'.*
*Known by the courtesy name Zijing [Tz'ee-jing]

Lu Xun [Loo Shoon] – *a long-serving vassal of the Sun clan; he joined the southern state's government at some point prior to the 'Battle of Red Cliffs' (the author has him join during Sun Ce's short reign). Lu Xun's impressive career is partially covered in 'Crouching Dragon: The Journey of Zhuge Liang'.*
*Known by the courtesy name Boyan [P'oh-yarn]

Lu Zhi [Loo Ch'ee] – *a scholar of the Han court; he tutored the warlords Liu Bei and Gongsun Zan and was lauded for his military efforts against the Yellow Turbans.*
*Known by the courtesy name Zigan [Tz'ee-garn]

Lü Bu [L' Boo] – *one of the most famous – or, more appropriately, notorious – men of the era; he is known particularly for his disloyalty, inconstancy, and inevitable downfall. In fiction, he is portrayed as a near-invincible warrior – a 'Man among men' – that rides the unparalleled horse, 'Red Hare' (one popular adage is 'Among horses, Red Hare; among men, Lü Bu); Lü Bu's career forms part of several story threads in '"Yellow Sky": Crisis for the Han Dynasty', and he serves as a major antagonist for Sun Jian and a political nuisance for Sun Ce in this work.*
*Known by the courtesy name Fengxian [Fung-shee-arn]

Lü Dai [L' T'eye] – *a long-serving vassal of the Sun clan; while he is relatively unimportant in this work and is not seen to join the cause until Yuan Shu's declaration of sovereignty (when Dai actually joined the Sun faction is debatable, but the author added him here), he is a high-ranking official in later years and actually outlived Sun Quan by 4 years, dying at the age of 95/96.*
*Known by the courtesy name Dinggong [T'ing-k'ong]

Lü Fan [L' Farn] – *a long-serving vassal of the Sun clan and personal friend of Sun Ce: the author almost contemplated referring to him by his style name 'Ziheng' as a result, but refrained from doing so to highlight the importance of Sun Ce and Zhou Yu's closer relationship. The author chose to include a variant on the popular story that he gained his important role by demonstrating his skill through a game of weiqi ('Chinese chess'),*

although he is depicted as already knowing Sun Ce well at that point. It is Fan that accompanies Sun Ce on almost every campaign as his chief strategist, while Zhou Yu is often trusted with guarding Danyang or is otherwise preoccupied: in fiction, Zhou Yu often replaces Fan as the main strategist.
*Known by the courtesy name Ziheng [Tz'ee-hung]

Lü Meng [L' Mung] – *a long-serving vassal of the Sun clan; as per the adaption in this work, his first contributions were as an unwanted follower of his brother-in-law Deng Dang. The author was unable to provide anything close to a complete picture of this complicated man in this work, but Lü Meng's later brilliance and triumph over Guan Yu form part of 'Crouching Dragon'.*
*Known by the courtesy name Ziming [Tz'ee-ming]
*Ridiculed in his early career as A'Meng [Ah Mung]

Ma Midi [Mah Mee-t'ee] – *Han official that is noted for two things: as Grand Tutor he assisted the career of Sun clan ally Zhu Zhi, and he was one of only a very small number of men – possibly two – that paid respects to Dong Zhuo after the latter's death.*

Ma Teng [Mah Tung] – *a mid-ranking officer in the Han imperial army that defected to the Liang Province rebels; he later married a Qiang woman and became the father of the famous Qiang warlord Ma Chao. He was forced to seek refuge with Cao Cao after a feud with fellow warlord Han Sui, whereupon he was put under house arrest by the Han Prime Minister; when his son rebelled against the Han in the wake of the 'Battle of Red Cliffs', Ma Teng and all of the family that he had brought with him to the capital were executed. In fiction, his death is sometimes moved to before Ma Chao's uprising so that Chao is not responsible for the death of his own family. Ma Teng is only mentioned in this work, but his role in the Liang Province Rebellion is featured in '"Yellow Sky"'.*
*Known by the courtesy name Shoucheng [S'oh-t'ung]

Magistrate Hao [Hah-oh] – *NAMED FOR NARRATIVE COHESION: the Magistrate of Hougan that aids Wang Lang during the second phase of Sun Ce's campaign in Kuaiji. He contemplated surrender to Sun Ce's officers but was killed by Zhang Ya, a rebel leader that was aiding Wang Lang.*

Major Yuan [Yoo-arn] – *the historical Yuan Xiong [Yoo-arn Shee-ong] that Lü Meng surrendered to after killing one of Sun Ce's officials in anger.*

Mister Dai [T'eye] – *NAMED FOR NARRATIVE COHESION: the heckling official that Lü Meng killed in anger.*

Niu Fu [Nee-oo Foo] – *Dong Zhuo's son-in-law and minor warlord in his own right: he was Jia Xu's second significant lord. Niu was in a city to the east of Chang'an when Dong Zhuo was assassinated, and Lü Bu was forced to send Li Su to kill Niu before he could organise Dong's loyalists and retaliate: Li Su failed due to Jia Xu's ability as a strategist, so Lü Bu personally marched against Niu. Jia Xu was busy rallying other former vassals of Dong*

Zhuo when Bu attacked Niu, and another adviser – sensing defeat – tricked Niu into gathering his family and belongings and fleeing the city, whereupon the adviser murdered Niu and his family and surrendered to Lü Bu. Jia Xu then became adviser to Li Jue and Guo Si, paving the way for their takeover of the capital and the subsequent regency government.

Older Lady Qiao – *see Lady Qiao (Older)*

Ou Xing [Oh Shing] – *bandit and-or rebel leader in Changsha County that Sun Jian was sent to the region to quell*

Qi Ji [Chee Jee] – *an officer in Yuan Shu's army; he defected to Cao Cao (after being won over by Liu Fu) at some point after Emperor Xian arrived in Yan Province.*

Qiao Mao [Chee-ow Mah-oh] – *Han official that was appointed as Administrator of Dong Prefecture by Han loyalists prior to the creation of the Eastern Pass Coalition; Qiao Mao wrote the edict that condemned Dong Zhuo and called on others to rise up against him. He later suffered a difficult working relationship with his superior, Yan Governor Liu Dai, who eventually killed him.*
*Known by the courtesy name Yuanwei [Yoo-arn-way]

Qiao Xuan [Chee-ow Shoo-arn] – *an infamous scholar and senior government official of the later years of the Han Dynasty; some fictional accounts have Xuan as the father of the Qiao sisters that Sun Ce and Zhou Yu married, but he died before the Yellow Turban Rebellion, making this impossible since the Qiao's father was still alive at the time of the marriage (15 years later).*
*Known by the courtesy name Gongzu [K'ong-tz'oo]

Qin Song [Chin Song] – *adviser to Sun Ce.*
*Known by the courtesy name Wenbiao [Wern-p'ee-ow]

Qin Yi [Chin Yee] – *an officer in Yuan Shu's army; he defected to Cao Cao (after being won over by Liu Fu) at some point after Emperor Xian arrived in Yan Province.*

Qu Yi [Choo Yee] – *a military officer during the time of the Yellow Turban Rebellion, Qu already had experience fighting rebels and tribes and lent his experience to the loyalist cause. He later worked for the Ji Governor Han Fu and his successor Yuan Shao: he was Shao's vanguard general during a major battle with Gongsun Zan, and he overcame Gongsun's famed cavalry to deliver a stunning and decisive victory. Yuan Shao took a sudden dislike to Qu's lofty behaviour in the wake of the victory over Gongsun Zan and decided to have him arrested, but accounts differ as to what happened next: Qu Yi was either caught and executed or forced to flee and live as a fugitive. Qu Yi's career and fate forms part of a story thread in '"Yellow Sky": Crisis for the Han Dynasty'.*

Quan Rou [Choo-arn Roh] – *adviser to Sun Ce and his successor Sun Quan: Quan Rou is used as an adviser to Sun Fu on the* *latter's campaigns against Yuan Shu, but the author did this for narrative cohesion. His son Quan Song – who is not mentioned or seen in this work – was born a year before this novel ends and went on to marry Sun Quan's daughter and fight for Eastern Wu as a senior officer.*

Sheng Xian [S'ung Shee-arn] – *the Administrator of Wu Prefecture during the reigns of Emperors Shao and Xian: he was ousted by a popular figure called Xu Gong and forced to seek refuge with a retired general called Xu Zhao. Sheng Xian is trapped in Xu Zhao's estate for most of the novel, and he might therefore seem irrelevant: he is assassinated after Sun Ce's death, which leads to his loyal allies, Dai Guan and Gui Lan, hatching a plot to kill prominent members of the Sun family. There is a level of creativity when approaching Sheng Xian, as the information about him is rather patchy, but he provides a third layer to Wu Prefecture's complicated political structure that needs explaining.*
*Known by the courtesy name Xiaozhang [Shee-ow-ch'arng]

Shi Xie [S'ee Shee-er] – *the Governor of Jiaozhi, the region to the south of Yang Province (which includes part of Northern Vietnam); he plays no important part in this novel (other than promising a safe haven to the fugitive Wang Lang and his adviser Xu Jing after Kuaiji is lost), but he and his descendants have a lot of dealings with the Sun clan in subsequent decades.*
*Known by the courtesy name Weiyan [Way-yarn]

Shi Ran [S'ee Rarn] – *see Zhu Ran*

Song Jian [Song Jee'arn] – *a Liang Province rebel leader that eventually formed his own independent state that lasted for decades; he is only mentioned in this work, but his role in the Liang Province Rebellion is featured in '"Yellow Sky"'.*

Song Qian [Song Chee-arn] – *a vassal of Sun Ce and Sun Quan that served as an officer; the author depicts him as alternating between a field officer and a bodyguard to Sun Ce, and he might well have occupied both roles. He was said to have been present when Sun Ce fought his duel with Taishi Ci at Shen Town.*

Su Fei [Soo Fay] – *an officer serving the Jiangxia Administrator Huang Zu; he is briefly shown at a meeting but is otherwise unused. He was an associate of Gan Ning, a pirate that later earned fame for his actions against and later for the Sun clan. The author took the liberty of combining this Su Fei with a Su Fei that supposedly tried to convince Guan Yu to defect to Sun Quan: that event is shown in 'Crouching Dragon'.*

Sun Ben [Soon P'ern] – *the eldest son of Sun Jian's twin brother, who died suddenly; Sun Jian took Ben and his younger brother Fu into his own home and cared for them as though they were his sons. Sun Ben accompanied Jian on campaigns and became acting head of the clan when Jian died during the Jing Province campaign: he also inherited Jian's appointments from Yuan Shu, although their actual value is debatable. Sun Ben yielded to Sun*

Ce and continued to follow him as he consolidated southern Yang Prefecture. His relationship with Sun Quan was not as good, and he fell out of favour after being seen to ponder his loyalties.
*Known by the courtesy name Boyang [P'oh-yarng]

Sun Ce [Soon Ts'er] – *referred to as 'Bofu' once he reaches adulthood and becomes a protagonist in the main narrative (from Act IV onward) but is called Sun Ce in Acts I-III and the prologue/epilogue. Sun Ce is the second protagonist of this novel, which ends before his death, which was partly caused by followers of Xu Gong, a usurper-administrator in Wu Prefecture that tried to coerce Cao Cao into attacking Ce and paid with his life (Xu Gong is supposed to have been the source of the nickname 'Little Conqueror' that was attached to Sun Ce over time). Sun Ce died at the start of the 3rd Century, leaving his legacy to his younger brother Sun Quan. Sun Ce's death is another great mystery, like that of his father: historically, Ce was attacked whilst out hunting with inadequate security (how long he lived after the attempt on his life is unknown exactly); he survives that assassination attempt in fiction, but is then persecuted to the grave by the spirit of a Taoist saint that he had executed earlier. The author does highlight some other possibilities regarding motive and suspects as the narrative draws to a close.*
*Known by the courtesy name Bofu [P'oh-foo]
*Known later by the epithet 'Little Conqueror' (mainly by enemies)

Sun Fu [Soon Foo] – *the younger son of Sun Jian's twin brother, who died suddenly; Sun Jian took Fu and his older brother Ben into his own home and cared for them as though they were his sons. Sun Fu later accompanied his brother on campaigns, by which time Sun Ce was head of the clan.*
*Known by the courtesy name Guoyi [K'oo-oh-yee]

Sun Hao [Soon Hah-oh] – *the eldest son of Sun Jian's younger brother Sun Jing; he accompanied Jing on campaigns, but is relatively unimportant to the narrative. Two of Sun Hao's grandchildren – Sun Chen [Soon T'ern] and Sun Jun [Soon Ch'oon] – individually became regents during the later years of the Sun Wu Empire and were highly controversial.*

Sun Hè [Soon Her] – *a cousin from the related Yu clan, he came to live in the Sun household and was made an honorary member of the clan, going so far as to take the Sun name (whether this happened during Sun Jian's lifetime is debatable – some accounts suggest that it was Sun Ce that inducted him – but the author made the choice to have him as a Sun at the start). Sun Hè served Sun Ce as a bodyguard throughout the latter's life, but he fatefully missed an opportunity to save Sun Ce from an assassination attempt by followers of Xu Gong. Sun Hè served Sun Quan as an official, but he was a victim of a revenge attack by followers of the former Wu Administrator, Sheng Xian.*
*Known by the courtesy name Bohai [P'oh-h'eye]
*Known as Yu Hè [Yoo Her] before his admission into the Sun clan

Sun Hè's brother – *mentioned briefly in the narrative; he would* *have been a Yu [Yoo] rather than a Sun. He is the ancestor of a few prominent figures in Eastern Wu (that all took the name 'Sun' at some point, as Sun Hè had).*

Sun Jian [Soon Jee-arn] – *a southern man whose well-known military career began during the Yellow Turban Rebellion and continued with a sizeable role in the Liang Province pacification campaign, Changsha pacification campaign and the campaign against Dong Zhuo. His progeny –beginning with his eldest son Sun Ce – would found the state of Eastern Wu (and later the Sun Wu Empire) and improve the fortunes of the beleaguered south of China, but Jian himself would die an ignominious death in Jing Province; the circumstances surrounding his death would become a major factor in events for years to come.*
*Known by the courtesy name Wentai [Wern-tigh]

Sun Jian's (two) younger daughters – *neither of the two are named in history, and little is known about them*

Sun Jian's second consort – *this character is never named, and may not have existed; she is included as a possible mother to some of Sun Jian's younger children – Sun Lang and-or one of Sun Jian's daughters – and dies 'off-stage'*

Sun Jing [Soon Ch'ing] – *the younger brother of Sun Jian; he aided his nephew Sun Ce on campaigns.*
*Known by the courtesy name Youtai [Yoh-tigh]

Sun Kuang [Soon Koo-arng] – *a younger son of Sun Jian by his wife Lady Wu; when Jian died, Kuang was given his father's marquisate as an act of generosity by Sun Ce. Kuang was not a military might like his elder brothers Ce and Yi: he was married to a niece of the warlord Cao Cao as part of a general peacekeeping exercise, although Cao Cao and Sun Quan would later clash at Red Cliffs. Sun Kuang died young, around four years after his elder brother Ce.*
*Known by the courtesy name Jizuo [Ch'ee-tz'oo-oh]

Sun Lang [Soon Larng] – *a younger son of Sun Jian; his mother's identity is not known at the time of writing, but it is likely to be Lady Chen or Sun Jian's possible second consort. He is a very young child during the timeline of this novel: he later has a disaster-prone career whilst serving his brother Quan.*
*Known by the courtesy name Zao'an [Tz'ah-oh Arn]

Sun Quan [Soon Choo-arn] – *Sun Jian's second son; he initially aided Sun Ce's administration, but when Sun Ce died without a male heir (his wife Daqiao was pregnant with his only son at the time of his death) Quan inherited his brother's role, responsibilities and power. Sun Quan would rule Jiangdong – later expanded to the state of Eastern Wu – for 50 years and have a significant role in some of the most important events of the time, such as the 'Battle of Red Cliffs' (as the main opponent of Cao Cao), the 'Battle of Xiaoting' (as the target of Liu Bei's wrath) and the creation of the 'Three Kingdoms' era itself (as one of the three*

644

rulers). He was made a king by the Cao Wei emperor Cao Pi (as a placatory gesture), but he later became First Emperor of the Sun Wu Empire. As he aged, his sanity appears to have eroded: he became increasingly unstable, turning against early allies and even having some of them executed. He left the management of Sun Wu and the welfare of his heir to Regent Zhuge Ke upon his death, which did not turn out to be a sound decision.
*Known by the courtesy name Zhongmou [Ch'ong-moh]

Sun Shangxiang [Soon S'arng-shee-arng] – *the eldest daughter of the Han Dynasty officer Sun Jian; she is famous (although this might just be embellishment by scholars or folklore) for being a tomboy that surrounded herself with weapons and an elite force of female bodyguards, one of whom married her brother Sun Quan. She later married the warlord Liu Bei but they were forced to separate when her husband's ambitions conflicted with those of her family. In fiction, she is sometimes called Shangxiang since, like most women in ancient China, her given name is unknown (the name 'Shangxiang' seemingly originates from folklore, and she is simply known (like her sisters) as 'Lady Sun' when mentioned in historical texts); the author has used this name in order to allow family members to refer to her as something other than 'Lady Sun'. Sun Shangxiang's marriage to Liu Bei is part of a major plot thread in the author's first 'Three Kingdoms' work, 'Crouching Dragon' (where she is referred to as 'Lady Sun').*

Sun Yi [Soon Yee] – *Sun Jian's third son; he was said to be similar in appearance and nature to his older brother Sun Ce, and many considered him a preferable heir to Ce's legacy. Sun Yi served Quan as an official, but his easy-going nature made him an easy first victim of a revenge plot by followers of former Wu Administrator Sheng Xian.*
*Known by the courtesy name Shubi [S'oo-bee]

Sun Yu [Soon Yoo] – *Sun Jing's second son and Sun Ce's cousin; he served as an official and officer.*
*Known by the courtesy name Zhongyi [Ch'ong-yee]

Taishi Ci [Tigh-sher Ts'eh] – *a famous 'lone wolf' that had a mixed career; Taishi Ci died only a few years after his eventual lord Sun Ce, although fiction would award him another decade of incredible service and a more fitting end in battle.*
*Known by the courtesy name Ziyi [Tz'ee-yee]

Taishi Ci's mother – *she is seen as the person that sends him on most of his missions*

Tao Qian [T'ow Chee-arn] – *Inspector and later Governor of Xu Province; Tao Qian is revered in some fiction as a morally upstanding man, but historical accounts suggest a wily, jealous man that hankered for talented subordinates and reacted badly to any that rejected his work offers. He once employed the official Wang Lang, who advised him to avoid fighting Dong Zhuo or the subsequent regency government and instead focus on defending his borders. Tao Qian is famous for being held responsible for the*

robbing and death of Cao Cao's father, Cao Song; Cao Cao took a force into Xu Province and massacred 100,000 of its inhabitants in reaction to the affront, and Tao Qian died shortly thereafter of an illness. Tao Qian briefly allied to the ambitious Yuan Shu but soon became another target for Yuan's growing desire for land. Tao's successor as Governor, Liu Bei (whose succession is supposedly desired by Tao Qian in fiction, but that is more murky in historical accounts), surrendered the province to Yuan Shu's rival, Yuan Shao in order to force Cao Cao – who was to all intents and purposes a vassal of Yuan Shao – to retreat. Tao Qian is briefly featured in this work as an ally of Sun Jian and later an enemy of Sun Ce: the rest of his career and eventual fate forms part of a story thread in '"Yellow Sky": Crisis for the Han Dynasty'.
*Known by the courtesy name Gongzu [K'ong-tz'oo]

Tian Kai [Tee-arn K'eye] – *officer and trusted offical serving Gongsun Zan; Gongsun made him Inspector of Qing Province.*

Wang Can [Warng Ts'arn] – *a Han Dynasty official that later served Cao Cao; his family were prestigious enough for his grandfather and great-grandfather to be Excellences alongside the Yuan clan. He was said to possess an eidetic memory and have a fascination with donkeys, among other things, and the famed polymath Cai Yong was a vocal sponsor. Wang Can wrote a historical work, 'Record of Heroes', that serves as an alternative biographical compendium to the more famous 'Record of the Three Kingdoms', though it might be seen as biased toward Cao Cao's faction. It includes alternate fates (or even dates of death) for some notable figures, such as Sun Jian.*
*Known by the courtesy name Zhongxuan [Ch'ong-shoo-arn]

Wang Kuang [Warng Koo-arng] – *a subordinate of Commander-in-Chief Hè Jin at the end of Emperor Ling's reign; he later became the Administrator of Henei at the suggestion of Han loyalists in Dong Zhuo's government and joined the Eastern Pass Coalition. He was defeated by Dong Zhuo and retired from military service.*
*Known by the courtesy name Gongjie [K'ong-Jee-er]

Wang Lang [Warng Larng] – *official that served the Han Dynasty; he was a friend of men like Kong Rong. He was appointed as Administrator of Kuaiji by the court, and he allied himself to Governor Liu Yao, although he was not averse to forging alliance with bandits, anti-Han rebels and hostile tribes as well. He served as a major antagonist to Sun Ce during the latter's Kuaiji Campaign; he fled to the north after his defeat and was brought into Cao Cao's court by Kong Rong. Wang Lang served Cao's administration and received many promotions. He was (allegedly) a proponent of Han Emperor Xian's abdication in favour of Cao Cao's son Cao Pi: he served the Cao Wei Empire until death. He had an influence on the next political transition through his progeny: his granddaughter Wang Yuanji [Warng Yoo-arn-jee] was the mother of the first Jin Dynasty Emperor, Sima Yan [Ss'mah Yarn].*
*Known by the courtesy name Jingxing [Jing-shing]

Wang Yun [Warng Yoon] – *a Han Dynasty official; he was Inspector of Yu Province around the time of the Yellow Turban Rebellion (whether he was Inspector during the actual rebellion is not entirely clear, but the author has placed him there to introduce him). When Dong Zhuo seized the court and relocated the capital to Chang'an, Wang Yun decided to plot against the tyrant (there is an elaborate fictional version that is recounted in Wang Yun's bio in '"Yellow Sky"'). Wang Yun managed to convince Lü Bu to betray Dong Zhuo, and once Dong was dead, Wang Yun took charge in Chang'an, condemning most of Dong's former aides as traitors and executing the renowned scholar Cai Yong for collaboration. Wang Yun was eventually isolated and murdered by some of Dong Zhuo's former vassals when they realised that they would not receive amnesty from him; they then seized control and formed their own regency government led by Li Jue and Guo Si. Wang Yun's exploits form part of a plot thread in '"Yellow Sky"'.*
*Known by the courtesy name Zishi [Tz'ee-s'ee]

Wei Teng [Way Tung] – *an official that joined Sun Ce's government at some point (the author's choice is arbitrary); he angered Sun Ce with his criticisms and was only saved from death when Lady Wu, Sun Ce's mother, intervened. This (supposedly historical) event is dramatized and used as the final chapter of this novel: it does not necessarily portray Sun Ce in a positive light (the author argues that he is rightly frustrated but chooses, briefly, to manifest that frustration wrongly) and does not necessarily serve as the best image to leave an audience with, but it indicates that there is friction (like the preceding 'Gan Ji incident') and foreshadows Sun Ce's fate.*

Wei Xu [Way Shoo] – *a trusted relative of Lü Bu that served him as a military officer; he later defected to Cao Cao.*

"White Tiger" Yan [Yarn] – *a 'khan' of the Shanyue tribes in Wu Prefecture; he is referred to in many texts as 'Yan Baihu' [Yarn P'eye-hoo], where 'Baihu' translates to 'White Tiger': the author used the translated form to make him stand out. He is a major antagonist to Sun Ce for much of the middle of the novel, as he and his tribal allies repeatedly rise up in revolt, sometimes alone and sometimes in alliance with others. It is said that Yang Governor Liu Yao and Kuaiji Administrator Wang Lang were secretly funding and supplying him at various points. He was repeatedly defeated, and he eventually contented himself with fuelling unrest from the shadows: in fiction he is often killed by Sun Ce or one of Sun Ce's generals, but he probably outlived Ce.*

Wu Fen [Woo Fern] – *the elder son of Sun Jian's brother-in-law Wu Jing; he is briefly shown at a family gathering.*

Wu Jing [Woo Ch'ing] – *Sun Jian's brother-in-law; he served Jian and then his sons as an officer and official until his death.*

Wu Qi [Woo Chee] – *the younger son of Sun Jian's brother-in-law Wu Jing; he is briefly shown at a family gathering.*

Xiaoqiao [Shee-ow-chee-ow] – *see Lady Qiao (Younger)*

Xu Gong [Shoo K'ong] – *an official in Wu Prefecture; his contribution to the story was pivotal but difficult to present because the information is so unhelpful at times. The author pieced it together as follows: Sheng Xian was the court-appointed Administrator of Wu Prefecture; Xu Gong overthrew Sheng Xian (by, it is implied, popular demand), but was then recognised by the regency court led by Li Jue and Guo Si; Xu Gong then lent his support to the regency court's appointed Governor of Yang Province (of which Wu is a part), Liu Yao; both Liu Yao and Xu Gong were then defeated by Sun Ce; Xu Gong went into exile (the author has him shelter with the same Xu Zhao that is sheltering Sheng Xian, for better or worse); Xu Gong is then recognised again, this time by Sun Ce (the author states that this is because Sheng Xian will not cooperate); Xu Gong plots secretly against Sun Ce, is discovered and then killed by Sun Ce's agents. Xu Gong's followers then plotted to assassinate Sun Ce: they attacked him and left him with mortal injuries within a year of Xu Gong's death, but they did not live to enjoy their victory.*

Xu Gong's son – *appears briefly in the scene where Xu Gong is going to seek refuge with Xu Zhao.*

Xu Jing [Shoo Jing] – *an official in the Han court that aided Yuan Shao and secretly conspired against Dong Zhuo; he was the brother of the famous appraiser Xu Shao that supposedly told Cao Cao that he was a 'Hero of Chaos' or 'Crafty Villain'. He fled Luoyang when Dong Zhuo began his purge of the intelligentsia and went to the south to serve Kong Zhuo in Yu Province and then Wang Lang in Kuaiji. He fled to Jiaozhi after Wang Lang's defeat and eventually travelled to Yi Province, where he served in Liu Zhang's government. When Liu Zhang ceded Yi to Liu Bei, Xu Jing held a high degree of respect and authority, even demanding deference from the likes of the Shu Han Prime Minister Zhuge Liang (a fact that is mentioned in passing in chapter 101 of the author's earlier work 'Crouching Dragon: the Journey of Zhuge Liang', although Xu Jing does not feature prominently otherwise) Xu Jing's earlier career (the part that leads into this work) is shown in '"Yellow Sky": Crisis for the Han Dynasty'.*
*Known by the courtesy name Wenxiu [Wern-shee-oo]

Xu Kun [Shoo Koon] – *Sun Jian's nephew (his sister's son); he appears sporadically throughout the novel as a field officer and guest at family gatherings. His daughter later married his cousin Sun Quan.*

Xu Rong [Shoo Rong] – *a general serving Dong Zhuo. Historically his ability is considerable, as he defeats many notable figures during the siege of Luoyang, including Sun Jian: he joined Lü Bu and Wang Yun's Han faction after Dong Zhuo's assassination, but he was subsequently outwitted by Jia Xu and killed in battle.*

Xu Shao [Shoo S'ah-oh] – *a famous appraiser who was known for fearless frankness; it was said that men feared his judgement and*

would try to curry favour with him in the hope that it would result in a career-boosting response. He is famous for having supposedly judged Cao Cao to be 'An able statesman in times of peace, and a 'jianxiong' (meaning a 'crafty villain', more or less) in chaotic times'. He later travelled to Xu Province, where he supposedly rated its governor Tao Qian poorly; after that, he went to Yang Province and served the court-appointed governor Liu Yao. He serves as a semi-antagonist to the Sun clan when they are trying to wrest Danyang Prefecture from Liu Yao: he fled with Liu Yao after the latter's resounding defeat and died whilst in exile in Yuzhang.
*Known by the courtesy name Zijiang [Tz'ee-jee-arng]

Xu Zhao [Shoo Ch'ah-oh] – *a retired Han general that gave sanctuary to any officials that were down on their luck. His motivations are hard to fathom, and the list of figures that he did supposedly shelter is strange (perhaps it is even nonsensical).*

Xue Li [Shoo-er Lee] – *one of Xu Province Governor Tao Qian's staunchest allies and the Chancellor of Tao's original capital, Peng City; he left Xu Province and travelled to Yang Province to aid the regency court's appointed governor, Liu Yao: that inadvertently reunited him with Ze Rong, the Buddhist cultist that had governed Xiapi for Tao Qian. The two worked together against Sun Ce, but ultimately it was Sun Ce that was to win: Xue Li was later murdered by Ze Rong.*

Xue Zhou [Shoo-er Ch'oh] – *a pirate king that was active along Guangling Prefecture's waterways: he may or may not have been an antagonist to Wu Jing prior to Yuan Shu's declaration of sovereignty, and he may or may not have been in the employ of Yuan Shu afterward.*

Xun Yu [Shoon Yoo] – *a descendant of numerous prominent Han officials; he was also an official in the Han court before joining Yuan Shao as an emissary and adviser. He later 'defected' to Cao Cao and started to find more officials to serve his new lord, including Xi Zhicai, his own nephew Xun Gongda and Guo Jia. He later advocated Cao Cao bringing the isolated Emperor Xian to Yan Province, and he remained Cao's staunch supporter through the 'Girdle Edict Crisis' (wherein several high-ranking figures put their names to a petition condemning Cao as a threat to the emperor and calling for military action against him) and the 'Battle of Guandu' (where Cao was pitted against Xun's former lord Yuan Shao); none of this was to save him when he questioned Cao Cao's decision to go along with plans to petition the sovereign to make him a duke. Xun Yu was soundly rebuked by Cao, fell out of favour, was beset by a mysterious illness and died shortly thereafter.*
*Known by the courtesy name Wenruo [Wern-roo-oh]

Yan Baihu [Yarn P'eye-hoo] – *see "White Tiger" Yan*

Yan Xiang [Yarn Shee-arng] – *an adviser to the nobleman-warlord Yuan Shu; he was loyal to Yuan in most instances, but he* remonstrated when Yuan wanted to declare that he was mandated to rule China as an emperor. His final fate is unknown, but he is depicted by the author as staying at Yuan Shu's side through the 'dynastic crisis' and being 'lost in action' somehow.

Yan Yu [Yarn Yoo] – the brother of 'White Tiger Yan', the khan of the Shanyue tribes in Wu Prefecture: he supposedly died fighting Sun Ce (the event is dramatized in this novel).

Yang Hong [Yarng Hong] – an adviser to the nobleman-warlord Yuan Shu; he survived the last battles between Yuan Shu's loyalists and Cao Cao's forces and was part of the refugee group that reached Lujiang Prefecture, whereupon he was captured by Liu Xun, the man that had initially promised refuge. His final fate is unknown and outside the timeframe of this work.

Yang Si [Yarng See] – a respected elder statesman and teacher/mentor to Wang Lang; it might be implied that he was the Chief of Staff, since the official Wang Lang served as an assistant to the holder of that role and retired when Yang Si died.

Younger Lady Qiao [Chee-ow] – see Lady Qiao (Younger)

Yu Fan [Yoo Farn] – a Han 'Officer of Merit' serving Kuaiji Administrator Wang Lang; he surrendered to Sun Ce after Wang Lang's first defeat and joined Sun Ce's faction. The author has him aid Sun Ce's recruitment of Dong Xi and Hè Qi and support Dong Xi's pacification of Shanyin (neither of which is unlikely).
*Known by the courtesy name Zhongxiang [Ch'ong-shee-arng]

Yu Mi [Yoo Mee] – a Han general serving Yang Governor Liu Yao; he was defeated repeatedly by Sun Ce's army. The author has him die 'off-stage' prior to Liu Ji's surrender.

Yu Zi [Yoo Tz-ee] – a trusted acolyte and subordinate of the cultist Ze Rong; he fought Sun Ce's army, but his fate is unknown: he is given a lieutenant role in this novel that may vastly outweigh his historical role. The author has him die alongside his master.

Yuan Huan [Yoo-arn Hoo-arn] – a vassal of Yuan Shu that served him as an adviser; he was said to have served Liu Bei prior to that in some accounts. He later abandoned Yuan Shu (the author has him do this when Yuan Shu declared his own mandate to rule) and joined Lü Bu: he surrendered to Cao Cao when Bu was defeated and served the Han court until his death.
*Known by the courtesy name Yaoqing [Yah-oh-ching]

Yuan Shao [Yoo-arn S'ah-oh] – one of the most important figures of the later years of the Han Dynasty: he was the descendant of numerous high-ranking court officials (one, Yuan An, had statues commemorating him) and (as the adopted son of the heir) heir apparent to a vast fortune that then made him one of the most powerful and influential men in China. Yuan Shao was born at a time when political power was shifting: the 'Ten Attendants' – a clique of court eunuchs – were so powerful that they could select

650

key government figures and have anyone – even empresses and princes – slandered and-or killed. Yuan Shao protected many officials and scholars that were slandered as enemies of the state during the so-called 'Partisan Crisis', and he later became the closest ally of Commander-in-Chief Hè Jin, whose nephew was heir to the Han throne. Jin oversaw his nephew's ascension and fought off a rival claim by supporters of Emperor Ling's widow, Dowager Dong, but he was then murdered by the 'Ten' after a failed attempt to purge them: Yuan Shao was the man that avenged Jin, slaughtering many allies of the 'Ten' and hundreds more eunuchs besides. Dong Zhuo then seized power, and Yuan Shao opposed his plan to depose Emperor Shao – Hè Jin's nephew – and replace him (with Emperor Xian): Yuan formed the 'Eastern Pass Coalition' to blockade the capital and force Dong to reinstate Emperor Shao. Dong's response was to kill the deposed emperor and then torture and execute the families of the coalition leaders, including Yuan's. The coalition failed to have a decisive victory over Dong, who fled east with Emperor Xian: Yuan Shao's brother Shu had declared that he should be clan chieftain, and Shao and Shu began a military feud that engulfed the east of China for the next eight years. By the time of Yuan Shu's death, Yuan Shao was ruler of most of the north of China: he then declared war of his childhood friend Cao Cao, who by then had Emperor Xian in his protective custody and a petition labelling him as a seditionist hanging over his head. Yuan and Cao eventually met in a series of military encounters known collectively as the 'Battle of Guandu': Yuan lost to Cao Cao and died shortly thereafter. Yuan Shao is a prominent character in '"Yellow Sky"'.
*Known by the courtesy name Benchu [P'ern-t'oo]

Yuan Shu [Yoo-arn S'oo] – *one of the most important figures of the later years of the Eastern Han Dynasty: he was the eldest legitimate son of the brother of the heir to the Yuan clan chieftainship. His half-brother, Yuan Shao, was older but born to a maidservant: Yuan Shu argued that Shao was therefore excluded from the succession, but when their heirless uncle - the clan chieftain – adopted Shao, that ended Shu's dreams of being the heir, and it caused deep resentment that never eased. His tale is told in this work and in '"Yellow Sky": Crisis for the Han Dynasty'.*
*Known by the courtesy name Gonglu [K'ong-loo]

Yuan Tan [Yoo-arn Tarn] – *the eldest son of the powerful and influential warlord Yuan Shao; he served his father as a general in Qing Province and fought allies of Gongsun Zan and his (biological) uncle Yuan Shu on his father's behalf.*
*Known by the courtesy name Xiansi [Shee-an-see]

Yuan Yao [Yoo-arn Yah-oh] – *the eldest son of the warlord Yuan Shu; he was named as Crown Prince when Yuan Shu declared that he was First Emperor of the Zhong Dynasty. Yuan Shu was defeated by Cao Cao and tried to find refuge with his half-brother Yuan Shao: Yao accompanied him to the border, but they were forced to turn back to Shouchun and Shu died during the return trip. Yuan Yao then travelled to Lujiang Prefecture with the remainder of his father's loyalists, but he was then captured by*

Lujiang's ruler (and former vassal of Yuan Shu) Liu Xun. Sun Ce defeated Liu Xun, and Yuan Yao went to Jiangdong, where he eventually earned a place in Sun Quan's court.

Yuan Yi [Yoo-arn Yee] – a cousin of Yuan Shao and Yuan Shu that later served as Administrator of Shanyang Prefecture, Yan Province; he was a founder member of Yuan Shao's Eastern Pass Coalition against Dong Zhuo, serving under his provincial governor Liu Dai. Cao Cao was said to respect him greatly. He was later defeated by Yuan Shu's forces and killed as he retreated through Xu Province.
*Known by the courtesy name Boye [P'oh-yer]

Yuan Yin [Yoo-arn Yin] – a cousin of Yuan Shu that served him as an adviser; he remained in Shu's service until Shu's death, whereupon he defended the remnants of Shu's loyalists as they made their way to Lujiang Prefecture. His fate after that is unclear: in some accounts, the ruler of Lujiang, Liu Xun – who captured the refugees and declared independence – somehow coerced Yuan Yin to serve him, but some accounts have him die in battle with Cao Cao on the way to Lujiang.

Yufuluo [Yoo-foo-loo-oh] – the chieftain of a breakaway faction of Southern Xiongnu; he had been selected as the Chanyu (king) of his people by a meddling Han court, but instead of accepting Yufuluo the Southern Xiongnu exiled him and his followers (although his brother stayed and was actually elected as the next Chanyu by the Xiongnu themselves). Yufuluo then became a wandering warlord of sorts, but he joined Yuan Shao's Eastern Pass Coalition very briefly; he tired of the inactivity and rebelled, capturing Shangdang Administrator Zhang Yang and forging alliances with the Black Mountain Bandits and groups of Yellow Turbans at varying points in time. He was the father of future Southern Xiongnu Chanyu Liu Bao, whose progeny would enjoy great power in northern China. Yufuluo is a secondary antagonist in '"Yellow Sky": Crisis for the Han Dynasty'.

Zang Ba [Tz'arng P'ah] – resident of northeast Xu Province that began his career as a Yellow Turban suppressor in Qing Province but later took over an entire region of Xu and ruled it as an independent 'crime haven'.
*Known by the courtesy name Xuangao [Shoo-arng-k'ao]

Ze Rong [Tz'er Rong] – a 'Buddhist cleric' in Xu Province: he is a major antagonist for Sun Ce during the Danyang Campaign.

Zhang Bao [Ch'arng P'ao] – a brother of the founder of the 'Way of Peace', Zhang Jue, and dubbed 'General of the Land' during the Yellow Turban Rebellion. He was defeated and killed a few months after his brother Jue.

Zhang Fei [Ch'arng Fay] – an early ally and sponsor of Liu Bei, and frequently paired with Guan Yu. He only appears briefly in this work: his early career under Liu Bei is covered in '"Yellow Sky": Crisis for the Han Dynasty', while his later career and death are

chronicled in 'Crouching Dragon: The Journey of Zhuge Liang'.
*Known by the courtesy name Yide [Yee-der]

Zhang Hong [Ch'arng Hong] – *one of the 'Two Zhangs' (the other was his more famous brother Zhang Zhao) and an adviser/envoy/politician that served Sun Ce and Sun Quan in succession; he spent a lot of time in the Han capital as Sun Quan's representative but he returned to the south prior to the outbreak of hostilities (the 'Battle of Red Cliffs') and remained there afterward. He died four years after Red Cliffs, but his descendants continued to serve the Sun clan.*
*Known by the courtesy name Zigang [Tz'ee-k'arng]

Zhang Huan [Ch'ang Hoo-arn] – *a famed general who was in semi-retirement at the time of the 'Partisan Crisis'; he was once Dong Zhuo's superior during a pacification campaign in Liang Province, and other notable officers (such as Qu Yi) probably served with him as well. He unintentionally prevented the 'Ten Attendants' from being ousted when he opposed the empress's father's plot against them.*

Zhang Ji [Ch'arng Jee] – *a general serving Dong Zhuo; he was envied for his beautiful wife, Lady Zhou. He later served the regents Li Jue and Guo Ji and was part of the Emperor's escort to Luoyang: the escort was defeated by Han loyalists and Zhang fled to nearby Nan County, Jing Province. Zhang Ji died taking Nan County from Liu Biao's forces and his nephew, Zhang Xiu, and the adviser Jia Xu 'inherited' the county.*

Zhang Jue [Ch'arng J'oo-er] – *The founder of the Taoist sect 'The Way of Peace' (his name is sometimes Romanised to Zhang Jiao [Ch'arng J'ee-ah-oh], but the author has chosen the older, more traditional version); he also instigated the first Yellow Turban Rebellion but died before it ended. The initial and subsequent rebellions are a fundamental part – and inspired the title of – '"Yellow Sky": Crisis for the Han Dynasty'.*

Zhang Liang [Ch'arng Lee-arng] – *a brother of the founder of the 'Way of Peace', Zhang Jue, and dubbed 'General of the People' during the Yellow Turban Rebellion; he was forced to carry on after Zhang Jue died, but he lacked the charisma to lead the religious movement or the peasant armies as well as his brother had done, and he was defeated less than a year later.*

Zhang Liao [Ch'arng Lee-ow] – *a subordinate of Lü Bu; he went on to serve Cao Cao and earn greater fame as dangerous enemy of the Sun clan in eastern China. His most famous exploit is his defence of the Hefei fortress in Lujiang Prefecture: he almost succeeded in killing Sun Quan (and, in fiction, he is partially responsible for the death of Taishi Ci in the same encounter) and earned a fearsome reputation in the south and was used as a bogeyman to scare naughty children.*
*Known by the courtesy name Wenyuan [Wern-yoo-arn]

Zhang Mancheng [Ch'arng Marn-t'erng] – *a Yellow Turban* *commander; he crushed the forces defending northern Jing and paved the way for the seizure of the strategically important city of Wan that Sun Jian was subsequently tasked with liberating again. Zhang was eventually defeated by forces under the joint command of Huangfu Song and Zhu Jun.*

Zhang Miao [Ch'arng Mee-ow] – *friend of Cao Cao and Yuan Shao; he is later made Administrator of Chenliu Prefecture/Principality. Zhang Miao is a primary protagonist in '"Yellow Sky"'.*
*Known by the courtesy name Mengzhuo [Mung-ch'oo-oh]

Zhang Wen [Ch'arng Wern] – *Excellency of Works in the Han court, later appointed as General of Chariots and Cavalry on the Left after Huangfu Song was removed from the post by slander during the Liang Province Rebellion. Sun Jian's secondment to Zhou Shen forms part of this work, and Zhang Wen's later career and death are dramatized in '"Yellow Sky"'.*
*Known by the courtesy name Boshen [P'oh-s'ern]

Zhang Xiu [Ch'arng Shee-oo] – *nephew of Dong Zhuo's ally Zhang Ji; he later received Jia Xu's service after occupying Wan City in Jing Province. Cao Cao made 'pacifying' Jing Governor Liu Biao his next major project after defeating the Xiongnu renegade Yufuluo and the Yellow Turbans in Yu Province, and he started that Jing campaign by attacking Nan County. Jia Xu advised surrender, and Zhang Xiu complied: Cao Cao then behaved unprofessionally, going so far as to take Zhang Xiu's aunt, Lady Zhou (who had recently been widowed) as his consort. The enraged Zhang Xiu vented his feelings privately, but Cao's spies heard and reported it to Cao, who then plotted to kill him: Jia Xu's spies reported that, and Jia Xu launched a pre-emptive attack that robbed Cao of his eldest son and bodyguard. Zhang Xiu later surrendered to Cao Cao again: Jia Xu joined Cao on that occasion, and Zhang enjoyed a short career as a Han official before dying (cause unknown, probably illness).*

Zhang Ya [Ch'arng Yah] – *a rebel leader in Hougan County, Kuaiji Prefecture that allied to a desperate Wang Lang during the second phase of Sun Ce's Kuaiji Campaign. He was initially successful, but Sun Ce's ally Hè Qi divided him from his son-in-law (named 'Liao' in this work) and defeated him.*

Zhang Ya's brother - *ADDED FOR NARRATIVE COHESION; a brother of Hougan County rebel leader Zhang Ya*

Zhang Yang [Ch'arng Yarng] – *a general that served Bing Province Inspector Ding Yuan; his colleague Lü Bu betrayed and killed Ding Yuan, but he never lost faith in Lü Bu and defended him many times, despite also lending his army to the Eastern Pass Coalition, which was dedicated to the destruction of Lü Bu's new master Dong Zhuo. His contribution to the coalition ended when he was captured by his own ally Yufuluo, who had tired of aiding Yuan Shao (who then had to rescue Zhang Yang). He was then made Administrator of Henei by Dong Zhuo's court in Chang'an, and later gave safe haven to the fugitive official Dong Zhao [T'ong*

Ch'ah-oh]: neither aided his professional relationship with Yuan Shao. He later played a key role in the restoration of the imperial palace in the capital Luoyang, but when he ordered his forces to prepare for a march to Xu Province to save Lü Bu from Cao Cao's army, a disgruntled subordinate killed him.
*Known by the courtesy name Zhishu [Ch'ee-s'oo]

Zhang Ying [Ch'arng Ying] – *a Han general that served Yang Governor Liu Yao; he was repeatedly defeated by Sun Ce's forces. The author has him die in a duel with Chen Wu, but he has no concrete historical date (or cause) of death.*

Zhang Yun [Ch'arng Yoon] – *an officer serving Jing Governor Liu Biao; he was the nephew of Cai Mao.*

Zhang Zhao [Ch'arng Hong] – *one of the 'Two Zhangs' (the other was his less famous brother Zhang Hong) and an adviser/politician that served Sun Ce and Sun Quan in succession; he was a highly-talented debater and could destroy a man's reputation with ease if allowed to. He was one of the most vocal supporters of surrendering to Cao Cao during the political tension leading up to the 'Battle of Red Cliffs', and many – including Zhou Yu, Cheng Pu, Lu Su and Liu Bei's adviser Zhuge Liang – were forced to debate with him on the issue. He later plotted against Liu Bei, Cao Cao and whoever else was considered to be a threat to Eastern Wu: he is often portrayed as a spiteful antagonist of sorts in popular fiction (this author tends to as well) but in his defence, he had Eastern Wu's best interests at heart. He is a recurring character in 'Crouching Dragon: the Journey of Zhuge Liang'.*
*Known by the courtesy name Zibu [Tz'ee-p'oo]

Zhao Yu [Ch'ah-oh Yoo] – *the Administrator of Guangling*

Zhen Bao [Ch'ern P'ah-oh] – *a rebellious general in Huainan that Liu Ye defeated through a ruse; Zhen's troops then ceased to be a threat to Liu Xun and became Xun's to command. The story is mentioned in passing when Liu Ye is rebuking Liu Xun for failing to heed his advice.*

Zhou Ang [Ch'oh Arng] – *brother of Zhou Yu (Renming) and Zhou Xin that served Yuan Shao: he was tasked with guarding Jiujiang but was defeated by Yuan Shu*

Zhou Ba [Ch'oh P'ah] – *a bandit leader in Shanyin*

Zhou Chou [Ch'oh T'oh] – *a bandit leader in Changsha*

Zhou Shang [Ch'oh S'arng] – *the uncle of Zhou Yu (Gongjin)*

Zhou Shen [Ch'oh S'ern] – *appointed as 'General that strikes fear into the unlawful' during the middle stage of the ill-fated campaign against the Liang Province rebels. He had Sun Jian as a consultant on his march, but he failed to heed any of Sun's advice and was routed as a consequence.*

Zhou Tai [Ch'oh Tigh] – *a former pirate that joined Sun Ce and served as an officer and bodyguard; he later became Sun Quan's personal bodyguard and almost lost his life defending Quan during a Shanyue attack on Xuan City. When Zhou Tai recovered he became an official and vanguard general that participated in many of Sun Ce's final campaigns. He became Sun Quan's bodyguard yet again after Sun Ce's death, and he almost died saving him yet again when a campaign to take Hefei Fortress went horribly wrong. Sun Quan valued him and did not allow anyone to treat him disrespectfully, despite his poor background.*
*Known by the courtesy name Youping [Yoh-ping]

Zhou Xin [Ch'oh Shin] – *brother of Zhou Yu (Renming) and Zhou Ang that served Yuan Shao and Wang Lang in succession: he is a secondary antagonist during Sun Ce's campaigns in Danyang and Kuaiji, although his appearance in Danyang is not necessarily historically accurate (he was defeated earlier by Wu Jing and may have fled to Kuaiji immediately, but the author wanted to introduce him slowly).*
*Known by the courtesy name Daming [T'ah-ming]

Zhou Yi [Ch'oh Yee] – *the father of Zhou Yu (Gongjin); he was Magistrate of Luoyang around the time of Emperor Ling's death and fled Luoyang when Dong Zhuo took power, settling in Shu City in Lujiang Prefecture. He had Sun Jian's family stay in his vast home during Sun Jian's time in the Eastern Pass Coalition, and his son Zhou Yu went on to become Sun Ce's closest friend and ally.*

Zhou Yu (Gongjin) [Ch'oh Yoo] – *referred to as 'Gongjin' once he reaches adulthood and becomes a protagonist in the main narrative (from Act IV onward) but is called Zhou Yu in Acts I-III and the prologue/epilogue. When Sun Ce died in the middle of a campaign to annex the north of Yang Province, Zhou Yu chose to continue serving the state under its new ruler, Sun Quan. He was the senior mastermind behind the 'Battle of Red Cliffs' (although Huang Gai suggested the surrender ruse) and the subsequent conquest of southern Jing Province: he had plans to ally with northern rebels and pincer Cao Cao, but fate favoured the warlord Liu Bei, whom Zhou Yu deeply distrusted. Zhou reluctantly accepted Liu Bei being allowed to occupy parts of Jing, but he continued pursuing other plans until his premature death two years after Red Cliffs, whereupon his responsibilities passed to his friend and benefactor Lu Su.*
*Known by the courtesy name Gongjin [K'ong-jin]

Zhou Yu (Renming) [Ch'oh Yoo] – *an adviser to Cao Cao that defected to Yuan Shao; he was later appointed Inspector of Yu Province as a rival to Sun Jian, which led to the Battle of Yang City (which is depicted in this novel). His brothers, Ang and Xin, also served Yuan Shao. Not to be confused with the more famous Zhou Yu (Gongjin) that was an ally of the Sun clan.*
*Known by the courtesy name Renming [Rern-ming]

Zhu Hao [Ch'oo Ha-oh] – *the Administrator of Yuzhang when Ze*

Rong fled there after abandoning Moling; Ze Rong killed him and occupied the prefectural capital.

Zhu Jun [Ch'oo J'oon] – *a prominent Han official; he was Sun Jian's 'sponsor' and recommended him for campaigns whenever he could. His career was affected by his opposition to the 'Ten Attendants': although he was handsomely rewarded for his role in defeating the Yellow Turban rebels, he also suffered slander and endured periods of hardship. He ended his days as a harassed landowner in Central Province.*
*Known by the courtesy name Gongwei [K'ong-way]

Zhu Ran [Ch'oo Rarn] – *introduced into the narrative as Shi Ran; he is later adopted by Sun Jian's chief strategist Zhu Zhi. Zhu Ran was a close friend of Sun Quan, who later inherited the state from Sun Ce: Ran became very important as an official and officer. He is most famous for his role in the 'Battle of Xiaoting', where his fire attack decimated Liu Bei's poorly-organised forces while they camped, rather foolishly, in a forest at the height of summer (the 'Battle of Xiaoting' is an event in 'Crouching Dragon: the Journey of Zhuge Liang').*
*Known by the courtesy name Yifeng [Yee-fung]

Zhu Zhi [Ch'oo Ch'ee] – *a Han official that joined Sun Jian during his middle career; he was a capable administrator and strategist, and his adopted son Zhu Ran would be a pivotal figure in future times. He spends most of this work thanklessly defending Wu Prefecture from Shanyue attacks.*
*Known by the courtesy name Junli [Ch'oon-lee]

Zhuge Jin [Ch'oo-ker Jin] – *the eldest of three brothers that were descendants of prominent Han officials; his family fled the troubles in Qing, Yan and Xu Provinces to the east and settled in Jing Province. Jin then travelled to Yang Province to find work and eventually found reasonable employment under Sun Ce and Sun Quan, despite the political suspicions surrounding the family (Jing was governed by an enemy of the Sun clan, and Jin's sisters were married to prominent politicians in the Jing regime). Zhuge Jin was eventually trusted by Sun Quan, who gave him ever-higher ranks, and he tried, repeatedly, to get his talented brother Liang – known as 'Crouching Dragon' – to join him. Zhuge Liang chose to serve the wandering warlord Liu Bei, which often placed Liang and Jin on opposite sides of a feud, but the two remained close. When a lasting peace was established between Liu Bei's son and Sun Quan, Jin allowed the childless Liang to adopt his younger son, but that young man died within a few years of the adoption. Jin's eldest son, Zhuge Ke, was eventually trusted as a regent to Sun Quan's young son, despite many – including Zhuge Liang and Jin himself – questioning Ke's character, and the worst suspicions were proved correct. Zhuge Jin is a prominent character in 'Crouching Dragon': the Journey of Zhuge Liang'.*
*Known by the courtesy name Ziyu [Tz'ee-yoo]

Zhuge Jun [Ch'oo-ker Joon] and Zhuge Liang [Ch'oo-ker Lee-arng] – *referenced together but never seen in this work, these two are Zhuge Jin's younger brothers. The latter's story is the main subject of 'Crouching Dragon: the Journey of Zhuge Liang'.*

Zu Lang [Tz'oo Larng] – a bandit leader in southern Yang Province that is a minor antagonist to Sun Ce.

Zu Mao [Tz'oo Mah-oh] – an early ally of Sun Jian; he often travelled with his master and seems to have been a bodyguard of sorts. Little was known of him at the time of writing; the author chose to sidestep the absence of his style name (he is awarded one in fiction, but where it came from is unknown) and any detail on his early service under Sun Jian by having him act as a 'shadow' that follows Sun everywhere and giving him enigmatic reactions to familiarity or curiosity about his past. He was mentioned during the campaign against Dong Zhuo as having acted as a decoy when Sun Jian suffered a critical loss against forces led by Dong Zhuo's best generals; some fictional accounts kill him there, but the author chose to let him survive until Sun Jian's death in northern Jing, perishing 'off-stage' alongside his master.

UNNAMED QING PROVINCIAL OFFICE MESSENGER – *unnamed courier that Taishi Ci is forced to outwit as part of his first mission.*

HISTORICAL CHINESE FIGURES

Confucius (Romanisation of Kong Fusha, lit. Master Kong) – *a famous scholar and philosopher whose beliefs and teachings became a philosophy in their own right, with many noted figures throughout Chinese history adopting 'Confucianism' as a way of life. Confucius' 'analects' were seen as the model for a morally correct way of living: their teachings usually sat alongside any other moral or spiritual beliefs that the practitioner had.*

Daji [T'ah-jee] – *famous evil and sadistic concubine of King Zhou [Ch'oh] during the Shang Dynasty. A fantastical version of the fall of the Shang Dynasty/rise of the Zhou Dynasty was written during the Ming Dynasty: it is called 'Fengshen Yanyi' (a.k.a. Fengshen Bang, known sometimes as 'Creation/Investiture/ of the Gods' or 'Apotheosis of Heroes' in english).*

Lao Tzu [Lao Tz'oo] (sometimes Romanised to Laozi [Lao-tz-er], but the author has opted for the older form) – *famous philosopher and founder of Taoism (again, this can be Romanised to Daoism, but the author has opted for one over the other). Li Jue apparently claimed to be his descendant.*

Liu Bang [Lee-oo P'arng] – *the founder of the Han Dynasty; his region of influence, Hanzhong, gave his dynasty its name. One of his descendants was eventually overthrown by the chancellor Wang Mang; Wang was defeated in turn by a popular uprising led by Liu clan members, and the Han Dynasty was restored. The second of the new line of Han Emperors, Liu Xiu/Emperor Guangwu, moved the capital to the eastern city of Luoyang to create distance between his government and the foreign tribes that threatened to devour the western provinces. As such, some historians tend refer to a Western Han (pre-Wang Mang) and an Eastern Han (post-Wang Mang).*

Sun Tzu [Soon Tz'oo] (sometimes Romanised to Sunzi [Soon-tz'er], but the author has opted for the older form) – *a legendary scholar, famed for his work 'The Art of War'; while new technologies outdated some strategies and forced later scholars such as Zhuge Liang to annotate the work, his understanding of the psychological aspects of warfare were used to great effect, and unlike technology, those references remained relevant since people, unlike their inventions, did not and do not change. The 2nd Century warlord Sun Jian and his progeny claimed descent from Sun Tzu, though this was never completely proven or disputed.*

Wang Mang [Warng Marng] – *the regent and Chancellor to the last Chang'an-based Han Emperor and founder of his own short-lived Xin Dynasty. He created the idea of the Mandate of Heaven that later regimes kept despite the reputation of its conceptualist. He was eventually overthrown by members of Liu clan, who revived the Han Dynasty. Wang Mang is treated as a villain by Han loyalists and subsequent imperial regimes, while some historians argue that his government was not entirely malevolent. His name was typically used in Han times as a slander to imply that a person was seditious – or, more typically, make a specific accusation of evil ambition.*

Yuan An [Yoo-arn Arn] – *an ancestor of Yuan Shao that provided much support to the Han Dynasty; he was rewarded with grand titles that his descendants inherited, and there were many statues erected to honour him.*

PLACES

In this book, land locations are sorted by their provincial-level location and other landmarks – rivers and such – trail the list. Most of the novel takes place in Yang Province, but other places (Jing, Yu and Liang Provinces in particular) are the stages for important events.

Luoyang [Loo-oh-yarng] – *the eastern and current capital, used by Han Emperor Guangwu (Liu Xiu) onwards during the second phase of the Han Dynasty; the capital is the scene of many dramas, including the Partisan Crisis, a series of attempted coups (including one by the 'Way of Peace'), and a war between the court eunuchs and followers of assassinated Commander-in-Chief Hè Jin before it is finally pillaged and burned to the ground by Dong Zhuo and his allies, prior to their move to the former capital Chang'an. Luoyang does not enjoy a revival until the early 3rd Century, when it becomes the seat of a new dynasty, Cao Wei.*

Chang'an [T'arng Arn] – *the western and former capital, designated so by the Han Dynasty founder Liu Bang and used until the usurper Wang Mang temporarily ended the Han Dynasty and founded his own Xin [Shin] Dynasty. It was still considered to be the capital for a very short time after the restoration of the Han, but for a number of reasons (primarily that the Qiang and other tribes in the west were a constant threat, and Emperor Guangwu had an established power base in the east), a new capital – Luoyang – was created. Dong Zhuo moves the court back to Chang'an during his time as Chancellor of State, and the regency court maintained Chang'an as their capital despite a new threat from the Qiang tribes of Liang Province (this is because the east is more hostile and Luoyang had been looted and gutted by Dong Zhuo during his move to the west) By the end of the text, Cao Cao has moved Emperor Xian to Xuchang (see below).*

Xuchang [Shoo-t'arng] – *located in northwest Yan Province; Cao Cao's chosen imperial capital while Luoyang was being rebuilt (sometimes known as Xu [Shoo] but that leads to confusion with Xu Province). Cao Cao was Governor of Yan, so the vast majority of the officials in Xuchang were Cao Cao's loyalists (even more so after the purge of men that followed Zhang Miao and Chen Gong's rebellion, and in addition, many of Emperor Xian's loyalists were killed by the regents or died on route to Luoyang): this would later lead to accusations of plotting sedition (the 'Girdle Edict Crisis' of 200 that eventually led to the 'Battle of Guandu')*

Central Province – *known at the time as 'Sili' [See-lee], but the author chose to refer to the province by its political purpose and geographical location. Luoyang is to the east of the region, and Chang'an is to the west, bordering (and also inhabiting, technically) Liang Province. Notable places include White Wave Gorge, the base of operations of the White Wave Bandits, who are obviously named for the place.*

Other places that are mentioned during the Eastern Pass Coalition's blockade of Luoyang include (or may include, due to boundary changes): Xingyang [Shing-yarng] (where Cao Cao fought Xu Rong after Dong Zhuo fled the capital); Suanzao [Soo-arn-tz'ao] where Yan Governor Liu Dai camped (it may be in Central Province, or it may be in Yan); Heyang [Her-yarng] Ford (which is probably located to the northwest of Luoyang), where Wang Kuang was based; Yangren [Yarng-rern] (located to the south of Luoyang), where Sun Jian had a battle with Dong Zhuo's forces (it may be in Central Province, or it may be in Yu); Liangdong [Lee-arng-t'ong] (located to the southeast of Luoyang), where Sun Jian had a battle with Dong Zhuo's forces (it may be in Central Province, or it may be in Yu); Huayin [Hoo-ah-yin] and Mianchi [Mee-an-t'ee] (both located in western Central Province), which become strategic bases for Dong Zhuo's followers after the end of the Dong Zhuo Campaign; Anyi [Arn-yee] (located in western Central Province) which becomes a strategic base for Dong Zhuo's son-in-law Niu Fu after the end of the Dong Zhuo Campaign; and Zhongmu [Ch'ong-moo] (located in eastern Central Province, to the southeast of Luoyang and near the Yan Province border), where Dong Zhuo's followers defeat Zhu Jun and attack Yan after the end of the Dong Zhuo Campaign.

Henei [Her-nay] Prefecture – *the capital prefecture of Central Province; Henei City, the northern capital of Henei Prefecture (and later the overall capital after Luoyang's destruction), is located between Central Province, Bing Province and Ji Province; it is south of the Yellow River and north of Luoyang. Yuan Shao is based here during the Dong Zhuo Campaign, and Zhang Yang later becomes prefectural administrator and runs the region from here. Luoyang, the overall capital until Dong Zhuo moves Emperor Xian to Chang'an, is in Henei.*

Yang [Yarng] Province – *located in the southeast of China, east of southern Jing and south of everything else; it is quite a large province, and can be divided into two as the Yangtze/Great River bisects the province. The southern part is also considered to be east of the Great River, and is sometimes known as Jiangdong [Jee-arng-t'ong] (lit. river-east, or 'east of the river'). Lujiang and Jiujiang Prefectures comprise the majority of the northern part, although Guangling and Danyang could be partially included (and were often considered as annexed into Xu Province as well). The northern part of the province is the only part featured.*

Jiujiang [Jee-oo-jee-arng] Prefecture – *located in the northeast of Yang Province, 'above' the Great River; the provincial capital Shouchun [S'oh-t'oon] is based here (SHouchun is also Yuan Shu's 'Imperial capital' when he reinvents himself as First Emperor of the Zhong Dynasty. There are land borders with Yan and Xu Provinces to the north. Sun Ce fought Liu Yao's forces at Hengjiang [Hung-ch'ee-arng] and Danglikou [T'arng-lee-koh] (both located on the riverbank) and Zhou Yu was later made Magistrate of Juchao [Ch'oo-t'ow] to the north of Hengjiang.*
    The Huai [Hoo-eye] River runs to the north of the prefecture: Shouchun County is part of Huainan [Hoo-eye-narn]. Lu Su's home region, Dongcheng [T'ong-t'erng], is to the east of here. The Qian [Chee-arn] Hills are somewhere close to Shouchun, and served as a base for bandits and deserters from Yuan Shu's army (such as Chen Lan and Lei Bo).

Lujiang [Loo-jiang] Prefecture – *located in the northwest of Yang, 'above' the Great River; there are land borders with Jing, Yu and Yan Provinces. Zhou Yu (Gongjin) hailed from Lujiang. The capital, Huancheng [Hoo-arn-t'eng], was the site of several sieges.*
    Hefei [Her-fay] is located in the south of Lujiang Prefecture; this strategically useful area was eventually fortified by Cao Cao. The resultant fortress was a major obstacle to the Sun clan's plans to reclaim northern Yang Province. Lu [Loo County] County is to the northwest of Hefei; Yuan Shu camped here during the campaign against Dong Zhuo. Shu [S'oo] City was the home of Zhou Yu's family after fleeing Luoyang, and Sun Jian settled his family here while he went to fight Dong Zhuo.

Wu [Woo] Prefecture – *located in the east of Yang Province, south of Guangling and west of Wu Prefecture, 'below' the Yangtze/Great River; the Sun clan hailed from this region, and the scholar Cai Yong hid here for 12 years. NOTE: Wu and Danyang tend to overlap and the boundaries change as different parts fall into different hands.*

Moling [Moh-ling] was located in the north of Wu Prefecture; Liu Yao stationed his forces here when he became the court-appointed Governor of Yang, as Yuan Shu had control of the real capital Shouchun. Moling later became known as Jianye [Jee-an-yer], the seat of the ruler of Eastern Wu. Fuchun [Foo-t'oon] County – located in the south of Wu Prefecture – was the ancestral home of the famous Sun clan that founded Eastern Wu. Xuan City was the site of one of Sun Quan's early tactical blunders and the setting of a major battle between Sun Ce and 'White Tiger' Yan of the Shanyue

Danyang [T'arn-yarng] Prefecture – *located in the centre of Yang Province, south of Jiujiang and 'below' the Yangtze/Great River; the region was famous for producing good cavalrymen, and it becomes the focus of intense fighting between Yuan Shu's vassals (including the Suns), Yuan Shao's vassals and court-appointed Governor Liu Yao. Its capital varied, but Qu'e was typical at the time of this text. Jing [Ch'ing] County was a base for Zu Lang's bandits (Sun Ce fought his first major battle as a warlord here, against the same Zu Lang). Key battles against Liu Yao were fought at (from west to east along the riverbank) Niuzhu [Nee-oo-ch'oo] and Hushu [Hoo-s'oo]. Sun Ce and Taishi Ci duelled outside Shen [S'ern] Town.*

Guangling [K'oo-arng-ling] Prefecture – *located in the east of Yang Province, on the coast, north of Wu Prefecture and south of Xiapi in eastern Xu Province; it appears to be controlled by various warlords (Tao Qian and whoever controls most of the rest of Yang) most of the time.*

Kuaiji [Koo-eye-jee] Prefecture – *located in the southeast of Yang Province, on the coast, south of Wu Prefecture; Wang Lang was Administrator of this prefecture when Yuan Shu sent Sun Ce to seize it. Shanyin [S'arn-yin] County was the capital (and the site of a sizeable rebellion). Other notable locations include Hougan County (the site of one major battle), Gaoqian [K'ow-chee-arn] (Wang Lang fortifies the area but loses to Sun Ce, and Dong Xi joins Sun Ce here as well) the Qiantang [Chee-arn-tarng] River near Gaoqian (which was used as a natural defensive line by Wang Lang) and Dongye [T'ong-yer] (Wang Lang fled here after losing Gaoqian, but later relocated to Hougan, where he received the aid of Zhang Ya). Hè Qi is recruited by Sun Ce in Yan [Yarn] County and given Yongning [Yong-ning] County to protect from Shanyue raiders and bandits.*

Yuzhang [Yoo-ch'arng] Prefecture – *located in the southwest of Yang Province, west of Danyang and Kuaiji and on the border with Jiangxia in southern Jing Province; Nanchang [Narn-t'arng] is the capital. Liu Yao and Ze Rong flee here after their defeats (Liu Yao is said to have gone to Pengze [Pung-tz'er]) and Taishi Ci is sent here as part of one of his three 'labours'. Sun Ben was 'given' the remote Luling County [Loo-ling] (to the far southwest) by Yuan Shu (with the probable intention of a pincer attack on the capital Nanchang), but he did not go there whilst serving Shu (his brother*

Fu went instead). Po [Poh] County and Hukou [Hoo-koh] are located to the northwest (they are harassed by Liu Pan and later used as bases by Sun Ce forces).

Liang [Lee-arng] Province – *located in the far northwest of China; the region is visited by Sun Jian in Act I, when he is seconded to a general charged with pacifying the rebellion there. The region is home to the Qiang and Yuezhi peoples, who rose up against the Han government in semi-organised revolt; many of the local Han Chinese people in the region were as dissatisfied with the government as the Qiang, so they joined the uprising, turning it into a full-blown rebellion that is never truly pacified during the course of the text (it would take many decades for the Han government to do that).*

Mei [May] County – *located in the southeast of Liang Province; it was Dong Zhuo's power base, though it appears to have been ceded to Ma Teng after Dong's death.*

Longxi [Long-shee] Prefecture – *located in western Liang Province; its capital Didao [T'ee-t'ao] County was the site of a siege that led to Han officer Ma Teng defecting to the rebels. Wangyuan [Warng-yoo-arn] (where Dong Zhuo was almost routed during the Liang Province Rebellion) is near or in this prefecture.*

Yu [Yoo] Province – *located south and east of Central Province; the Yuan clan's ancestral home, Ru County, is here. Sun Jian was once made Inspector of the province by his lord Yuan Shu, and Wang Yun held the role at some point. Yang [Yarng] City in the west of the province was the site of the first battle between the forces of the feuding Yuan brothers.*

Runan [Roo-narn] Prefecture – *the capital prefecture of Yu Province, located in its centre; the Yuan clan's ancestral home, Ru [Roo] County, is located here, and one of the final battles of the original Yellow Turban Rebellion is fought in Xihua [Shee-hoo-ah] County.*

Jing [Jing] Province – *a province located in the centre of Han China; it has borders with Yi, Hanzhong, Yu, Yan and Central provinces, which makes it strategically desirable to a would-be conqueror. A very important event occurs here, despite the region being 'irrelevant' in act II and acts IV to VIII.*

Nan [Narn] County – *a county located in the far north of Jing Province; it borders Yan Province, Yu Province and Central Province, making it strategically invaluable for conquering the north of China. The Yellow Turbans prioritised Nan County and almost took it during their first rebellion; Yuan Shu's vassal Sun Jian saved it during that campaign and later seized it for his lord, and Zhang Xiu later governed from the capital Wan [Wahn] City with surprising popularity.*
    Wan [Wahn] City has its own story; it is strategically important, so it suffers from repeated seizure attempts. Sun Jian liberated Wan from the Yellow Turbans during their rebellion, but

later returned to the province to seize it for Yuan Shu; Shu then lost it and fled to Fengqiu in Yan Province. Dong Zhuo's former vassal Zhang Ji seized the city after leaving Chang'an, but died and left the place in the hands of his nephew Zhang Xiu and the adviser Jia Xu. The two fugitives were then forced to fight Cao Cao's army: that event is famous for its outcome.

Xiangyang [Shee-arng-yarng] – *a county (and city named for the county) located in the lower north of Jing Province; it straddles the south bank of the River Han. The city of Xiangyang later becomes the location of numerous sieges: Sun Jian sieges the city and fights land battles here before his death, and Guan Yu sieged Xiangyang as part of his attack on Fan, a campaign that became his last great exploit (that is chronicled in 'Crouching Dragon').*

Fan [Farn] – *a county (and city named for the county) located in the lower north of Jing Province; it straddles the north bank of the River Han, which occasionally swells and floods the region. The city of Fan later becomes the location of numerous sieges: the most famous is the one conducted by Guan Yu that became his last great exploit (that is chronicled in 'Crouching Dragon'). Sun Jian fought Cai Mao at Deng [T'erng] to the east of the city.*

Nan [Narn] Prefecture – *located in southern Jing Province; this region is taken by Cao Cao after the death of Liu Biao, but it is subsequently taken by Sun Quan's strategist Zhou Yu (Gongjin) after a year-long siege of the prefectural capital Jiangling. It is then 'loaned' to Liu Bei's by his ally Sun Quan so that Bei has a base of operations, but it then becomes a source of contention (that is explored in 'Crouching Dragon'). Jiangling [Jee-arng-ling] was the capital of Nan Prefecture and southern capital of Jing Province: it is not featured heavily in this book, but a famous siege battle is fought here after the Battle of Red Cliffs (that is covered in 'Crouching Dragon'). Zhangling [Ch'arng-ling] is briefly mentioned as the administrative responsibility of Kuai Yue.*

Jiangxia [Jee-arng-shee-ah] Prefecture – *located in southeast Jing Province; this is Huang Zu's power base, and is the site of many battles between Huang Zu and the Sun clan: Xiakou [Shee-ah-koh] seems to serve as the capital. The novel ends with a battle at Three Rivers, a port region in eastern Jiangxia; Wulin [Woo-lin] is mentioned, and is later the site of battles prior to the fateful ones at Red Cliffs (also in Jiangxia). Ba Qiu [P'ah Chee-oo] is briefly mentioned, and this is in Jiangxia as well.*

Changsha [T'arng-s'ah] "County" – *located south of Jing Province and technically part of Jing; Changsha is more a commandery/prefecture, but is often referred to as a county, perhaps because it is sparsely inhabited and therefore has a county's population. Changsha was administrated by Sun Jian after the Yellow Turban Rebellion; it is later wanted by Liu Bei's faction and Sun Quan's faction (after Red Cliffs), but it is Liu Bei that triumphs initially (that is explored in 'Crouching Dragon').*

Wuling [Woo-ling] "County", Lingling [Ling-ling] "County" and

Guiyang [K'oo-ee-yarng] "County" – *located south of Jing Province and technically part of Jing; they are all better described in terms of size as commanderies/prefectures, but are often referred to as counties, perhaps because they are sparsely inhabited and therefore have county-sized populations. Huang Gai hails from Lingling, and Sun Jian is forced to expand his pacification campaign to these counties after calming Changsha.*

Qing [Ching] Province – *located in the northeast of China, east of Ji Province and south of Yòu Province; there is a large 'information hole' when it comes to Qing Province. The region seems to suffer from high crime and corruption, despite several principalities. Linzi [Lin-tz'er] – located in the centre-north of Qing Province – served as the provincial capital, although the fighting places Pingyuan at the centre of politics at times*

Donglai [T'ong-l'eye] Prefecture – *located to the east, this is where Taishi Ci's home village, Huangxian, is located.*

Beihai [P'ay-high] – *located in the centre-north of Qing Province, south of Linzi; Kong Rong is made Chancellor of the capital around the time of the death of Emperor Ling. Kong Rong famously required rescuing when an army of Yellow Turbans sieged the city; Taishi Ci borrowed an army from Liu Bei and saved him.*

Mount Tai [Tigh] Prefecture – *located in the northwest of Qing Province, near the actual Mount Tai; Huaxian [Hoo-ah-shee-an] was the home region of future minor warlord Zang Ba: at one point in time prior to the Yellow Turban Rebellion, Zang Ba's father was arrested after criticising the corrupt administrator, leading to his son becoming a criminal to free him.*

Ji'nan [Jee Narn] Prefecture – *located in the west of Qing Province, near the Ji River; Cao Cao was sent here by the court, but he could not cope with the pressure and retired*

Langya [Larng-yah] Prefecture – *located in the centre of Qing Province, southeast of Beihai; Yangdu [Yarng-t'oo], located in the southwest of Langya Prefecture, was the famous Zhuge clan's ancestral home.*

Pingyuan [Ping-yoo-arn] County – *located in the far northwest of Qing Province, near the border with Yòu Province; Gongsun Zan's appointed Inspector of Qing, Tian Kai, and Yuan Shao's son Yuan Tan fought here. Liu Bei was invited to Pingyuan by Gongsun Zan.*

Yan [Yarn] Province – *located in central China, to the east of Central and Jing Provinces, west of Xu Province and south of Ji Province; it was entrusted to Liu Dai prior to the death of Emperor Ling, but was later given to Cao Cao by Yuan Shao. Xuchang, the third capital that Emperor Xian 'ruled' from, is here, but is detailed at the start of the 'PLACES' section.*

Dong [T'ong] Prefecture – *located in northeast Yan Province; it is the provincial capital. Pan Zhang claims to hail from here.*

Yingchuan [Ying-t'oo-arn] – *located in southwest Yan Province and northeast Yu Province; it is the border between the provinces.*

Fengqiu [Ferng-chee-oo] – *located in northwest Yan Province; the Black Mountain Bandits and the Southern Xiongu exile Yufuluo repeatedly attacked and settled in this region, and Yuan Shu tries to occupy this region after being chased out of Jing Province by Liu Biao, leading to the Battle of Fengqiu.*
   Notable locations during the Battle of Fengqiu (that may or may not be actual parts of Fengqiu include: Kuang [Koo-arng] Town, which Yuan Shu's officers try (and fail) to take during Shu's attempted occupation; Xiangyi [Shee-arng-yee], a point of retreat for Yuan Shu; Tianshou [Tee-an-s'oh], where Cao Cao had a river diverted to foil Yuan Shu's plans to occupy Xiangyi; Ning [Ning] Hill, Yuan Shu's last point of retreat before fleeing Yan Province.

Xu [Shoo] Province – *located in the centre-east of China, south of Qing Province and east of Yan Province; it is governed by Tao Qian until Cao Cao's campaign.*
   The capital prior to Cao Cao's campaign was Peng [Perng] City; Tao Qian later relocated to Tan [Tarn], which offered greater defence, and then to Xiapi, which became the new capital.

Xiapi [Shee-ah-pee] Prefecture – *located in the east of Xu Province, east of the Si River; it is administrated by Ze Rong prior to Cao Cao's campaign.* Xiapi [Shee-ah-pee] City was *the capital of Xiapi Prefecture; the Buddhist cult leader Ze Rong runs the city as a 'Buddhist Utopia' prior to Cao Cao's campaign, whereupon Ze Rong flees the city and Tao Qian retreats to it, turning it into his new provincial capital.*

Kaiyang [K-eye-yarng] County – *located somewhere in the far north-northeast of Xu Province; in the wake of the Yellow Turban Rebellion, the minor warlord Zang Ba occupied this place and made it into an independent state with few rules.*

Ji [Jee] Province – *located in the northeast of China, south of Yòu Province, east of Bing Province and west of Qing Province; this later becomes Yuan Shao's power base. Its first capital is Xindu [Shin-t'oo] in the centre of the province, but Yuan Shao later relocates the capital to the southern city of Yè [Yer].*

Julu [Joo-luu] Prefecture – *located in the centre of Ji Province, south of Xindu; the prefectural capital, Yingtao [Ying-tao], was occupied by Zhang Jue, founder of the 'Way of Peace' and organiser of the nationwide Yellow Turban Rebellion.*

Yòu [Yoh] Province – *located in the northeast of China, on the frontier; it is therefore prone to frequent attacks by Northern Xiongnu, Wuhuan and other tribes. Liu Yu was made Governor, and the famous warlord Gongsun Zan was based here. Its capital is Fanyang [Farn-yarng]. Cheng Pu hails from (Yòu)Beiping [Yoh-p'ei-ping] in the far northeast, and Han Dang hails from nearby Liaoxi [Lee-ow-shee].*

Bing [P'ing] Province – *located in the centre-north of China, north of Central Province; it is relatively unimportant to the narrative. Ding Yuan is Inspector of the province, the Southern Xiongnu mainly live in Bing, and the Black Mountain Bandits are very active here.*

Yi [Yee] Province – *a province located in the centre-west of Han China, south of Hanzhong and west of Jing; it is a relatively harsh and unforgiving place at this point (now it is Szechuan), but Liu Yan craved the governorship precisely because it was isolated enough for him to have complete autonomy. Liu Bei later sets his sights on making Yi his first base (after the loaned piece of Jing that he has obtained by that point) and seizes it from Liu Yan's son Zhang after a long campaign that robbed Bei of his adviser Pang Tong (the entire affair is chronicled in 'Crouching Dragon'). Its first capital was Mianzhu [Mee-an-ch'oo], a city located in the centre-west of Yi Prefecture; it is protected by mountains, hills and valleys. After a series of events that Governor Liu Yan deemed inauspicious, he moved the capital to Chengdu [T'erng-doo], in the south of Yi Province; that place was protected by a complex natural defensive barrier of rivers, hills and mountains.*

Hanzhong [Harn-ch'ong] Province – *later known as (The Taoist State of) Han'ning [Harn Ning]; this region was the fief of sorts of Liu Bang, founder of the Han Dynasty, and he named his dynasty for this region. When Zhang Lu occupied Hanzhong, he renamed it: if Hanzhong is read as meaning 'Amidst/In Han', Han'ning could, when taking individual characters, mean 'Tranqil Han' or, possibly, 'Rather than Han/Preferable to Han', which fits perfectly with Zhang Lu's beliefs. The region serves as little more than a place that people must journey through in this text, but it becomes a battleground for Cao Cao and Liu Bei in later years.*

Jiaozhi [Ch'ee-ow-ch'ee] (Province) – *a region to the south of Kuaiji Prefecture (in Yang Province) that includes part of Northern Vietnam: Xu Jing fled here after Wang Lang's defeat, and the Sun clan later stake a claim on the region as part of the expansion of the state of Eastern Wu.*

Liaodong [Lee-ow-t'ong] Peninsula – *a region to the northeast of Qing Province: Taishi Ci lived here when in exile.*

Great Wall [a.k.a. 'The Endless Wall'] – *commissioned by various rulers throughout history to repel the Xiongnu and other tribal invaders; it spans the entire northern border.*

Bian [P'ee-an] River – *runs through southeast Central Province at the very least; Xingyang is close to this river*

Ji [Jee] River – *ran parallel to (and east of) the Yellow River from the coast to Chenliu.*

Qing [Ching] River – *located in Ji Province, to the north of Yè*

Si [See] River – *located in Qing and Xu Provinces; it flows south and east toward the east coast. Xiapi is east of its banks.*

Wei [Way] River – *spawns from the Yellow River near Chang'an and runs west to Longxi, where it turns north and ends at Didao.*

Yangtze [Yarng-tz'ee] River – *spoken of in the text as the Great River, it runs from the west of China to the east, separating the land naturally into north and south.*

Yellow River – *located in the centre-north of China; this vibrant river – which literally runs yellow with sand – runs south and west from the northeast coast to the lands east of Luoyang, whereupon it turns west and runs north of Luoyang as far as the lands east of Chang'an, whereupon it splits and runs north and west.*

MISCELLANEOUS

Di [Dee] – *a northern, non-Han Chinese race, broken down further into tribes; they were indigenous to the mountains of Hanzhong.*

Qiang [Chee-arng] – *non-Chinese ethnic tribes that lived in the northwest on either side of the Great Wall. The various tribes were typically enemies of the Han Dynasty. Ma Teng and Han Sui famously joined the tribes, and the eldest son of the former, Ma Chao, became a notorious historical warrior king.*

Shanyue [S'arn-yoo-er] – *non-Chinese tribes that lived in and around various regions: they lived in Yang Province in large numbers. They resented Han rule, but their allegiances shifted dramatically through the eras.*

The 'Ten Attendants' – *a clique of eunuchs in the imperial capital Luoyang; they began life as loyalists that helped Emperor Huan to purge Liang Ji and Empress Dowager Liang's influence, but over time they formed a power base of their own. By the year 166, they were almost untouchable, and anyone that crossed them, deliberately or otherwise, was dealt with in the harshest fashion: hundreds of non-compliant intelligentsia were labelled as traitors and persecuted, an event known as the 'Partisan Crisis'. They were finally purged after thwarted political action by Commander-in-Chief Hè Jin and decisive military action by his ally Yuan Shao.*

'The Way of Five Pecks' – *a religious cult that was led by Zhang Lu, the ruler of Han'ning; their doctrine was based around a non-monetary system where rice was the currency and community was paramount, although many decried the way that potentially troublesome elements were kept loyal by providing them with whatever they needed at the expense of others.*

'The Way of Peace' – *the religious group that started the Yellow Turban Rebellion; although it can probably be said that many of those that fought were not followers of this Taoist cult, they had a 16-character mantra that was a simple, inspirational way to gather followers and rally other forms of support.*

Wuhuan [Woo-hoo-arn] – *non-Chinese tribes that lived across China and the surrounding territories*

Xiongnu [Shee-ong-noo] – *non-Chinese ethnic tribes that lived in the north on either side of the Great Wall; the various tribes were enemies, economic trading partners or allies of the Han Dynasty. The Southern Xiongnu provided troops to the Han army.*

Xianbei [Shee-an-p'ay] – *a confederacy of mostly Xiongnu tribes that became a powerful force in the lands north of the Great Wall.*

Yellow Turbans – *a common army that earned their name from the yellow scarves that they used to cover their hair. They were mostly made up of peasants that were tired of heavy taxation and poor treatment by the state. The founder was a Taoist cultist, Zhang Jue. The rebellion was eventually crushed by a combination of government forces and local militias, but they reappeared many times over the next decade before they were finally suppressed by the Han government.*

Nan(man) [Narn(-marn)] – *a southern, non-Chinese race, broken down further into tribes; they were indigenous to Nanzhong, which once included Yi Province until the Han Chinese expanded into their territory. They play no role in this book, but they are mentioned by Lu Su and Zhou Yu. The western state of Shu Han was forced to launch a military campaign to 'pacify' them in the early 3rd Century (this is dramatized in the author's earlier work, 'Crouching Dragon: the Journey of Zhuge Liang').*

Yuezhi [Yoo-er-ch'ee] – *a northern, non-Han Chinese race, broken down further into tribes; they were indigenous to Liang Province. They sided with the Qiang and the rebels during the Liang Province Rebellion.*

****

www.ingramcontent.com/pod-product-compliance
Lightning Source LLC
Chambersburg PA
CBHW050607110726
47899CB00001B/7